PEANUTS™
The Gang's All Here!

Other *Peanuts* Kids' Collections

Charlie Brown: Pow!

Woodstock: Master of Disguise

Snoopy: Contact!

Snoopy: Party Animal

Charlie Brown: Here We Go Again

Snoopy to the Rescue

Snoopy: What's Wrong with Dog Lips?

I'm Not Your Sweet Babboo!

Snoopy: Boogie Down!

Lucy: Speak Out!

Charlie Brown: All Tied Up

Snoopy: First Beagle in Space

PEANUTS ™

The Gang's All Here!

A PEANUTS ™ Collection

CHARLES M. SCHULZ

A special *Peanuts* collection featuring comics from
Snoopy: Cowabunga! and *Charlie Brown and Friends*

Andrews McMeel
PUBLISHING®

Peanuts is distributed internationally by Andrews McMeel Syndication.

Peanuts: The Gang's All Here! copyright © 2020 by Peanuts Worldwide, LLC. This 2020 edition is a compilation of two previously published books: *Snoopy: Cowabunga!* © 2013 and *Charlie Brown and Friends* © 2014. All rights reserved. Printed in China. No part of this book may be used or reproduced in any manner whatsoever without written permission except in the case of reprints in the context of reviews.

Andrews McMeel Publishing
a division of Andrews McMeel Universal
1130 Walnut Street, Kansas City, Missouri 64106

www.andrewsmcmeel.com

www.peanuts.com

22 23 24 25 26 SDB 10 9 8 7 6 5

ISBN: 978-1-5248-6179-7

Made by:
King Yip (Dongguan) Printing & Packaging Factory Ltd.
Address and location of manufacturer:
Daning Administrative District, Humen Town
Dongguan Guangdong, China 523930
5th Printing—9/20/21

ATTENTION: SCHOOLS AND BUSINESSES

SNOOPY ™
COWABUNGA!

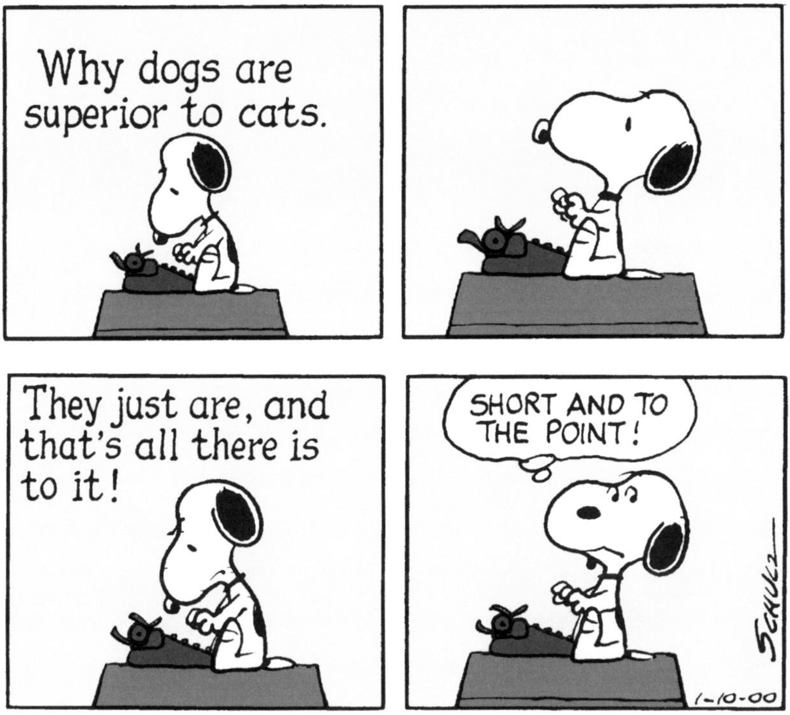
Why dogs are superior to cats.
They just are, and that's all there is to it!
SHORT AND TO THE POINT!
SCHULZ
1-10-00

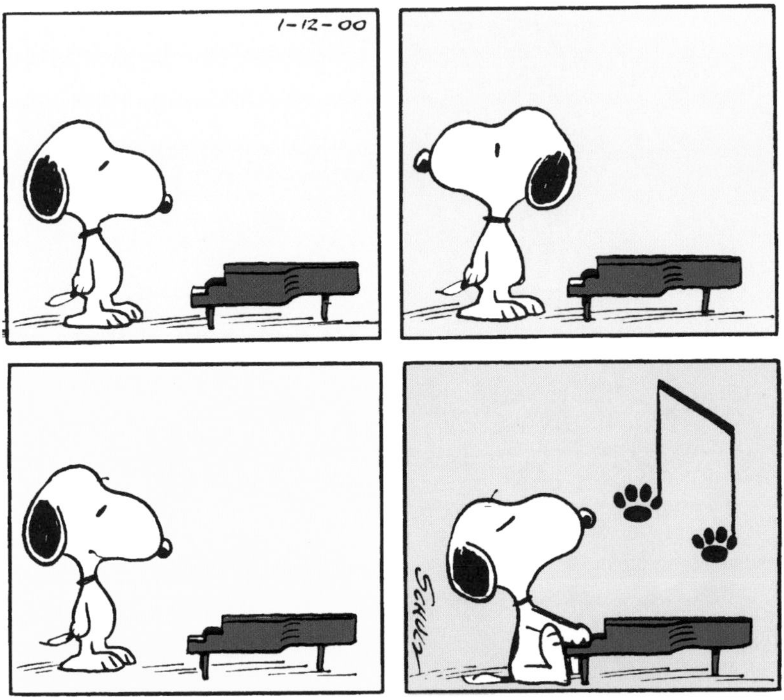
1-12-00
SCHULZ

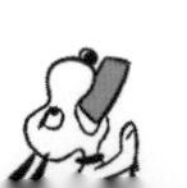

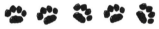

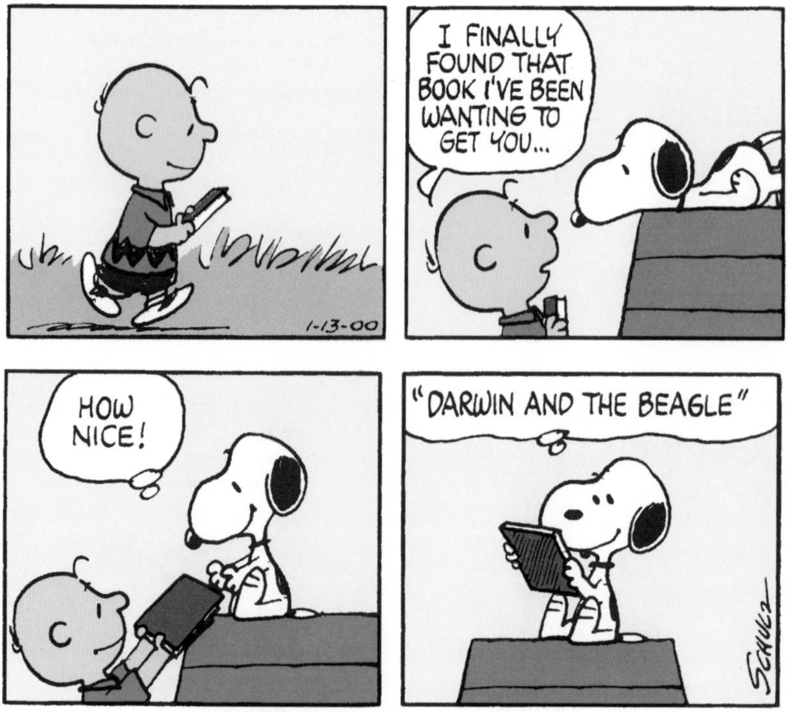
1-13-00
I FINALLY FOUND THAT BOOK I'VE BEEN WANTING TO GET YOU...
HOW NICE!
"DARWIN AND THE BEAGLE"
SCHULZ

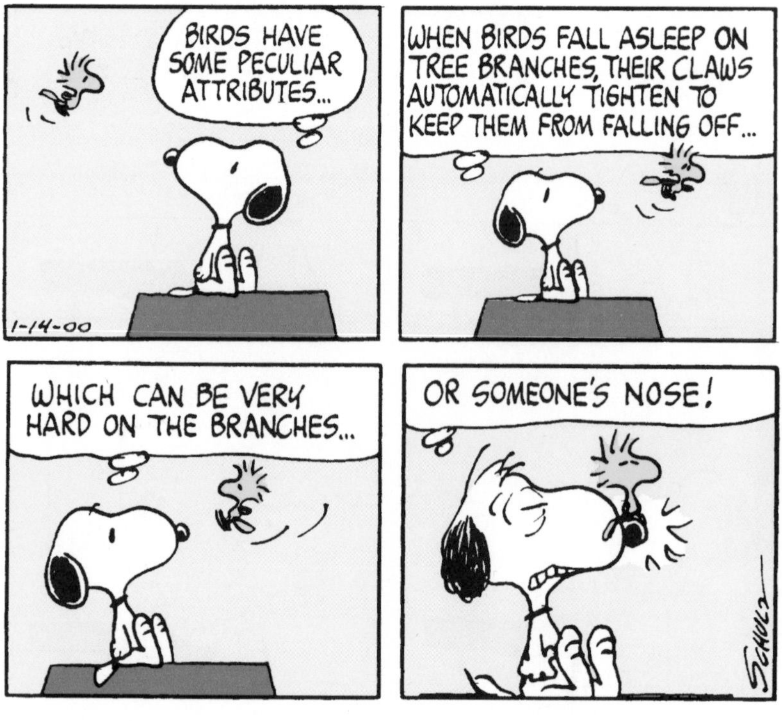
BIRDS HAVE SOME PECULIAR ATTRIBUTES...
1-14-00
WHEN BIRDS FALL ASLEEP ON TREE BRANCHES, THEIR CLAWS AUTOMATICALLY TIGHTEN TO KEEP THEM FROM FALLING OFF...
WHICH CAN BE VERY HARD ON THE BRANCHES...
OR SOMEONE'S NOSE!
SCHULZ

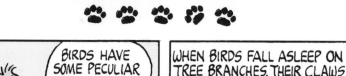

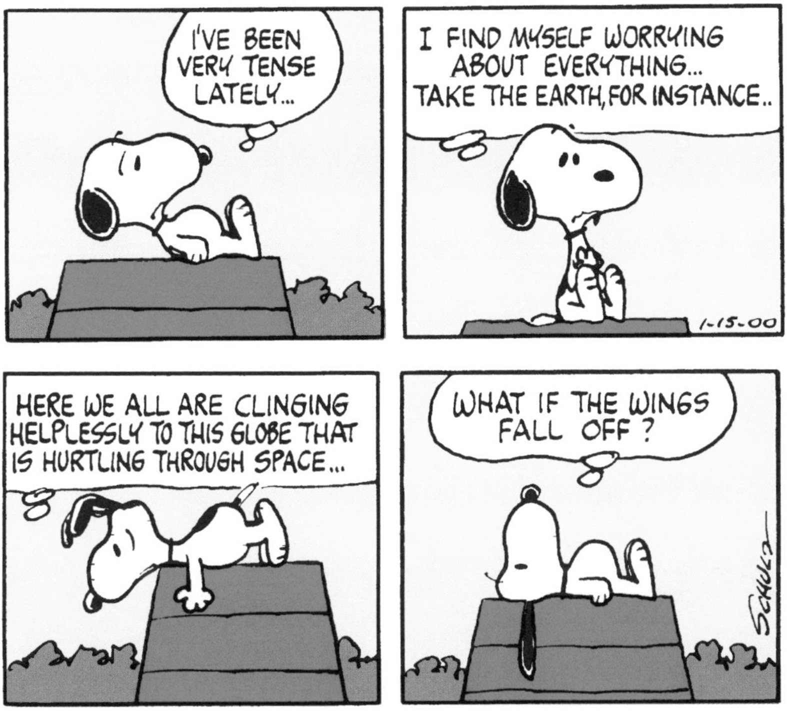
I'VE BEEN VERY TENSE LATELY...
I FIND MYSELF WORRYING ABOUT EVERYTHING... TAKE THE EARTH, FOR INSTANCE..
1-15-00
HERE WE ALL ARE CLINGING HELPLESSLY TO THIS GLOBE THAT IS HURTLING THROUGH SPACE...
WHAT IF THE WINGS FALL OFF?
SCHULZ

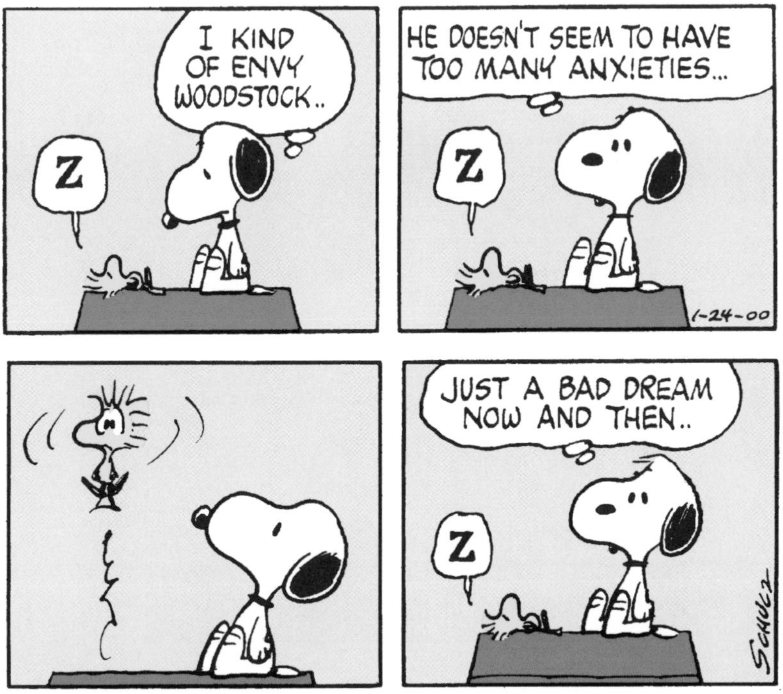
I KIND OF ENVY WOODSTOCK..
Z
HE DOESN'T SEEM TO HAVE TOO MANY ANXIETIES...
Z
1-24-00
JUST A BAD DREAM NOW AND THEN..
Z
SCHULZ

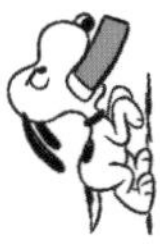

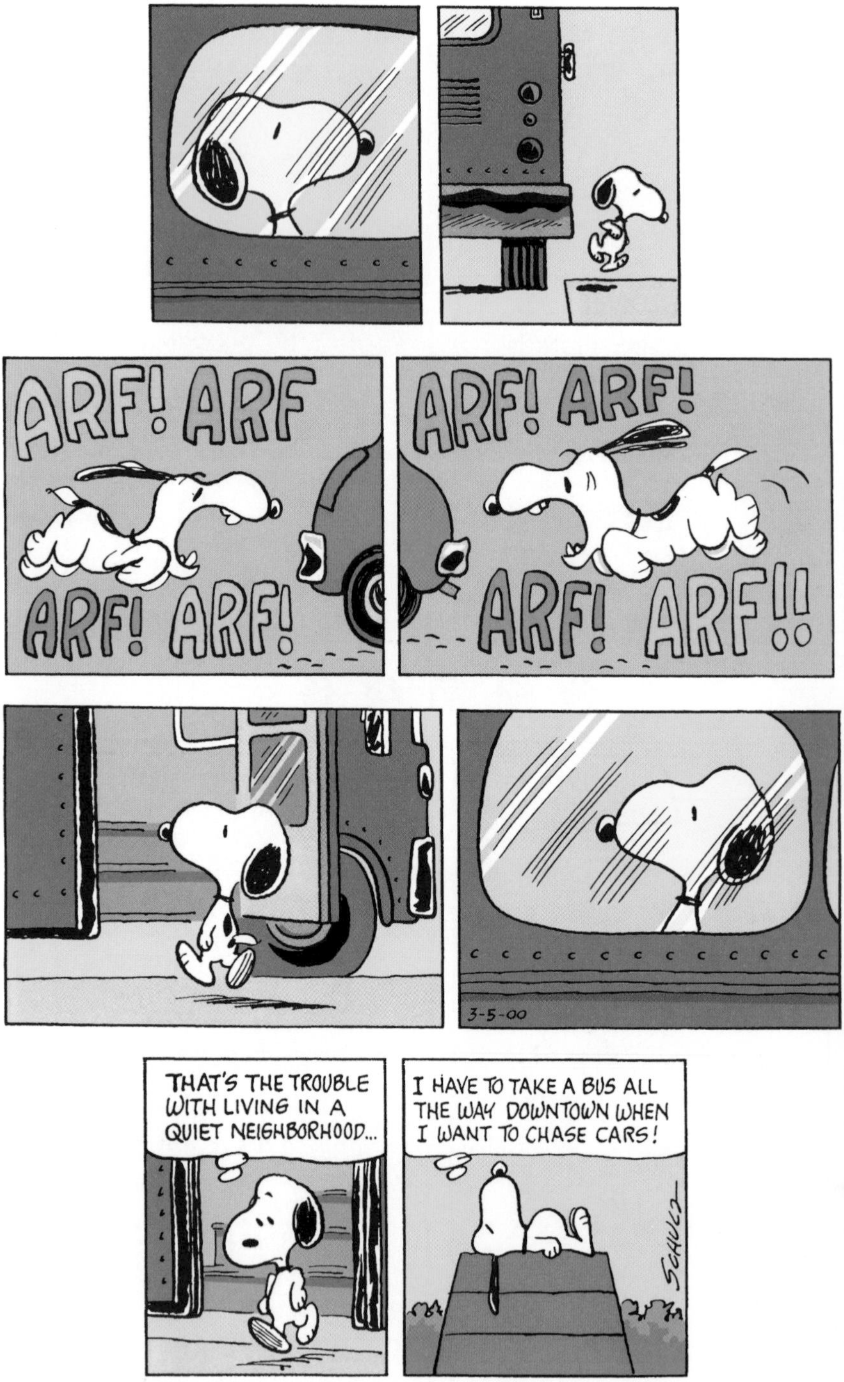
ARF! ARF
ARF! ARF!
ARF! ARF!
ARF! ARF!!
3-5-00
THAT'S THE TROUBLE WITH LIVING IN A QUIET NEIGHBORHOOD...
I HAVE TO TAKE A BUS ALL THE WAY DOWNTOWN WHEN I WANT TO CHASE CARS!
SCHULZ

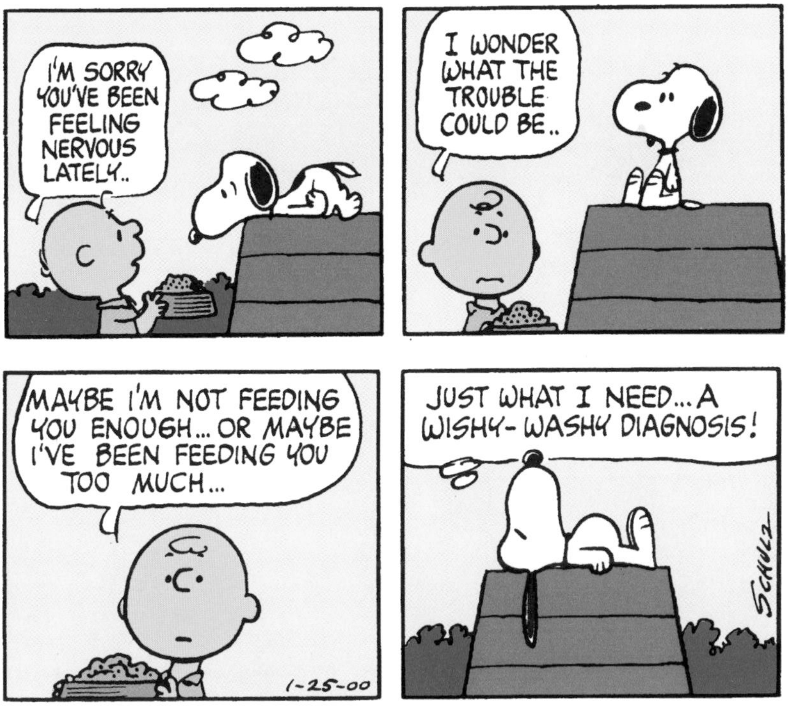
I'M SORRY YOU'VE BEEN FEELING NERVOUS LATELY..
I WONDER WHAT THE TROUBLE COULD BE..
MAYBE I'M NOT FEEDING YOU ENOUGH... OR MAYBE I'VE BEEN FEEDING YOU TOO MUCH...
1-25-00
JUST WHAT I NEED... A WISHY-WASHY DIAGNOSIS!
SCHULZ

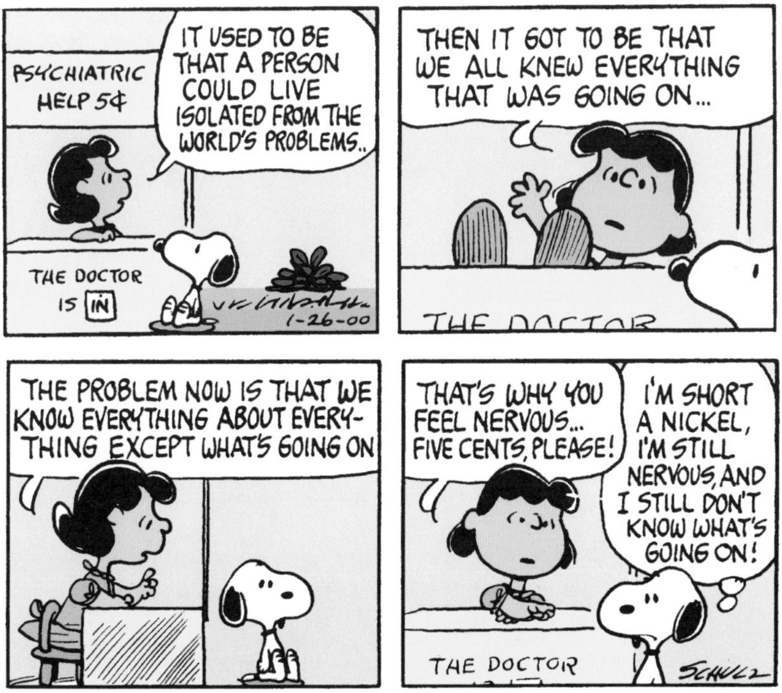
PSYCHIATRIC HELP 5¢
IT USED TO BE THAT A PERSON COULD LIVE ISOLATED FROM THE WORLD'S PROBLEMS..
THE DOCTOR IS IN
1-26-00
THEN IT GOT TO BE THAT WE ALL KNEW EVERYTHING THAT WAS GOING ON...
THE PROBLEM NOW IS THAT WE KNOW EVERYTHING ABOUT EVERYTHING EXCEPT WHAT'S GOING ON
THAT'S WHY YOU FEEL NERVOUS... FIVE CENTS, PLEASE!
I'M SHORT A NICKEL, I'M STILL NERVOUS, AND I STILL DON'T KNOW WHAT'S GOING ON!
THE DOCTOR
SCHULZ

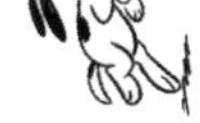

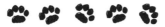

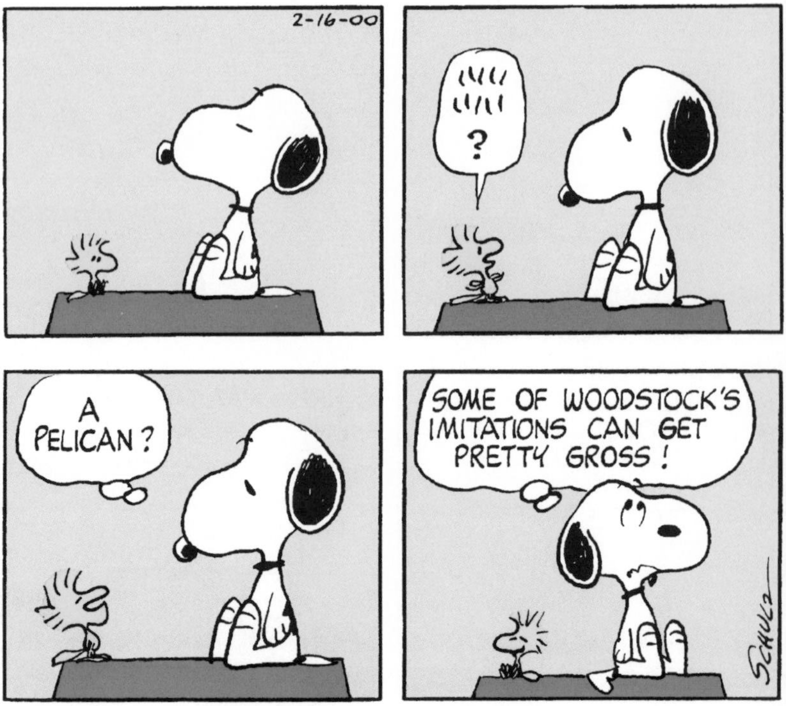
2-16-00
?
A PELICAN?
SOME OF WOODSTOCK'S IMITATIONS CAN GET PRETTY GROSS!
SCHULZ

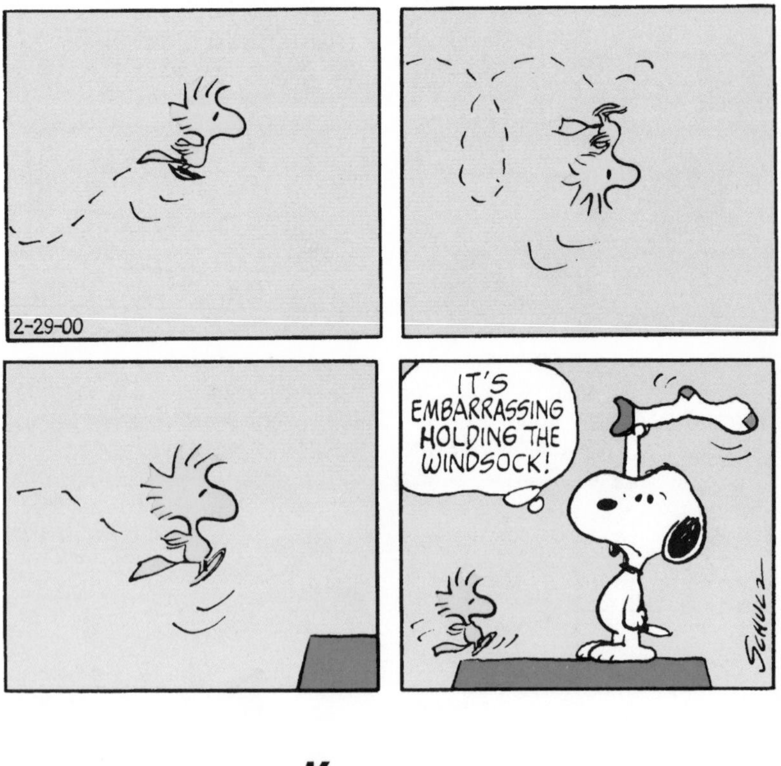
2-29-00
IT'S EMBARRASSING HOLDING THE WINDSOCK!
SCHULZ

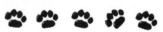

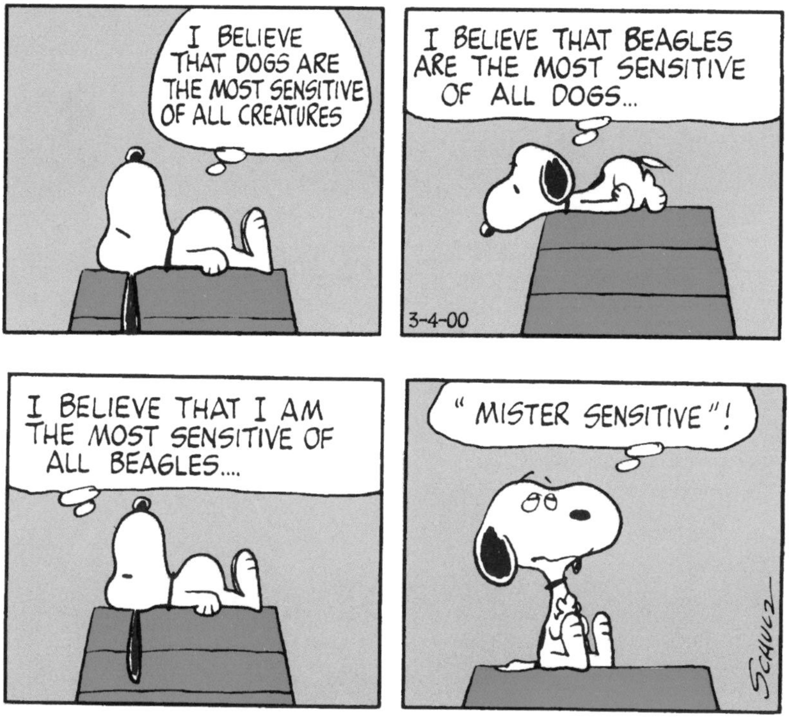
I BELIEVE THAT DOGS ARE THE MOST SENSITIVE OF ALL CREATURES
I BELIEVE THAT BEAGLES ARE THE MOST SENSITIVE OF ALL DOGS...
3-4-00
I BELIEVE THAT I AM THE MOST SENSITIVE OF ALL BEAGLES....
" MISTER SENSITIVE "!
SCHULZ

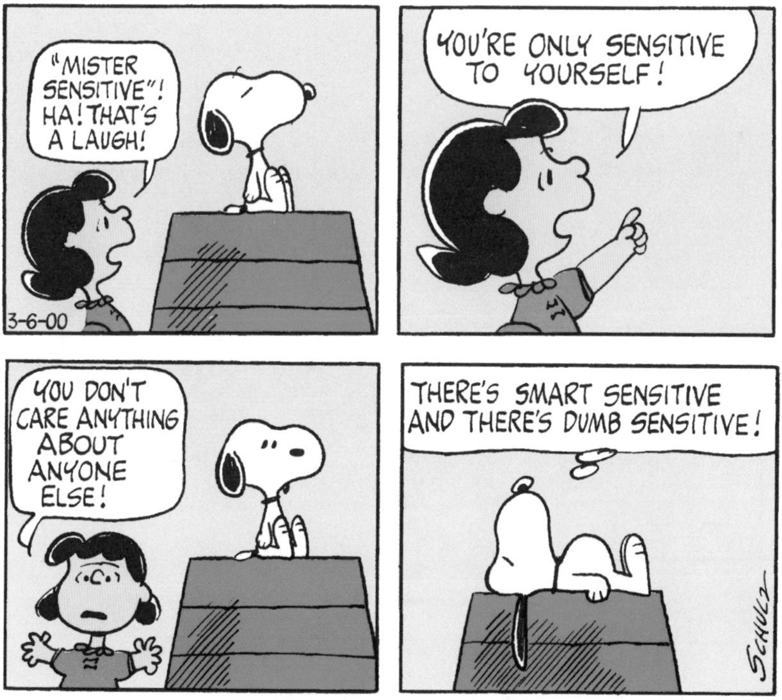
"MISTER SENSITIVE"! HA! THAT'S A LAUGH!
3-6-00
YOU'RE ONLY SENSITIVE TO YOURSELF!
YOU DON'T CARE ANYTHING ABOUT ANYONE ELSE!
THERE'S SMART SENSITIVE AND THERE'S DUMB SENSITIVE!
SCHULZ

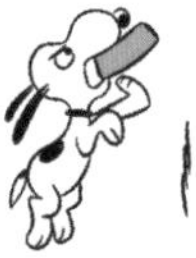

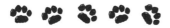

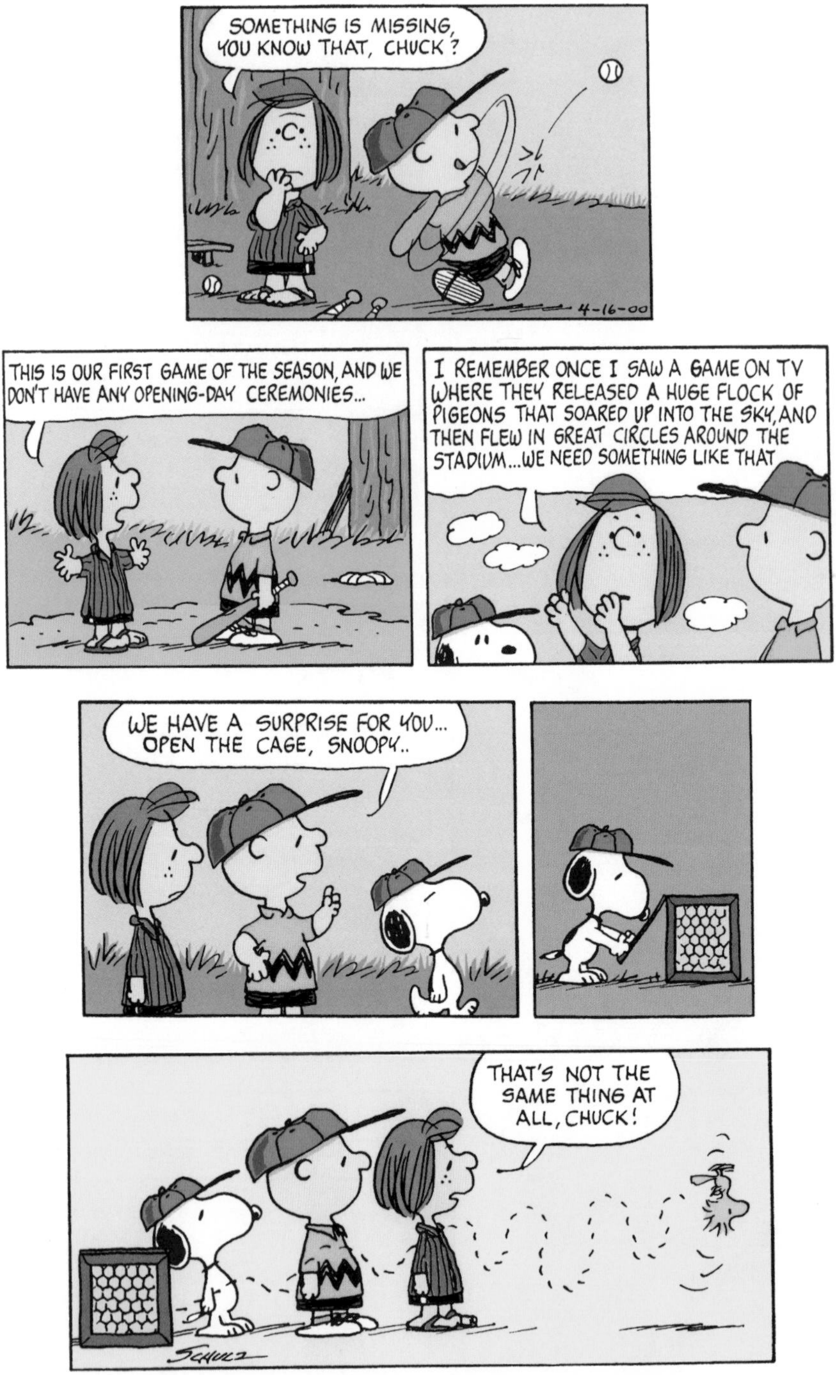
SOMETHING IS MISSING, YOU KNOW THAT, CHUCK?
4-16-00
THIS IS OUR FIRST GAME OF THE SEASON, AND WE DON'T HAVE ANY OPENING-DAY CEREMONIES...
I REMEMBER ONCE I SAW A GAME ON TV WHERE THEY RELEASED A HUGE FLOCK OF PIGEONS THAT SOARED UP INTO THE SKY, AND THEN FLEW IN GREAT CIRCLES AROUND THE STADIUM...WE NEED SOMETHING LIKE THAT
WE HAVE A SURPRISE FOR YOU... OPEN THE CAGE, SNOOPY..
THAT'S NOT THE SAME THING AT ALL, CHUCK!
SCHULZ

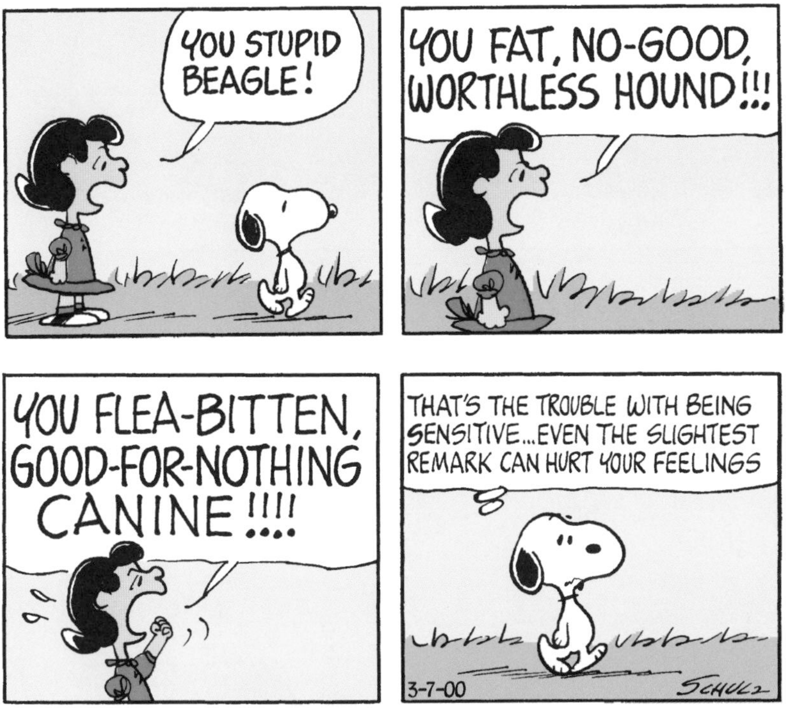
YOU STUPID BEAGLE!
YOU FAT, NO-GOOD, WORTHLESS HOUND!!!
YOU FLEA-BITTEN, GOOD-FOR-NOTHING CANINE!!!!
THAT'S THE TROUBLE WITH BEING SENSITIVE...EVEN THE SLIGHTEST REMARK CAN HURT YOUR FEELINGS
3-7-00
SCHULZ

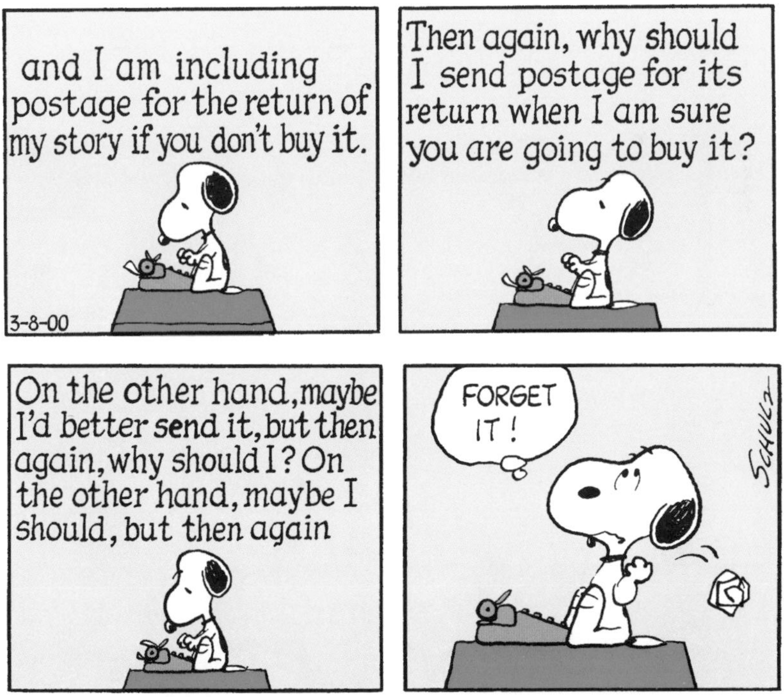
and I am including postage for the return of my story if you don't buy it.
3-8-00
Then again, why should I send postage for its return when I am sure you are going to buy it?
On the other hand, maybe I'd better send it, but then again, why should I? On the other hand, maybe I should, but then again
FORGET IT!
SCHULZ

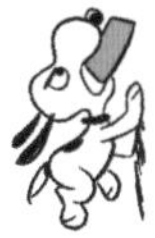

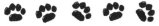

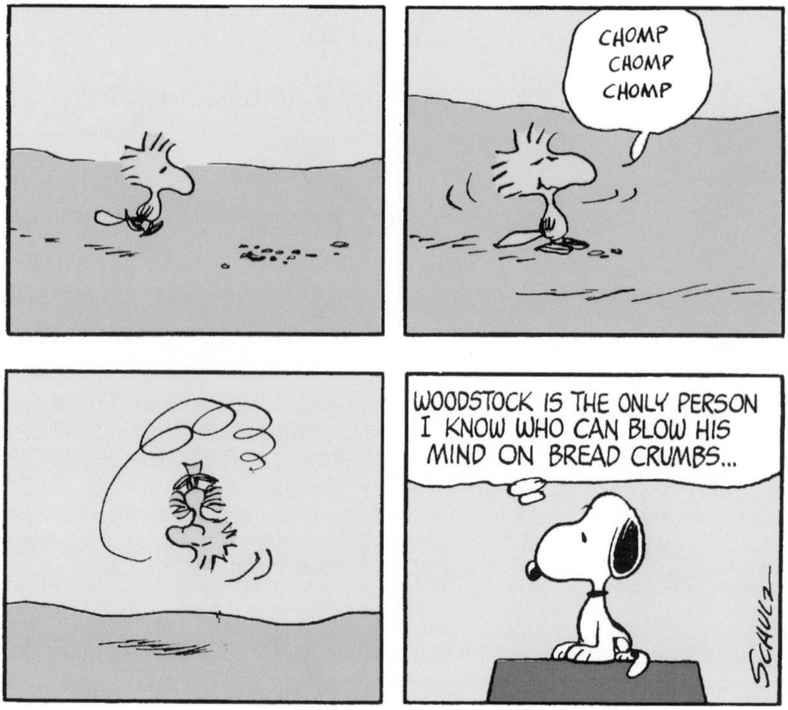
CHOMP CHOMP CHOMP
WOODSTOCK IS THE ONLY PERSON I KNOW WHO CAN BLOW HIS MIND ON BREAD CRUMBS...
SCHULZ

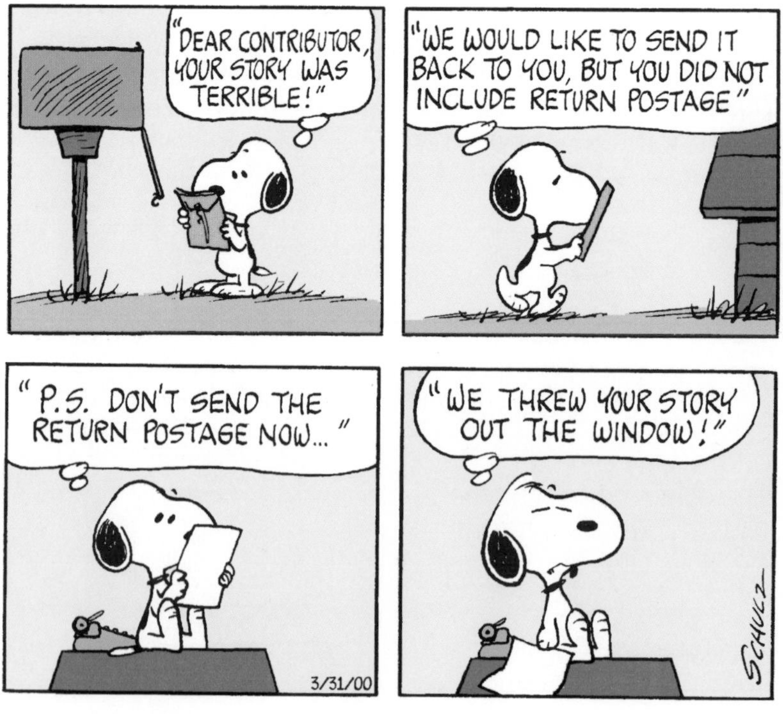
"DEAR CONTRIBUTOR, YOUR STORY WAS TERRIBLE!"
"WE WOULD LIKE TO SEND IT BACK TO YOU, BUT YOU DID NOT INCLUDE RETURN POSTAGE"
" P.S. DON'T SEND THE RETURN POSTAGE NOW... "
3/31/00
"WE THREW YOUR STORY OUT THE WINDOW!"
SCHULZ

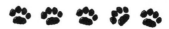

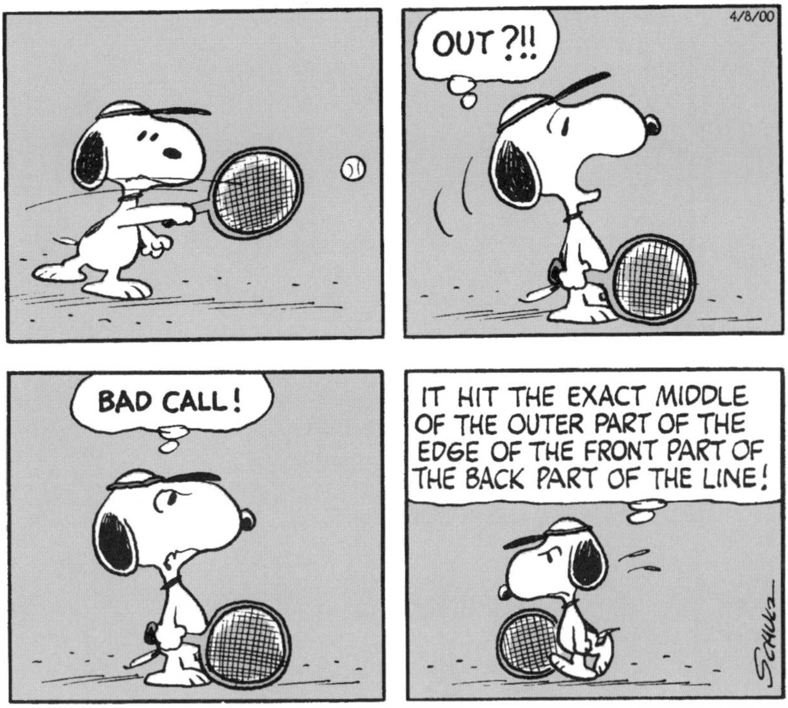
4/8/00
OUT ?!!
BAD CALL!
IT HIT THE EXACT MIDDLE OF THE OUTER PART OF THE EDGE OF THE FRONT PART OF THE BACK PART OF THE LINE!
SCHULZ

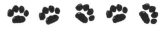

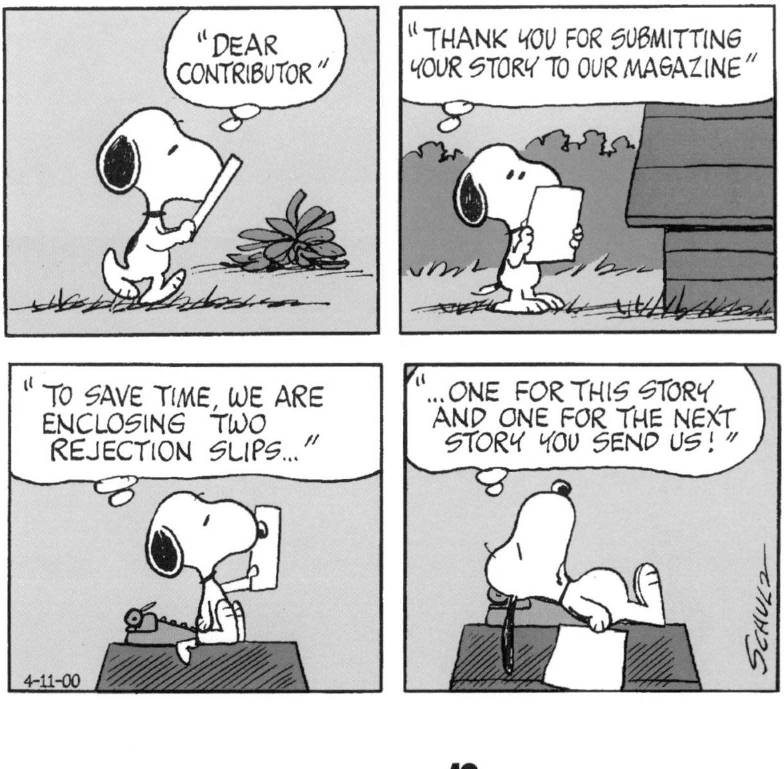
"DEAR CONTRIBUTOR"
"THANK YOU FOR SUBMITTING YOUR STORY TO OUR MAGAZINE"
"TO SAVE TIME, WE ARE ENCLOSING TWO REJECTION SLIPS..."
"...ONE FOR THIS STORY AND ONE FOR THE NEXT STORY YOU SEND US!"
4-11-00
SCHULZ

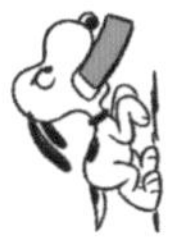

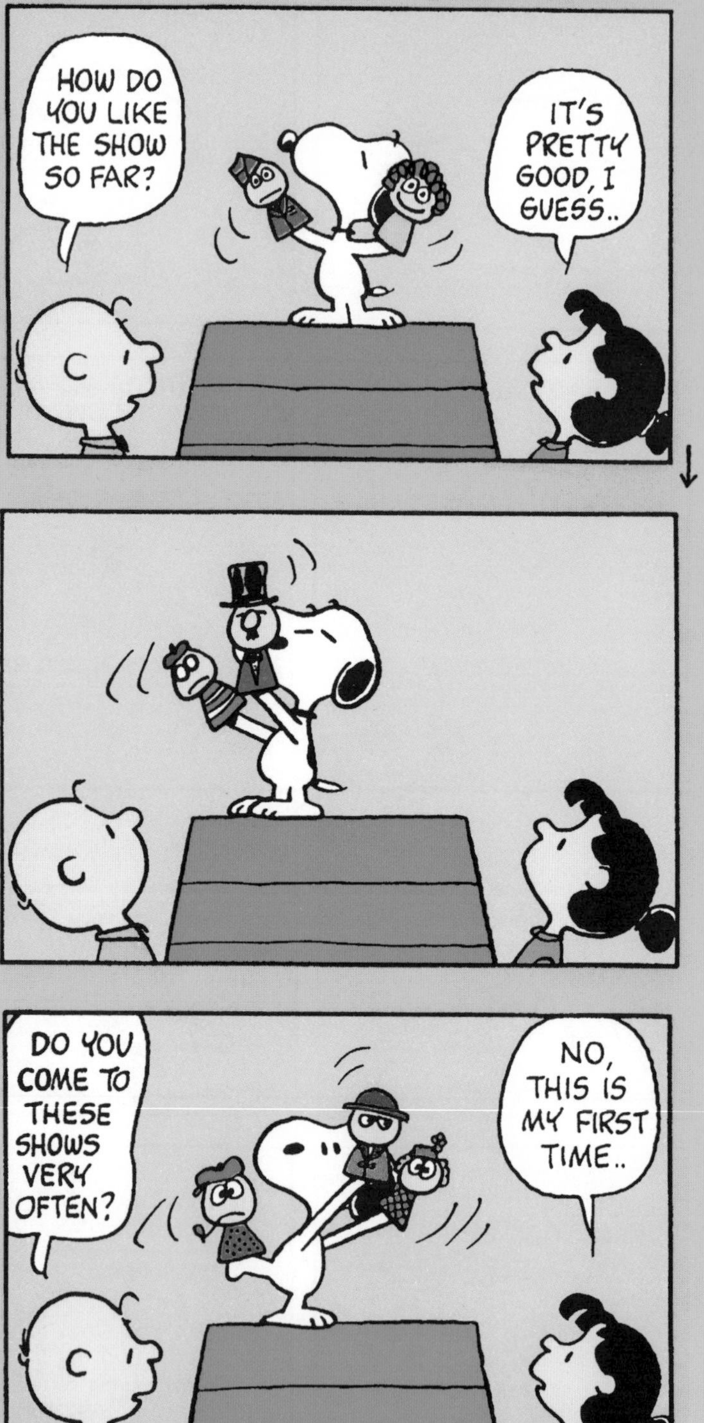
HOW DO YOU LIKE THE SHOW SO FAR?
IT'S PRETTY GOOD, I GUESS..
DO YOU COME TO THESE SHOWS VERY OFTEN?
NO, THIS IS MY FIRST TIME..

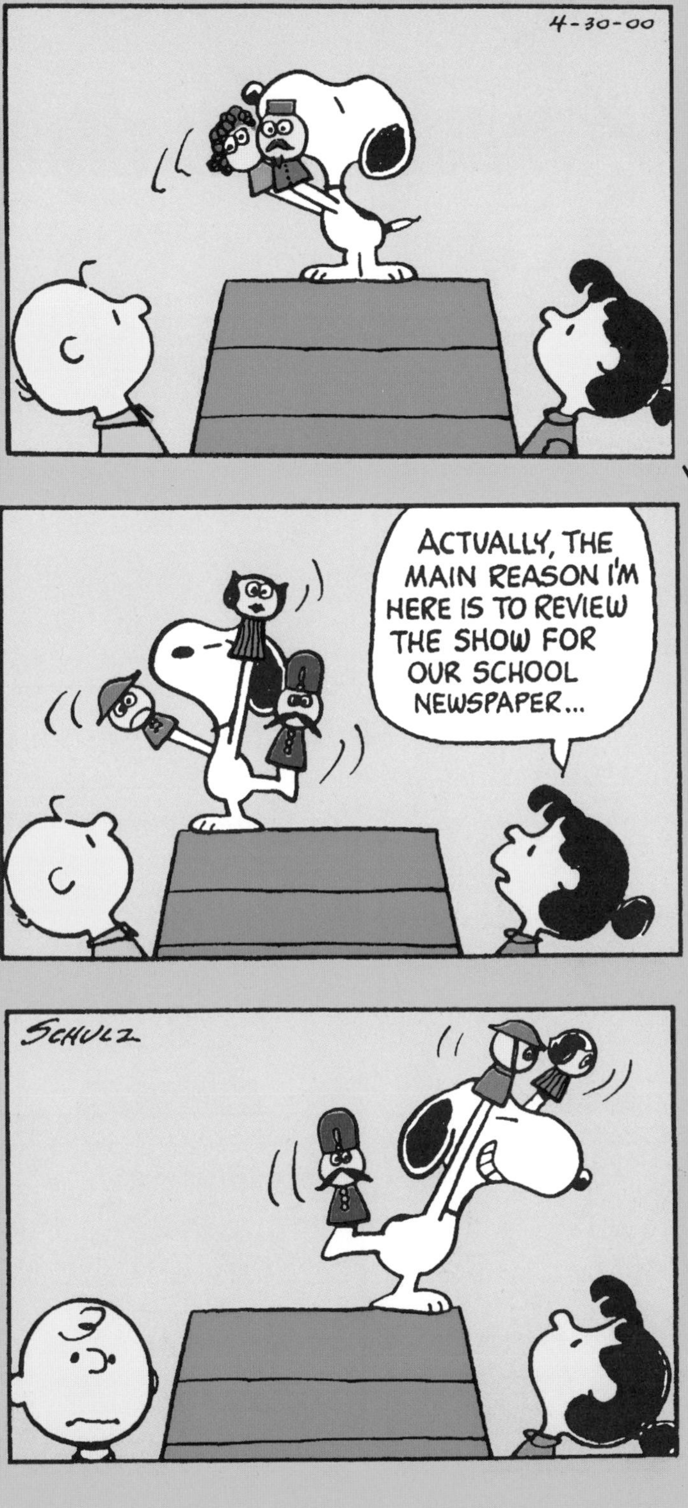
4-30-00
ACTUALLY, THE MAIN REASON I'M HERE IS TO REVIEW THE SHOW FOR OUR SCHOOL NEWSPAPER...
SCHULZ

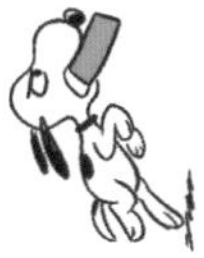

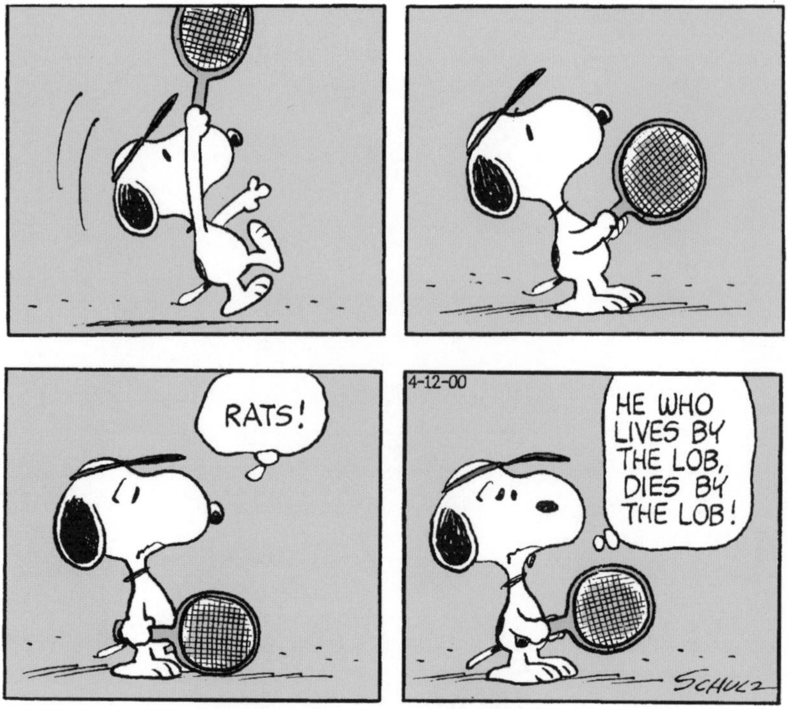
RATS!
4-12-00
HE WHO LIVES BY THE LOB, DIES BY THE LOB!
SCHULZ

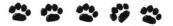

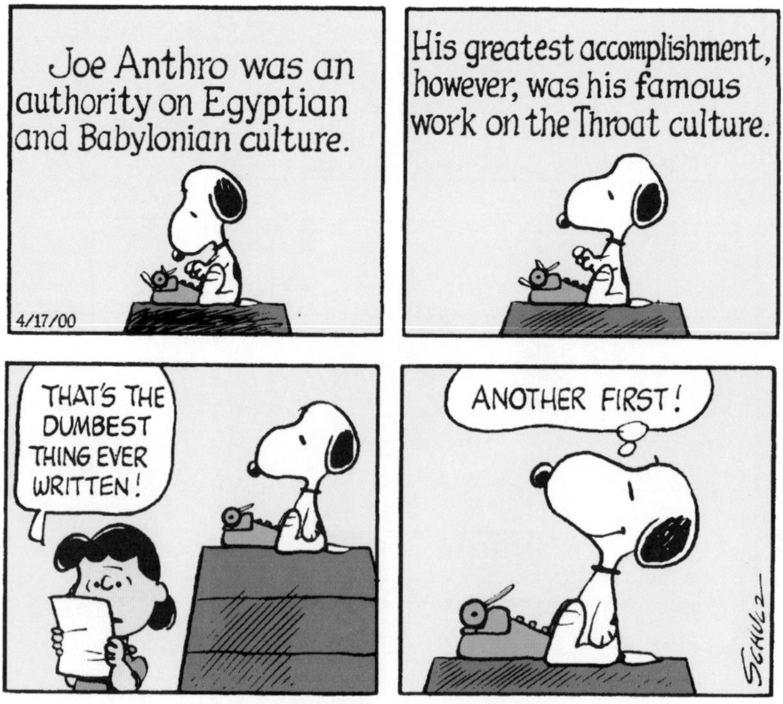
Joe Anthro was an authority on Egyptian and Babylonian culture.
4/17/00
His greatest accomplishment, however, was his famous work on the Throat culture.
THAT'S THE DUMBEST THING EVER WRITTEN!
ANOTHER FIRST!
SCHULZ

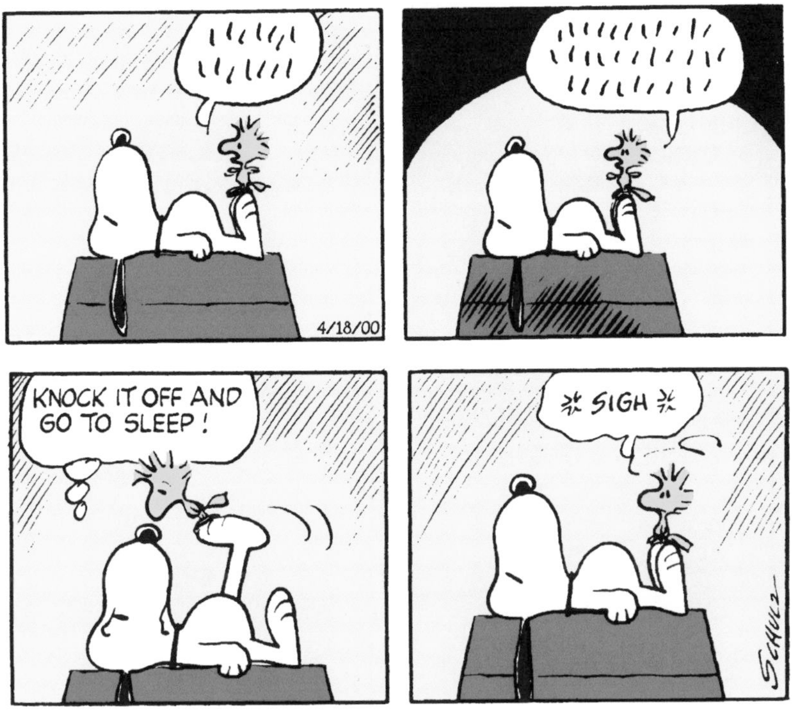
4/18/00
KNOCK IT OFF AND GO TO SLEEP!
SIGH
SCHULZ

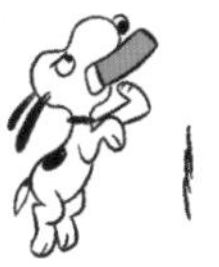

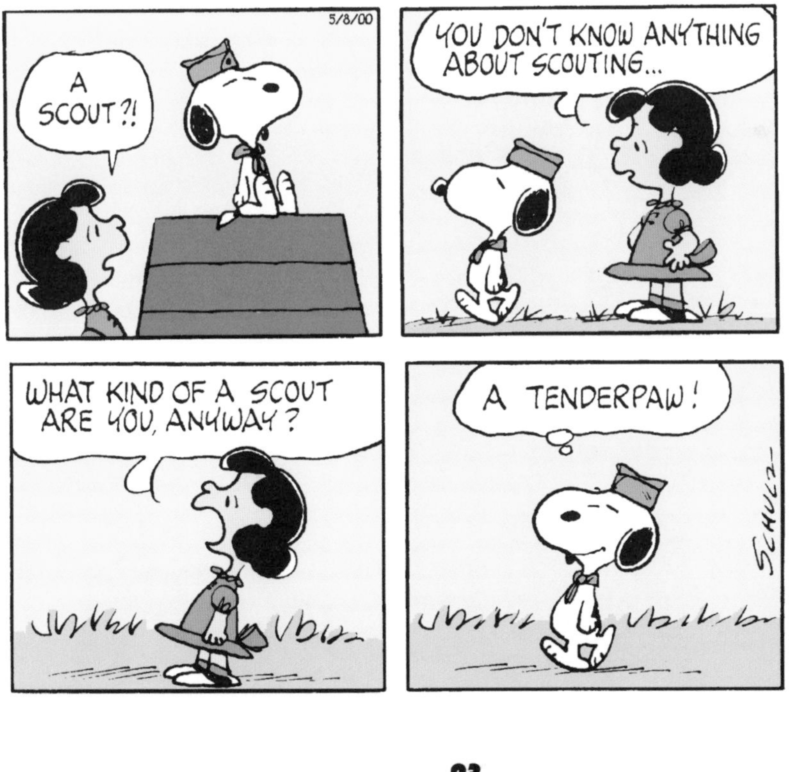
5/8/00
A SCOUT?!
YOU DON'T KNOW ANYTHING ABOUT SCOUTING...
WHAT KIND OF A SCOUT ARE YOU, ANYWAY?
A TENDERPAW!
SCHULZ

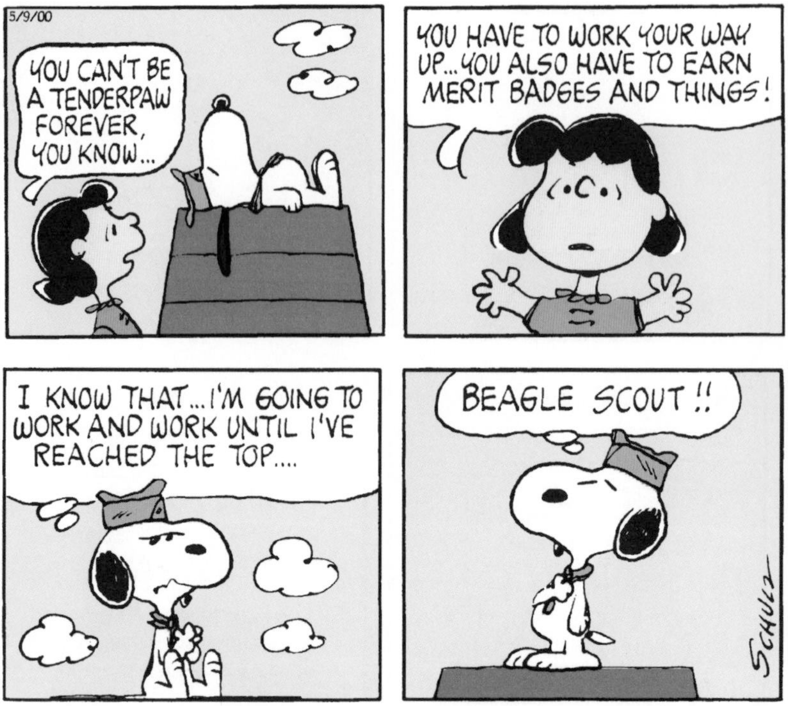
5/9/00
YOU CAN'T BE A TENDERPAW FOREVER, YOU KNOW...
YOU HAVE TO WORK YOUR WAY UP...YOU ALSO HAVE TO EARN MERIT BADGES AND THINGS!
I KNOW THAT...I'M GOING TO WORK AND WORK UNTIL I'VE REACHED THE TOP....
BEAGLE SCOUT!!
SCHULZ

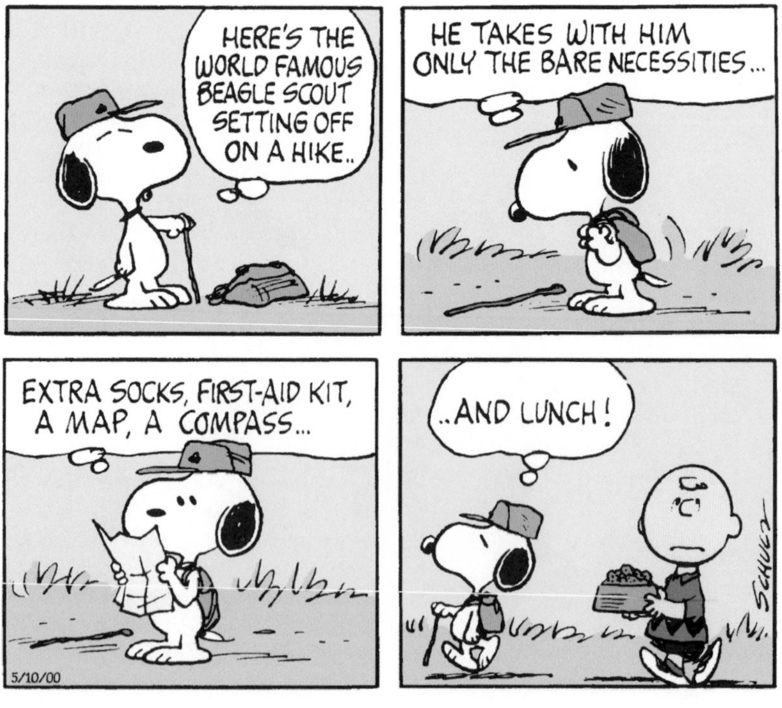
HERE'S THE WORLD FAMOUS BEAGLE SCOUT SETTING OFF ON A HIKE..
HE TAKES WITH HIM ONLY THE BARE NECESSITIES...
EXTRA SOCKS, FIRST-AID KIT, A MAP, A COMPASS...
..AND LUNCH!
SCHULZ
5/10/00

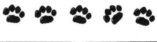

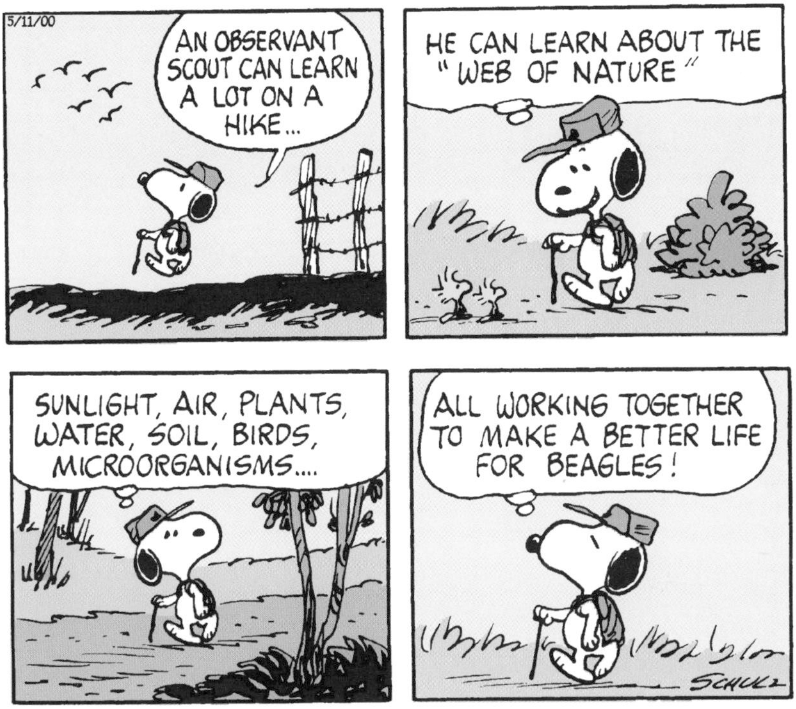
5/11/00
AN OBSERVANT SCOUT CAN LEARN A LOT ON A HIKE...
HE CAN LEARN ABOUT THE "WEB OF NATURE"
SUNLIGHT, AIR, PLANTS, WATER, SOIL, BIRDS, MICROORGANISMS....
ALL WORKING TOGETHER TO MAKE A BETTER LIFE FOR BEAGLES!
SCHULZ

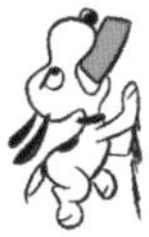

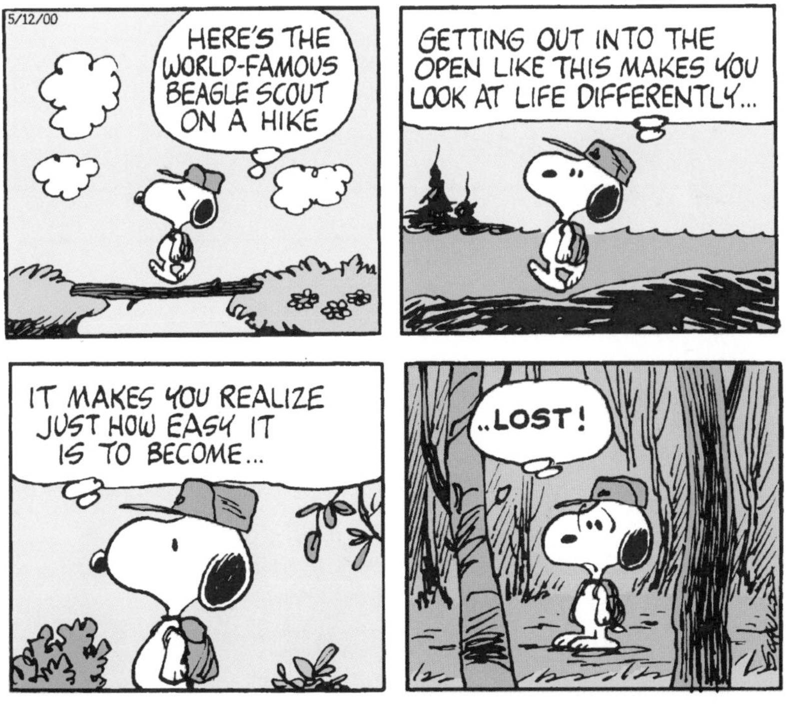
5/12/00
HERE'S THE WORLD-FAMOUS BEAGLE SCOUT ON A HIKE
GETTING OUT INTO THE OPEN LIKE THIS MAKES YOU LOOK AT LIFE DIFFERENTLY...
IT MAKES YOU REALIZE JUST HOW EASY IT IS TO BECOME...
..LOST!

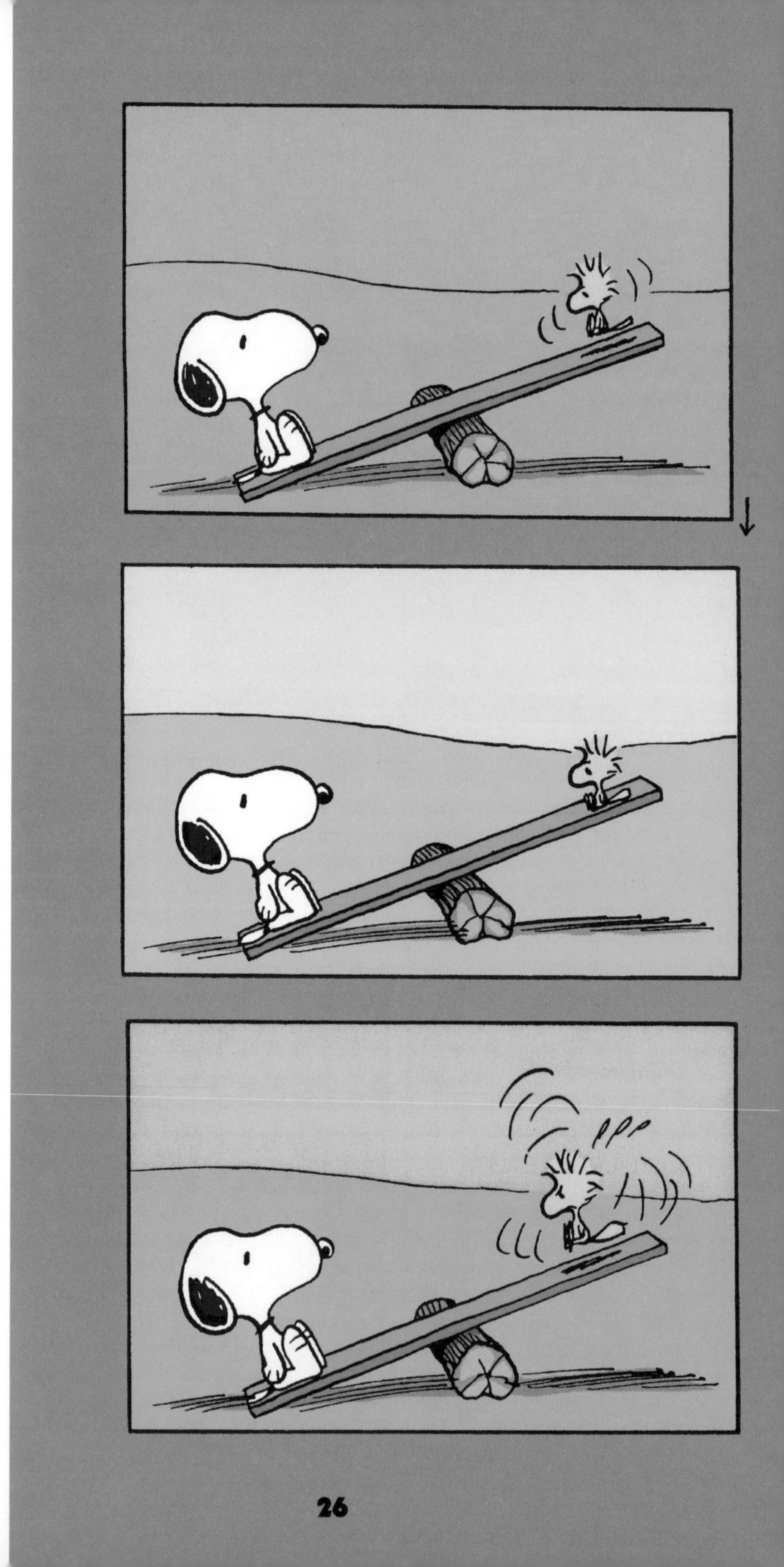

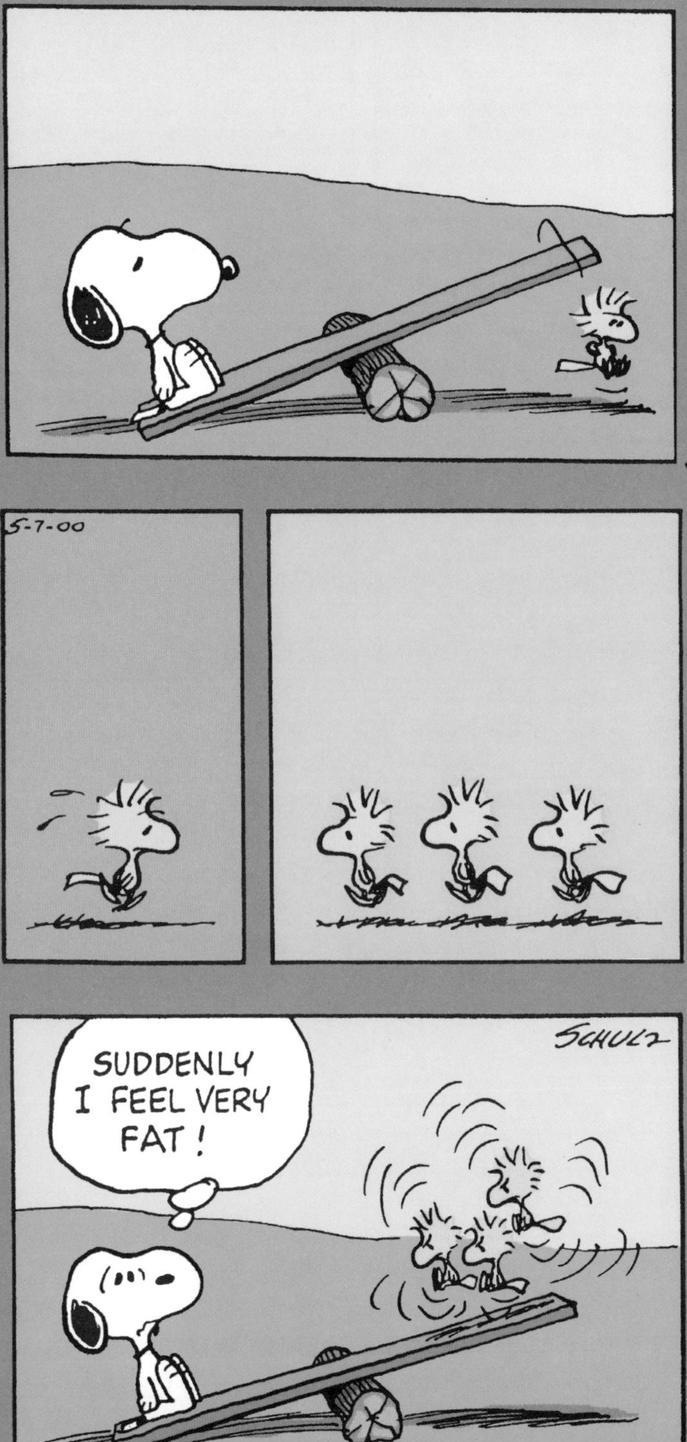
5-7-00
SUDDENLY I FEEL VERY FAT!
SCHULZ

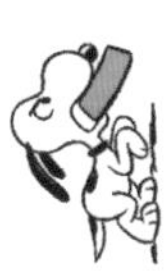

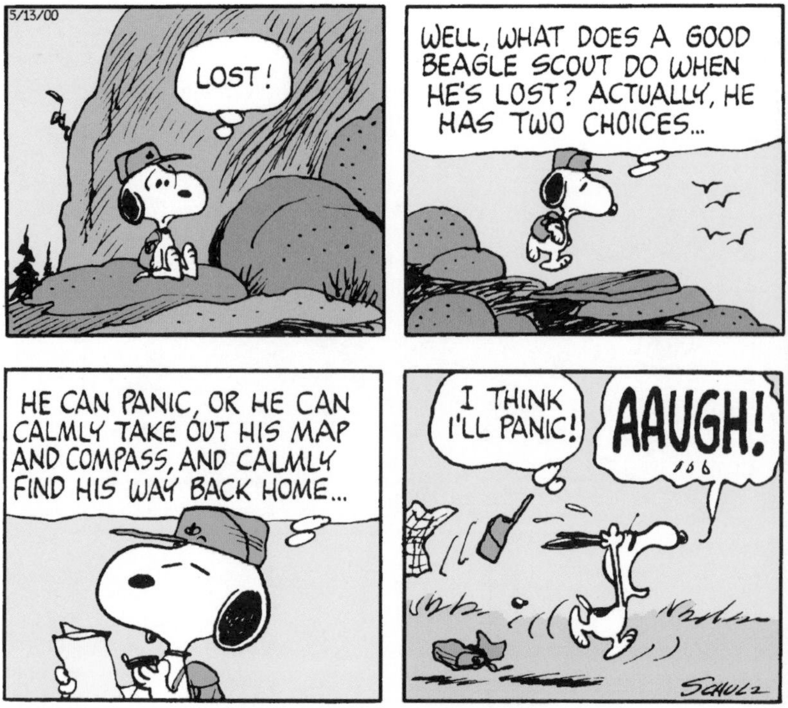
5/13/00
LOST!
WELL, WHAT DOES A GOOD BEAGLE SCOUT DO WHEN HE'S LOST? ACTUALLY, HE HAS TWO CHOICES...
HE CAN PANIC, OR HE CAN CALMLY TAKE OUT HIS MAP AND COMPASS, AND CALMLY FIND HIS WAY BACK HOME...
I THINK I'LL PANIC!
AAUGH!
SCHULZ

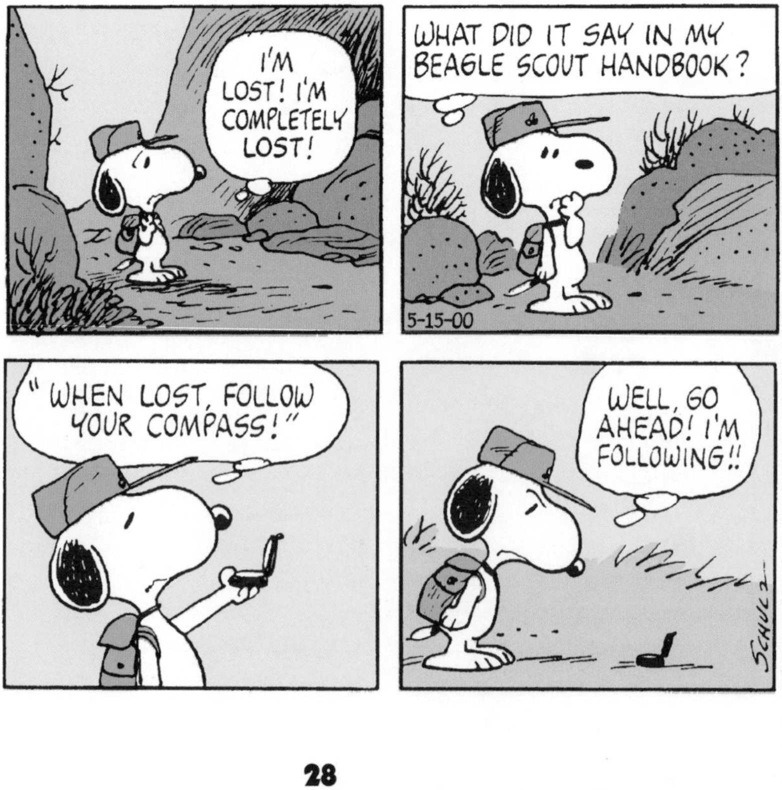
I'M LOST! I'M COMPLETELY LOST!
WHAT DID IT SAY IN MY BEAGLE SCOUT HANDBOOK?
5-15-00
"WHEN LOST, FOLLOW YOUR COMPASS!"
WELL, GO AHEAD! I'M FOLLOWING!!
SCHULZ

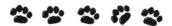

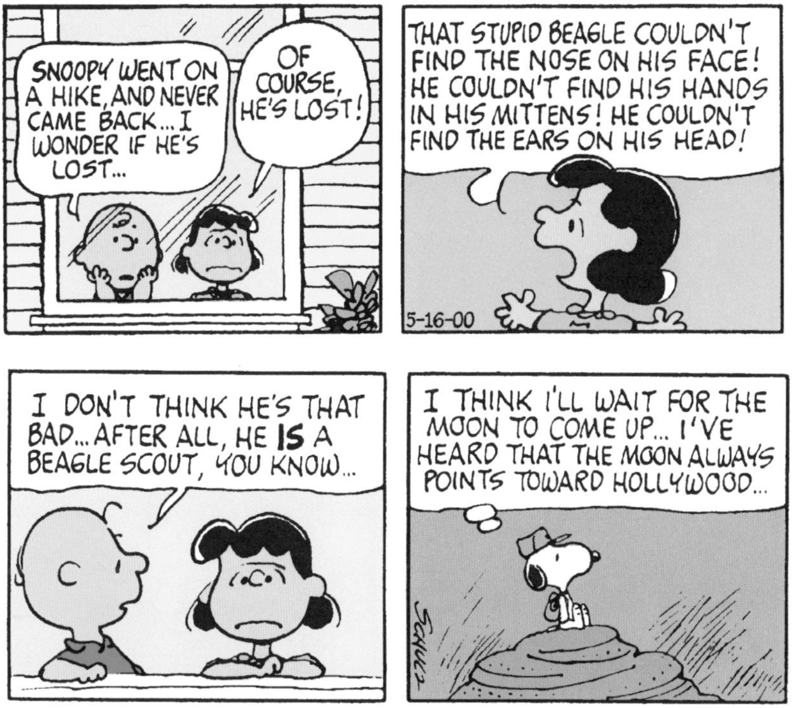
SNOOPY WENT ON A HIKE, AND NEVER CAME BACK... I WONDER IF HE'S LOST...
OF COURSE, HE'S LOST!
THAT STUPID BEAGLE COULDN'T FIND THE NOSE ON HIS FACE! HE COULDN'T FIND HIS HANDS IN HIS MITTENS! HE COULDN'T FIND THE EARS ON HIS HEAD!
5-16-00
I DON'T THINK HE'S THAT BAD... AFTER ALL, HE IS A BEAGLE SCOUT, YOU KNOW...
I THINK I'LL WAIT FOR THE MOON TO COME UP... I'VE HEARD THAT THE MOON ALWAYS POINTS TOWARD HOLLYWOOD...
SCHULZ

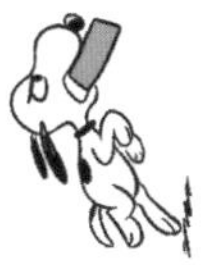

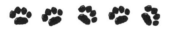

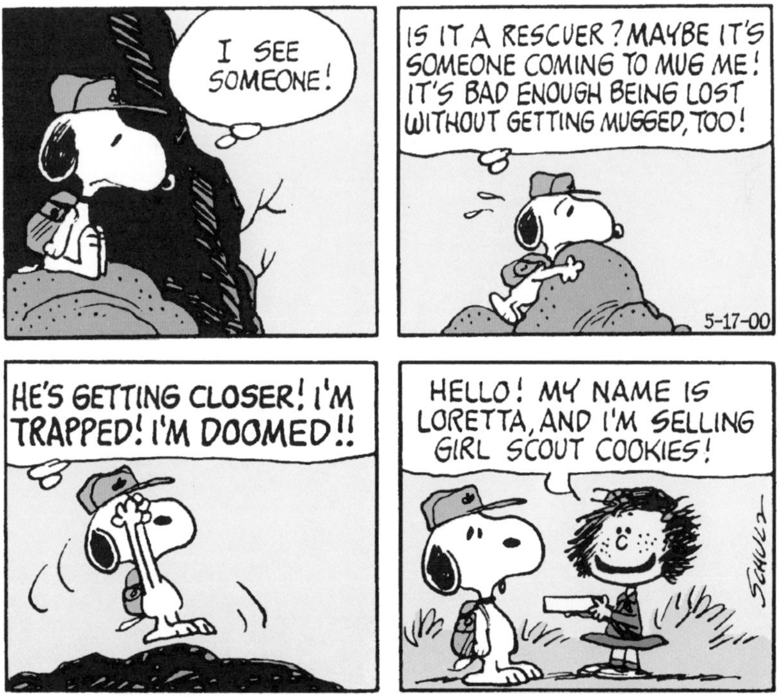
I SEE SOMEONE!
IS IT A RESCUER? MAYBE IT'S SOMEONE COMING TO MUG ME! IT'S BAD ENOUGH BEING LOST WITHOUT GETTING MUGGED, TOO!
5-17-00
HE'S GETTING CLOSER! I'M TRAPPED! I'M DOOMED!!
HELLO! MY NAME IS LORETTA, AND I'M SELLING GIRL SCOUT COOKIES!
SCHULZ

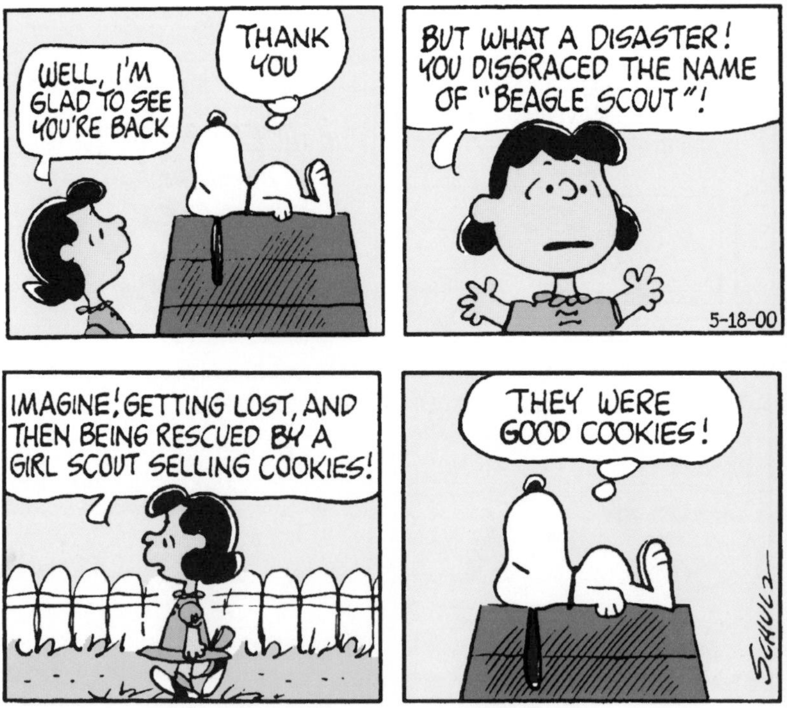
WELL, I'M GLAD TO SEE YOU'RE BACK
THANK YOU
BUT WHAT A DISASTER! YOU DISGRACED THE NAME OF "BEAGLE SCOUT"!
5-18-00
IMAGINE! GETTING LOST, AND THEN BEING RESCUED BY A GIRL SCOUT SELLING COOKIES!
THEY WERE GOOD COOKIES!
SCHULZ

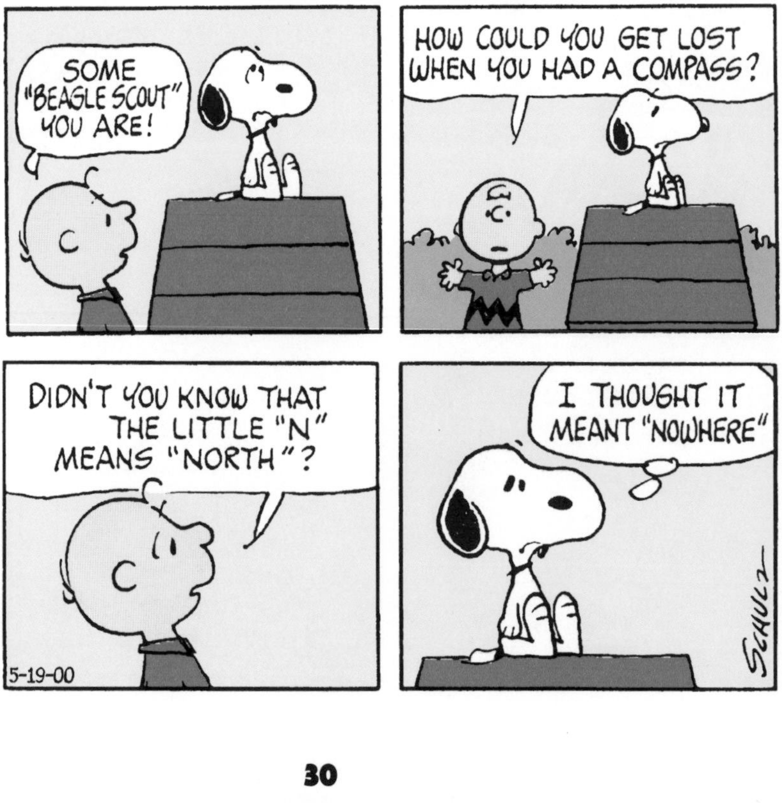
SOME "BEAGLE SCOUT" YOU ARE!
HOW COULD YOU GET LOST WHEN YOU HAD A COMPASS?
DIDN'T YOU KNOW THAT THE LITTLE "N" MEANS "NORTH"?
5-19-00
I THOUGHT IT MEANT "NOWHERE"
SCHULZ

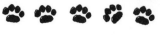

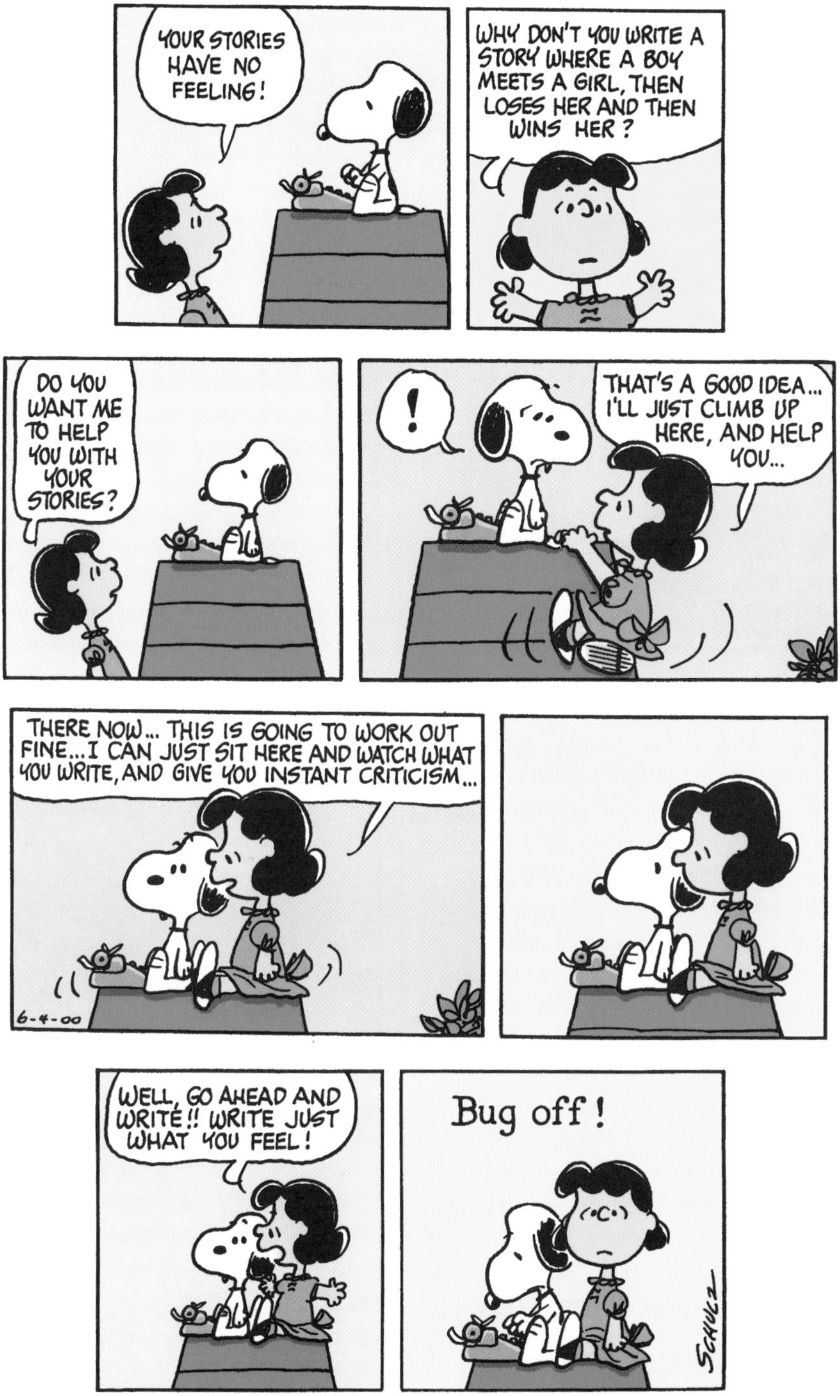
YOUR STORIES HAVE NO FEELING!
WHY DON'T YOU WRITE A STORY WHERE A BOY MEETS A GIRL, THEN LOSES HER AND THEN WINS HER?
DO YOU WANT ME TO HELP YOU WITH YOUR STORIES?
!
THAT'S A GOOD IDEA... I'LL JUST CLIMB UP HERE, AND HELP YOU...
THERE NOW... THIS IS GOING TO WORK OUT FINE... I CAN JUST SIT HERE AND WATCH WHAT YOU WRITE, AND GIVE YOU INSTANT CRITICISM...
6-4-00
WELL, GO AHEAD AND WRITE!! WRITE JUST WHAT YOU FEEL!
Bug off!
SCHULZ

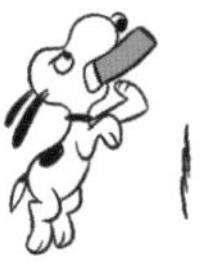

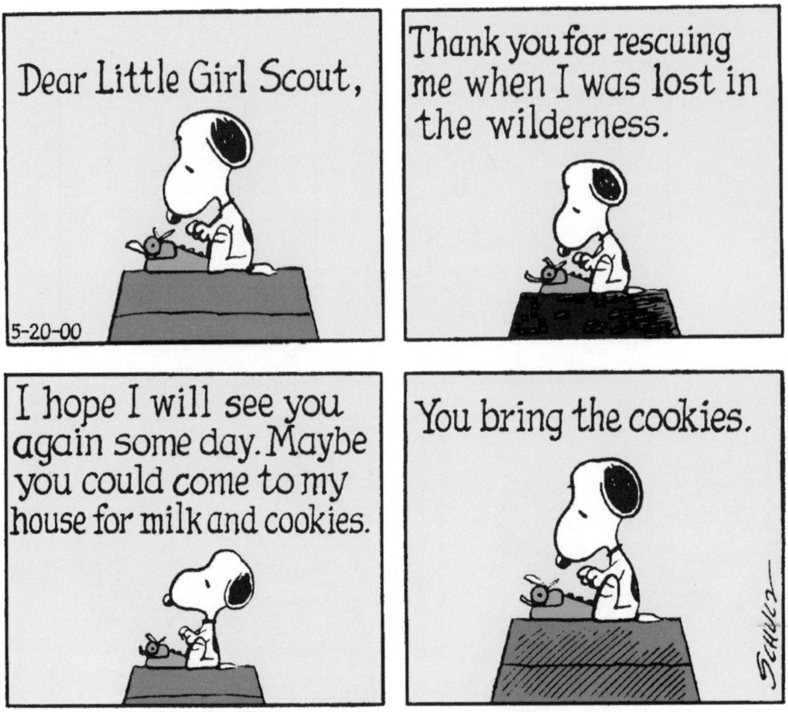
Dear Little Girl Scout,
5-20-00
Thank you for rescuing me when I was lost in the wilderness.
I hope I will see you again some day. Maybe you could come to my house for milk and cookies.
You bring the cookies.
SCHULZ

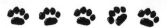

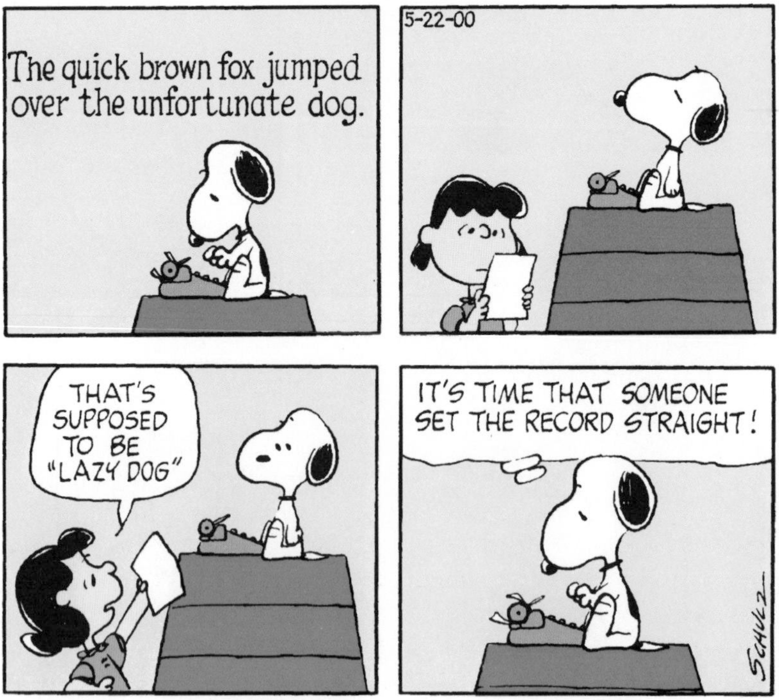
The quick brown fox jumped over the unfortunate dog.
5-22-00
THAT'S SUPPOSED TO BE "LAZY DOG"
IT'S TIME THAT SOMEONE SET THE RECORD STRAIGHT!
SCHULZ

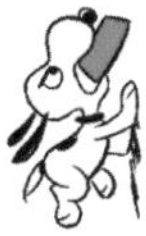

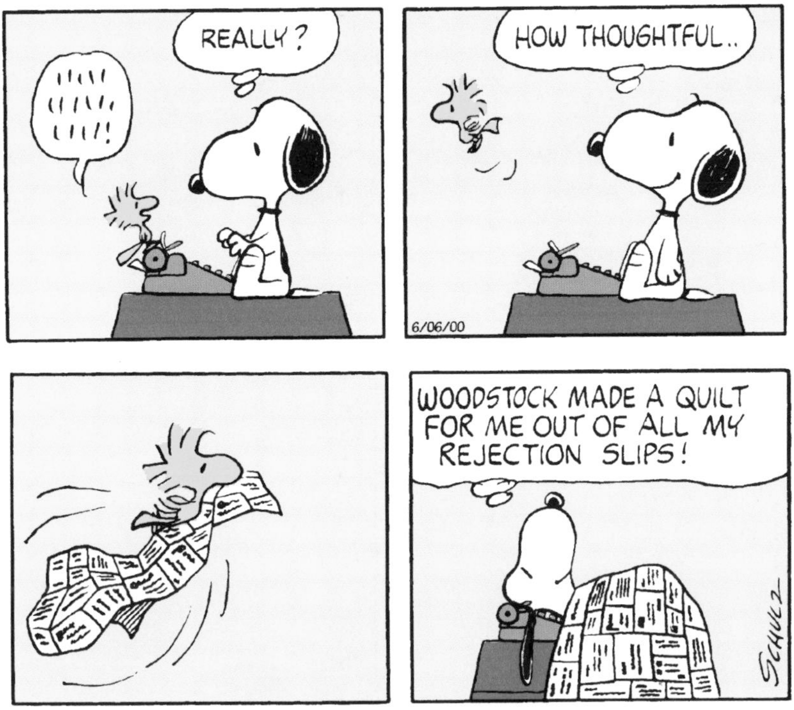
REALLY?
HOW THOUGHTFUL..
6/06/00
WOODSTOCK MADE A QUILT FOR ME OUT OF ALL MY REJECTION SLIPS!
SCHULZ

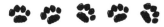

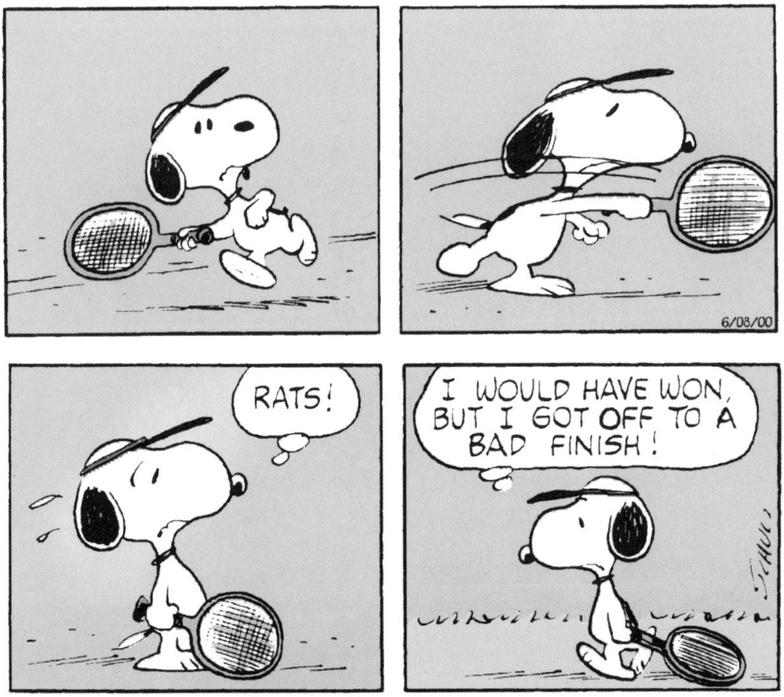
6/08/00
RATS!
I WOULD HAVE WON, BUT I GOT OFF TO A BAD FINISH!
SCHULZ

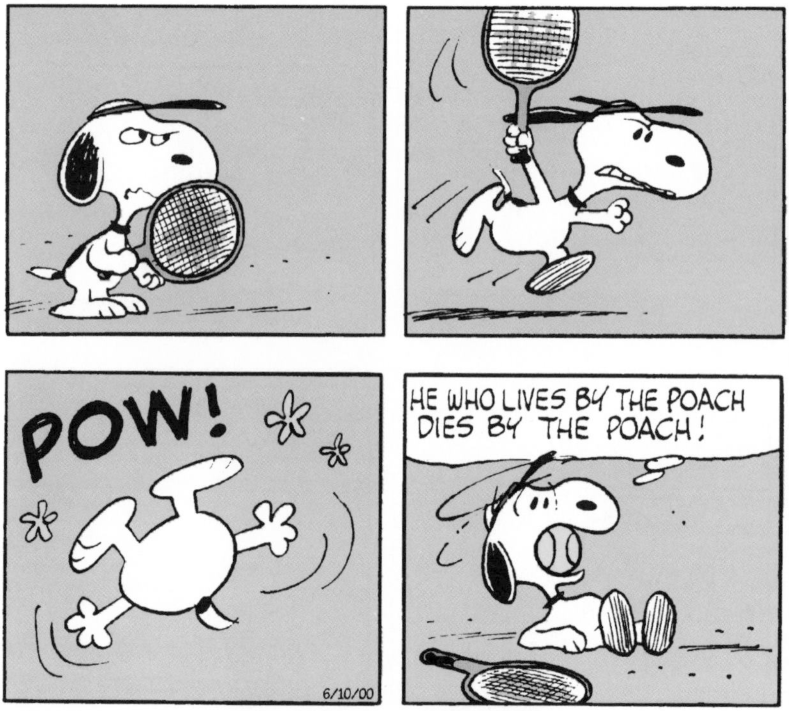
POW!
HE WHO LIVES BY THE POACH DIES BY THE POACH!
6/10/00

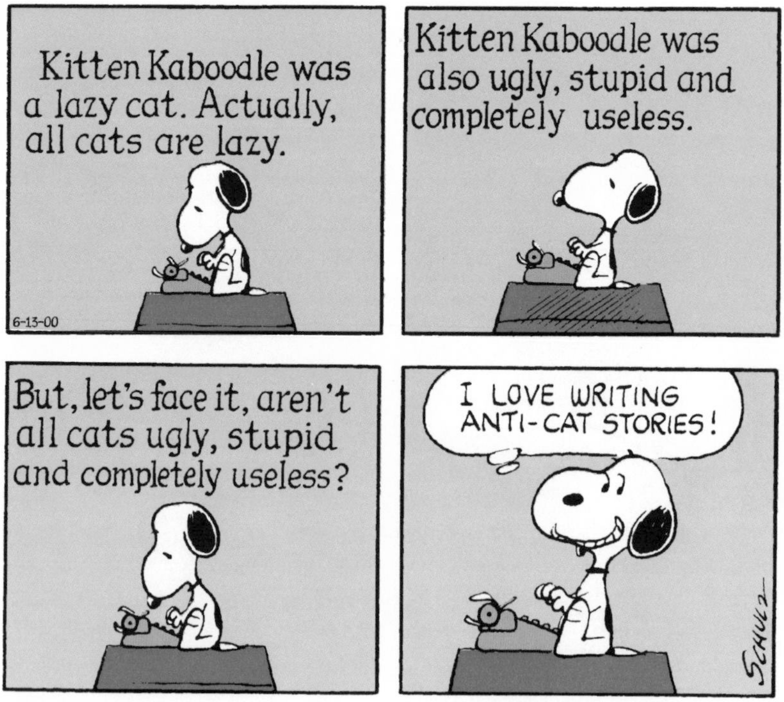
Kitten Kaboodle was a lazy cat. Actually, all cats are lazy.
6-13-00
Kitten Kaboodle was also ugly, stupid and completely useless.
But, let's face it, aren't all cats ugly, stupid and completely useless?
I LOVE WRITING ANTI-CAT STORIES!
SCHULZ

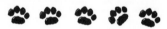

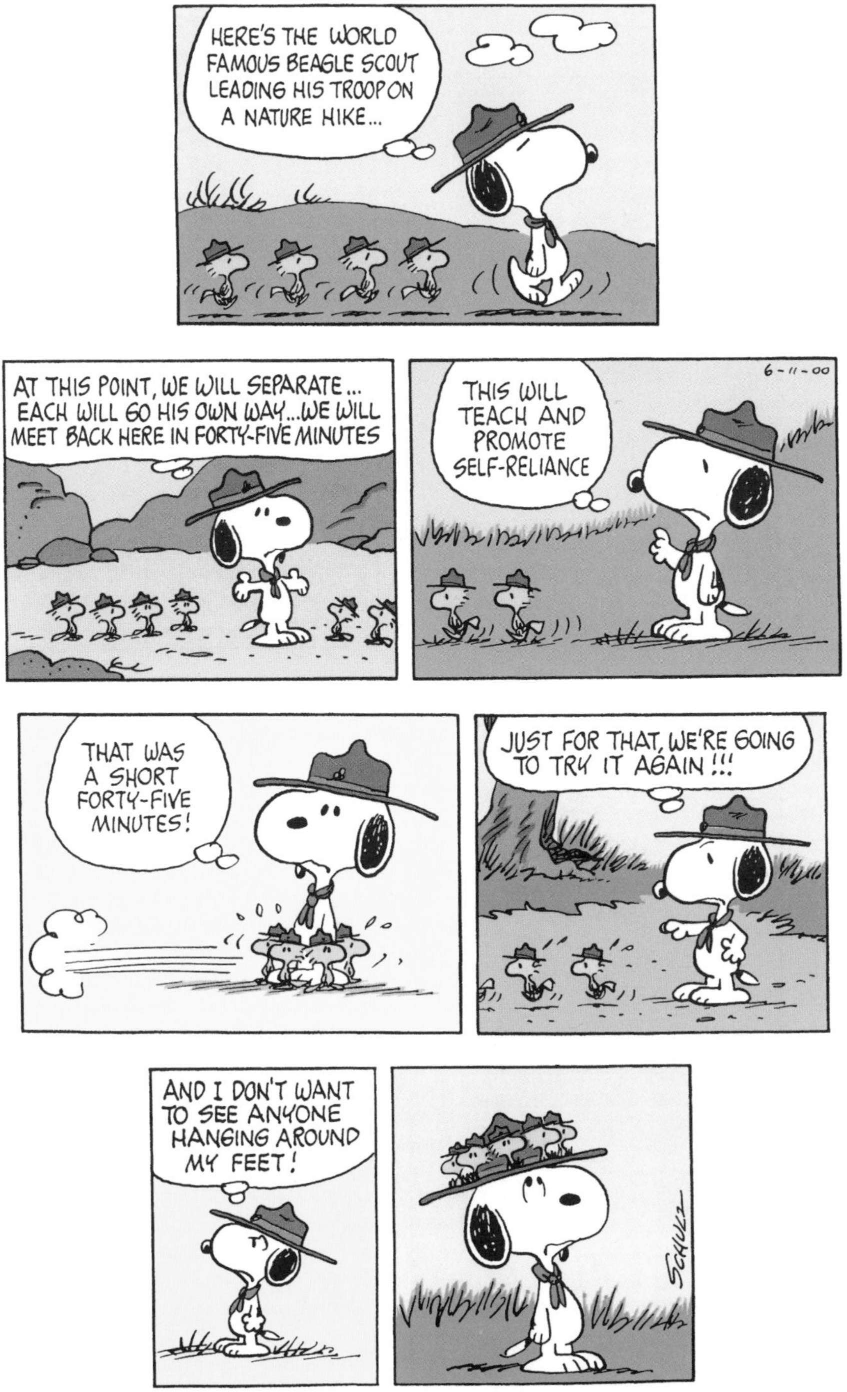
HERE'S THE WORLD FAMOUS BEAGLE SCOUT LEADING HIS TROOP ON A NATURE HIKE...
AT THIS POINT, WE WILL SEPARATE... EACH WILL GO HIS OWN WAY...WE WILL MEET BACK HERE IN FORTY-FIVE MINUTES
6-11-00
THIS WILL TEACH AND PROMOTE SELF-RELIANCE
THAT WAS A SHORT FORTY-FIVE MINUTES!
JUST FOR THAT, WE'RE GOING TO TRY IT AGAIN!!!
AND I DON'T WANT TO SEE ANYONE HANGING AROUND MY FEET!

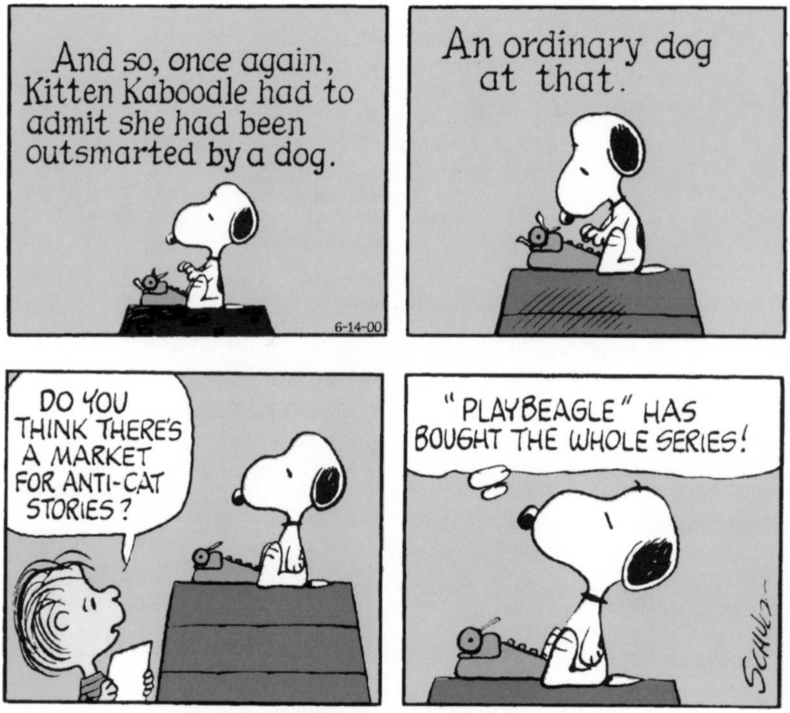
And so, once again, Kitten Kaboodle had to admit she had been outsmarted by a dog.
6-14-00
An ordinary dog at that.
DO YOU THINK THERE'S A MARKET FOR ANTI-CAT STORIES?
"PLAYBEAGLE" HAS BOUGHT THE WHOLE SERIES!
SCHULZ

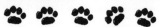

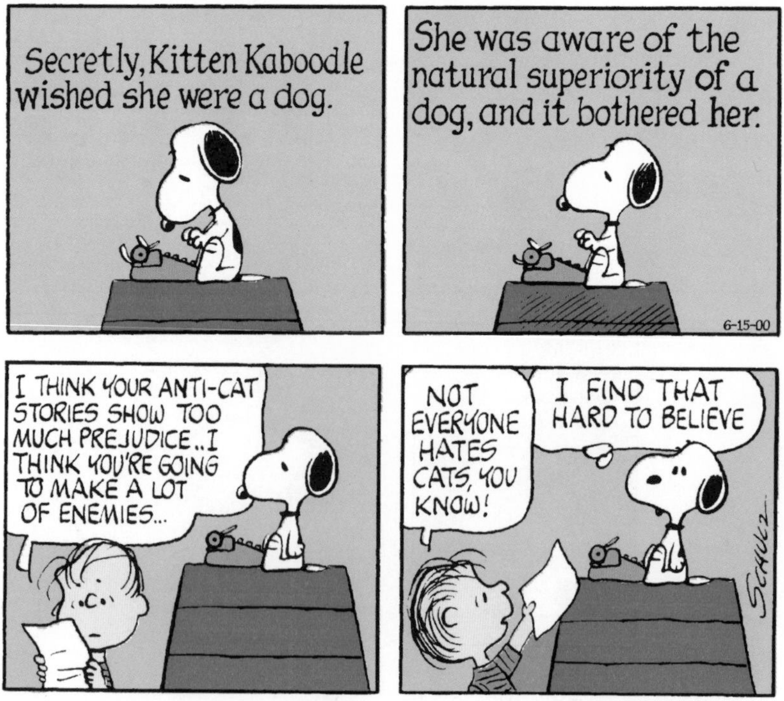
Secretly, Kitten Kaboodle wished she were a dog.
She was aware of the natural superiority of a dog, and it bothered her.
6-15-00
I THINK YOUR ANTI-CAT STORIES SHOW TOO MUCH PREJUDICE..I THINK YOU'RE GOING TO MAKE A LOT OF ENEMIES...
NOT EVERYONE HATES CATS, YOU KNOW!
I FIND THAT HARD TO BELIEVE
SCHULZ

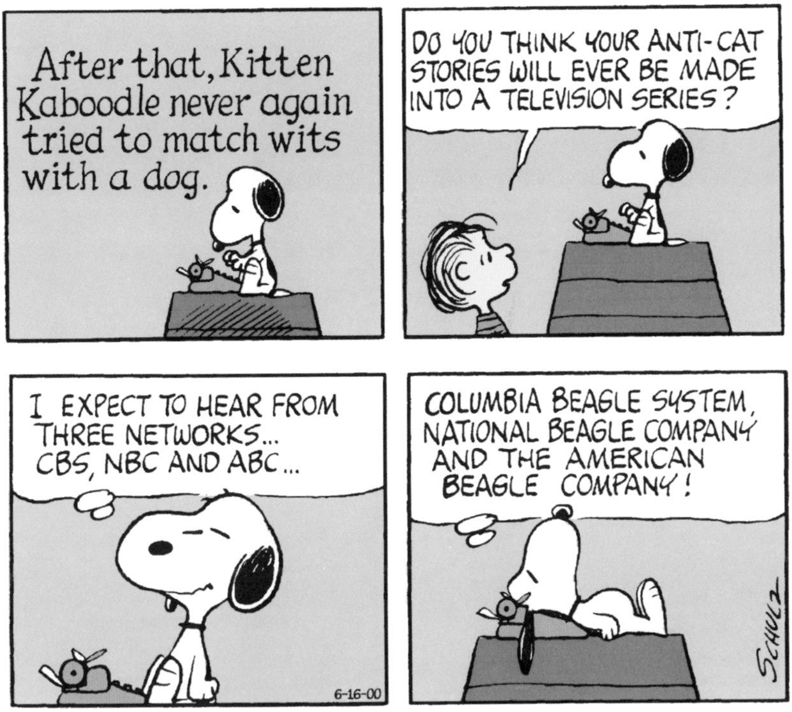
After that, Kitten Kaboodle never again tried to match wits with a dog.
DO YOU THINK YOUR ANTI-CAT STORIES WILL EVER BE MADE INTO A TELEVISION SERIES?
I EXPECT TO HEAR FROM THREE NETWORKS... CBS, NBC AND ABC...
6-16-00
COLUMBIA BEAGLE SYSTEM, NATIONAL BEAGLE COMPANY AND THE AMERICAN BEAGLE COMPANY!
SCHULZ

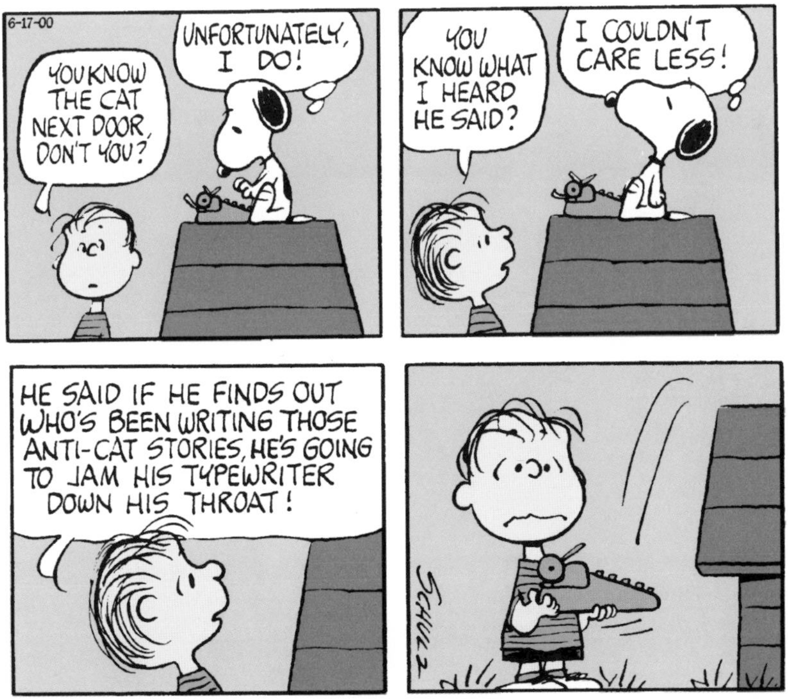
6-17-00
YOU KNOW THE CAT NEXT DOOR, DON'T YOU?
UNFORTUNATELY, I DO!
YOU KNOW WHAT I HEARD HE SAID?
I COULDN'T CARE LESS!
HE SAID IF HE FINDS OUT WHO'S BEEN WRITING THOSE ANTI-CAT STORIES, HE'S GOING TO JAM HIS TYPEWRITER DOWN HIS THROAT!
SCHULZ

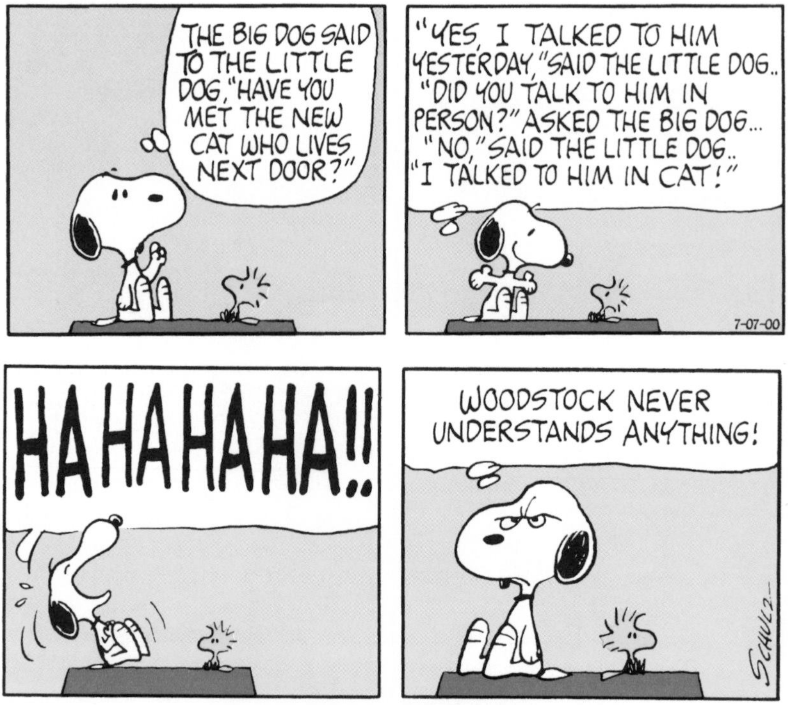
THE BIG DOG SAID TO THE LITTLE DOG, "HAVE YOU MET THE NEW CAT WHO LIVES NEXT DOOR?"
"YES, I TALKED TO HIM YESTERDAY," SAID THE LITTLE DOG.. "DID YOU TALK TO HIM IN PERSON?" ASKED THE BIG DOG... "NO," SAID THE LITTLE DOG.. "I TALKED TO HIM IN CAT!"
7-07-00
HAHAHAHA!!
WOODSTOCK NEVER UNDERSTANDS ANYTHING!
SCHULZ

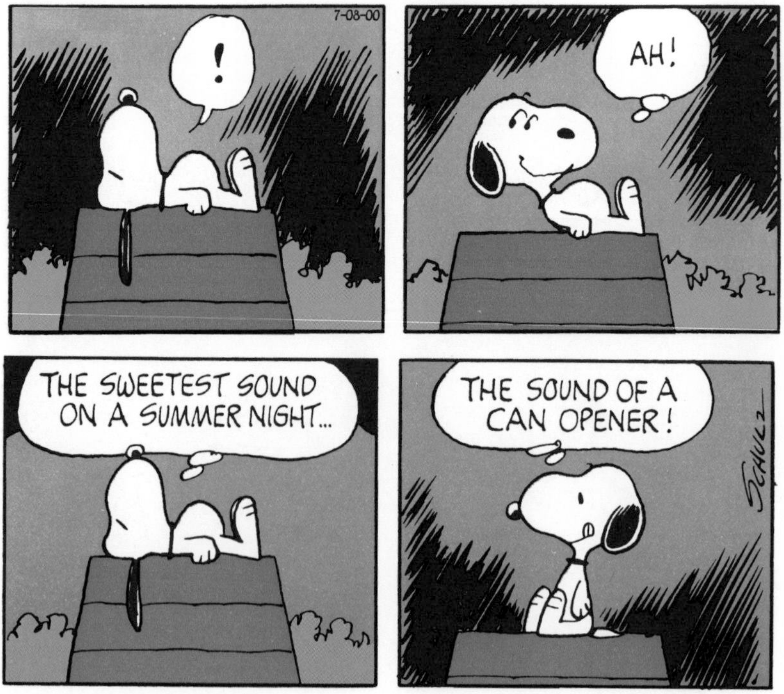
7-08-00
!
AH!
THE SWEETEST SOUND ON A SUMMER NIGHT...
THE SOUND OF A CAN OPENER!
SCHULZ

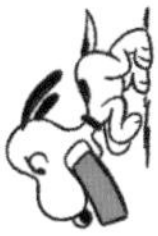

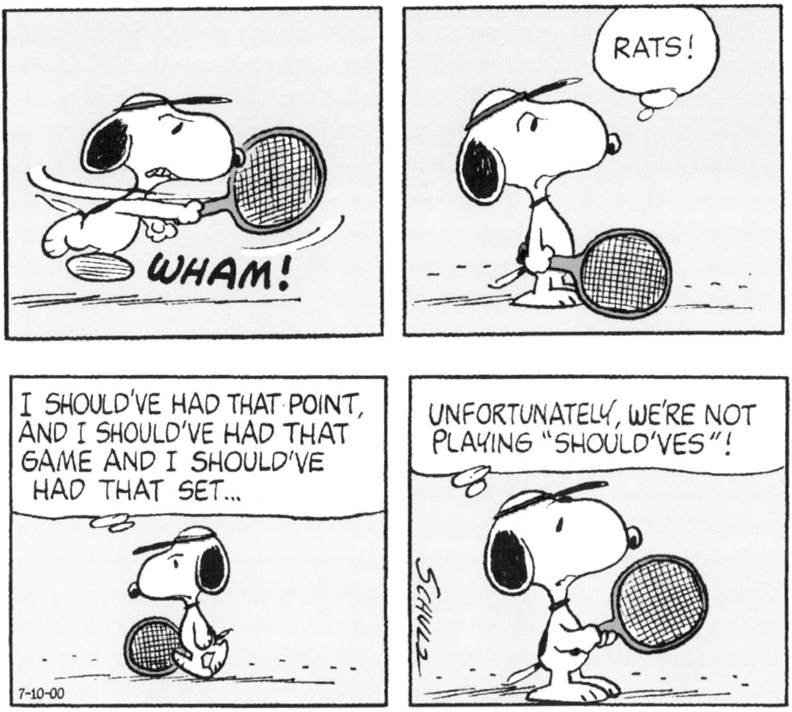
WHAM!
RATS!
I SHOULD'VE HAD THAT POINT, AND I SHOULD'VE HAD THAT GAME AND I SHOULD'VE HAD THAT SET...
7-10-00
UNFORTUNATELY, WE'RE NOT PLAYING "SHOULD'VES"!
SCHULZ

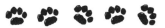

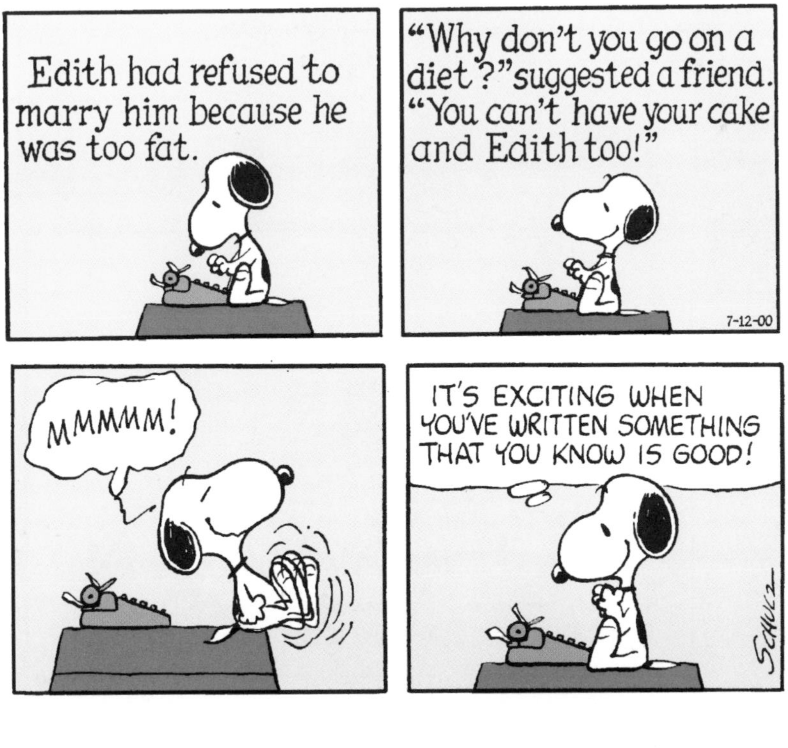
Edith had refused to marry him because he was too fat.
"Why don't you go on a diet?" suggested a friend. "You can't have your cake and Edith too!"
7-12-00
MMMMM!
IT'S EXCITING WHEN YOU'VE WRITTEN SOMETHING THAT YOU KNOW IS GOOD!
SCHULZ

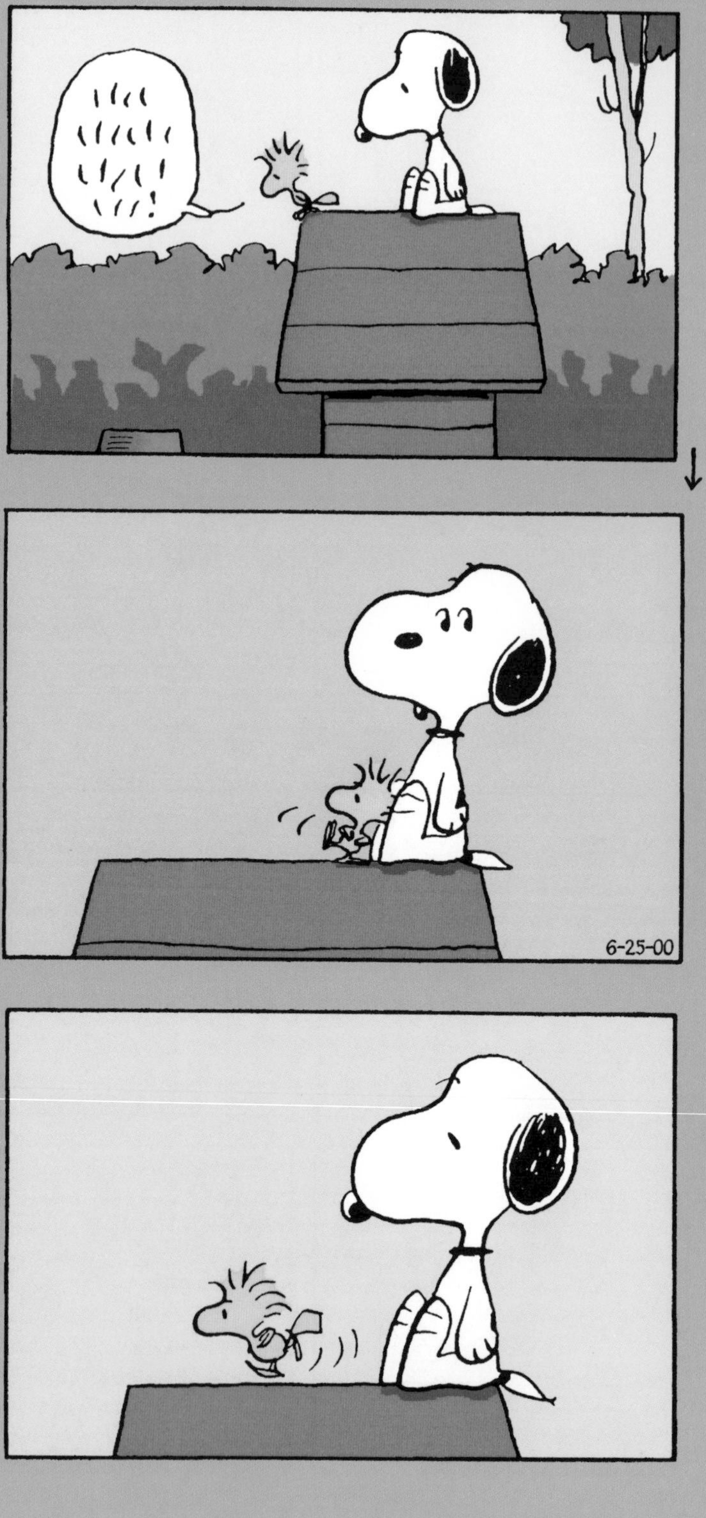
6-25-00

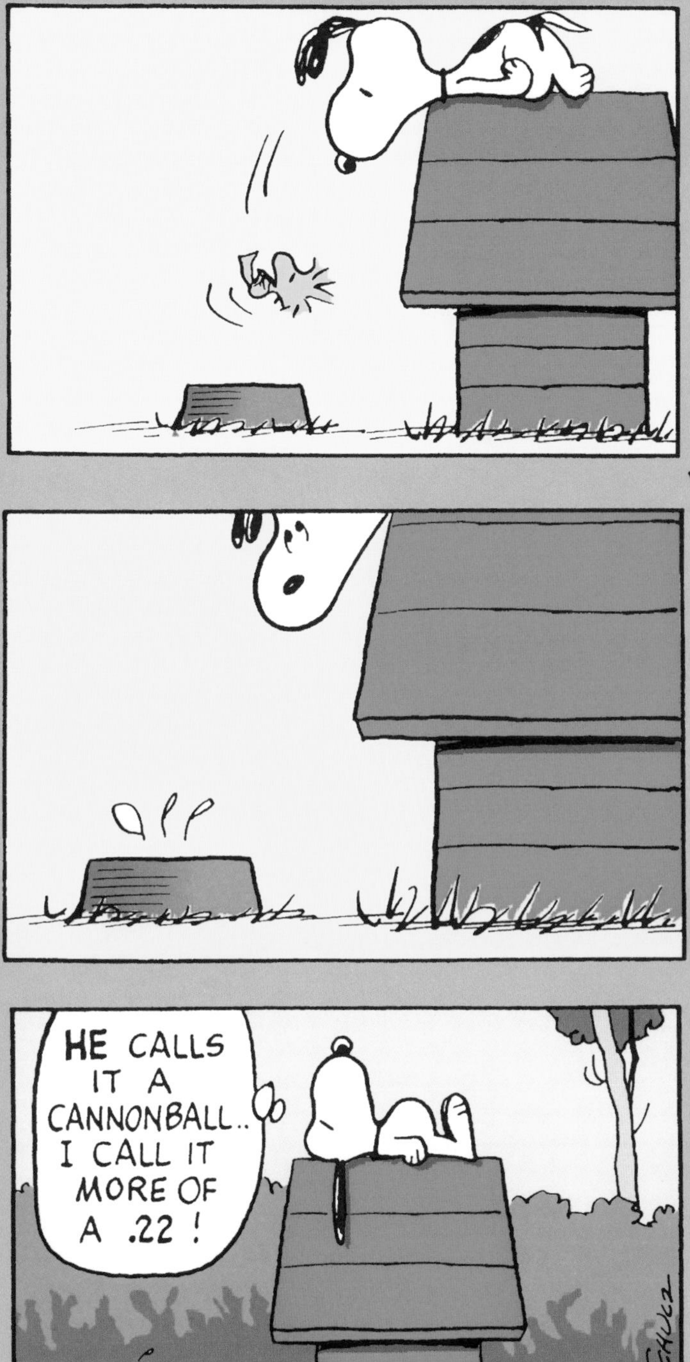
HE CALLS IT A CANNONBALL.. I CALL IT MORE OF A .22 !
SCHULZ

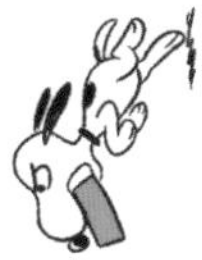

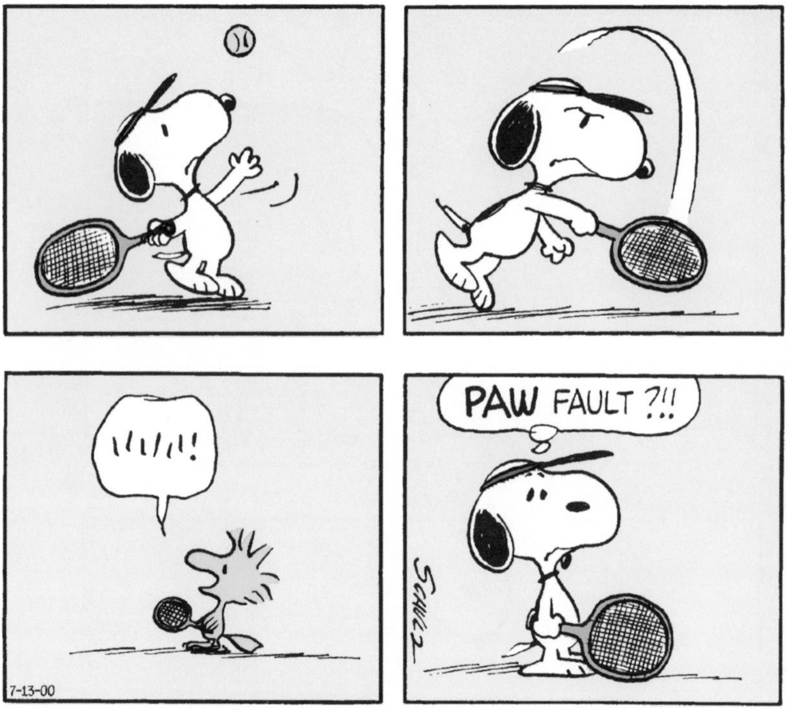
PAW FAULT ?!!
7-13-00

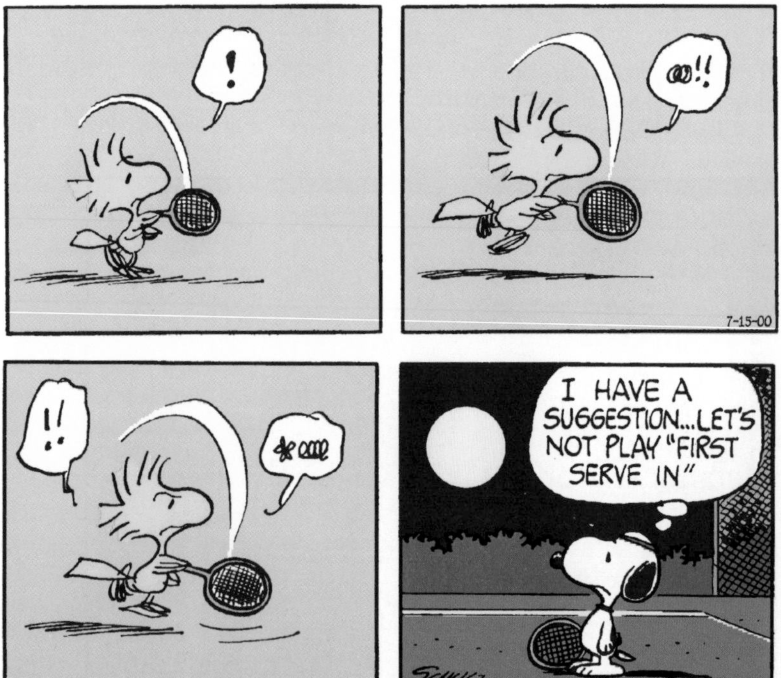
!
7-15-00
!!
I HAVE A SUGGESTION...LET'S NOT PLAY "FIRST SERVE IN"

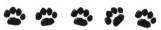

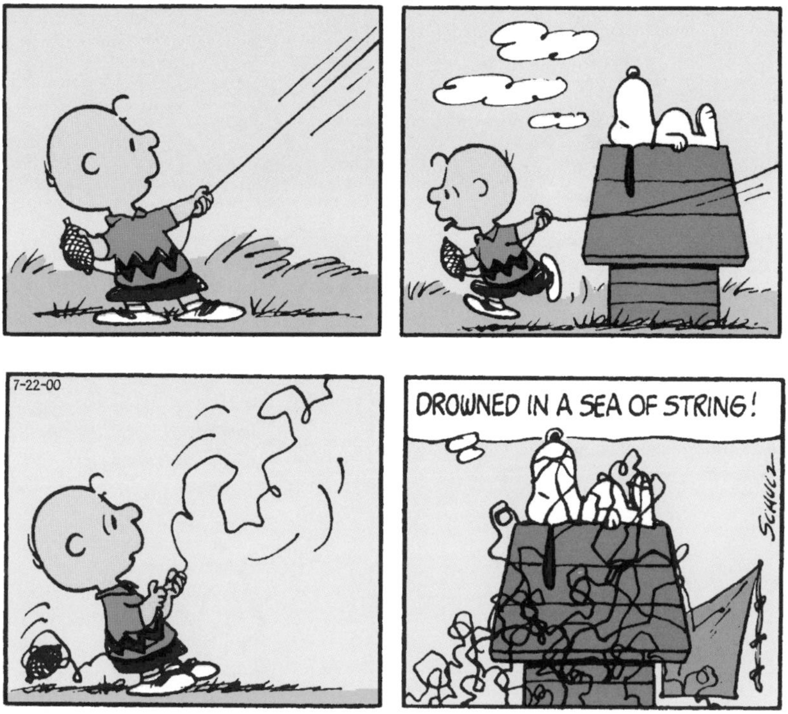

7-22-00
DROWNED IN A SEA OF STRING!

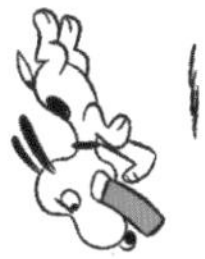

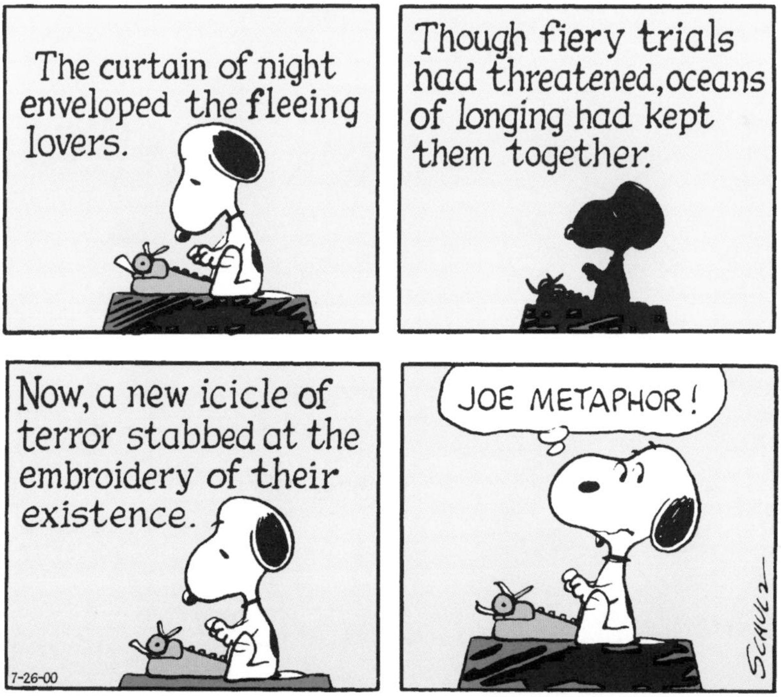

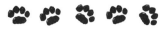

The curtain of night enveloped the fleeing lovers.
Though fiery trials had threatened, oceans of longing had kept them together.
Now, a new icicle of terror stabbed at the embroidery of their existence.
7-26-00
JOE METAPHOR!

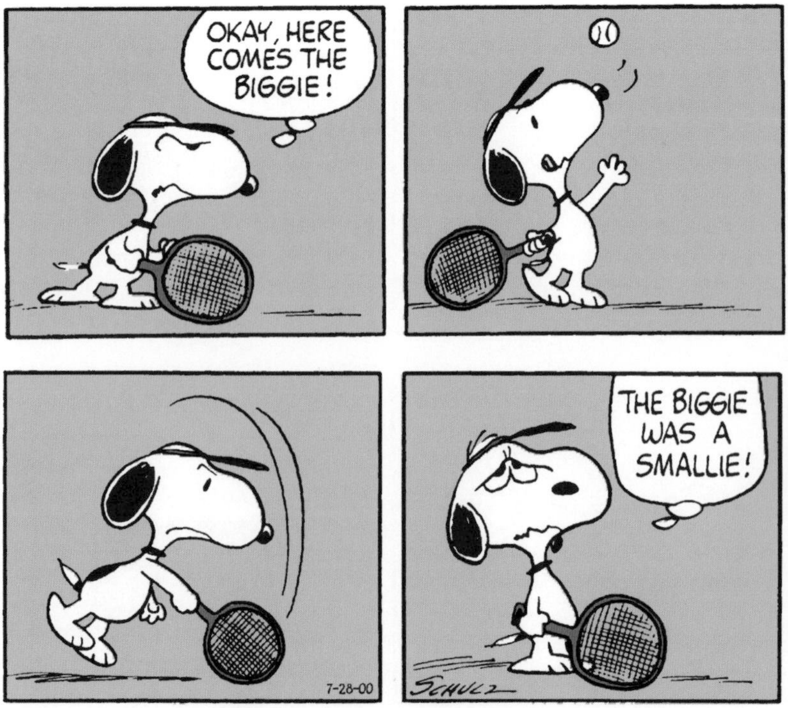
OKAY, HERE COMES THE BIGGIE!
THE BIGGIE WAS A SMALLIE!
7-28-00
SCHULZ

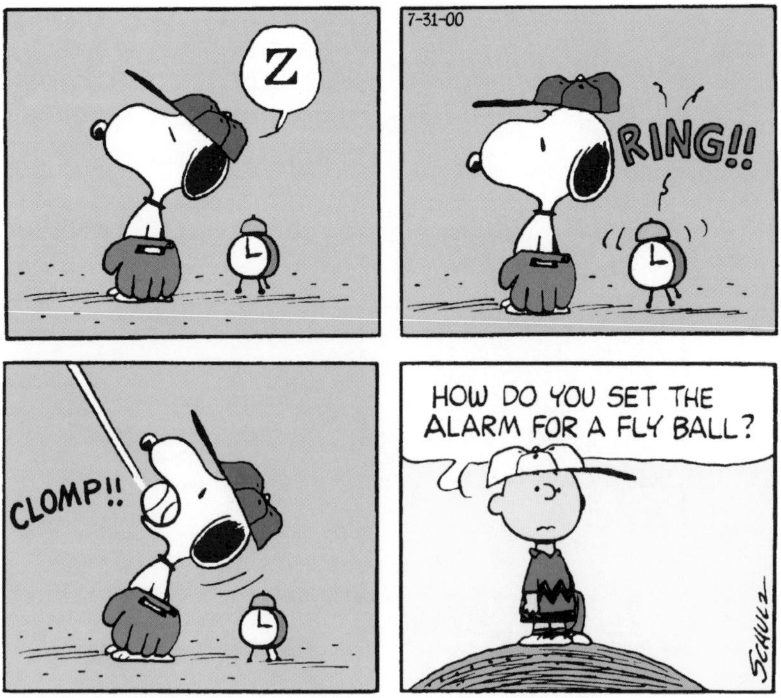
7-31-00
Z
RING!!
CLOMP!!
HOW DO YOU SET THE ALARM FOR A FLY BALL?
SCHULZ

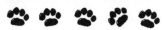

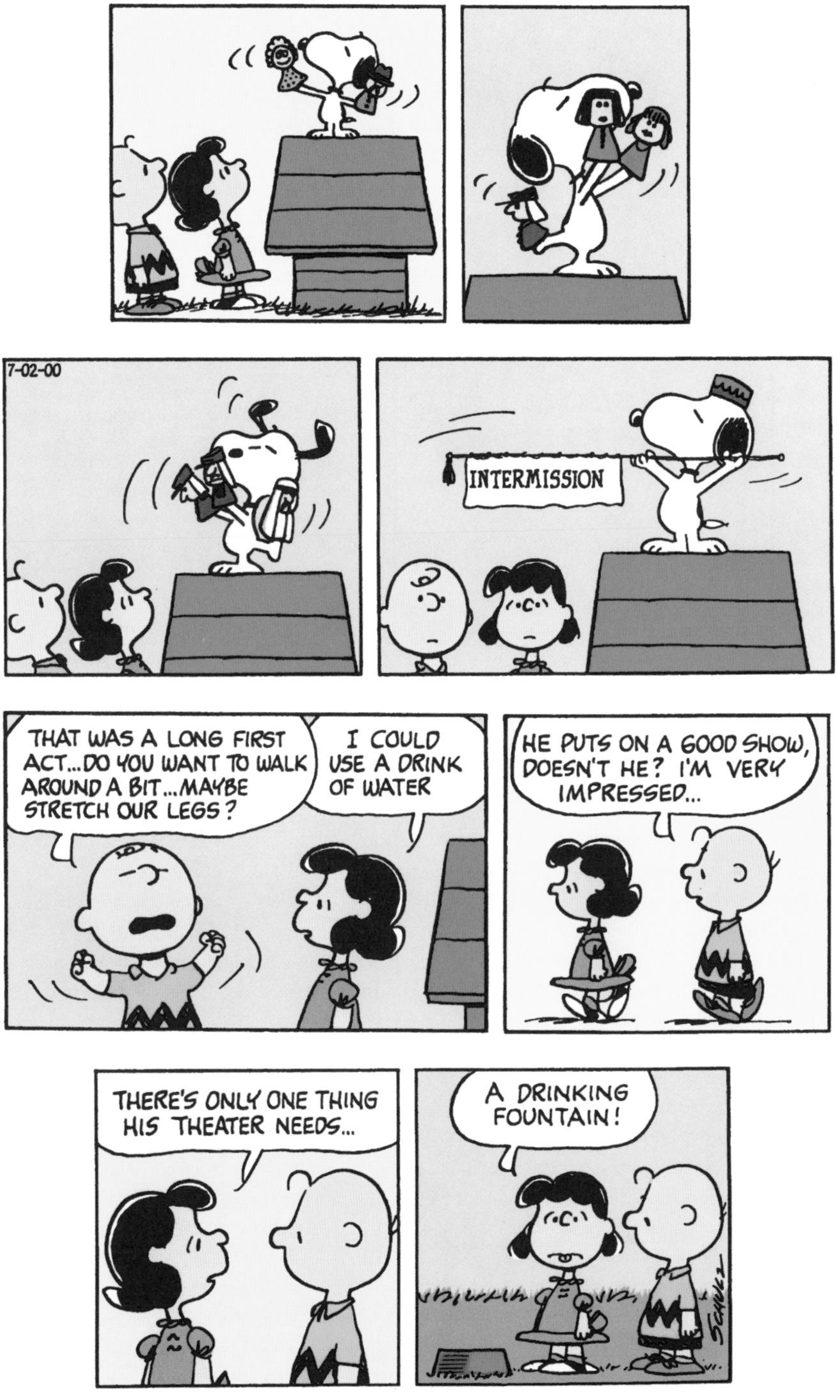
7-02-00
INTERMISSION
THAT WAS A LONG FIRST ACT...DO YOU WANT TO WALK AROUND A BIT...MAYBE STRETCH OUR LEGS?
I COULD USE A DRINK OF WATER
HE PUTS ON A GOOD SHOW, DOESN'T HE? I'M VERY IMPRESSED...
THERE'S ONLY ONE THING HIS THEATER NEEDS...
A DRINKING FOUNTAIN!
SCHULZ

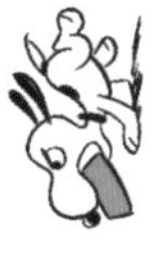

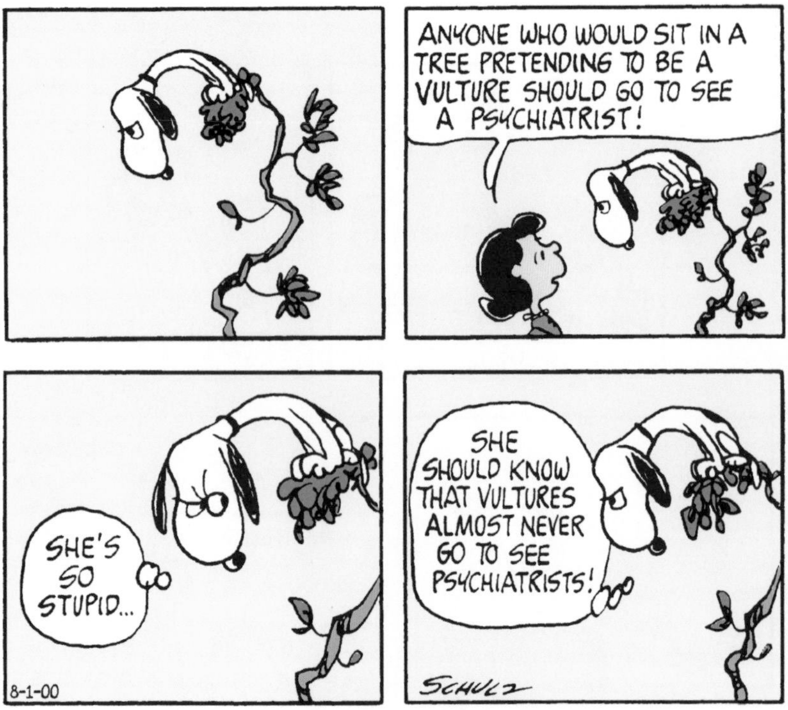
ANYONE WHO WOULD SIT IN A TREE PRETENDING TO BE A VULTURE SHOULD GO TO SEE A PSYCHIATRIST!
SHE'S SO STUPID...
SHE SHOULD KNOW THAT VULTURES ALMOST NEVER GO TO SEE PSYCHIATRISTS!
8-1-00
SCHULZ

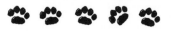

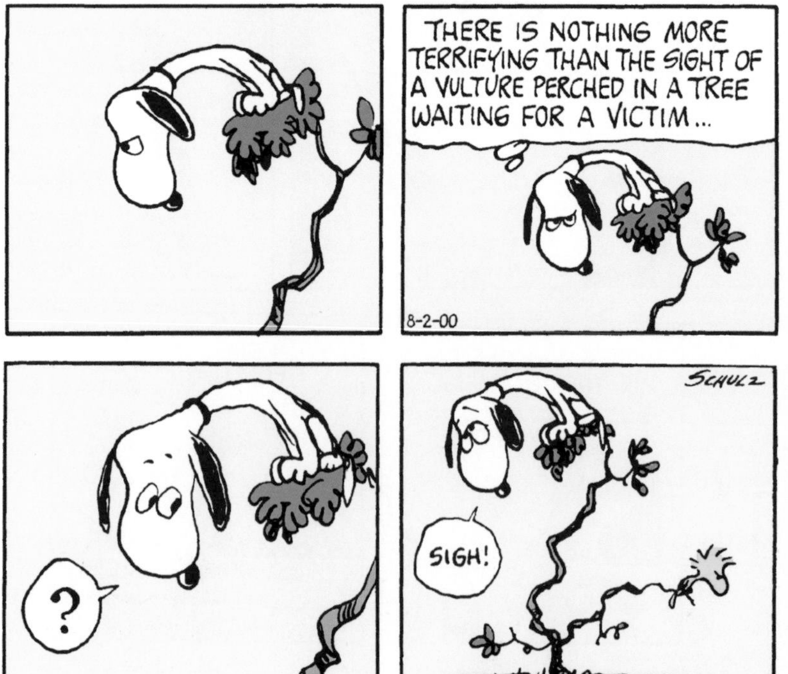
THERE IS NOTHING MORE TERRIFYING THAN THE SIGHT OF A VULTURE PERCHED IN A TREE WAITING FOR A VICTIM...
8-2-00
?
SCHULZ
SIGH!

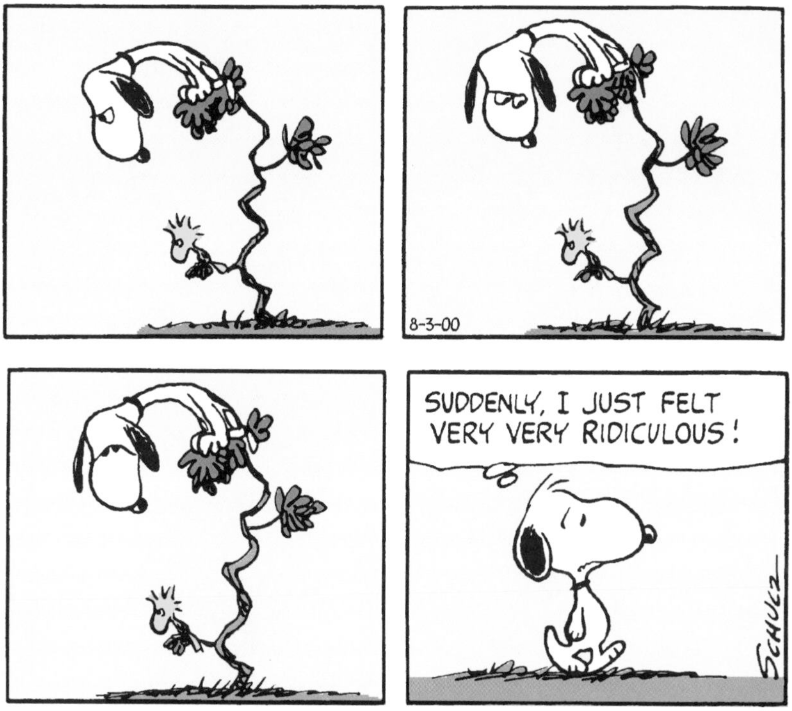
8-3-00
SUDDENLY, I JUST FELT VERY VERY RIDICULOUS!
SCHULZ

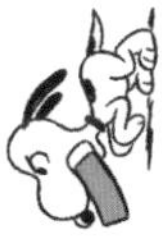

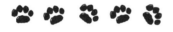

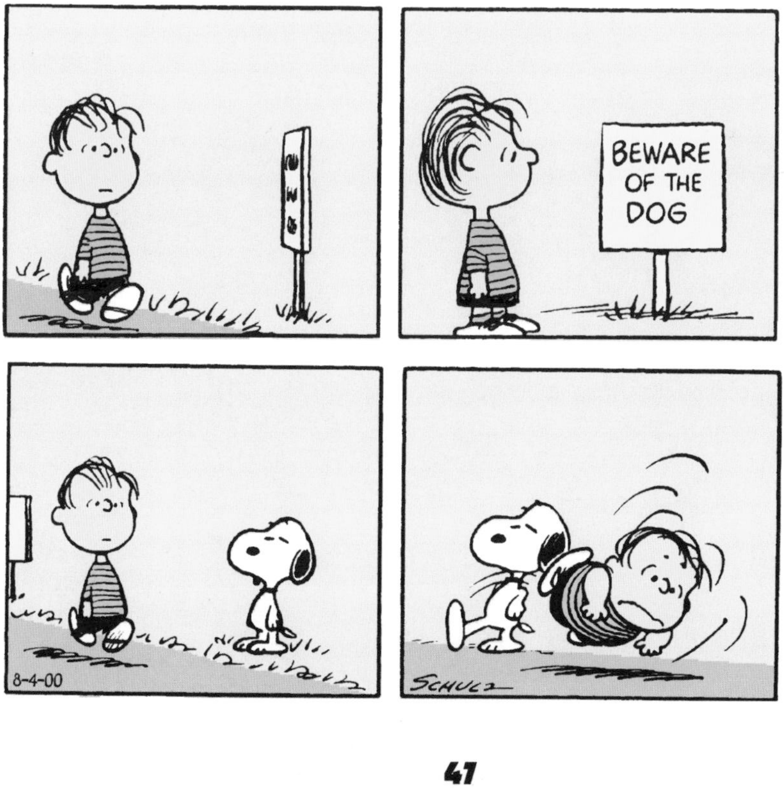
BEWARE OF THE DOG
8-4-00
SCHULZ

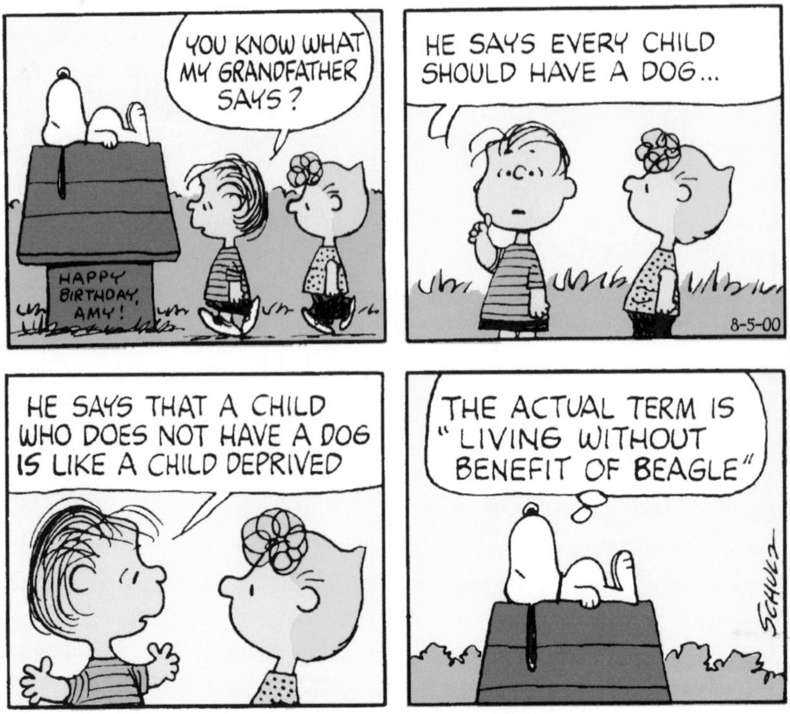
YOU KNOW WHAT MY GRANDFATHER SAYS?
HAPPY BIRTHDAY, AMY!
HE SAYS EVERY CHILD SHOULD HAVE A DOG...
8-5-00
HE SAYS THAT A CHILD WHO DOES NOT HAVE A DOG IS LIKE A CHILD DEPRIVED
THE ACTUAL TERM IS "LIVING WITHOUT BENEFIT OF BEAGLE"
SCHULZ

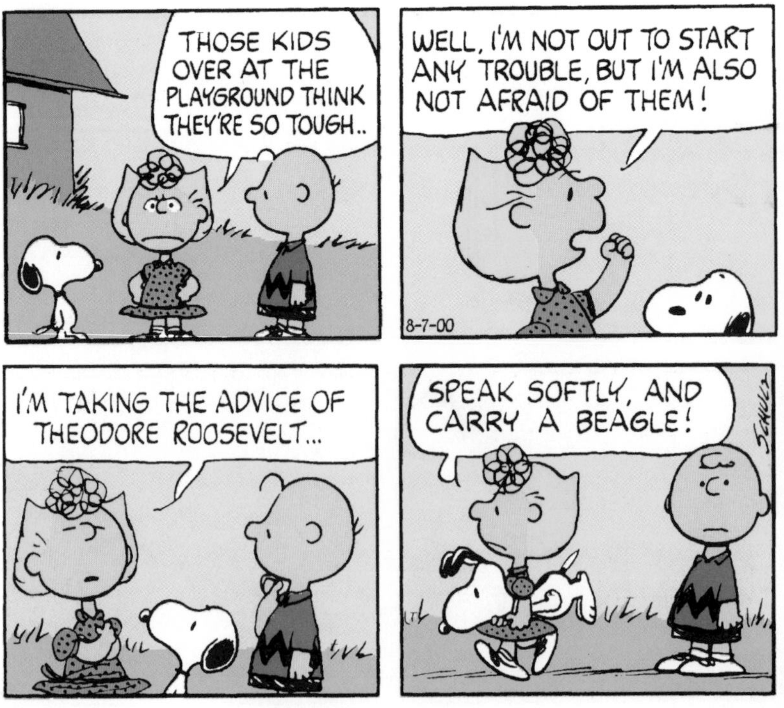
THOSE KIDS OVER AT THE PLAYGROUND THINK THEY'RE SO TOUGH..
WELL, I'M NOT OUT TO START ANY TROUBLE, BUT I'M ALSO NOT AFRAID OF THEM!
8-7-00
I'M TAKING THE ADVICE OF THEODORE ROOSEVELT...
SPEAK SOFTLY, AND CARRY A BEAGLE!
SCHULZ

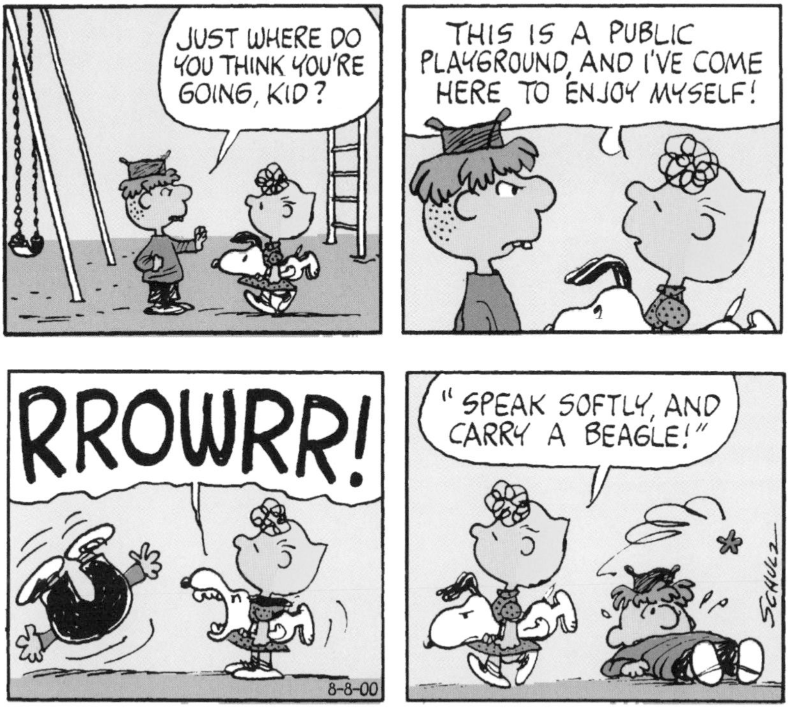
JUST WHERE DO YOU THINK YOU'RE GOING, KID?
THIS IS A PUBLIC PLAYGROUND, AND I'VE COME HERE TO ENJOY MYSELF!
RROWRR!
8-8-00
"SPEAK SOFTLY, AND CARRY A BEAGLE!"
SCHULZ

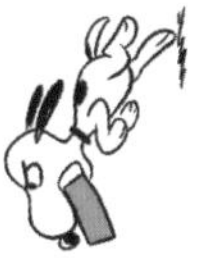

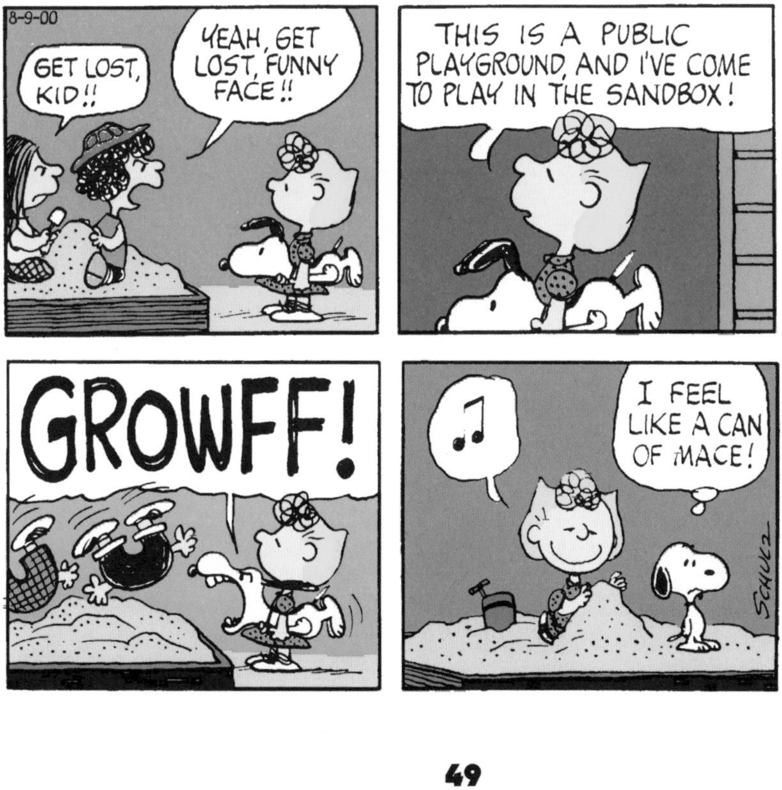
8-9-00
GET LOST, KID!!
YEAH, GET LOST, FUNNY FACE!!
THIS IS A PUBLIC PLAYGROUND, AND I'VE COME TO PLAY IN THE SANDBOX!
GROWFF!
I FEEL LIKE A CAN OF MACE!
SCHULZ

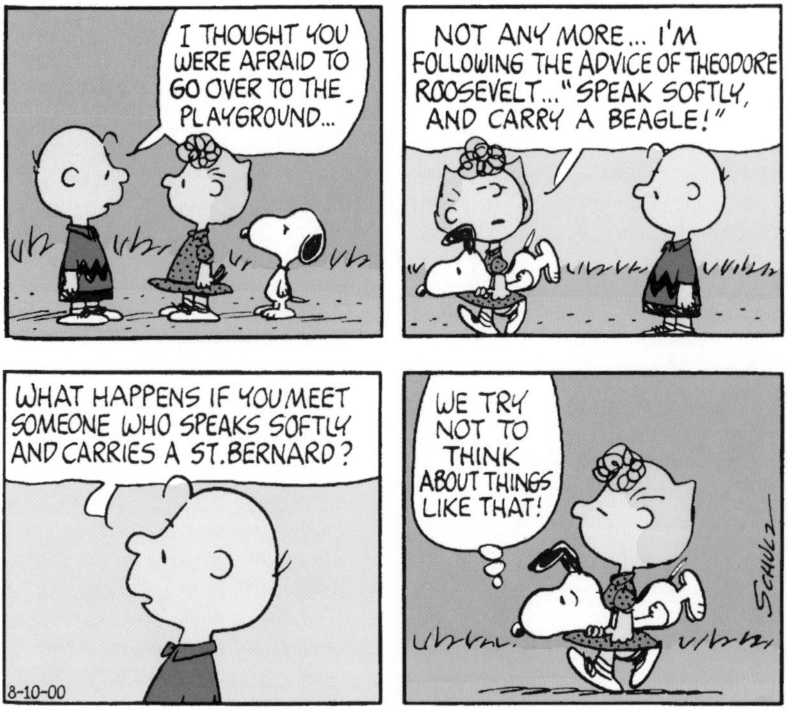
I THOUGHT YOU WERE AFRAID TO GO OVER TO THE PLAYGROUND...
NOT ANY MORE... I'M FOLLOWING THE ADVICE OF THEODORE ROOSEVELT..."SPEAK SOFTLY, AND CARRY A BEAGLE!"
WHAT HAPPENS IF YOU MEET SOMEONE WHO SPEAKS SOFTLY AND CARRIES A ST. BERNARD?
8-10-00
WE TRY NOT TO THINK ABOUT THINGS LIKE THAT!
SCHULZ

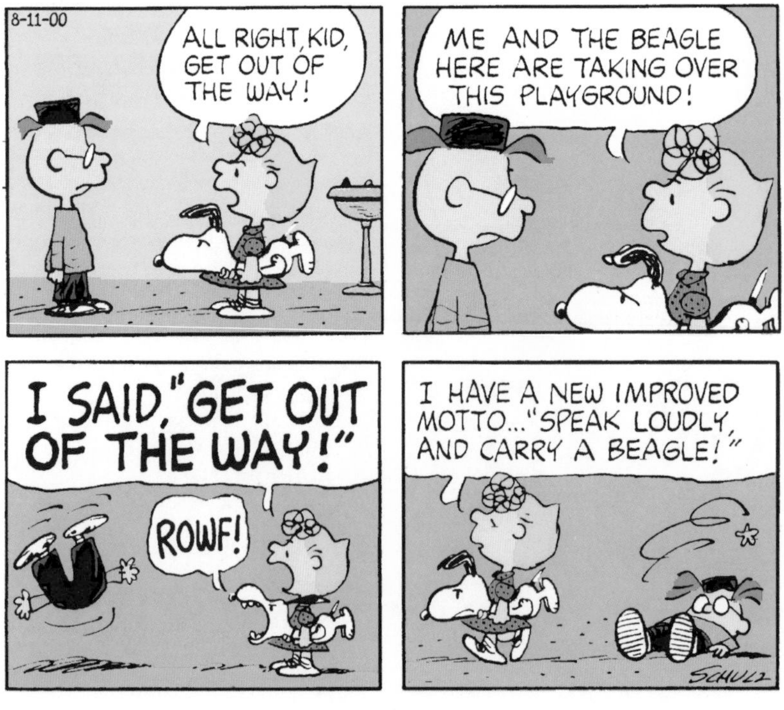
8-11-00
ALL RIGHT, KID, GET OUT OF THE WAY!
ME AND THE BEAGLE HERE ARE TAKING OVER THIS PLAYGROUND!
I SAID, "GET OUT OF THE WAY!"
ROWF!
I HAVE A NEW IMPROVED MOTTO..."SPEAK LOUDLY, AND CARRY A BEAGLE!"
SCHULZ

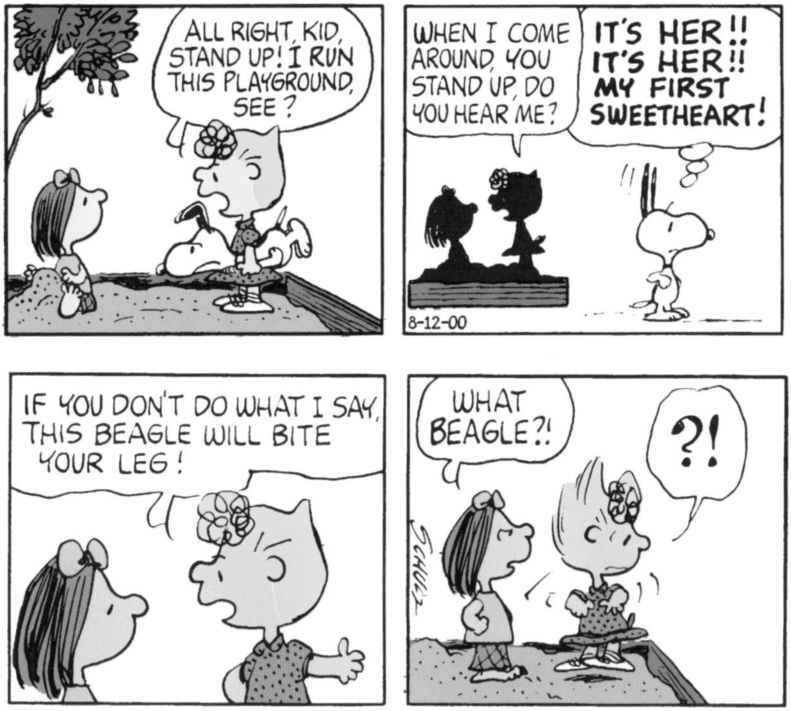
ALL RIGHT, KID, STAND UP! I RUN THIS PLAYGROUND, SEE?
WHEN I COME AROUND, YOU STAND UP, DO YOU HEAR ME?
IT'S HER!! IT'S HER!! MY FIRST SWEETHEART!
8-12-00
IF YOU DON'T DO WHAT I SAY, THIS BEAGLE WILL BITE YOUR LEG!
WHAT BEAGLE?!
?!
SCHULZ

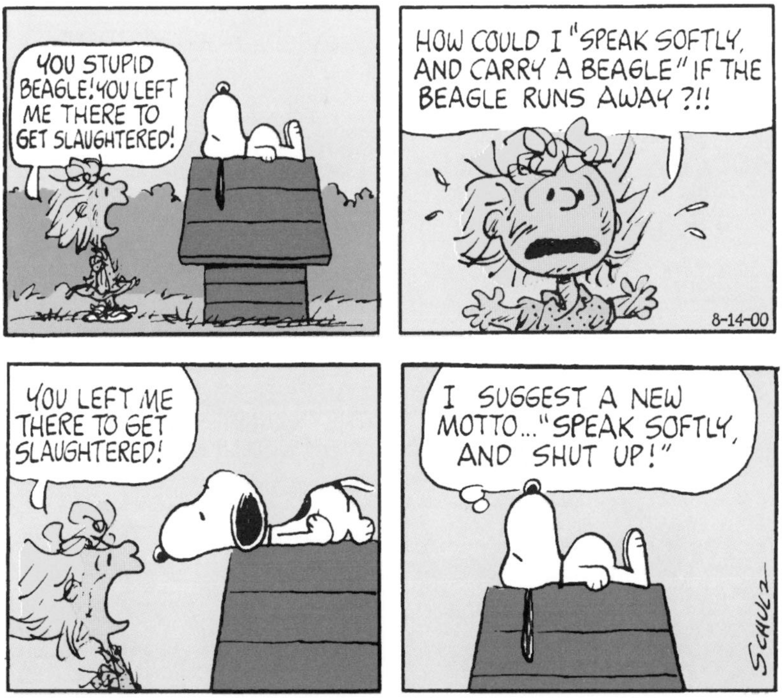
YOU STUPID BEAGLE! YOU LEFT ME THERE TO GET SLAUGHTERED!
HOW COULD I "SPEAK SOFTLY, AND CARRY A BEAGLE" IF THE BEAGLE RUNS AWAY?!!
8-14-00
YOU LEFT ME THERE TO GET SLAUGHTERED!
I SUGGEST A NEW MOTTO..."SPEAK SOFTLY, AND SHUT UP!"
SCHULZ

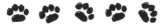

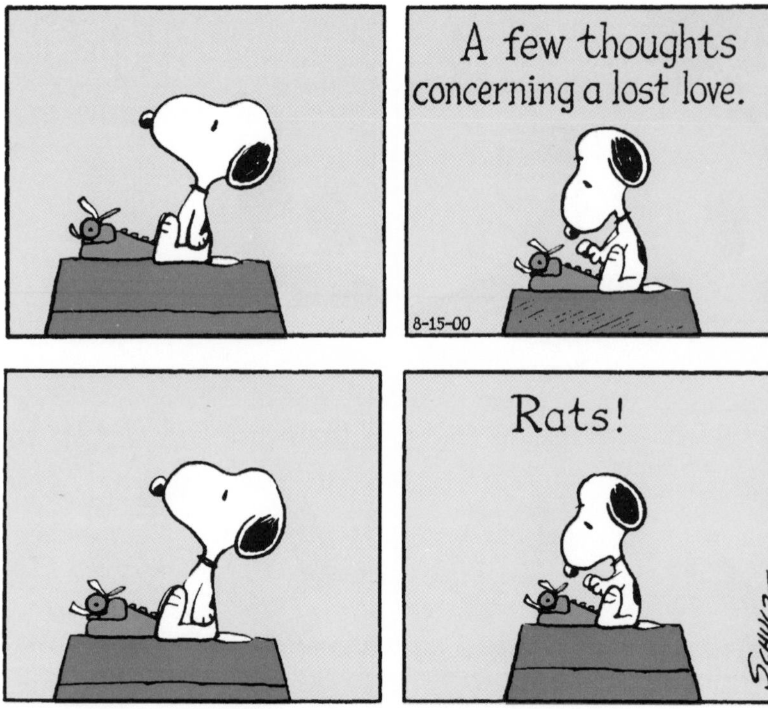
A few thoughts concerning a lost love.
8-15-00
Rats!
SCHULZ

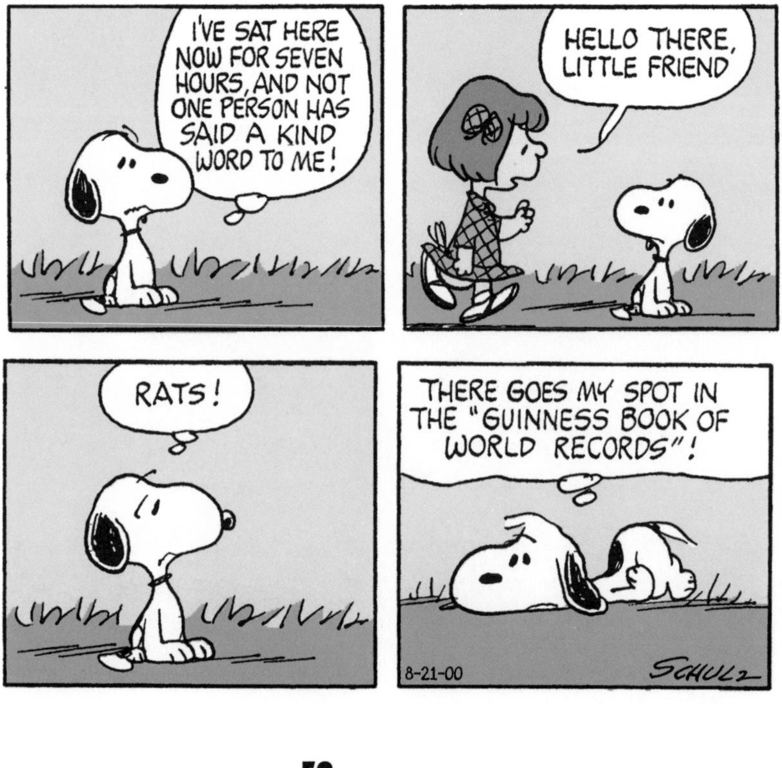
I'VE SAT HERE NOW FOR SEVEN HOURS, AND NOT ONE PERSON HAS SAID A KIND WORD TO ME!
HELLO THERE, LITTLE FRIEND
RATS!
THERE GOES MY SPOT IN THE "GUINNESS BOOK OF WORLD RECORDS"!
8-21-00
SCHULZ

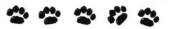

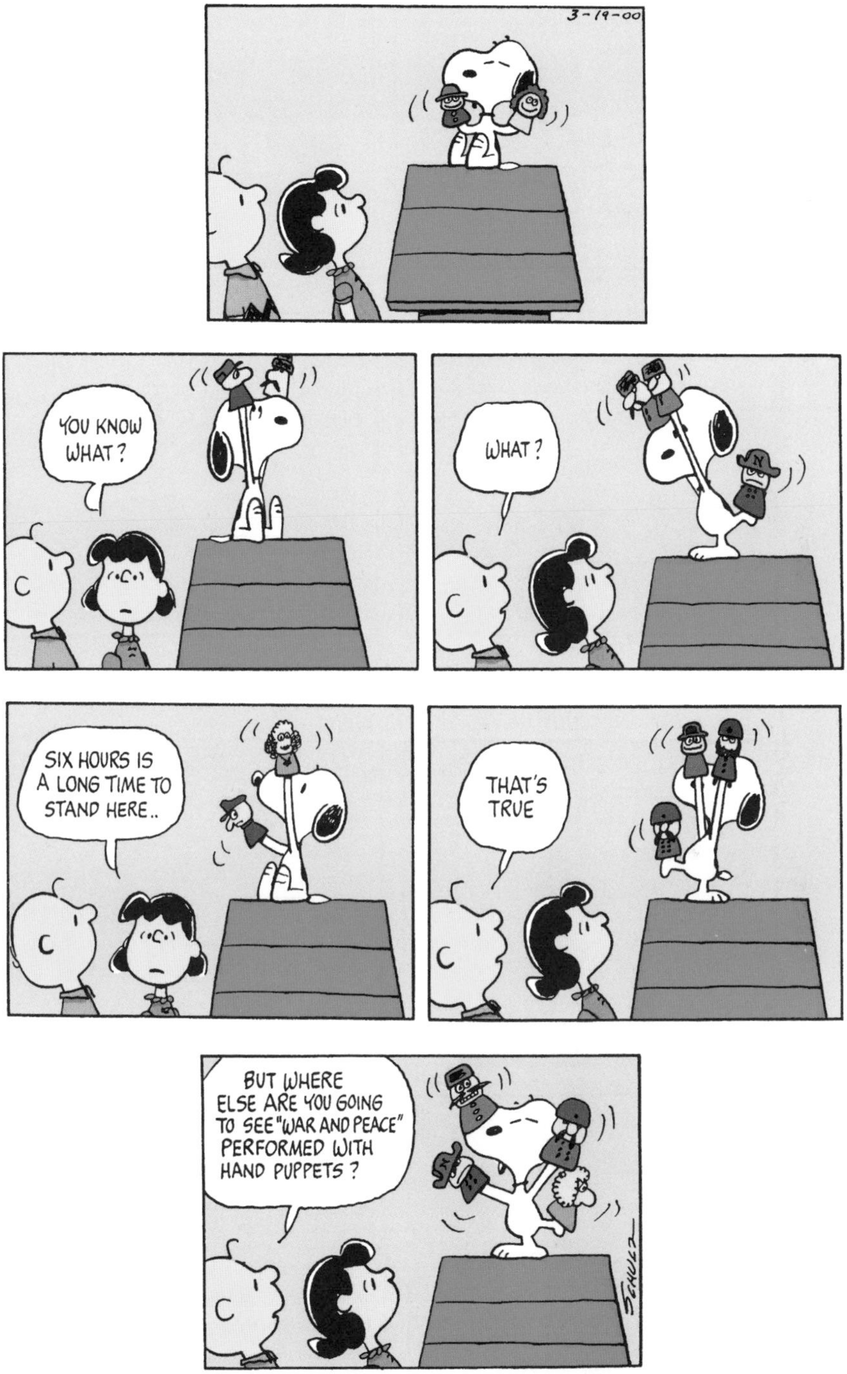
3-19-00
YOU KNOW WHAT?
WHAT?
SIX HOURS IS A LONG TIME TO STAND HERE..
THAT'S TRUE
BUT WHERE ELSE ARE YOU GOING TO SEE "WAR AND PEACE" PERFORMED WITH HAND PUPPETS?
SCHULZ

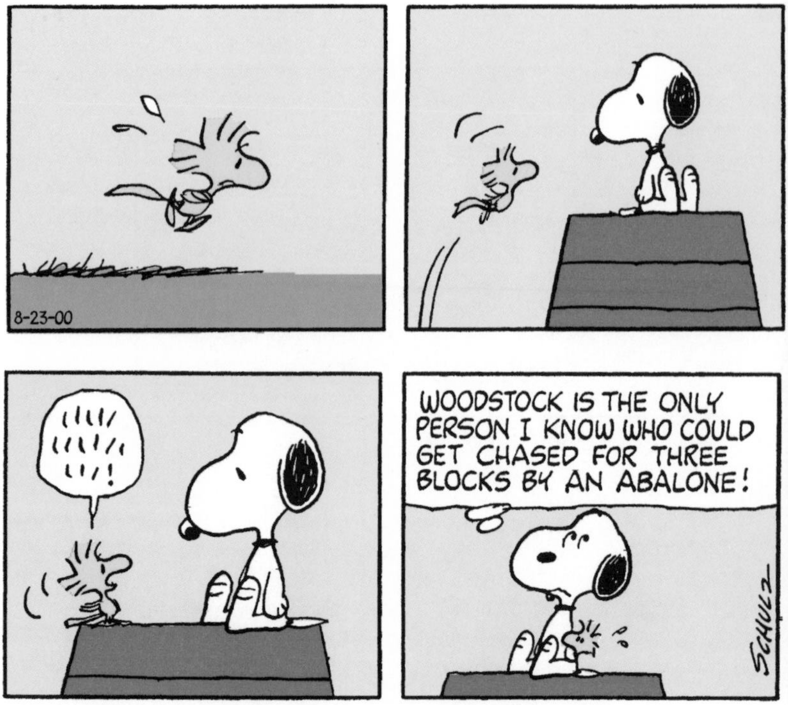
8-23-00
WOODSTOCK IS THE ONLY PERSON I KNOW WHO COULD GET CHASED FOR THREE BLOCKS BY AN ABALONE!
SCHULZ

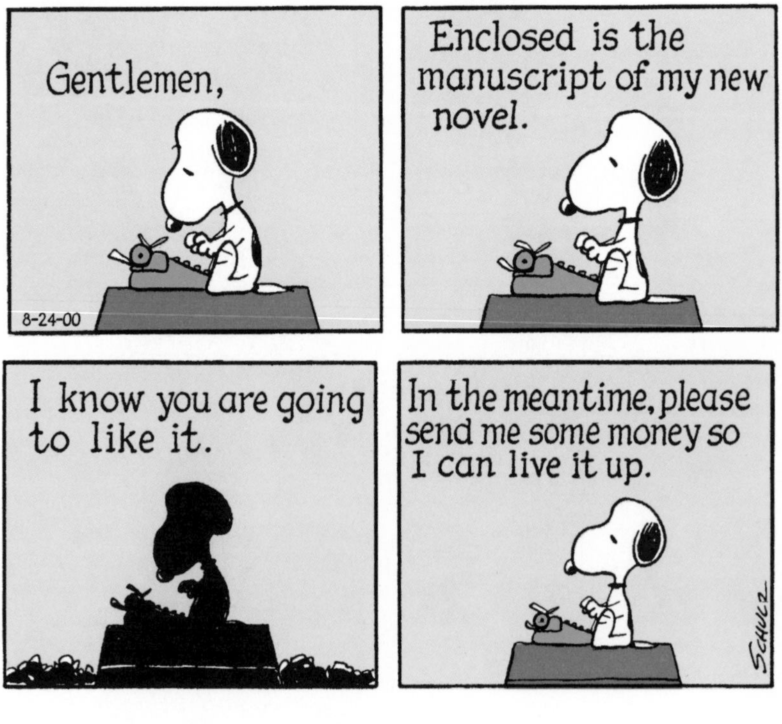
Gentlemen,
8-24-00
Enclosed is the manuscript of my new novel.
I know you are going to like it.
In the meantime, please send me some money so I can live it up.
SCHULZ

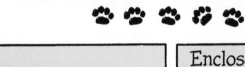

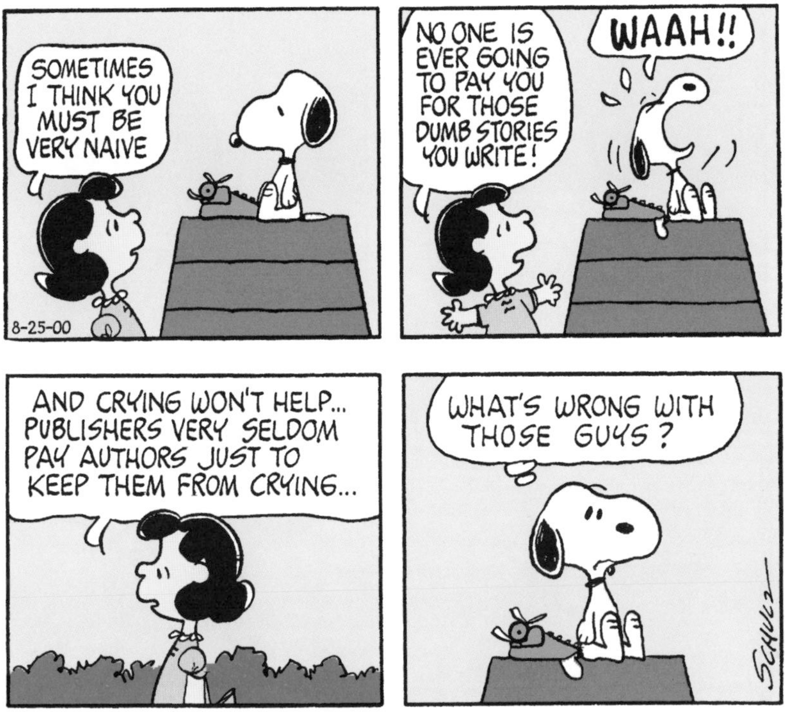
SOMETIMES I THINK YOU MUST BE VERY NAIVE
8-25-00
NO ONE IS EVER GOING TO PAY YOU FOR THOSE DUMB STORIES YOU WRITE!
WAAH!!
AND CRYING WON'T HELP... PUBLISHERS VERY SELDOM PAY AUTHORS JUST TO KEEP THEM FROM CRYING...
WHAT'S WRONG WITH THOSE GUYS?
SCHULZ

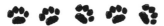

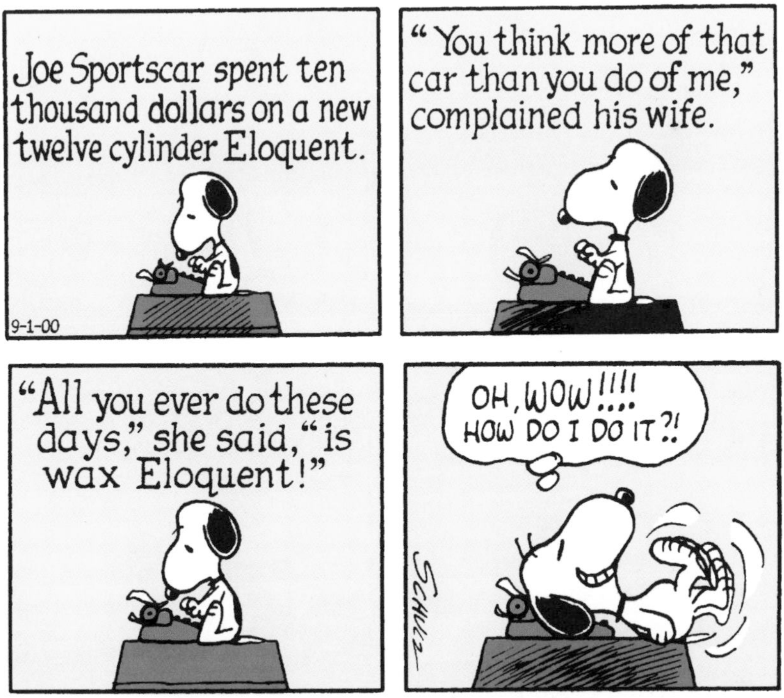
Joe Sportscar spent ten thousand dollars on a new twelve cylinder Eloquent.
9-1-00
"You think more of that car than you do of me," complained his wife.
"All you ever do these days," she said, "is wax Eloquent!"
OH, WOW!!!!.... HOW DO I DO IT?!
SCHULZ

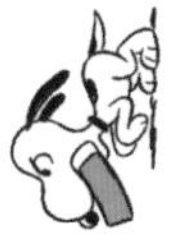

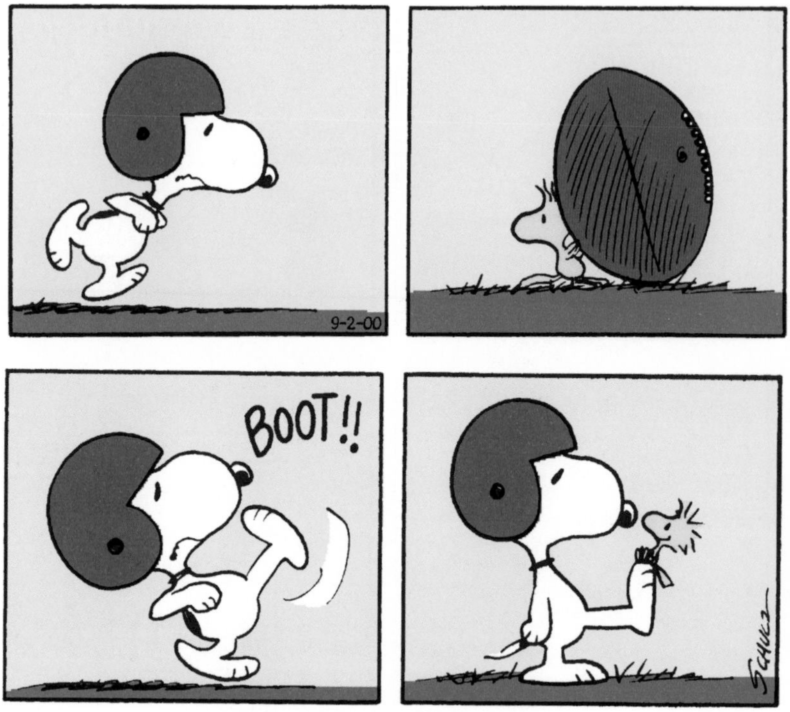
9-2-00
BOOT!!
SCHULZ

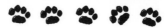

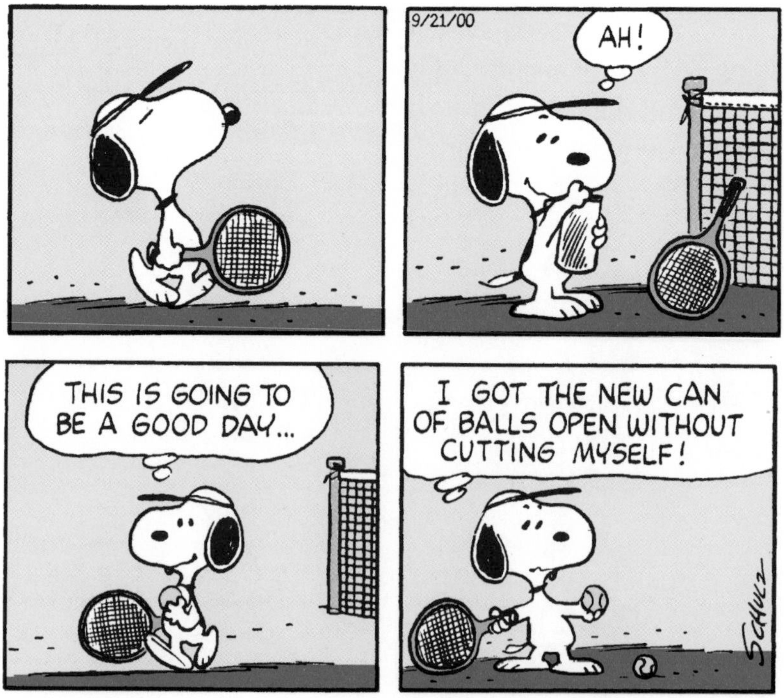
9/21/00
AH!
THIS IS GOING TO BE A GOOD DAY...
I GOT THE NEW CAN OF BALLS OPEN WITHOUT CUTTING MYSELF!
SCHULZ

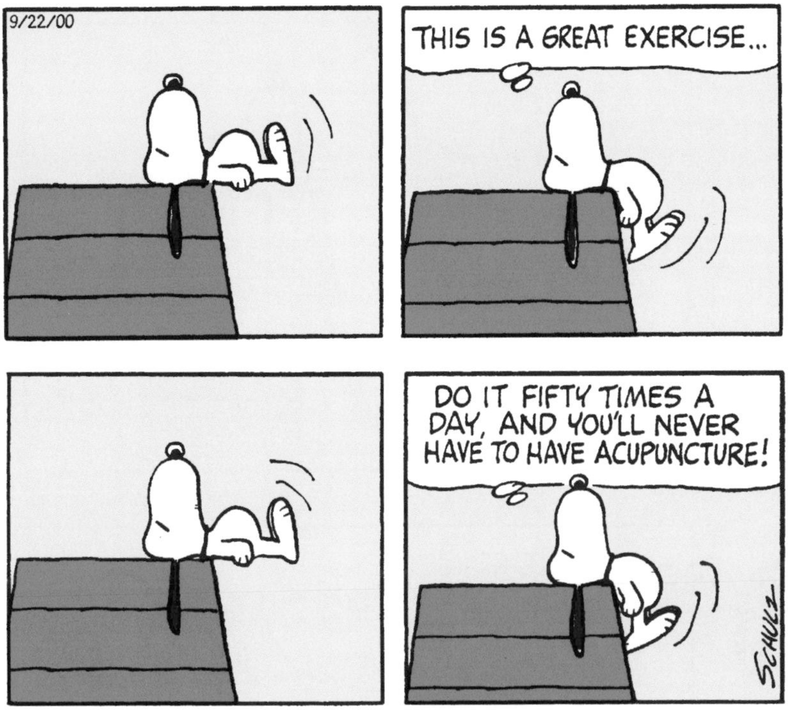
9/22/00
THIS IS A GREAT EXERCISE...
DO IT FIFTY TIMES A DAY, AND YOU'LL NEVER HAVE TO HAVE ACUPUNCTURE!
SCHULZ

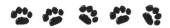

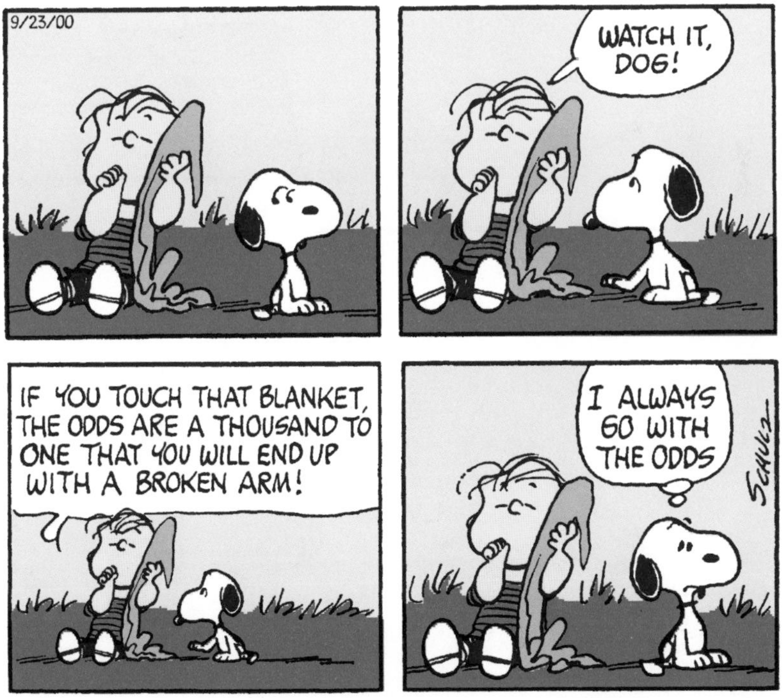
9/23/00
WATCH IT, DOG!
IF YOU TOUCH THAT BLANKET, THE ODDS ARE A THOUSAND TO ONE THAT YOU WILL END UP WITH A BROKEN ARM!
I ALWAYS GO WITH THE ODDS
SCHULZ

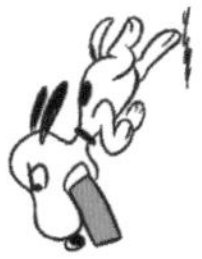

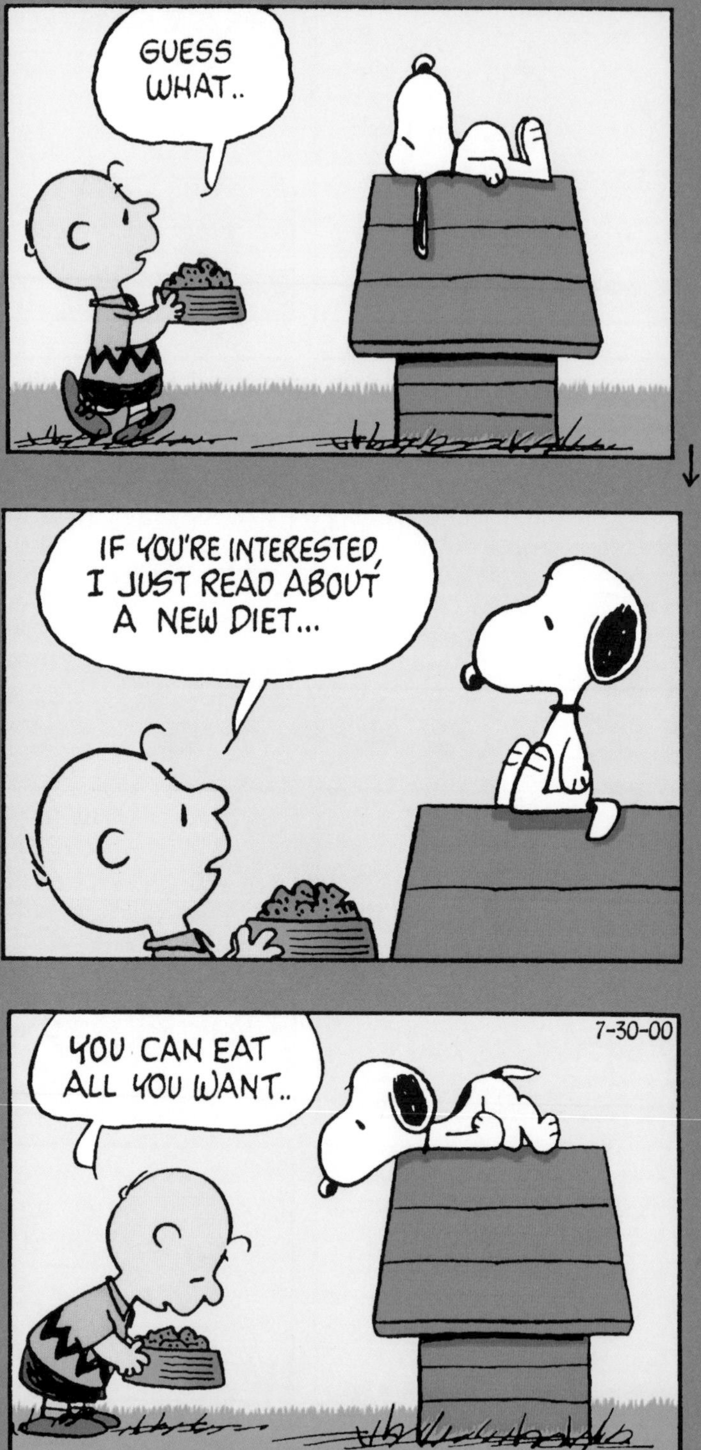
GUESS WHAT..
IF YOU'RE INTERESTED, I JUST READ ABOUT A NEW DIET...
7-30-00
YOU CAN EAT ALL YOU WANT..

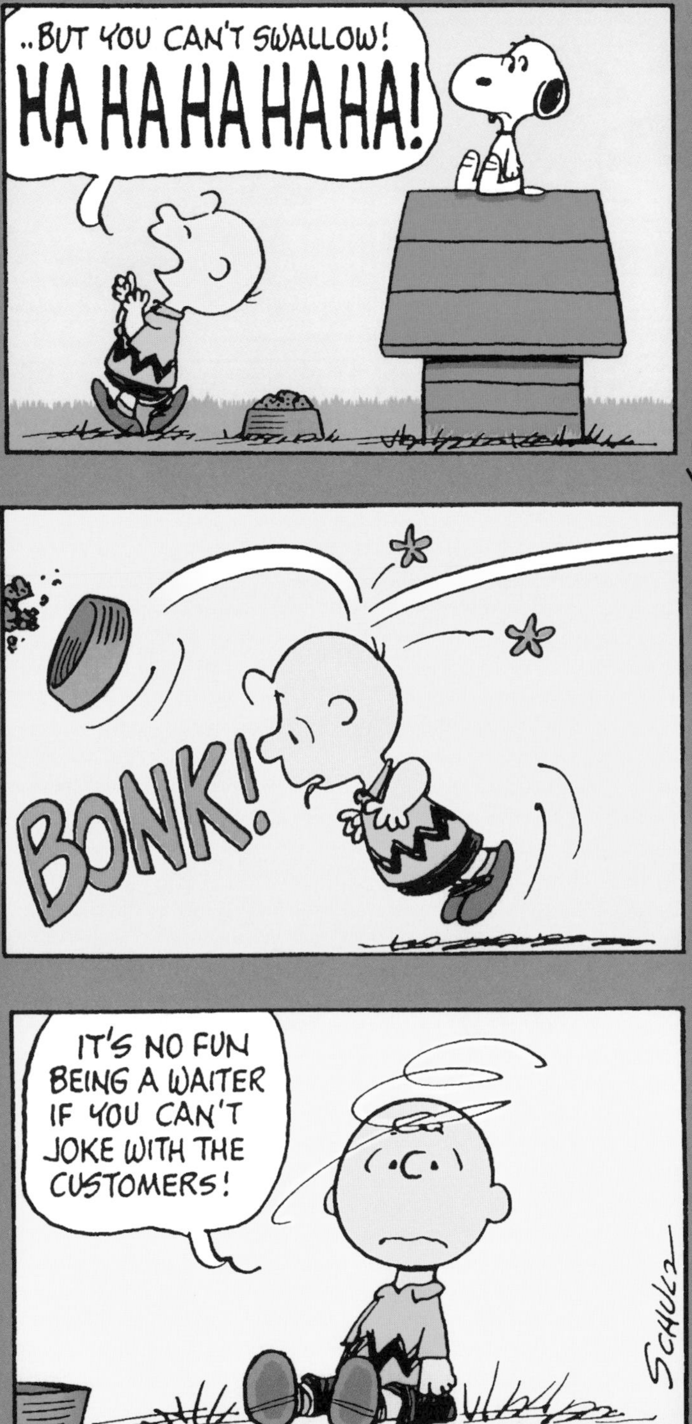
..BUT YOU CAN'T SWALLOW!
HA HA HA HA HA!
BONK!
IT'S NO FUN BEING A WAITER IF YOU CAN'T JOKE WITH THE CUSTOMERS!
SCHULZ

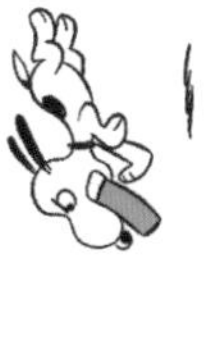

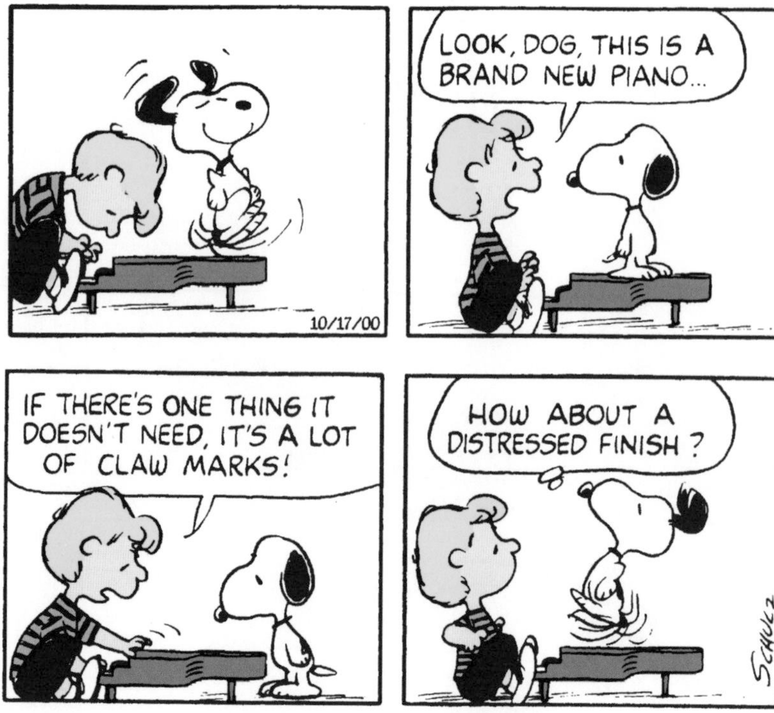
10/17/00
LOOK, DOG, THIS IS A BRAND NEW PIANO...
IF THERE'S ONE THING IT DOESN'T NEED, IT'S A LOT OF CLAW MARKS!
HOW ABOUT A DISTRESSED FINISH ?
SCHULZ

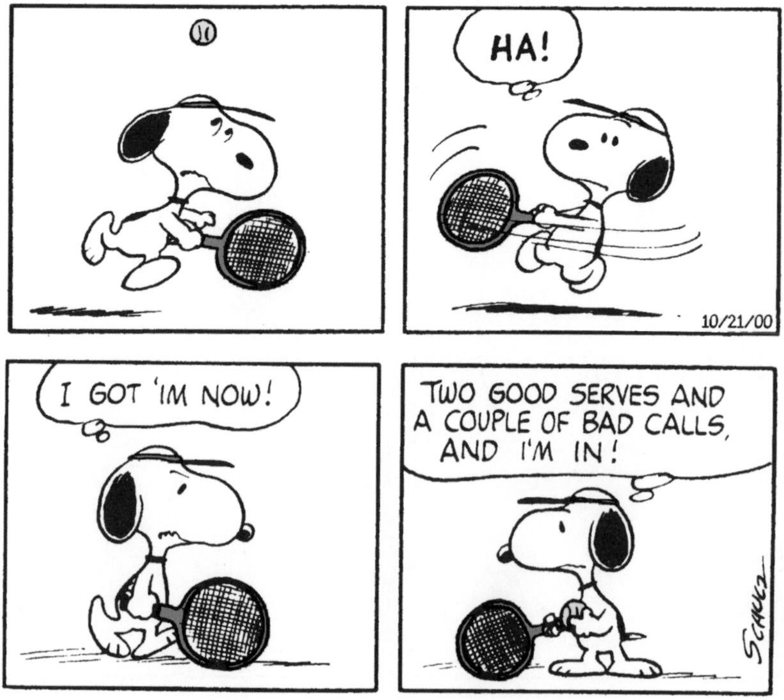
HA!
10/21/00
I GOT 'IM NOW!
TWO GOOD SERVES AND A COUPLE OF BAD CALLS, AND I'M IN!
SCHULZ

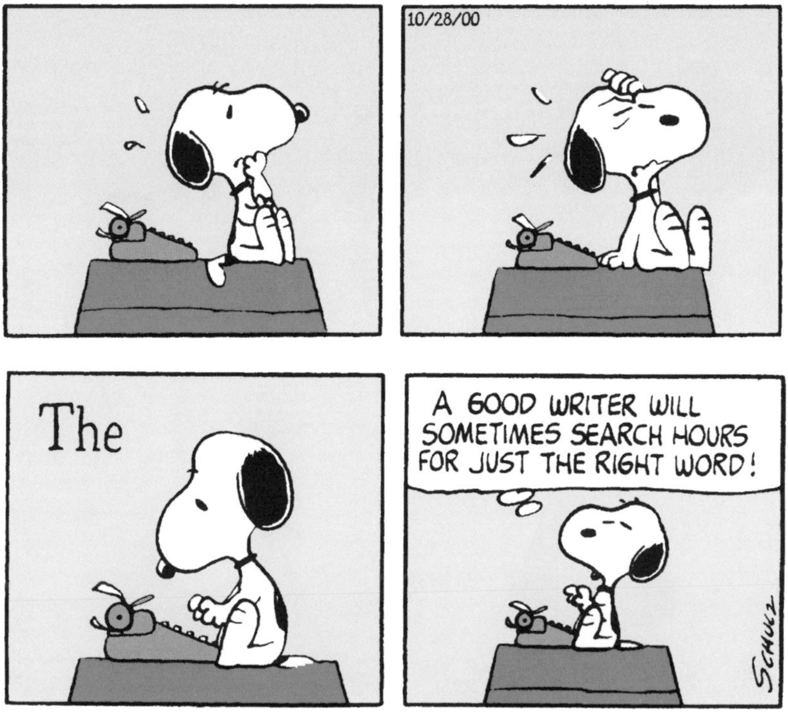
10/28/00
The
A GOOD WRITER WILL SOMETIMES SEARCH HOURS FOR JUST THE RIGHT WORD!
SCHULZ

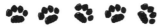

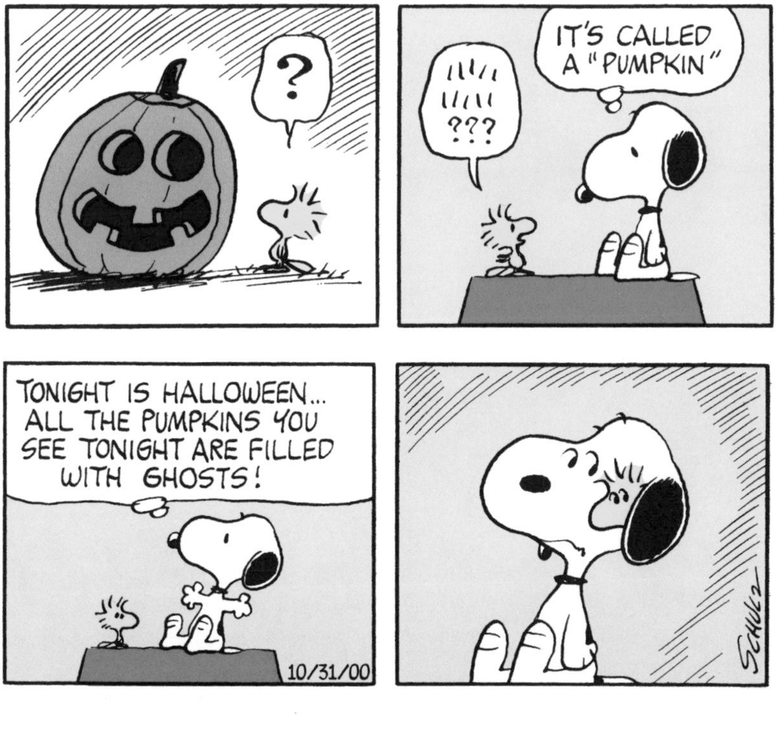
?
???
IT'S CALLED A "PUMPKIN"
TONIGHT IS HALLOWEEN... ALL THE PUMPKINS YOU SEE TONIGHT ARE FILLED WITH GHOSTS!
10/31/00
SCHULZ

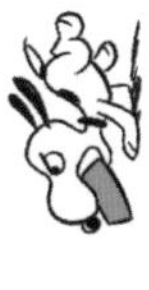

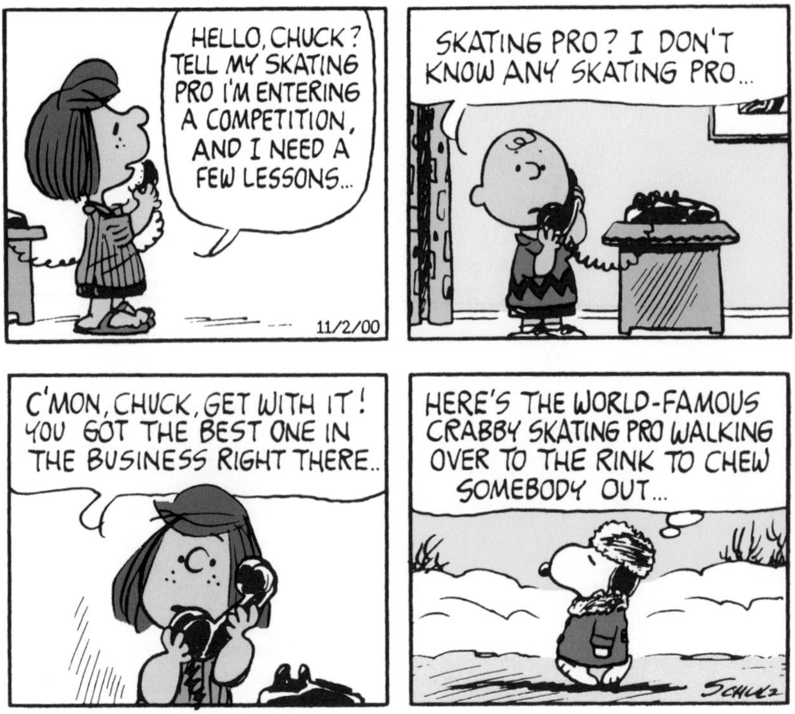
HELLO, CHUCK? TELL MY SKATING PRO I'M ENTERING A COMPETITION, AND I NEED A FEW LESSONS...
11/2/00
SKATING PRO? I DON'T KNOW ANY SKATING PRO...
C'MON, CHUCK, GET WITH IT! YOU GOT THE BEST ONE IN THE BUSINESS RIGHT THERE..
HERE'S THE WORLD-FAMOUS CRABBY SKATING PRO WALKING OVER TO THE RINK TO CHEW SOMEBODY OUT...
SCHULZ

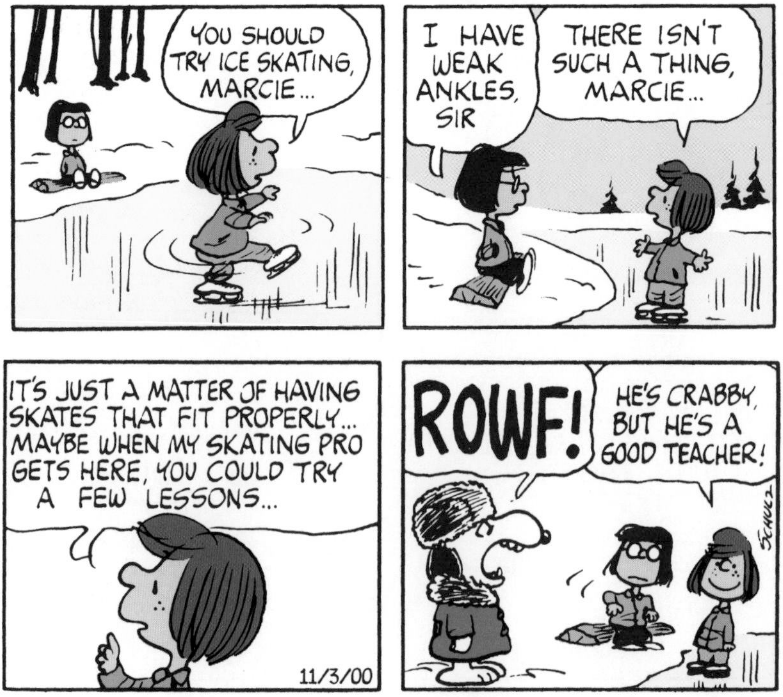
YOU SHOULD TRY ICE SKATING, MARCIE...
I HAVE WEAK ANKLES, SIR
THERE ISN'T SUCH A THING, MARCIE...
IT'S JUST A MATTER OF HAVING SKATES THAT FIT PROPERLY... MAYBE WHEN MY SKATING PRO GETS HERE, YOU COULD TRY A FEW LESSONS...
11/3/00
ROWF!
HE'S CRABBY, BUT HE'S A GOOD TEACHER!
SCHULZ

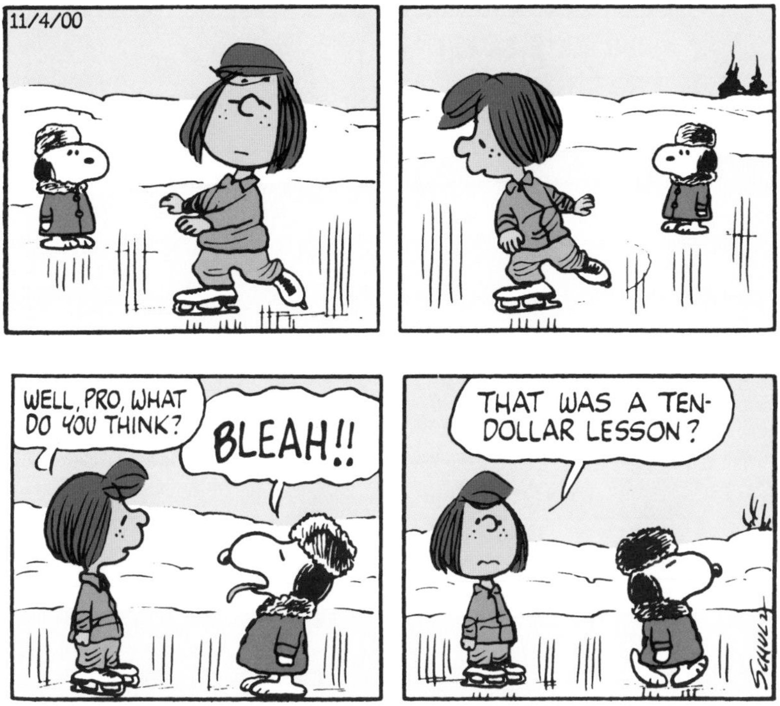
11/4/00
WELL, PRO, WHAT DO YOU THINK?
BLEAH!!
THAT WAS A TEN-DOLLAR LESSON?
SCHULZ

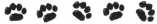

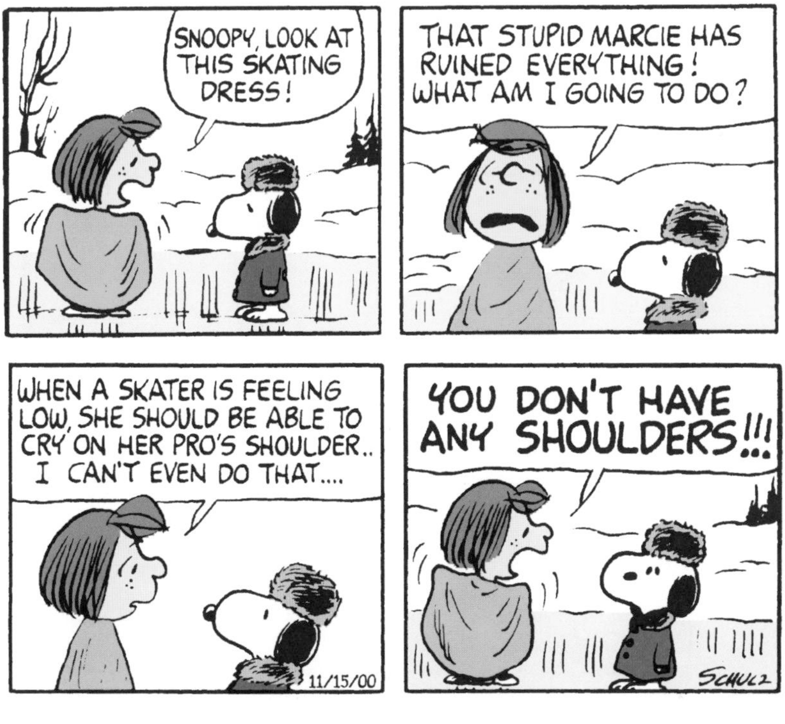
SNOOPY, LOOK AT THIS SKATING DRESS!
THAT STUPID MARCIE HAS RUINED EVERYTHING! WHAT AM I GOING TO DO?
WHEN A SKATER IS FEELING LOW, SHE SHOULD BE ABLE TO CRY ON HER PRO'S SHOULDER.. I CAN'T EVEN DO THAT....
11/15/00
YOU DON'T HAVE ANY SHOULDERS!!!
SCHULZ

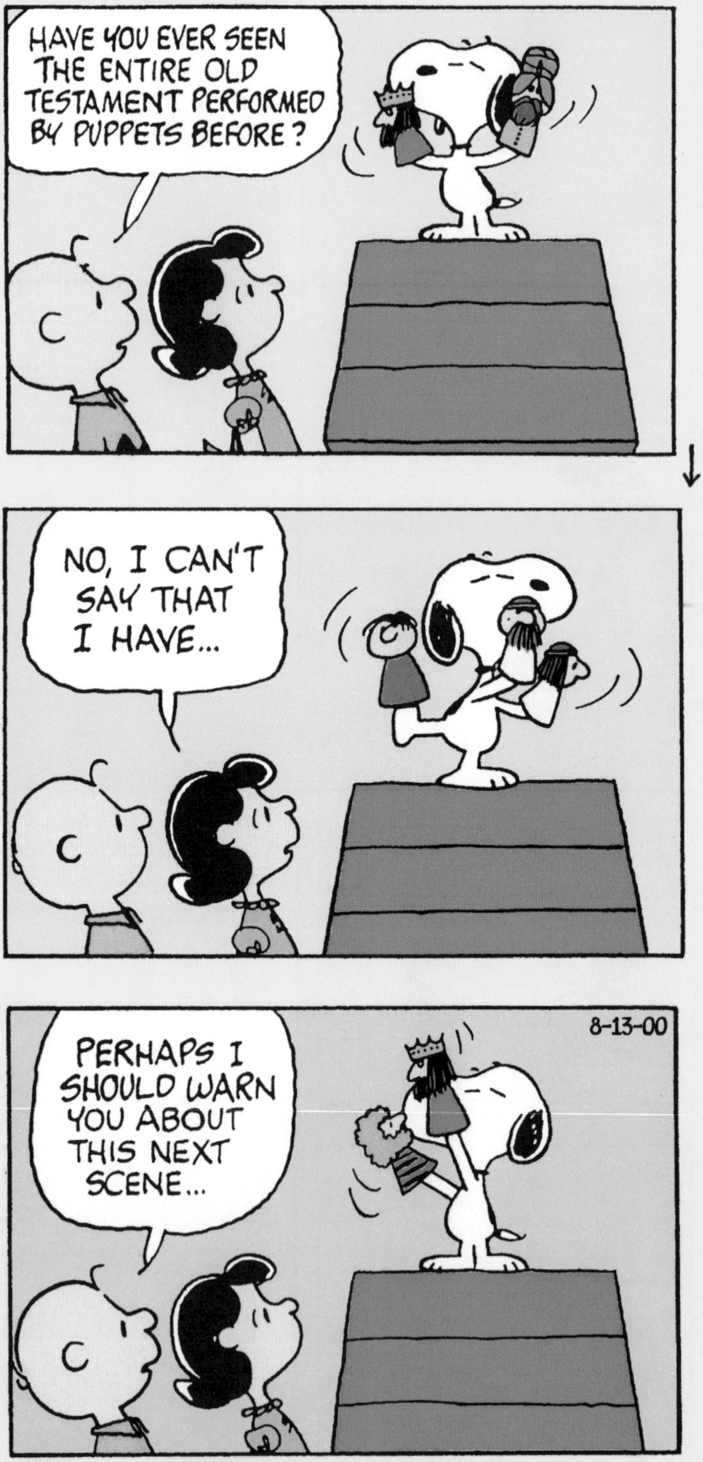
HAVE YOU EVER SEEN THE ENTIRE OLD TESTAMENT PERFORMED BY PUPPETS BEFORE?
NO, I CAN'T SAY THAT I HAVE...
PERHAPS I SHOULD WARN YOU ABOUT THIS NEXT SCENE...
8-13-00

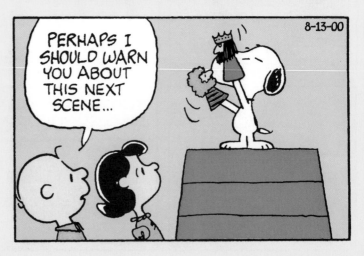

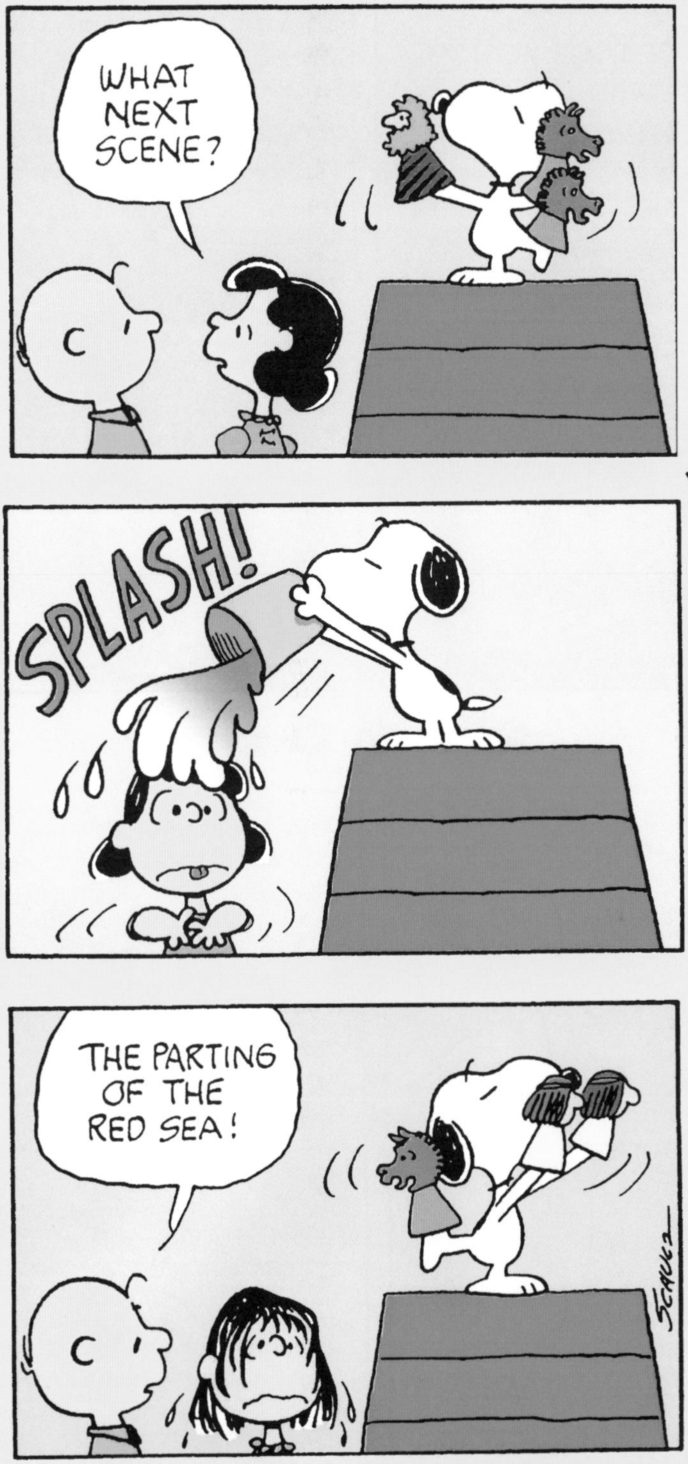
WHAT NEXT SCENE?
SPLASH!
THE PARTING OF THE RED SEA!
SCHULZ

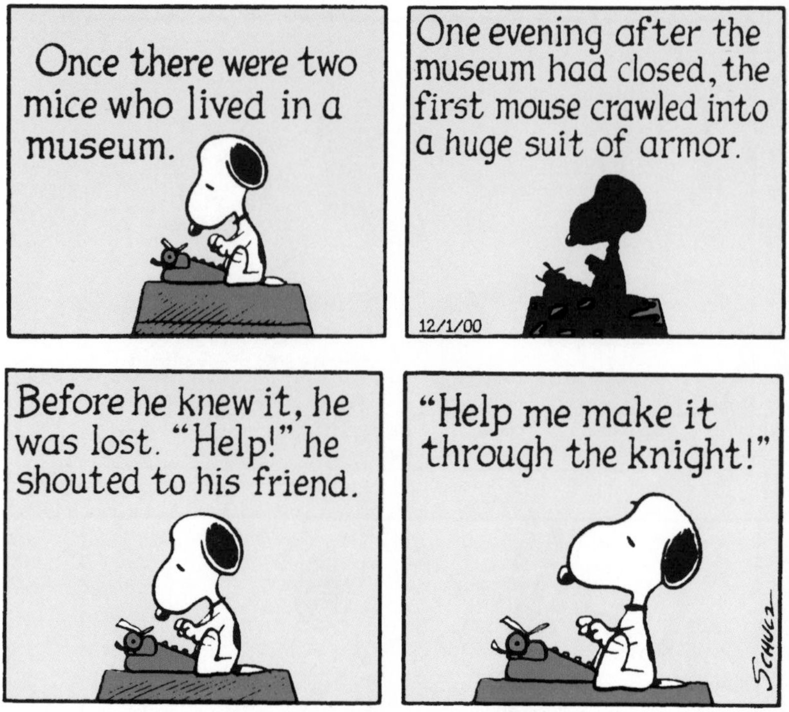
Once there were two mice who lived in a museum.
One evening after the museum had closed, the first mouse crawled into a huge suit of armor.
12/1/00
Before he knew it, he was lost. "Help!" he shouted to his friend.
"Help me make it through the knight!"
SCHULZ

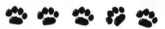

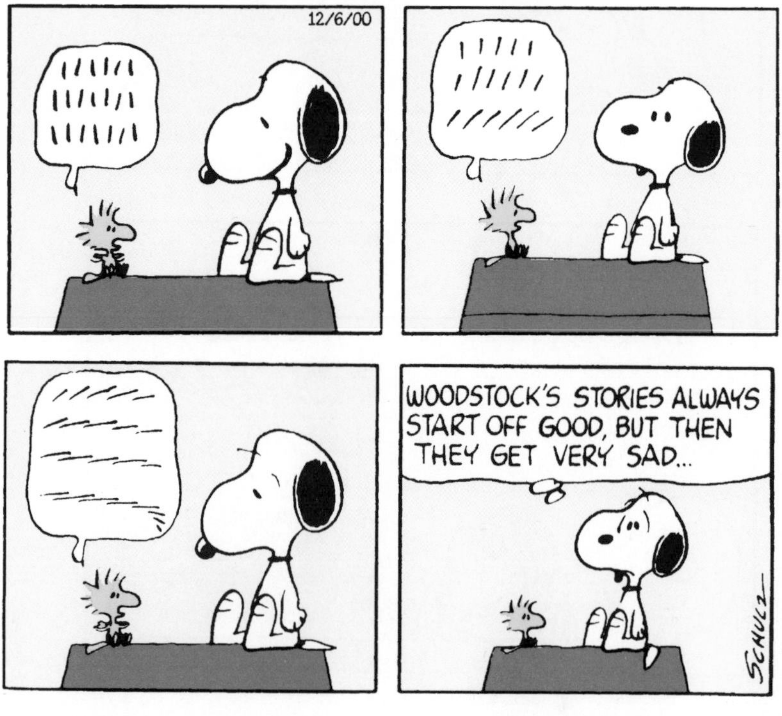
12/6/00
WOODSTOCK'S STORIES ALWAYS START OFF GOOD, BUT THEN THEY GET VERY SAD...
SCHULZ

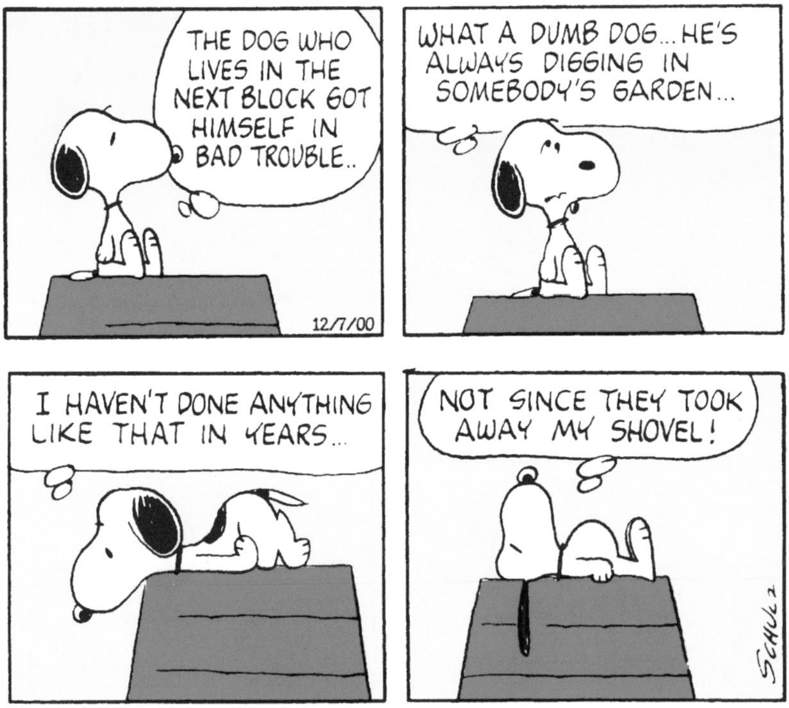
THE DOG WHO LIVES IN THE NEXT BLOCK GOT HIMSELF IN BAD TROUBLE..
12/7/00
WHAT A DUMB DOG... HE'S ALWAYS DIGGING IN SOMEBODY'S GARDEN...
I HAVEN'T DONE ANYTHING LIKE THAT IN YEARS...
NOT SINCE THEY TOOK AWAY MY SHOVEL!
SCHULZ

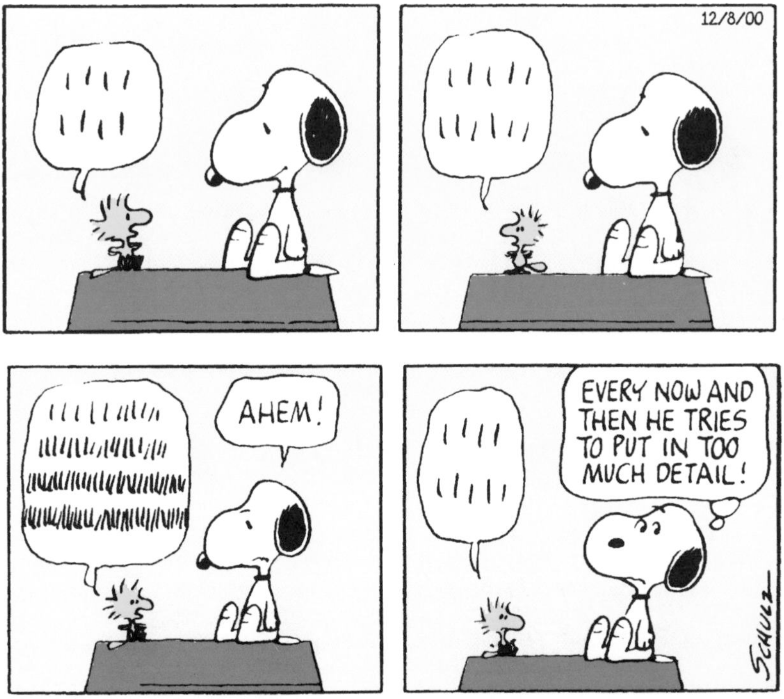
12/8/00
AHEM!
EVERY NOW AND THEN HE TRIES TO PUT IN TOO MUCH DETAIL!
SCHULZ

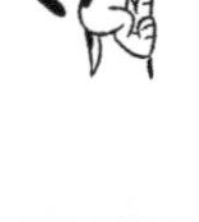

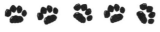

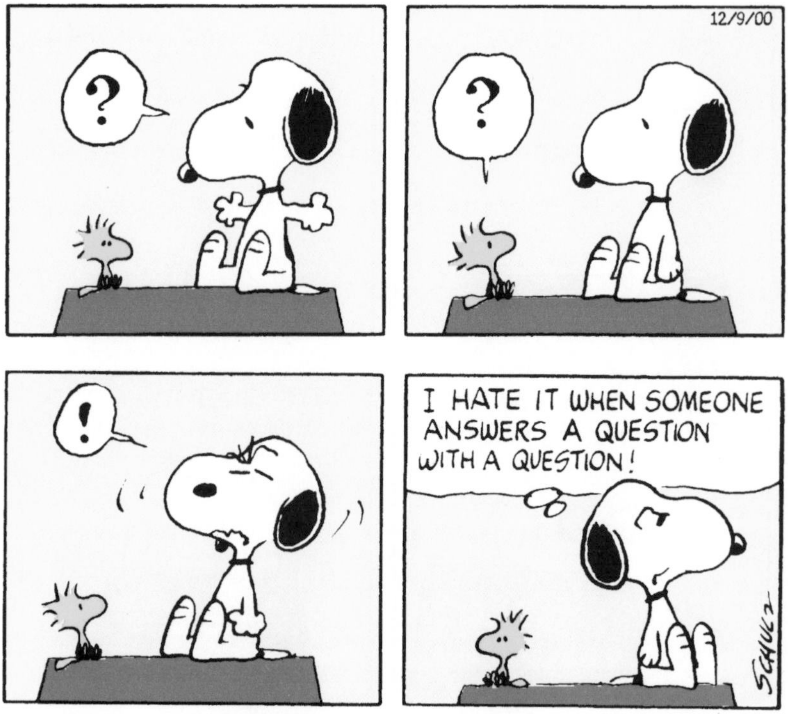
12/9/00
?
?
!
I HATE IT WHEN SOMEONE ANSWERS A QUESTION WITH A QUESTION!
SCHULZ

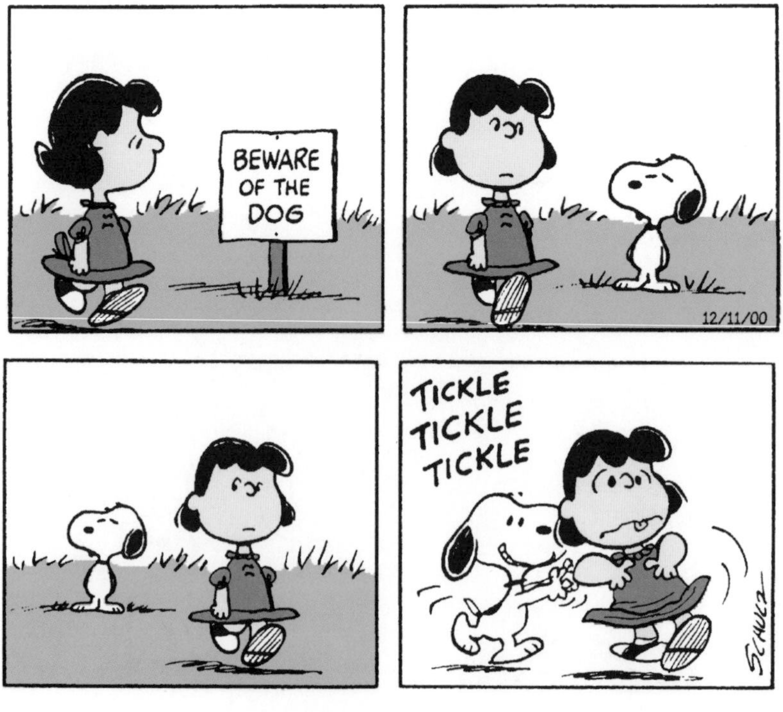
BEWARE OF THE DOG
12/11/00
TICKLE TICKLE TICKLE
SCHULZ

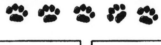

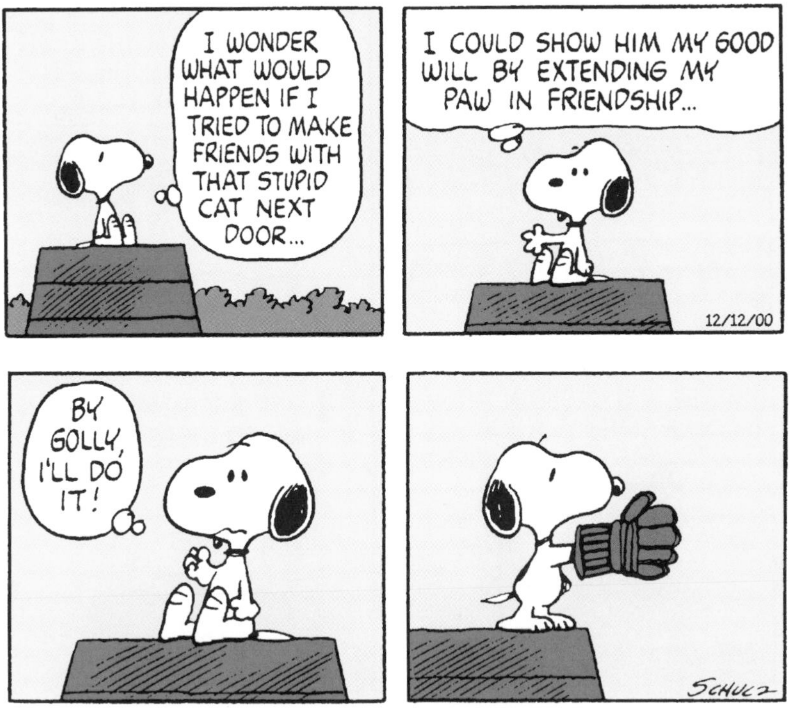
I WONDER WHAT WOULD HAPPEN IF I TRIED TO MAKE FRIENDS WITH THAT STUPID CAT NEXT DOOR...
I COULD SHOW HIM MY GOOD WILL BY EXTENDING MY PAW IN FRIENDSHIP...
12/12/00
BY GOLLY, I'LL DO IT!
SCHULZ

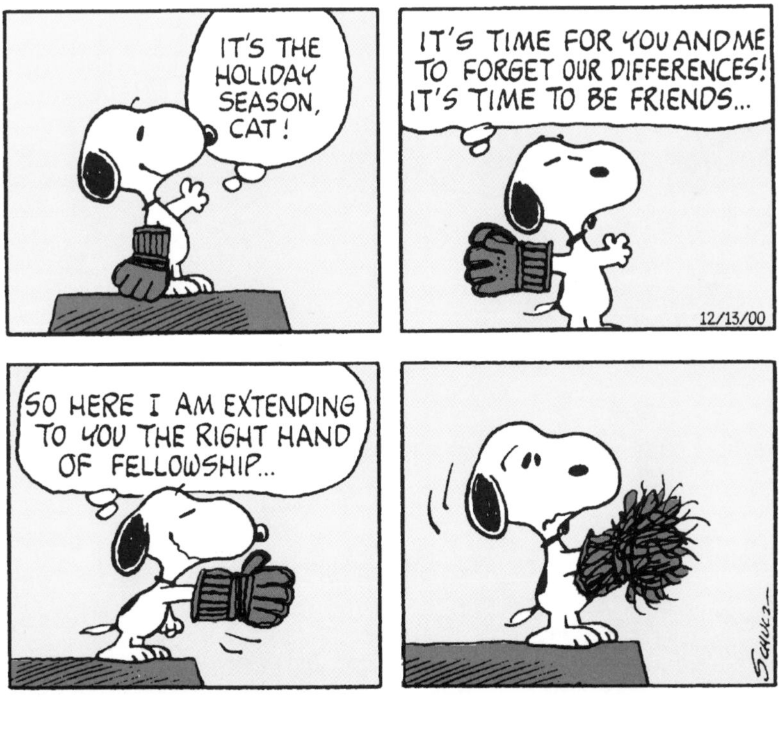
IT'S THE HOLIDAY SEASON, CAT!
IT'S TIME FOR YOU AND ME TO FORGET OUR DIFFERENCES! IT'S TIME TO BE FRIENDS...
12/13/00
SO HERE I AM EXTENDING TO YOU THE RIGHT HAND OF FELLOWSHIP...
SCHULZ

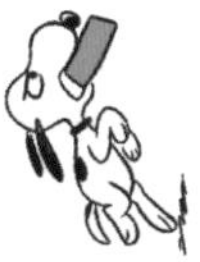

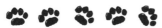

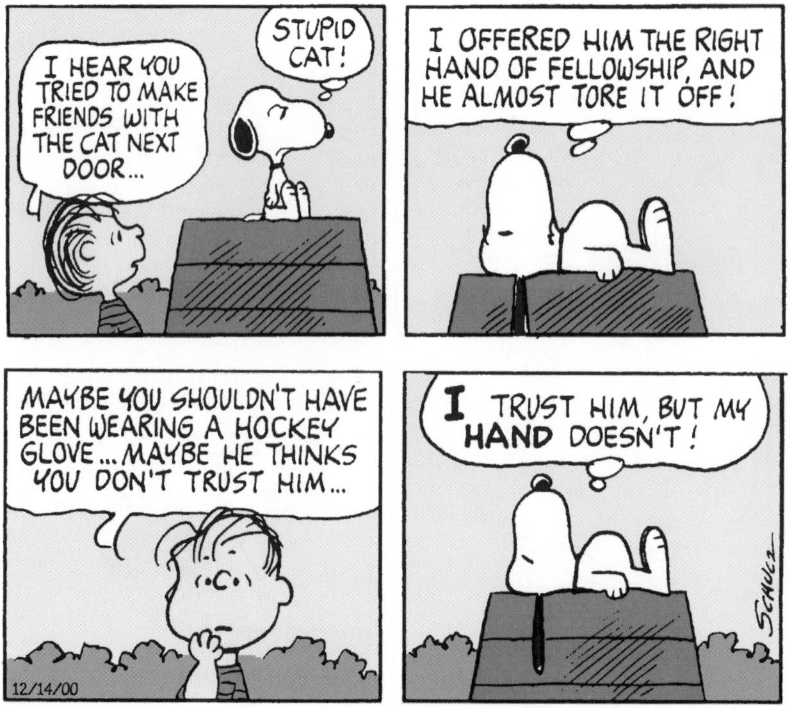
I HEAR YOU TRIED TO MAKE FRIENDS WITH THE CAT NEXT DOOR...
STUPID CAT!
I OFFERED HIM THE RIGHT HAND OF FELLOWSHIP, AND HE ALMOST TORE IT OFF!
MAYBE YOU SHOULDN'T HAVE BEEN WEARING A HOCKEY GLOVE... MAYBE HE THINKS YOU DON'T TRUST HIM...
I TRUST HIM, BUT MY HAND DOESN'T!
12/14/00

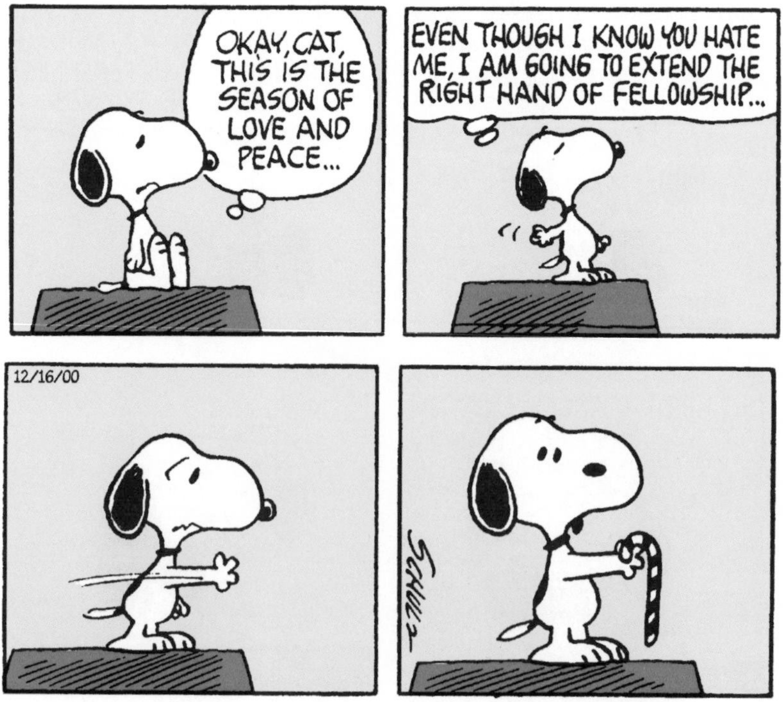
OKAY, CAT, THIS IS THE SEASON OF LOVE AND PEACE...
EVEN THOUGH I KNOW YOU HATE ME, I AM GOING TO EXTEND THE RIGHT HAND OF FELLOWSHIP...
12/16/00

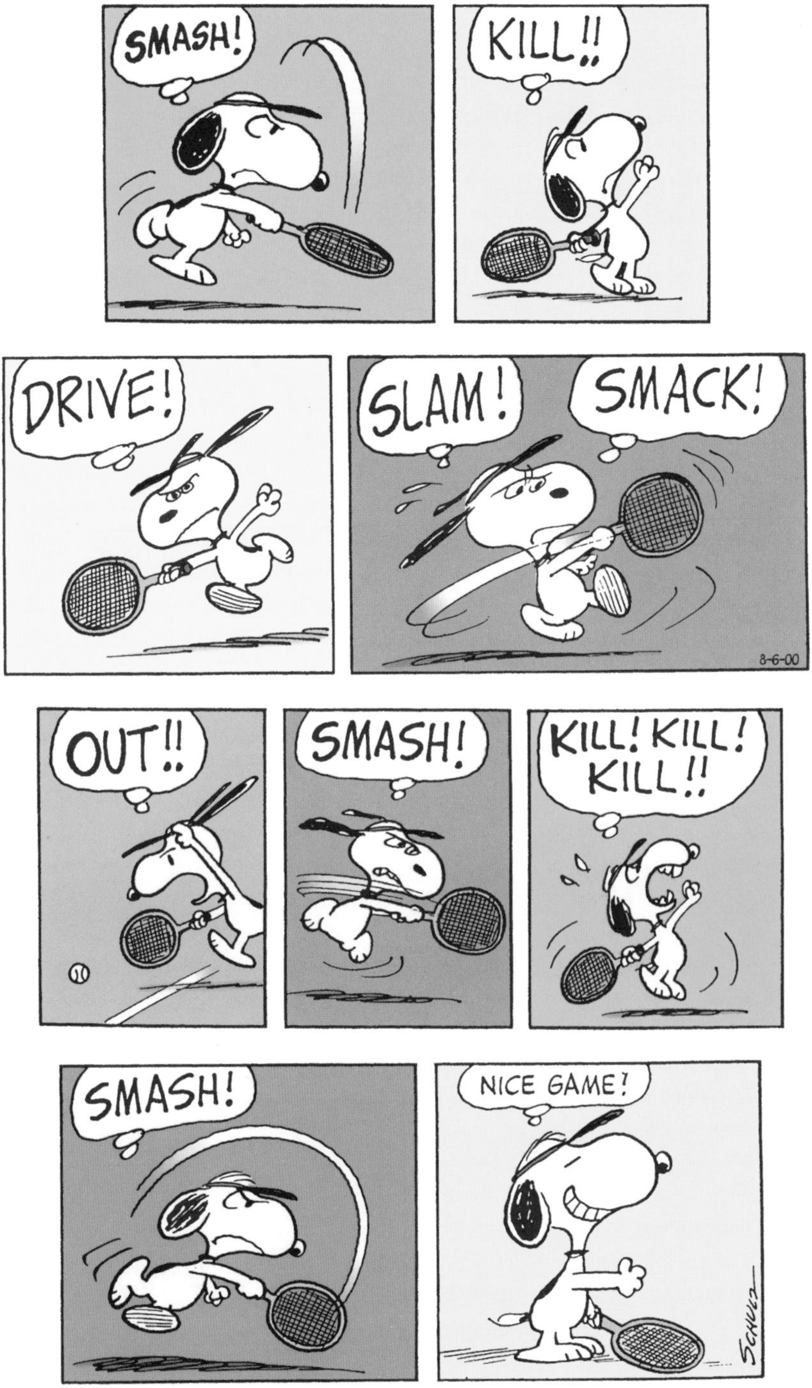
SMASH!
KILL!!
DRIVE!
SLAM!
SMACK!
8-6-00
OUT!!
SMASH!
KILL! KILL! KILL!!
SMASH!
NICE GAME!
SCHULZ

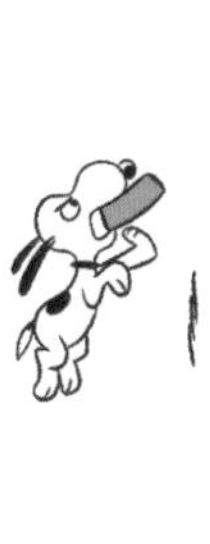

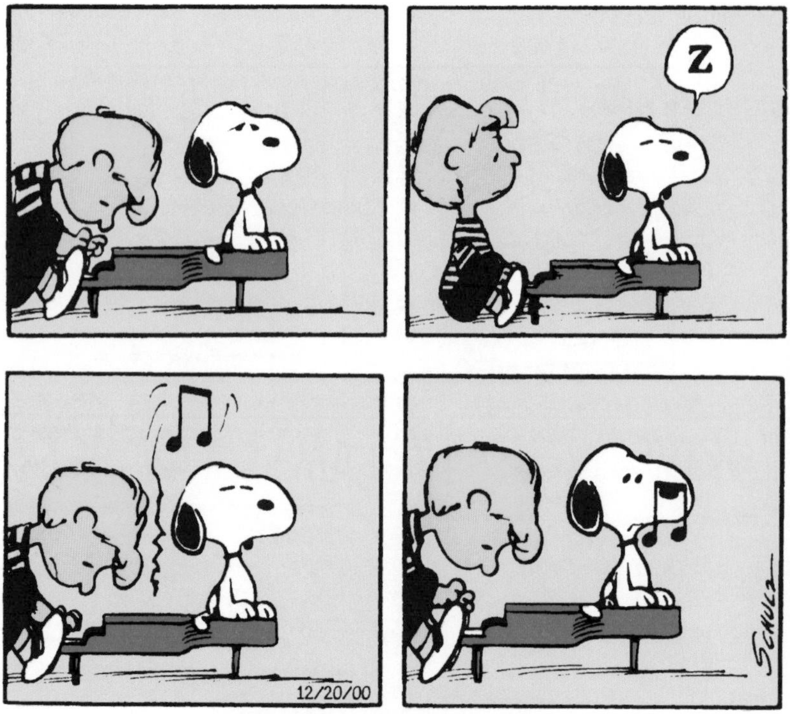
Z
12/20/00
SCHULZ

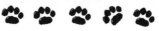

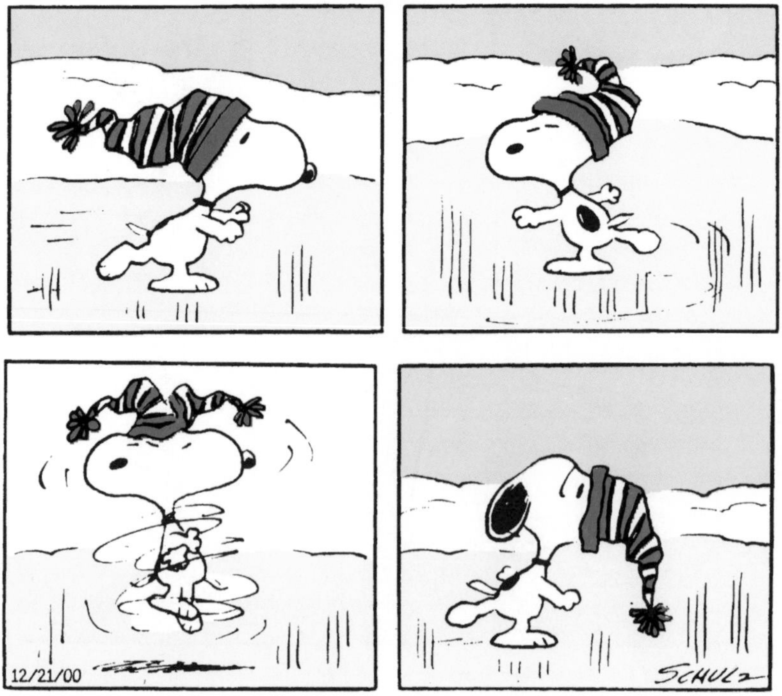
12/21/00
SCHULZ

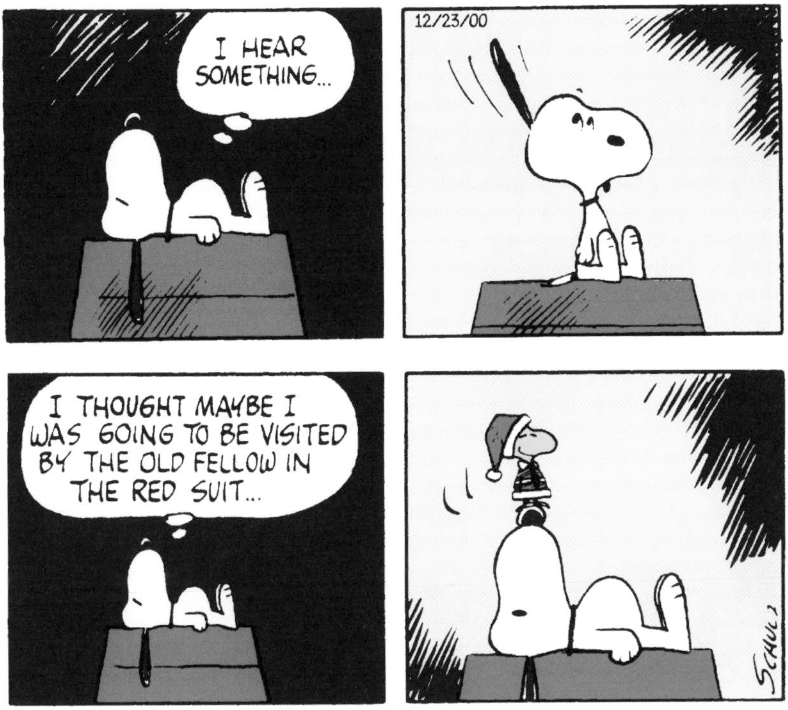
I HEAR SOMETHING...
12/23/00
I THOUGHT MAYBE I WAS GOING TO BE VISITED BY THE OLD FELLOW IN THE RED SUIT...
SCHULZ

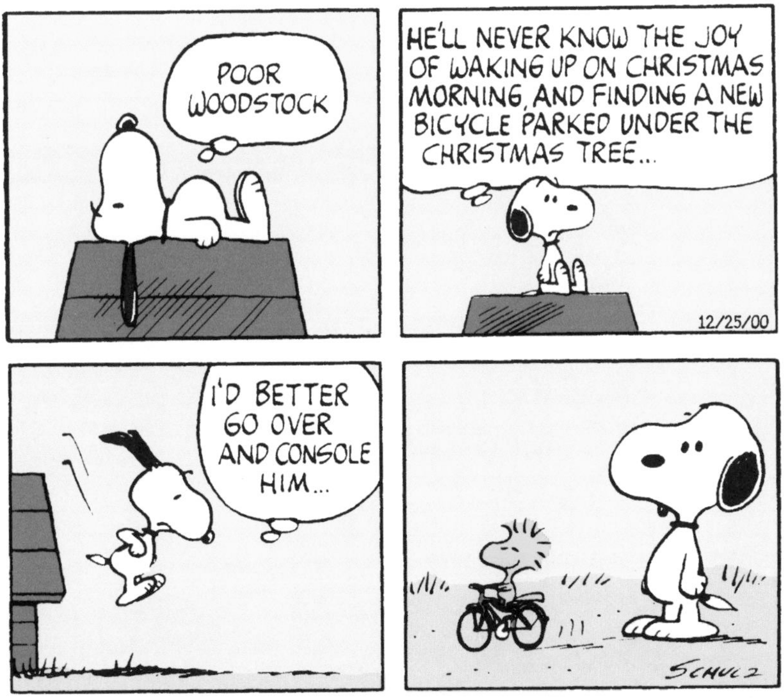
POOR WOODSTOCK
HE'LL NEVER KNOW THE JOY OF WAKING UP ON CHRISTMAS MORNING, AND FINDING A NEW BICYCLE PARKED UNDER THE CHRISTMAS TREE...
12/25/00
I'D BETTER GO OVER AND CONSOLE HIM...
SCHULZ

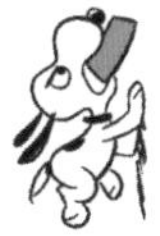

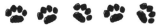

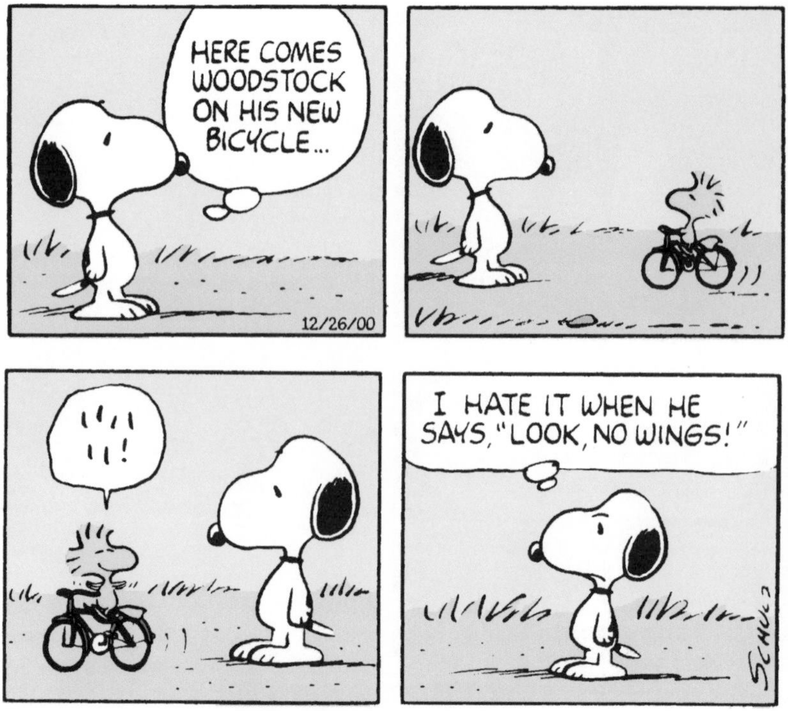
HERE COMES WOODSTOCK ON HIS NEW BICYCLE...
12/26/00
I HATE IT WHEN HE SAYS, "LOOK, NO WINGS!"

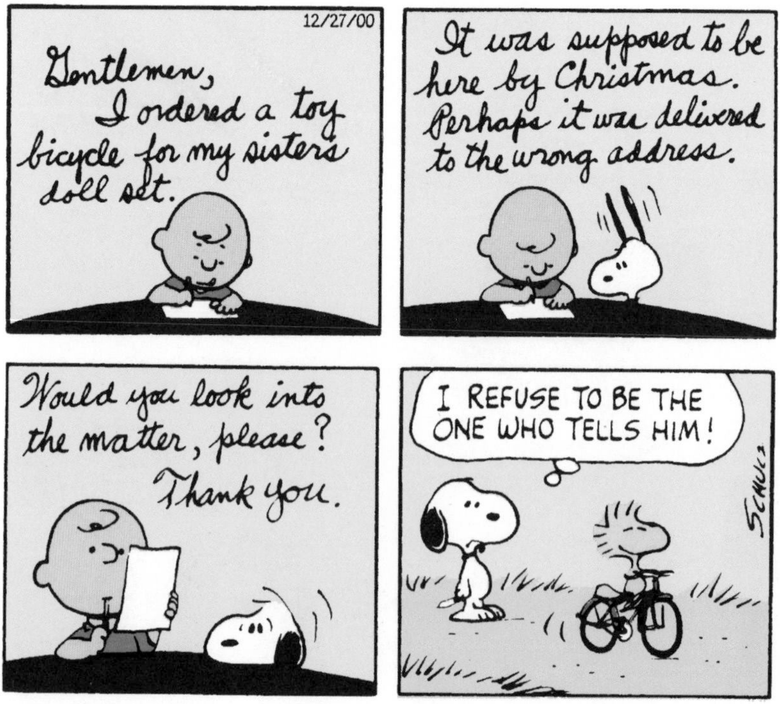
12/27/00
Gentlemen,
I ordered a toy bicycle for my sister's doll set.
It was supposed to be here by Christmas. Perhaps it was delivered to the wrong address.
Would you look into the matter, please?
Thank you.
I REFUSE TO BE THE ONE WHO TELLS HIM!

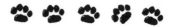

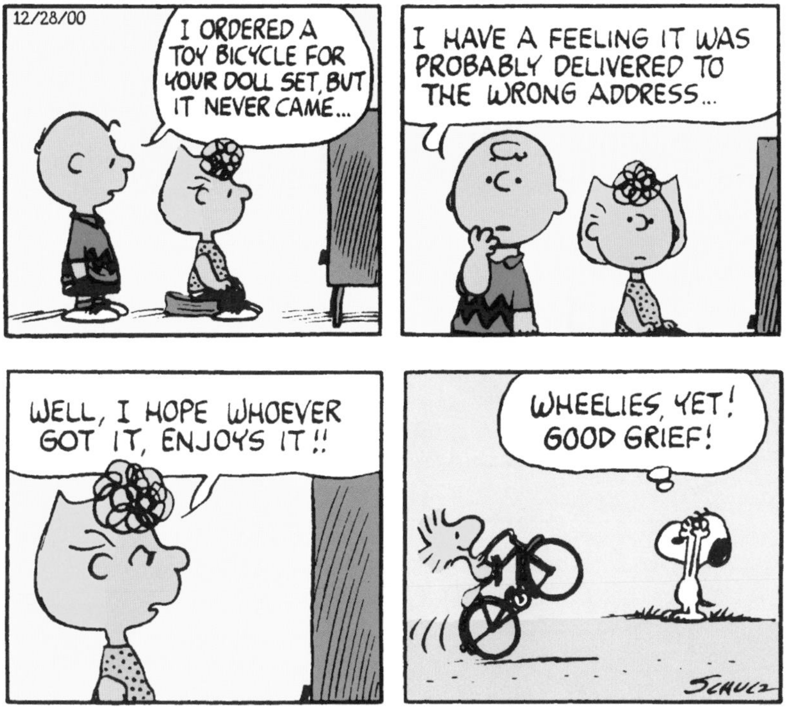
12/28/00
I ORDERED A TOY BICYCLE FOR YOUR DOLL SET, BUT IT NEVER CAME...
I HAVE A FEELING IT WAS PROBABLY DELIVERED TO THE WRONG ADDRESS...
WELL, I HOPE WHOEVER GOT IT, ENJOYS IT!!
WHEELIES, YET! GOOD GRIEF!
SCHULZ

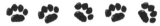

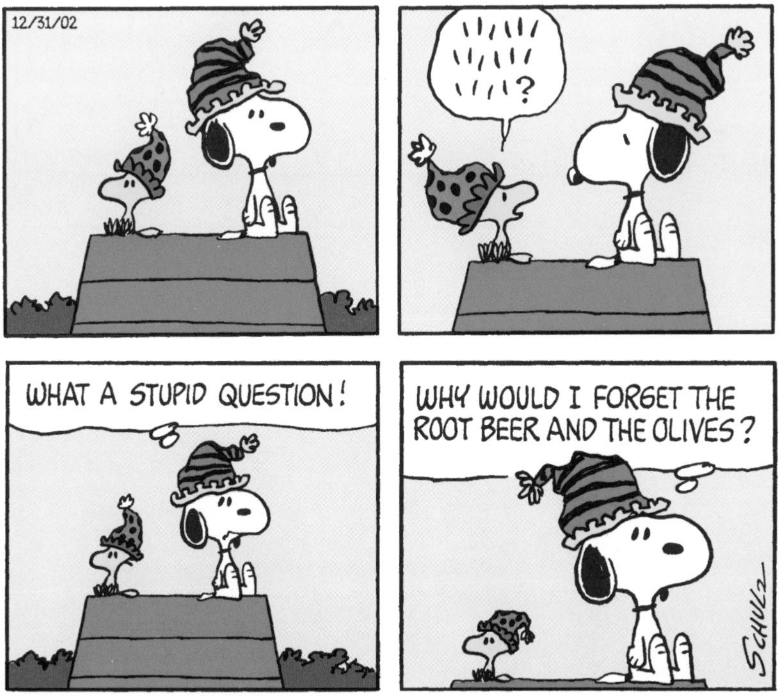
12/31/02
?
WHAT A STUPID QUESTION!
WHY WOULD I FORGET THE ROOT BEER AND THE OLIVES?
SCHULZ

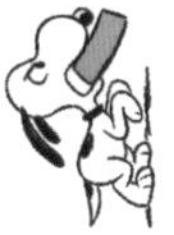

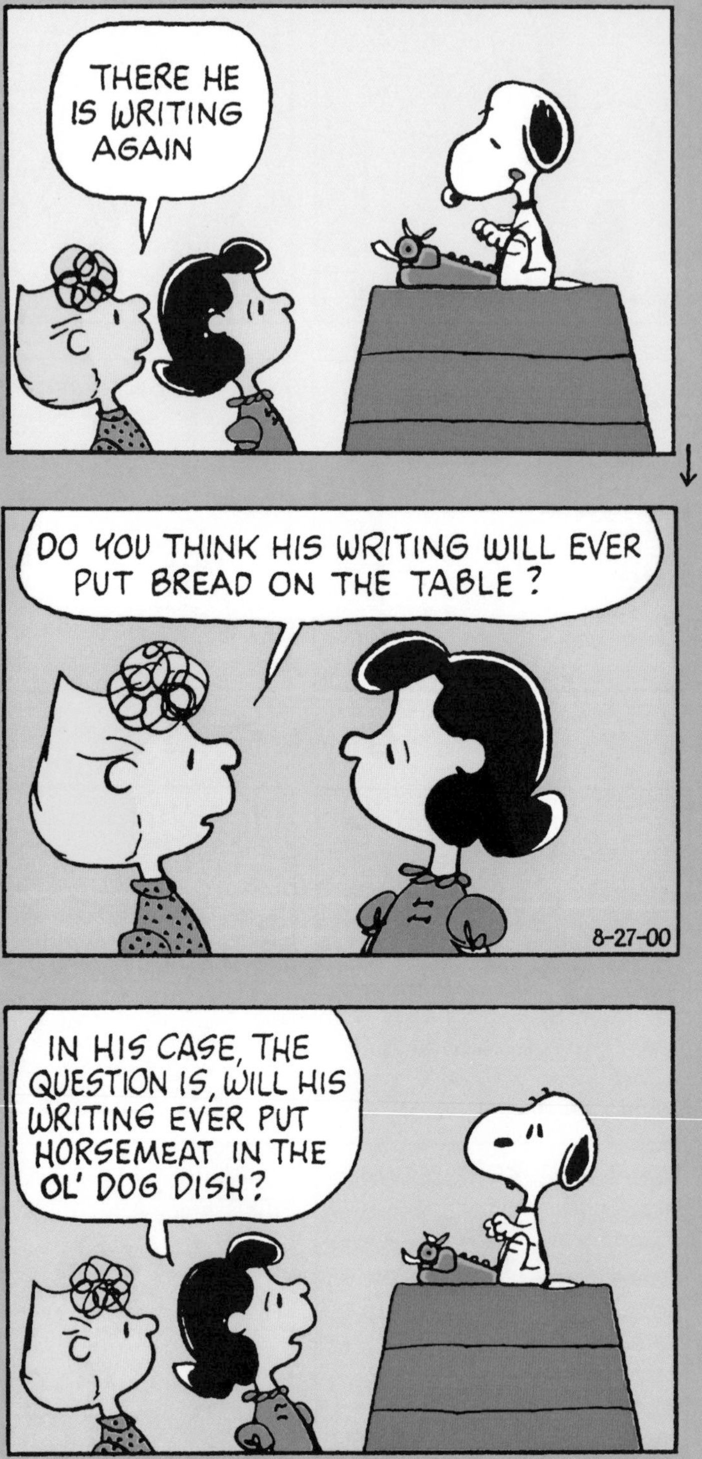
THERE HE IS WRITING AGAIN
DO YOU THINK HIS WRITING WILL EVER PUT BREAD ON THE TABLE?
8-27-00
IN HIS CASE, THE QUESTION IS, WILL HIS WRITING EVER PUT HORSEMEAT IN THE OL' DOG DISH?

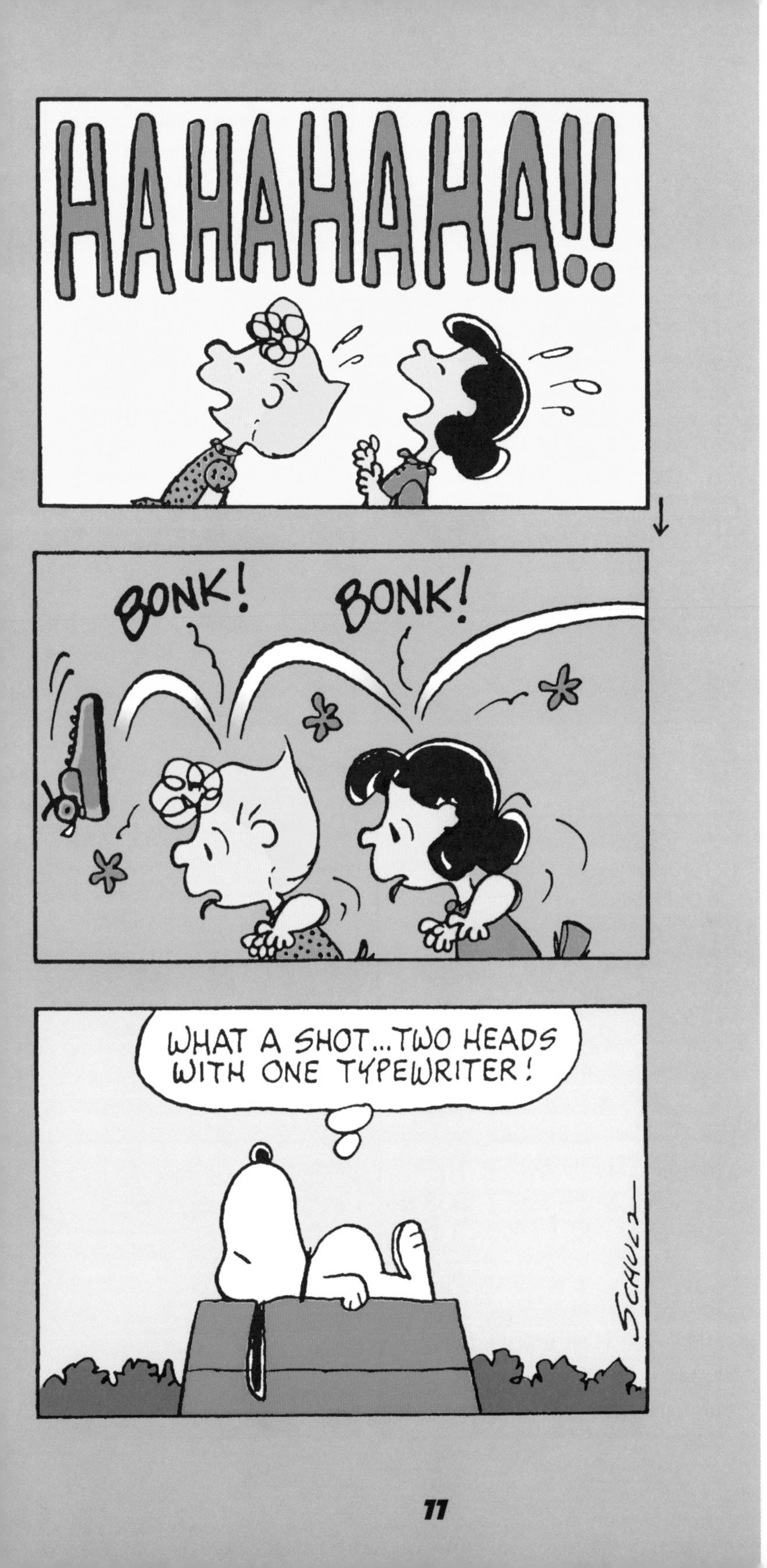
HAHAHAHA!!
BONK! BONK!
WHAT A SHOT...TWO HEADS WITH ONE TYPEWRITER!
SCHULZ

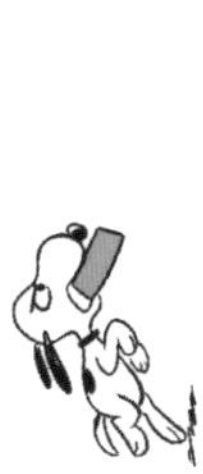

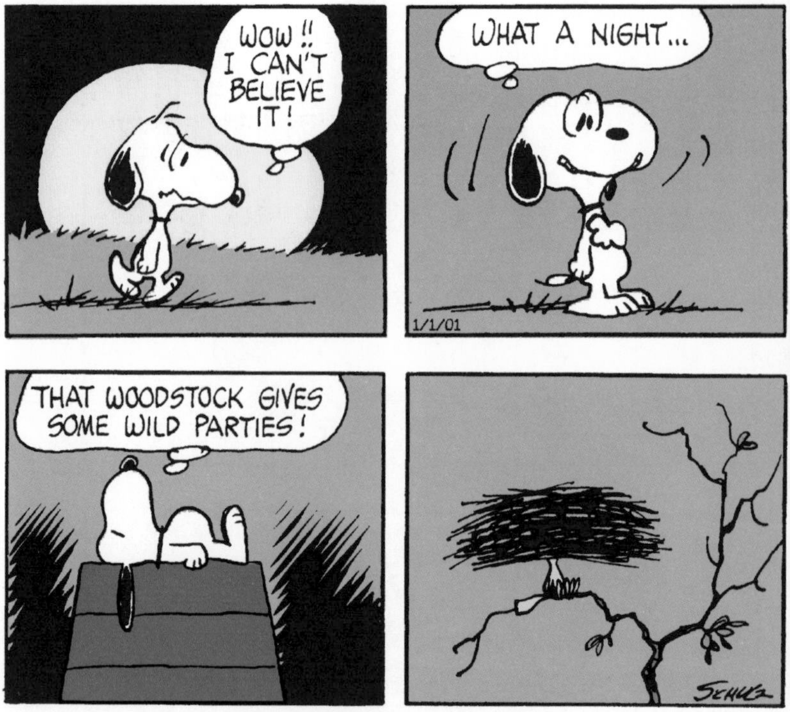
WOW!! I CAN'T BELIEVE IT!
WHAT A NIGHT...
1/1/01
THAT WOODSTOCK GIVES SOME WILD PARTIES!
SCHULZ

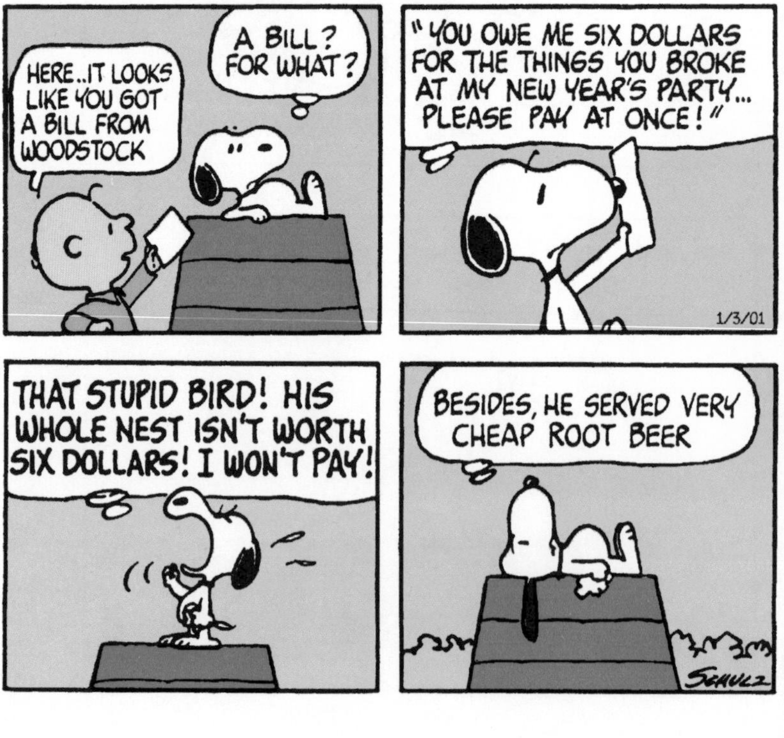
HERE..IT LOOKS LIKE YOU GOT A BILL FROM WOODSTOCK
A BILL? FOR WHAT?
"YOU OWE ME SIX DOLLARS FOR THE THINGS YOU BROKE AT MY NEW YEAR'S PARTY... PLEASE PAY AT ONCE!"
1/3/01
THAT STUPID BIRD! HIS WHOLE NEST ISN'T WORTH SIX DOLLARS! I WON'T PAY!
BESIDES, HE SERVED VERY CHEAP ROOT BEER
SCHULZ

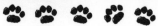

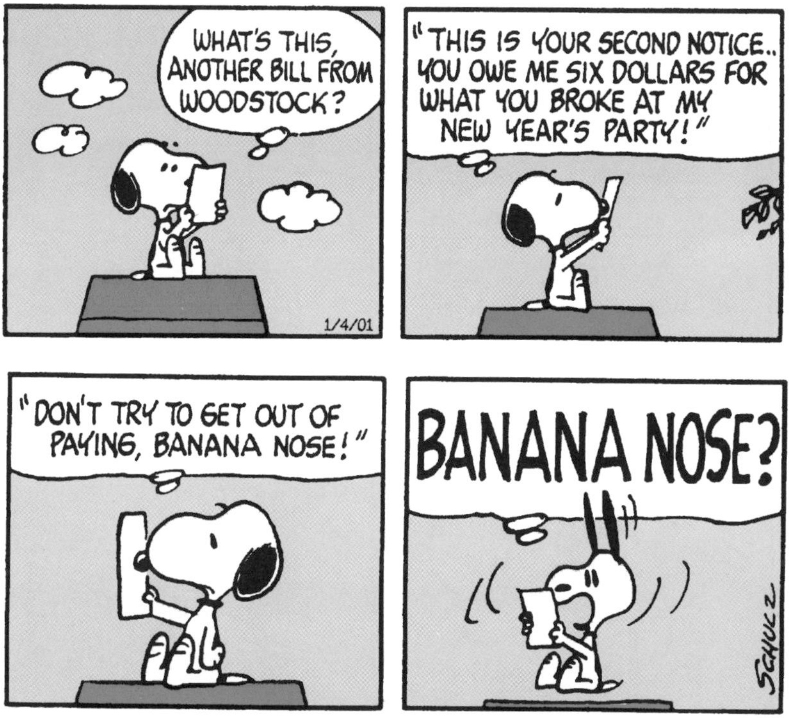
WHAT'S THIS, ANOTHER BILL FROM WOODSTOCK?
1/4/01
"THIS IS YOUR SECOND NOTICE.. YOU OWE ME SIX DOLLARS FOR WHAT YOU BROKE AT MY NEW YEAR'S PARTY!"
"DON'T TRY TO GET OUT OF PAYING, BANANA NOSE!"
BANANA NOSE?
SCHULZ

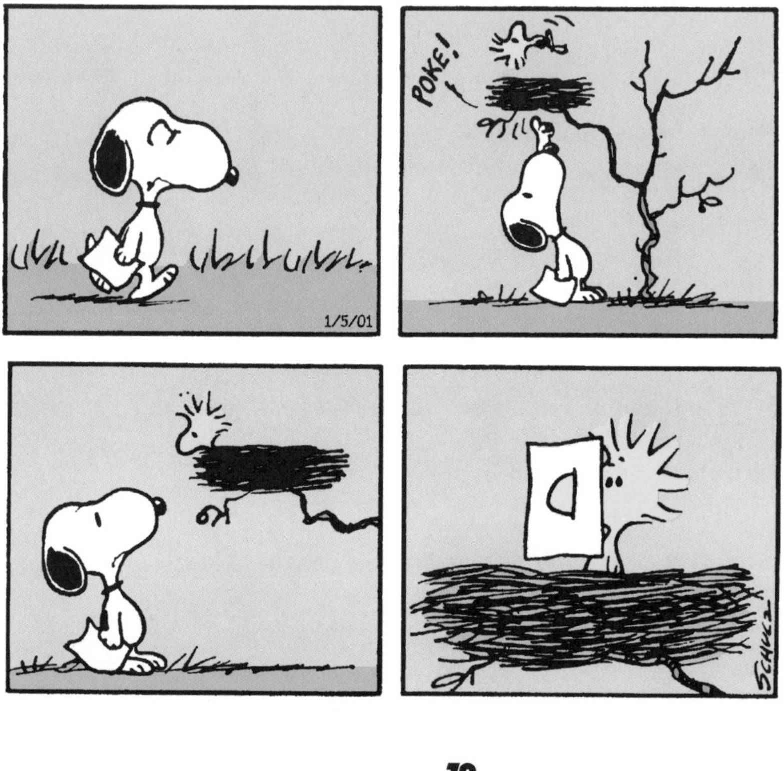
1/5/01
POKE!
SCHULZ

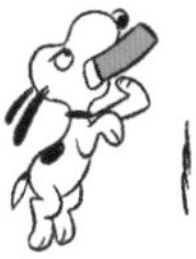

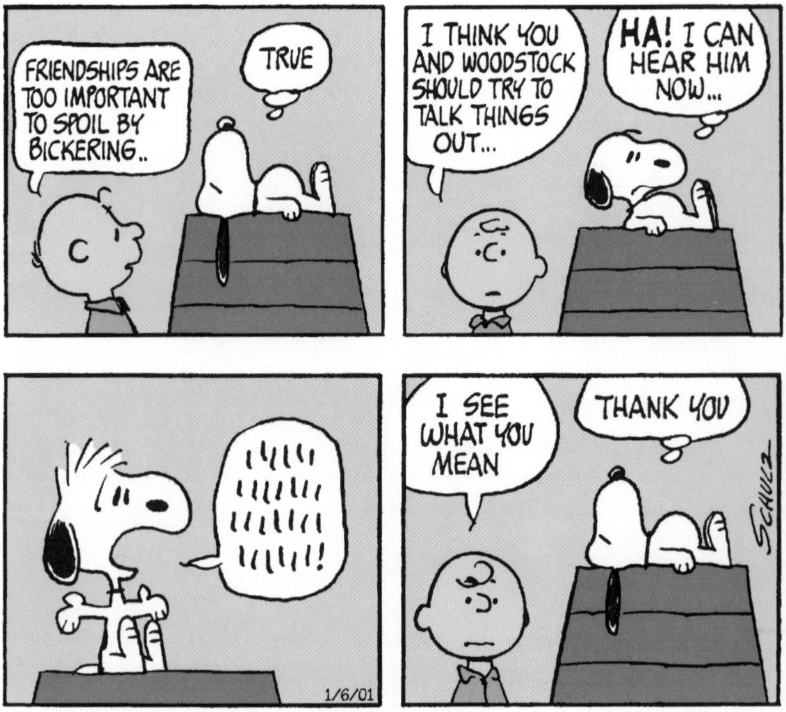
FRIENDSHIPS ARE TOO IMPORTANT TO SPOIL BY BICKERING..
TRUE
I THINK YOU AND WOODSTOCK SHOULD TRY TO TALK THINGS OUT...
HA! I CAN HEAR HIM NOW...
1/6/01
I SEE WHAT YOU MEAN
THANK YOU
SCHULZ

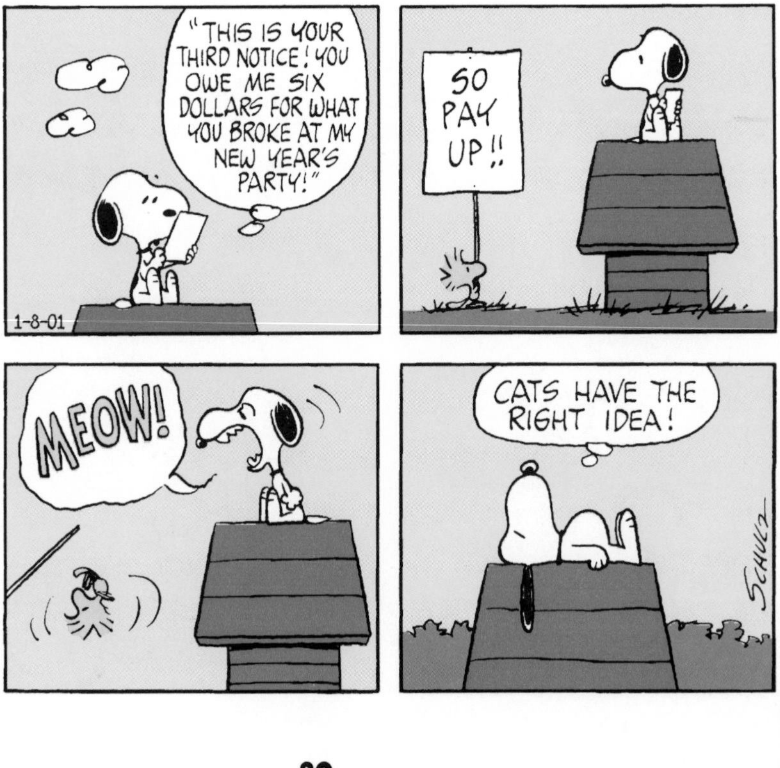
"THIS IS YOUR THIRD NOTICE! YOU OWE ME SIX DOLLARS FOR WHAT YOU BROKE AT MY NEW YEAR'S PARTY!"
1-8-01
SO PAY UP!!
MEOW!
CATS HAVE THE RIGHT IDEA!
SCHULZ

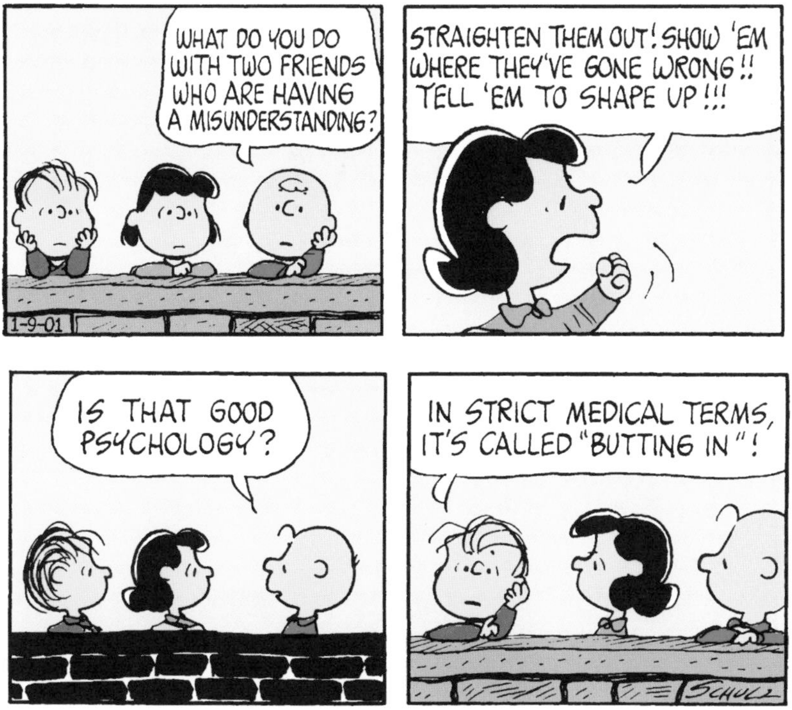
WHAT DO YOU DO WITH TWO FRIENDS WHO ARE HAVING A MISUNDERSTANDING?
1-9-01
STRAIGHTEN THEM OUT! SHOW 'EM WHERE THEY'VE GONE WRONG!! TELL 'EM TO SHAPE UP!!!
IS THAT GOOD PSYCHOLOGY?
IN STRICT MEDICAL TERMS, IT'S CALLED "BUTTING IN"!
SCHULZ

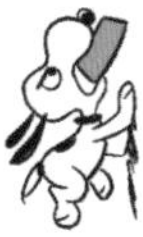

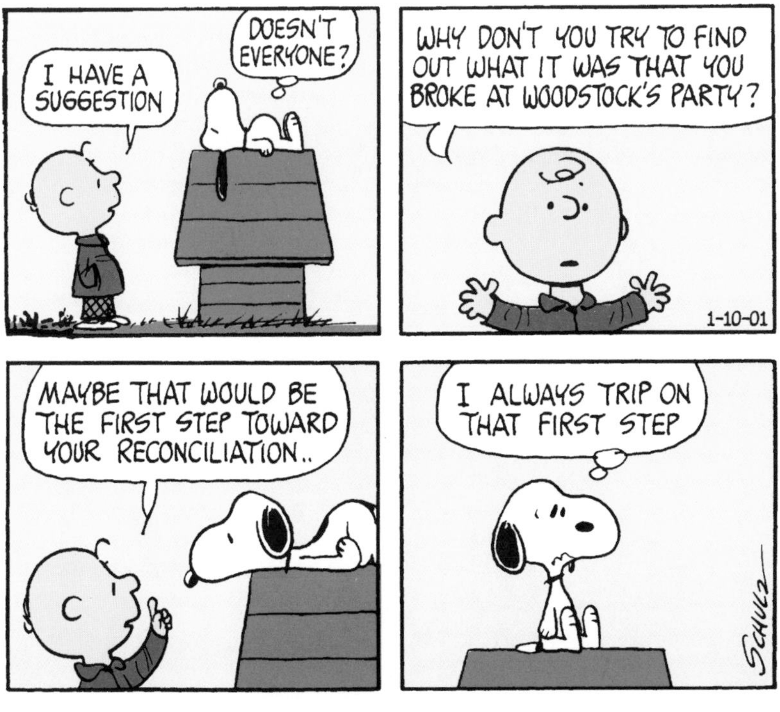
I HAVE A SUGGESTION
DOESN'T EVERYONE?
WHY DON'T YOU TRY TO FIND OUT WHAT IT WAS THAT YOU BROKE AT WOODSTOCK'S PARTY?
1-10-01
MAYBE THAT WOULD BE THE FIRST STEP TOWARD YOUR RECONCILIATION..
I ALWAYS TRIP ON THAT FIRST STEP
SCHULZ

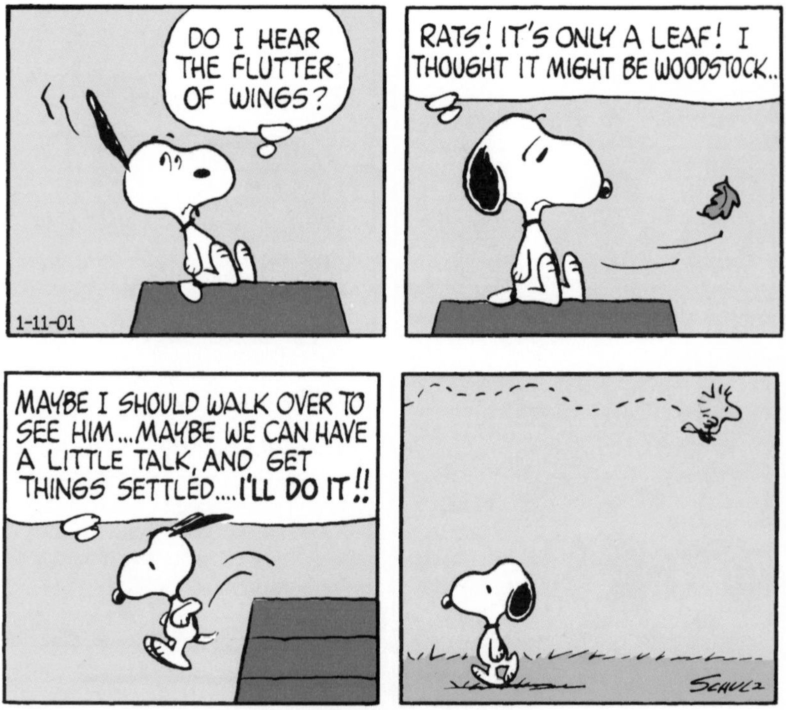
DO I HEAR THE FLUTTER OF WINGS?
1-11-01
RATS! IT'S ONLY A LEAF! I THOUGHT IT MIGHT BE WOODSTOCK..
MAYBE I SHOULD WALK OVER TO SEE HIM...MAYBE WE CAN HAVE A LITTLE TALK, AND GET THINGS SETTLED....I'LL DO IT!!

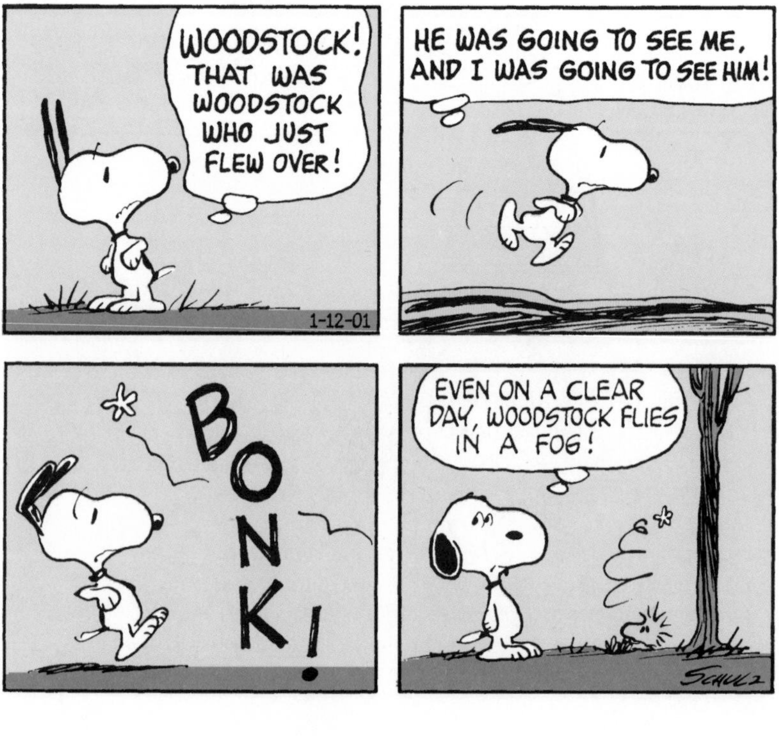
WOODSTOCK! THAT WAS WOODSTOCK WHO JUST FLEW OVER!
1-12-01
HE WAS GOING TO SEE ME, AND I WAS GOING TO SEE HIM!
BONK!
EVEN ON A CLEAR DAY, WOODSTOCK FLIES IN A FOG!

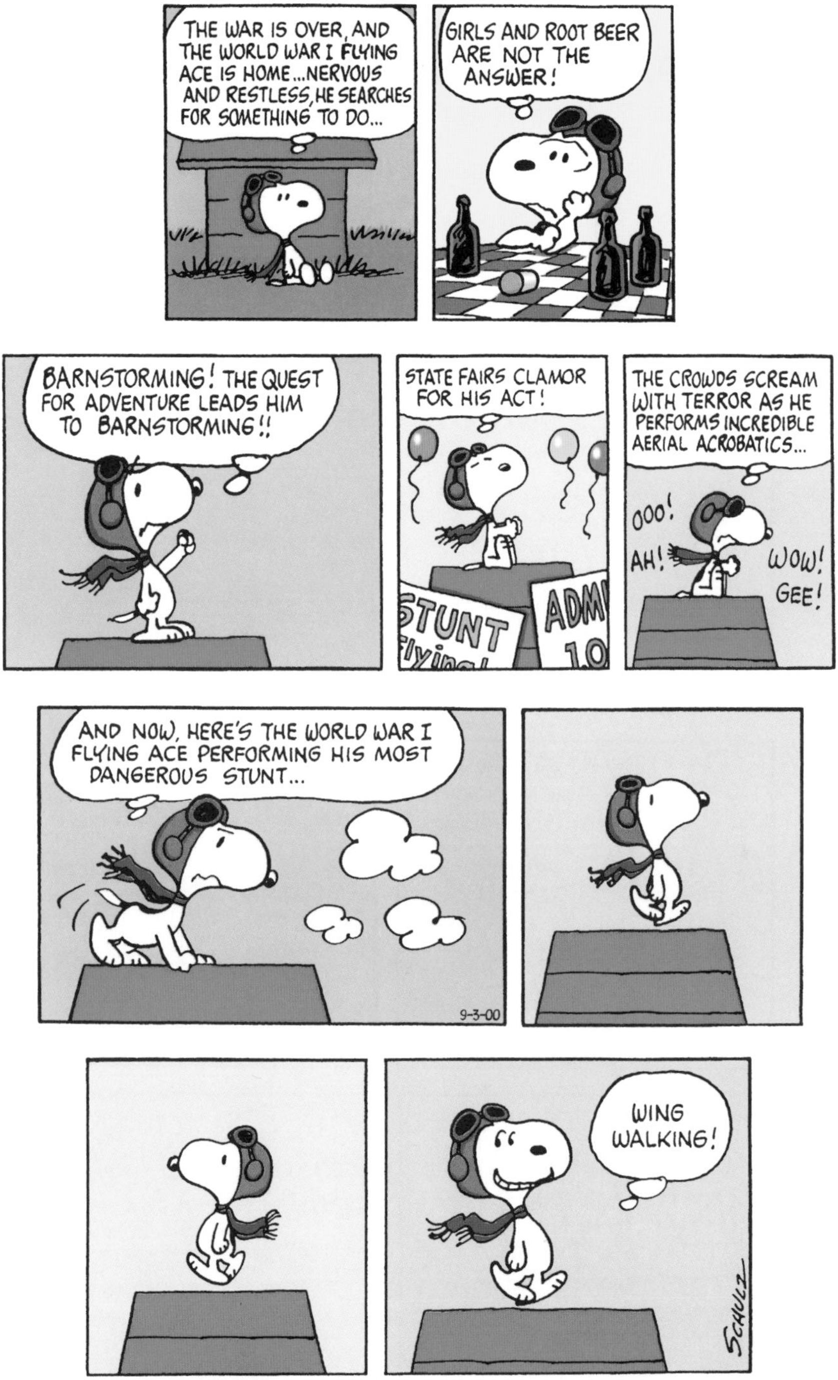
THE WAR IS OVER, AND THE WORLD WAR I FLYING ACE IS HOME...NERVOUS AND RESTLESS, HE SEARCHES FOR SOMETHING TO DO...
GIRLS AND ROOT BEER ARE NOT THE ANSWER!
BARNSTORMING! THE QUEST FOR ADVENTURE LEADS HIM TO BARNSTORMING!!
STATE FAIRS CLAMOR FOR HIS ACT!
STUNT
THE CROWDS SCREAM WITH TERROR AS HE PERFORMS INCREDIBLE AERIAL ACROBATICS...
OOO!
AH!
WOW!
GEE!
AND NOW, HERE'S THE WORLD WAR I FLYING ACE PERFORMING HIS MOST DANGEROUS STUNT...
9-3-00
WING WALKING!
SCHULZ

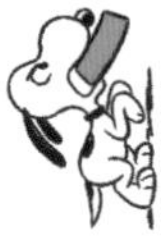

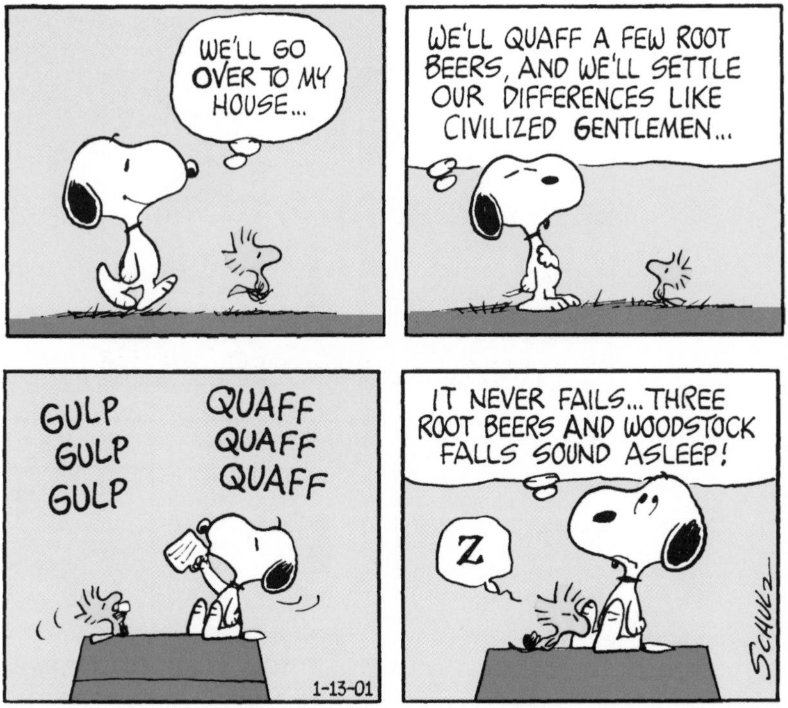
WE'LL GO OVER TO MY HOUSE...
WE'LL QUAFF A FEW ROOT BEERS, AND WE'LL SETTLE OUR DIFFERENCES LIKE CIVILIZED GENTLEMEN...
GULP GULP GULP
QUAFF QUAFF QUAFF
1-13-01
IT NEVER FAILS...THREE ROOT BEERS AND WOODSTOCK FALLS SOUND ASLEEP!
Z
SCHULZ

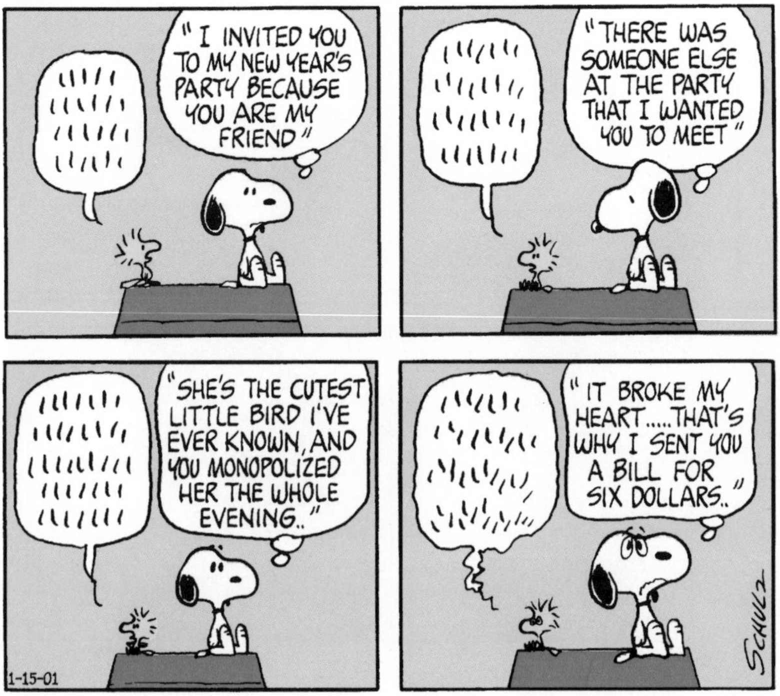
"I INVITED YOU TO MY NEW YEAR'S PARTY BECAUSE YOU ARE MY FRIEND"
"THERE WAS SOMEONE ELSE AT THE PARTY THAT I WANTED YOU TO MEET"
"SHE'S THE CUTEST LITTLE BIRD I'VE EVER KNOWN, AND YOU MONOPOLIZED HER THE WHOLE EVENING.."
1-15-01
"IT BROKE MY HEART.....THAT'S WHY I SENT YOU A BILL FOR SIX DOLLARS.."
SCHULZ

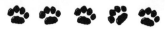

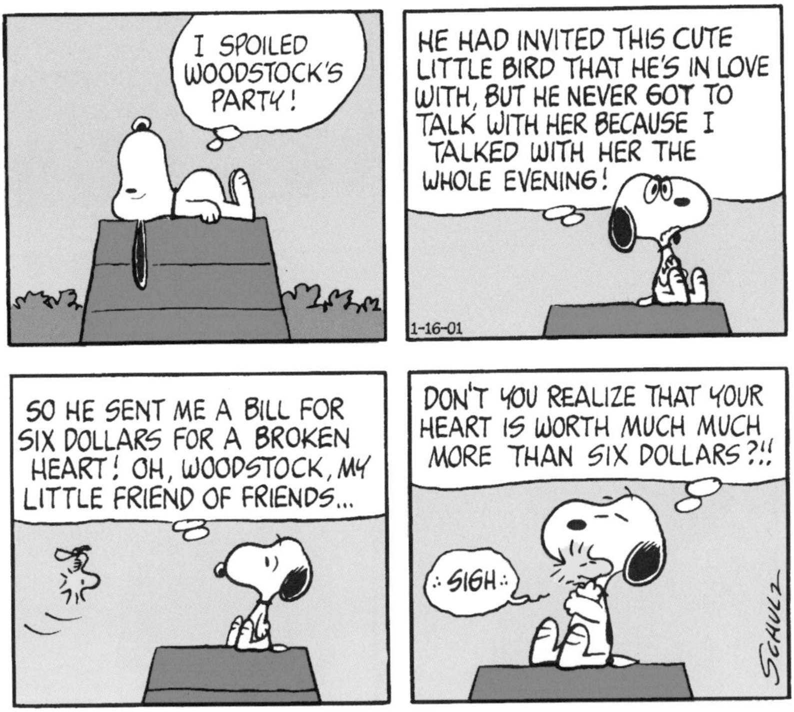
I SPOILED WOODSTOCK'S PARTY!
HE HAD INVITED THIS CUTE LITTLE BIRD THAT HE'S IN LOVE WITH, BUT HE NEVER GOT TO TALK WITH HER BECAUSE I TALKED WITH HER THE WHOLE EVENING!
1-16-01
SO HE SENT ME A BILL FOR SIX DOLLARS FOR A BROKEN HEART! OH, WOODSTOCK, MY LITTLE FRIEND OF FRIENDS...
DON'T YOU REALIZE THAT YOUR HEART IS WORTH MUCH MUCH MORE THAN SIX DOLLARS?!!
SIGH
SCHULZ

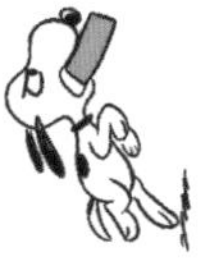

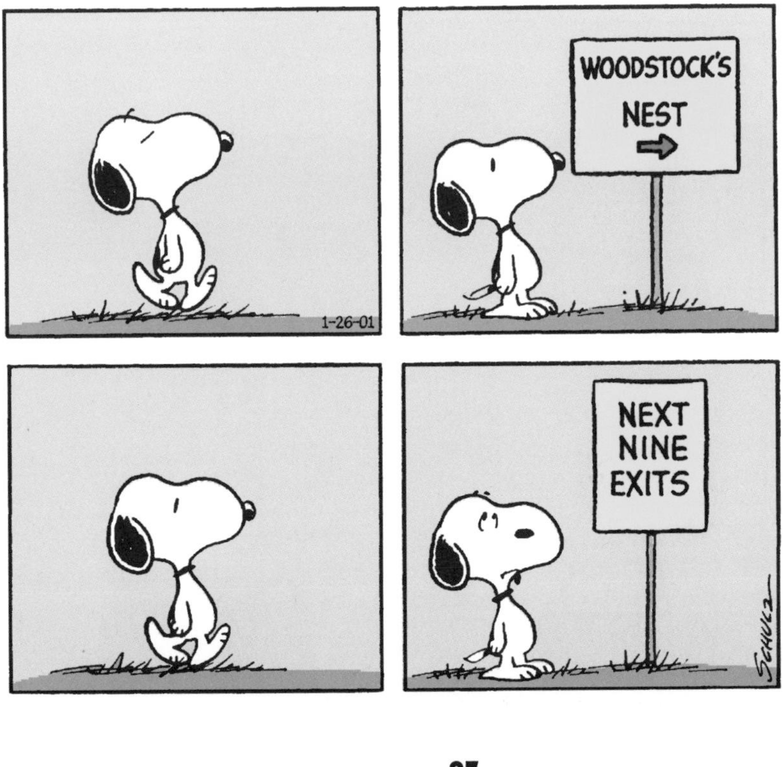
1-26-01
WOODSTOCK'S NEST
NEXT NINE EXITS
SCHULZ

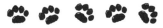

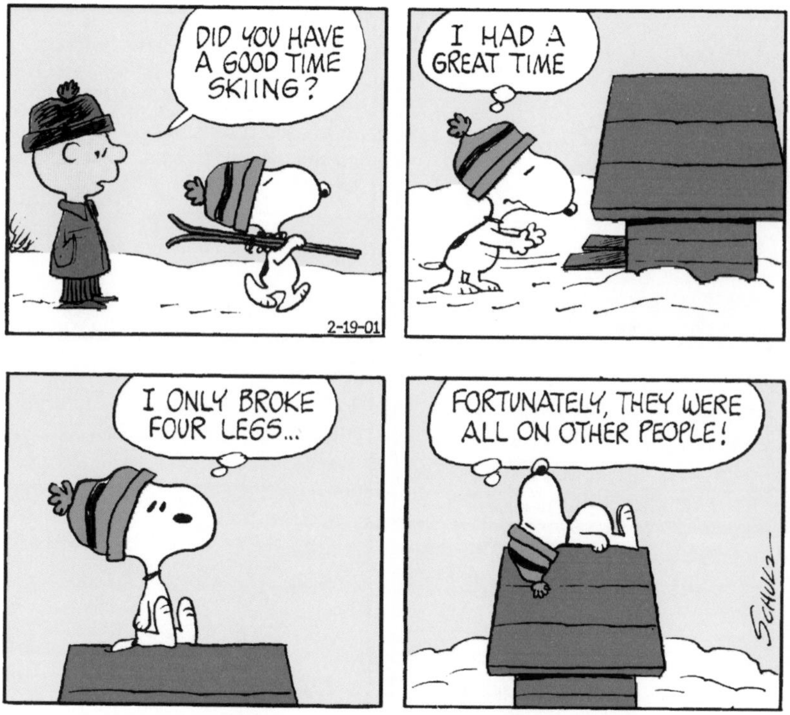
DID YOU HAVE A GOOD TIME SKIING?
2-19-01
I HAD A GREAT TIME
I ONLY BROKE FOUR LEGS...
FORTUNATELY, THEY WERE ALL ON OTHER PEOPLE!
SCHULZ

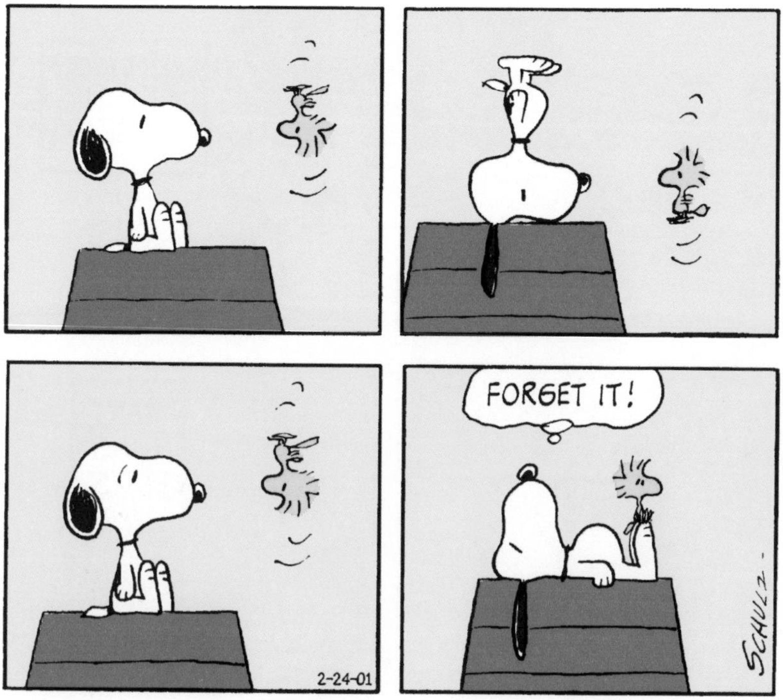
2-24-01
FORGET IT!
SCHULZ

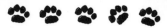

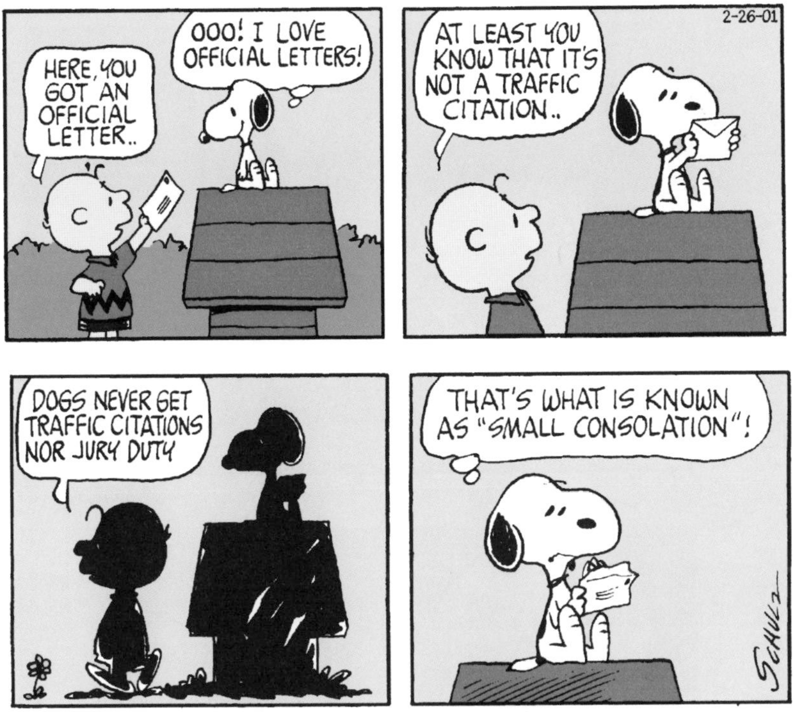
2-26-01
HERE, YOU GOT AN OFFICIAL LETTER..
OOO! I LOVE OFFICIAL LETTERS!
AT LEAST YOU KNOW THAT IT'S NOT A TRAFFIC CITATION..
DOGS NEVER GET TRAFFIC CITATIONS NOR JURY DUTY
THAT'S WHAT IS KNOWN AS "SMALL CONSOLATION"!
SCHULZ

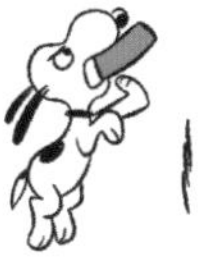

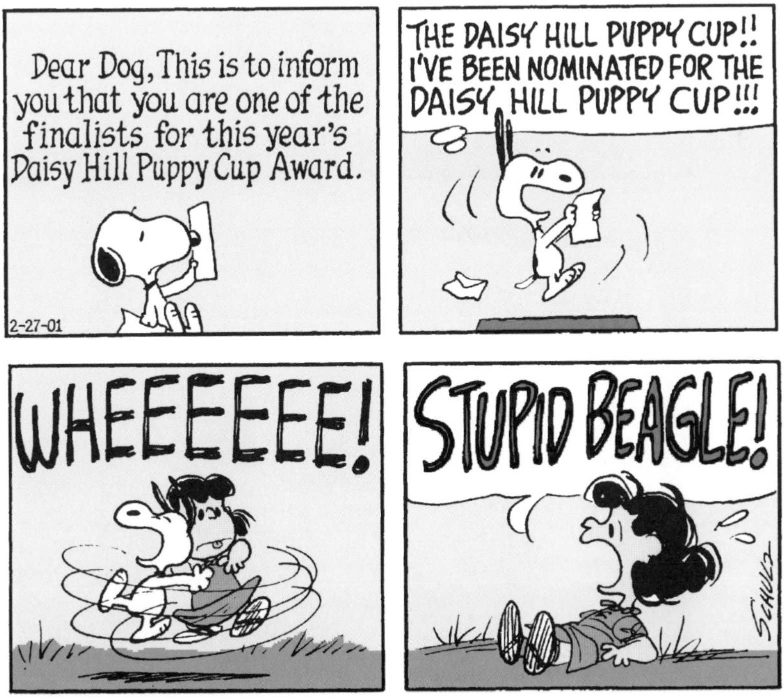
Dear Dog, This is to inform you that you are one of the finalists for this year's Daisy Hill Puppy Cup Award.
2-27-01
THE DAISY HILL PUPPY CUP!! I'VE BEEN NOMINATED FOR THE DAISY HILL PUPPY CUP!!!
WHEEEEEE!
STUPID BEAGLE!
SCHULZ

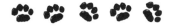

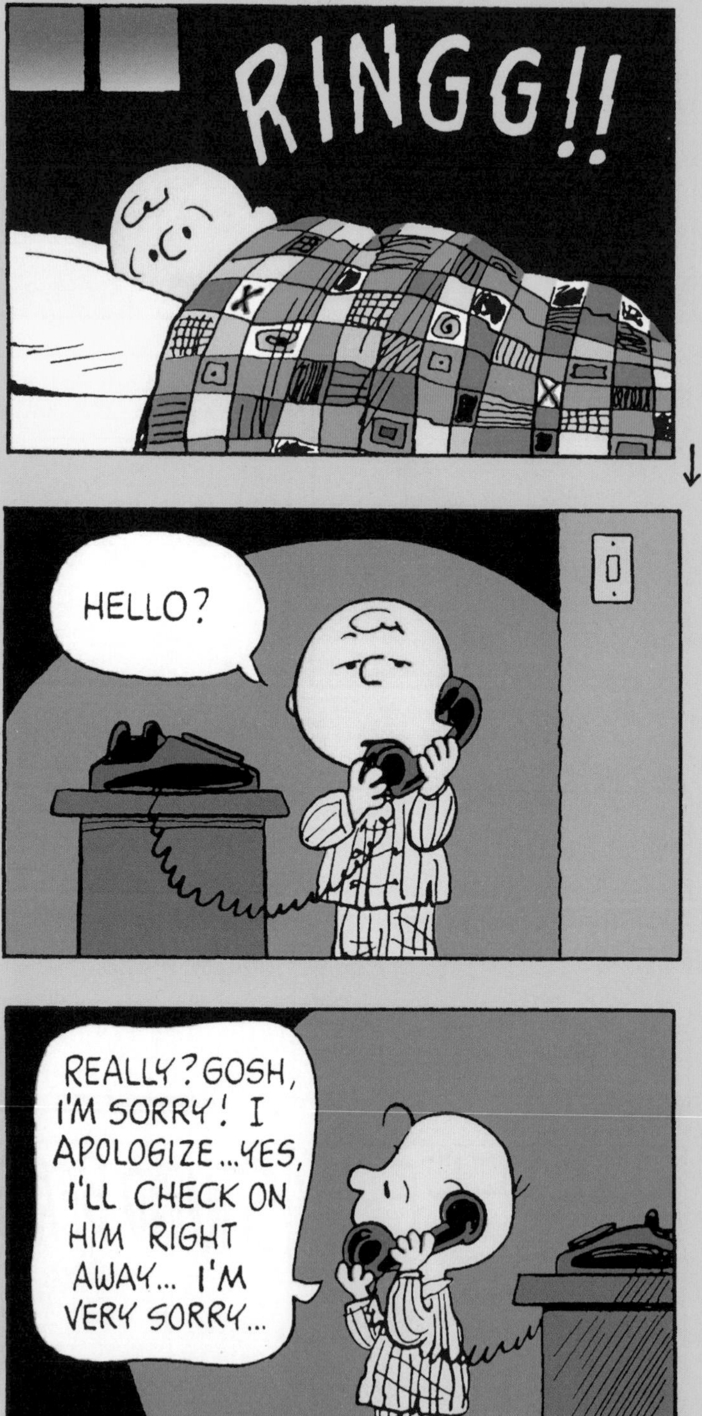
RINGG!!
HELLO?
REALLY? GOSH, I'M SORRY! I APOLOGIZE...YES, I'LL CHECK ON HIM RIGHT AWAY... I'M VERY SORRY...

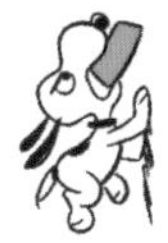

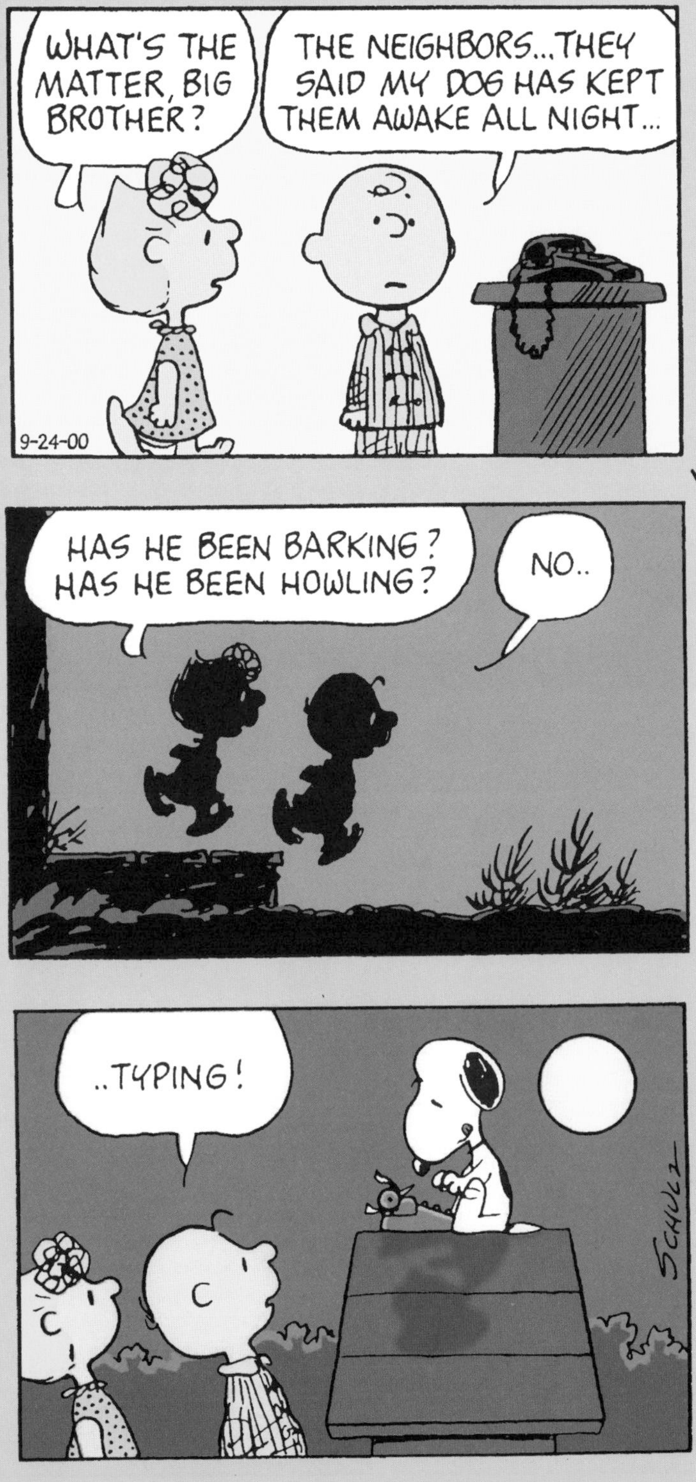
WHAT'S THE MATTER, BIG BROTHER?
THE NEIGHBORS...THEY SAID MY DOG HAS KEPT THEM AWAKE ALL NIGHT...
9-24-00
HAS HE BEEN BARKING? HAS HE BEEN HOWLING?
NO..
..TYPING!
SCHULZ

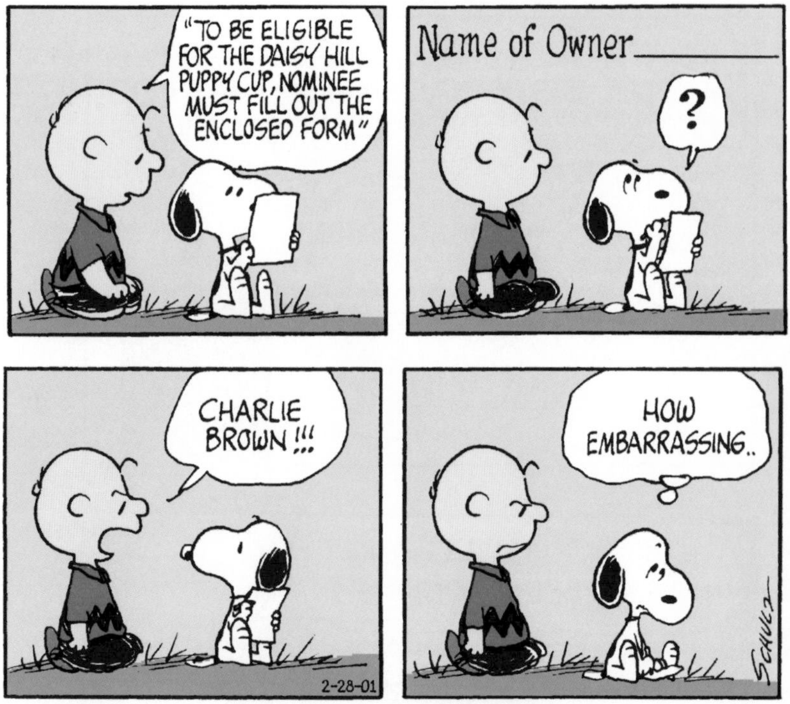
"TO BE ELIGIBLE FOR THE DAISY HILL PUPPY CUP, NOMINEE MUST FILL OUT THE ENCLOSED FORM"
Name of Owner________
?
CHARLIE BROWN !!!
HOW EMBARRASSING..
2-28-01
SCHULZ

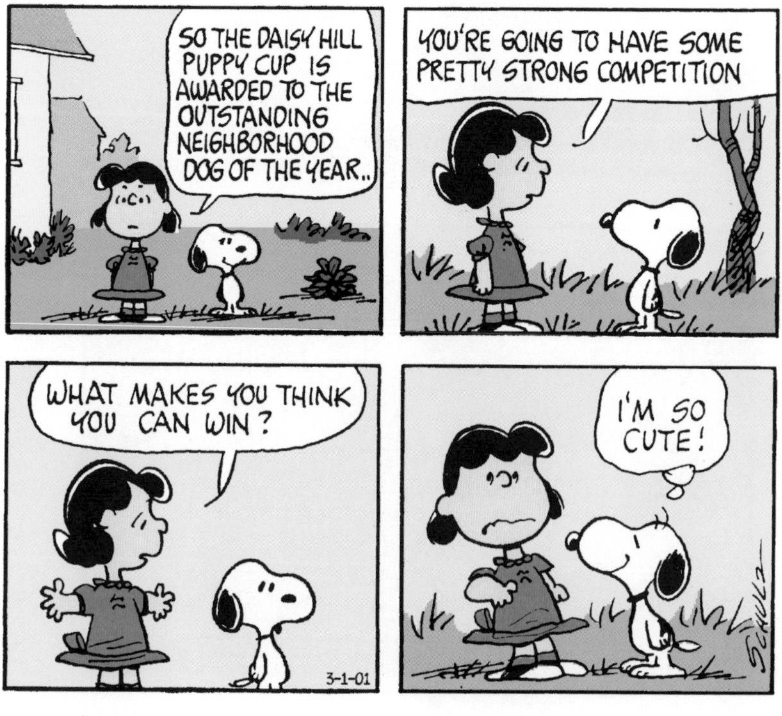
SO THE DAISY HILL PUPPY CUP IS AWARDED TO THE OUTSTANDING NEIGHBORHOOD DOG OF THE YEAR..
YOU'RE GOING TO HAVE SOME PRETTY STRONG COMPETITION
WHAT MAKES YOU THINK YOU CAN WIN?
I'M SO CUTE!
3-1-01
SCHULZ

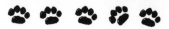

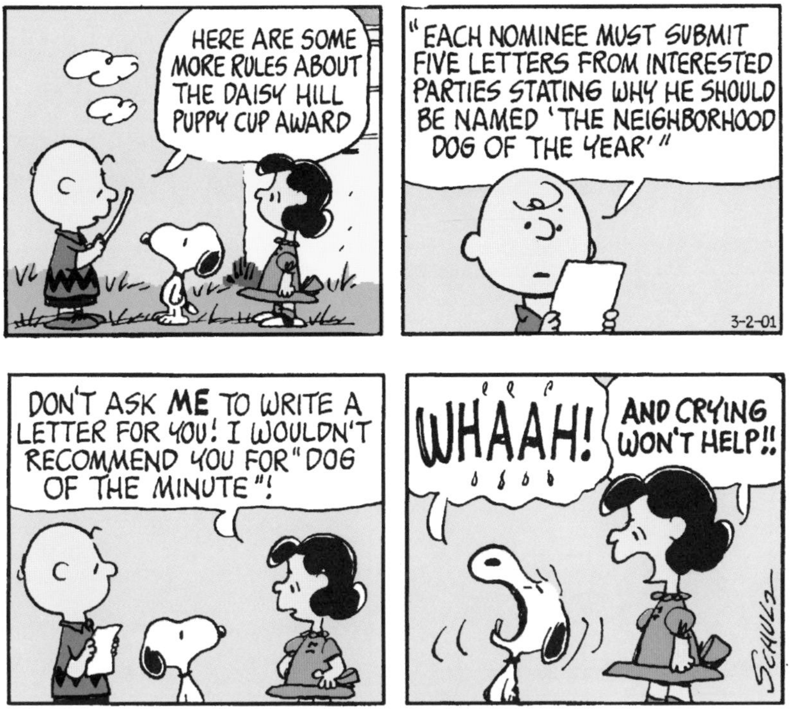
HERE ARE SOME MORE RULES ABOUT THE DAISY HILL PUPPY CUP AWARD
"EACH NOMINEE MUST SUBMIT FIVE LETTERS FROM INTERESTED PARTIES STATING WHY HE SHOULD BE NAMED ‘THE NEIGHBORHOOD DOG OF THE YEAR’"
3-2-01
DON'T ASK ME TO WRITE A LETTER FOR YOU! I WOULDN'T RECOMMEND YOU FOR "DOG OF THE MINUTE"!
WHAAH!
AND CRYING WON'T HELP!!
SCHULZ

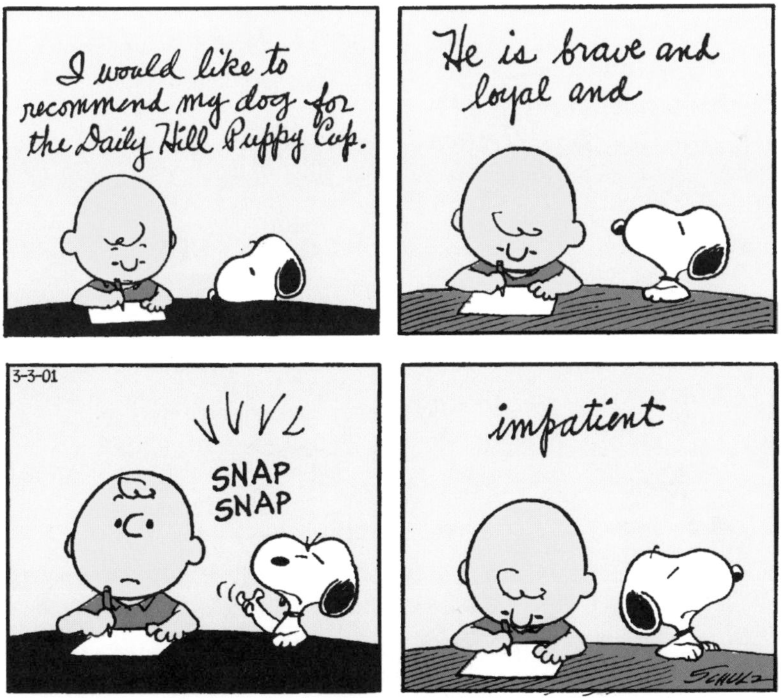
I would like to recommend my dog for the Daisy Hill Puppy Cup.
He is brave and loyal and
3-3-01
SNAP SNAP
impatient
SCHULZ

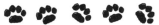

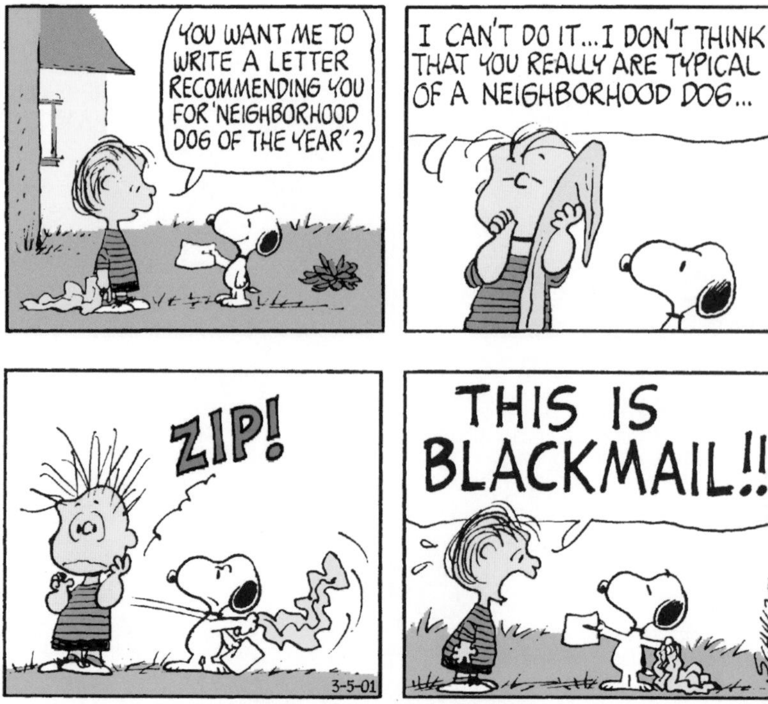
YOU WANT ME TO WRITE A LETTER RECOMMENDING YOU FOR 'NEIGHBORHOOD DOG OF THE YEAR'?
I CAN'T DO IT... I DON'T THINK THAT YOU REALLY ARE TYPICAL OF A NEIGHBORHOOD DOG...
ZIP!
3-5-01
THIS IS BLACKMAIL!!
SCHULZ

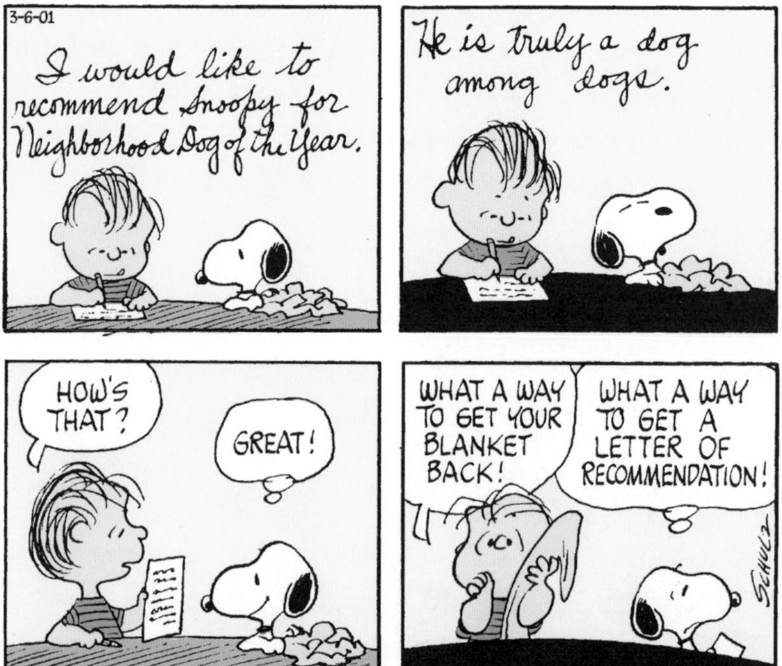
3-6-01
I would like to recommend Snoopy for Neighborhood Dog of the Year.
He is truly a dog among dogs.
HOW'S THAT?
GREAT!
WHAT A WAY TO GET YOUR BLANKET BACK!
WHAT A WAY TO GET A LETTER OF RECOMMENDATION!
SCHULZ

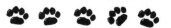

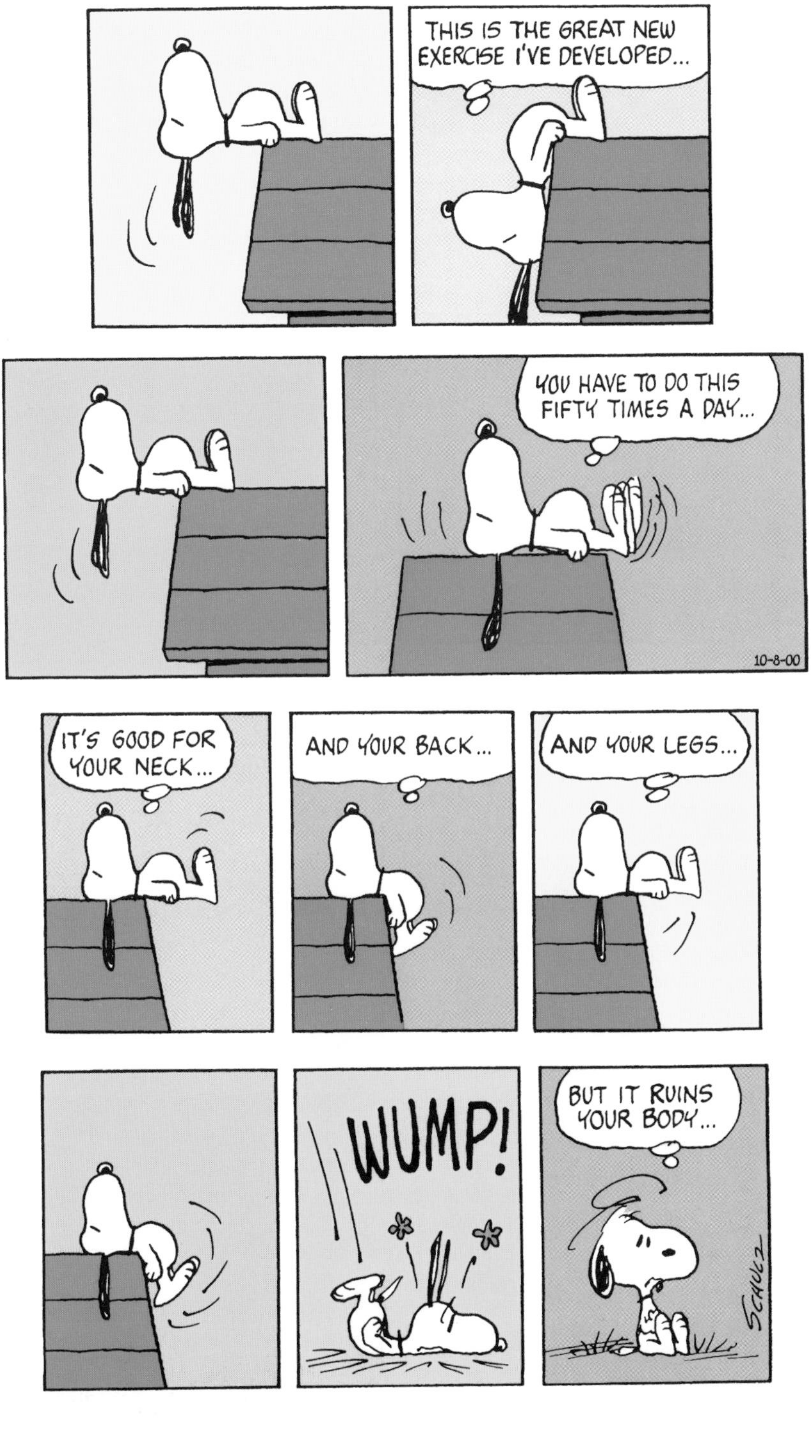
THIS IS THE GREAT NEW EXERCISE I'VE DEVELOPED...
YOU HAVE TO DO THIS FIFTY TIMES A DAY...
10-8-00
IT'S GOOD FOR YOUR NECK...
AND YOUR BACK...
AND YOUR LEGS...
WUMP!
BUT IT RUINS YOUR BODY...
SCHULZ

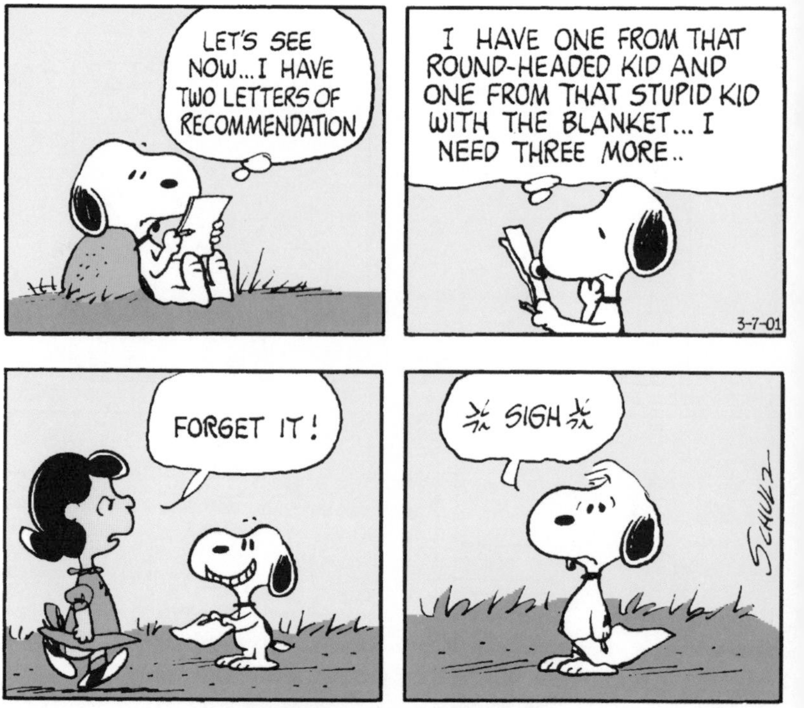
LET'S SEE NOW...I HAVE TWO LETTERS OF RECOMMENDATION
I HAVE ONE FROM THAT ROUND-HEADED KID AND ONE FROM THAT STUPID KID WITH THE BLANKET... I NEED THREE MORE..
3-7-01
FORGET IT!
SIGH

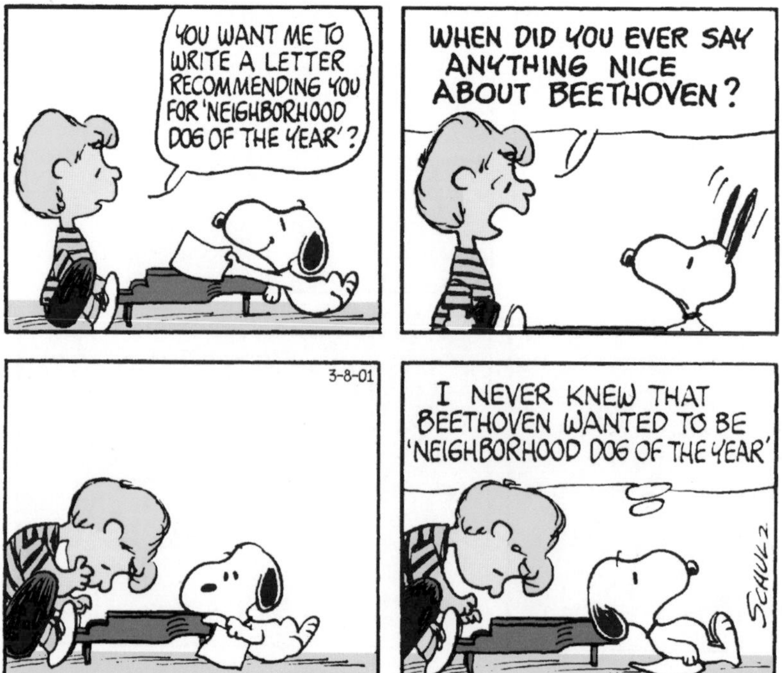
YOU WANT ME TO WRITE A LETTER RECOMMENDING YOU FOR 'NEIGHBORHOOD DOG OF THE YEAR'?
WHEN DID YOU EVER SAY ANYTHING NICE ABOUT BEETHOVEN?
3-8-01
I NEVER KNEW THAT BEETHOVEN WANTED TO BE 'NEIGHBORHOOD DOG OF THE YEAR'

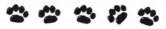

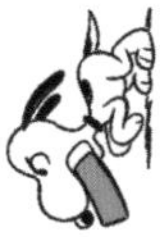

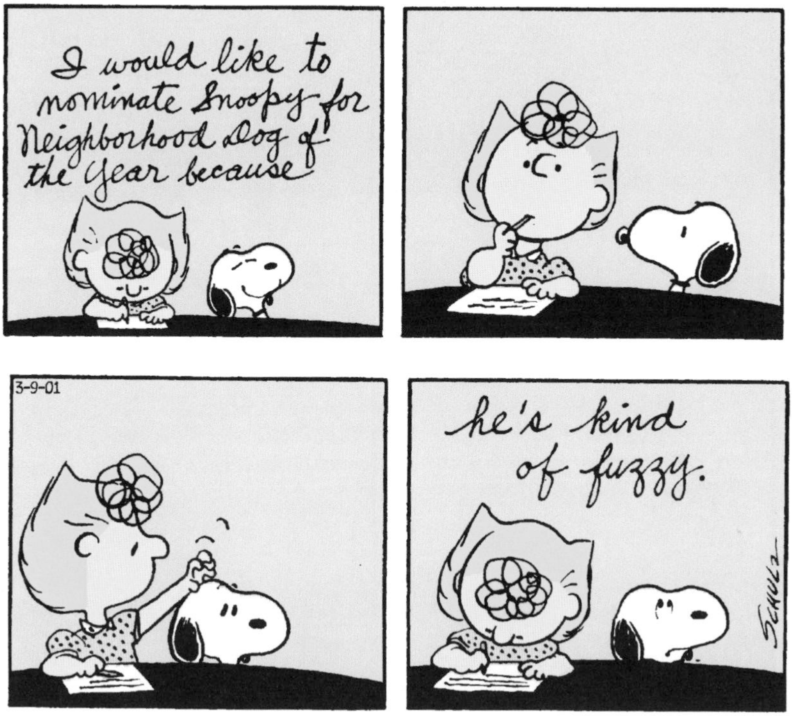
I would like to nominate Snoopy for Neighborhood Dog of the Year because
3-9-01
he's kind of fuzzy.
SCHULZ

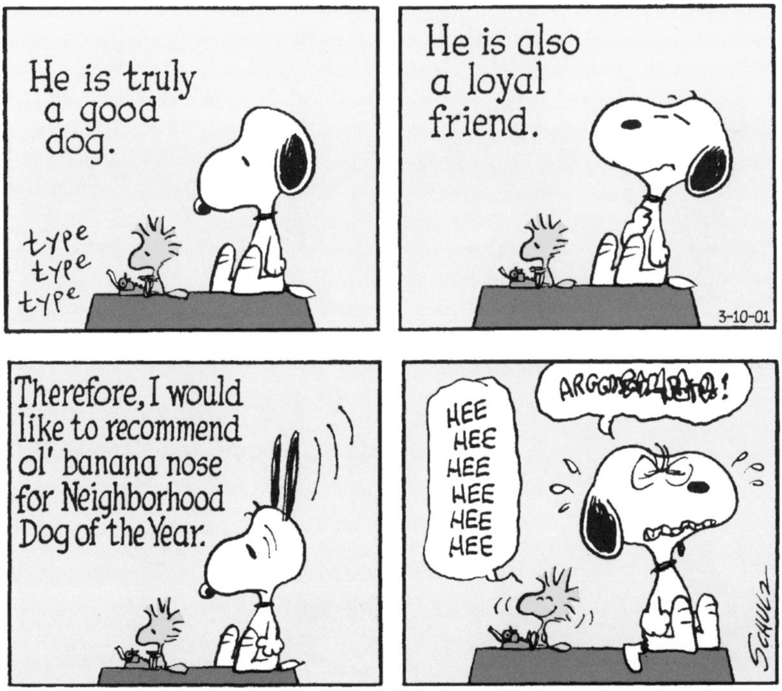
He is truly a good dog.
type type type
He is also a loyal friend.
3-10-01
Therefore, I would like to recommend ol' banana nose for Neighborhood Dog of the Year.
HEE HEE HEE HEE HEE HEE
ARGG
SCHULZ

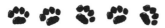

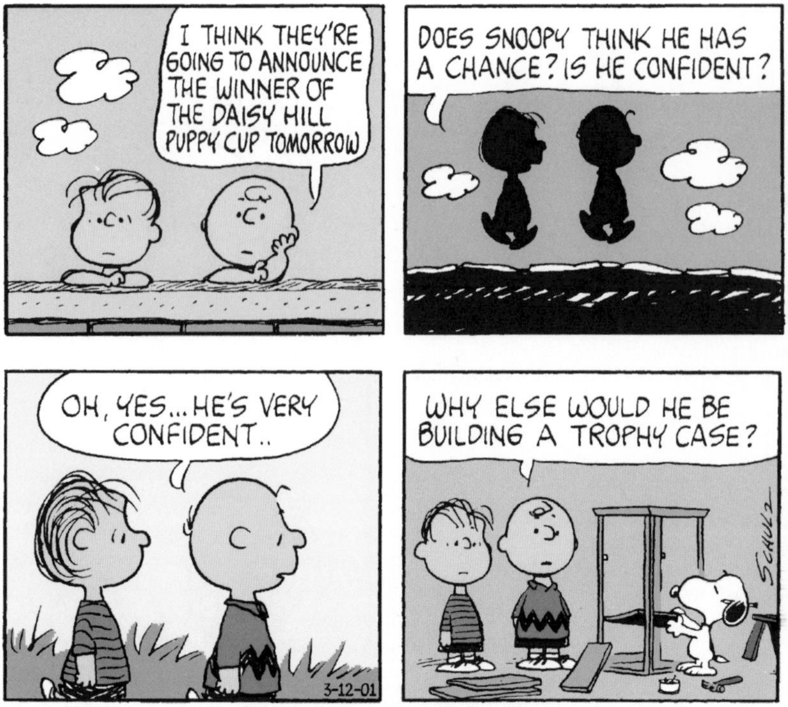
I THINK THEY'RE GOING TO ANNOUNCE THE WINNER OF THE DAISY HILL PUPPY CUP TOMORROW
DOES SNOOPY THINK HE HAS A CHANCE? IS HE CONFIDENT?
OH, YES...HE'S VERY CONFIDENT..
WHY ELSE WOULD HE BE BUILDING A TROPHY CASE?
SCHULZ
3-12-01

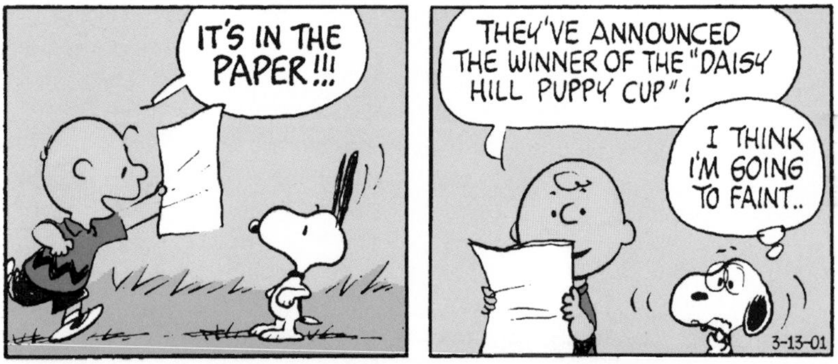
IT'S IN THE PAPER!!!
THEY'VE ANNOUNCED THE WINNER OF THE "DAISY HILL PUPPY CUP"!
I THINK I'M GOING TO FAINT..
3-13-01

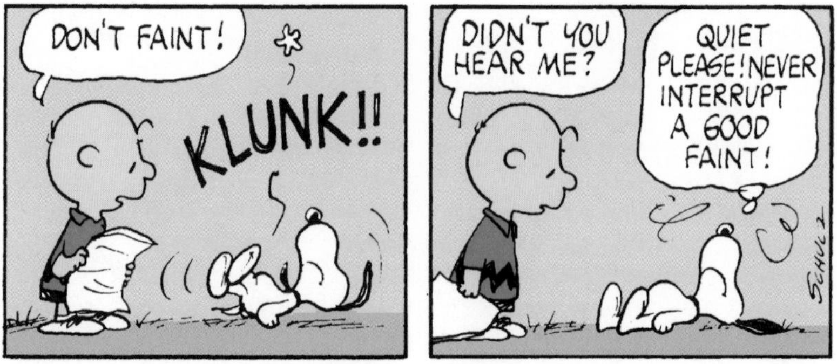
DON'T FAINT!
KLUNK!!
DIDN'T YOU HEAR ME?
QUIET PLEASE! NEVER INTERRUPT A GOOD FAINT!
SCHULZ

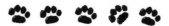

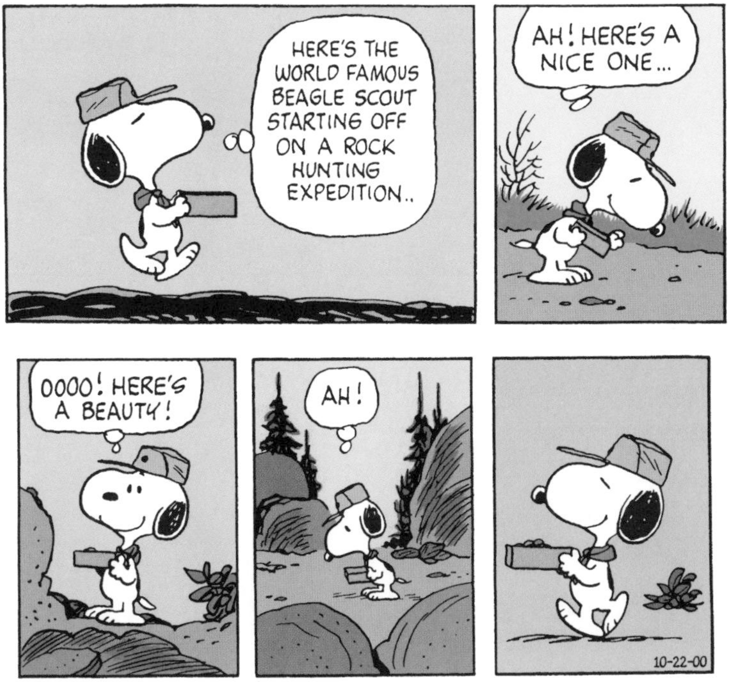
HERE'S THE WORLD FAMOUS BEAGLE SCOUT STARTING OFF ON A ROCK HUNTING EXPEDITION..
AH! HERE'S A NICE ONE...
OOOO! HERE'S A BEAUTY!
AH!
10-22-00

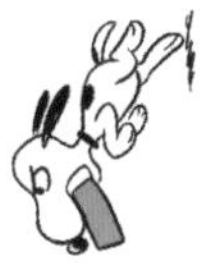

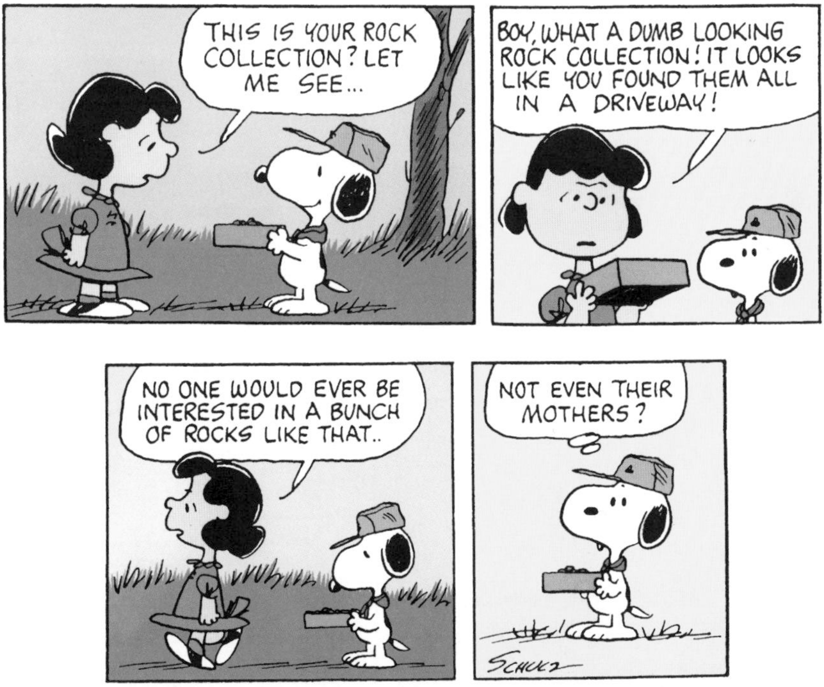
THIS IS YOUR ROCK COLLECTION? LET ME SEE...
BOY, WHAT A DUMB LOOKING ROCK COLLECTION! IT LOOKS LIKE YOU FOUND THEM ALL IN A DRIVEWAY!
NO ONE WOULD EVER BE INTERESTED IN A BUNCH OF ROCKS LIKE THAT..
NOT EVEN THEIR MOTHERS?
SCHULZ

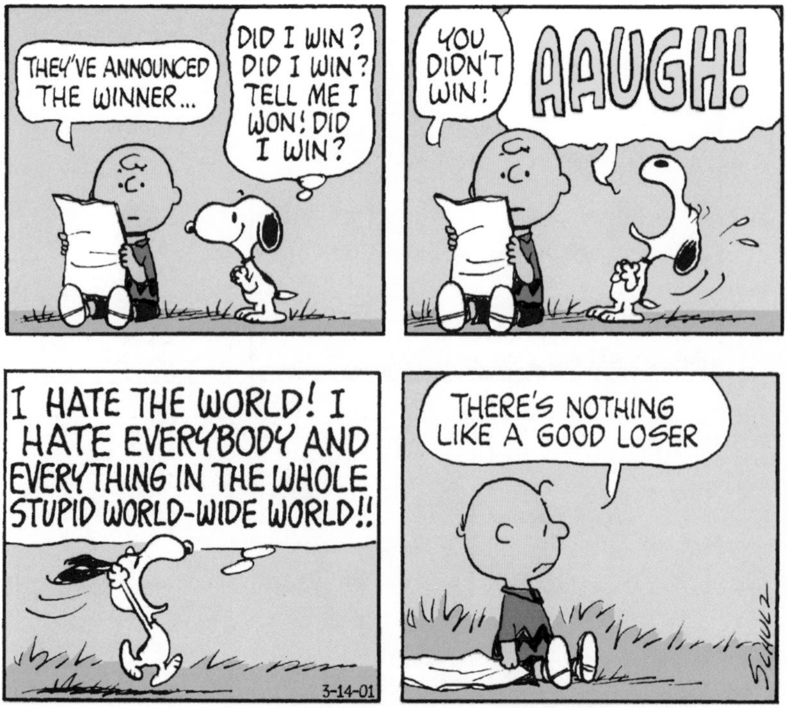
THEY'VE ANNOUNCED THE WINNER...
DID I WIN? DID I WIN? TELL ME I WON! DID I WIN?
YOU DIDN'T WIN!
AAUGH!
I HATE THE WORLD! I HATE EVERYBODY AND EVERYTHING IN THE WHOLE STUPID WORLD-WIDE WORLD!!
3-14-01
THERE'S NOTHING LIKE A GOOD LOSER
SCHULZ

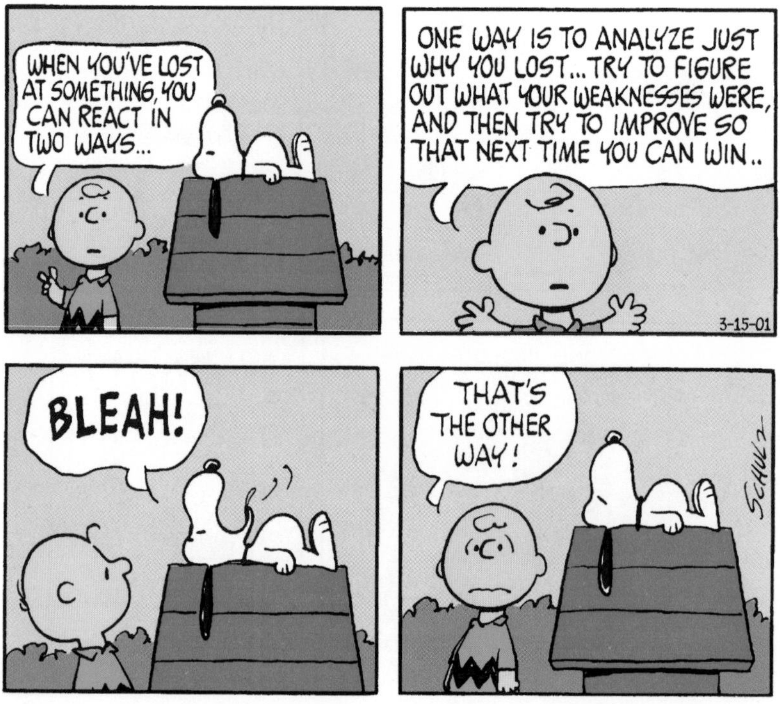
WHEN YOU'VE LOST AT SOMETHING, YOU CAN REACT IN TWO WAYS...
ONE WAY IS TO ANALYZE JUST WHY YOU LOST...TRY TO FIGURE OUT WHAT YOUR WEAKNESSES WERE, AND THEN TRY TO IMPROVE SO THAT NEXT TIME YOU CAN WIN..
3-15-01
BLEAH!
THAT'S THE OTHER WAY!
SCHULZ

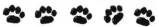

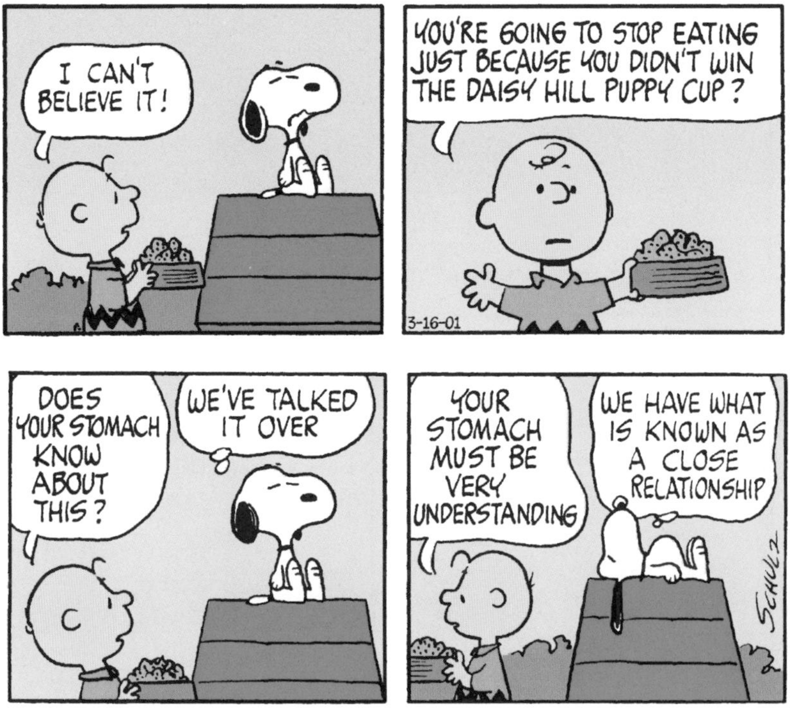
I CAN'T BELIEVE IT!
YOU'RE GOING TO STOP EATING JUST BECAUSE YOU DIDN'T WIN THE DAISY HILL PUPPY CUP?
3-16-01
DOES YOUR STOMACH KNOW ABOUT THIS?
WE'VE TALKED IT OVER
YOUR STOMACH MUST BE VERY UNDERSTANDING
WE HAVE WHAT IS KNOWN AS A CLOSE RELATIONSHIP
SCHULZ

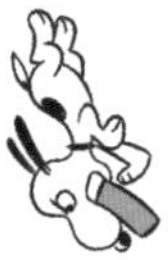

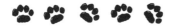

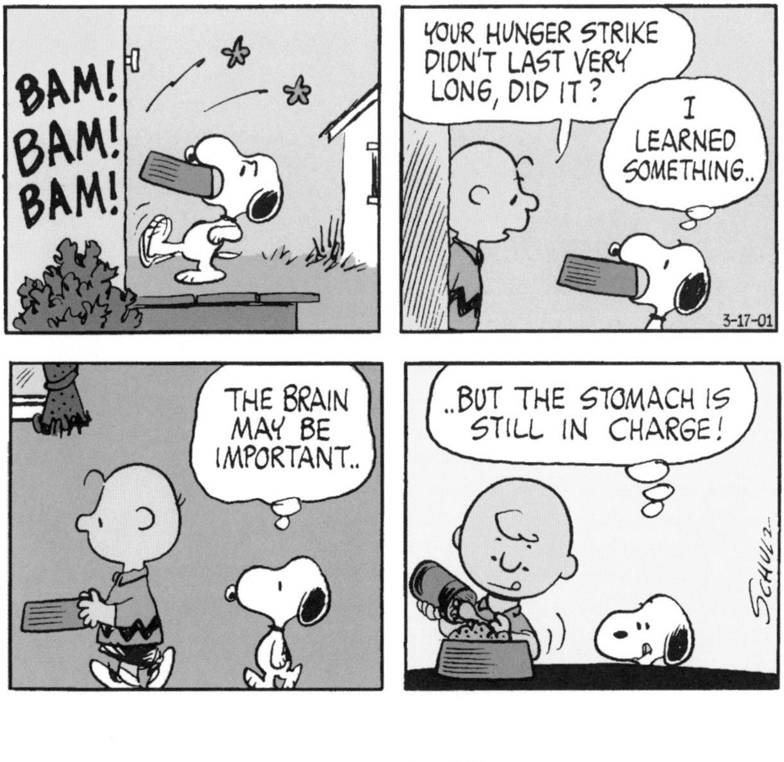
BAM! BAM! BAM!
YOUR HUNGER STRIKE DIDN'T LAST VERY LONG, DID IT?
I LEARNED SOMETHING..
3-17-01
THE BRAIN MAY BE IMPORTANT..
..BUT THE STOMACH IS STILL IN CHARGE!
SCHULZ

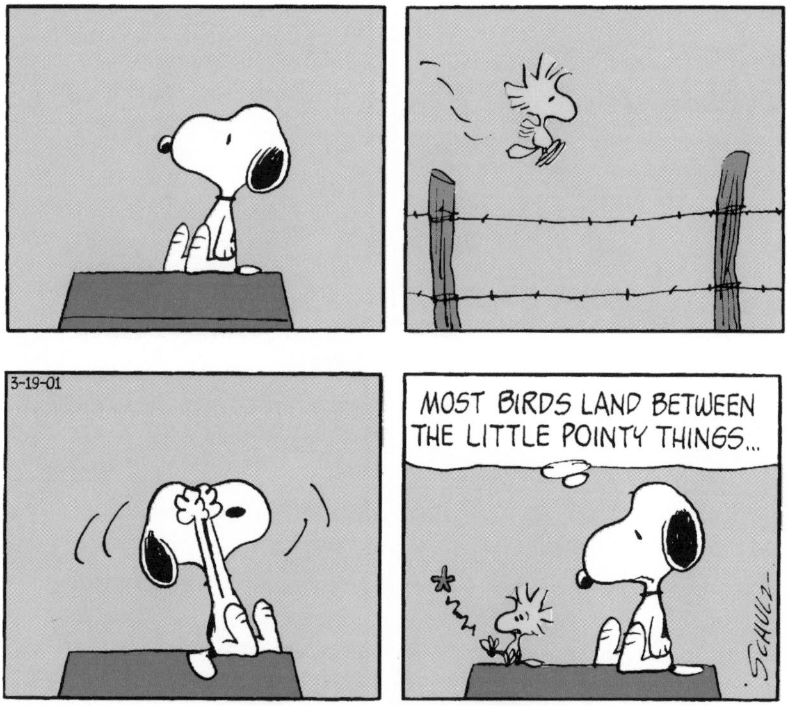
3-19-01
MOST BIRDS LAND BETWEEN THE LITTLE POINTY THINGS...
SCHULZ

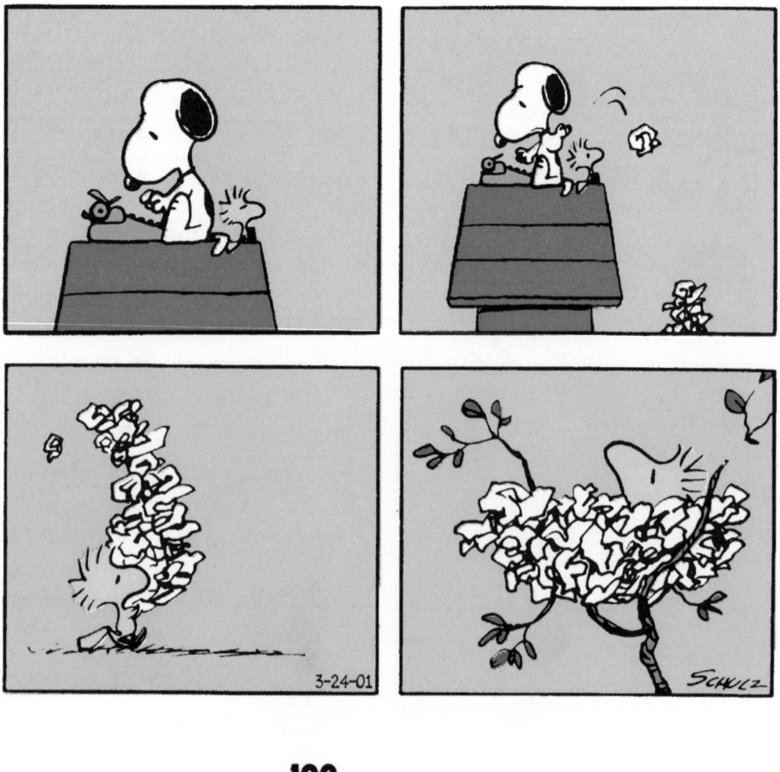
3-24-01
SCHULZ

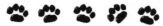

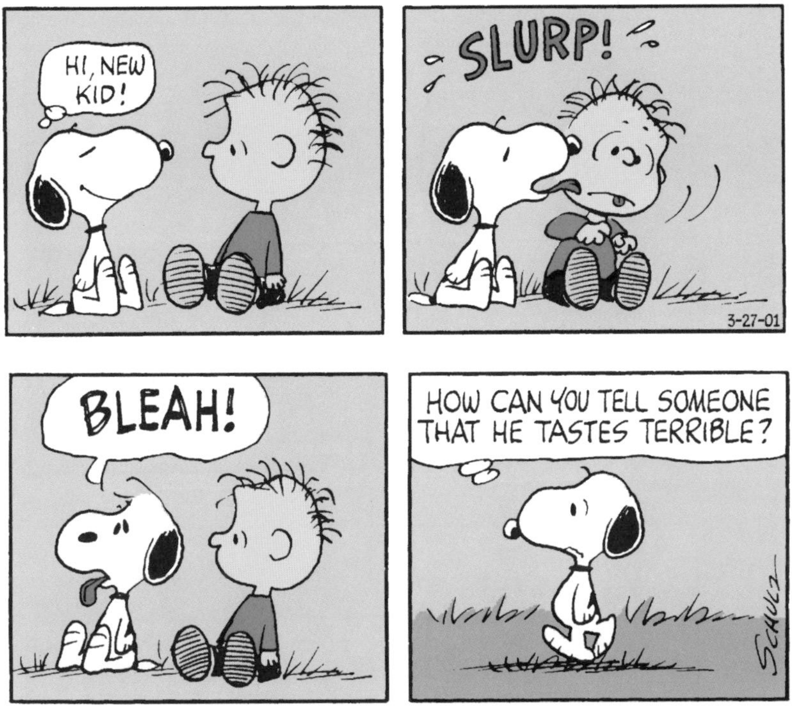
HI, NEW KID!
SLURP!
3-27-01
BLEAH!
HOW CAN YOU TELL SOMEONE THAT HE TASTES TERRIBLE?
SCHULZ

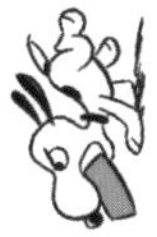

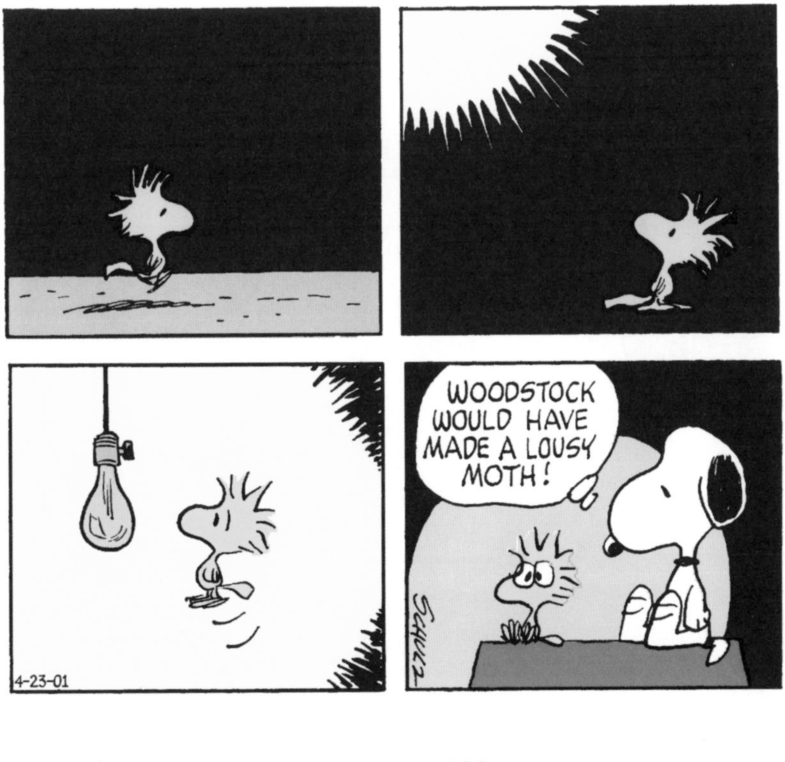
4-23-01
WOODSTOCK WOULD HAVE MADE A LOUSY MOTH!
SCHULZ

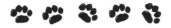

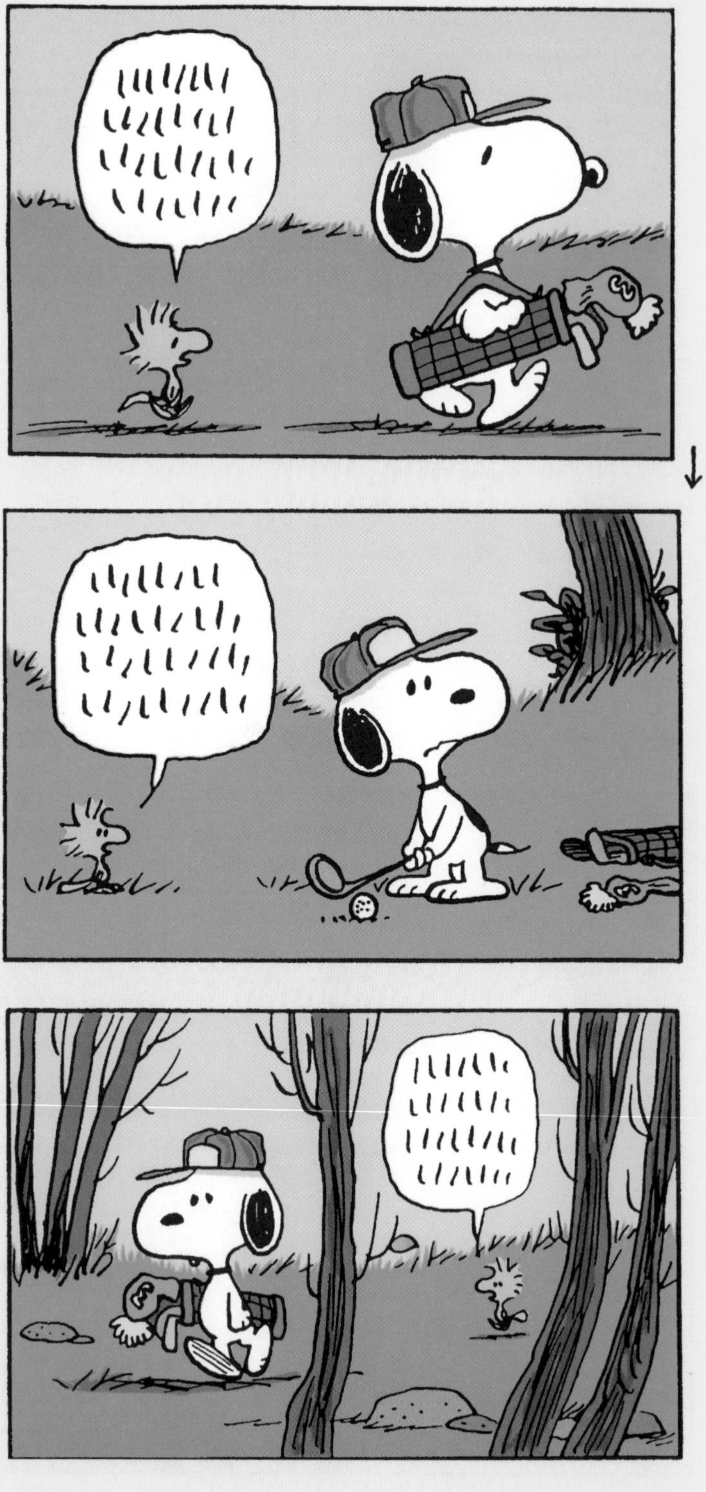

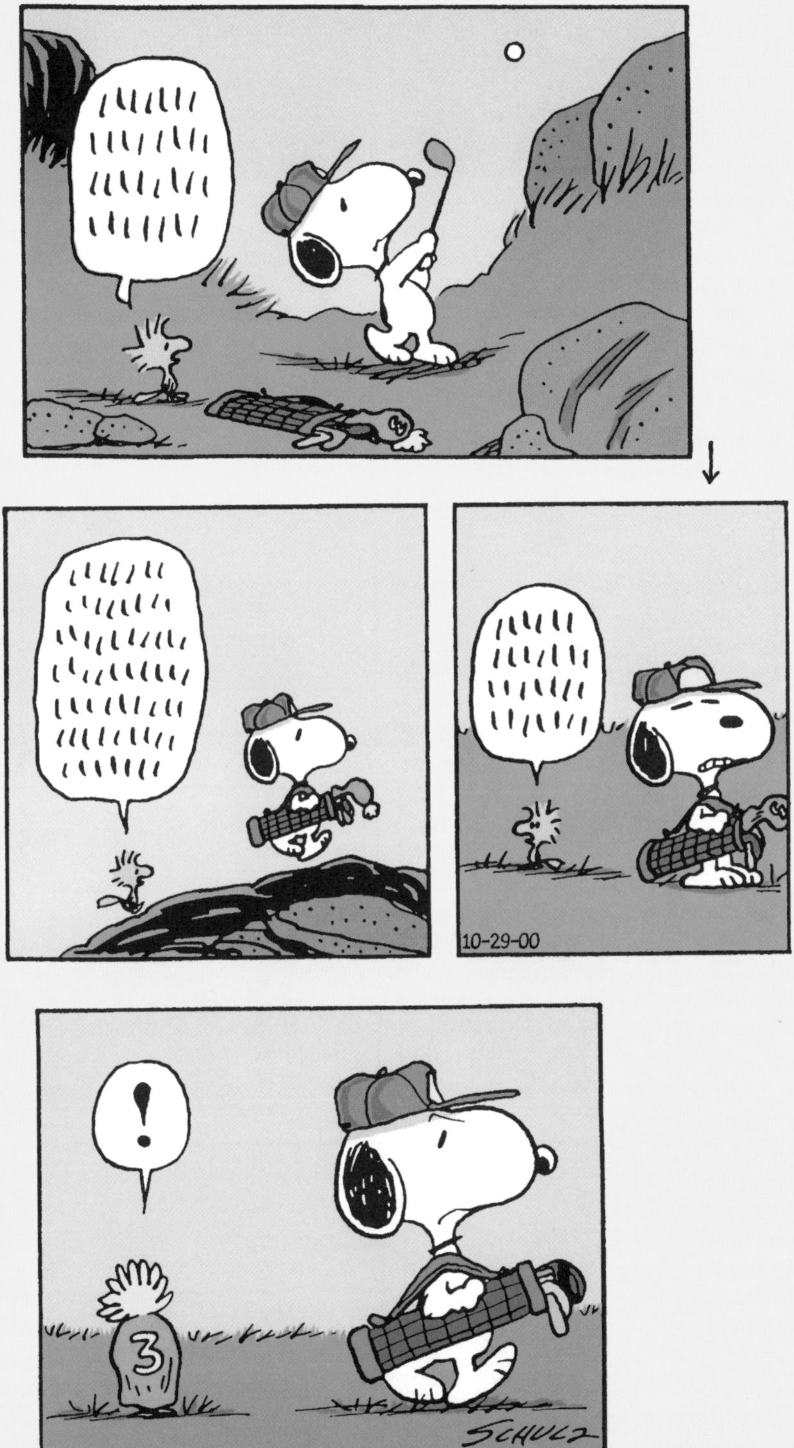
10-29-00
!
3
SCHULZ

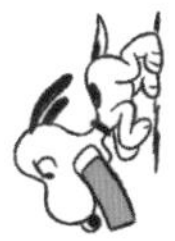

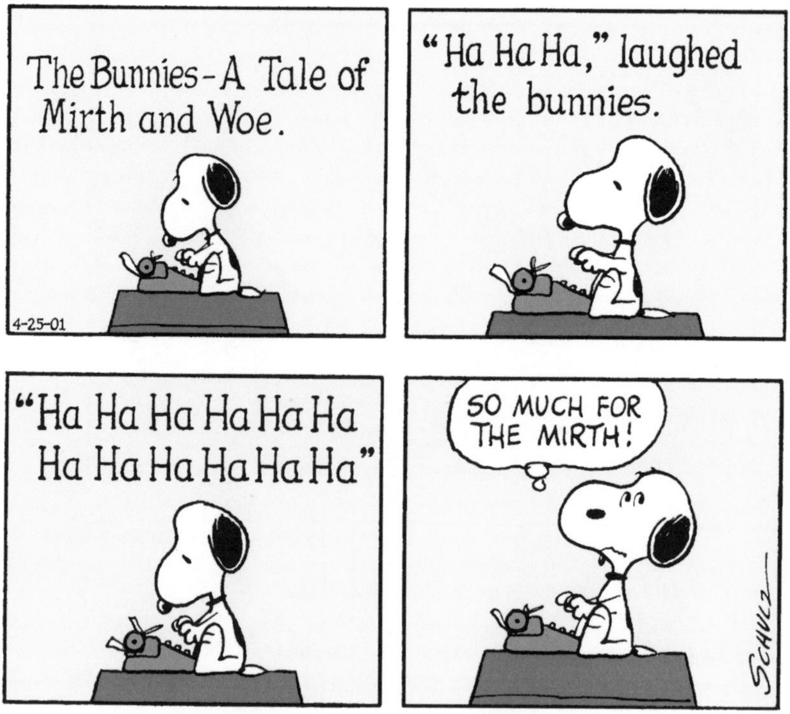
The Bunnies - A Tale of Mirth and Woe.
4-25-01
"Ha Ha Ha," laughed the bunnies.
"Ha Ha Ha Ha Ha Ha Ha Ha Ha Ha Ha Ha"
SO MUCH FOR THE MIRTH!
SCHULZ

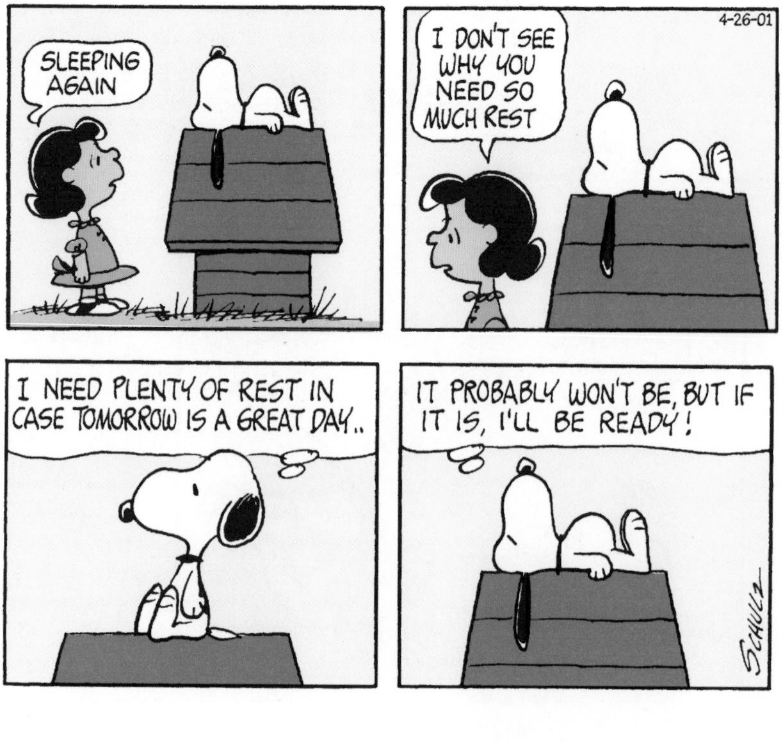
SLEEPING AGAIN
4-26-01
I DON'T SEE WHY YOU NEED SO MUCH REST
I NEED PLENTY OF REST IN CASE TOMORROW IS A GREAT DAY..
IT PROBABLY WON'T BE, BUT IF IT IS, I'LL BE READY!
SCHULZ

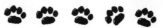

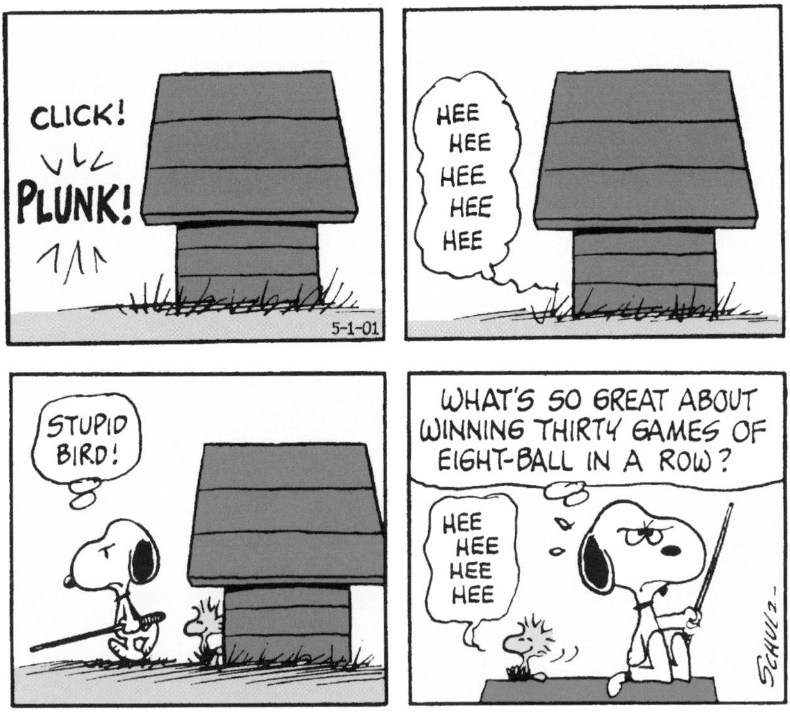
CLICK!
PLUNK!
5-1-01
HEE HEE HEE HEE HEE
STUPID BIRD!
WHAT'S SO GREAT ABOUT WINNING THIRTY GAMES OF EIGHT-BALL IN A ROW?
HEE HEE HEE HEE
SCHULZ

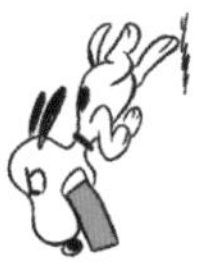

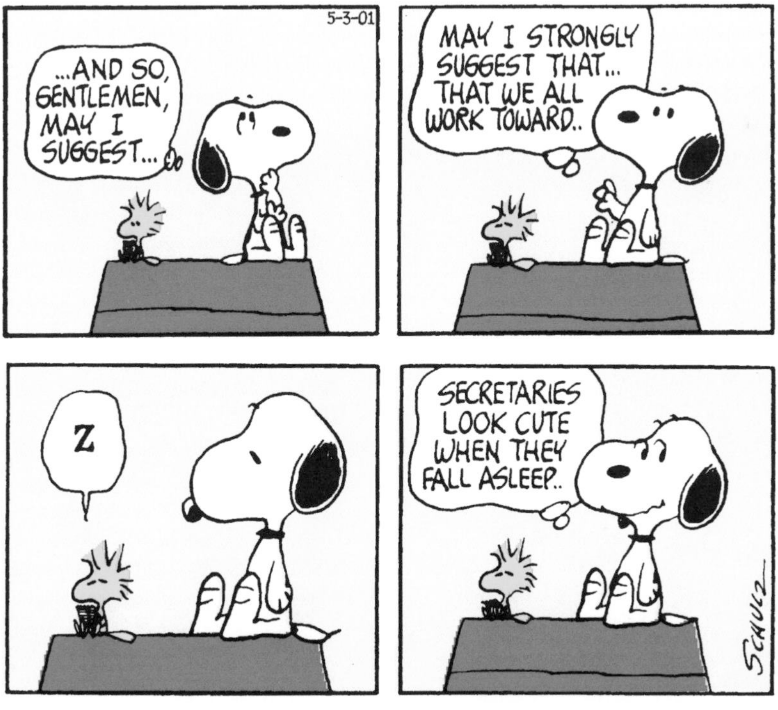
5-3-01
...AND SO, GENTLEMEN, MAY I SUGGEST...
MAY I STRONGLY SUGGEST THAT... THAT WE ALL WORK TOWARD..
Z
SECRETARIES LOOK CUTE WHEN THEY FALL ASLEEP..
SCHULZ

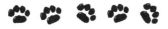

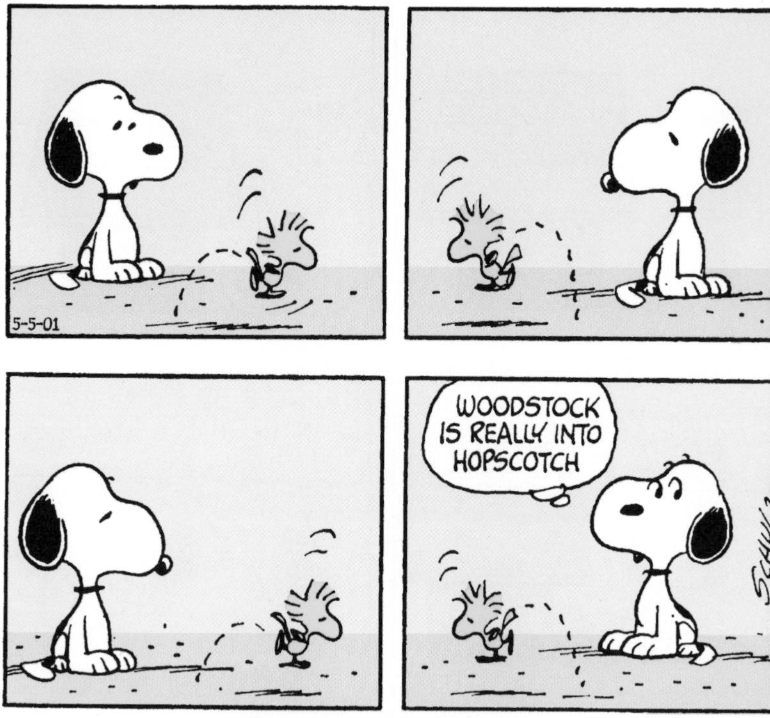
5-5-01
WOODSTOCK IS REALLY INTO HOPSCOTCH
SCHULZ

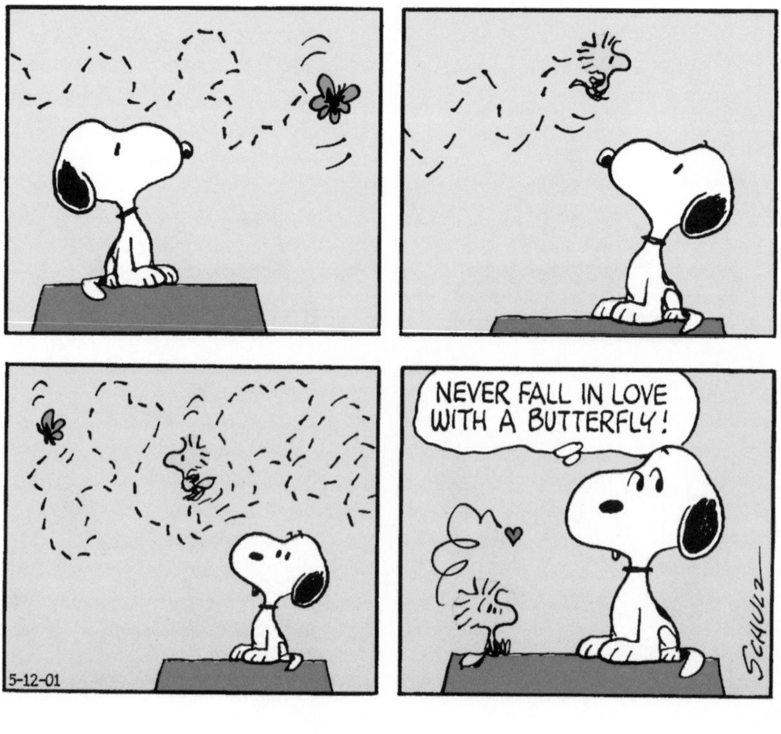
NEVER FALL IN LOVE WITH A BUTTERFLY!
5-12-01
SCHULZ

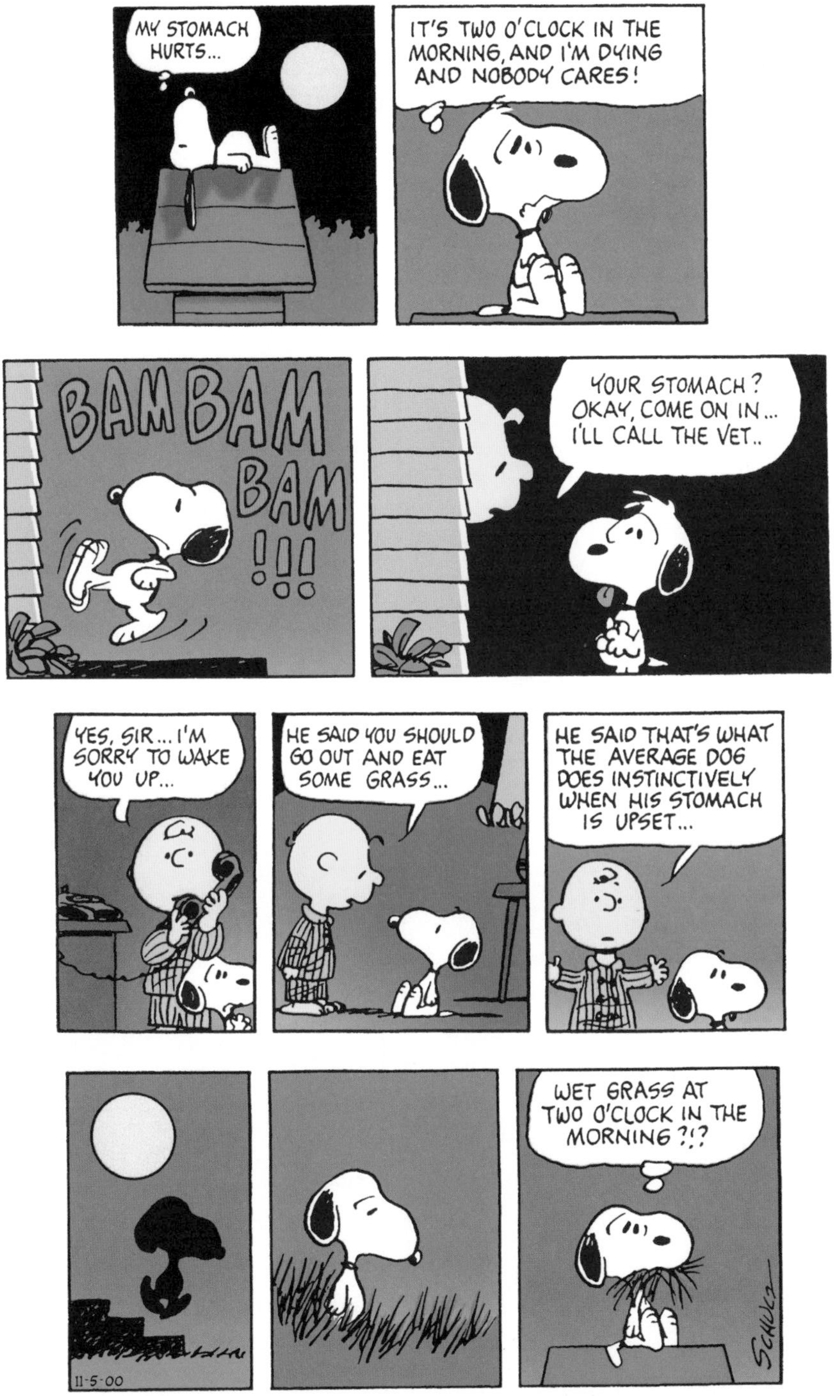
MY STOMACH HURTS...
IT'S TWO O'CLOCK IN THE MORNING, AND I'M DYING AND NOBODY CARES!
BAM BAM BAM!!!
YOUR STOMACH? OKAY, COME ON IN... I'LL CALL THE VET..
YES, SIR... I'M SORRY TO WAKE YOU UP...
HE SAID YOU SHOULD GO OUT AND EAT SOME GRASS...
HE SAID THAT'S WHAT THE AVERAGE DOG DOES INSTINCTIVELY WHEN HIS STOMACH IS UPSET...
11-5-00
WET GRASS AT TWO O'CLOCK IN THE MORNING?!?
SCHULZ

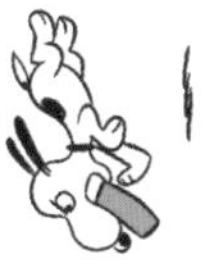

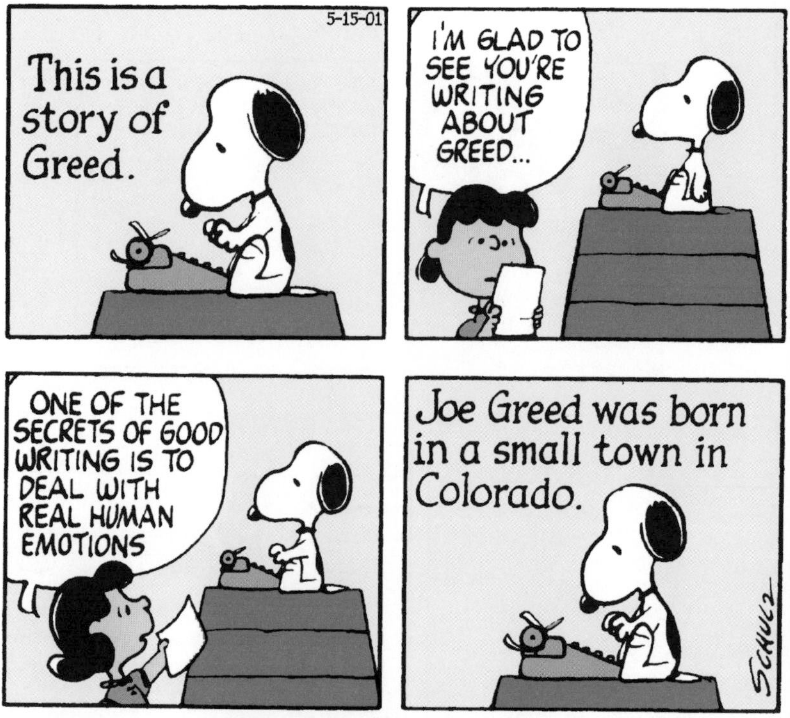
5-15-01
This is a story of Greed.
I'M GLAD TO SEE YOU'RE WRITING ABOUT GREED...
ONE OF THE SECRETS OF GOOD WRITING IS TO DEAL WITH REAL HUMAN EMOTIONS
Joe Greed was born in a small town in Colorado.
SCHULZ

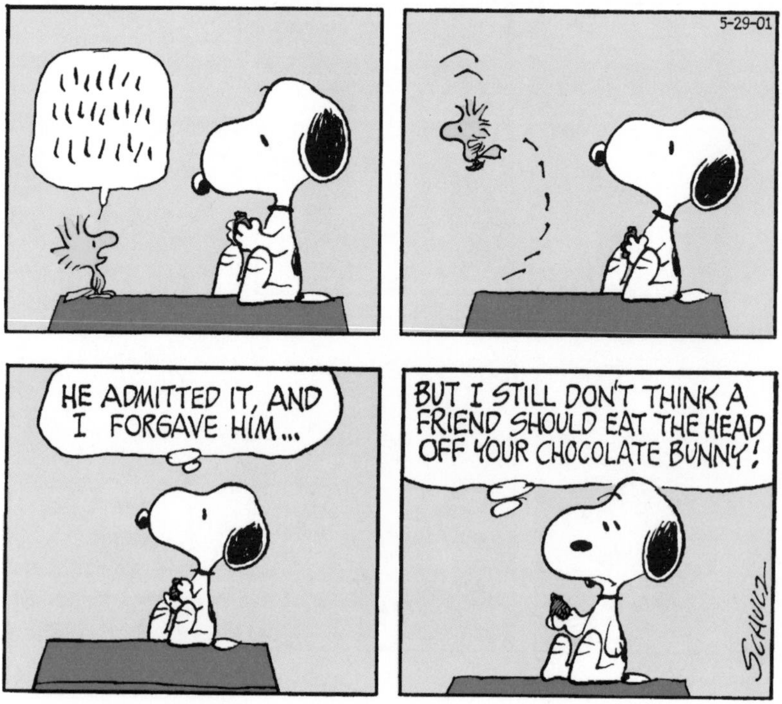
5-29-01
HE ADMITTED IT, AND I FORGAVE HIM...
BUT I STILL DON'T THINK A FRIEND SHOULD EAT THE HEAD OFF YOUR CHOCOLATE BUNNY!
SCHULZ

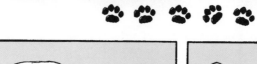

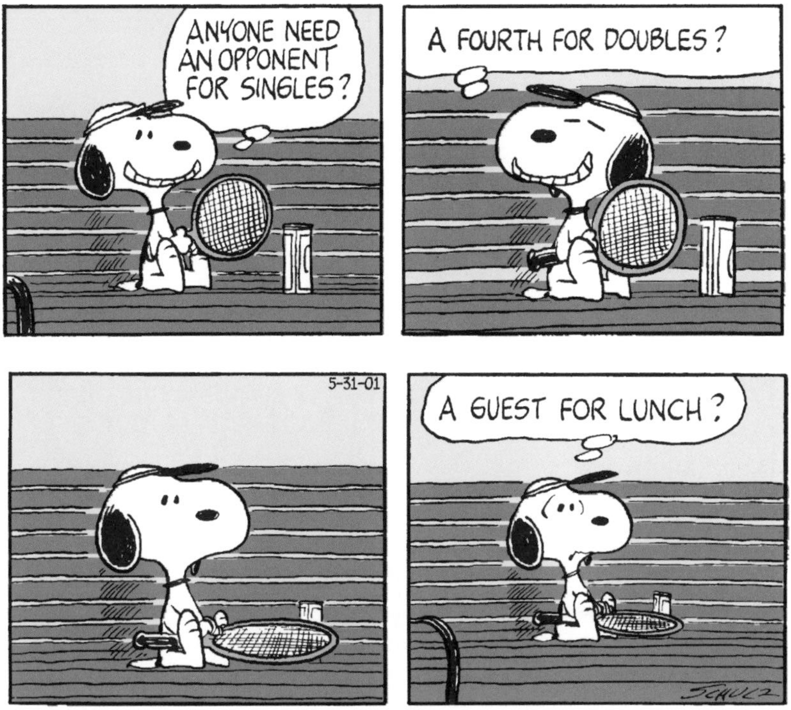
ANYONE NEED AN OPPONENT FOR SINGLES?
A FOURTH FOR DOUBLES?
5-31-01
A GUEST FOR LUNCH?
SCHULZ

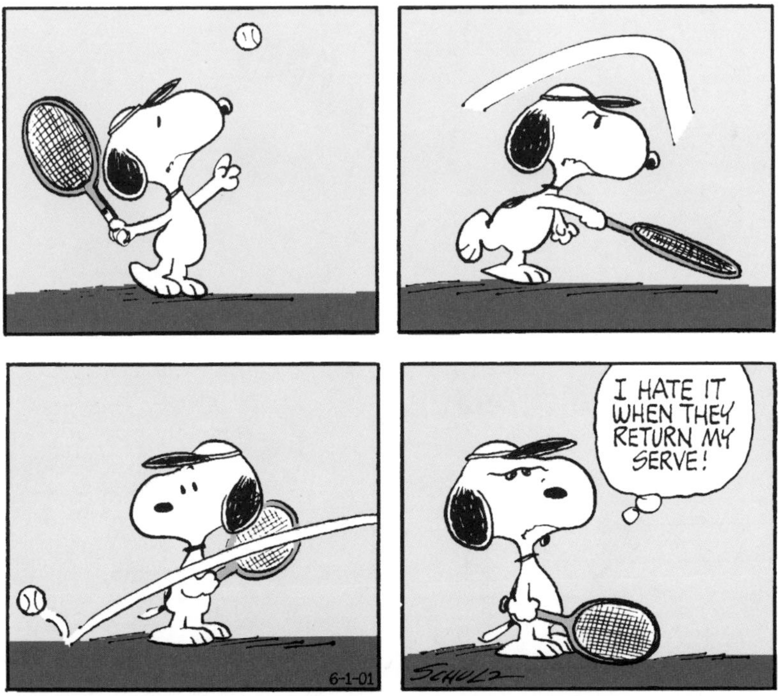
6-1-01
SCHULZ
I HATE IT WHEN THEY RETURN MY SERVE!

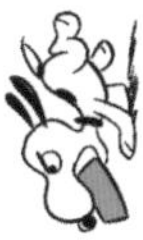

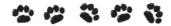

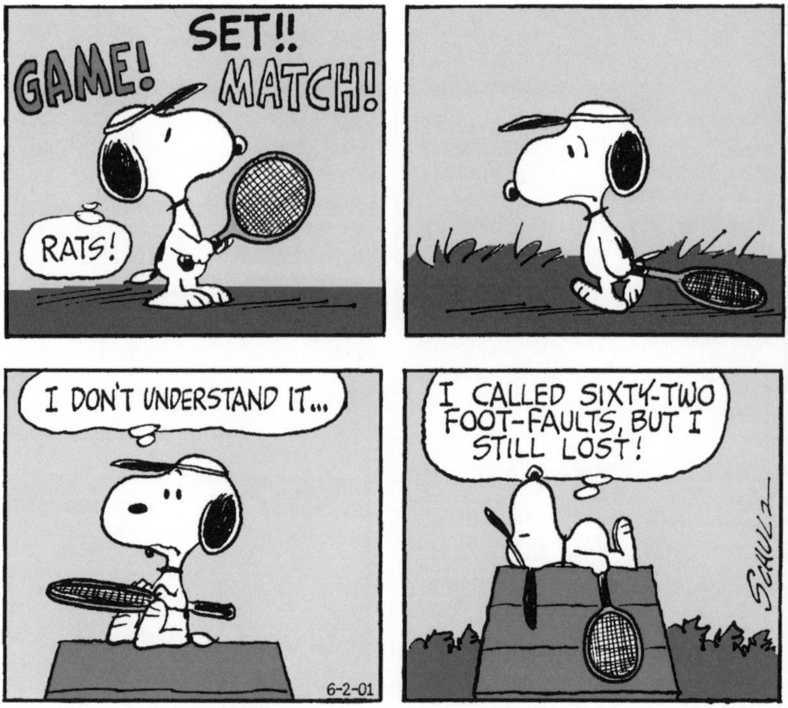
GAME! SET!! MATCH!
RATS!
I DON'T UNDERSTAND IT...
I CALLED SIXTY-TWO FOOT-FAULTS, BUT I STILL LOST!
SCHULZ
6-2-01

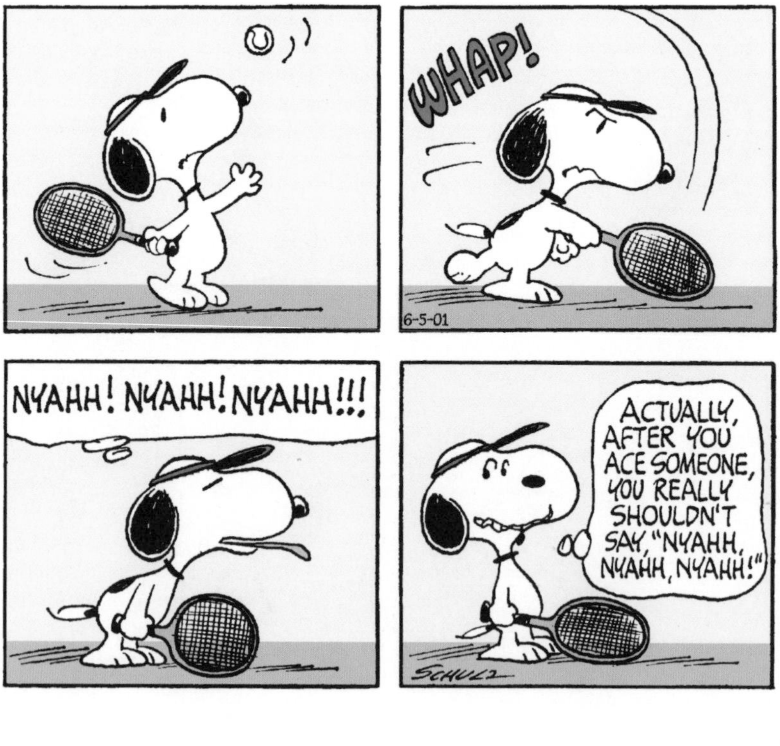
WHAP!
6-5-01
NYAHH! NYAHH! NYAHH!!!
ACTUALLY, AFTER YOU ACE SOMEONE, YOU REALLY SHOULDN'T SAY, "NYAHH, NYAHH, NYAHH!"
SCHULZ

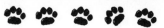

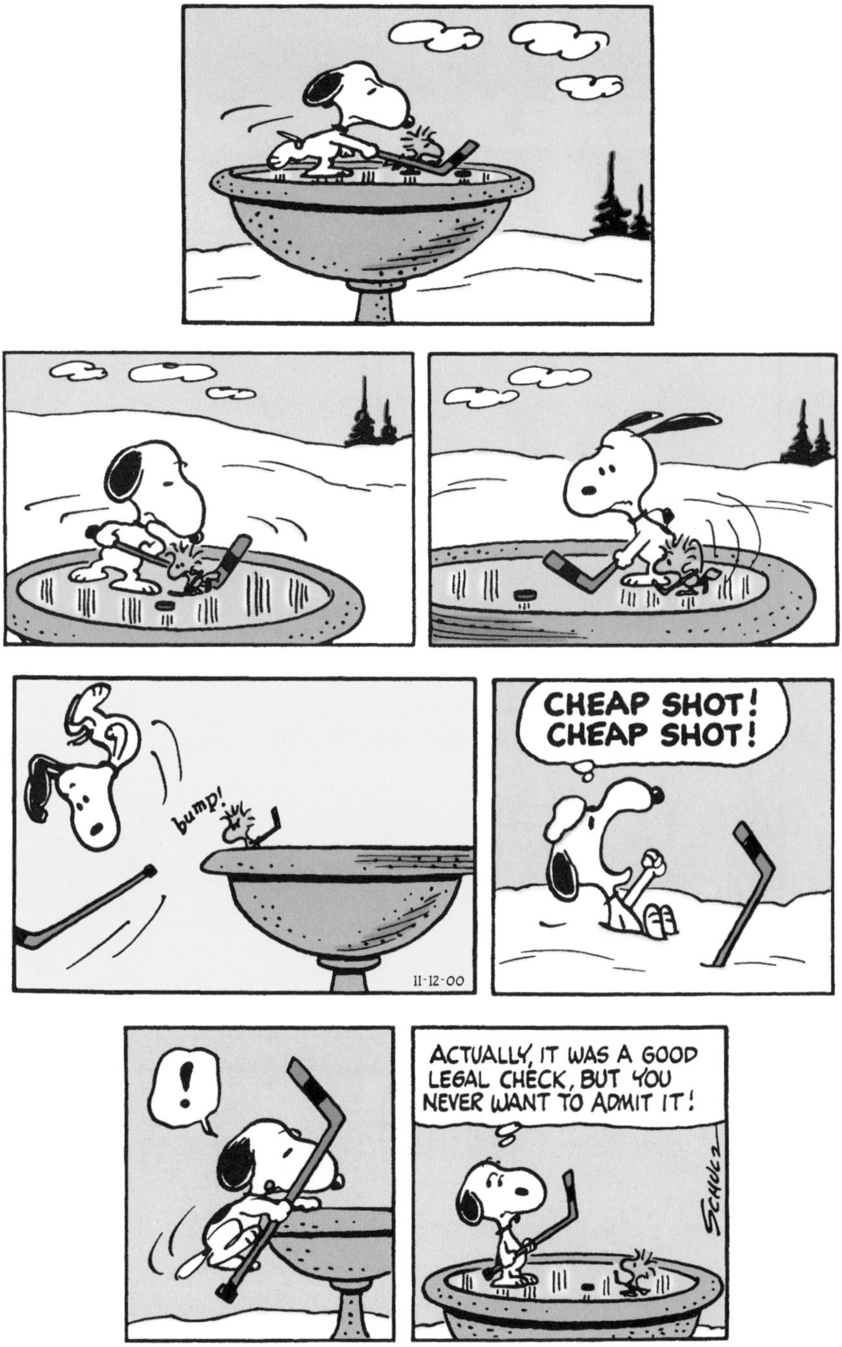
bump!
11-12-00
CHEAP SHOT! CHEAP SHOT!
!
ACTUALLY, IT WAS A GOOD LEGAL CHECK, BUT YOU NEVER WANT TO ADMIT IT!
SCHULZ

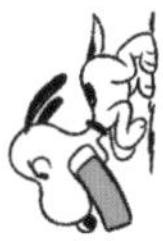

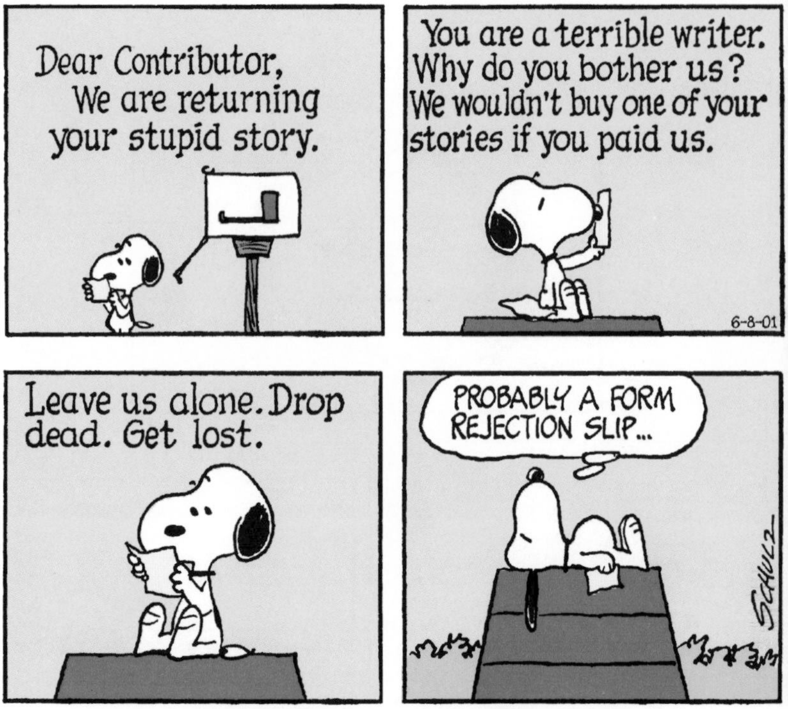
Dear Contributor,
We are returning your stupid story.
You are a terrible writer. Why do you bother us? We wouldn't buy one of your stories if you paid us.
6-8-01
Leave us alone. Drop dead. Get lost.
PROBABLY A FORM REJECTION SLIP...
SCHULZ

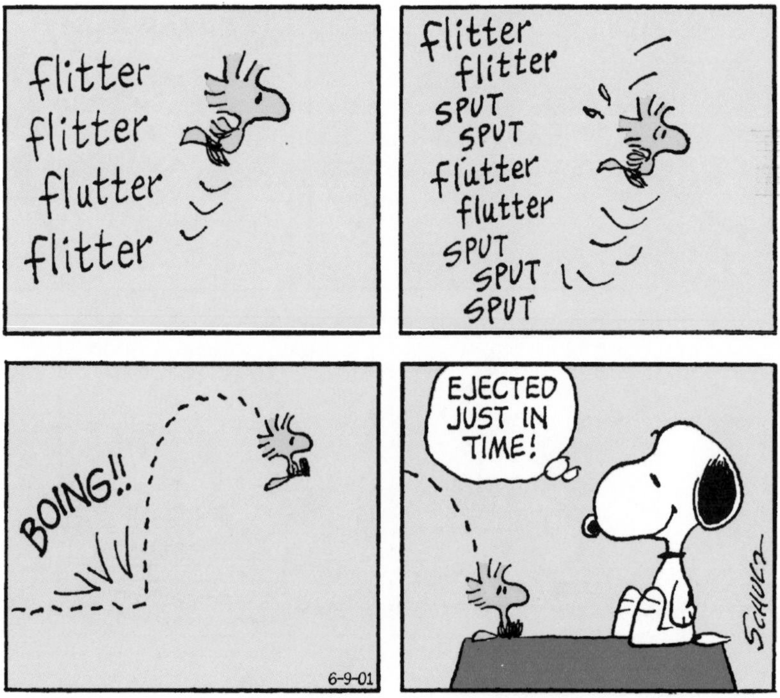
flitter
flitter
flutter
flitter
flitter
flitter
SPUT
SPUT
flutter
flutter
SPUT
SPUT
SPUT
BOING!!
6-9-01
EJECTED JUST IN TIME!
SCHULZ

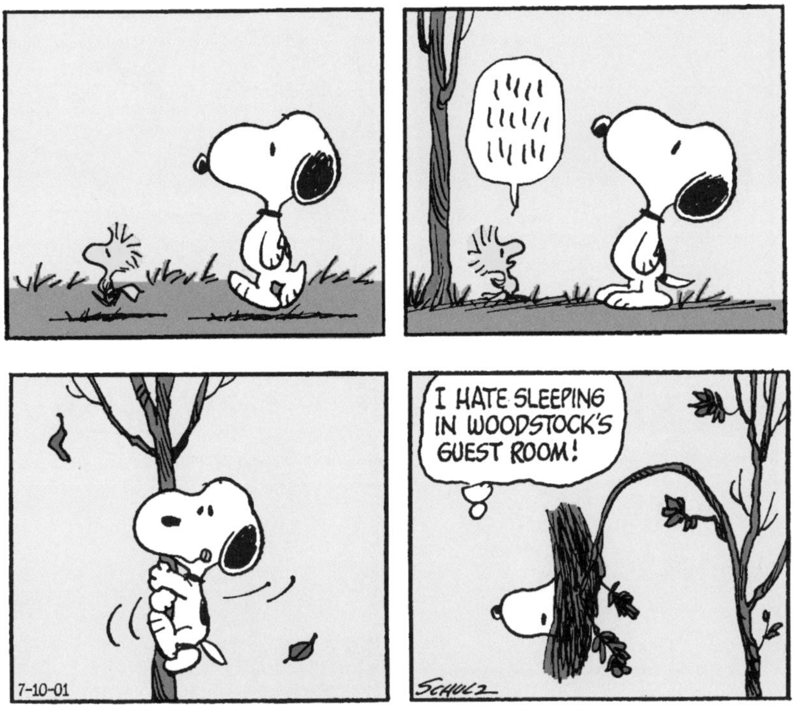
I HATE SLEEPING IN WOODSTOCK'S GUEST ROOM!
7-10-01
SCHULZ

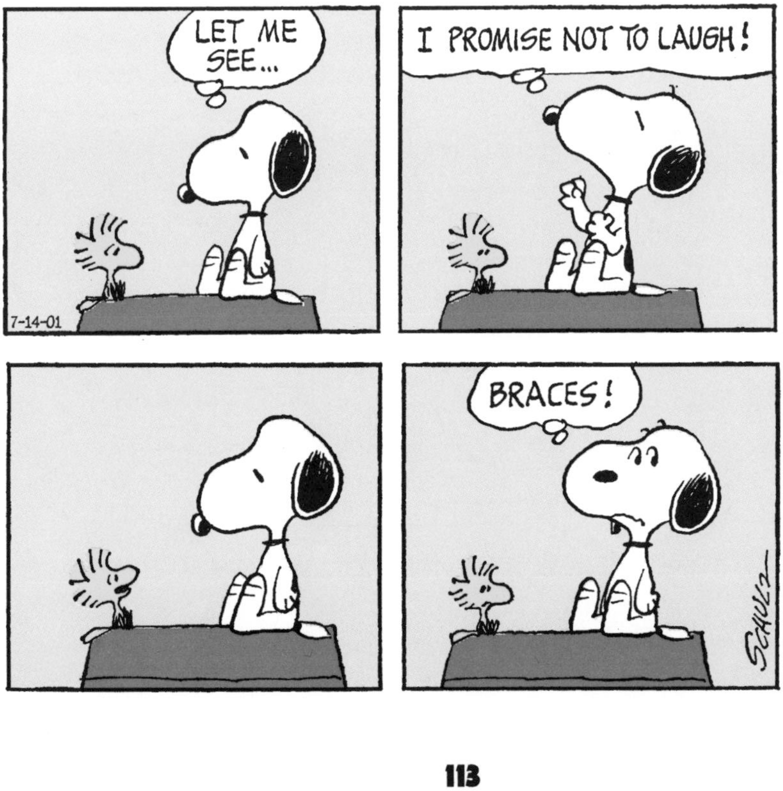
LET ME SEE...
I PROMISE NOT TO LAUGH!
BRACES!
7-14-01
SCHULZ

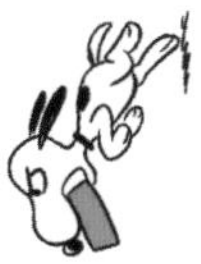

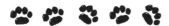

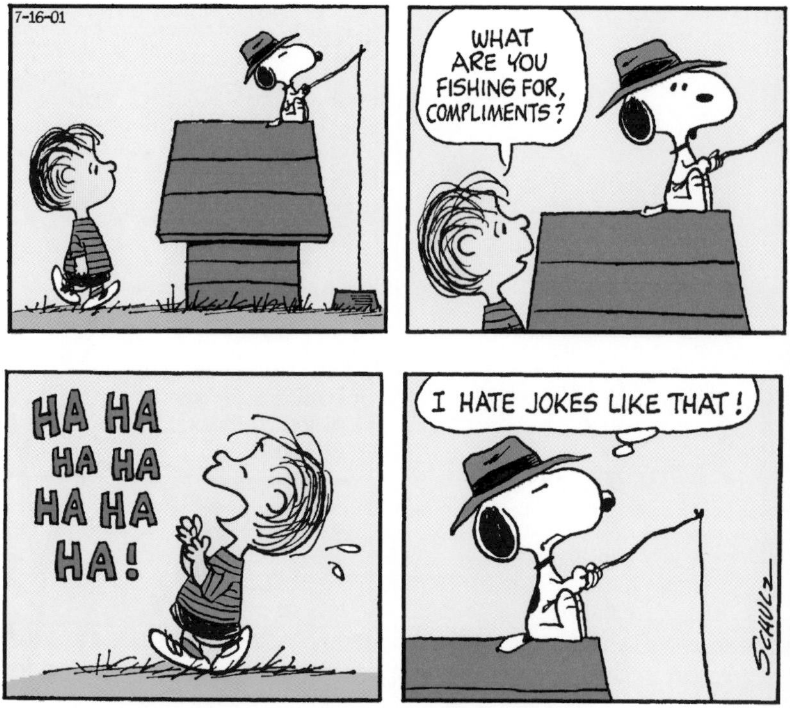
7-16-01
WHAT ARE YOU FISHING FOR, COMPLIMENTS?
HA HA HA HA HA HA HA!
I HATE JOKES LIKE THAT!

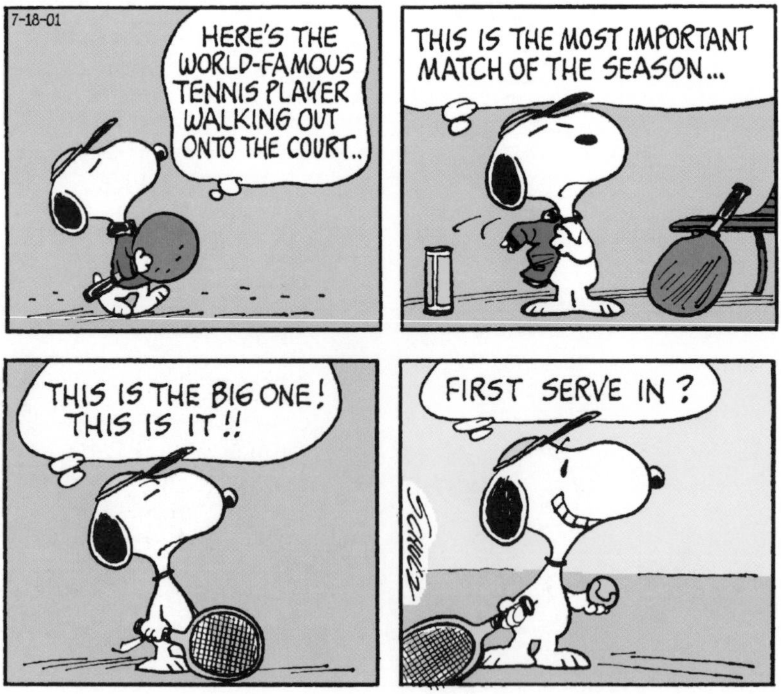
7-18-01
HERE'S THE WORLD-FAMOUS TENNIS PLAYER WALKING OUT ONTO THE COURT..
THIS IS THE MOST IMPORTANT MATCH OF THE SEASON...
THIS IS THE BIG ONE! THIS IS IT!!
FIRST SERVE IN?

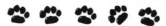

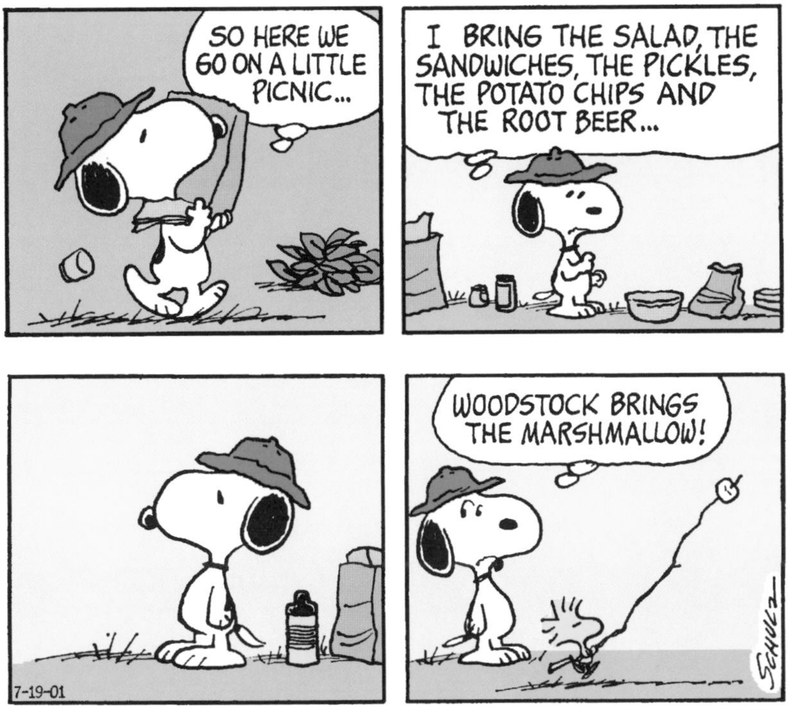
SO HERE WE GO ON A LITTLE PICNIC...
I BRING THE SALAD, THE SANDWICHES, THE PICKLES, THE POTATO CHIPS AND THE ROOT BEER...
7-19-01
WOODSTOCK BRINGS THE MARSHMALLOW!
SCHULZ

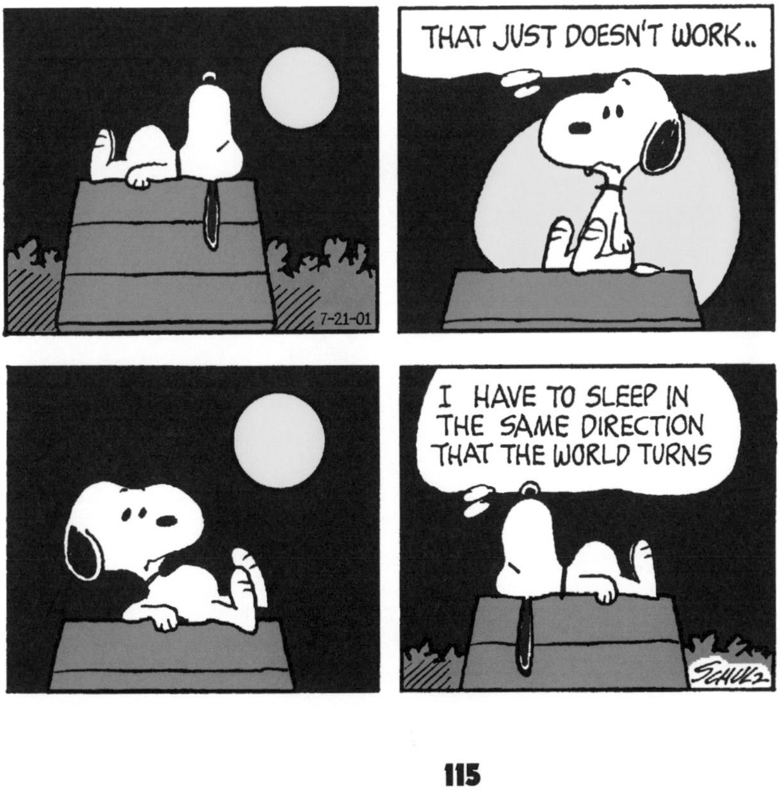
7-21-01
THAT JUST DOESN'T WORK..
I HAVE TO SLEEP IN THE SAME DIRECTION THAT THE WORLD TURNS
SCHULZ

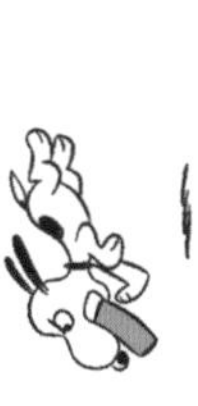

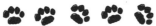

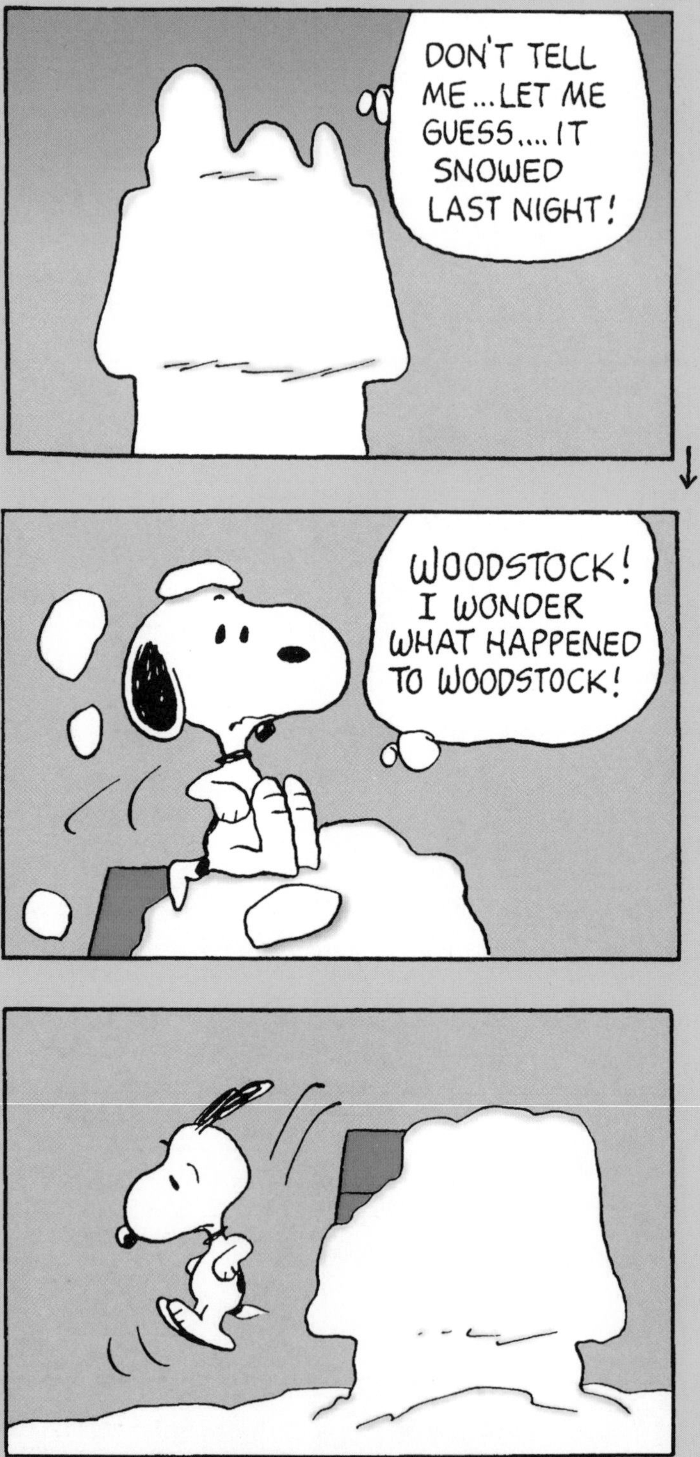
DON'T TELL ME...LET ME GUESS.... IT SNOWED LAST NIGHT!
WOODSTOCK! I WONDER WHAT HAPPENED TO WOODSTOCK!

POOR WOODSTOCK DOESN'T KNOW HOW TO TAKE CARE OF HIMSELF IN EMERGENCIES...
11-26-00
HE'S PROBABLY SNOWED UNDER, OR FROZEN STIFF, OR...
SCHULZ

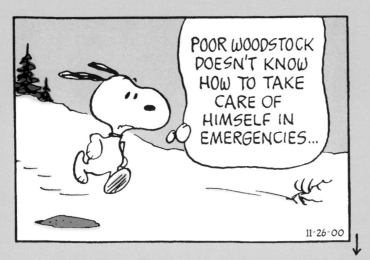

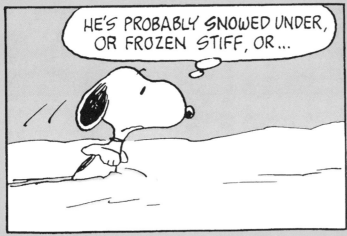

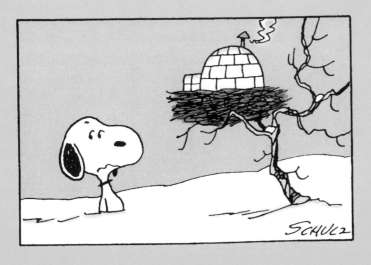

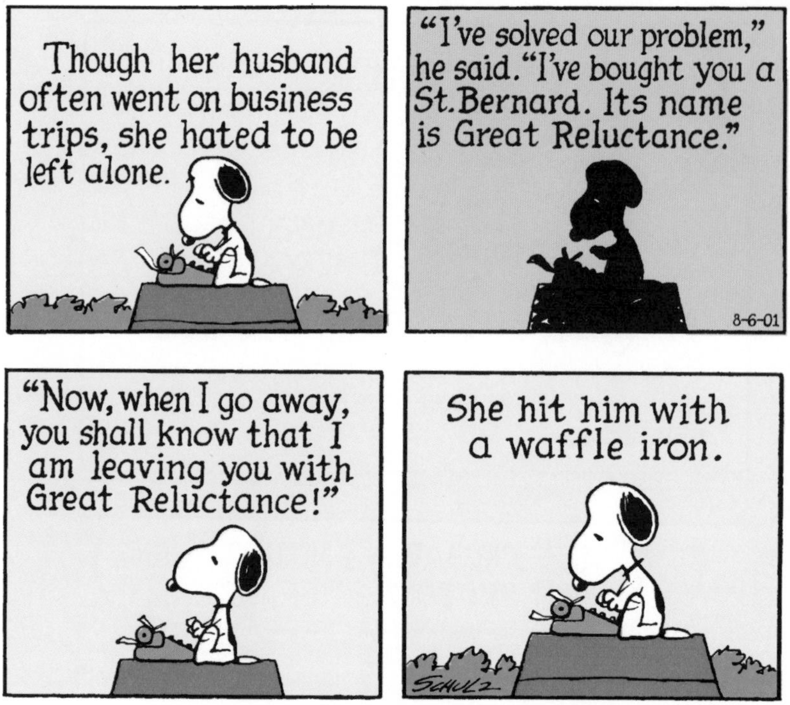
Though her husband often went on business trips, she hated to be left alone.
"I've solved our problem," he said. "I've bought you a St. Bernard. Its name is Great Reluctance."
8-6-01
"Now, when I go away, you shall know that I am leaving you with Great Reluctance!"
She hit him with a waffle iron.
SCHULZ

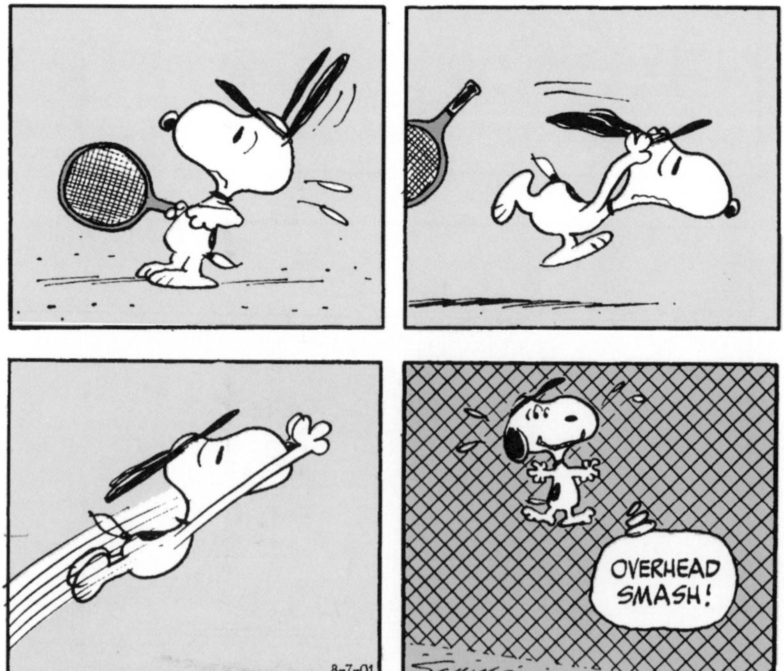
8-7-01
OVERHEAD SMASH!
SCHULZ

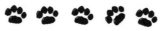

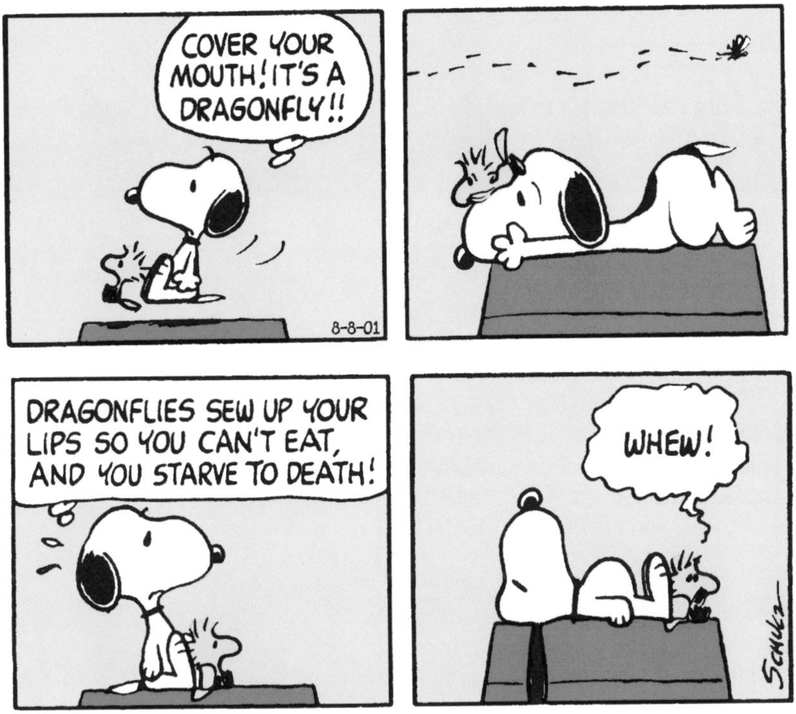
COVER YOUR MOUTH! IT'S A DRAGONFLY!!
8-8-01
DRAGONFLIES SEW UP YOUR LIPS SO YOU CAN'T EAT, AND YOU STARVE TO DEATH!
WHEW!
SCHULZ

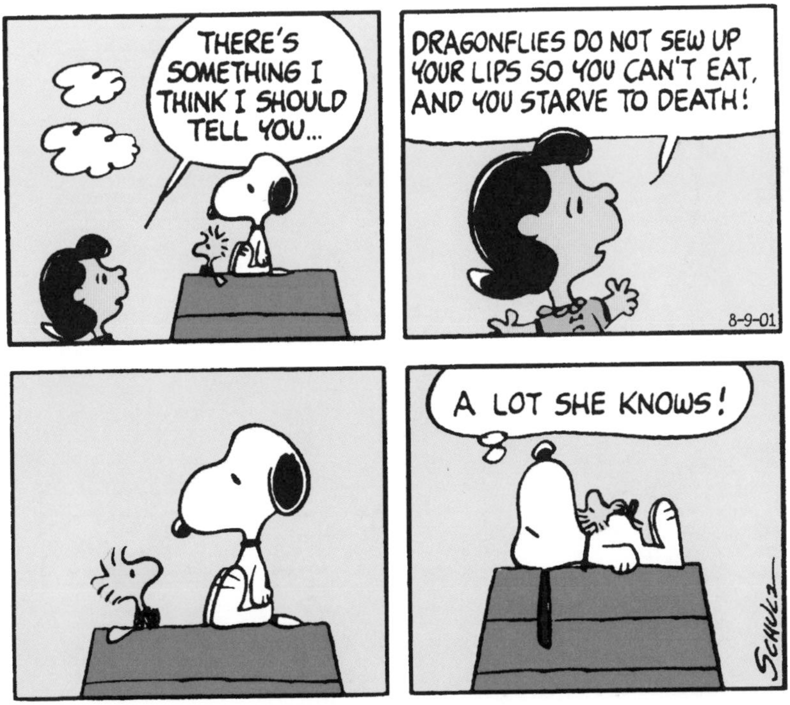
THERE'S SOMETHING I THINK I SHOULD TELL YOU...
DRAGONFLIES DO NOT SEW UP YOUR LIPS SO YOU CAN'T EAT, AND YOU STARVE TO DEATH!
8-9-01
A LOT SHE KNOWS!
SCHULZ

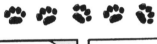

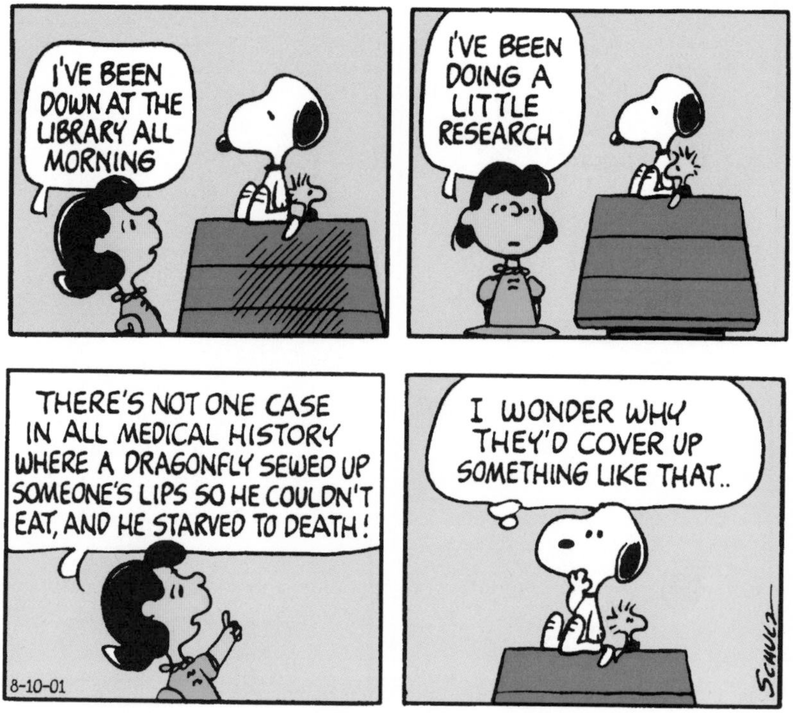
I'VE BEEN DOWN AT THE LIBRARY ALL MORNING
I'VE BEEN DOING A LITTLE RESEARCH
THERE'S NOT ONE CASE IN ALL MEDICAL HISTORY WHERE A DRAGONFLY SEWED UP SOMEONE'S LIPS SO HE COULDN'T EAT, AND HE STARVED TO DEATH!
8-10-01
I WONDER WHY THEY'D COVER UP SOMETHING LIKE THAT..
SCHULZ

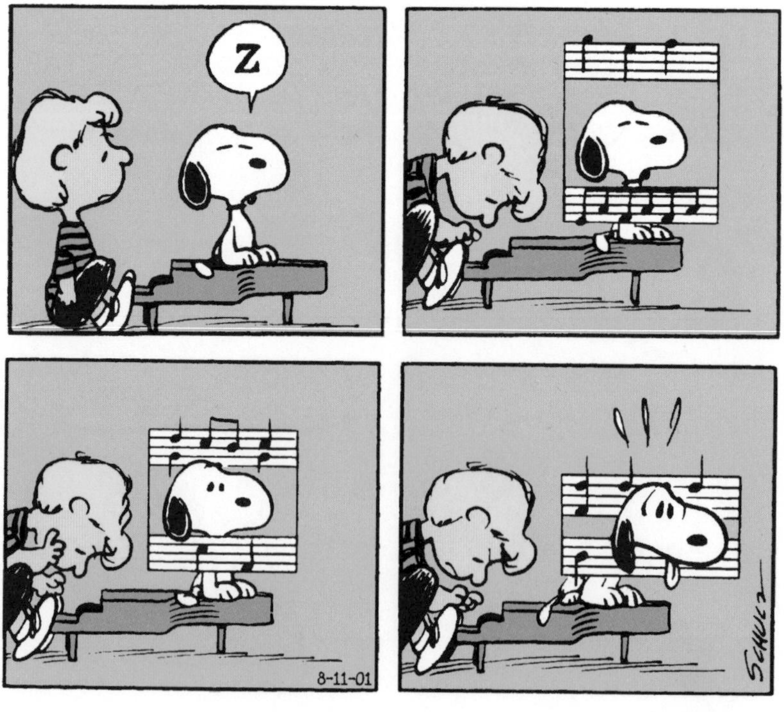
Z
8-11-01
SCHULZ

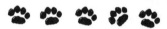

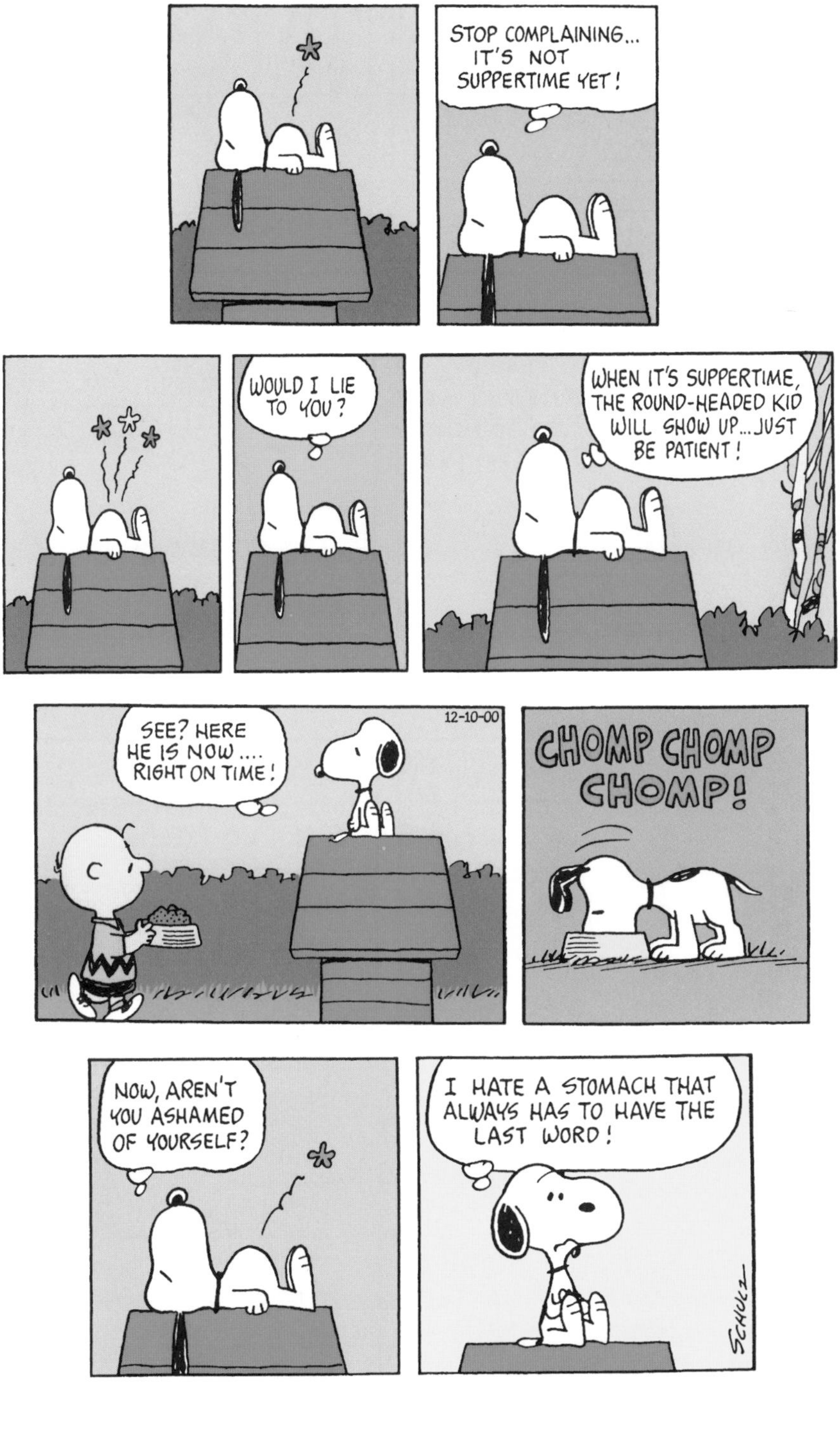
STOP COMPLAINING... IT'S NOT SUPPERTIME YET!
WOULD I LIE TO YOU?
WHEN IT'S SUPPERTIME, THE ROUND-HEADED KID WILL SHOW UP... JUST BE PATIENT!
12-10-00
SEE? HERE HE IS NOW.... RIGHT ON TIME!
CHOMP CHOMP CHOMP!
NOW, AREN'T YOU ASHAMED OF YOURSELF?
I HATE A STOMACH THAT ALWAYS HAS TO HAVE THE LAST WORD!
SCHULZ

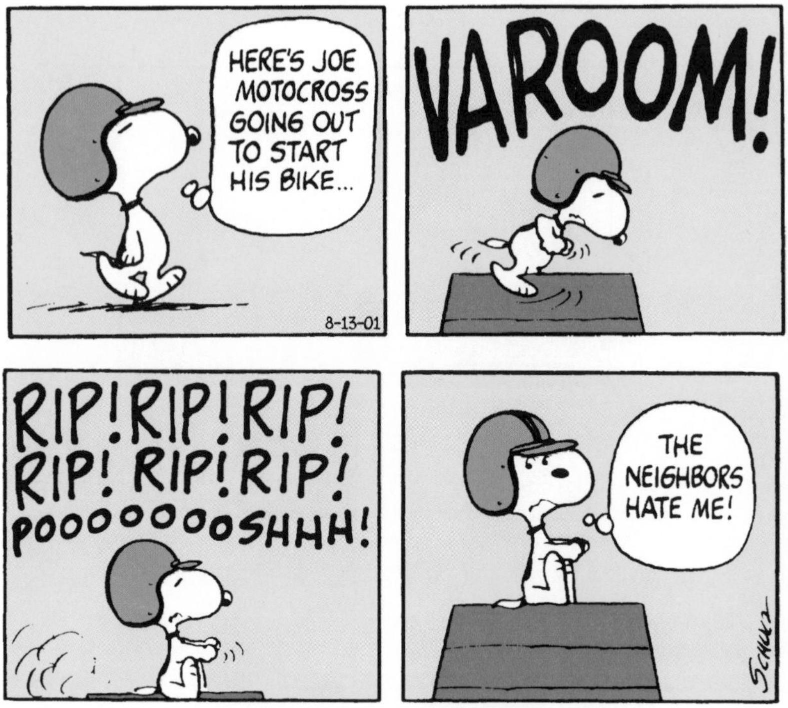
HERE'S JOE MOTOCROSS GOING OUT TO START HIS BIKE...
8-13-01
VAROOM!
RIP! RIP! RIP! RIP! RIP! RIP! POOOOOOOOSHHH!
THE NEIGHBORS HATE ME!
SCHULZ

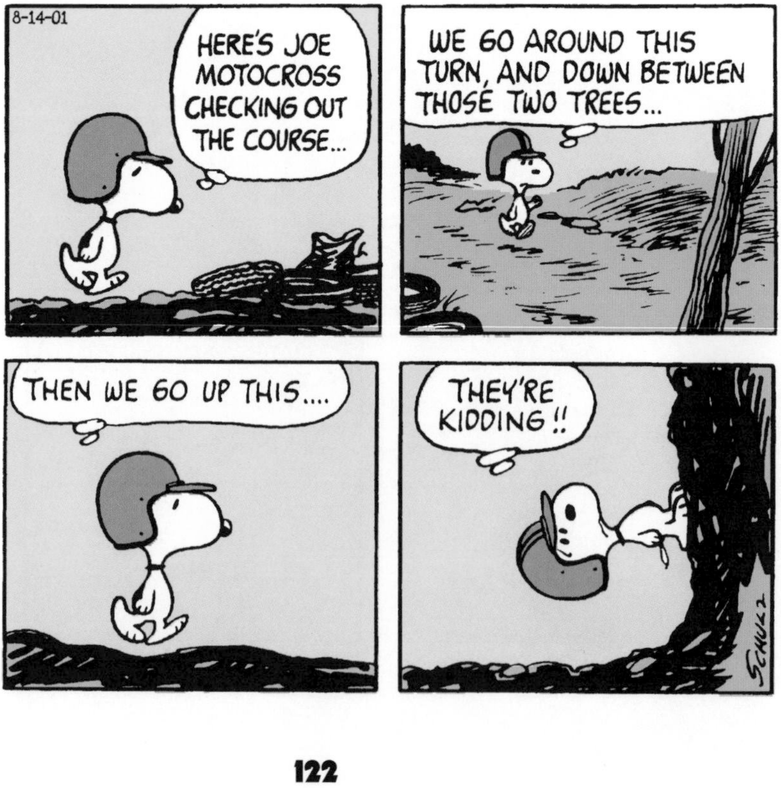
8-14-01
HERE'S JOE MOTOCROSS CHECKING OUT THE COURSE...
WE GO AROUND THIS TURN, AND DOWN BETWEEN THOSE TWO TREES...
THEN WE GO UP THIS....
THEY'RE KIDDING!!
SCHULZ

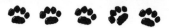

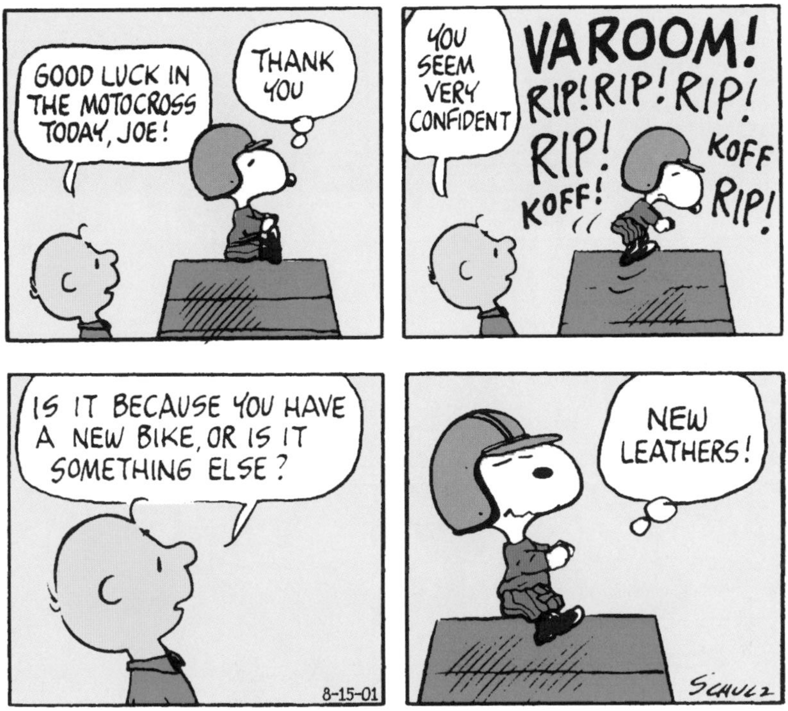
GOOD LUCK IN THE MOTOCROSS TODAY, JOE!
THANK YOU
YOU SEEM VERY CONFIDENT
VAROOM!
RIP! RIP! RIP!
RIP!
KOFF!
KOFF
RIP!
IS IT BECAUSE YOU HAVE A NEW BIKE, OR IS IT SOMETHING ELSE?
8-15-01
NEW LEATHERS!
SCHULZ

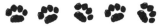

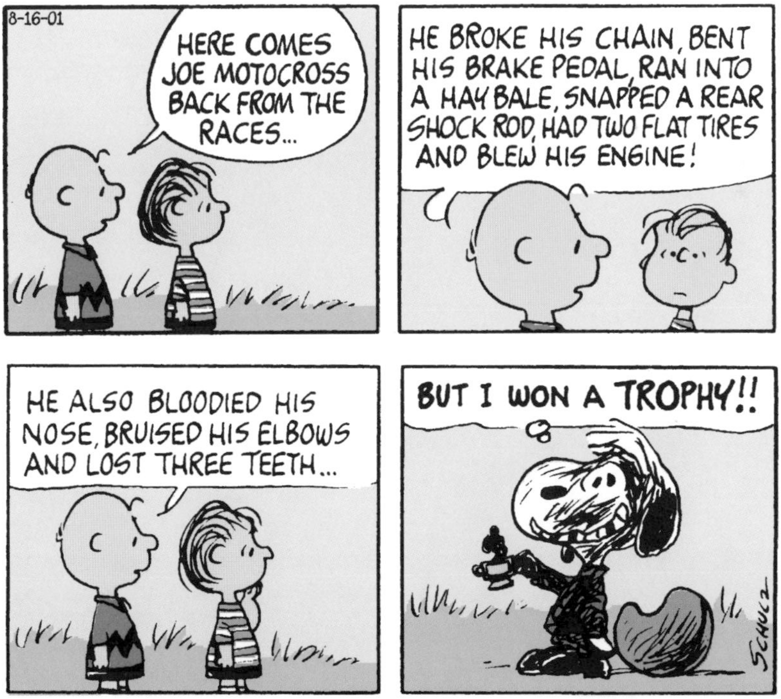
8-16-01
HERE COMES JOE MOTOCROSS BACK FROM THE RACES...
HE BROKE HIS CHAIN, BENT HIS BRAKE PEDAL, RAN INTO A HAY BALE, SNAPPED A REAR SHOCK ROD, HAD TWO FLAT TIRES AND BLEW HIS ENGINE!
HE ALSO BLOODIED HIS NOSE, BRUISED HIS ELBOWS AND LOST THREE TEETH...
BUT I WON A TROPHY!!
SCHULZ

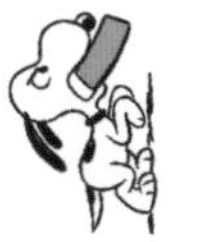

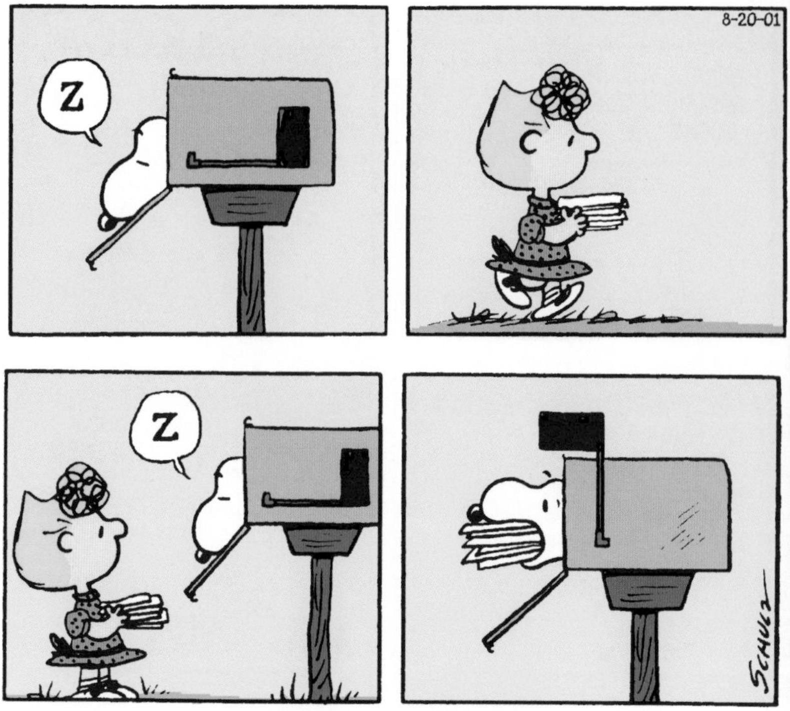
Z
8-20-01
Z
SCHULZ

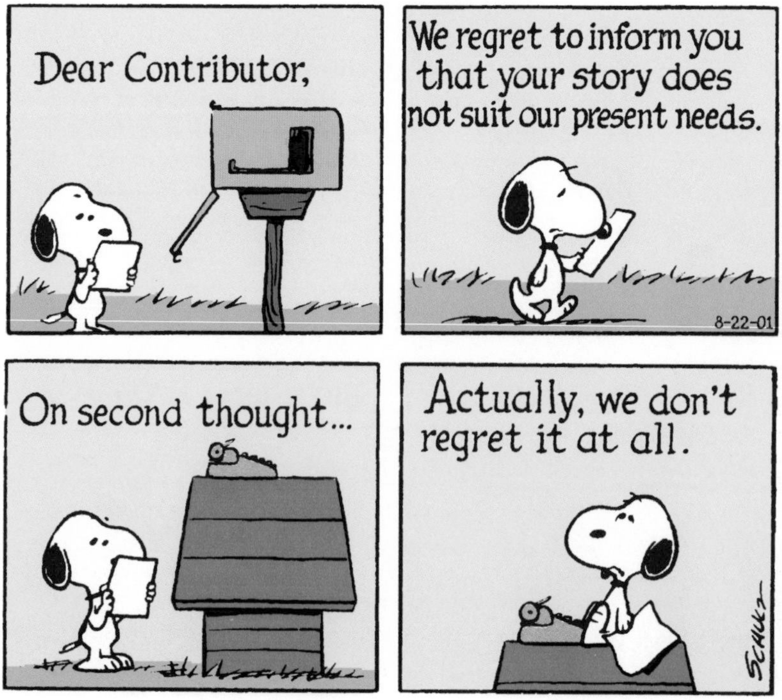
Dear Contributor,
We regret to inform you that your story does not suit our present needs.
8-22-01
On second thought...
Actually, we don't regret it at all.
SCHULZ

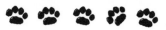

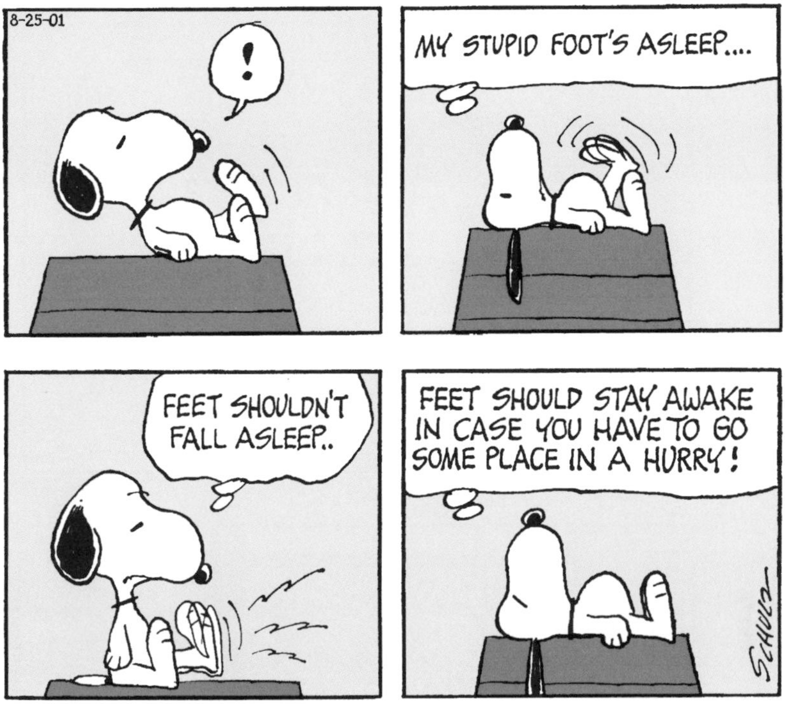
8-25-01
!
MY STUPID FOOT'S ASLEEP....
FEET SHOULDN'T FALL ASLEEP..
FEET SHOULD STAY AWAKE IN CASE YOU HAVE TO GO SOME PLACE IN A HURRY!
SCHULZ

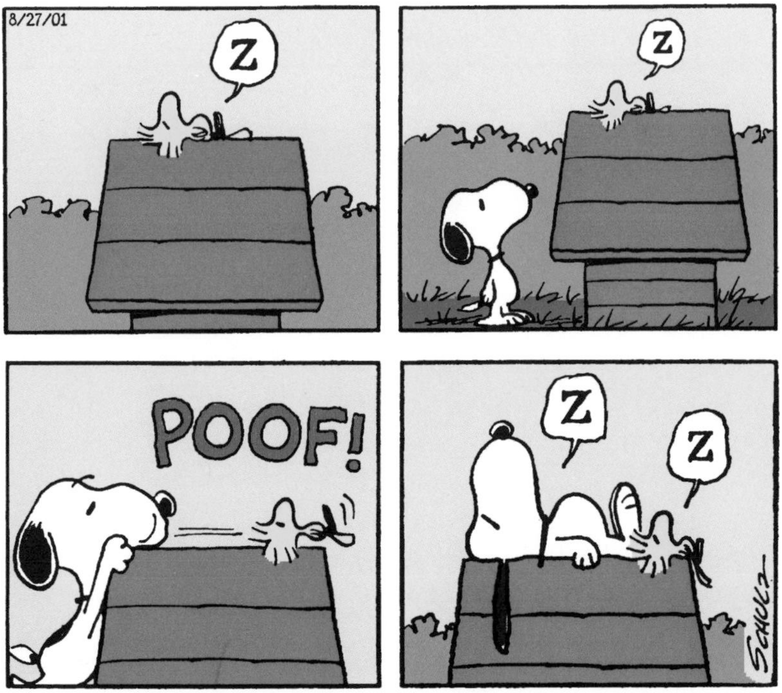
8/27/01
Z
Z
POOF!
Z
Z
SCHULZ

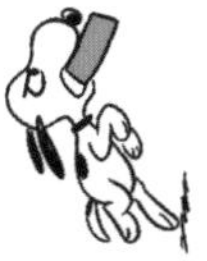

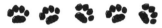

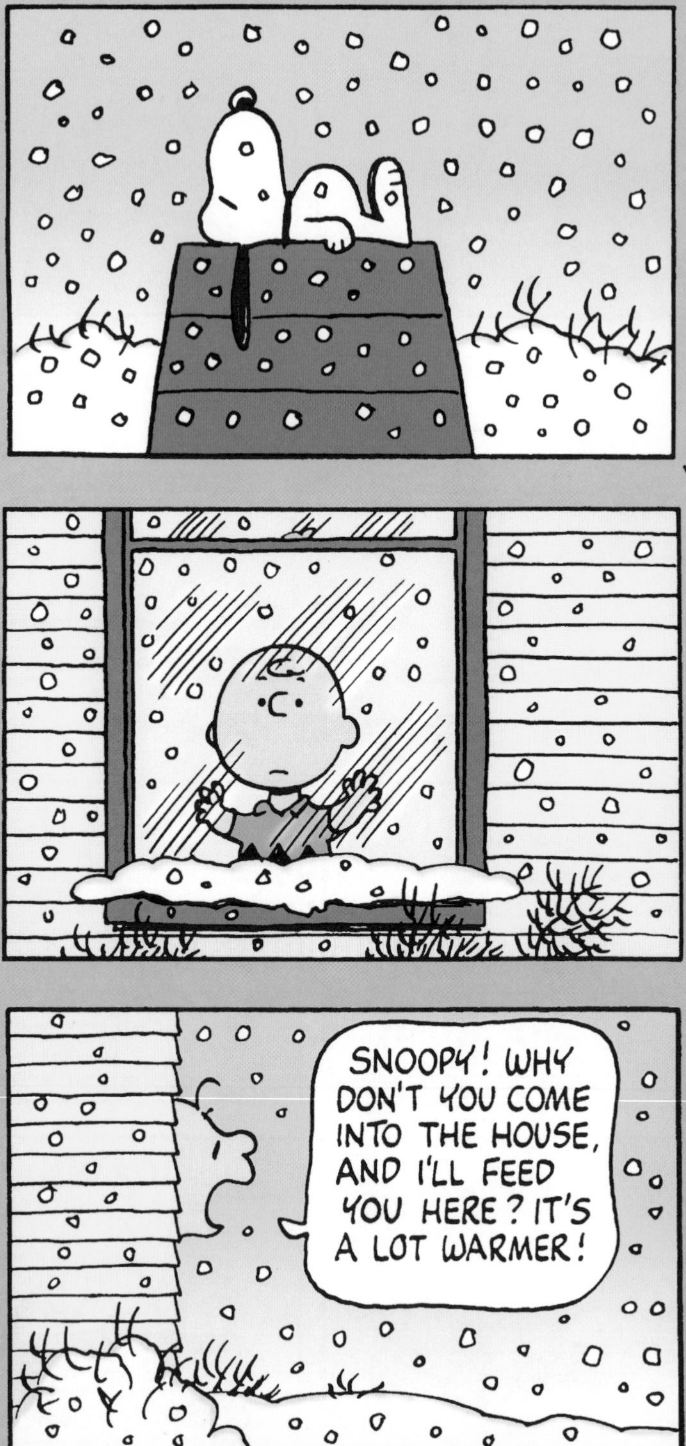
SNOOPY! WHY DON'T YOU COME INTO THE HOUSE, AND I'LL FEED YOU HERE? IT'S A LOT WARMER!

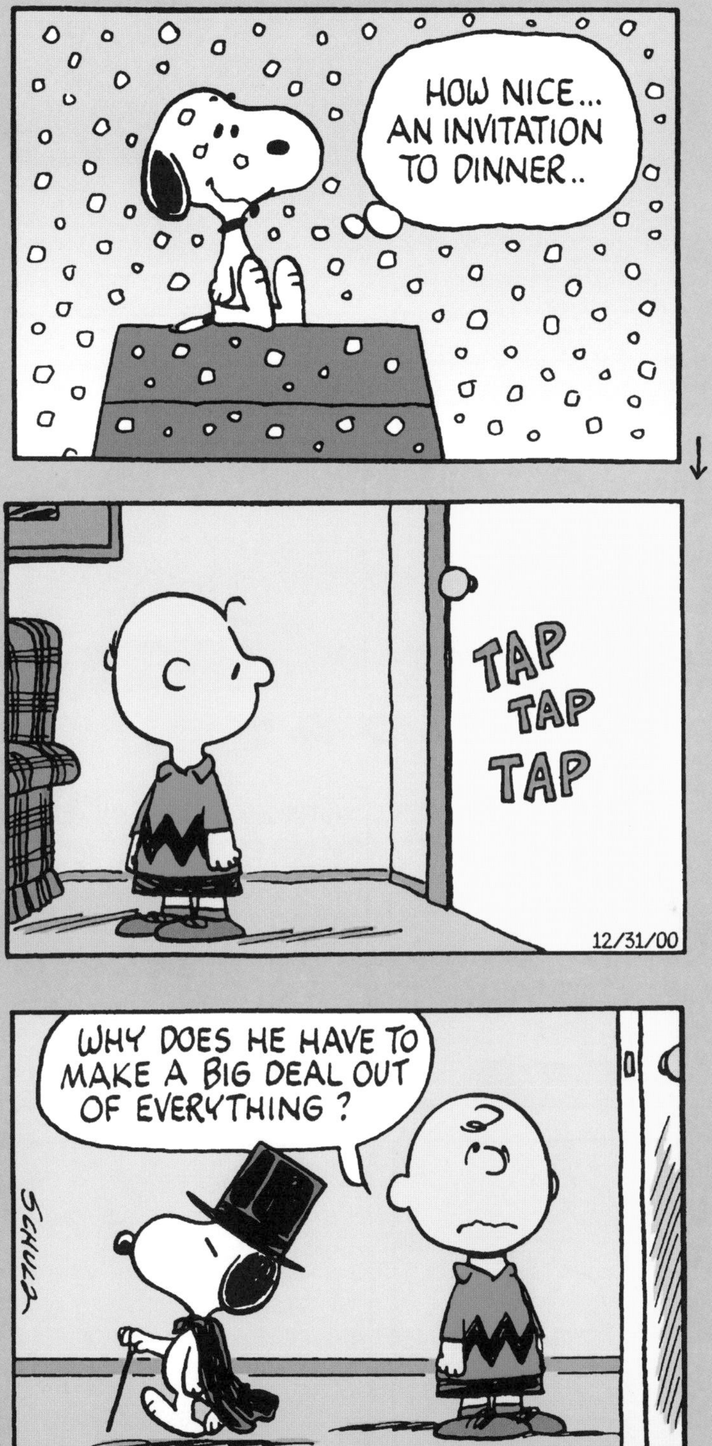
HOW NICE... AN INVITATION TO DINNER..
TAP
TAP
TAP
12/31/00
WHY DOES HE HAVE TO MAKE A BIG DEAL OUT OF EVERYTHING ?
SCHULZ

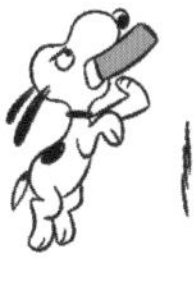

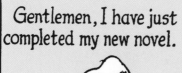
Gentlemen, I have just completed my new novel.

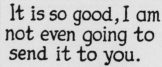
It is so good, I am not even going to send it to you.

8/29/01

Why don't you just come and get it?

Gentlemen,

Yesterday, I waited all day for you to come and get my novel and to publish it and make me rich and famous.

8/30/01

You did not show up.

Were you not feeling well?

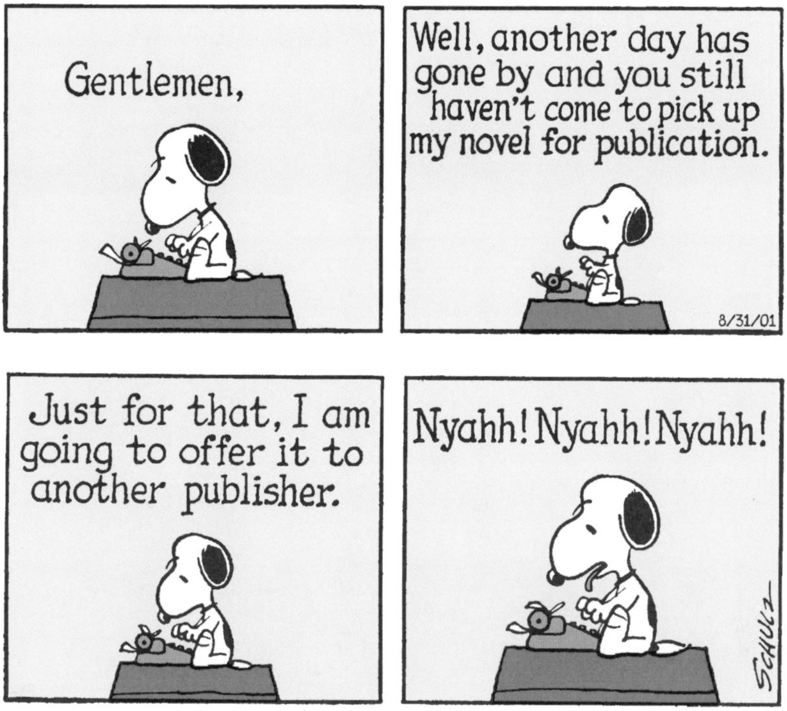
Gentlemen,
Well, another day has gone by and you still haven't come to pick up my novel for publication.
8/31/01
Just for that, I am going to offer it to another publisher.
Nyahh! Nyahh! Nyahh!

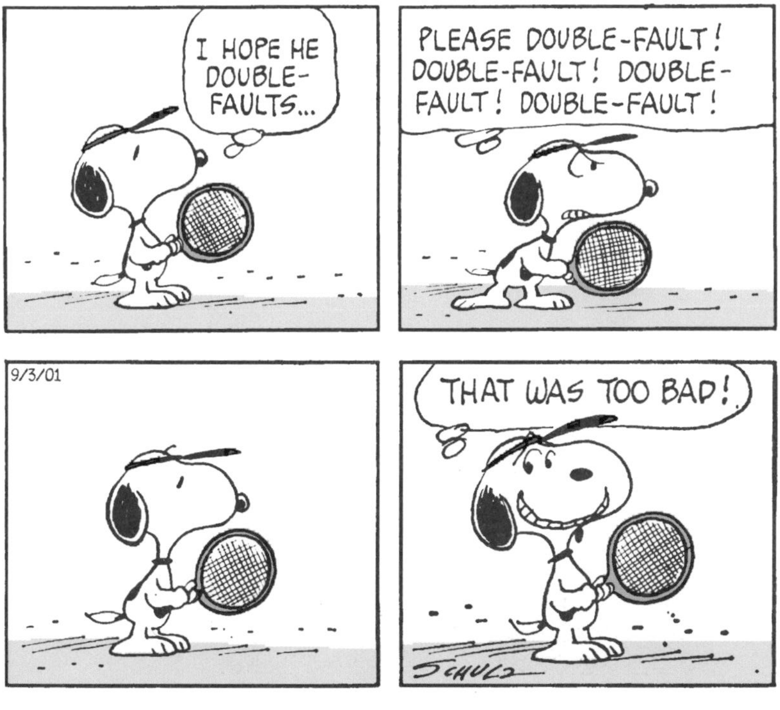
I HOPE HE DOUBLE-FAULTS...
PLEASE DOUBLE-FAULT! DOUBLE-FAULT! DOUBLE-FAULT! DOUBLE-FAULT!
9/3/01
THAT WAS TOO BAD!

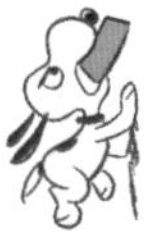

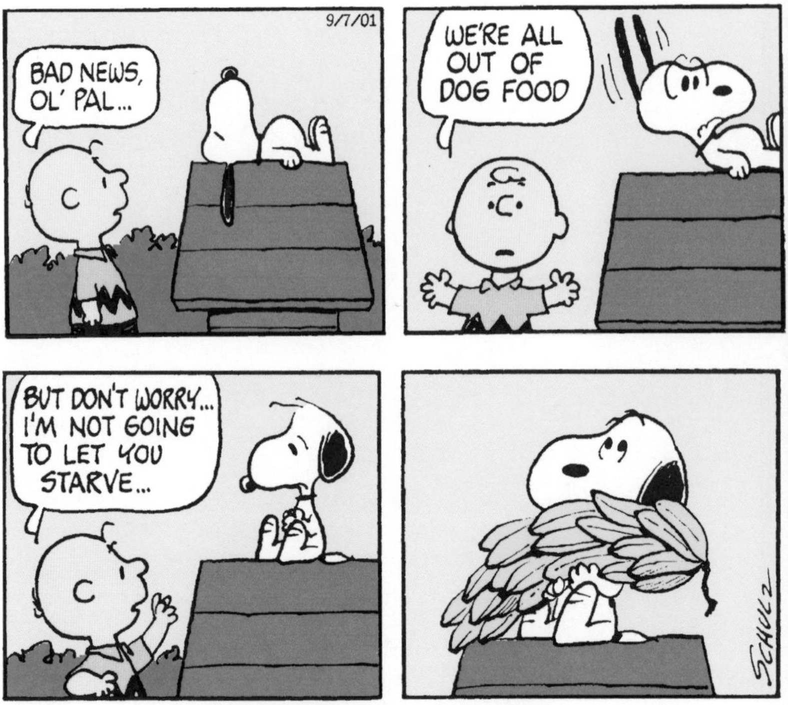
9/7/01
BAD NEWS, OL' PAL...
WE'RE ALL OUT OF DOG FOOD
BUT DON'T WORRY... I'M NOT GOING TO LET YOU STARVE...
SCHULZ

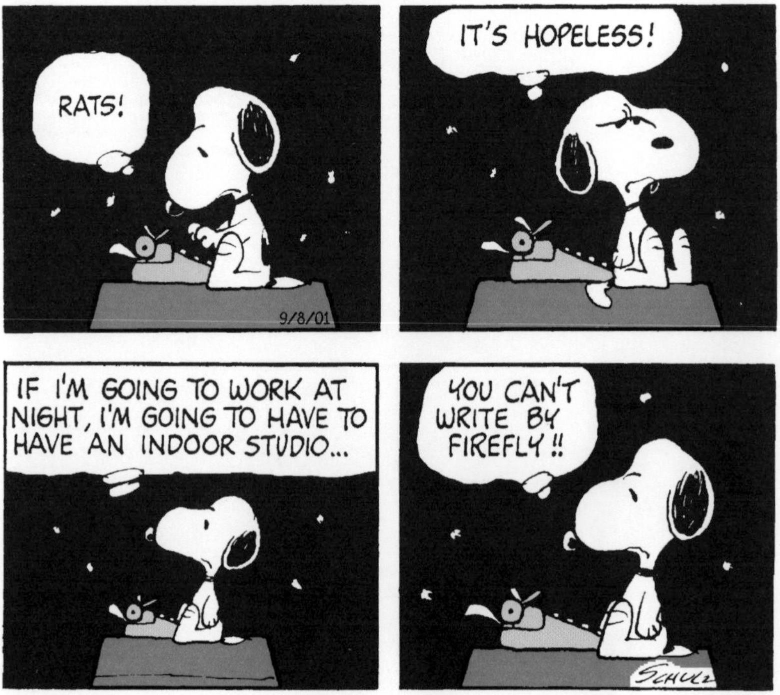
RATS!
9/8/01
IT'S HOPELESS!
IF I'M GOING TO WORK AT NIGHT, I'M GOING TO HAVE TO HAVE AN INDOOR STUDIO...
YOU CAN'T WRITE BY FIREFLY !!
SCHULZ

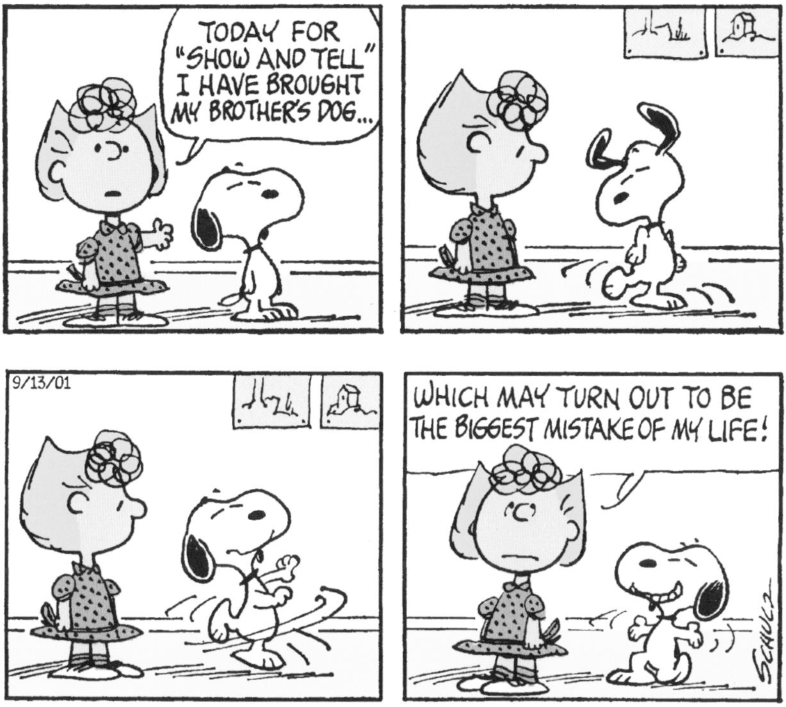
TODAY FOR "SHOW AND TELL" I HAVE BROUGHT MY BROTHER'S DOG...
9/13/01
WHICH MAY TURN OUT TO BE THE BIGGEST MISTAKE OF MY LIFE!
SCHULZ

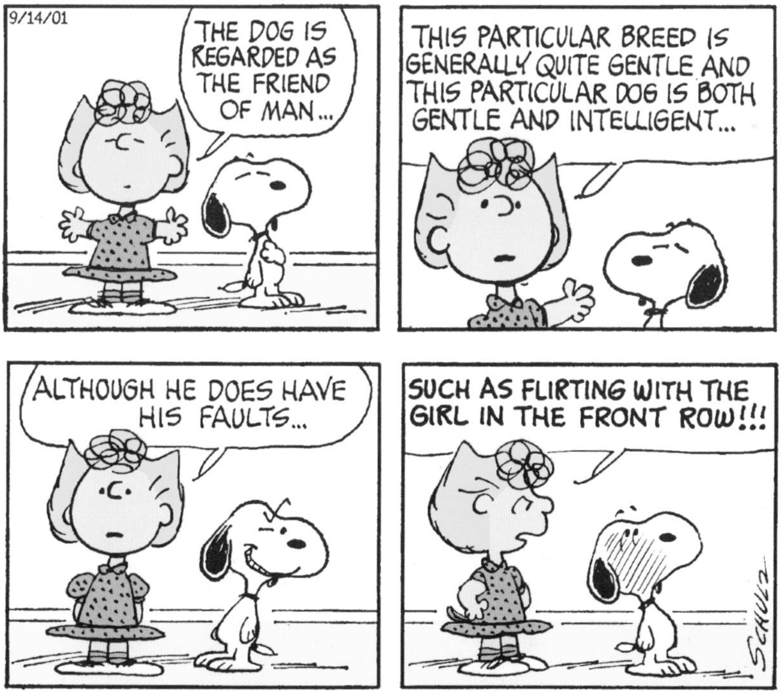
9/14/01
THE DOG IS REGARDED AS THE FRIEND OF MAN...
THIS PARTICULAR BREED IS GENERALLY QUITE GENTLE AND THIS PARTICULAR DOG IS BOTH GENTLE AND INTELLIGENT...
ALTHOUGH HE DOES HAVE HIS FAULTS...
SUCH AS FLIRTING WITH THE GIRL IN THE FRONT ROW!!!
SCHULZ

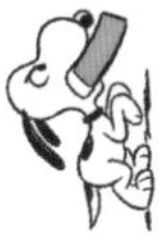

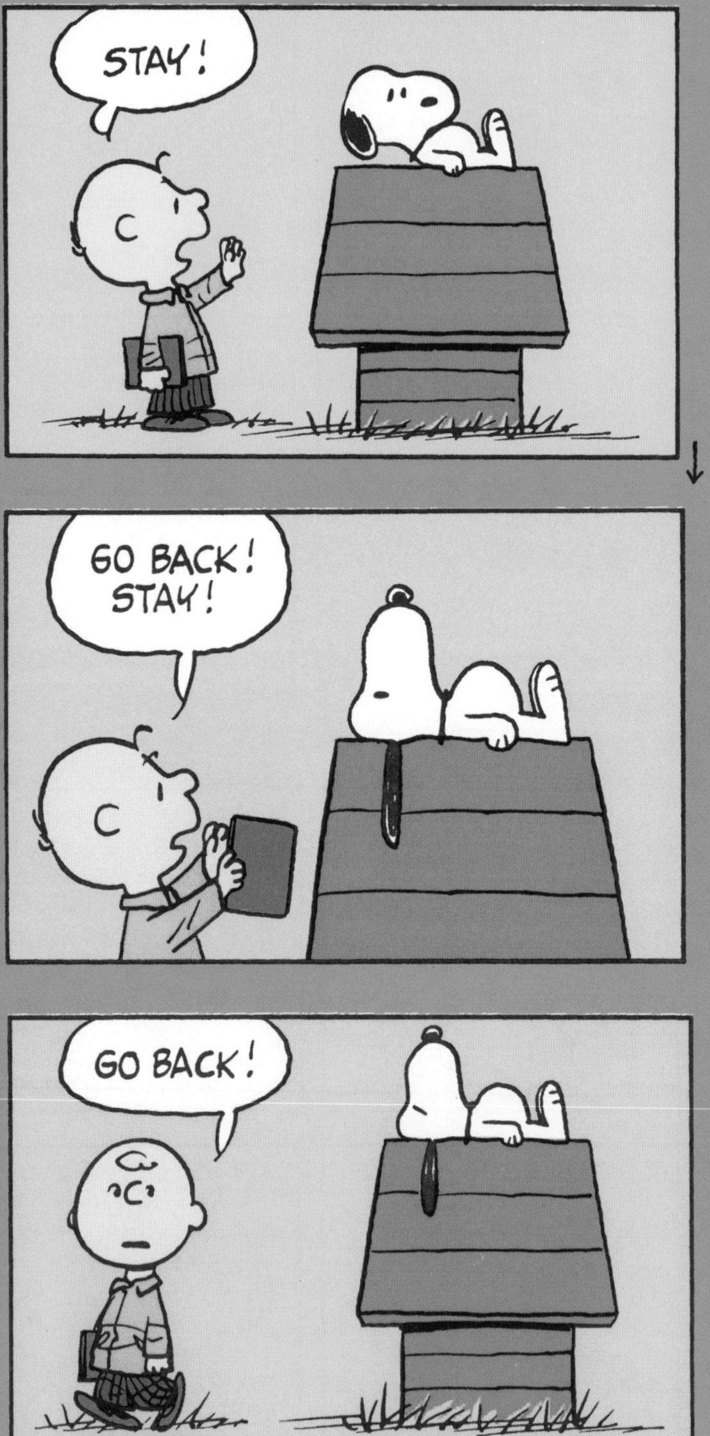
STAY!
GO BACK! STAY!
GO BACK!

BACK, I SAY! BACK!
SIGH SOME KIDS HAVE DOGS WHO TRY TO FOLLOW THEM TO SCHOOL...
1-14-01
SCHULZ

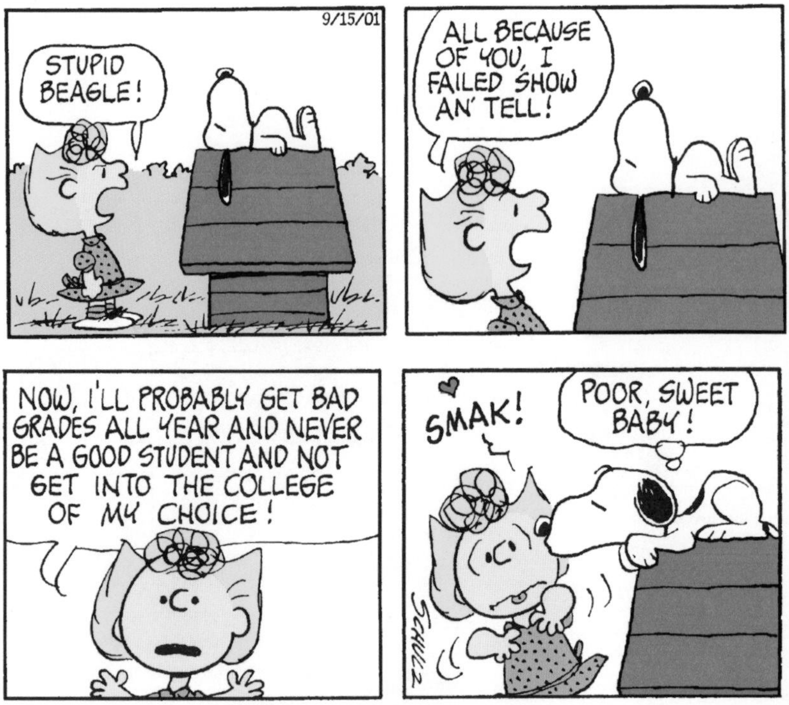

9/15/01
STUPID BEAGLE!
ALL BECAUSE OF YOU, I FAILED SHOW AN' TELL!
NOW, I'LL PROBABLY GET BAD GRADES ALL YEAR AND NEVER BE A GOOD STUDENT AND NOT GET INTO THE COLLEGE OF MY CHOICE!
SMAK!
POOR, SWEET BABY!
SCHULZ

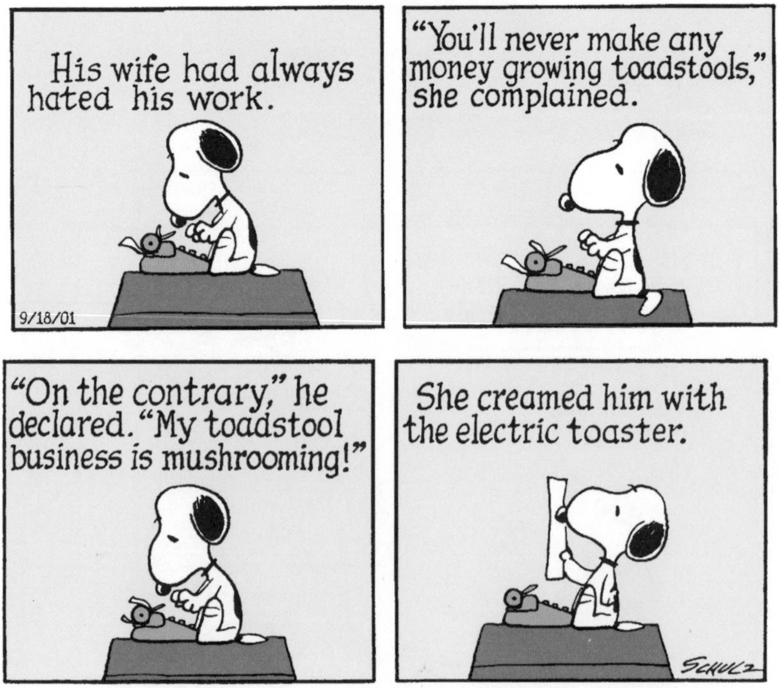

His wife had always hated his work.
9/18/01
"You'll never make any money growing toadstools," she complained.
"On the contrary," he declared. "My toadstool business is mushrooming!"
She creamed him with the electric toaster.
SCHULZ

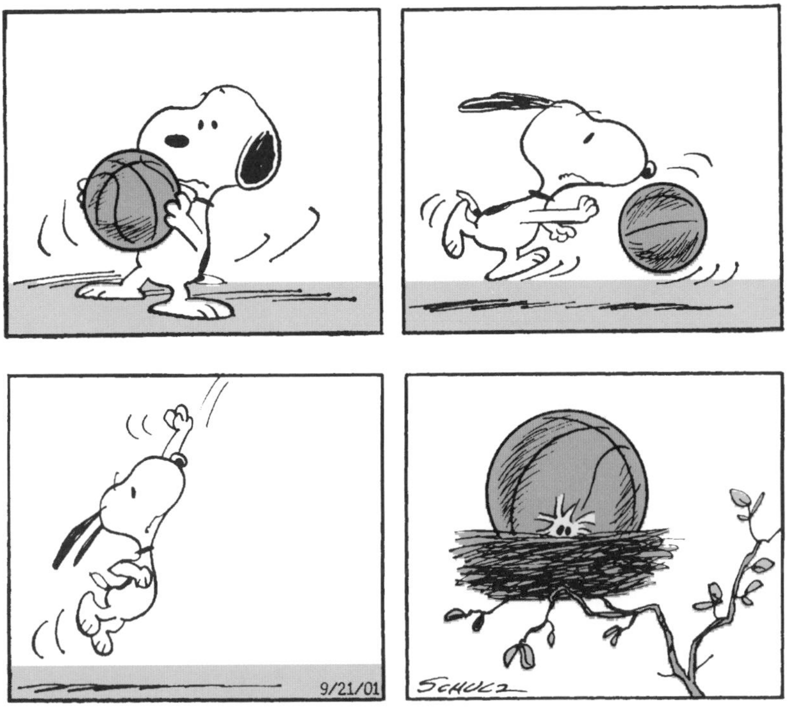
9/21/01
SCHULZ

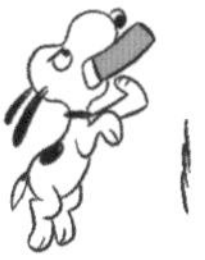

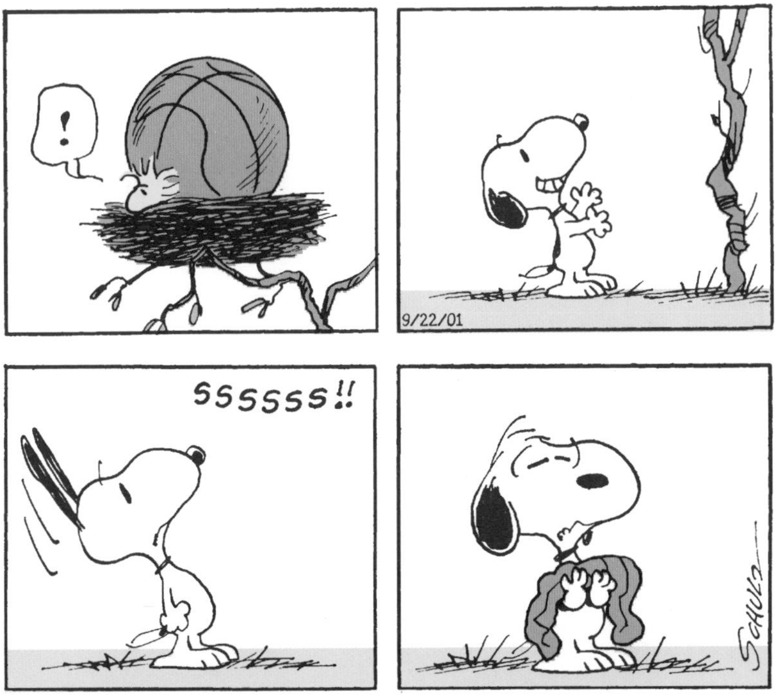
!
9/22/01
SSSSSS!!
SCHULZ

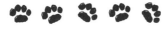

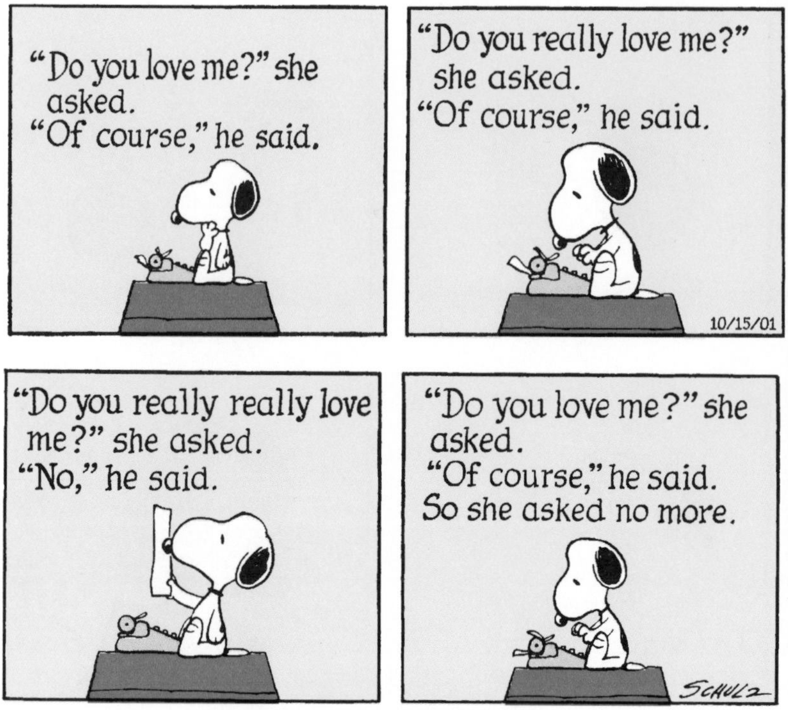
"Do you love me?" she asked.
"Of course," he said.
"Do you really love me?" she asked.
"Of course," he said.
10/15/01
"Do you really really love me?" she asked.
"No," he said.
"Do you love me?" she asked.
"Of course," he said.
So she asked no more.
SCHULZ

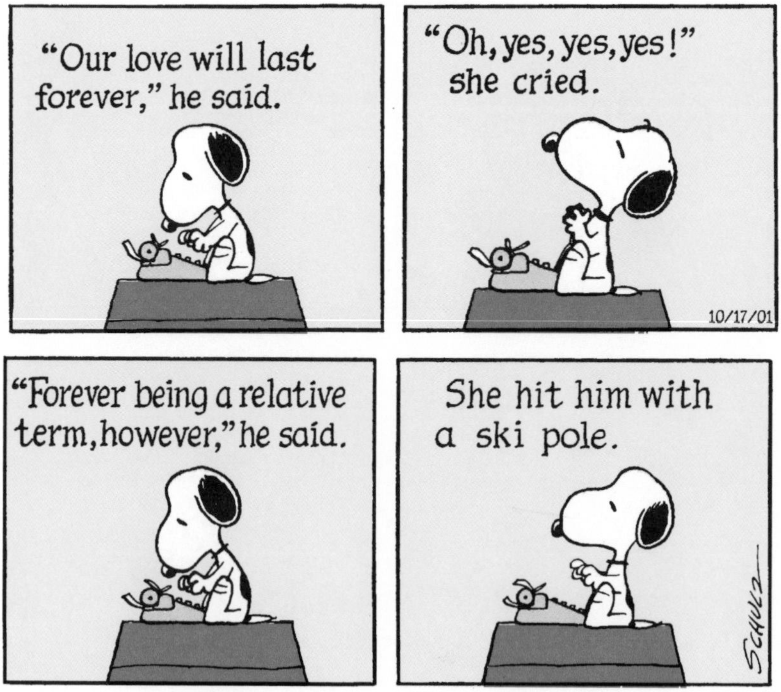
"Our love will last forever," he said.
"Oh, yes, yes, yes!" she cried.
10/17/01
"Forever being a relative term, however," he said.
She hit him with a ski pole.
SCHULZ

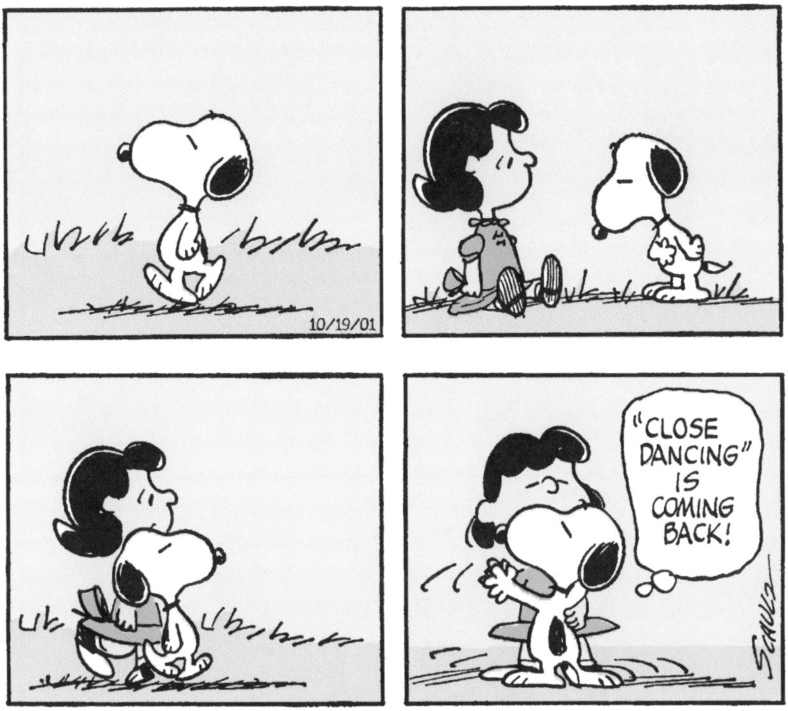
10/19/01
"CLOSE DANCING" IS COMING BACK!
SCHULZ

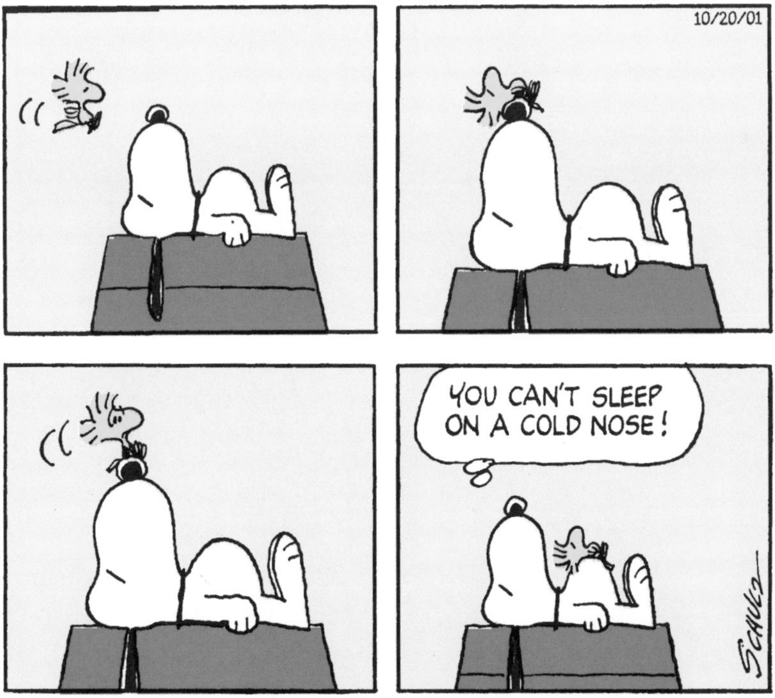
10/20/01
YOU CAN'T SLEEP ON A COLD NOSE!
SCHULZ

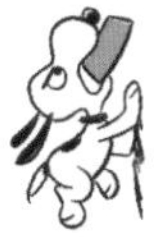

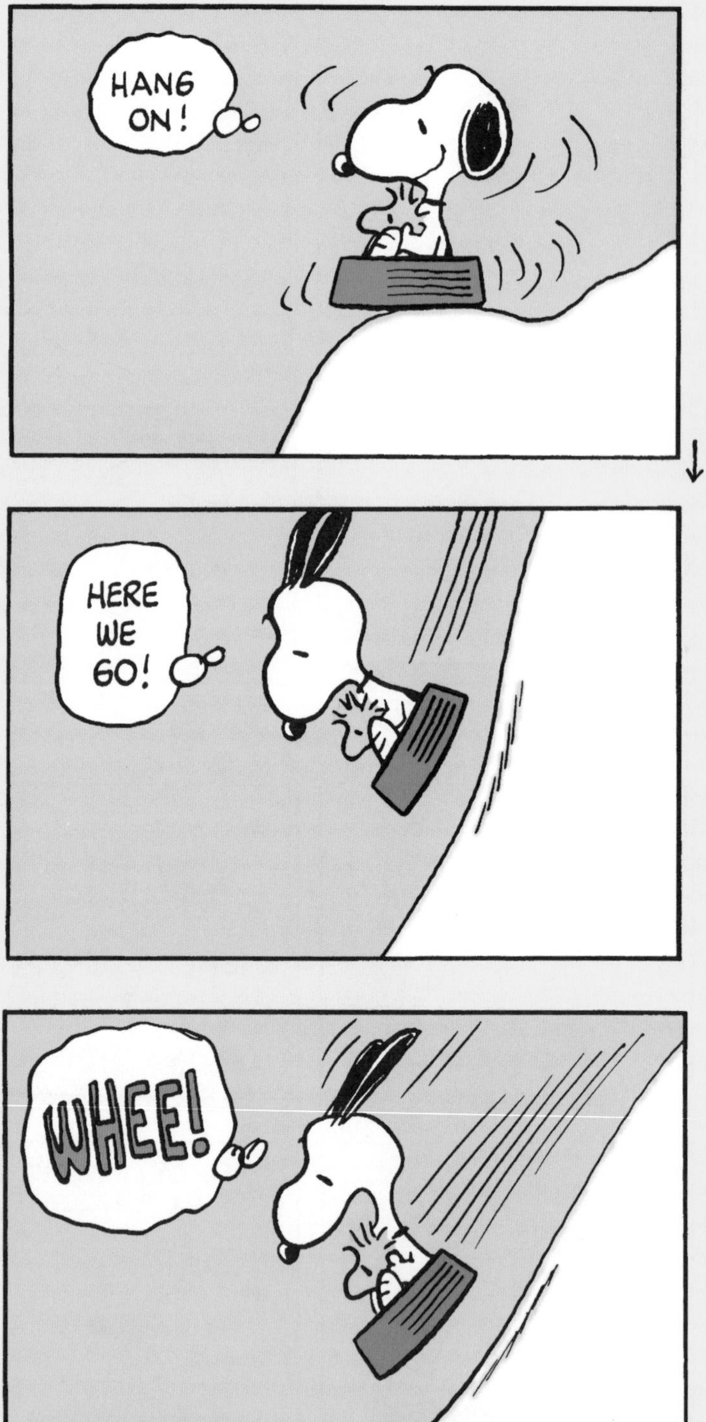
HANG ON!
HERE WE GO!
WHEE!
1-28-01

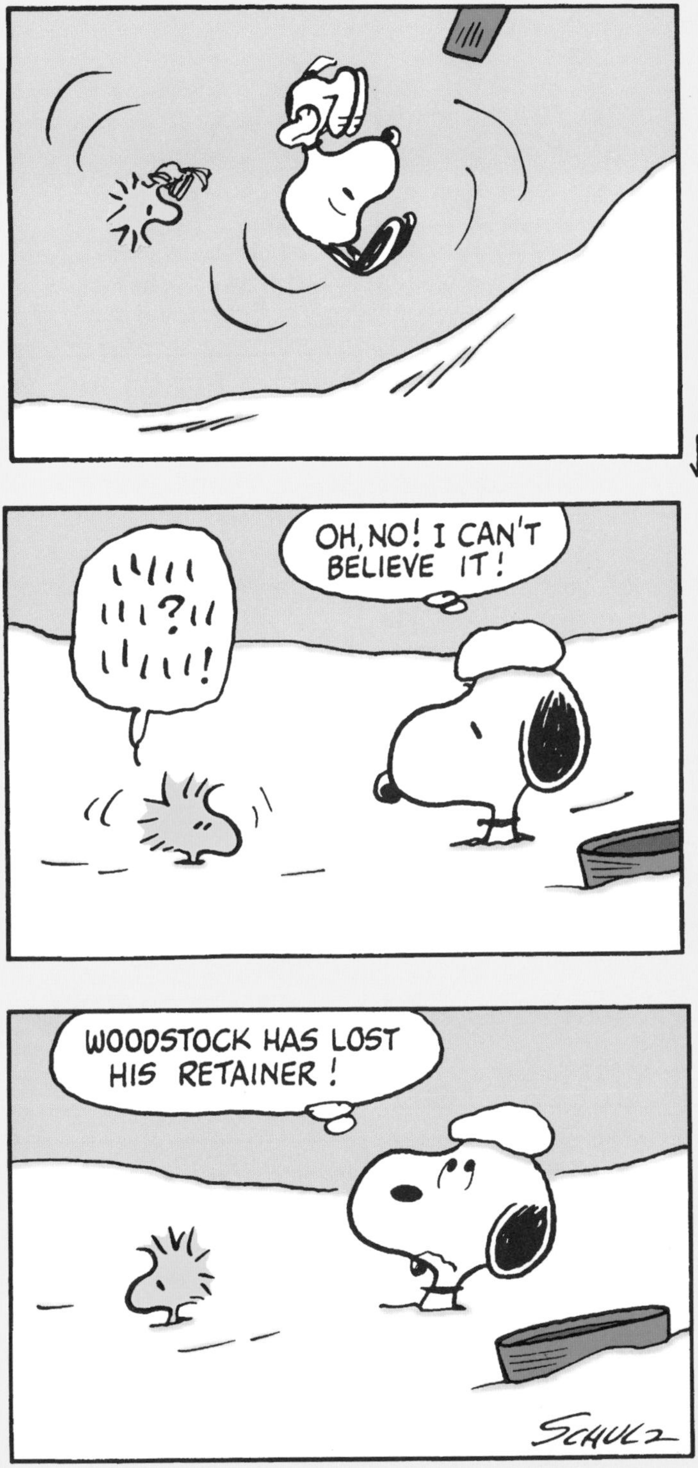
OH, NO! I CAN'T BELIEVE IT!
WOODSTOCK HAS LOST HIS RETAINER!
SCHULZ

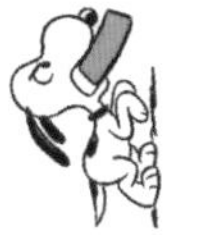

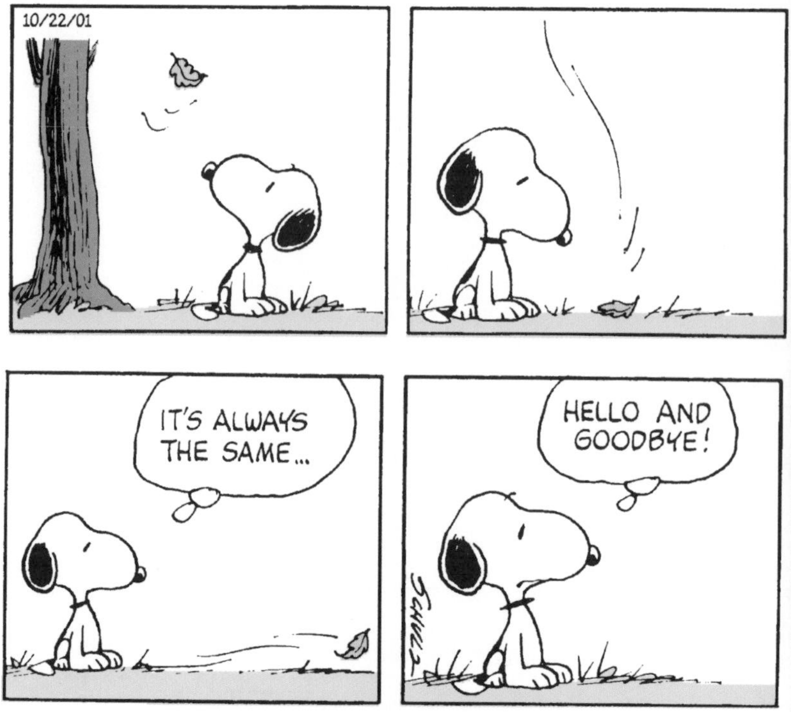
10/22/01
IT'S ALWAYS THE SAME...
HELLO AND GOODBYE!
SCHULZ

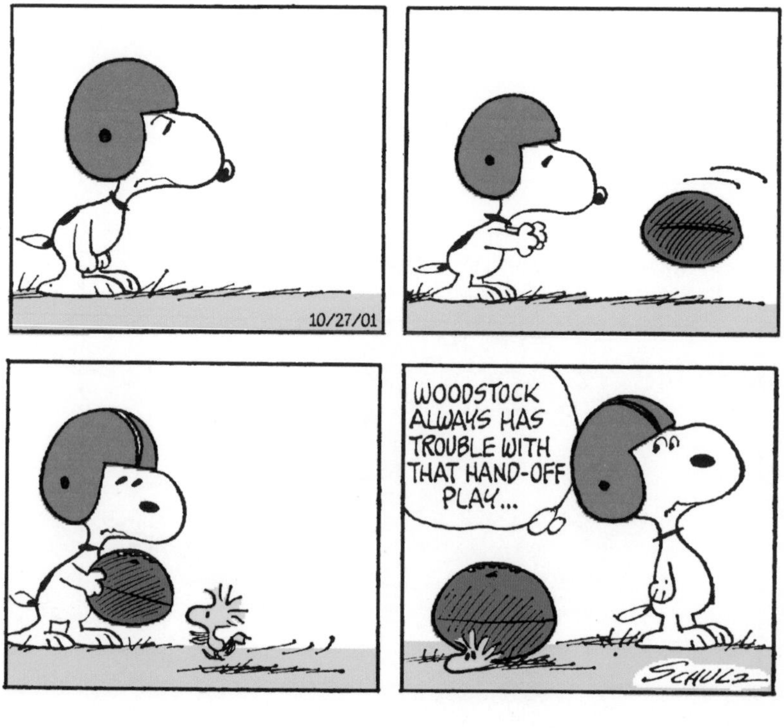
10/27/01
WOODSTOCK ALWAYS HAS TROUBLE WITH THAT HAND-OFF PLAY...
SCHULZ

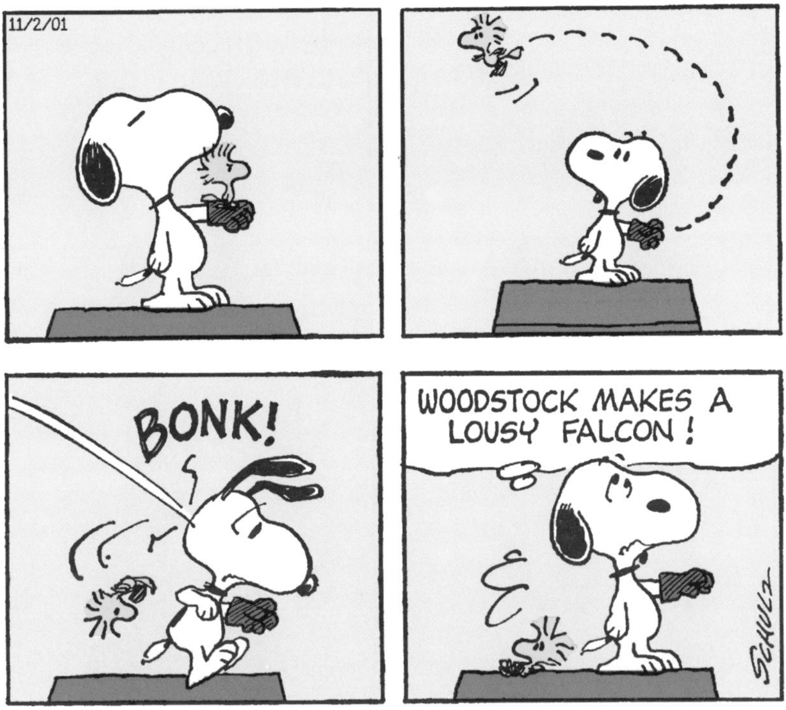
11/2/01
BONK!
WOODSTOCK MAKES A LOUSY FALCON!
SCHULZ

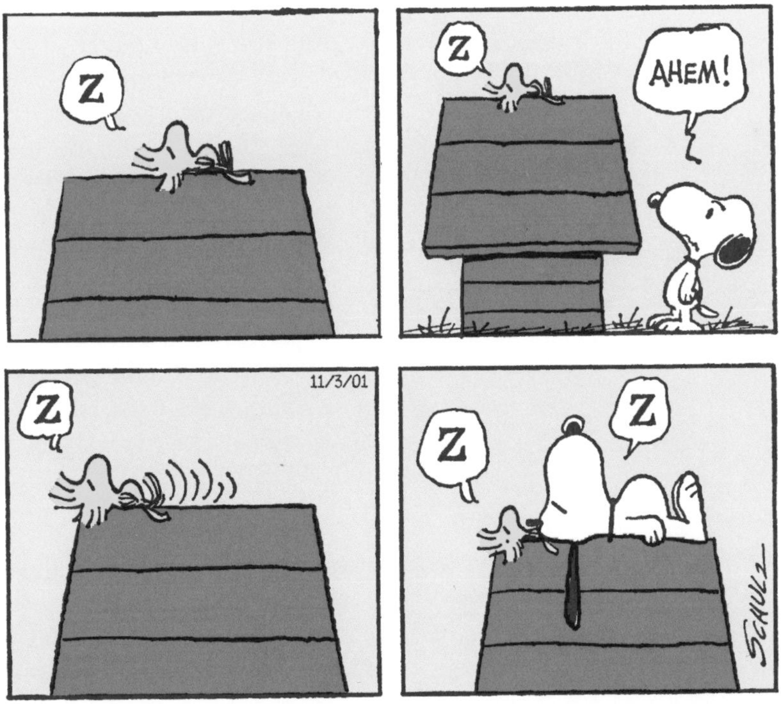
Z
Z
AHEM!
11/3/01
Z
Z
Z
SCHULZ

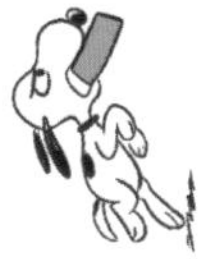

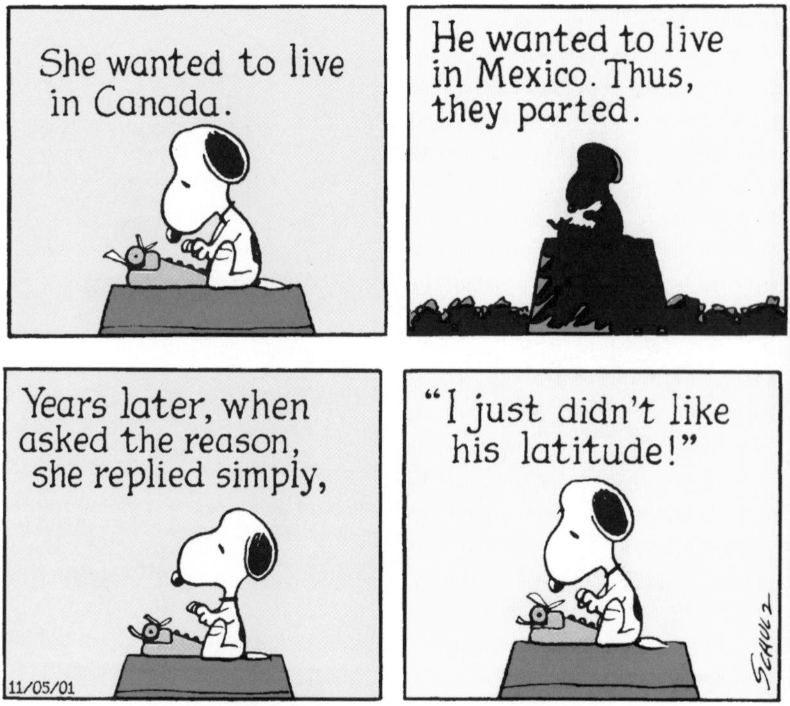
She wanted to live in Canada.
He wanted to live in Mexico. Thus, they parted.
Years later, when asked the reason, she replied simply,
11/05/01
"I just didn't like his latitude!"
SCHULZ

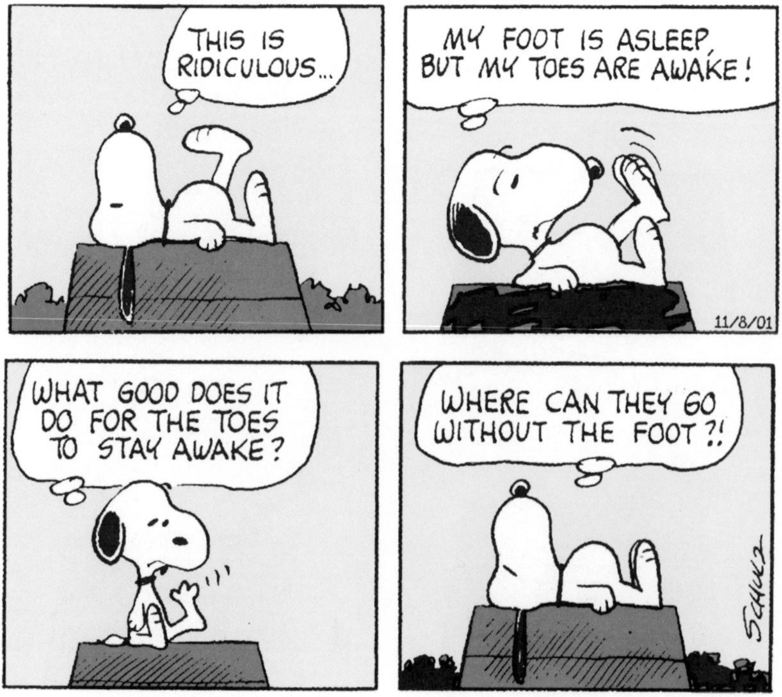
THIS IS RIDICULOUS...
MY FOOT IS ASLEEP, BUT MY TOES ARE AWAKE!
11/8/01
WHAT GOOD DOES IT DO FOR THE TOES TO STAY AWAKE?
WHERE CAN THEY GO WITHOUT THE FOOT?!
SCHULZ

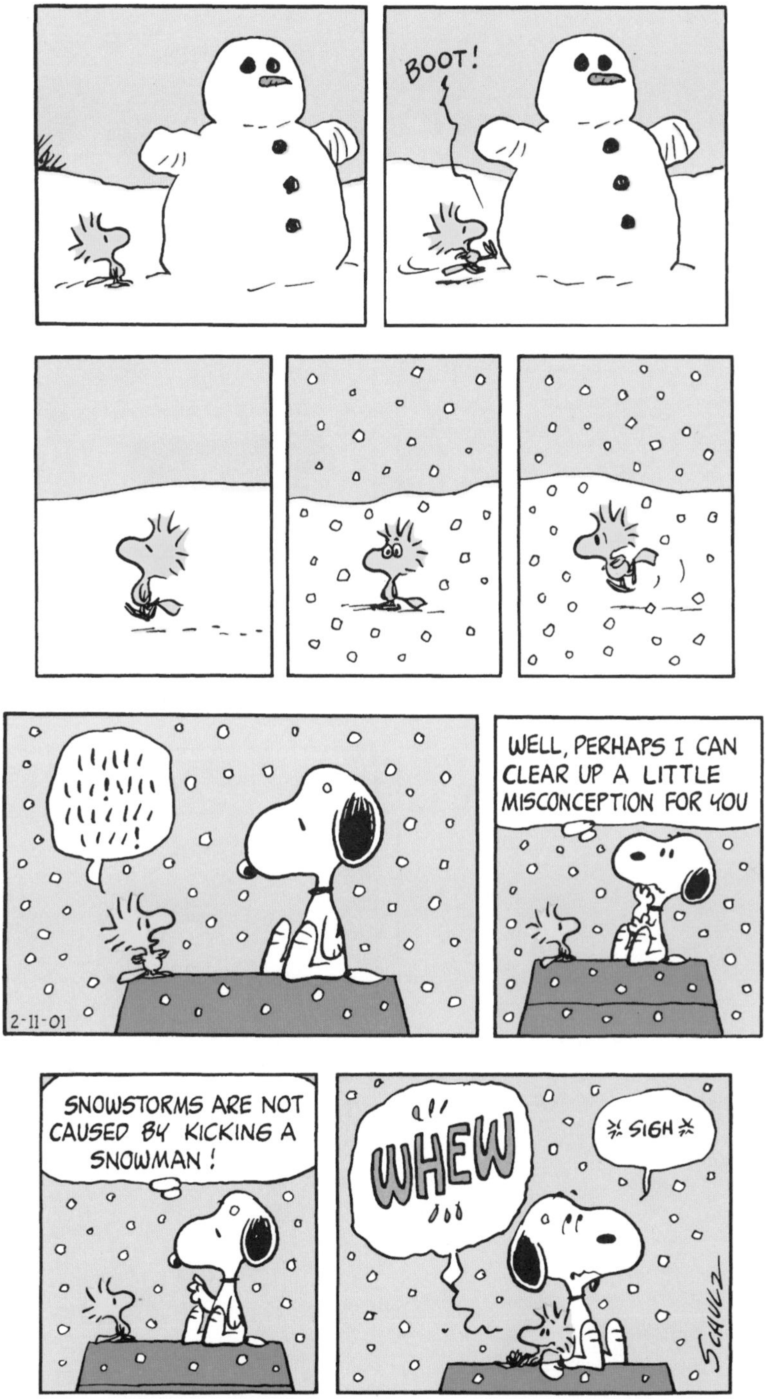
BOOT!
2-11-01
WELL, PERHAPS I CAN CLEAR UP A LITTLE MISCONCEPTION FOR YOU
SNOWSTORMS ARE NOT CAUSED BY KICKING A SNOWMAN!
WHEW
SIGH
SCHULZ

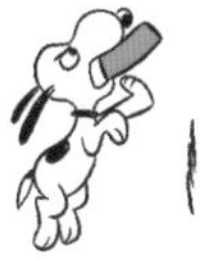

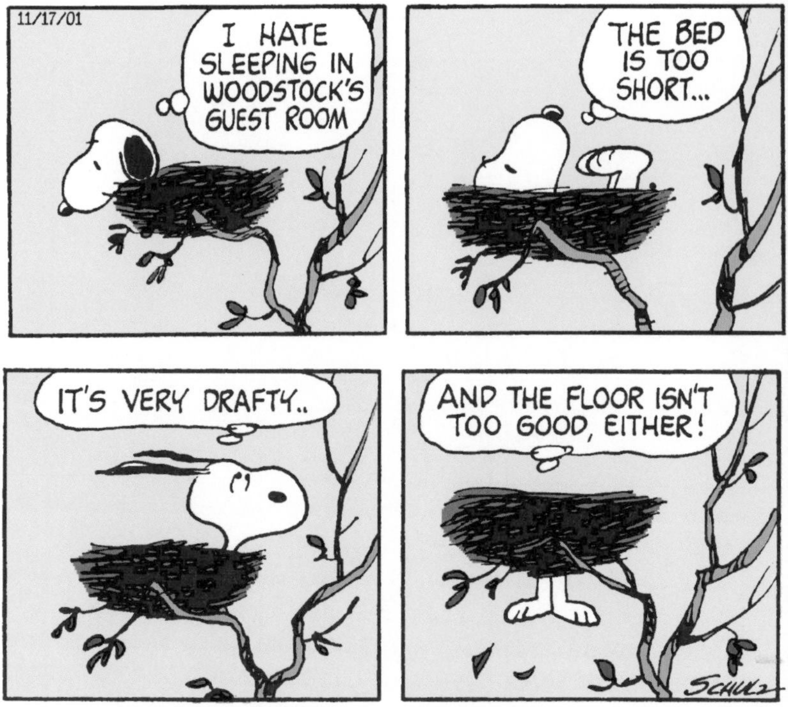
11/17/01
I HATE SLEEPING IN WOODSTOCK'S GUEST ROOM
THE BED IS TOO SHORT...
IT'S VERY DRAFTY..
AND THE FLOOR ISN'T TOO GOOD, EITHER!
SCHULZ

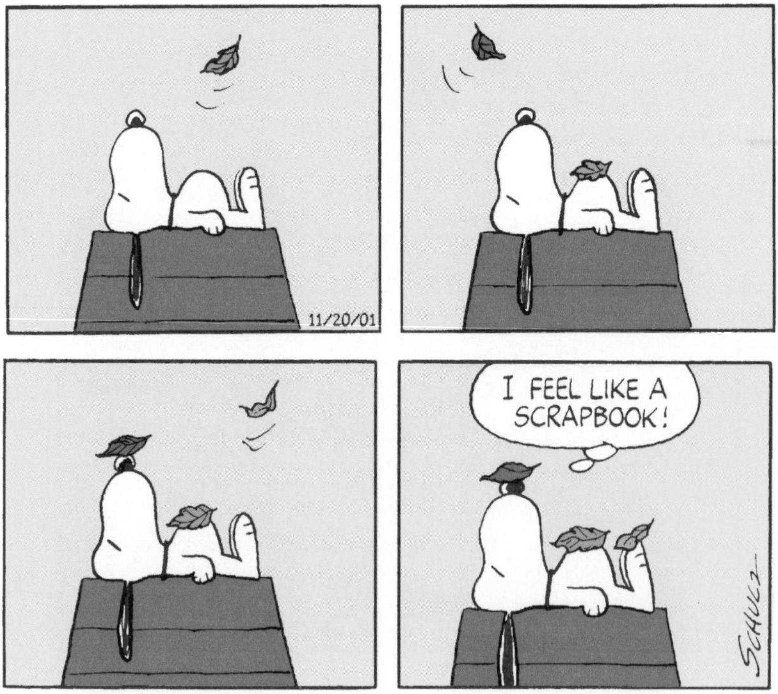
11/20/01
I FEEL LIKE A SCRAPBOOK!
SCHULZ

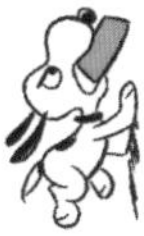

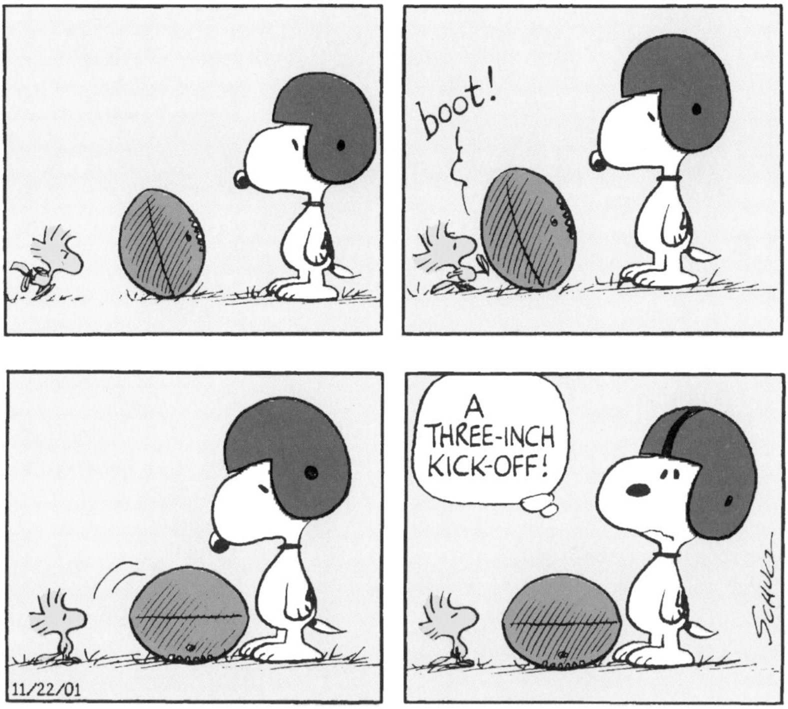
boot!
A THREE-INCH KICK-OFF!
SCHULZ
11/22/01

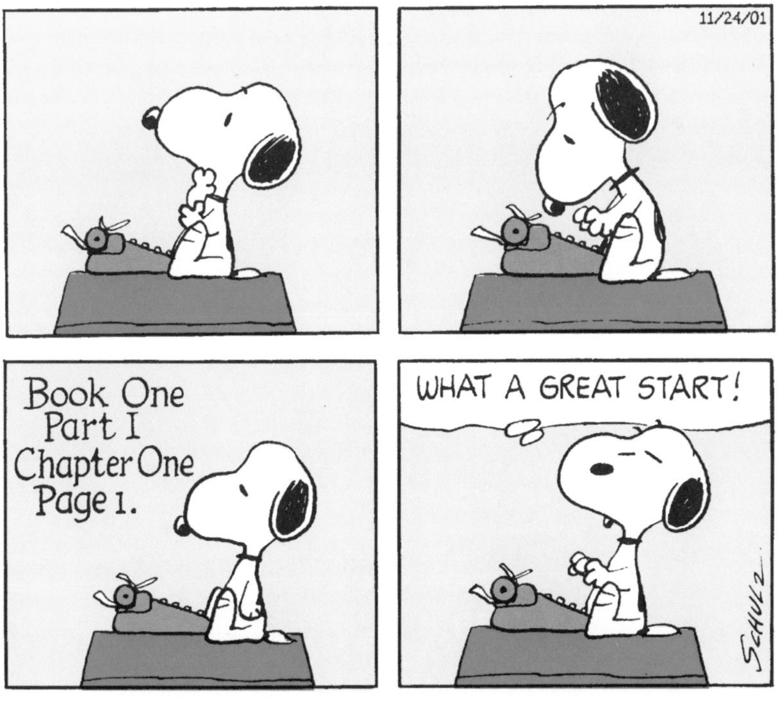
11/24/01
Book One
Part I
Chapter One
Page 1.
WHAT A GREAT START!
SCHULZ

I THINK YOUR STORIES ARE STUPID!
IF THEY'RE EVER PRINTED IN A BOOK, I REFUSE TO WASTE MY MONEY ON IT...
12/11/01
HOWEVER, IF YOU GET SOME FREE AUTHOR'S COPIES, I'LL BE GLAD TO TAKE ONE!
BONK!
SCHULZ

The Monster and the Bunnies
A Tale of Terror and Suspense
12/15/01
"Boo!" said the Monster.
WOW!!
SCHULZ

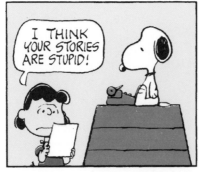

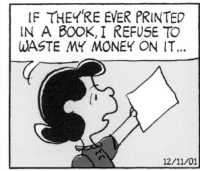

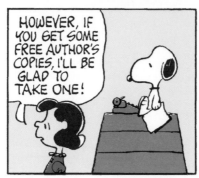

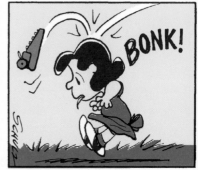

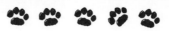

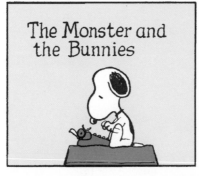

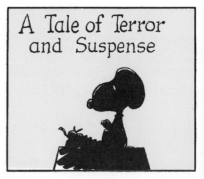

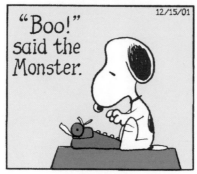

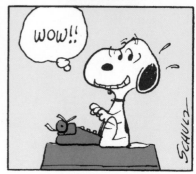

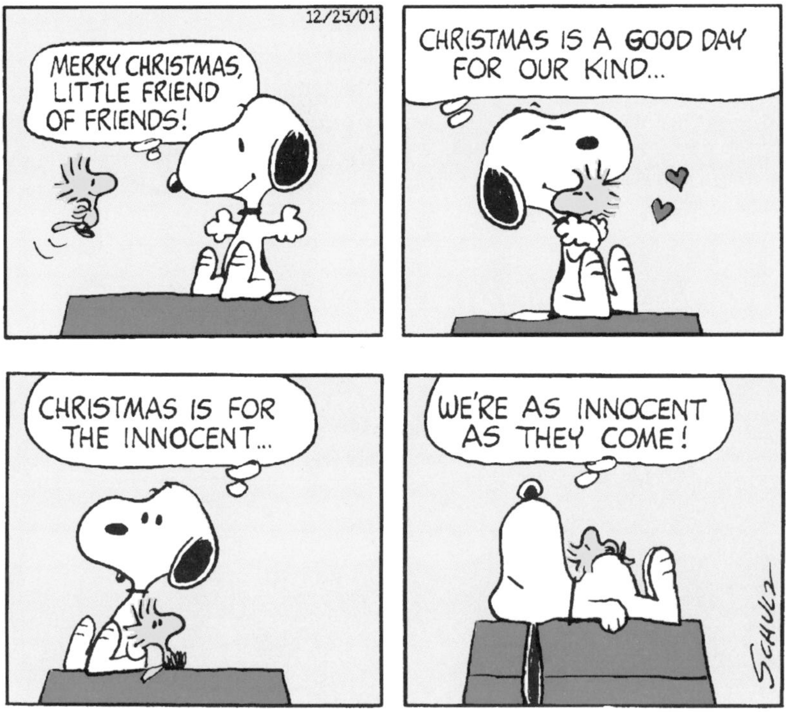
12/25/01
MERRY CHRISTMAS, LITTLE FRIEND OF FRIENDS!
CHRISTMAS IS A GOOD DAY FOR OUR KIND...
CHRISTMAS IS FOR THE INNOCENT...
WE'RE AS INNOCENT AS THEY COME!
SCHULZ

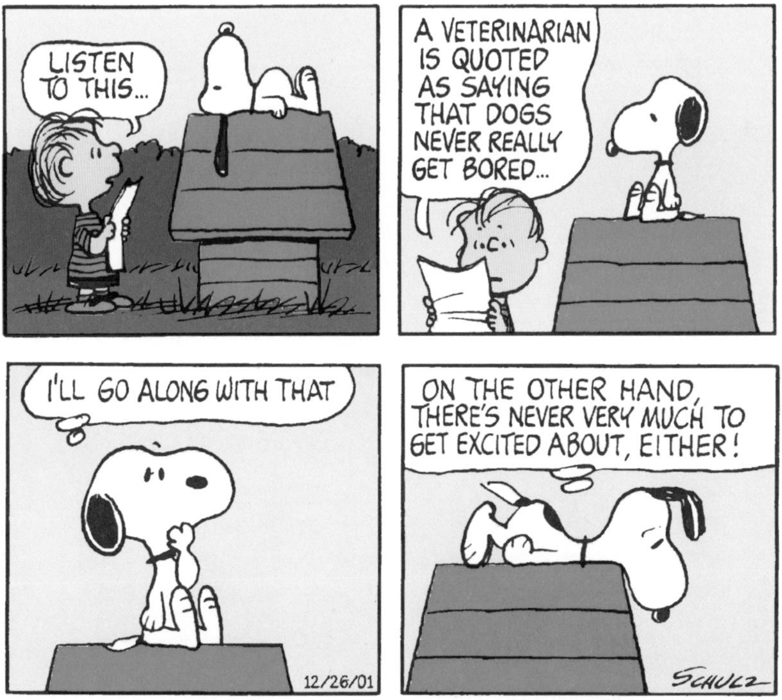
LISTEN TO THIS...
A VETERINARIAN IS QUOTED AS SAYING THAT DOGS NEVER REALLY GET BORED...
I'LL GO ALONG WITH THAT
12/26/01
ON THE OTHER HAND, THERE'S NEVER VERY MUCH TO GET EXCITED ABOUT, EITHER!
SCHULZ

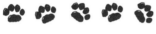

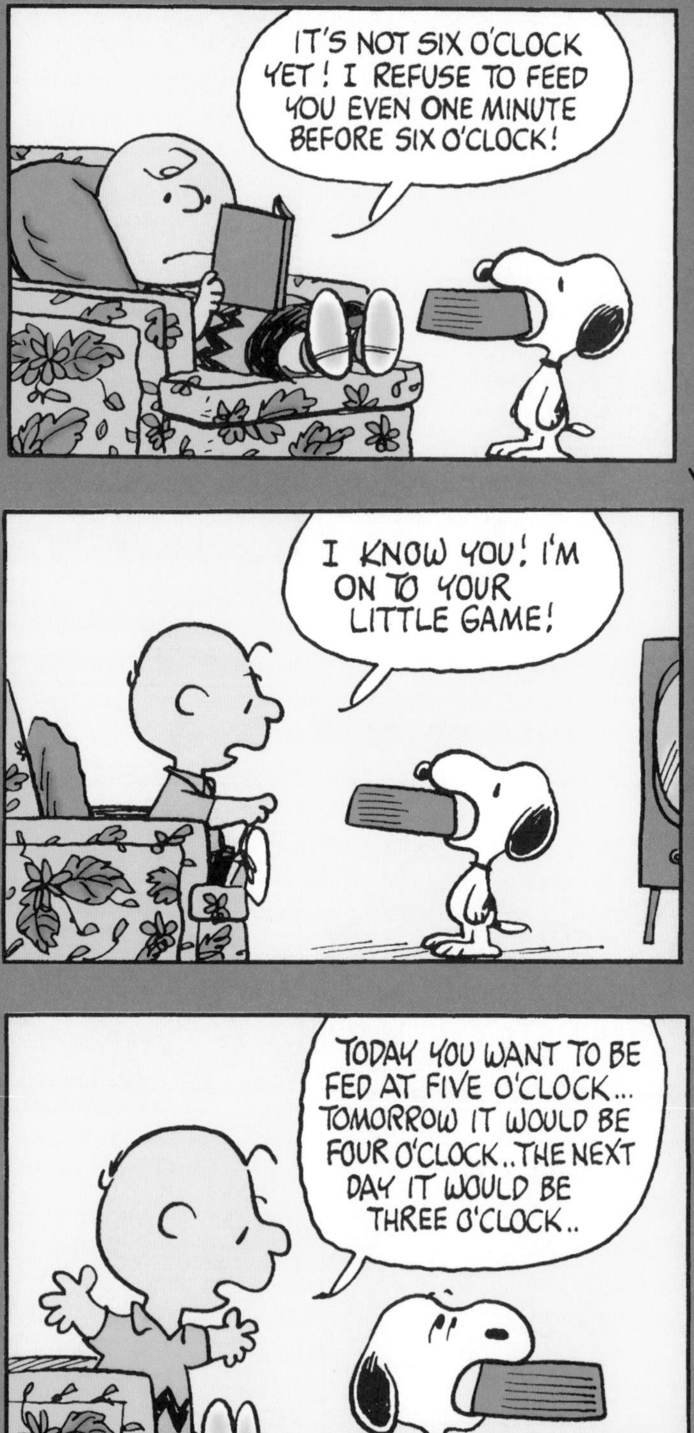
IT'S NOT SIX O'CLOCK YET! I REFUSE TO FEED YOU EVEN ONE MINUTE BEFORE SIX O'CLOCK!
I KNOW YOU! I'M ON TO YOUR LITTLE GAME!
TODAY YOU WANT TO BE FED AT FIVE O'CLOCK... TOMORROW IT WOULD BE FOUR O'CLOCK..THE NEXT DAY IT WOULD BE THREE O'CLOCK..

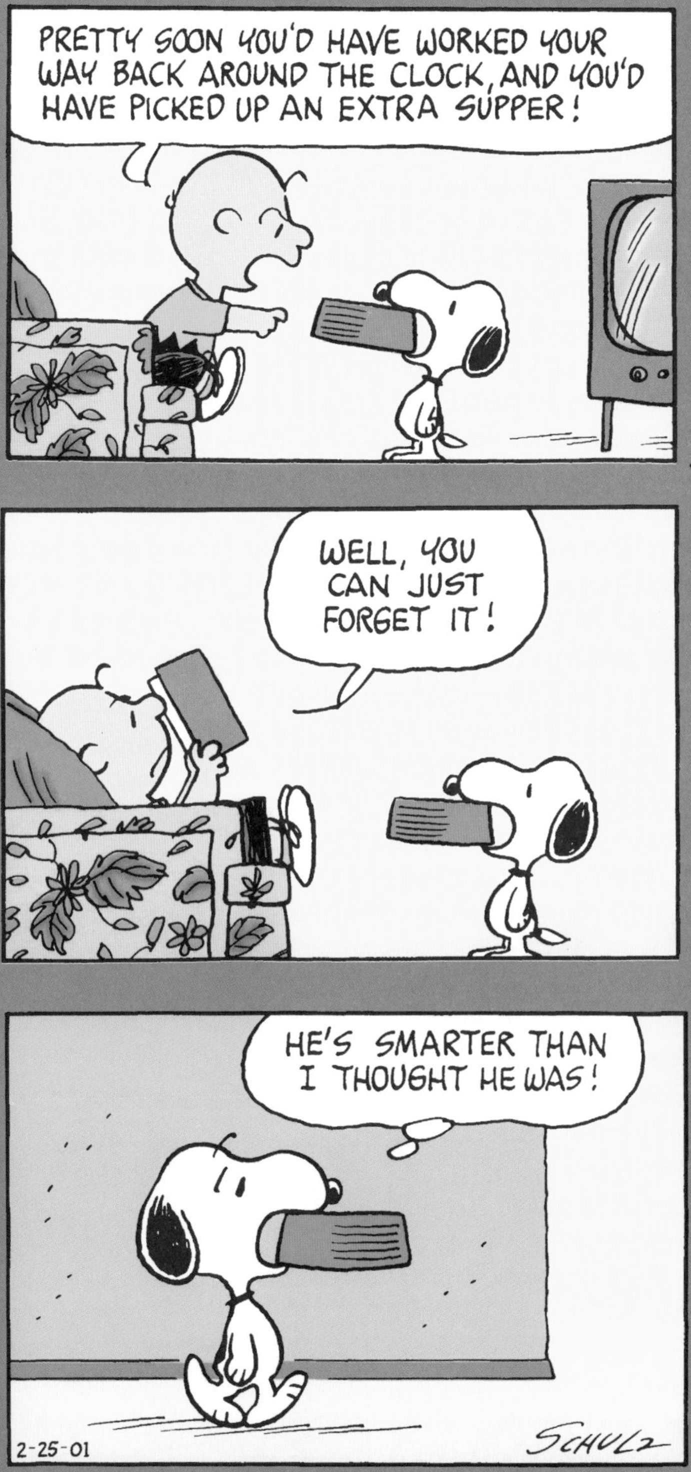
PRETTY SOON YOU'D HAVE WORKED YOUR WAY BACK AROUND THE CLOCK, AND YOU'D HAVE PICKED UP AN EXTRA SUPPER!
WELL, YOU CAN JUST FORGET IT!
HE'S SMARTER THAN I THOUGHT HE WAS!
2-25-01
SCHULZ

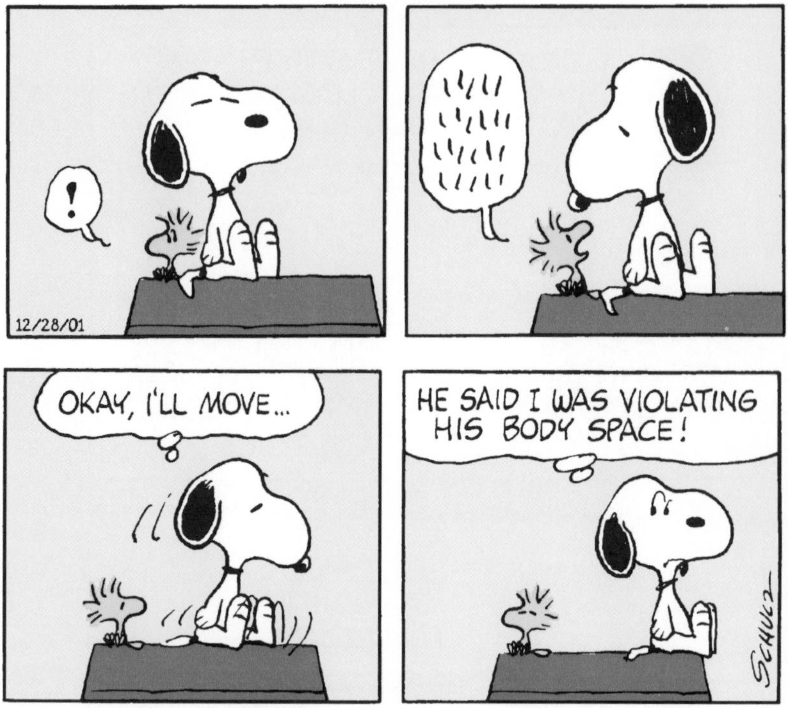
!
12/28/01
OKAY, I'LL MOVE...
HE SAID I WAS VIOLATING HIS BODY SPACE!
SCHULZ

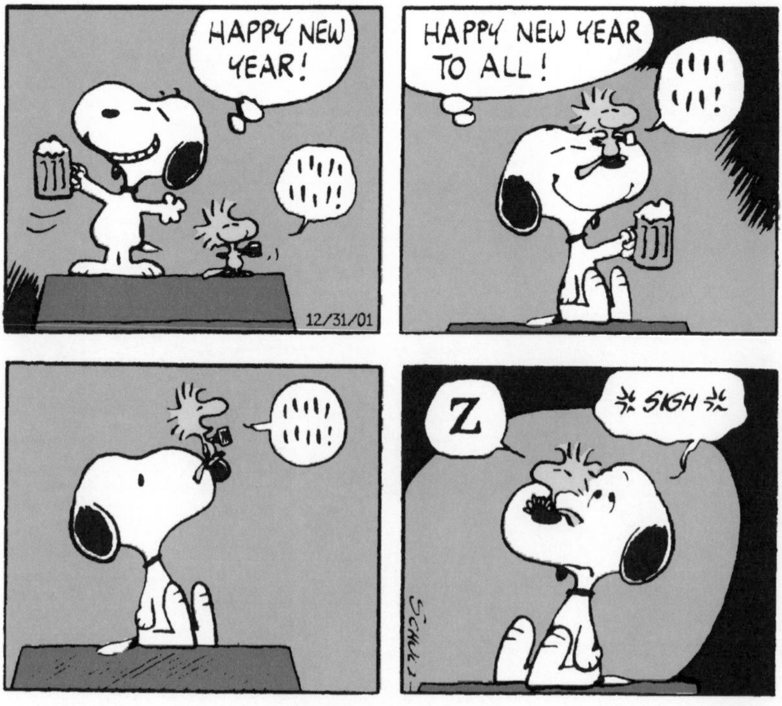
HAPPY NEW YEAR!
12/31/01
HAPPY NEW YEAR TO ALL!
Z
SIGH
SCHULZ

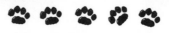

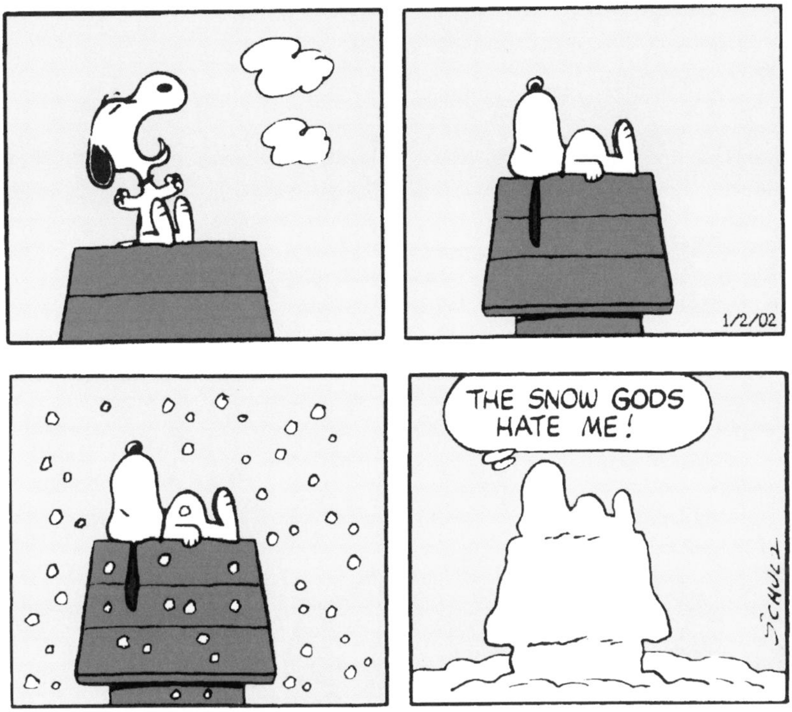
1/2/02
THE SNOW GODS HATE ME!
SCHULZ

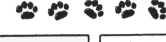

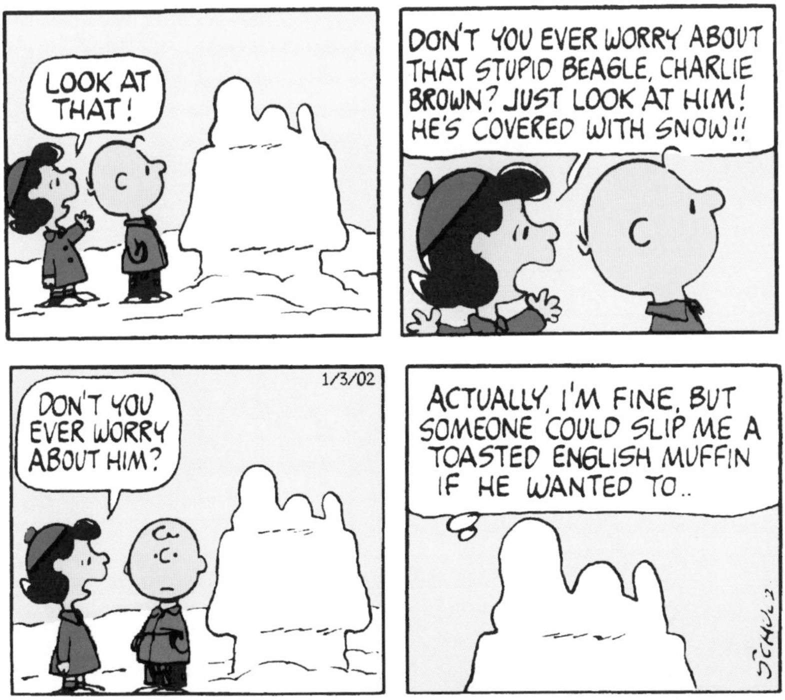
LOOK AT THAT!
DON'T YOU EVER WORRY ABOUT THAT STUPID BEAGLE, CHARLIE BROWN? JUST LOOK AT HIM! HE'S COVERED WITH SNOW!!
1/3/02
DON'T YOU EVER WORRY ABOUT HIM?
ACTUALLY, I'M FINE, BUT SOMEONE COULD SLIP ME A TOASTED ENGLISH MUFFIN IF HE WANTED TO..
SCHULZ

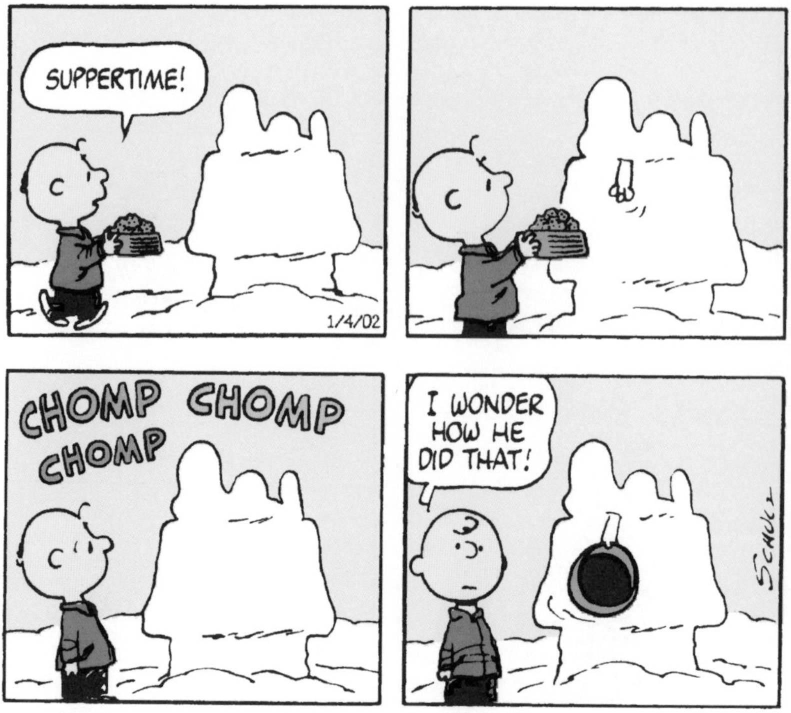
SUPPERTIME!
1/4/02
CHOMP CHOMP CHOMP
I WONDER HOW HE DID THAT!
SCHULZ

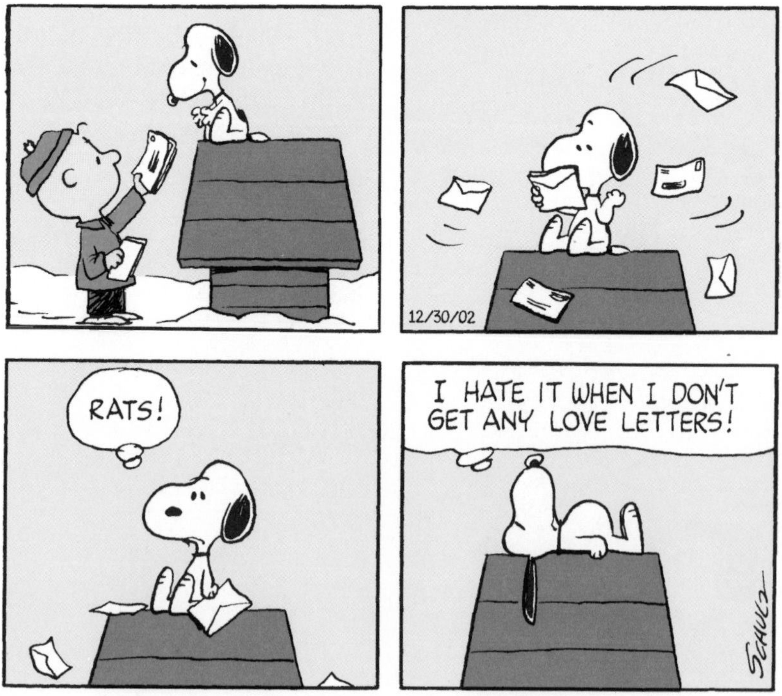
12/30/02
RATS!
I HATE IT WHEN I DON'T GET ANY LOVE LETTERS!
SCHULZ

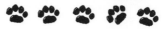

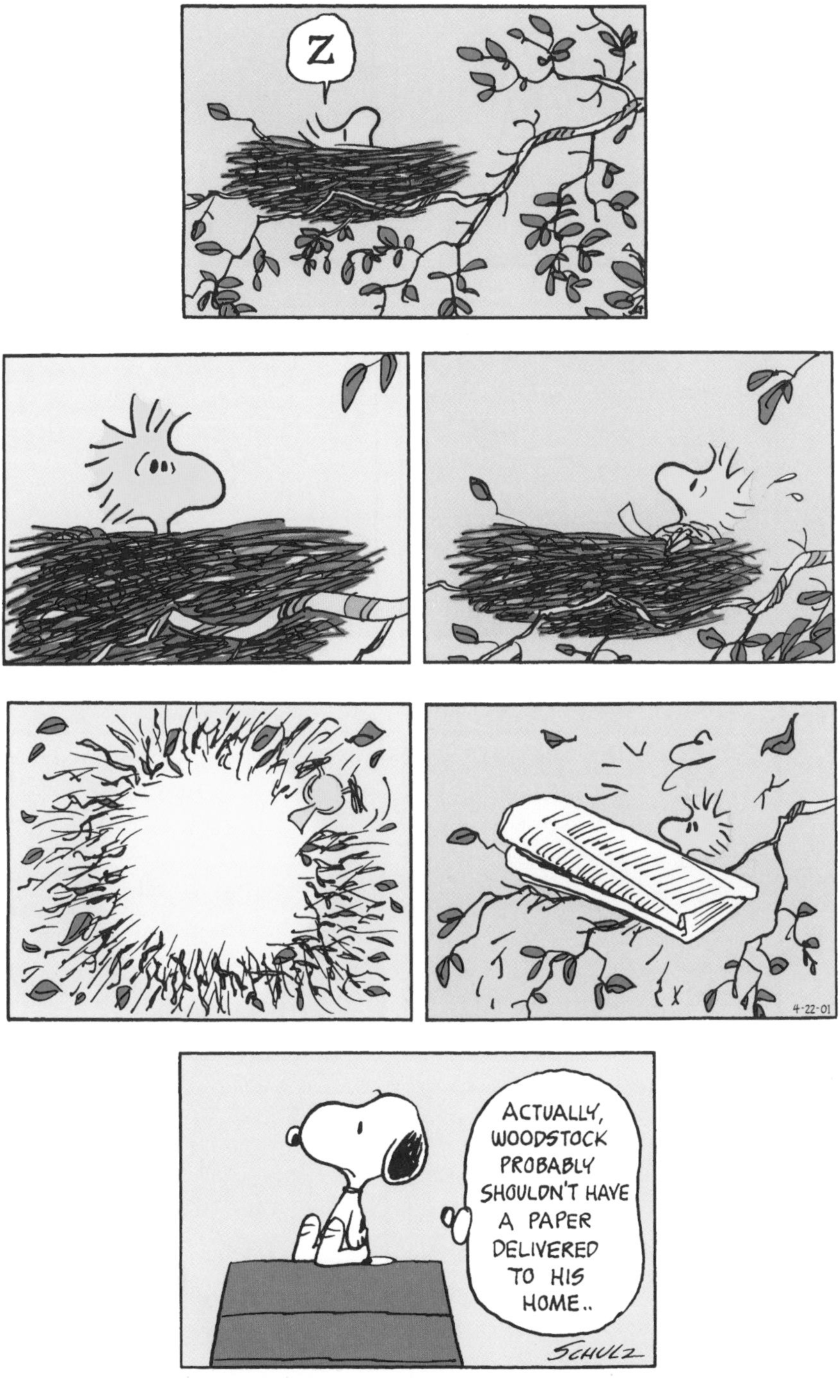
Z
4-22-01
ACTUALLY, WOODSTOCK PROBABLY SHOULDN'T HAVE A PAPER DELIVERED TO HIS HOME..
SCHULZ

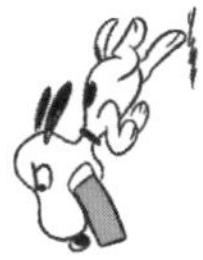

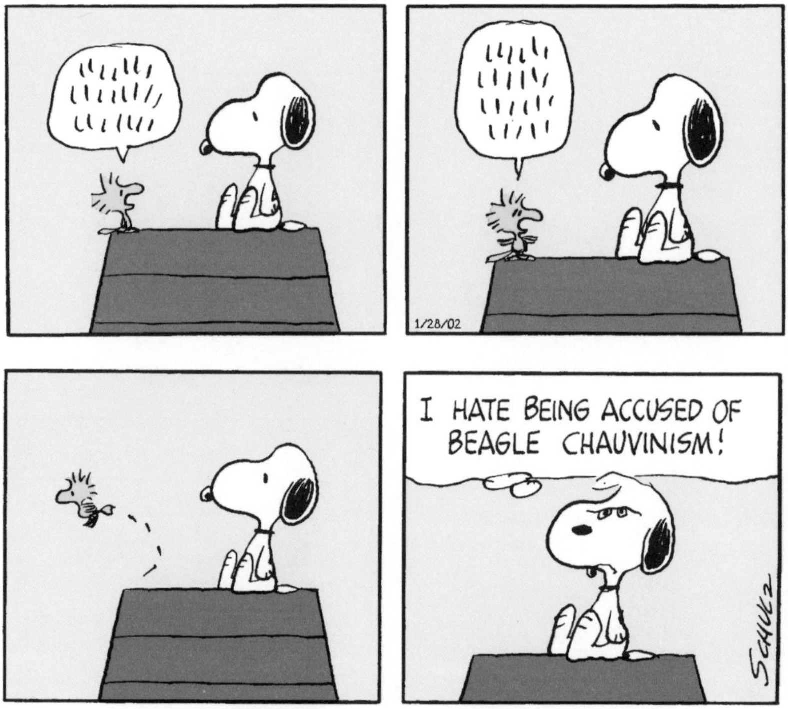
1/28/02
I HATE BEING ACCUSED OF BEAGLE CHAUVINISM!
SCHULZ

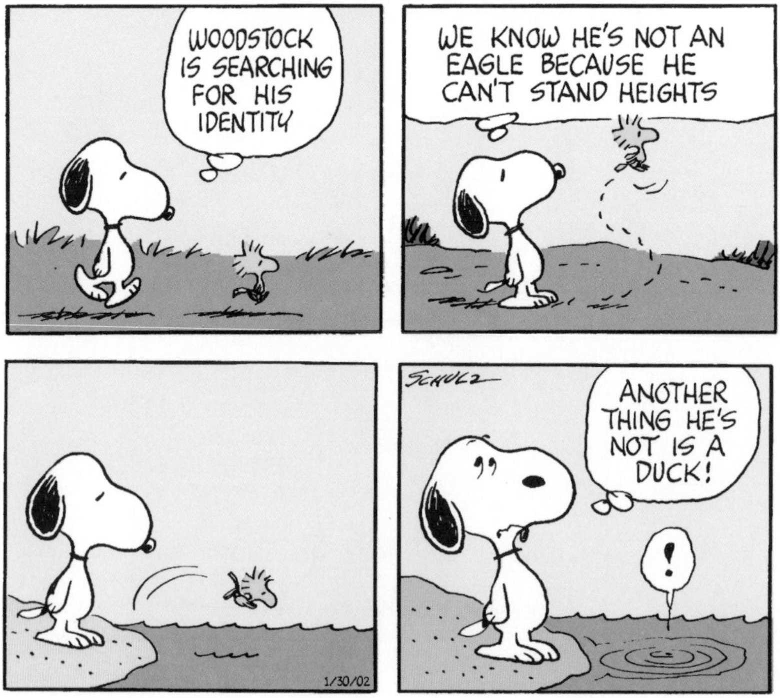
WOODSTOCK IS SEARCHING FOR HIS IDENTITY
WE KNOW HE'S NOT AN EAGLE BECAUSE HE CAN'T STAND HEIGHTS
1/30/02
SCHULZ
ANOTHER THING HE'S NOT IS A DUCK!
!

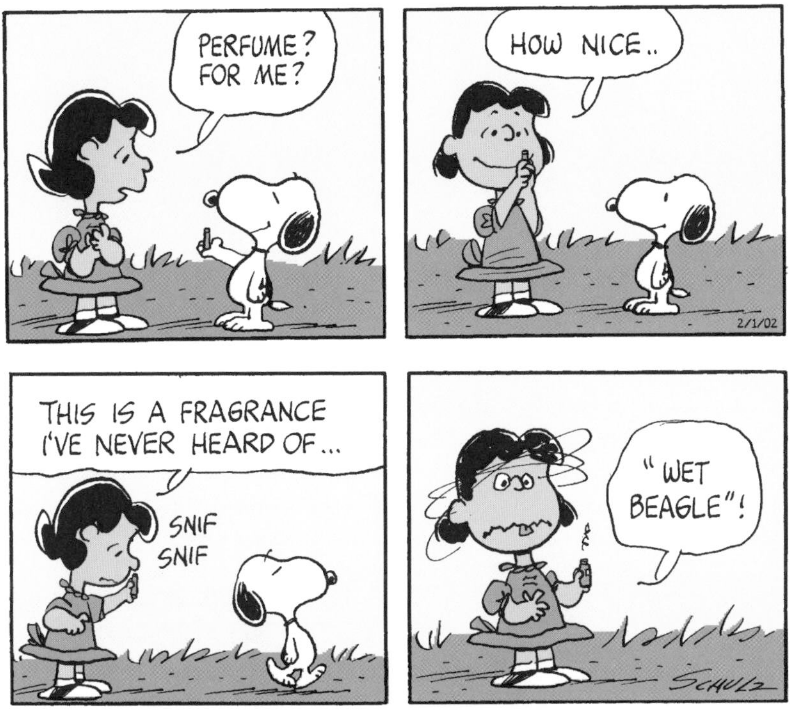
PERFUME? FOR ME?
HOW NICE..
2/1/02
THIS IS A FRAGRANCE I'VE NEVER HEARD OF...
SNIF SNIF
"WET BEAGLE"!
SCHULZ

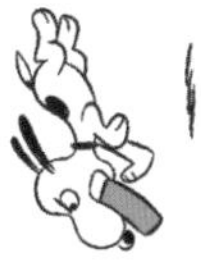

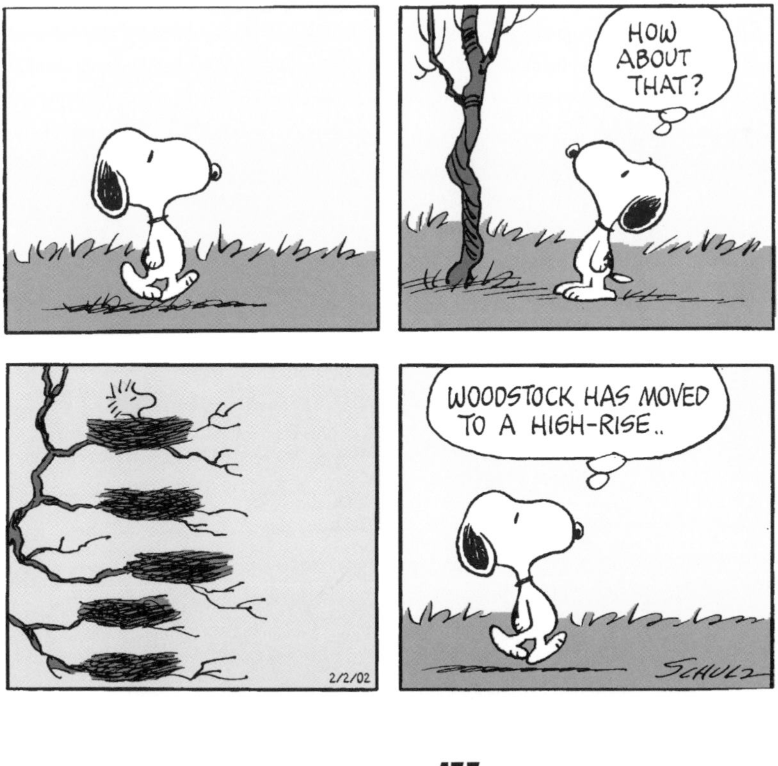
HOW ABOUT THAT?
2/2/02
WOODSTOCK HAS MOVED TO A HIGH-RISE..
SCHULZ

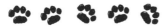

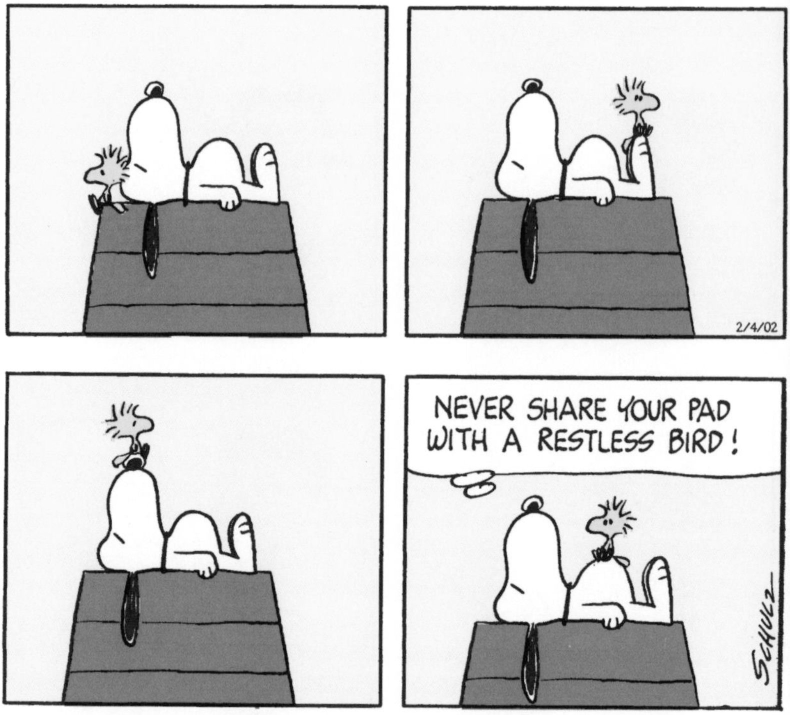
2/4/02
NEVER SHARE YOUR PAD WITH A RESTLESS BIRD!
SCHULZ

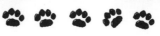

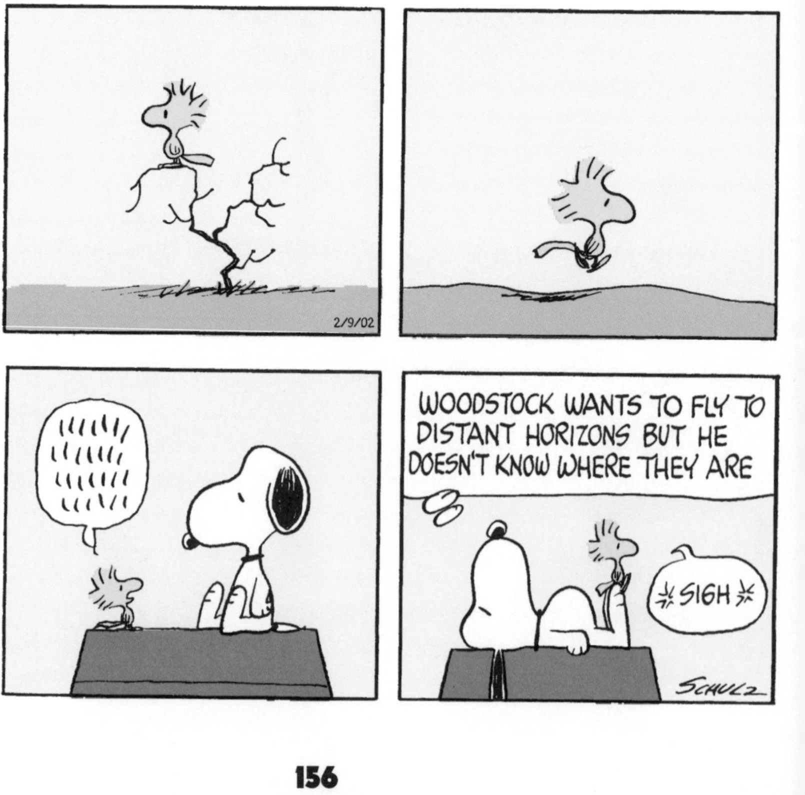
2/9/02
WOODSTOCK WANTS TO FLY TO DISTANT HORIZONS BUT HE DOESN'T KNOW WHERE THEY ARE
SIGH
SCHULZ

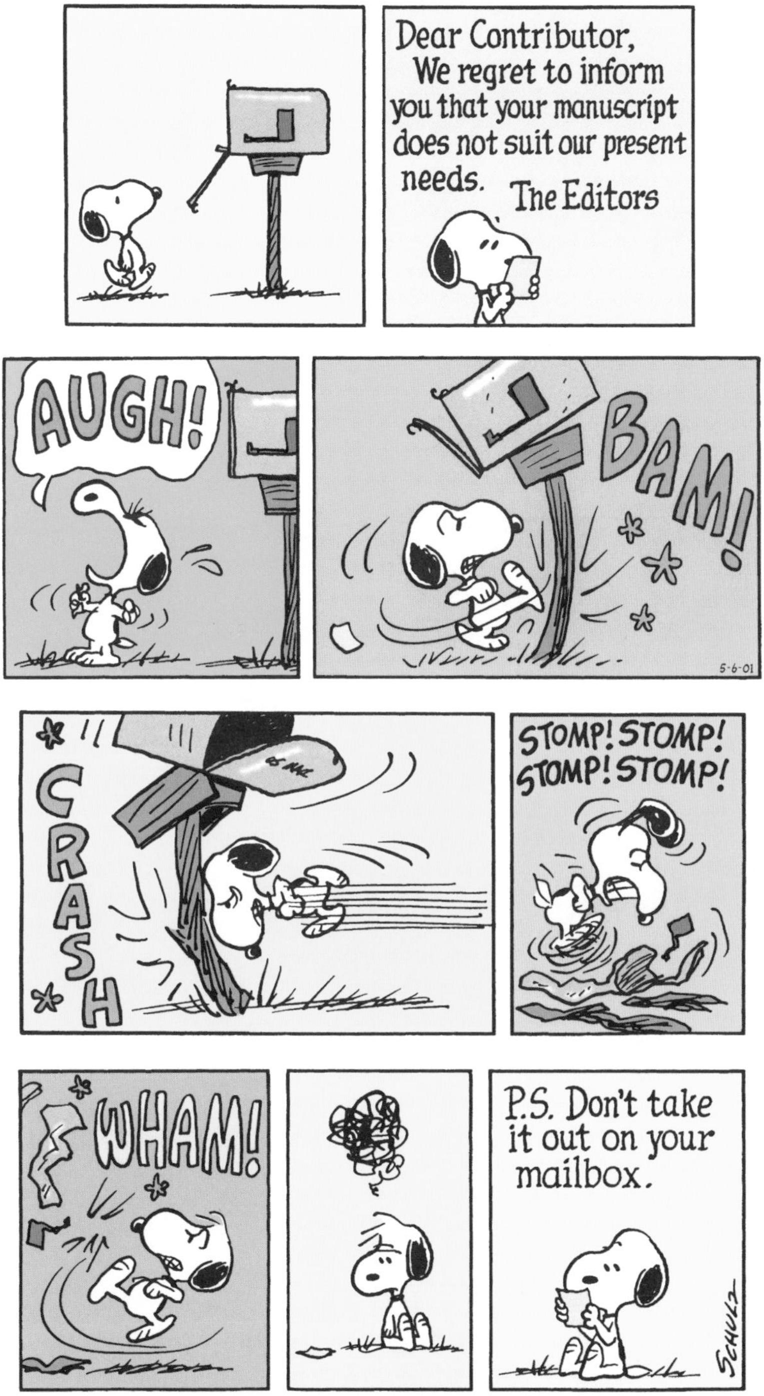

Dear Contributor,
We regret to inform you that your manuscript does not suit our present needs.
The Editors
AUGH!
BAM!
5-6-01
CRASH
STOMP! STOMP! STOMP! STOMP!
WHAM!
P.S. Don't take it out on your mailbox.
SCHULZ

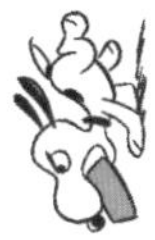

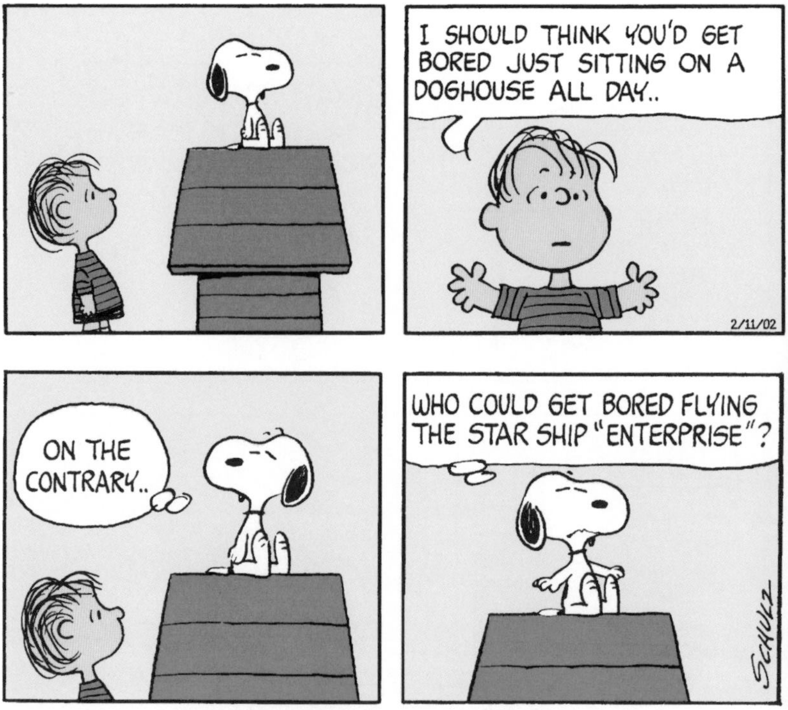
I SHOULD THINK YOU'D GET BORED JUST SITTING ON A DOGHOUSE ALL DAY..
2/11/02
ON THE CONTRARY..
WHO COULD GET BORED FLYING THE STAR SHIP "ENTERPRISE"?
SCHULZ

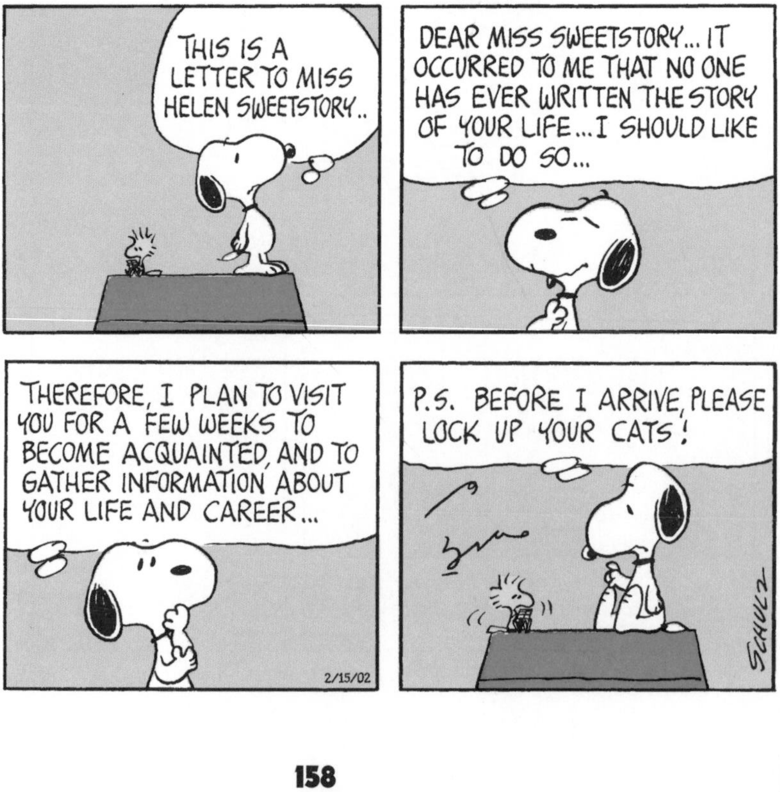
THIS IS A LETTER TO MISS HELEN SWEETSTORY..
DEAR MISS SWEETSTORY... IT OCCURRED TO ME THAT NO ONE HAS EVER WRITTEN THE STORY OF YOUR LIFE...I SHOULD LIKE TO DO SO...
THEREFORE, I PLAN TO VISIT YOU FOR A FEW WEEKS TO BECOME ACQUAINTED, AND TO GATHER INFORMATION ABOUT YOUR LIFE AND CAREER...
2/15/02
P.S. BEFORE I ARRIVE, PLEASE LOCK UP YOUR CATS!
SCHULZ

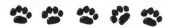

MISS SWEETSTORY ANSWERED MY LETTER!
"DEAR FRIEND, THANK YOU FOR WRITING... SINCERELY, HELEN SWEETSTORY"
SHE WANTS ME TO VISIT HER!
THIS IS A **FORM** LETTER!
2/16/02
MISS SWEETSTORY HAS INVITED ME TO HER HOME, AND WANTS ME TO WRITE THE STORY OF HER LIFE!
THIS IS A FORM LETTER!!
SOME PEOPLE JUST CAN'T READ BETWEEN THE LINES!
SCHULZ

YOU'RE GOING TO VISIT MISS SWEETSTORY?
I'M GOING TO INTERVIEW HER, AND WRITE HER BIOGRAPHY
YOU DON'T EVEN KNOW WHERE SHE LIVES!
I'M SURE SHE LIVES IN A WHITE VINE-COVERED COTTAGE WITH ROSE BUSHES, A PICKET FENCE AND A WILLOW TREE...
I'LL KNOW IT WHEN I SEE IT!
SCHULZ
2/18/02

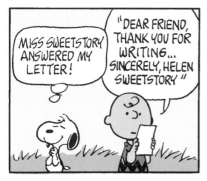

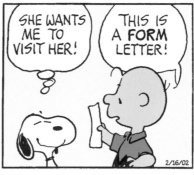

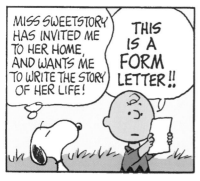

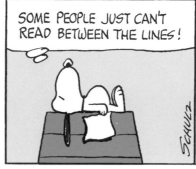

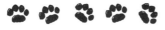

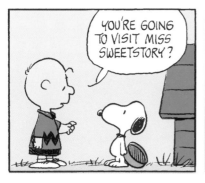

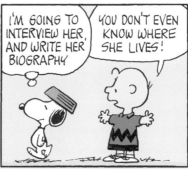

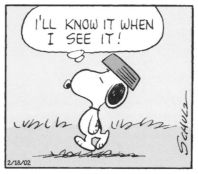

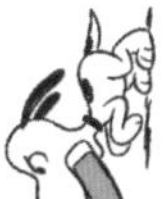

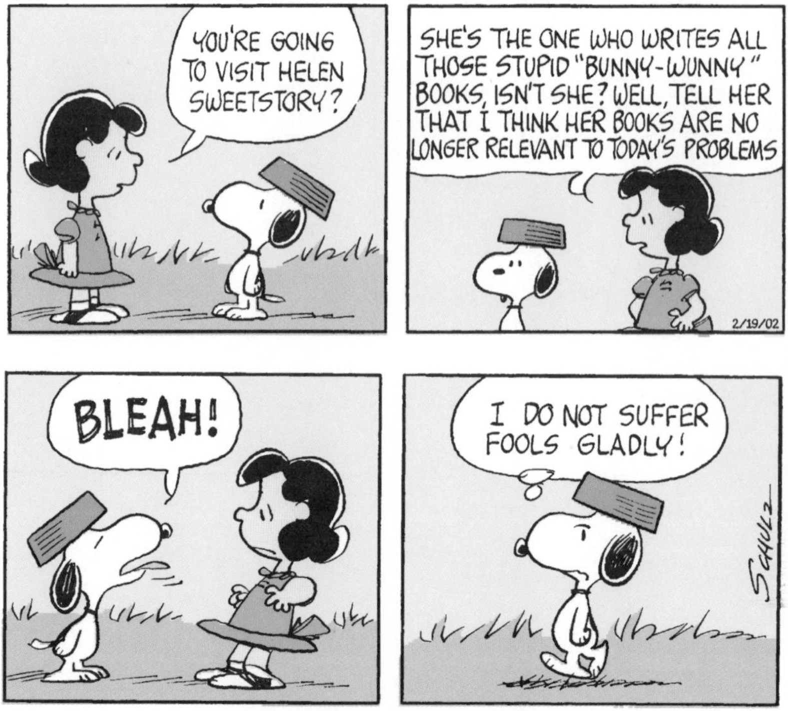
YOU'RE GOING TO VISIT HELEN SWEETSTORY?
SHE'S THE ONE WHO WRITES ALL THOSE STUPID "BUNNY-WUNNY" BOOKS, ISN'T SHE? WELL, TELL HER THAT I THINK HER BOOKS ARE NO LONGER RELEVANT TO TODAY'S PROBLEMS
2/19/02
BLEAH!
I DO NOT SUFFER FOOLS GLADLY!
SCHULZ

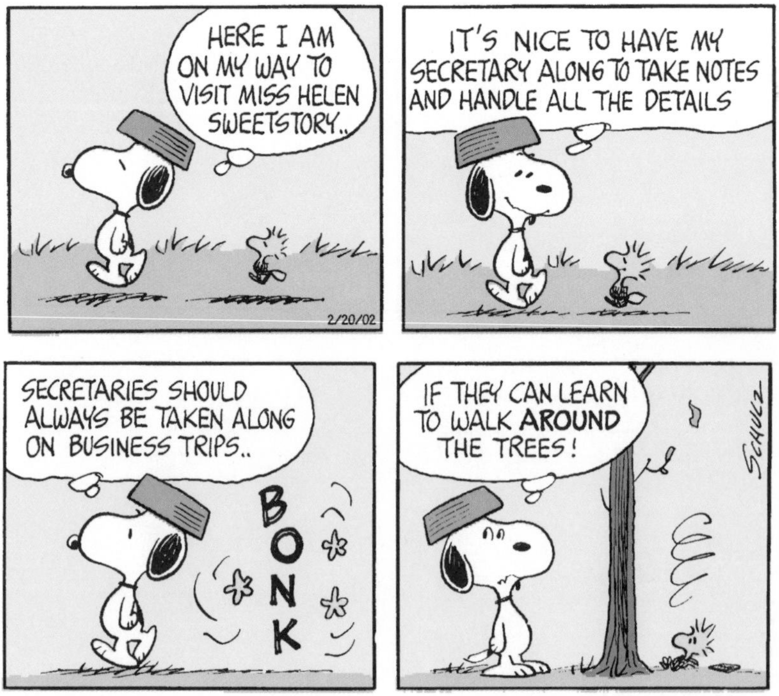
HERE I AM ON MY WAY TO VISIT MISS HELEN SWEETSTORY..
2/20/02
IT'S NICE TO HAVE MY SECRETARY ALONG TO TAKE NOTES AND HANDLE ALL THE DETAILS
SECRETARIES SHOULD ALWAYS BE TAKEN ALONG ON BUSINESS TRIPS..
BONK
IF THEY CAN LEARN TO WALK AROUND THE TREES!
SCHULZ

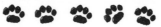

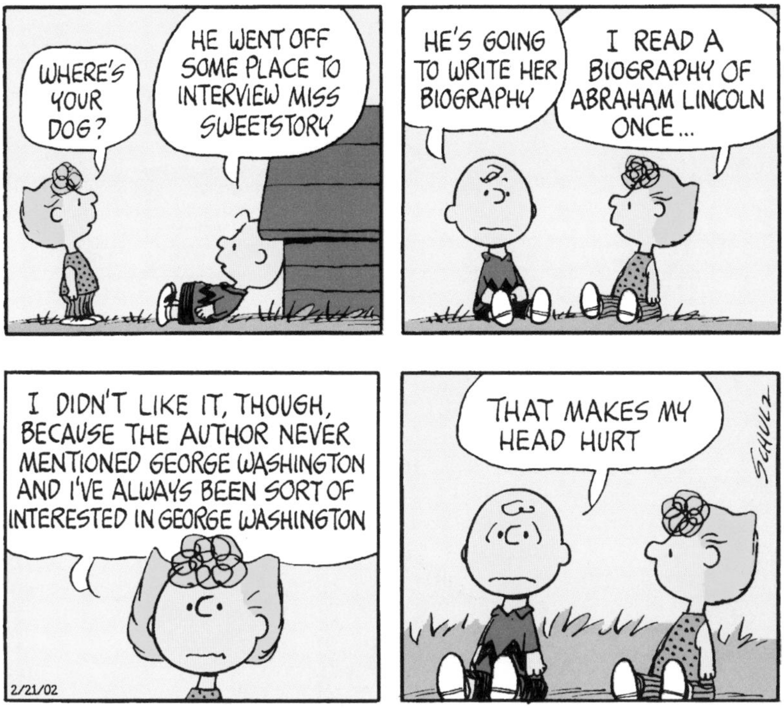
WHERE'S YOUR DOG?
HE WENT OFF SOME PLACE TO INTERVIEW MISS SWEETSTORY
HE'S GOING TO WRITE HER BIOGRAPHY
I READ A BIOGRAPHY OF ABRAHAM LINCOLN ONCE...
I DIDN'T LIKE IT, THOUGH, BECAUSE THE AUTHOR NEVER MENTIONED GEORGE WASHINGTON AND I'VE ALWAYS BEEN SORT OF INTERESTED IN GEORGE WASHINGTON
2/21/02
THAT MAKES MY HEAD HURT
SCHULZ

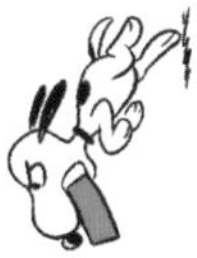

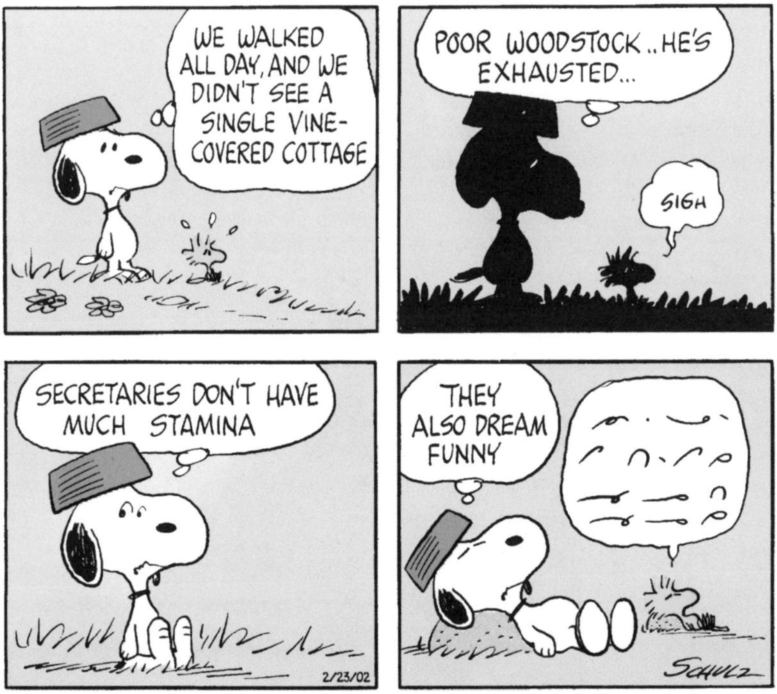
WE WALKED ALL DAY, AND WE DIDN'T SEE A SINGLE VINE-COVERED COTTAGE
POOR WOODSTOCK.. HE'S EXHAUSTED...
SIGH
SECRETARIES DON'T HAVE MUCH STAMINA
2/23/02
THEY ALSO DREAM FUNNY
SCHULZ

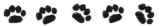

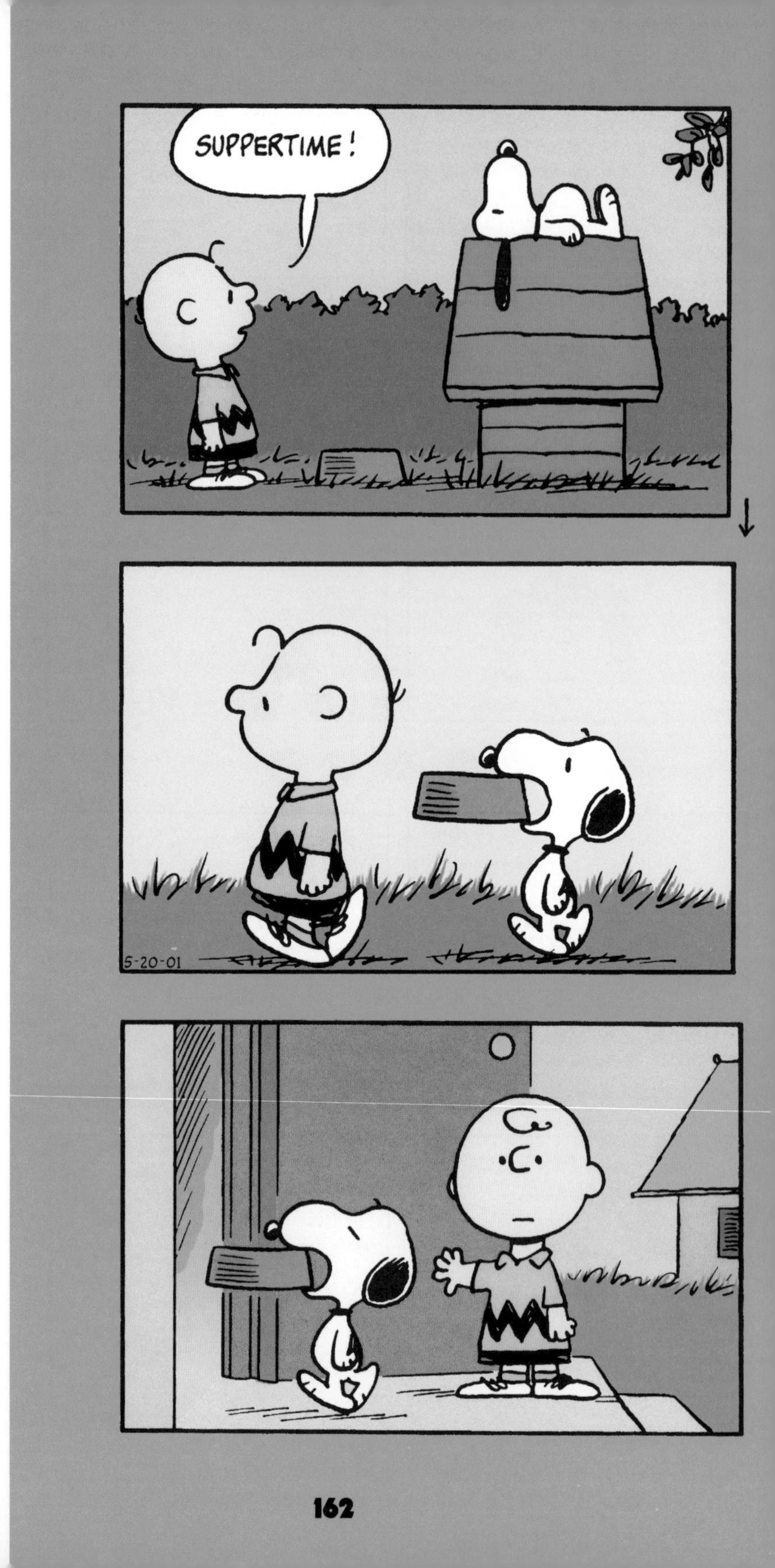
SUPPERTIME!
5-20-01

THANK YOU
YOU DON'T GET A TIP FOR CARRYING IN YOUR OWN DISH!
SCHULZ

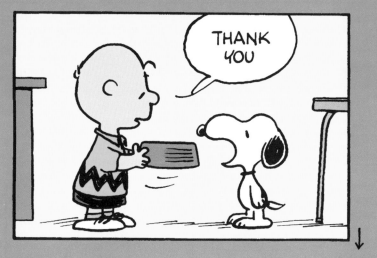

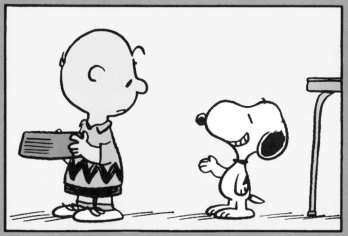

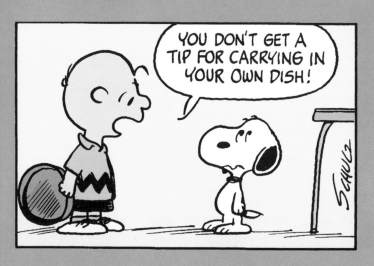

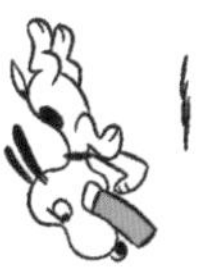

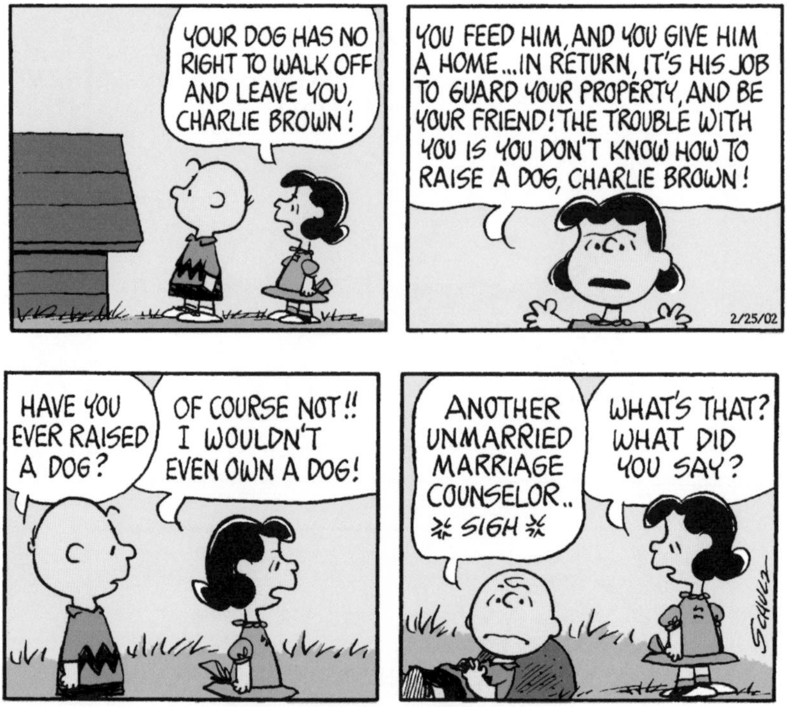
YOUR DOG HAS NO RIGHT TO WALK OFF AND LEAVE YOU, CHARLIE BROWN!
YOU FEED HIM, AND YOU GIVE HIM A HOME...IN RETURN, IT'S HIS JOB TO GUARD YOUR PROPERTY, AND BE YOUR FRIEND! THE TROUBLE WITH YOU IS YOU DON'T KNOW HOW TO RAISE A DOG, CHARLIE BROWN!
2/25/02
HAVE YOU EVER RAISED A DOG?
OF COURSE NOT!! I WOULDN'T EVEN OWN A DOG!
ANOTHER UNMARRIED MARRIAGE COUNSELOR.. SIGH
WHAT'S THAT? WHAT DID YOU SAY?
SCHULZ

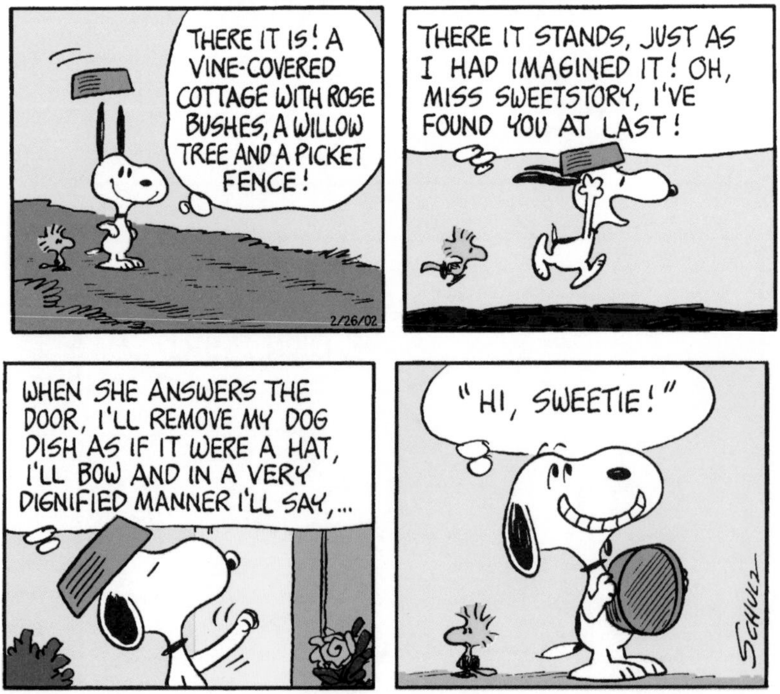
THERE IT IS! A VINE-COVERED COTTAGE WITH ROSE BUSHES, A WILLOW TREE AND A PICKET FENCE!
2/26/02
THERE IT STANDS, JUST AS I HAD IMAGINED IT! OH, MISS SWEETSTORY, I'VE FOUND YOU AT LAST!
WHEN SHE ANSWERS THE DOOR, I'LL REMOVE MY DOG DISH AS IF IT WERE A HAT, I'LL BOW AND IN A VERY DIGNIFIED MANNER I'LL SAY,...
"HI, SWEETIE!"
SCHULZ

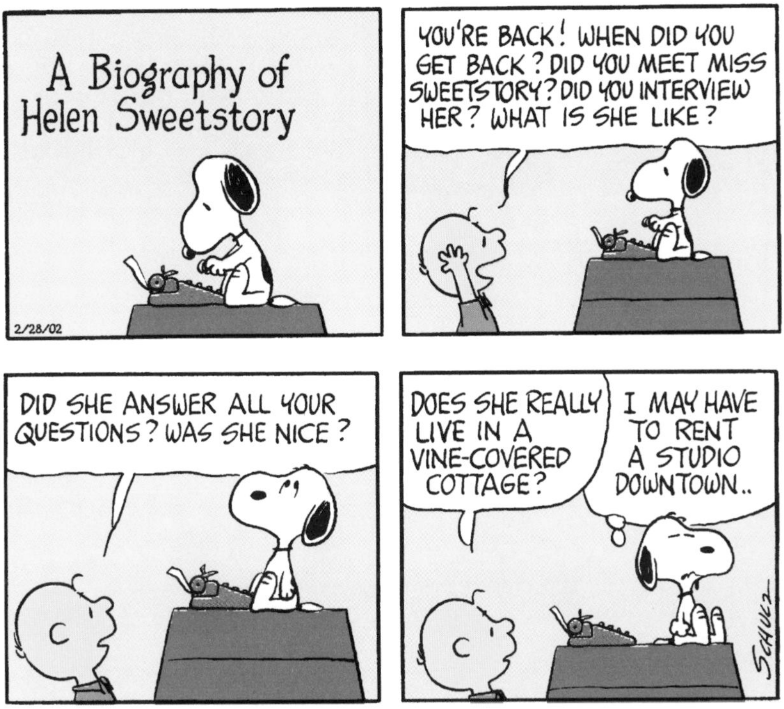
A Biography of Helen Sweetstory
2/28/02
YOU'RE BACK! WHEN DID YOU GET BACK? DID YOU MEET MISS SWEETSTORY? DID YOU INTERVIEW HER? WHAT IS SHE LIKE?
DID SHE ANSWER ALL YOUR QUESTIONS? WAS SHE NICE?
DOES SHE REALLY LIVE IN A VINE-COVERED COTTAGE?
I MAY HAVE TO RENT A STUDIO DOWNTOWN..
SCHULZ

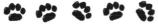

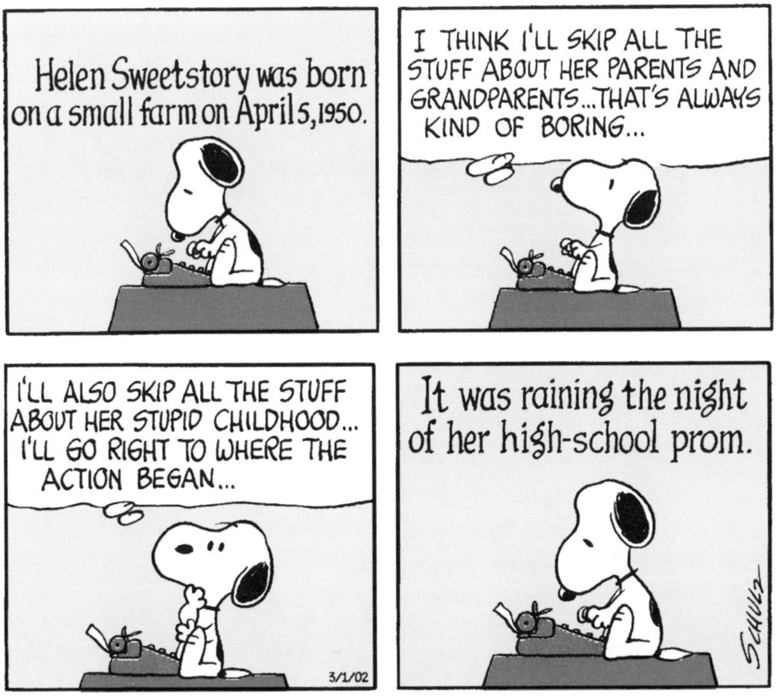
Helen Sweetstory was born on a small farm on April 5, 1950.
I THINK I'LL SKIP ALL THE STUFF ABOUT HER PARENTS AND GRANDPARENTS...THAT'S ALWAYS KIND OF BORING...
I'LL ALSO SKIP ALL THE STUFF ABOUT HER STUPID CHILDHOOD... I'LL GO RIGHT TO WHERE THE ACTION BEGAN...
3/1/02
It was raining the night of her high-school prom.
SCHULZ

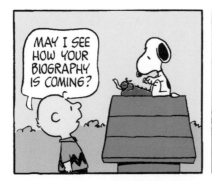

MAY I SEE HOW YOUR BIOGRAPHY IS COMING?

"HELEN SWEETSTORY WAS BORN ON A SMALL FARM ON APRIL 5, 1950... IT WAS RAINING THE NIGHT OF HER HIGH-SCHOOL PROM...LATER THAT SUMMER SHE WAS THROWN FROM A HORSE..."

3/2/02

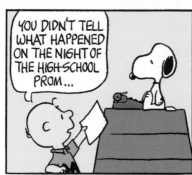

YOU DIDN'T TELL WHAT HAPPENED ON THE NIGHT OF THE HIGH-SCHOOL PROM...

THAT'S NOBODY'S BUSINESS!

THIS IS KIND OF AN INTERESTING ARTICLE

"MISS HELEN SWEETSTORY, AUTHOR OF THE 'BUNNY-WUNNY' SERIES, DENIED THAT THE STORY OF HER LIFE WAS BEING WRITTEN..'SUCH A BIOGRAPHY IS COMPLETELY UNAUTHORIZED,' SHE SAID..."

3/8/02

WELL! WHAT DO YOU THINK OF THAT?

HERE'S THE WORLD WAR I FLYING ACE ZOOMING THROUGH THE AIR IN HIS SOPWITH CAMEL!

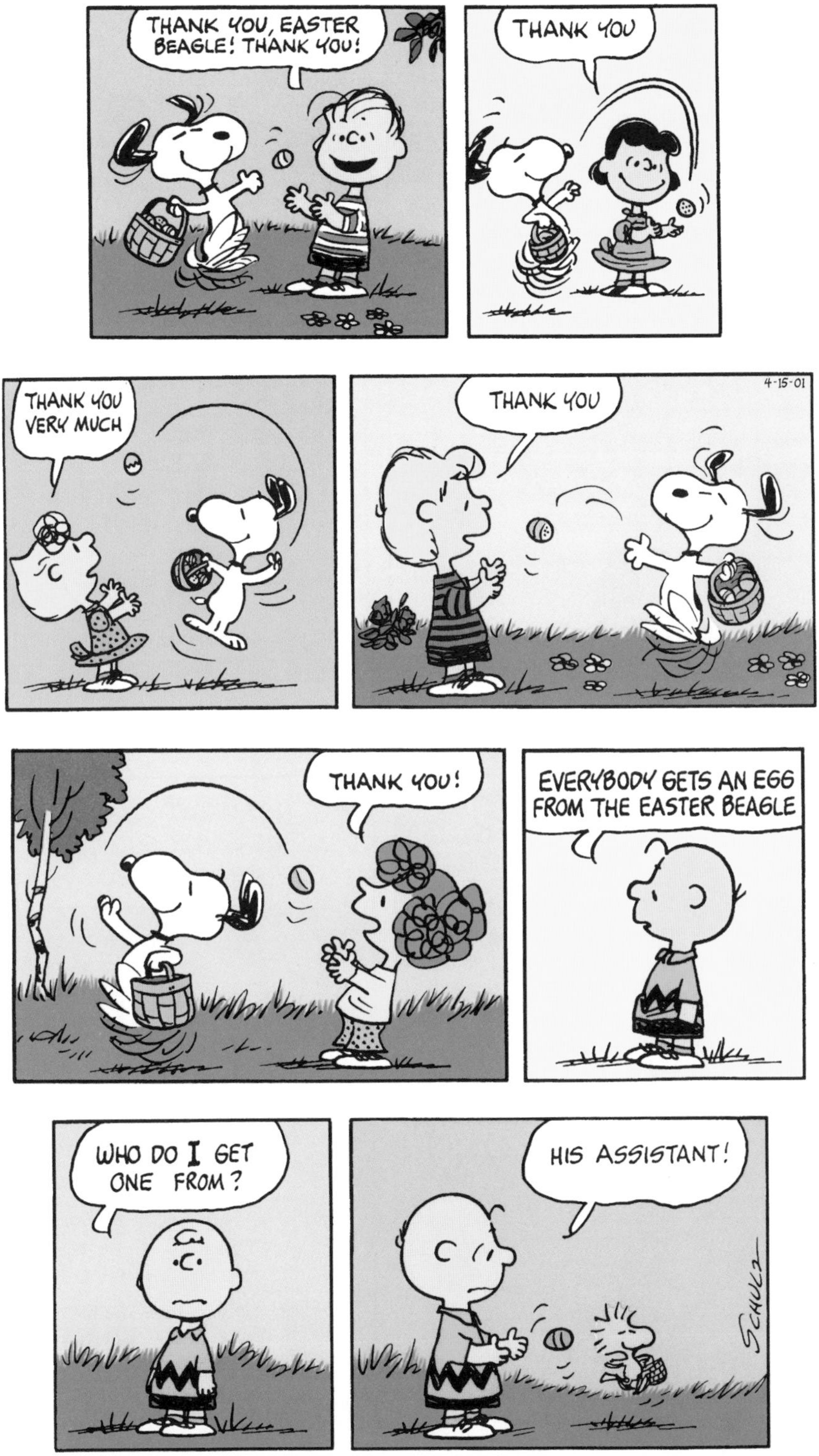
THANK YOU, EASTER BEAGLE! THANK YOU!
THANK YOU
THANK YOU VERY MUCH
THANK YOU
4-15-01
THANK YOU!
EVERYBODY GETS AN EGG FROM THE EASTER BEAGLE
WHO DO I GET ONE FROM?
HIS ASSISTANT!
SCHULZ

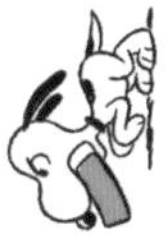

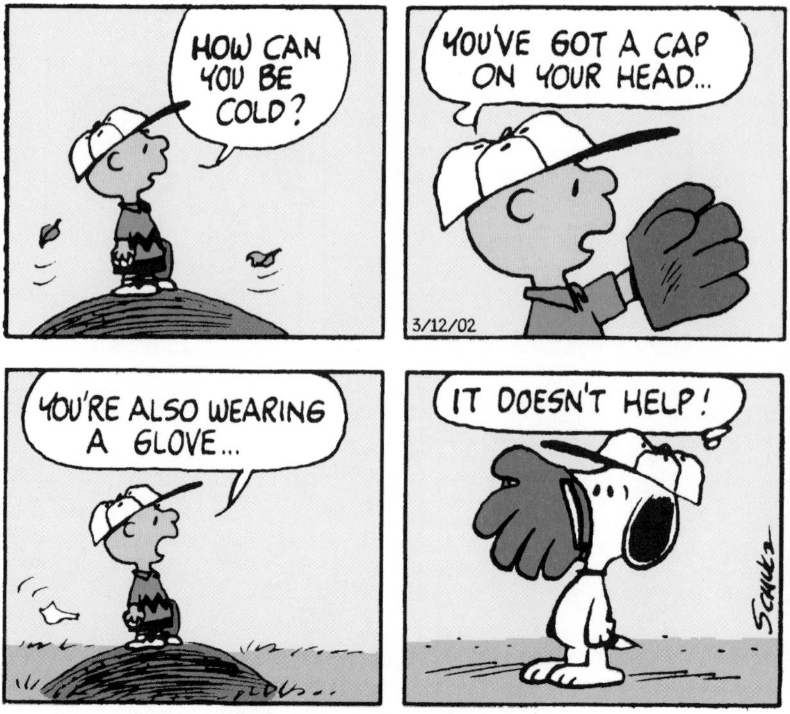
HOW CAN YOU BE COLD?
YOU'VE GOT A CAP ON YOUR HEAD...
3/12/02
YOU'RE ALSO WEARING A GLOVE...
IT DOESN'T HELP!

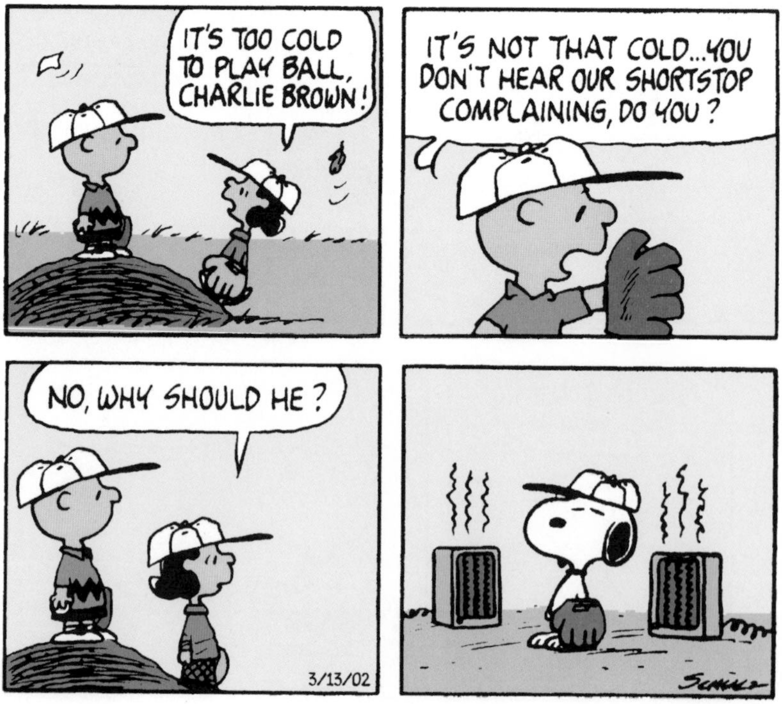
IT'S TOO COLD TO PLAY BALL, CHARLIE BROWN!
IT'S NOT THAT COLD...YOU DON'T HEAR OUR SHORTSTOP COMPLAINING, DO YOU?
NO, WHY SHOULD HE?
3/13/02

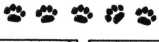

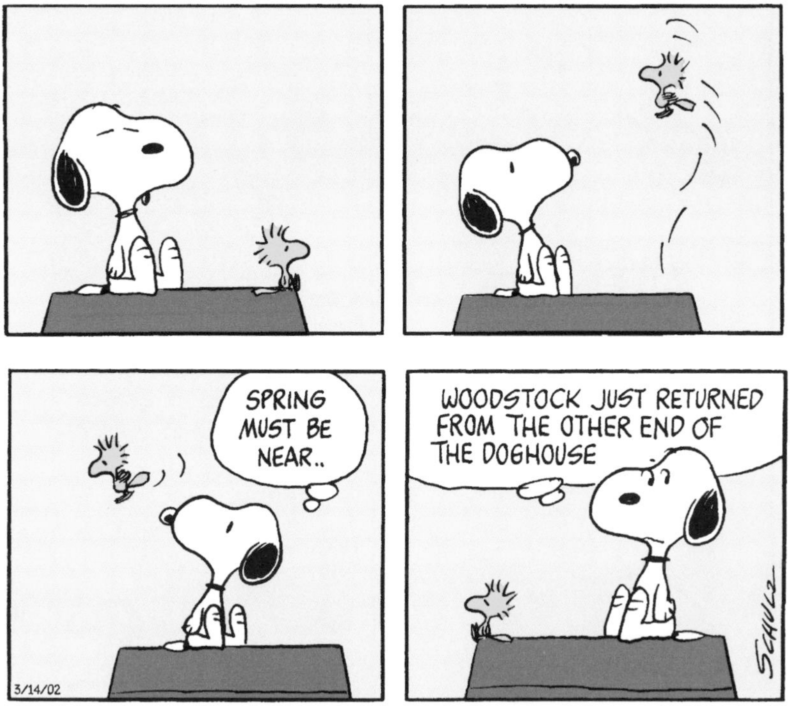
SPRING MUST BE NEAR..
3/14/02
WOODSTOCK JUST RETURNED FROM THE OTHER END OF THE DOGHOUSE
SCHULZ

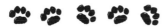

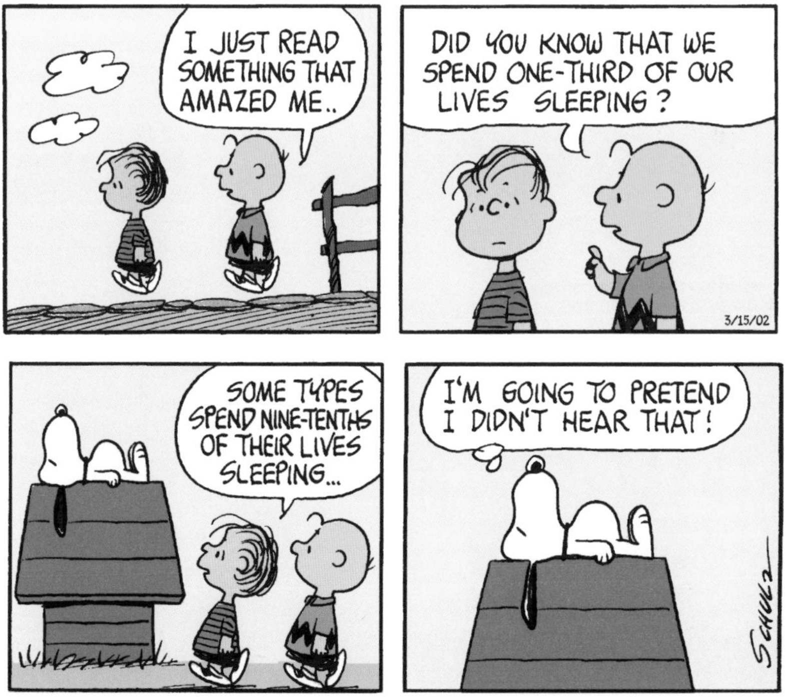
I JUST READ SOMETHING THAT AMAZED ME..
DID YOU KNOW THAT WE SPEND ONE-THIRD OF OUR LIVES SLEEPING ?
3/15/02
SOME TYPES SPEND NINE-TENTHS OF THEIR LIVES SLEEPING...
I'M GOING TO PRETEND I DIDN'T HEAR THAT !
SCHULZ

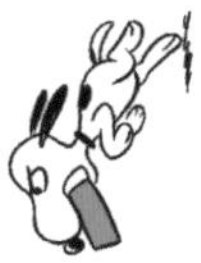

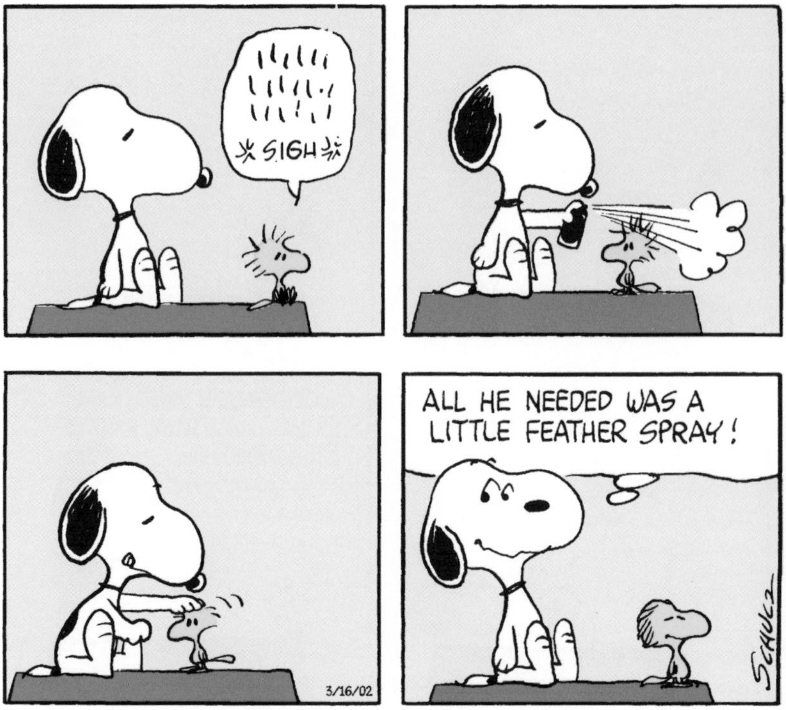
SIGH
ALL HE NEEDED WAS A LITTLE FEATHER SPRAY!
3/16/02
SCHULZ

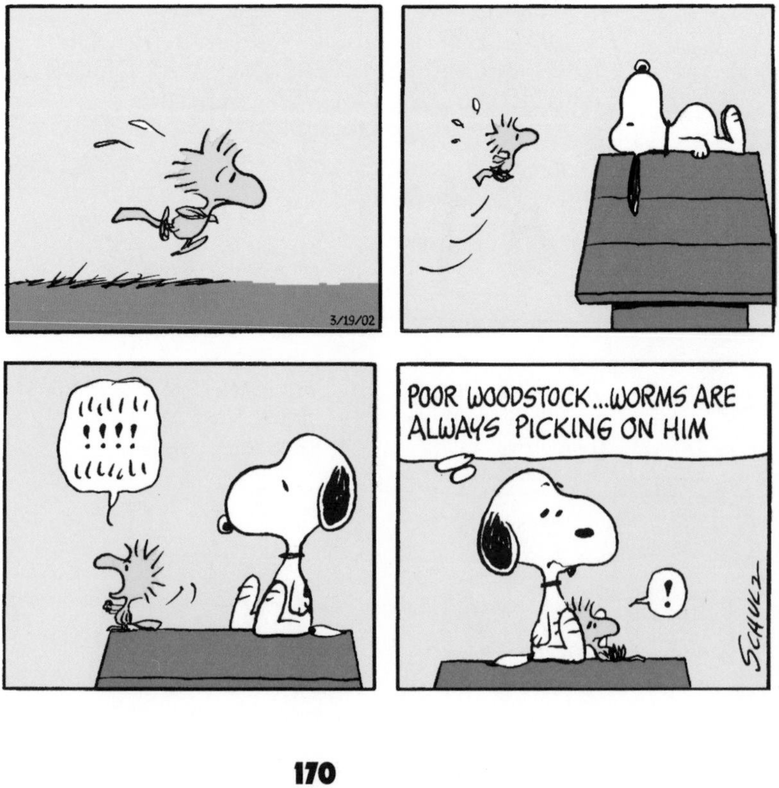
!!!!
POOR WOODSTOCK...WORMS ARE ALWAYS PICKING ON HIM
!
3/19/02
SCHULZ

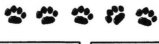

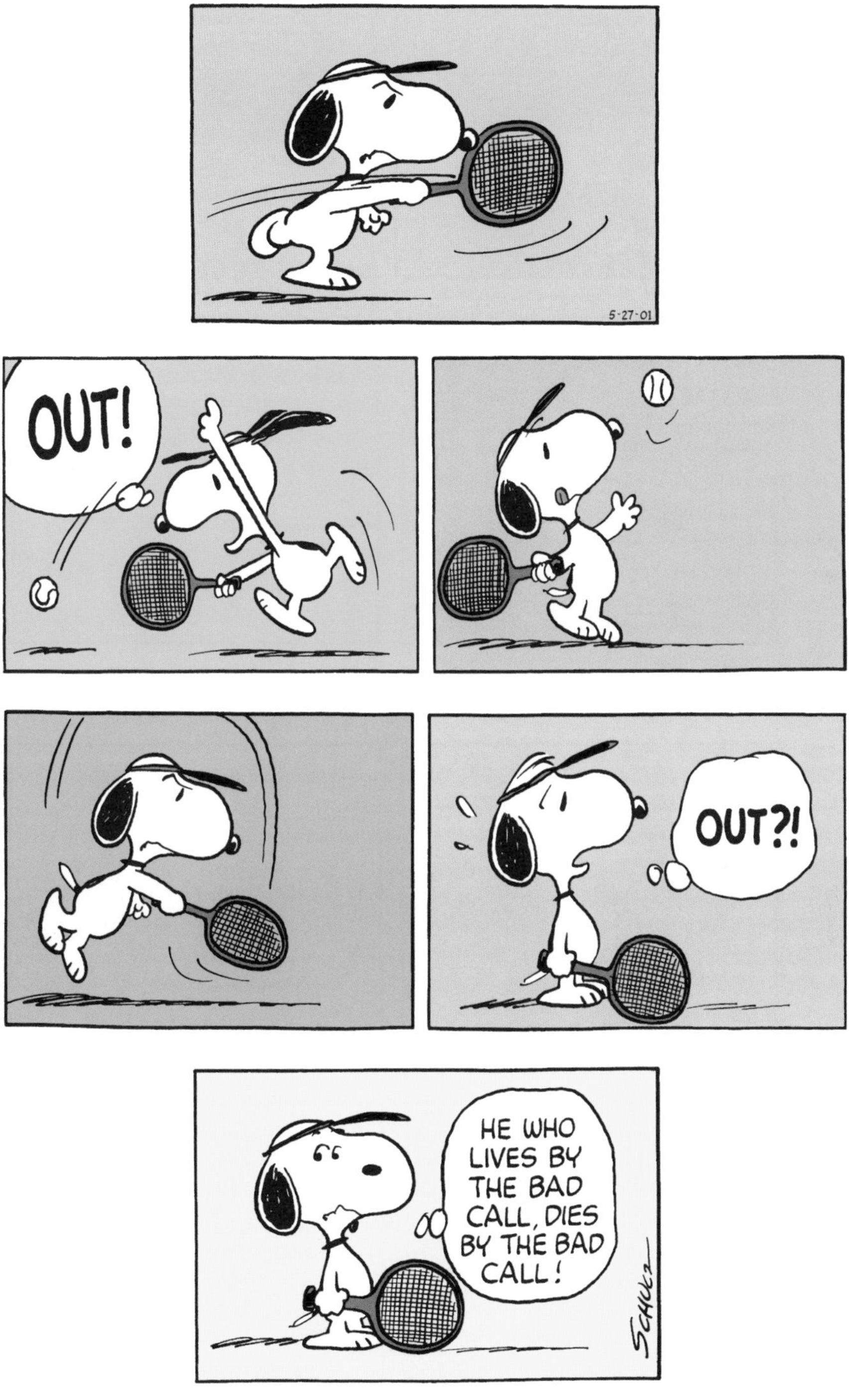
5-27-01
OUT!
OUT?!
HE WHO LIVES BY THE BAD CALL, DIES BY THE BAD CALL!
SCHULZ

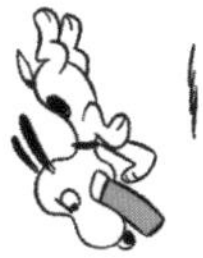

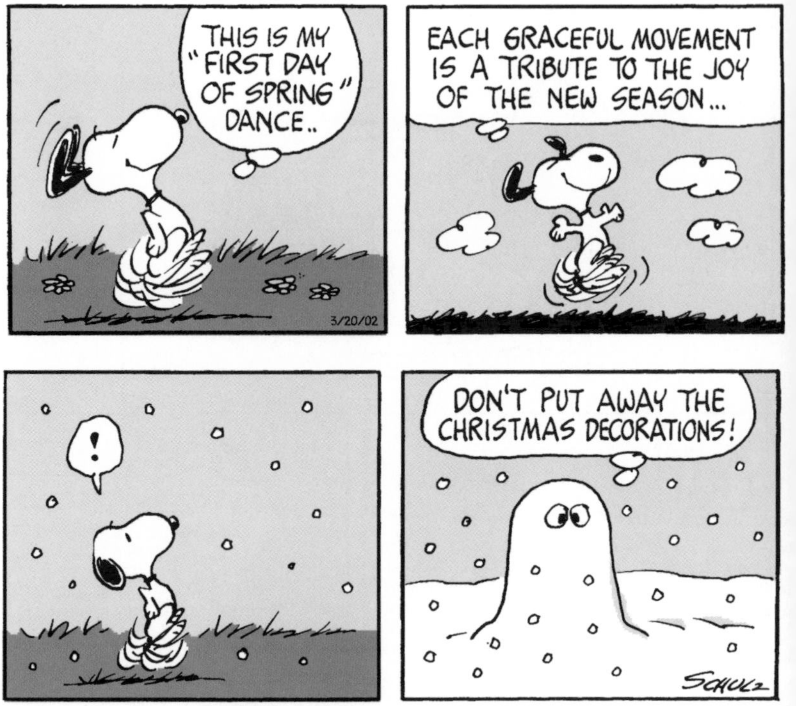
THIS IS MY "FIRST DAY OF SPRING" DANCE..
3/20/02
EACH GRACEFUL MOVEMENT IS A TRIBUTE TO THE JOY OF THE NEW SEASON...
!
DON'T PUT AWAY THE CHRISTMAS DECORATIONS!
SCHULZ

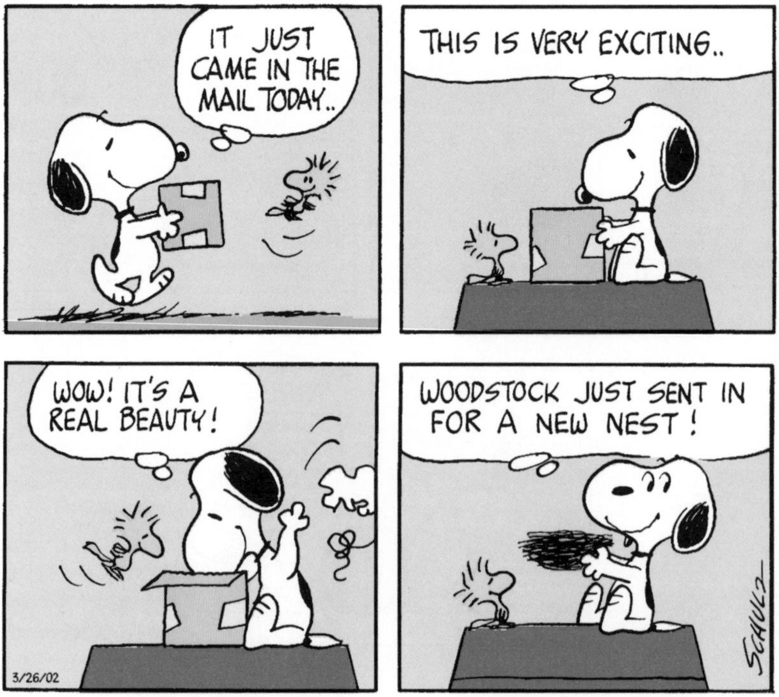
IT JUST CAME IN THE MAIL TODAY..
THIS IS VERY EXCITING..
WOW! IT'S A REAL BEAUTY!
3/26/02
WOODSTOCK JUST SENT IN FOR A NEW NEST!
SCHULZ

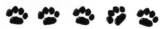

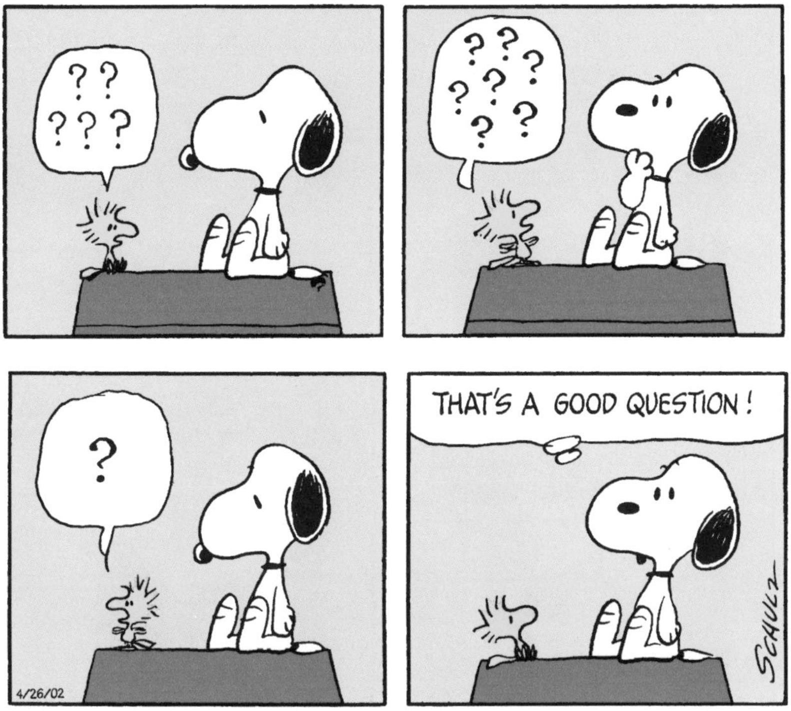
? ? ? ? ?
? ? ? ? ? ? ?
?
THAT'S A GOOD QUESTION!
4/26/02
SCHULZ

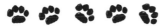

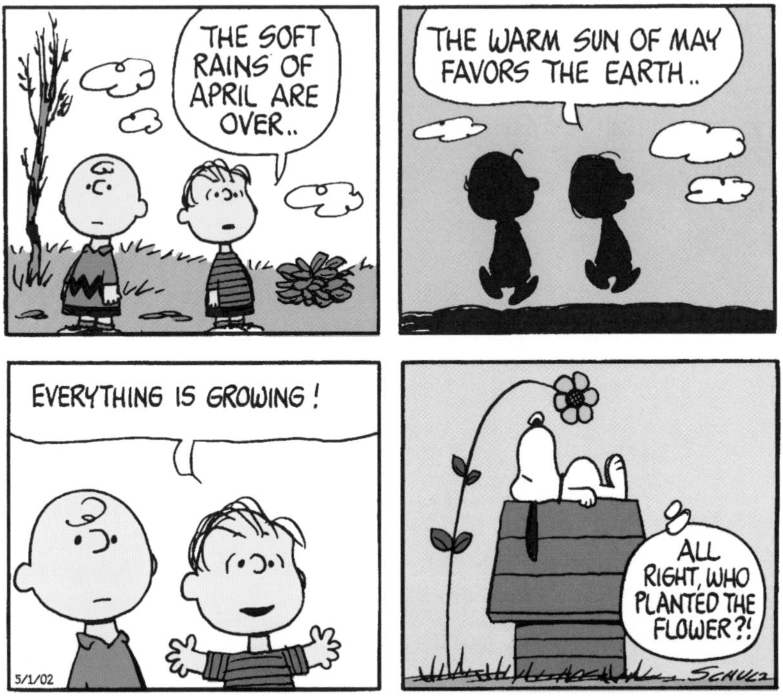
THE SOFT RAINS OF APRIL ARE OVER..
THE WARM SUN OF MAY FAVORS THE EARTH..
EVERYTHING IS GROWING!
5/1/02
ALL RIGHT, WHO PLANTED THE FLOWER?!
SCHULZ

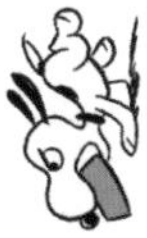

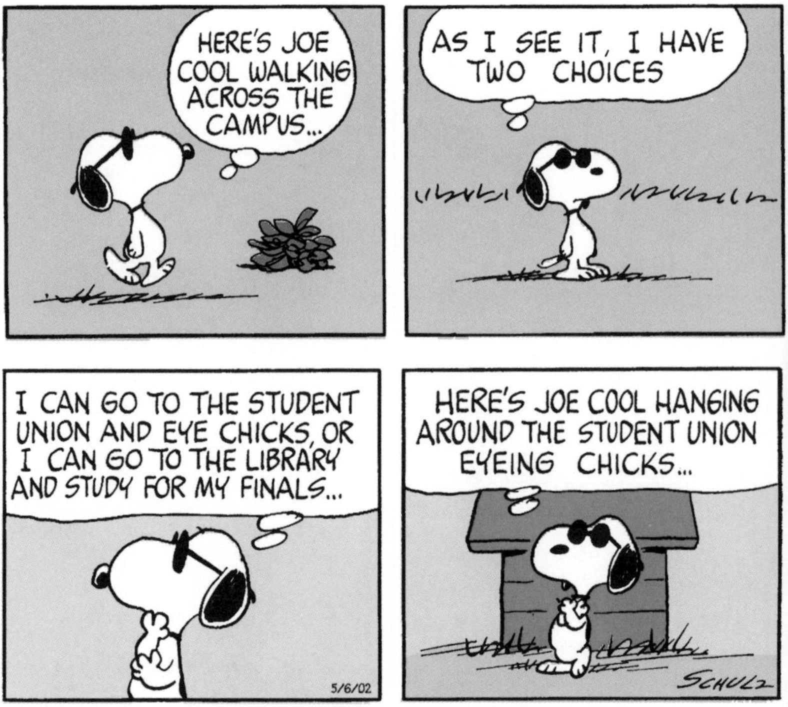
HERE'S JOE COOL WALKING ACROSS THE CAMPUS...
AS I SEE IT, I HAVE TWO CHOICES
I CAN GO TO THE STUDENT UNION AND EYE CHICKS, OR I CAN GO TO THE LIBRARY AND STUDY FOR MY FINALS...
5/6/02
HERE'S JOE COOL HANGING AROUND THE STUDENT UNION EYEING CHICKS...
SCHULZ

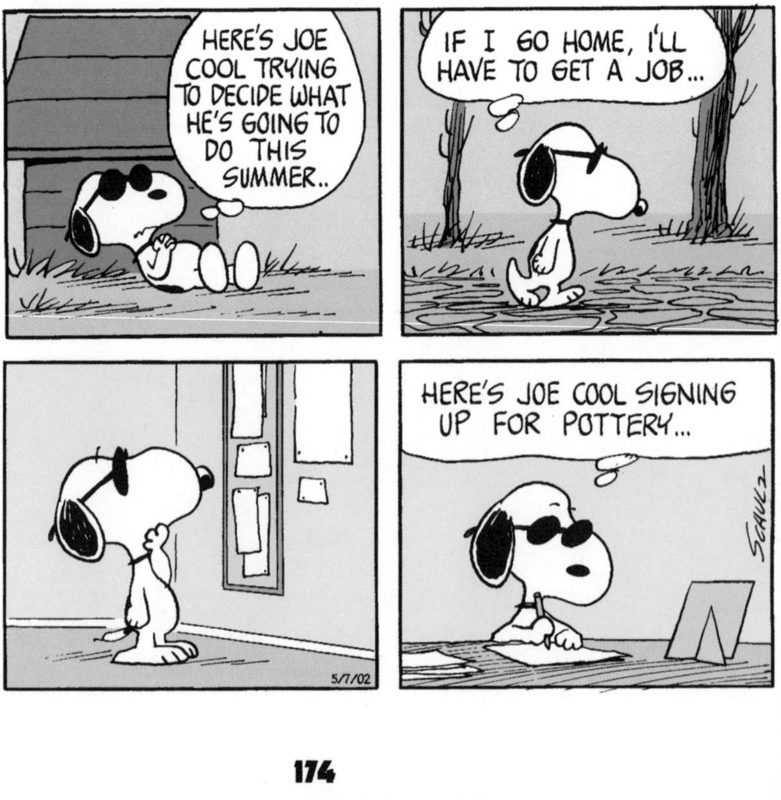
HERE'S JOE COOL TRYING TO DECIDE WHAT HE'S GOING TO DO THIS SUMMER..
IF I GO HOME, I'LL HAVE TO GET A JOB...
5/7/02
HERE'S JOE COOL SIGNING UP FOR POTTERY...
SCHULZ

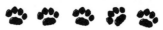

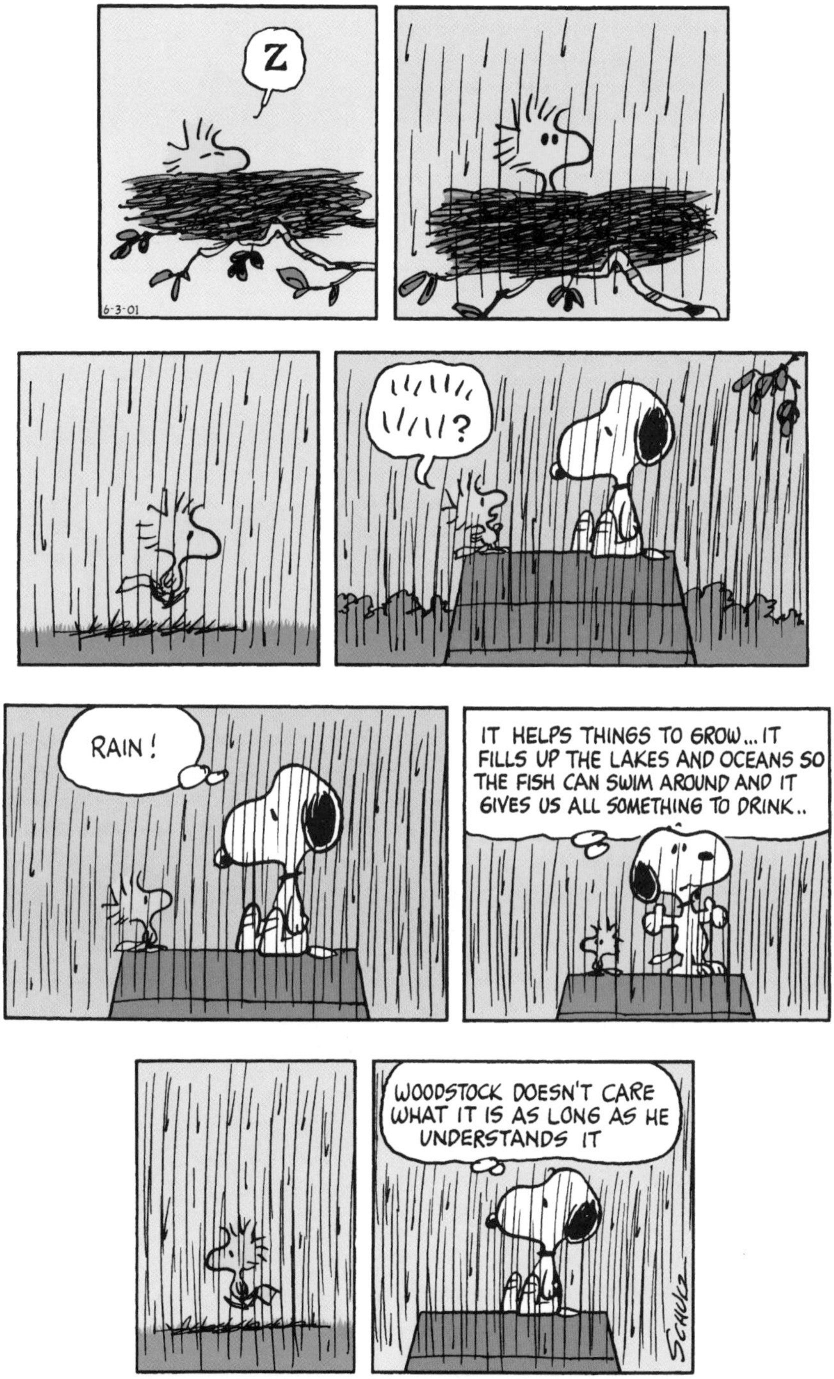
Z
6-3-01
RAIN!
IT HELPS THINGS TO GROW... IT FILLS UP THE LAKES AND OCEANS SO THE FISH CAN SWIM AROUND AND IT GIVES US ALL SOMETHING TO DRINK..
WOODSTOCK DOESN'T CARE WHAT IT IS AS LONG AS HE UNDERSTANDS IT
SCHULZ

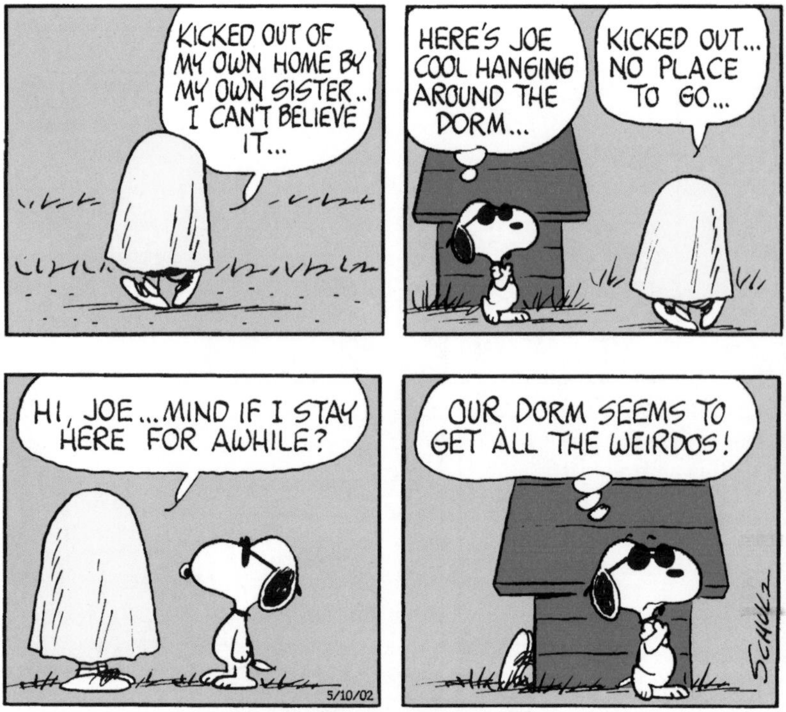
KICKED OUT OF MY OWN HOME BY MY OWN SISTER.. I CAN'T BELIEVE IT...
HERE'S JOE COOL HANGING AROUND THE DORM...
KICKED OUT... NO PLACE TO GO...
HI, JOE...MIND IF I STAY HERE FOR AWHILE?
OUR DORM SEEMS TO GET ALL THE WEIRDOS!
5/10/02
SCHULZ

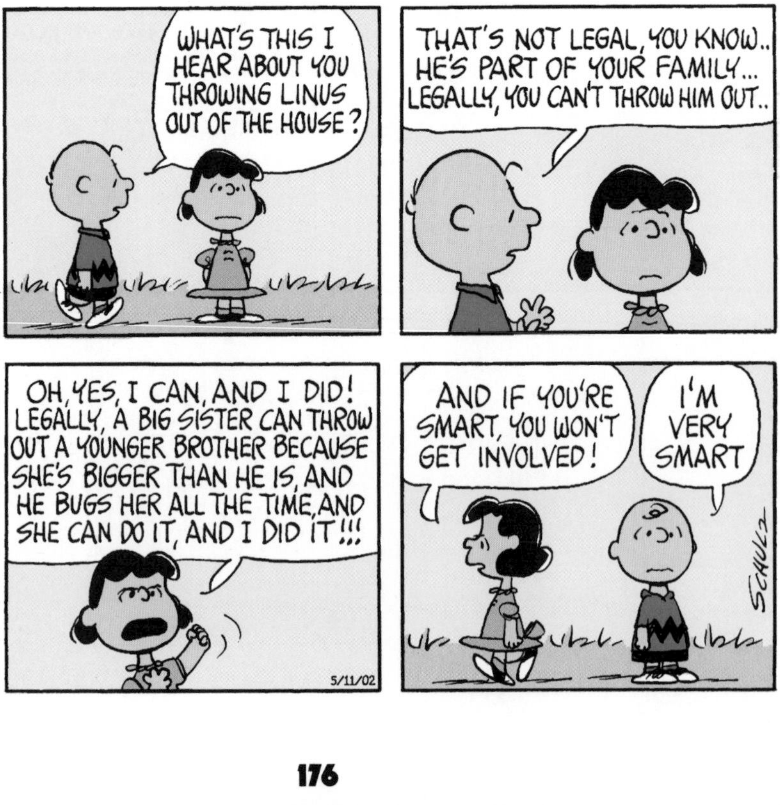
WHAT'S THIS I HEAR ABOUT YOU THROWING LINUS OUT OF THE HOUSE?
THAT'S NOT LEGAL, YOU KNOW.. HE'S PART OF YOUR FAMILY... LEGALLY, YOU CAN'T THROW HIM OUT..
OH, YES, I CAN, AND I DID! LEGALLY, A BIG SISTER CAN THROW OUT A YOUNGER BROTHER BECAUSE SHE'S BIGGER THAN HE IS, AND HE BUGS HER ALL THE TIME, AND SHE CAN DO IT, AND I DID IT!!!
5/11/02
AND IF YOU'RE SMART, YOU WON'T GET INVOLVED!
I'M VERY SMART
SCHULZ

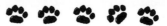

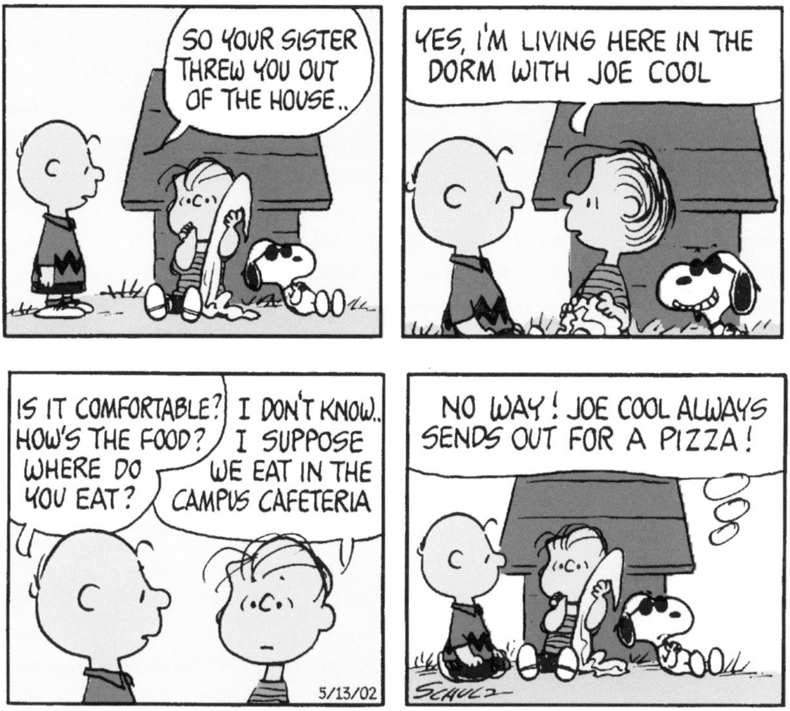
SO YOUR SISTER THREW YOU OUT OF THE HOUSE..
YES, I'M LIVING HERE IN THE DORM WITH JOE COOL
IS IT COMFORTABLE? HOW'S THE FOOD? WHERE DO YOU EAT?
I DON'T KNOW.. I SUPPOSE WE EAT IN THE CAMPUS CAFETERIA
5/13/02
NO WAY! JOE COOL ALWAYS SENDS OUT FOR A PIZZA!
SCHULZ

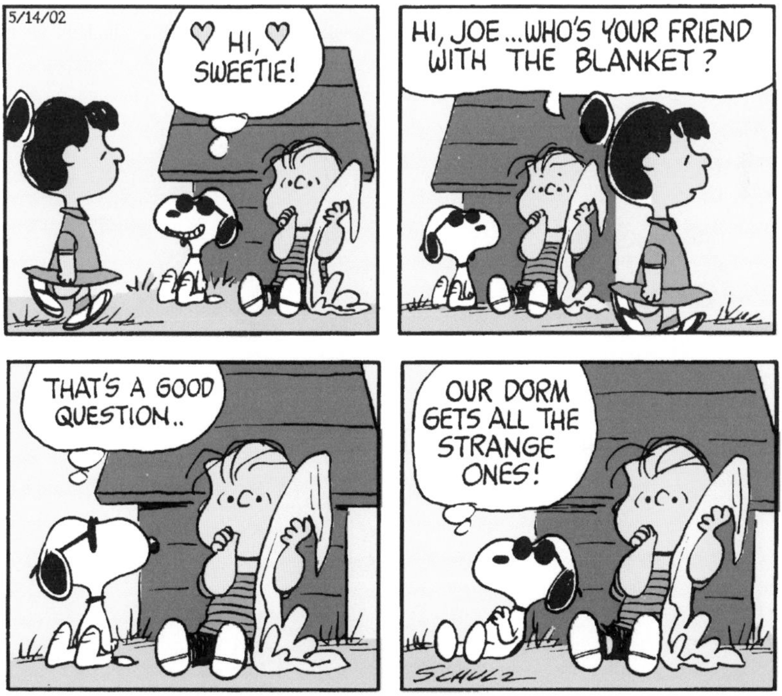
5/14/02
♡ HI, ♡ SWEETIE!
HI, JOE...WHO'S YOUR FRIEND WITH THE BLANKET?
THAT'S A GOOD QUESTION..
OUR DORM GETS ALL THE STRANGE ONES!
SCHULZ

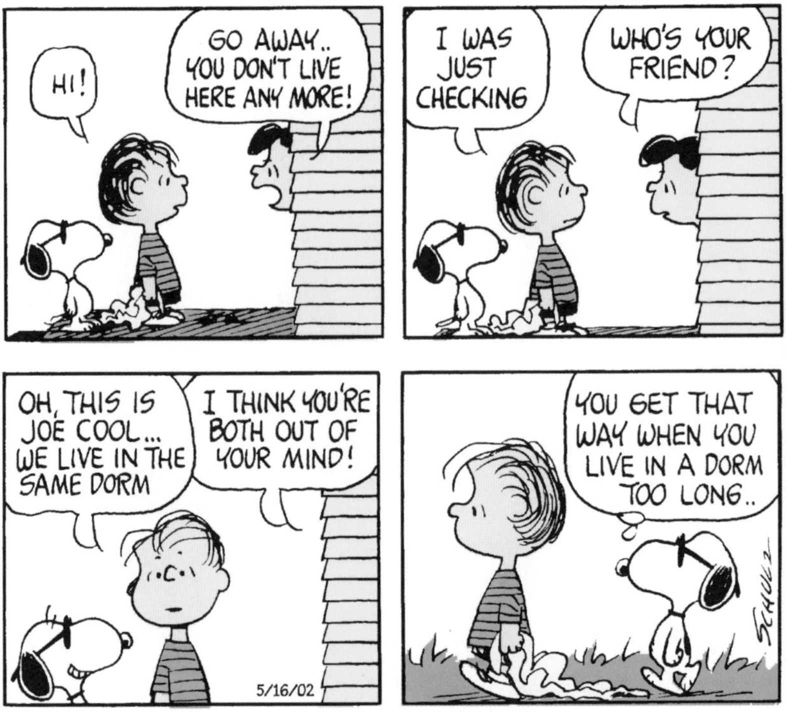
HI!
GO AWAY.. YOU DON'T LIVE HERE ANY MORE!
I WAS JUST CHECKING
WHO'S YOUR FRIEND?
OH, THIS IS JOE COOL... WE LIVE IN THE SAME DORM
I THINK YOU'RE BOTH OUT OF YOUR MIND!
5/16/02
YOU GET THAT WAY WHEN YOU LIVE IN A DORM TOO LONG..
SCHULZ

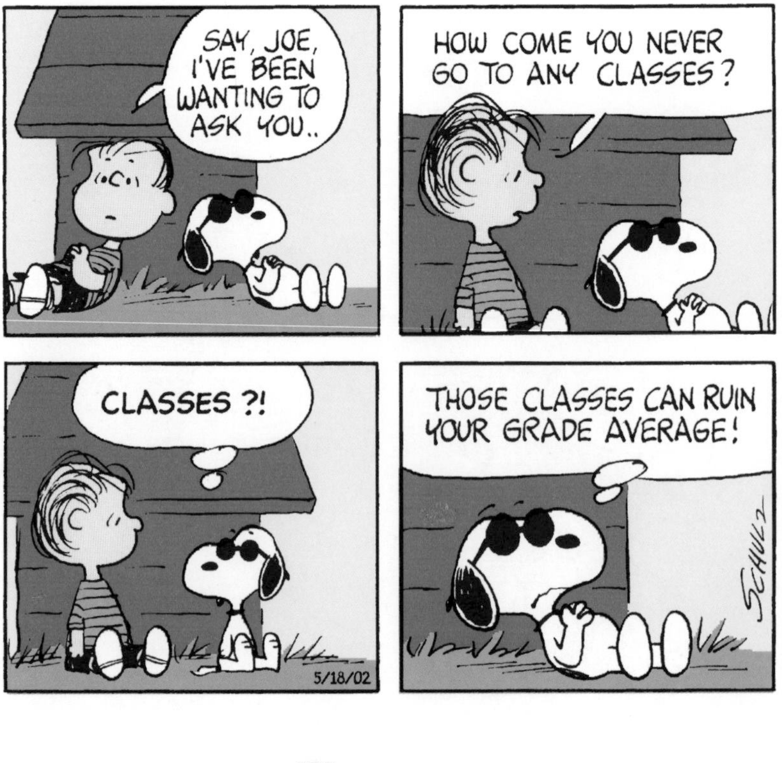
SAY, JOE, I'VE BEEN WANTING TO ASK YOU..
HOW COME YOU NEVER GO TO ANY CLASSES?
CLASSES ?!
5/18/02
THOSE CLASSES CAN RUIN YOUR GRADE AVERAGE!
SCHULZ

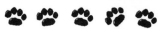

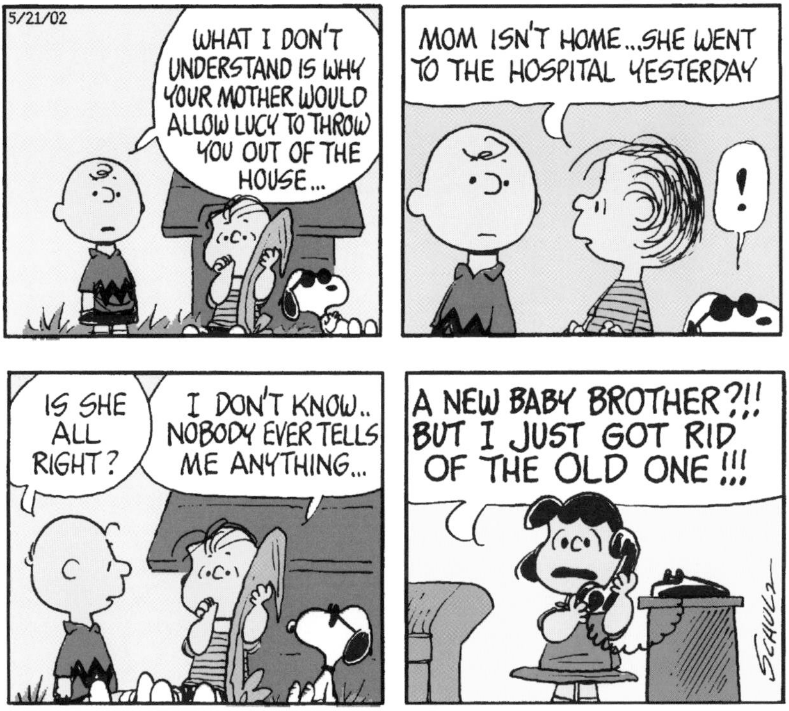

5/21/02
WHAT I DON'T UNDERSTAND IS WHY YOUR MOTHER WOULD ALLOW LUCY TO THROW YOU OUT OF THE HOUSE...
MOM ISN'T HOME...SHE WENT TO THE HOSPITAL YESTERDAY
!
IS SHE ALL RIGHT?
I DON'T KNOW.. NOBODY EVER TELLS ME ANYTHING...
A NEW BABY BROTHER?!! BUT I JUST GOT RID OF THE OLD ONE!!!
SCHULZ

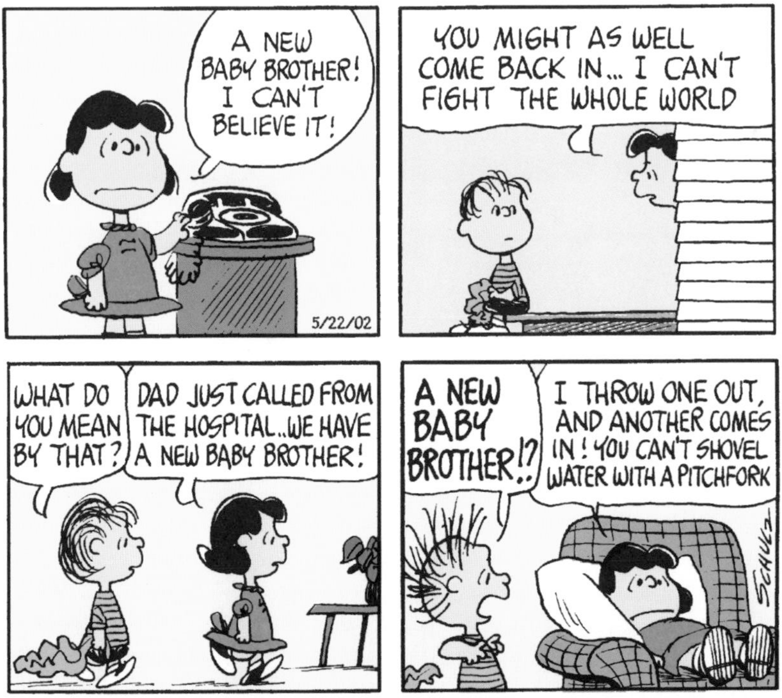

A NEW BABY BROTHER! I CAN'T BELIEVE IT!
5/22/02
YOU MIGHT AS WELL COME BACK IN... I CAN'T FIGHT THE WHOLE WORLD
WHAT DO YOU MEAN BY THAT?
DAD JUST CALLED FROM THE HOSPITAL..WE HAVE A NEW BABY BROTHER!
A NEW BABY BROTHER!?
I THROW ONE OUT, AND ANOTHER COMES IN! YOU CAN'T SHOVEL WATER WITH A PITCHFORK
SCHULZ

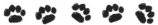

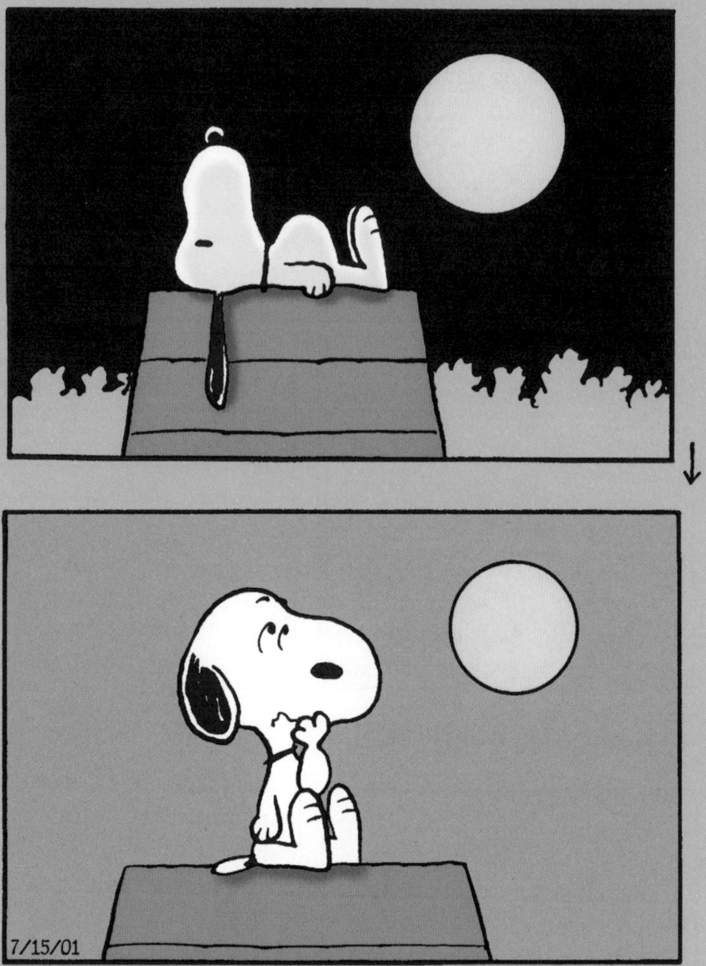
7/15/01

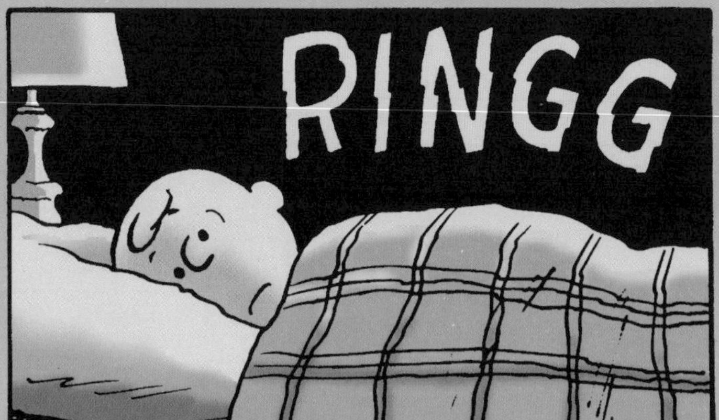
RINGG

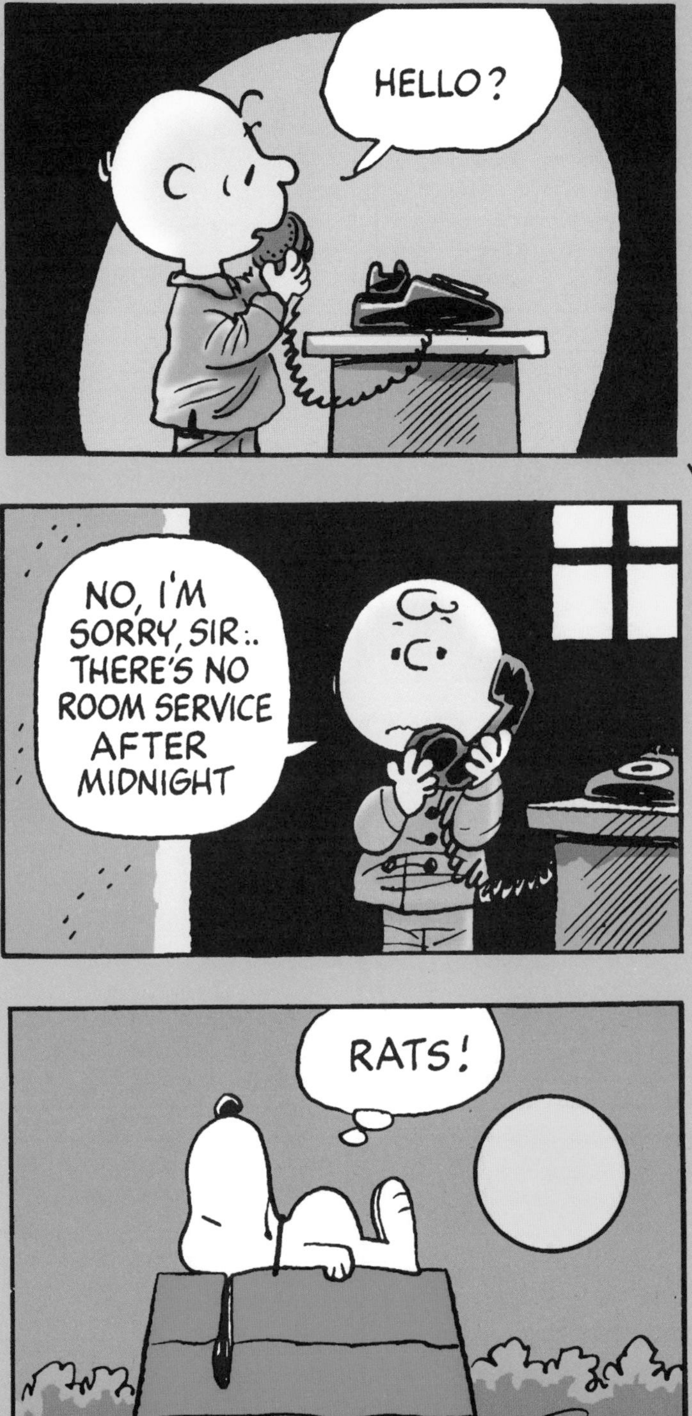
HELLO?
NO, I'M SORRY, SIR.. THERE'S NO ROOM SERVICE AFTER MIDNIGHT
RATS!
SCHULZ

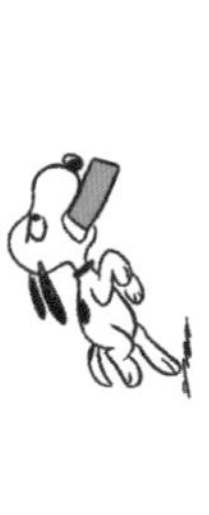

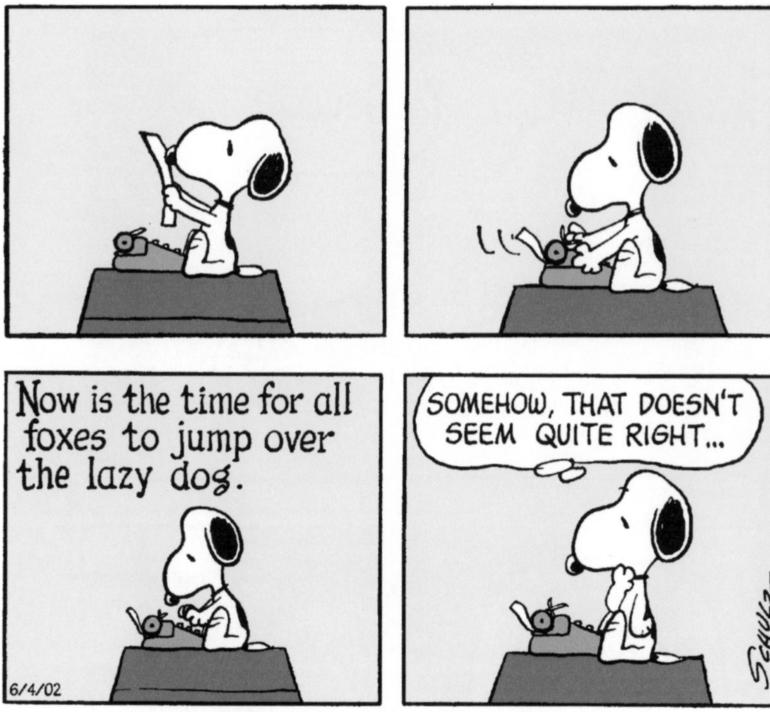
Now is the time for all foxes to jump over the lazy dog.
6/4/02
SOMEHOW, THAT DOESN'T SEEM QUITE RIGHT...
SCHULZ

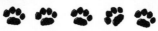

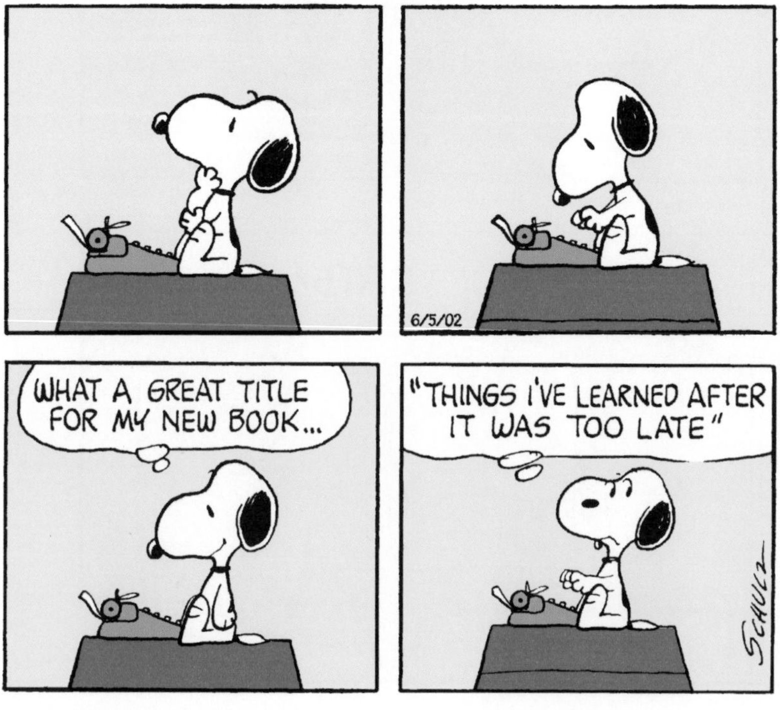
6/5/02
WHAT A GREAT TITLE FOR MY NEW BOOK...
"THINGS I'VE LEARNED AFTER IT WAS TOO LATE"
SCHULZ

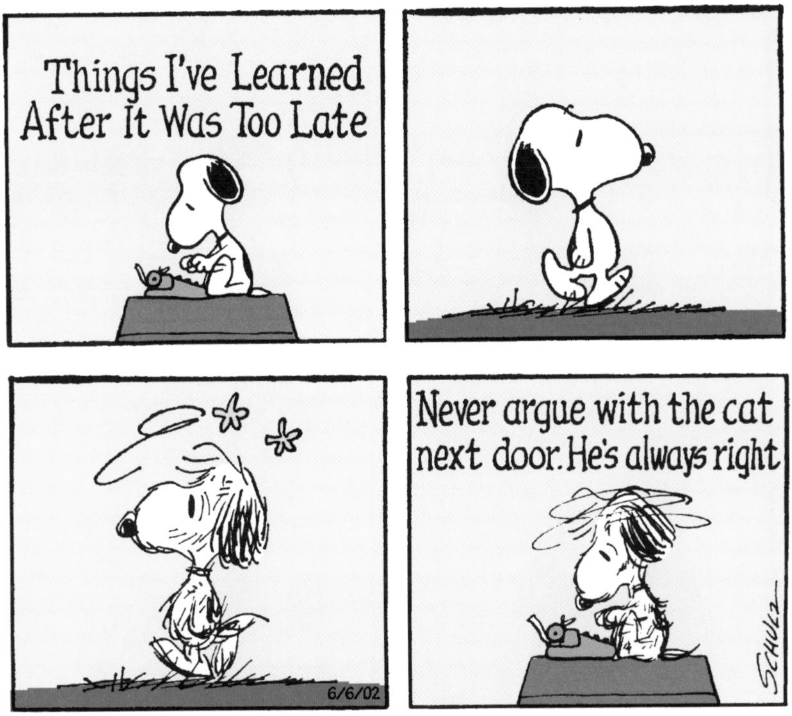
Things I've Learned After It Was Too Late
Never argue with the cat next door. He's always right
6/6/02
SCHULZ

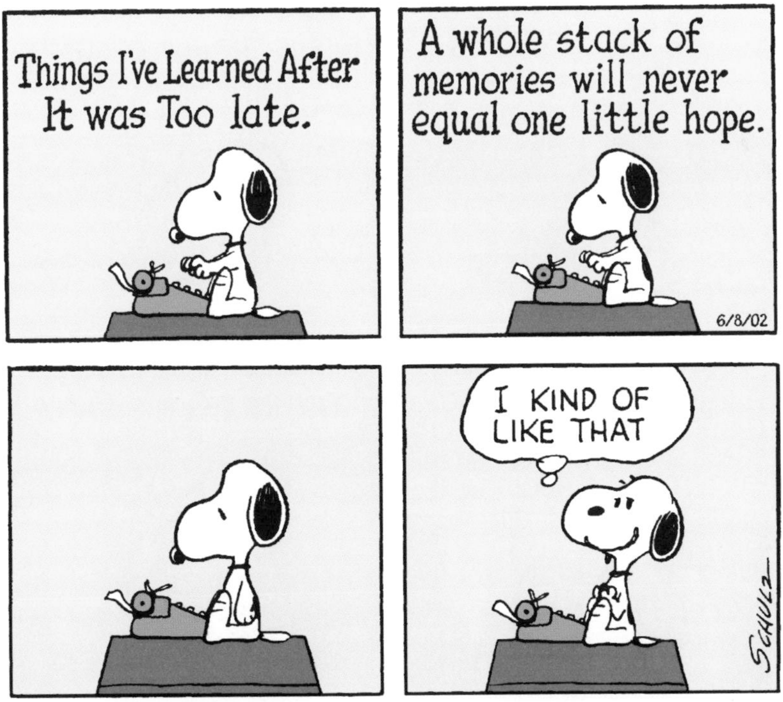
Things I've Learned After It was Too late.
A whole stack of memories will never equal one little hope.
6/8/02
I KIND OF LIKE THAT
SCHULZ

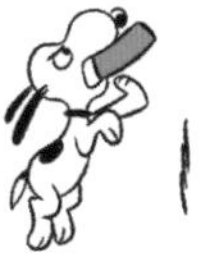

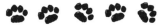

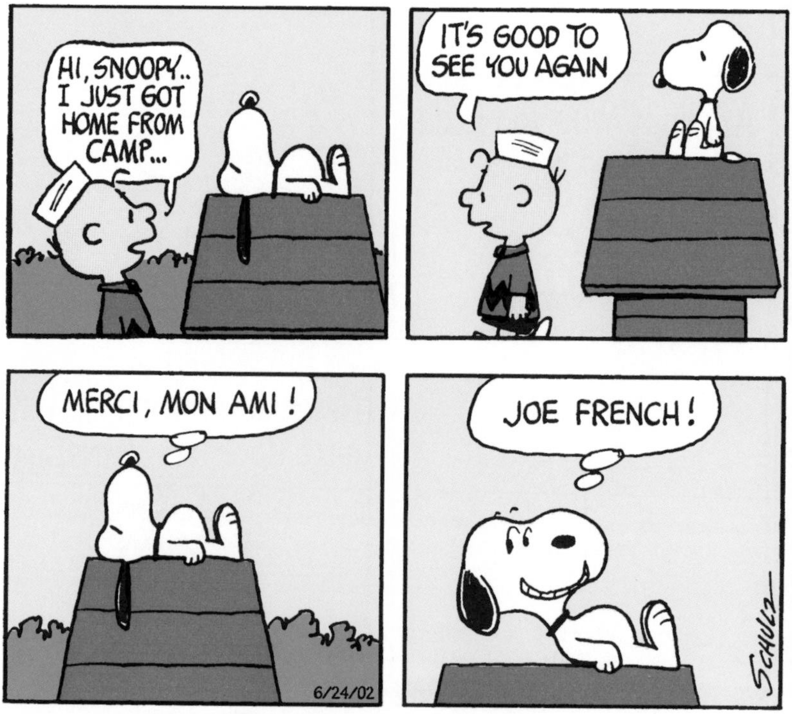
HI, SNOOPY.. I JUST GOT HOME FROM CAMP...
IT'S GOOD TO SEE YOU AGAIN
MERCI, MON AMI!
6/24/02
JOE FRENCH!
SCHULZ

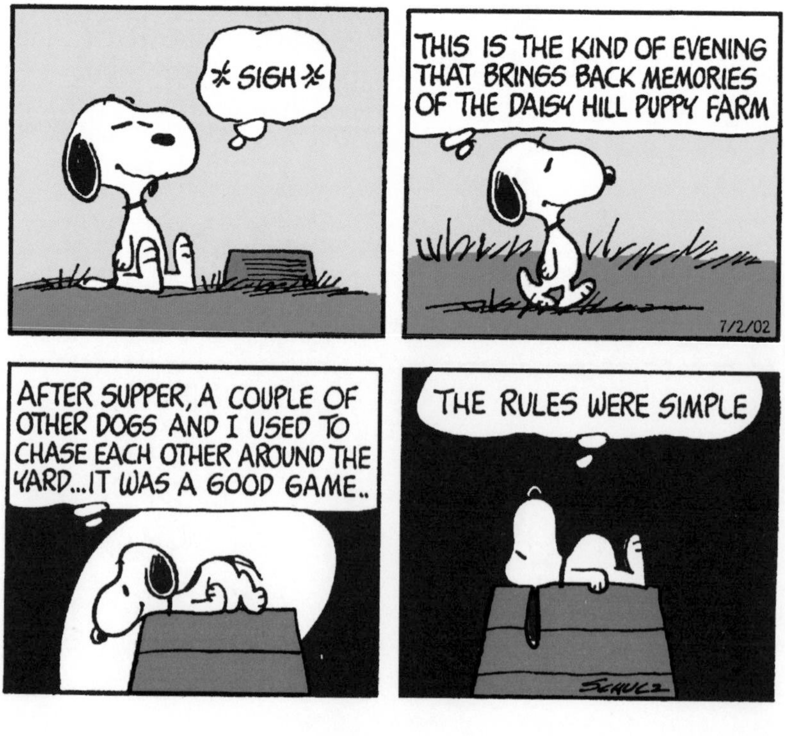
SIGH
THIS IS THE KIND OF EVENING THAT BRINGS BACK MEMORIES OF THE DAISY HILL PUPPY FARM
7/2/02
AFTER SUPPER, A COUPLE OF OTHER DOGS AND I USED TO CHASE EACH OTHER AROUND THE YARD...IT WAS A GOOD GAME..
THE RULES WERE SIMPLE
SCHULZ

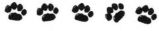

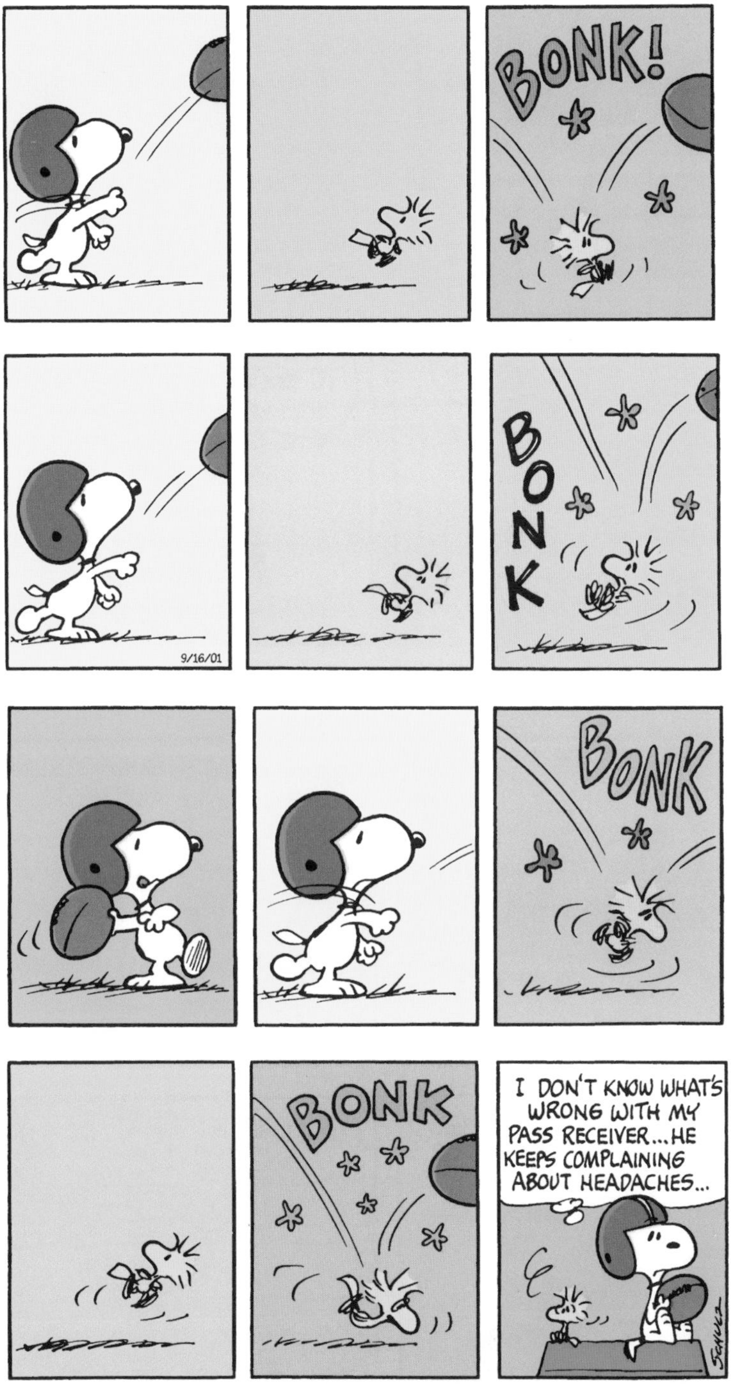
BONK!
9/16/01
BONK
BONK
BONK
I DON'T KNOW WHAT'S WRONG WITH MY PASS RECEIVER...HE KEEPS COMPLAINING ABOUT HEADACHES...
SCHULZ

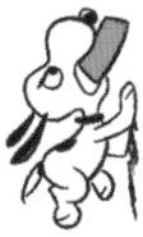

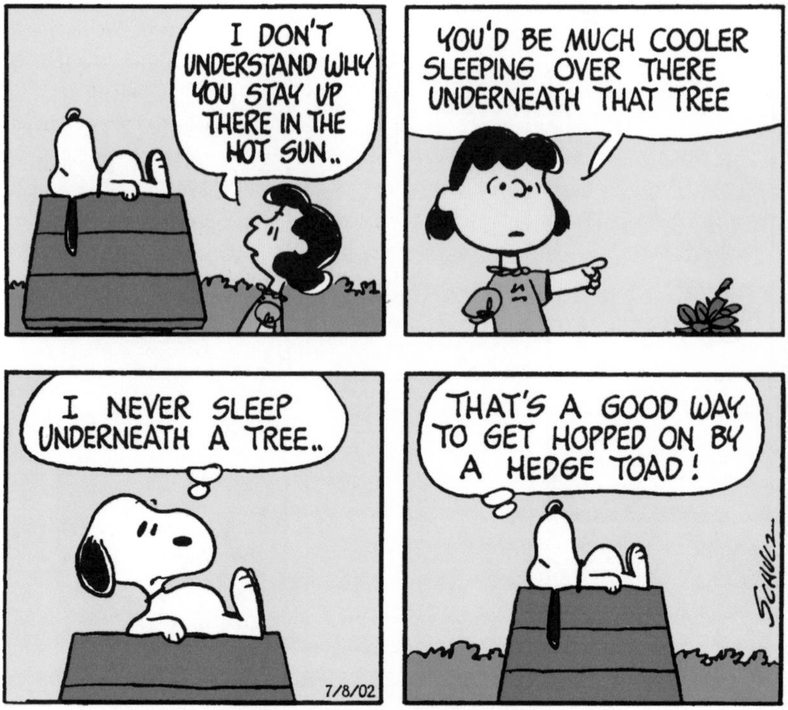
I DON'T UNDERSTAND WHY YOU STAY UP THERE IN THE HOT SUN..
YOU'D BE MUCH COOLER SLEEPING OVER THERE UNDERNEATH THAT TREE
I NEVER SLEEP UNDERNEATH A TREE..
7/8/02
THAT'S A GOOD WAY TO GET HOPPED ON BY A HEDGE TOAD!
SCHULZ

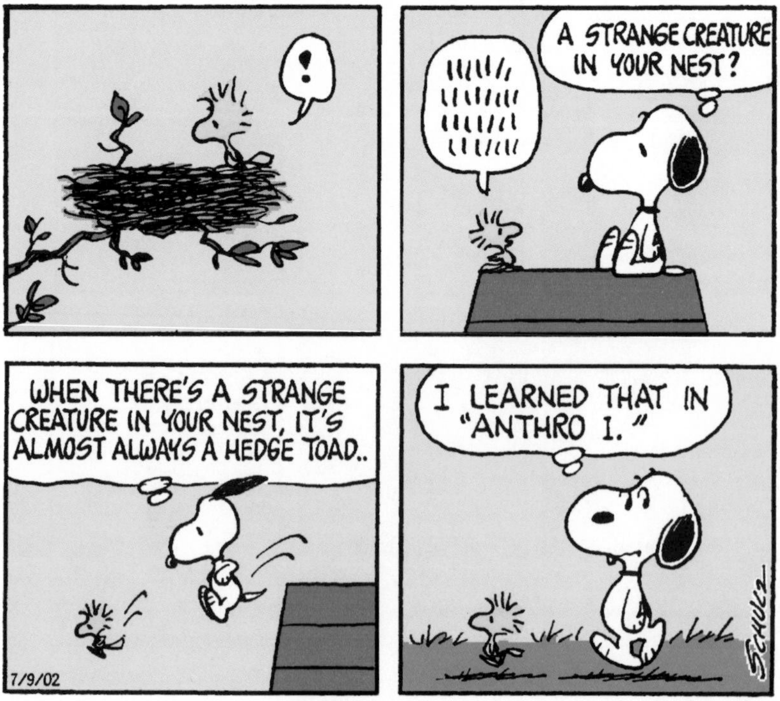
!
A STRANGE CREATURE IN YOUR NEST?
WHEN THERE'S A STRANGE CREATURE IN YOUR NEST, IT'S ALMOST ALWAYS A HEDGE TOAD..
7/9/02
I LEARNED THAT IN "ANTHRO I."
SCHULZ

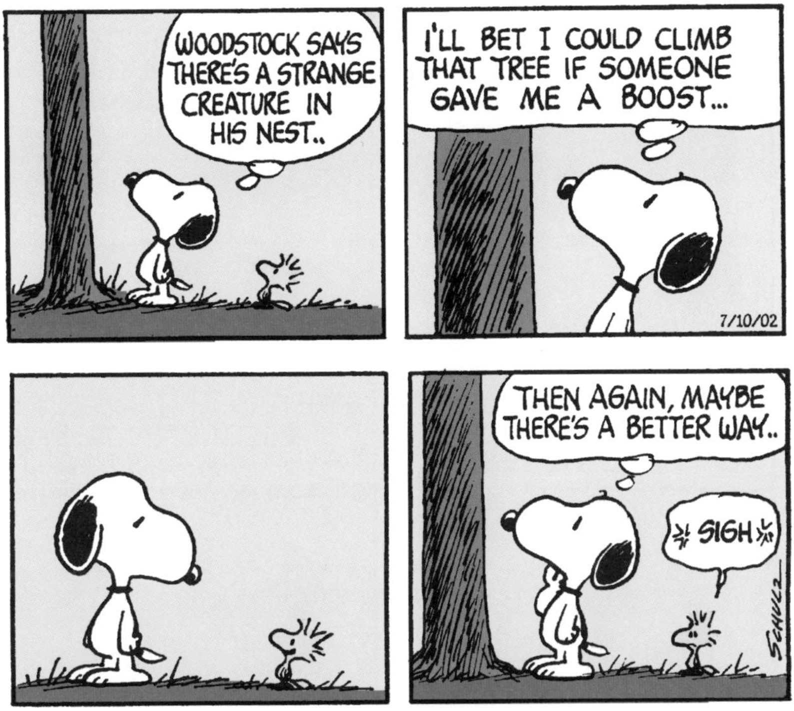
WOODSTOCK SAYS THERE'S A STRANGE CREATURE IN HIS NEST..
I'LL BET I COULD CLIMB THAT TREE IF SOMEONE GAVE ME A BOOST...
7/10/02
THEN AGAIN, MAYBE THERE'S A BETTER WAY..
SIGH
SCHULZ

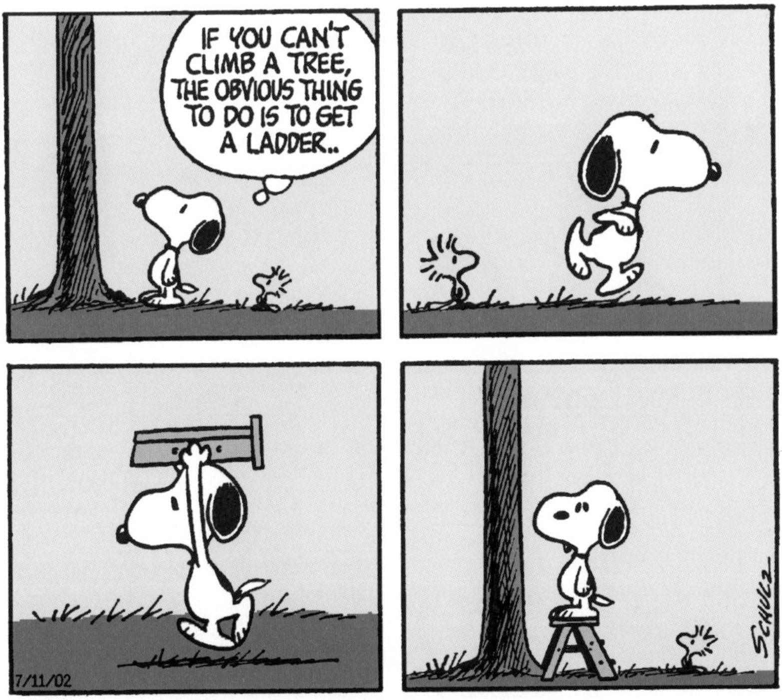
IF YOU CAN'T CLIMB A TREE, THE OBVIOUS THING TO DO IS TO GET A LADDER..
7/11/02
SCHULZ

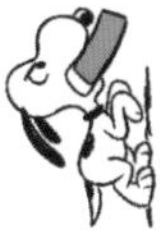

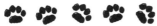

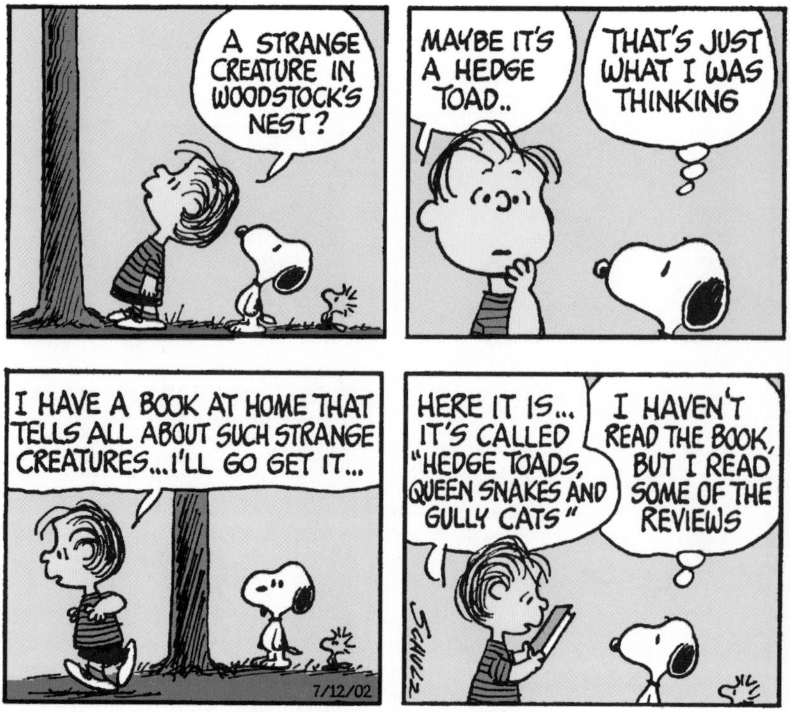
A STRANGE CREATURE IN WOODSTOCK'S NEST?
MAYBE IT'S A HEDGE TOAD..
THAT'S JUST WHAT I WAS THINKING
I HAVE A BOOK AT HOME THAT TELLS ALL ABOUT SUCH STRANGE CREATURES...I'LL GO GET IT...
HERE IT IS... IT'S CALLED "HEDGE TOADS, QUEEN SNAKES AND GULLY CATS"
I HAVEN'T READ THE BOOK, BUT I READ SOME OF THE REVIEWS
SCHULZ
7/12/02

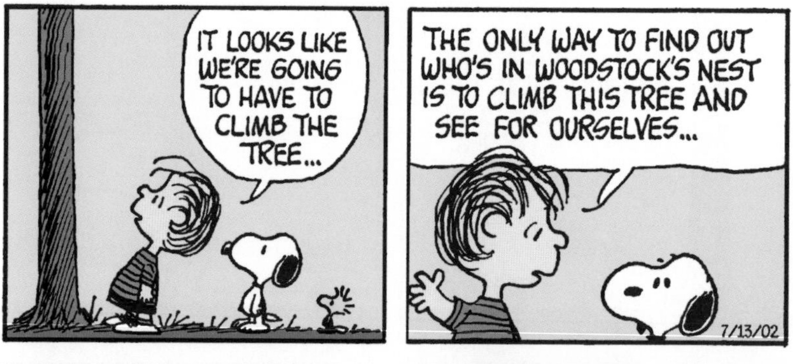
IT LOOKS LIKE WE'RE GOING TO HAVE TO CLIMB THE TREE...
THE ONLY WAY TO FIND OUT WHO'S IN WOODSTOCK'S NEST IS TO CLIMB THIS TREE AND SEE FOR OURSELVES...
7/13/02

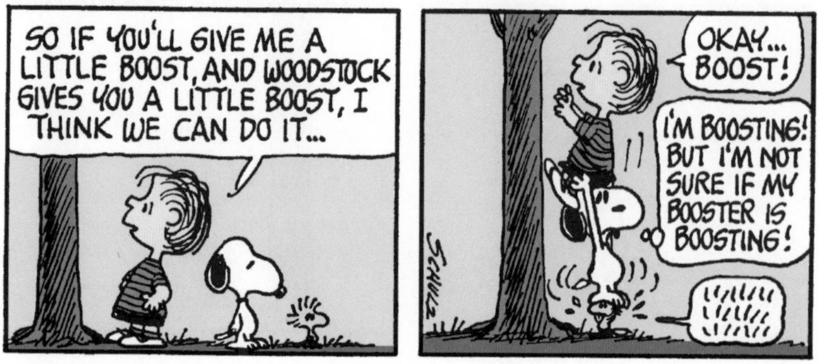
SO IF YOU'LL GIVE ME A LITTLE BOOST, AND WOODSTOCK GIVES YOU A LITTLE BOOST, I THINK WE CAN DO IT...
OKAY... BOOST!
I'M BOOSTING! BUT I'M NOT SURE IF MY BOOSTER IS BOOSTING!
SCHULZ

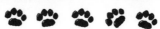

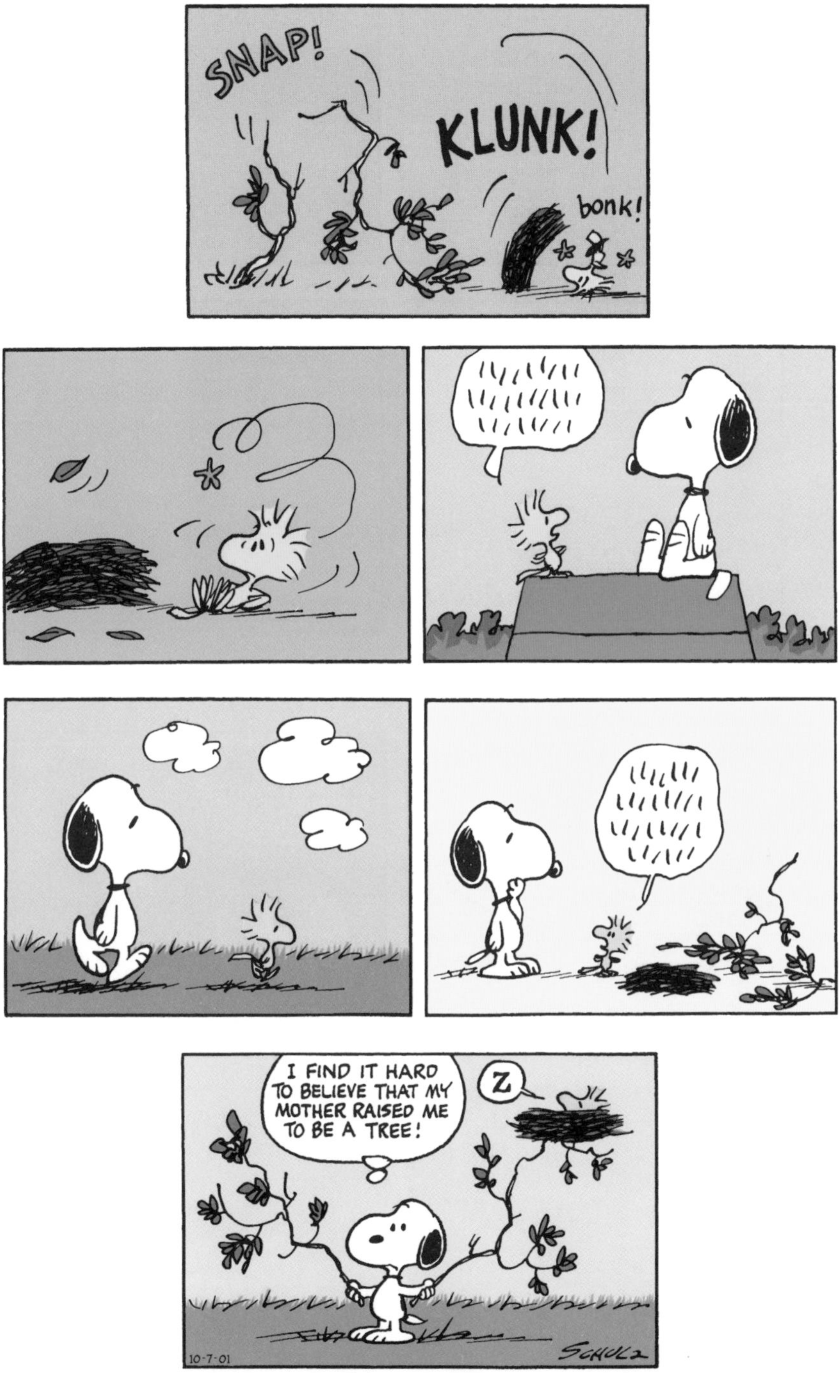
SNAP!
KLUNK!
bonk!
I FIND IT HARD TO BELIEVE THAT MY MOTHER RAISED ME TO BE A TREE!
Z
10-7-01
SCHULZ

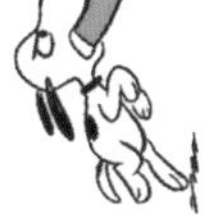

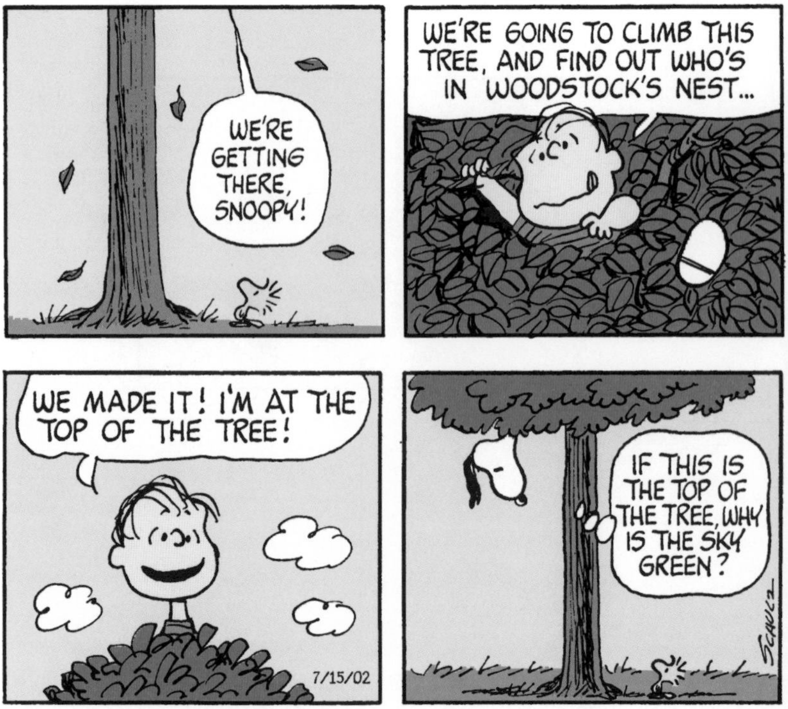
WE'RE GETTING THERE, SNOOPY!
WE'RE GOING TO CLIMB THIS TREE, AND FIND OUT WHO'S IN WOODSTOCK'S NEST...
WE MADE IT! I'M AT THE TOP OF THE TREE!
7/15/02
IF THIS IS THE TOP OF THE TREE, WHY IS THE SKY GREEN?
SCHULZ

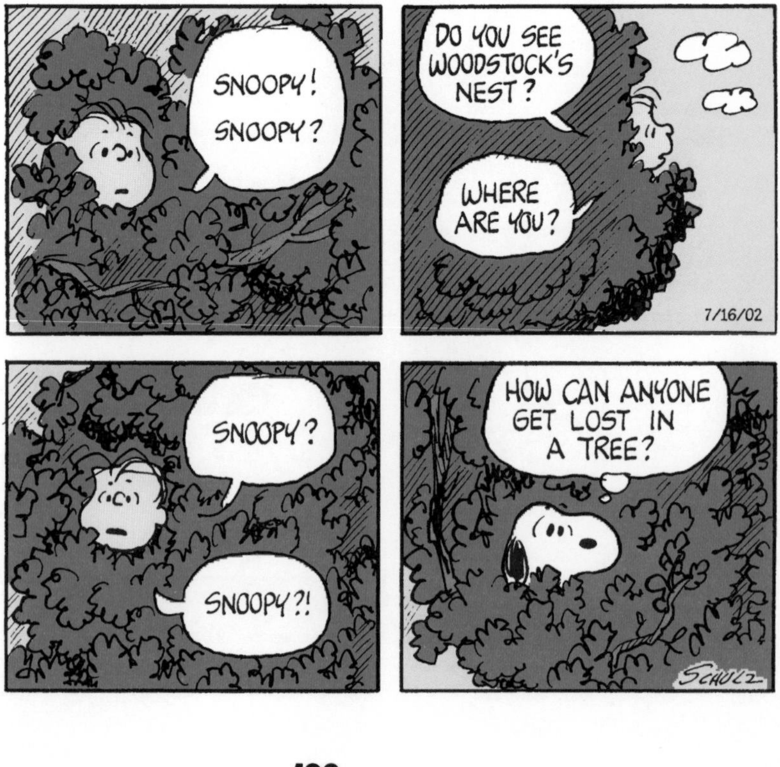
SNOOPY!
SNOOPY?
DO YOU SEE WOODSTOCK'S NEST?
WHERE ARE YOU?
7/16/02
SNOOPY?
SNOOPY?!
HOW CAN ANYONE GET LOST IN A TREE?
SCHULZ

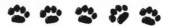

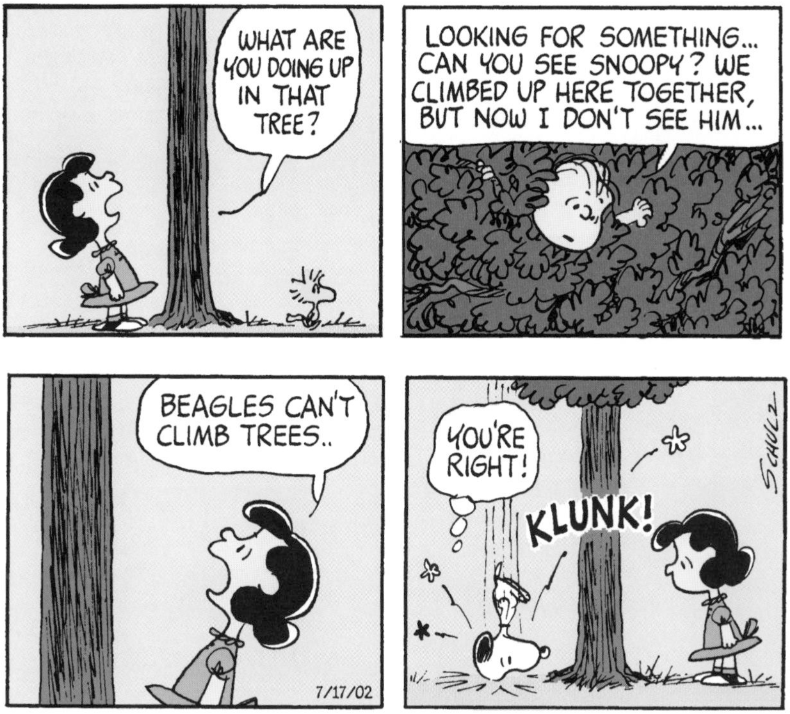
WHAT ARE YOU DOING UP IN THAT TREE?
LOOKING FOR SOMETHING... CAN YOU SEE SNOOPY? WE CLIMBED UP HERE TOGETHER, BUT NOW I DON'T SEE HIM...
BEAGLES CAN'T CLIMB TREES..
7/17/02
YOU'RE RIGHT!
KLUNK!
SCHULZ

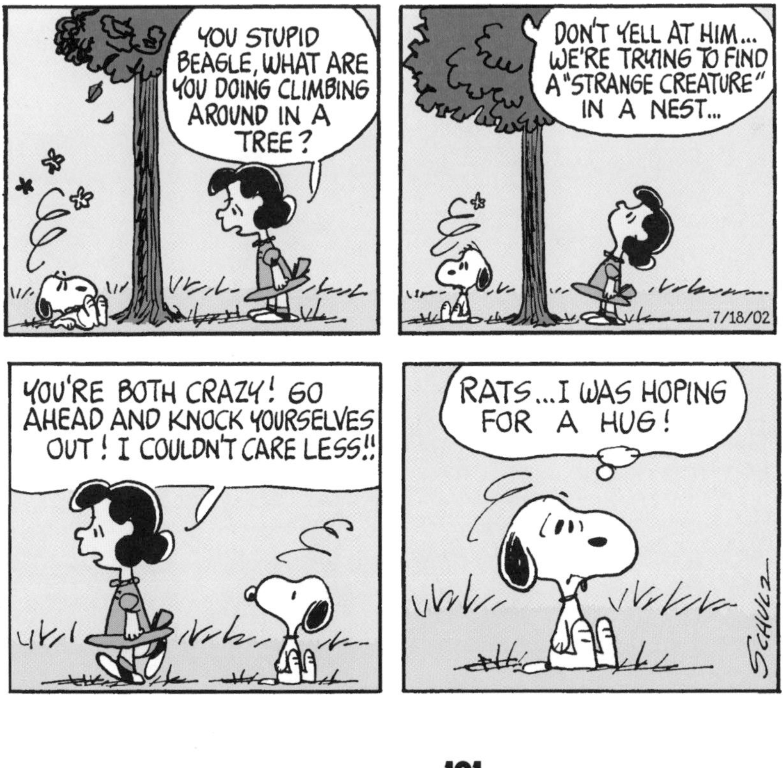
YOU STUPID BEAGLE, WHAT ARE YOU DOING CLIMBING AROUND IN A TREE?
DON'T YELL AT HIM... WE'RE TRYING TO FIND A "STRANGE CREATURE" IN A NEST...
7/18/02
YOU'RE BOTH CRAZY! GO AHEAD AND KNOCK YOURSELVES OUT! I COULDN'T CARE LESS!!
RATS...I WAS HOPING FOR A HUG!
SCHULZ

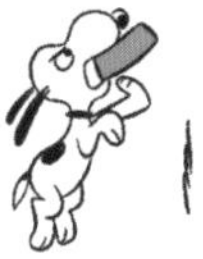

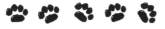

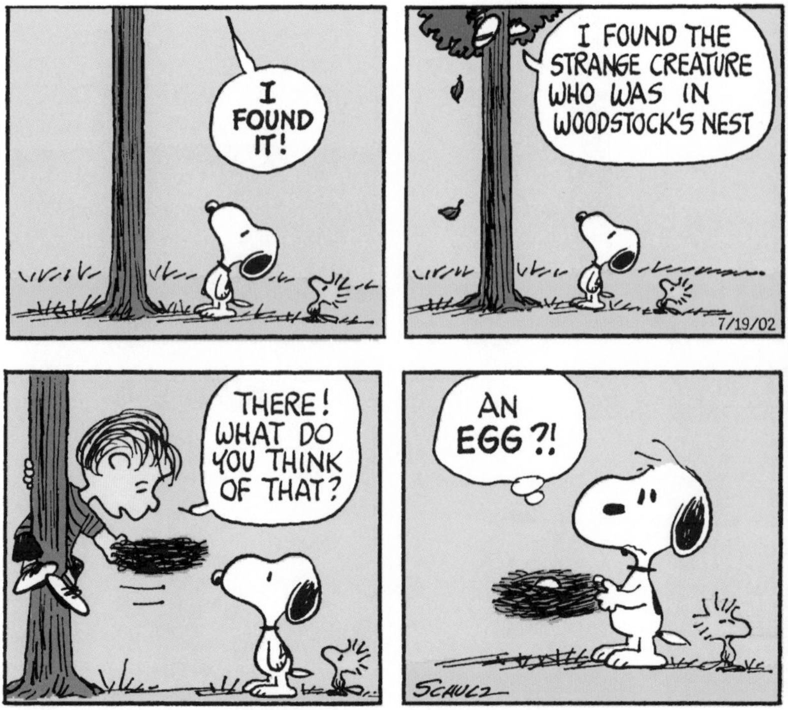
I FOUND IT!
I FOUND THE STRANGE CREATURE WHO WAS IN WOODSTOCK'S NEST
7/19/02
THERE! WHAT DO YOU THINK OF THAT?
AN EGG?!
SCHULZ

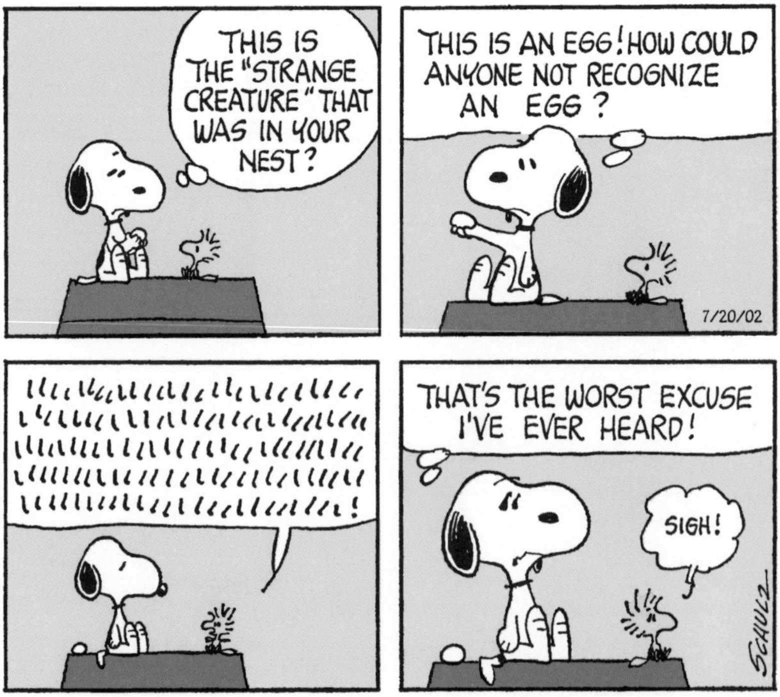
THIS IS THE "STRANGE CREATURE" THAT WAS IN YOUR NEST?
THIS IS AN EGG! HOW COULD ANYONE NOT RECOGNIZE AN EGG?
7/20/02
THAT'S THE WORST EXCUSE I'VE EVER HEARD!
SIGH!
SCHULZ

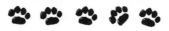

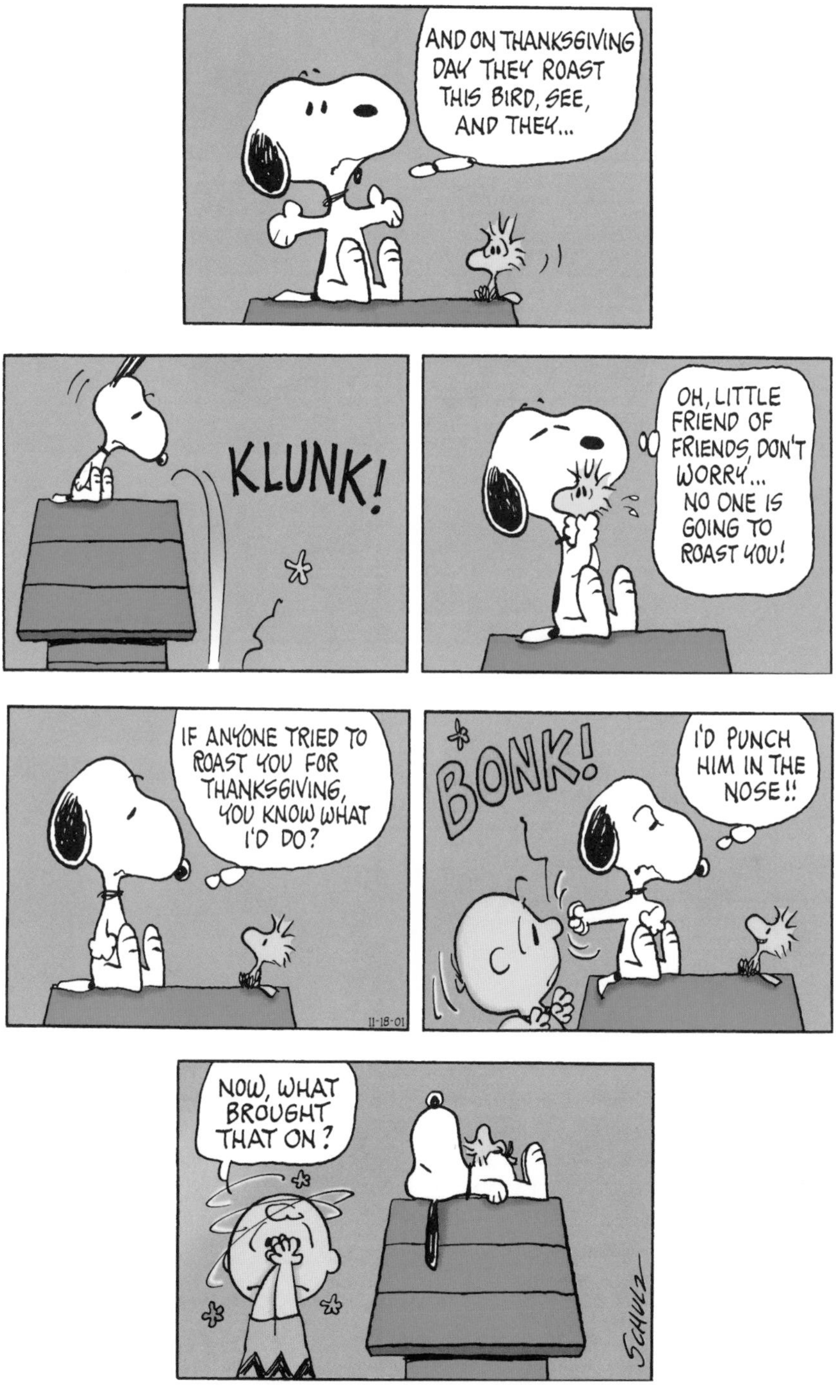
AND ON THANKSGIVING DAY THEY ROAST THIS BIRD, SEE, AND THEY...
KLUNK!
OH, LITTLE FRIEND OF FRIENDS, DON'T WORRY... NO ONE IS GOING TO ROAST YOU!
IF ANYONE TRIED TO ROAST YOU FOR THANKSGIVING, YOU KNOW WHAT I'D DO?
11-18-01
BONK!
I'D PUNCH HIM IN THE NOSE!!
NOW, WHAT BROUGHT THAT ON?
SCHULZ

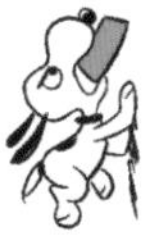

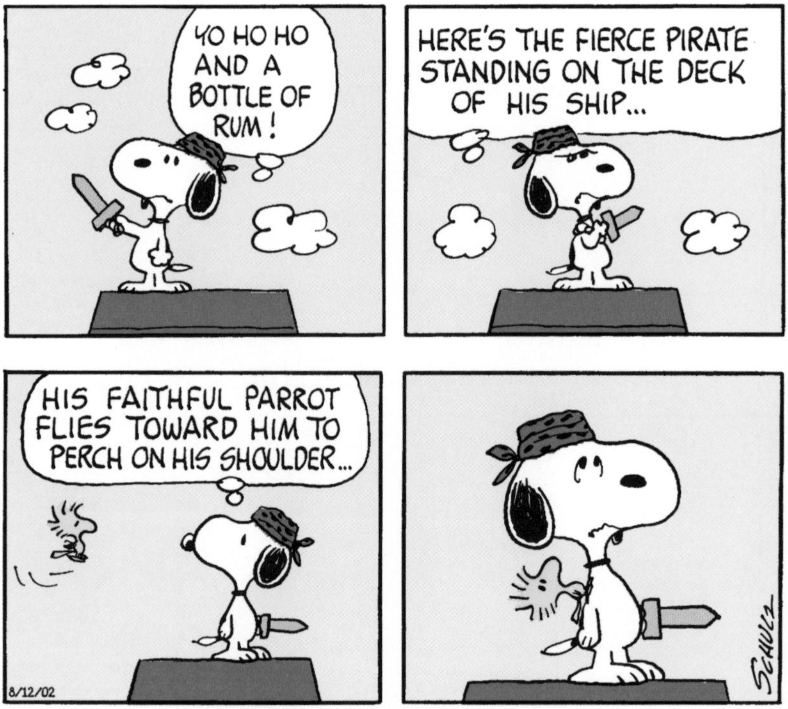
YO HO HO AND A BOTTLE OF RUM!
HERE'S THE FIERCE PIRATE STANDING ON THE DECK OF HIS SHIP...
HIS FAITHFUL PARROT FLIES TOWARD HIM TO PERCH ON HIS SHOULDER...
8/12/02
SCHULZ

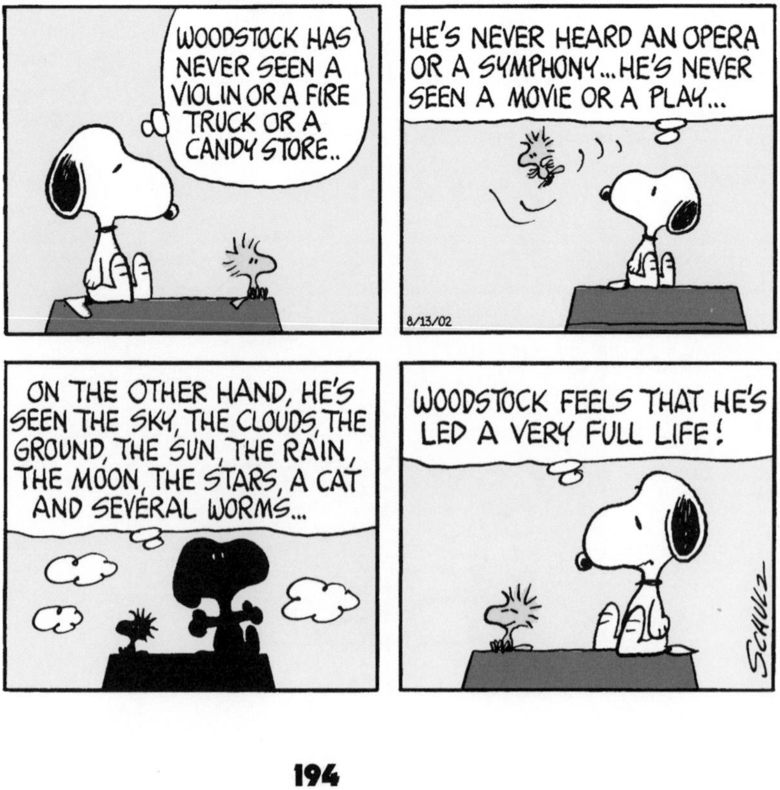
WOODSTOCK HAS NEVER SEEN A VIOLIN OR A FIRE TRUCK OR A CANDY STORE..
HE'S NEVER HEARD AN OPERA OR A SYMPHONY...HE'S NEVER SEEN A MOVIE OR A PLAY...
8/13/02
ON THE OTHER HAND, HE'S SEEN THE SKY, THE CLOUDS, THE GROUND, THE SUN, THE RAIN, THE MOON, THE STARS, A CAT AND SEVERAL WORMS...
WOODSTOCK FEELS THAT HE'S LED A VERY FULL LIFE!
SCHULZ

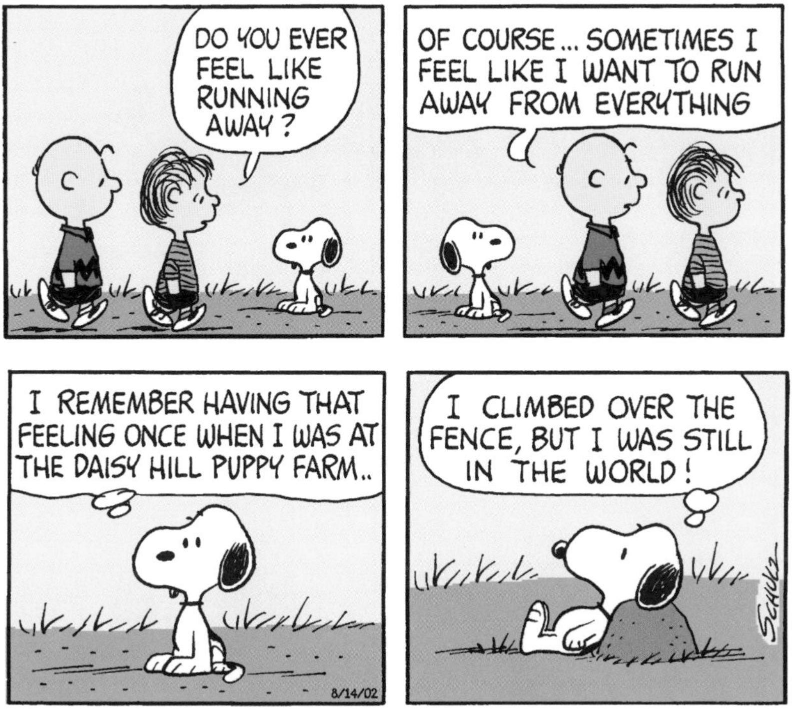
DO YOU EVER FEEL LIKE RUNNING AWAY?
OF COURSE... SOMETIMES I FEEL LIKE I WANT TO RUN AWAY FROM EVERYTHING
I REMEMBER HAVING THAT FEELING ONCE WHEN I WAS AT THE DAISY HILL PUPPY FARM..
I CLIMBED OVER THE FENCE, BUT I WAS STILL IN THE WORLD!

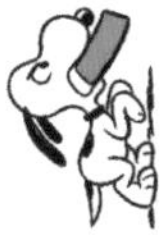

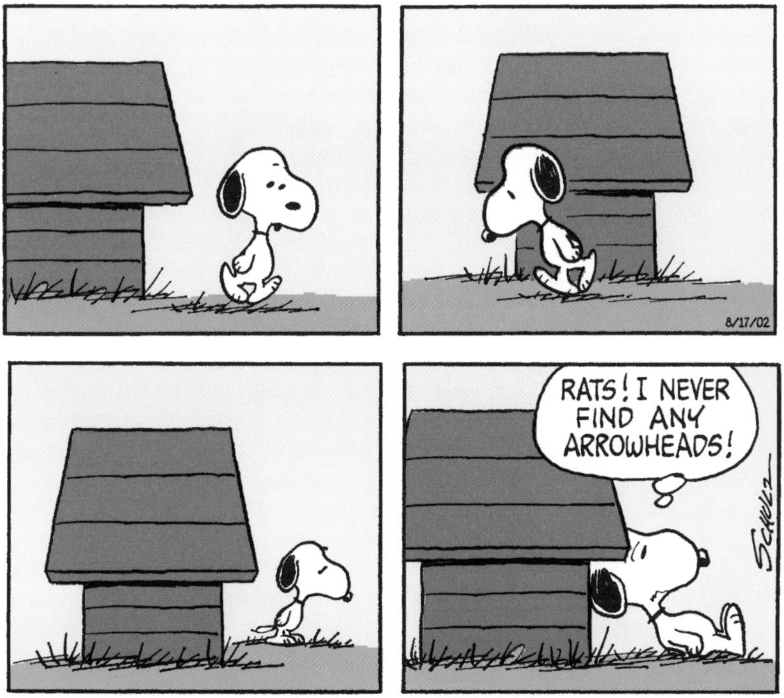
RATS! I NEVER FIND ANY ARROWHEADS!

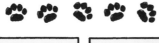

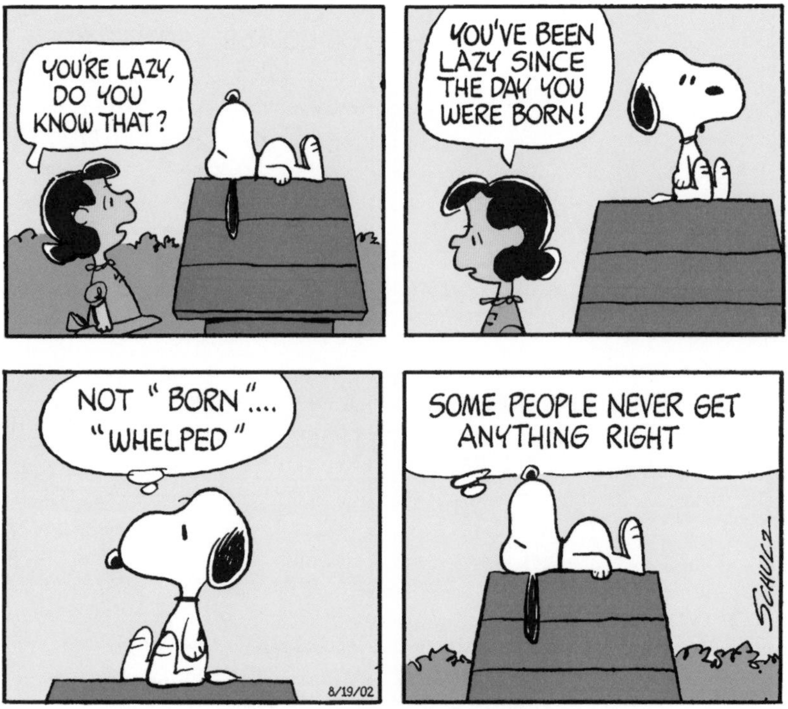
YOU'RE LAZY, DO YOU KNOW THAT?
YOU'VE BEEN LAZY SINCE THE DAY YOU WERE BORN!
NOT "BORN".... "WHELPED"
8/19/02
SOME PEOPLE NEVER GET ANYTHING RIGHT
SCHULZ

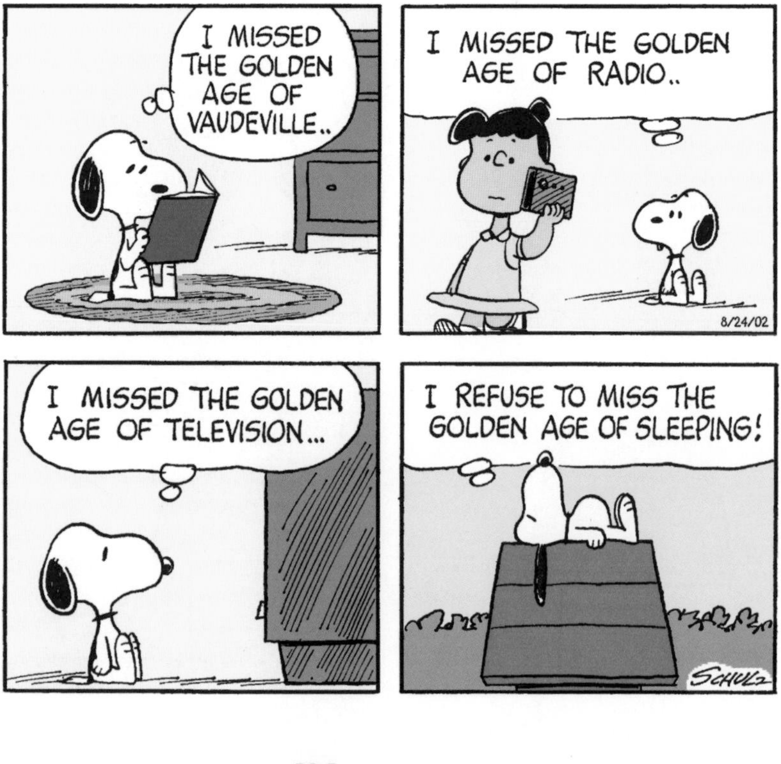
I MISSED THE GOLDEN AGE OF VAUDEVILLE..
I MISSED THE GOLDEN AGE OF RADIO..
8/24/02
I MISSED THE GOLDEN AGE OF TELEVISION...
I REFUSE TO MISS THE GOLDEN AGE OF SLEEPING!
SCHULZ

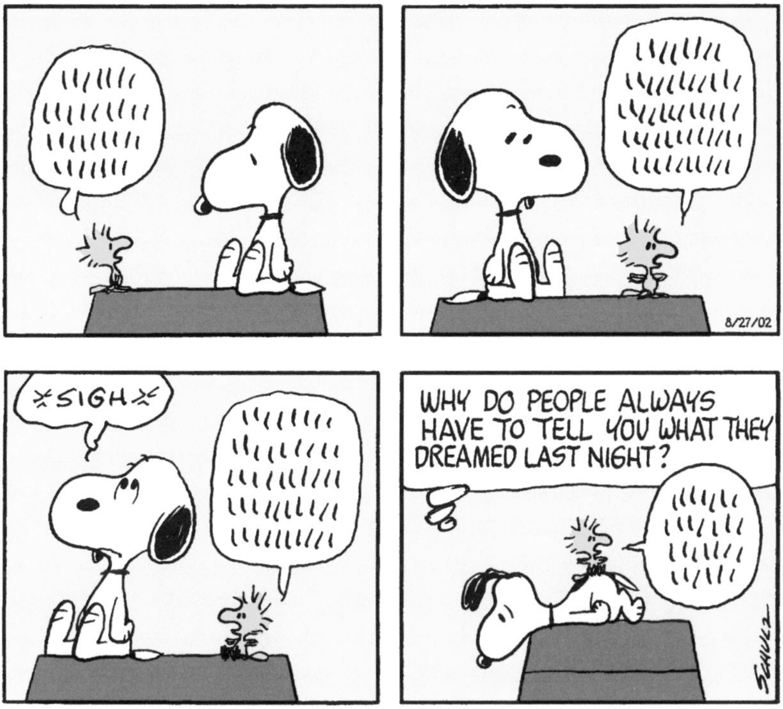
8/27/02
SIGH
WHY DO PEOPLE ALWAYS HAVE TO TELL YOU WHAT THEY DREAMED LAST NIGHT?
SCHULZ

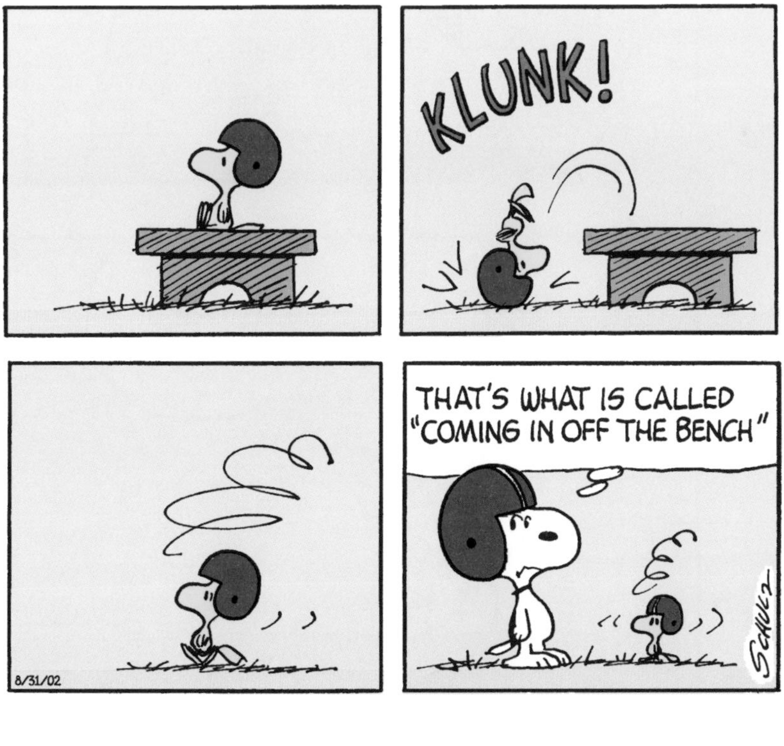
KLUNK!
8/31/02
THAT'S WHAT IS CALLED "COMING IN OFF THE BENCH"
SCHULZ

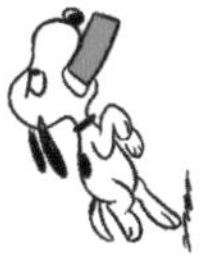

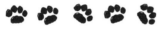

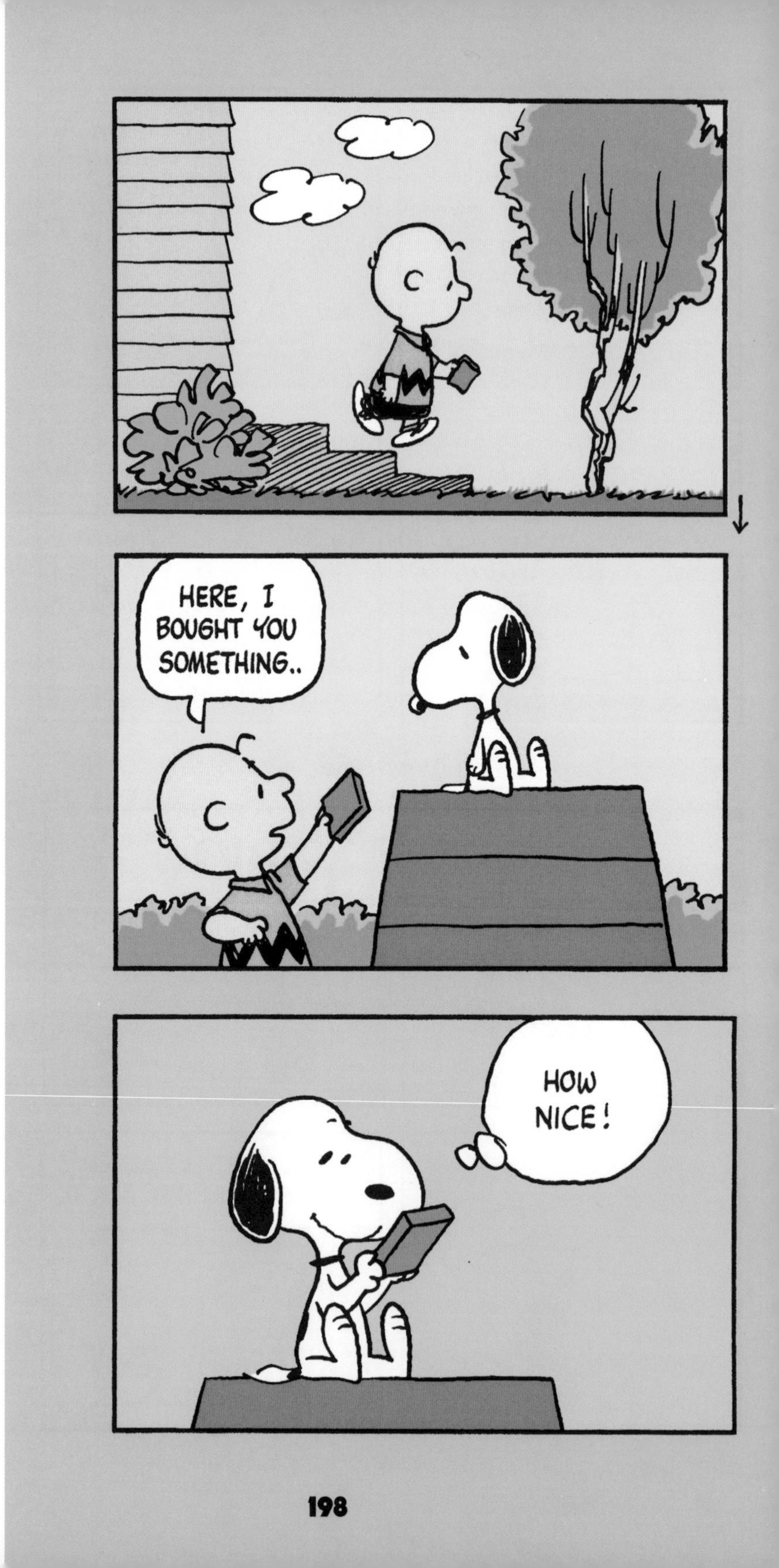
HERE, I BOUGHT YOU SOMETHING..
HOW NICE!

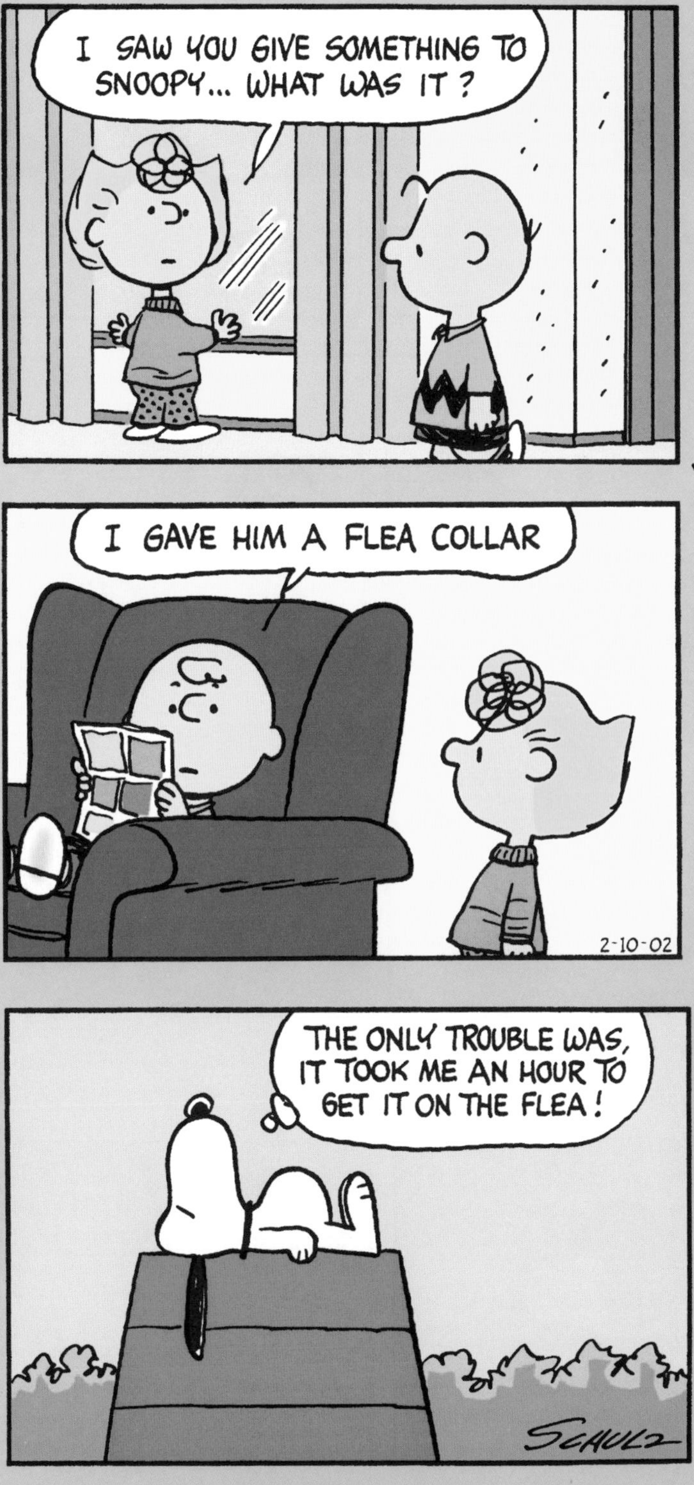
I SAW YOU GIVE SOMETHING TO SNOOPY... WHAT WAS IT ?
I GAVE HIM A FLEA COLLAR
2-10-02
THE ONLY TROUBLE WAS, IT TOOK ME AN HOUR TO GET IT ON THE FLEA !
SCHULZ

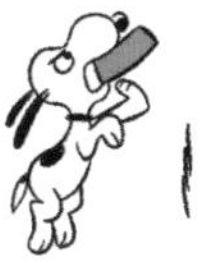

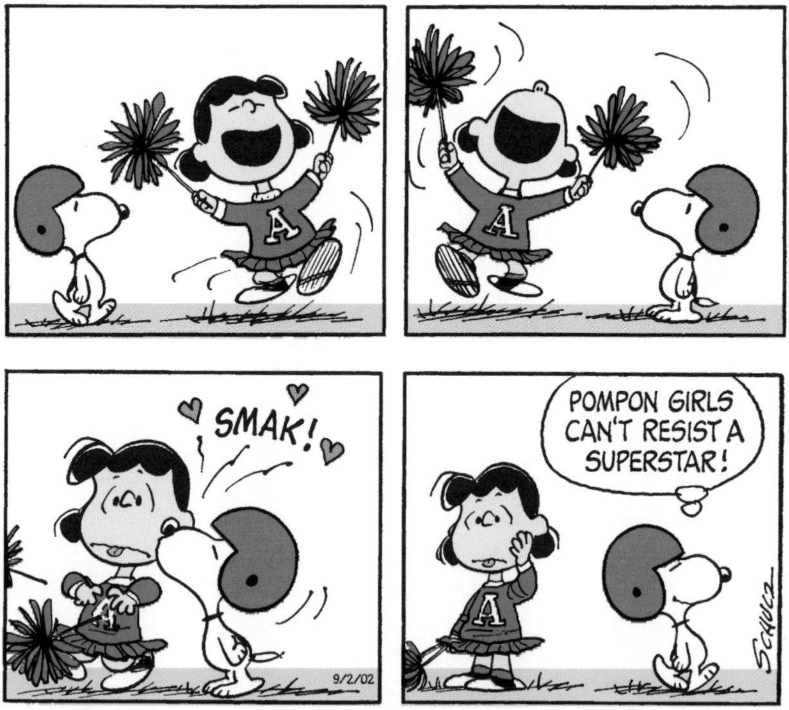
SMAK!
POMPON GIRLS CAN'T RESIST A SUPERSTAR!
9/2/02
SCHULZ

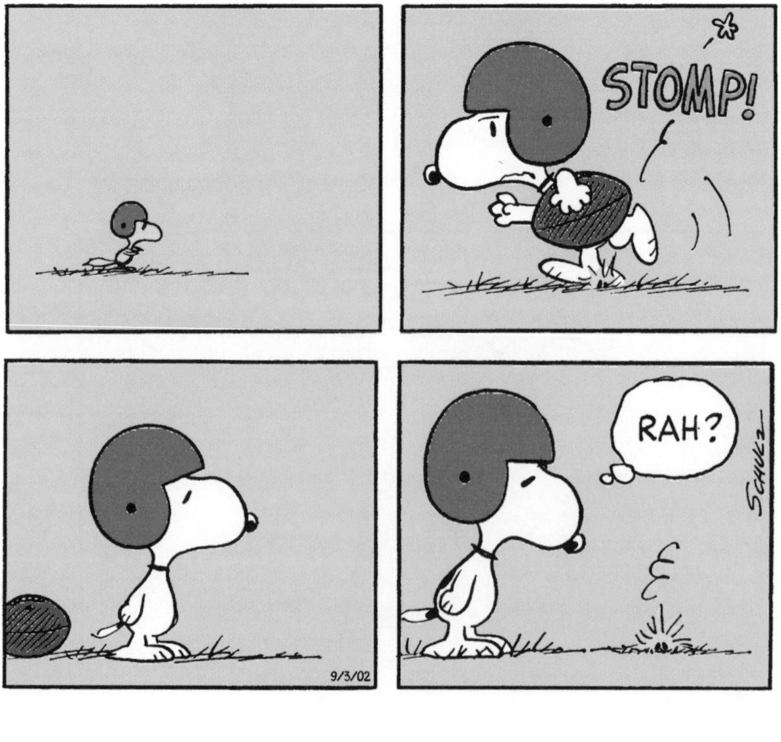
STOMP!
9/3/02
RAH?
SCHULZ

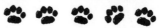

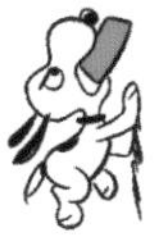

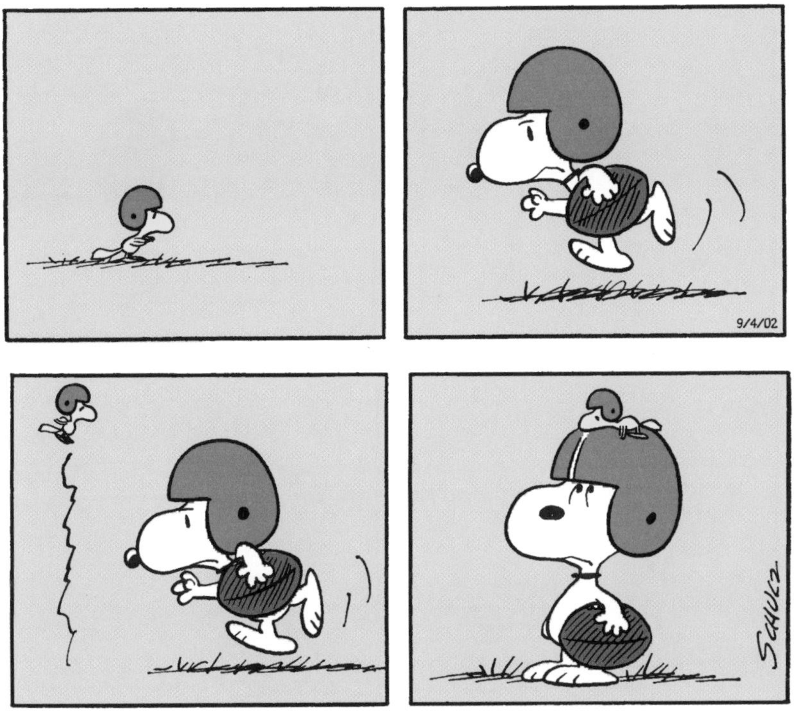
9/4/02
SCHULZ

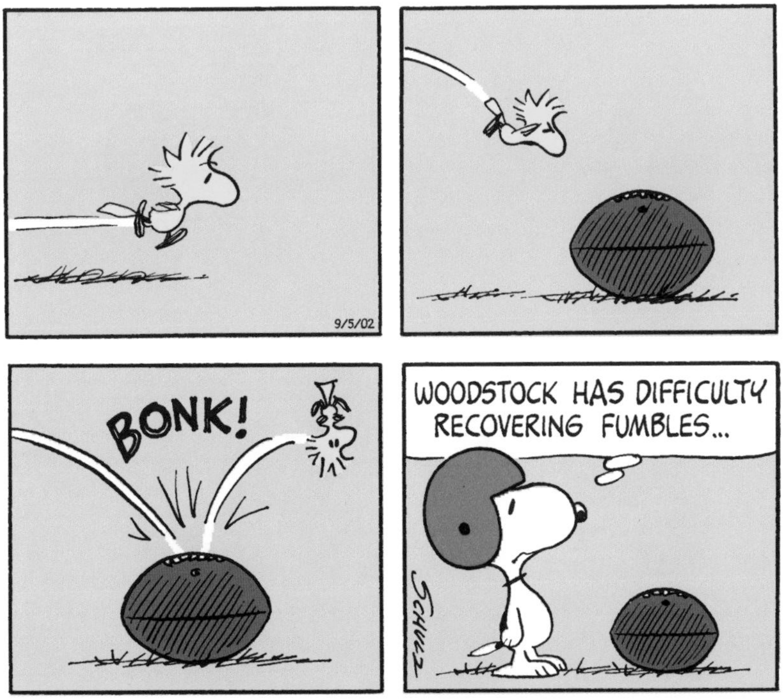
9/5/02
BONK!
WOODSTOCK HAS DIFFICULTY RECOVERING FUMBLES...
SCHULZ

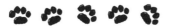

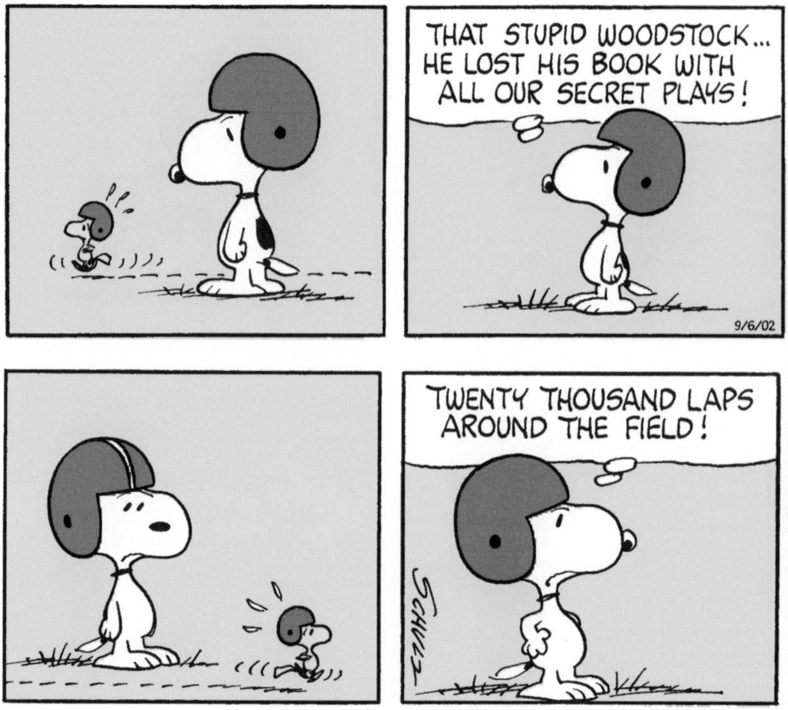
THAT STUPID WOODSTOCK... HE LOST HIS BOOK WITH ALL OUR SECRET PLAYS!
9/6/02
TWENTY THOUSAND LAPS AROUND THE FIELD!
SCHULZ

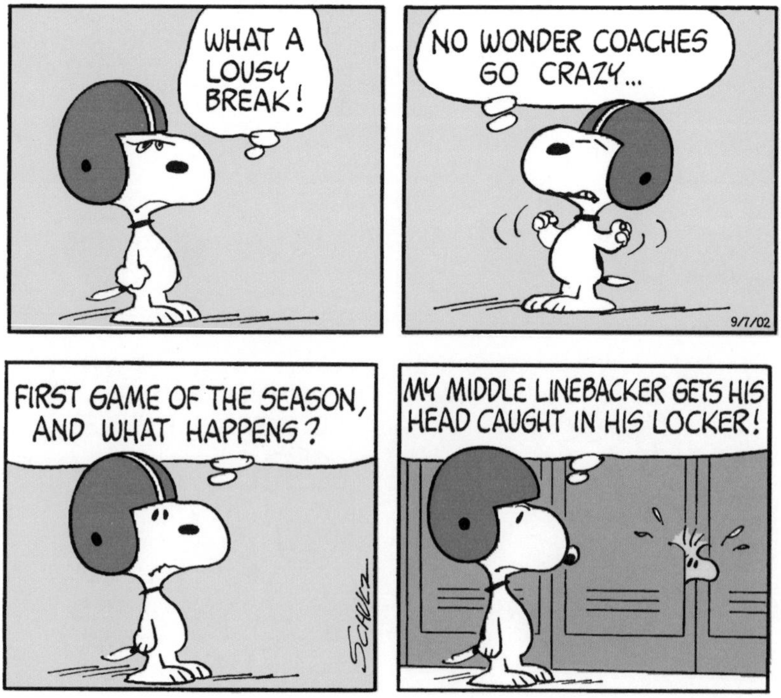
WHAT A LOUSY BREAK!
NO WONDER COACHES GO CRAZY...
9/7/02
FIRST GAME OF THE SEASON, AND WHAT HAPPENS?
SCHULZ
MY MIDDLE LINEBACKER GETS HIS HEAD CAUGHT IN HIS LOCKER!

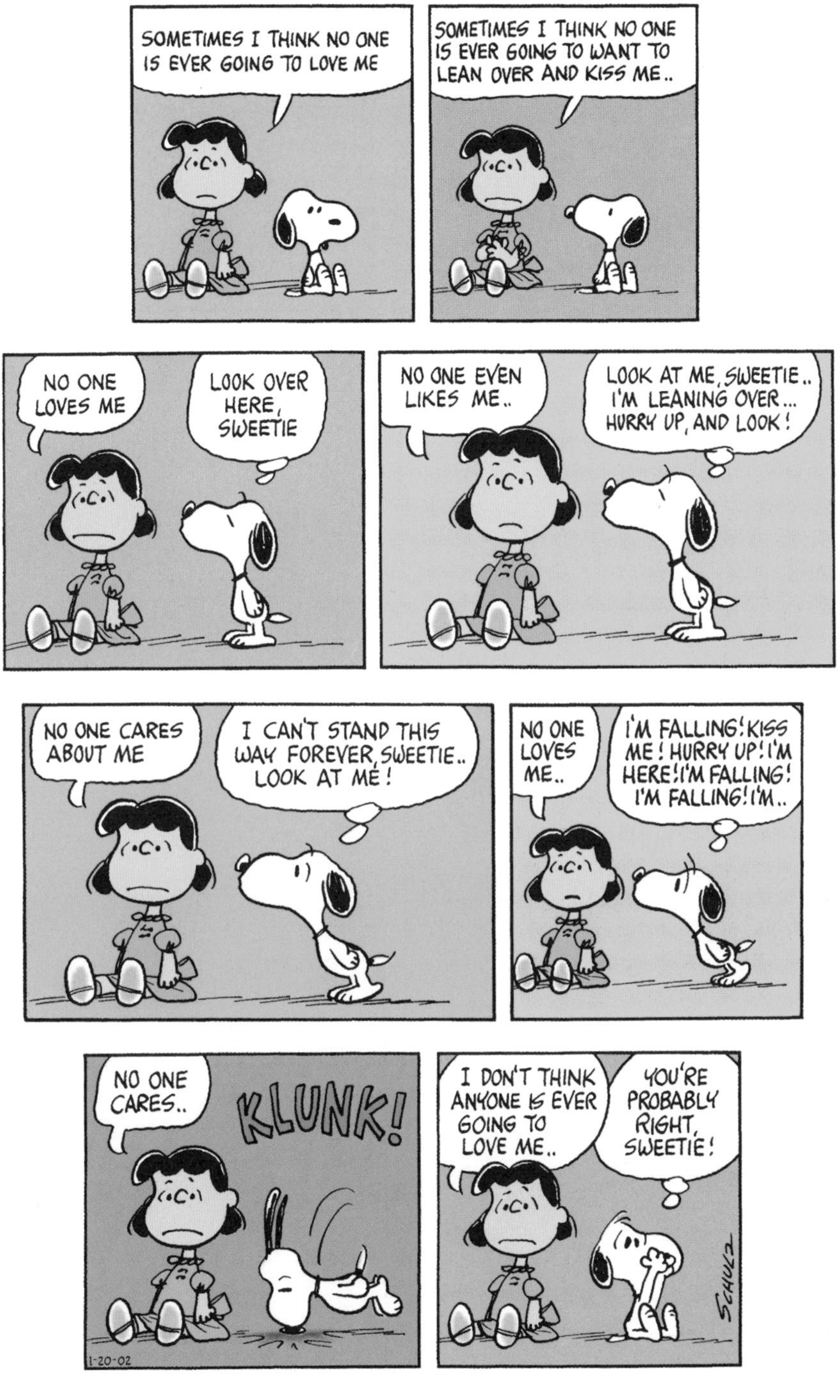
SOMETIMES I THINK NO ONE IS EVER GOING TO LOVE ME
SOMETIMES I THINK NO ONE IS EVER GOING TO WANT TO LEAN OVER AND KISS ME..
NO ONE LOVES ME
LOOK OVER HERE, SWEETIE
NO ONE EVEN LIKES ME..
LOOK AT ME, SWEETIE.. I'M LEANING OVER... HURRY UP, AND LOOK!
NO ONE CARES ABOUT ME
I CAN'T STAND THIS WAY FOREVER, SWEETIE.. LOOK AT ME!
NO ONE LOVES ME..
I'M FALLING! KISS ME! HURRY UP! I'M HERE! I'M FALLING! I'M FALLING! I'M..
NO ONE CARES..
KLUNK!
1-20-02
I DON'T THINK ANYONE IS EVER GOING TO LOVE ME..
YOU'RE PROBABLY RIGHT, SWEETIE!
SCHULZ

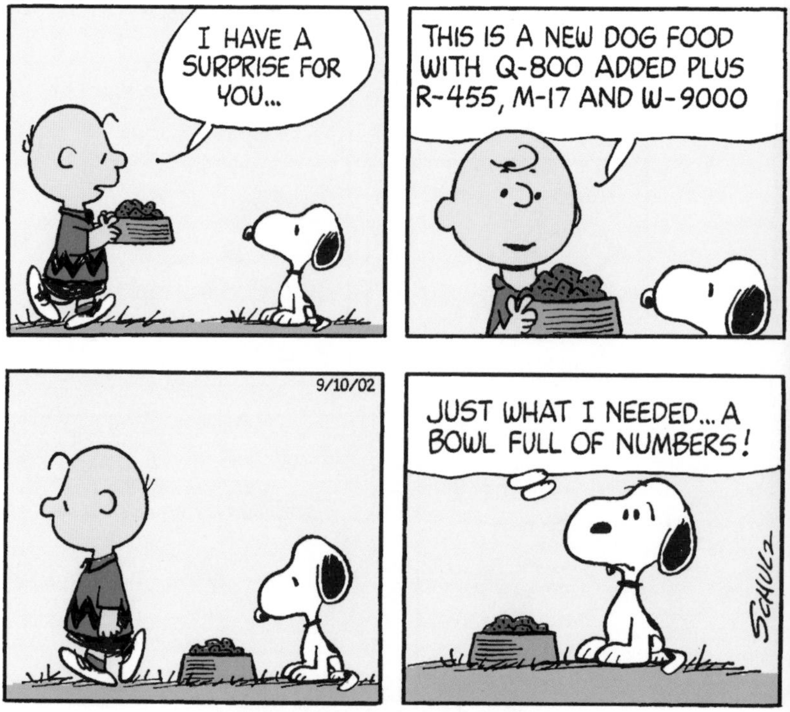
I HAVE A SURPRISE FOR YOU...
THIS IS A NEW DOG FOOD WITH Q-800 ADDED PLUS R-455, M-17 AND W-9000
9/10/02
JUST WHAT I NEEDED... A BOWL FULL OF NUMBERS!
SCHULZ

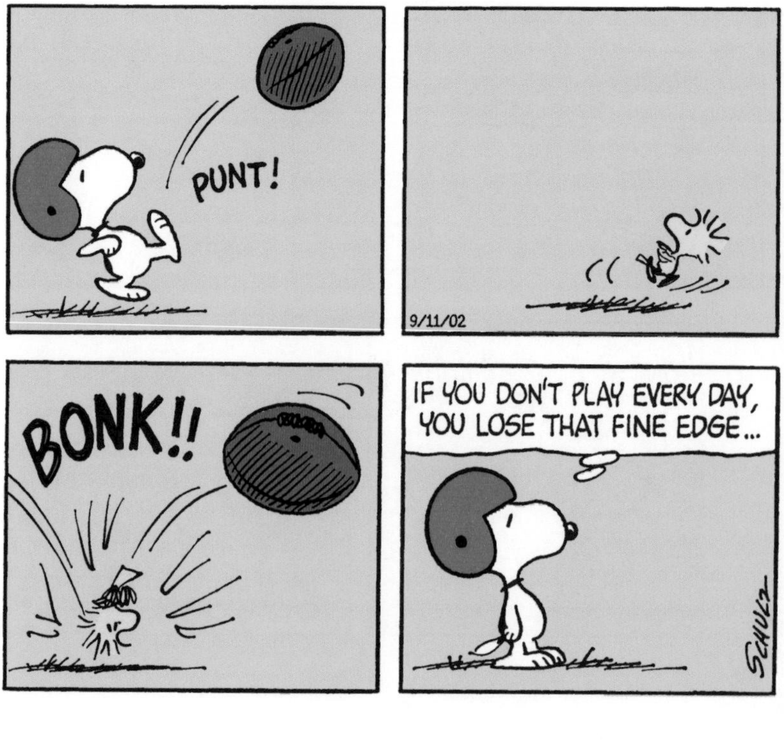
PUNT!
9/11/02
BONK!!
IF YOU DON'T PLAY EVERY DAY, YOU LOSE THAT FINE EDGE...
SCHULZ

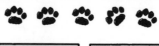

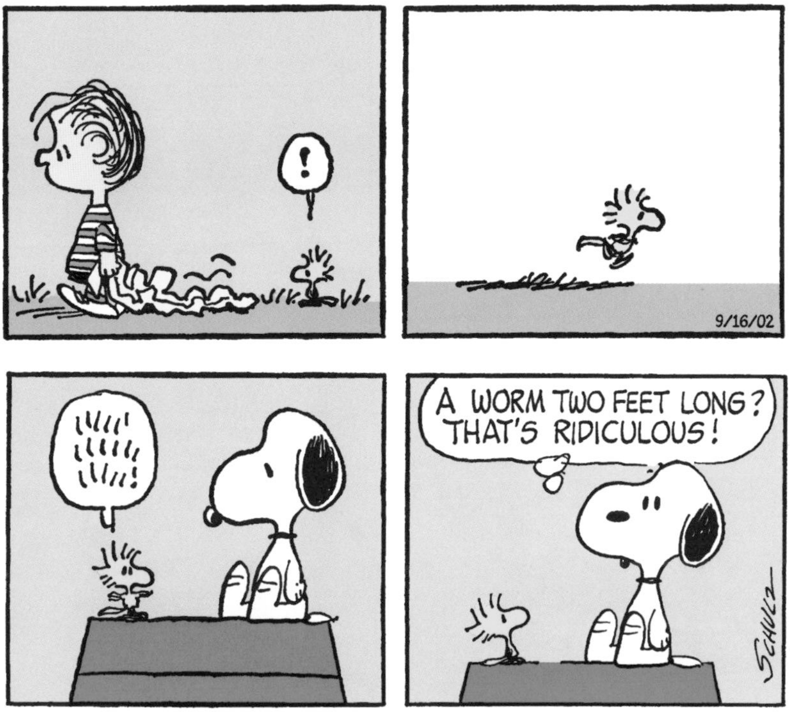
!
9/16/02
A WORM TWO FEET LONG? THAT'S RIDICULOUS!
SCHULZ

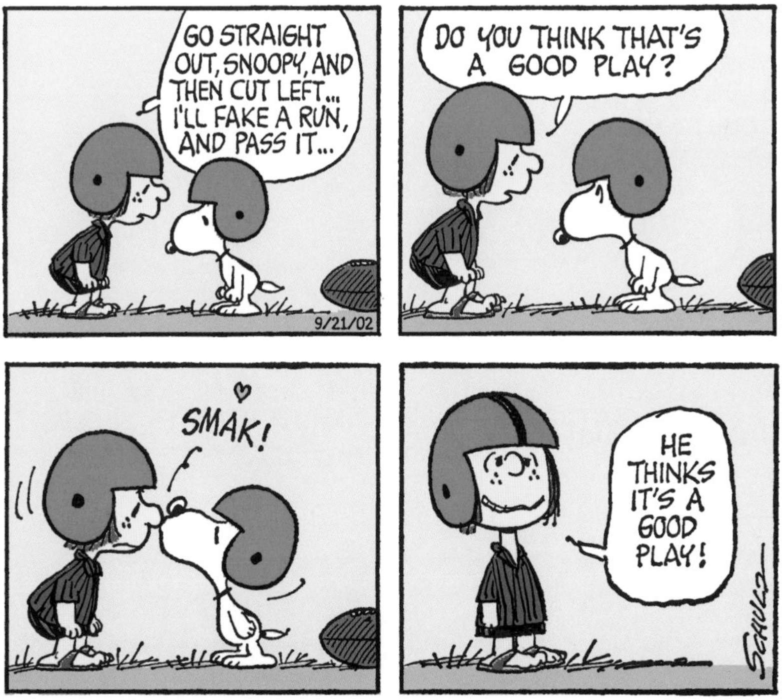
GO STRAIGHT OUT, SNOOPY, AND THEN CUT LEFT... I'LL FAKE A RUN, AND PASS IT...
9/21/02
DO YOU THINK THAT'S A GOOD PLAY?
SMAK!
HE THINKS IT'S A GOOD PLAY!
SCHULZ

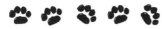

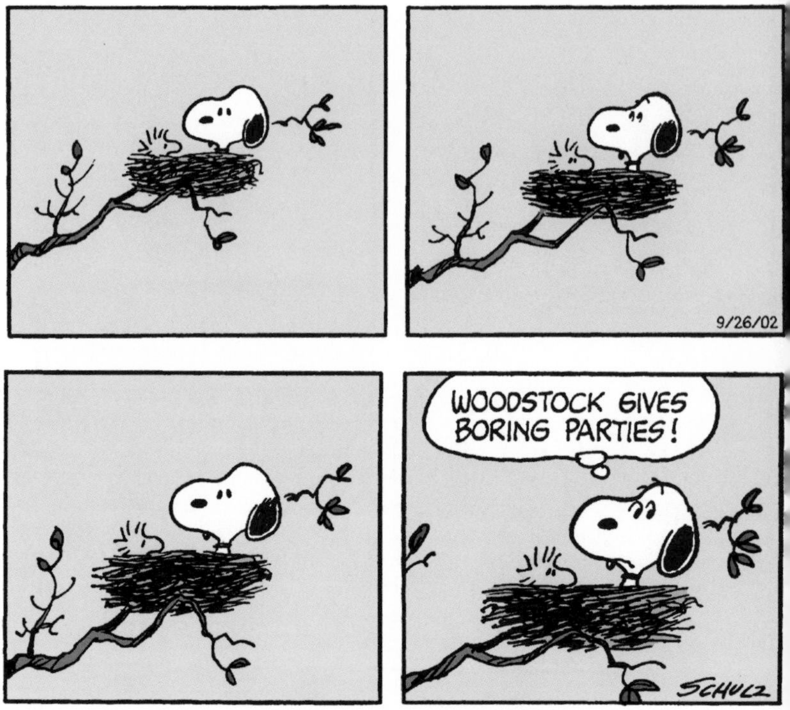
9/26/02
WOODSTOCK GIVES BORING PARTIES!
SCHULZ

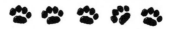

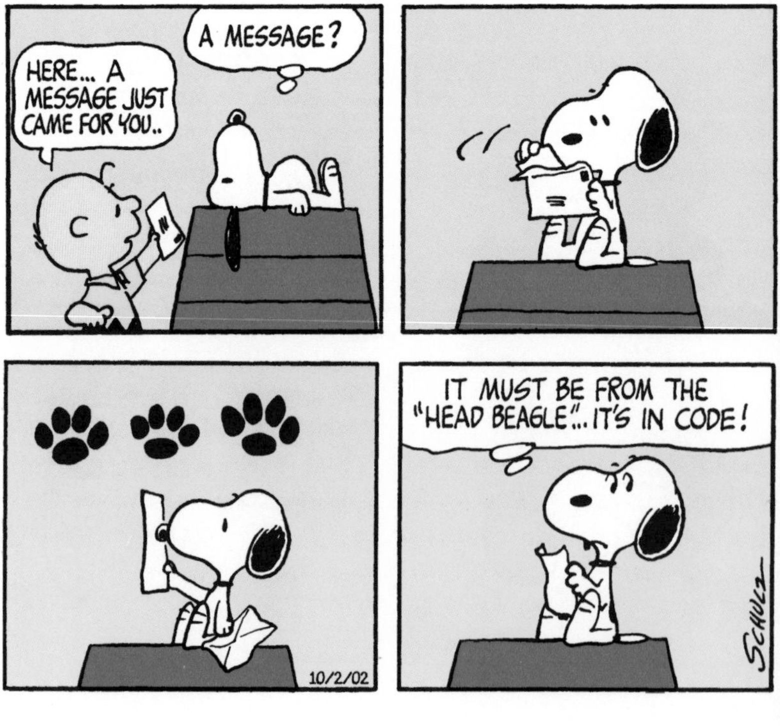
HERE... A MESSAGE JUST CAME FOR YOU..
A MESSAGE?
10/2/02
IT MUST BE FROM THE "HEAD BEAGLE"... IT'S IN CODE!
SCHULZ

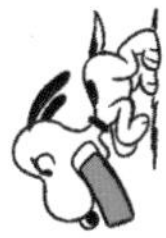

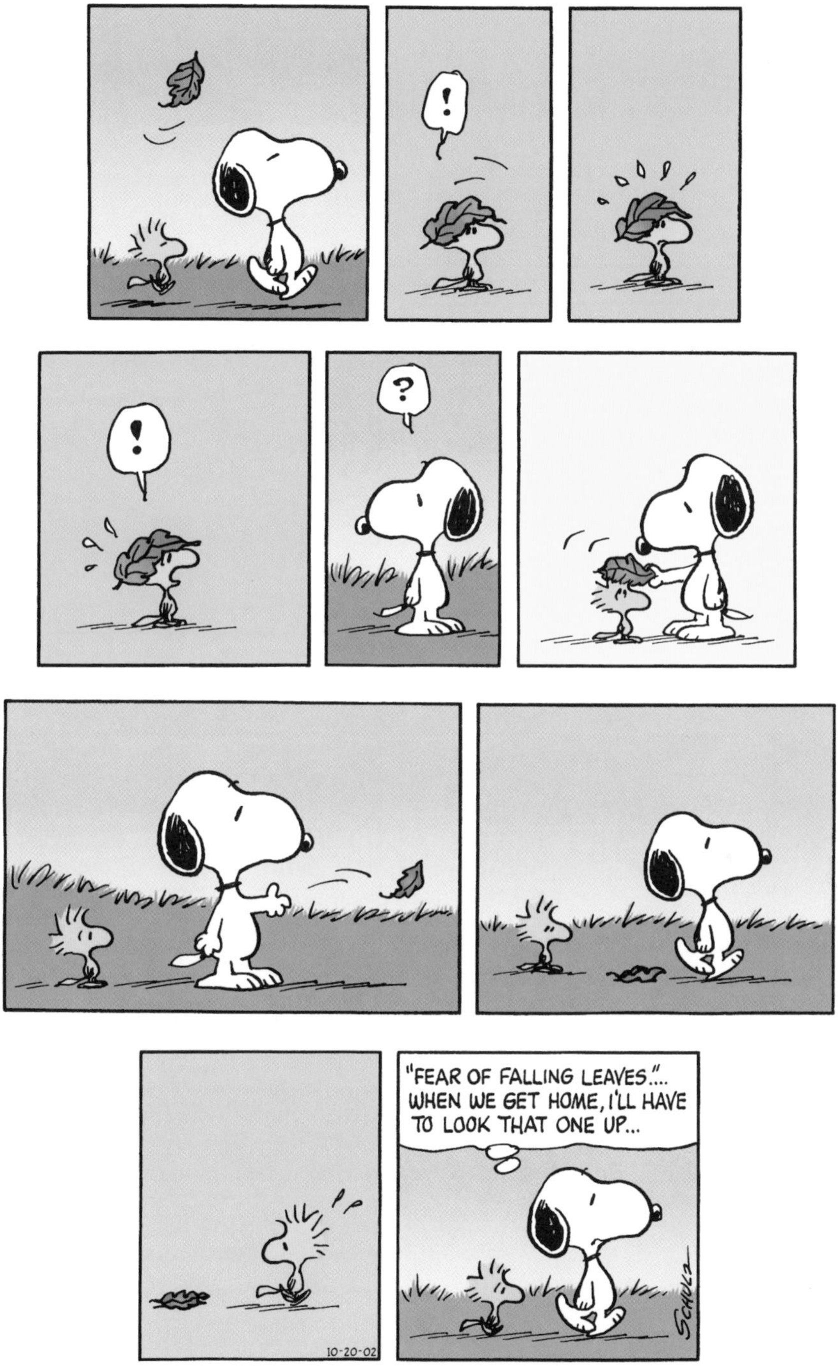
!
!
?
10-20-02
"FEAR OF FALLING LEAVES."... WHEN WE GET HOME, I'LL HAVE TO LOOK THAT ONE UP...
SCHULZ

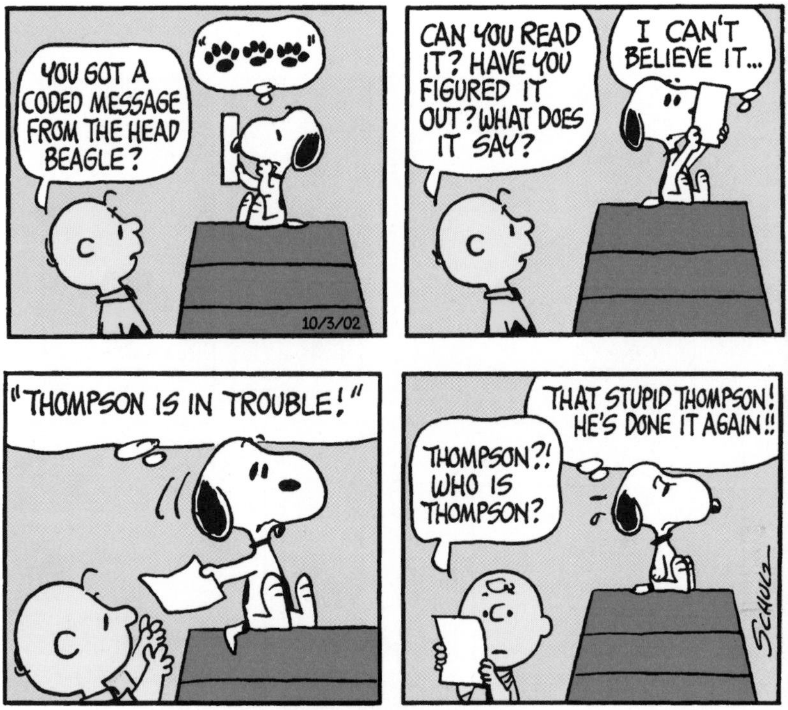
YOU GOT A CODED MESSAGE FROM THE HEAD BEAGLE?
10/3/02
CAN YOU READ IT? HAVE YOU FIGURED IT OUT? WHAT DOES IT SAY?
I CAN'T BELIEVE IT...
"THOMPSON IS IN TROUBLE!"
THAT STUPID THOMPSON! HE'S DONE IT AGAIN!!
THOMPSON?! WHO IS THOMPSON?
SCHULZ

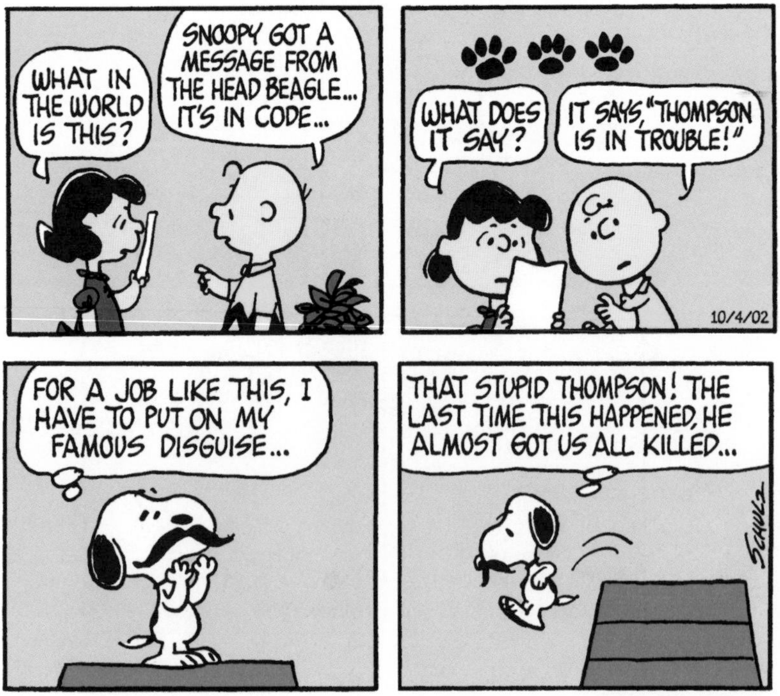
WHAT IN THE WORLD IS THIS?
SNOOPY GOT A MESSAGE FROM THE HEAD BEAGLE... IT'S IN CODE...
WHAT DOES IT SAY?
IT SAYS, "THOMPSON IS IN TROUBLE!"
10/4/02
FOR A JOB LIKE THIS, I HAVE TO PUT ON MY FAMOUS DISGUISE...
THAT STUPID THOMPSON! THE LAST TIME THIS HAPPENED, HE ALMOST GOT US ALL KILLED...
SCHULZ

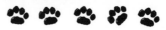

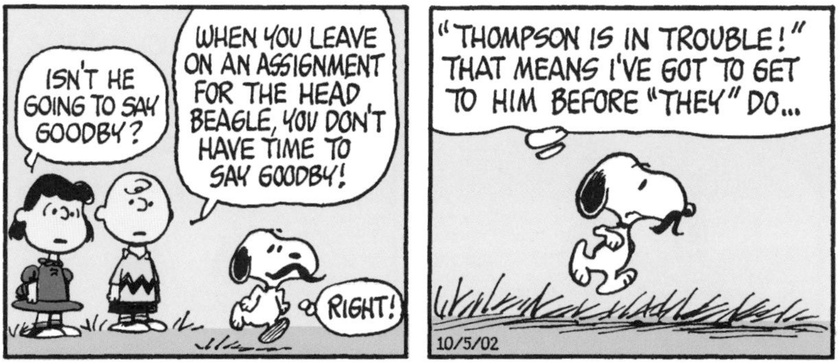
ISN'T HE GOING TO SAY GOODBY?
WHEN YOU LEAVE ON AN ASSIGNMENT FOR THE HEAD BEAGLE, YOU DON'T HAVE TIME TO SAY GOODBY!
RIGHT!
"THOMPSON IS IN TROUBLE!" THAT MEANS I'VE GOT TO GET TO HIM BEFORE "THEY" DO...
10/5/02

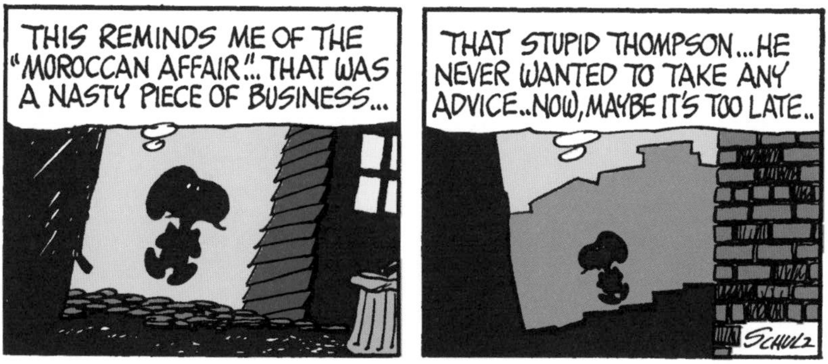
THIS REMINDS ME OF THE "MOROCCAN AFFAIR"... THAT WAS A NASTY PIECE OF BUSINESS...
THAT STUPID THOMPSON... HE NEVER WANTED TO TAKE ANY ADVICE.. NOW, MAYBE IT'S TOO LATE..
SCHULZ

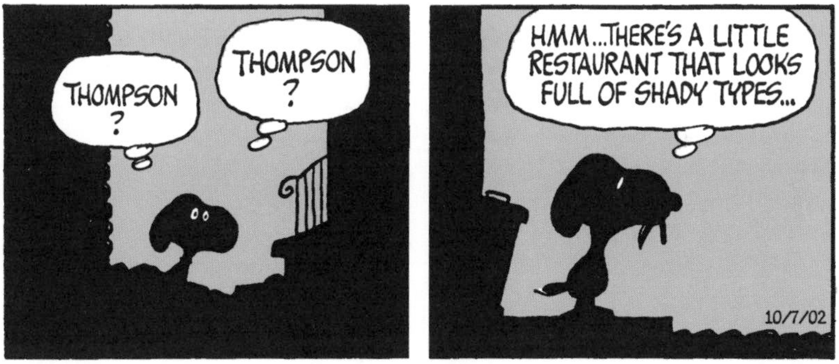
THOMPSON ?
THOMPSON ?
HMM... THERE'S A LITTLE RESTAURANT THAT LOOKS FULL OF SHADY TYPES...
10/7/02

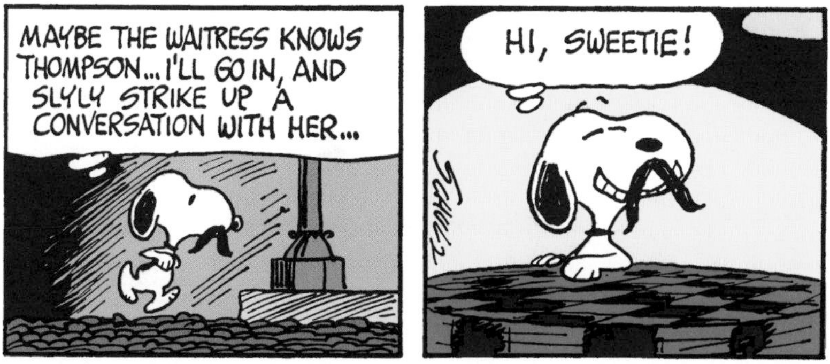
MAYBE THE WAITRESS KNOWS THOMPSON... I'LL GO IN, AND SLYLY STRIKE UP A CONVERSATION WITH HER...
HI, SWEETIE!
SCHULZ

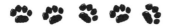

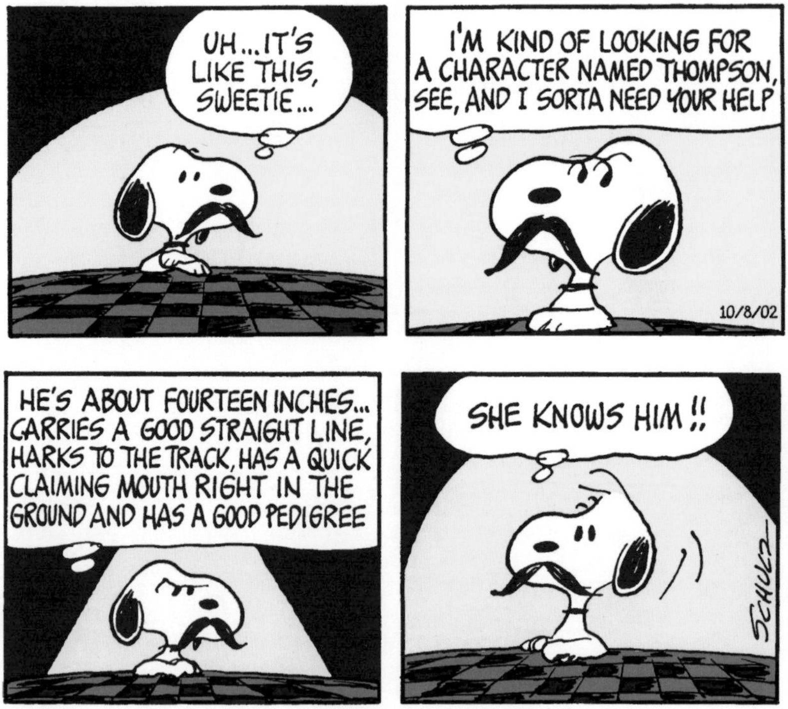
UH...IT'S LIKE THIS, SWEETIE...
I'M KIND OF LOOKING FOR A CHARACTER NAMED THOMPSON, SEE, AND I SORTA NEED YOUR HELP
10/8/02
HE'S ABOUT FOURTEEN INCHES... CARRIES A GOOD STRAIGHT LINE, HARKS TO THE TRACK, HAS A QUICK CLAIMING MOUTH RIGHT IN THE GROUND AND HAS A GOOD PEDIGREE
SHE KNOWS HIM !!
SCHULZ

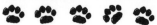

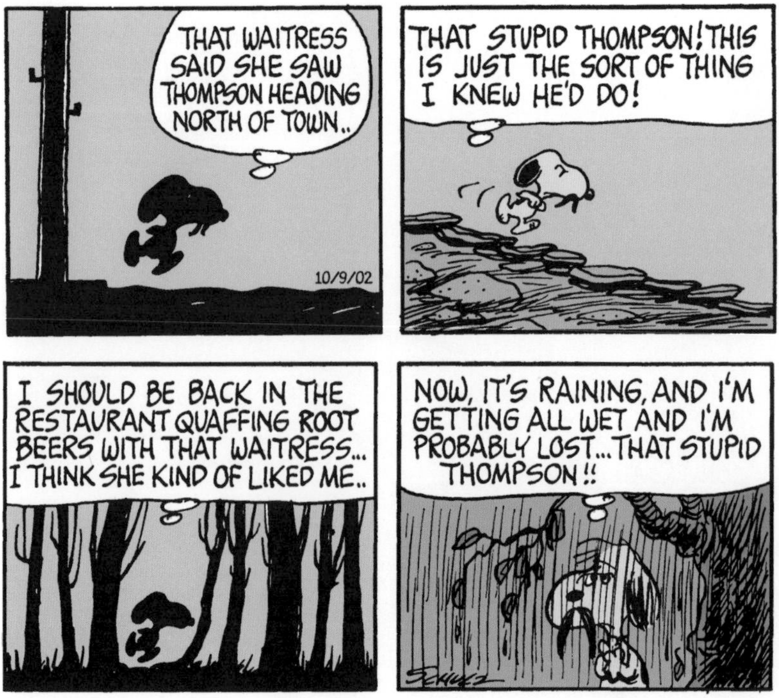
THAT WAITRESS SAID SHE SAW THOMPSON HEADING NORTH OF TOWN..
10/9/02
THAT STUPID THOMPSON! THIS IS JUST THE SORT OF THING I KNEW HE'D DO!
I SHOULD BE BACK IN THE RESTAURANT QUAFFING ROOT BEERS WITH THAT WAITRESS... I THINK SHE KIND OF LIKED ME..
NOW, IT'S RAINING, AND I'M GETTING ALL WET AND I'M PROBABLY LOST...THAT STUPID THOMPSON !!
SCHULZ

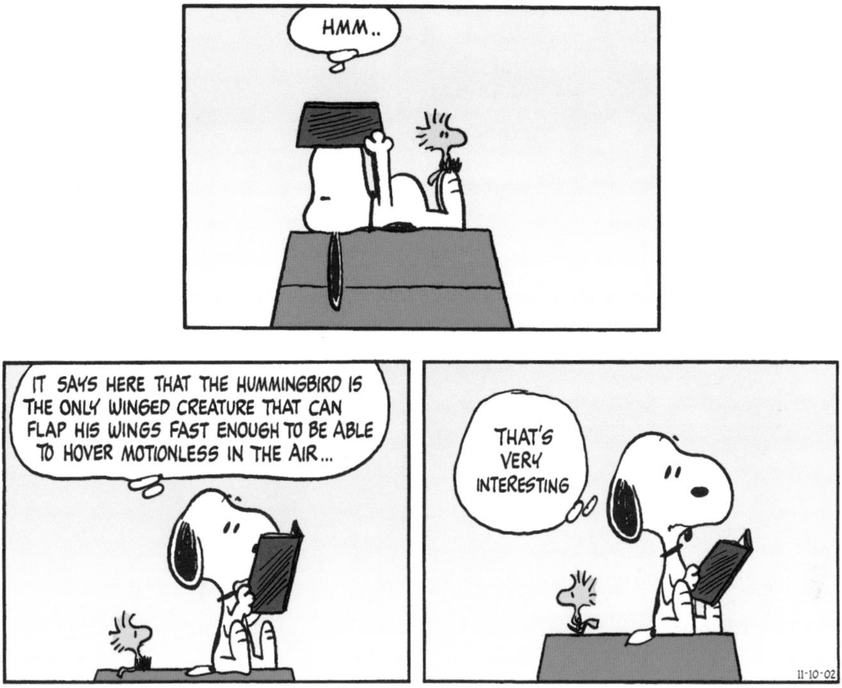
HMM..
IT SAYS HERE THAT THE HUMMINGBIRD IS THE ONLY WINGED CREATURE THAT CAN FLAP HIS WINGS FAST ENOUGH TO BE ABLE TO HOVER MOTIONLESS IN THE AIR...
THAT'S VERY INTERESTING
11-10-02

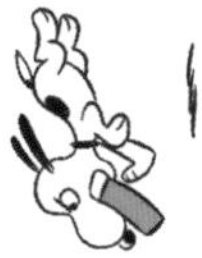

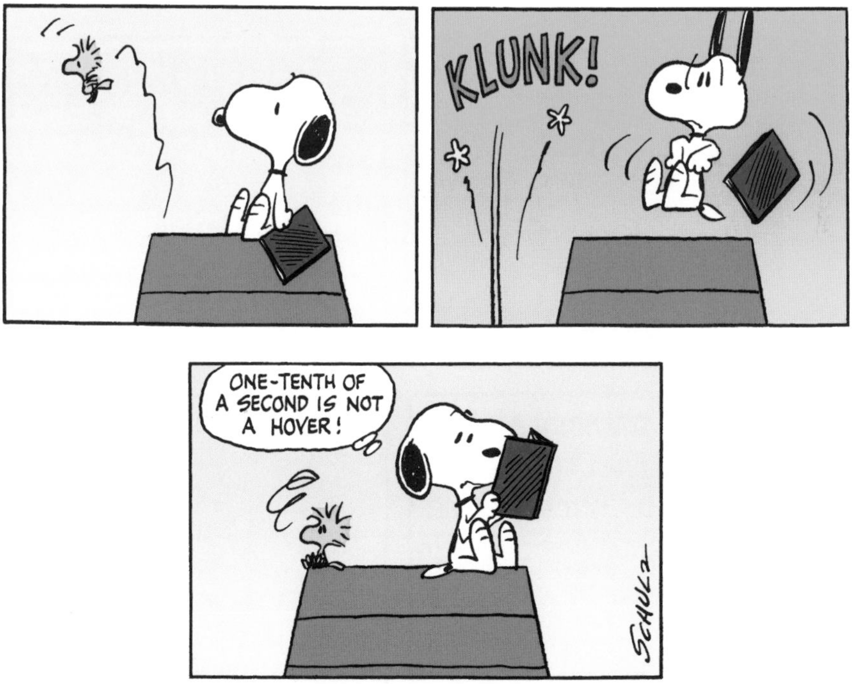
KLUNK!
ONE-TENTH OF A SECOND IS NOT A HOVER!
SCHULZ

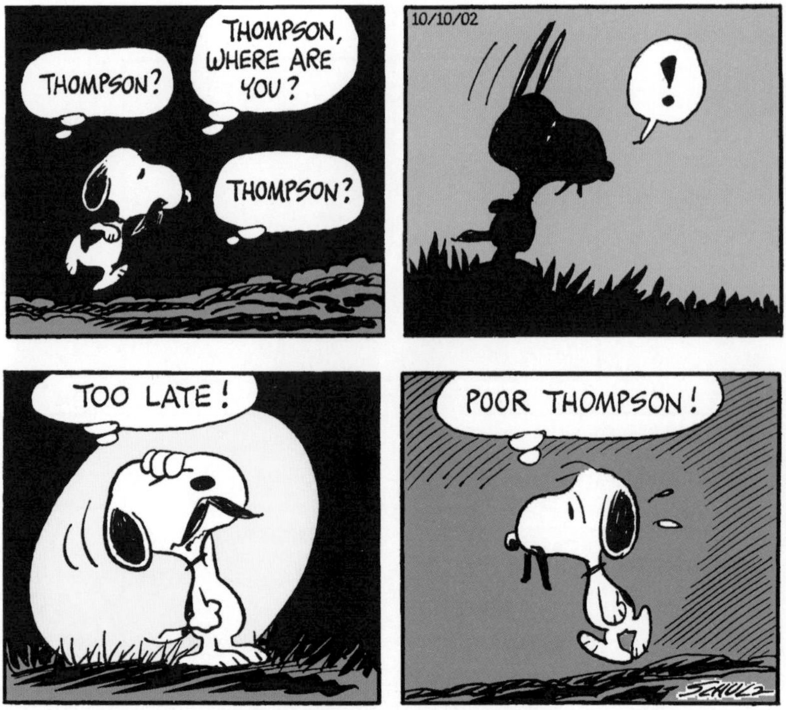
THOMPSON?
THOMPSON, WHERE ARE YOU?
THOMPSON?
10/10/02
!
TOO LATE!
POOR THOMPSON!
SCHULZ

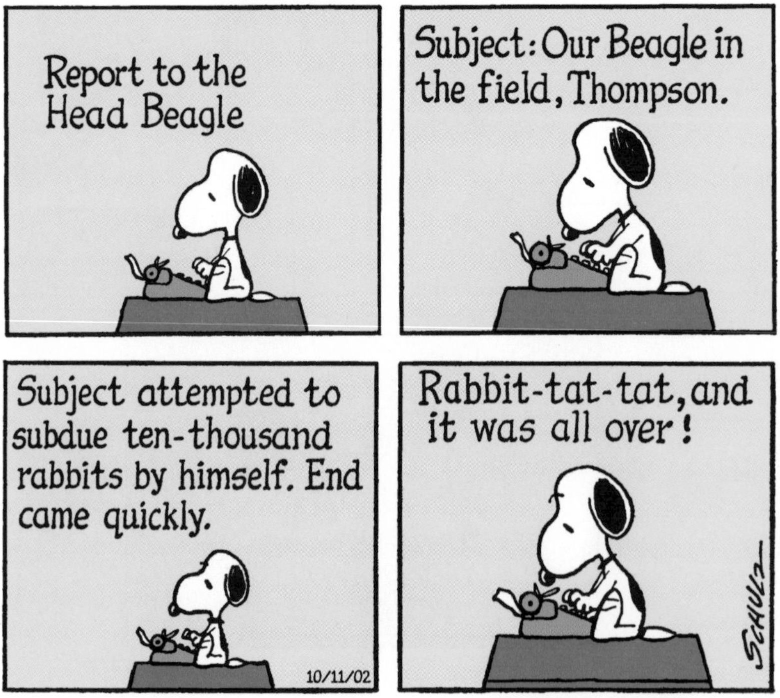
Report to the Head Beagle
Subject: Our Beagle in the field, Thompson.
Subject attempted to subdue ten-thousand rabbits by himself. End came quickly.
10/11/02
Rabbit-tat-tat, and it was all over!
SCHULZ

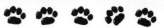

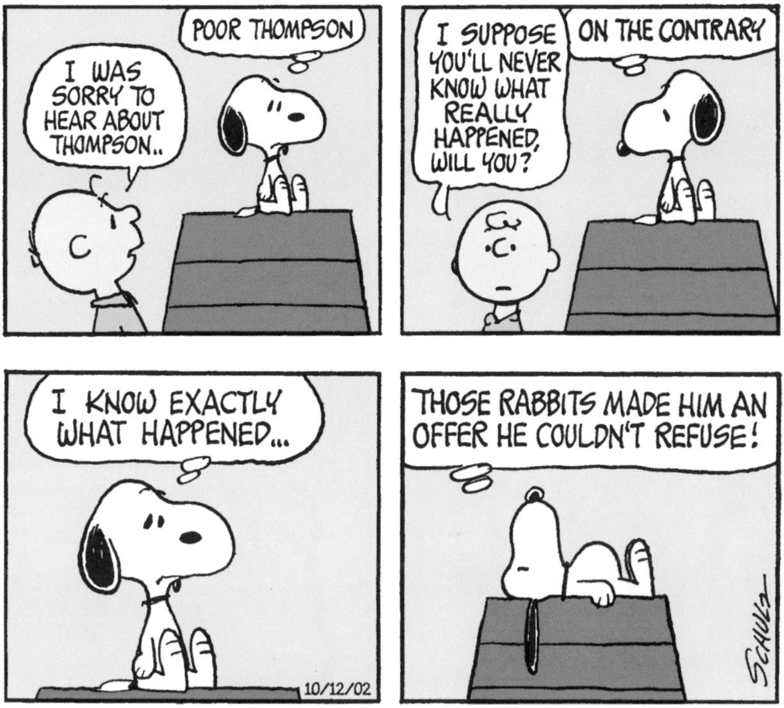
I WAS SORRY TO HEAR ABOUT THOMPSON..
POOR THOMPSON
I SUPPOSE YOU'LL NEVER KNOW WHAT REALLY HAPPENED, WILL YOU?
ON THE CONTRARY
I KNOW EXACTLY WHAT HAPPENED...
10/12/02
THOSE RABBITS MADE HIM AN OFFER HE COULDN'T REFUSE!
SCHULZ

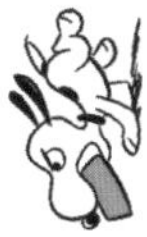

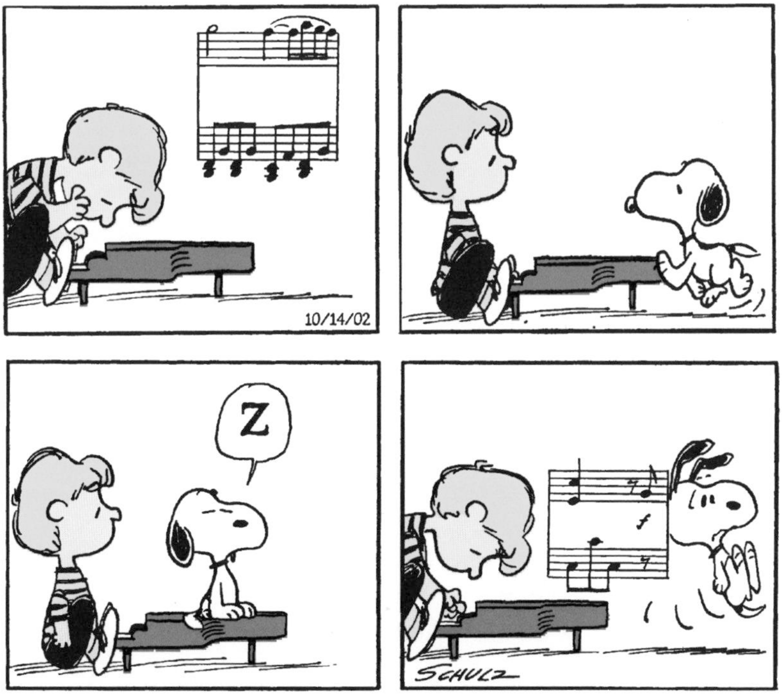
10/14/02
Z
SCHULZ

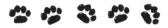

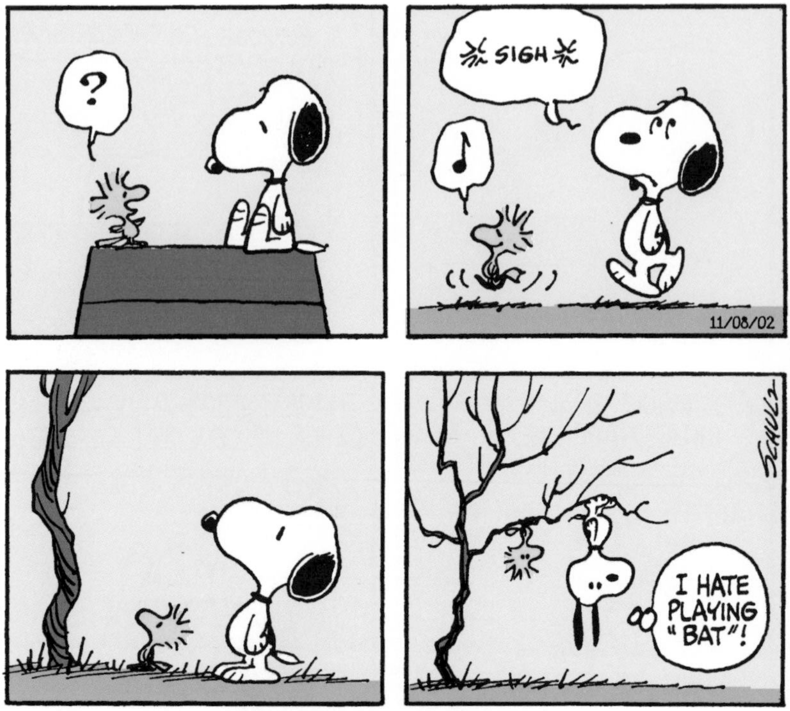
?
SIGH
11/08/02
SCHULZ
I HATE PLAYING "BAT"!

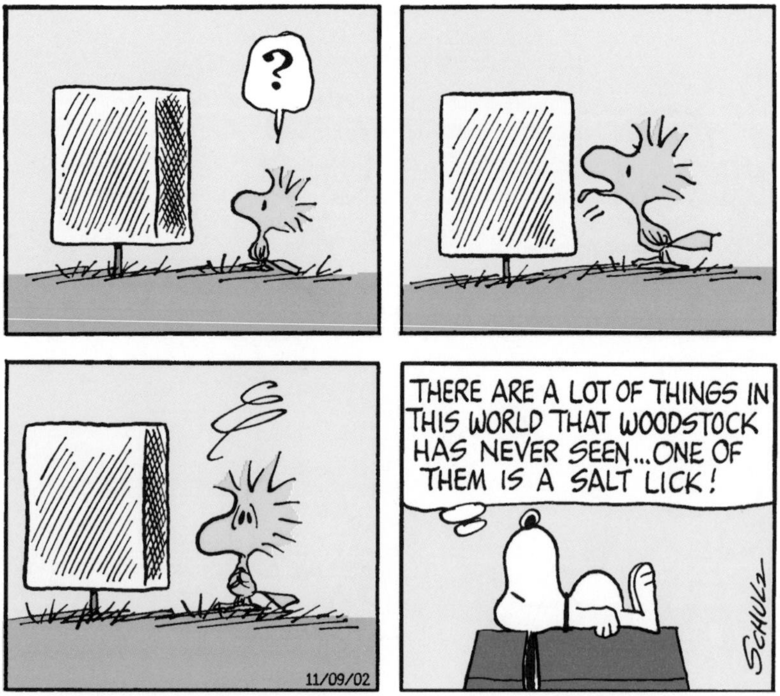
?
11/09/02
THERE ARE A LOT OF THINGS IN THIS WORLD THAT WOODSTOCK HAS NEVER SEEN...ONE OF THEM IS A SALT LICK!
SCHULZ

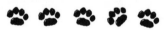

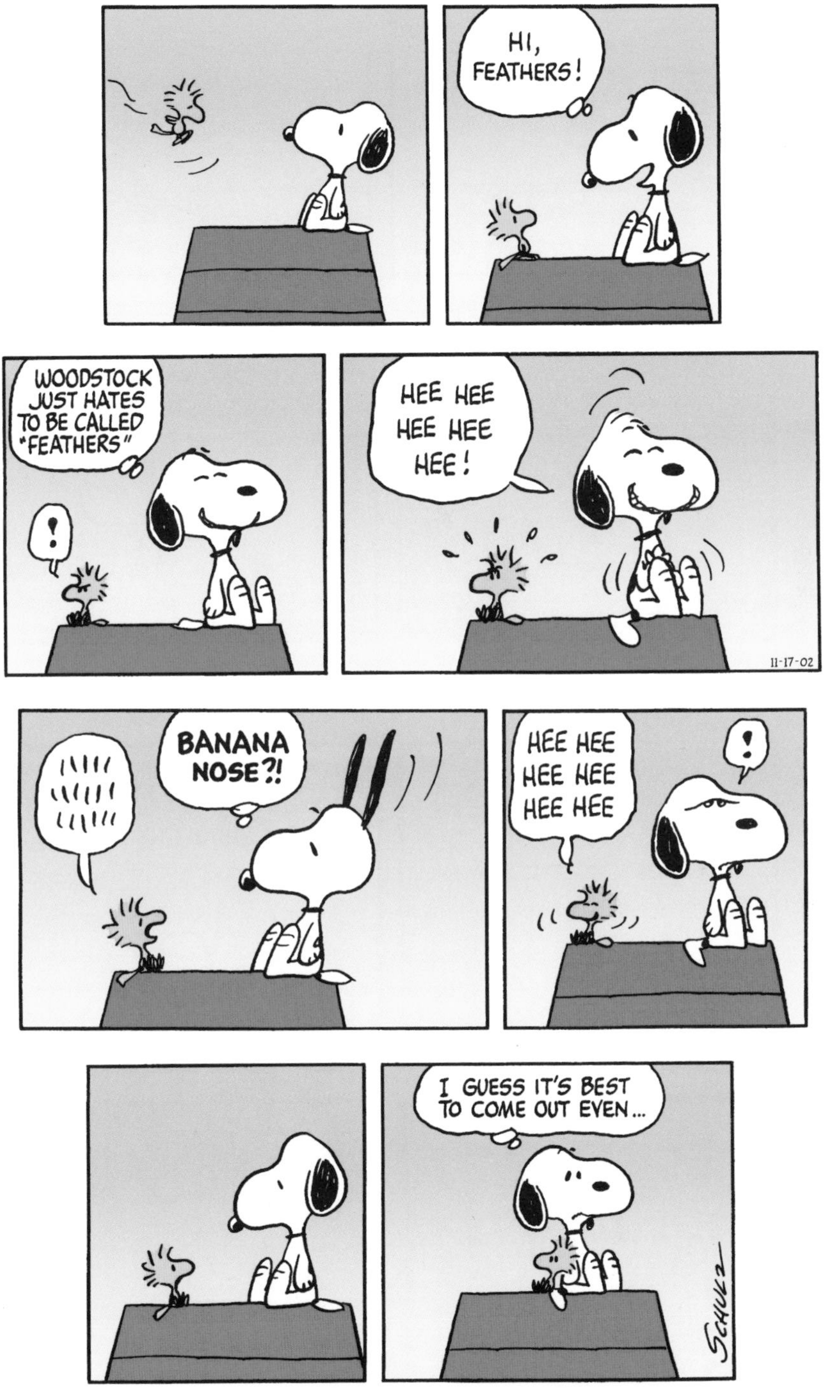
HI, FEATHERS!
WOODSTOCK JUST HATES TO BE CALLED "FEATHERS"
!
HEE HEE HEE HEE HEE!
11-17-02
BANANA NOSE?!
HEE HEE HEE HEE HEE HEE
!
I GUESS IT'S BEST TO COME OUT EVEN...
SCHULZ

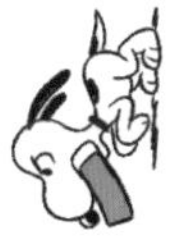

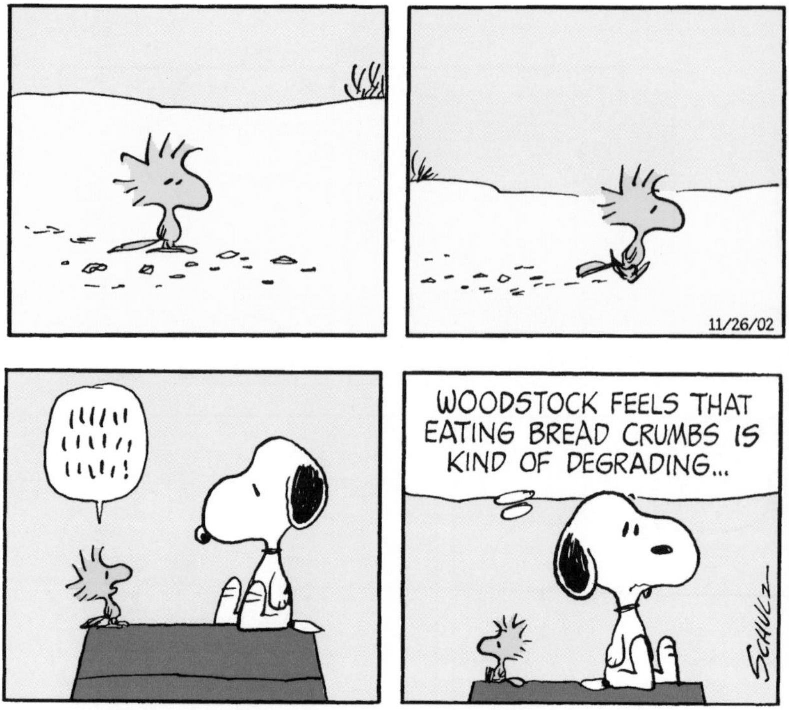
11/26/02
WOODSTOCK FEELS THAT EATING BREAD CRUMBS IS KIND OF DEGRADING...
SCHULZ

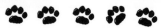

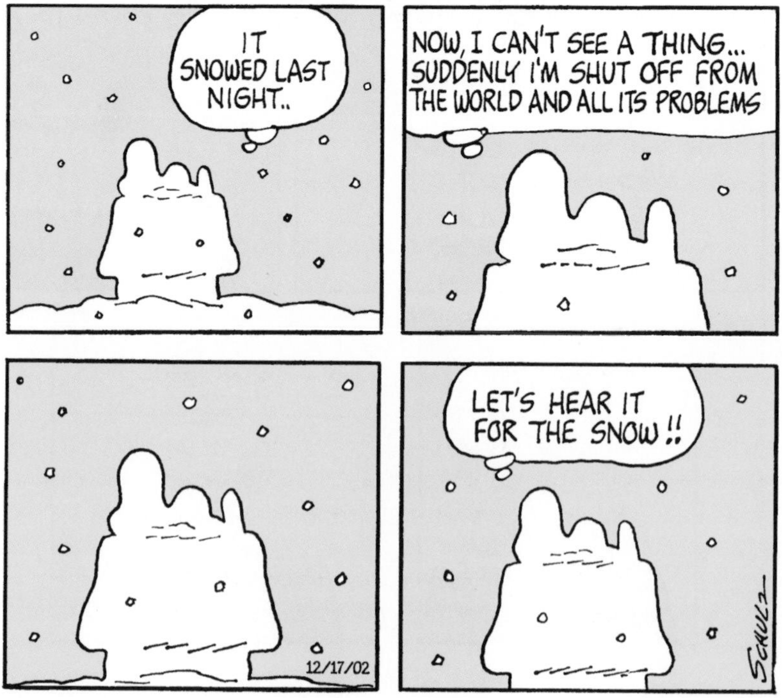
IT SNOWED LAST NIGHT..
NOW, I CAN'T SEE A THING... SUDDENLY I'M SHUT OFF FROM THE WORLD AND ALL ITS PROBLEMS
12/17/02
LET'S HEAR IT FOR THE SNOW!!
SCHULZ

In addition to all these great Snoopy cartoons, here are some cool activities and fun facts for you. Thanks to our friends at the Charles M. Schulz Museum and Research Center in Santa Rosa, California, for letting us share these with you!

Make a Recycled Bird Feeder for Woodstock and His Friends

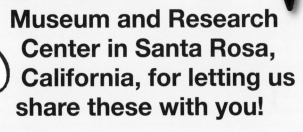

MATERIALS: empty plastic water bottle, Popsicle stick, birdseed, scissors, tape

INSTRUCTIONS:

1 Cut an opening in one side of the bottle and fill it with birdseed.

2 Decorate the bottle with paint or markers. Tape a Popsicle stick to the opening for a bird perch.

3 Tie a ribbon on top of the bottle for a hanger and hang it outside for birds to enjoy.

Make Snoopy's Dog House

MATERIALS: an 8.5 x 11 inch piece of paper, scissors, tracing paper

Start with the piece of paper. The best paper to use is colored on BOTH sides, but in the illustrations, the side of the sheet that will end up INSIDE the doghouse is white, just to make it easier to see the folds. Match corners and edges carefully and crease well.

1 Bring bottom edge to top. Crease flat.

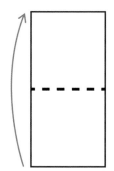

2 Rotate so open edge is at the bottom. Bring bottom edge of top layer to the top. Crease flat.

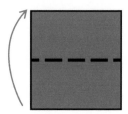

3 Turn over and repeat on other side, then rotate so open edges face down.

4 Lift the bottom edge of one side and make a fold upwards, along an imaginary line about one-half inch below the top fold.

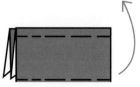

It should look like this. ⟶

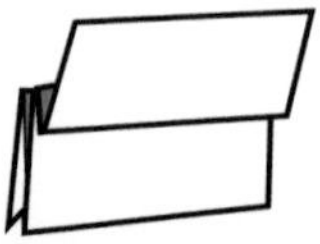

5 Turn over. Bring corners of second side up to meet corners of folded side. When pressed flat, it will crease in the right place.

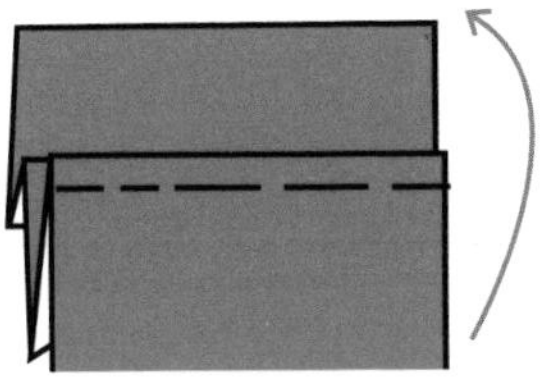

It will look like this:

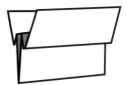

Now rotate:

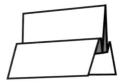

6 Lay it flat, and turn down (dog-ear) the corners of the middle fold, as squarely as you can. Crease well! Turn over and repeat.

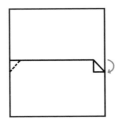

Hint: Try for *square corners* like this:

Not like this:

7 UNFOLD the corners, and poke them INSIDE the fold, along the creases you just made. Press flat.

Does it look like this? Congratulations!

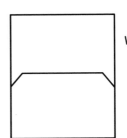

8 Fold back each edge of the top layer by opening the little corners and creasing a fold parallel to the vertical sides. Fold both edges, then turn over and repeat on other side.

It should look like this:

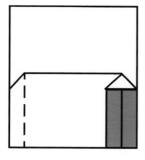

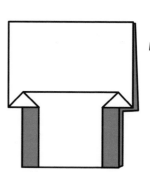

9 Re-fold the TOP of the house in the other direction, putting all your work INSIDE. Yay! A house! Now we just have to make the roof edges slant.

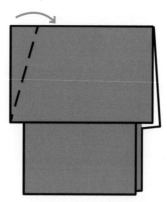

10 Fold a narrow slanted edge on each side, as shown. Crease well, unfold, and poke inside. Flatten.

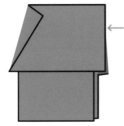

Leave room for Snoopy!

11 Open the ends a little and apply tape.

Trace the Snoopy art below, color it in, cut it out, and put Snoopy on his roof!

Charles M. Schulz and *Peanuts* Fun Facts

- Charles Schulz drew 17,897 comic strips throughout his career.
- Schulz was first published in Ripley's newspaper feature = in 1937. He was fifteen years old and the drawing was of the family dog.
- From birth, comics played a large role in Schulz's life. At just two days old, an uncle nicknamed Schulz "Sparky" after the horse Spark Plug from the *Barney Google* comic strip. And that's what he was called for the rest of his life.
- In a bit of foreshadowing, Schulz's kindergarten teacher told him, "Someday, Charles, you're going to be an artist."
- Growing up, Schulz had a black-and-white dog that later became the inspiration for Snoopy—the same dog that Schulz drew for Ripley's *Believe It or Not*. The dog's name was Spike.

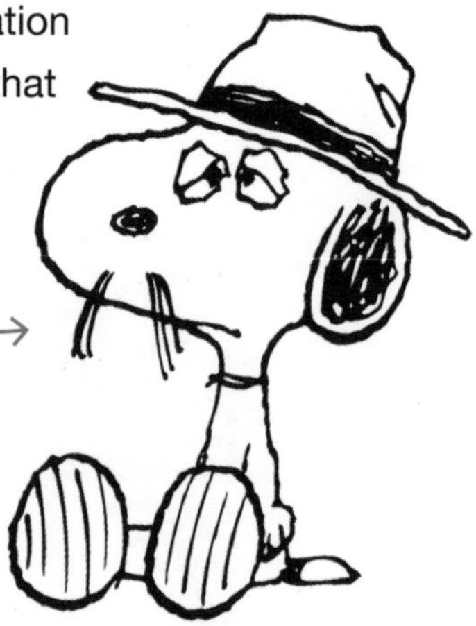

- Charles Schulz earned a star on the Hollywood Walk of Fame in 1996.

Learn How Comics Can Reflect Life

MATERIALS: blank piece of paper, pencil, markers or colored pencils

1. Make four blank cartoon panels, all the same size, on the piece of paper.
2. Look at the example below to see how Charles Schulz used his own life in his strips—even painful experiences like that of loss—and turned them into strips. Think of something that has happened to you at home or school that had a big impact on you.
3. Once you have decided on a story you want to tell, draw it in four panels. Remember, it should have a beginning, a middle, and an end.

An example from Schulz's life:

In 1966, a fire destroyed Schulz's Sebastopol studio. He translated his feelings into a strip about Snoopy's doghouse catching fire:

PEANUTS
SNIF?
I SMELL SMOKE!
SNIF SNIF
9-19
BAM! BAM! BAM! BAM!
Tm. Reg. U. S. Pat. Off.—All rights reserved ©1966 by United Feature Syndicate, Inc.
WHAT IN THE WORLD.....
GOOD GRIEF!
MY BOOKS! MY RECORDS! MY POOL TABLE! MY VAN GOGH!
SOB!
SCHULZ

Make a Snoopy Finger Puppet

MATERIALS: an 8.5 x 11 piece of paper, black construction paper, red or pink construction paper, scissors, tape, black marker

1. Fold paper into thirds, lengthwise.

2. Fold the paper in half by bringing one of the open ends to the other and creasing a fold in the middle.

3. Bring one of the open ends up to the middle and crease flat.

4. Turn the paper over.

5. Bring the second open end up to the middle and crease flat.

6. The finished folded square should look like an "M" or "W" when placed on its side on a flat surface.

7. Hold the square with the open ends facing you.

8. Use your thumb and index finger to gently pinch the folded points toward each other so the open ends open up.

9. Pull the two inside pages together.

10. Place a piece of tape over the middle of the inside pages.

11. Put your index finger and middle finger inside one of the pockets you have created.

12 Put your thumb inside the pocket below.

13 Close the puppet mouth by bringing your thumb to your index and middle finger. Open the puppet mouth by opening your fingers.

14 Cut out two ears from black construction paper and glue them to the face of your Snoopy.

15 Cut out one tongue from red or pink construction paper and glue it inside Snoopy's mouth.

16 Use a black marker to give Snoopy eyes.

It should look like this!

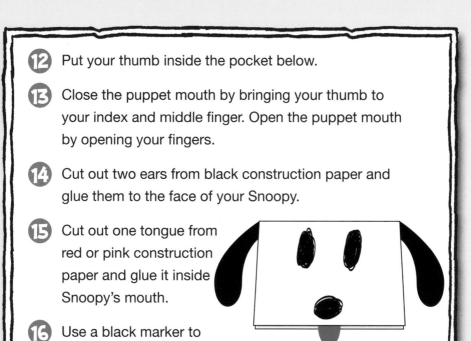

A round-headed boy named Charlie Brown, a security blanket, and a five-cent psychiatrist—just some of the classics you will find when you visit the largest collection of *Peanuts* artwork in the world. Laugh at Schulz's original comic strips, learn about the art of cartooning, and Schulz's role in its development, watch documentaries and animated *Peanuts* specials in the theater, and draw your own cartoons in the hands-on education room. The Museum features changing exhibitions, a re-creation of Schulz's art studio, outdoor gardens, holiday workshops. and special events. Take a virtual tour of the Museum at schulzmuseum.org!

CHARLES M. SCHULZ MUSEUM

CHARLIE BROWN
AND FRIENDS

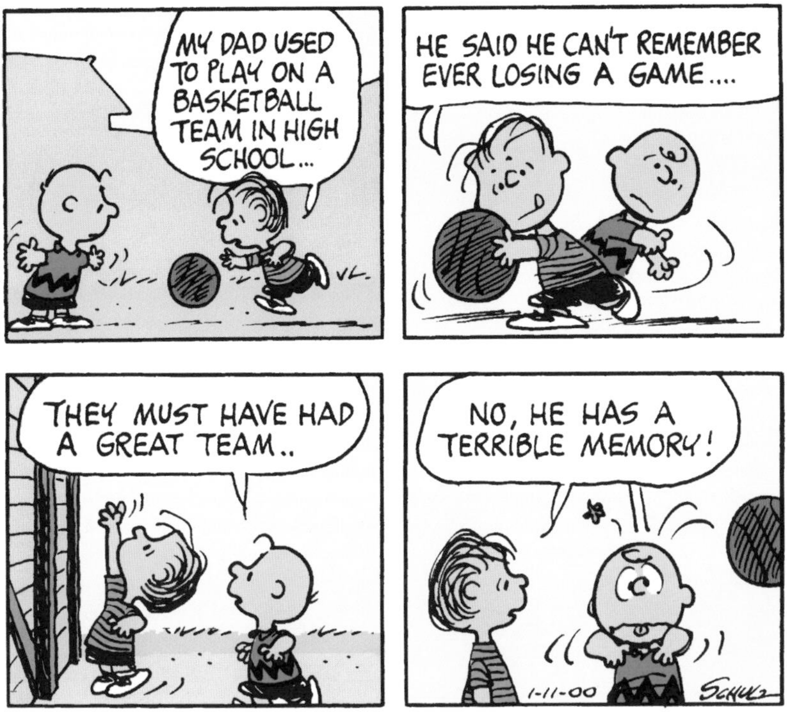
MY DAD USED TO PLAY ON A BASKETBALL TEAM IN HIGH SCHOOL...
HE SAID HE CAN'T REMEMBER EVER LOSING A GAME....
THEY MUST HAVE HAD A GREAT TEAM..
NO, HE HAS A TERRIBLE MEMORY!
1-11-00
SCHULZ

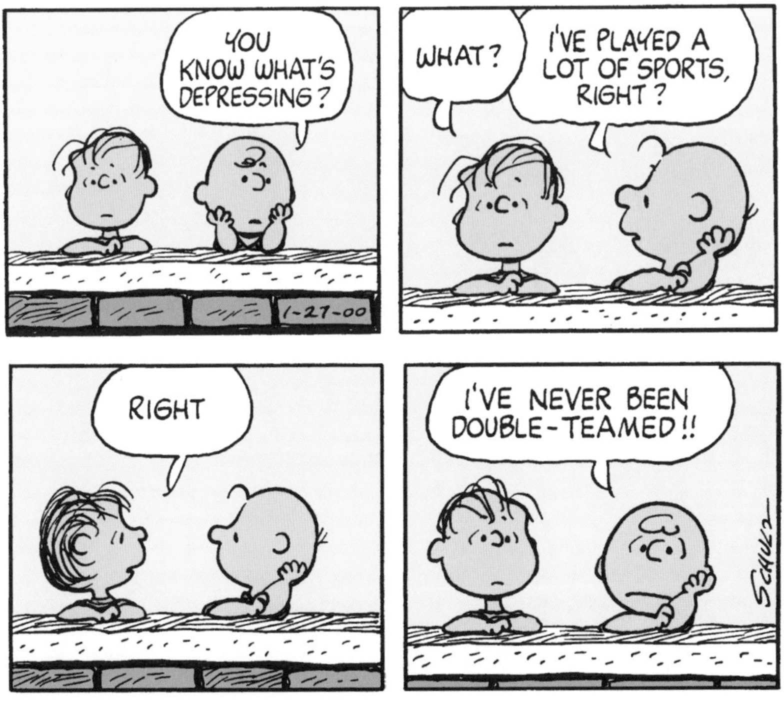
YOU KNOW WHAT'S DEPRESSING?
1-27-00
WHAT?
I'VE PLAYED A LOT OF SPORTS, RIGHT?
RIGHT
I'VE NEVER BEEN DOUBLE-TEAMED!!
SCHULZ

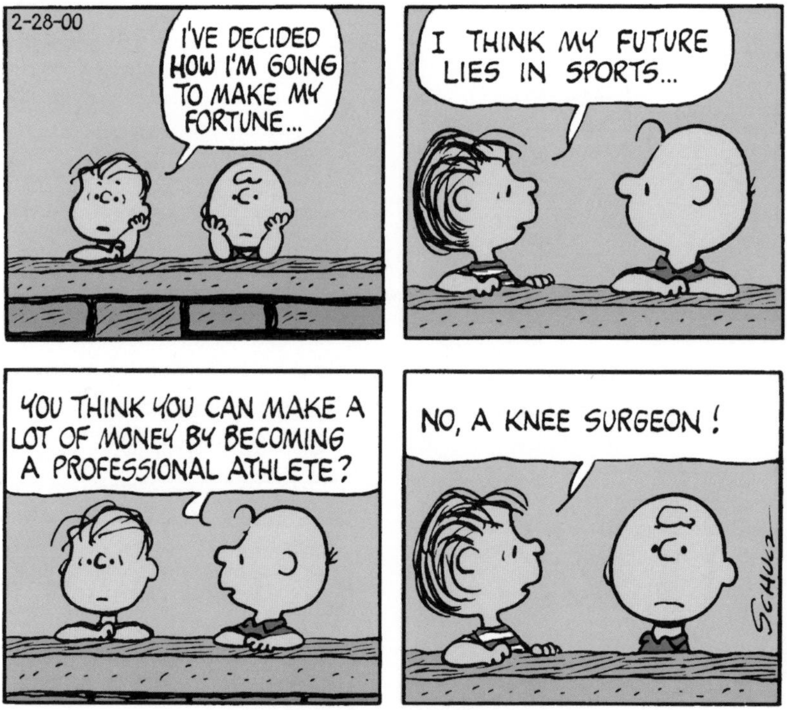
2-28-00
I'VE DECIDED HOW I'M GOING TO MAKE MY FORTUNE...
I THINK MY FUTURE LIES IN SPORTS...
YOU THINK YOU CAN MAKE A LOT OF MONEY BY BECOMING A PROFESSIONAL ATHLETE?
NO, A KNEE SURGEON!
SCHULZ

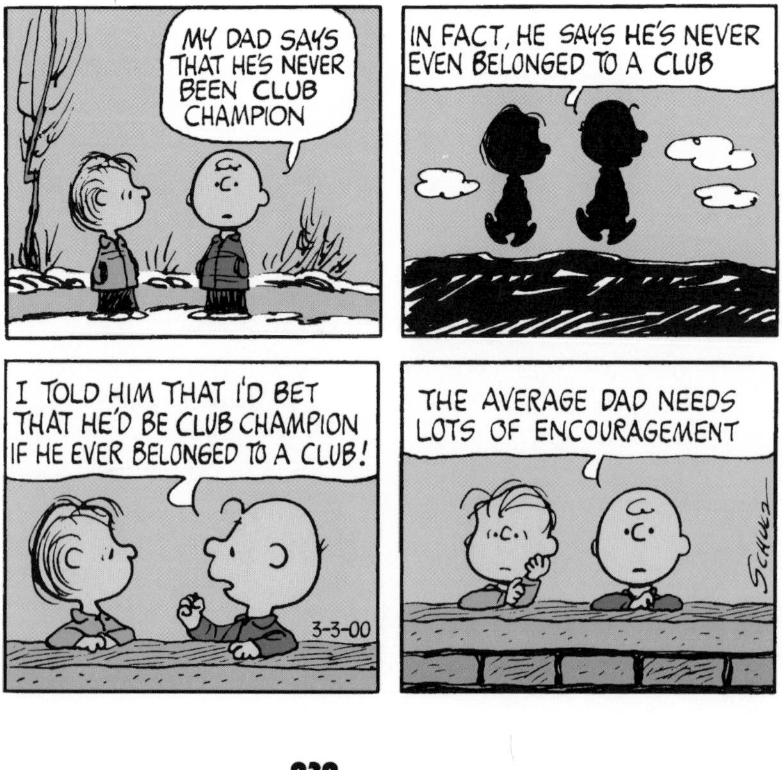
MY DAD SAYS THAT HE'S NEVER BEEN CLUB CHAMPION
IN FACT, HE SAYS HE'S NEVER EVEN BELONGED TO A CLUB
I TOLD HIM THAT I'D BET THAT HE'D BE CLUB CHAMPION IF HE EVER BELONGED TO A CLUB!
3-3-00
THE AVERAGE DAD NEEDS LOTS OF ENCOURAGEMENT
SCHULZ

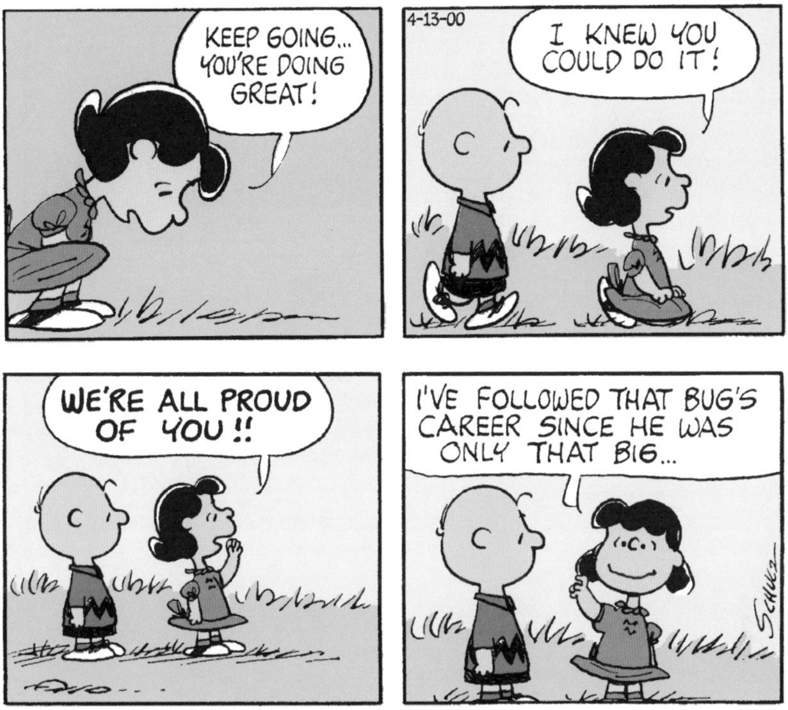
KEEP GOING... YOU'RE DOING GREAT!
4-13-00
I KNEW YOU COULD DO IT!
WE'RE ALL PROUD OF YOU!!
I'VE FOLLOWED THAT BUG'S CAREER SINCE HE WAS ONLY THAT BIG...
SCHULZ

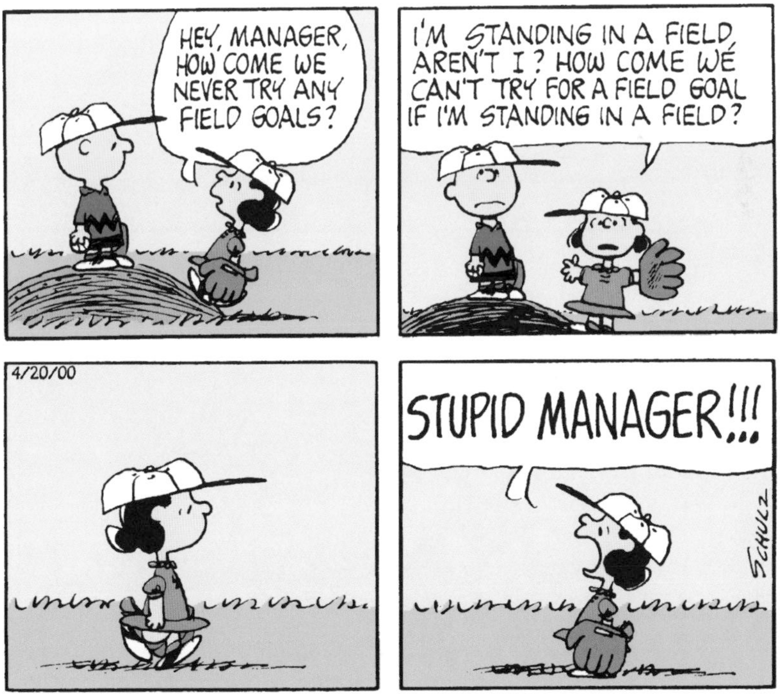
HEY, MANAGER, HOW COME WE NEVER TRY ANY FIELD GOALS?
I'M STANDING IN A FIELD, AREN'T I? HOW COME WE CAN'T TRY FOR A FIELD GOAL IF I'M STANDING IN A FIELD?
4/20/00
STUPID MANAGER!!!
SCHULZ

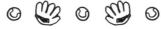

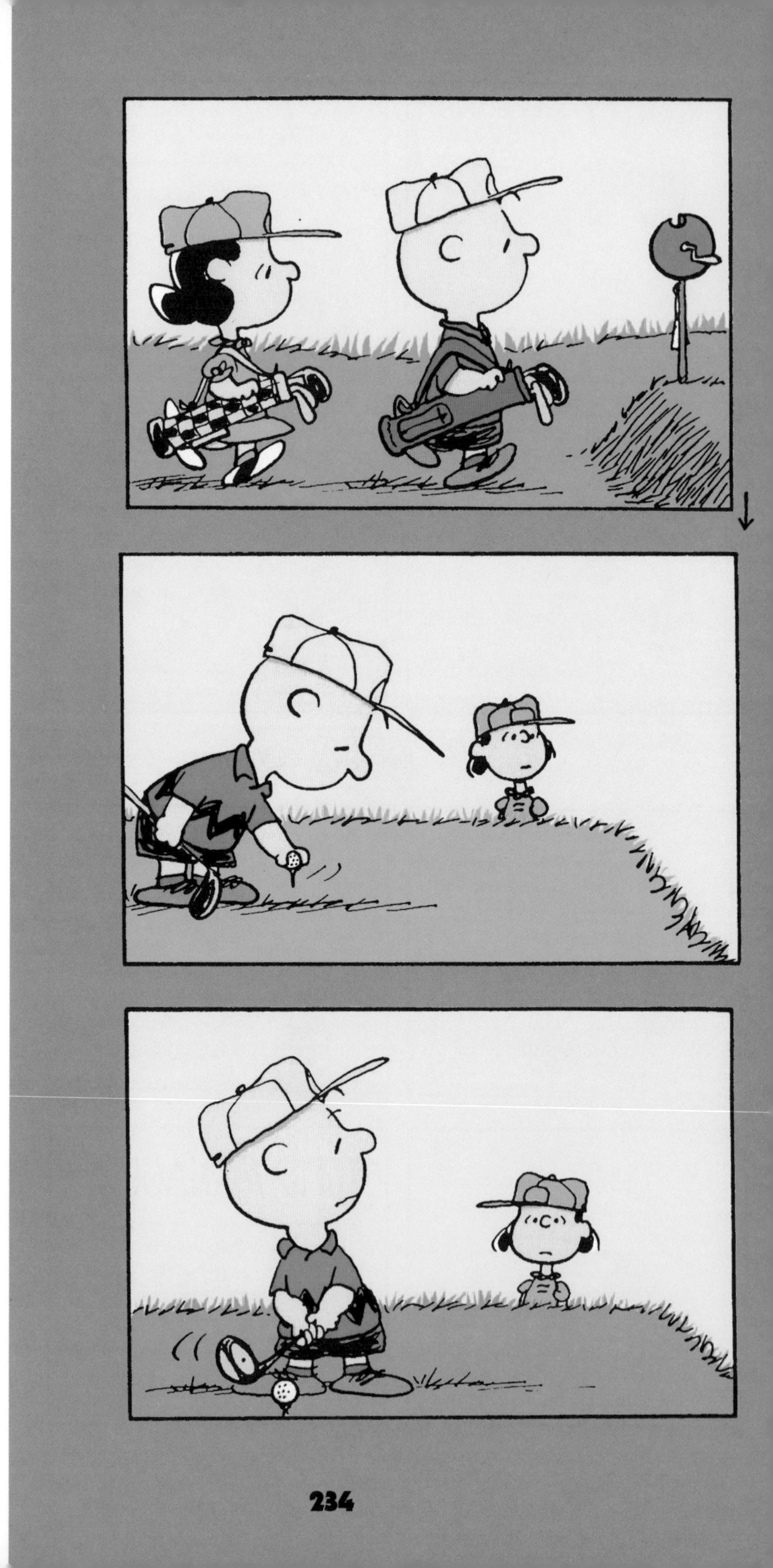

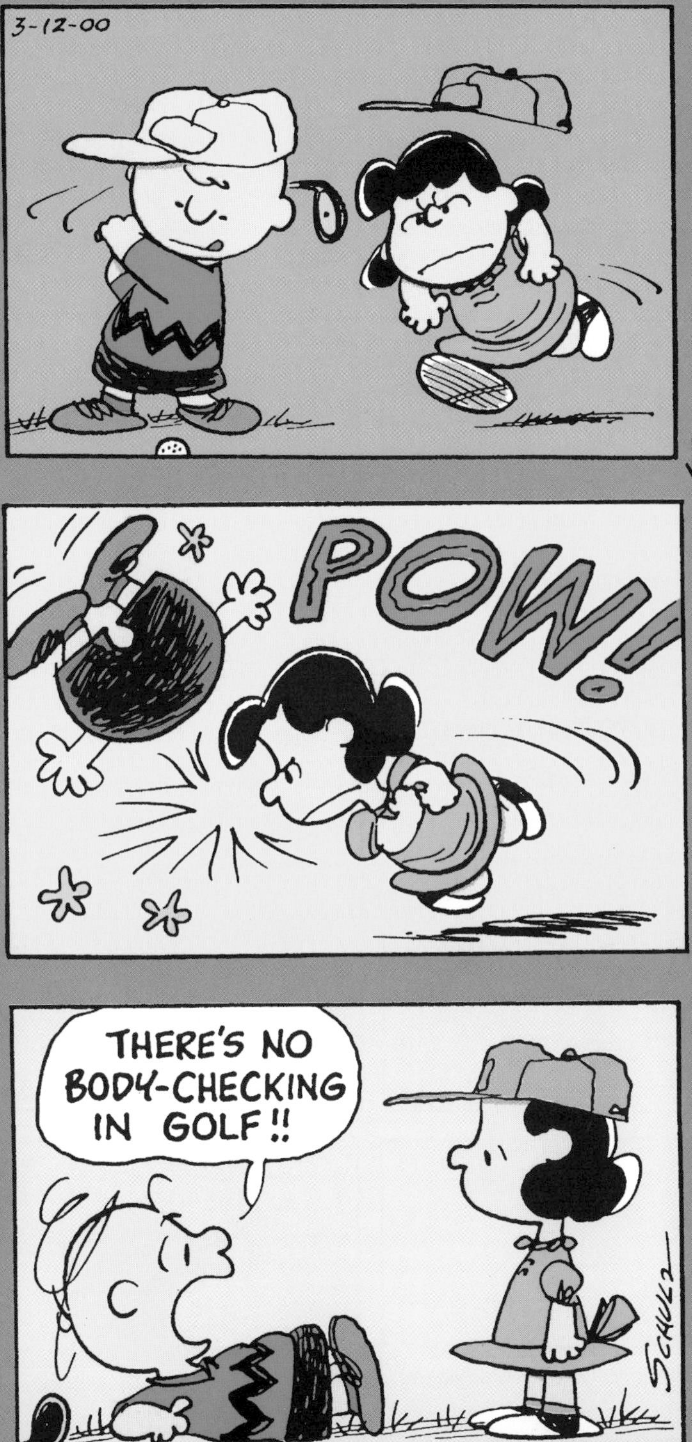
3-12-00
POW!
THERE'S NO BODY-CHECKING IN GOLF!!
SCHULZ

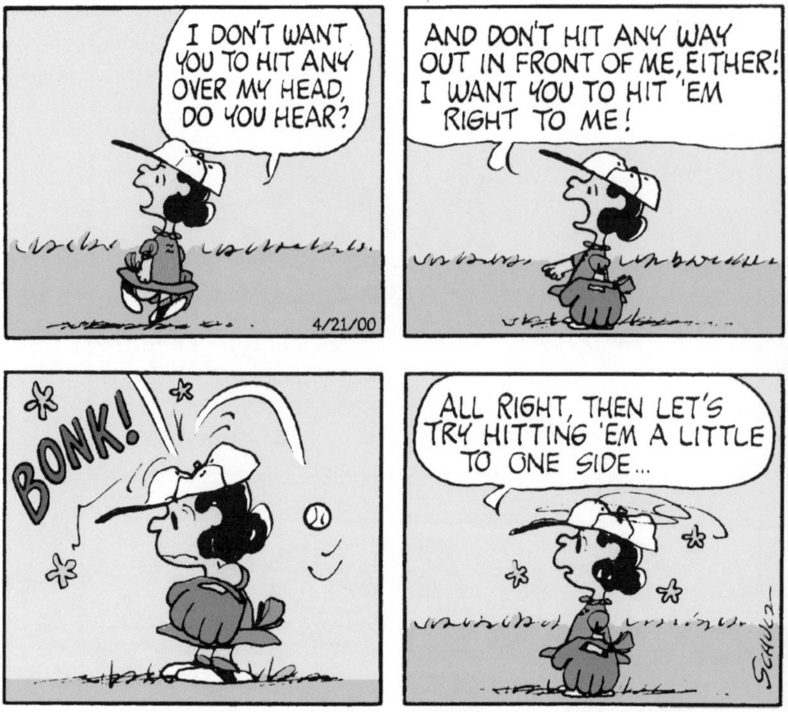
I DON'T WANT YOU TO HIT ANY OVER MY HEAD, DO YOU HEAR?
4/21/00
AND DON'T HIT ANY WAY OUT IN FRONT OF ME, EITHER! I WANT YOU TO HIT 'EM RIGHT TO ME!
BONK!
ALL RIGHT, THEN LET'S TRY HITTING 'EM A LITTLE TO ONE SIDE...
SCHULZ

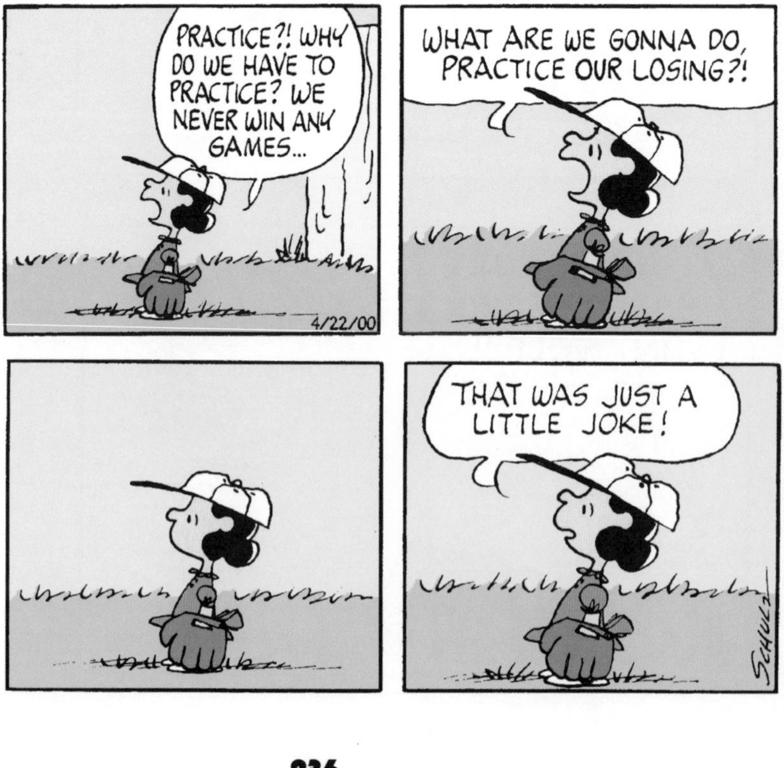
PRACTICE?! WHY DO WE HAVE TO PRACTICE? WE NEVER WIN ANY GAMES...
4/22/00
WHAT ARE WE GONNA DO, PRACTICE OUR LOSING?!
THAT WAS JUST A LITTLE JOKE!
SCHULZ

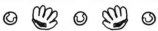

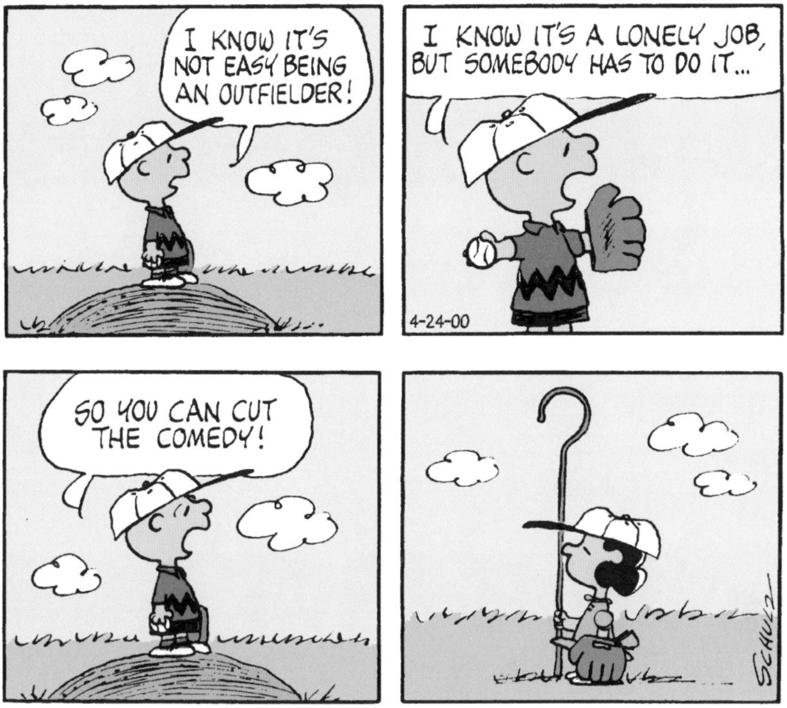
I KNOW IT'S NOT EASY BEING AN OUTFIELDER!
I KNOW IT'S A LONELY JOB, BUT SOMEBODY HAS TO DO IT...
4-24-00
SO YOU CAN CUT THE COMEDY!
SCHULZ

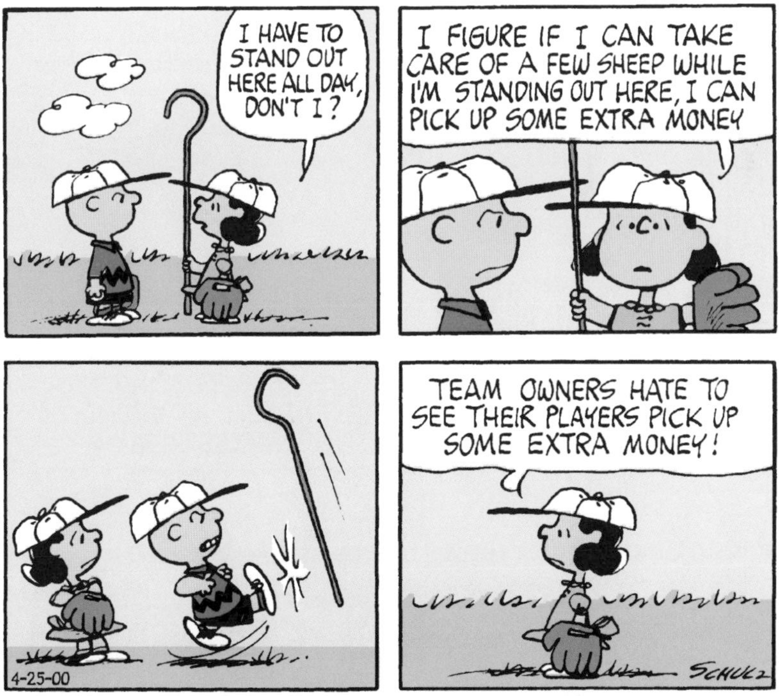
I HAVE TO STAND OUT HERE ALL DAY, DON'T I?
I FIGURE IF I CAN TAKE CARE OF A FEW SHEEP WHILE I'M STANDING OUT HERE, I CAN PICK UP SOME EXTRA MONEY
4-25-00
TEAM OWNERS HATE TO SEE THEIR PLAYERS PICK UP SOME EXTRA MONEY!
SCHULZ

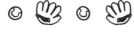

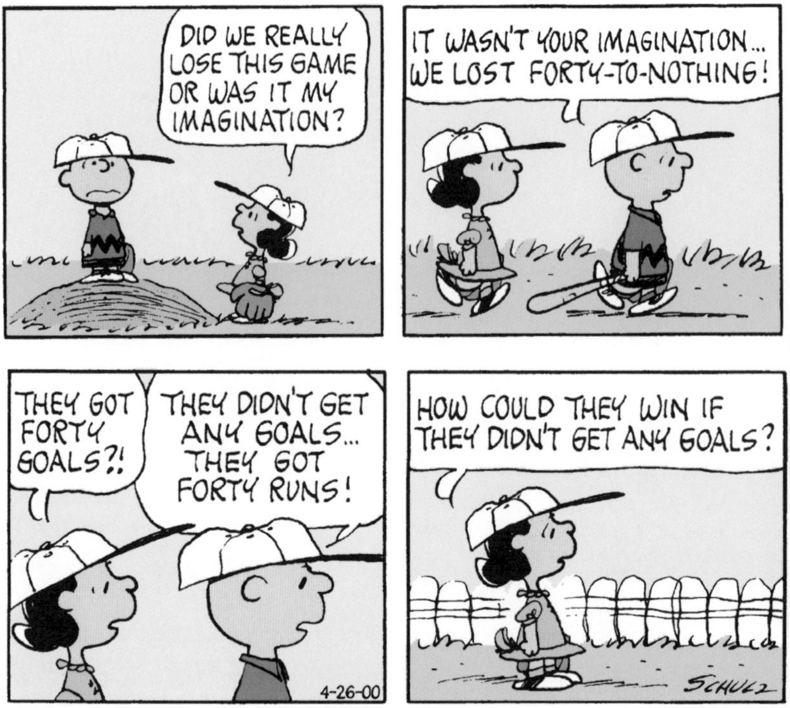
DID WE REALLY LOSE THIS GAME OR WAS IT MY IMAGINATION?
IT WASN'T YOUR IMAGINATION... WE LOST FORTY-TO-NOTHING!
THEY GOT FORTY GOALS?!
THEY DIDN'T GET ANY GOALS... THEY GOT FORTY RUNS!
4-26-00
HOW COULD THEY WIN IF THEY DIDN'T GET ANY GOALS?
SCHULZ

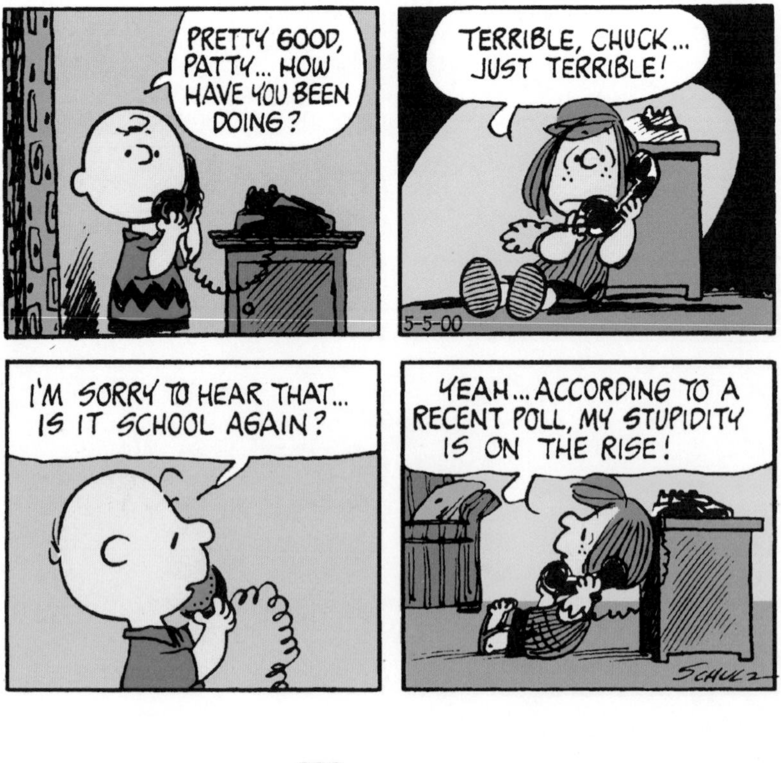
PRETTY GOOD, PATTY... HOW HAVE YOU BEEN DOING?
TERRIBLE, CHUCK... JUST TERRIBLE!
5-5-00
I'M SORRY TO HEAR THAT... IS IT SCHOOL AGAIN?
YEAH... ACCORDING TO A RECENT POLL, MY STUPIDITY IS ON THE RISE!
SCHULZ

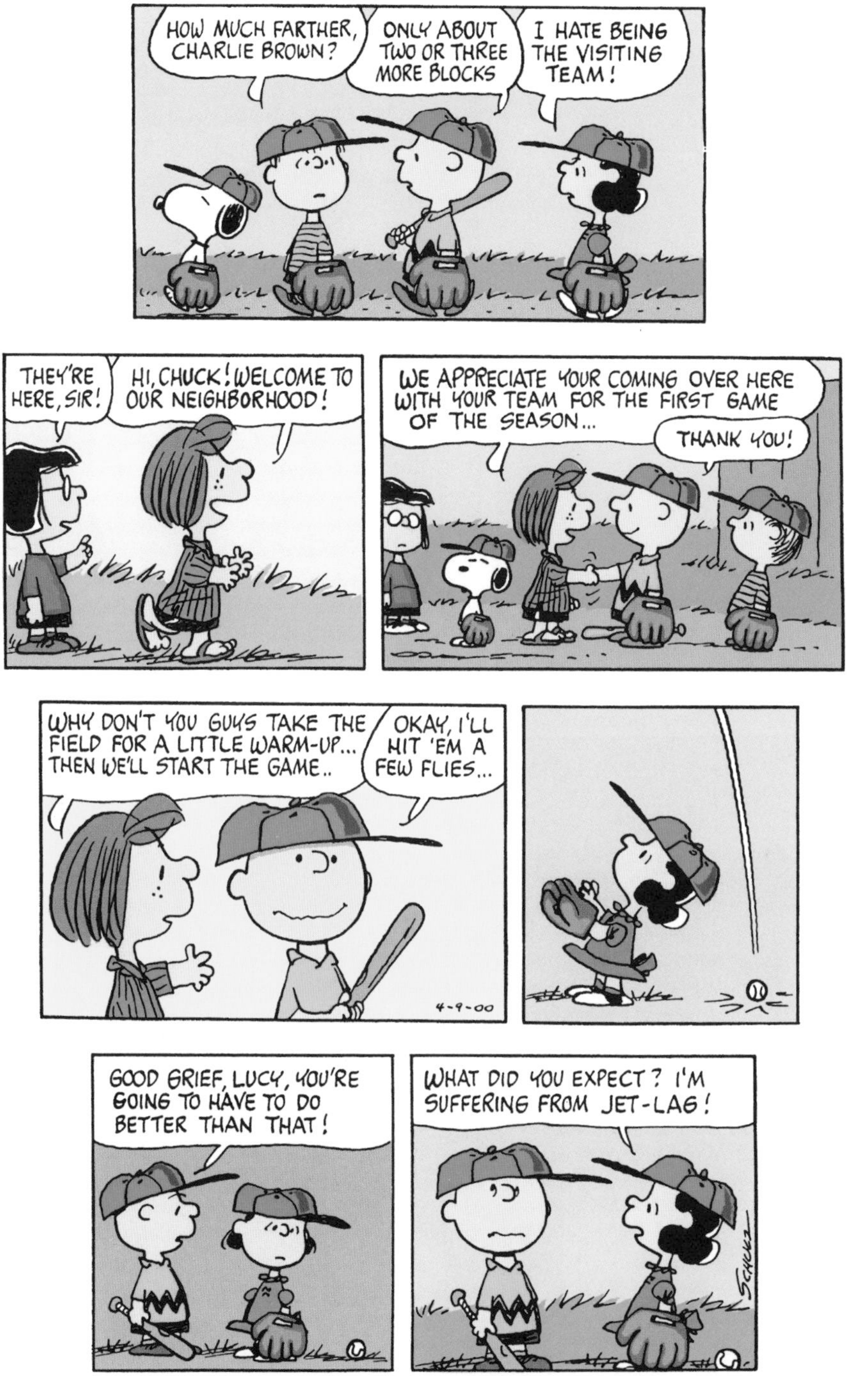
HOW MUCH FARTHER, CHARLIE BROWN?
ONLY ABOUT TWO OR THREE MORE BLOCKS
I HATE BEING THE VISITING TEAM!
THEY'RE HERE, SIR!
HI, CHUCK! WELCOME TO OUR NEIGHBORHOOD!
WE APPRECIATE YOUR COMING OVER HERE WITH YOUR TEAM FOR THE FIRST GAME OF THE SEASON...
THANK YOU!
WHY DON'T YOU GUYS TAKE THE FIELD FOR A LITTLE WARM-UP... THEN WE'LL START THE GAME..
OKAY, I'LL HIT 'EM A FEW FLIES...
4-9-00
GOOD GRIEF, LUCY, YOU'RE GOING TO HAVE TO DO BETTER THAN THAT!
WHAT DID YOU EXPECT? I'M SUFFERING FROM JET-LAG!
SCHULZ

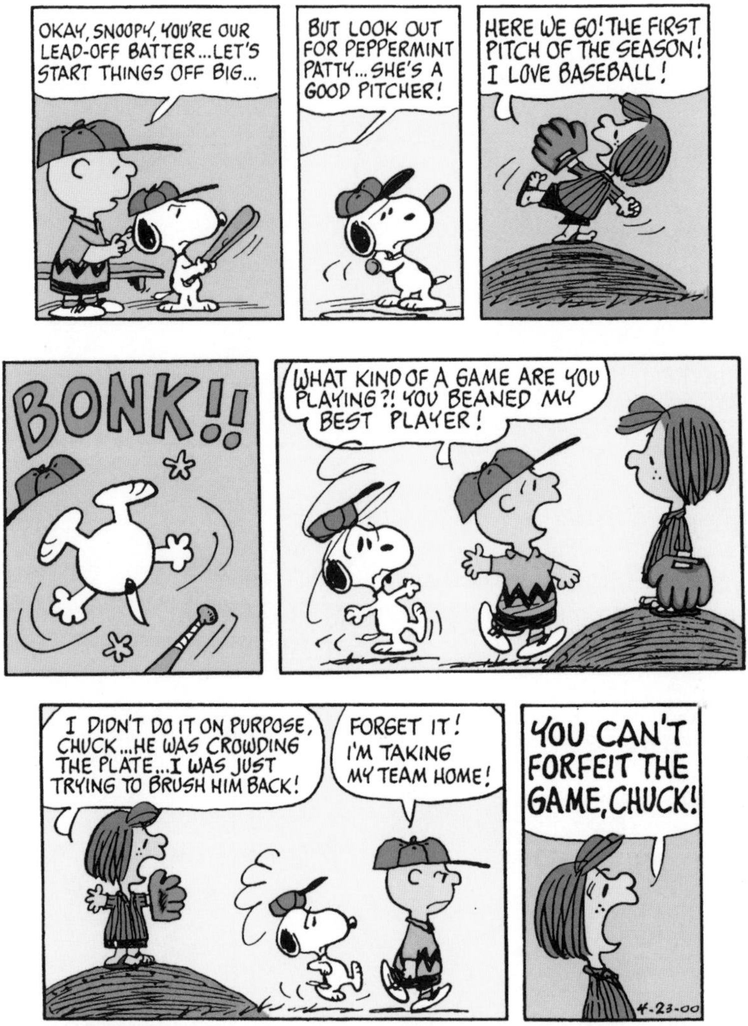
OKAY, SNOOPY, YOU'RE OUR LEAD-OFF BATTER...LET'S START THINGS OFF BIG...
BUT LOOK OUT FOR PEPPERMINT PATTY...SHE'S A GOOD PITCHER!
HERE WE GO! THE FIRST PITCH OF THE SEASON! I LOVE BASEBALL!
BONK!!
WHAT KIND OF A GAME ARE YOU PLAYING?! YOU BEANED MY BEST PLAYER!
I DIDN'T DO IT ON PURPOSE, CHUCK...HE WAS CROWDING THE PLATE...I WAS JUST TRYING TO BRUSH HIM BACK!
FORGET IT! I'M TAKING MY TEAM HOME!
YOU CAN'T FORFEIT THE GAME, CHUCK!
4-23-00

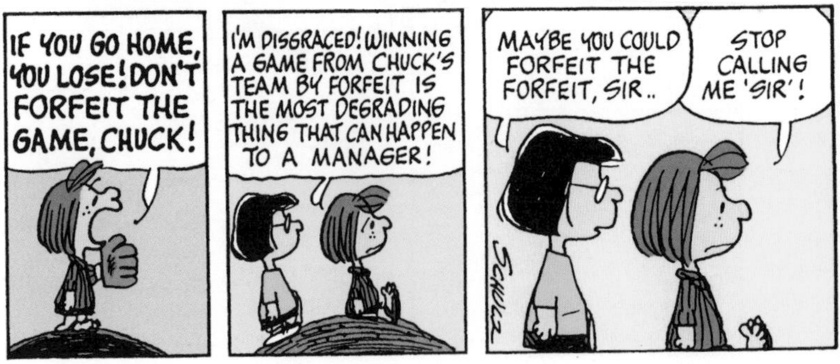
IF YOU GO HOME, YOU LOSE! DON'T FORFEIT THE GAME, CHUCK!
I'M DISGRACED! WINNING A GAME FROM CHUCK'S TEAM BY FORFEIT IS THE MOST DEGRADING THING THAT CAN HAPPEN TO A MANAGER!
MAYBE YOU COULD FORFEIT THE FORFEIT, SIR..
STOP CALLING ME 'SIR'!
SCHULZ

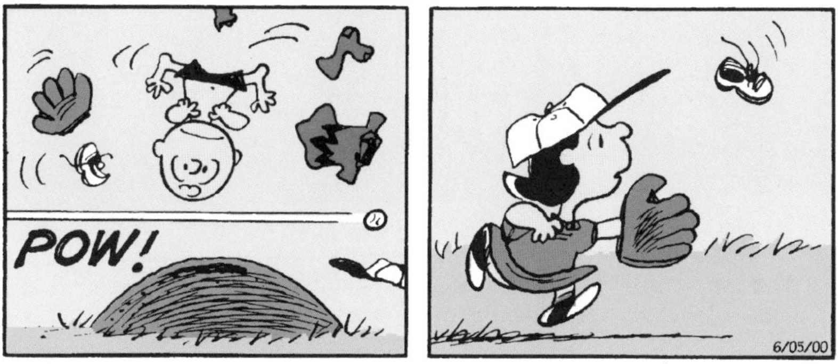
POW!
6/05/00

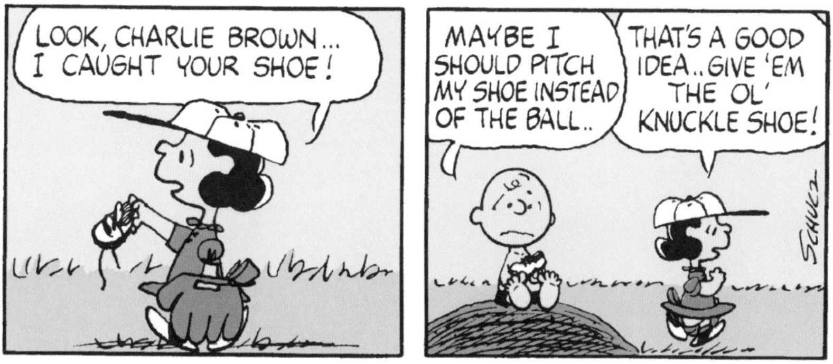
LOOK, CHARLIE BROWN... I CAUGHT YOUR SHOE!
MAYBE I SHOULD PITCH MY SHOE INSTEAD OF THE BALL..
THAT'S A GOOD IDEA..GIVE 'EM THE OL' KNUCKLE SHOE!
SCHULZ

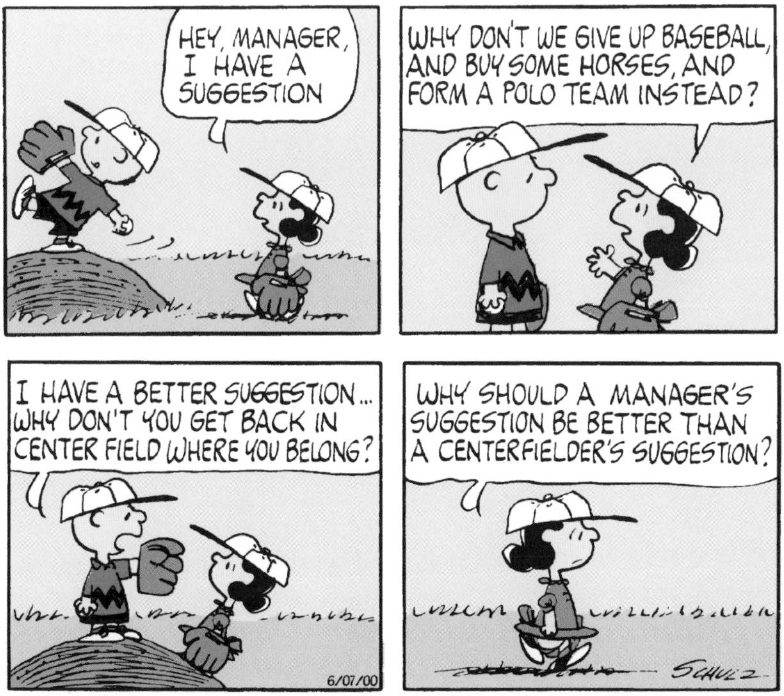
HEY, MANAGER, I HAVE A SUGGESTION
WHY DON'T WE GIVE UP BASEBALL, AND BUY SOME HORSES, AND FORM A POLO TEAM INSTEAD?
I HAVE A BETTER SUGGESTION... WHY DON'T YOU GET BACK IN CENTER FIELD WHERE YOU BELONG?
6/07/00
WHY SHOULD A MANAGER'S SUGGESTION BE BETTER THAN A CENTERFIELDER'S SUGGESTION?
SCHULZ

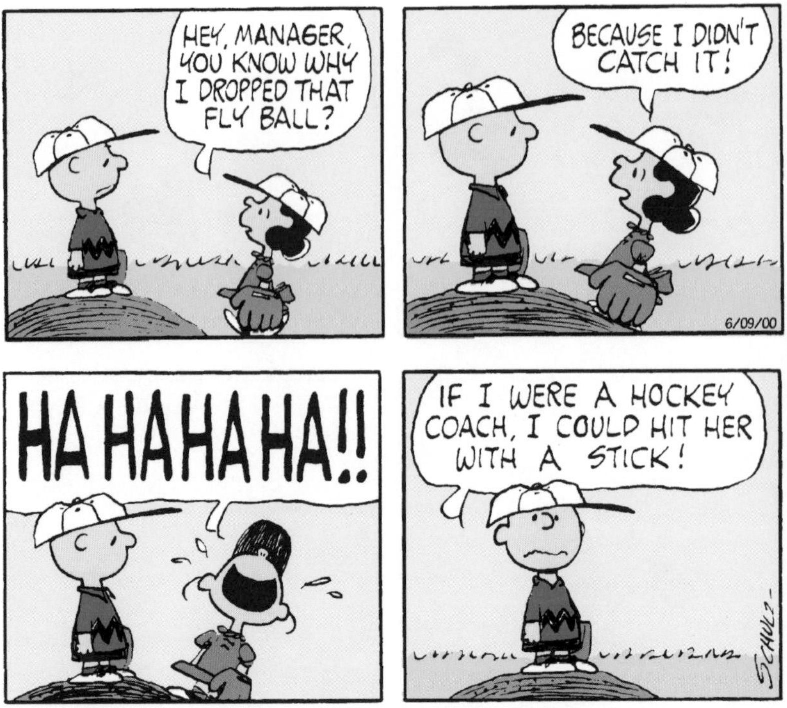
HEY, MANAGER, YOU KNOW WHY I DROPPED THAT FLY BALL?
BECAUSE I DIDN'T CATCH IT!
6/09/00
HA HA HA HA HA!!
IF I WERE A HOCKEY COACH, I COULD HIT HER WITH A STICK!
SCHULZ

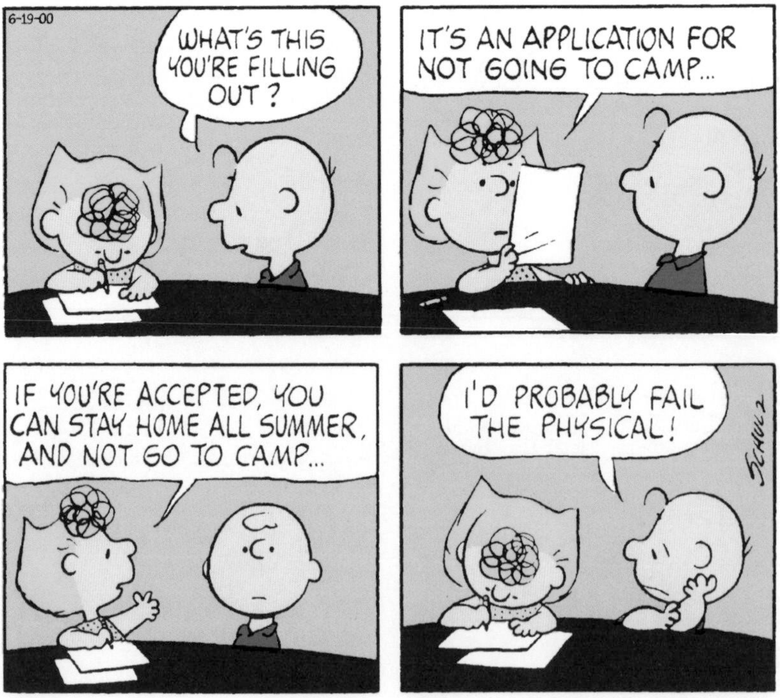
6-19-00
WHAT'S THIS YOU'RE FILLING OUT?
IT'S AN APPLICATION FOR NOT GOING TO CAMP...
IF YOU'RE ACCEPTED, YOU CAN STAY HOME ALL SUMMER, AND NOT GO TO CAMP...
I'D PROBABLY FAIL THE PHYSICAL!
SCHULZ

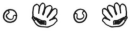

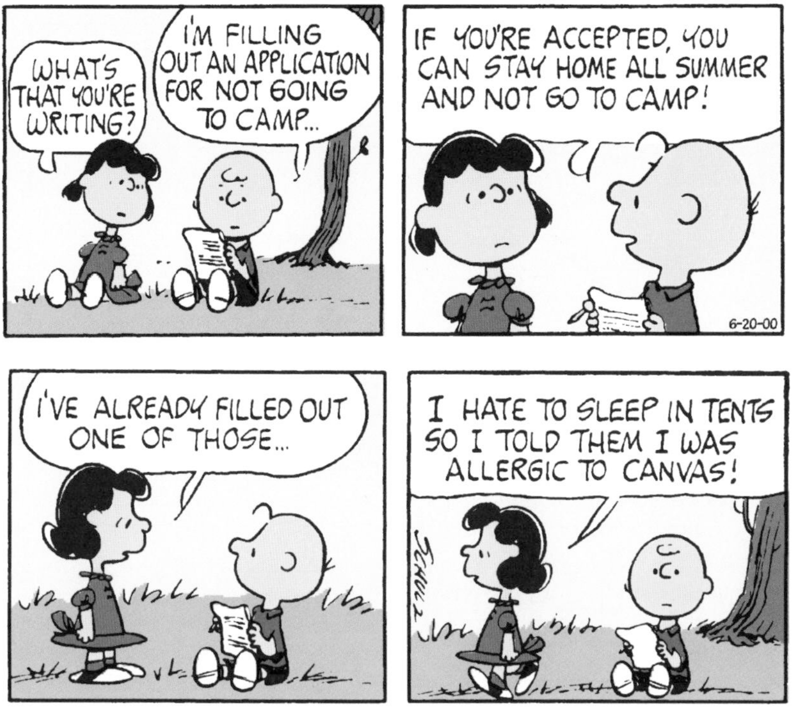
WHAT'S THAT YOU'RE WRITING?
I'M FILLING OUT AN APPLICATION FOR NOT GOING TO CAMP...
IF YOU'RE ACCEPTED, YOU CAN STAY HOME ALL SUMMER AND NOT GO TO CAMP!
6-20-00
I'VE ALREADY FILLED OUT ONE OF THOSE...
I HATE TO SLEEP IN TENTS SO I TOLD THEM I WAS ALLERGIC TO CANVAS!
SCHULZ

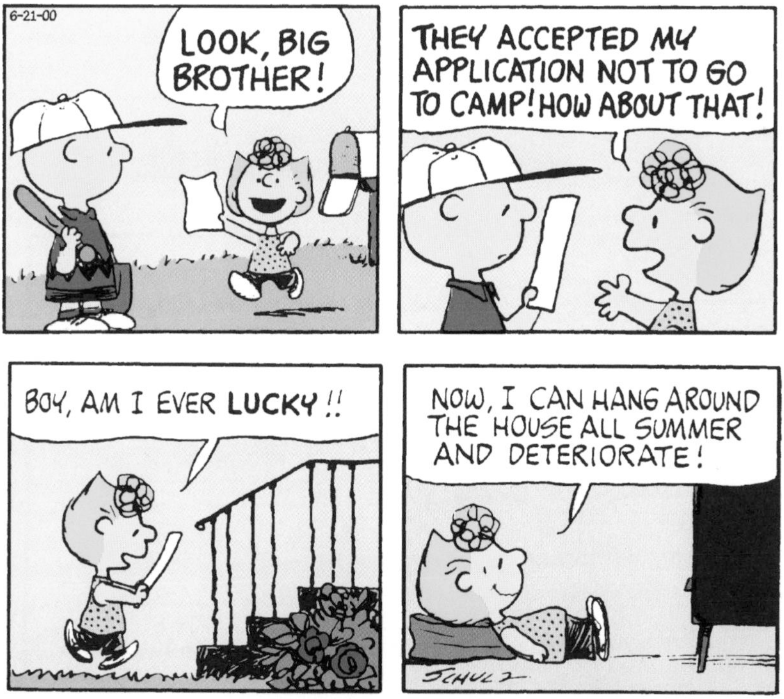
6-21-00
LOOK, BIG BROTHER!
THEY ACCEPTED MY APPLICATION NOT TO GO TO CAMP! HOW ABOUT THAT!
BOY, AM I EVER **LUCKY**!!
NOW, I CAN HANG AROUND THE HOUSE ALL SUMMER AND DETERIORATE!
SCHULZ

OKAY, CHARLIE BROWN...LET'S GET THIS NEXT HITTER...
WHERE'S THE BALL?
I CAN'T PITCH WITHOUT THE BALL!
NOT SO LOUD, YOU DUMMY!

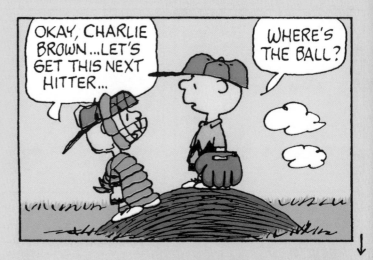

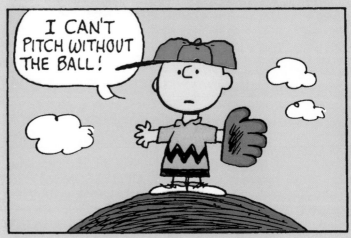

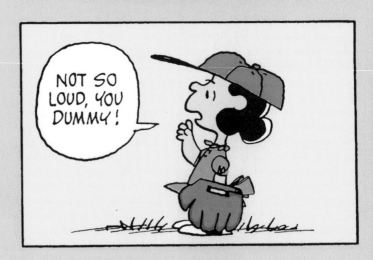

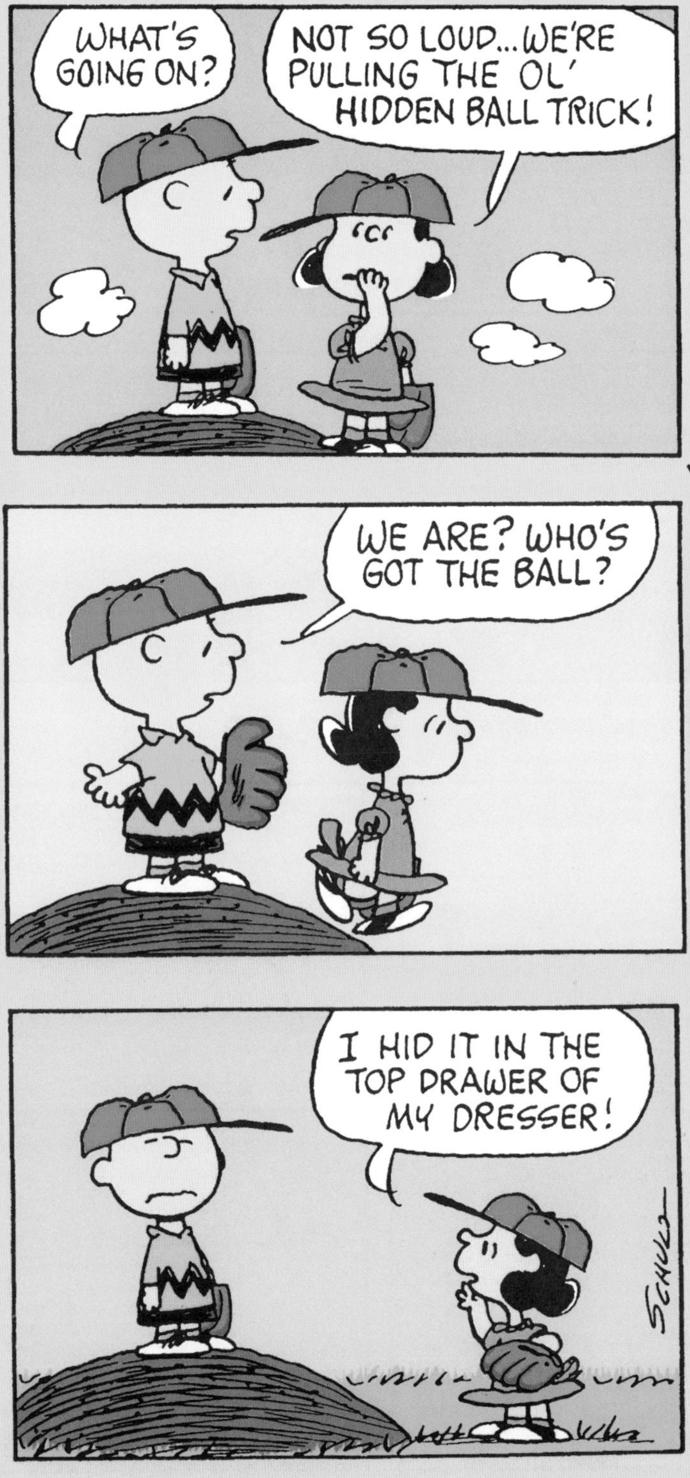
WHAT'S GOING ON?
NOT SO LOUD...WE'RE PULLING THE OL' HIDDEN BALL TRICK!
WE ARE? WHO'S GOT THE BALL?
I HID IT IN THE TOP DRAWER OF MY DRESSER!
SCHULZ

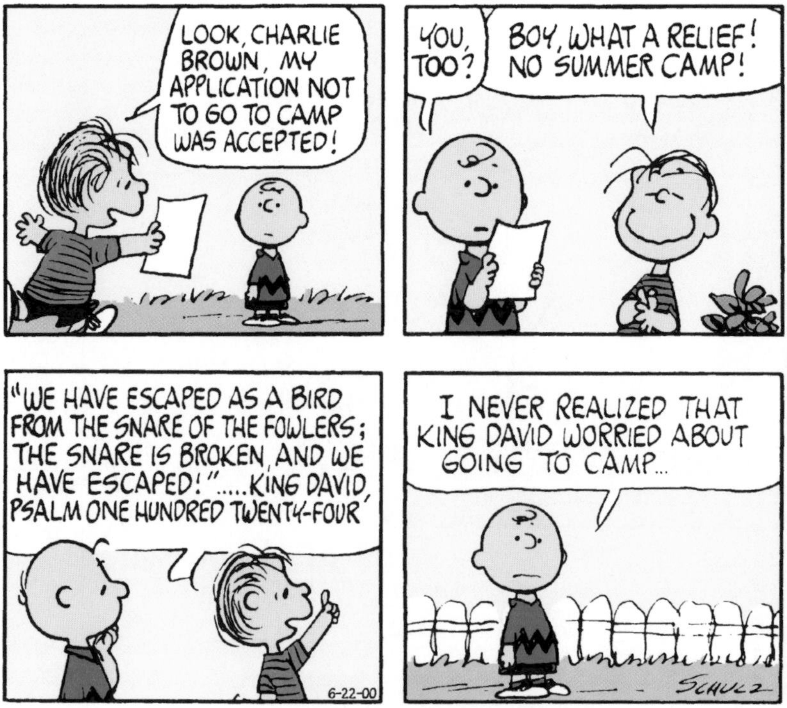
LOOK, CHARLIE BROWN, MY APPLICATION NOT TO GO TO CAMP WAS ACCEPTED!
YOU, TOO?
BOY, WHAT A RELIEF! NO SUMMER CAMP!
"WE HAVE ESCAPED AS A BIRD FROM THE SNARE OF THE FOWLERS; THE SNARE IS BROKEN, AND WE HAVE ESCAPED!"....KING DAVID, PSALM ONE HUNDRED TWENTY-FOUR
6-22-00
I NEVER REALIZED THAT KING DAVID WORRIED ABOUT GOING TO CAMP...
SCHULZ

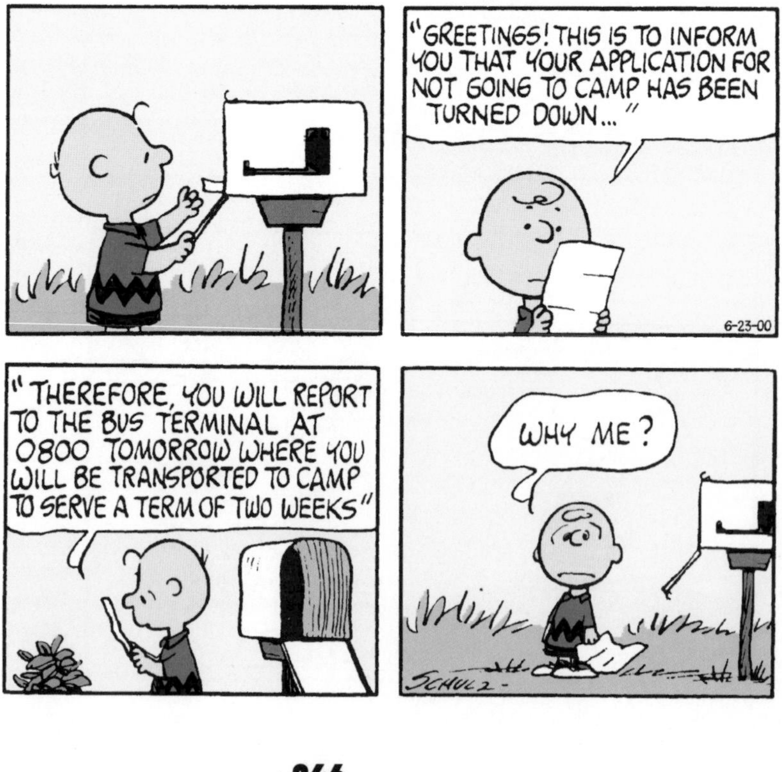
"GREETINGS! THIS IS TO INFORM YOU THAT YOUR APPLICATION FOR NOT GOING TO CAMP HAS BEEN TURNED DOWN..."
6-23-00
"THEREFORE, YOU WILL REPORT TO THE BUS TERMINAL AT 0800 TOMORROW WHERE YOU WILL BE TRANSPORTED TO CAMP TO SERVE A TERM OF TWO WEEKS"
WHY ME?
SCHULZ

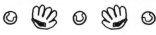

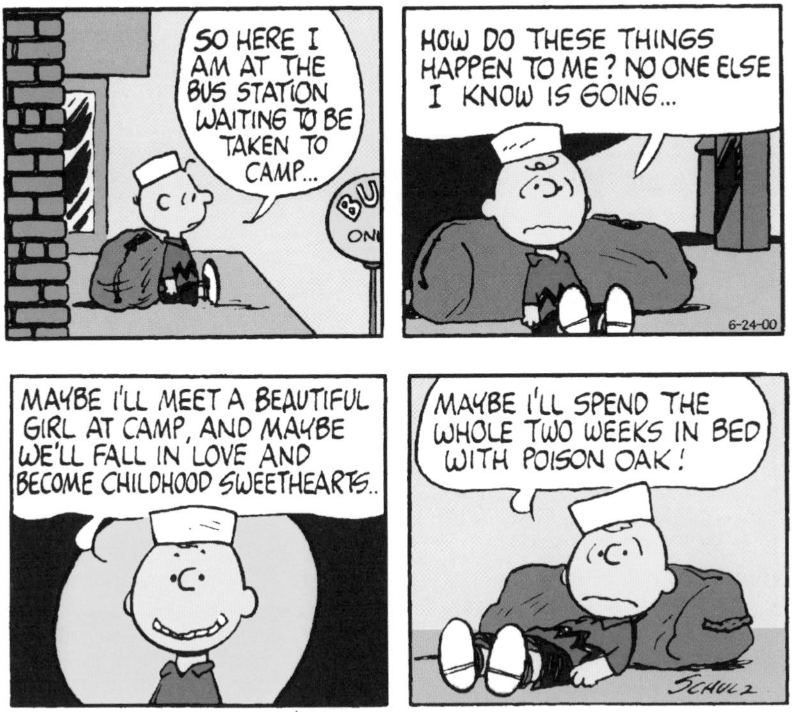
SO HERE I AM AT THE BUS STATION WAITING TO BE TAKEN TO CAMP...
BU
ON
HOW DO THESE THINGS HAPPEN TO ME? NO ONE ELSE I KNOW IS GOING...
6-24-00
MAYBE I'LL MEET A BEAUTIFUL GIRL AT CAMP, AND MAYBE WE'LL FALL IN LOVE AND BECOME CHILDHOOD SWEETHEARTS..
MAYBE I'LL SPEND THE WHOLE TWO WEEKS IN BED WITH POISON OAK!
SCHULZ

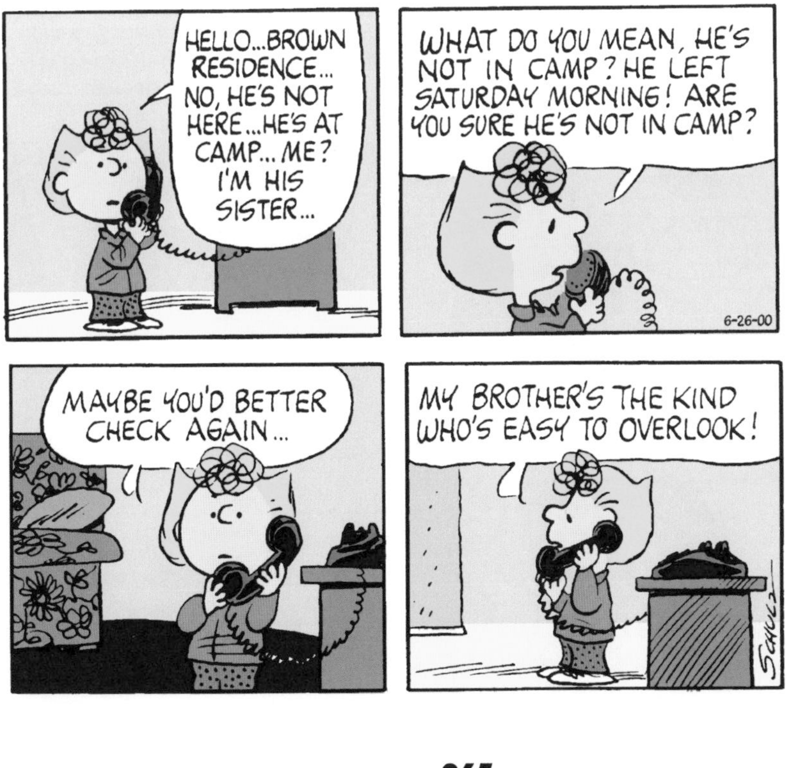
HELLO...BROWN RESIDENCE... NO, HE'S NOT HERE...HE'S AT CAMP... ME? I'M HIS SISTER...
WHAT DO YOU MEAN, HE'S NOT IN CAMP? HE LEFT SATURDAY MORNING! ARE YOU SURE HE'S NOT IN CAMP?
6-26-00
MAYBE YOU'D BETTER CHECK AGAIN...
MY BROTHER'S THE KIND WHO'S EASY TO OVERLOOK!
SCHULZ

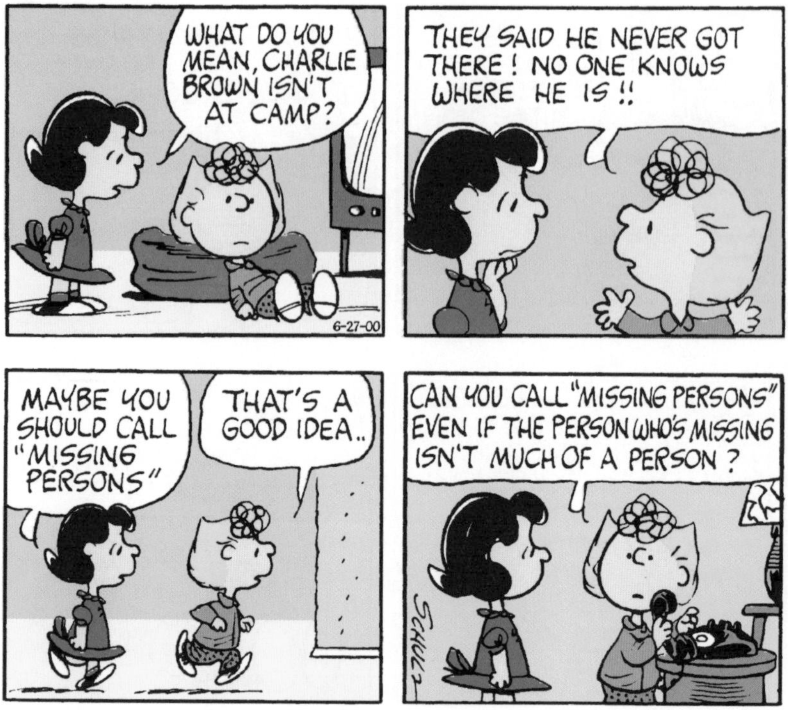
WHAT DO YOU MEAN, CHARLIE BROWN ISN'T AT CAMP?
6-27-00
THEY SAID HE NEVER GOT THERE! NO ONE KNOWS WHERE HE IS!!
MAYBE YOU SHOULD CALL "MISSING PERSONS"
THAT'S A GOOD IDEA..
CAN YOU CALL "MISSING PERSONS" EVEN IF THE PERSON WHO'S MISSING ISN'T MUCH OF A PERSON?
SCHULZ

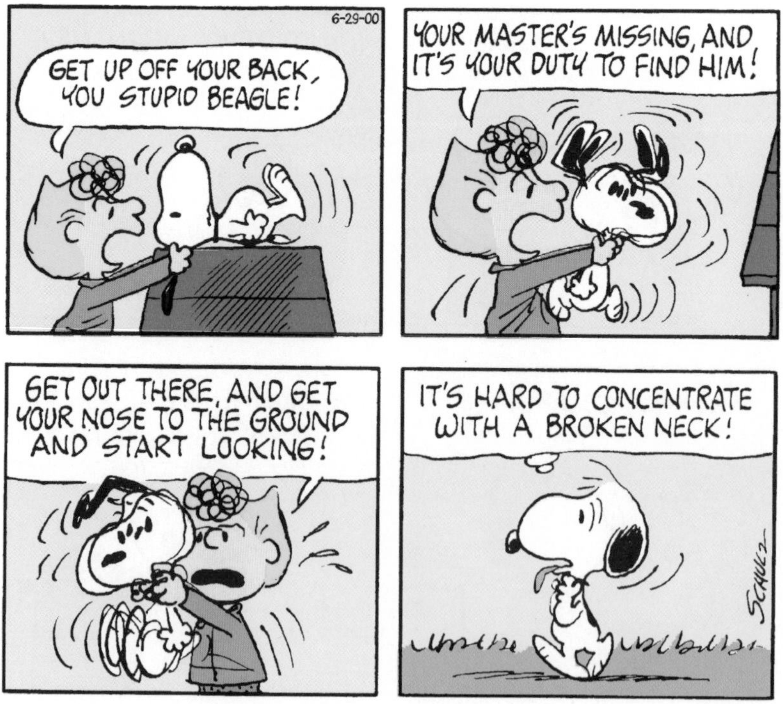
6-29-00
GET UP OFF YOUR BACK, YOU STUPID BEAGLE!
YOUR MASTER'S MISSING, AND IT'S YOUR DUTY TO FIND HIM!
GET OUT THERE, AND GET YOUR NOSE TO THE GROUND AND START LOOKING!
IT'S HARD TO CONCENTRATE WITH A BROKEN NECK!
SCHULZ

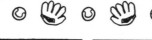

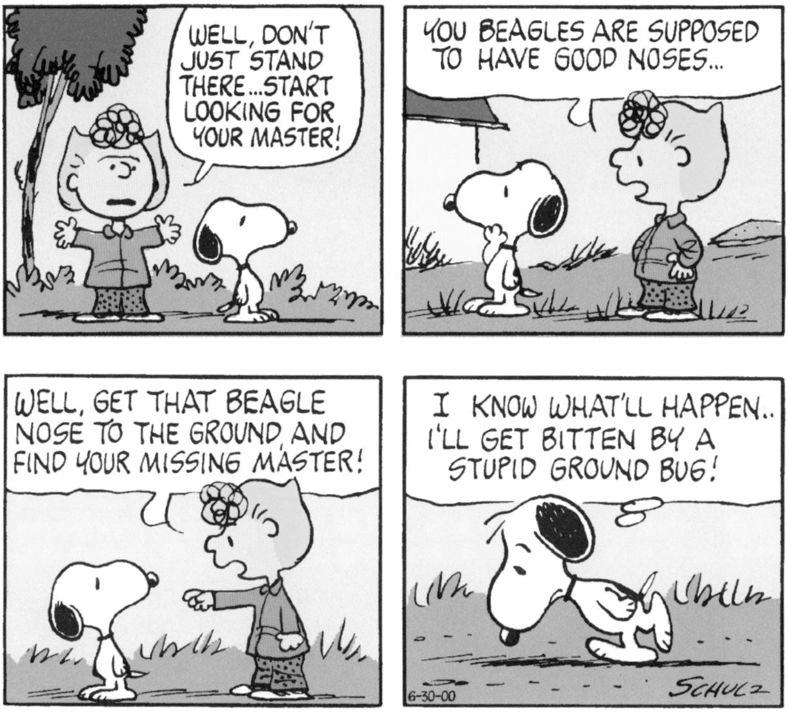
WELL, DON'T JUST STAND THERE...START LOOKING FOR YOUR MASTER!
YOU BEAGLES ARE SUPPOSED TO HAVE GOOD NOSES...
WELL, GET THAT BEAGLE NOSE TO THE GROUND, AND FIND YOUR MISSING MASTER!
I KNOW WHAT'LL HAPPEN.. I'LL GET BITTEN BY A STUPID GROUND BUG!
6-30-00
SCHULZ

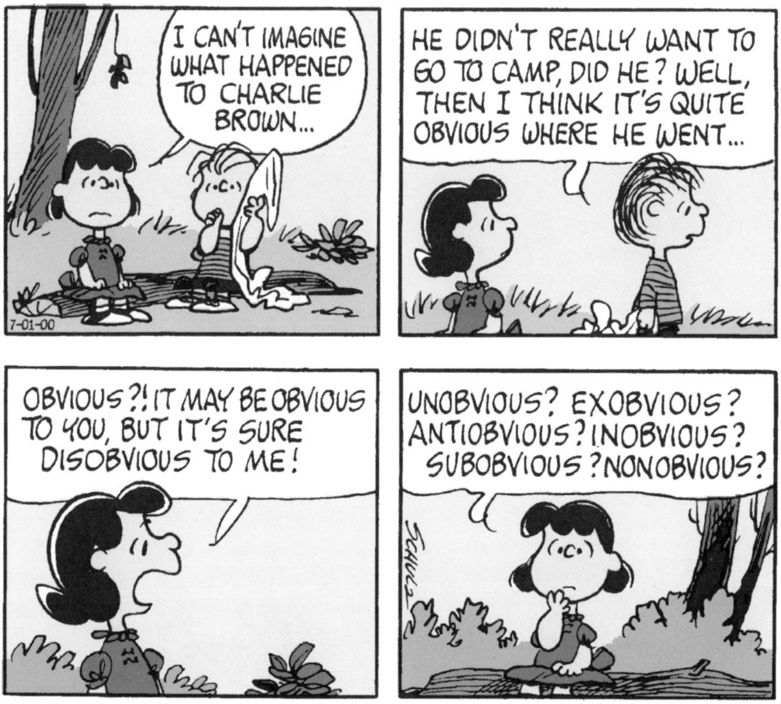
I CAN'T IMAGINE WHAT HAPPENED TO CHARLIE BROWN...
7-01-00
HE DIDN'T REALLY WANT TO GO TO CAMP, DID HE? WELL, THEN I THINK IT'S QUITE OBVIOUS WHERE HE WENT...
OBVIOUS?! IT MAY BE OBVIOUS TO YOU, BUT IT'S SURE DISOBVIOUS TO ME!
UNOBVIOUS? EXOBVIOUS? ANTIOBVIOUS? INOBVIOUS? SUBOBVIOUS? NONOBVIOUS?
SCHULZ

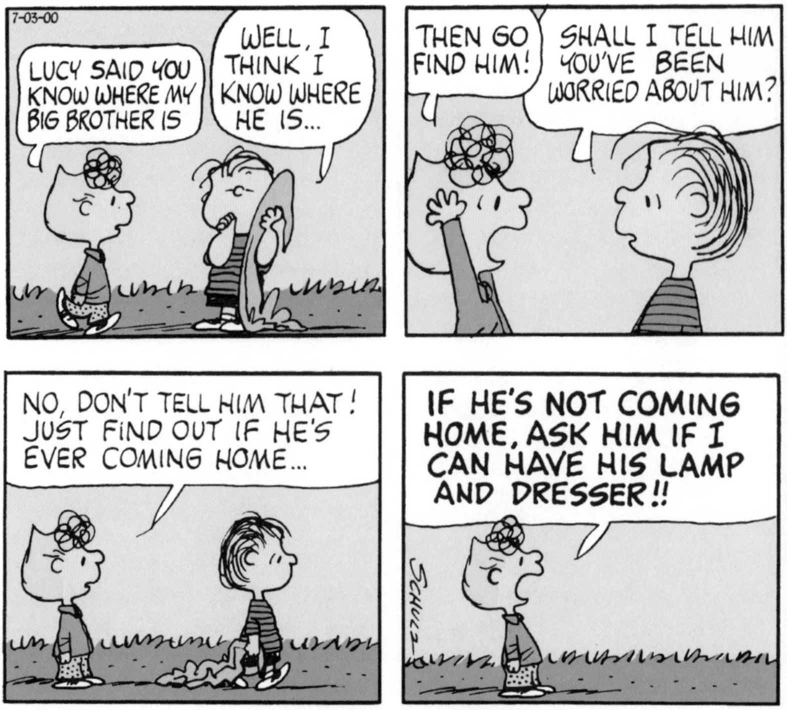
7-03-00
LUCY SAID YOU KNOW WHERE MY BIG BROTHER IS
WELL, I THINK I KNOW WHERE HE IS...
THEN GO FIND HIM!
SHALL I TELL HIM YOU'VE BEEN WORRIED ABOUT HIM?
NO, DON'T TELL HIM THAT! JUST FIND OUT IF HE'S EVER COMING HOME...
IF HE'S NOT COMING HOME, ASK HIM IF I CAN HAVE HIS LAMP AND DRESSER!!
SCHULZ

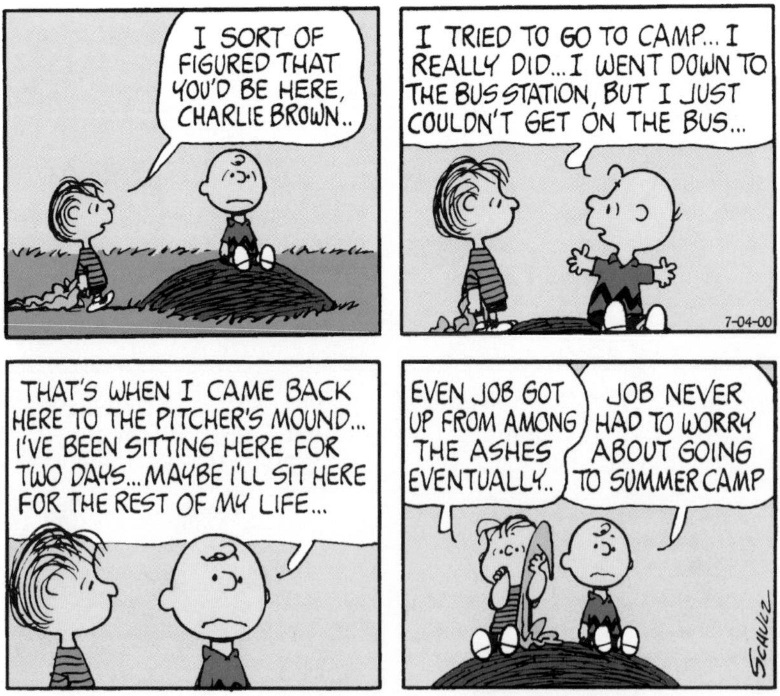
I SORT OF FIGURED THAT YOU'D BE HERE, CHARLIE BROWN..
I TRIED TO GO TO CAMP... I REALLY DID... I WENT DOWN TO THE BUS STATION, BUT I JUST COULDN'T GET ON THE BUS...
7-04-00
THAT'S WHEN I CAME BACK HERE TO THE PITCHER'S MOUND... I'VE BEEN SITTING HERE FOR TWO DAYS... MAYBE I'LL SIT HERE FOR THE REST OF MY LIFE...
EVEN JOB GOT UP FROM AMONG THE ASHES EVENTUALLY..
JOB NEVER HAD TO WORRY ABOUT GOING TO SUMMER CAMP
SCHULZ

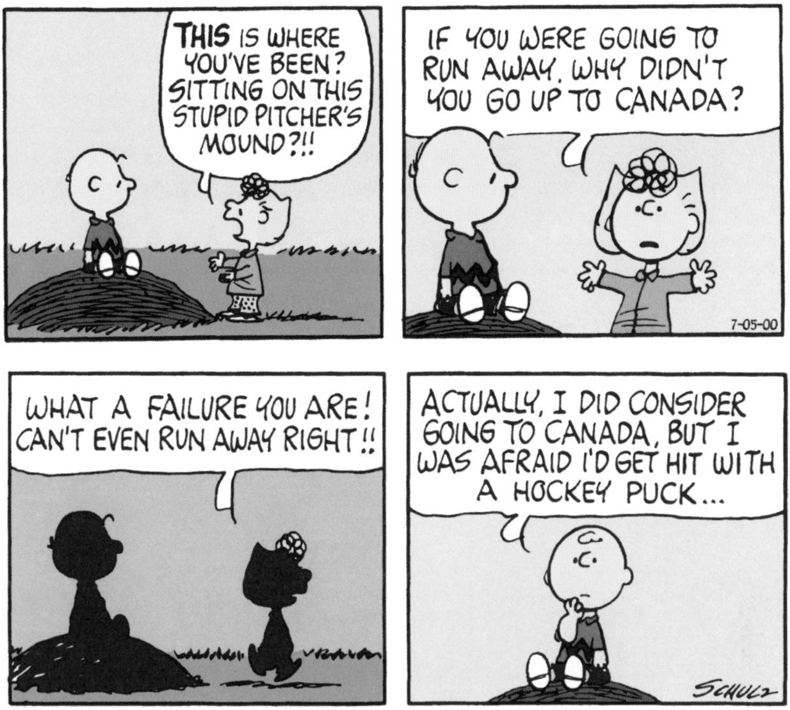
THIS IS WHERE YOU'VE BEEN? SITTING ON THIS STUPID PITCHER'S MOUND?!!
IF YOU WERE GOING TO RUN AWAY, WHY DIDN'T YOU GO UP TO CANADA?
7-05-00
WHAT A FAILURE YOU ARE! CAN'T EVEN RUN AWAY RIGHT!!
ACTUALLY, I DID CONSIDER GOING TO CANADA, BUT I WAS AFRAID I'D GET HIT WITH A HOCKEY PUCK...
SCHULZ

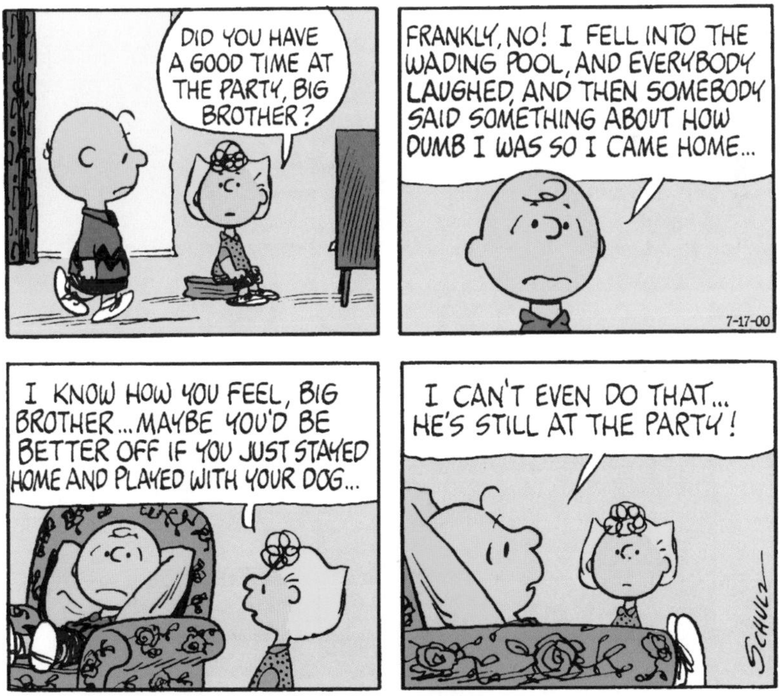
DID YOU HAVE A GOOD TIME AT THE PARTY, BIG BROTHER?
FRANKLY, NO! I FELL INTO THE WADING POOL, AND EVERYBODY LAUGHED, AND THEN SOMEBODY SAID SOMETHING ABOUT HOW DUMB I WAS SO I CAME HOME...
7-17-00
I KNOW HOW YOU FEEL, BIG BROTHER...MAYBE YOU'D BE BETTER OFF IF YOU JUST STAYED HOME AND PLAYED WITH YOUR DOG...
I CAN'T EVEN DO THAT... HE'S STILL AT THE PARTY!
SCHULZ

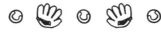

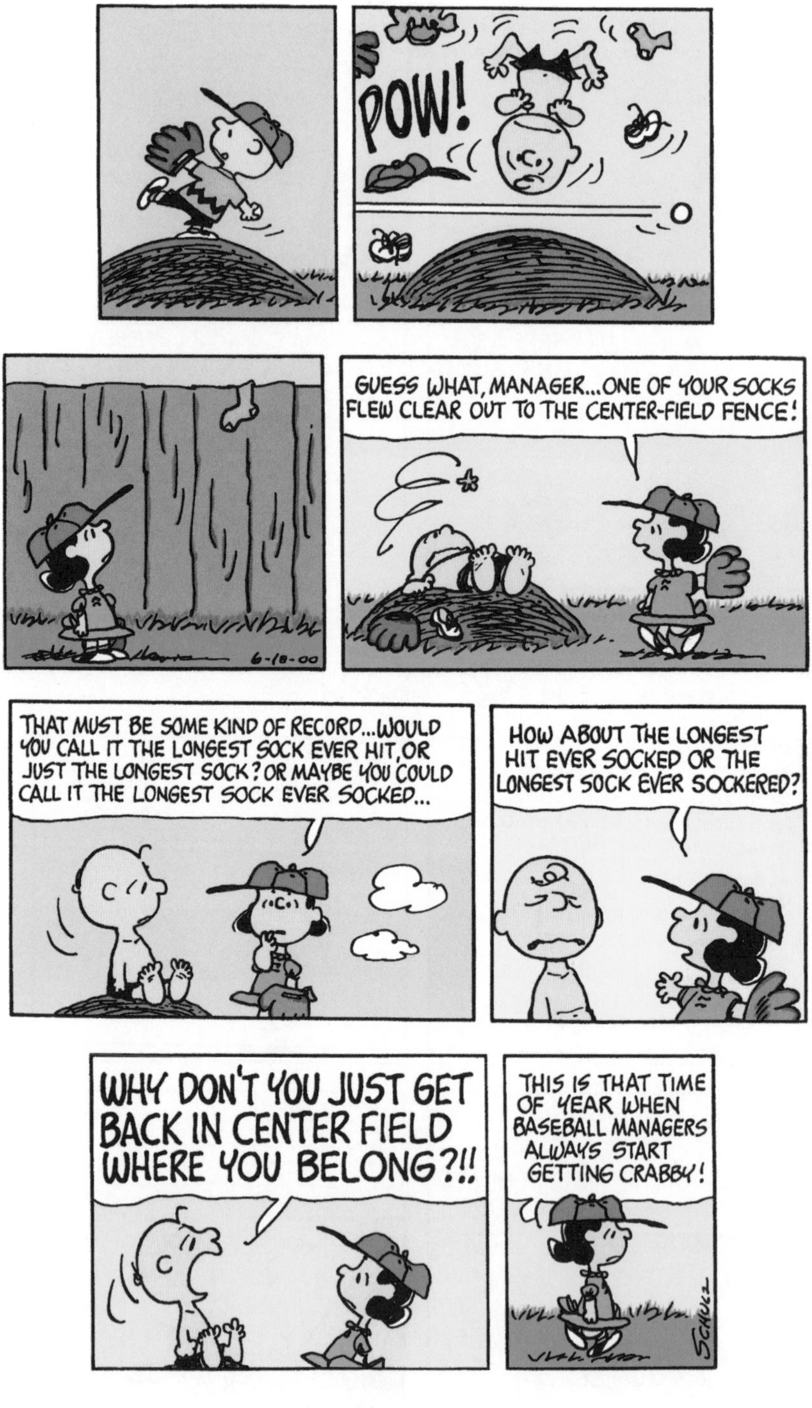
POW!
GUESS WHAT, MANAGER...ONE OF YOUR SOCKS FLEW CLEAR OUT TO THE CENTER-FIELD FENCE!
6-18-00
THAT MUST BE SOME KIND OF RECORD...WOULD YOU CALL IT THE LONGEST SOCK EVER HIT, OR JUST THE LONGEST SOCK? OR MAYBE YOU COULD CALL IT THE LONGEST SOCK EVER SOCKED...
HOW ABOUT THE LONGEST HIT EVER SOCKED OR THE LONGEST SOCK EVER SOCKERED?
WHY DON'T YOU JUST GET BACK IN CENTER FIELD WHERE YOU BELONG?!!
THIS IS THAT TIME OF YEAR WHEN BASEBALL MANAGERS ALWAYS START GETTING CRABBY!
SCHULZ

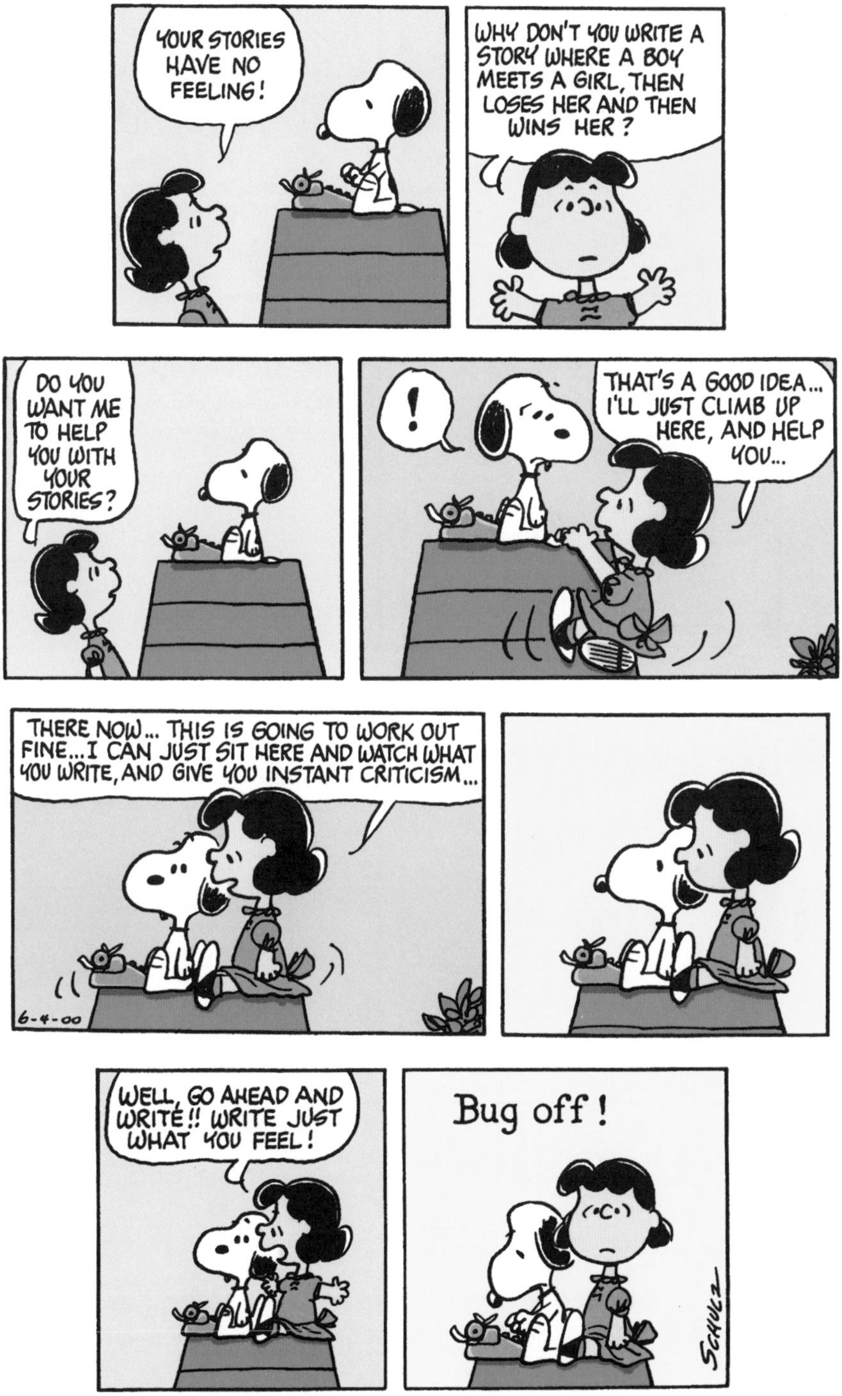
YOUR STORIES HAVE NO FEELING!
WHY DON'T YOU WRITE A STORY WHERE A BOY MEETS A GIRL, THEN LOSES HER AND THEN WINS HER?
DO YOU WANT ME TO HELP YOU WITH YOUR STORIES?
!
THAT'S A GOOD IDEA... I'LL JUST CLIMB UP HERE, AND HELP YOU...
THERE NOW... THIS IS GOING TO WORK OUT FINE...I CAN JUST SIT HERE AND WATCH WHAT YOU WRITE, AND GIVE YOU INSTANT CRITICISM...
6-4-00
WELL, GO AHEAD AND WRITE!! WRITE JUST WHAT YOU FEEL!
Bug off!
SCHULZ

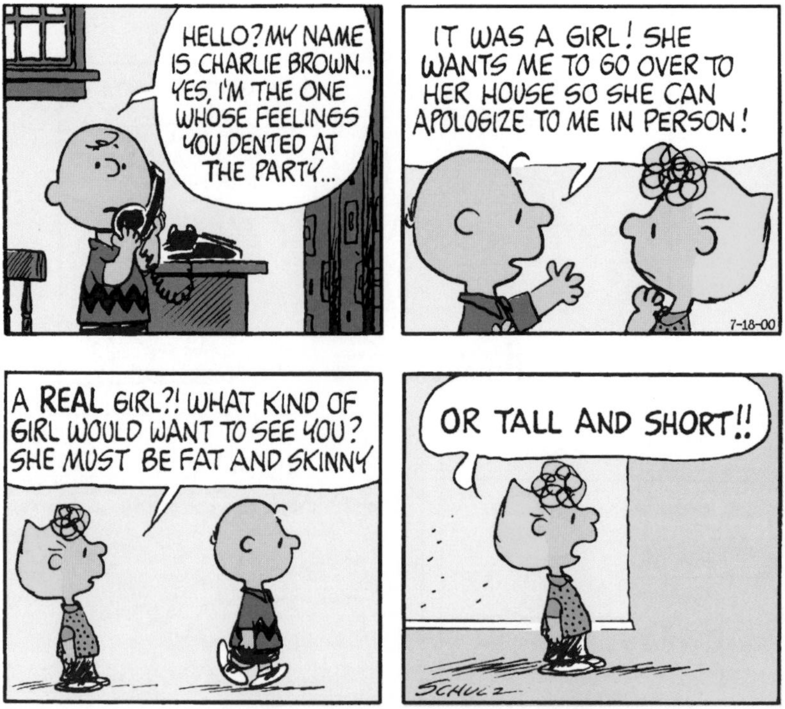
HELLO? MY NAME IS CHARLIE BROWN.. YES, I'M THE ONE WHOSE FEELINGS YOU DENTED AT THE PARTY...
IT WAS A GIRL! SHE WANTS ME TO GO OVER TO HER HOUSE SO SHE CAN APOLOGIZE TO ME IN PERSON!
7-18-00
A REAL GIRL?! WHAT KIND OF GIRL WOULD WANT TO SEE YOU? SHE MUST BE FAT AND SKINNY
OR TALL AND SHORT!!
SCHULZ

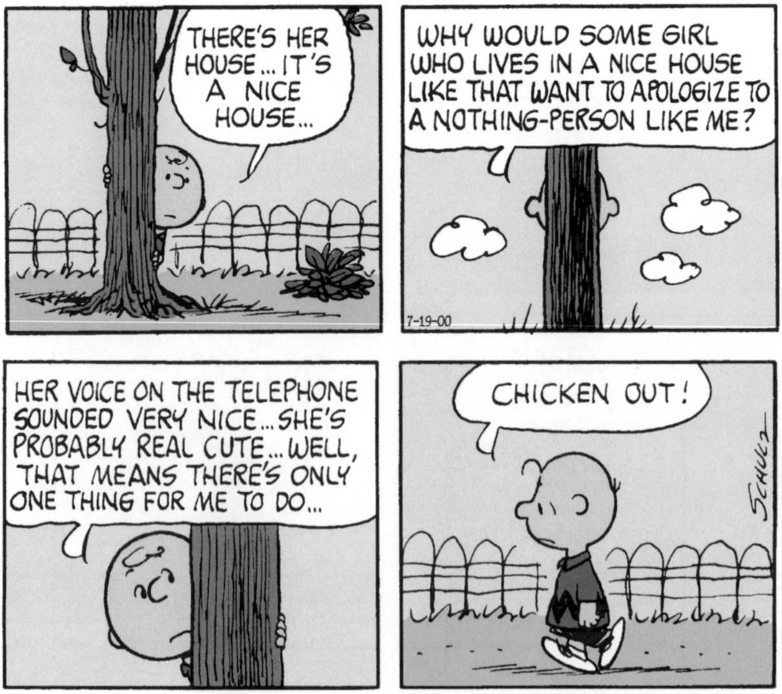
THERE'S HER HOUSE... IT'S A NICE HOUSE...
WHY WOULD SOME GIRL WHO LIVES IN A NICE HOUSE LIKE THAT WANT TO APOLOGIZE TO A NOTHING-PERSON LIKE ME?
7-19-00
HER VOICE ON THE TELEPHONE SOUNDED VERY NICE... SHE'S PROBABLY REAL CUTE... WELL, THAT MEANS THERE'S ONLY ONE THING FOR ME TO DO...
CHICKEN OUT!
SCHULZ

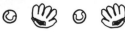

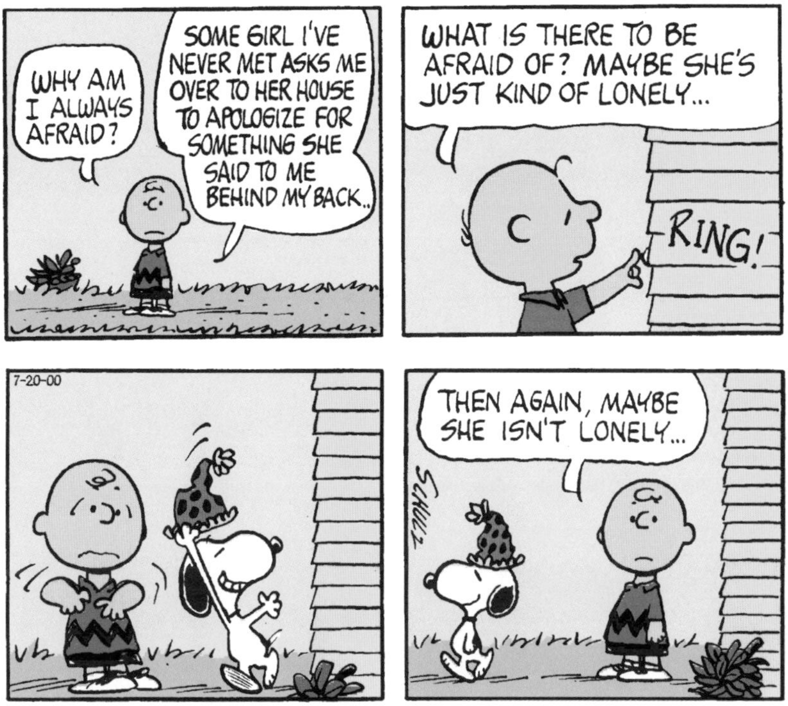
WHY AM I ALWAYS AFRAID?
SOME GIRL I'VE NEVER MET ASKS ME OVER TO HER HOUSE TO APOLOGIZE FOR SOMETHING SHE SAID TO ME BEHIND MY BACK..
WHAT IS THERE TO BE AFRAID OF? MAYBE SHE'S JUST KIND OF LONELY...
RING!
7-20-00
THEN AGAIN, MAYBE SHE ISN'T LONELY...
SCHULZ

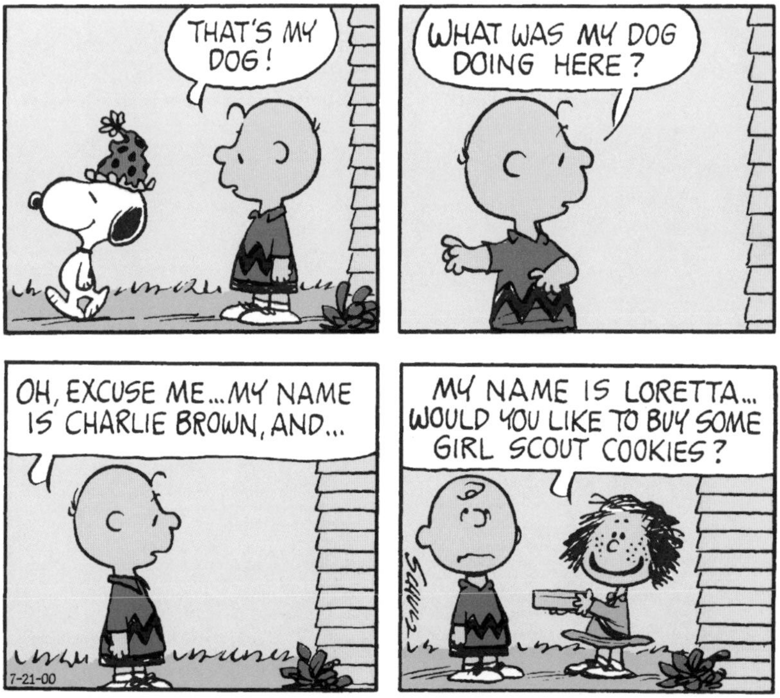
THAT'S MY DOG!
WHAT WAS MY DOG DOING HERE?
OH, EXCUSE ME...MY NAME IS CHARLIE BROWN, AND...
7-21-00
MY NAME IS LORETTA... WOULD YOU LIKE TO BUY SOME GIRL SCOUT COOKIES?
SCHULZ

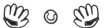

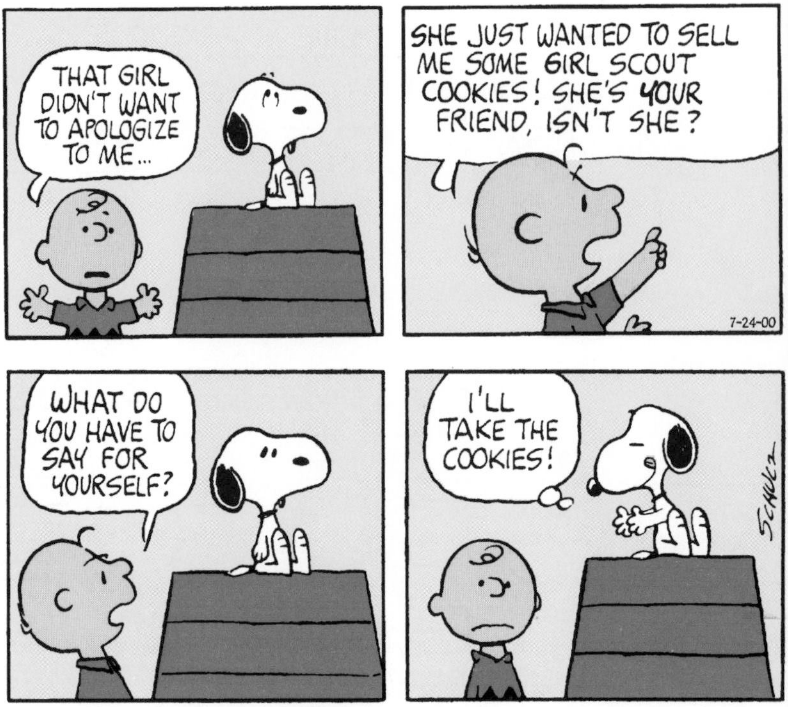
THAT GIRL DIDN'T WANT TO APOLOGIZE TO ME...
SHE JUST WANTED TO SELL ME SOME GIRL SCOUT COOKIES! SHE'S YOUR FRIEND, ISN'T SHE?
7-24-00
WHAT DO YOU HAVE TO SAY FOR YOURSELF?
I'LL TAKE THE COOKIES!
SCHULZ

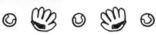

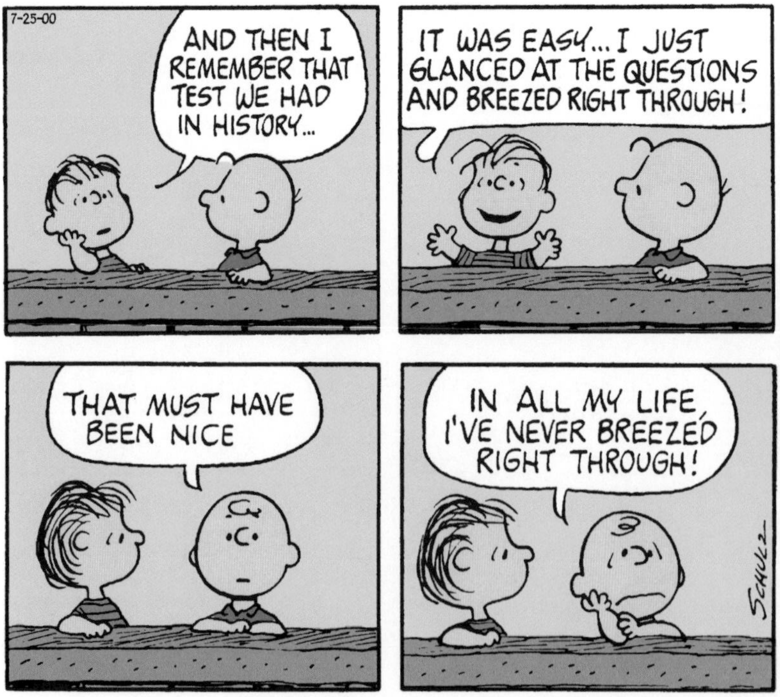
7-25-00
AND THEN I REMEMBER THAT TEST WE HAD IN HISTORY...
IT WAS EASY... I JUST GLANCED AT THE QUESTIONS AND BREEZED RIGHT THROUGH!
THAT MUST HAVE BEEN NICE
IN ALL MY LIFE, I'VE NEVER BREEZED RIGHT THROUGH!
SCHULZ

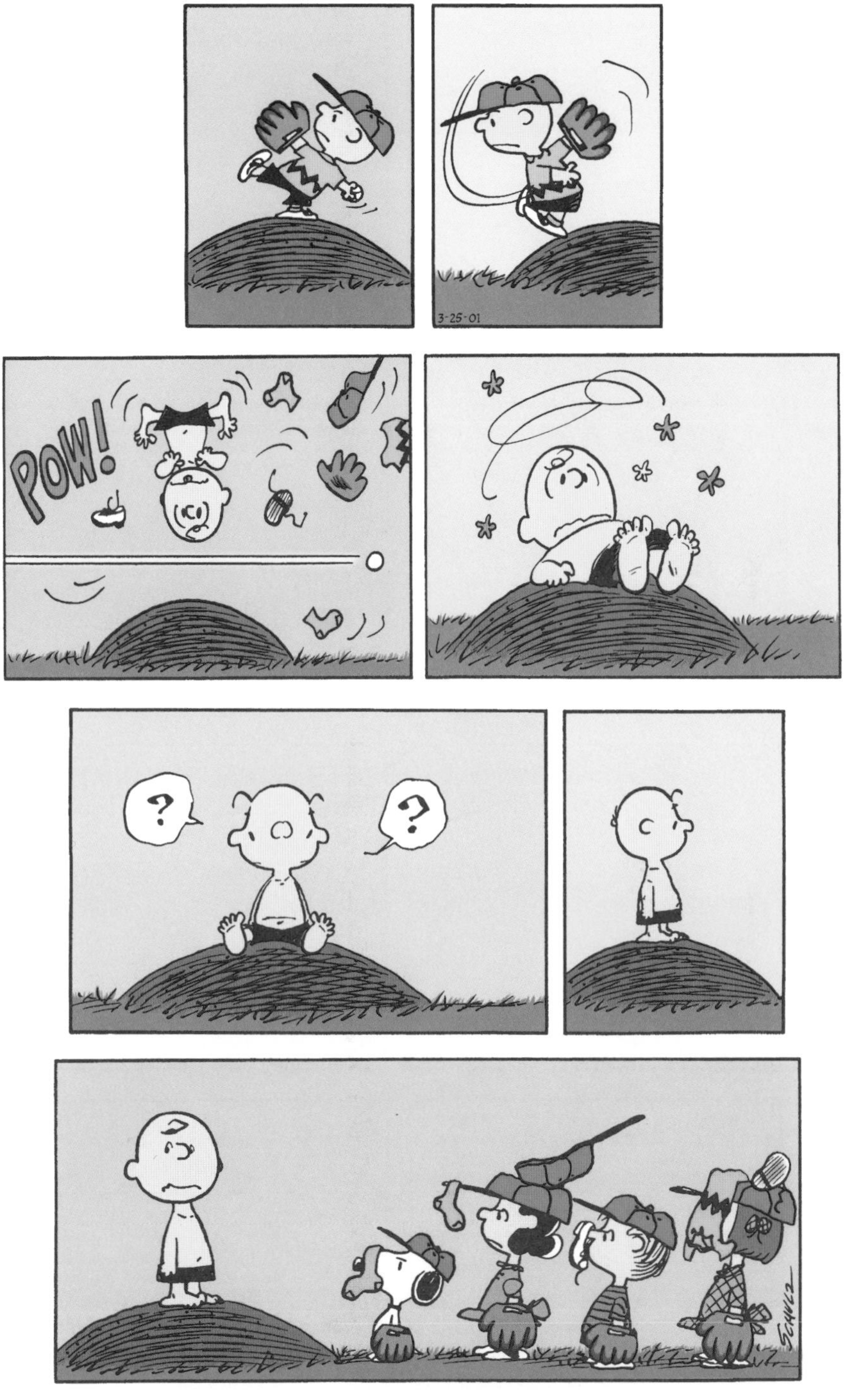
3-25-01
POW!
?
?
SCHULZ

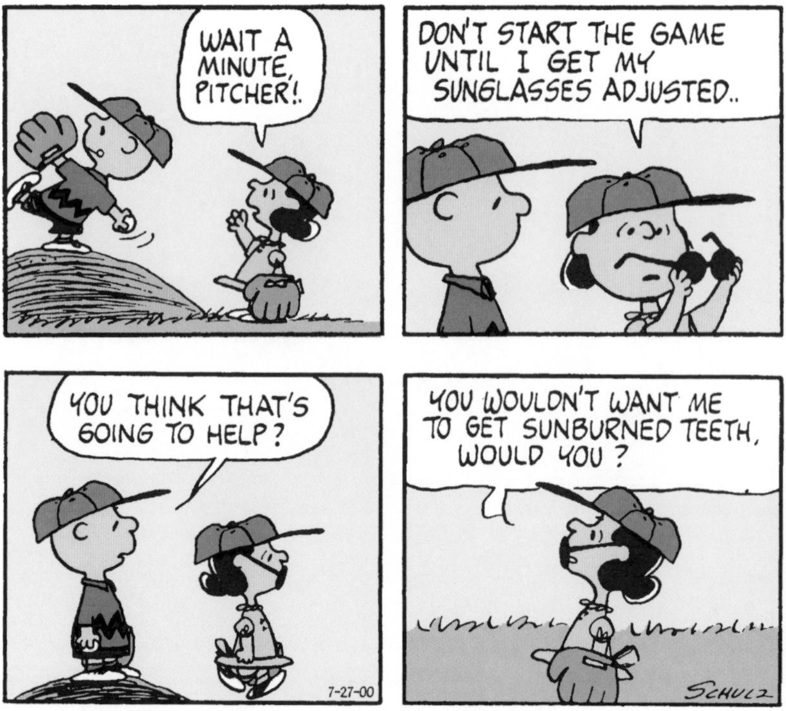
WAIT A MINUTE, PITCHER!.
DON'T START THE GAME UNTIL I GET MY SUNGLASSES ADJUSTED..
YOU THINK THAT'S GOING TO HELP?
YOU WOULDN'T WANT ME TO GET SUNBURNED TEETH, WOULD YOU?
7-27-00

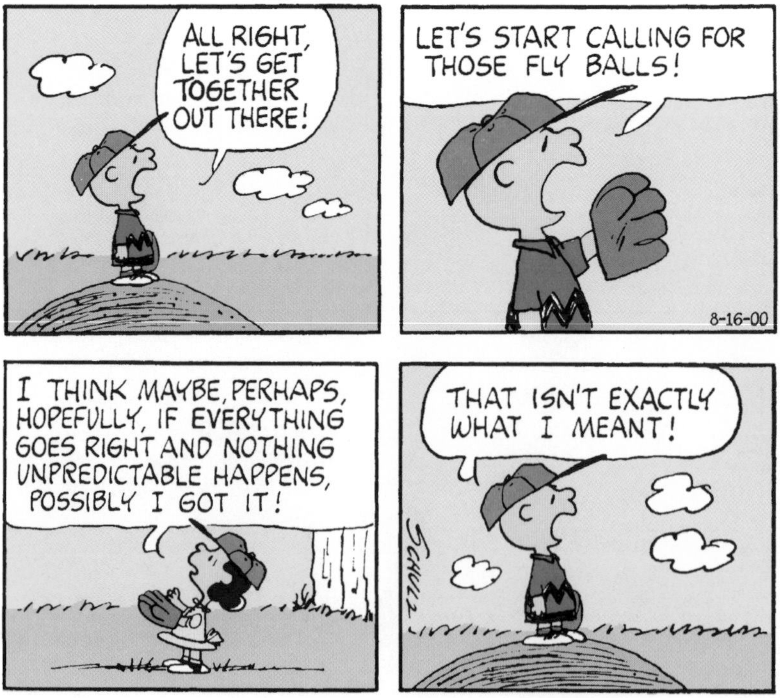
ALL RIGHT, LET'S GET TOGETHER OUT THERE!
LET'S START CALLING FOR THOSE FLY BALLS!
8-16-00
I THINK MAYBE, PERHAPS, HOPEFULLY, IF EVERYTHING GOES RIGHT AND NOTHING UNPREDICTABLE HAPPENS, POSSIBLY I GOT IT!
THAT ISN'T EXACTLY WHAT I MEANT!

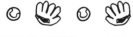

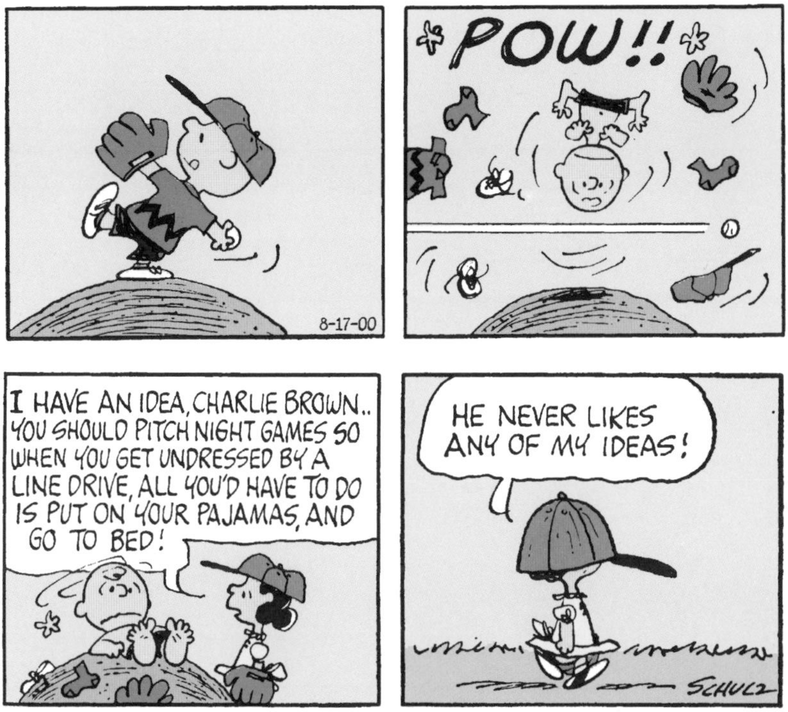

8-17-00
POW!!
I HAVE AN IDEA, CHARLIE BROWN.. YOU SHOULD PITCH NIGHT GAMES SO WHEN YOU GET UNDRESSED BY A LINE DRIVE, ALL YOU'D HAVE TO DO IS PUT ON YOUR PAJAMAS, AND GO TO BED!
HE NEVER LIKES ANY OF MY IDEAS!
SCHULZ

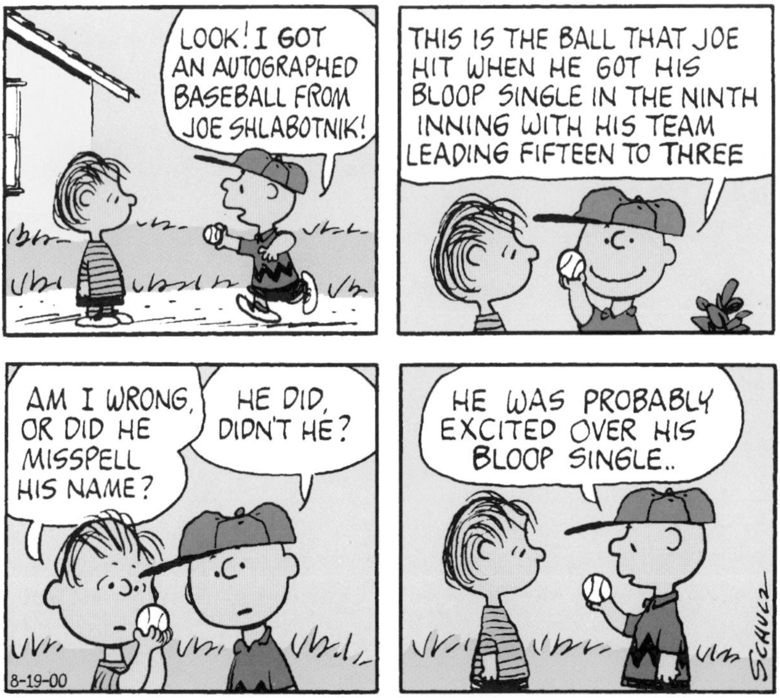

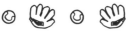

LOOK! I GOT AN AUTOGRAPHED BASEBALL FROM JOE SHLABOTNIK!
THIS IS THE BALL THAT JOE HIT WHEN HE GOT HIS BLOOP SINGLE IN THE NINTH INNING WITH HIS TEAM LEADING FIFTEEN TO THREE
AM I WRONG, OR DID HE MISSPELL HIS NAME?
HE DID, DIDN'T HE?
8-19-00
HE WAS PROBABLY EXCITED OVER HIS BLOOP SINGLE..
SCHULZ

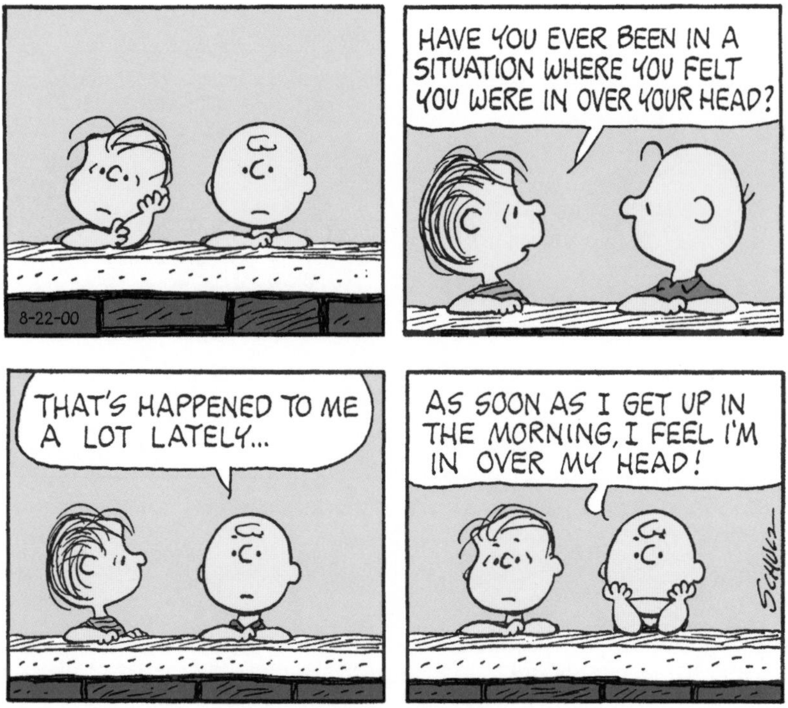
8-22-00
HAVE YOU EVER BEEN IN A SITUATION WHERE YOU FELT YOU WERE IN OVER YOUR HEAD?
THAT'S HAPPENED TO ME A LOT LATELY...
AS SOON AS I GET UP IN THE MORNING, I FEEL I'M IN OVER MY HEAD!
SCHULZ

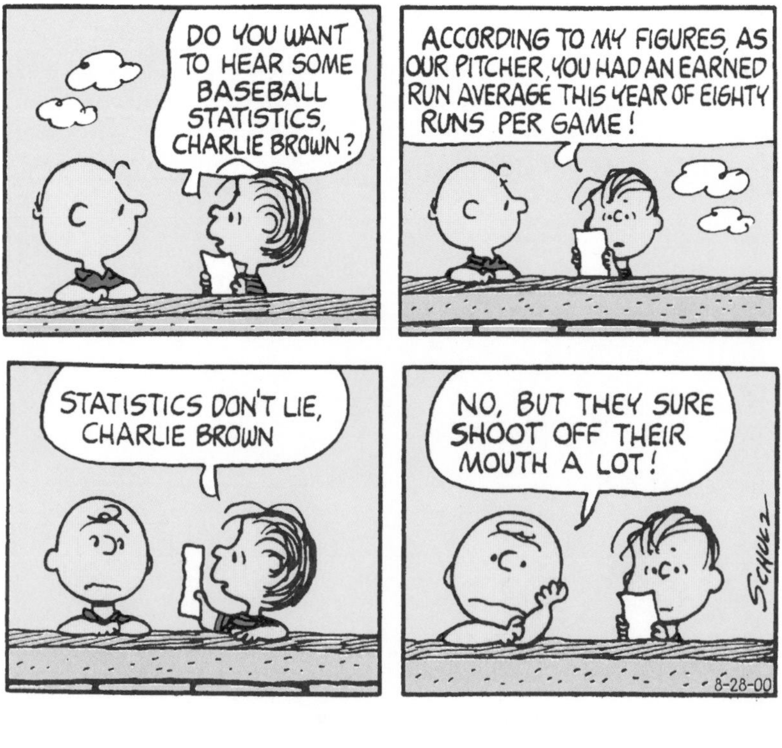
DO YOU WANT TO HEAR SOME BASEBALL STATISTICS, CHARLIE BROWN?
ACCORDING TO MY FIGURES, AS OUR PITCHER, YOU HAD AN EARNED RUN AVERAGE THIS YEAR OF EIGHTY RUNS PER GAME!
STATISTICS DON'T LIE, CHARLIE BROWN
NO, BUT THEY SURE SHOOT OFF THEIR MOUTH A LOT!
SCHULZ
8-28-00

PSYCHIATRIC HELP 5¢

THE DOCTOR IS IN

MY TROUBLE IS I NEVER KNOW IF I'M DOING THE RIGHT THING

I NEED TO HAVE SOMEONE AROUND WHO CAN TELL ME WHEN I'M DOING THE RIGHT THING...

6-10-01

OKAY... YOU'RE DOING THE RIGHT THING... THAT'LL BE FIVE CENTS, PLEASE!

THE DOCTOR IS IN

PSYCHIATRIC HELP 5¢

THE DOCTOR IS IN

BACK ALREADY? WHAT HAPPENED?

THE DOCTOR IS IN

I WAS WRONG... IT DIDN'T HELP..

YOU NEED MORE IN LIFE THAN JUST HAVING SOMEONE AROUND TO TELL YOU WHEN YOU'RE DOING THE RIGHT THING...

NOW, YOU'VE **REALLY** LEARNED SOMETHING! THAT'LL BE ANOTHER FIVE CENTS, PLEASE!

THE DOCTOR IS IN

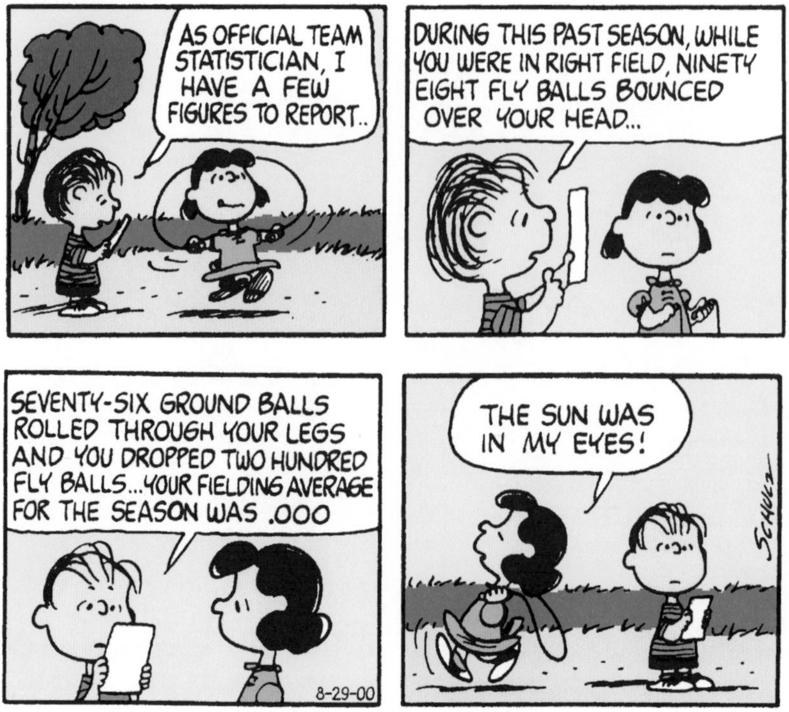
AS OFFICIAL TEAM STATISTICIAN, I HAVE A FEW FIGURES TO REPORT..
DURING THIS PAST SEASON, WHILE YOU WERE IN RIGHT FIELD, NINETY EIGHT FLY BALLS BOUNCED OVER YOUR HEAD...
SEVENTY-SIX GROUND BALLS ROLLED THROUGH YOUR LEGS AND YOU DROPPED TWO HUNDRED FLY BALLS...YOUR FIELDING AVERAGE FOR THE SEASON WAS .000
8-29-00
THE SUN WAS IN MY EYES!
SCHULZ

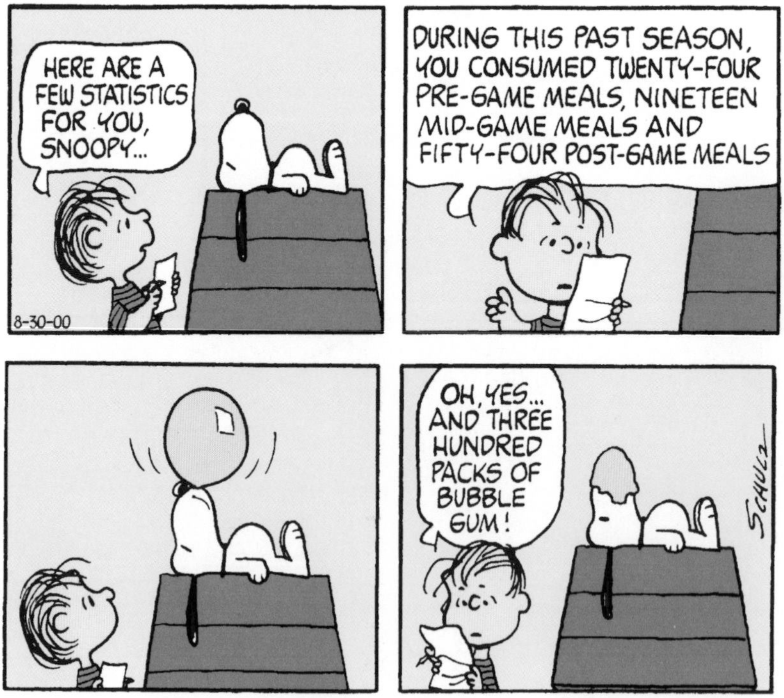
HERE ARE A FEW STATISTICS FOR YOU, SNOOPY...
8-30-00
DURING THIS PAST SEASON, YOU CONSUMED TWENTY-FOUR PRE-GAME MEALS, NINETEEN MID-GAME MEALS AND FIFTY-FOUR POST-GAME MEALS
OH, YES... AND THREE HUNDRED PACKS OF BUBBLE GUM!
SCHULZ

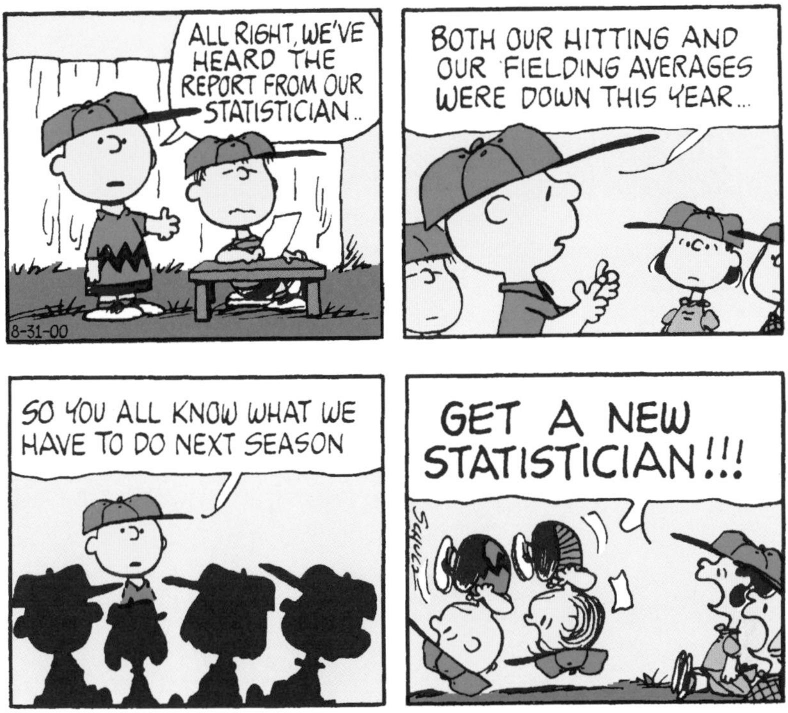
ALL RIGHT, WE'VE HEARD THE REPORT FROM OUR STATISTICIAN..
8-31-00
BOTH OUR HITTING AND OUR FIELDING AVERAGES WERE DOWN THIS YEAR...
SO YOU ALL KNOW WHAT WE HAVE TO DO NEXT SEASON
GET A NEW STATISTICIAN!!!
SCHULZ

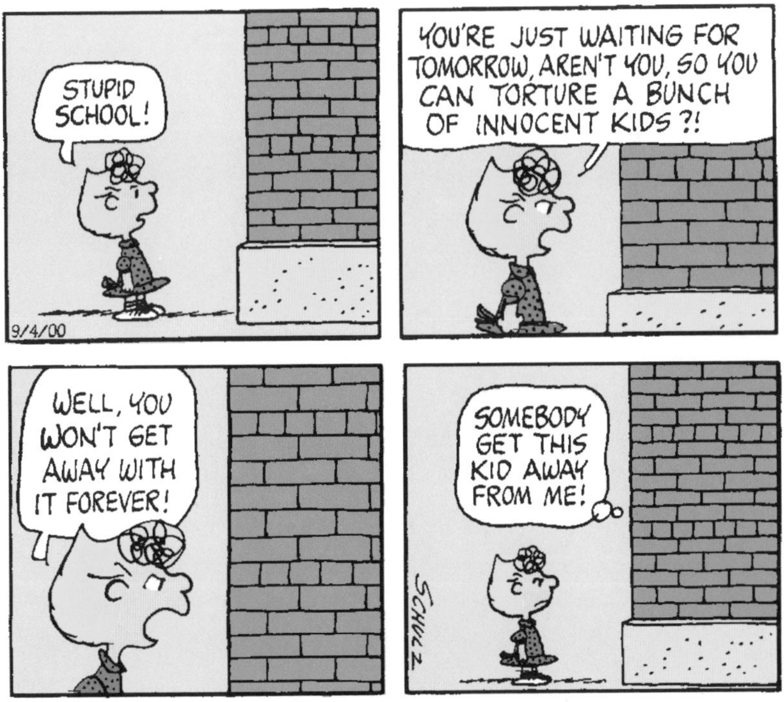
STUPID SCHOOL!
9/4/00
YOU'RE JUST WAITING FOR TOMORROW, AREN'T YOU, SO YOU CAN TORTURE A BUNCH OF INNOCENT KIDS?!
WELL, YOU WON'T GET AWAY WITH IT FOREVER!
SOMEBODY GET THIS KID AWAY FROM ME!
SCHULZ

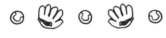

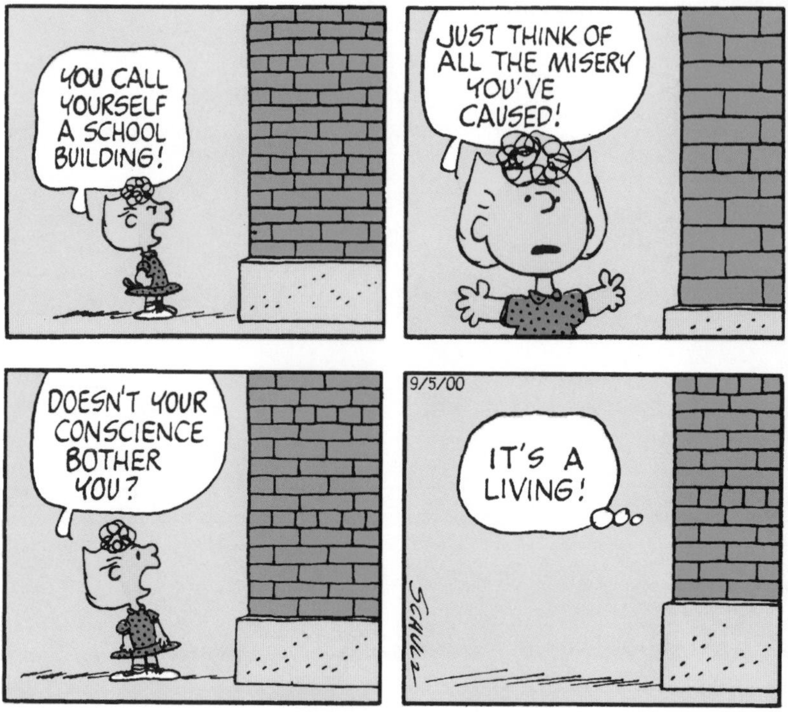
YOU CALL YOURSELF A SCHOOL BUILDING!
JUST THINK OF ALL THE MISERY YOU'VE CAUSED!
DOESN'T YOUR CONSCIENCE BOTHER YOU?
9/5/00
IT'S A LIVING!
SCHULZ

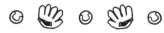

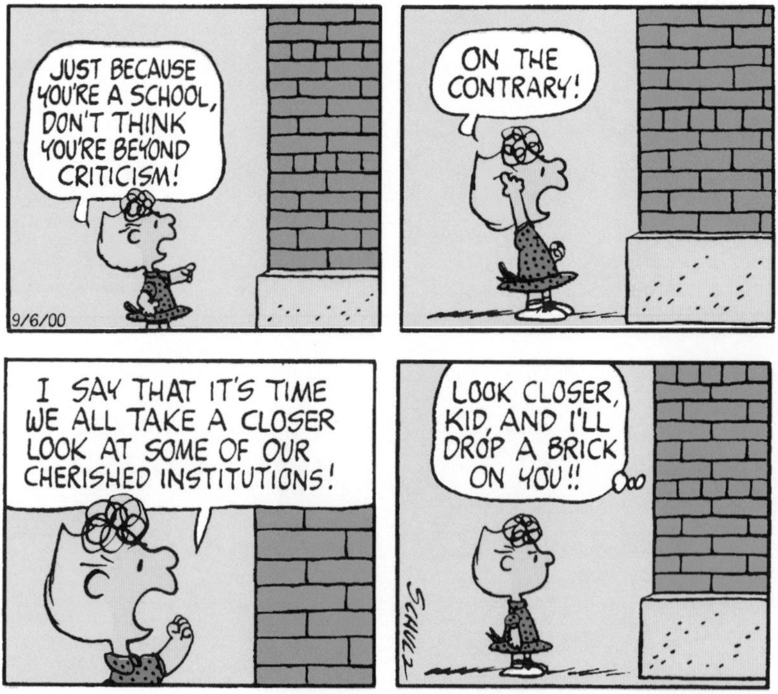
JUST BECAUSE YOU'RE A SCHOOL, DON'T THINK YOU'RE BEYOND CRITICISM!
9/6/00
ON THE CONTRARY!
I SAY THAT IT'S TIME WE ALL TAKE A CLOSER LOOK AT SOME OF OUR CHERISHED INSTITUTIONS!
LOOK CLOSER, KID, AND I'LL DROP A BRICK ON YOU!!
SCHULZ

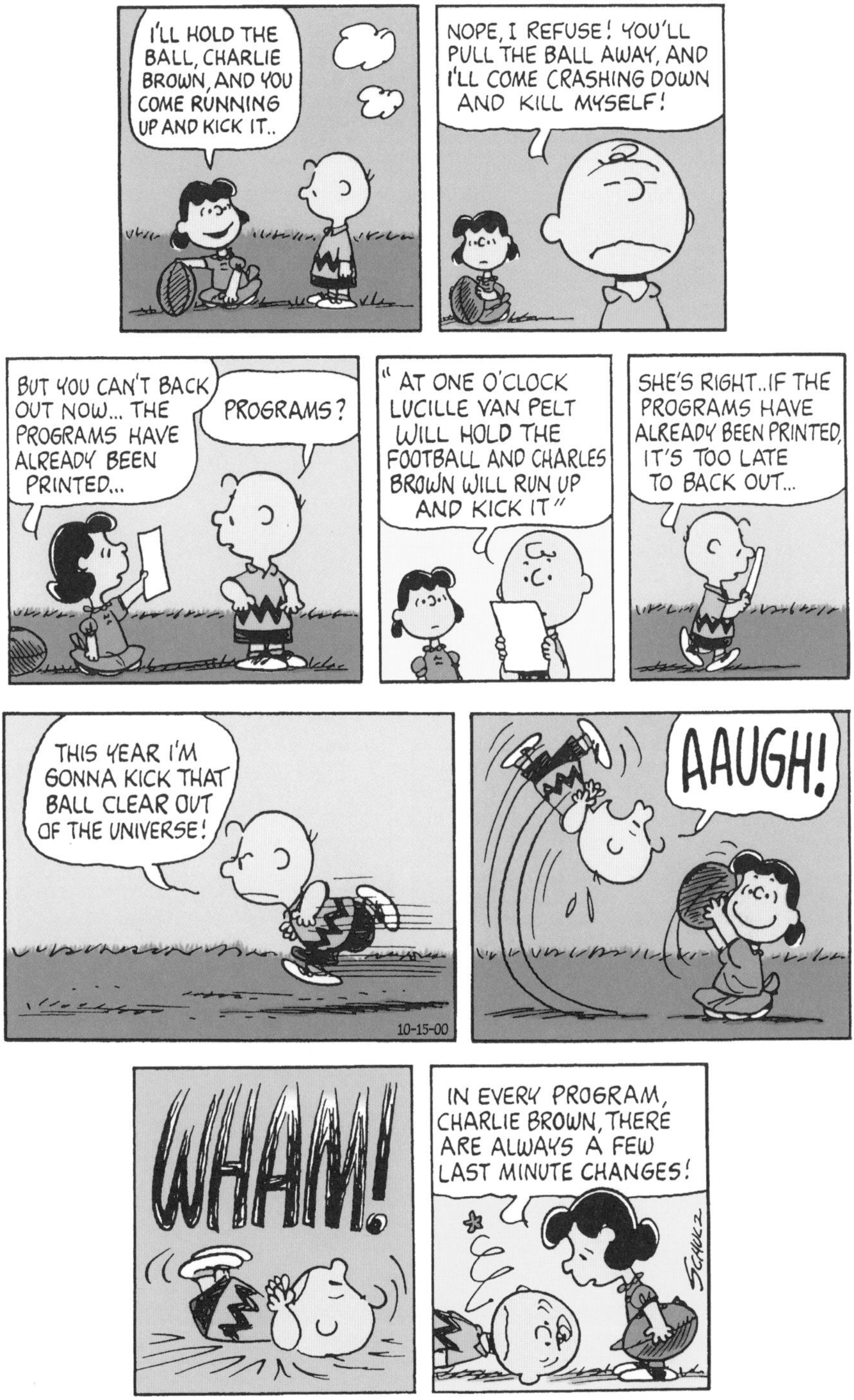
I'LL HOLD THE BALL, CHARLIE BROWN, AND YOU COME RUNNING UP AND KICK IT..
NOPE, I REFUSE! YOU'LL PULL THE BALL AWAY, AND I'LL COME CRASHING DOWN AND KILL MYSELF!
BUT YOU CAN'T BACK OUT NOW... THE PROGRAMS HAVE ALREADY BEEN PRINTED...
PROGRAMS?
"AT ONE O'CLOCK LUCILLE VAN PELT WILL HOLD THE FOOTBALL AND CHARLES BROWN WILL RUN UP AND KICK IT"
SHE'S RIGHT..IF THE PROGRAMS HAVE ALREADY BEEN PRINTED, IT'S TOO LATE TO BACK OUT...
THIS YEAR I'M GONNA KICK THAT BALL CLEAR OUT OF THE UNIVERSE!
10-15-00
AAUGH!
WHAM!
IN EVERY PROGRAM, CHARLIE BROWN, THERE ARE ALWAYS A FEW LAST MINUTE CHANGES!
SCHULZ

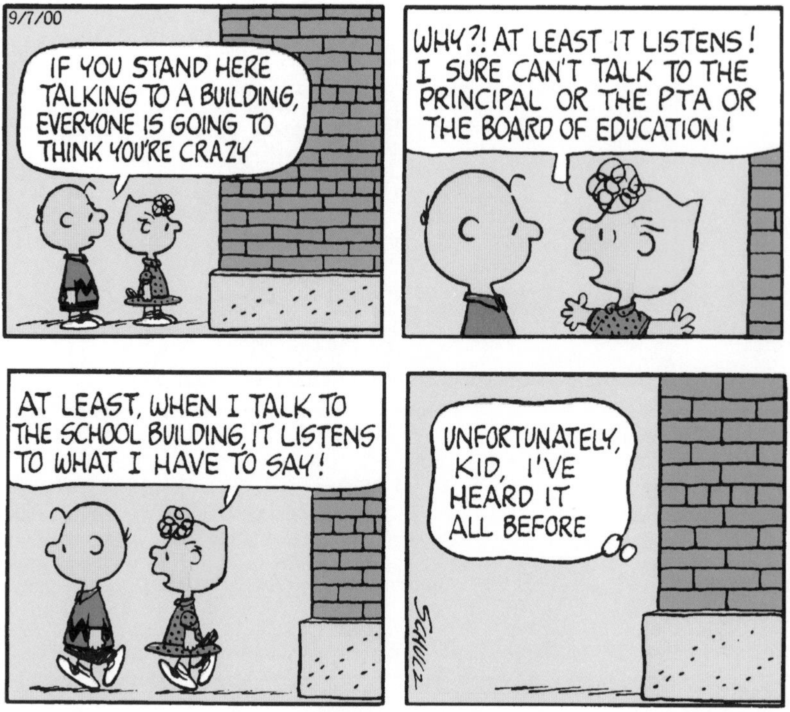
9/7/00
IF YOU STAND HERE TALKING TO A BUILDING, EVERYONE IS GOING TO THINK YOU'RE CRAZY
WHY?! AT LEAST IT LISTENS! I SURE CAN'T TALK TO THE PRINCIPAL OR THE PTA OR THE BOARD OF EDUCATION!
AT LEAST, WHEN I TALK TO THE SCHOOL BUILDING, IT LISTENS TO WHAT I HAVE TO SAY!
UNFORTUNATELY, KID, I'VE HEARD IT ALL BEFORE
SCHULZ

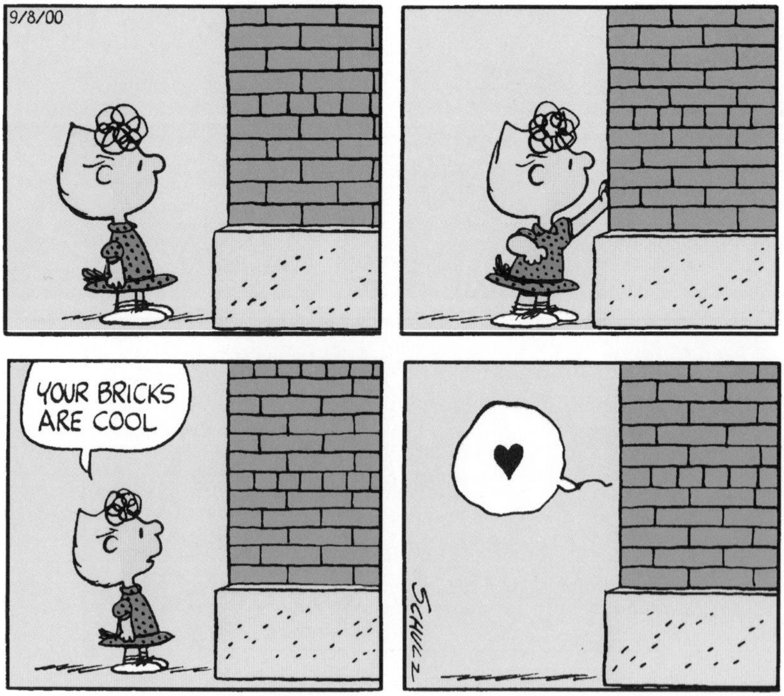
9/8/00
YOUR BRICKS ARE COOL
SCHULZ

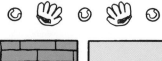

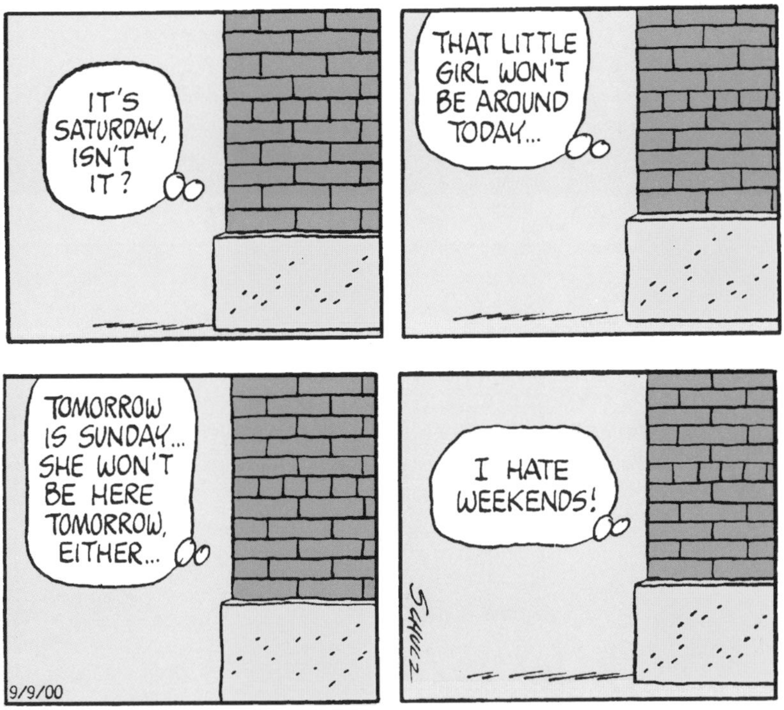
IT'S SATURDAY, ISN'T IT?
THAT LITTLE GIRL WON'T BE AROUND TODAY...
TOMORROW IS SUNDAY... SHE WON'T BE HERE TOMORROW, EITHER...
I HATE WEEKENDS!
9/9/00
SCHULZ

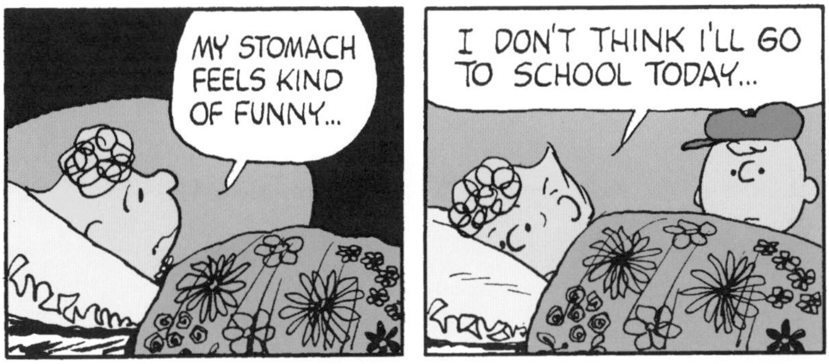
MY STOMACH FEELS KIND OF FUNNY...
I DON'T THINK I'LL GO TO SCHOOL TODAY...

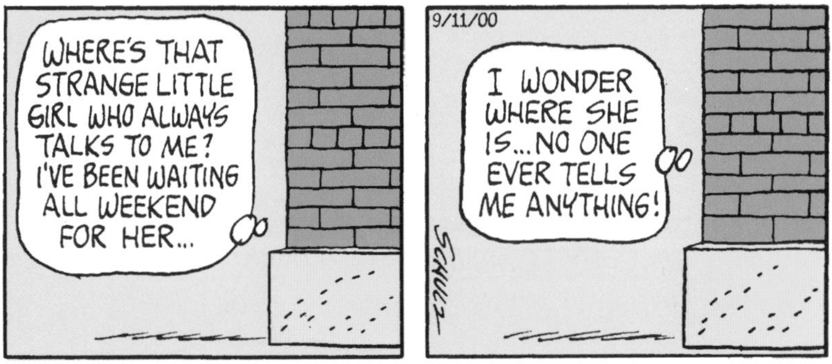
WHERE'S THAT STRANGE LITTLE GIRL WHO ALWAYS TALKS TO ME? I'VE BEEN WAITING ALL WEEKEND FOR HER...
9/11/00
I WONDER WHERE SHE IS...NO ONE EVER TELLS ME ANYTHING!
SCHULZ

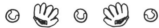

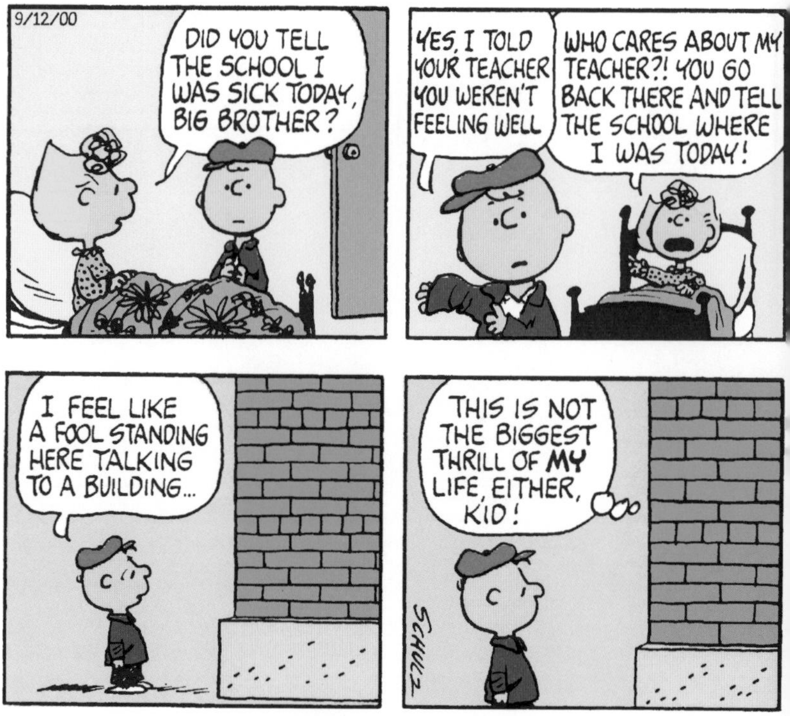
9/12/00
DID YOU TELL THE SCHOOL I WAS SICK TODAY, BIG BROTHER?
YES, I TOLD YOUR TEACHER YOU WEREN'T FEELING WELL
WHO CARES ABOUT MY TEACHER?! YOU GO BACK THERE AND TELL THE SCHOOL WHERE I WAS TODAY!
I FEEL LIKE A FOOL STANDING HERE TALKING TO A BUILDING...
THIS IS NOT THE BIGGEST THRILL OF MY LIFE, EITHER, KID!
SCHULZ

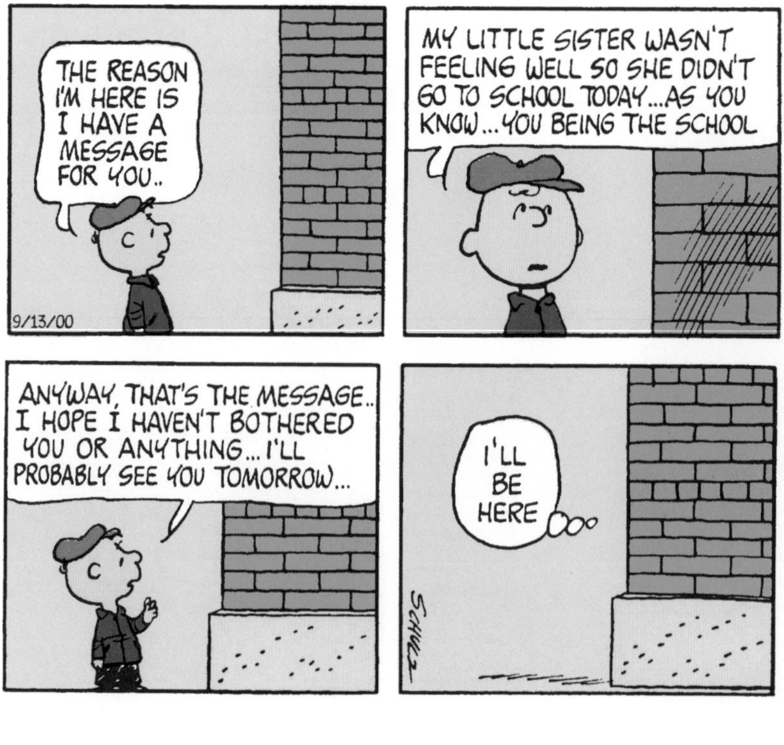
THE REASON I'M HERE IS I HAVE A MESSAGE FOR YOU..
9/13/00
MY LITTLE SISTER WASN'T FEELING WELL SO SHE DIDN'T GO TO SCHOOL TODAY...AS YOU KNOW...YOU BEING THE SCHOOL
ANYWAY, THAT'S THE MESSAGE.. I HOPE I HAVEN'T BOTHERED YOU OR ANYTHING... I'LL PROBABLY SEE YOU TOMORROW...
I'LL BE HERE
SCHULZ

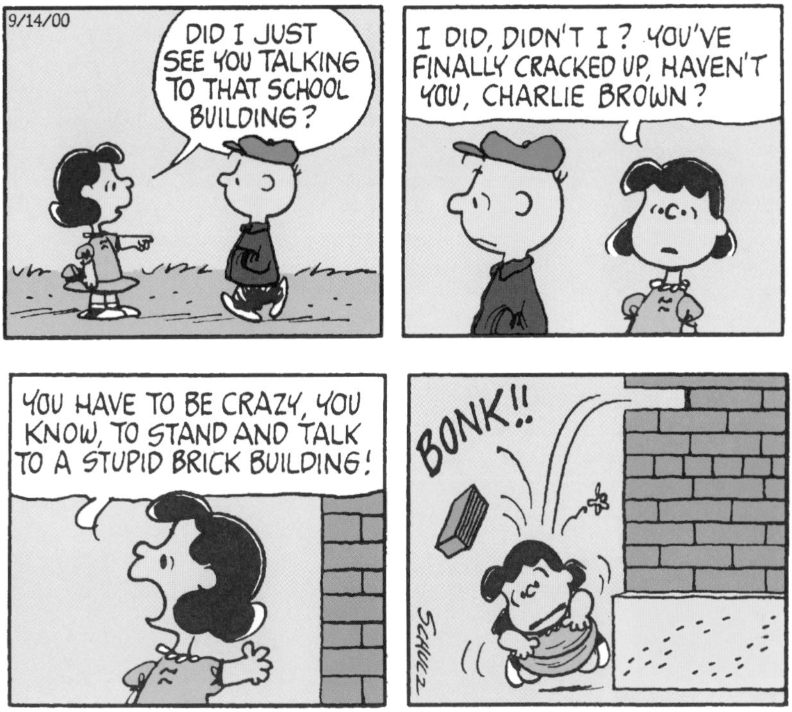
9/14/00
DID I JUST SEE YOU TALKING TO THAT SCHOOL BUILDING?
I DID, DIDN'T I? YOU'VE FINALLY CRACKED UP, HAVEN'T YOU, CHARLIE BROWN?
YOU HAVE TO BE CRAZY, YOU KNOW, TO STAND AND TALK TO A STUPID BRICK BUILDING!
BONK!!
SCHULZ

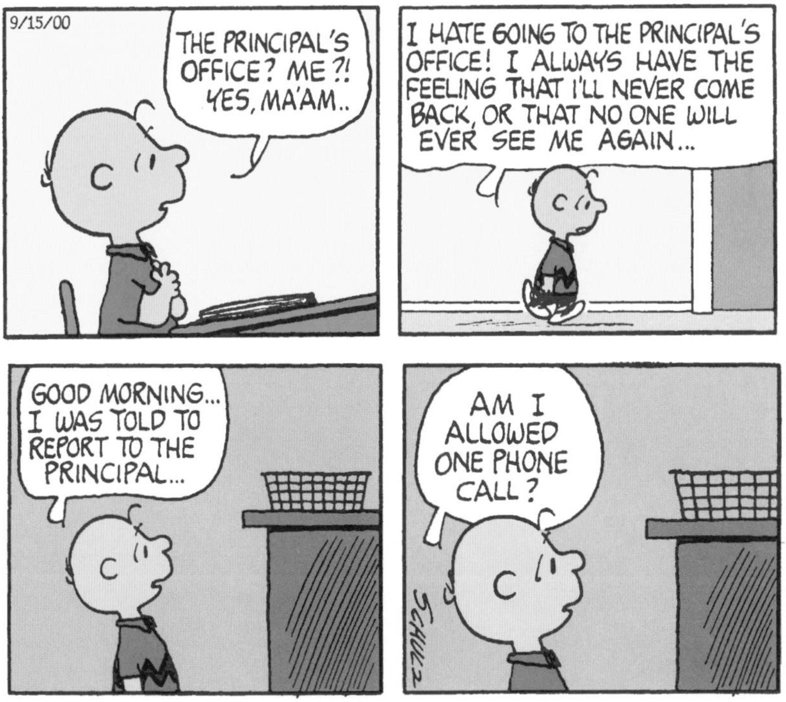
9/15/00
THE PRINCIPAL'S OFFICE? ME?! YES, MA'AM..
I HATE GOING TO THE PRINCIPAL'S OFFICE! I ALWAYS HAVE THE FEELING THAT I'LL NEVER COME BACK, OR THAT NO ONE WILL EVER SEE ME AGAIN...
GOOD MORNING... I WAS TOLD TO REPORT TO THE PRINCIPAL...
AM I ALLOWED ONE PHONE CALL?
SCHULZ

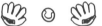

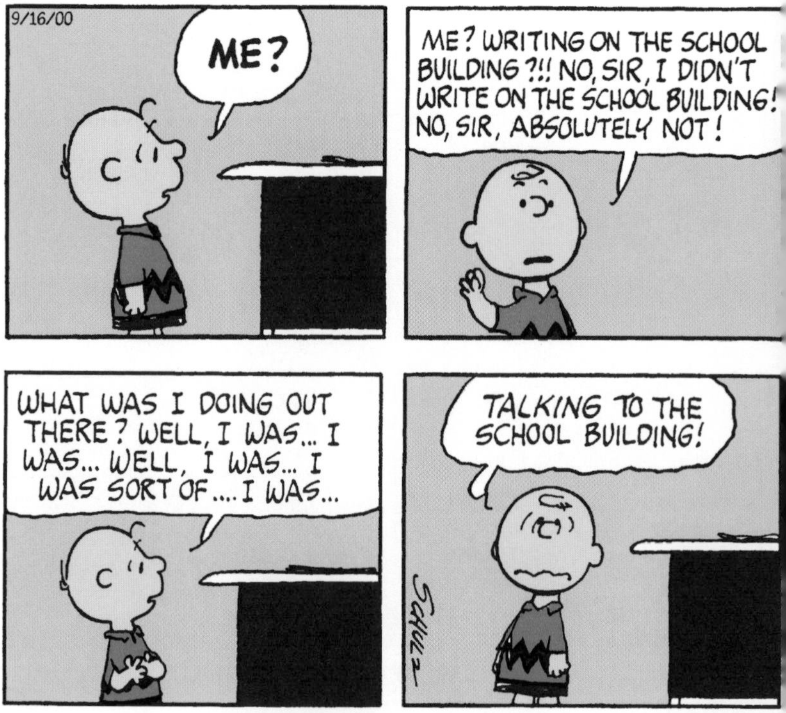
9/16/00
ME?
ME? WRITING ON THE SCHOOL BUILDING?!! NO, SIR, I DIDN'T WRITE ON THE SCHOOL BUILDING! NO, SIR, ABSOLUTELY NOT!
WHAT WAS I DOING OUT THERE? WELL, I WAS... I WAS... WELL, I WAS... I WAS SORT OF.... I WAS...
TALKING TO THE SCHOOL BUILDING!
SCHULZ

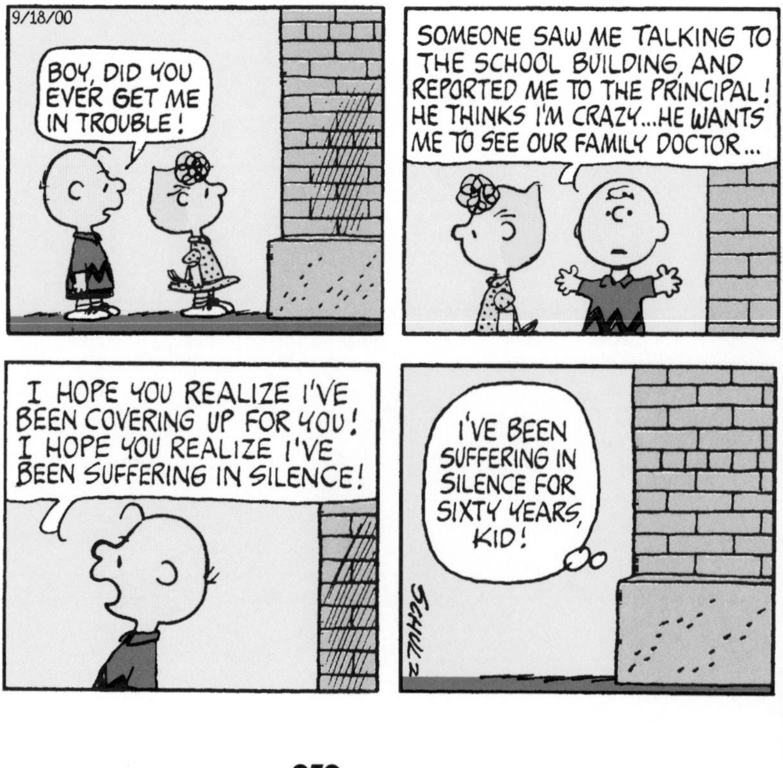
9/18/00
BOY, DID YOU EVER GET ME IN TROUBLE!
SOMEONE SAW ME TALKING TO THE SCHOOL BUILDING, AND REPORTED ME TO THE PRINCIPAL! HE THINKS I'M CRAZY...HE WANTS ME TO SEE OUR FAMILY DOCTOR...
I HOPE YOU REALIZE I'VE BEEN COVERING UP FOR YOU! I HOPE YOU REALIZE I'VE BEEN SUFFERING IN SILENCE!
I'VE BEEN SUFFERING IN SILENCE FOR SIXTY YEARS, KID!
SCHULZ

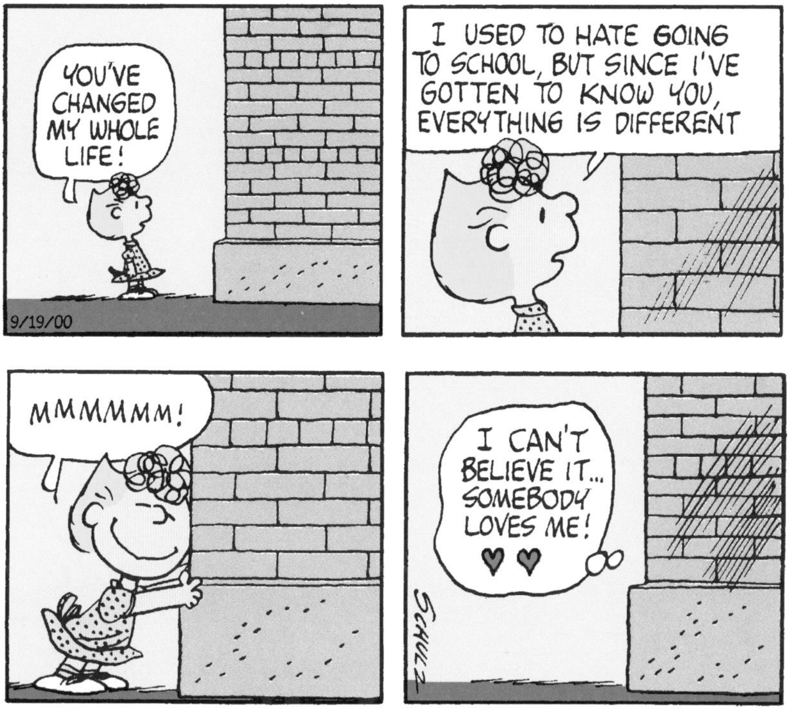
9/19/00
YOU'VE CHANGED MY WHOLE LIFE!
I USED TO HATE GOING TO SCHOOL, BUT SINCE I'VE GOTTEN TO KNOW YOU, EVERYTHING IS DIFFERENT
MMMMMM!
I CAN'T BELIEVE IT... SOMEBODY LOVES ME!
SCHULZ

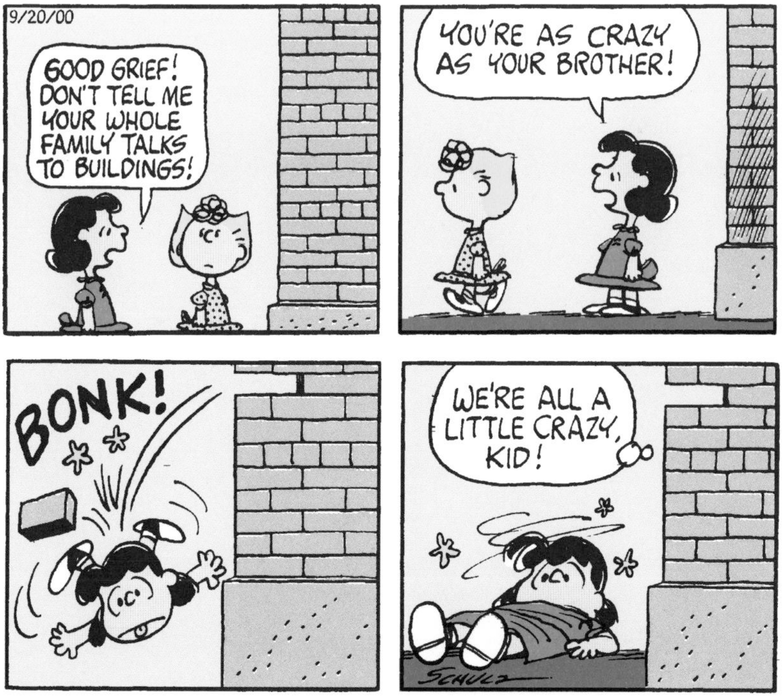
9/20/00
GOOD GRIEF! DON'T TELL ME YOUR WHOLE FAMILY TALKS TO BUILDINGS!
YOU'RE AS CRAZY AS YOUR BROTHER!
BONK!
WE'RE ALL A LITTLE CRAZY, KID!
SCHULZ

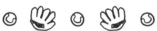

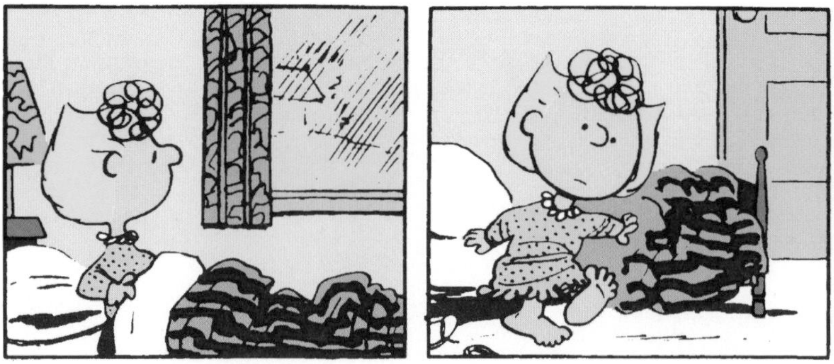

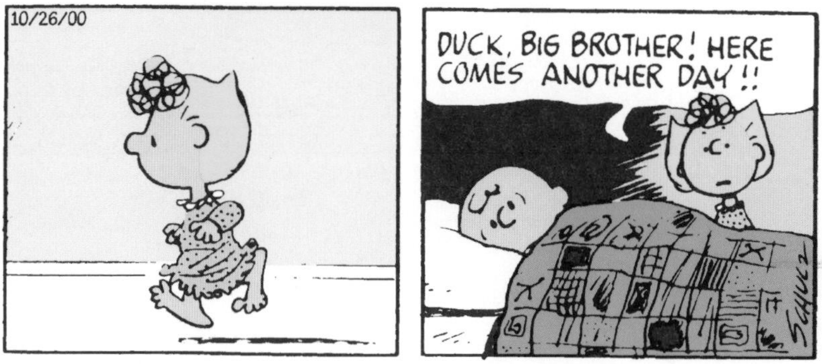
10/26/00
DUCK, BIG BROTHER! HERE COMES ANOTHER DAY!!
SCHULZ

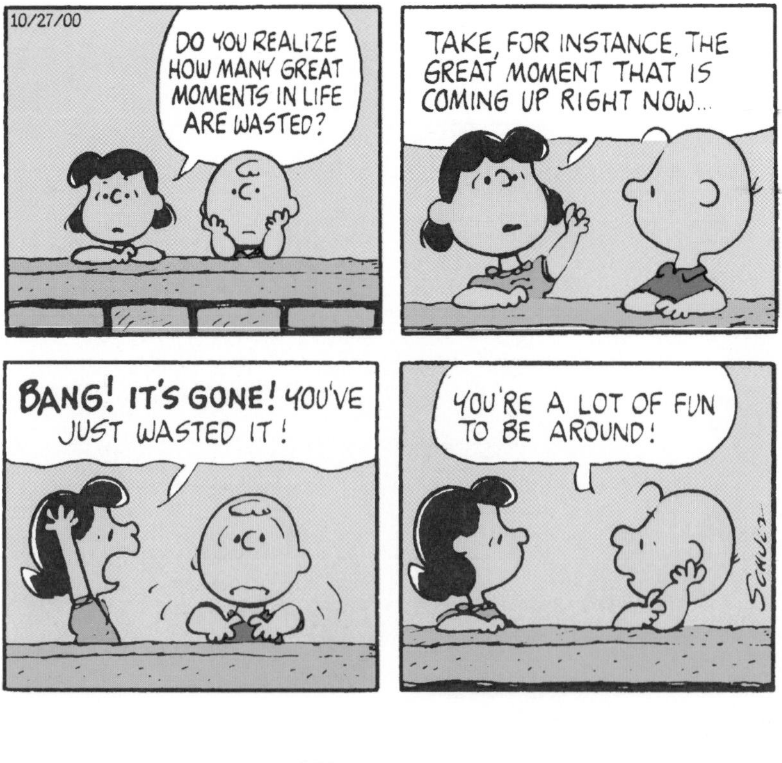
10/27/00
DO YOU REALIZE HOW MANY GREAT MOMENTS IN LIFE ARE WASTED?
TAKE, FOR INSTANCE, THE GREAT MOMENT THAT IS COMING UP RIGHT NOW...
BANG! IT'S GONE! YOU'VE JUST WASTED IT!
YOU'RE A LOT OF FUN TO BE AROUND!
SCHULZ

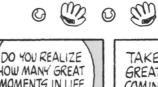

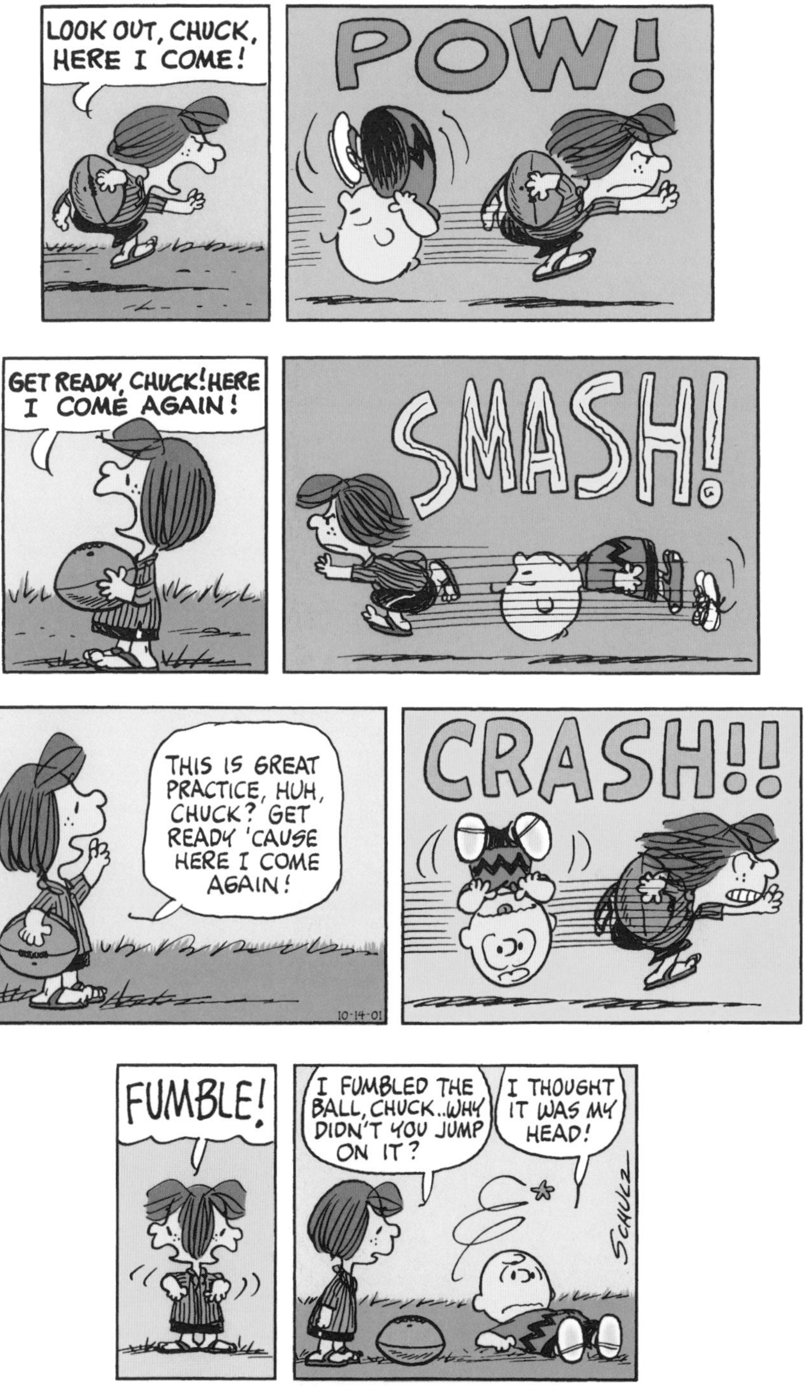
LOOK OUT, CHUCK, HERE I COME!
POW!
GET READY, CHUCK! HERE I COME AGAIN!
SMASH!
THIS IS GREAT PRACTICE, HUH, CHUCK? GET READY 'CAUSE HERE I COME AGAIN!
10-14-01
CRASH!!
FUMBLE!
I FUMBLED THE BALL, CHUCK..WHY DIDN'T YOU JUMP ON IT?
I THOUGHT IT WAS MY HEAD!
SCHULZ

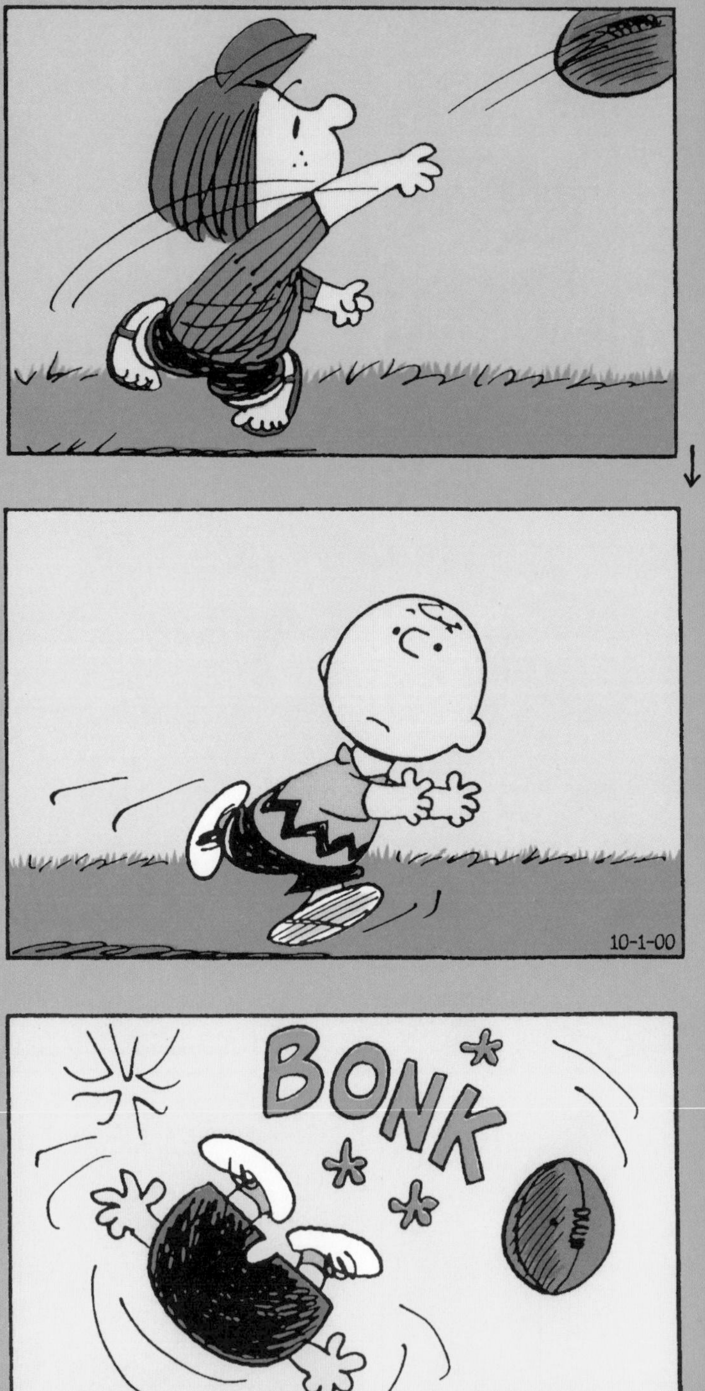
10-1-00
BONK

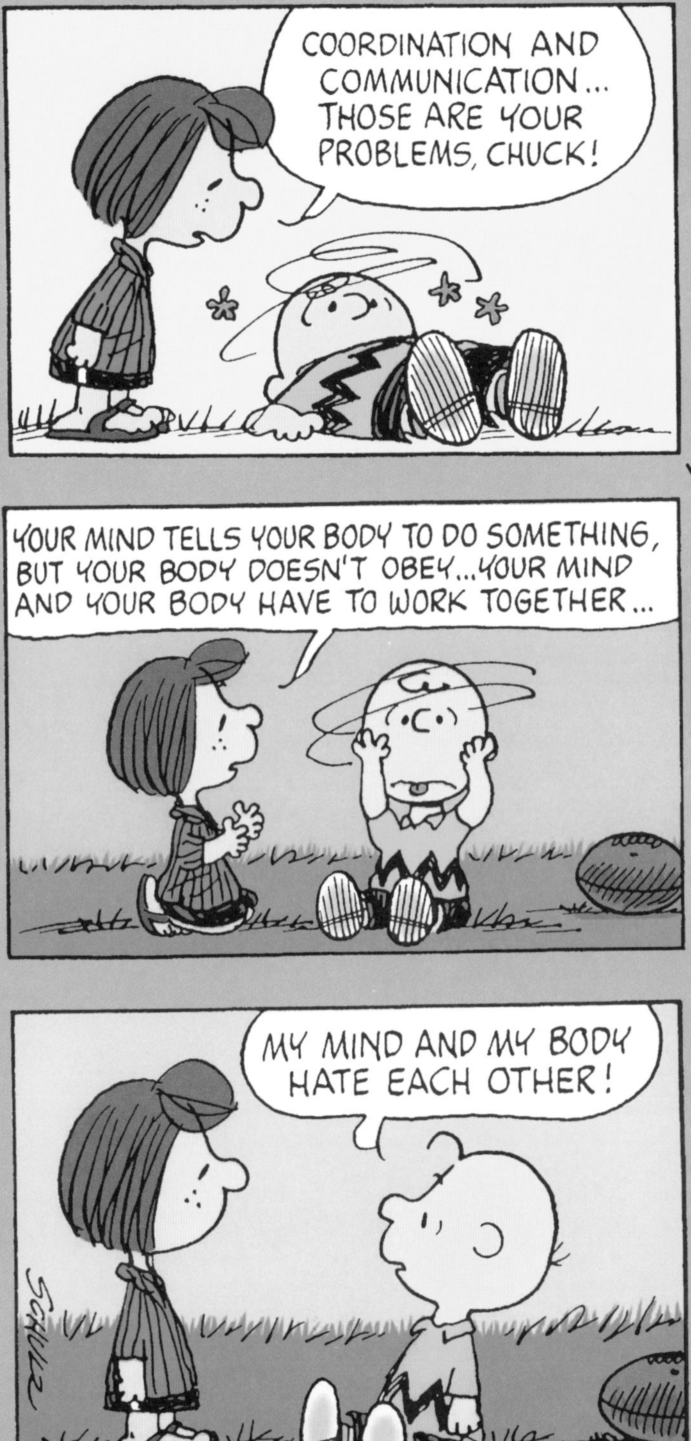
COORDINATION AND COMMUNICATION... THOSE ARE YOUR PROBLEMS, CHUCK!
YOUR MIND TELLS YOUR BODY TO DO SOMETHING, BUT YOUR BODY DOESN'T OBEY...YOUR MIND AND YOUR BODY HAVE TO WORK TOGETHER...
MY MIND AND MY BODY HATE EACH OTHER!
SCHULZ

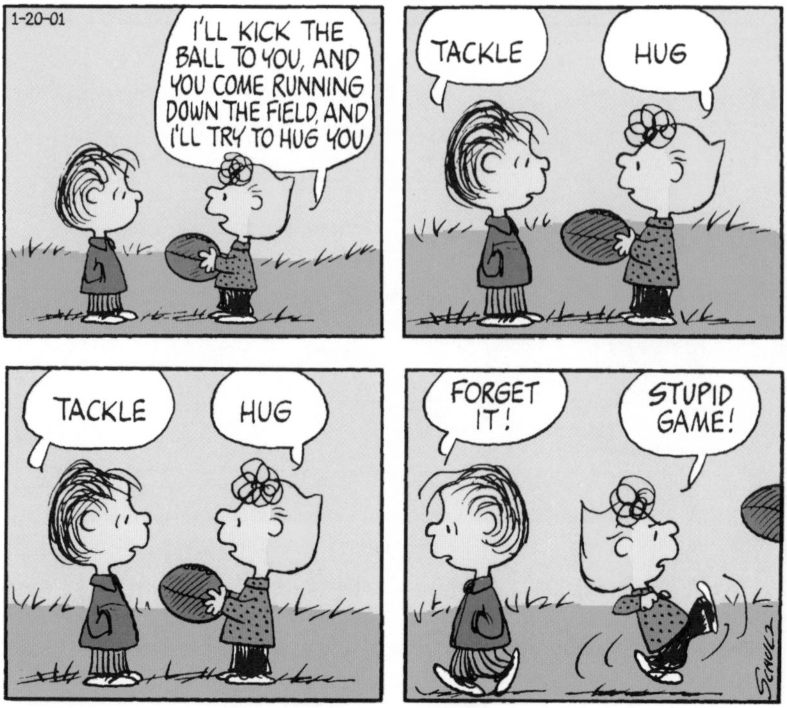
1-20-01
I'LL KICK THE BALL TO YOU, AND YOU COME RUNNING DOWN THE FIELD, AND I'LL TRY TO HUG YOU
TACKLE
HUG
TACKLE
HUG
FORGET IT!
STUPID GAME!
SCHULZ

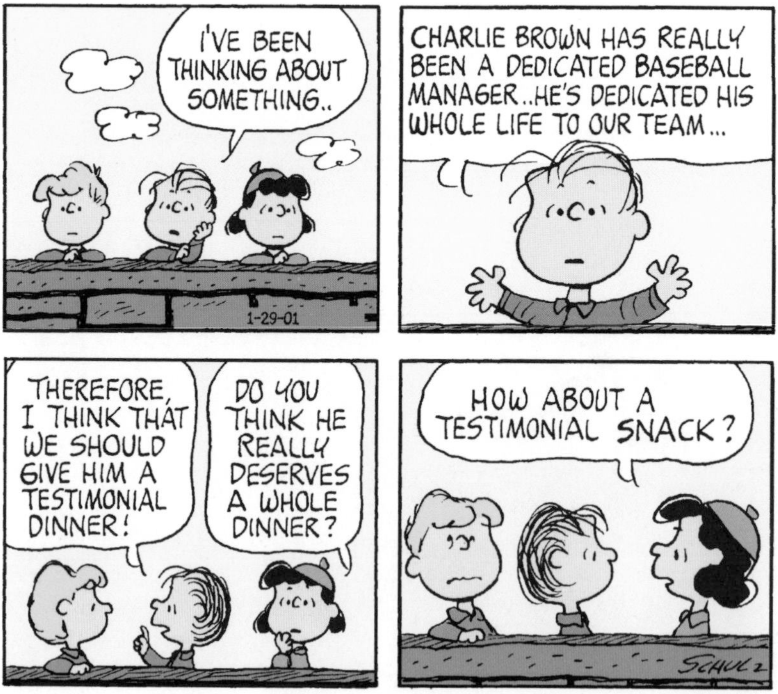
I'VE BEEN THINKING ABOUT SOMETHING..
1-29-01
CHARLIE BROWN HAS REALLY BEEN A DEDICATED BASEBALL MANAGER..HE'S DEDICATED HIS WHOLE LIFE TO OUR TEAM...
THEREFORE, I THINK THAT WE SHOULD GIVE HIM A TESTIMONIAL DINNER!
DO YOU THINK HE REALLY DESERVES A WHOLE DINNER?
HOW ABOUT A TESTIMONIAL SNACK?
SCHULZ

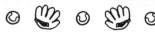

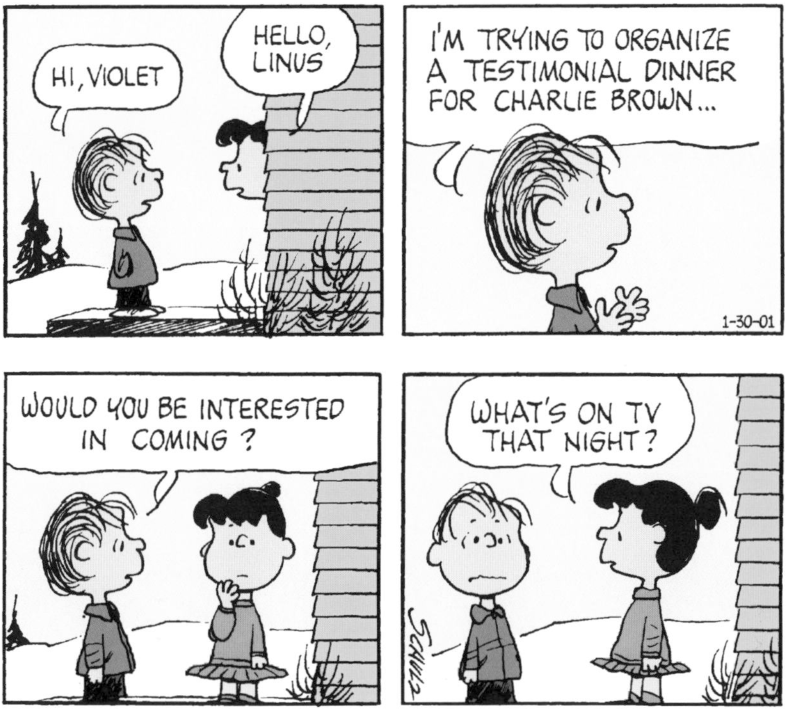
HI, VIOLET
HELLO, LINUS
I'M TRYING TO ORGANIZE A TESTIMONIAL DINNER FOR CHARLIE BROWN...
1-30-01
WOULD YOU BE INTERESTED IN COMING ?
WHAT'S ON TV THAT NIGHT ?
SCHULZ

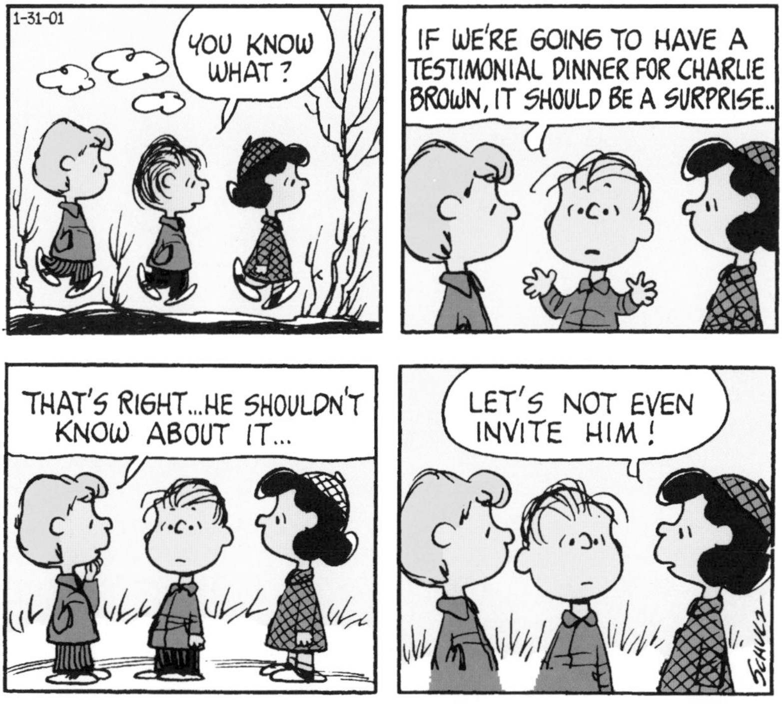
1-31-01
YOU KNOW WHAT ?
IF WE'RE GOING TO HAVE A TESTIMONIAL DINNER FOR CHARLIE BROWN, IT SHOULD BE A SURPRISE..
THAT'S RIGHT...HE SHOULDN'T KNOW ABOUT IT...
LET'S NOT EVEN INVITE HIM !
SCHULZ

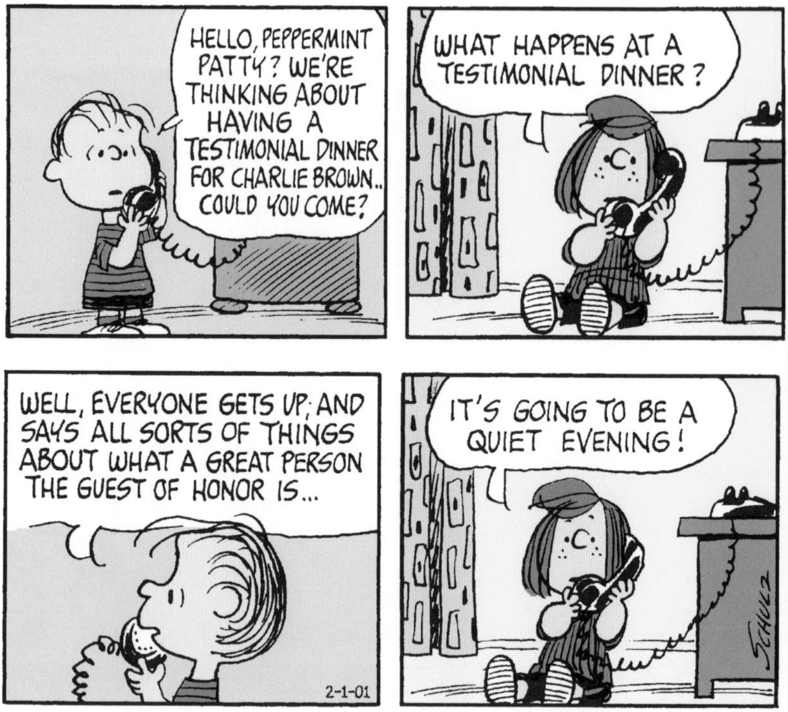
HELLO, PEPPERMINT PATTY? WE'RE THINKING ABOUT HAVING A TESTIMONIAL DINNER FOR CHARLIE BROWN.. COULD YOU COME?
WHAT HAPPENS AT A TESTIMONIAL DINNER?
WELL, EVERYONE GETS UP, AND SAYS ALL SORTS OF THINGS ABOUT WHAT A GREAT PERSON THE GUEST OF HONOR IS...
2-1-01
IT'S GOING TO BE A QUIET EVENING!
SCHULZ

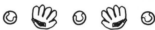

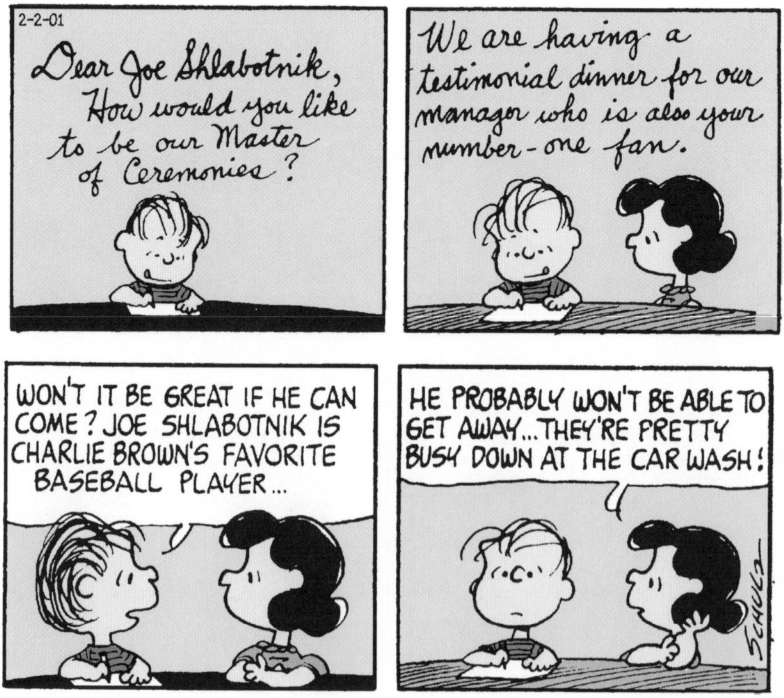
2-2-01
Dear Joe Shlabotnik,
How would you like to be our Master of Ceremonies?
We are having a testimonial dinner for our manager who is also your number-one fan.
WON'T IT BE GREAT IF HE CAN COME? JOE SHLABOTNIK IS CHARLIE BROWN'S FAVORITE BASEBALL PLAYER...
HE PROBABLY WON'T BE ABLE TO GET AWAY...THEY'RE PRETTY BUSY DOWN AT THE CAR WASH!
SCHULZ

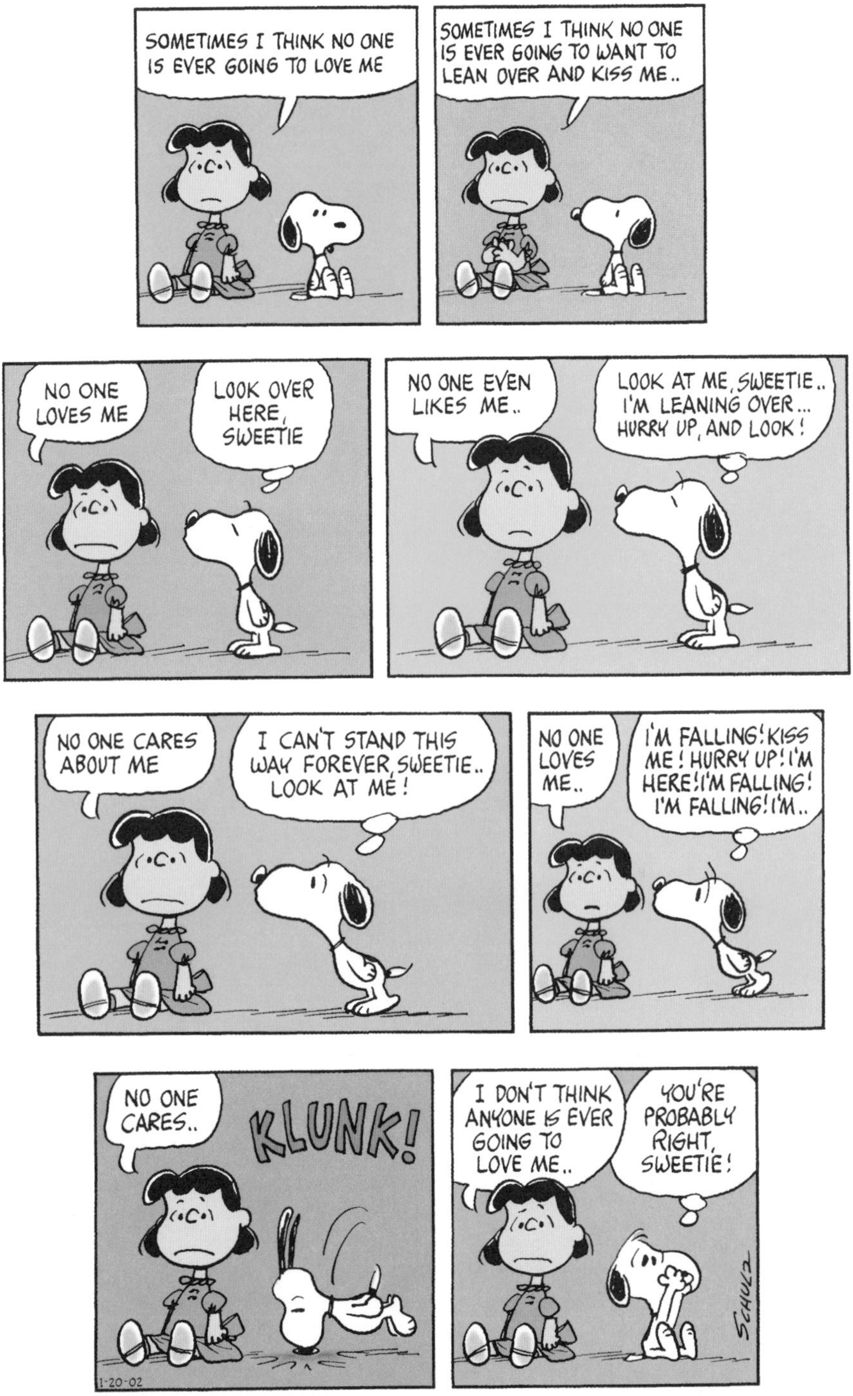
SOMETIMES I THINK NO ONE IS EVER GOING TO LOVE ME
SOMETIMES I THINK NO ONE IS EVER GOING TO WANT TO LEAN OVER AND KISS ME..
NO ONE LOVES ME
LOOK OVER HERE, SWEETIE
NO ONE EVEN LIKES ME..
LOOK AT ME, SWEETIE.. I'M LEANING OVER... HURRY UP, AND LOOK!
NO ONE CARES ABOUT ME
I CAN'T STAND THIS WAY FOREVER, SWEETIE.. LOOK AT ME!
NO ONE LOVES ME..
I'M FALLING! KISS ME! HURRY UP! I'M HERE! I'M FALLING! I'M FALLING! I'M..
NO ONE CARES..
KLUNK!
I DON'T THINK ANYONE IS EVER GOING TO LOVE ME..
YOU'RE PROBABLY RIGHT, SWEETIE!
SCHULZ
1-20-02

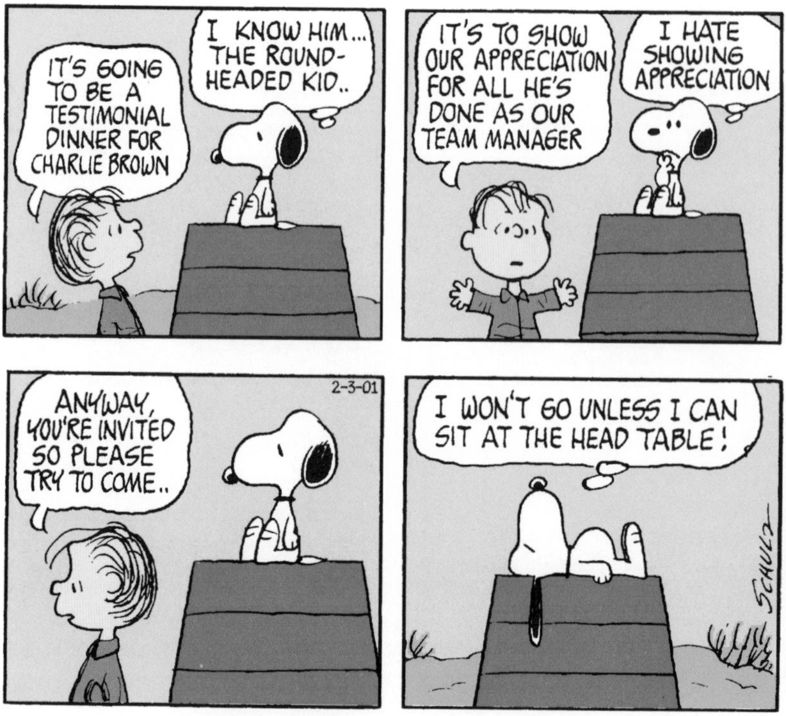
IT'S GOING TO BE A TESTIMONIAL DINNER FOR CHARLIE BROWN
I KNOW HIM... THE ROUND-HEADED KID..
IT'S TO SHOW OUR APPRECIATION FOR ALL HE'S DONE AS OUR TEAM MANAGER
I HATE SHOWING APPRECIATION
2-3-01
ANYWAY, YOU'RE INVITED SO PLEASE TRY TO COME..
I WON'T GO UNLESS I CAN SIT AT THE HEAD TABLE!
SCHULZ

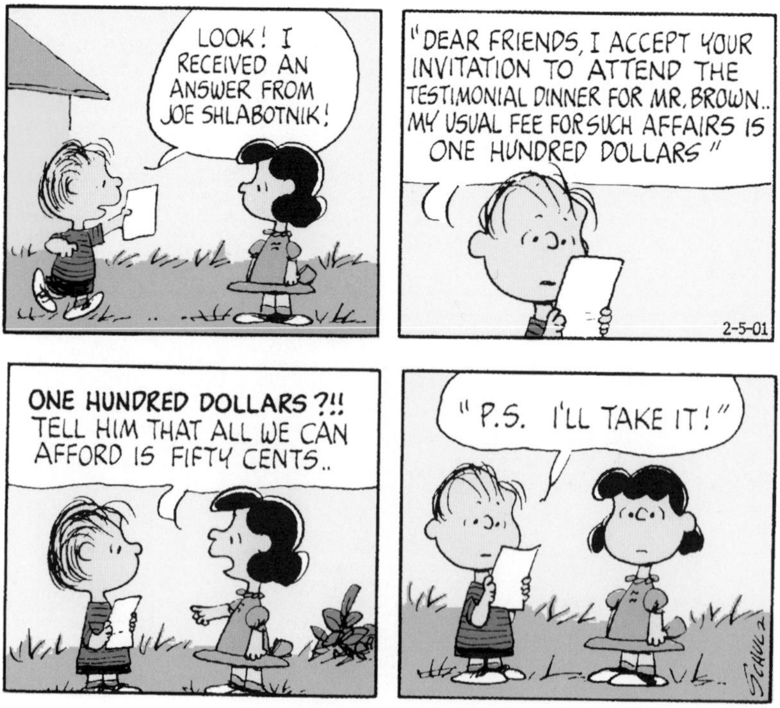
LOOK! I RECEIVED AN ANSWER FROM JOE SHLABOTNIK!
"DEAR FRIENDS, I ACCEPT YOUR INVITATION TO ATTEND THE TESTIMONIAL DINNER FOR MR. BROWN.. MY USUAL FEE FOR SUCH AFFAIRS IS ONE HUNDRED DOLLARS"
2-5-01
ONE HUNDRED DOLLARS?!! TELL HIM THAT ALL WE CAN AFFORD IS FIFTY CENTS..
"P.S. I'LL TAKE IT!"
SCHULZ

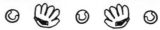

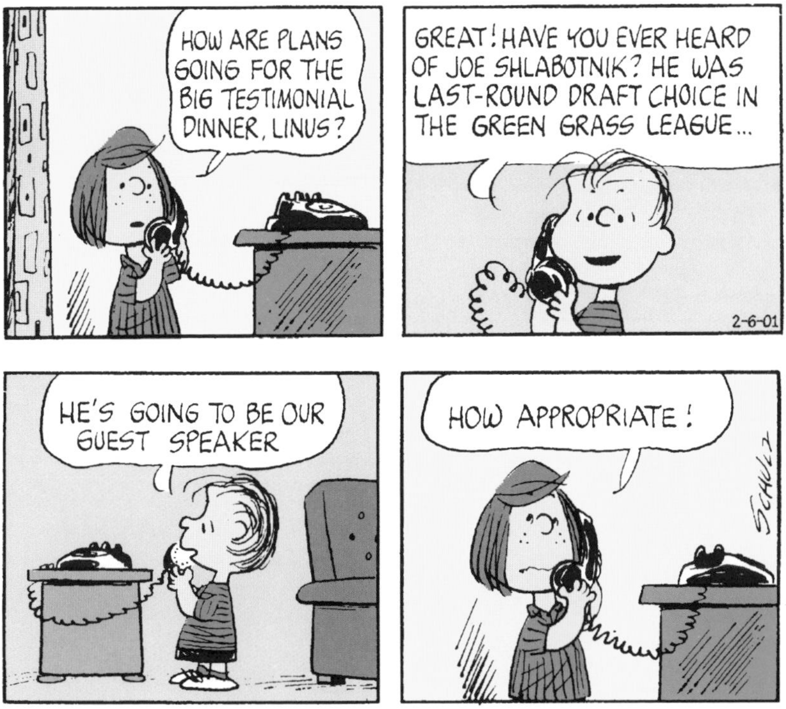
HOW ARE PLANS GOING FOR THE BIG TESTIMONIAL DINNER, LINUS?
GREAT! HAVE YOU EVER HEARD OF JOE SHLABOTNIK? HE WAS LAST-ROUND DRAFT CHOICE IN THE GREEN GRASS LEAGUE...
2-6-01
HE'S GOING TO BE OUR GUEST SPEAKER
HOW APPROPRIATE!
SCHULZ

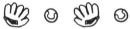

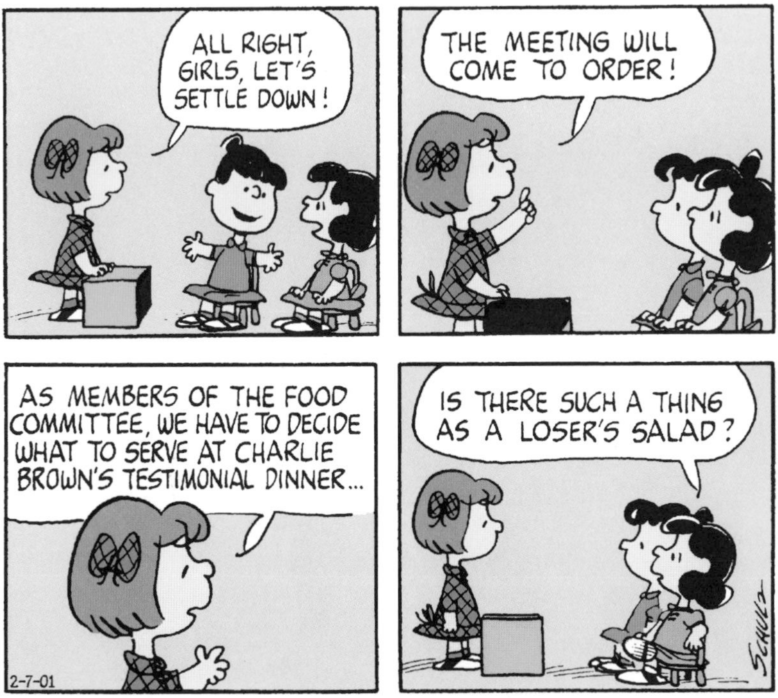
ALL RIGHT, GIRLS, LET'S SETTLE DOWN!
THE MEETING WILL COME TO ORDER!
AS MEMBERS OF THE FOOD COMMITTEE, WE HAVE TO DECIDE WHAT TO SERVE AT CHARLIE BROWN'S TESTIMONIAL DINNER...
2-7-01
IS THERE SUCH A THING AS A LOSER'S SALAD?
SCHULZ

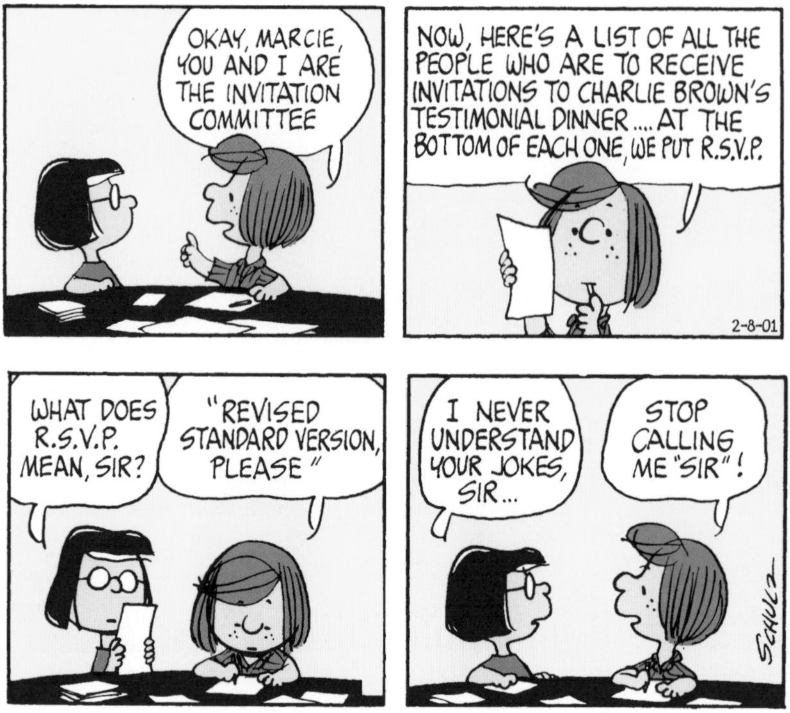
OKAY, MARCIE, YOU AND I ARE THE INVITATION COMMITTEE
NOW, HERE'S A LIST OF ALL THE PEOPLE WHO ARE TO RECEIVE INVITATIONS TO CHARLIE BROWN'S TESTIMONIAL DINNER.... AT THE BOTTOM OF EACH ONE, WE PUT R.S.V.P.
2-8-01
WHAT DOES R.S.V.P. MEAN, SIR?
"REVISED STANDARD VERSION, PLEASE"
I NEVER UNDERSTAND YOUR JOKES, SIR...
STOP CALLING ME "SIR"!
SCHULZ

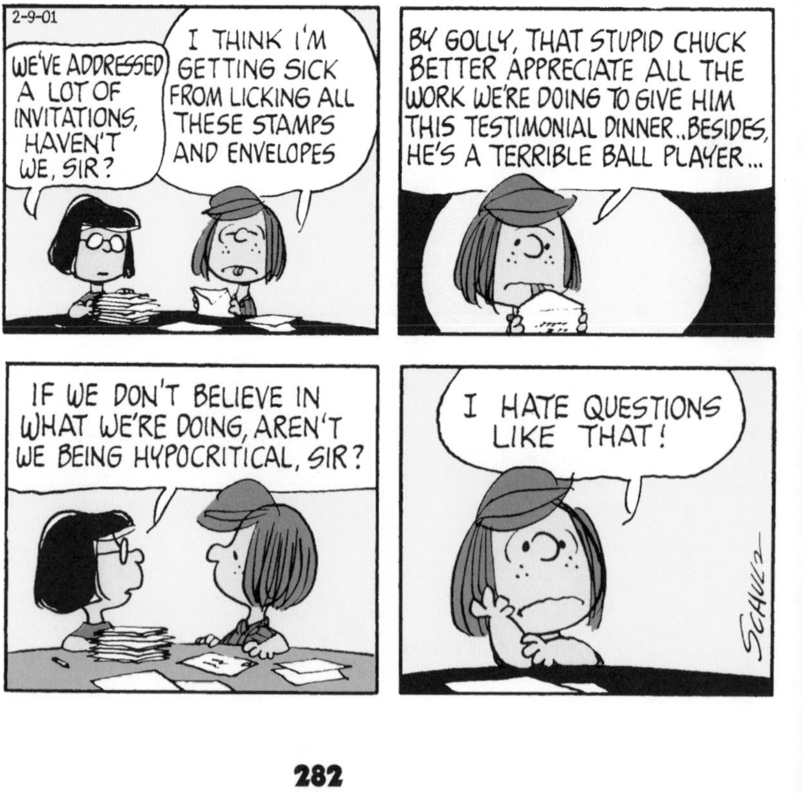
2-9-01
WE'VE ADDRESSED A LOT OF INVITATIONS, HAVEN'T WE, SIR?
I THINK I'M GETTING SICK FROM LICKING ALL THESE STAMPS AND ENVELOPES
BY GOLLY, THAT STUPID CHUCK BETTER APPRECIATE ALL THE WORK WE'RE DOING TO GIVE HIM THIS TESTIMONIAL DINNER..BESIDES, HE'S A TERRIBLE BALL PLAYER...
IF WE DON'T BELIEVE IN WHAT WE'RE DOING, AREN'T WE BEING HYPOCRITICAL, SIR?
I HATE QUESTIONS LIKE THAT!
SCHULZ

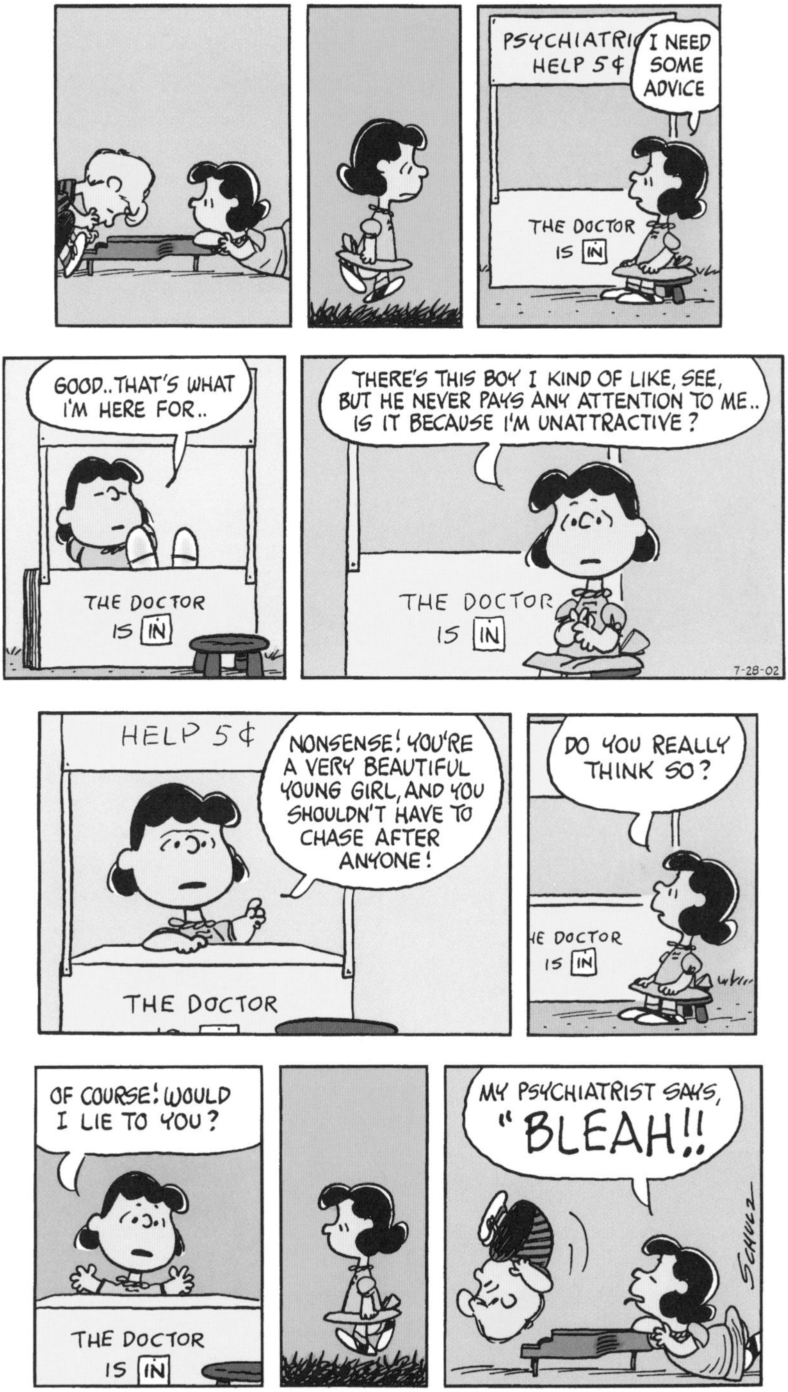
PSYCHIATRIC HELP 5¢
I NEED SOME ADVICE
THE DOCTOR IS IN
GOOD..THAT'S WHAT I'M HERE FOR..
THE DOCTOR IS IN
THERE'S THIS BOY I KIND OF LIKE, SEE, BUT HE NEVER PAYS ANY ATTENTION TO ME.. IS IT BECAUSE I'M UNATTRACTIVE?
THE DOCTOR IS IN
7-28-02
HELP 5¢
NONSENSE! YOU'RE A VERY BEAUTIFUL YOUNG GIRL, AND YOU SHOULDN'T HAVE TO CHASE AFTER ANYONE!
THE DOCTOR
DO YOU REALLY THINK SO?
HE DOCTOR IS IN
OF COURSE! WOULD I LIE TO YOU?
THE DOCTOR IS IN
MY PSYCHIATRIST SAYS, "BLEAH!!
SCHULZ

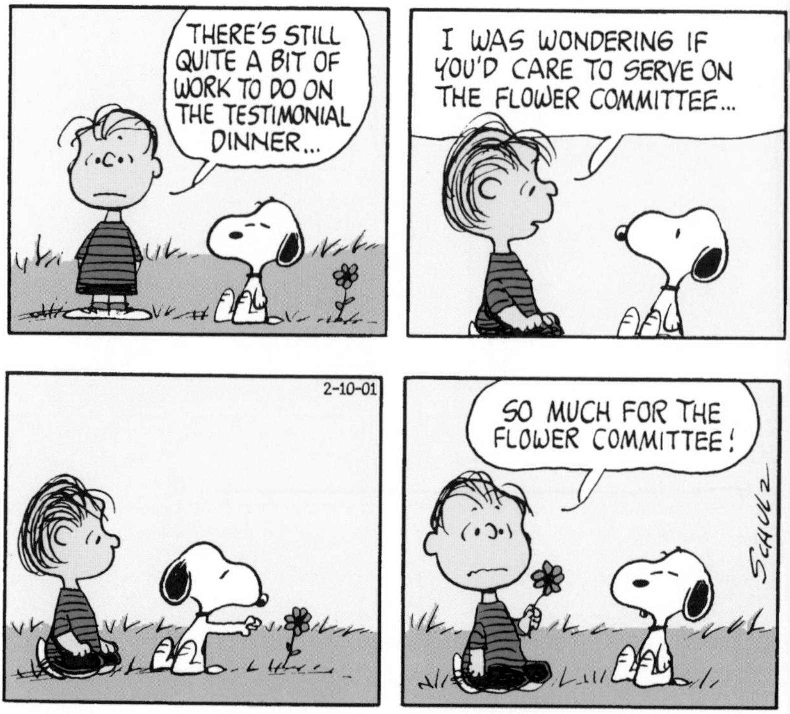
THERE'S STILL QUITE A BIT OF WORK TO DO ON THE TESTIMONIAL DINNER...
I WAS WONDERING IF YOU'D CARE TO SERVE ON THE FLOWER COMMITTEE...
2-10-01
SO MUCH FOR THE FLOWER COMMITTEE!
SCHULZ

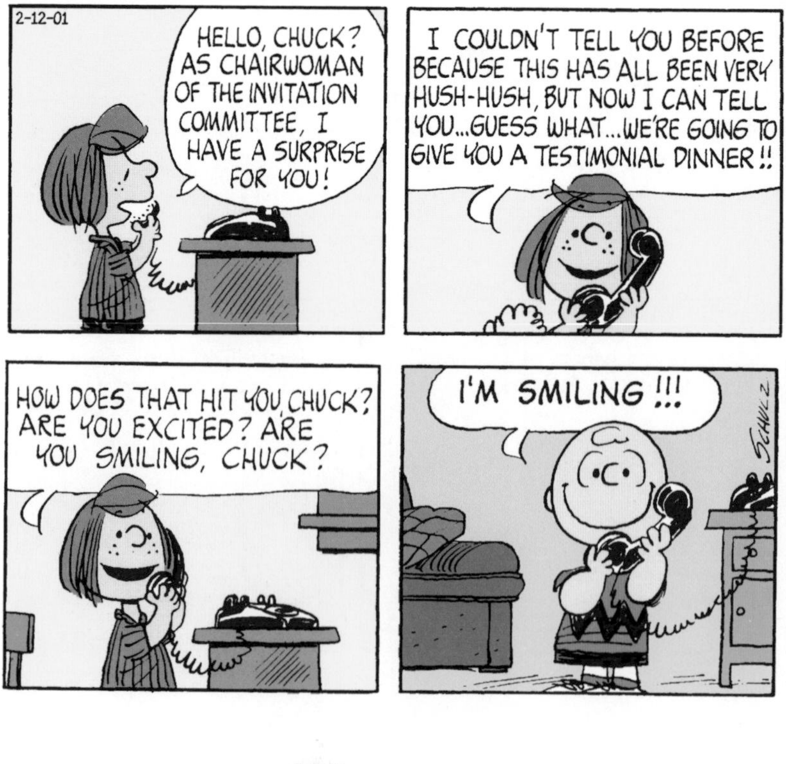
2-12-01
HELLO, CHUCK? AS CHAIRWOMAN OF THE INVITATION COMMITTEE, I HAVE A SURPRISE FOR YOU!
I COULDN'T TELL YOU BEFORE BECAUSE THIS HAS ALL BEEN VERY HUSH-HUSH, BUT NOW I CAN TELL YOU...GUESS WHAT...WE'RE GOING TO GIVE YOU A TESTIMONIAL DINNER!!
HOW DOES THAT HIT YOU, CHUCK? ARE YOU EXCITED? ARE YOU SMILING, CHUCK?
I'M SMILING!!!
SCHULZ

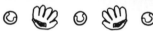

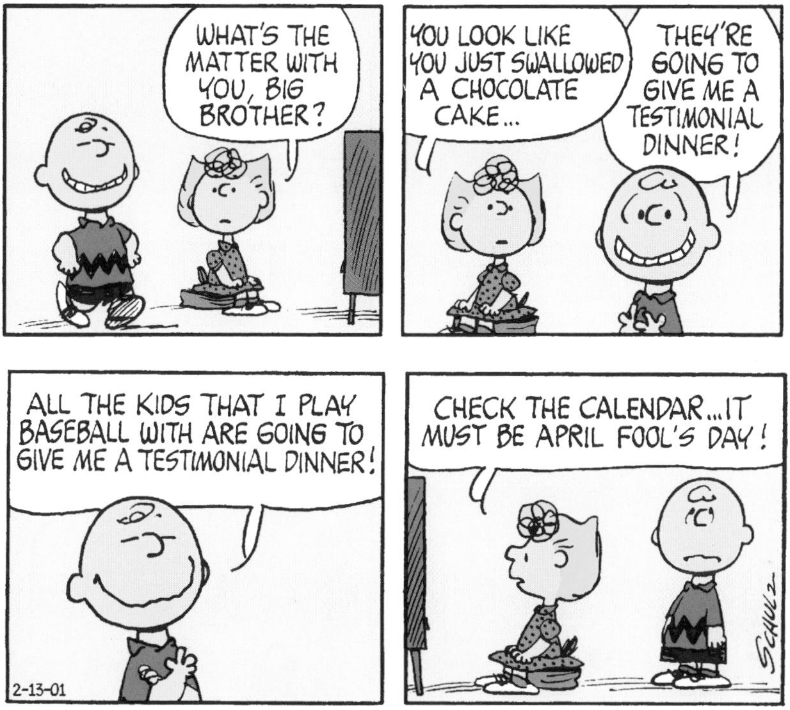
WHAT'S THE MATTER WITH YOU, BIG BROTHER?
YOU LOOK LIKE YOU JUST SWALLOWED A CHOCOLATE CAKE...
THEY'RE GOING TO GIVE ME A TESTIMONIAL DINNER!
ALL THE KIDS THAT I PLAY BASEBALL WITH ARE GOING TO GIVE ME A TESTIMONIAL DINNER!
2-13-01
CHECK THE CALENDAR...IT MUST BE APRIL FOOL'S DAY!
SCHULZ

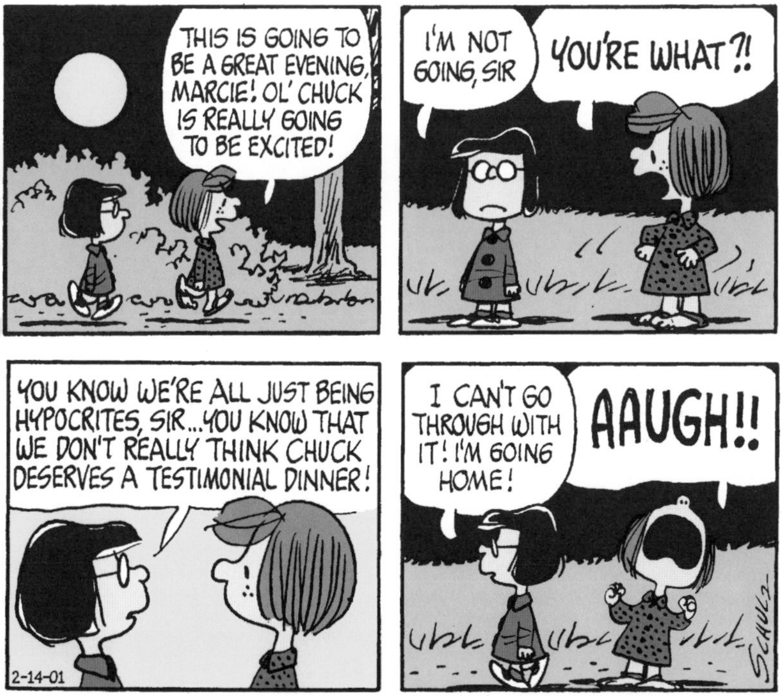
THIS IS GOING TO BE A GREAT EVENING, MARCIE! OL' CHUCK IS REALLY GOING TO BE EXCITED!
I'M NOT GOING, SIR
YOU'RE WHAT?!
YOU KNOW WE'RE ALL JUST BEING HYPOCRITES, SIR...YOU KNOW THAT WE DON'T REALLY THINK CHUCK DESERVES A TESTIMONIAL DINNER!
2-14-01
I CAN'T GO THROUGH WITH IT! I'M GOING HOME!
AAUGH!!
SCHULZ

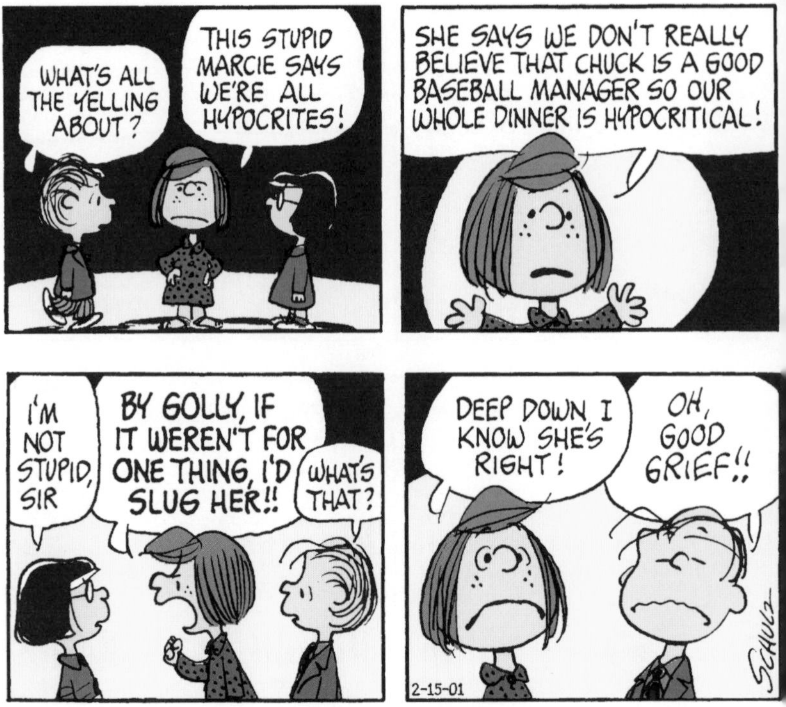
WHAT'S ALL THE YELLING ABOUT ?
THIS STUPID MARCIE SAYS WE'RE ALL HYPOCRITES!
SHE SAYS WE DON'T REALLY BELIEVE THAT CHUCK IS A GOOD BASEBALL MANAGER SO OUR WHOLE DINNER IS HYPOCRITICAL!
I'M NOT STUPID, SIR
BY GOLLY, IF IT WEREN'T FOR ONE THING, I'D SLUG HER!!
WHAT'S THAT?
DEEP DOWN I KNOW SHE'S RIGHT!
OH, GOOD GRIEF!!
2-15-01

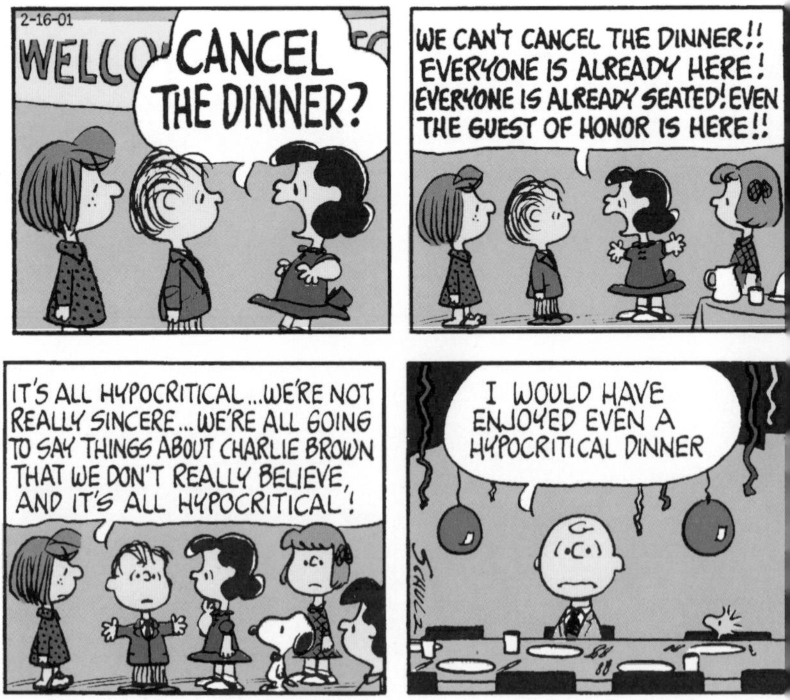
2-16-01
CANCEL THE DINNER?
WE CAN'T CANCEL THE DINNER!! EVERYONE IS ALREADY HERE! EVERYONE IS ALREADY SEATED! EVEN THE GUEST OF HONOR IS HERE!!
IT'S ALL HYPOCRITICAL...WE'RE NOT REALLY SINCERE...WE'RE ALL GOING TO SAY THINGS ABOUT CHARLIE BROWN THAT WE DON'T REALLY BELIEVE, AND IT'S ALL HYPOCRITICAL!
I WOULD HAVE ENJOYED EVEN A HYPOCRITICAL DINNER

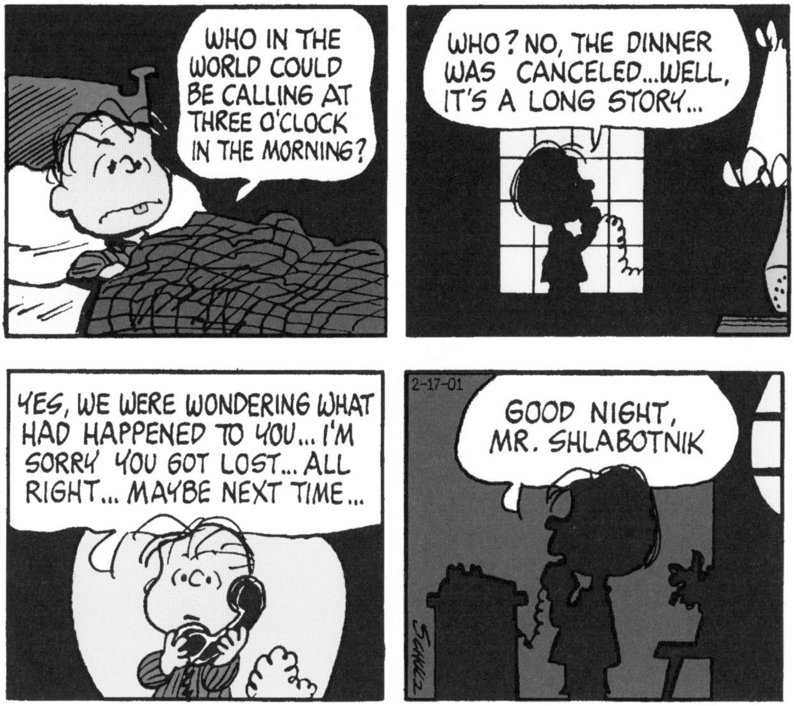
WHO IN THE WORLD COULD BE CALLING AT THREE O'CLOCK IN THE MORNING?
WHO? NO, THE DINNER WAS CANCELED...WELL, IT'S A LONG STORY...
YES, WE WERE WONDERING WHAT HAD HAPPENED TO YOU... I'M SORRY YOU GOT LOST... ALL RIGHT... MAYBE NEXT TIME...
2-17-01
GOOD NIGHT, MR. SHLABOTNIK
SCHULZ

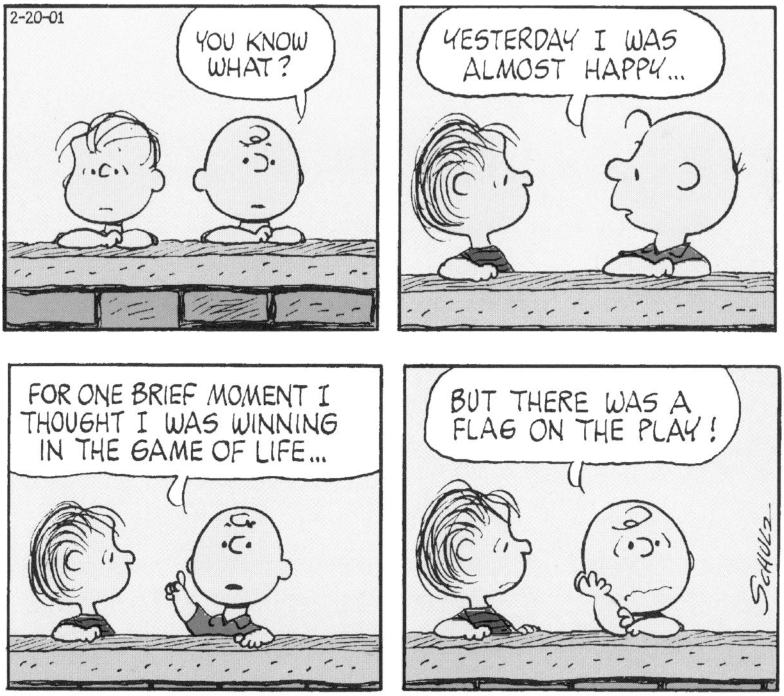
2-20-01
YOU KNOW WHAT?
YESTERDAY I WAS ALMOST HAPPY...
FOR ONE BRIEF MOMENT I THOUGHT I WAS WINNING IN THE GAME OF LIFE...
BUT THERE WAS A FLAG ON THE PLAY!
SCHULZ

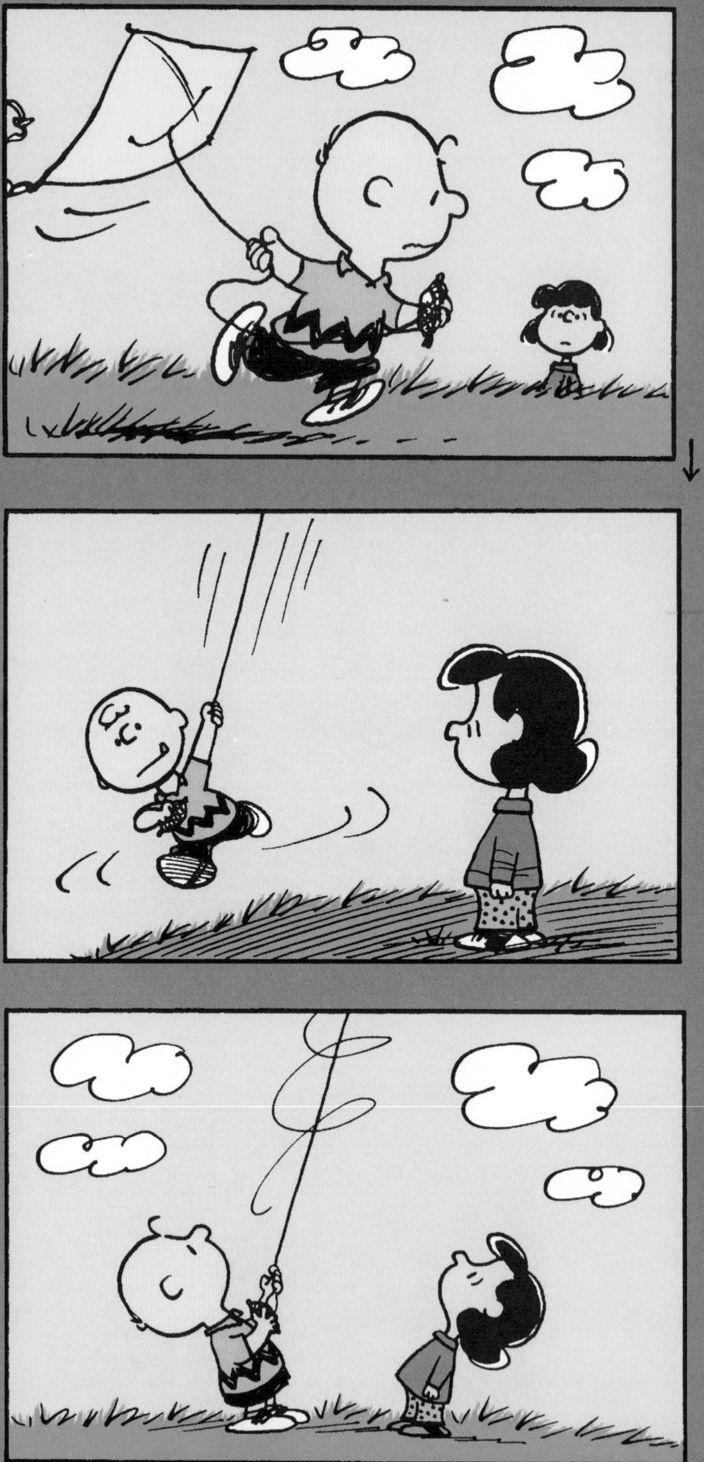

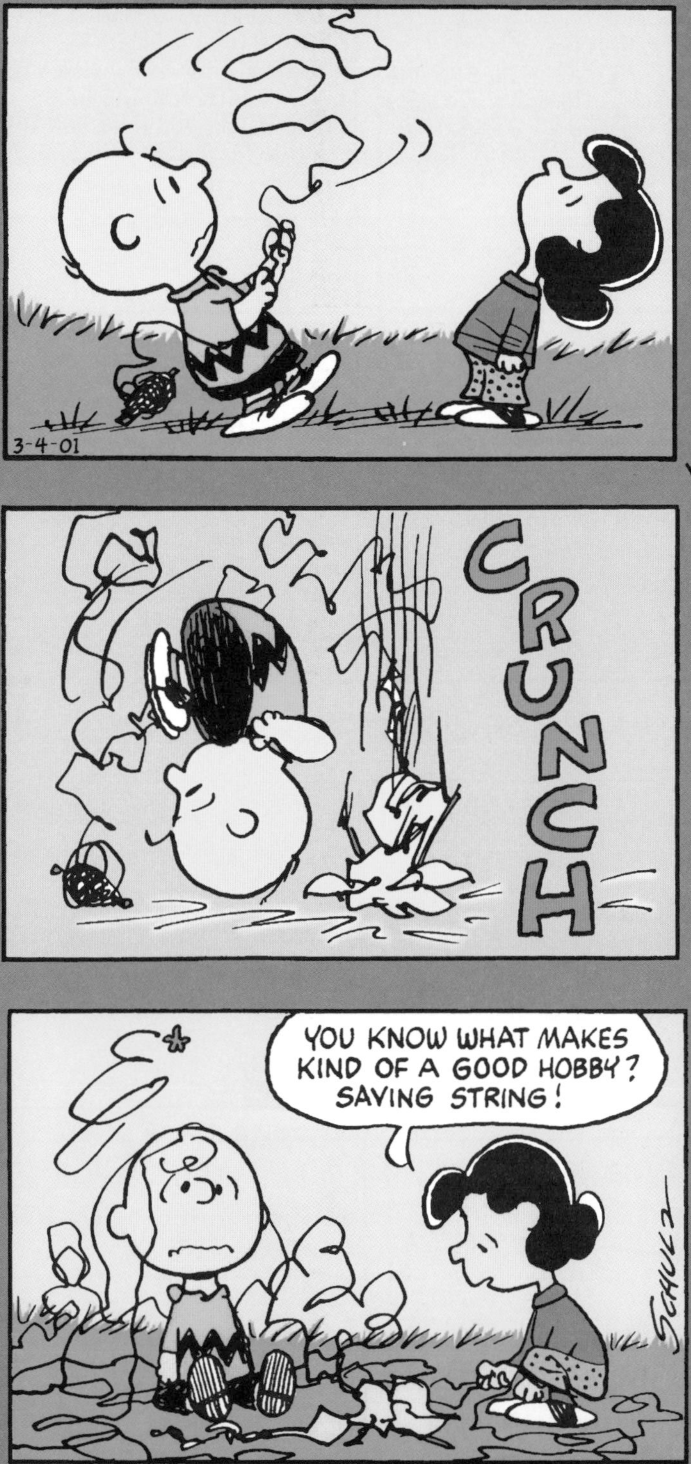
3-4-01
CRUNCH
YOU KNOW WHAT MAKES KIND OF A GOOD HOBBY? SAVING STRING!
SCHULZ

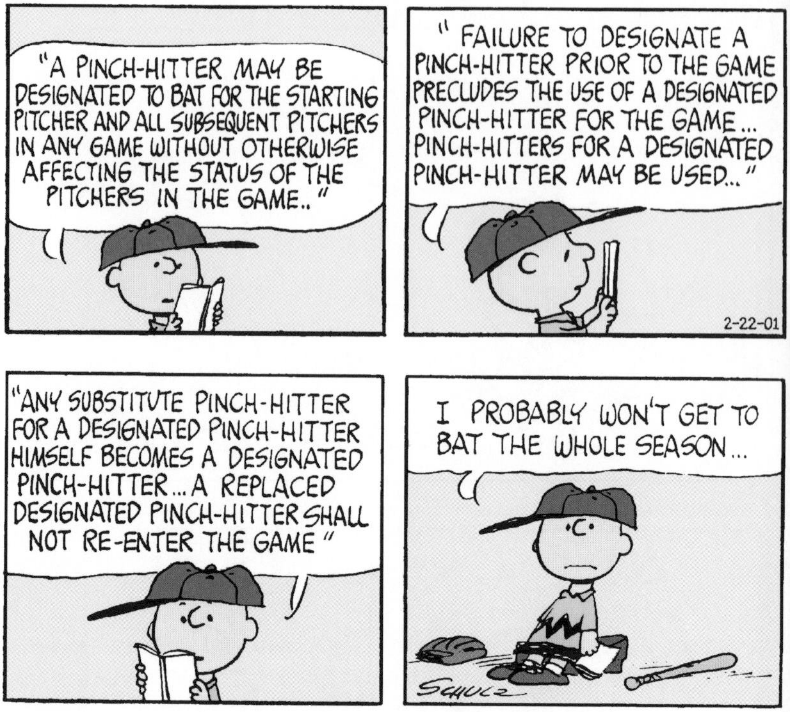
"A PINCH-HITTER MAY BE DESIGNATED TO BAT FOR THE STARTING PITCHER AND ALL SUBSEQUENT PITCHERS IN ANY GAME WITHOUT OTHERWISE AFFECTING THE STATUS OF THE PITCHERS IN THE GAME.."
"FAILURE TO DESIGNATE A PINCH-HITTER PRIOR TO THE GAME PRECLUDES THE USE OF A DESIGNATED PINCH-HITTER FOR THE GAME... PINCH-HITTERS FOR A DESIGNATED PINCH-HITTER MAY BE USED..."
2-22-01
"ANY SUBSTITUTE PINCH-HITTER FOR A DESIGNATED PINCH-HITTER HIMSELF BECOMES A DESIGNATED PINCH-HITTER... A REPLACED DESIGNATED PINCH-HITTER SHALL NOT RE-ENTER THE GAME"
I PROBABLY WON'T GET TO BAT THE WHOLE SEASON...
SCHULZ

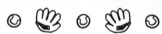

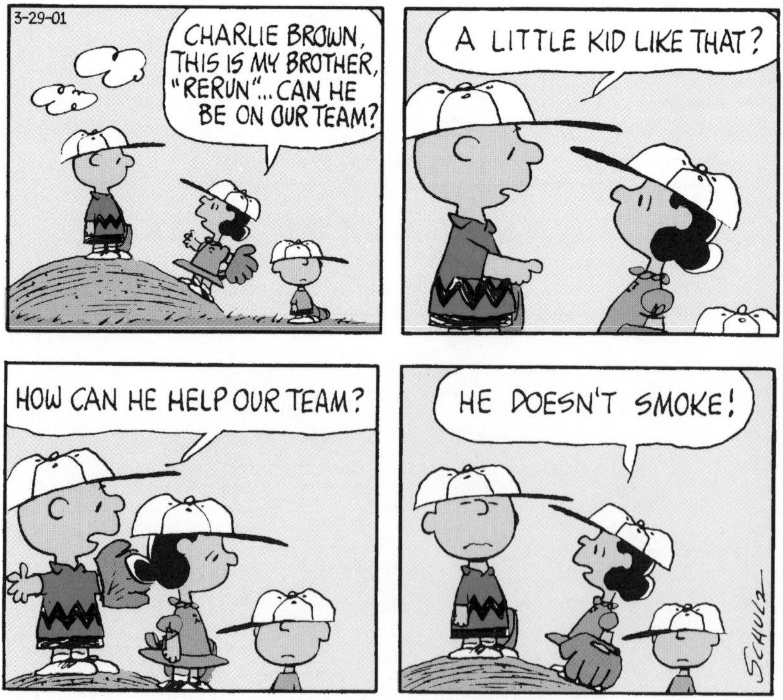
3-29-01
CHARLIE BROWN, THIS IS MY BROTHER, "RERUN"... CAN HE BE ON OUR TEAM?
A LITTLE KID LIKE THAT?
HOW CAN HE HELP OUR TEAM?
HE DOESN'T SMOKE!
SCHULZ

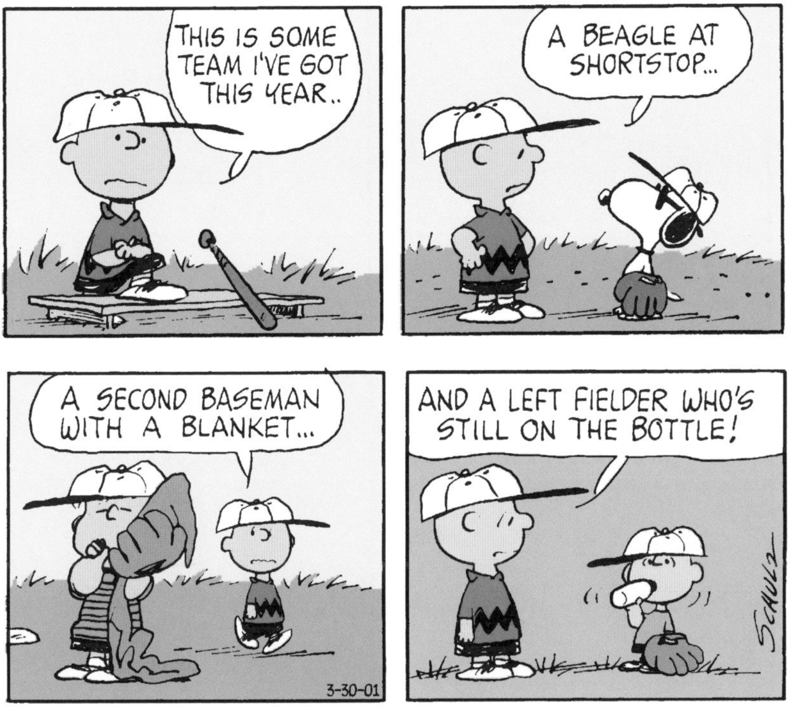
THIS IS SOME TEAM I'VE GOT THIS YEAR..
A BEAGLE AT SHORTSTOP...
A SECOND BASEMAN WITH A BLANKET...
AND A LEFT FIELDER WHO'S STILL ON THE BOTTLE!
SCHULZ
3-30-01

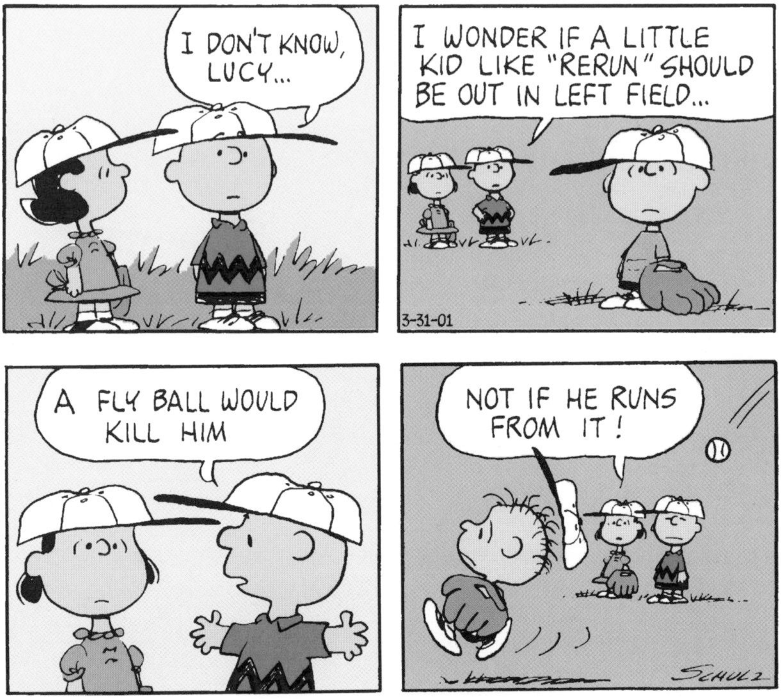
I DON'T KNOW, LUCY...
I WONDER IF A LITTLE KID LIKE "RERUN" SHOULD BE OUT IN LEFT FIELD...
3-31-01
A FLY BALL WOULD KILL HIM
NOT IF HE RUNS FROM IT!
SCHULZ

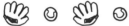

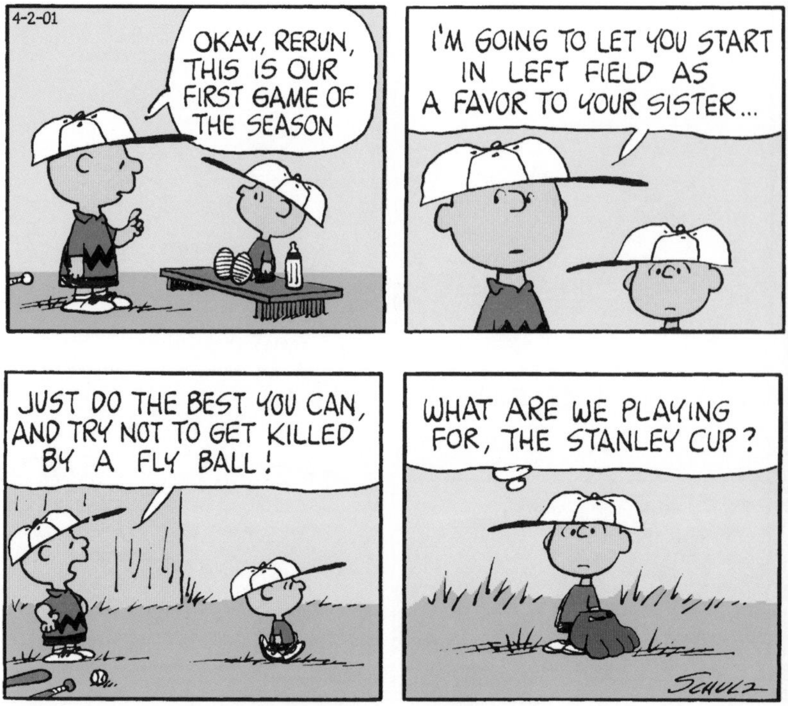
4-2-01
OKAY, RERUN, THIS IS OUR FIRST GAME OF THE SEASON
I'M GOING TO LET YOU START IN LEFT FIELD AS A FAVOR TO YOUR SISTER...
JUST DO THE BEST YOU CAN, AND TRY NOT TO GET KILLED BY A FLY BALL!
WHAT ARE WE PLAYING FOR, THE STANLEY CUP?
SCHULZ

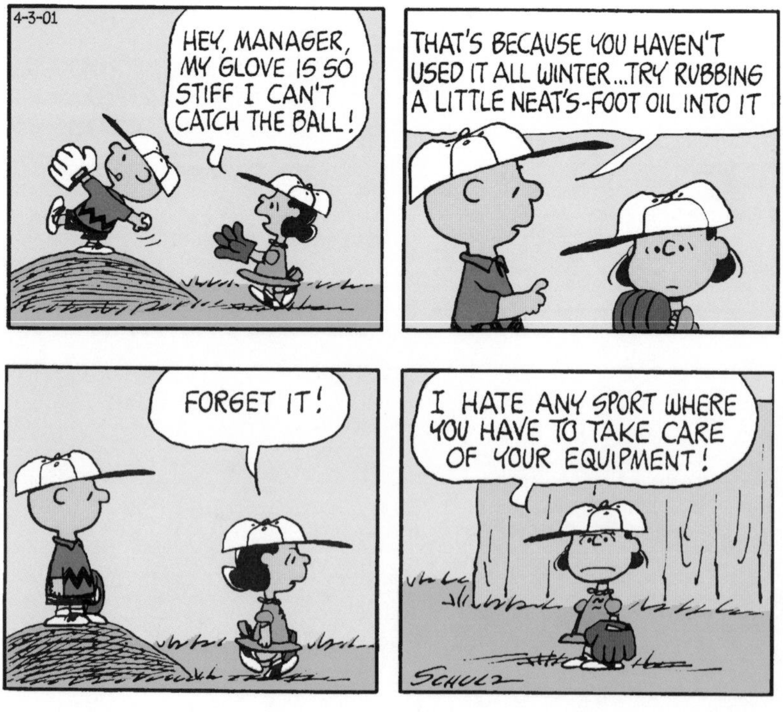
4-3-01
HEY, MANAGER, MY GLOVE IS SO STIFF I CAN'T CATCH THE BALL!
THAT'S BECAUSE YOU HAVEN'T USED IT ALL WINTER...TRY RUBBING A LITTLE NEAT'S-FOOT OIL INTO IT
FORGET IT!
I HATE ANY SPORT WHERE YOU HAVE TO TAKE CARE OF YOUR EQUIPMENT!
SCHULZ

WHY DO YOU ALWAYS PUT YOUR LEFT SHOE ON FIRST, BIG BROTHER?

WELL, ACTUALLY, I DON'T... I ONLY PUT IT ON FIRST ON DAYS WHEN WE HAVE A BASEBALL GAME...

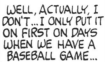

I GUESS IT'S KIND OF A SUPERSTITION... BASEBALL PLAYERS HAVE A LOT OF SUPERSTITIONS..

WHAT WOULD HAPPEN IF YOU DIDN'T DO IT?

WELL, WE'D PROBABLY LOSE THE GAME

HAVE YOU EVER WON?

WHERE'S OUR PITCHER?

I DON'T KNOW...I HAVEN'T SEEN HIM..

6-24-01

!?

I DON'T UNDERSTAND... THE GAME IS READY TO START, AND YOU'RE STILL SITTING HERE IN YOUR BEDROOM WITHOUT YOUR SHOES ON!

SCHULZ

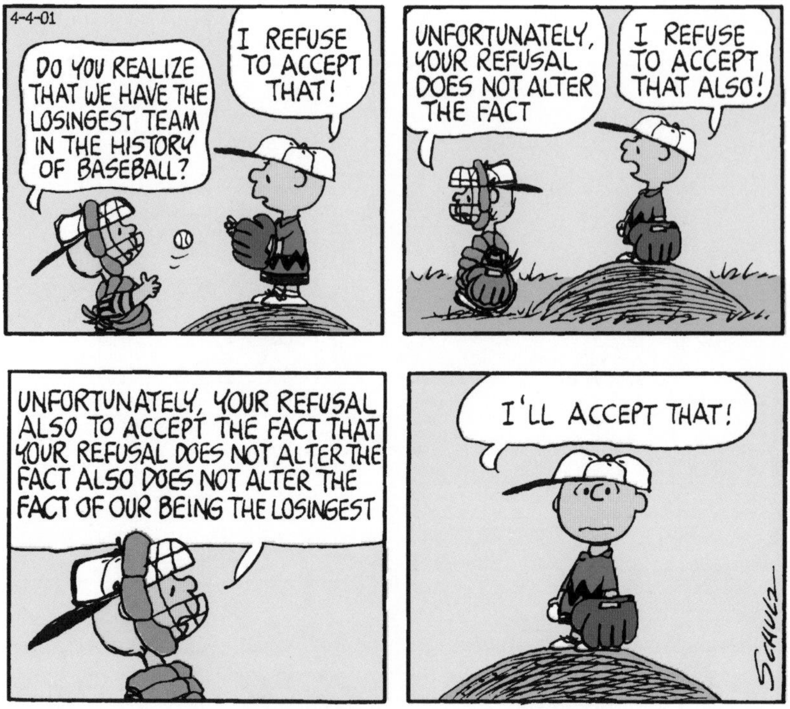
4-4-01
DO YOU REALIZE THAT WE HAVE THE LOSINGEST TEAM IN THE HISTORY OF BASEBALL?
I REFUSE TO ACCEPT THAT!
UNFORTUNATELY, YOUR REFUSAL DOES NOT ALTER THE FACT
I REFUSE TO ACCEPT THAT ALSO!
UNFORTUNATELY, YOUR REFUSAL ALSO TO ACCEPT THE FACT THAT YOUR REFUSAL DOES NOT ALTER THE FACT ALSO DOES NOT ALTER THE FACT OF OUR BEING THE LOSINGEST
I'LL ACCEPT THAT!
SCHULZ

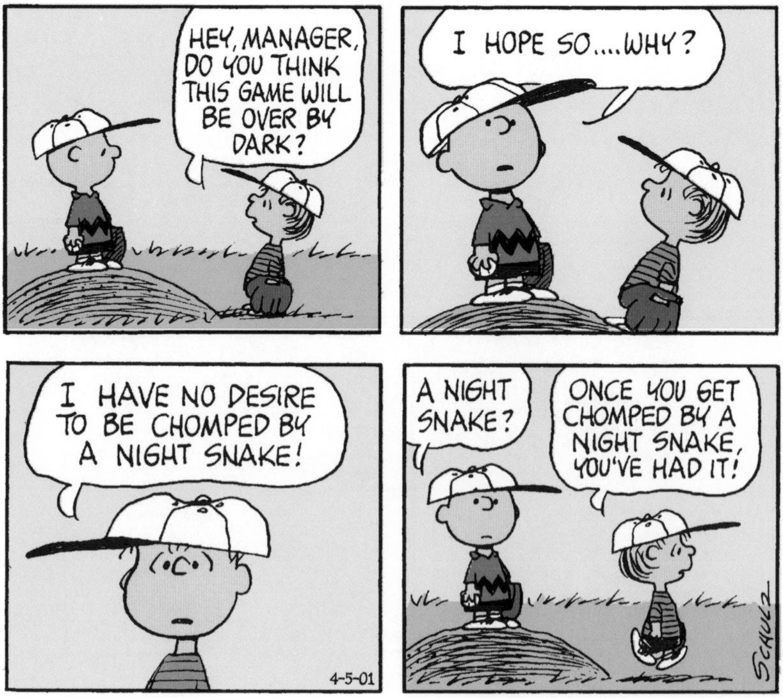
HEY, MANAGER, DO YOU THINK THIS GAME WILL BE OVER BY DARK?
I HOPE SO....WHY?
I HAVE NO DESIRE TO BE CHOMPED BY A NIGHT SNAKE!
4-5-01
A NIGHT SNAKE?
ONCE YOU GET CHOMPED BY A NIGHT SNAKE, YOU'VE HAD IT!
SCHULZ

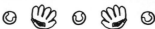

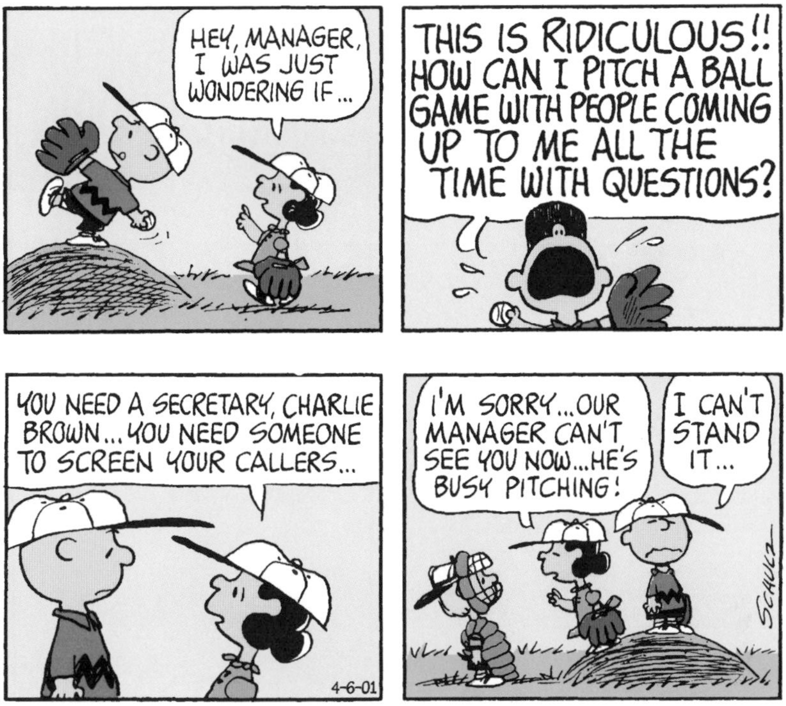
HEY, MANAGER, I WAS JUST WONDERING IF...
THIS IS RIDICULOUS!! HOW CAN I PITCH A BALL GAME WITH PEOPLE COMING UP TO ME ALL THE TIME WITH QUESTIONS?
YOU NEED A SECRETARY, CHARLIE BROWN... YOU NEED SOMEONE TO SCREEN YOUR CALLERS...
I'M SORRY...OUR MANAGER CAN'T SEE YOU NOW...HE'S BUSY PITCHING!
I CAN'T STAND IT...
SCHULZ
4-6-01

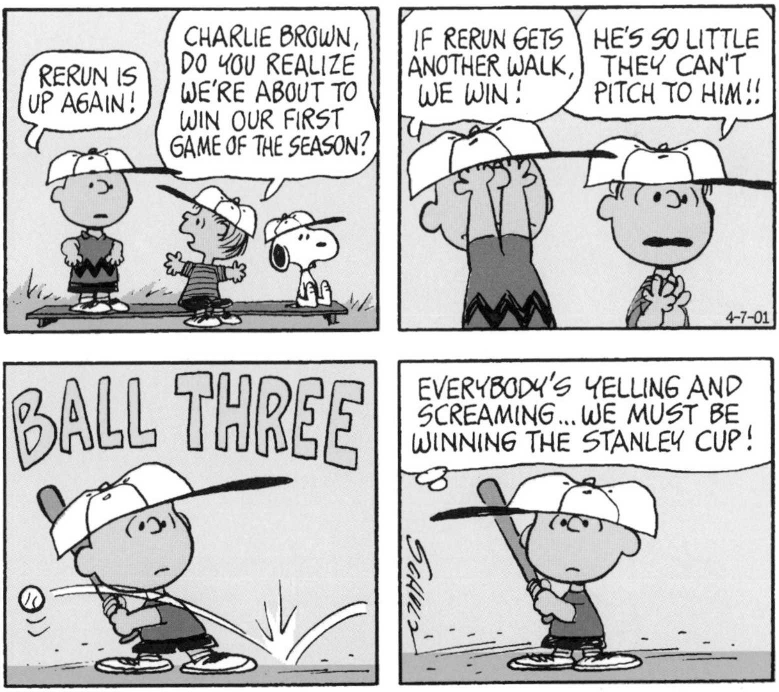
RERUN IS UP AGAIN!
CHARLIE BROWN, DO YOU REALIZE WE'RE ABOUT TO WIN OUR FIRST GAME OF THE SEASON?
IF RERUN GETS ANOTHER WALK, WE WIN!
HE'S SO LITTLE THEY CAN'T PITCH TO HIM!!
4-7-01
BALL THREE
EVERYBODY'S YELLING AND SCREAMING... WE MUST BE WINNING THE STANLEY CUP!
SCHULZ

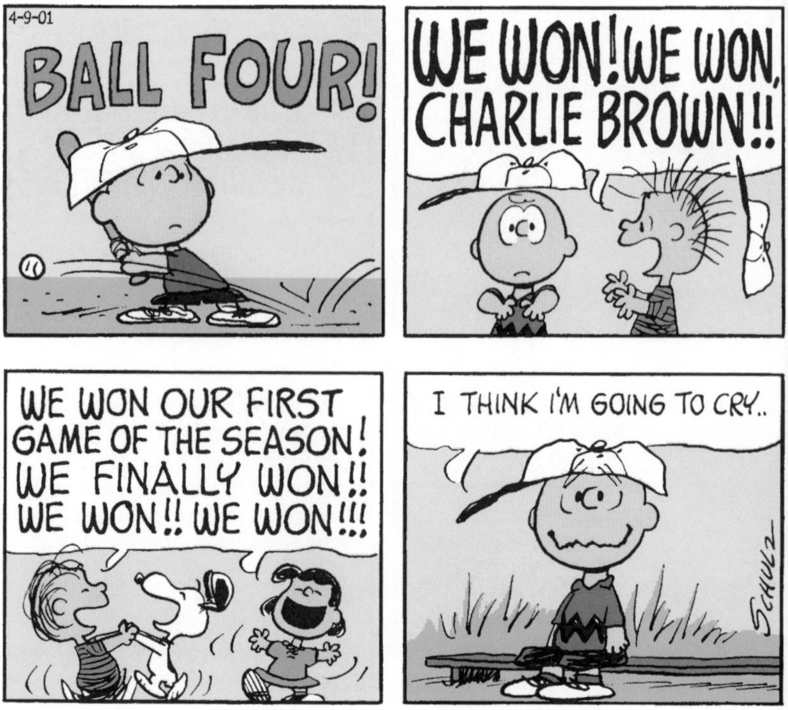
4-9-01
BALL FOUR!
WE WON! WE WON, WE WON, CHARLIE BROWN!!
WE WON OUR FIRST GAME OF THE SEASON! WE FINALLY WON!! WE WON!! WE WON!!!
I THINK I'M GOING TO CRY..
SCHULZ

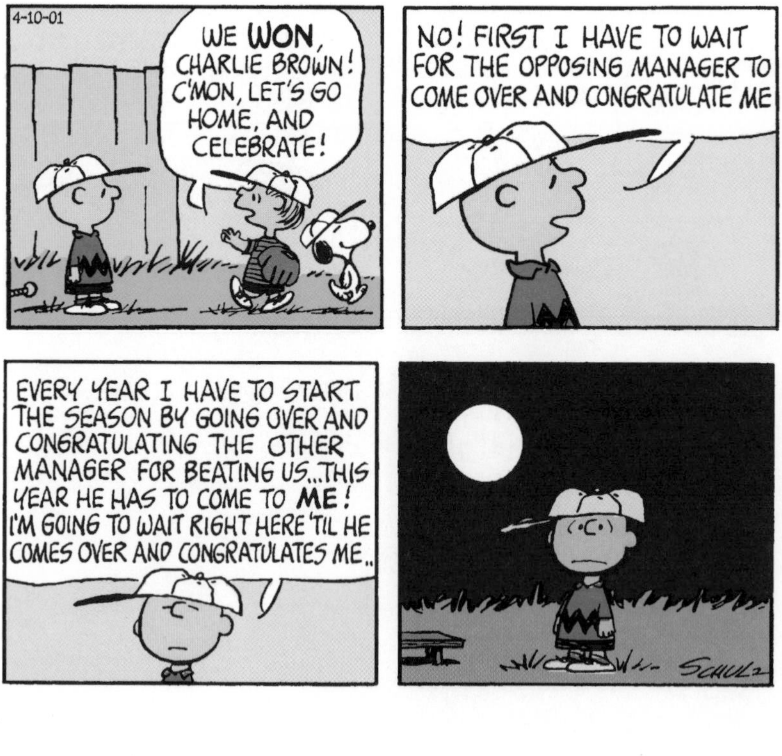
4-10-01
WE WON, CHARLIE BROWN! C'MON, LET'S GO HOME, AND CELEBRATE!
NO! FIRST I HAVE TO WAIT FOR THE OPPOSING MANAGER TO COME OVER AND CONGRATULATE ME
EVERY YEAR I HAVE TO START THE SEASON BY GOING OVER AND CONGRATULATING THE OTHER MANAGER FOR BEATING US...THIS YEAR HE HAS TO COME TO ME! I'M GOING TO WAIT RIGHT HERE 'TIL HE COMES OVER AND CONGRATULATES ME..
SCHULZ

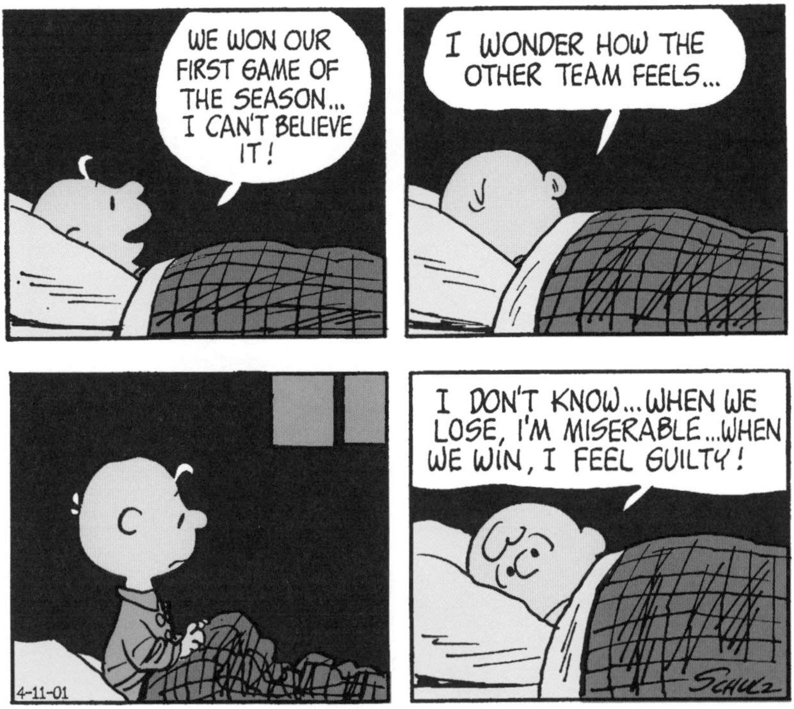
WE WON OUR FIRST GAME OF THE SEASON... I CAN'T BELIEVE IT!
I WONDER HOW THE OTHER TEAM FEELS...
I DON'T KNOW...WHEN WE LOSE, I'M MISERABLE...WHEN WE WIN, I FEEL GUILTY!
4-11-01
SCHULZ

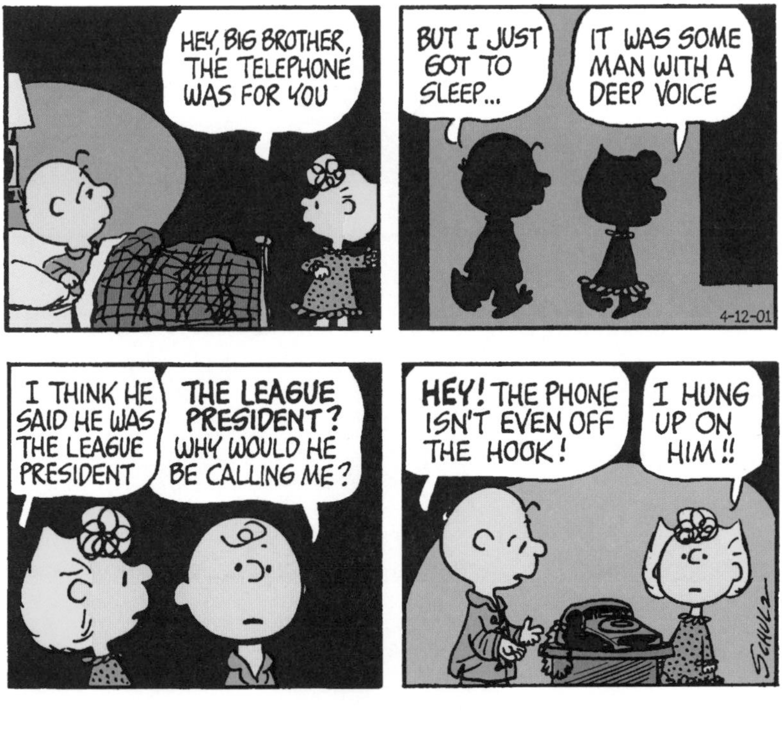
HEY, BIG BROTHER, THE TELEPHONE WAS FOR YOU
BUT I JUST GOT TO SLEEP...
IT WAS SOME MAN WITH A DEEP VOICE
4-12-01
I THINK HE SAID HE WAS THE LEAGUE PRESIDENT
THE LEAGUE PRESIDENT? WHY WOULD HE BE CALLING ME?
HEY! THE PHONE ISN'T EVEN OFF THE HOOK!
I HUNG UP ON HIM!!
SCHULZ

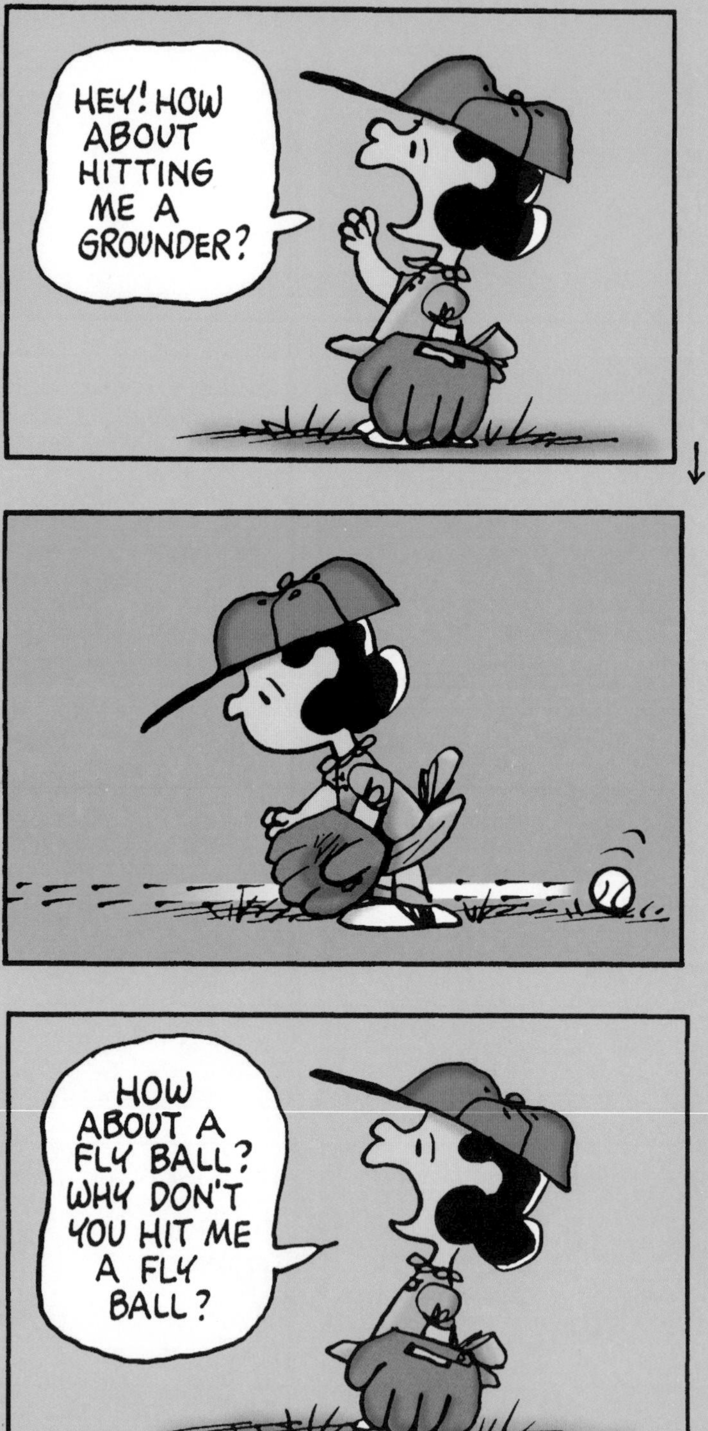
HEY! HOW ABOUT HITTING ME A GROUNDER?
HOW ABOUT A FLY BALL? WHY DON'T YOU HIT ME A FLY BALL?

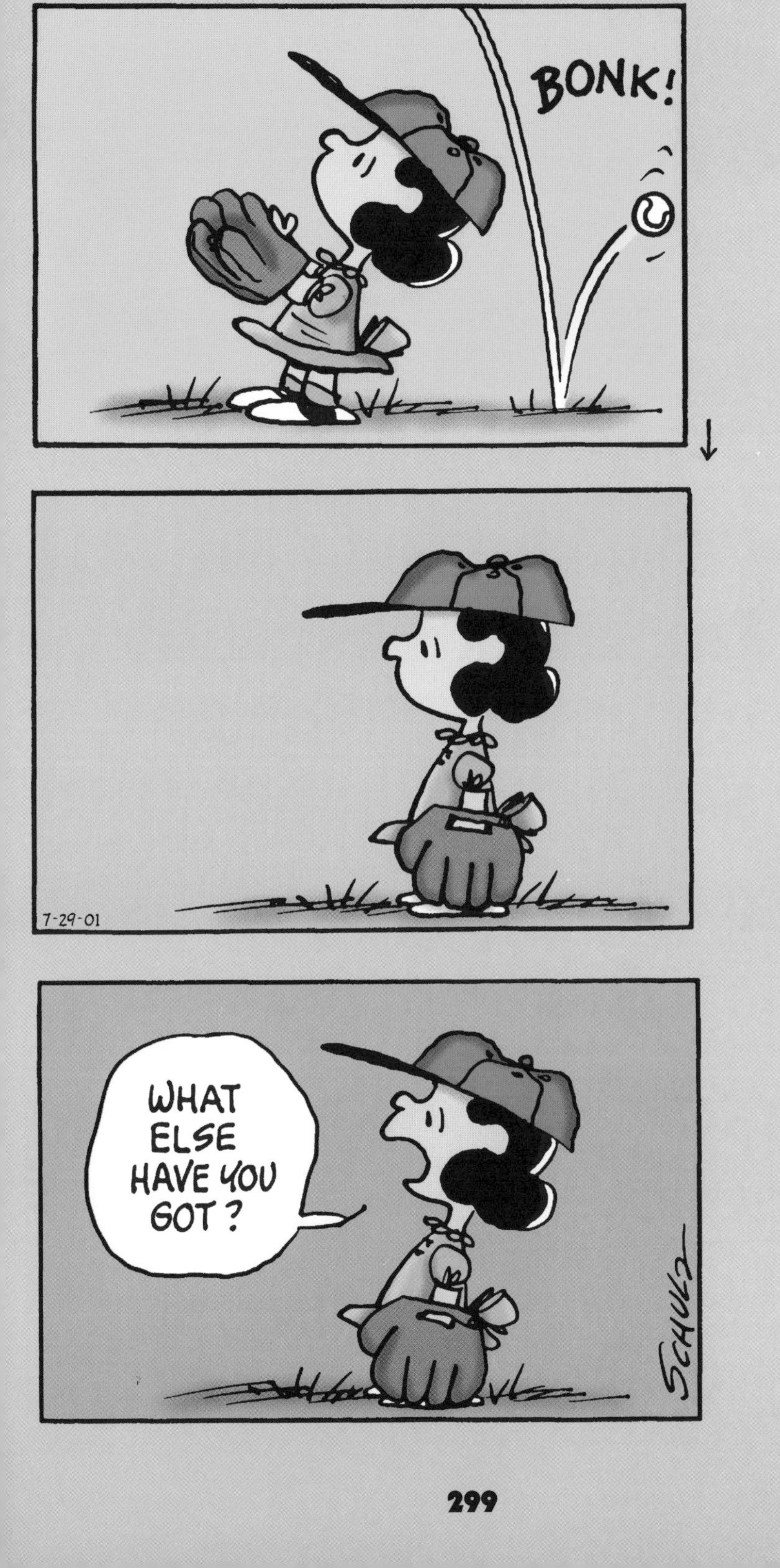
BONK!
7-29-01
WHAT ELSE HAVE YOU GOT ?
SCHULZ

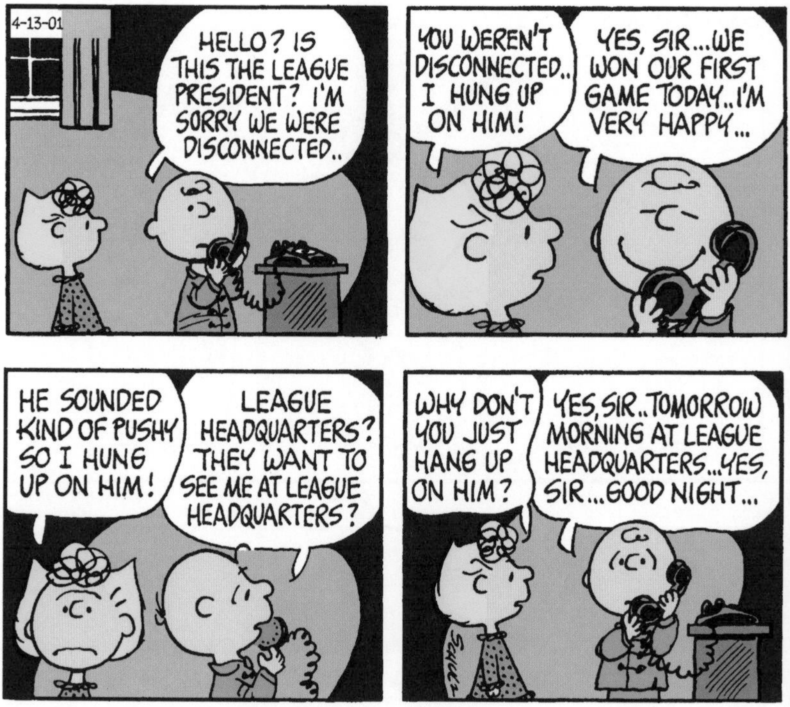
4-13-01
HELLO? IS THIS THE LEAGUE PRESIDENT? I'M SORRY WE WERE DISCONNECTED..
YOU WEREN'T DISCONNECTED.. I HUNG UP ON HIM!
YES, SIR...WE WON OUR FIRST GAME TODAY..I'M VERY HAPPY...
HE SOUNDED KIND OF PUSHY SO I HUNG UP ON HIM!
LEAGUE HEADQUARTERS? THEY WANT TO SEE ME AT LEAGUE HEADQUARTERS?
WHY DON'T YOU JUST HANG UP ON HIM?
YES, SIR..TOMORROW MORNING AT LEAGUE HEADQUARTERS...YES, SIR...GOOD NIGHT...
SCHULZ

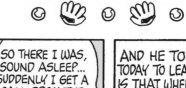

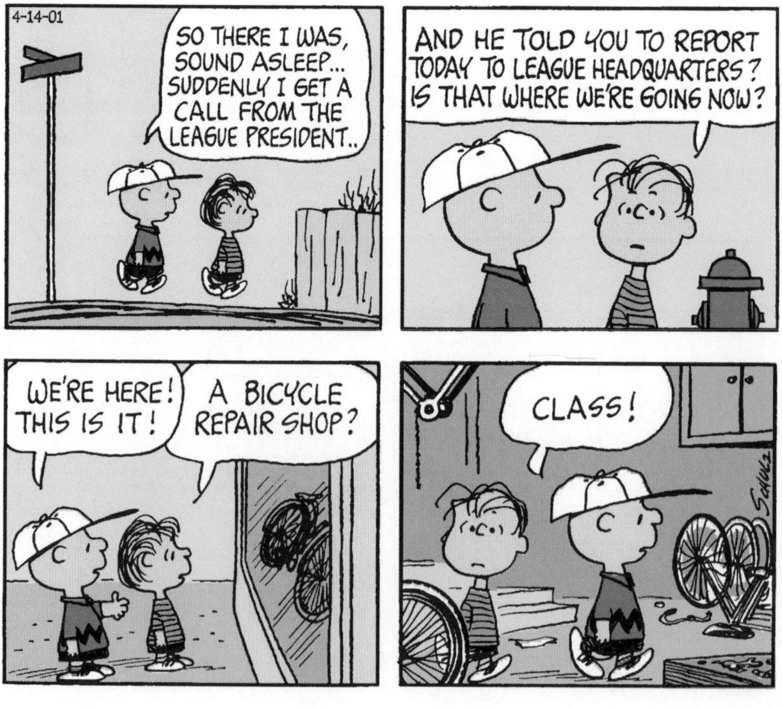
4-14-01
SO THERE I WAS, SOUND ASLEEP... SUDDENLY I GET A CALL FROM THE LEAGUE PRESIDENT..
AND HE TOLD YOU TO REPORT TODAY TO LEAGUE HEADQUARTERS? IS THAT WHERE WE'RE GOING NOW?
WE'RE HERE! THIS IS IT!
A BICYCLE REPAIR SHOP?
CLASS!
SCHULZ

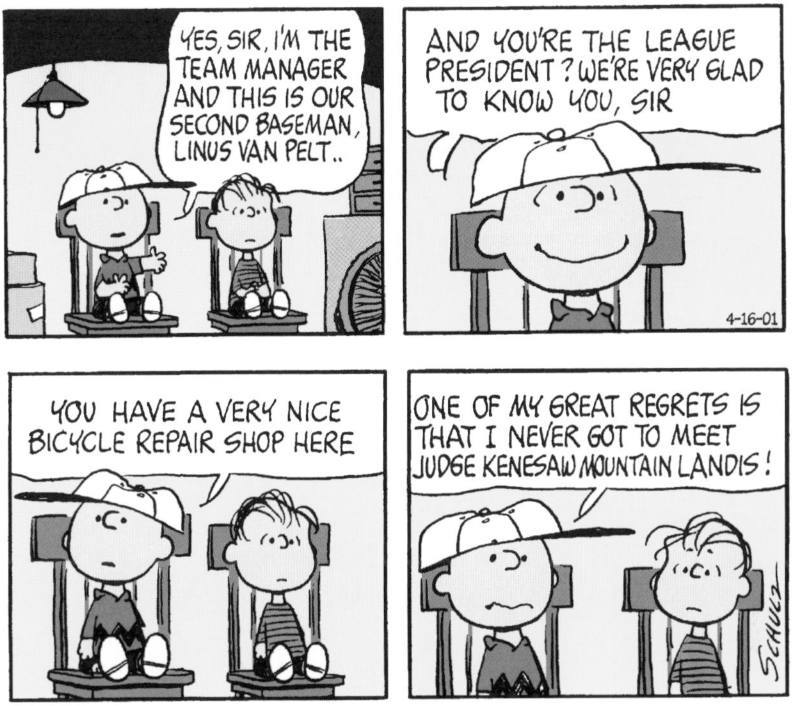
YES, SIR, I'M THE TEAM MANAGER AND THIS IS OUR SECOND BASEMAN, LINUS VAN PELT..
AND YOU'RE THE LEAGUE PRESIDENT? WE'RE VERY GLAD TO KNOW YOU, SIR
4-16-01
YOU HAVE A VERY NICE BICYCLE REPAIR SHOP HERE
ONE OF MY GREAT REGRETS IS THAT I NEVER GOT TO MEET JUDGE KENESAW MOUNTAIN LANDIS!
SCHULZ

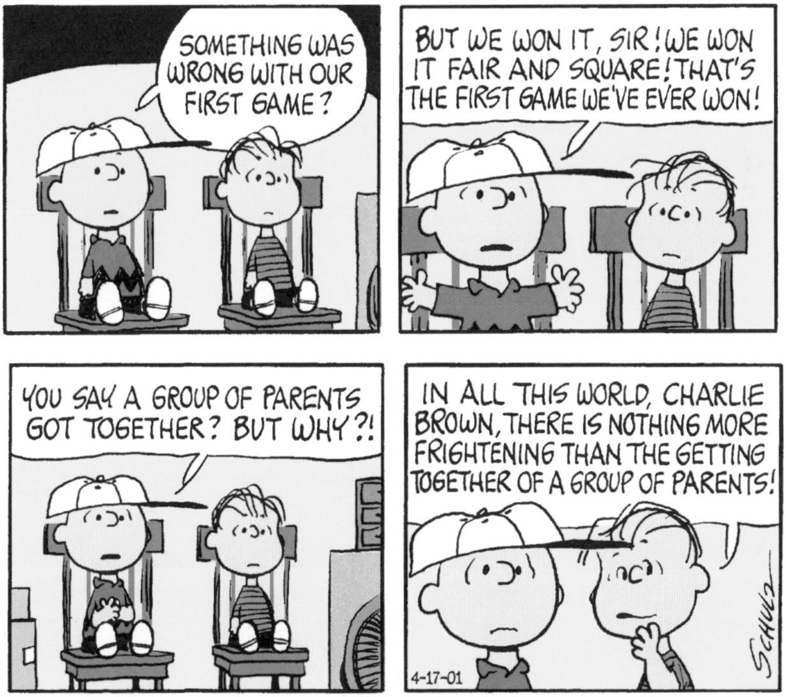
SOMETHING WAS WRONG WITH OUR FIRST GAME?
BUT WE WON IT, SIR! WE WON IT FAIR AND SQUARE! THAT'S THE FIRST GAME WE'VE EVER WON!
YOU SAY A GROUP OF PARENTS GOT TOGETHER? BUT WHY?!
IN ALL THIS WORLD, CHARLIE BROWN, THERE IS NOTHING MORE FRIGHTENING THAN THE GETTING TOGETHER OF A GROUP OF PARENTS!
4-17-01
SCHULZ

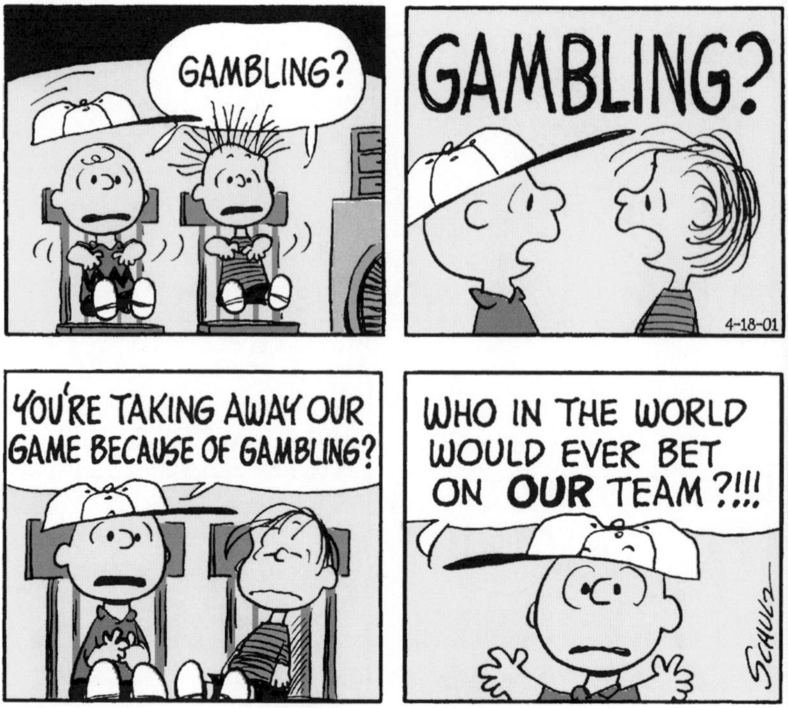
GAMBLING?
GAMBLING?
4-18-01
YOU'RE TAKING AWAY OUR GAME BECAUSE OF GAMBLING?
WHO IN THE WORLD WOULD EVER BET ON **OUR** TEAM?!!!
SCHULZ

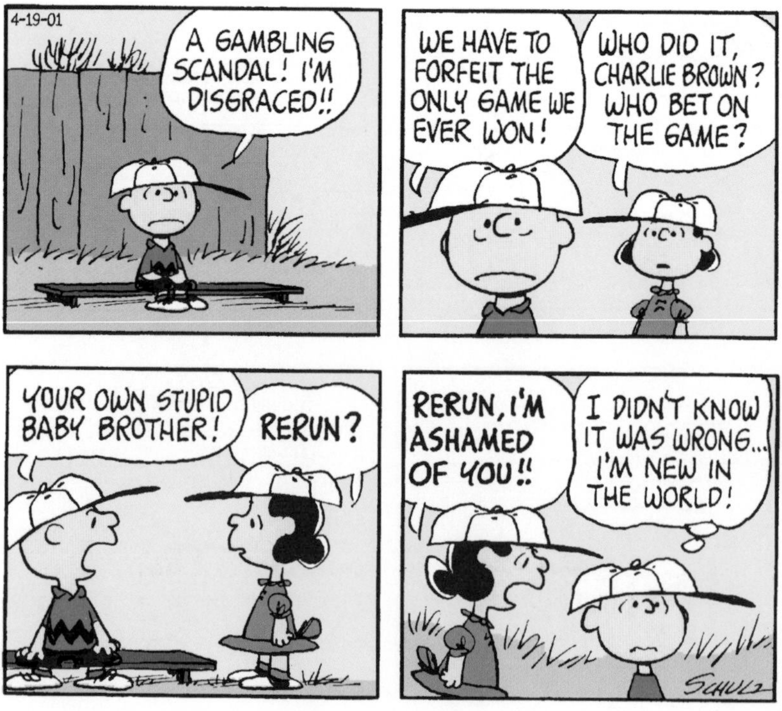
4-19-01
A GAMBLING SCANDAL! I'M DISGRACED!!
WE HAVE TO FORFEIT THE ONLY GAME WE EVER WON!
WHO DID IT, CHARLIE BROWN? WHO BET ON THE GAME?
YOUR OWN STUPID BABY BROTHER!
RERUN?
RERUN, I'M ASHAMED OF YOU!!
I DIDN'T KNOW IT WAS WRONG... I'M NEW IN THE WORLD!
SCHULZ

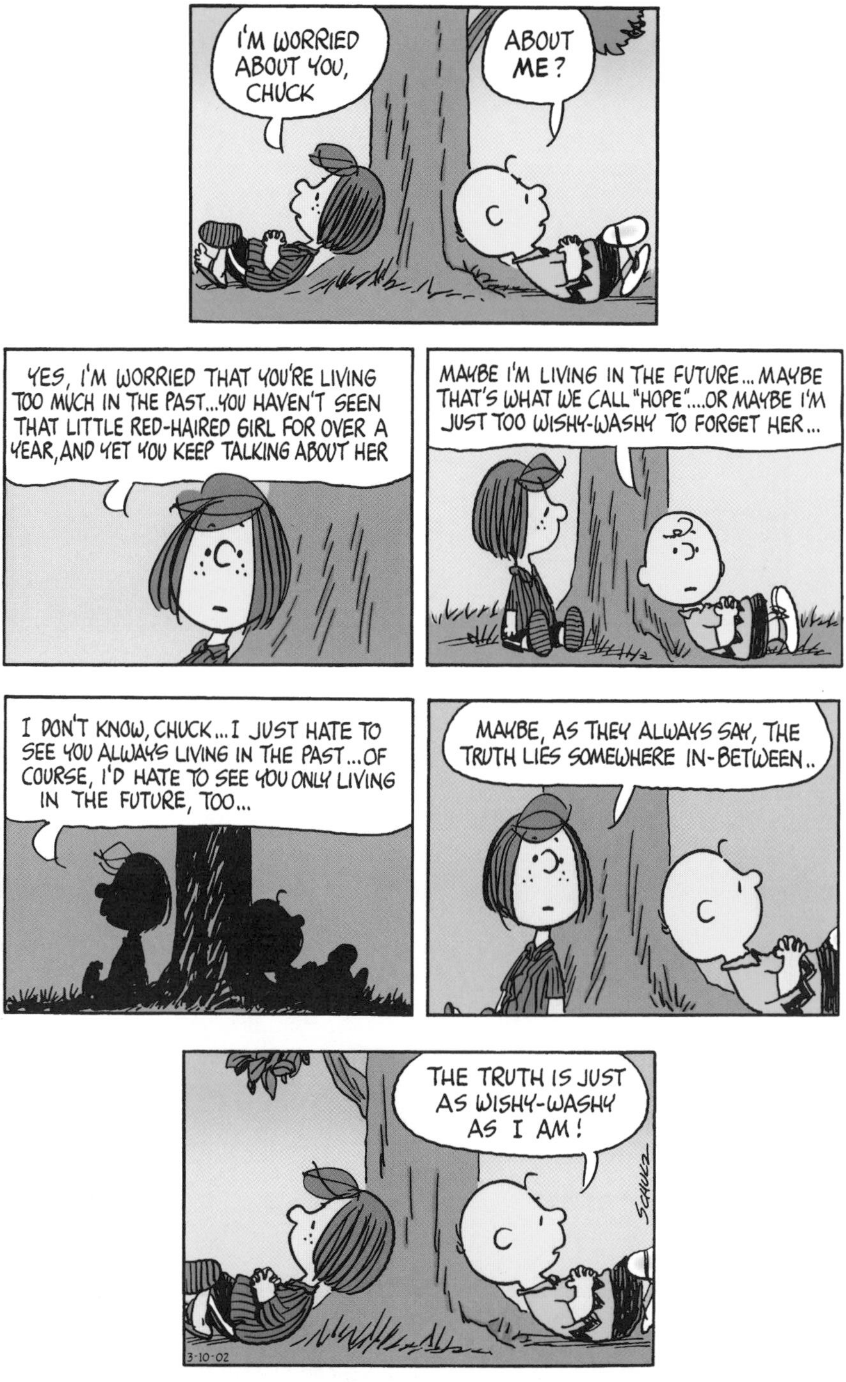
I'M WORRIED ABOUT YOU, CHUCK
ABOUT ME?
YES, I'M WORRIED THAT YOU'RE LIVING TOO MUCH IN THE PAST...YOU HAVEN'T SEEN THAT LITTLE RED-HAIRED GIRL FOR OVER A YEAR, AND YET YOU KEEP TALKING ABOUT HER
MAYBE I'M LIVING IN THE FUTURE... MAYBE THAT'S WHAT WE CALL "HOPE"....OR MAYBE I'M JUST TOO WISHY-WASHY TO FORGET HER...
I DON'T KNOW, CHUCK...I JUST HATE TO SEE YOU ALWAYS LIVING IN THE PAST...OF COURSE, I'D HATE TO SEE YOU ONLY LIVING IN THE FUTURE, TOO...
MAYBE, AS THEY ALWAYS SAY, THE TRUTH LIES SOMEWHERE IN-BETWEEN..
THE TRUTH IS JUST AS WISHY-WASHY AS I AM!
SCHULZ
3-10-02

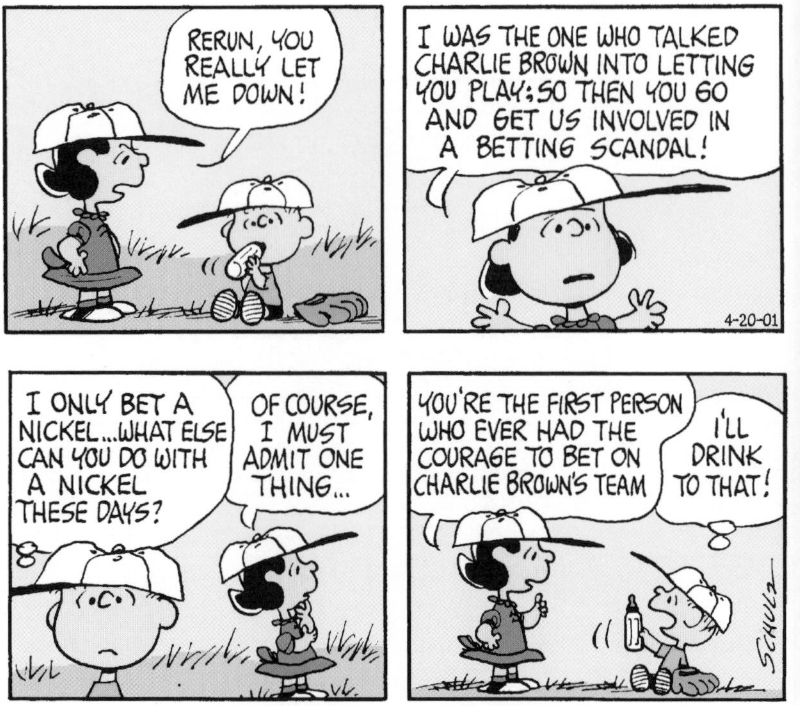
RERUN, YOU REALLY LET ME DOWN!
I WAS THE ONE WHO TALKED CHARLIE BROWN INTO LETTING YOU PLAY; SO THEN YOU GO AND GET US INVOLVED IN A BETTING SCANDAL!
4-20-01
I ONLY BET A NICKEL...WHAT ELSE CAN YOU DO WITH A NICKEL THESE DAYS?
OF COURSE, I MUST ADMIT ONE THING...
YOU'RE THE FIRST PERSON WHO EVER HAD THE COURAGE TO BET ON CHARLIE BROWN'S TEAM
I'LL DRINK TO THAT!
SCHULZ

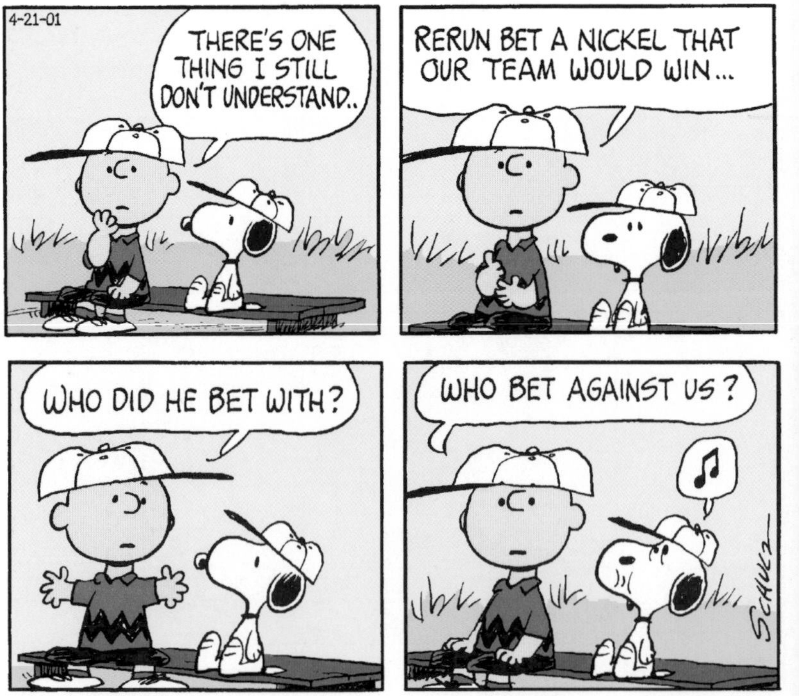
4-21-01
THERE'S ONE THING I STILL DON'T UNDERSTAND..
RERUN BET A NICKEL THAT OUR TEAM WOULD WIN...
WHO DID HE BET WITH?
WHO BET AGAINST US?
SCHULZ

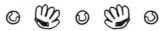

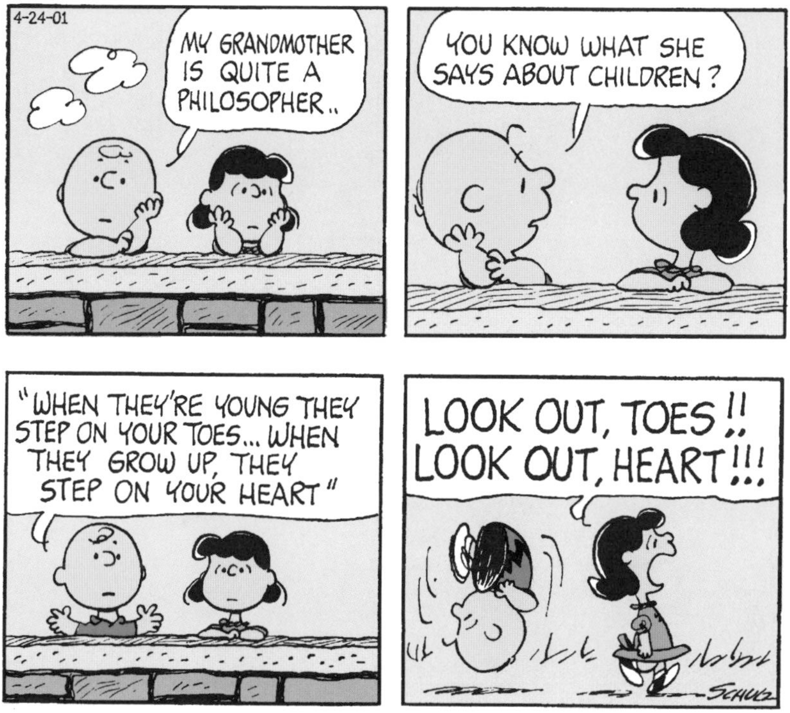
4-24-01
MY GRANDMOTHER IS QUITE A PHILOSOPHER..
YOU KNOW WHAT SHE SAYS ABOUT CHILDREN?
"WHEN THEY'RE YOUNG THEY STEP ON YOUR TOES... WHEN THEY GROW UP, THEY STEP ON YOUR HEART"
LOOK OUT, TOES!! LOOK OUT, HEART!!!
SCHULZ

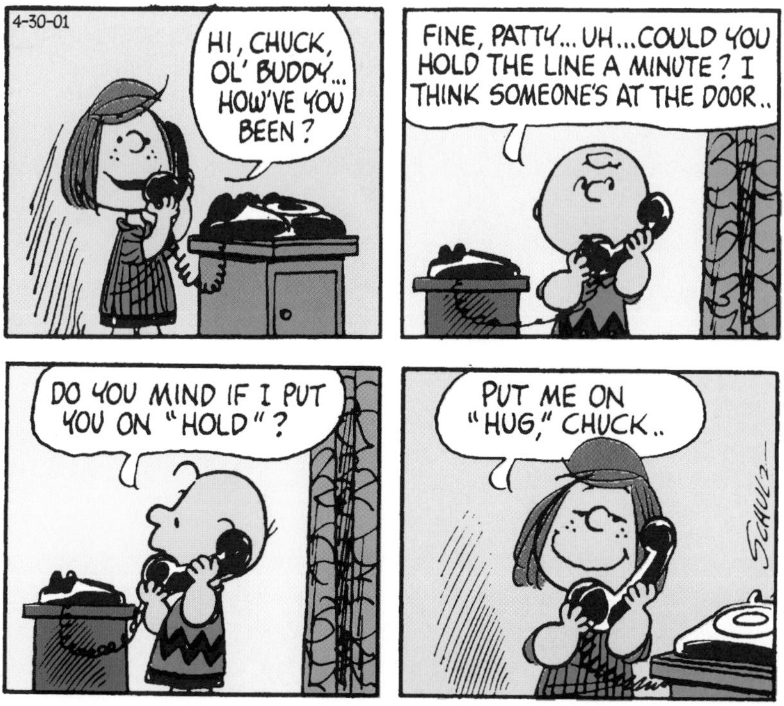
4-30-01
HI, CHUCK, OL' BUDDY... HOW'VE YOU BEEN?
FINE, PATTY... UH... COULD YOU HOLD THE LINE A MINUTE? I THINK SOMEONE'S AT THE DOOR..
DO YOU MIND IF I PUT YOU ON "HOLD"?
PUT ME ON "HUG," CHUCK..
SCHULZ

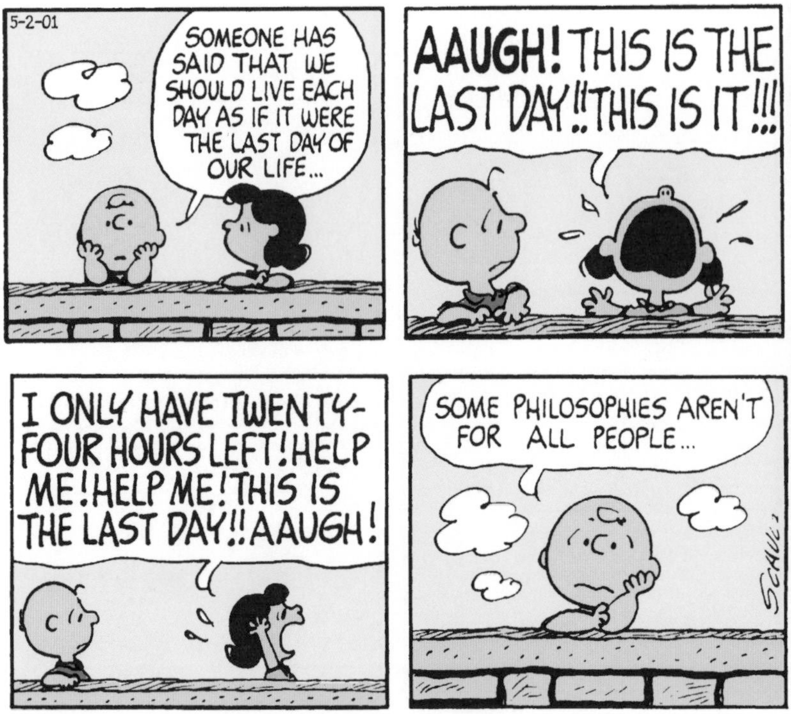
5-2-01
SOMEONE HAS SAID THAT WE SHOULD LIVE EACH DAY AS IF IT WERE THE LAST DAY OF OUR LIFE...
AAUGH! THIS IS THE LAST DAY!! THIS IS IT!!!
I ONLY HAVE TWENTY-FOUR HOURS LEFT! HELP ME! HELP ME! THIS IS THE LAST DAY!! AAUGH!
SOME PHILOSOPHIES AREN'T FOR ALL PEOPLE...
SCHULZ

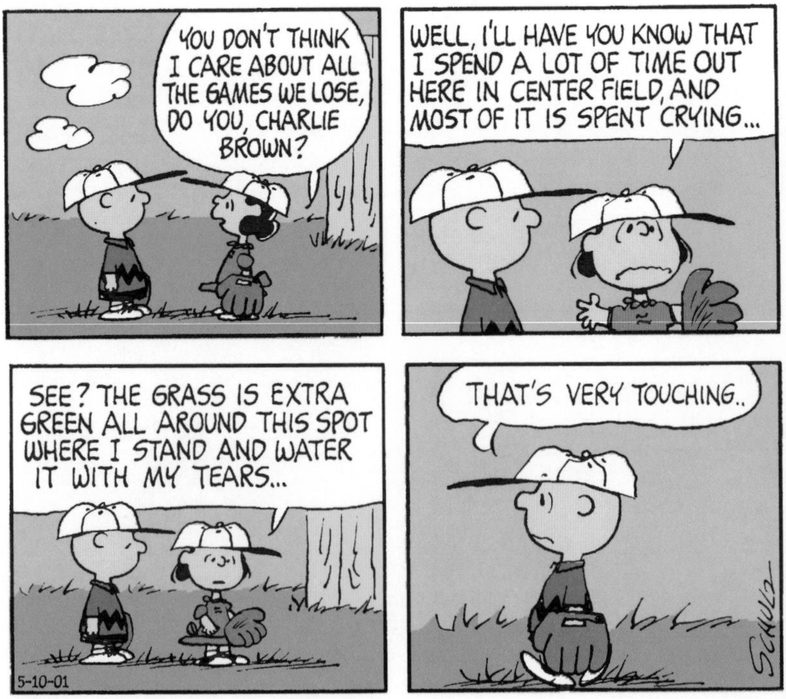
YOU DON'T THINK I CARE ABOUT ALL THE GAMES WE LOSE, DO YOU, CHARLIE BROWN?
WELL, I'LL HAVE YOU KNOW THAT I SPEND A LOT OF TIME OUT HERE IN CENTER FIELD, AND MOST OF IT IS SPENT CRYING...
SEE? THE GRASS IS EXTRA GREEN ALL AROUND THIS SPOT WHERE I STAND AND WATER IT WITH MY TEARS...
5-10-01
THAT'S VERY TOUCHING..
SCHULZ

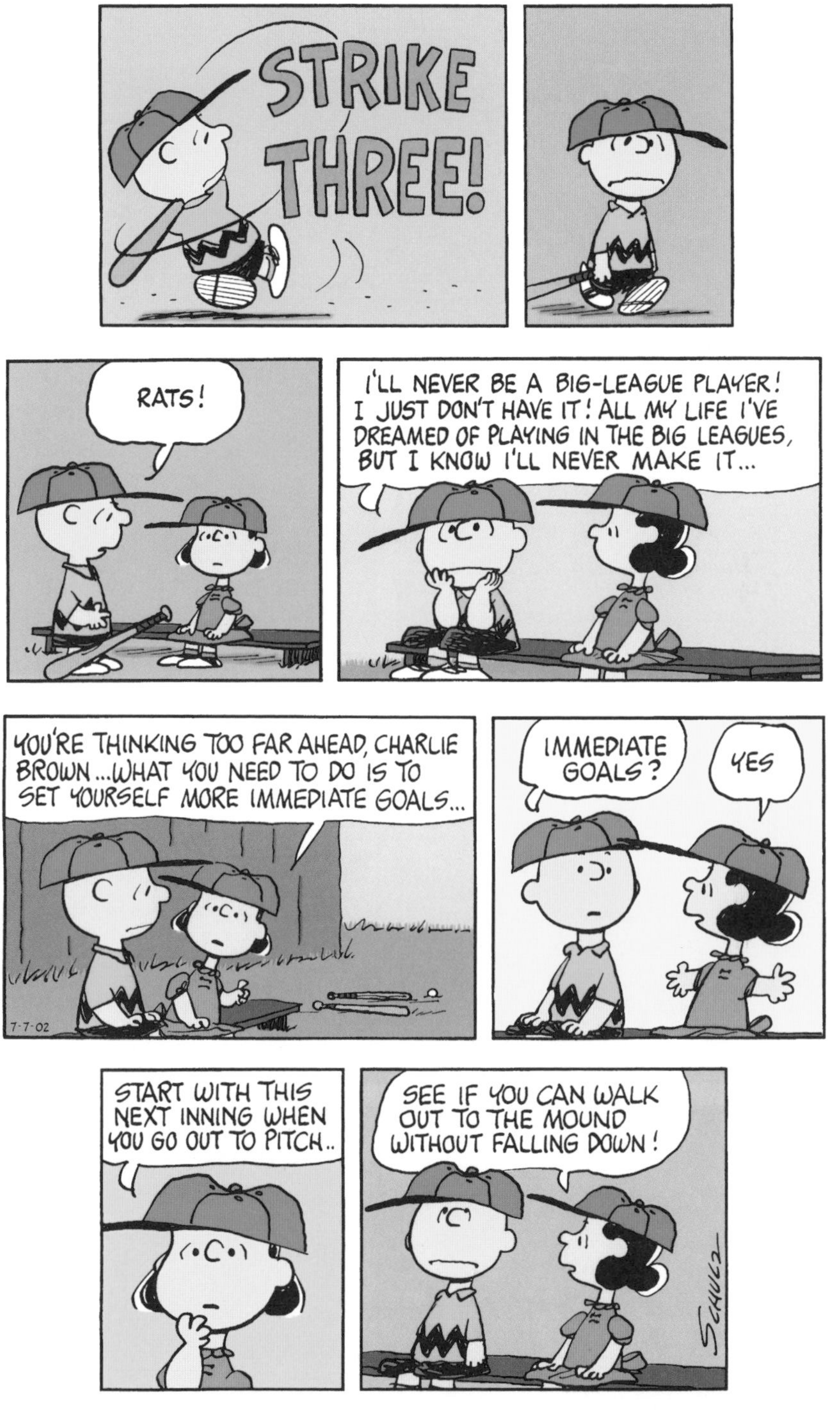
STRIKE THREE!
RATS!
I'LL NEVER BE A BIG-LEAGUE PLAYER! I JUST DON'T HAVE IT! ALL MY LIFE I'VE DREAMED OF PLAYING IN THE BIG LEAGUES, BUT I KNOW I'LL NEVER MAKE IT...
YOU'RE THINKING TOO FAR AHEAD, CHARLIE BROWN...WHAT YOU NEED TO DO IS TO SET YOURSELF MORE IMMEDIATE GOALS...
7-7-02
IMMEDIATE GOALS?
YES
START WITH THIS NEXT INNING WHEN YOU GO OUT TO PITCH..
SEE IF YOU CAN WALK OUT TO THE MOUND WITHOUT FALLING DOWN!
SCHULZ

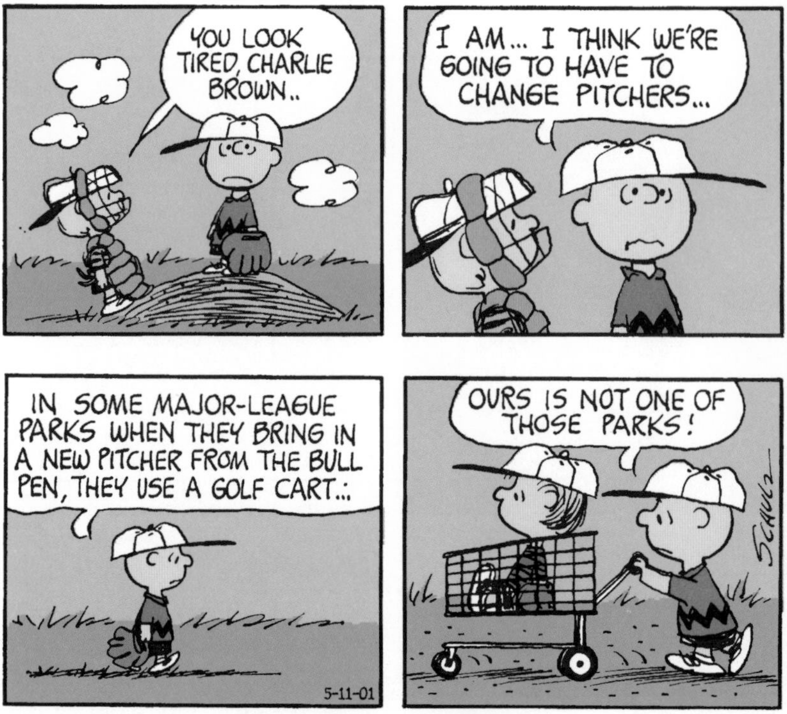
YOU LOOK TIRED, CHARLIE BROWN..
I AM... I THINK WE'RE GOING TO HAVE TO CHANGE PITCHERS...
IN SOME MAJOR-LEAGUE PARKS WHEN THEY BRING IN A NEW PITCHER FROM THE BULL PEN, THEY USE A GOLF CART..:
5-11-01
OURS IS NOT ONE OF THOSE PARKS!

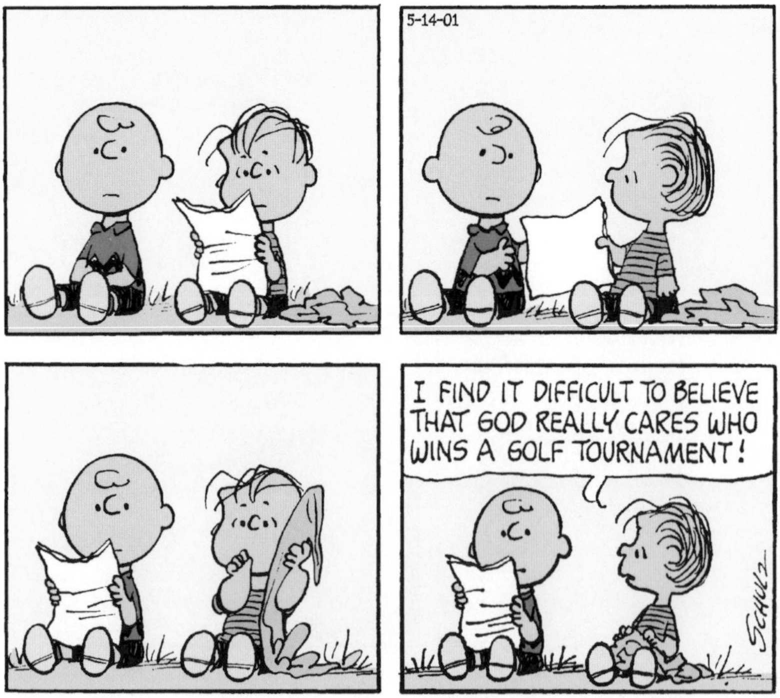
5-14-01
I FIND IT DIFFICULT TO BELIEVE THAT GOD REALLY CARES WHO WINS A GOLF TOURNAMENT!

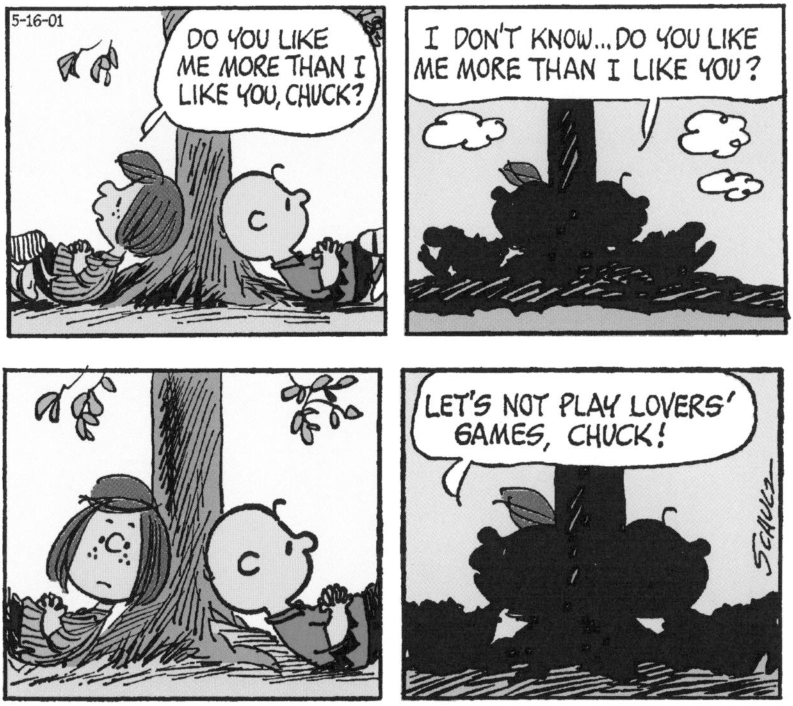
5-16-01
DO YOU LIKE ME MORE THAN I LIKE YOU, CHUCK?
I DON'T KNOW...DO YOU LIKE ME MORE THAN I LIKE YOU?
LET'S NOT PLAY LOVERS' GAMES, CHUCK!
SCHULZ

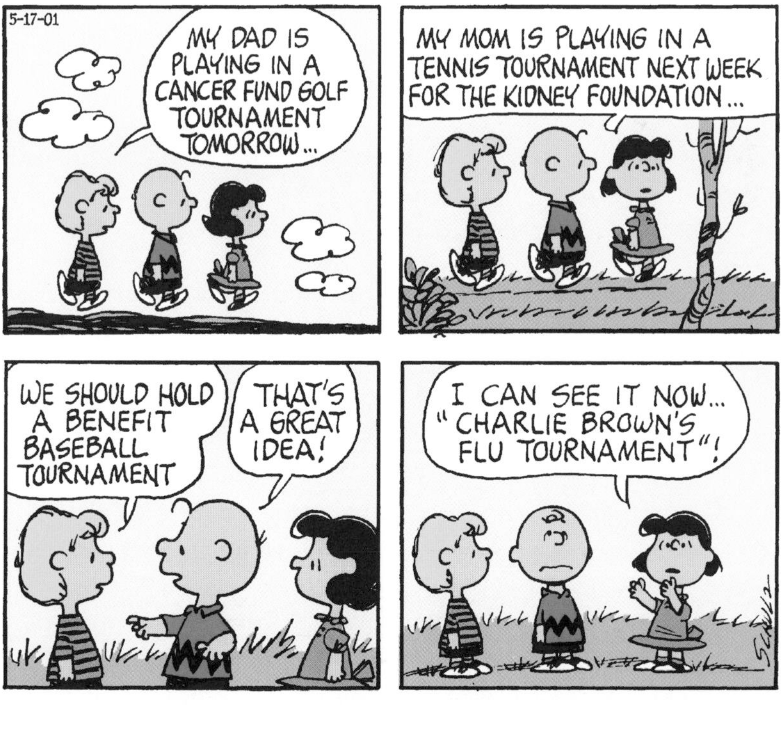
5-17-01
MY DAD IS PLAYING IN A CANCER FUND GOLF TOURNAMENT TOMORROW...
MY MOM IS PLAYING IN A TENNIS TOURNAMENT NEXT WEEK FOR THE KIDNEY FOUNDATION...
WE SHOULD HOLD A BENEFIT BASEBALL TOURNAMENT
THAT'S A GREAT IDEA!
I CAN SEE IT NOW... "CHARLIE BROWN'S FLU TOURNAMENT"!
SCHULZ

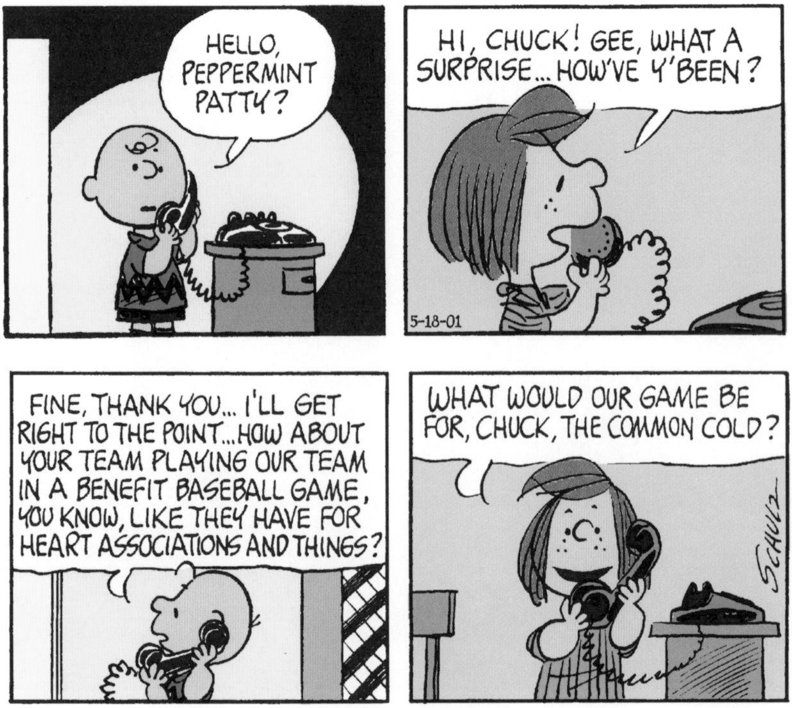
HELLO, PEPPERMINT PATTY?
HI, CHUCK! GEE, WHAT A SURPRISE... HOW'VE Y'BEEN?
5-18-01
FINE, THANK YOU... I'LL GET RIGHT TO THE POINT...HOW ABOUT YOUR TEAM PLAYING OUR TEAM IN A BENEFIT BASEBALL GAME, YOU KNOW, LIKE THEY HAVE FOR HEART ASSOCIATIONS AND THINGS?
WHAT WOULD OUR GAME BE FOR, CHUCK, THE COMMON COLD?
SCHULZ

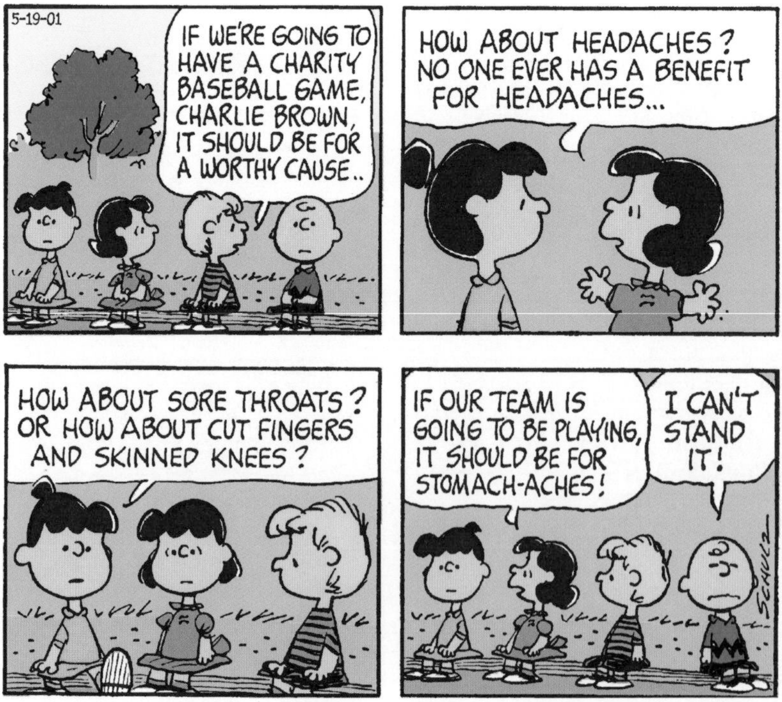
5-19-01
IF WE'RE GOING TO HAVE A CHARITY BASEBALL GAME, CHARLIE BROWN, IT SHOULD BE FOR A WORTHY CAUSE..
HOW ABOUT HEADACHES? NO ONE EVER HAS A BENEFIT FOR HEADACHES...
HOW ABOUT SORE THROATS? OR HOW ABOUT CUT FINGERS AND SKINNED KNEES?
IF OUR TEAM IS GOING TO BE PLAYING, IT SHOULD BE FOR STOMACH-ACHES!
I CAN'T STAND IT!
SCHULZ

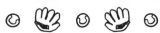

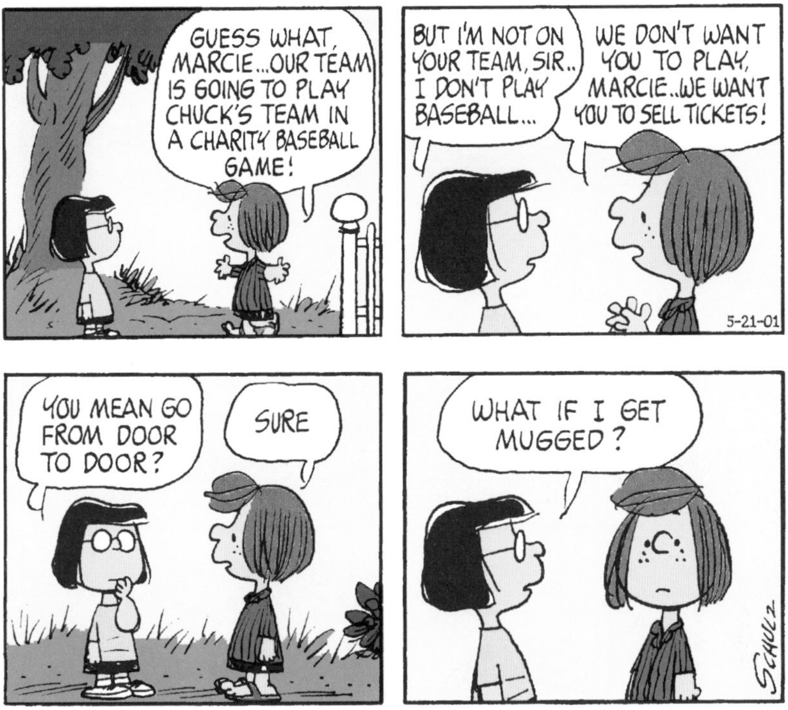
GUESS WHAT, MARCIE...OUR TEAM IS GOING TO PLAY CHUCK'S TEAM IN A CHARITY BASEBALL GAME!
BUT I'M NOT ON YOUR TEAM, SIR.. I DON'T PLAY BASEBALL...
WE DON'T WANT YOU TO PLAY, MARCIE..WE WANT YOU TO SELL TICKETS!
5-21-01
YOU MEAN GO FROM DOOR TO DOOR?
SURE
WHAT IF I GET MUGGED?
SCHULZ

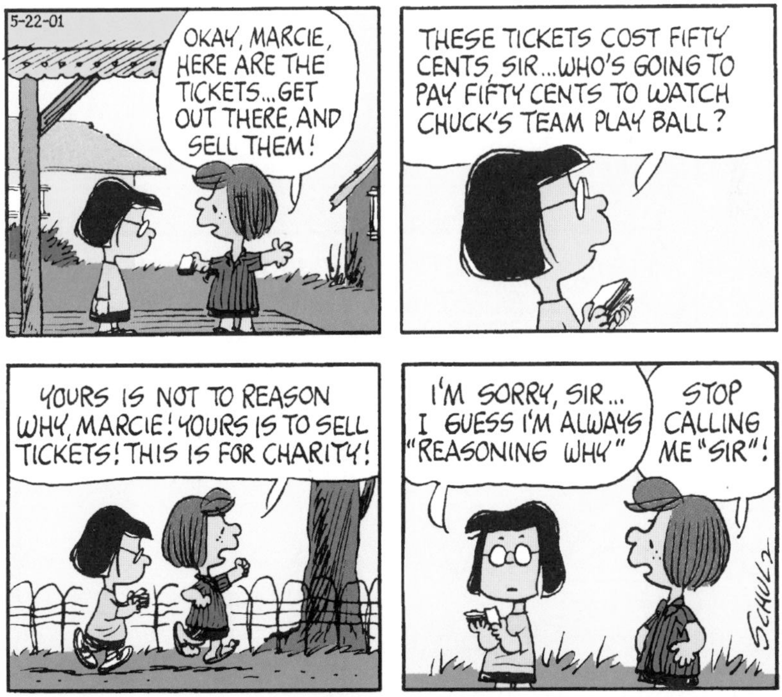
5-22-01
OKAY, MARCIE, HERE ARE THE TICKETS...GET OUT THERE, AND SELL THEM!
THESE TICKETS COST FIFTY CENTS, SIR...WHO'S GOING TO PAY FIFTY CENTS TO WATCH CHUCK'S TEAM PLAY BALL?
YOURS IS NOT TO REASON WHY, MARCIE! YOURS IS TO SELL TICKETS! THIS IS FOR CHARITY!
I'M SORRY, SIR... I GUESS I'M ALWAYS "REASONING WHY"
STOP CALLING ME "SIR"!
SCHULZ

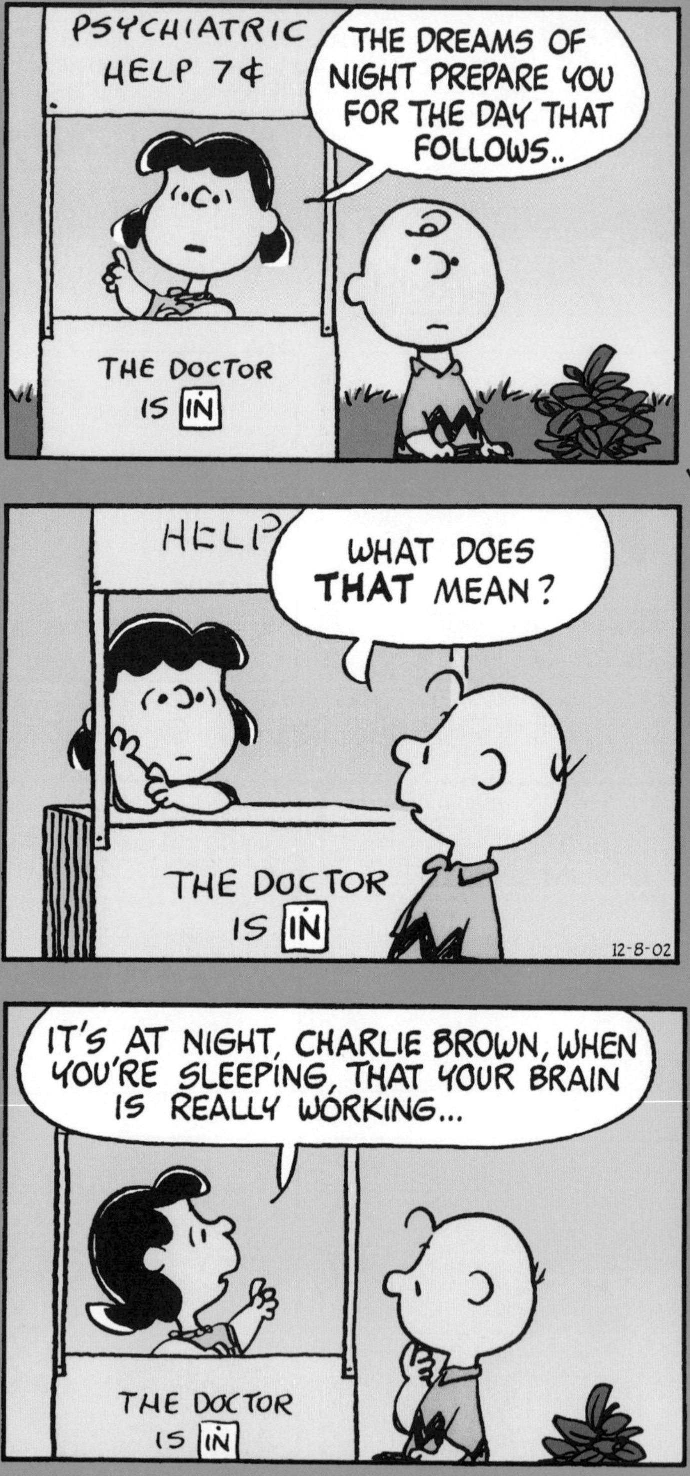
PSYCHIATRIC HELP 7¢
THE DREAMS OF NIGHT PREPARE YOU FOR THE DAY THAT FOLLOWS..
THE DOCTOR IS IN
HELP
WHAT DOES **THAT** MEAN?
THE DOCTOR IS IN
12-8-02
IT'S AT NIGHT, CHARLIE BROWN, WHEN YOU'RE SLEEPING, THAT YOUR BRAIN IS REALLY WORKING...
THE DOCTOR IS IN

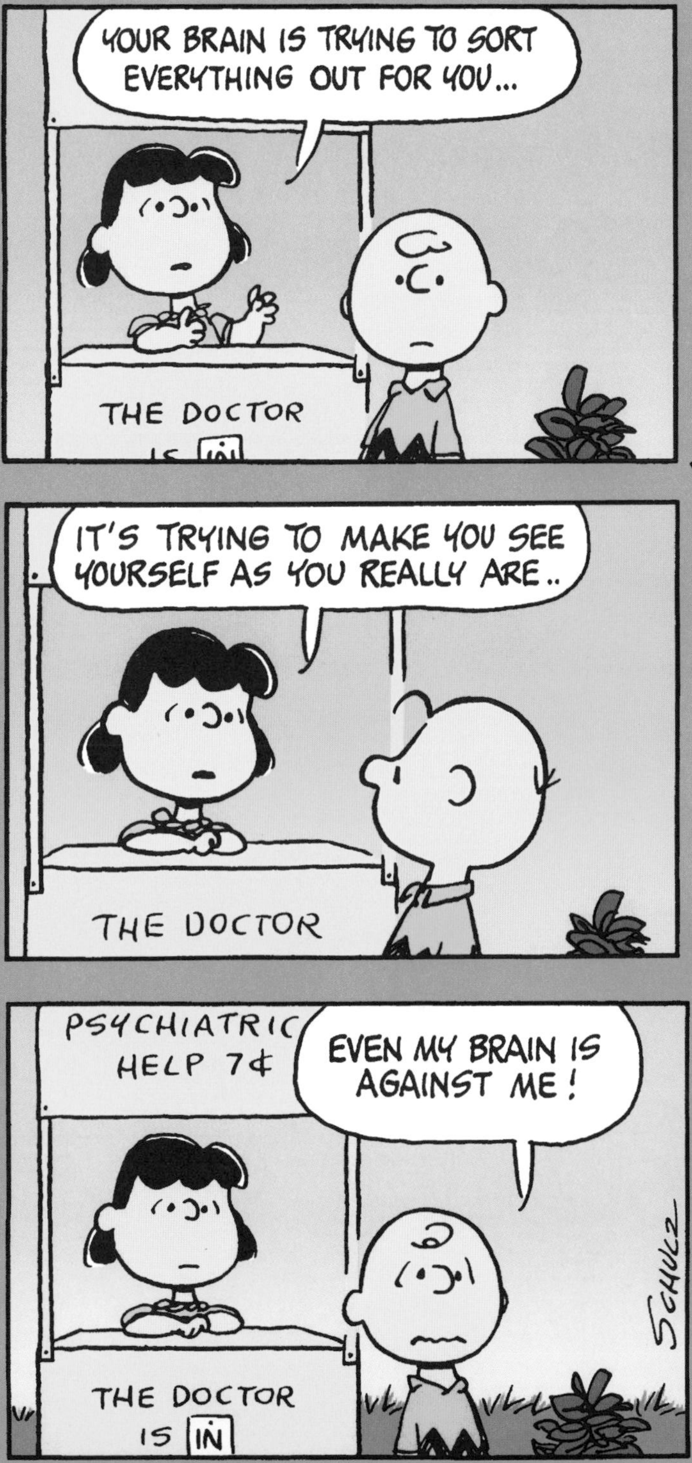
YOUR BRAIN IS TRYING TO SORT EVERYTHING OUT FOR YOU...
THE DOCTOR
IT'S TRYING TO MAKE YOU SEE YOURSELF AS YOU REALLY ARE..
THE DOCTOR
PSYCHIATRIC HELP 7¢
EVEN MY BRAIN IS AGAINST ME!
THE DOCTOR IS IN
SCHULZ

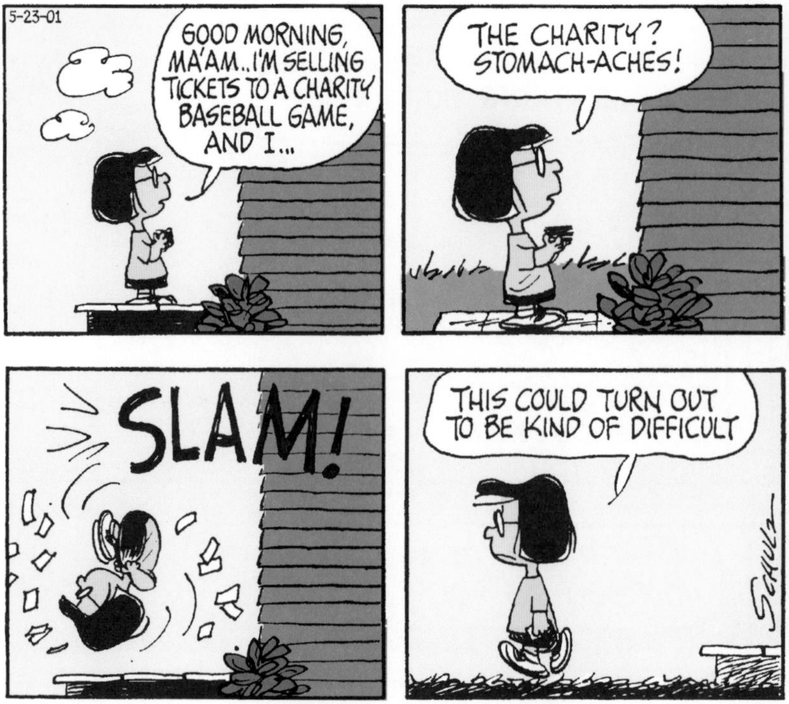
5-23-01
GOOD MORNING, MA'AM..I'M SELLING TICKETS TO A CHARITY BASEBALL GAME, AND I...
THE CHARITY? STOMACH-ACHES!
SLAM!
THIS COULD TURN OUT TO BE KIND OF DIFFICULT
SCHULZ

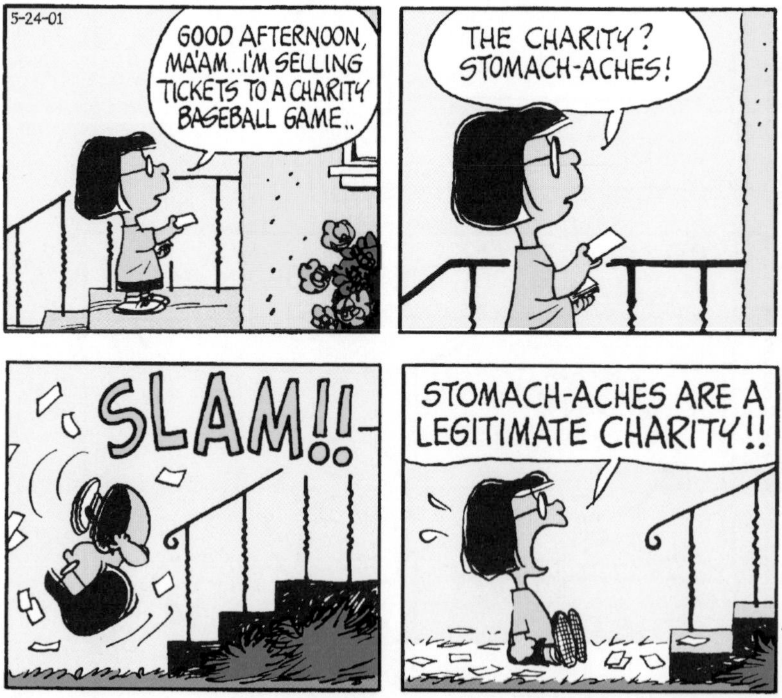
5-24-01
GOOD AFTERNOON, MA'AM..I'M SELLING TICKETS TO A CHARITY BASEBALL GAME..
THE CHARITY? STOMACH-ACHES!
SLAM!!
STOMACH-ACHES ARE A LEGITIMATE CHARITY!!

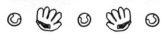

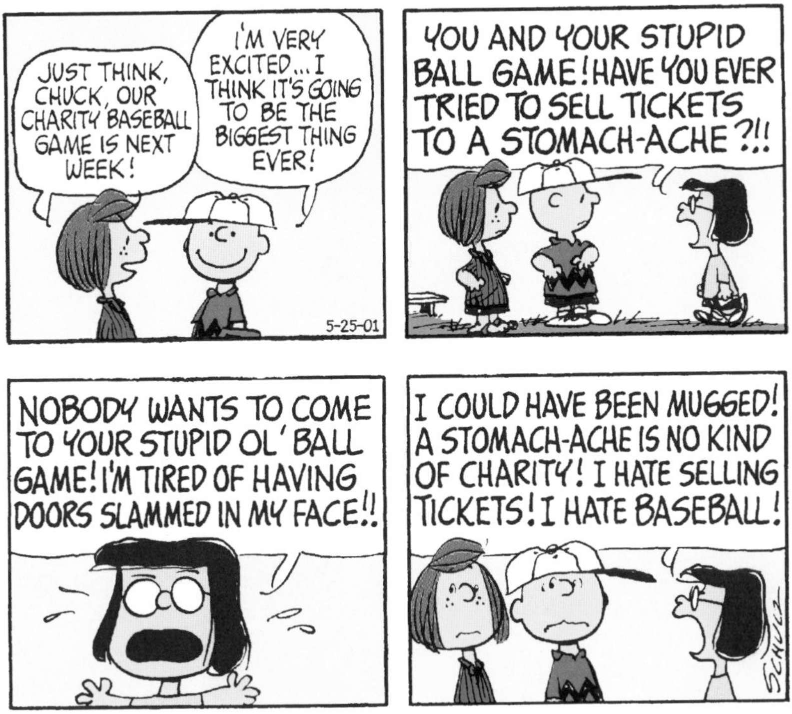
JUST THINK, CHUCK, OUR CHARITY BASEBALL GAME IS NEXT WEEK!
I'M VERY EXCITED... I THINK IT'S GOING TO BE THE BIGGEST THING EVER!
5-25-01
YOU AND YOUR STUPID BALL GAME! HAVE YOU EVER TRIED TO SELL TICKETS TO A STOMACH-ACHE?!!
NOBODY WANTS TO COME TO YOUR STUPID OL' BALL GAME! I'M TIRED OF HAVING DOORS SLAMMED IN MY FACE!!
I COULD HAVE BEEN MUGGED! A STOMACH-ACHE IS NO KIND OF CHARITY! I HATE SELLING TICKETS! I HATE BASEBALL!
SCHULZ

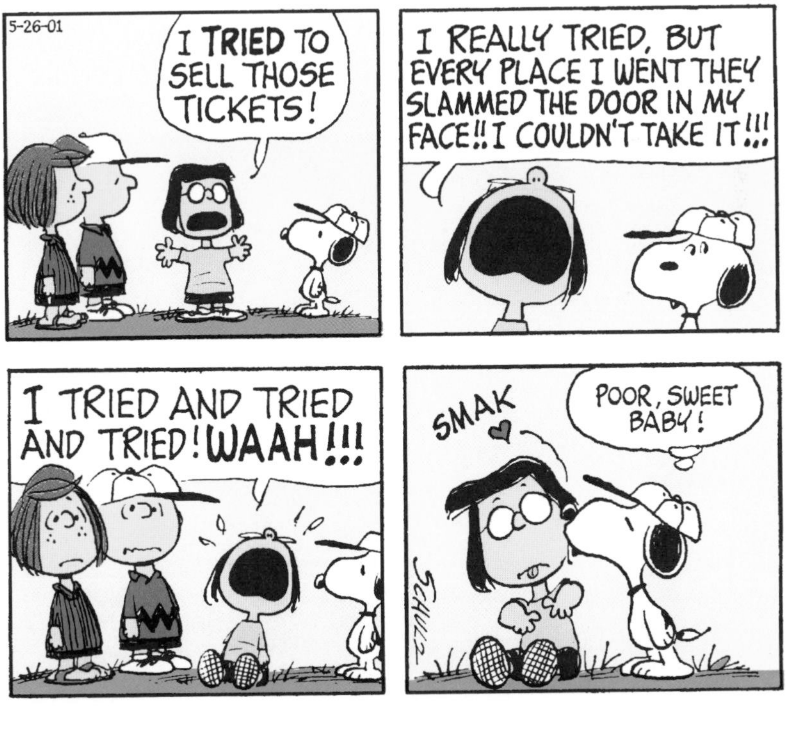
5-26-01
I TRIED TO SELL THOSE TICKETS!
I REALLY TRIED, BUT EVERY PLACE I WENT THEY SLAMMED THE DOOR IN MY FACE!! I COULDN'T TAKE IT!!!
I TRIED AND TRIED AND TRIED! WAAH!!!
SCHULZ
SMAK
POOR, SWEET BABY!

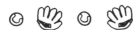

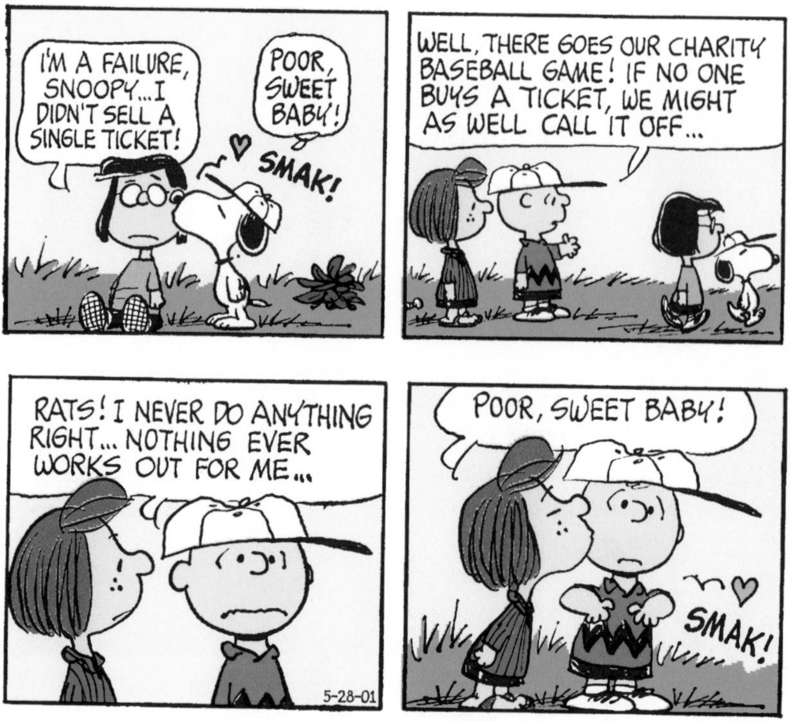
I'M A FAILURE, SNOOPY...I DIDN'T SELL A SINGLE TICKET!
POOR, SWEET BABY!
SMAK!
WELL, THERE GOES OUR CHARITY BASEBALL GAME! IF NO ONE BUYS A TICKET, WE MIGHT AS WELL CALL IT OFF...
RATS! I NEVER DO ANYTHING RIGHT... NOTHING EVER WORKS OUT FOR ME...
5-28-01
POOR, SWEET BABY!
SMAK!

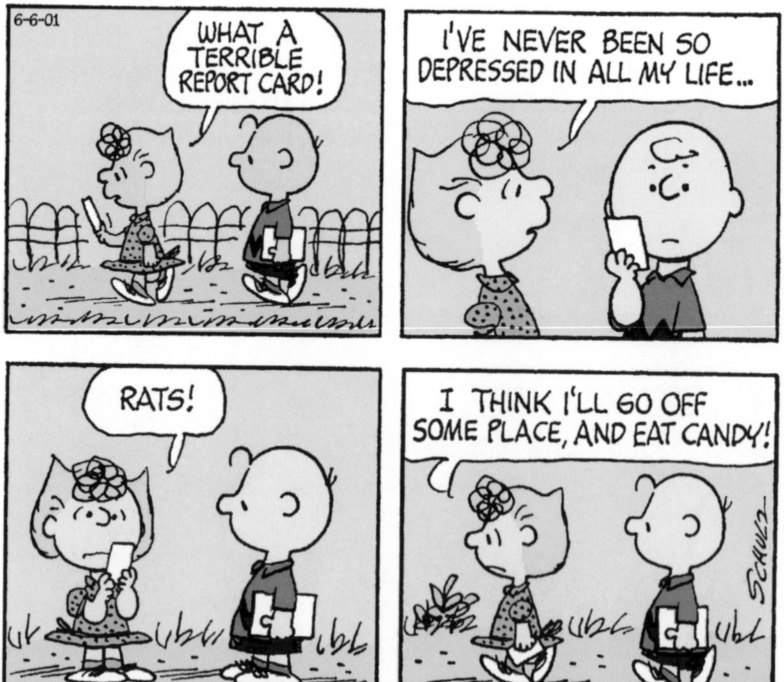
6-6-01
WHAT A TERRIBLE REPORT CARD!
I'VE NEVER BEEN SO DEPRESSED IN ALL MY LIFE...
RATS!
I THINK I'LL GO OFF SOME PLACE, AND EAT CANDY!
SCHULZ

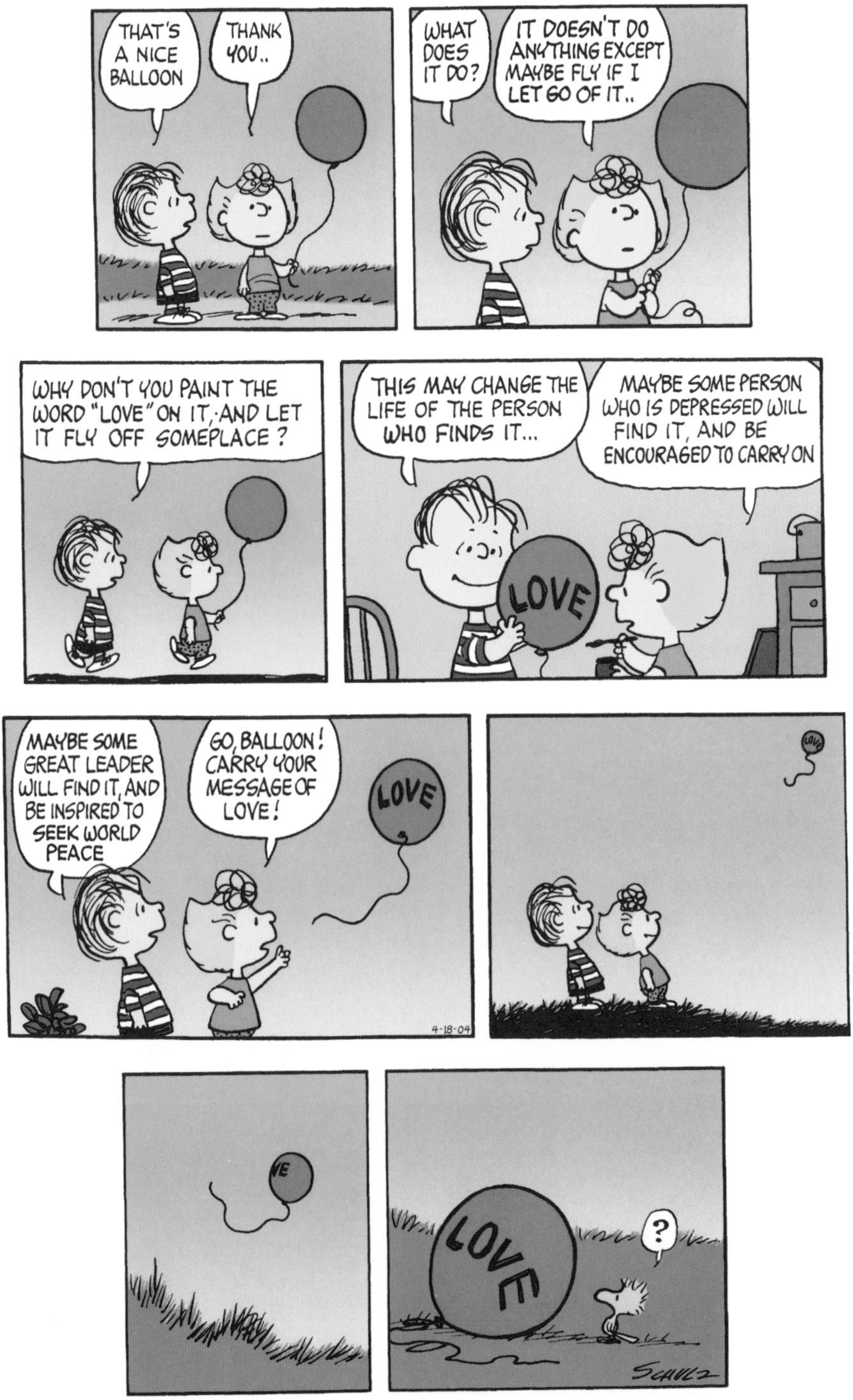
THAT'S A NICE BALLOON
THANK YOU..
WHAT DOES IT DO?
IT DOESN'T DO ANYTHING EXCEPT MAYBE FLY IF I LET GO OF IT..
WHY DON'T YOU PAINT THE WORD "LOVE" ON IT, AND LET IT FLY OFF SOMEPLACE?
THIS MAY CHANGE THE LIFE OF THE PERSON WHO FINDS IT...
MAYBE SOME PERSON WHO IS DEPRESSED WILL FIND IT, AND BE ENCOURAGED TO CARRY ON
LOVE
MAYBE SOME GREAT LEADER WILL FIND IT, AND BE INSPIRED TO SEEK WORLD PEACE
GO, BALLOON! CARRY YOUR MESSAGE OF LOVE!
LOVE
4-18-04
LOVE
?
LOVE
SCHULZ

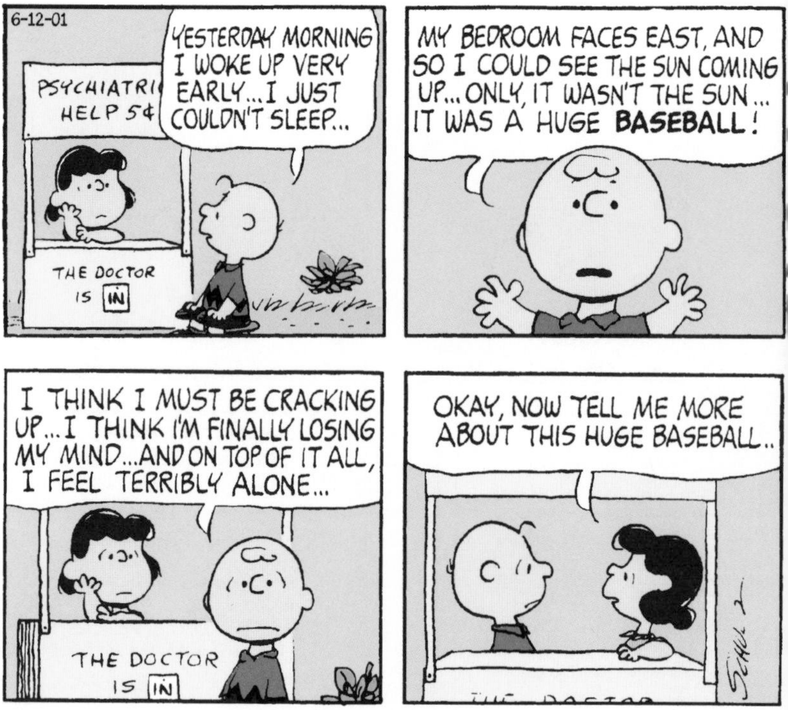
6-12-01
PSYCHIATRIC HELP 5¢
THE DOCTOR IS IN
YESTERDAY MORNING I WOKE UP VERY EARLY...I JUST COULDN'T SLEEP...
MY BEDROOM FACES EAST, AND SO I COULD SEE THE SUN COMING UP...ONLY, IT WASN'T THE SUN... IT WAS A HUGE **BASEBALL**!
I THINK I MUST BE CRACKING UP...I THINK I'M FINALLY LOSING MY MIND...AND ON TOP OF IT ALL, I FEEL TERRIBLY ALONE...
THE DOCTOR IS IN
OKAY, NOW TELL ME MORE ABOUT THIS HUGE BASEBALL..

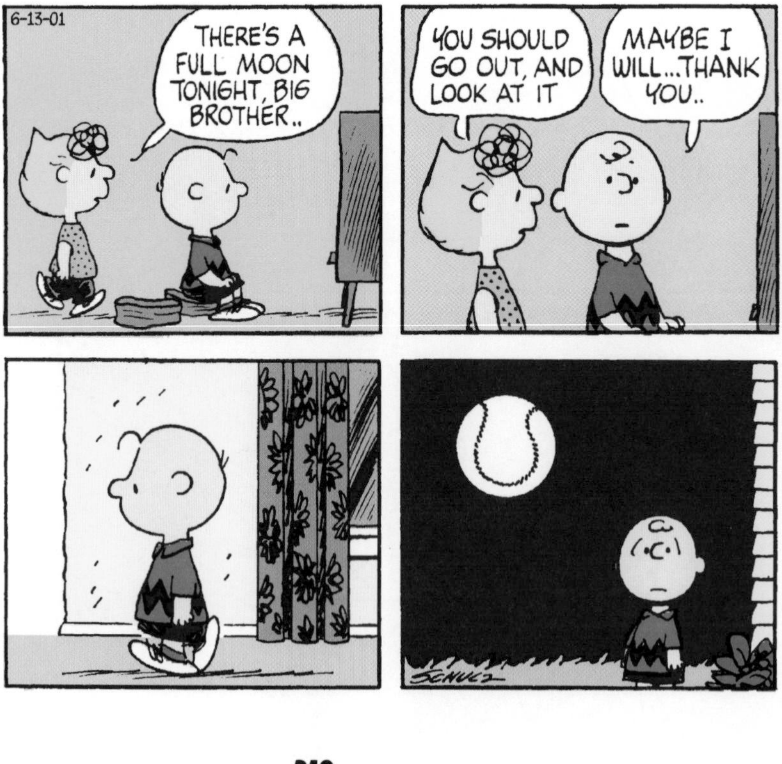
6-13-01
THERE'S A FULL MOON TONIGHT, BIG BROTHER..
YOU SHOULD GO OUT, AND LOOK AT IT
MAYBE I WILL...THANK YOU..

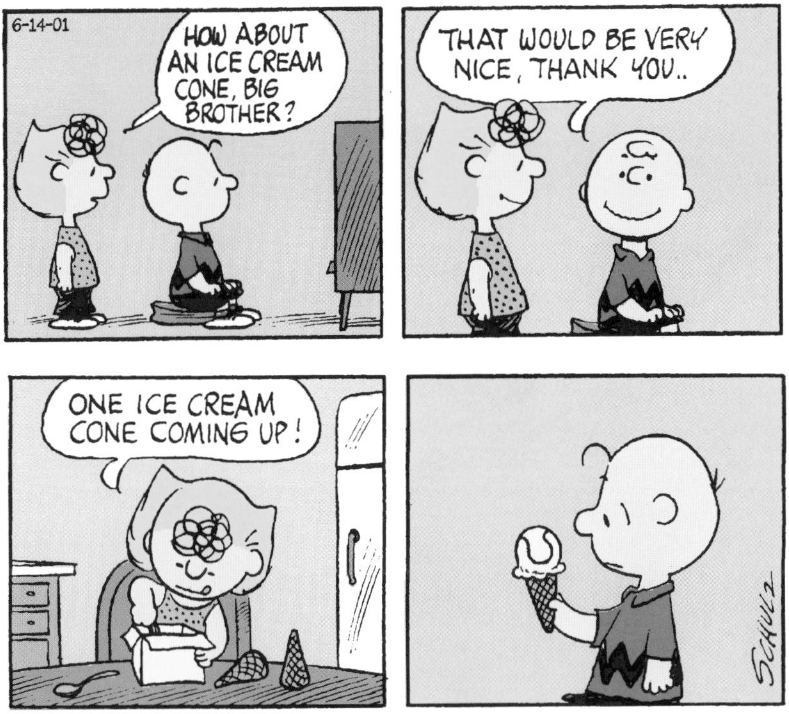
6-14-01
HOW ABOUT AN ICE CREAM CONE, BIG BROTHER?
THAT WOULD BE VERY NICE, THANK YOU..
ONE ICE CREAM CONE COMING UP!
SCHULZ

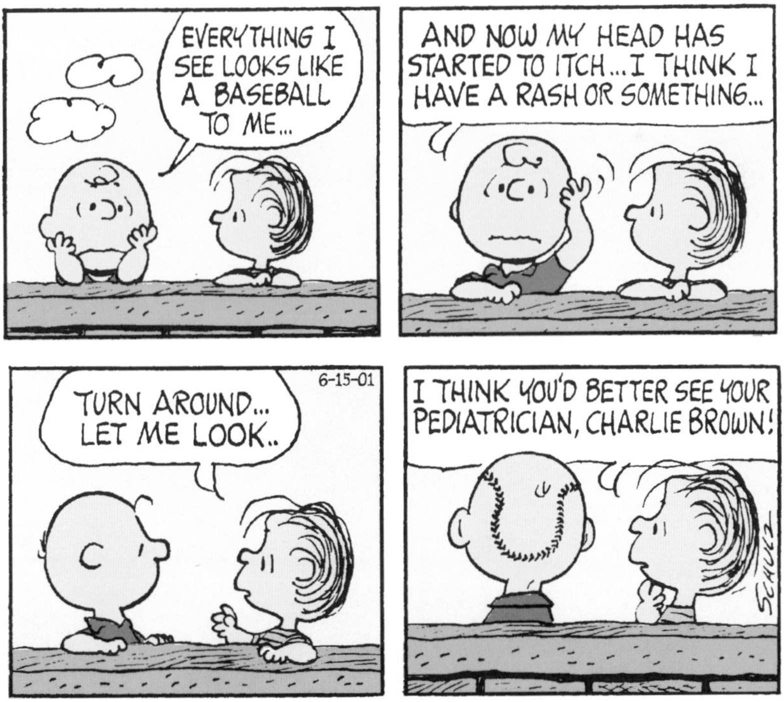
EVERYTHING I SEE LOOKS LIKE A BASEBALL TO ME...
AND NOW MY HEAD HAS STARTED TO ITCH...I THINK I HAVE A RASH OR SOMETHING...
6-15-01
TURN AROUND... LET ME LOOK..
I THINK YOU'D BETTER SEE YOUR PEDIATRICIAN, CHARLIE BROWN!
SCHULZ

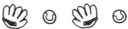

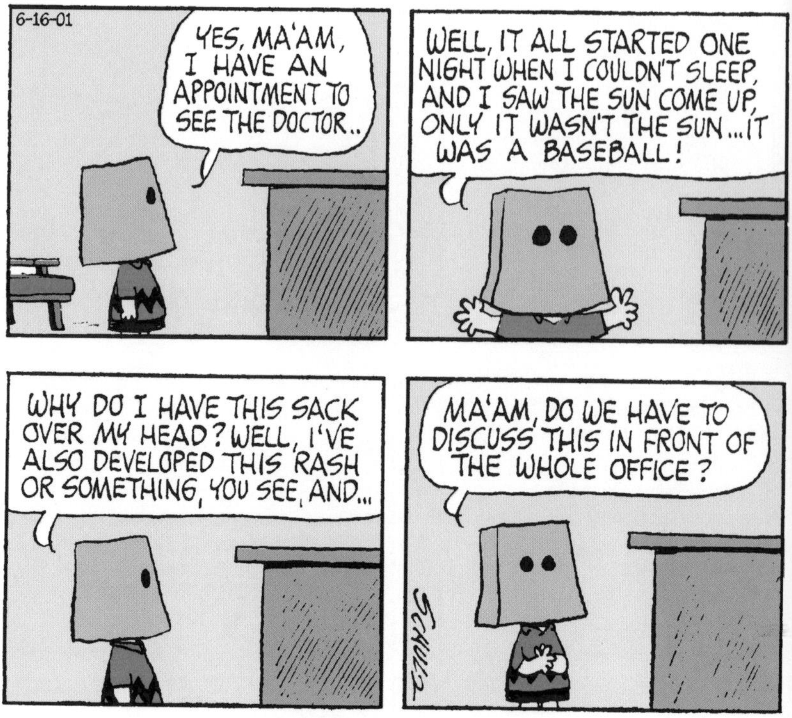
6-16-01
YES, MA'AM, I HAVE AN APPOINTMENT TO SEE THE DOCTOR..
WELL, IT ALL STARTED ONE NIGHT WHEN I COULDN'T SLEEP, AND I SAW THE SUN COME UP, ONLY IT WASN'T THE SUN...IT WAS A BASEBALL!
WHY DO I HAVE THIS SACK OVER MY HEAD? WELL, I'VE ALSO DEVELOPED THIS RASH OR SOMETHING, YOU SEE, AND...
MA'AM, DO WE HAVE TO DISCUSS THIS IN FRONT OF THE WHOLE OFFICE?
SCHULZ

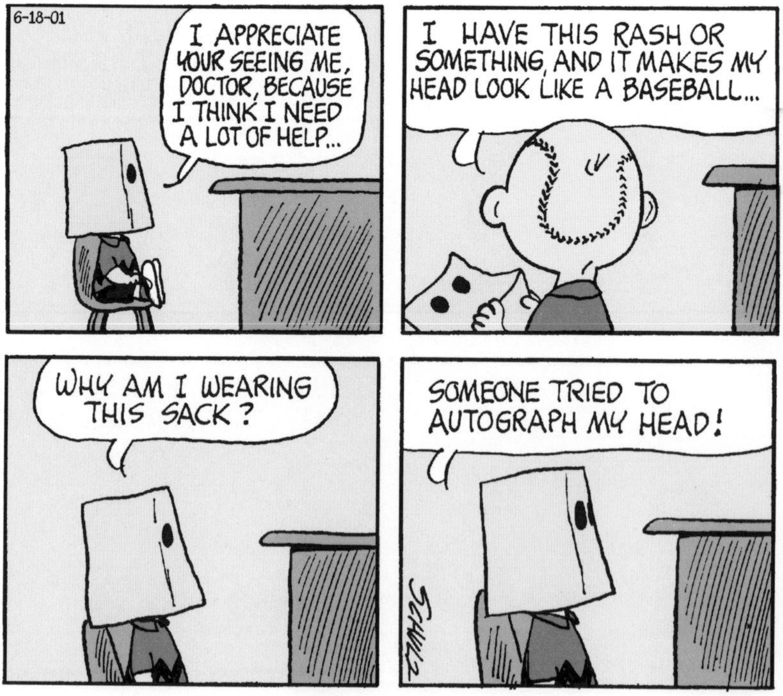
6-18-01
I APPRECIATE YOUR SEEING ME, DOCTOR, BECAUSE I THINK I NEED A LOT OF HELP...
I HAVE THIS RASH OR SOMETHING, AND IT MAKES MY HEAD LOOK LIKE A BASEBALL...
WHY AM I WEARING THIS SACK?
SOMEONE TRIED TO AUTOGRAPH MY HEAD!
SCHULZ

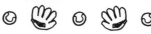

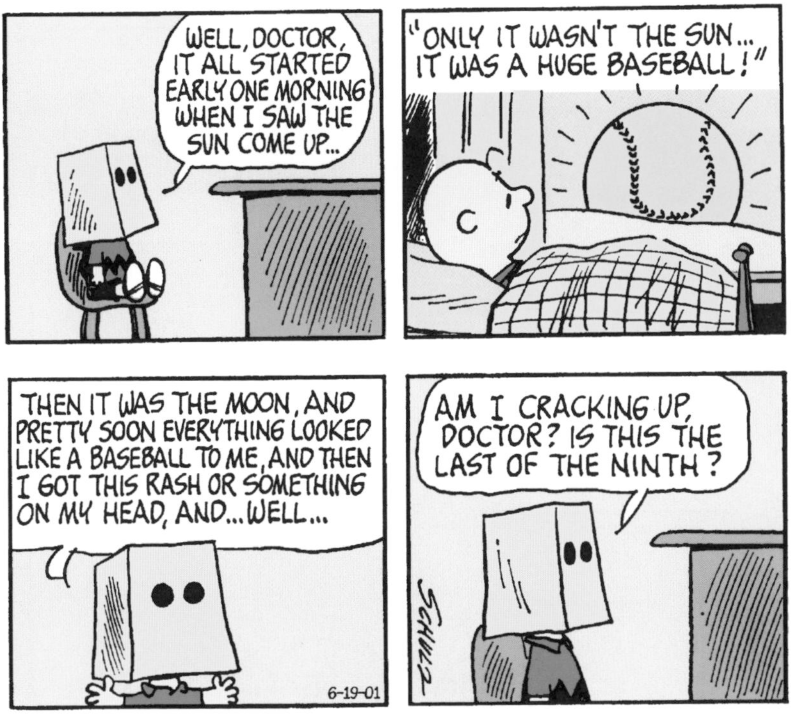

WELL, DOCTOR, IT ALL STARTED EARLY ONE MORNING WHEN I SAW THE SUN COME UP...
"ONLY IT WASN'T THE SUN... IT WAS A HUGE BASEBALL!"
THEN IT WAS THE MOON, AND PRETTY SOON EVERYTHING LOOKED LIKE A BASEBALL TO ME, AND THEN I GOT THIS RASH OR SOMETHING ON MY HEAD, AND...WELL...
6-19-01
AM I CRACKING UP, DOCTOR? IS THIS THE LAST OF THE NINTH?
SCHULZ

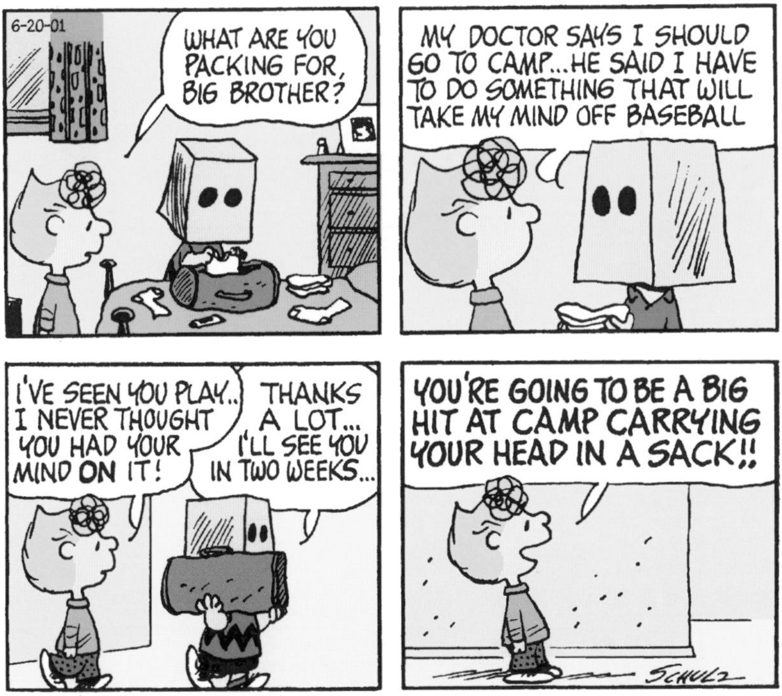

6-20-01
WHAT ARE YOU PACKING FOR, BIG BROTHER?
MY DOCTOR SAYS I SHOULD GO TO CAMP...HE SAID I HAVE TO DO SOMETHING THAT WILL TAKE MY MIND OFF BASEBALL
I'VE SEEN YOU PLAY.. I NEVER THOUGHT YOU HAD YOUR MIND ON IT!
THANKS A LOT... I'LL SEE YOU IN TWO WEEKS...
YOU'RE GOING TO BE A BIG HIT AT CAMP CARRYING YOUR HEAD IN A SACK!!
SCHULZ

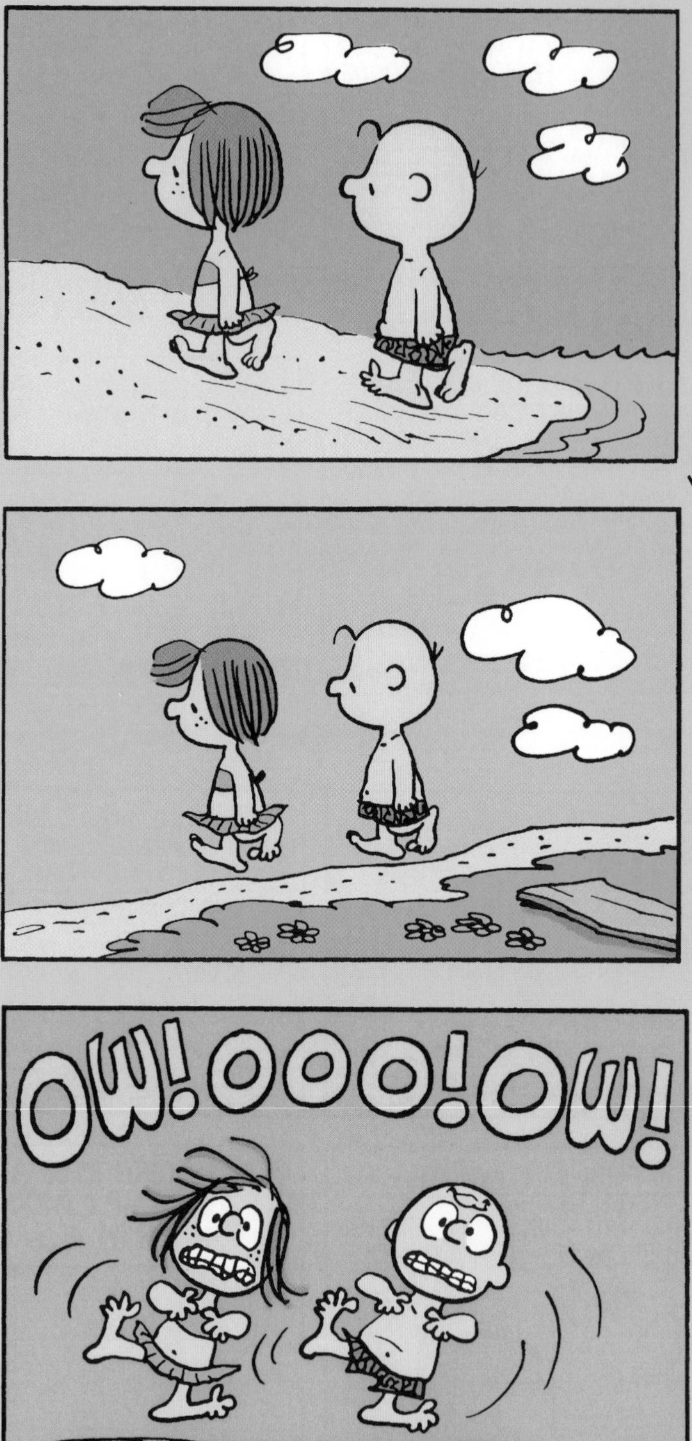
OW! OOO! OW!

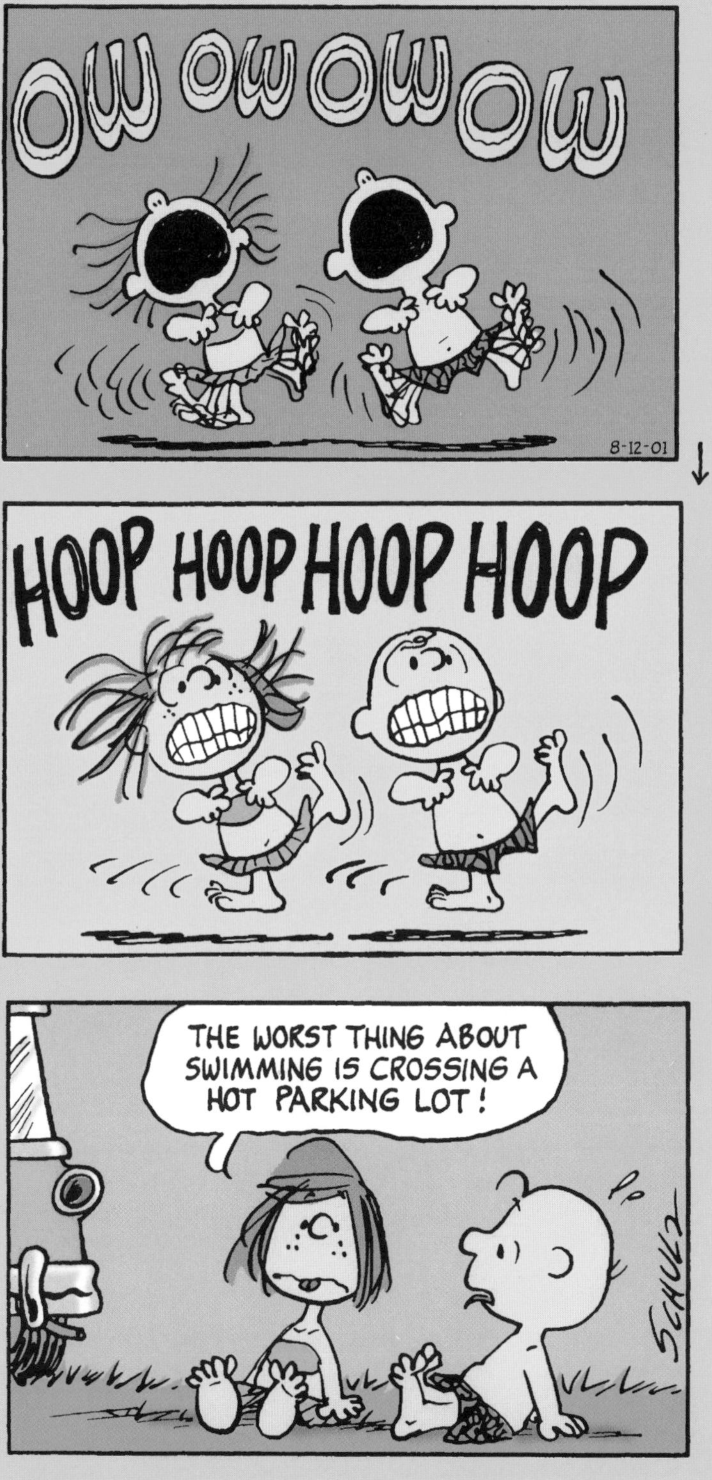
OW OW OW OW OW
8-12-01
HOOP HOOP HOOP HOOP
THE WORST THING ABOUT SWIMMING IS CROSSING A HOT PARKING LOT!
SCHULZ

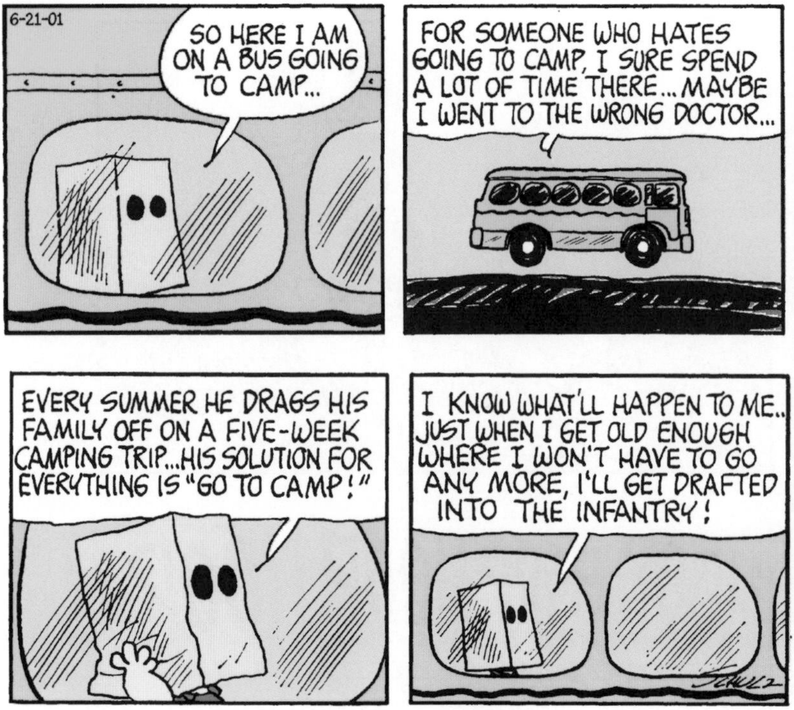
6-21-01
SO HERE I AM ON A BUS GOING TO CAMP...
FOR SOMEONE WHO HATES GOING TO CAMP, I SURE SPEND A LOT OF TIME THERE... MAYBE I WENT TO THE WRONG DOCTOR...
EVERY SUMMER HE DRAGS HIS FAMILY OFF ON A FIVE-WEEK CAMPING TRIP...HIS SOLUTION FOR EVERYTHING IS "GO TO CAMP!"
I KNOW WHAT'LL HAPPEN TO ME.. JUST WHEN I GET OLD ENOUGH WHERE I WON'T HAVE TO GO ANY MORE, I'LL GET DRAFTED INTO THE INFANTRY!

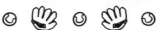

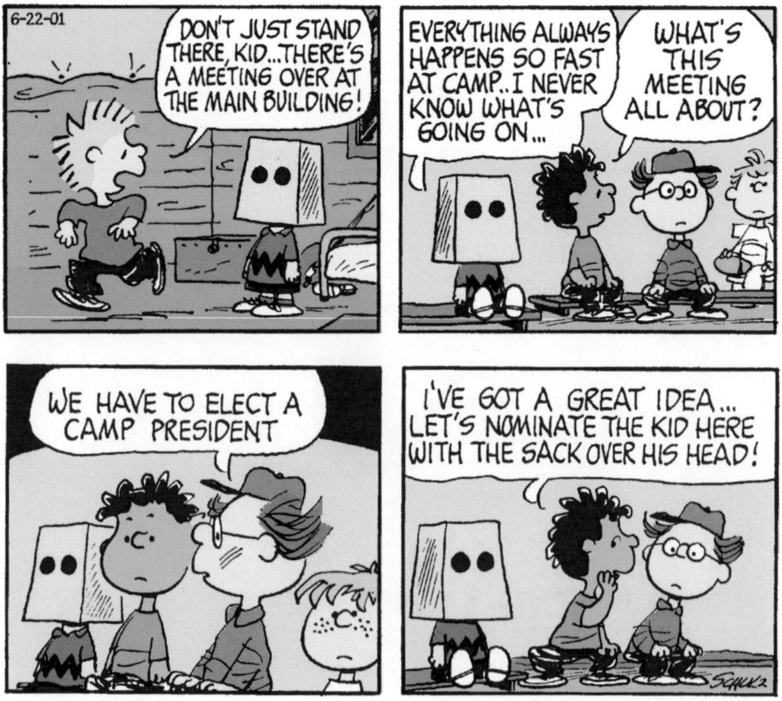
6-22-01
DON'T JUST STAND THERE, KID...THERE'S A MEETING OVER AT THE MAIN BUILDING!
EVERYTHING ALWAYS HAPPENS SO FAST AT CAMP..I NEVER KNOW WHAT'S GOING ON...
WHAT'S THIS MEETING ALL ABOUT?
WE HAVE TO ELECT A CAMP PRESIDENT
I'VE GOT A GREAT IDEA... LET'S NOMINATE THE KID HERE WITH THE SACK OVER HIS HEAD!

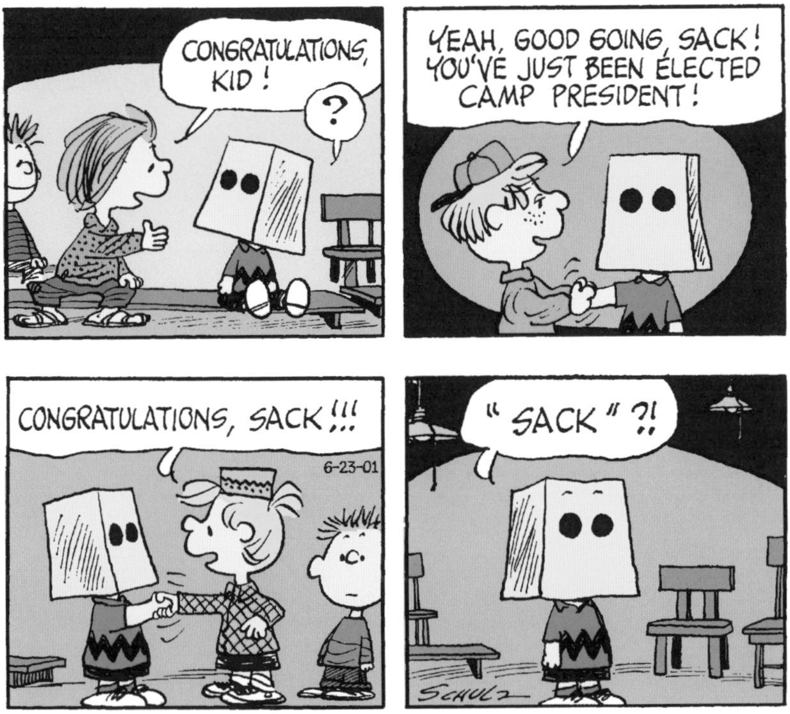
CONGRATULATIONS, KID!
?
YEAH, GOOD GOING, SACK! YOU'VE JUST BEEN ELECTED CAMP PRESIDENT!
CONGRATULATIONS, SACK!!!
6-23-01
"SACK"?!
SCHULZ

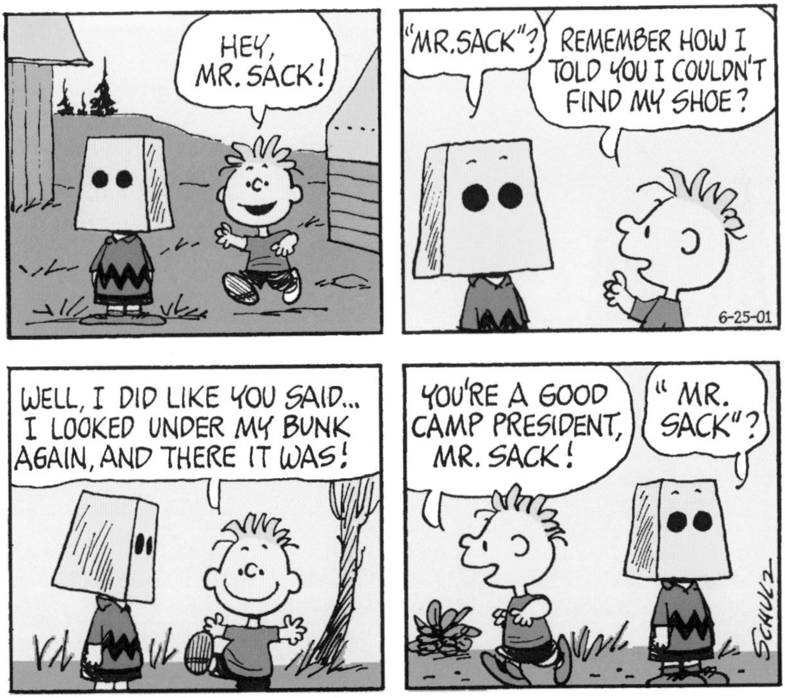
HEY, MR. SACK!
"MR.SACK"?
REMEMBER HOW I TOLD YOU I COULDN'T FIND MY SHOE?
6-25-01
WELL, I DID LIKE YOU SAID... I LOOKED UNDER MY BUNK AGAIN, AND THERE IT WAS!
YOU'RE A GOOD CAMP PRESIDENT, MR. SACK!
"MR. SACK"?
SCHULZ

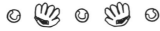

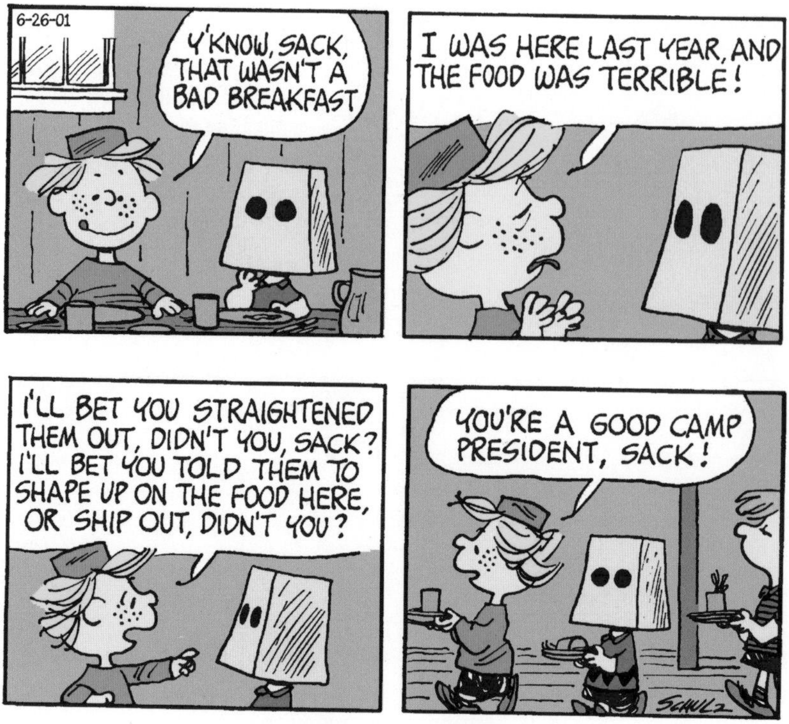
6-26-01
Y'KNOW, SACK, THAT WASN'T A BAD BREAKFAST
I WAS HERE LAST YEAR, AND THE FOOD WAS TERRIBLE!
I'LL BET YOU STRAIGHTENED THEM OUT, DIDN'T YOU, SACK? I'LL BET YOU TOLD THEM TO SHAPE UP ON THE FOOD HERE, OR SHIP OUT, DIDN'T YOU?
YOU'RE A GOOD CAMP PRESIDENT, SACK!
SCHULZ

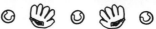

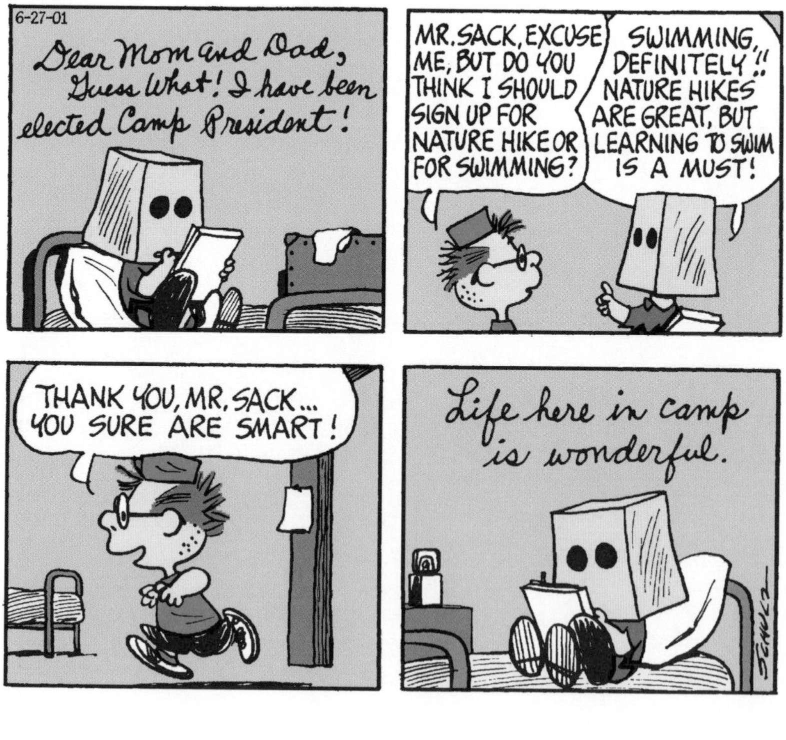
6-27-01
Dear Mom and Dad, Guess What! I have been elected Camp President!
MR. SACK, EXCUSE ME, BUT DO YOU THINK I SHOULD SIGN UP FOR NATURE HIKE OR FOR SWIMMING?
SWIMMING, DEFINITELY!! NATURE HIKES ARE GREAT, BUT LEARNING TO SWIM IS A MUST!
THANK YOU, MR. SACK... YOU SURE ARE SMART!
Life here in camp is wonderful.
SCHULZ

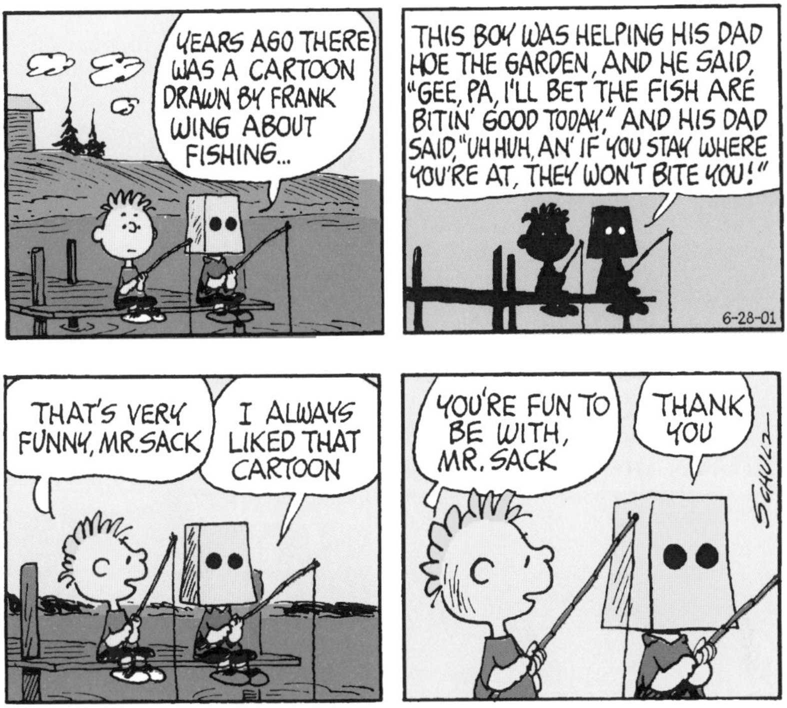
YEARS AGO THERE WAS A CARTOON DRAWN BY FRANK WING ABOUT FISHING...
THIS BOY WAS HELPING HIS DAD HOE THE GARDEN, AND HE SAID, "GEE, PA, I'LL BET THE FISH ARE BITIN' GOOD TODAY," AND HIS DAD SAID, "UH HUH, AN' IF YOU STAY WHERE YOU'RE AT, THEY WON'T BITE YOU!"
6-28-01
THAT'S VERY FUNNY, MR. SACK
I ALWAYS LIKED THAT CARTOON
YOU'RE FUN TO BE WITH, MR. SACK
THANK YOU
SCHULZ

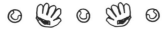

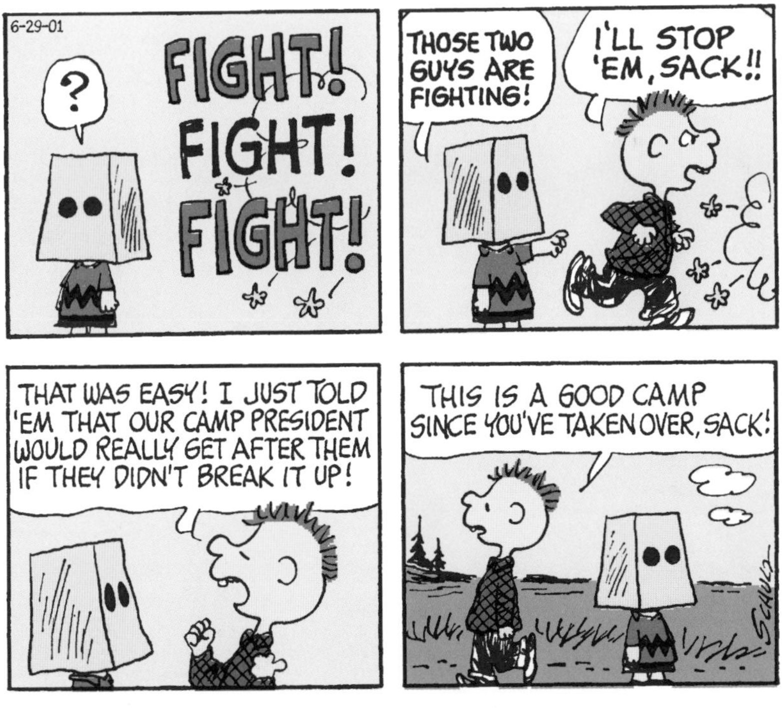
6-29-01
?
FIGHT! FIGHT! FIGHT!
THOSE TWO GUYS ARE FIGHTING!
I'LL STOP 'EM, SACK!!
THAT WAS EASY! I JUST TOLD 'EM THAT OUR CAMP PRESIDENT WOULD REALLY GET AFTER THEM IF THEY DIDN'T BREAK IT UP!
THIS IS A GOOD CAMP SINCE YOU'VE TAKEN OVER, SACK!
SCHULZ

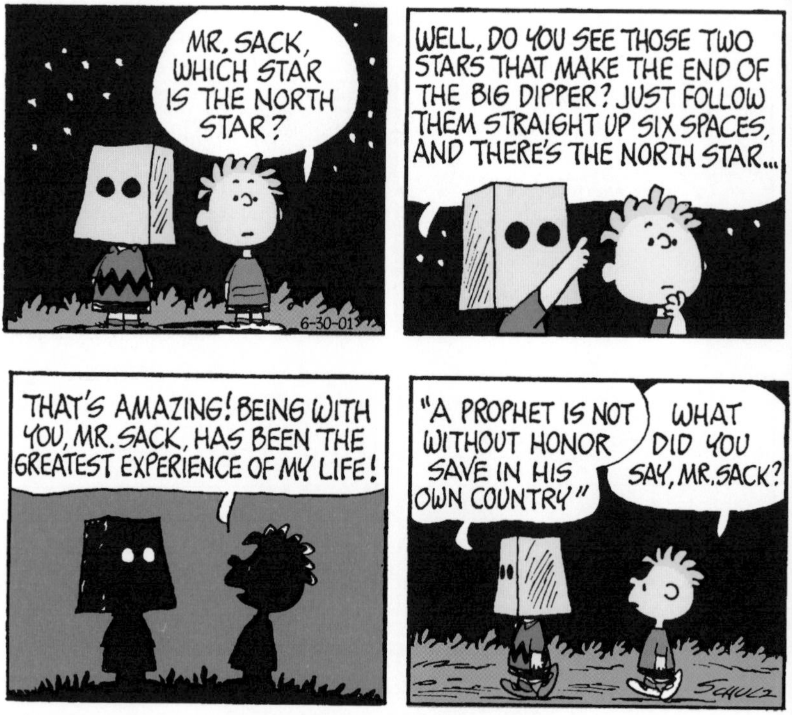
MR. SACK, WHICH STAR IS THE NORTH STAR?
6-30-01
WELL, DO YOU SEE THOSE TWO STARS THAT MAKE THE END OF THE BIG DIPPER? JUST FOLLOW THEM STRAIGHT UP SIX SPACES, AND THERE'S THE NORTH STAR...
THAT'S AMAZING! BEING WITH YOU, MR. SACK, HAS BEEN THE GREATEST EXPERIENCE OF MY LIFE!
"A PROPHET IS NOT WITHOUT HONOR SAVE IN HIS OWN COUNTRY"
WHAT DID YOU SAY, MR. SACK?
SCHULZ

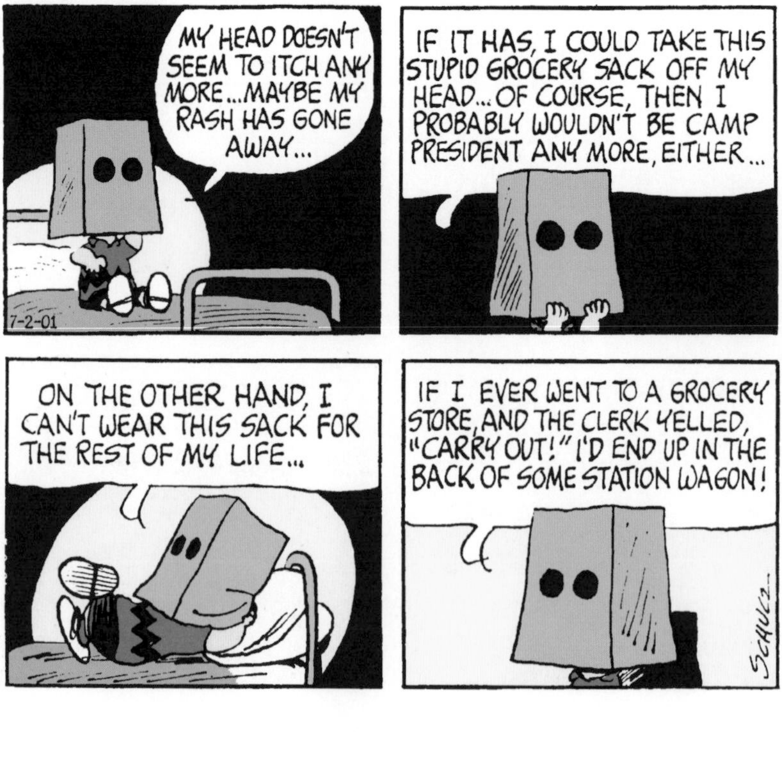
MY HEAD DOESN'T SEEM TO ITCH ANY MORE...MAYBE MY RASH HAS GONE AWAY...
7-2-01
IF IT HAS, I COULD TAKE THIS STUPID GROCERY SACK OFF MY HEAD...OF COURSE, THEN I PROBABLY WOULDN'T BE CAMP PRESIDENT ANY MORE, EITHER...
ON THE OTHER HAND, I CAN'T WEAR THIS SACK FOR THE REST OF MY LIFE...
IF I EVER WENT TO A GROCERY STORE, AND THE CLERK YELLED, "CARRY OUT!" I'D END UP IN THE BACK OF SOME STATION WAGON!
SCHULZ

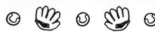

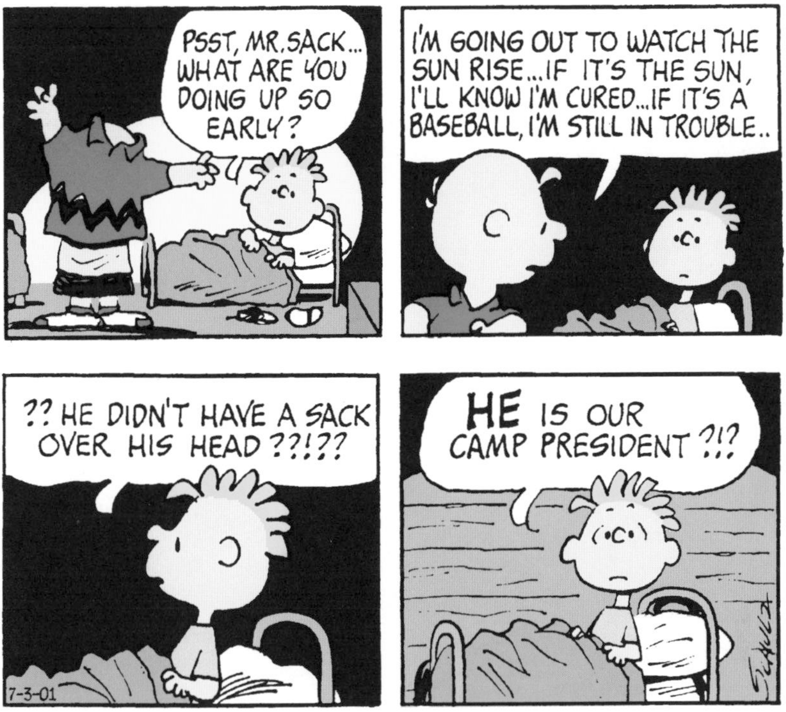
PSST, MR. SACK... WHAT ARE YOU DOING UP SO EARLY?
I'M GOING OUT TO WATCH THE SUN RISE...IF IT'S THE SUN, I'LL KNOW I'M CURED...IF IT'S A BASEBALL, I'M STILL IN TROUBLE..
?? HE DIDN'T HAVE A SACK OVER HIS HEAD ??!??
7-3-01
HE IS OUR CAMP PRESIDENT ?!?

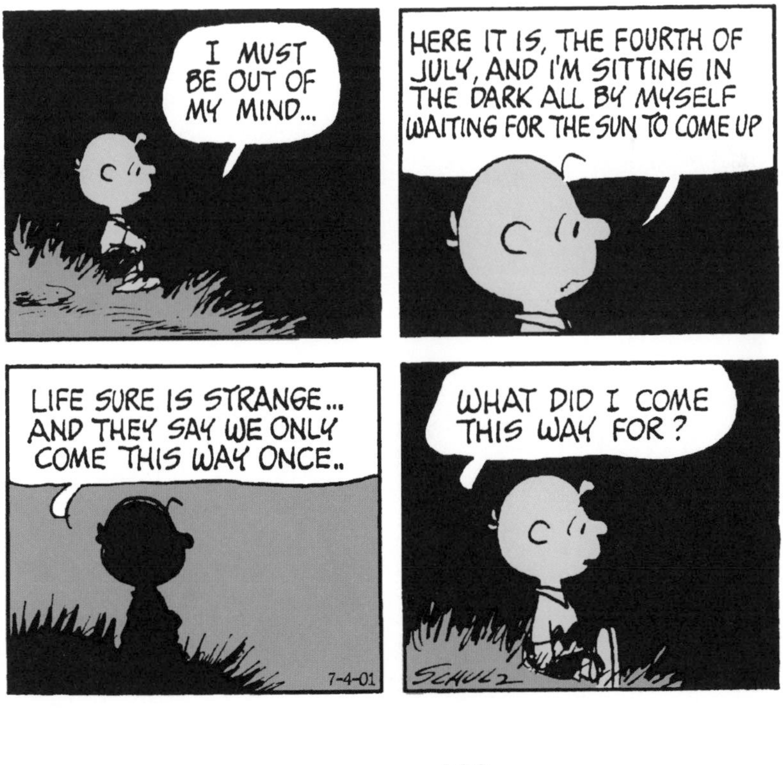
I MUST BE OUT OF MY MIND...
HERE IT IS, THE FOURTH OF JULY, AND I'M SITTING IN THE DARK ALL BY MYSELF WAITING FOR THE SUN TO COME UP
LIFE SURE IS STRANGE... AND THEY SAY WE ONLY COME THIS WAY ONCE..
7-4-01
WHAT DID I COME THIS WAY FOR?
SCHULZ

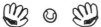

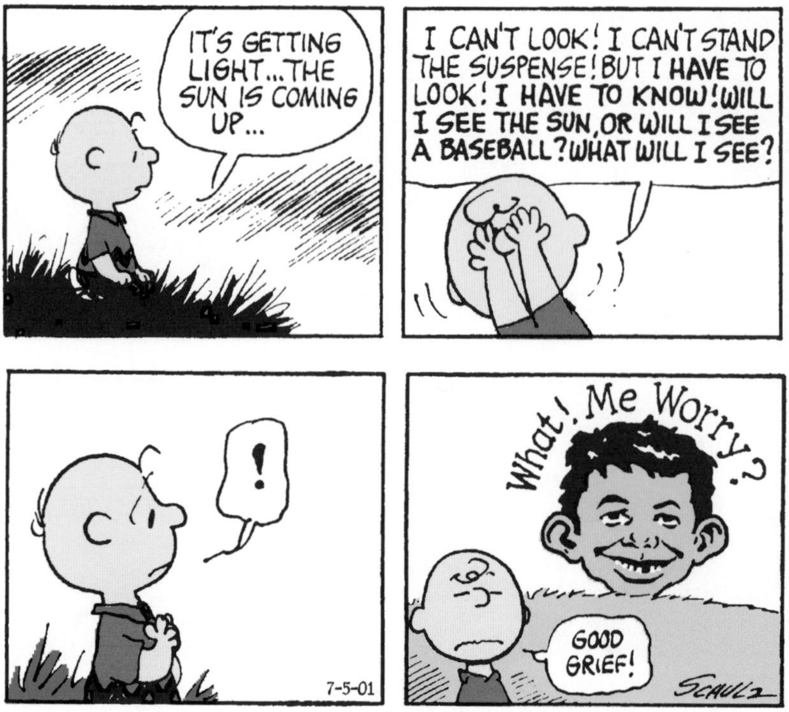

IT'S GETTING LIGHT...THE SUN IS COMING UP...
I CAN'T LOOK! I CAN'T STAND THE SUSPENSE! BUT I HAVE TO LOOK! I HAVE TO KNOW! WILL I SEE THE SUN, OR WILL I SEE A BASEBALL? WHAT WILL I SEE?
!
7-5-01
What, Me Worry?
GOOD GRIEF!
SCHULZ

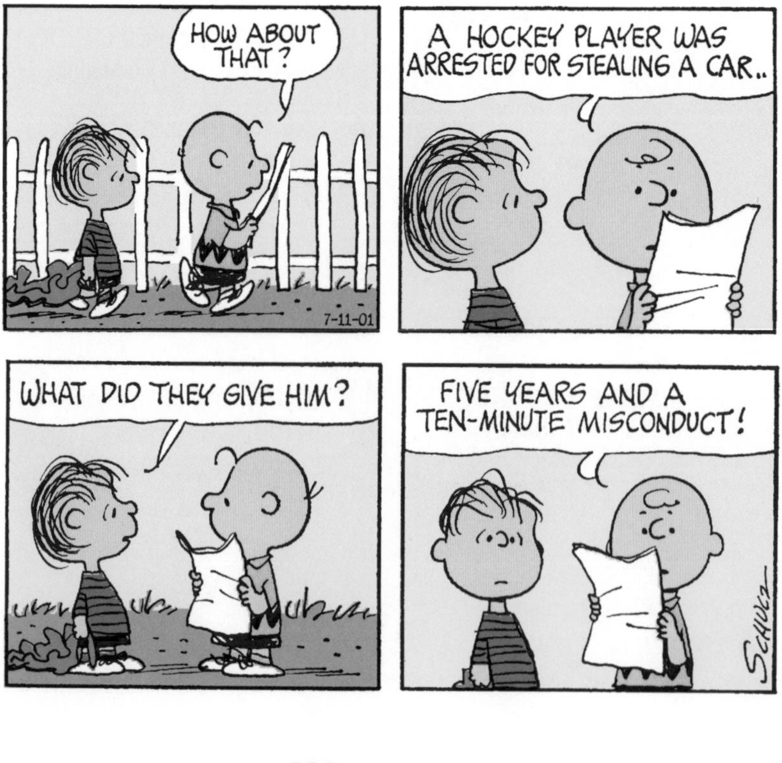

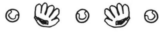

HOW ABOUT THAT?
7-11-01
A HOCKEY PLAYER WAS ARRESTED FOR STEALING A CAR..
WHAT DID THEY GIVE HIM?
FIVE YEARS AND A TEN-MINUTE MISCONDUCT!
SCHULZ

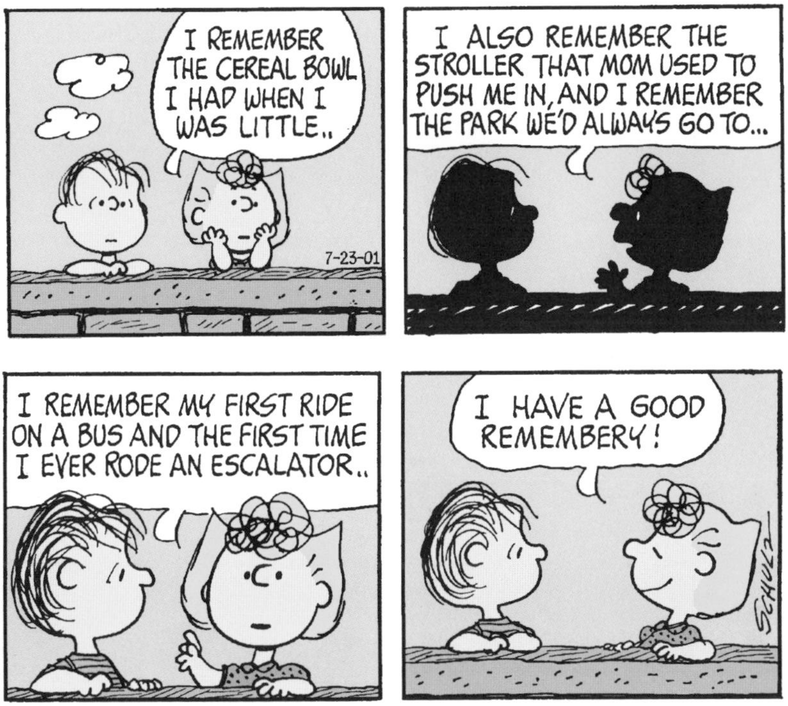
I REMEMBER THE CEREAL BOWL I HAD WHEN I WAS LITTLE..
7-23-01
I ALSO REMEMBER THE STROLLER THAT MOM USED TO PUSH ME IN, AND I REMEMBER THE PARK WE'D ALWAYS GO TO...
I REMEMBER MY FIRST RIDE ON A BUS AND THE FIRST TIME I EVER RODE AN ESCALATOR..
I HAVE A GOOD REMEMBERY!
SCHULZ

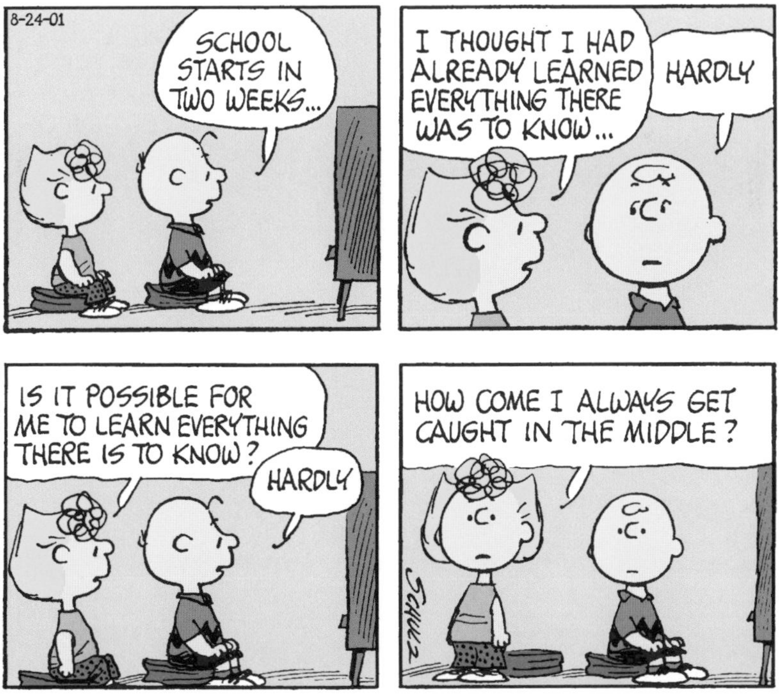
8-24-01
SCHOOL STARTS IN TWO WEEKS...
I THOUGHT I HAD ALREADY LEARNED EVERYTHING THERE WAS TO KNOW...
HARDLY
IS IT POSSIBLE FOR ME TO LEARN EVERYTHING THERE IS TO KNOW?
HARDLY
HOW COME I ALWAYS GET CAUGHT IN THE MIDDLE?
SCHULZ

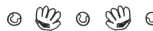

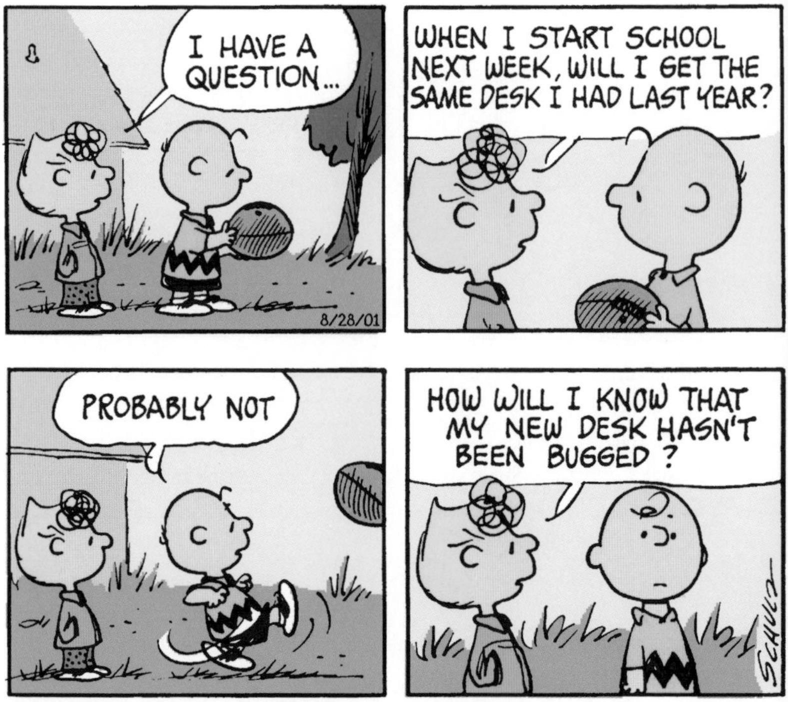
I HAVE A QUESTION...
8/28/01
WHEN I START SCHOOL NEXT WEEK, WILL I GET THE SAME DESK I HAD LAST YEAR?
PROBABLY NOT
HOW WILL I KNOW THAT MY NEW DESK HASN'T BEEN BUGGED?
SCHULZ

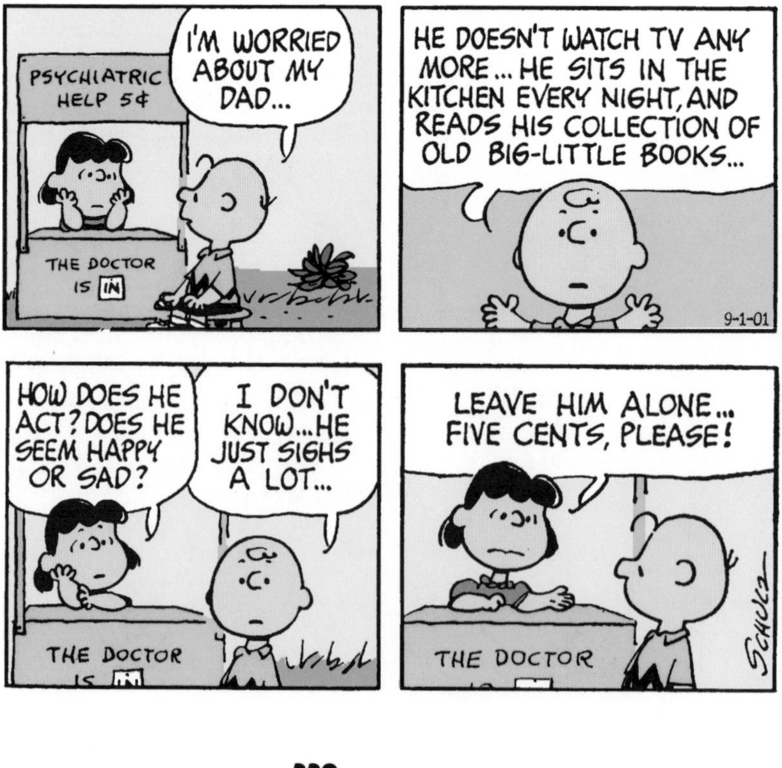
PSYCHIATRIC HELP 5¢
THE DOCTOR IS IN
I'M WORRIED ABOUT MY DAD...
HE DOESN'T WATCH TV ANY MORE... HE SITS IN THE KITCHEN EVERY NIGHT, AND READS HIS COLLECTION OF OLD BIG-LITTLE BOOKS...
9-1-01
HOW DOES HE ACT? DOES HE SEEM HAPPY OR SAD?
I DON'T KNOW...HE JUST SIGHS A LOT...
THE DOCTOR
LEAVE HIM ALONE... FIVE CENTS, PLEASE!
THE DOCTOR
SCHULZ

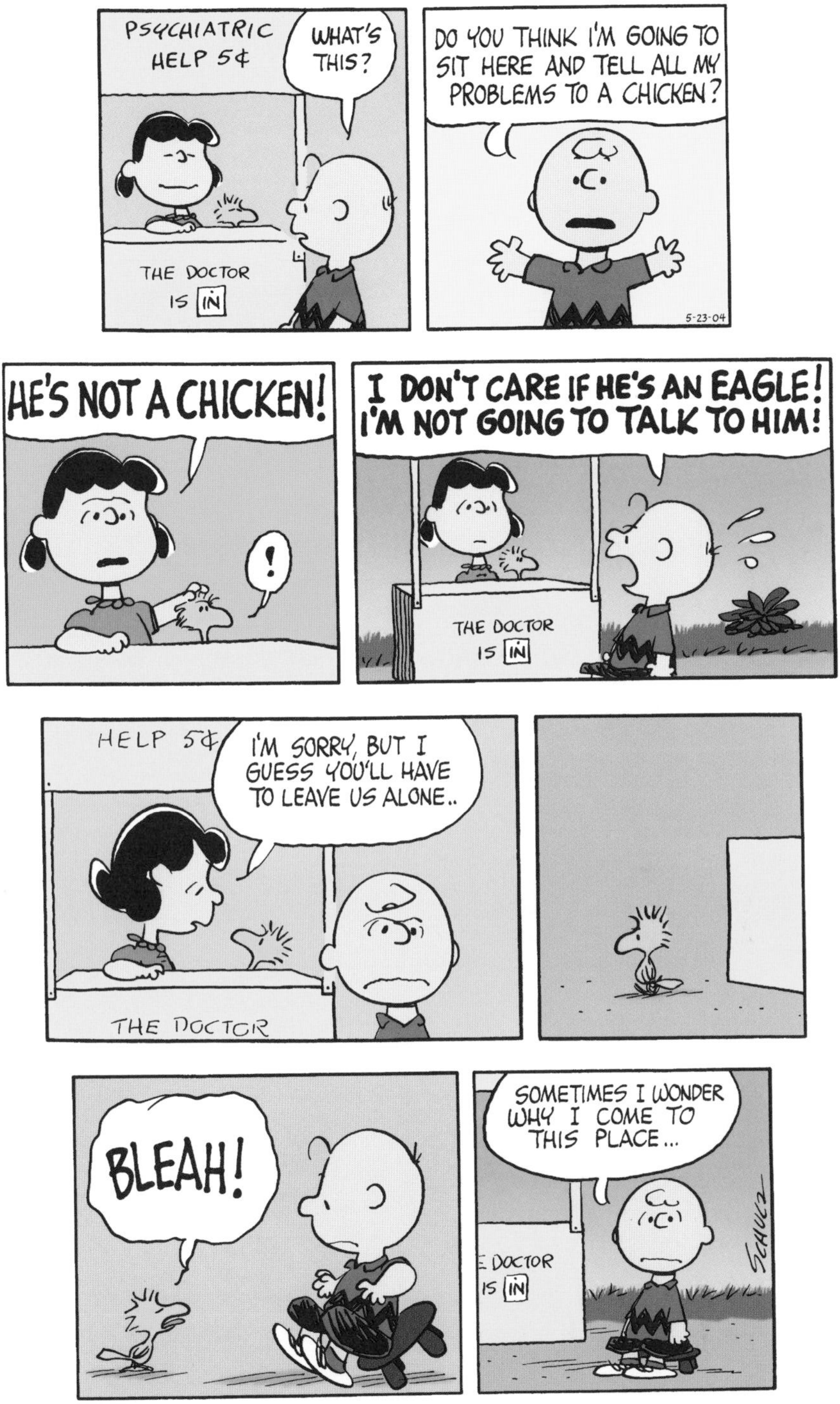
PSYCHIATRIC HELP 5¢
WHAT'S THIS?
THE DOCTOR IS IN
DO YOU THINK I'M GOING TO SIT HERE AND TELL ALL MY PROBLEMS TO A CHICKEN?
5-23-04
HE'S NOT A CHICKEN!
!
I DON'T CARE IF HE'S AN EAGLE! I'M NOT GOING TO TALK TO HIM!
THE DOCTOR IS IN
HELP 5¢
I'M SORRY, BUT I GUESS YOU'LL HAVE TO LEAVE US ALONE..
THE DOCTOR
BLEAH!
SOMETIMES I WONDER WHY I COME TO THIS PLACE...
E DOCTOR IS IN
SCHULZ

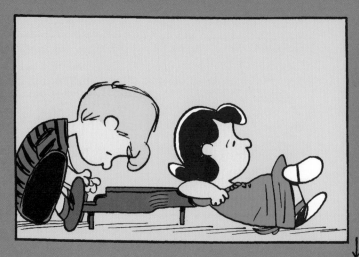

I'LL BET I KNOW SOMETHING YOU DON'T KNOW...

WHAT'S THAT?

8-15-04

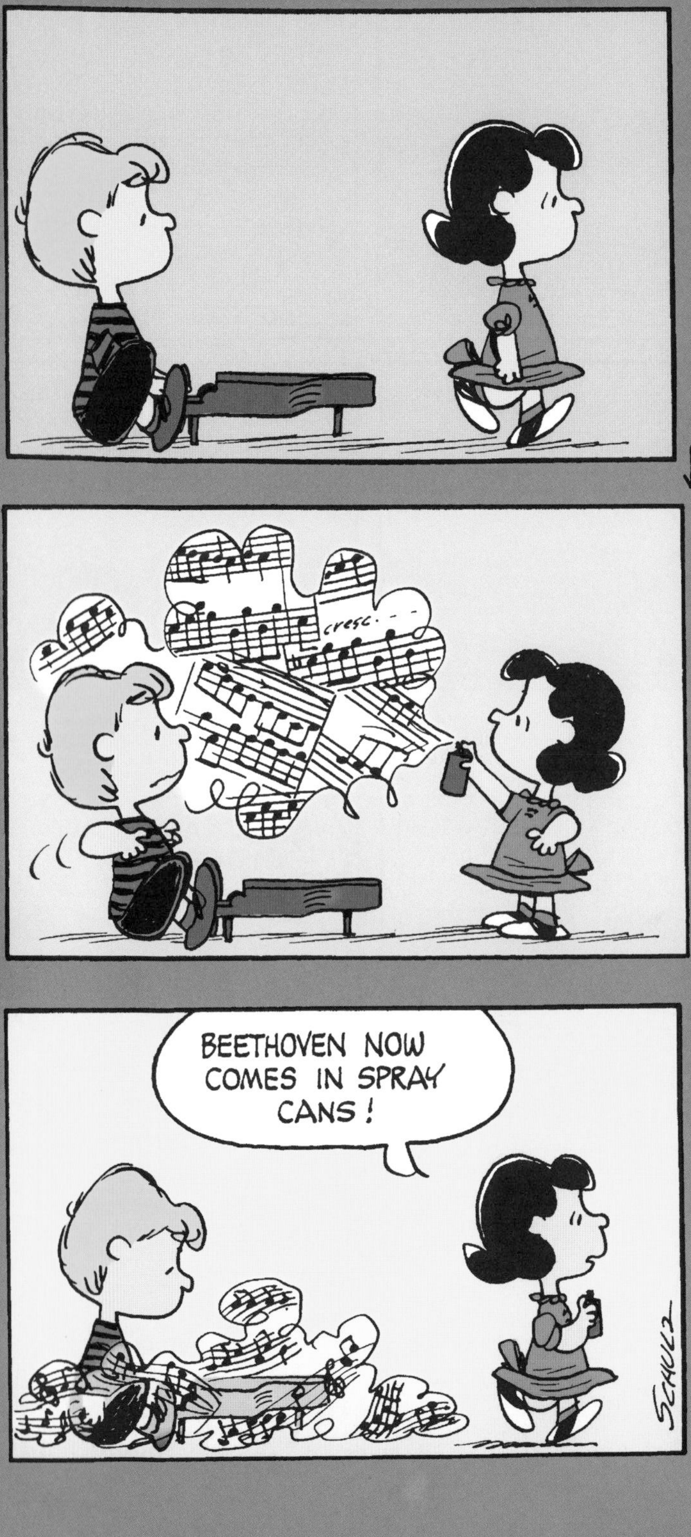
cresc.
BEETHOVEN NOW COMES IN SPRAY CANS!
SCHULZ

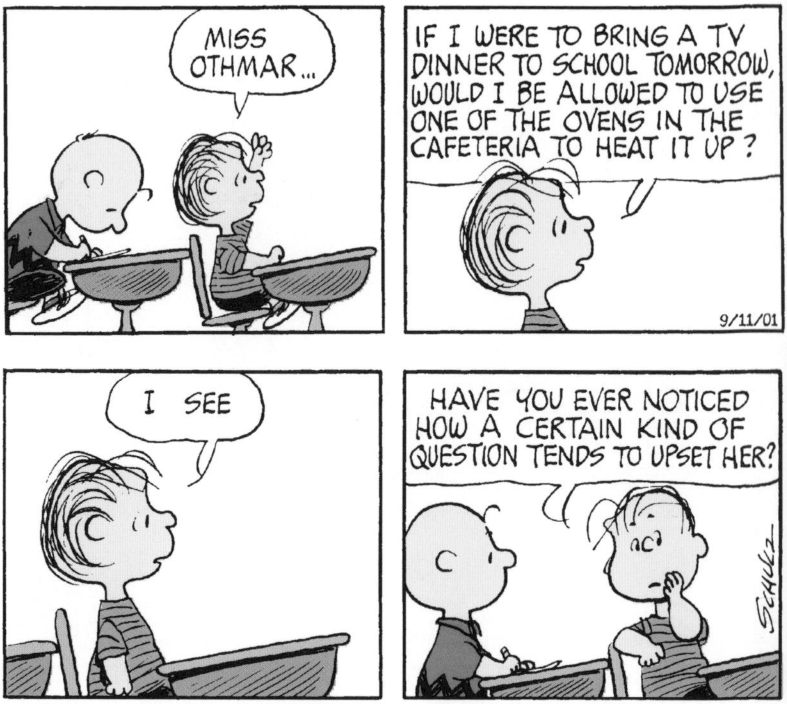
MISS OTHMAR...
IF I WERE TO BRING A TV DINNER TO SCHOOL TOMORROW, WOULD I BE ALLOWED TO USE ONE OF THE OVENS IN THE CAFETERIA TO HEAT IT UP?
9/11/01
I SEE
HAVE YOU EVER NOTICED HOW A CERTAIN KIND OF QUESTION TENDS TO UPSET HER?
SCHULZ

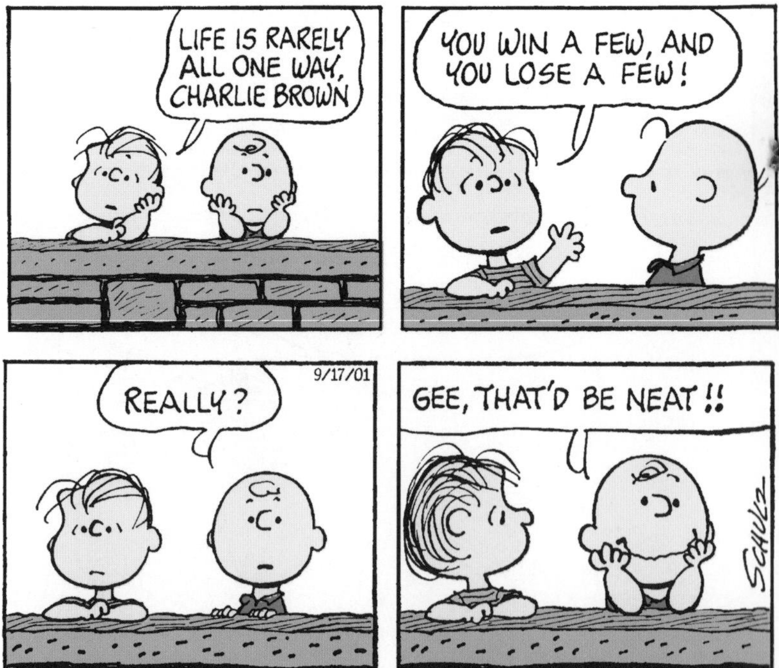
LIFE IS RARELY ALL ONE WAY, CHARLIE BROWN
YOU WIN A FEW, AND YOU LOSE A FEW!
9/17/01
REALLY?
GEE, THAT'D BE NEAT!!
SCHULZ

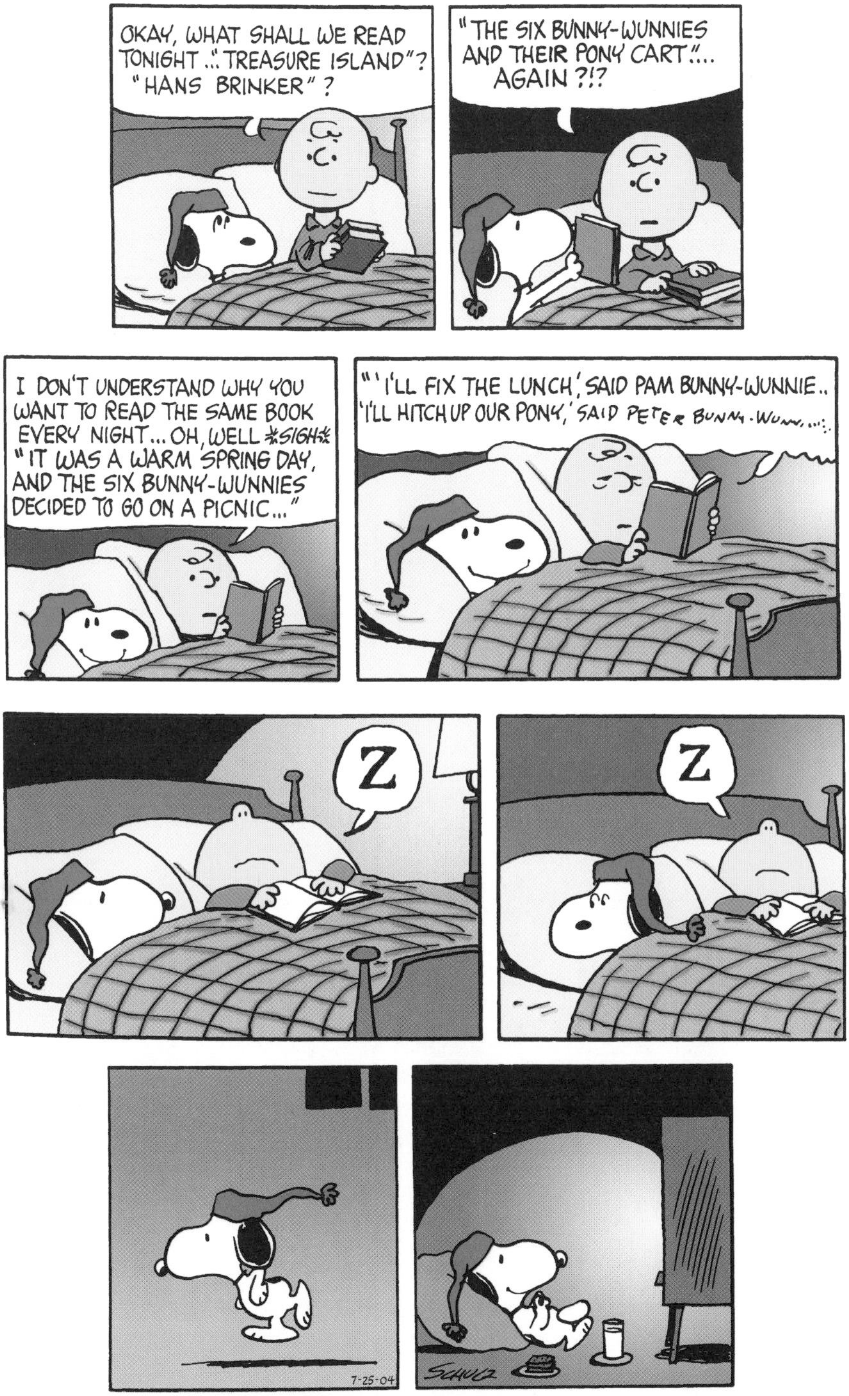

OKAY, WHAT SHALL WE READ TONIGHT ... "TREASURE ISLAND"? "HANS BRINKER"?
"THE SIX BUNNY-WUNNIES AND THEIR PONY CART"... AGAIN ?!?
I DON'T UNDERSTAND WHY YOU WANT TO READ THE SAME BOOK EVERY NIGHT... OH, WELL *SIGH* "IT WAS A WARM SPRING DAY, AND THE SIX BUNNY-WUNNIES DECIDED TO GO ON A PICNIC..."
"'I'LL FIX THE LUNCH,' SAID PAM BUNNY-WUNNIE.. 'I'LL HITCH UP OUR PONY,' SAID PETER BUNNY-WUNN...
Z
Z
7-25-04
SCHULZ

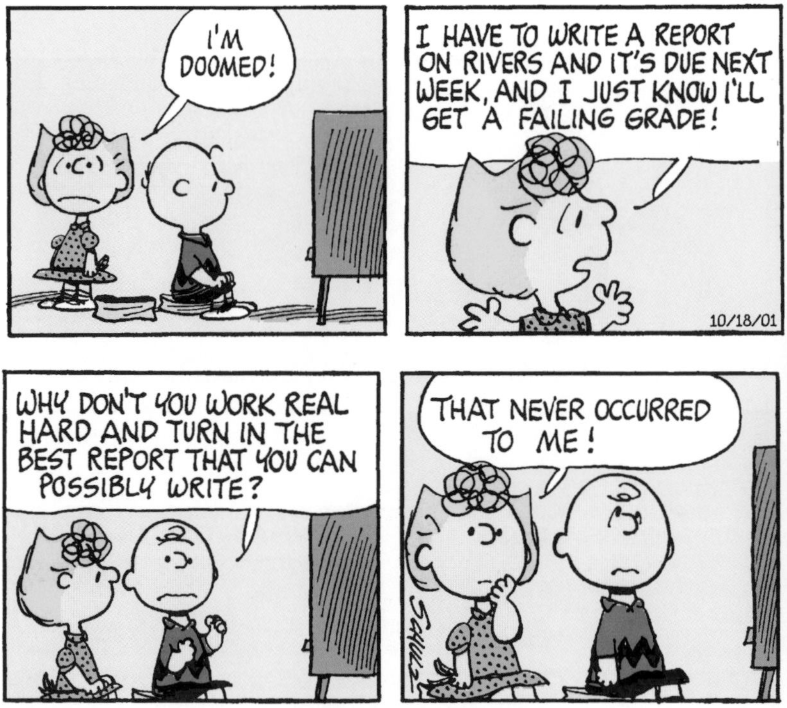
I'M DOOMED!
I HAVE TO WRITE A REPORT ON RIVERS AND IT'S DUE NEXT WEEK, AND I JUST KNOW I'LL GET A FAILING GRADE!
10/18/01
WHY DON'T YOU WORK REAL HARD AND TURN IN THE BEST REPORT THAT YOU CAN POSSIBLY WRITE?
THAT NEVER OCCURRED TO ME!
SCHULZ

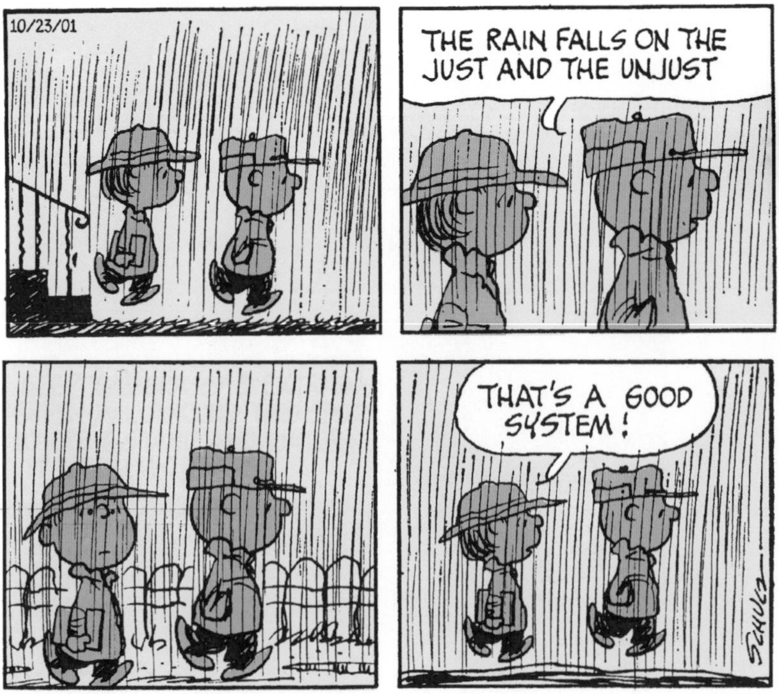
10/23/01
THE RAIN FALLS ON THE JUST AND THE UNJUST
THAT'S A GOOD SYSTEM!
SCHULZ

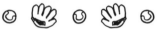

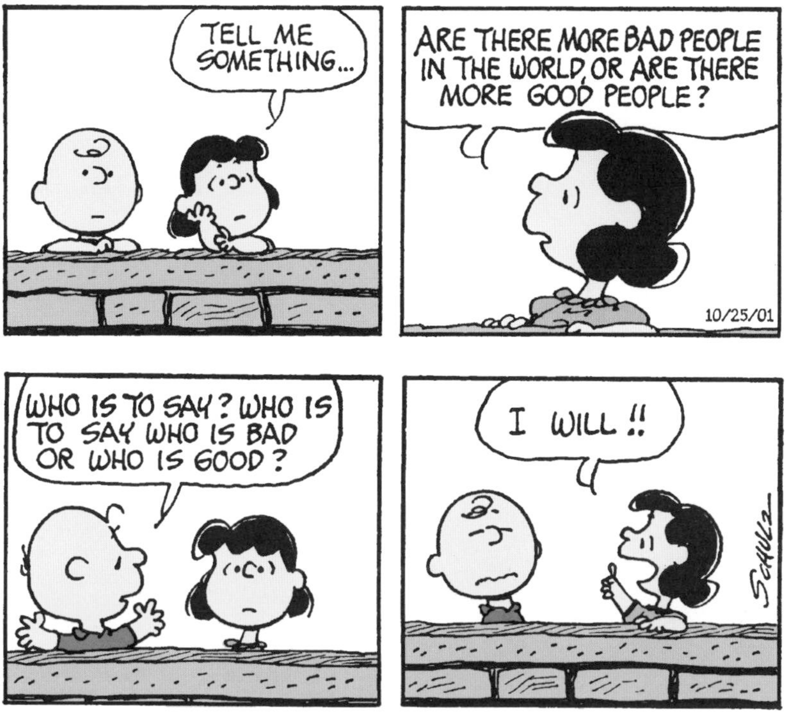
TELL ME SOMETHING...
ARE THERE MORE BAD PEOPLE IN THE WORLD, OR ARE THERE MORE GOOD PEOPLE?
10/25/01
WHO IS TO SAY? WHO IS TO SAY WHO IS BAD OR WHO IS GOOD?
I WILL!!
SCHULZ

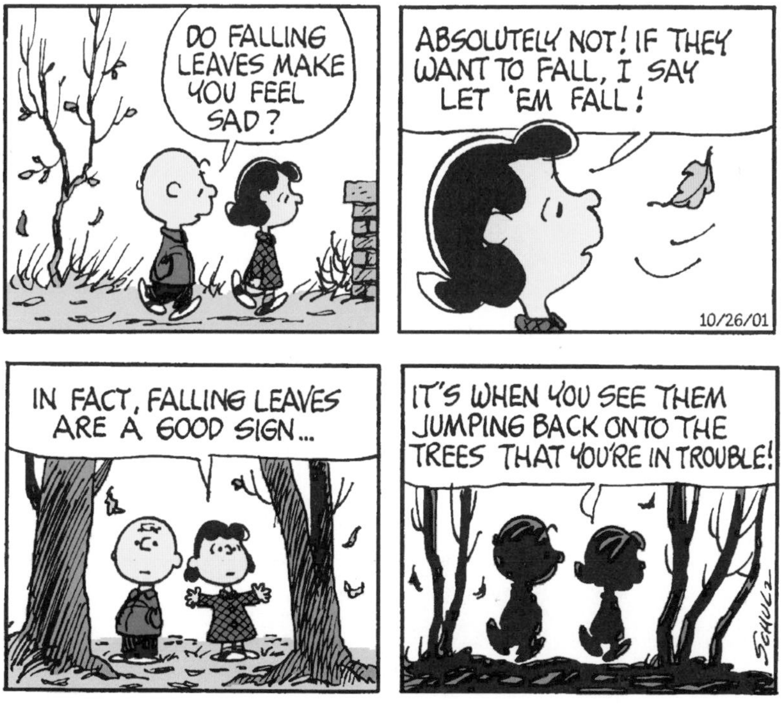
DO FALLING LEAVES MAKE YOU FEEL SAD?
ABSOLUTELY NOT! IF THEY WANT TO FALL, I SAY LET 'EM FALL!
10/26/01
IN FACT, FALLING LEAVES ARE A GOOD SIGN...
IT'S WHEN YOU SEE THEM JUMPING BACK ONTO THE TREES THAT YOU'RE IN TROUBLE!
SCHULZ

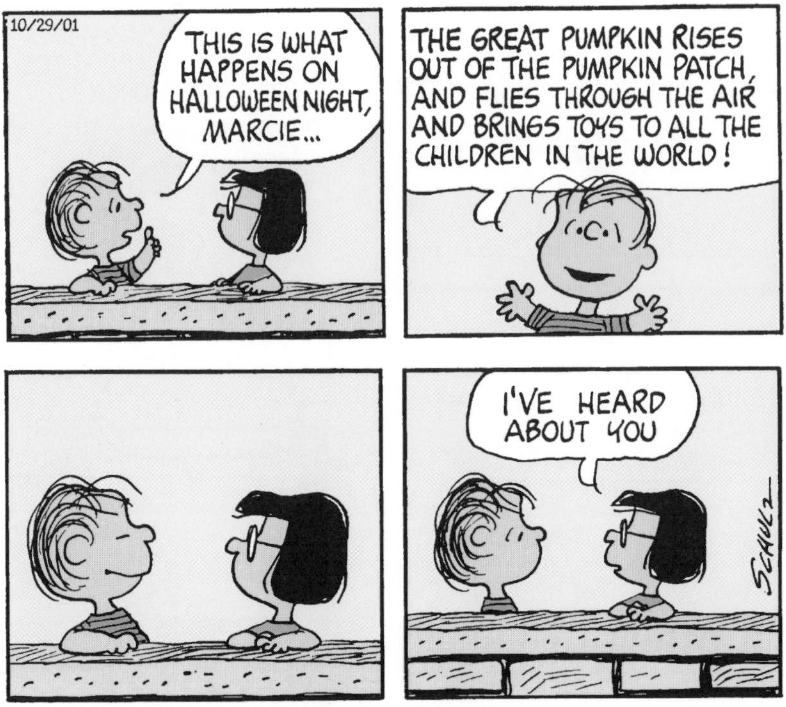
10/29/01
THIS IS WHAT HAPPENS ON HALLOWEEN NIGHT, MARCIE...
THE GREAT PUMPKIN RISES OUT OF THE PUMPKIN PATCH, AND FLIES THROUGH THE AIR AND BRINGS TOYS TO ALL THE CHILDREN IN THE WORLD!
I'VE HEARD ABOUT YOU

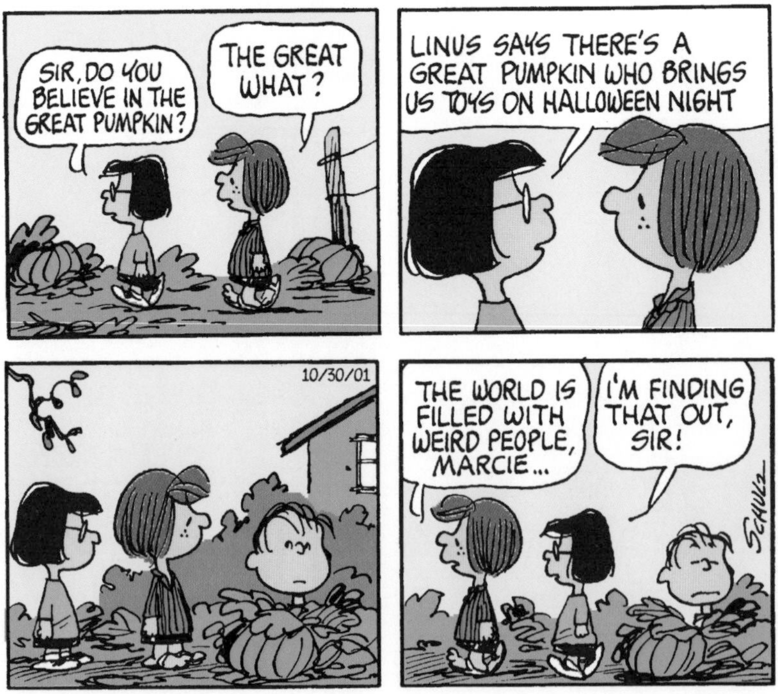
SIR, DO YOU BELIEVE IN THE GREAT PUMPKIN?
THE GREAT WHAT?
LINUS SAYS THERE'S A GREAT PUMPKIN WHO BRINGS US TOYS ON HALLOWEEN NIGHT
10/30/01
THE WORLD IS FILLED WITH WEIRD PEOPLE, MARCIE...
I'M FINDING THAT OUT, SIR!

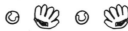

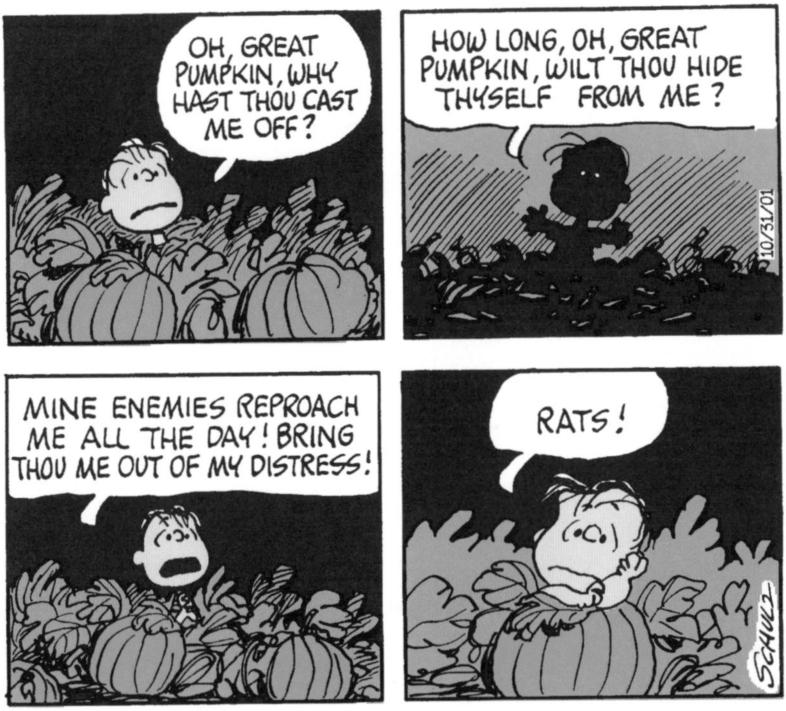
OH, GREAT PUMPKIN, WHY HAST THOU CAST ME OFF?
HOW LONG, OH, GREAT PUMPKIN, WILT THOU HIDE THYSELF FROM ME?
10/31/01
MINE ENEMIES REPROACH ME ALL THE DAY! BRING THOU ME OUT OF MY DISTRESS!
RATS!
SCHULZ

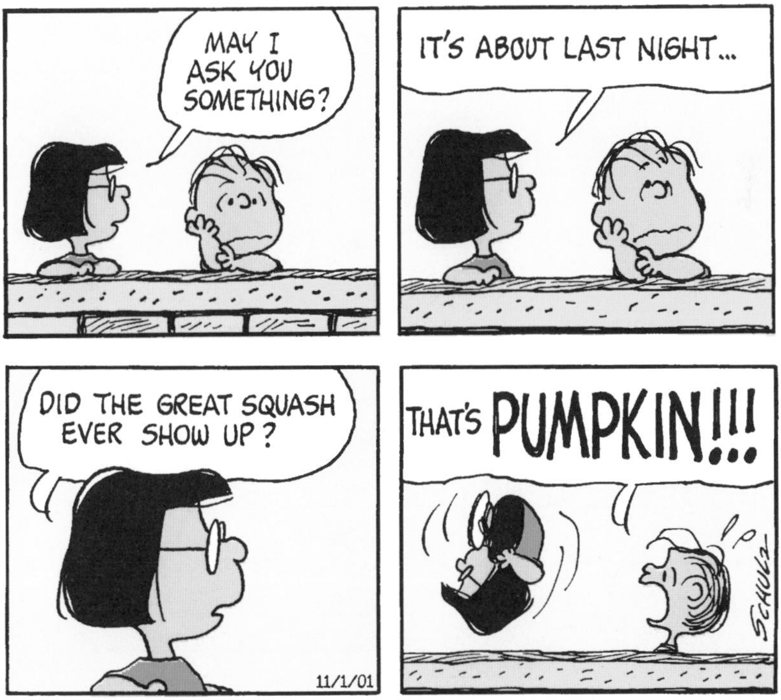
MAY I ASK YOU SOMETHING?
IT'S ABOUT LAST NIGHT...
DID THE GREAT SQUASH EVER SHOW UP?
11/1/01
THAT'S PUMPKIN!!!
SCHULZ

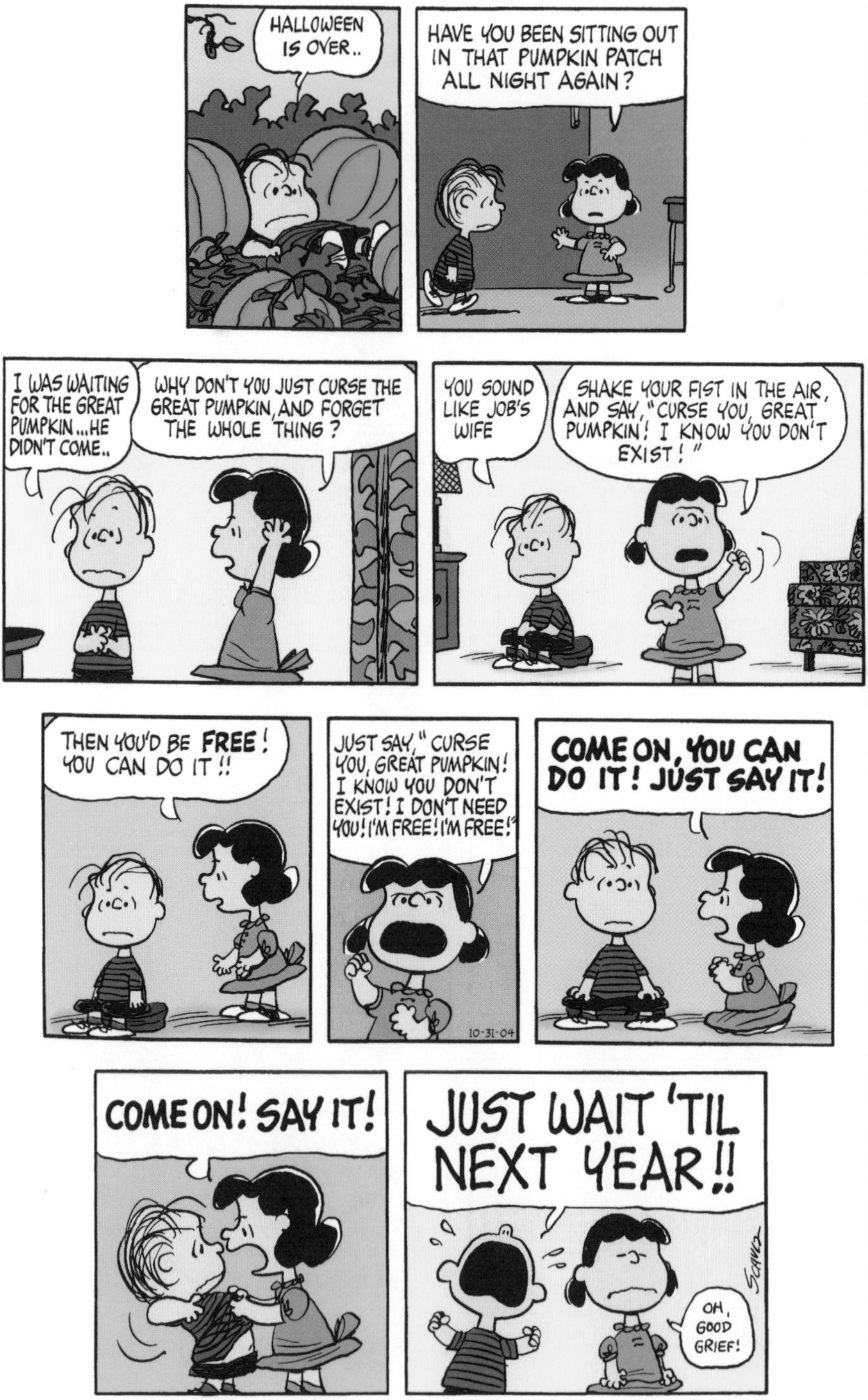
HALLOWEEN IS OVER..
HAVE YOU BEEN SITTING OUT IN THAT PUMPKIN PATCH ALL NIGHT AGAIN?
I WAS WAITING FOR THE GREAT PUMPKIN...HE DIDN'T COME..
WHY DON'T YOU JUST CURSE THE GREAT PUMPKIN, AND FORGET THE WHOLE THING?
YOU SOUND LIKE JOB'S WIFE
SHAKE YOUR FIST IN THE AIR, AND SAY, "CURSE YOU, GREAT PUMPKIN! I KNOW YOU DON'T EXIST!"
THEN YOU'D BE FREE! YOU CAN DO IT!!
JUST SAY, "CURSE YOU, GREAT PUMPKIN! I KNOW YOU DON'T EXIST! I DON'T NEED YOU! I'M FREE! I'M FREE!"
10-31-04
COME ON, YOU CAN DO IT! JUST SAY IT!
COME ON! SAY IT!
JUST WAIT 'TIL NEXT YEAR!!
OH, GOOD GRIEF!
SCHULZ

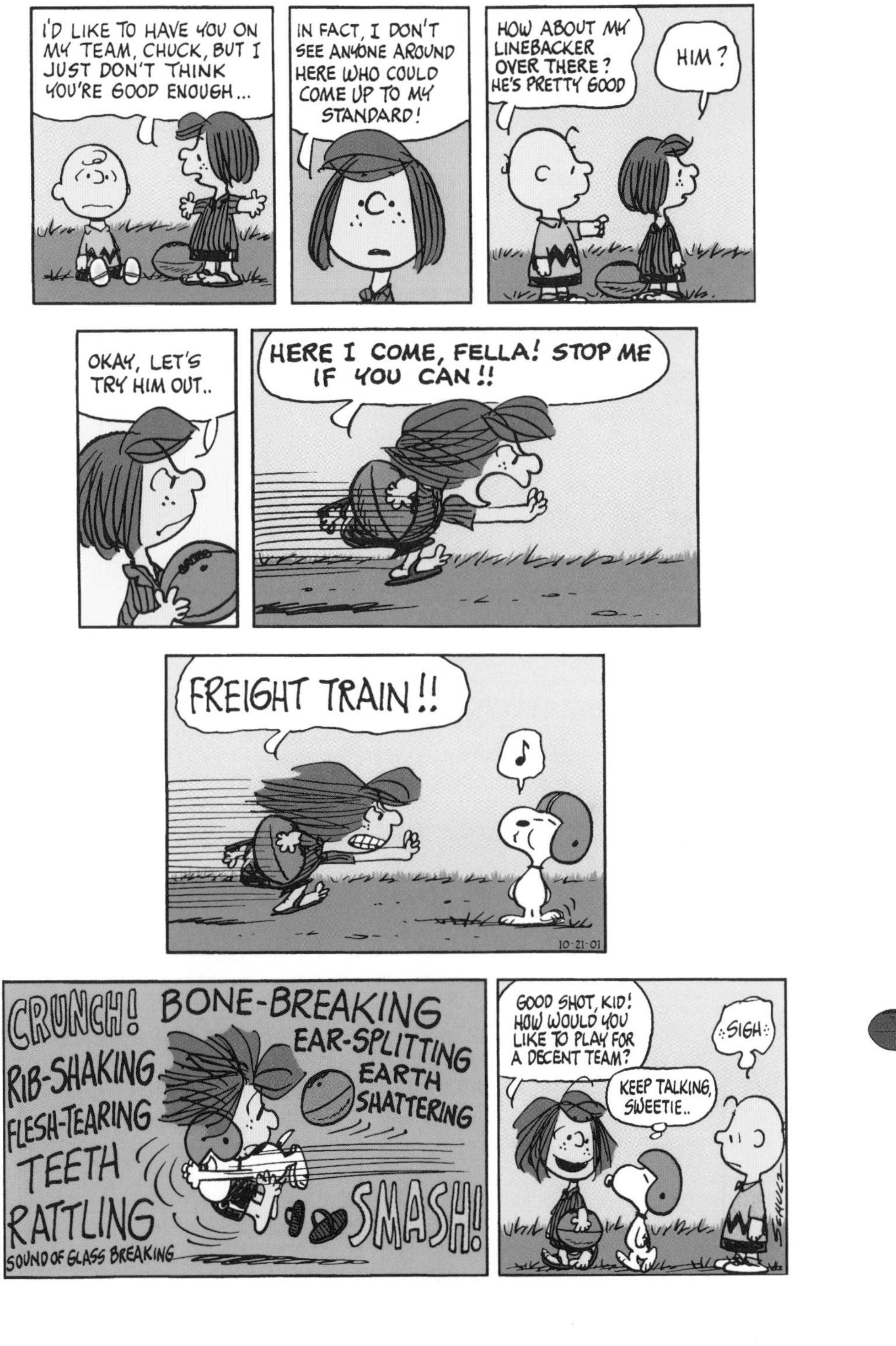

I'D LIKE TO HAVE YOU ON MY TEAM, CHUCK, BUT I JUST DON'T THINK YOU'RE GOOD ENOUGH...
IN FACT, I DON'T SEE ANYONE AROUND HERE WHO COULD COME UP TO MY STANDARD!
HOW ABOUT MY LINEBACKER OVER THERE? HE'S PRETTY GOOD
HIM?
OKAY, LET'S TRY HIM OUT..
HERE I COME, FELLA! STOP ME IF YOU CAN!!
FREIGHT TRAIN!!
♪
10-21-01
CRUNCH! BONE-BREAKING
EAR-SPLITTING
RIB-SHAKING
EARTH SHATTERING
FLESH-TEARING
TEETH RATTLING
SMASH!
SOUND OF GLASS BREAKING
GOOD SHOT, KID! HOW WOULD YOU LIKE TO PLAY FOR A DECENT TEAM?
SIGH
KEEP TALKING, SWEETIE..
SCHULZ

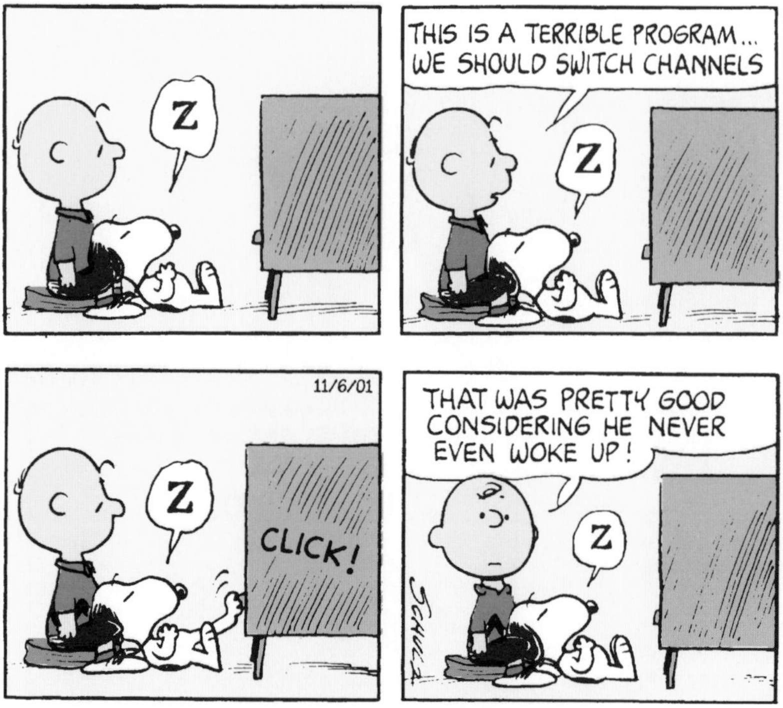
Z
THIS IS A TERRIBLE PROGRAM... WE SHOULD SWITCH CHANNELS
Z
11/6/01
Z
CLICK!
THAT WAS PRETTY GOOD CONSIDERING HE NEVER EVEN WOKE UP!
Z

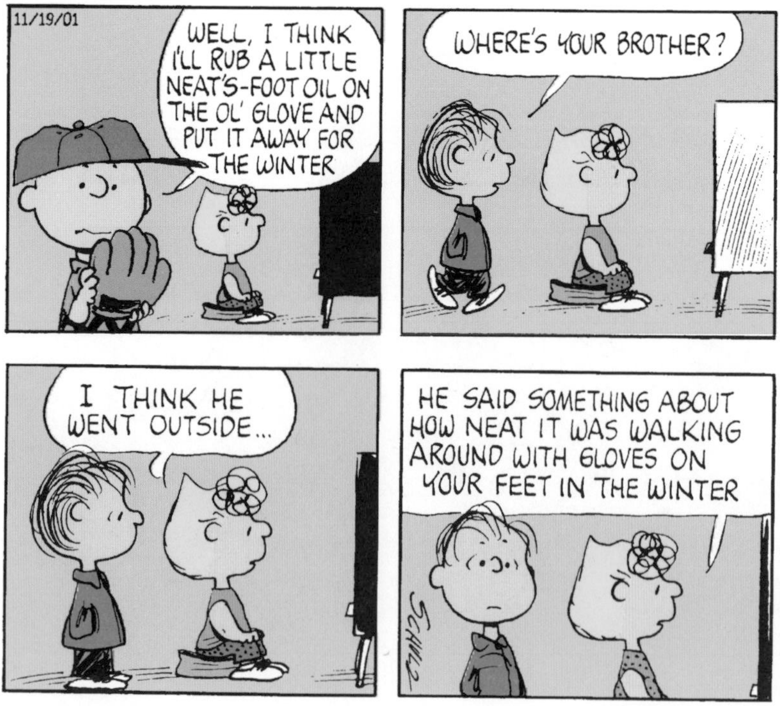
11/19/01
WELL, I THINK I'LL RUB A LITTLE NEAT'S-FOOT OIL ON THE OL' GLOVE AND PUT IT AWAY FOR THE WINTER
WHERE'S YOUR BROTHER?
I THINK HE WENT OUTSIDE...
HE SAID SOMETHING ABOUT HOW NEAT IT WAS WALKING AROUND WITH GLOVES ON YOUR FEET IN THE WINTER

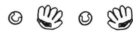

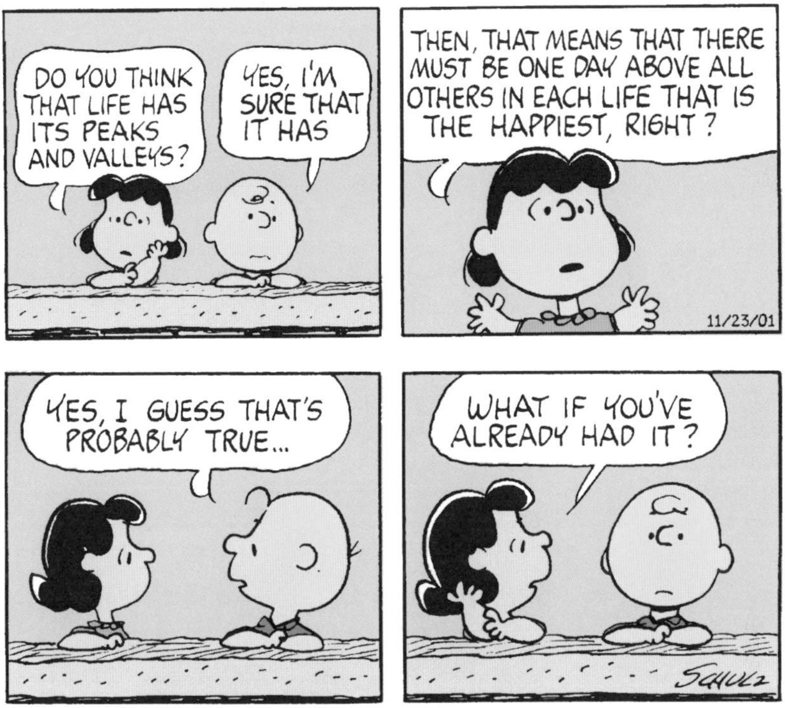
DO YOU THINK THAT LIFE HAS ITS PEAKS AND VALLEYS?
YES, I'M SURE THAT IT HAS
THEN, THAT MEANS THAT THERE MUST BE ONE DAY ABOVE ALL OTHERS IN EACH LIFE THAT IS THE HAPPIEST, RIGHT?
11/23/01
YES, I GUESS THAT'S PROBABLY TRUE...
WHAT IF YOU'VE ALREADY HAD IT?
SCHULZ

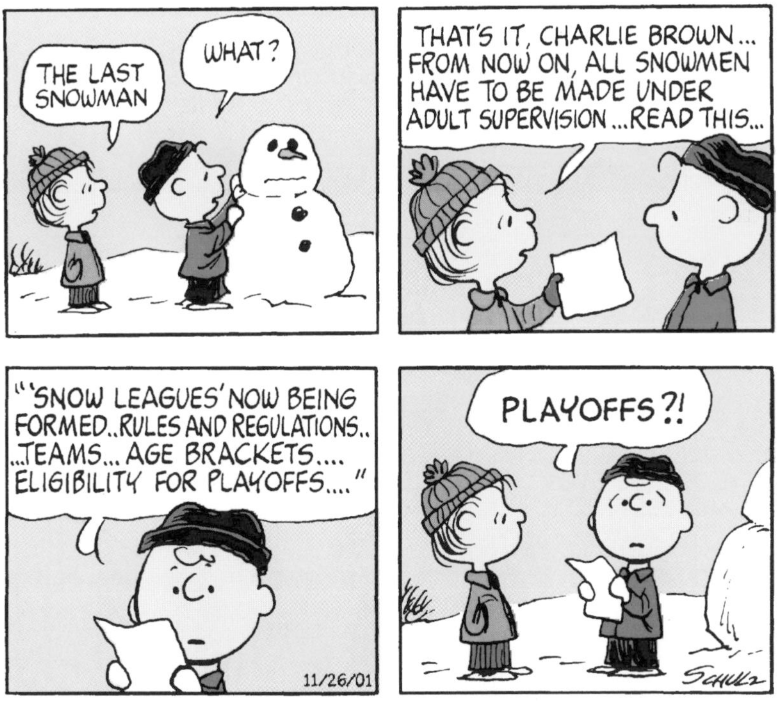
THE LAST SNOWMAN
WHAT?
THAT'S IT, CHARLIE BROWN... FROM NOW ON, ALL SNOWMEN HAVE TO BE MADE UNDER ADULT SUPERVISION...READ THIS...
"'SNOW LEAGUES' NOW BEING FORMED..RULES AND REGULATIONS.. ...TEAMS... AGE BRACKETS.... ELIGIBILITY FOR PLAYOFFS...."
11/26/01
PLAYOFFS?!
SCHULZ

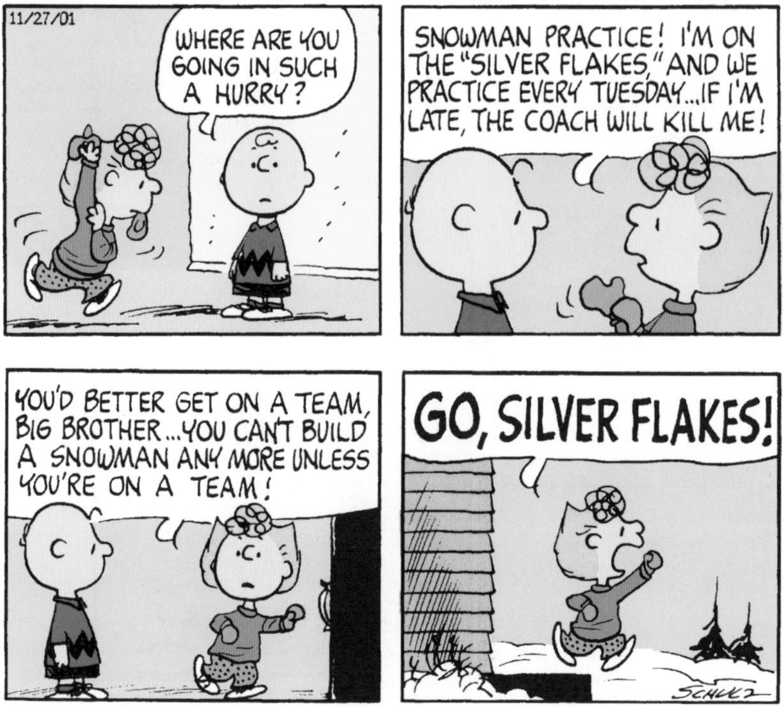
11/27/01
WHERE ARE YOU GOING IN SUCH A HURRY?
SNOWMAN PRACTICE! I'M ON THE "SILVER FLAKES," AND WE PRACTICE EVERY TUESDAY...IF I'M LATE, THE COACH WILL KILL ME!
YOU'D BETTER GET ON A TEAM, BIG BROTHER...YOU CAN'T BUILD A SNOWMAN ANY MORE UNLESS YOU'RE ON A TEAM!
GO, SILVER FLAKES!
SCHULZ

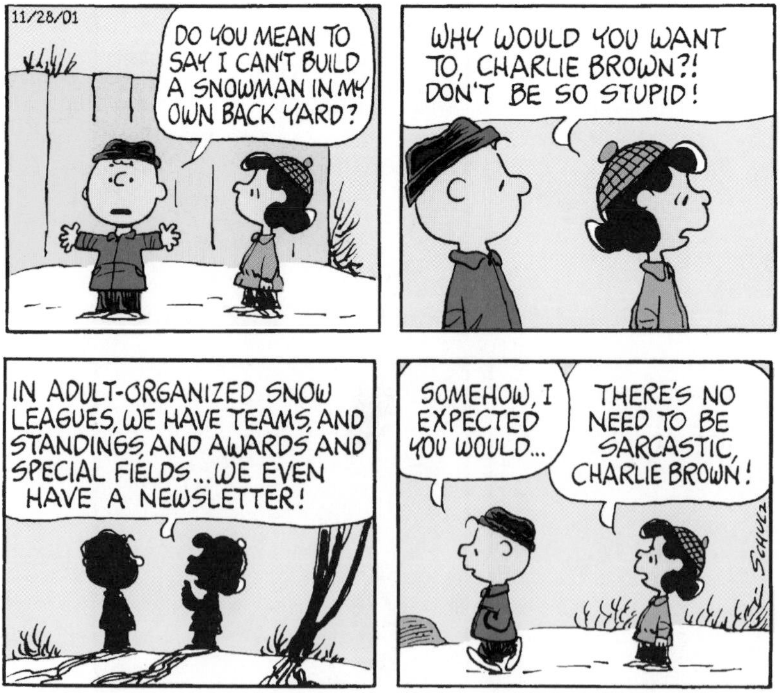
11/28/01
DO YOU MEAN TO SAY I CAN'T BUILD A SNOWMAN IN MY OWN BACK YARD?
WHY WOULD YOU WANT TO, CHARLIE BROWN?! DON'T BE SO STUPID!
IN ADULT-ORGANIZED SNOW LEAGUES, WE HAVE TEAMS, AND STANDINGS, AND AWARDS AND SPECIAL FIELDS...WE EVEN HAVE A NEWSLETTER!
SOMEHOW, I EXPECTED YOU WOULD...
THERE'S NO NEED TO BE SARCASTIC, CHARLIE BROWN!
SCHULZ

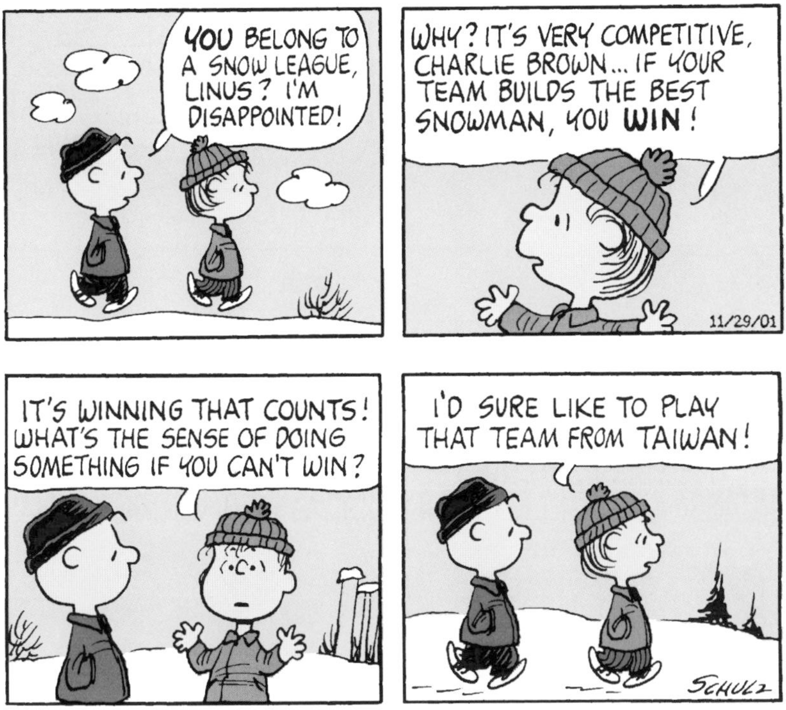
YOU BELONG TO A SNOW LEAGUE, LINUS? I'M DISAPPOINTED!
WHY? IT'S VERY COMPETITIVE, CHARLIE BROWN... IF YOUR TEAM BUILDS THE BEST SNOWMAN, YOU WIN!
11/29/01
IT'S WINNING THAT COUNTS! WHAT'S THE SENSE OF DOING SOMETHING IF YOU CAN'T WIN?
I'D SURE LIKE TO PLAY THAT TEAM FROM TAIWAN!
SCHULZ

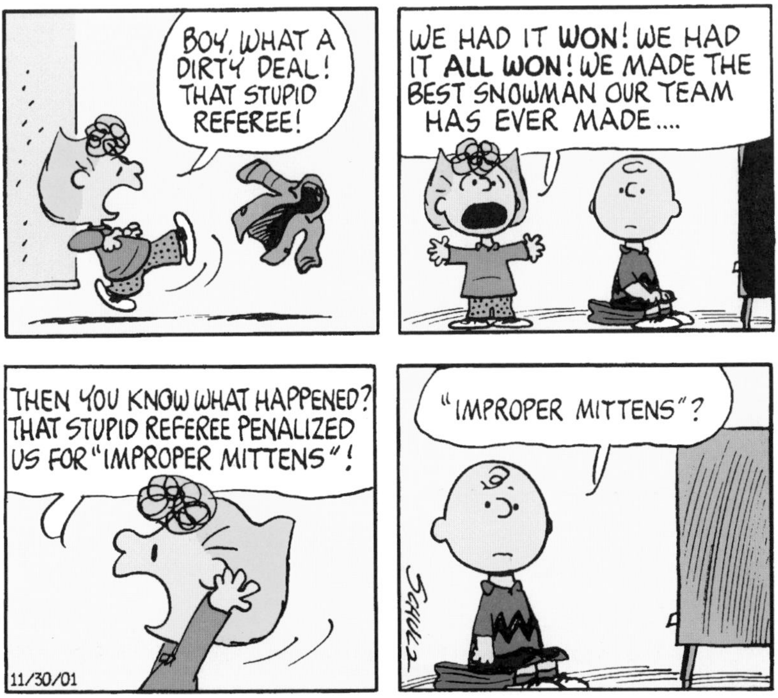
BOY, WHAT A DIRTY DEAL! THAT STUPID REFEREE!
WE HAD IT WON! WE HAD IT ALL WON! WE MADE THE BEST SNOWMAN OUR TEAM HAS EVER MADE....
THEN YOU KNOW WHAT HAPPENED? THAT STUPID REFEREE PENALIZED US FOR "IMPROPER MITTENS"!
11/30/01
"IMPROPER MITTENS"?
SCHULZ

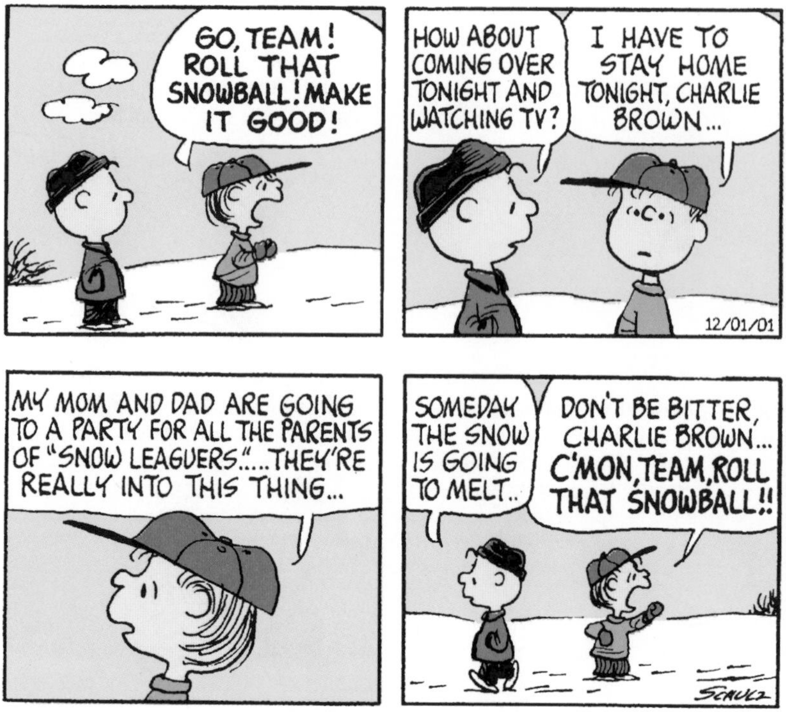
GO, TEAM! ROLL THAT SNOWBALL! MAKE IT GOOD!
HOW ABOUT COMING OVER TONIGHT AND WATCHING TV?
I HAVE TO STAY HOME TONIGHT, CHARLIE BROWN...
12/01/01
MY MOM AND DAD ARE GOING TO A PARTY FOR ALL THE PARENTS OF "SNOW LEAGUERS."...THEY'RE REALLY INTO THIS THING...
SOMEDAY THE SNOW IS GOING TO MELT..
DON'T BE BITTER, CHARLIE BROWN... C'MON, TEAM, ROLL THAT SNOWBALL!!
SCHULZ

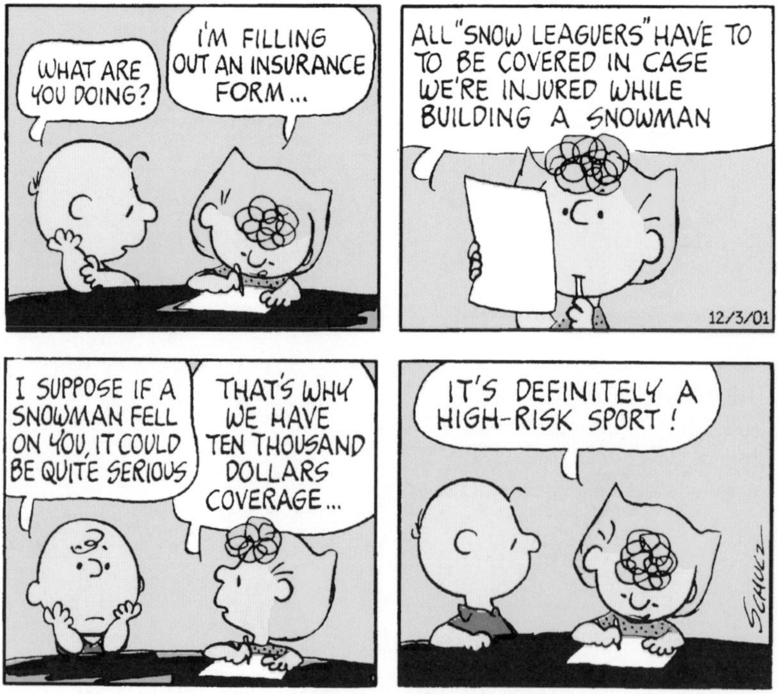
WHAT ARE YOU DOING?
I'M FILLING OUT AN INSURANCE FORM...
ALL "SNOW LEAGUERS" HAVE TO TO BE COVERED IN CASE WE'RE INJURED WHILE BUILDING A SNOWMAN
12/3/01
I SUPPOSE IF A SNOWMAN FELL ON YOU, IT COULD BE QUITE SERIOUS
THAT'S WHY WE HAVE TEN THOUSAND DOLLARS COVERAGE...
IT'S DEFINITELY A HIGH-RISK SPORT!
SCHULZ

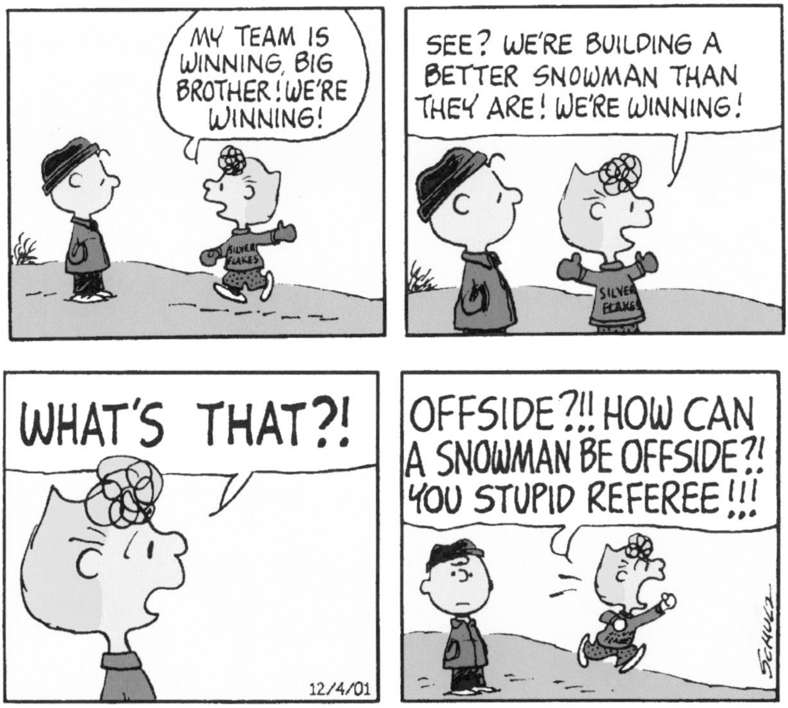
MY TEAM IS WINNING, BIG BROTHER! WE'RE WINNING!
SEE? WE'RE BUILDING A BETTER SNOWMAN THAN THEY ARE! WE'RE WINNING!
WHAT'S THAT?!
12/4/01
OFFSIDE?!! HOW CAN A SNOWMAN BE OFFSIDE?! YOU STUPID REFEREE!!!
SCHULZ

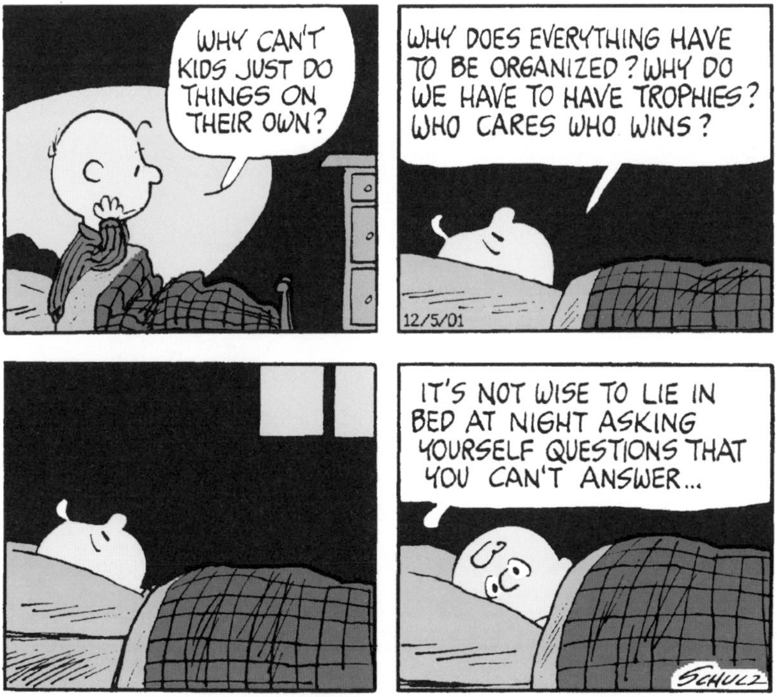
WHY CAN'T KIDS JUST DO THINGS ON THEIR OWN?
WHY DOES EVERYTHING HAVE TO BE ORGANIZED? WHY DO WE HAVE TO HAVE TROPHIES? WHO CARES WHO WINS?
12/5/01
IT'S NOT WISE TO LIE IN BED AT NIGHT ASKING YOURSELF QUESTIONS THAT YOU CAN'T ANSWER...
SCHULZ

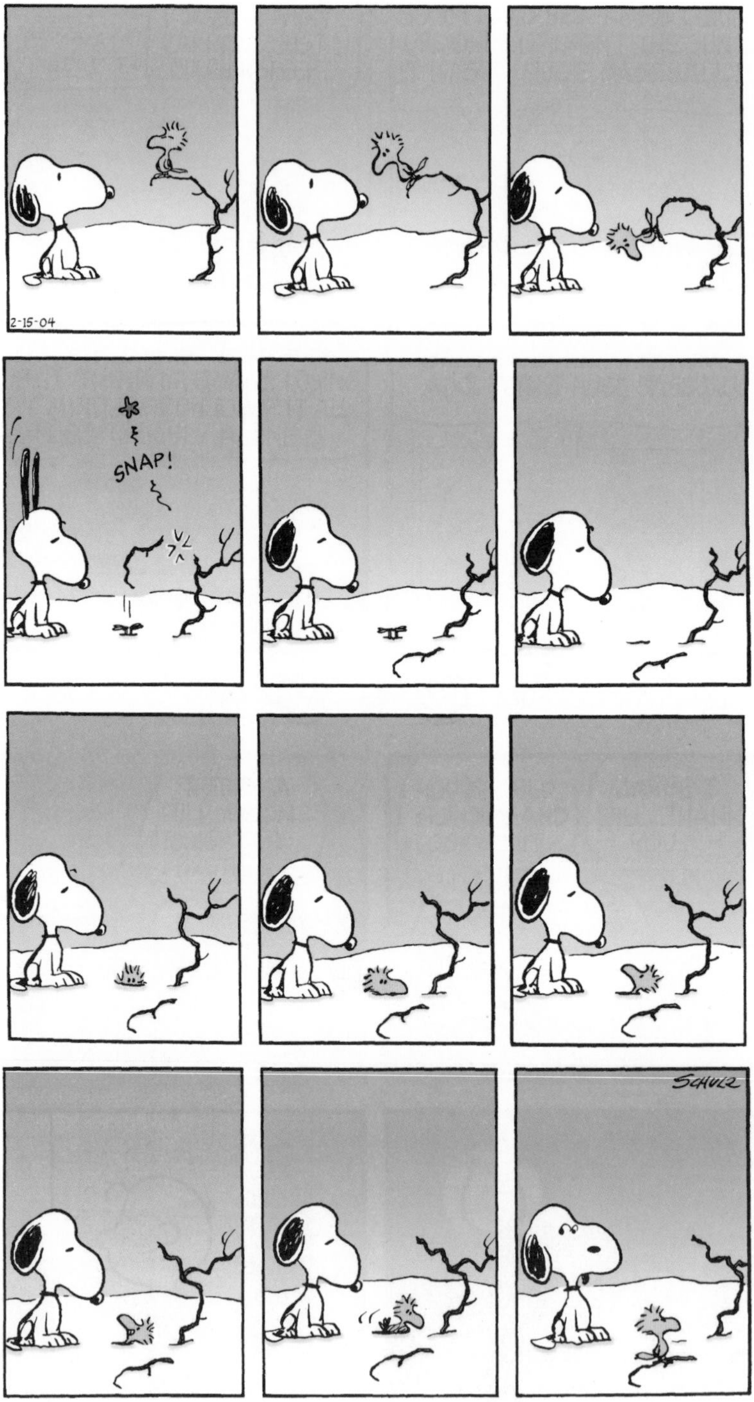
2-15-04
SNAP!
SCHULZ

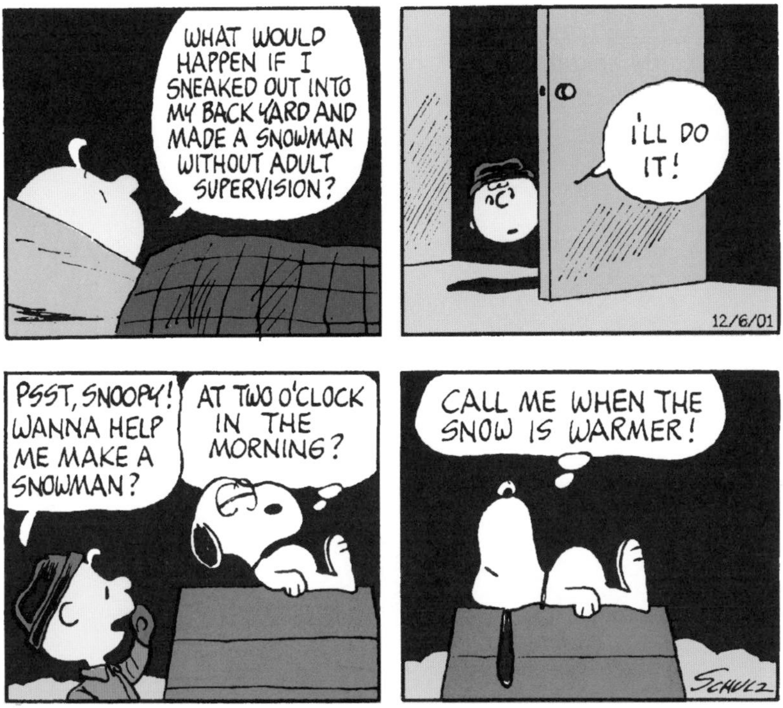
WHAT WOULD HAPPEN IF I SNEAKED OUT INTO MY BACK YARD AND MADE A SNOWMAN WITHOUT ADULT SUPERVISION?
I'LL DO IT!
12/6/01
PSST, SNOOPY! WANNA HELP ME MAKE A SNOWMAN?
AT TWO O'CLOCK IN THE MORNING?
CALL ME WHEN THE SNOW IS WARMER!
SCHULZ

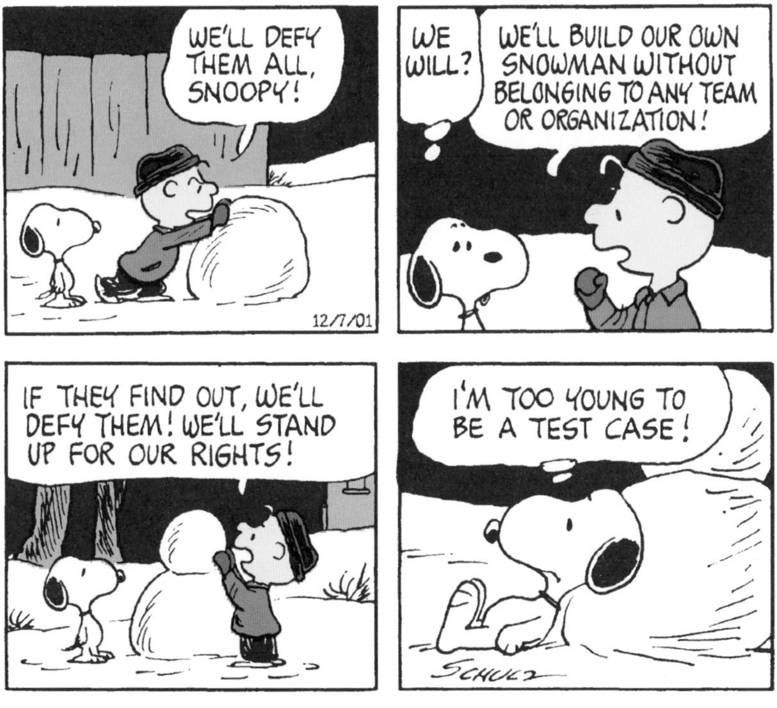
WE'LL DEFY THEM ALL, SNOOPY!
12/7/01
WE WILL?
WE'LL BUILD OUR OWN SNOWMAN WITHOUT BELONGING TO ANY TEAM OR ORGANIZATION!
IF THEY FIND OUT, WE'LL DEFY THEM! WE'LL STAND UP FOR OUR RIGHTS!
I'M TOO YOUNG TO BE A TEST CASE!
SCHULZ

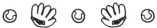

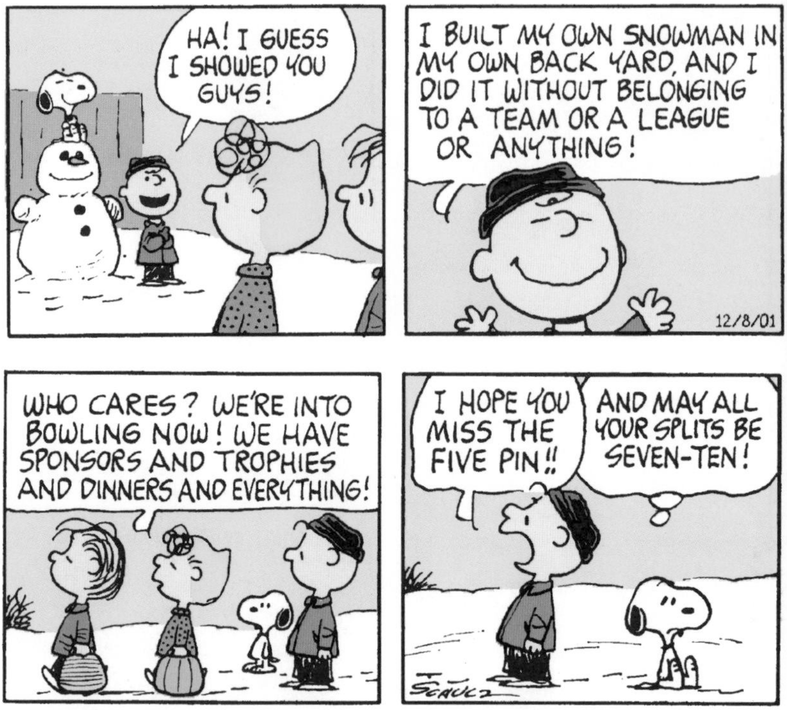
HA! I GUESS I SHOWED YOU GUYS!
I BUILT MY OWN SNOWMAN IN MY OWN BACK YARD, AND I DID IT WITHOUT BELONGING TO A TEAM OR A LEAGUE OR ANYTHING!
12/8/01
WHO CARES? WE'RE INTO BOWLING NOW! WE HAVE SPONSORS AND TROPHIES AND DINNERS AND EVERYTHING!
I HOPE YOU MISS THE FIVE PIN!!
AND MAY ALL YOUR SPLITS BE SEVEN-TEN!
SCHULZ

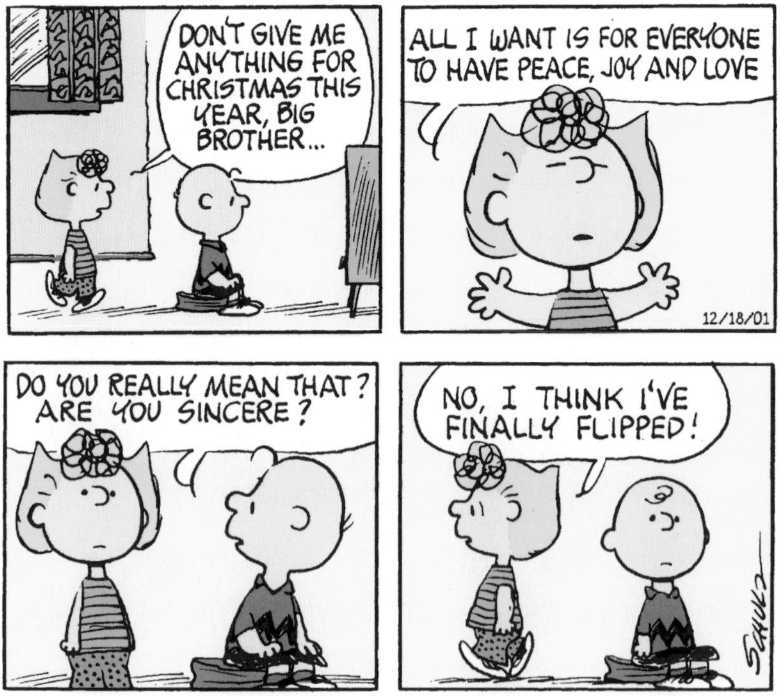
DON'T GIVE ME ANYTHING FOR CHRISTMAS THIS YEAR, BIG BROTHER...
ALL I WANT IS FOR EVERYONE TO HAVE PEACE, JOY AND LOVE
12/18/01
DO YOU REALLY MEAN THAT? ARE YOU SINCERE?
NO, I THINK I'VE FINALLY FLIPPED!
SCHULZ

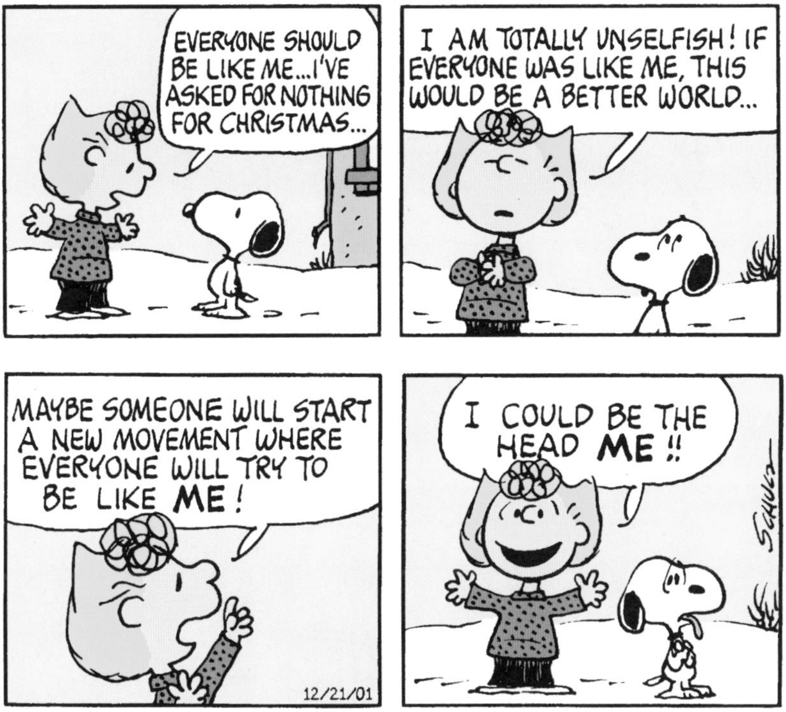
EVERYONE SHOULD BE LIKE ME...I'VE ASKED FOR NOTHING FOR CHRISTMAS...
I AM TOTALLY UNSELFISH! IF EVERYONE WAS LIKE ME, THIS WOULD BE A BETTER WORLD...
MAYBE SOMEONE WILL START A NEW MOVEMENT WHERE EVERYONE WILL TRY TO BE LIKE ME!
12/21/01
I COULD BE THE HEAD ME!!
SCHULZ

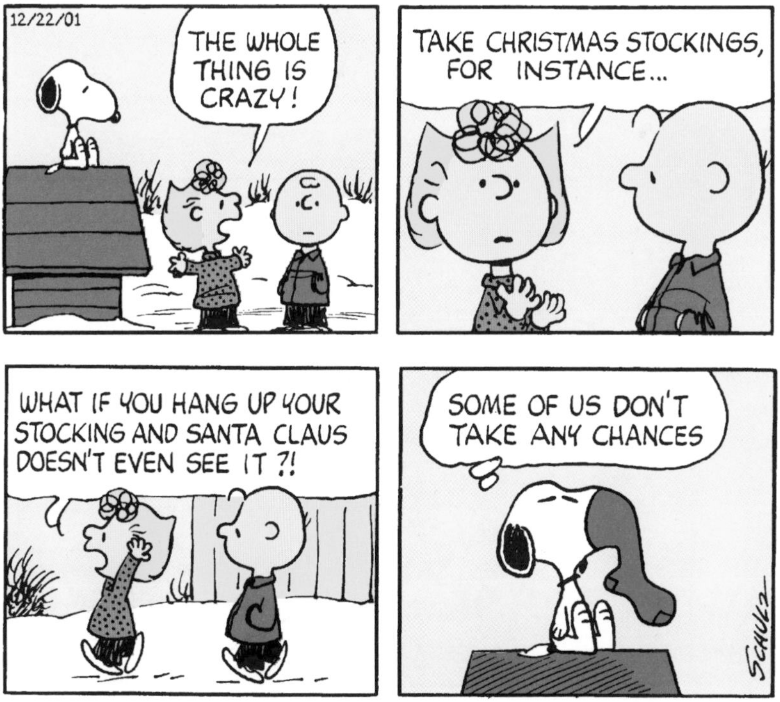
12/22/01
THE WHOLE THING IS CRAZY!
TAKE CHRISTMAS STOCKINGS, FOR INSTANCE...
WHAT IF YOU HANG UP YOUR STOCKING AND SANTA CLAUS DOESN'T EVEN SEE IT ?!
SOME OF US DON'T TAKE ANY CHANCES
SCHULZ

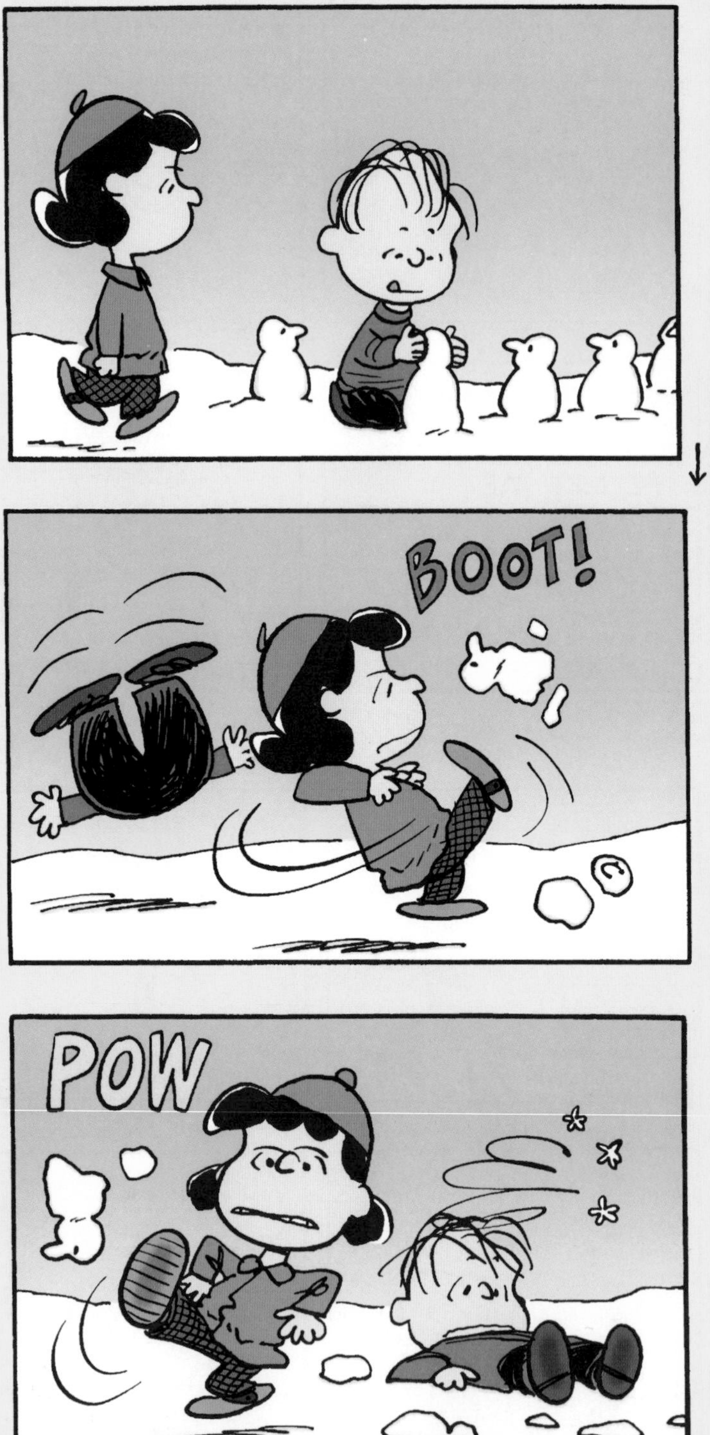
BOOT!
POW

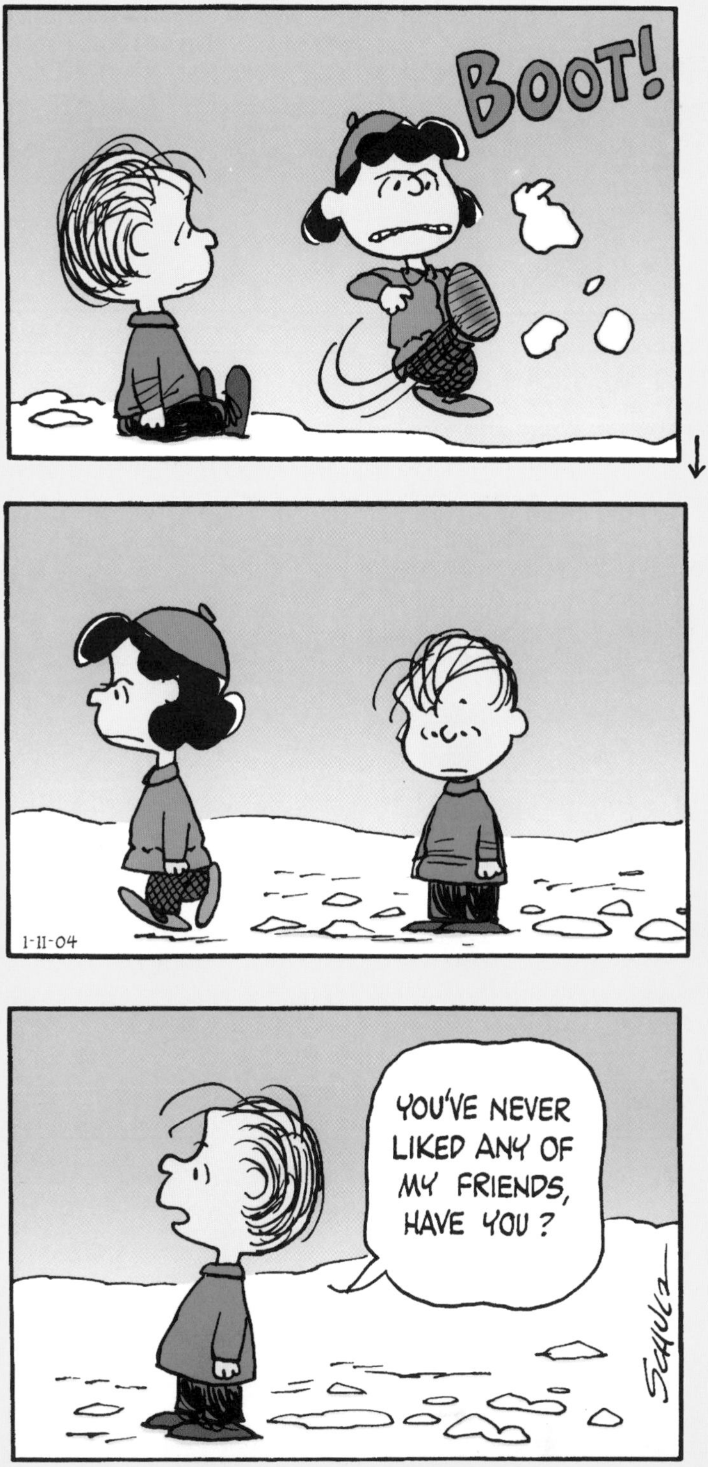
BOOT!
1-11-04
YOU'VE NEVER LIKED ANY OF MY FRIENDS, HAVE YOU ?
SCHULZ

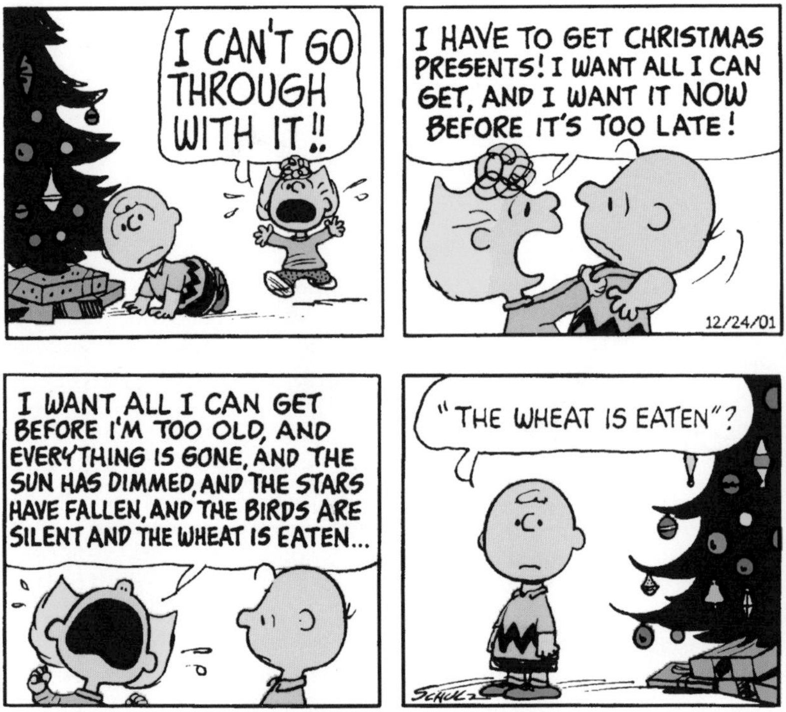
I CAN'T GO THROUGH WITH IT!!
I HAVE TO GET CHRISTMAS PRESENTS! I WANT ALL I CAN GET, AND I WANT IT NOW BEFORE IT'S TOO LATE!
12/24/01
I WANT ALL I CAN GET BEFORE I'M TOO OLD, AND EVERYTHING IS GONE, AND THE SUN HAS DIMMED, AND THE STARS HAVE FALLEN, AND THE BIRDS ARE SILENT AND THE WHEAT IS EATEN...
"THE WHEAT IS EATEN"?
SCHULZ

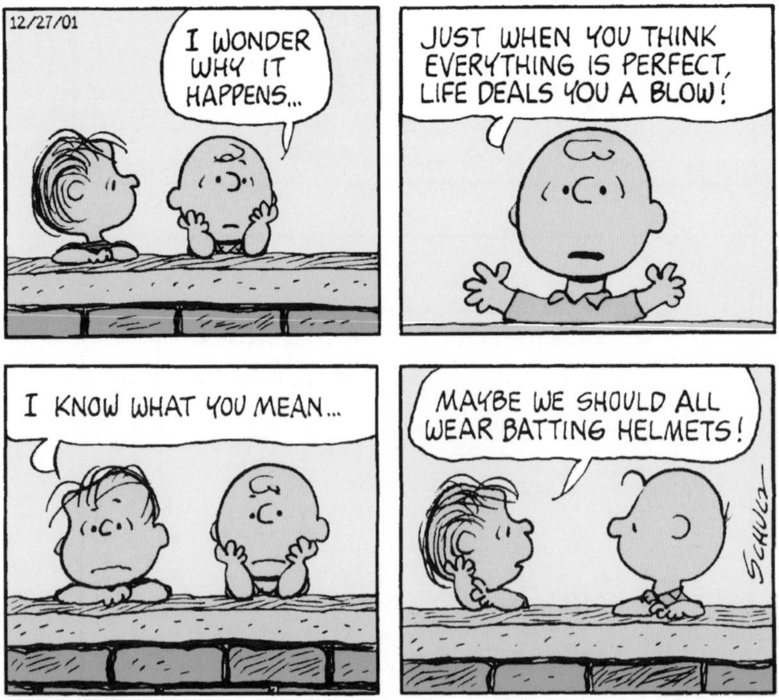
12/27/01
I WONDER WHY IT HAPPENS...
JUST WHEN YOU THINK EVERYTHING IS PERFECT, LIFE DEALS YOU A BLOW!
I KNOW WHAT YOU MEAN...
MAYBE WE SHOULD ALL WEAR BATTING HELMETS!
SCHULZ

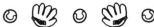

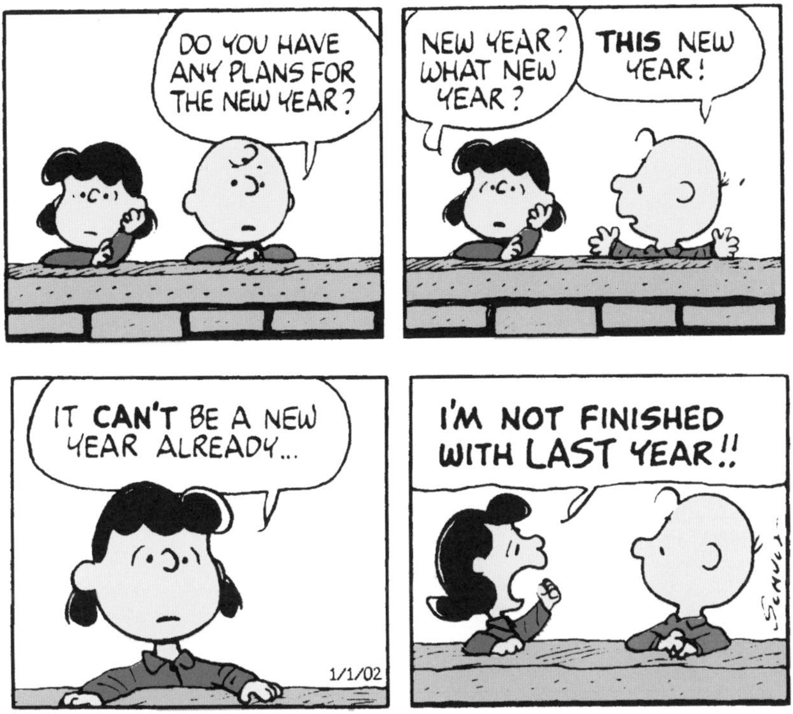
DO YOU HAVE ANY PLANS FOR THE NEW YEAR?
NEW YEAR? WHAT NEW YEAR?
THIS NEW YEAR!
IT CAN'T BE A NEW YEAR ALREADY...
1/1/02
I'M NOT FINISHED WITH LAST YEAR!!
SCHULZ

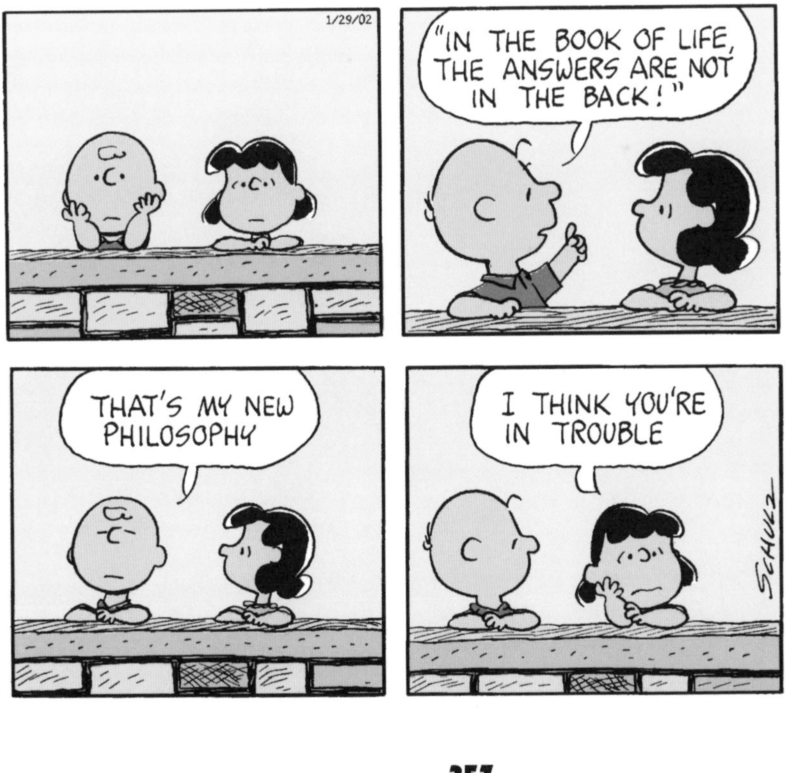
1/29/02
"IN THE BOOK OF LIFE, THE ANSWERS ARE NOT IN THE BACK!"
THAT'S MY NEW PHILOSOPHY
I THINK YOU'RE IN TROUBLE
SCHULZ

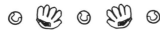

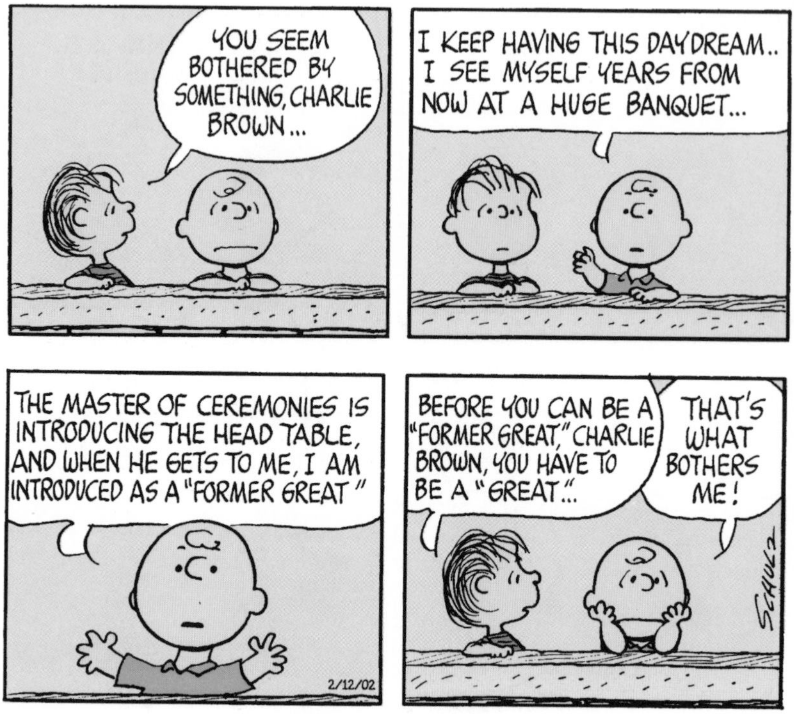
YOU SEEM BOTHERED BY SOMETHING, CHARLIE BROWN...
I KEEP HAVING THIS DAYDREAM.. I SEE MYSELF YEARS FROM NOW AT A HUGE BANQUET...
THE MASTER OF CEREMONIES IS INTRODUCING THE HEAD TABLE, AND WHEN HE GETS TO ME, I AM INTRODUCED AS A "FORMER GREAT"
2/12/02
BEFORE YOU CAN BE A "FORMER GREAT," CHARLIE BROWN, YOU HAVE TO BE A "GREAT."
THAT'S WHAT BOTHERS ME!
SCHULZ

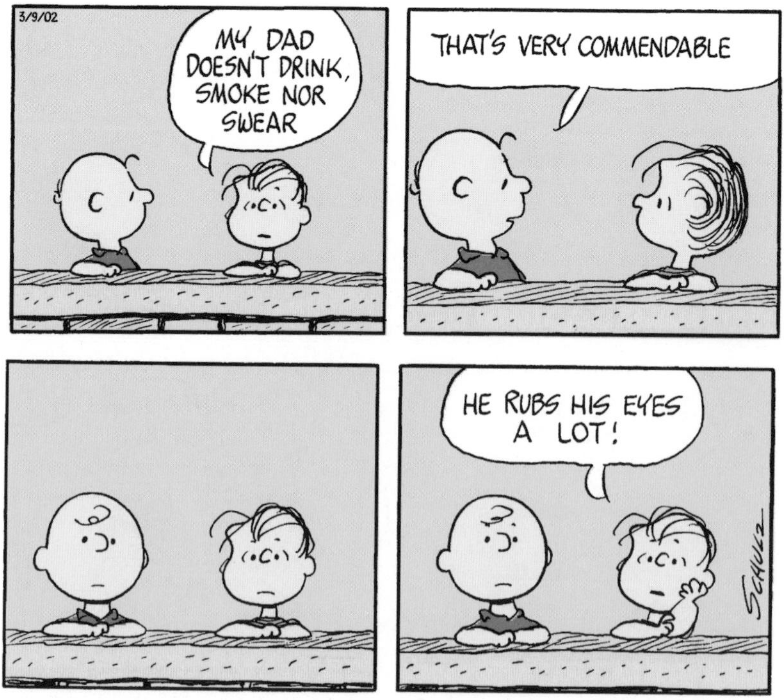
3/9/02
MY DAD DOESN'T DRINK, SMOKE NOR SWEAR
THAT'S VERY COMMENDABLE
HE RUBS HIS EYES A LOT!
SCHULZ

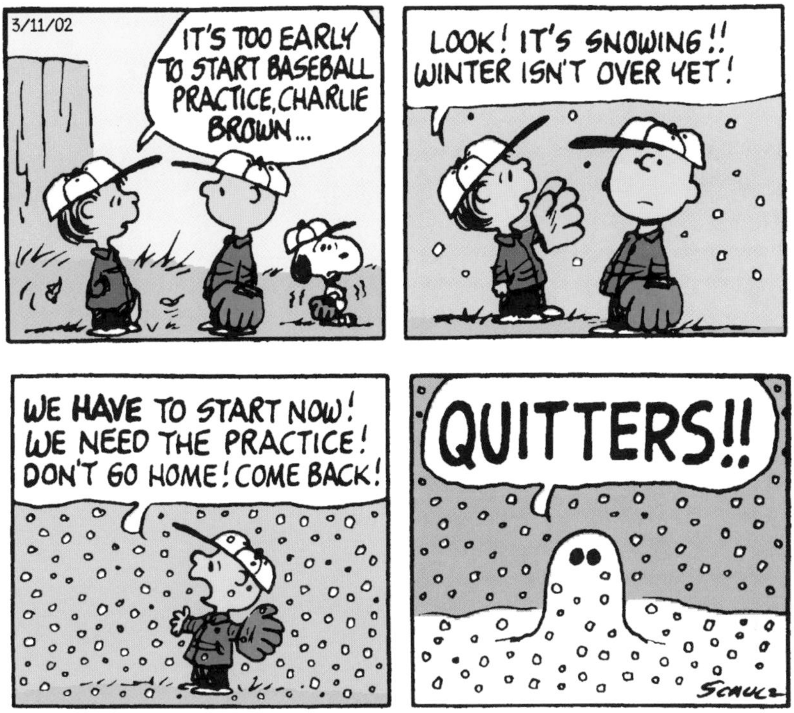
3/11/02
IT'S TOO EARLY TO START BASEBALL PRACTICE, CHARLIE BROWN...
LOOK! IT'S SNOWING!! WINTER ISN'T OVER YET!
WE **HAVE** TO START NOW! WE NEED THE PRACTICE! DON'T GO HOME! COME BACK!
QUITTERS!!
SCHULZ

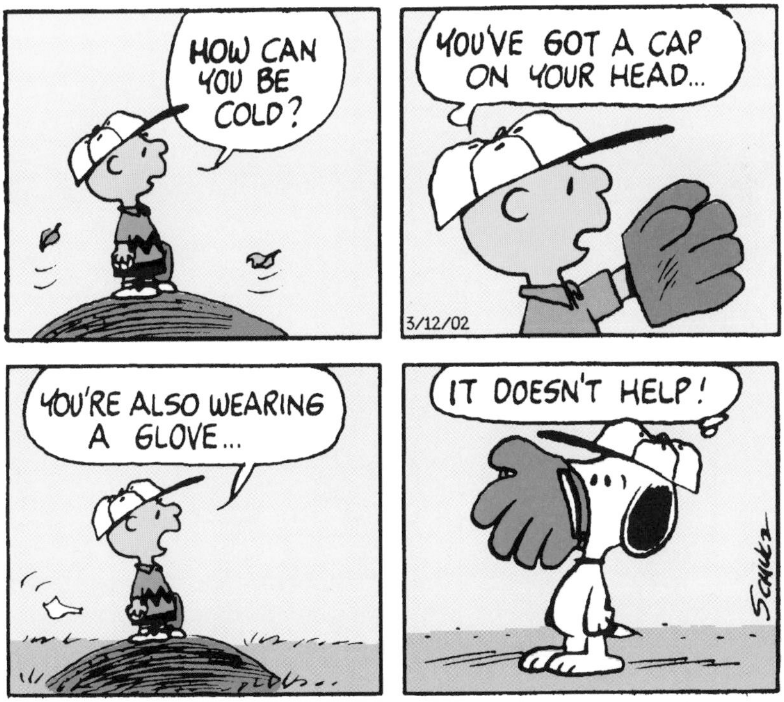
HOW CAN YOU BE COLD?
YOU'VE GOT A CAP ON YOUR HEAD...
3/12/02
YOU'RE ALSO WEARING A GLOVE...
IT DOESN'T HELP!
SCHULZ

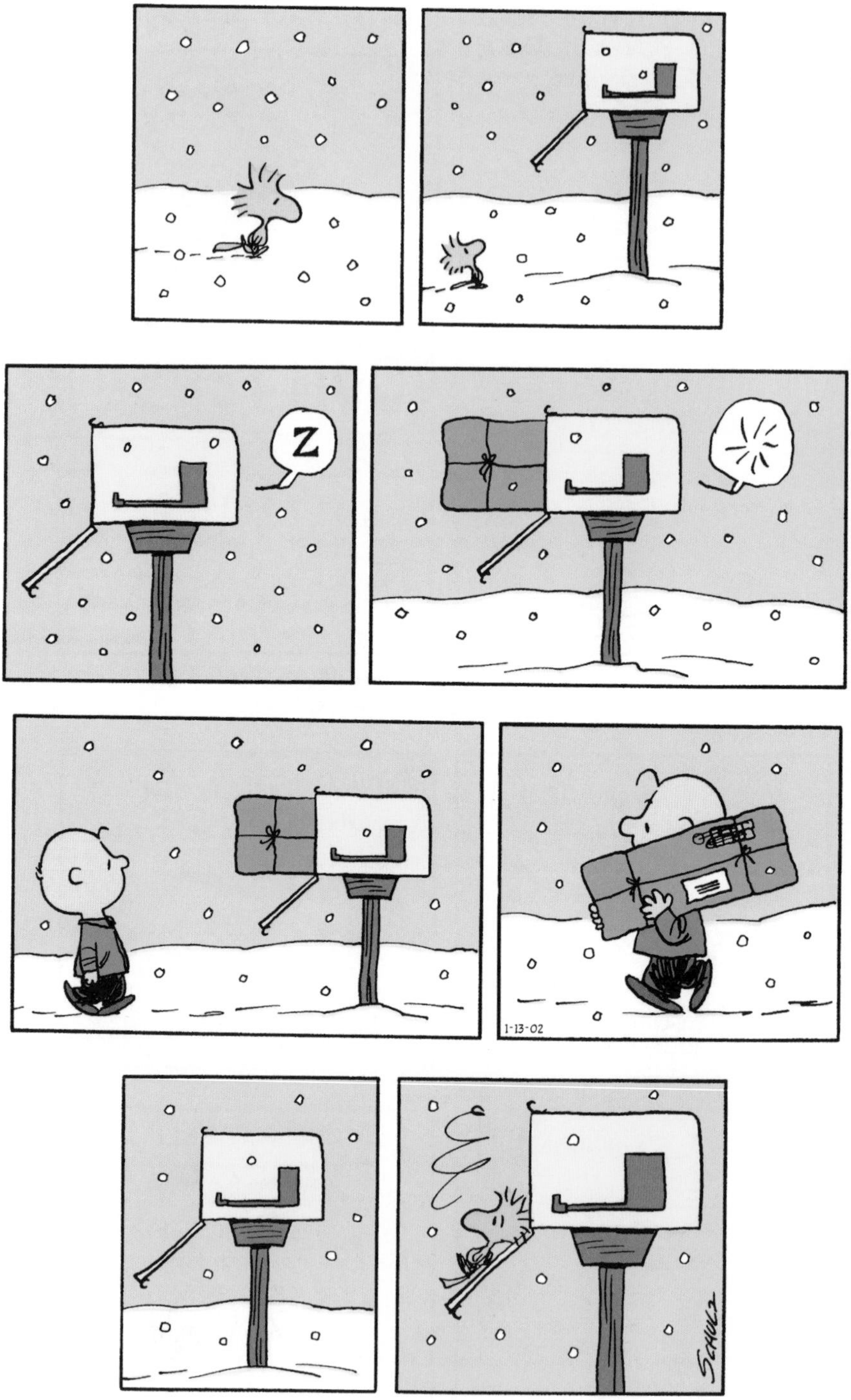
Z
1-13-02
SCHULZ

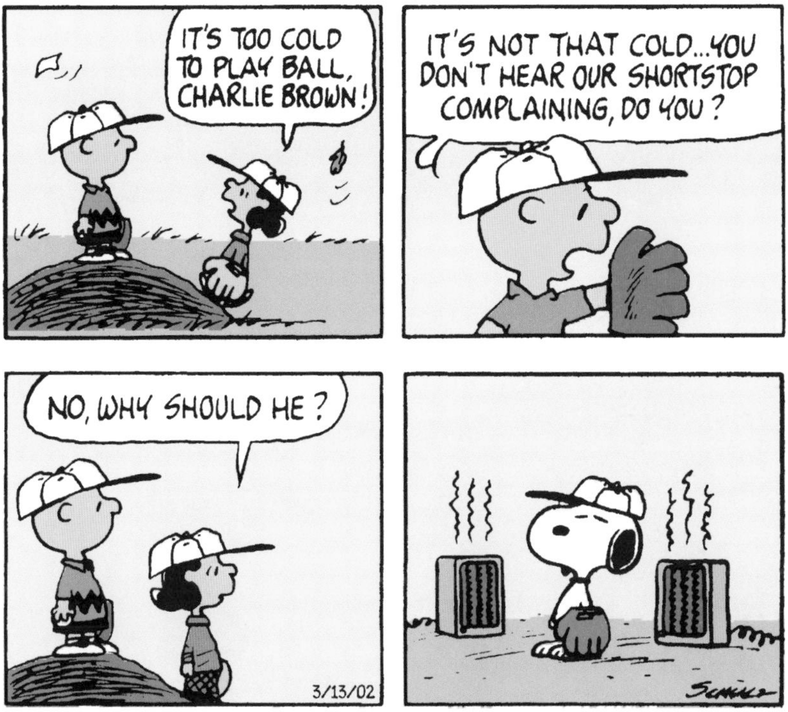
IT'S TOO COLD TO PLAY BALL, CHARLIE BROWN!
IT'S NOT THAT COLD...YOU DON'T HEAR OUR SHORTSTOP COMPLAINING, DO YOU?
NO, WHY SHOULD HE?
3/13/02

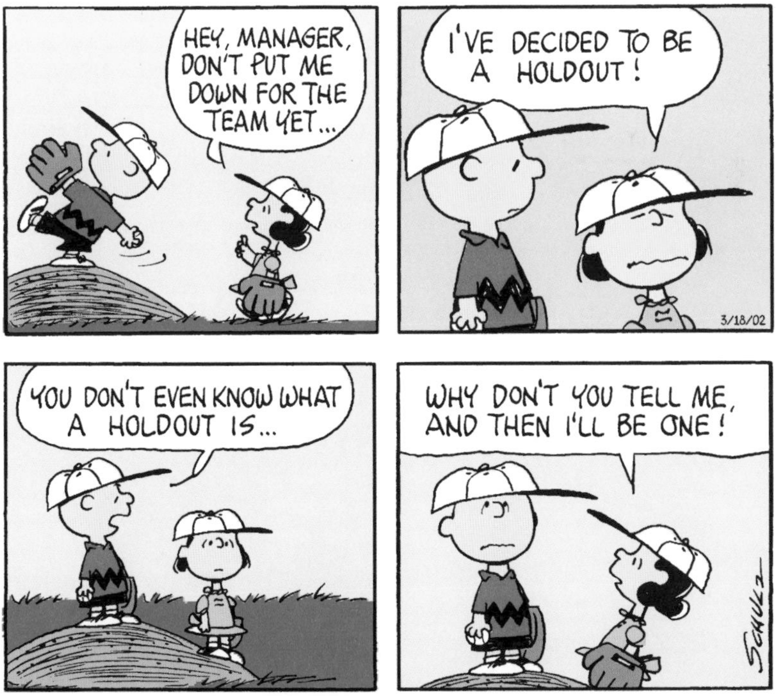
HEY, MANAGER, DON'T PUT ME DOWN FOR THE TEAM YET...
I'VE DECIDED TO BE A HOLDOUT!
3/18/02
YOU DON'T EVEN KNOW WHAT A HOLDOUT IS...
WHY DON'T YOU TELL ME, AND THEN I'LL BE ONE!

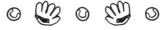

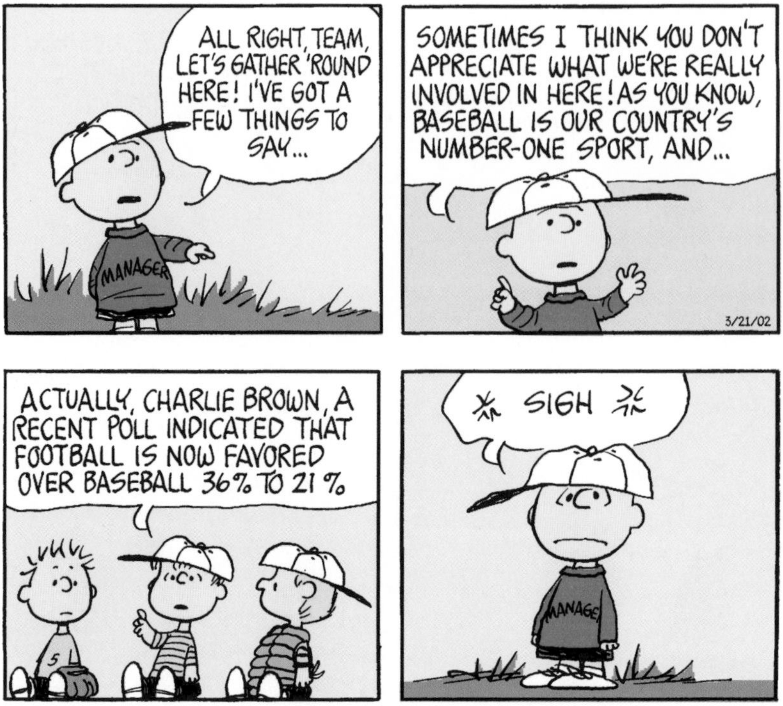
ALL RIGHT, TEAM, LET'S GATHER 'ROUND HERE! I'VE GOT A FEW THINGS TO SAY...
MANAGER
SOMETIMES I THINK YOU DON'T APPRECIATE WHAT WE'RE REALLY INVOLVED IN HERE! AS YOU KNOW, BASEBALL IS OUR COUNTRY'S NUMBER-ONE SPORT, AND...
3/21/02
ACTUALLY, CHARLIE BROWN, A RECENT POLL INDICATED THAT FOOTBALL IS NOW FAVORED OVER BASEBALL 36% TO 21%
SIGH

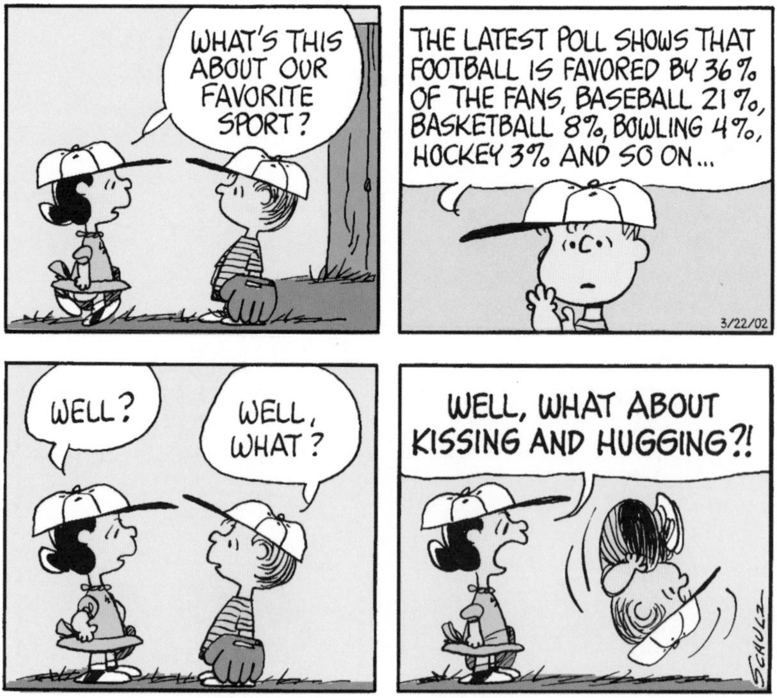
WHAT'S THIS ABOUT OUR FAVORITE SPORT?
THE LATEST POLL SHOWS THAT FOOTBALL IS FAVORED BY 36% OF THE FANS, BASEBALL 21%, BASKETBALL 8%, BOWLING 4%, HOCKEY 3% AND SO ON...
3/22/02
WELL?
WELL, WHAT?
WELL, WHAT ABOUT KISSING AND HUGGING?!
SCHULZ

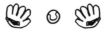

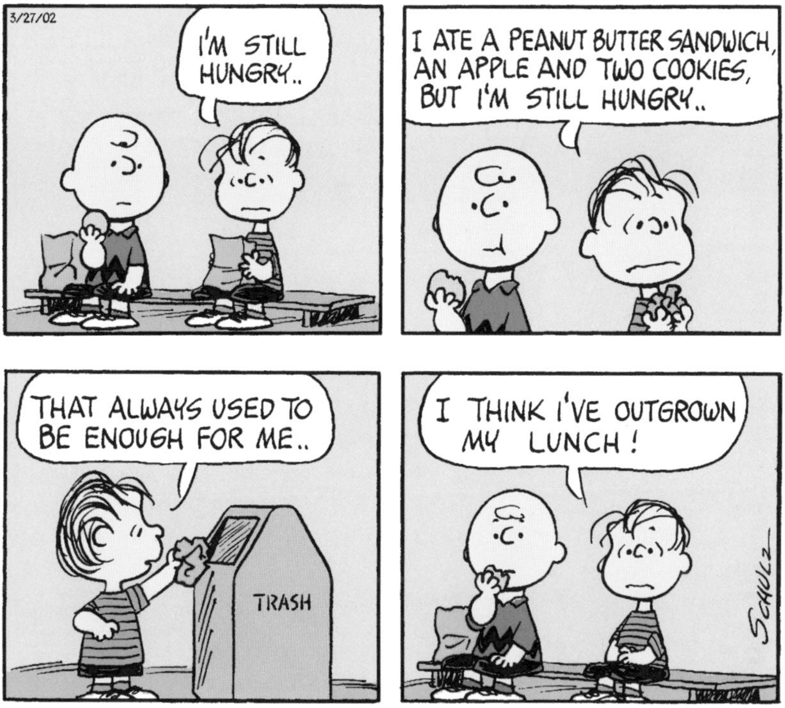
3/27/02
I'M STILL HUNGRY..
I ATE A PEANUT BUTTER SANDWICH, AN APPLE AND TWO COOKIES, BUT I'M STILL HUNGRY..
THAT ALWAYS USED TO BE ENOUGH FOR ME..
TRASH
I THINK I'VE OUTGROWN MY LUNCH!
SCHULZ

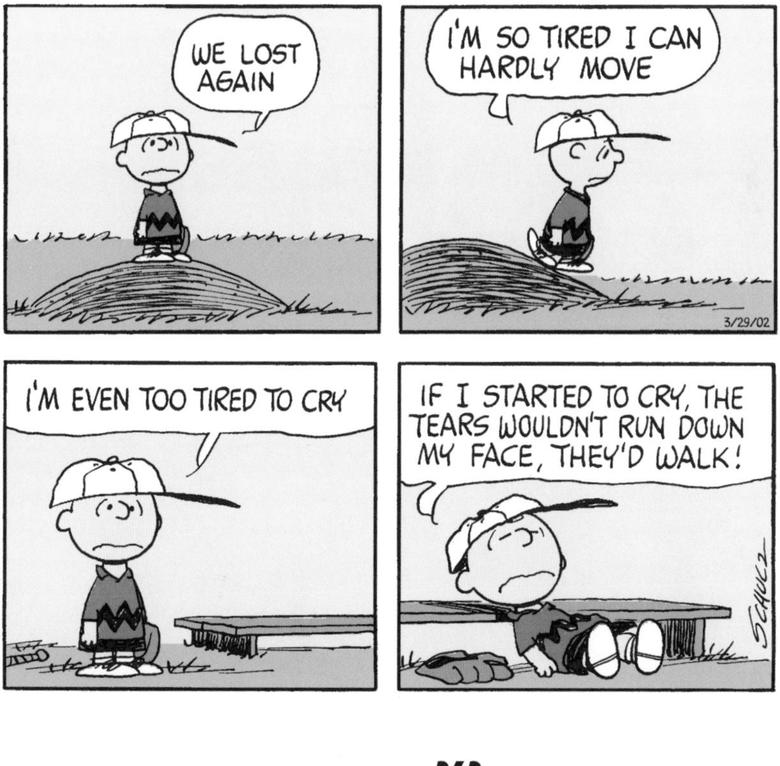
WE LOST AGAIN
I'M SO TIRED I CAN HARDLY MOVE
3/29/02
I'M EVEN TOO TIRED TO CRY
IF I STARTED TO CRY, THE TEARS WOULDN'T RUN DOWN MY FACE, THEY'D WALK!
SCHULZ

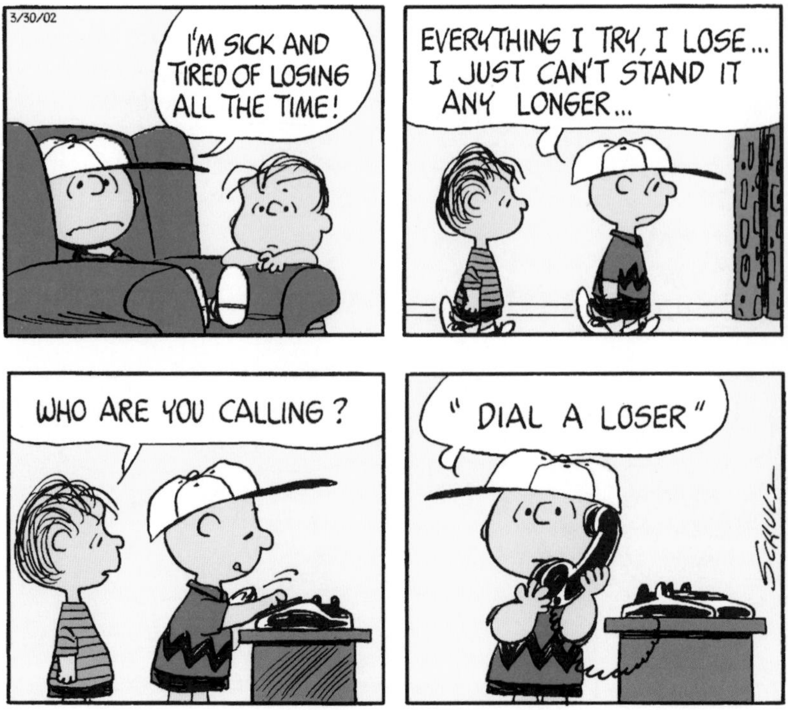
3/30/02
I'M SICK AND TIRED OF LOSING ALL THE TIME!
EVERYTHING I TRY, I LOSE... I JUST CAN'T STAND IT ANY LONGER...
WHO ARE YOU CALLING?
"DIAL A LOSER"
SCHULZ

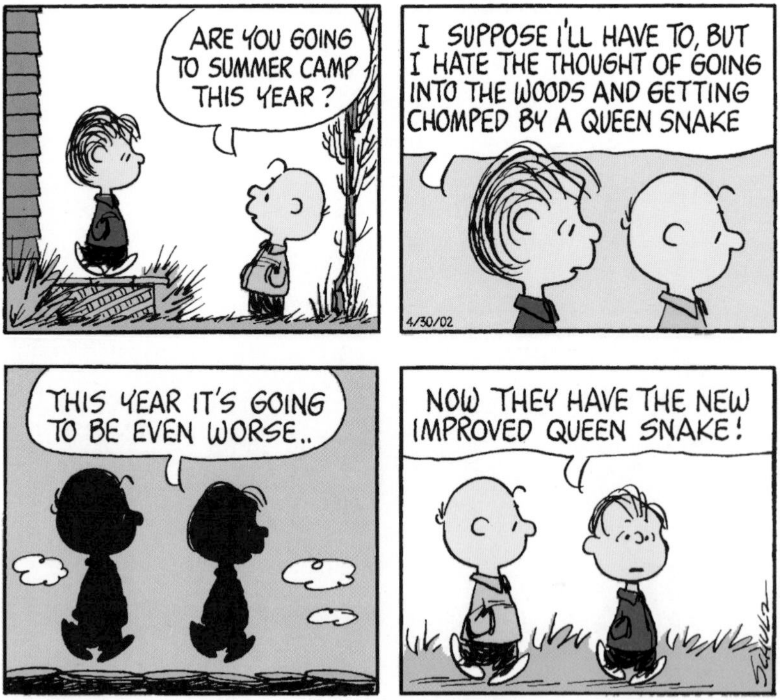
ARE YOU GOING TO SUMMER CAMP THIS YEAR?
I SUPPOSE I'LL HAVE TO, BUT I HATE THE THOUGHT OF GOING INTO THE WOODS AND GETTING CHOMPED BY A QUEEN SNAKE
4/30/02
THIS YEAR IT'S GOING TO BE EVEN WORSE..
NOW THEY HAVE THE NEW IMPROVED QUEEN SNAKE!
SCHULZ

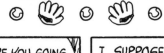

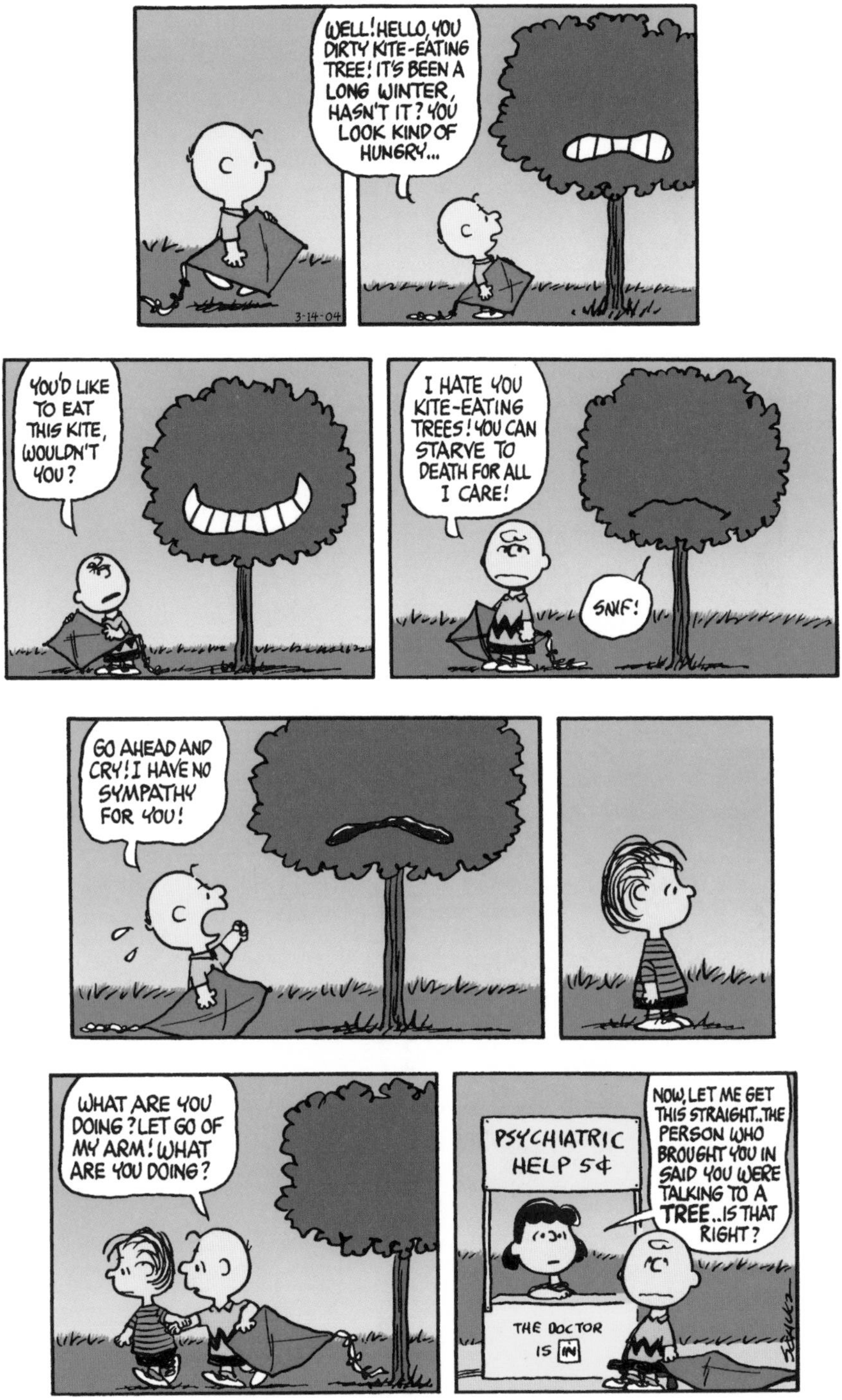
3-14-04
WELL! HELLO, YOU DIRTY KITE-EATING TREE! IT'S BEEN A LONG WINTER, HASN'T IT? YOU LOOK KIND OF HUNGRY...
YOU'D LIKE TO EAT THIS KITE, WOULDN'T YOU?
I HATE YOU KITE-EATING TREES! YOU CAN STARVE TO DEATH FOR ALL I CARE!
SNIF!
GO AHEAD AND CRY! I HAVE NO SYMPATHY FOR YOU!
WHAT ARE YOU DOING? LET GO OF MY ARM! WHAT ARE YOU DOING?
PSYCHIATRIC HELP 5¢
THE DOCTOR IS IN
NOW, LET ME GET THIS STRAIGHT..THE PERSON WHO BROUGHT YOU IN SAID YOU WERE TALKING TO A TREE..IS THAT RIGHT?
SCHULZ

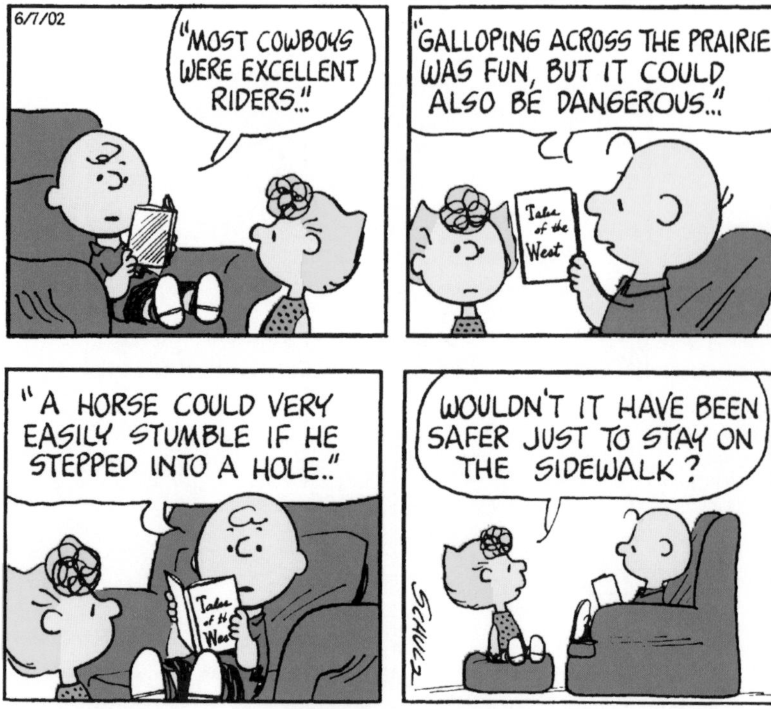
6/7/02
"MOST COWBOYS WERE EXCELLENT RIDERS."
"GALLOPING ACROSS THE PRAIRIE WAS FUN, BUT IT COULD ALSO BE DANGEROUS."
Tales of the West
"A HORSE COULD VERY EASILY STUMBLE IF HE STEPPED INTO A HOLE."
WOULDN'T IT HAVE BEEN SAFER JUST TO STAY ON THE SIDEWALK?
SCHULZ

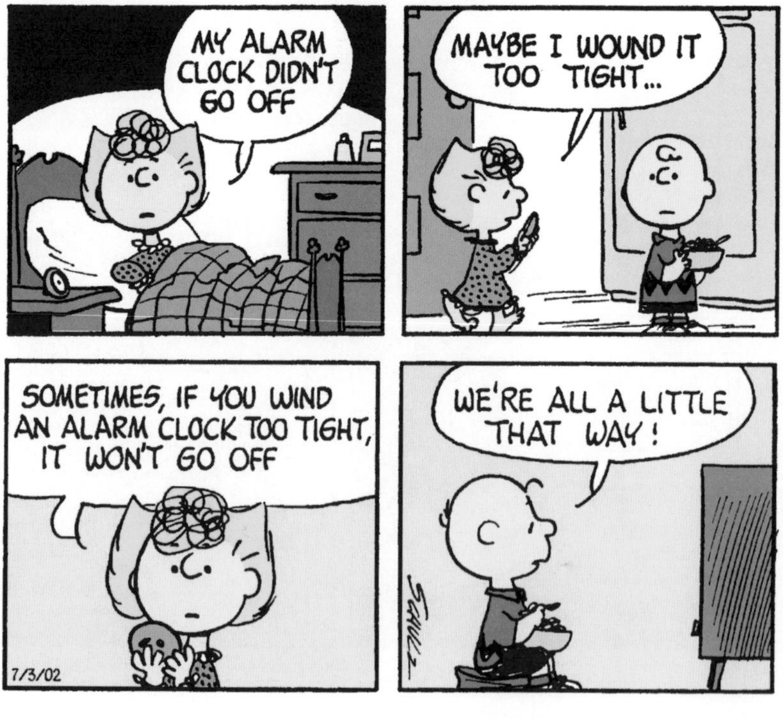
MY ALARM CLOCK DIDN'T GO OFF
MAYBE I WOUND IT TOO TIGHT...
SOMETIMES, IF YOU WIND AN ALARM CLOCK TOO TIGHT, IT WON'T GO OFF
7/3/02
WE'RE ALL A LITTLE THAT WAY!
SCHULZ

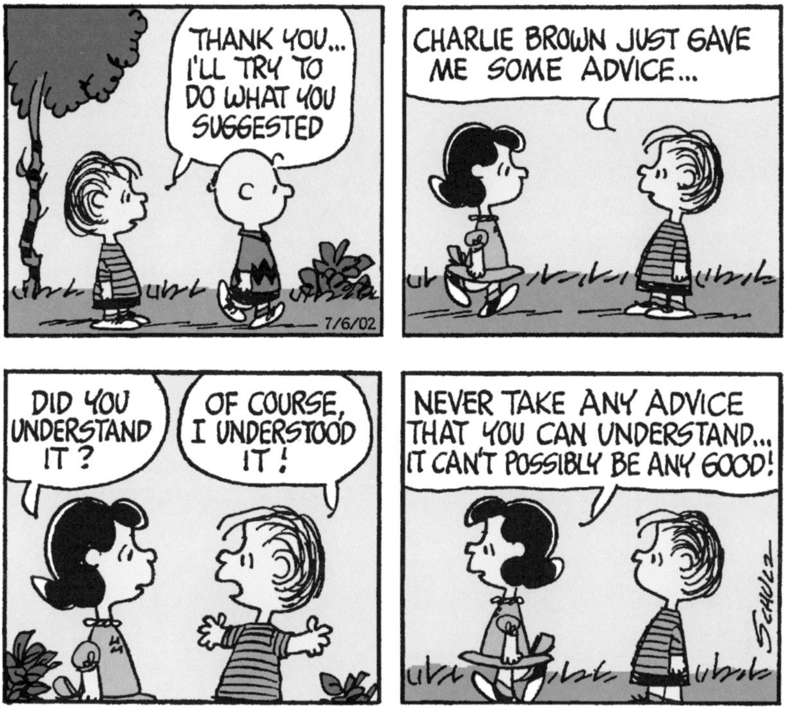
THANK YOU... I'LL TRY TO DO WHAT YOU SUGGESTED
7/6/02
CHARLIE BROWN JUST GAVE ME SOME ADVICE...
DID YOU UNDERSTAND IT ?
OF COURSE, I UNDERSTOOD IT !
NEVER TAKE ANY ADVICE THAT YOU CAN UNDERSTAND... IT CAN'T POSSIBLY BE ANY GOOD!
SCHULZ

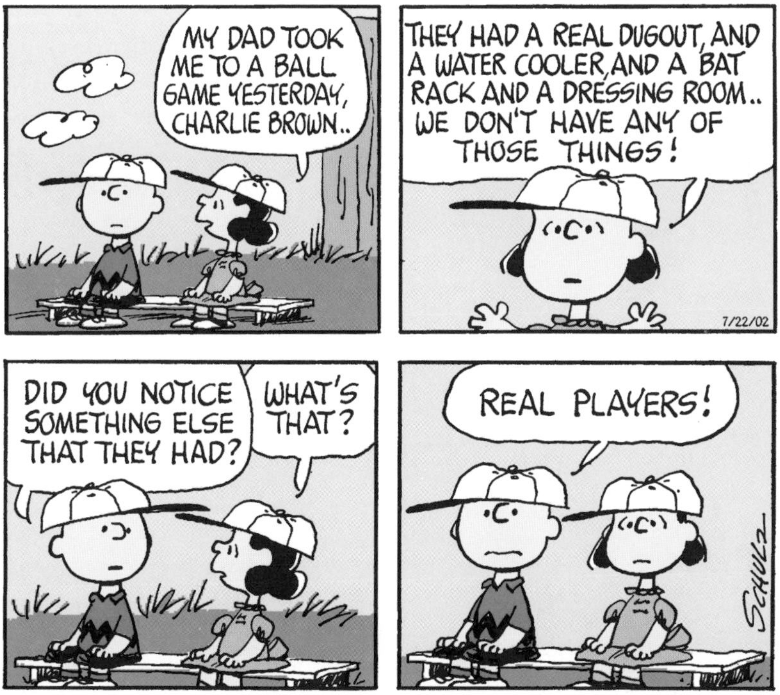
MY DAD TOOK ME TO A BALL GAME YESTERDAY, CHARLIE BROWN..
THEY HAD A REAL DUGOUT, AND A WATER COOLER, AND A BAT RACK AND A DRESSING ROOM.. WE DON'T HAVE ANY OF THOSE THINGS !
7/22/02
DID YOU NOTICE SOMETHING ELSE THAT THEY HAD?
WHAT'S THAT?
REAL PLAYERS!
SCHULZ

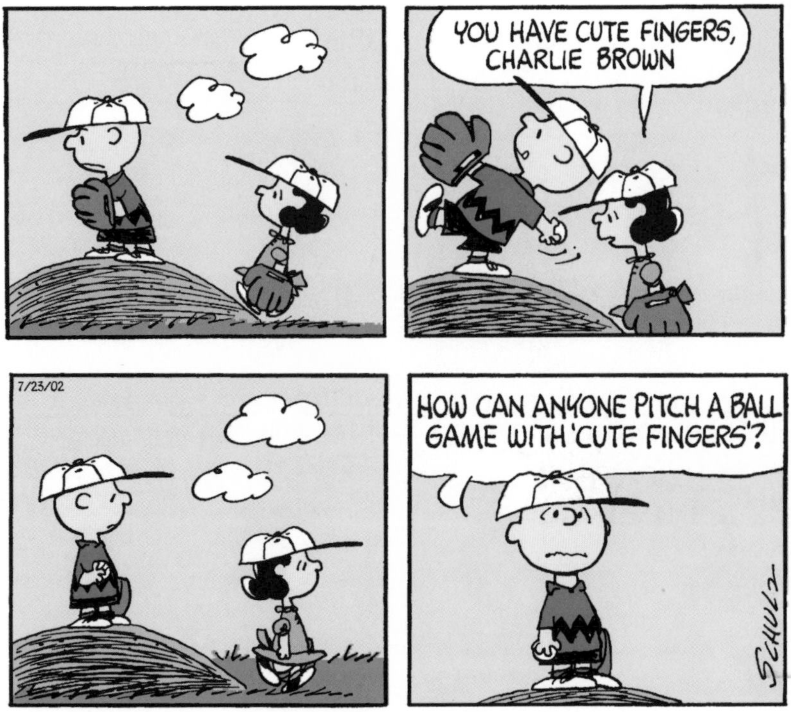
YOU HAVE CUTE FINGERS, CHARLIE BROWN
7/23/02
HOW CAN ANYONE PITCH A BALL GAME WITH 'CUTE FINGERS'?
SCHULZ

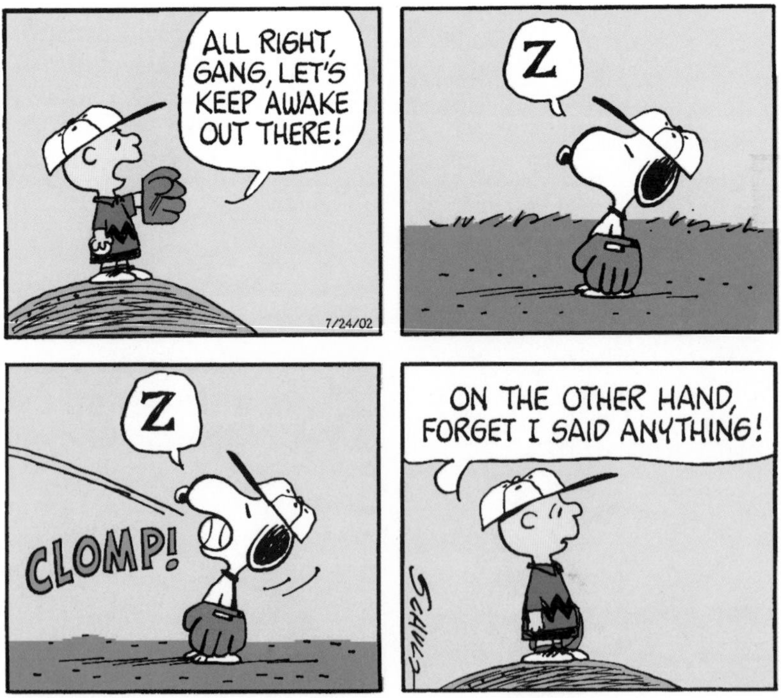
ALL RIGHT, GANG, LET'S KEEP AWAKE OUT THERE!
7/24/02
Z
Z
CLOMP!
ON THE OTHER HAND, FORGET I SAID ANYTHING!
SCHULZ

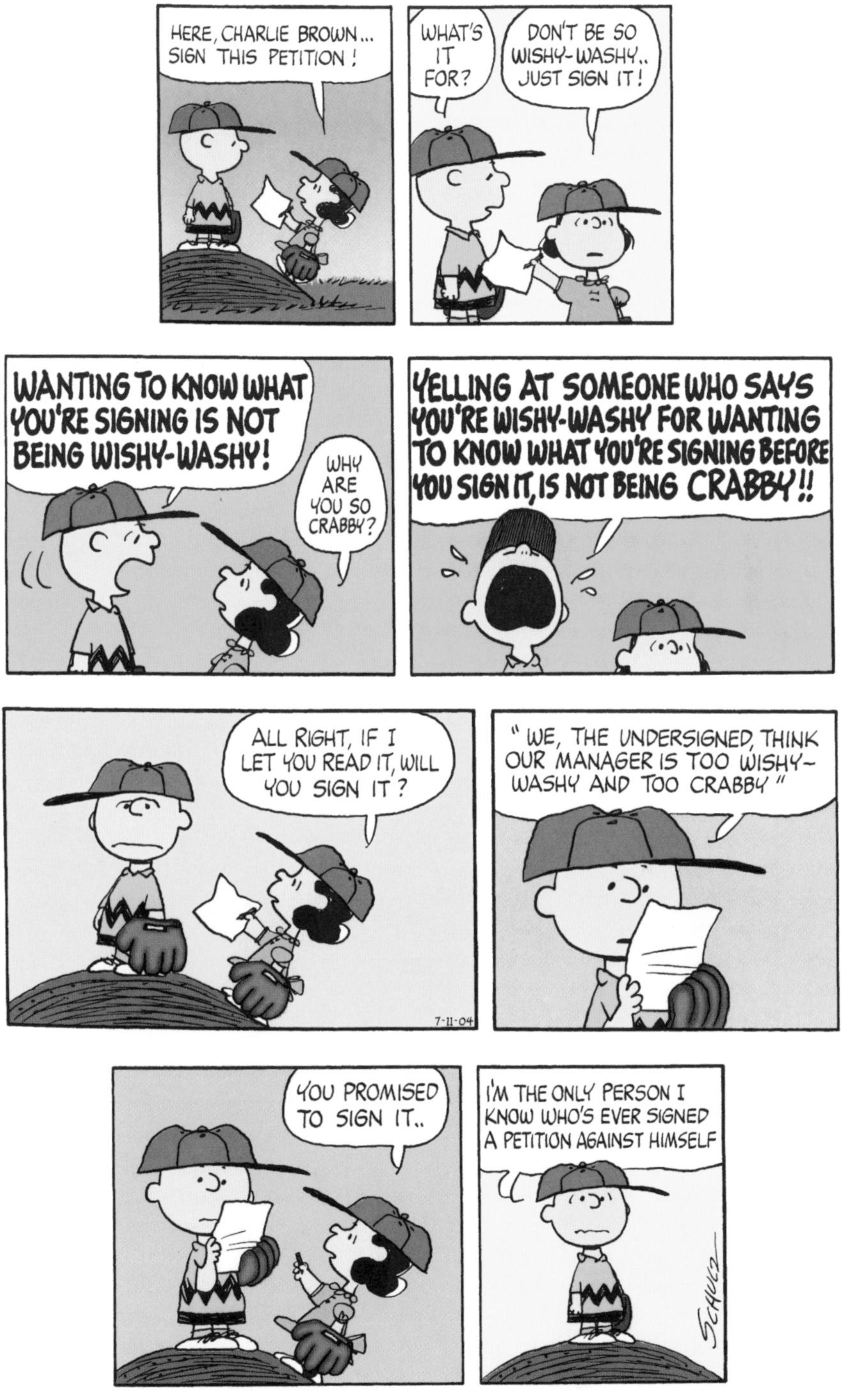

HERE, CHARLIE BROWN... SIGN THIS PETITION!
WHAT'S IT FOR?
DON'T BE SO WISHY-WASHY.. JUST SIGN IT!
WANTING TO KNOW WHAT YOU'RE SIGNING IS NOT BEING WISHY-WASHY!
WHY ARE YOU SO CRABBY?
YELLING AT SOMEONE WHO SAYS YOU'RE WISHY-WASHY FOR WANTING TO KNOW WHAT YOU'RE SIGNING BEFORE YOU SIGN IT, IS NOT BEING CRABBY!!
ALL RIGHT, IF I LET YOU READ IT, WILL YOU SIGN IT?
7-11-04
"WE, THE UNDERSIGNED, THINK OUR MANAGER IS TOO WISHY-WASHY AND TOO CRABBY"
YOU PROMISED TO SIGN IT..
I'M THE ONLY PERSON I KNOW WHO'S EVER SIGNED A PETITION AGAINST HIMSELF
SCHULZ

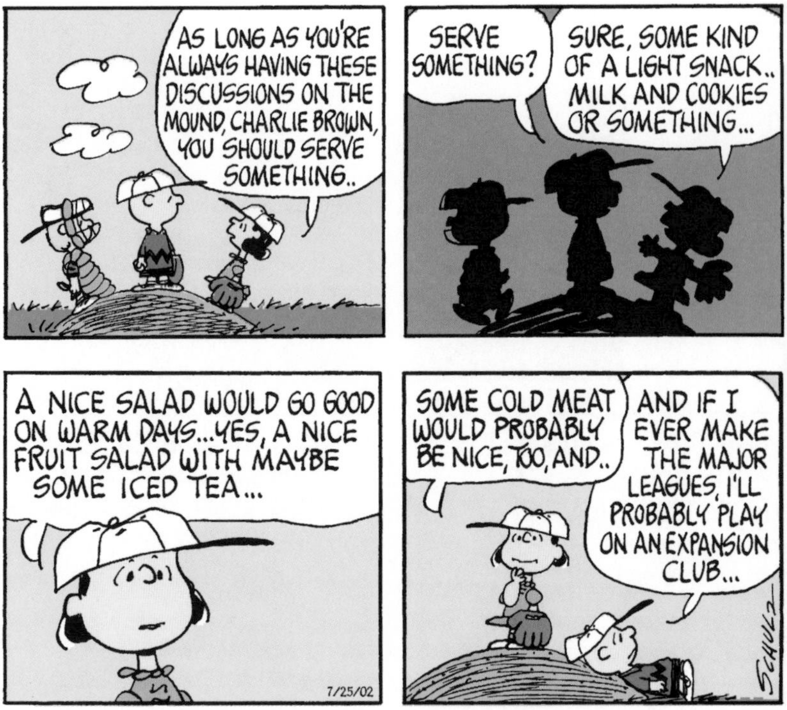
AS LONG AS YOU'RE ALWAYS HAVING THESE DISCUSSIONS ON THE MOUND, CHARLIE BROWN, YOU SHOULD SERVE SOMETHING..
SERVE SOMETHING?
SURE, SOME KIND OF A LIGHT SNACK.. MILK AND COOKIES OR SOMETHING...
A NICE SALAD WOULD GO GOOD ON WARM DAYS...YES, A NICE FRUIT SALAD WITH MAYBE SOME ICED TEA...
7/25/02
SOME COLD MEAT WOULD PROBABLY BE NICE, TOO, AND..
AND IF I EVER MAKE THE MAJOR LEAGUES, I'LL PROBABLY PLAY ON AN EXPANSION CLUB...
SCHULZ

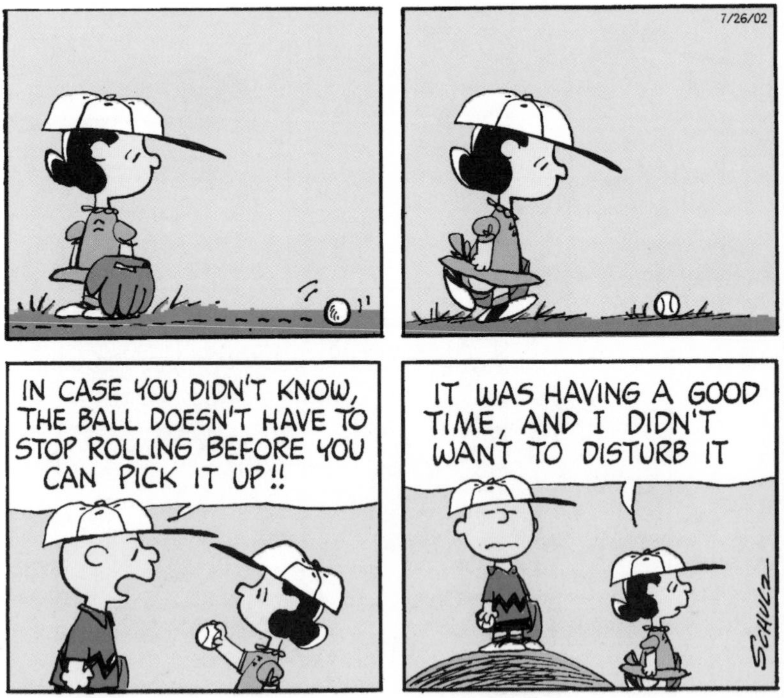
7/26/02
IN CASE YOU DIDN'T KNOW, THE BALL DOESN'T HAVE TO STOP ROLLING BEFORE YOU CAN PICK IT UP!!
IT WAS HAVING A GOOD TIME, AND I DIDN'T WANT TO DISTURB IT
SCHULZ

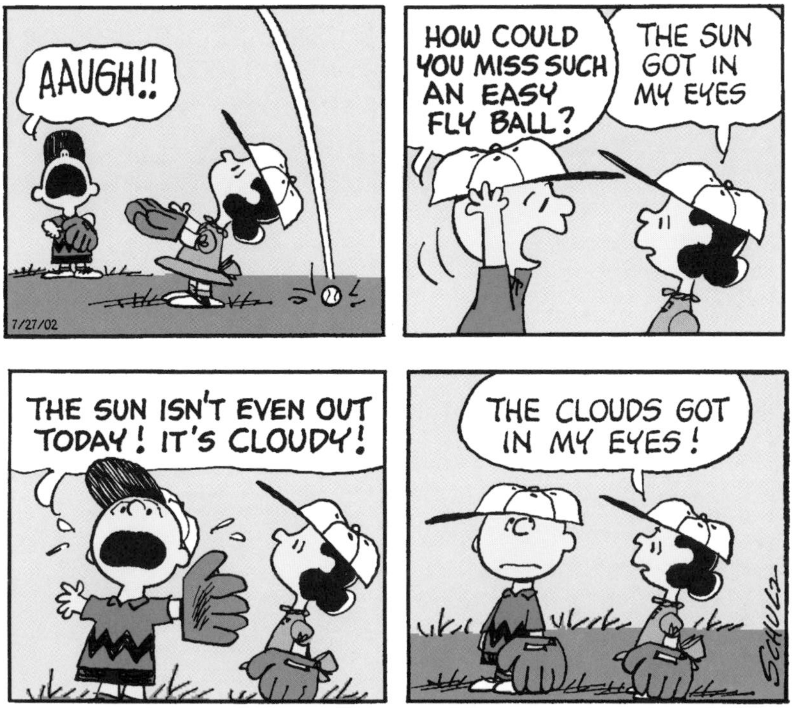
7/27/02
AAUGH!!
HOW COULD YOU MISS SUCH AN EASY FLY BALL?
THE SUN GOT IN MY EYES
THE SUN ISN'T EVEN OUT TODAY! IT'S CLOUDY!
THE CLOUDS GOT IN MY EYES!
SCHULZ

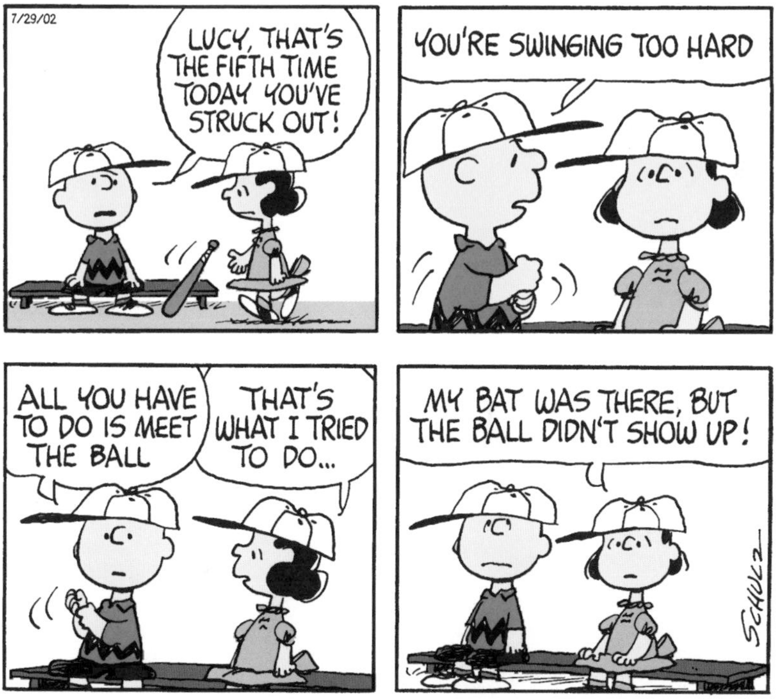
7/29/02
LUCY, THAT'S THE FIFTH TIME TODAY YOU'VE STRUCK OUT!
YOU'RE SWINGING TOO HARD
ALL YOU HAVE TO DO IS MEET THE BALL
THAT'S WHAT I TRIED TO DO...
MY BAT WAS THERE, BUT THE BALL DIDN'T SHOW UP!
SCHULZ

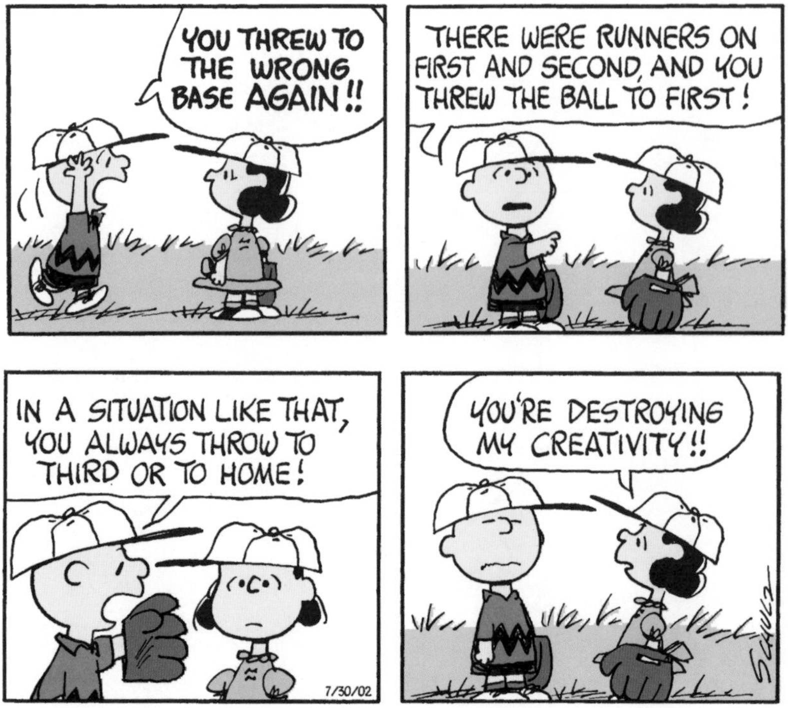
YOU THREW TO THE WRONG BASE AGAIN!!
THERE WERE RUNNERS ON FIRST AND SECOND, AND YOU THREW THE BALL TO FIRST!
IN A SITUATION LIKE THAT, YOU ALWAYS THROW TO THIRD OR TO HOME!
7/30/02
YOU'RE DESTROYING MY CREATIVITY!!
SCHULZ

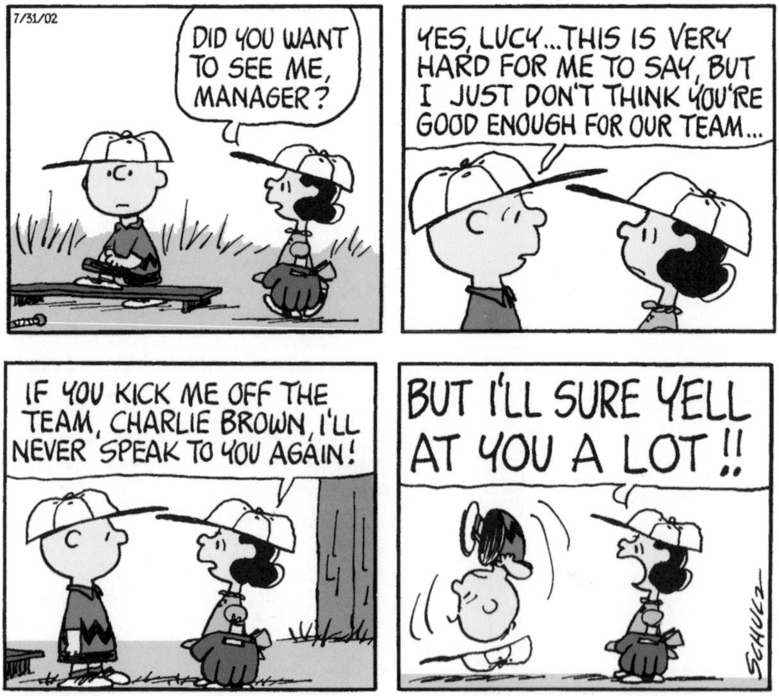
7/31/02
DID YOU WANT TO SEE ME, MANAGER?
YES, LUCY...THIS IS VERY HARD FOR ME TO SAY, BUT I JUST DON'T THINK YOU'RE GOOD ENOUGH FOR OUR TEAM...
IF YOU KICK ME OFF THE TEAM, CHARLIE BROWN, I'LL NEVER SPEAK TO YOU AGAIN!
BUT I'LL SURE YELL AT YOU A LOT!!
SCHULZ

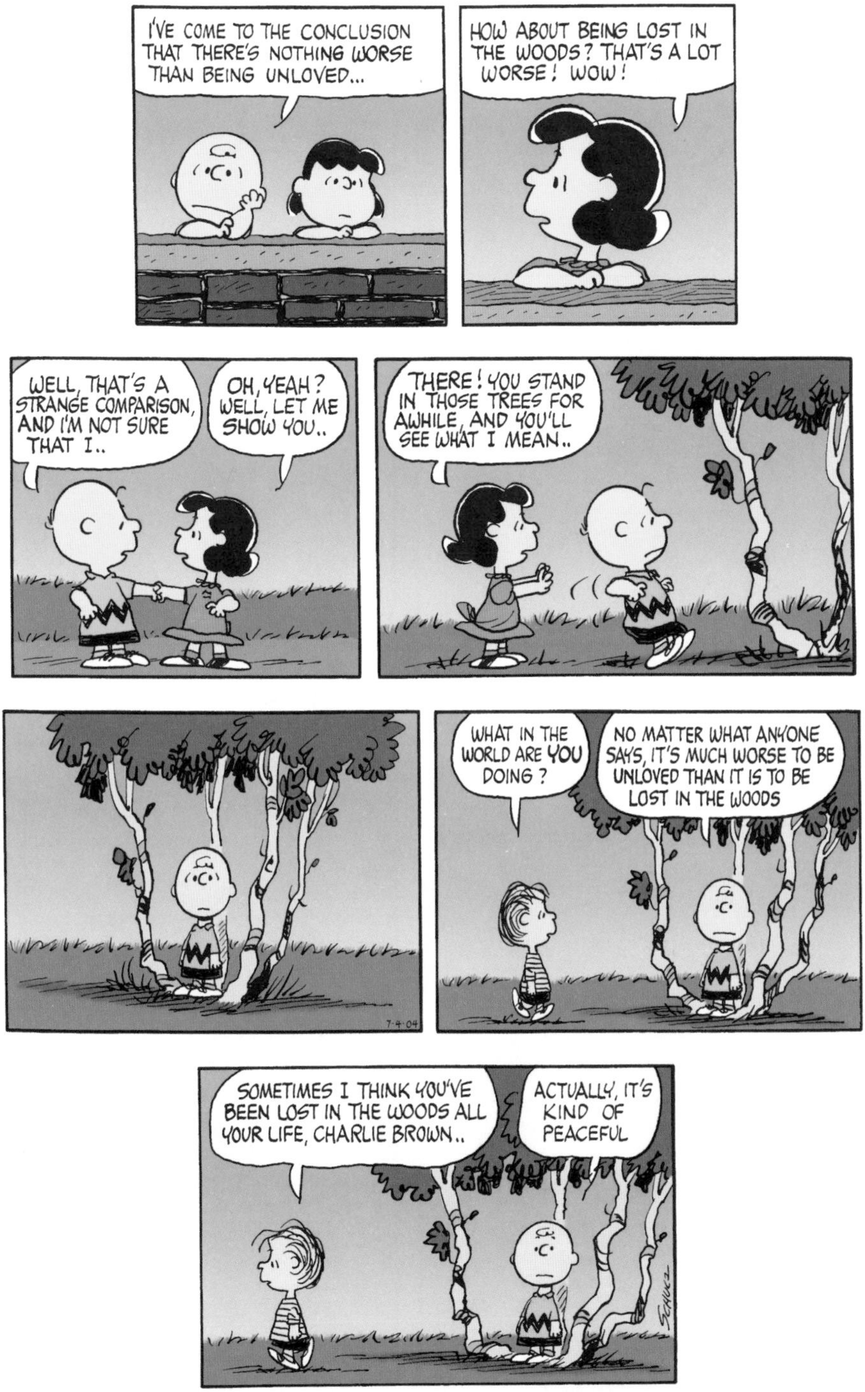
I'VE COME TO THE CONCLUSION THAT THERE'S NOTHING WORSE THAN BEING UNLOVED...
HOW ABOUT BEING LOST IN THE WOODS? THAT'S A LOT WORSE! WOW!
WELL, THAT'S A STRANGE COMPARISON, AND I'M NOT SURE THAT I..
OH, YEAH? WELL, LET ME SHOW YOU..
THERE! YOU STAND IN THOSE TREES FOR AWHILE, AND YOU'LL SEE WHAT I MEAN..
7-4-04
WHAT IN THE WORLD ARE YOU DOING?
NO MATTER WHAT ANYONE SAYS, IT'S MUCH WORSE TO BE UNLOVED THAN IT IS TO BE LOST IN THE WOODS
SOMETIMES I THINK YOU'VE BEEN LOST IN THE WOODS ALL YOUR LIFE, CHARLIE BROWN..
ACTUALLY, IT'S KIND OF PEACEFUL
SCHULZ

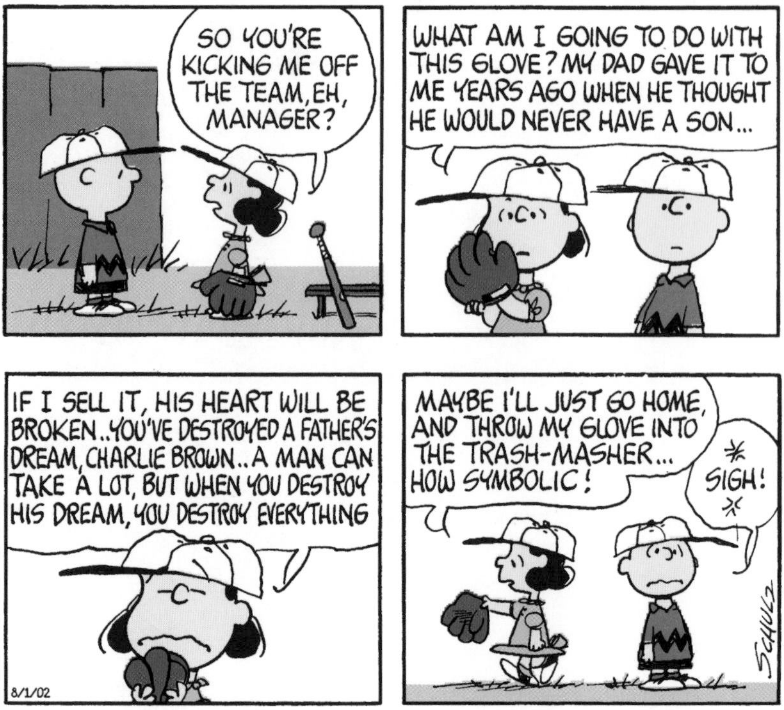
SO YOU'RE KICKING ME OFF THE TEAM, EH, MANAGER?
WHAT AM I GOING TO DO WITH THIS GLOVE? MY DAD GAVE IT TO ME YEARS AGO WHEN HE THOUGHT HE WOULD NEVER HAVE A SON...
IF I SELL IT, HIS HEART WILL BE BROKEN.. YOU'VE DESTROYED A FATHER'S DREAM, CHARLIE BROWN.. A MAN CAN TAKE A LOT, BUT WHEN YOU DESTROY HIS DREAM, YOU DESTROY EVERYTHING
8/1/02
MAYBE I'LL JUST GO HOME, AND THROW MY GLOVE INTO THE TRASH-MASHER... HOW SYMBOLIC!
SIGH!
SCHULZ

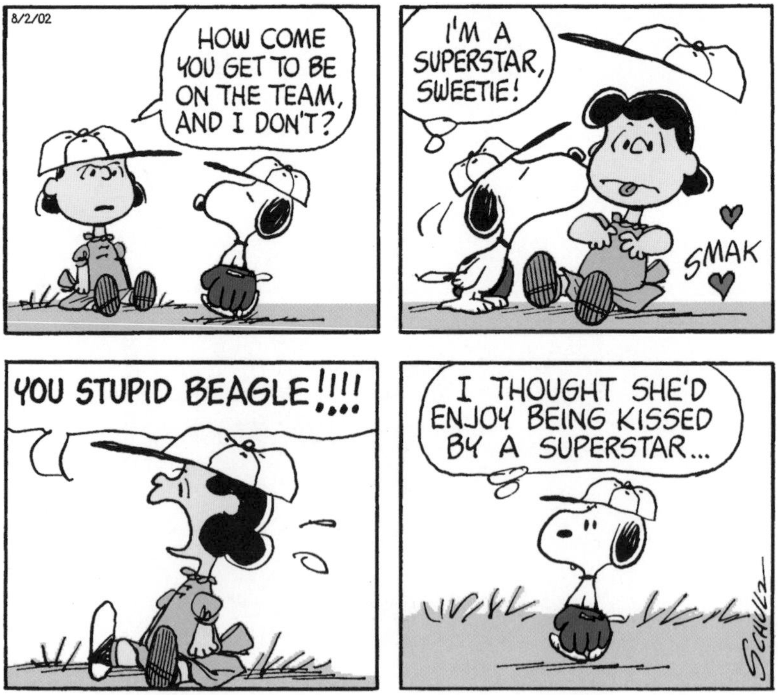
8/2/02
HOW COME YOU GET TO BE ON THE TEAM, AND I DON'T?
I'M A SUPERSTAR, SWEETIE!
SMAK
YOU STUPID BEAGLE!!!!
I THOUGHT SHE'D ENJOY BEING KISSED BY A SUPERSTAR...
SCHULZ

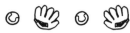

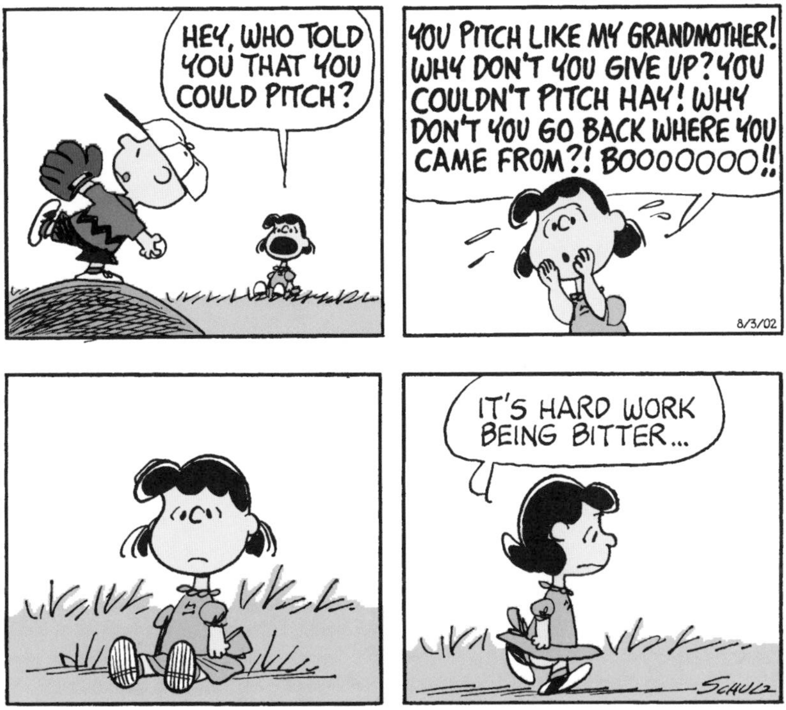
HEY, WHO TOLD YOU THAT YOU COULD PITCH?
YOU PITCH LIKE MY GRANDMOTHER! WHY DON'T YOU GIVE UP? YOU COULDN'T PITCH HAY! WHY DON'T YOU GO BACK WHERE YOU CAME FROM?! BOOOOOOO!!
8/3/02
IT'S HARD WORK BEING BITTER...
SCHULZ

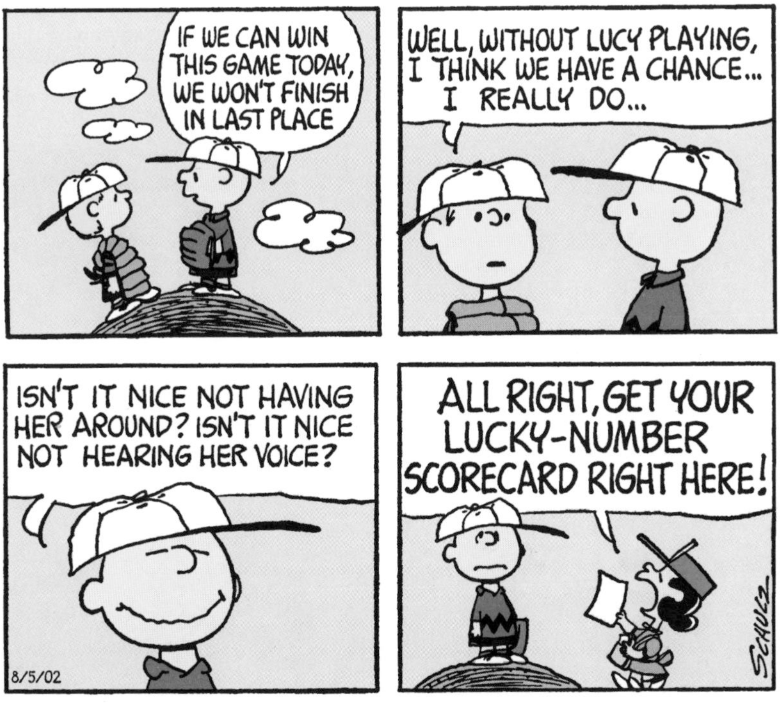
IF WE CAN WIN THIS GAME TODAY, WE WON'T FINISH IN LAST PLACE
WELL, WITHOUT LUCY PLAYING, I THINK WE HAVE A CHANCE... I REALLY DO...
ISN'T IT NICE NOT HAVING HER AROUND? ISN'T IT NICE NOT HEARING HER VOICE?
8/5/02
ALL RIGHT, GET YOUR LUCKY-NUMBER SCORECARD RIGHT HERE!
SCHULZ

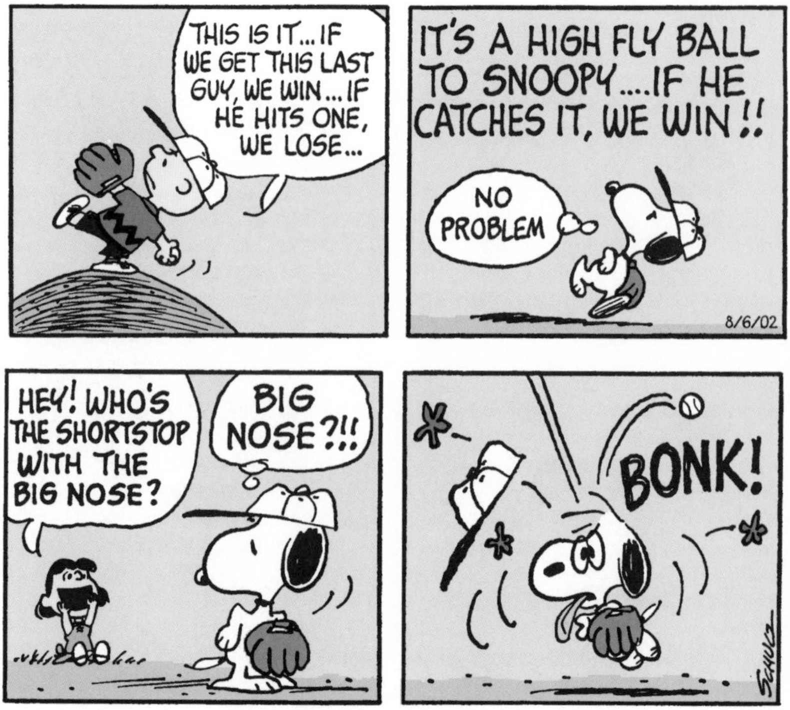
THIS IS IT... IF WE GET THIS LAST GUY, WE WIN... IF HE HITS ONE, WE LOSE...
IT'S A HIGH FLY BALL TO SNOOPY....IF HE CATCHES IT, WE WIN!!
NO PROBLEM
8/6/02
HEY! WHO'S THE SHORTSTOP WITH THE BIG NOSE?
BIG NOSE?!!
BONK!
SCHULZ

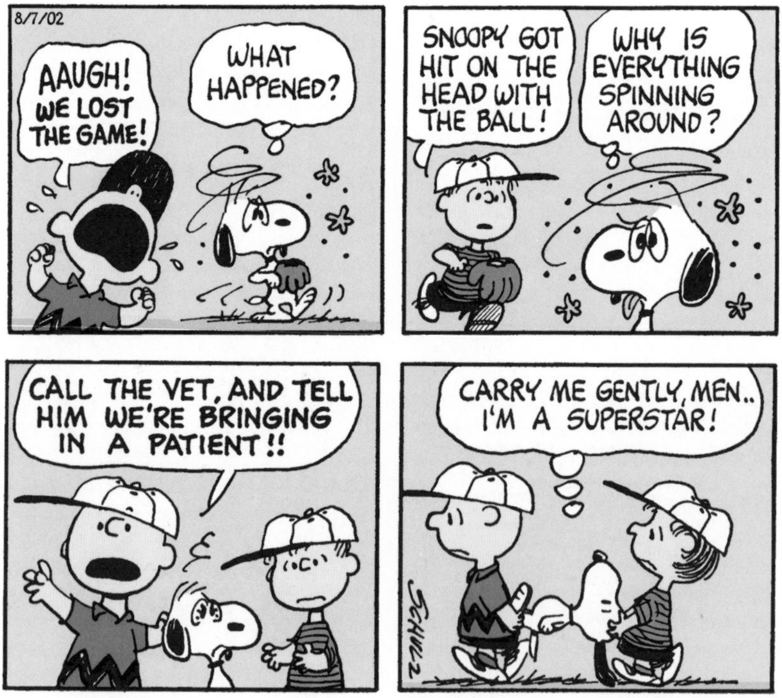
8/7/02
AAUGH! WE LOST THE GAME!
WHAT HAPPENED?
SNOOPY GOT HIT ON THE HEAD WITH THE BALL!
WHY IS EVERYTHING SPINNING AROUND?
CALL THE VET, AND TELL HIM WE'RE BRINGING IN A PATIENT!!
CARRY ME GENTLY, MEN.. I'M A SUPERSTAR!
SCHULZ

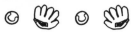

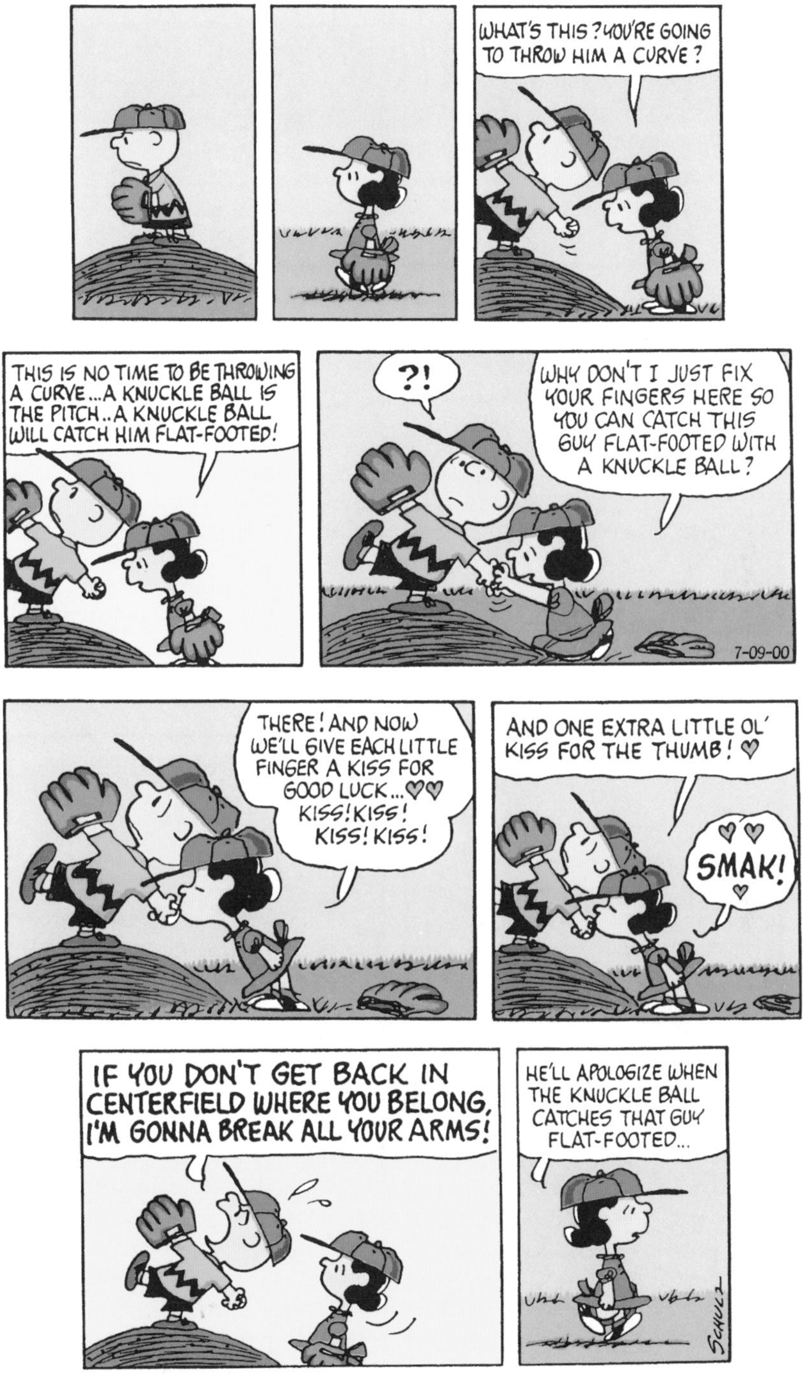
WHAT'S THIS? YOU'RE GOING TO THROW HIM A CURVE?
THIS IS NO TIME TO BE THROWING A CURVE...A KNUCKLE BALL IS THE PITCH..A KNUCKLE BALL WILL CATCH HIM FLAT-FOOTED!
?!
WHY DON'T I JUST FIX YOUR FINGERS HERE SO YOU CAN CATCH THIS GUY FLAT-FOOTED WITH A KNUCKLE BALL?
7-09-00
THERE! AND NOW WE'LL GIVE EACH LITTLE FINGER A KISS FOR GOOD LUCK... KISS! KISS! KISS! KISS!
AND ONE EXTRA LITTLE OL' KISS FOR THE THUMB!
SMAK!
IF YOU DON'T GET BACK IN CENTERFIELD WHERE YOU BELONG, I'M GONNA BREAK ALL YOUR ARMS!
HE'LL APOLOGIZE WHEN THE KNUCKLE BALL CATCHES THAT GUY FLAT-FOOTED...
SCHULZ

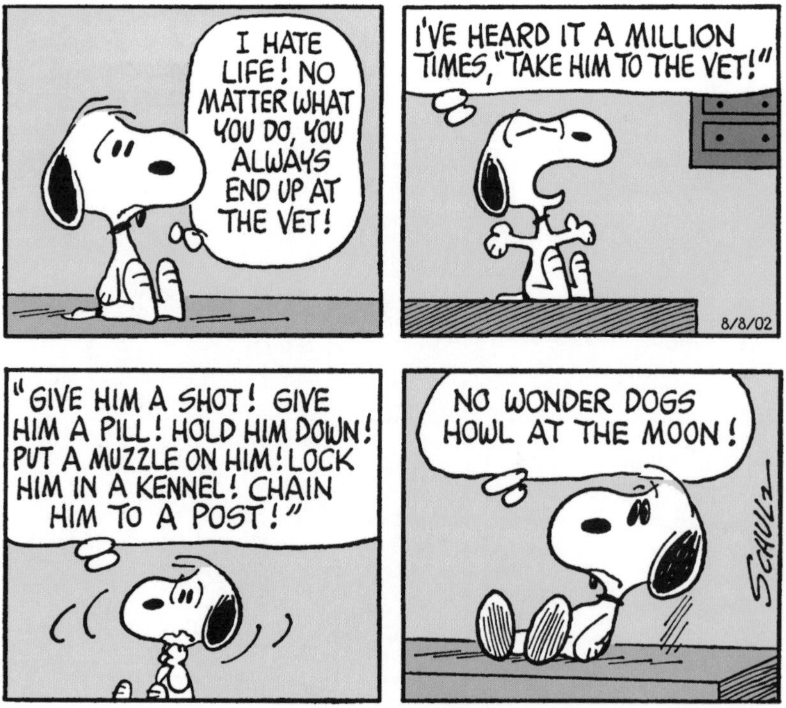
I HATE LIFE! NO MATTER WHAT YOU DO, YOU ALWAYS END UP AT THE VET!
I'VE HEARD IT A MILLION TIMES, "TAKE HIM TO THE VET!"
8/8/02
"GIVE HIM A SHOT! GIVE HIM A PILL! HOLD HIM DOWN! PUT A MUZZLE ON HIM! LOCK HIM IN A KENNEL! CHAIN HIM TO A POST!"
NO WONDER DOGS HOWL AT THE MOON!
SCHULZ

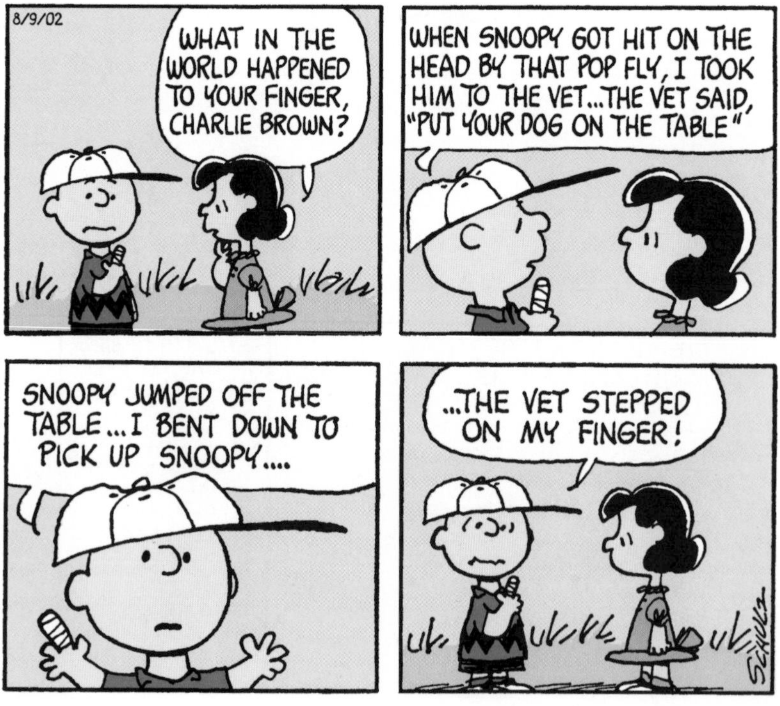
8/9/02
WHAT IN THE WORLD HAPPENED TO YOUR FINGER, CHARLIE BROWN?
WHEN SNOOPY GOT HIT ON THE HEAD BY THAT POP FLY, I TOOK HIM TO THE VET...THE VET SAID, "PUT YOUR DOG ON THE TABLE"
SNOOPY JUMPED OFF THE TABLE...I BENT DOWN TO PICK UP SNOOPY....
...THE VET STEPPED ON MY FINGER!
SCHULZ

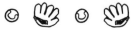

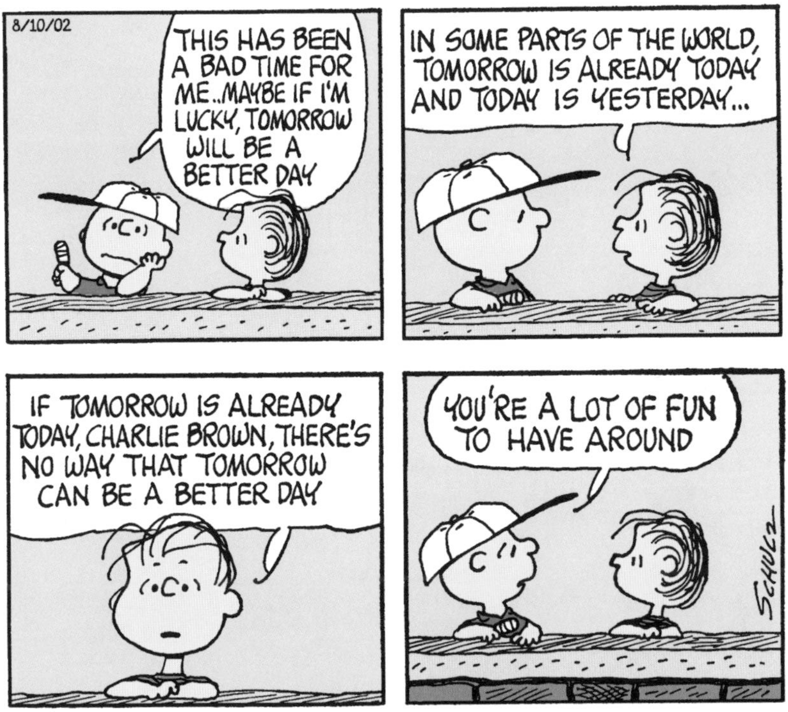
8/10/02
THIS HAS BEEN A BAD TIME FOR ME..MAYBE IF I'M LUCKY, TOMORROW WILL BE A BETTER DAY
IN SOME PARTS OF THE WORLD, TOMORROW IS ALREADY TODAY AND TODAY IS YESTERDAY...
IF TOMORROW IS ALREADY TODAY, CHARLIE BROWN, THERE'S NO WAY THAT TOMORROW CAN BE A BETTER DAY
YOU'RE A LOT OF FUN TO HAVE AROUND
SCHULZ

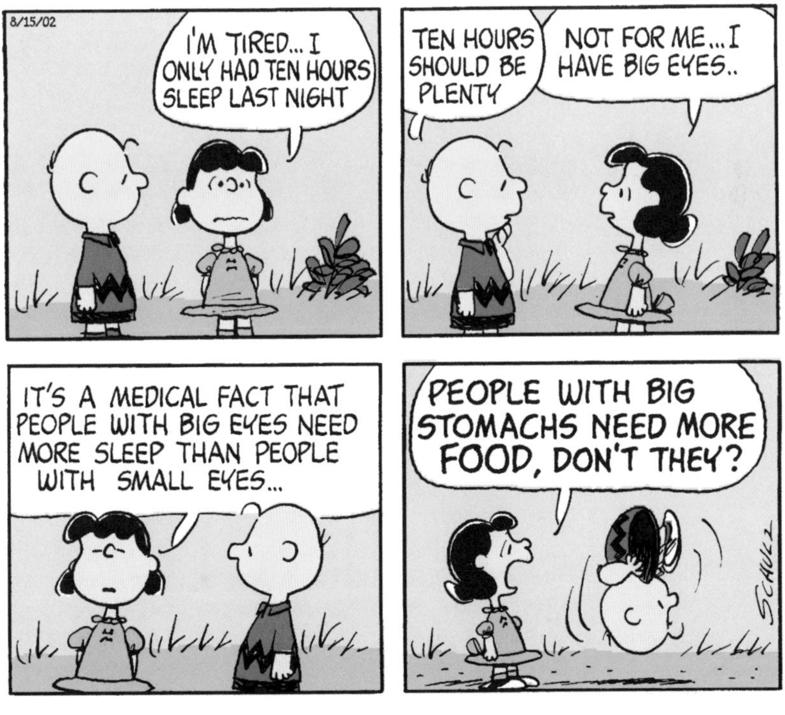
8/15/02
I'M TIRED... I ONLY HAD TEN HOURS SLEEP LAST NIGHT
TEN HOURS SHOULD BE PLENTY
NOT FOR ME... I HAVE BIG EYES..
IT'S A MEDICAL FACT THAT PEOPLE WITH BIG EYES NEED MORE SLEEP THAN PEOPLE WITH SMALL EYES...
PEOPLE WITH BIG STOMACHS NEED MORE FOOD, DON'T THEY?
SCHULZ

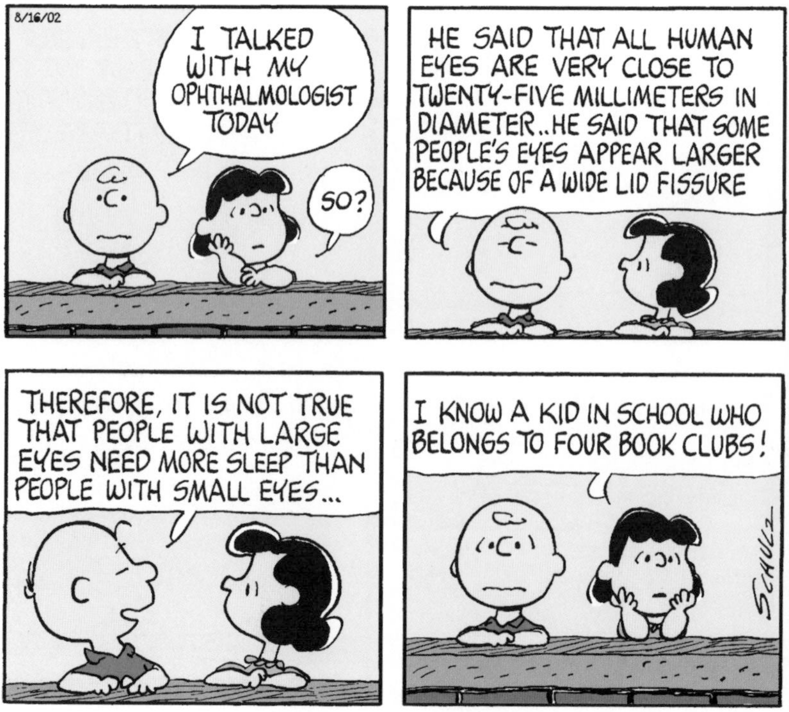
8/16/02
I TALKED WITH MY OPHTHALMOLOGIST TODAY
SO?
HE SAID THAT ALL HUMAN EYES ARE VERY CLOSE TO TWENTY-FIVE MILLIMETERS IN DIAMETER..HE SAID THAT SOME PEOPLE'S EYES APPEAR LARGER BECAUSE OF A WIDE LID FISSURE
THEREFORE, IT IS NOT TRUE THAT PEOPLE WITH LARGE EYES NEED MORE SLEEP THAN PEOPLE WITH SMALL EYES...
I KNOW A KID IN SCHOOL WHO BELONGS TO FOUR BOOK CLUBS!
SCHULZ

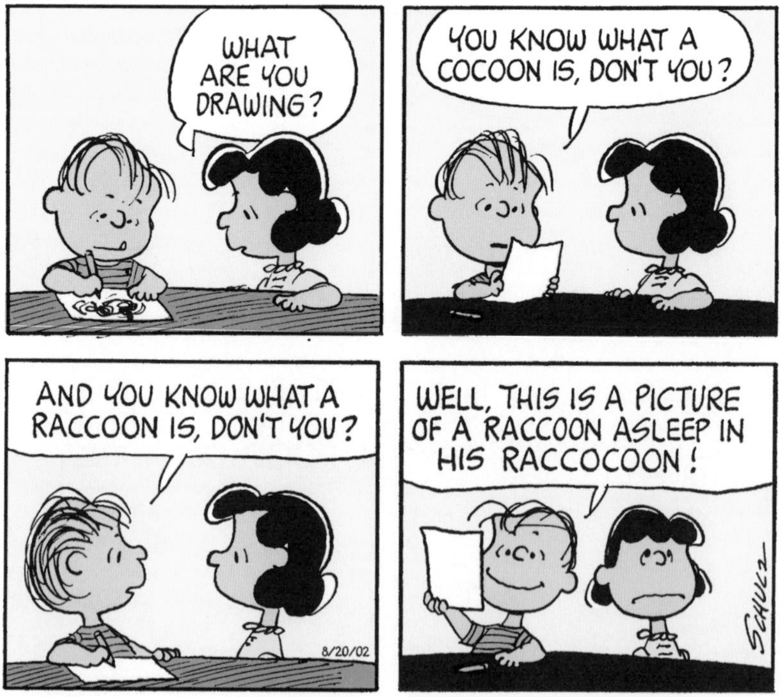
WHAT ARE YOU DRAWING?
YOU KNOW WHAT A COCOON IS, DON'T YOU?
AND YOU KNOW WHAT A RACCOON IS, DON'T YOU?
8/20/02
WELL, THIS IS A PICTURE OF A RACCOON ASLEEP IN HIS RACCOCOON!
SCHULZ

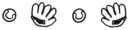

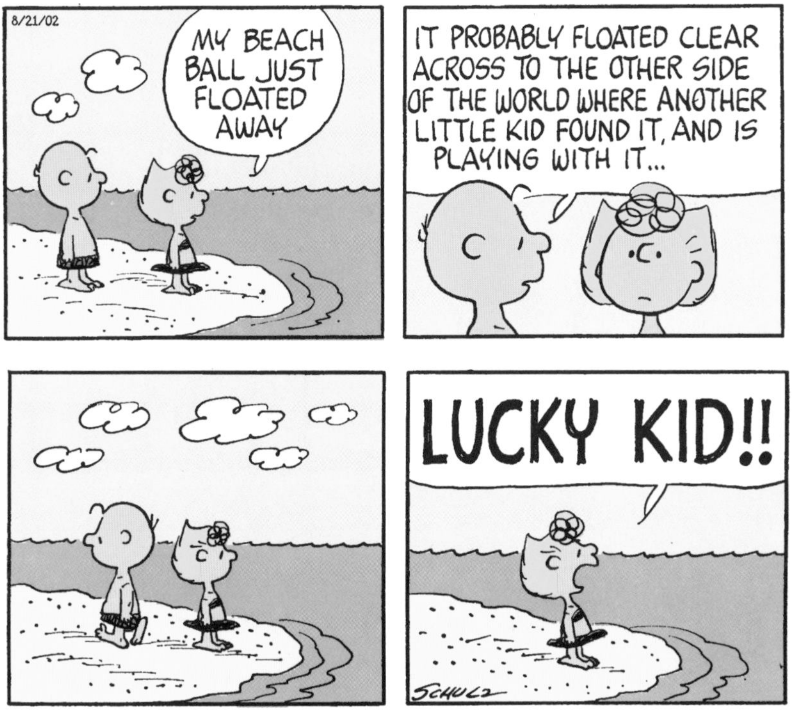
8/21/02
MY BEACH BALL JUST FLOATED AWAY
IT PROBABLY FLOATED CLEAR ACROSS TO THE OTHER SIDE OF THE WORLD WHERE ANOTHER LITTLE KID FOUND IT, AND IS PLAYING WITH IT...
LUCKY KID!!

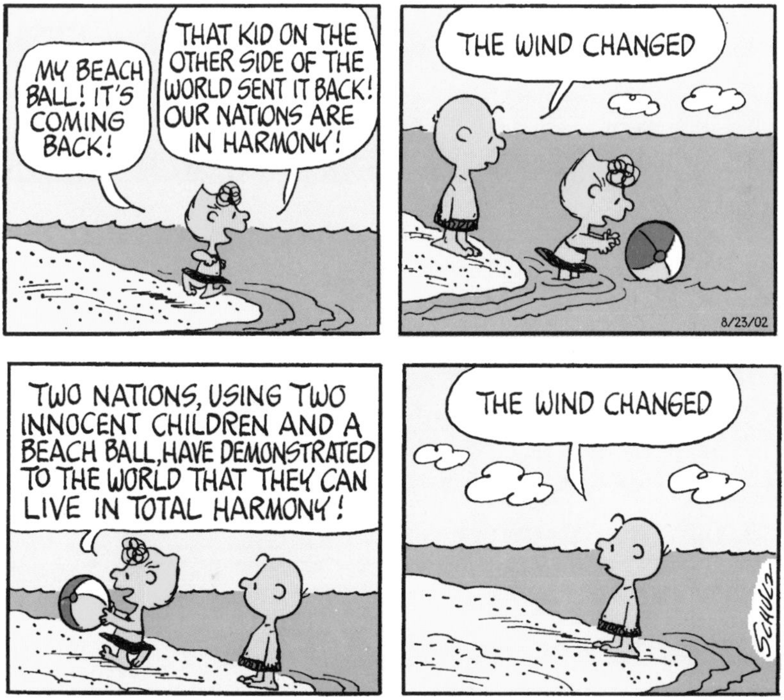
MY BEACH BALL! IT'S COMING BACK!
THAT KID ON THE OTHER SIDE OF THE WORLD SENT IT BACK! OUR NATIONS ARE IN HARMONY!
THE WIND CHANGED
8/23/02
TWO NATIONS, USING TWO INNOCENT CHILDREN AND A BEACH BALL, HAVE DEMONSTRATED TO THE WORLD THAT THEY CAN LIVE IN TOTAL HARMONY!
THE WIND CHANGED

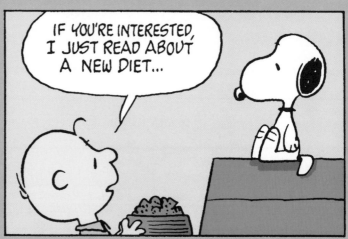

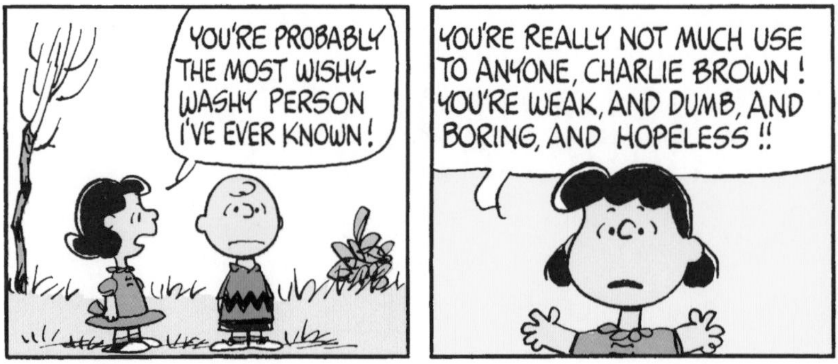
YOU'RE PROBABLY THE MOST WISHY-WASHY PERSON I'VE EVER KNOWN!
YOU'RE REALLY NOT MUCH USE TO ANYONE, CHARLIE BROWN! YOU'RE WEAK, AND DUMB, AND BORING, AND HOPELESS!!

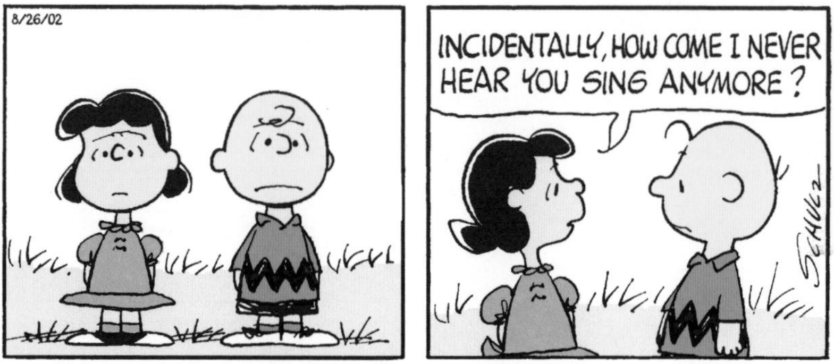
8/26/02
INCIDENTALLY, HOW COME I NEVER HEAR YOU SING ANYMORE?
SCHULZ

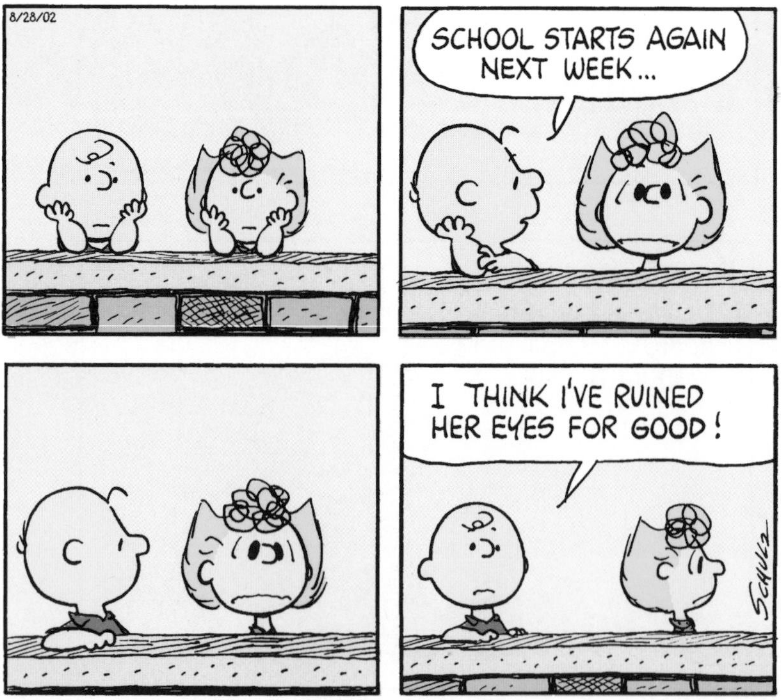
8/28/02
SCHOOL STARTS AGAIN NEXT WEEK...
I THINK I'VE RUINED HER EYES FOR GOOD!
SCHULZ

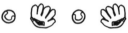

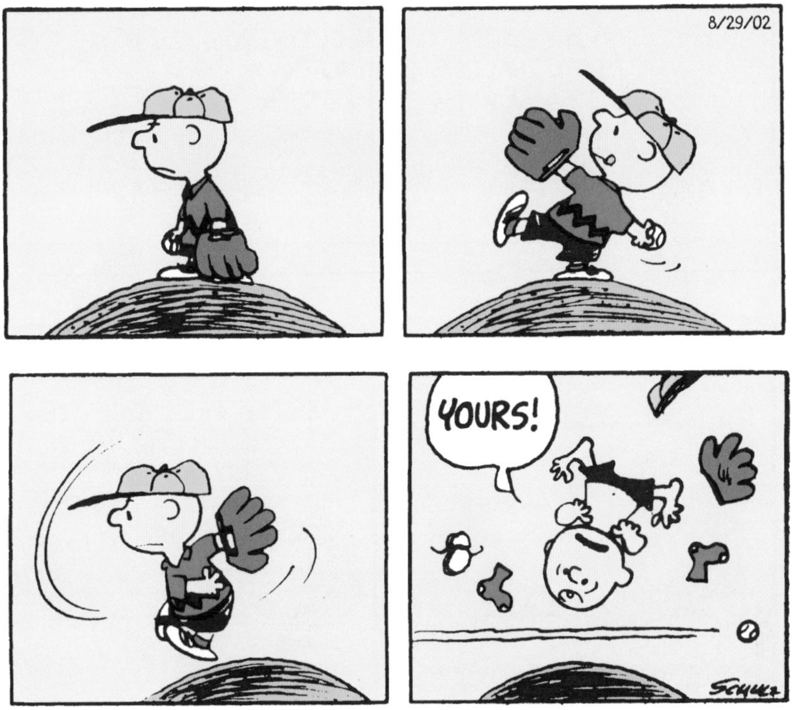
8/29/02
YOURS!
SCHULZ

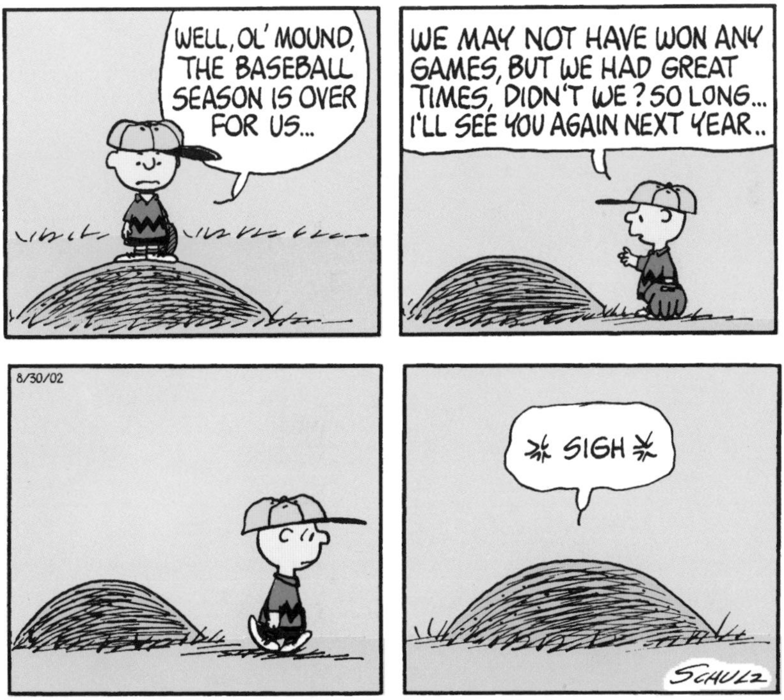
WELL, OL' MOUND, THE BASEBALL SEASON IS OVER FOR US...
WE MAY NOT HAVE WON ANY GAMES, BUT WE HAD GREAT TIMES, DIDN'T WE? SO LONG... I'LL SEE YOU AGAIN NEXT YEAR..
8/30/02
SIGH
SCHULZ

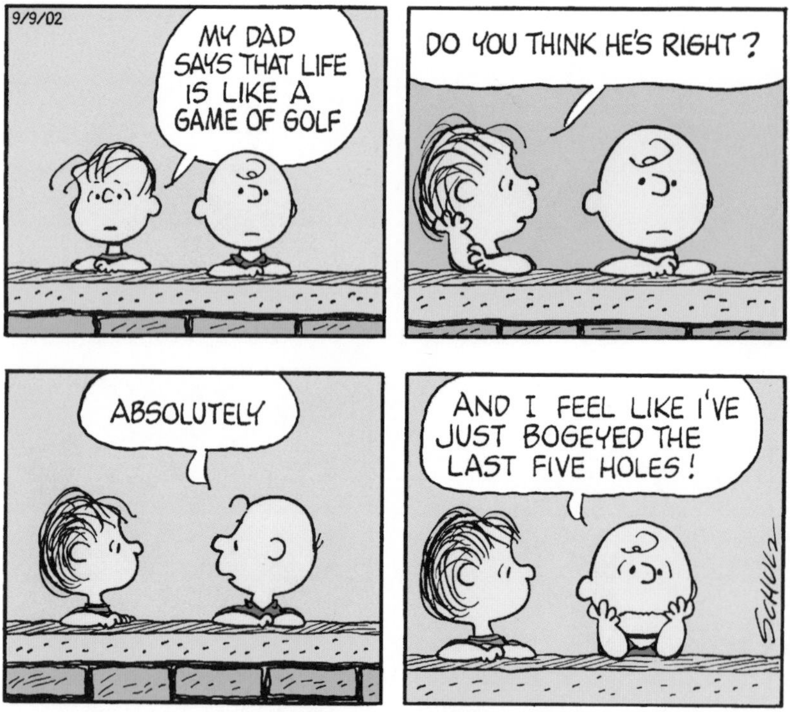
9/9/02
MY DAD SAYS THAT LIFE IS LIKE A GAME OF GOLF
DO YOU THINK HE'S RIGHT ?
ABSOLUTELY
AND I FEEL LIKE I'VE JUST BOGEYED THE LAST FIVE HOLES !
SCHULZ

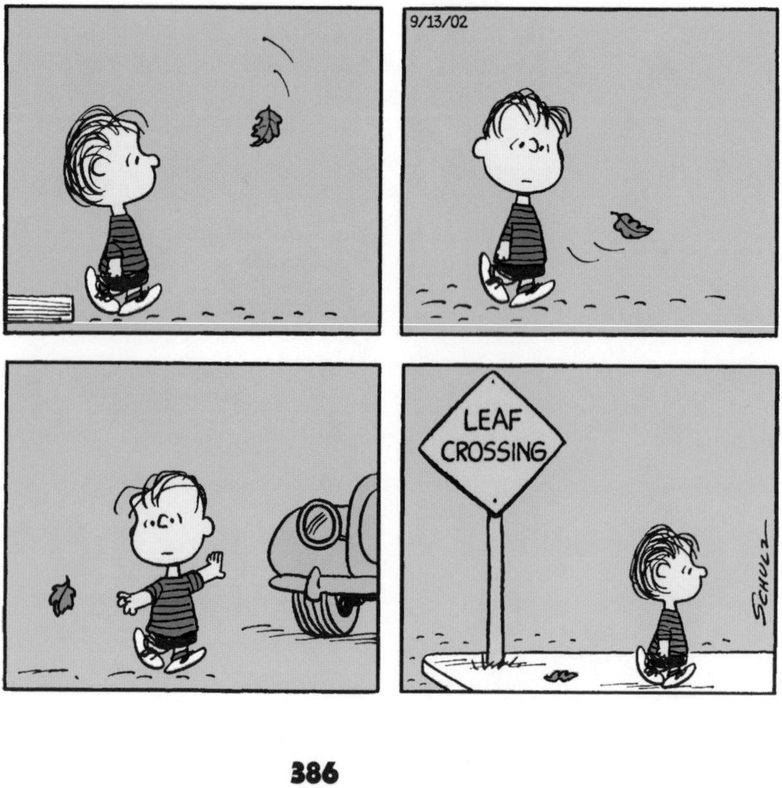
9/13/02
LEAF CROSSING
SCHULZ

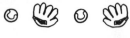

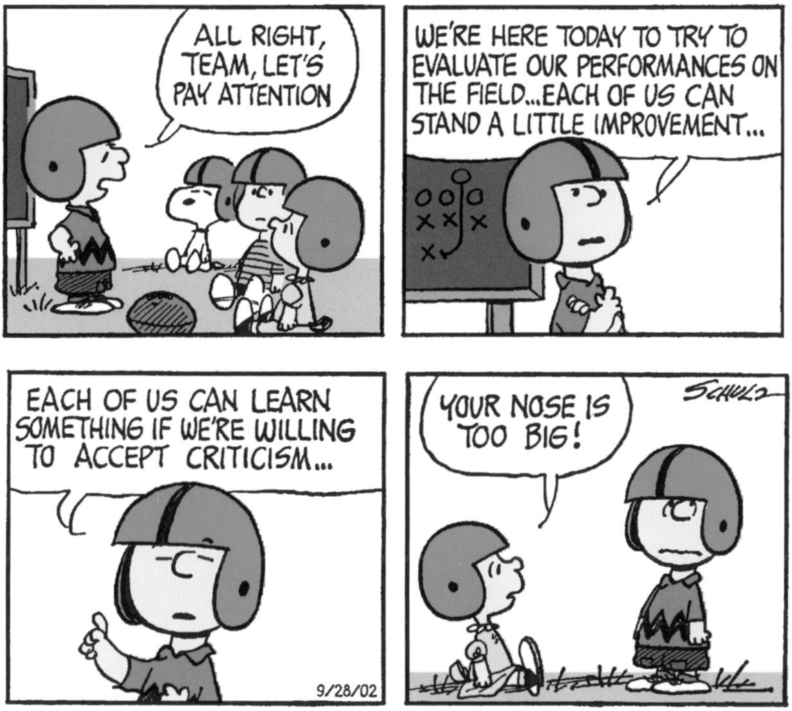
ALL RIGHT, TEAM, LET'S PAY ATTENTION
WE'RE HERE TODAY TO TRY TO EVALUATE OUR PERFORMANCES ON THE FIELD...EACH OF US CAN STAND A LITTLE IMPROVEMENT...
EACH OF US CAN LEARN SOMETHING IF WE'RE WILLING TO ACCEPT CRITICISM...
YOUR NOSE IS TOO BIG!
SCHULZ
9/28/02

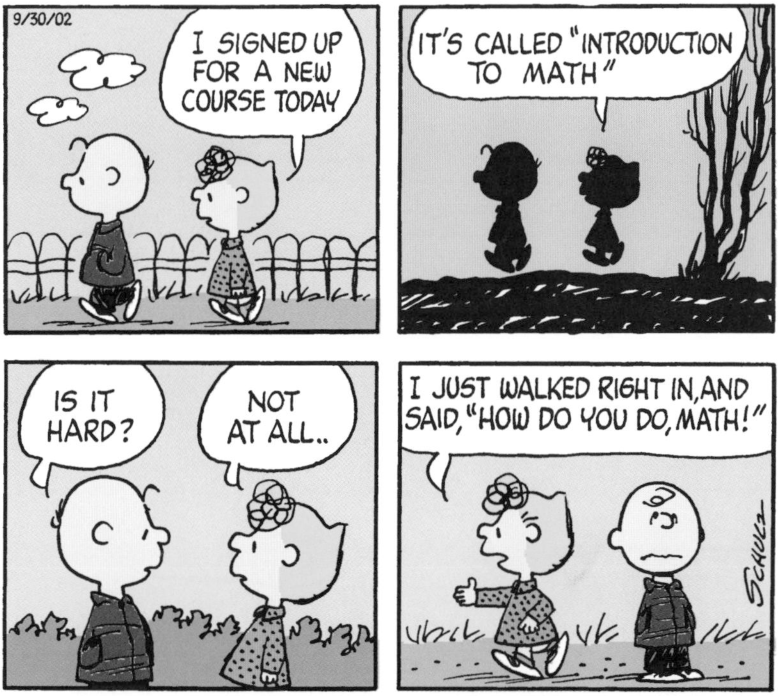
9/30/02
I SIGNED UP FOR A NEW COURSE TODAY
IT'S CALLED "INTRODUCTION TO MATH"
IS IT HARD?
NOT AT ALL..
I JUST WALKED RIGHT IN, AND SAID, "HOW DO YOU DO, MATH!"
SCHULZ

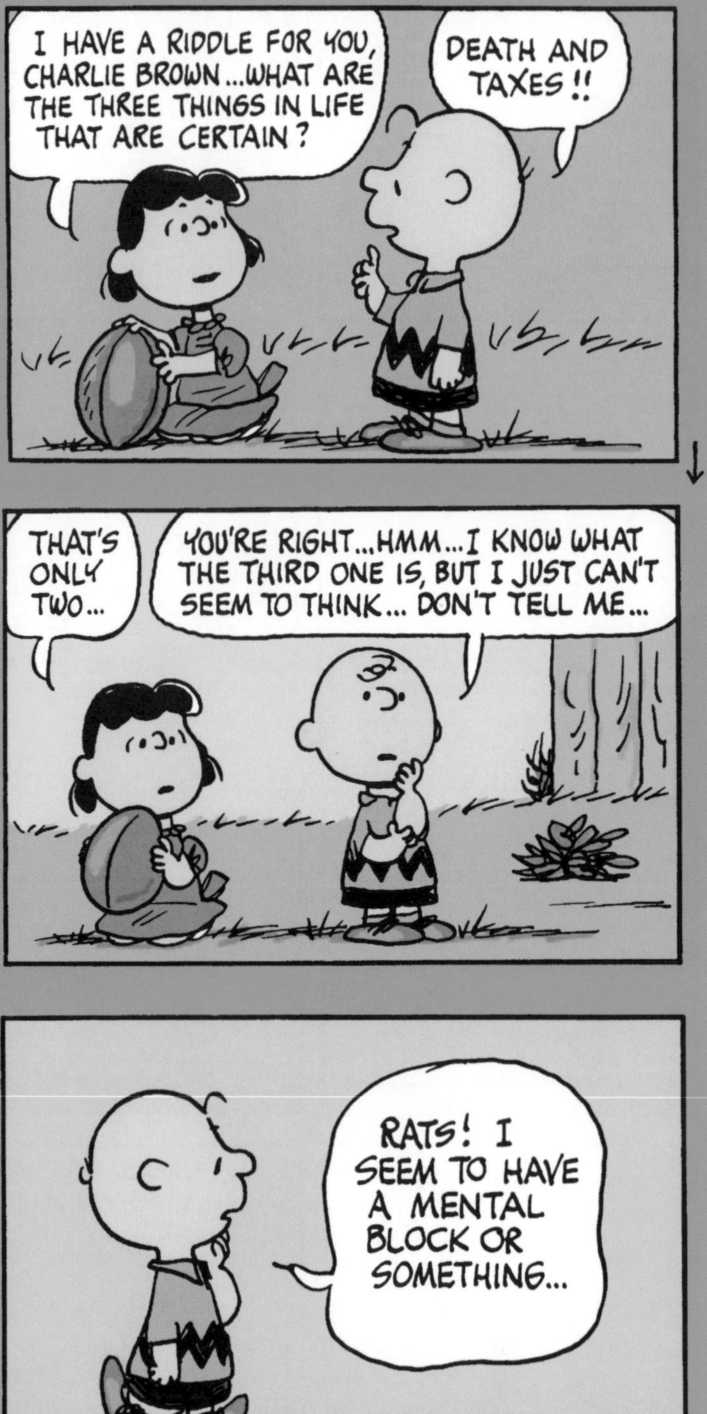
I HAVE A RIDDLE FOR YOU, CHARLIE BROWN...WHAT ARE THE THREE THINGS IN LIFE THAT ARE CERTAIN?
DEATH AND TAXES!!
THAT'S ONLY TWO...
YOU'RE RIGHT...HMM...I KNOW WHAT THE THIRD ONE IS, BUT I JUST CAN'T SEEM TO THINK... DON'T TELL ME...
RATS! I SEEM TO HAVE A MENTAL BLOCK OR SOMETHING...

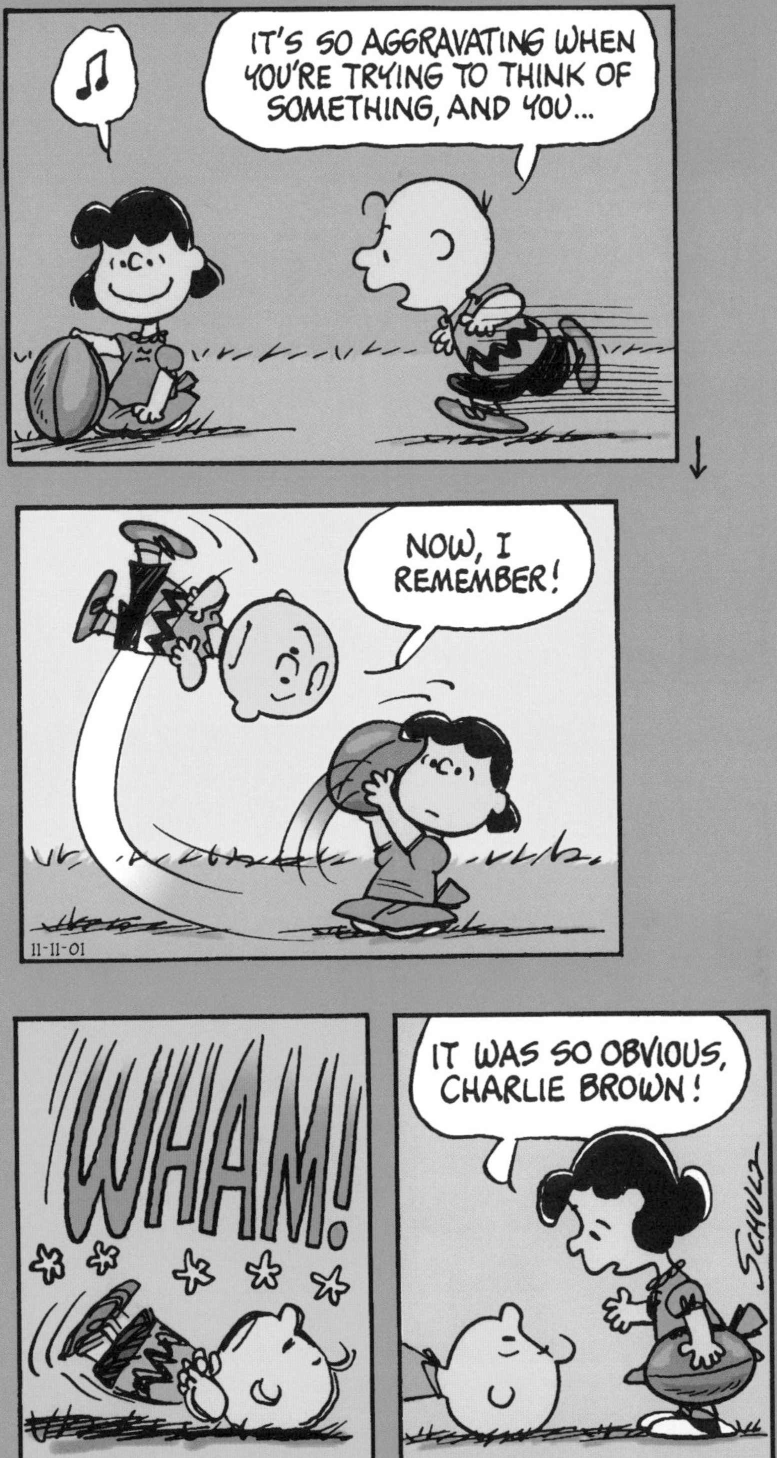
♫
IT'S SO AGGRAVATING WHEN YOU'RE TRYING TO THINK OF SOMETHING, AND YOU...
NOW, I REMEMBER!
11-11-01
WHAM!
IT WAS SO OBVIOUS, CHARLIE BROWN!
SCHULZ

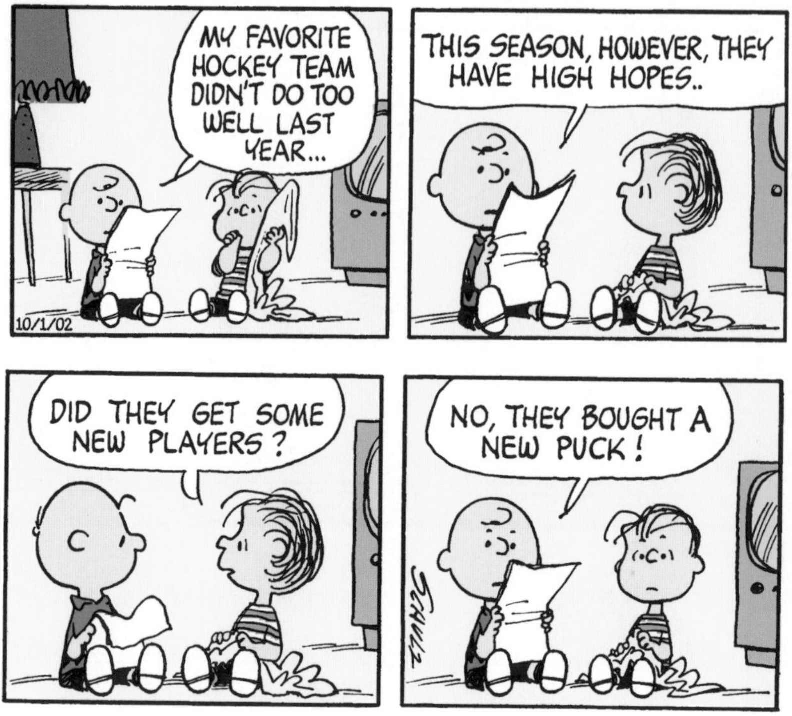
10/1/02
MY FAVORITE HOCKEY TEAM DIDN'T DO TOO WELL LAST YEAR...
THIS SEASON, HOWEVER, THEY HAVE HIGH HOPES..
DID THEY GET SOME NEW PLAYERS ?
NO, THEY BOUGHT A NEW PUCK !
SCHULZ

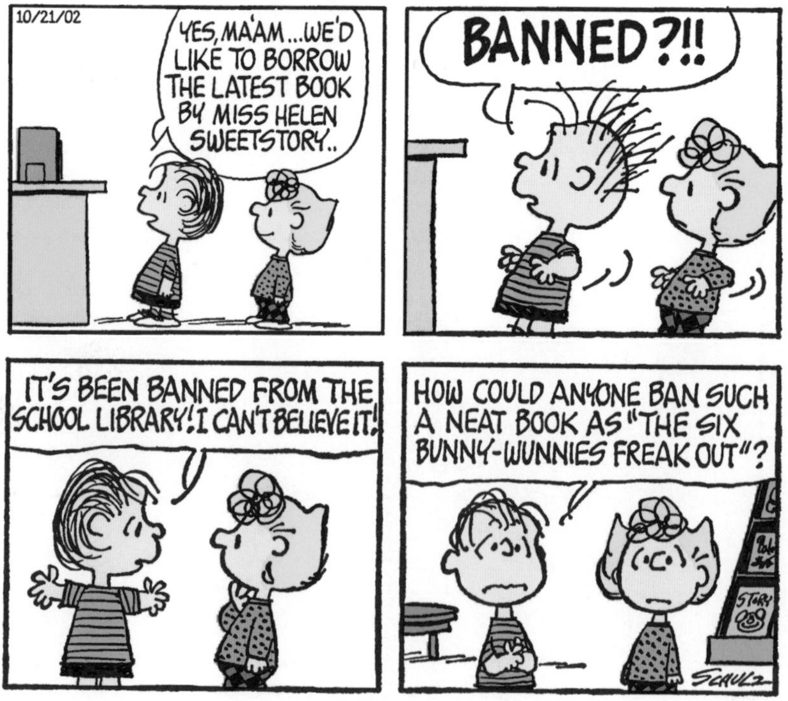
10/21/02
YES, MA'AM...WE'D LIKE TO BORROW THE LATEST BOOK BY MISS HELEN SWEETSTORY..
BANNED?!!
IT'S BEEN BANNED FROM THE SCHOOL LIBRARY! I CAN'T BELIEVE IT!
HOW COULD ANYONE BAN SUCH A NEAT BOOK AS "THE SIX BUNNY-WUNNIES FREAK OUT"?
SCHULZ

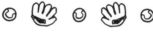

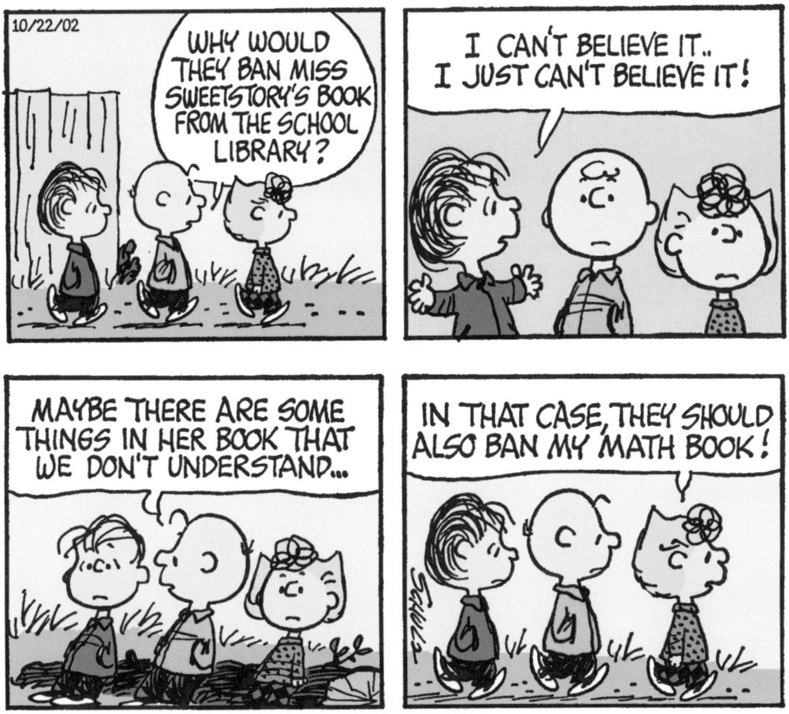
10/22/02
WHY WOULD THEY BAN MISS SWEETSTORY'S BOOK FROM THE SCHOOL LIBRARY?
I CAN'T BELIEVE IT.. I JUST CAN'T BELIEVE IT!
MAYBE THERE ARE SOME THINGS IN HER BOOK THAT WE DON'T UNDERSTAND...
IN THAT CASE, THEY SHOULD ALSO BAN MY MATH BOOK!
SCHULZ

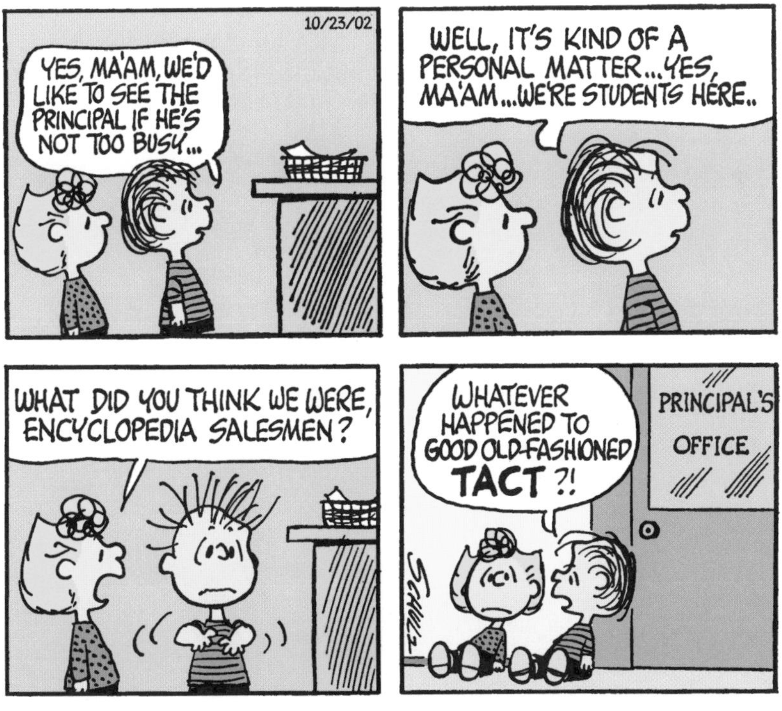
10/23/02
YES, MA'AM, WE'D LIKE TO SEE THE PRINCIPAL IF HE'S NOT TOO BUSY...
WELL, IT'S KIND OF A PERSONAL MATTER...YES, MA'AM...WE'RE STUDENTS HERE..
WHAT DID YOU THINK WE WERE, ENCYCLOPEDIA SALESMEN?
WHATEVER HAPPENED TO GOOD OLD-FASHIONED TACT?!
PRINCIPAL'S OFFICE
SCHULZ

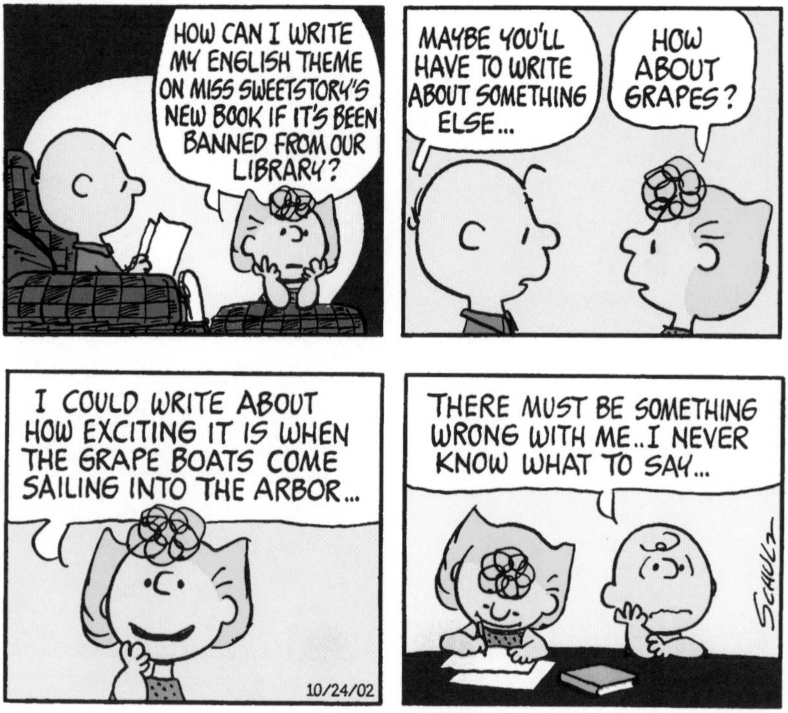
HOW CAN I WRITE MY ENGLISH THEME ON MISS SWEETSTORY'S NEW BOOK IF IT'S BEEN BANNED FROM OUR LIBRARY?
MAYBE YOU'LL HAVE TO WRITE ABOUT SOMETHING ELSE...
HOW ABOUT GRAPES?
I COULD WRITE ABOUT HOW EXCITING IT IS WHEN THE GRAPE BOATS COME SAILING INTO THE ARBOR...
10/24/02
THERE MUST BE SOMETHING WRONG WITH ME..I NEVER KNOW WHAT TO SAY...
SCHULZ

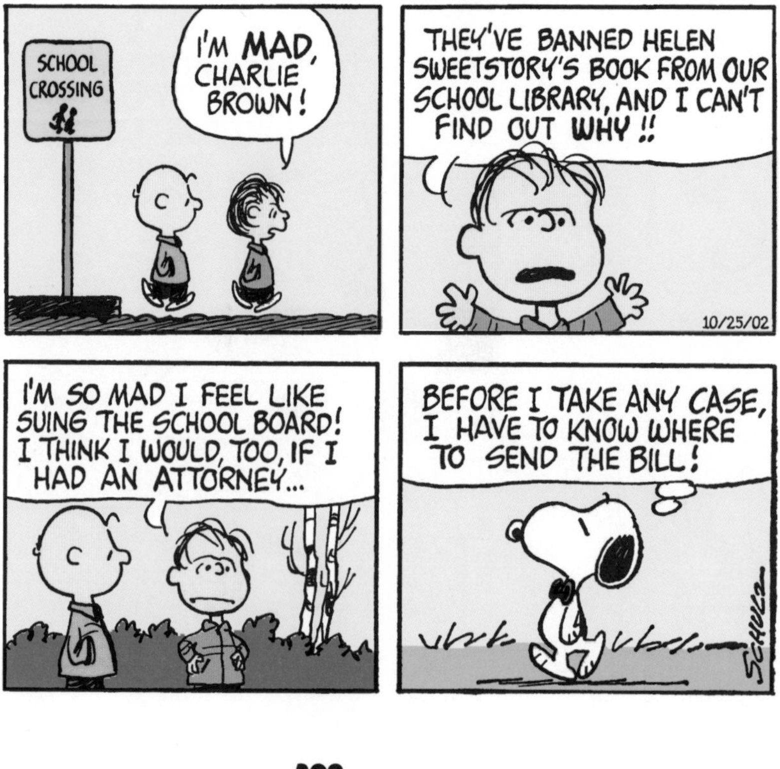
SCHOOL CROSSING
I'M MAD, CHARLIE BROWN!
THEY'VE BANNED HELEN SWEETSTORY'S BOOK FROM OUR SCHOOL LIBRARY, AND I CAN'T FIND OUT WHY!!
10/25/02
I'M SO MAD I FEEL LIKE SUING THE SCHOOL BOARD! I THINK I WOULD, TOO, IF I HAD AN ATTORNEY...
BEFORE I TAKE ANY CASE, I HAVE TO KNOW WHERE TO SEND THE BILL!
SCHULZ

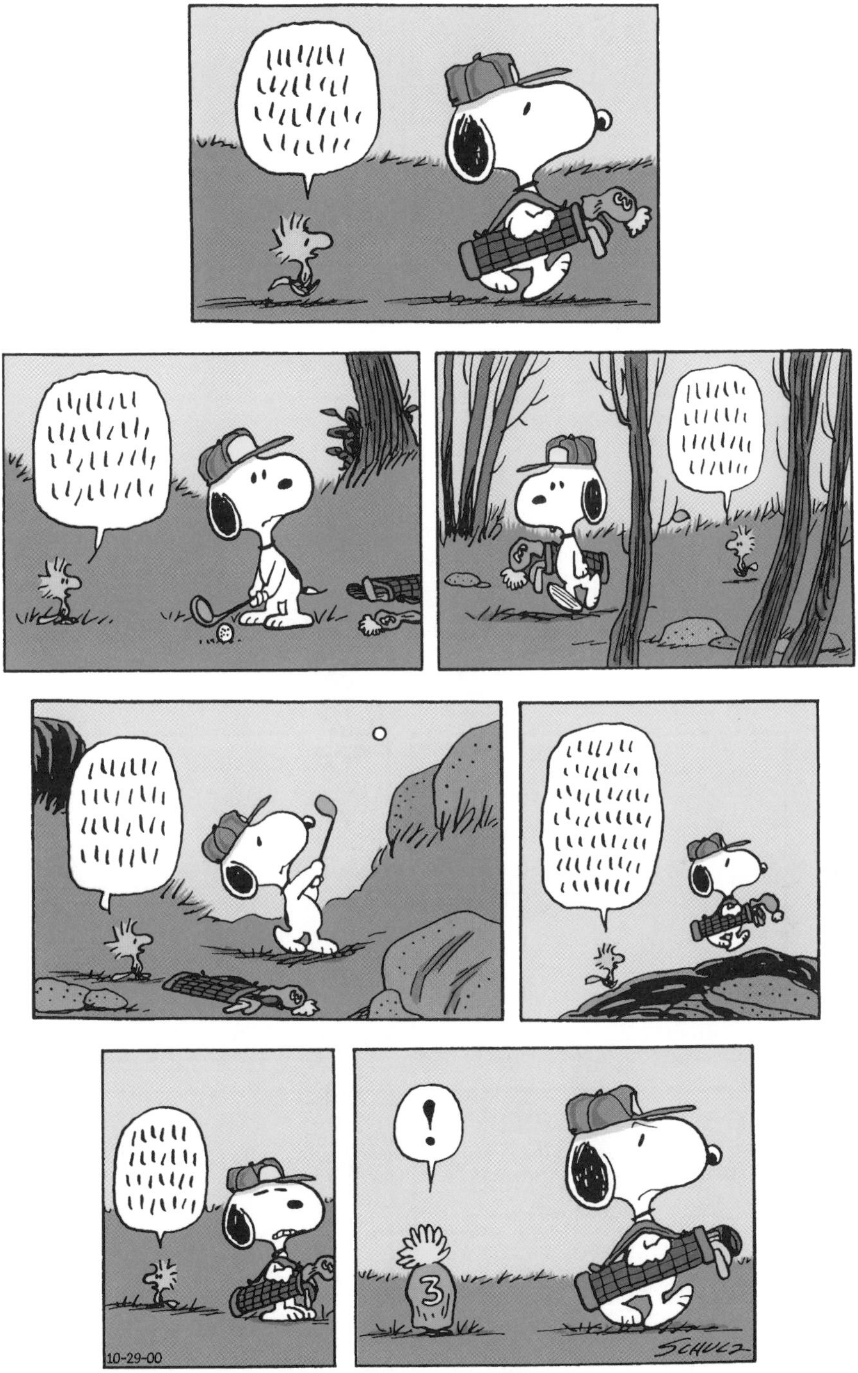
!
3
10-29-00
SCHULZ

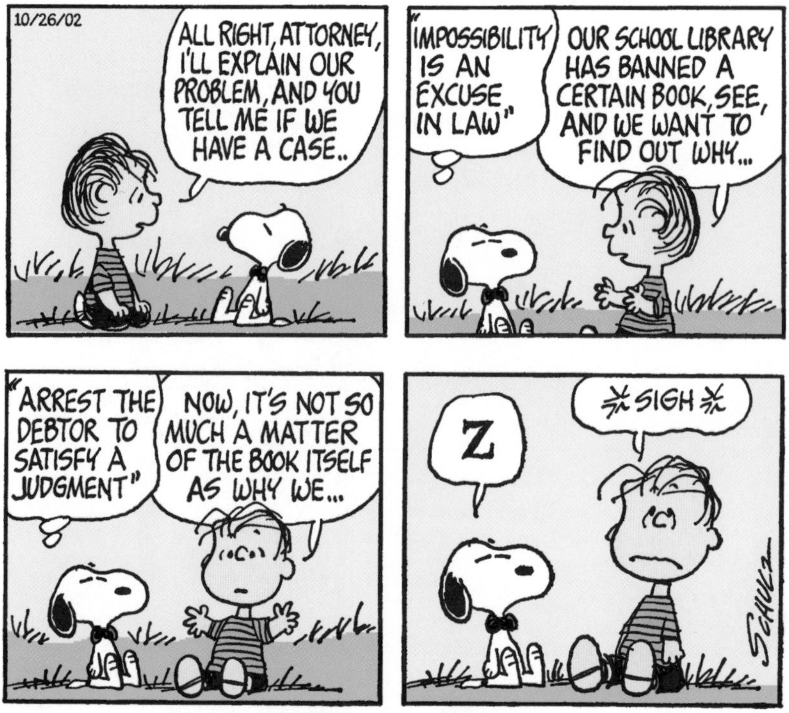
10/26/02
ALL RIGHT, ATTORNEY, I'LL EXPLAIN OUR PROBLEM, AND YOU TELL ME IF WE HAVE A CASE..
"IMPOSSIBILITY IS AN EXCUSE IN LAW"
OUR SCHOOL LIBRARY HAS BANNED A CERTAIN BOOK, SEE, AND WE WANT TO FIND OUT WHY...
"ARREST THE DEBTOR TO SATISFY A JUDGMENT"
NOW, IT'S NOT SO MUCH A MATTER OF THE BOOK ITSELF AS WHY WE...
Z
SIGH
SCHULZ

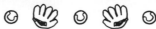

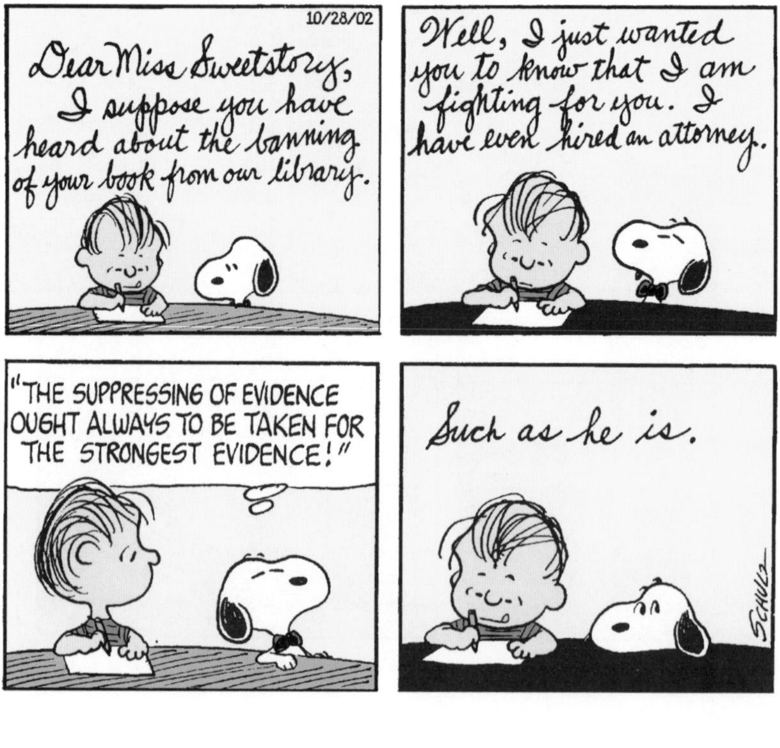
10/28/02
Dear Miss Sweetstory, I suppose you have heard about the banning of your book from our library.
Well, I just wanted you to know that I am fighting for you. I have even hired an attorney.
"THE SUPPRESSING OF EVIDENCE OUGHT ALWAYS TO BE TAKEN FOR THE STRONGEST EVIDENCE!"
Such as he is.
SCHULZ

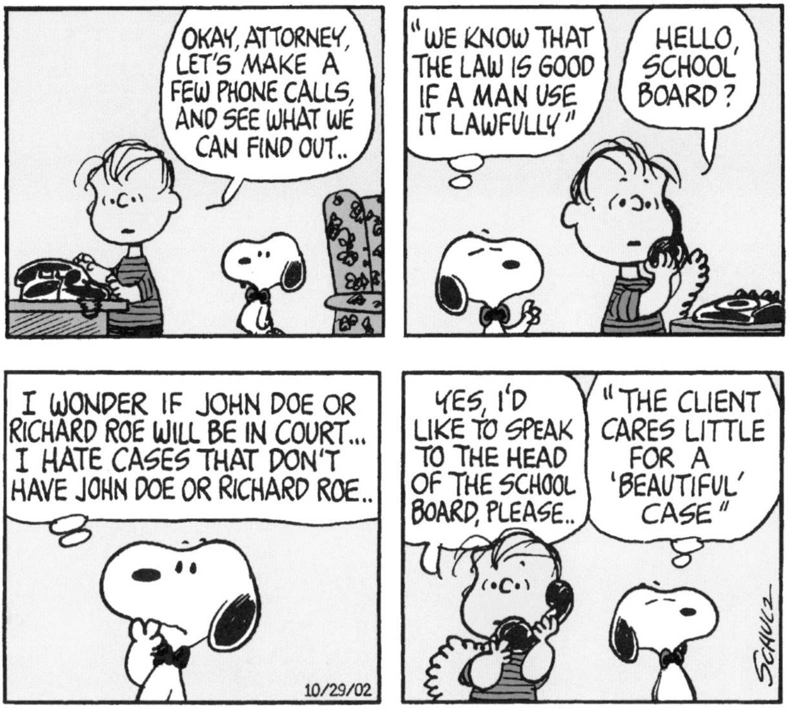
OKAY, ATTORNEY, LET'S MAKE A FEW PHONE CALLS, AND SEE WHAT WE CAN FIND OUT..
"WE KNOW THAT THE LAW IS GOOD IF A MAN USE IT LAWFULLY"
HELLO, SCHOOL BOARD?
I WONDER IF JOHN DOE OR RICHARD ROE WILL BE IN COURT... I HATE CASES THAT DON'T HAVE JOHN DOE OR RICHARD ROE..
10/29/02
YES, I'D LIKE TO SPEAK TO THE HEAD OF THE SCHOOL BOARD, PLEASE..
"THE CLIENT CARES LITTLE FOR A 'BEAUTIFUL' CASE"
SCHULZ

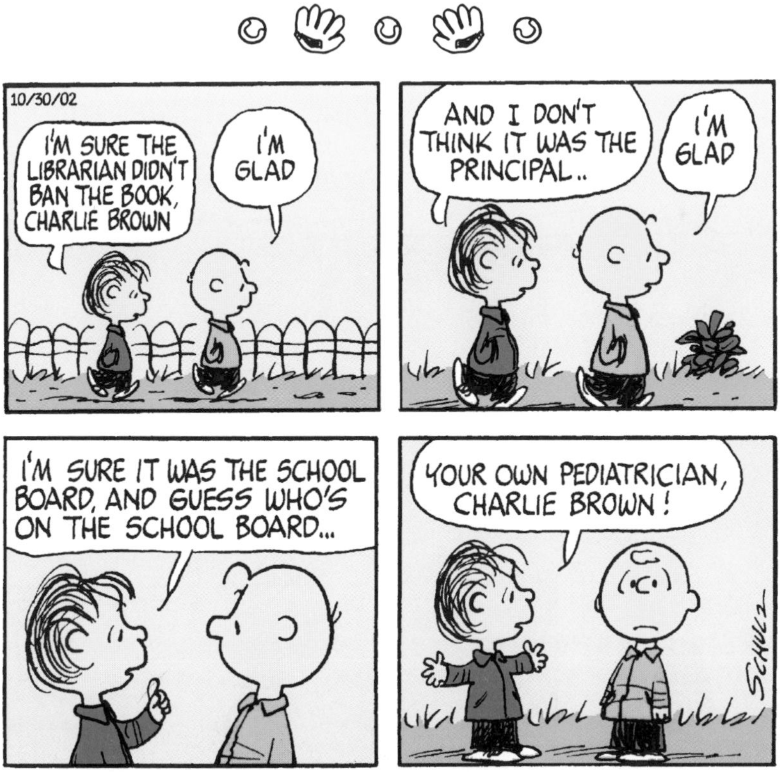
10/30/02
I'M SURE THE LIBRARIAN DIDN'T BAN THE BOOK, CHARLIE BROWN
I'M GLAD
AND I DON'T THINK IT WAS THE PRINCIPAL..
I'M GLAD
I'M SURE IT WAS THE SCHOOL BOARD, AND GUESS WHO'S ON THE SCHOOL BOARD...
YOUR OWN PEDIATRICIAN, CHARLIE BROWN!
SCHULZ

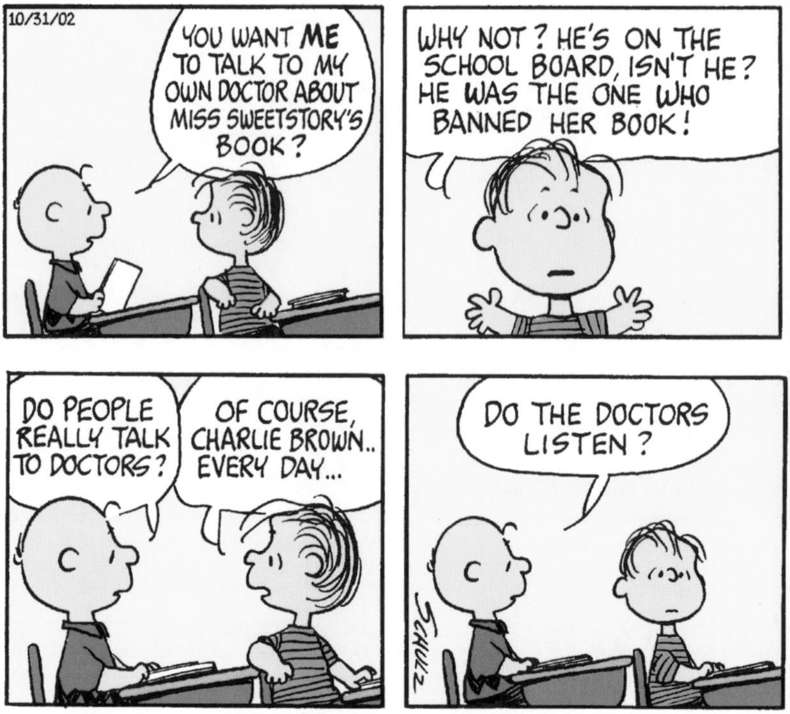
10/31/02
YOU WANT ME TO TALK TO MY OWN DOCTOR ABOUT MISS SWEETSTORY'S BOOK?
WHY NOT? HE'S ON THE SCHOOL BOARD, ISN'T HE? HE WAS THE ONE WHO BANNED HER BOOK!
DO PEOPLE REALLY TALK TO DOCTORS?
OF COURSE, CHARLIE BROWN.. EVERY DAY...
DO THE DOCTORS LISTEN?
SCHULZ

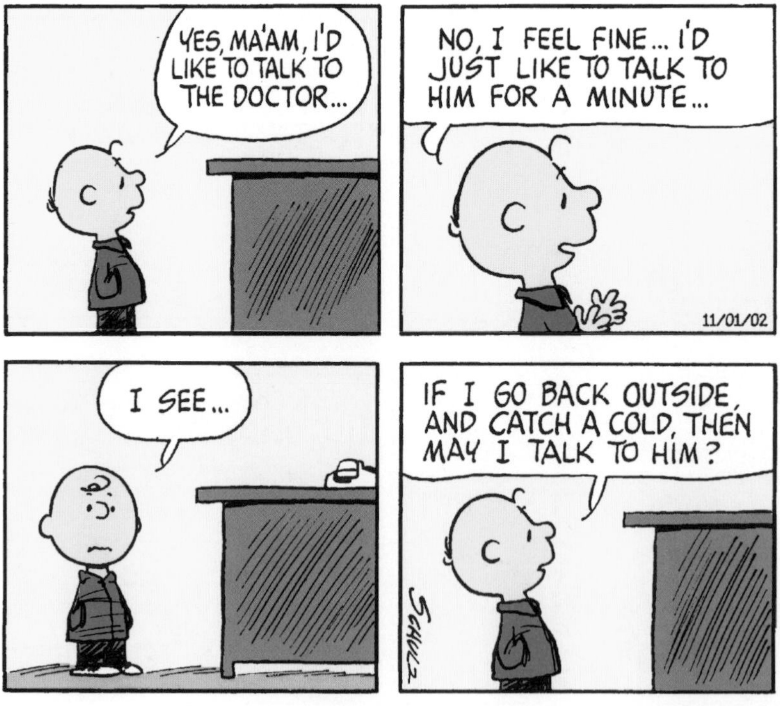
YES, MA'AM, I'D LIKE TO TALK TO THE DOCTOR...
NO, I FEEL FINE... I'D JUST LIKE TO TALK TO HIM FOR A MINUTE...
11/01/02
I SEE...
IF I GO BACK OUTSIDE, AND CATCH A COLD, THEN MAY I TALK TO HIM?
SCHULZ

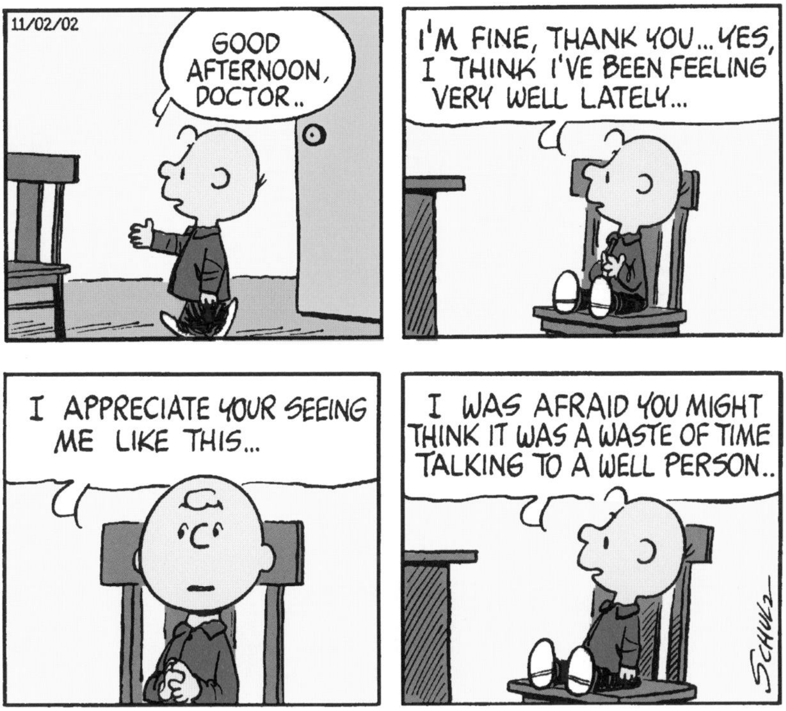
11/02/02
GOOD AFTERNOON, DOCTOR..
I'M FINE, THANK YOU... YES, I THINK I'VE BEEN FEELING VERY WELL LATELY...
I APPRECIATE YOUR SEEING ME LIKE THIS...
I WAS AFRAID YOU MIGHT THINK IT WAS A WASTE OF TIME TALKING TO A WELL PERSON..
SCHULZ

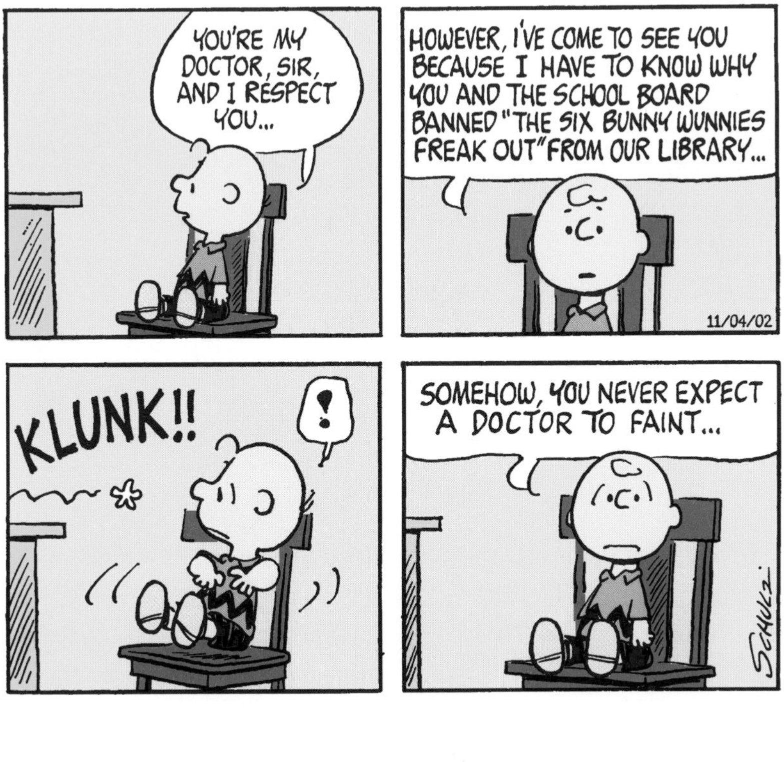
YOU'RE MY DOCTOR, SIR, AND I RESPECT YOU...
HOWEVER, I'VE COME TO SEE YOU BECAUSE I HAVE TO KNOW WHY YOU AND THE SCHOOL BOARD BANNED "THE SIX BUNNY WUNNIES FREAK OUT" FROM OUR LIBRARY...
11/04/02
KLUNK!!
!
SOMEHOW, YOU NEVER EXPECT A DOCTOR TO FAINT...
SCHULZ

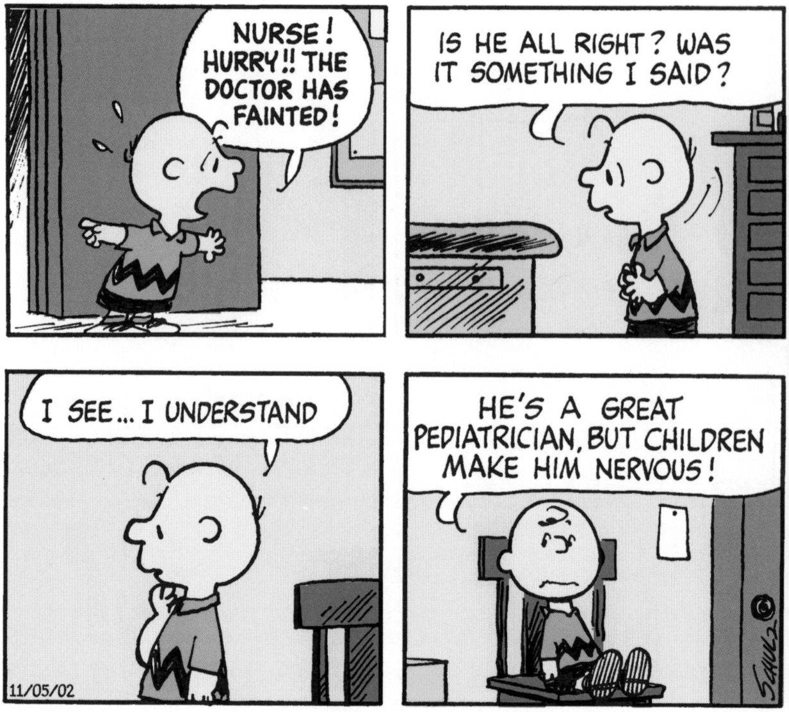
NURSE! HURRY!! THE DOCTOR HAS FAINTED!
IS HE ALL RIGHT? WAS IT SOMETHING I SAID?
I SEE... I UNDERSTAND
11/05/02
HE'S A GREAT PEDIATRICIAN, BUT CHILDREN MAKE HIM NERVOUS!
SCHULZ

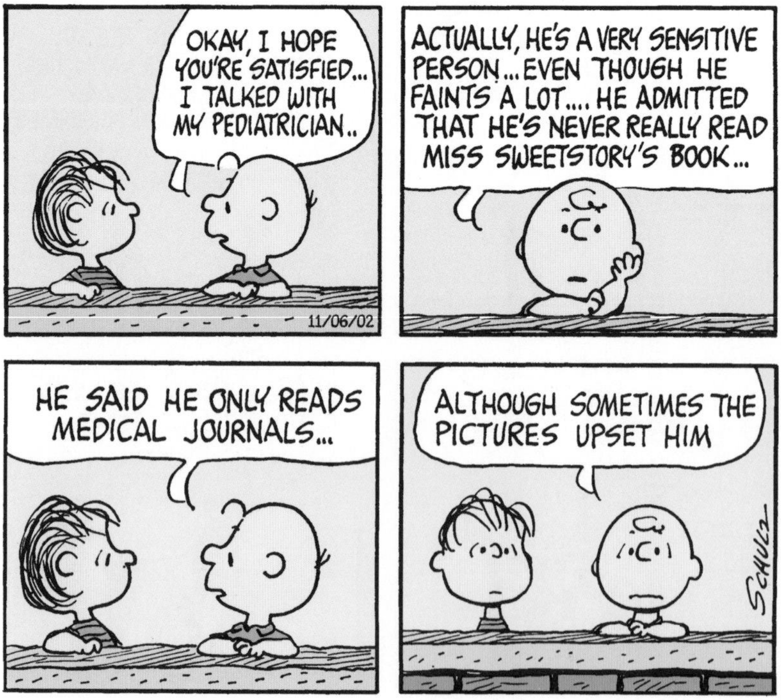
OKAY, I HOPE YOU'RE SATISFIED... I TALKED WITH MY PEDIATRICIAN..
11/06/02
ACTUALLY, HE'S A VERY SENSITIVE PERSON... EVEN THOUGH HE FAINTS A LOT.... HE ADMITTED THAT HE'S NEVER REALLY READ MISS SWEETSTORY'S BOOK...
HE SAID HE ONLY READS MEDICAL JOURNALS...
ALTHOUGH SOMETIMES THE PICTURES UPSET HIM
SCHULZ

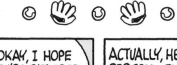

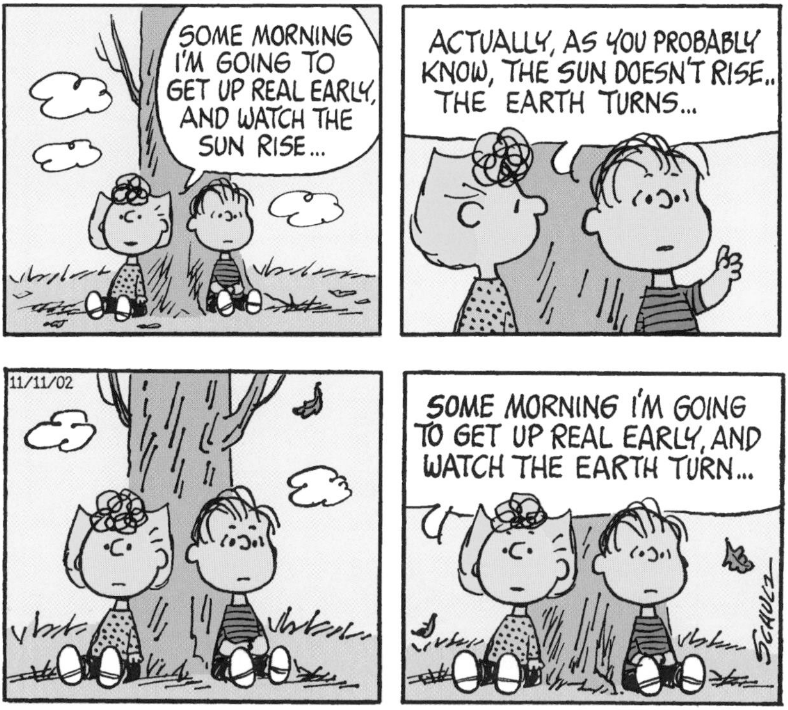
SOME MORNING I'M GOING TO GET UP REAL EARLY, AND WATCH THE SUN RISE...
ACTUALLY, AS YOU PROBABLY KNOW, THE SUN DOESN'T RISE.. THE EARTH TURNS...
11/11/02
SOME MORNING I'M GOING TO GET UP REAL EARLY, AND WATCH THE EARTH TURN...
SCHULZ

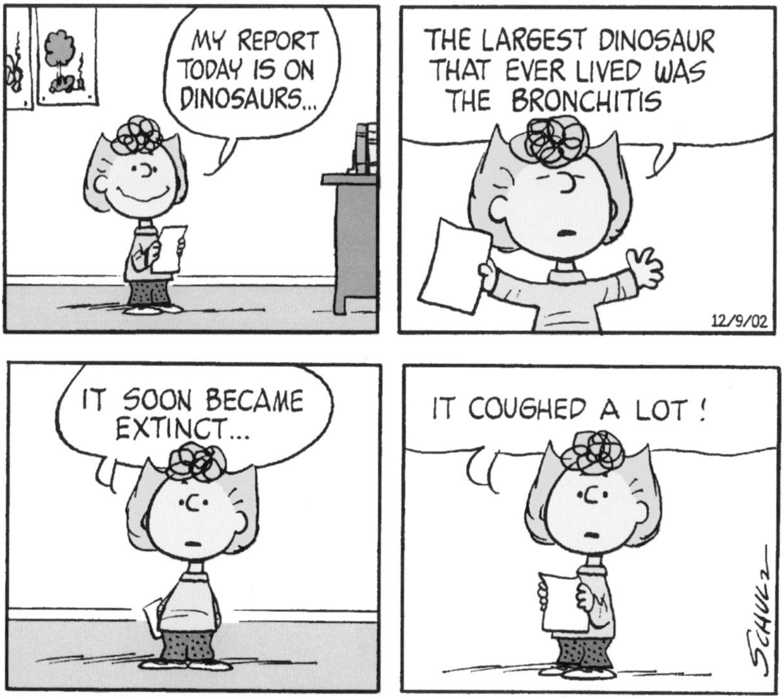
MY REPORT TODAY IS ON DINOSAURS...
THE LARGEST DINOSAUR THAT EVER LIVED WAS THE BRONCHITIS
12/9/02
IT SOON BECAME EXTINCT...
IT COUGHED A LOT !
SCHULZ

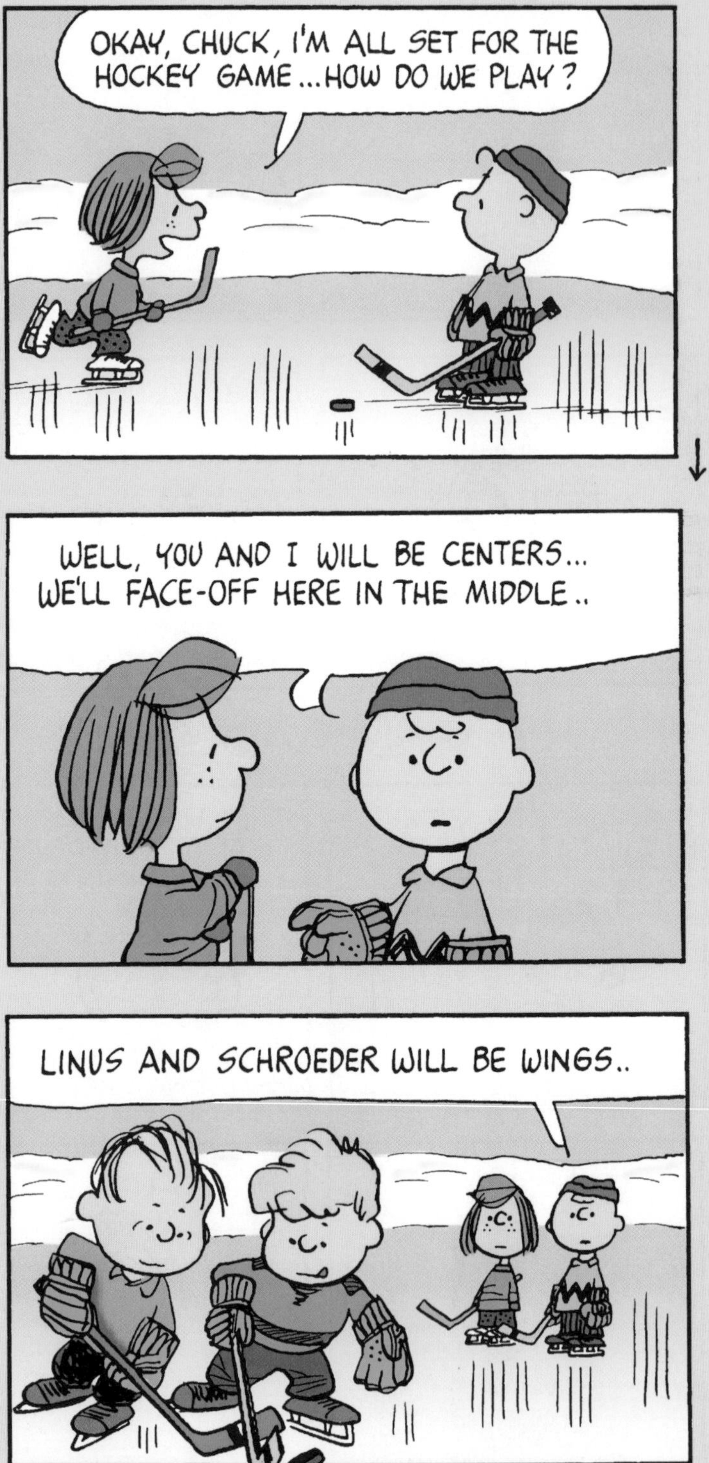
OKAY, CHUCK, I'M ALL SET FOR THE HOCKEY GAME...HOW DO WE PLAY?
WELL, YOU AND I WILL BE CENTERS... WE'LL FACE-OFF HERE IN THE MIDDLE..
LINUS AND SCHROEDER WILL BE WINGS..

THE IDEA IS TO SHOOT THE PUCK BETWEEN THOSE CHUNKS OF SNOW... THE GOALIE, OF COURSE, WILL TRY TO STOP YOU...
WHICH ONE IS THE GOALIE?
THE GOALIE IS THE ONE WEARING THOSE PADS...
SCHULZ
1-27-02

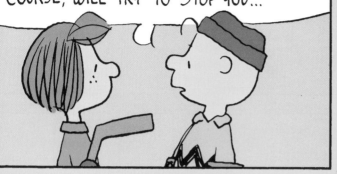

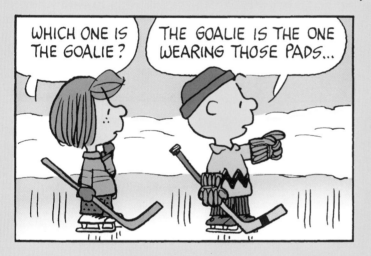

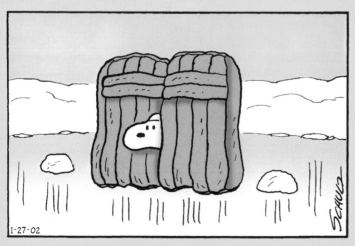

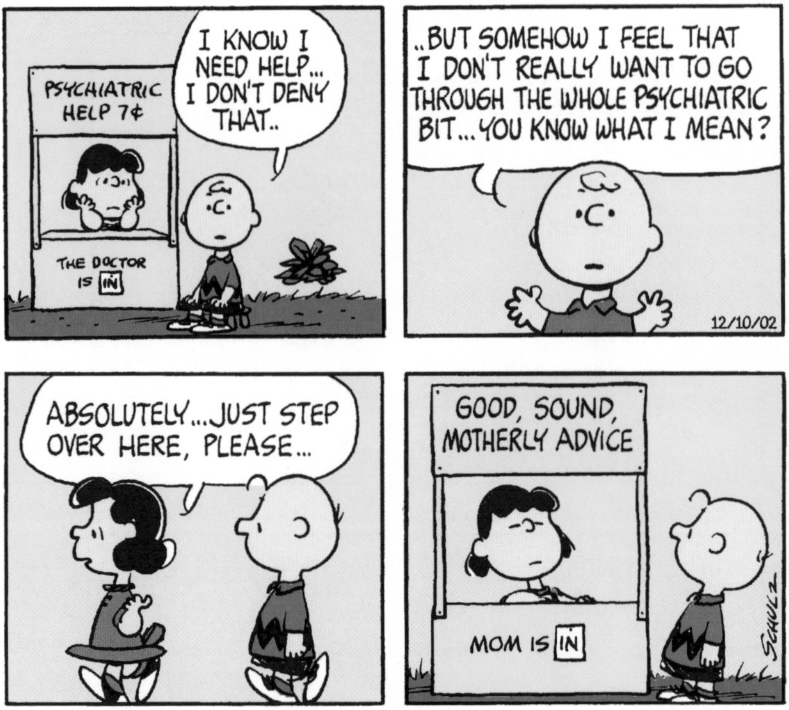
PSYCHIATRIC HELP 7¢
THE DOCTOR IS IN
I KNOW I NEED HELP... I DON'T DENY THAT..
..BUT SOMEHOW I FEEL THAT I DON'T REALLY WANT TO GO THROUGH THE WHOLE PSYCHIATRIC BIT...YOU KNOW WHAT I MEAN?
12/10/02
ABSOLUTELY...JUST STEP OVER HERE, PLEASE...
GOOD, SOUND, MOTHERLY ADVICE
MOM IS IN
SCHULZ

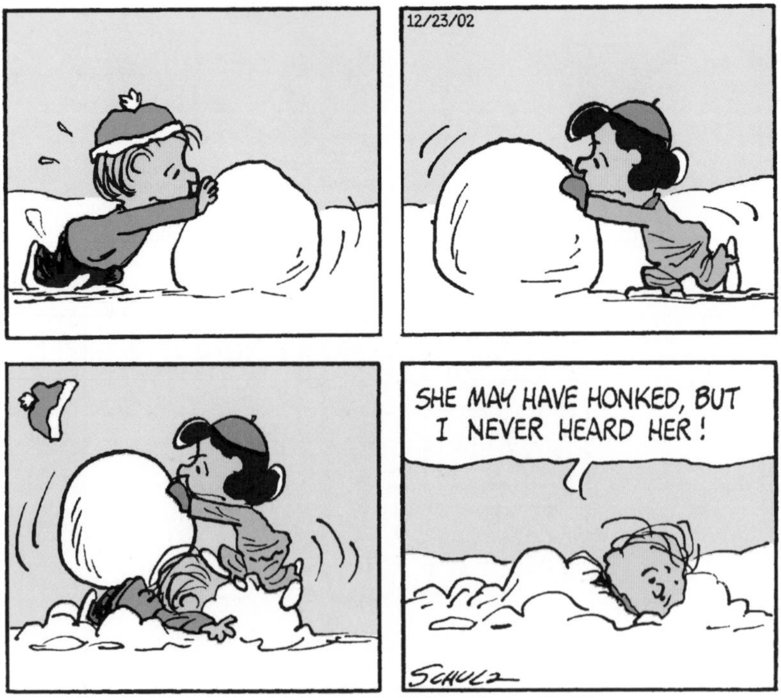
12/23/02
SHE MAY HAVE HONKED, BUT I NEVER HEARD HER!
SCHULZ

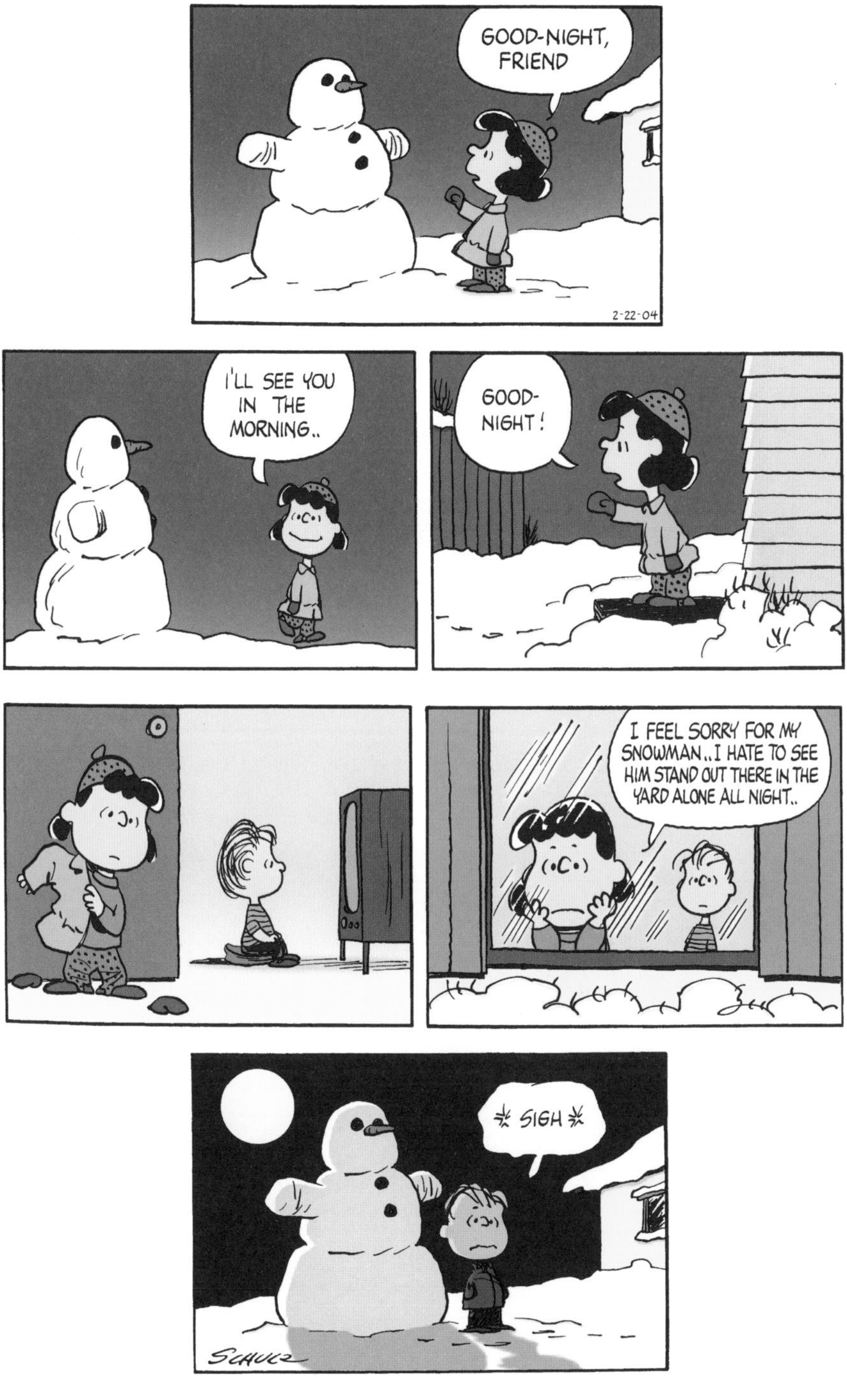
GOOD-NIGHT, FRIEND
2-22-04
I'LL SEE YOU IN THE MORNING..
GOOD-NIGHT!
I FEEL SORRY FOR MY SNOWMAN..I HATE TO SEE HIM STAND OUT THERE IN THE YARD ALONE ALL NIGHT..
SIGH
SCHULZ

1/1/03
DO YOU THINK THERE'S ANY TRUTH IN THE STATEMENT, "FOR EVERY SNOWFLAKE THAT FALLS A LIE IS BORN"?
I DON'T KNOW, LUCY... I'VE NEVER HEARD THAT ONE BEFORE
I JUST MADE IT UP
SCHULZ

I HATE HAVING SO MANY FAULTS...
I'D REALLY LIKE TO BE A BETTER PERSON
I WONDER WHAT IT WOULD BE LIKE TO KNOW THAT YOU WERE PERFECT?
1/8/03
TAKE IT FROM ME, IT'S A GREAT FEELING!
SCHULZ

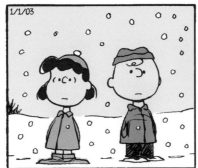

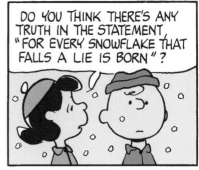

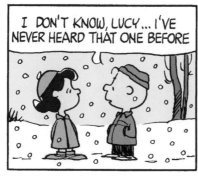

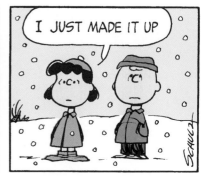

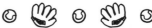

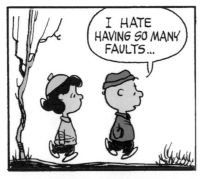

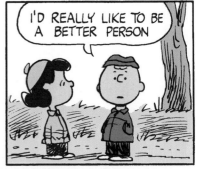

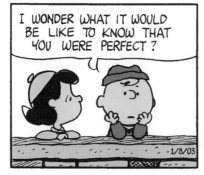

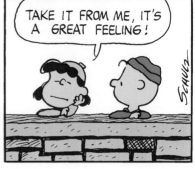

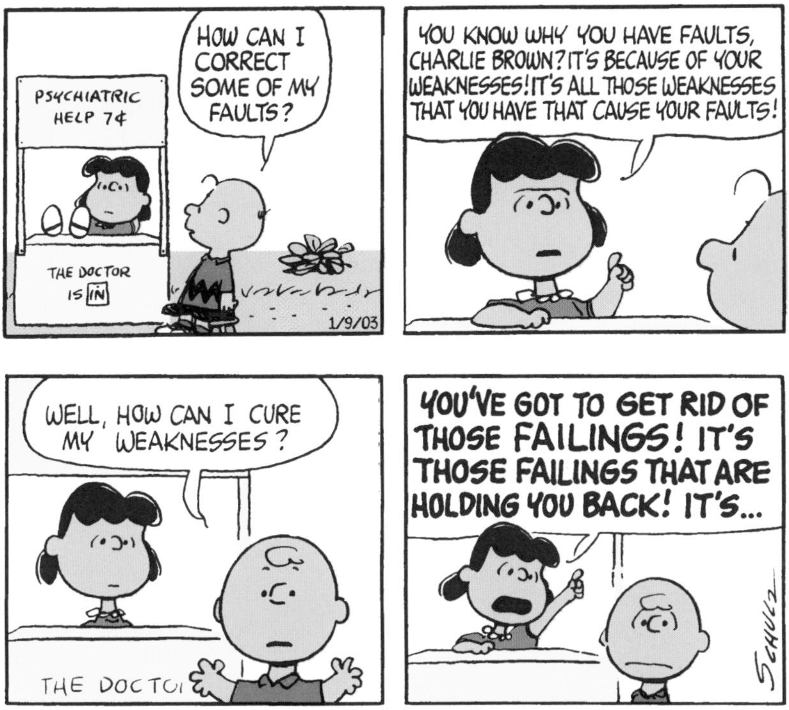
PSYCHIATRIC HELP 7¢
THE DOCTOR IS IN
HOW CAN I CORRECT SOME OF MY FAULTS?
1/9/03
YOU KNOW WHY YOU HAVE FAULTS, CHARLIE BROWN? IT'S BECAUSE OF YOUR WEAKNESSES! IT'S ALL THOSE WEAKNESSES THAT YOU HAVE THAT CAUSE YOUR FAULTS!
WELL, HOW CAN I CURE MY WEAKNESSES?
THE DOCTO
YOU'VE GOT TO GET RID OF THOSE FAILINGS! IT'S THOSE FAILINGS THAT ARE HOLDING YOU BACK! IT'S...
SCHULZ

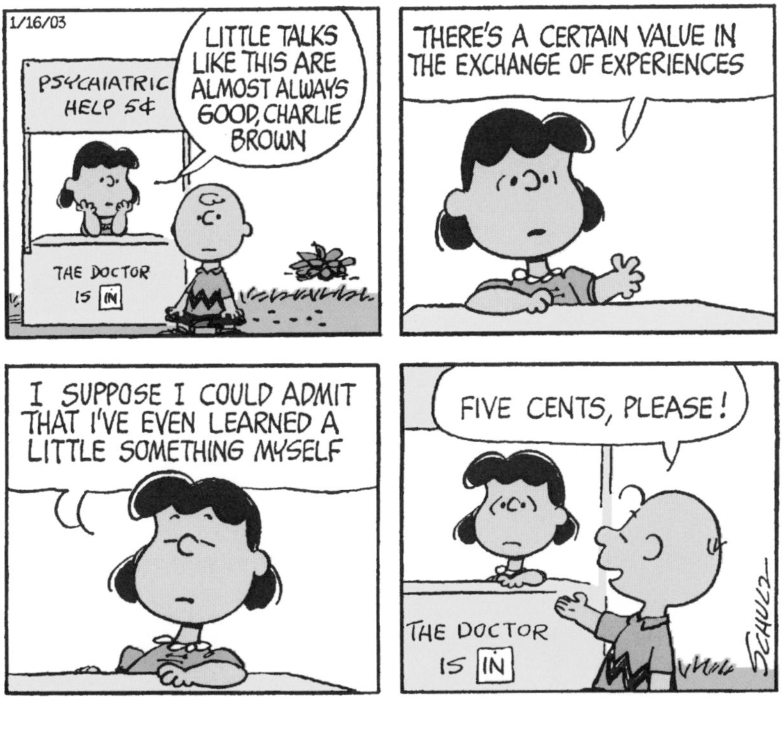
1/16/03
PSYCHIATRIC HELP 5¢
THE DOCTOR IS IN
LITTLE TALKS LIKE THIS ARE ALMOST ALWAYS GOOD, CHARLIE BROWN
THERE'S A CERTAIN VALUE IN THE EXCHANGE OF EXPERIENCES
I SUPPOSE I COULD ADMIT THAT I'VE EVEN LEARNED A LITTLE SOMETHING MYSELF
FIVE CENTS, PLEASE!
THE DOCTOR IS IN
SCHULZ

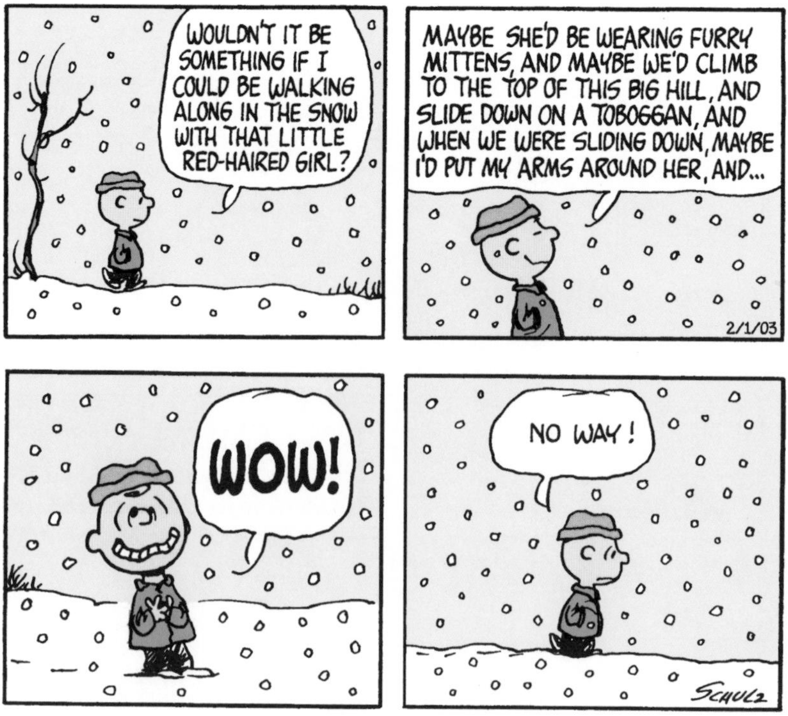
WOULDN'T IT BE SOMETHING IF I COULD BE WALKING ALONG IN THE SNOW WITH THAT LITTLE RED-HAIRED GIRL?
MAYBE SHE'D BE WEARING FURRY MITTENS, AND MAYBE WE'D CLIMB TO THE TOP OF THIS BIG HILL, AND SLIDE DOWN ON A TOBOGGAN, AND WHEN WE WERE SLIDING DOWN, MAYBE I'D PUT MY ARMS AROUND HER, AND...
2/1/03
WOW!
NO WAY!

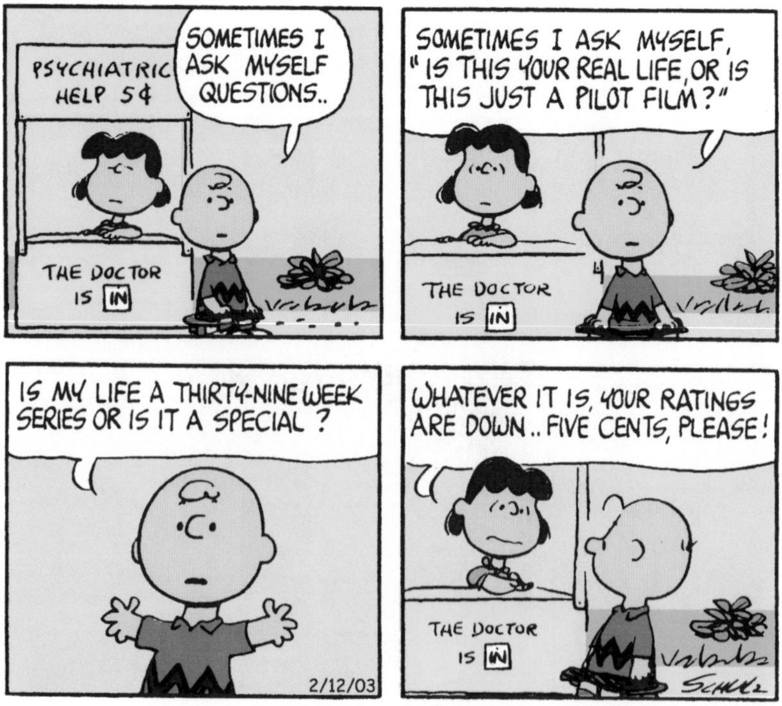
PSYCHIATRIC HELP 5¢
SOMETIMES I ASK MYSELF QUESTIONS..
THE DOCTOR IS IN
SOMETIMES I ASK MYSELF, "IS THIS YOUR REAL LIFE, OR IS THIS JUST A PILOT FILM?"
THE DOCTOR IS IN
IS MY LIFE A THIRTY-NINE WEEK SERIES OR IS IT A SPECIAL ?
2/12/03
WHATEVER IT IS, YOUR RATINGS ARE DOWN.. FIVE CENTS, PLEASE!
THE DOCTOR IS IN

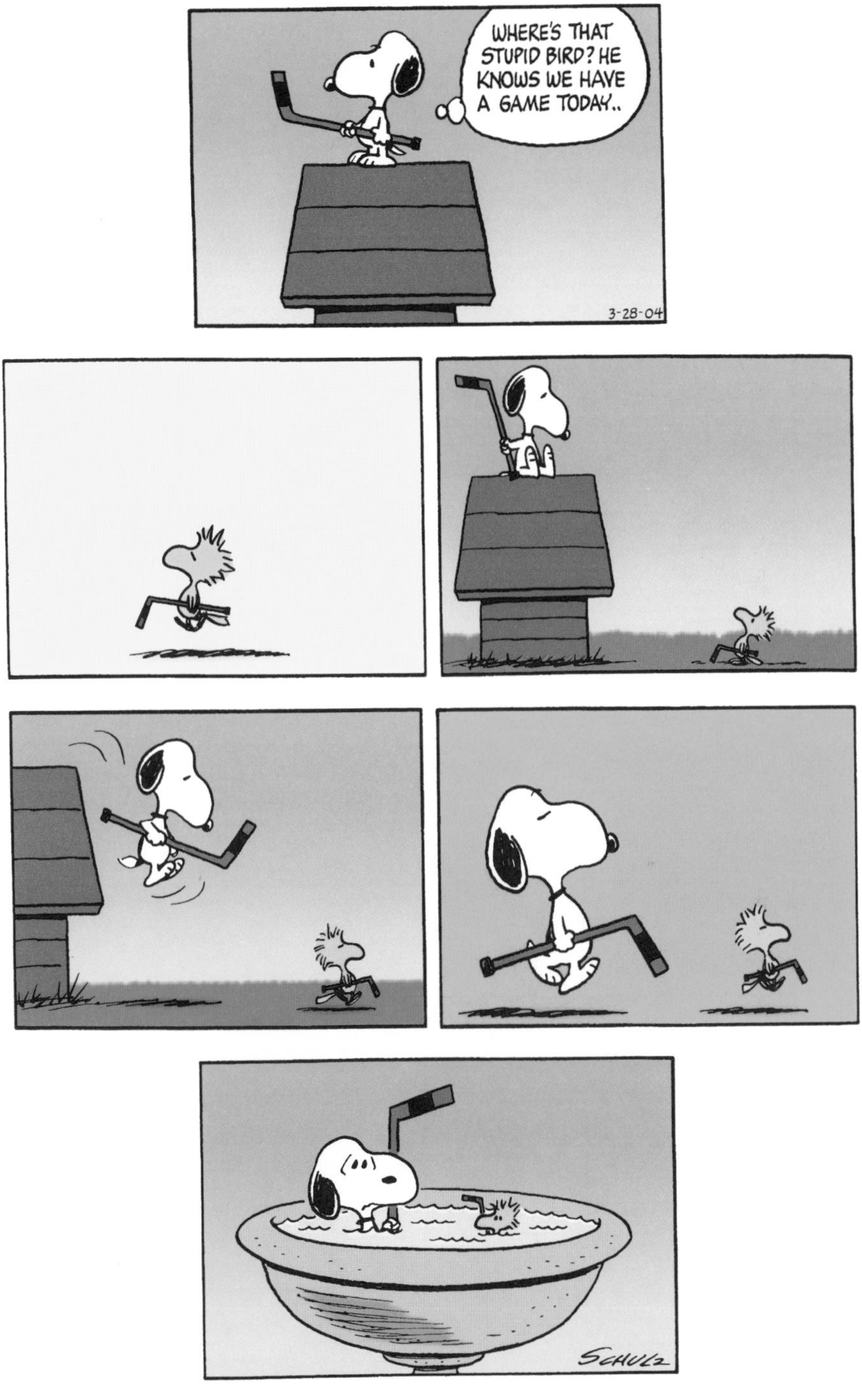
WHERE'S THAT STUPID BIRD? HE KNOWS WE HAVE A GAME TODAY..
3-28-04
SCHULZ

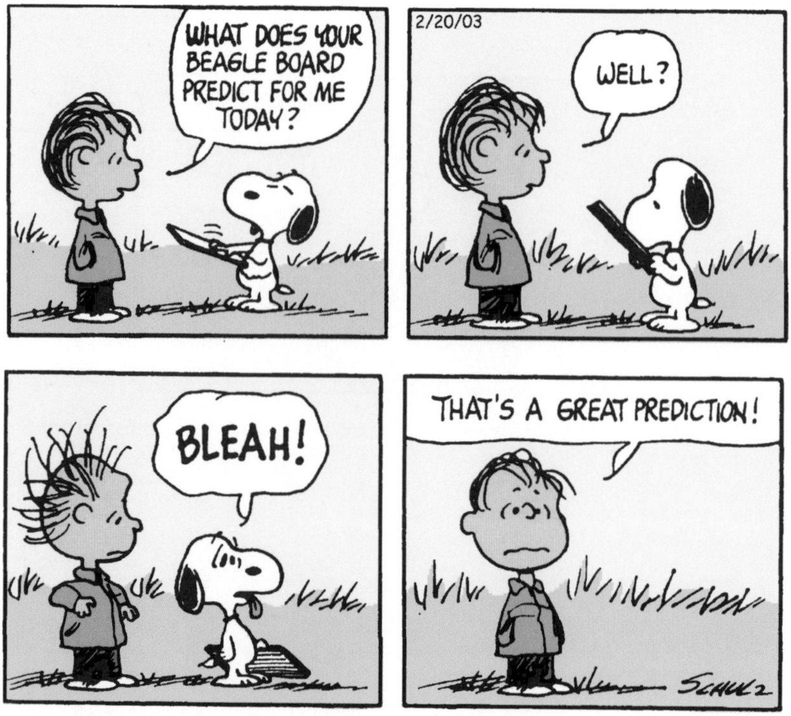
WHAT DOES YOUR BEAGLE BOARD PREDICT FOR ME TODAY?
2/20/03
WELL?
BLEAH!
THAT'S A GREAT PREDICTION!
SCHULZ

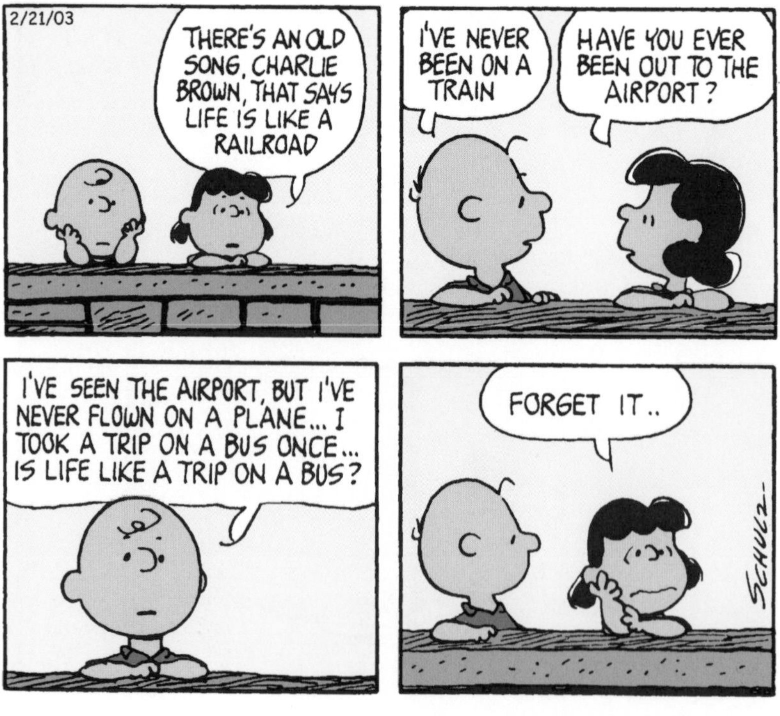
2/21/03
THERE'S AN OLD SONG, CHARLIE BROWN, THAT SAYS LIFE IS LIKE A RAILROAD
I'VE NEVER BEEN ON A TRAIN
HAVE YOU EVER BEEN OUT TO THE AIRPORT?
I'VE SEEN THE AIRPORT, BUT I'VE NEVER FLOWN ON A PLANE... I TOOK A TRIP ON A BUS ONCE... IS LIFE LIKE A TRIP ON A BUS?
FORGET IT..
SCHULZ

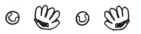

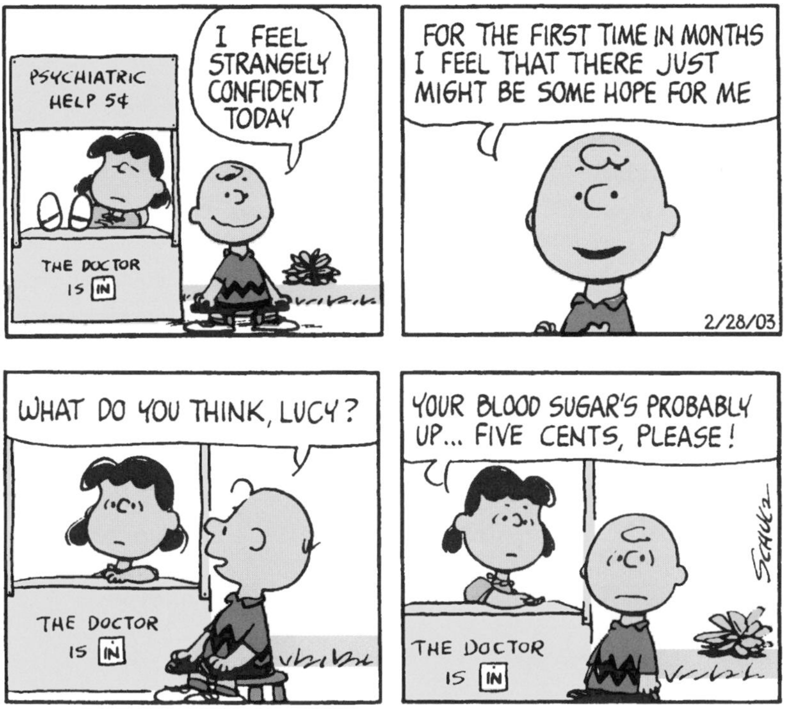
PSYCHIATRIC HELP 5¢
THE DOCTOR IS IN
I FEEL STRANGELY CONFIDENT TODAY
FOR THE FIRST TIME IN MONTHS I FEEL THAT THERE JUST MIGHT BE SOME HOPE FOR ME
2/28/03
WHAT DO YOU THINK, LUCY?
THE DOCTOR IS IN
YOUR BLOOD SUGAR'S PROBABLY UP... FIVE CENTS, PLEASE!
THE DOCTOR IS IN
SCHULZ

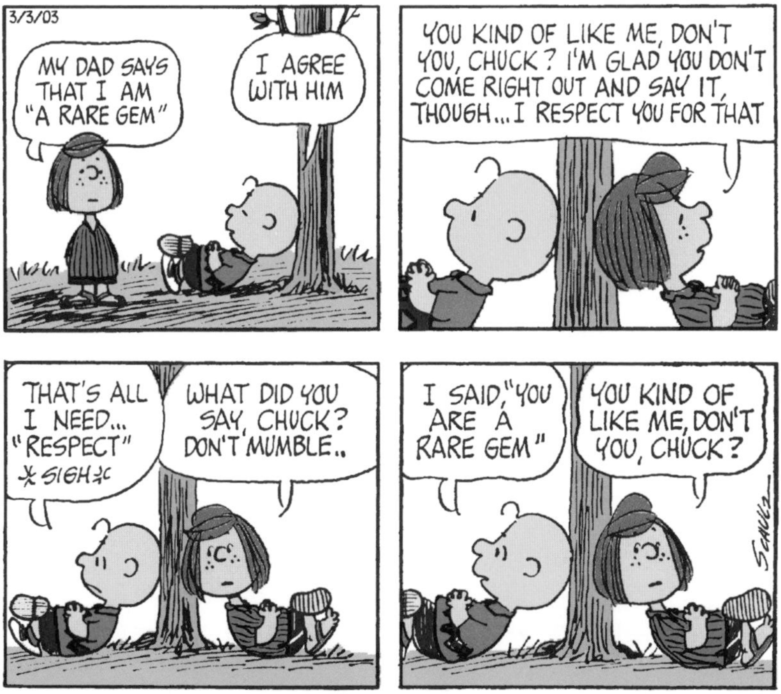
3/3/03
MY DAD SAYS THAT I AM "A RARE GEM"
I AGREE WITH HIM
YOU KIND OF LIKE ME, DON'T YOU, CHUCK? I'M GLAD YOU DON'T COME RIGHT OUT AND SAY IT, THOUGH... I RESPECT YOU FOR THAT
THAT'S ALL I NEED... "RESPECT" *SIGH*
WHAT DID YOU SAY, CHUCK? DON'T MUMBLE..
I SAID, "YOU ARE A RARE GEM"
YOU KIND OF LIKE ME, DON'T YOU, CHUCK?
SCHULZ

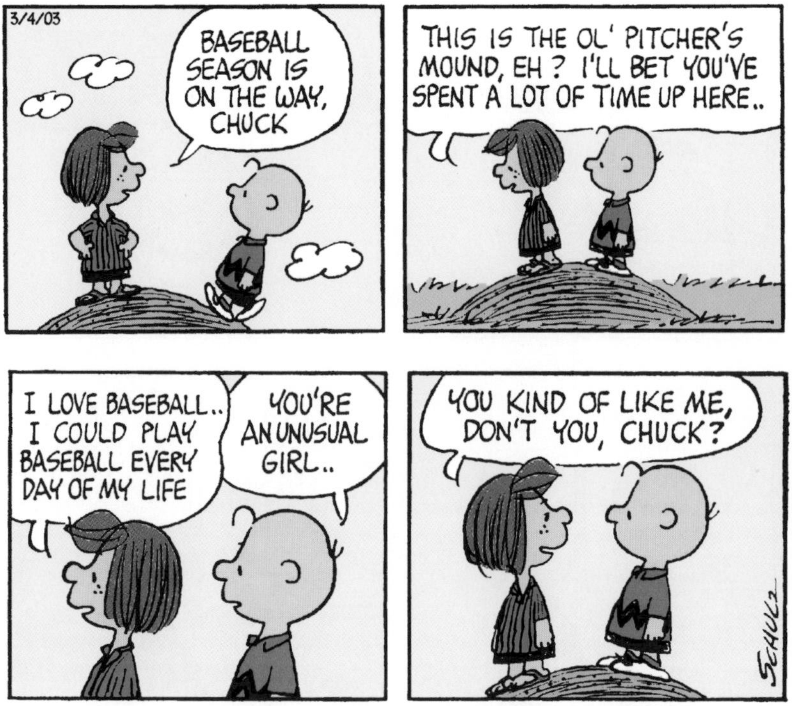
BASEBALL SEASON IS ON THE WAY, CHUCK
THIS IS THE OL' PITCHER'S MOUND, EH ? I'LL BET YOU'VE SPENT A LOT OF TIME UP HERE..
I LOVE BASEBALL.. I COULD PLAY BASEBALL EVERY DAY OF MY LIFE
YOU'RE AN UNUSUAL GIRL..
YOU KIND OF LIKE ME, DON'T YOU, CHUCK?

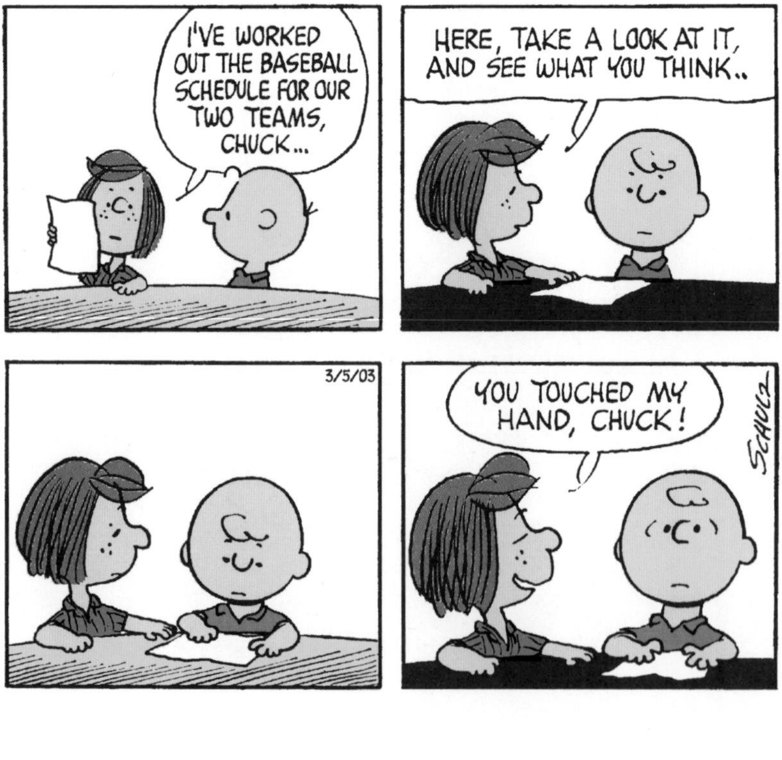
I'VE WORKED OUT THE BASEBALL SCHEDULE FOR OUR TWO TEAMS, CHUCK...
HERE, TAKE A LOOK AT IT, AND SEE WHAT YOU THINK..
YOU TOUCHED MY HAND, CHUCK!

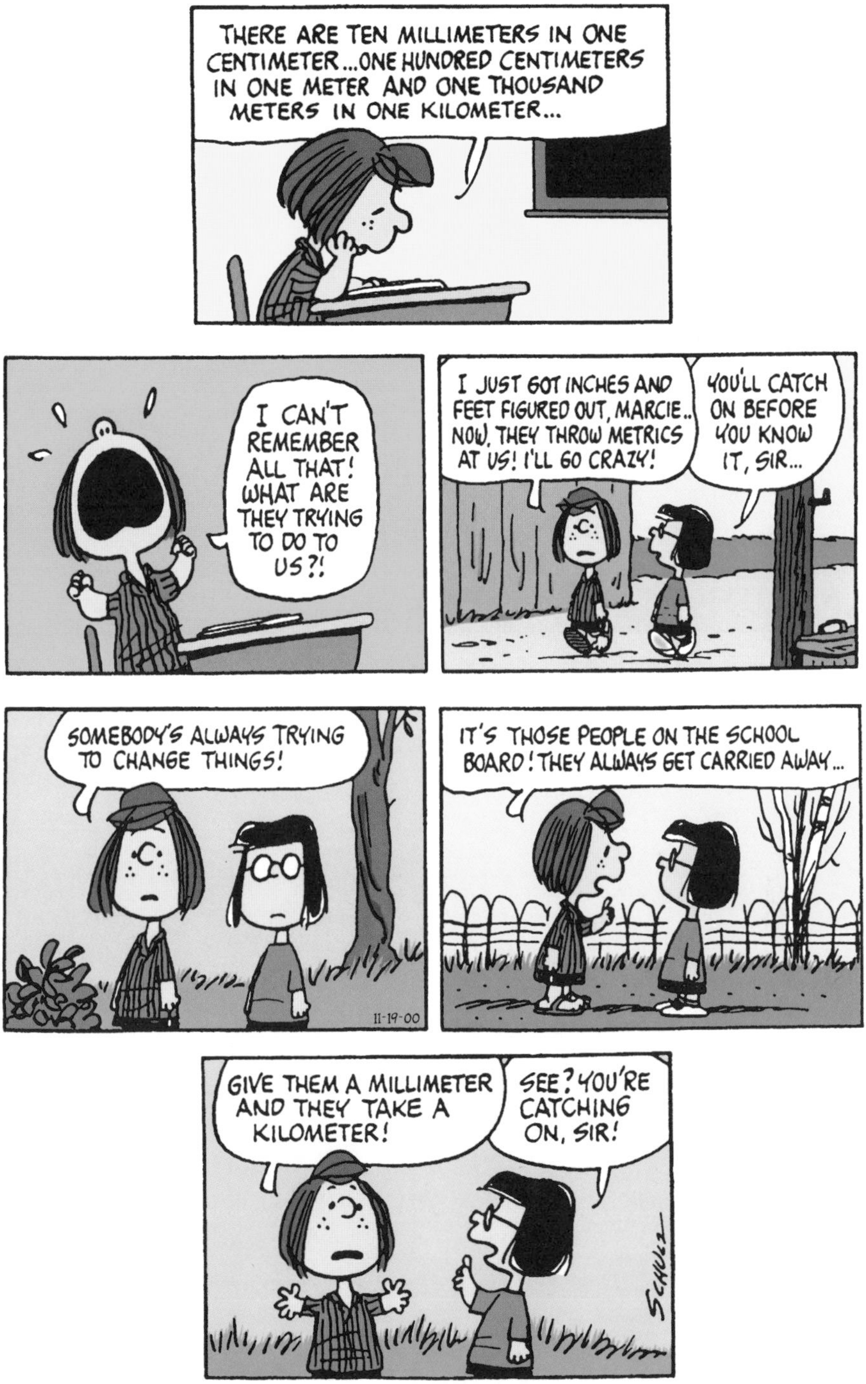
THERE ARE TEN MILLIMETERS IN ONE CENTIMETER...ONE HUNDRED CENTIMETERS IN ONE METER AND ONE THOUSAND METERS IN ONE KILOMETER...
I CAN'T REMEMBER ALL THAT! WHAT ARE THEY TRYING TO DO TO US?!
I JUST GOT INCHES AND FEET FIGURED OUT, MARCIE.. NOW, THEY THROW METRICS AT US! I'LL GO CRAZY!
YOU'LL CATCH ON BEFORE YOU KNOW IT, SIR...
SOMEBODY'S ALWAYS TRYING TO CHANGE THINGS!
11-19-00
IT'S THOSE PEOPLE ON THE SCHOOL BOARD! THEY ALWAYS GET CARRIED AWAY...
GIVE THEM A MILLIMETER AND THEY TAKE A KILOMETER!
SEE? YOU'RE CATCHING ON, SIR!
SCHULZ

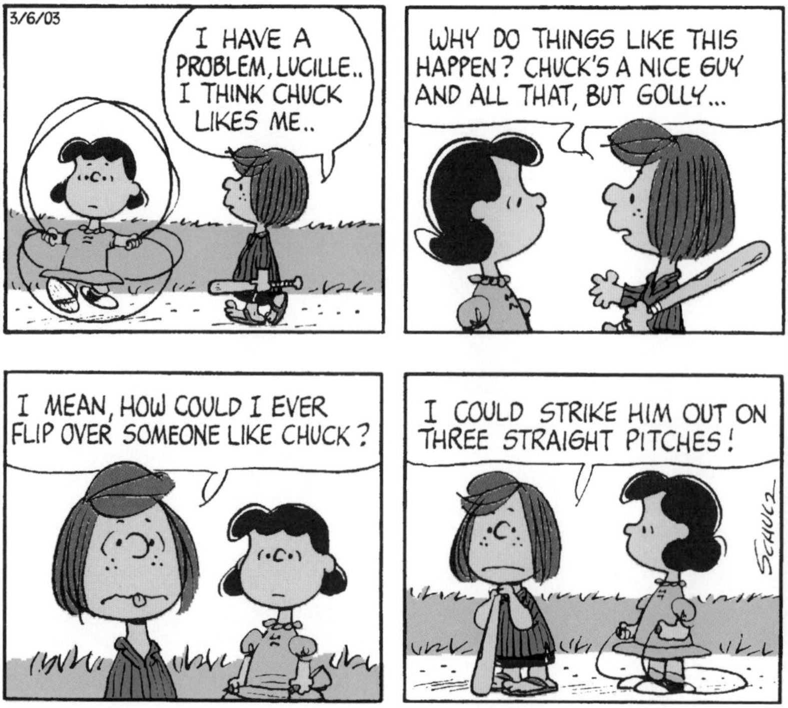
3/6/03
I HAVE A PROBLEM, LUCILLE.. I THINK CHUCK LIKES ME..
WHY DO THINGS LIKE THIS HAPPEN? CHUCK'S A NICE GUY AND ALL THAT, BUT GOLLY...
I MEAN, HOW COULD I EVER FLIP OVER SOMEONE LIKE CHUCK?
I COULD STRIKE HIM OUT ON THREE STRAIGHT PITCHES!
SCHULZ

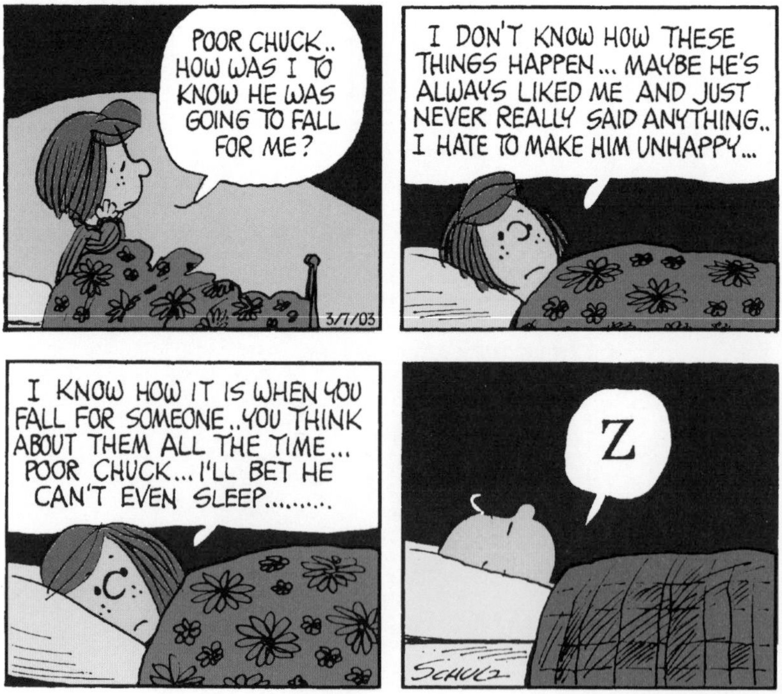
POOR CHUCK.. HOW WAS I TO KNOW HE WAS GOING TO FALL FOR ME?
3/7/03
I DON'T KNOW HOW THESE THINGS HAPPEN... MAYBE HE'S ALWAYS LIKED ME AND JUST NEVER REALLY SAID ANYTHING.. I HATE TO MAKE HIM UNHAPPY...
I KNOW HOW IT IS WHEN YOU FALL FOR SOMEONE..YOU THINK ABOUT THEM ALL THE TIME... POOR CHUCK... I'LL BET HE CAN'T EVEN SLEEP.........
Z
SCHULZ

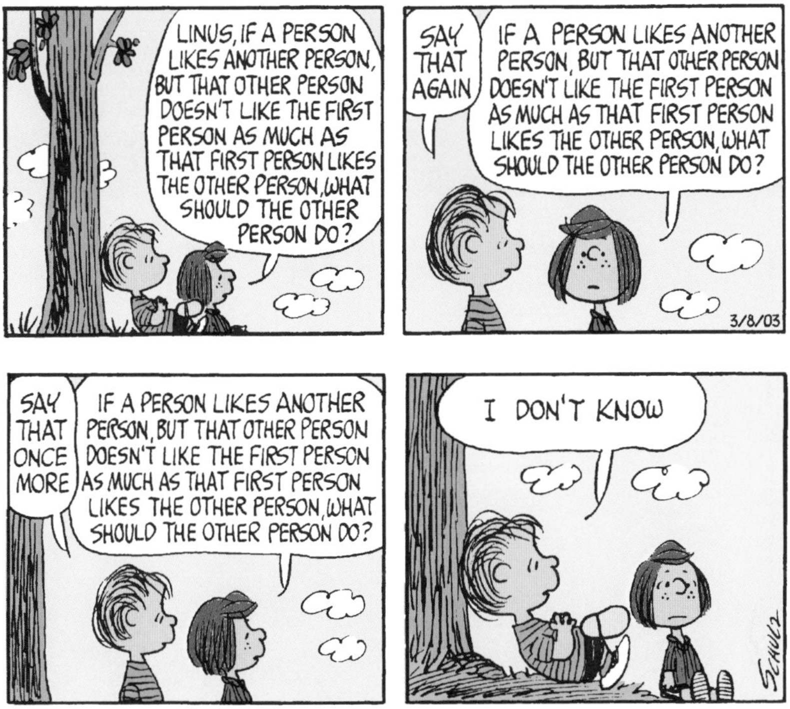
LINUS, IF A PERSON LIKES ANOTHER PERSON, BUT THAT OTHER PERSON DOESN'T LIKE THE FIRST PERSON AS MUCH AS THAT FIRST PERSON LIKES THE OTHER PERSON, WHAT SHOULD THE OTHER PERSON DO?
SAY THAT AGAIN
IF A PERSON LIKES ANOTHER PERSON, BUT THAT OTHER PERSON DOESN'T LIKE THE FIRST PERSON AS MUCH AS THAT FIRST PERSON LIKES THE OTHER PERSON, WHAT SHOULD THE OTHER PERSON DO?
3/8/03
SAY THAT ONCE MORE
IF A PERSON LIKES ANOTHER PERSON, BUT THAT OTHER PERSON DOESN'T LIKE THE FIRST PERSON AS MUCH AS THAT FIRST PERSON LIKES THE OTHER PERSON, WHAT SHOULD THE OTHER PERSON DO?
I DON'T KNOW
SCHULZ

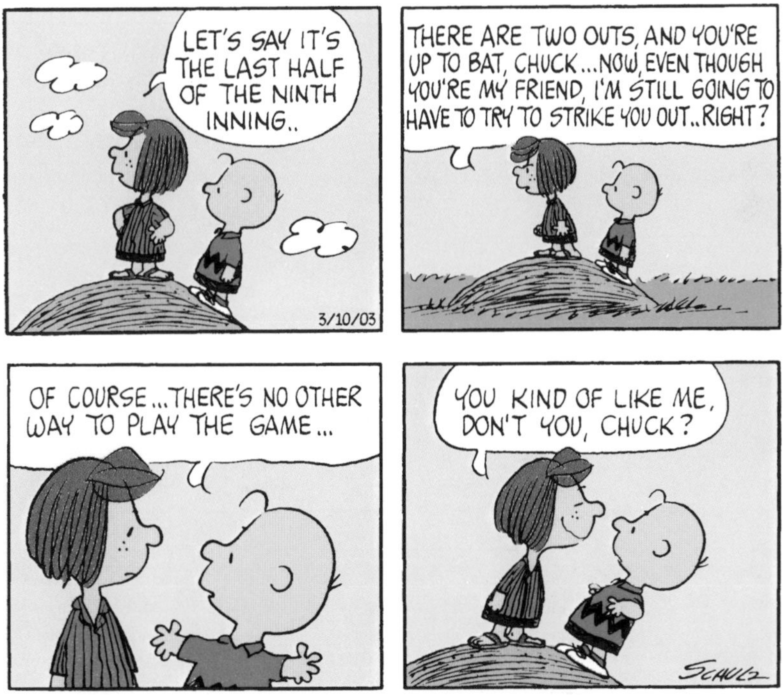
LET'S SAY IT'S THE LAST HALF OF THE NINTH INNING..
3/10/03
THERE ARE TWO OUTS, AND YOU'RE UP TO BAT, CHUCK...NOW, EVEN THOUGH YOU'RE MY FRIEND, I'M STILL GOING TO HAVE TO TRY TO STRIKE YOU OUT..RIGHT?
OF COURSE...THERE'S NO OTHER WAY TO PLAY THE GAME...
YOU KIND OF LIKE ME, DON'T YOU, CHUCK?
SCHULZ

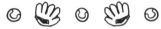

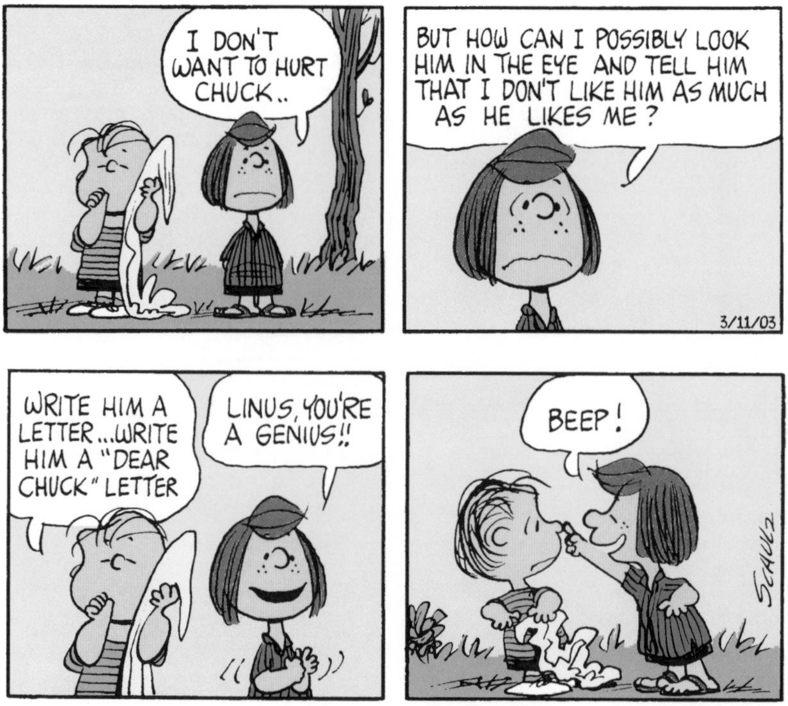
I DON'T WANT TO HURT CHUCK..
BUT HOW CAN I POSSIBLY LOOK HIM IN THE EYE AND TELL HIM THAT I DON'T LIKE HIM AS MUCH AS HE LIKES ME?
3/11/03
WRITE HIM A LETTER...WRITE HIM A "DEAR CHUCK" LETTER
LINUS, YOU'RE A GENIUS!!
BEEP!
SCHULZ

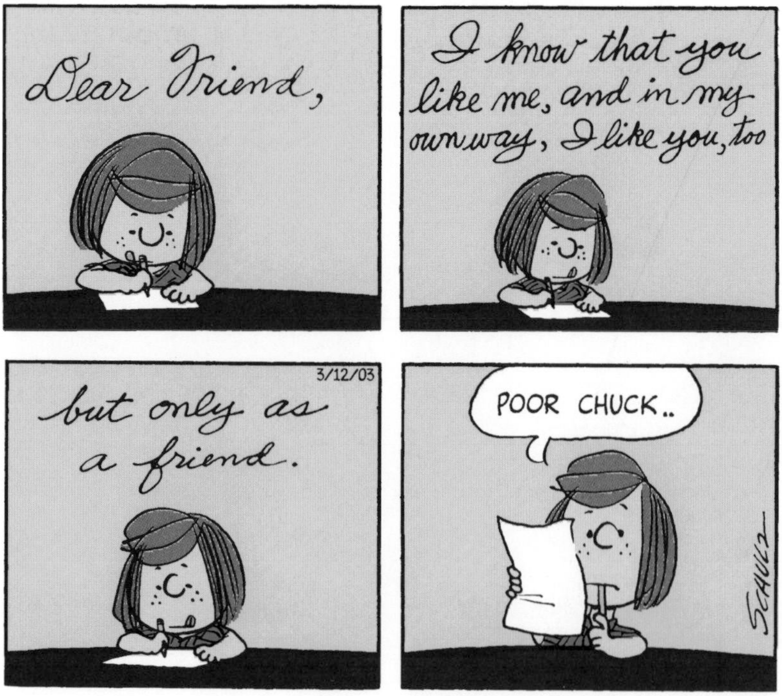
Dear Friend,
I know that you like me, and in my own way, I like you, too
3/12/03
but only as a friend.
POOR CHUCK..
SCHULZ

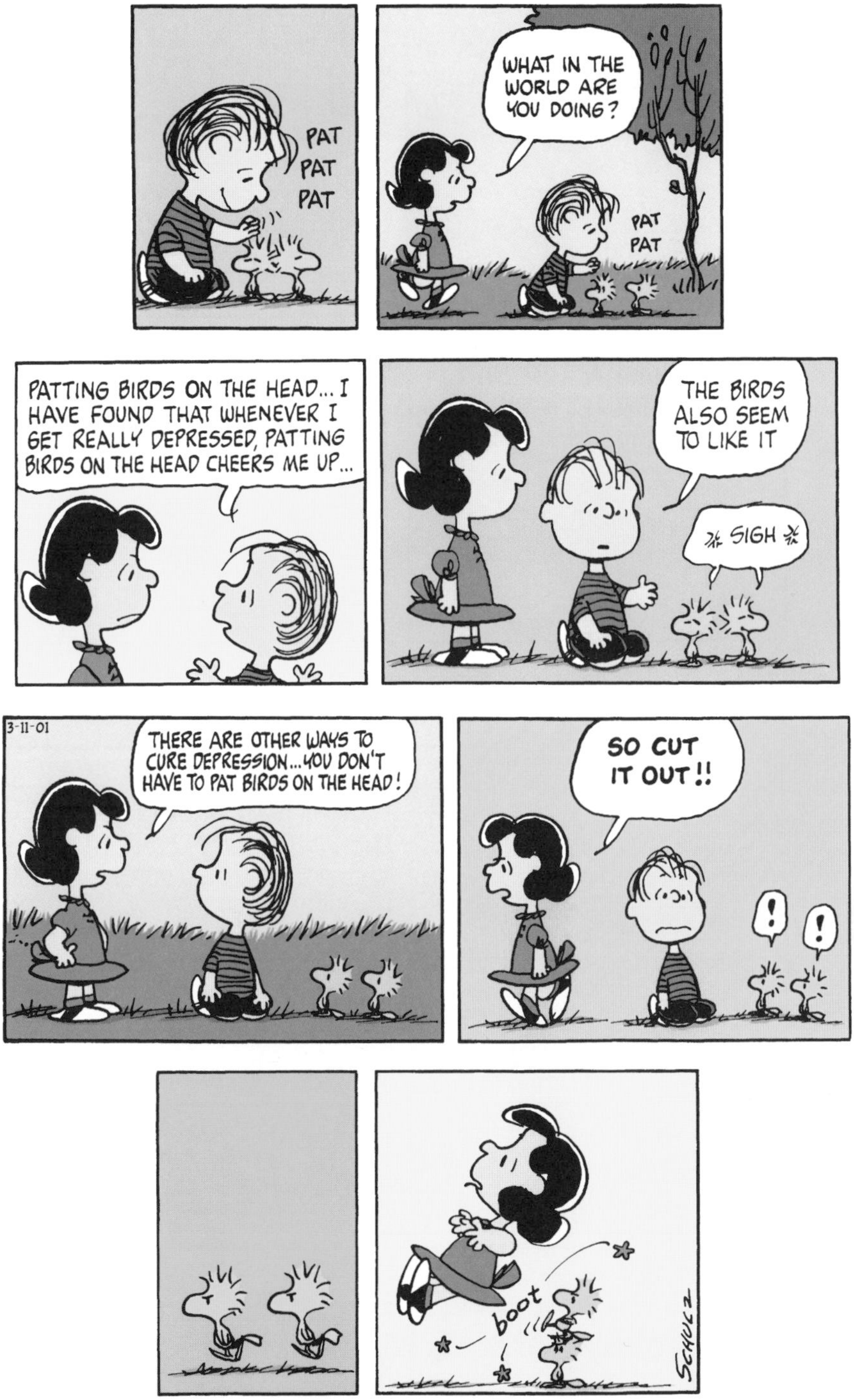

PAT
PAT
PAT
WHAT IN THE WORLD ARE YOU DOING?
PAT
PAT
PATTING BIRDS ON THE HEAD... I HAVE FOUND THAT WHENEVER I GET REALLY DEPRESSED, PATTING BIRDS ON THE HEAD CHEERS ME UP...
THE BIRDS ALSO SEEM TO LIKE IT
SIGH
3-11-01
THERE ARE OTHER WAYS TO CURE DEPRESSION...YOU DON'T HAVE TO PAT BIRDS ON THE HEAD!
SO CUT IT OUT!!
!
!
boot
SCHULZ

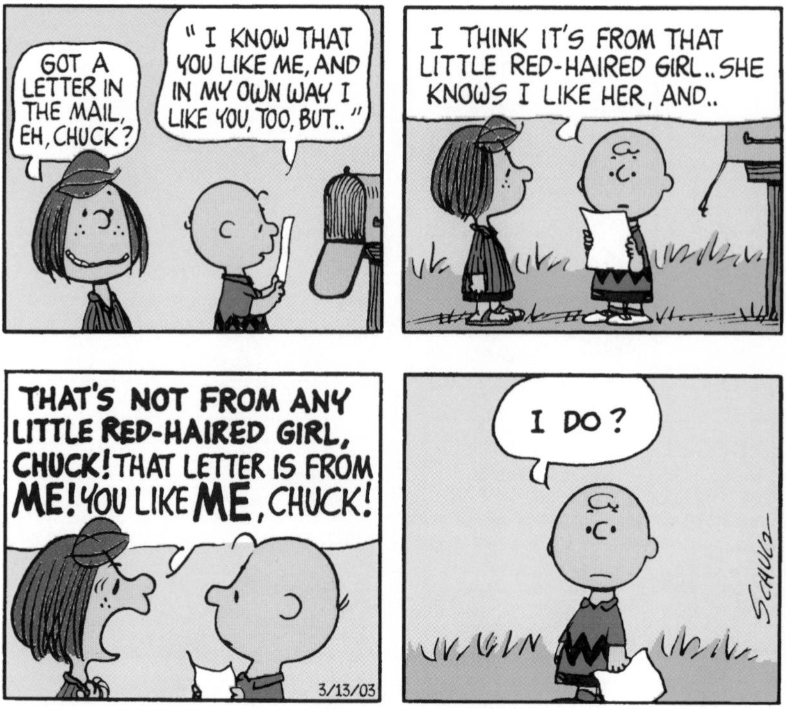
GOT A LETTER IN THE MAIL, EH, CHUCK?
"I KNOW THAT YOU LIKE ME, AND IN MY OWN WAY I LIKE YOU, TOO, BUT.."
I THINK IT'S FROM THAT LITTLE RED-HAIRED GIRL..SHE KNOWS I LIKE HER, AND..
THAT'S NOT FROM ANY LITTLE RED-HAIRED GIRL, CHUCK! THAT LETTER IS FROM ME! YOU LIKE ME, CHUCK!
3/13/03
I DO?
SCHULZ

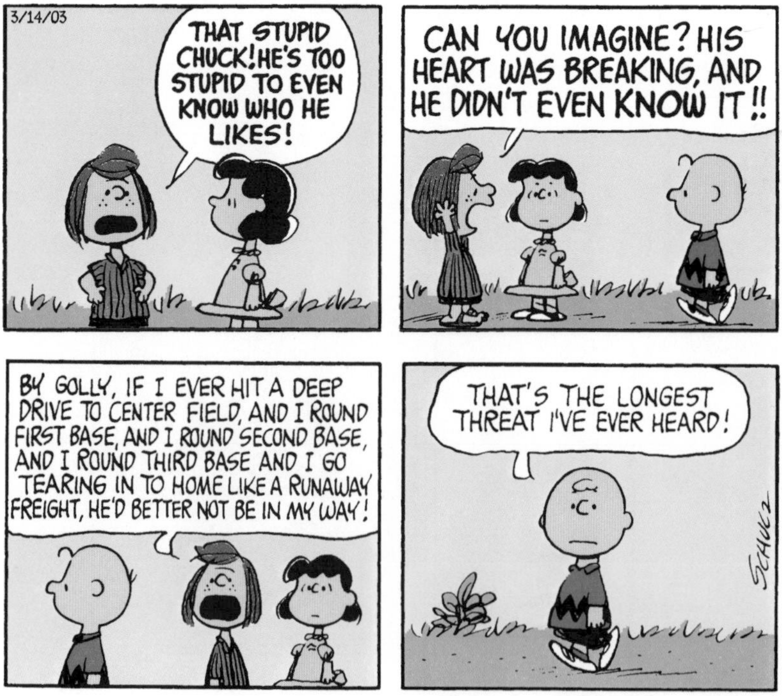
3/14/03
THAT STUPID CHUCK! HE'S TOO STUPID TO EVEN KNOW WHO HE LIKES!
CAN YOU IMAGINE? HIS HEART WAS BREAKING, AND HE DIDN'T EVEN KNOW IT!!
BY GOLLY, IF I EVER HIT A DEEP DRIVE TO CENTER FIELD, AND I ROUND FIRST BASE, AND I ROUND SECOND BASE, AND I ROUND THIRD BASE AND I GO TEARING IN TO HOME LIKE A RUNAWAY FREIGHT, HE'D BETTER NOT BE IN MY WAY!
THAT'S THE LONGEST THREAT I'VE EVER HEARD!
SCHULZ

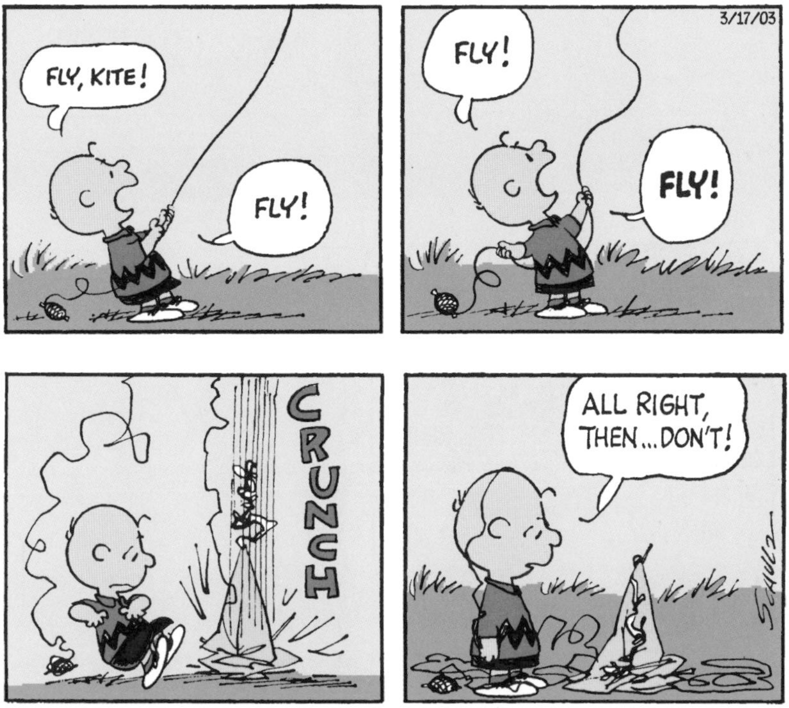
3/17/03
FLY, KITE!
FLY!
FLY!
FLY!
CRUNCH
ALL RIGHT, THEN...DON'T!
SCHULZ

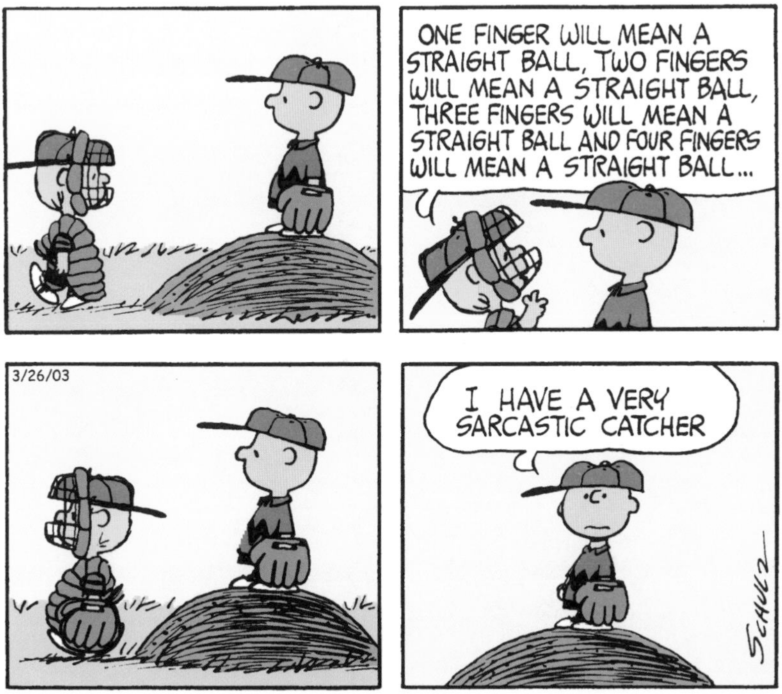
ONE FINGER WILL MEAN A STRAIGHT BALL, TWO FINGERS WILL MEAN A STRAIGHT BALL, THREE FINGERS WILL MEAN A STRAIGHT BALL AND FOUR FINGERS WILL MEAN A STRAIGHT BALL...
3/26/03
I HAVE A VERY SARCASTIC CATCHER
SCHULZ

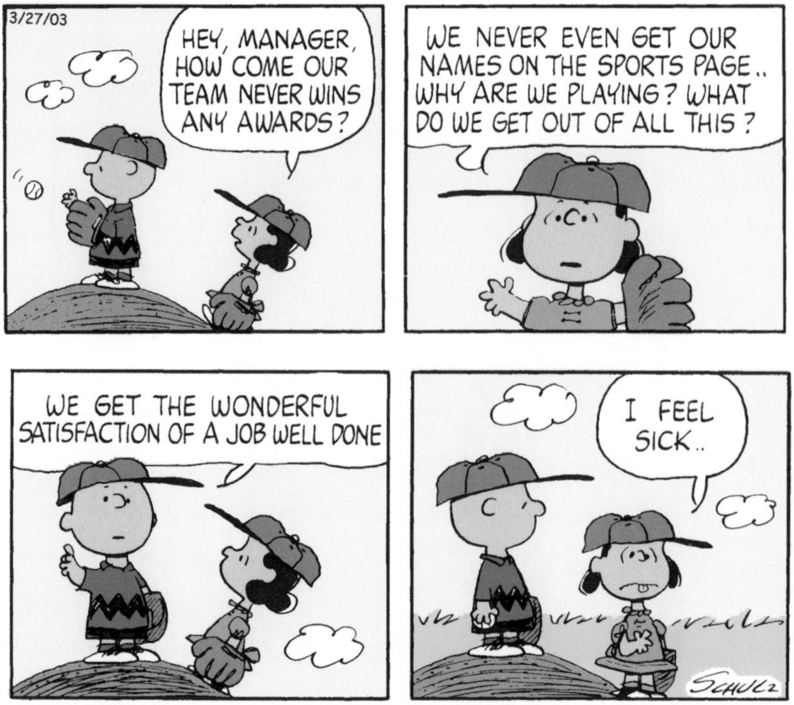
3/27/03
HEY, MANAGER, HOW COME OUR TEAM NEVER WINS ANY AWARDS?
WE NEVER EVEN GET OUR NAMES ON THE SPORTS PAGE.. WHY ARE WE PLAYING? WHAT DO WE GET OUT OF ALL THIS?
WE GET THE WONDERFUL SATISFACTION OF A JOB WELL DONE
I FEEL SICK..
SCHULZ

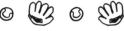

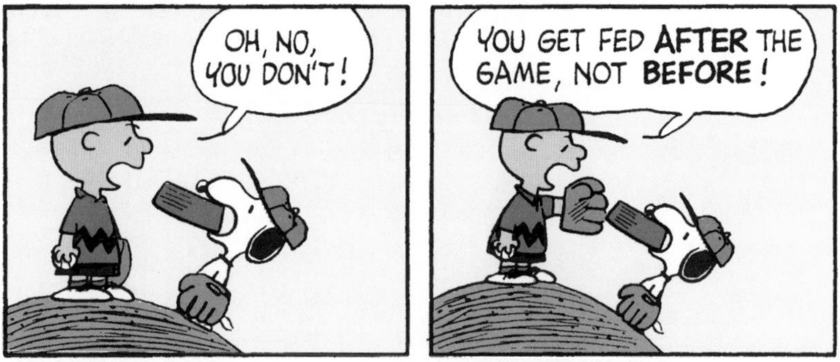
OH, NO, YOU DON'T!
YOU GET FED **AFTER** THE GAME, NOT **BEFORE**!

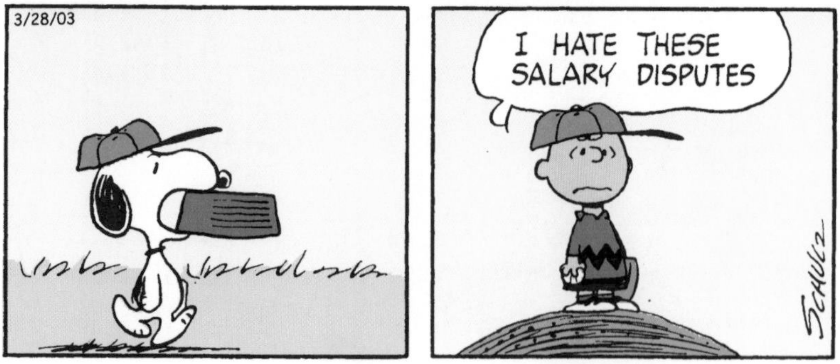
3/28/03
I HATE THESE SALARY DISPUTES
SCHULZ

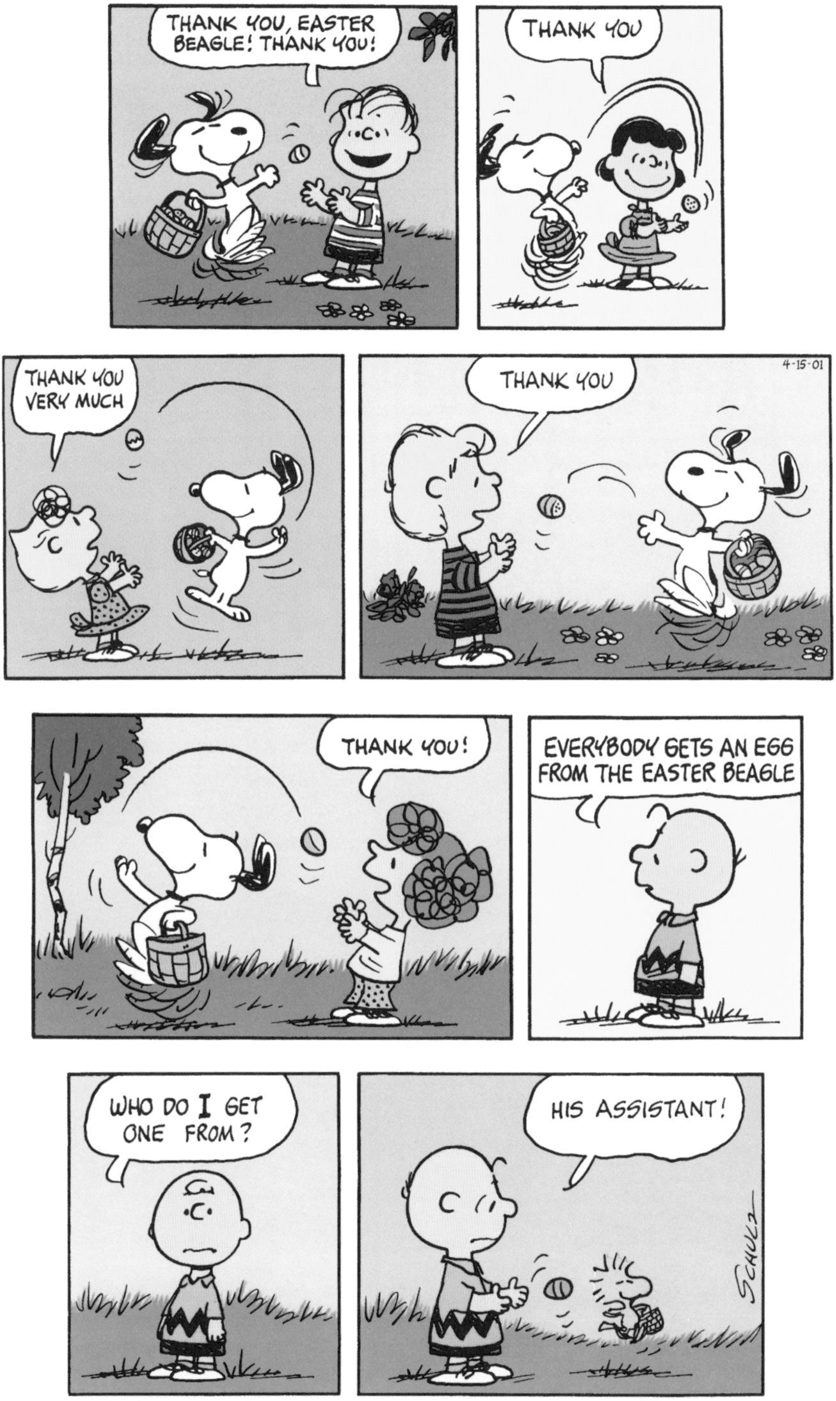
THANK YOU, EASTER BEAGLE! THANK YOU!
THANK YOU
THANK YOU VERY MUCH
THANK YOU
4-15-01
THANK YOU!
EVERYBODY GETS AN EGG FROM THE EASTER BEAGLE
WHO DO I GET ONE FROM?
HIS ASSISTANT!
SCHULZ

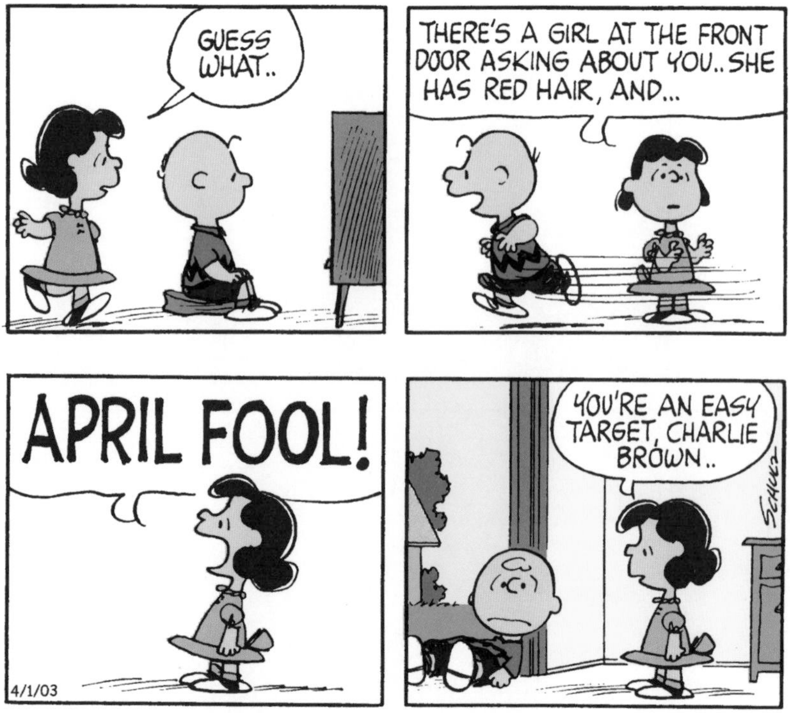
GUESS WHAT..
THERE'S A GIRL AT THE FRONT DOOR ASKING ABOUT YOU.. SHE HAS RED HAIR, AND...
APRIL FOOL!
4/1/03
YOU'RE AN EASY TARGET, CHARLIE BROWN..

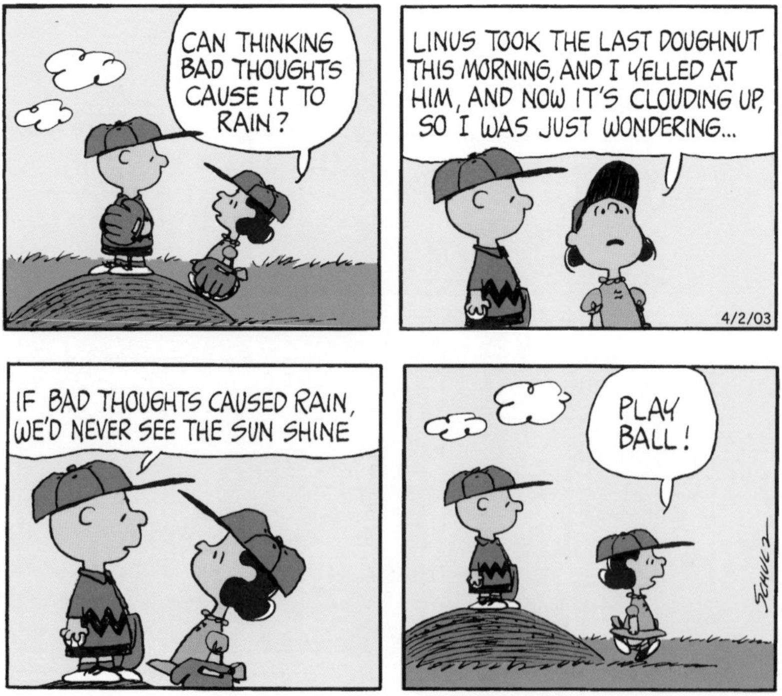
CAN THINKING BAD THOUGHTS CAUSE IT TO RAIN?
LINUS TOOK THE LAST DOUGHNUT THIS MORNING, AND I YELLED AT HIM, AND NOW IT'S CLOUDING UP, SO I WAS JUST WONDERING...
4/2/03
IF BAD THOUGHTS CAUSED RAIN, WE'D NEVER SEE THE SUN SHINE
PLAY BALL!

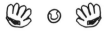

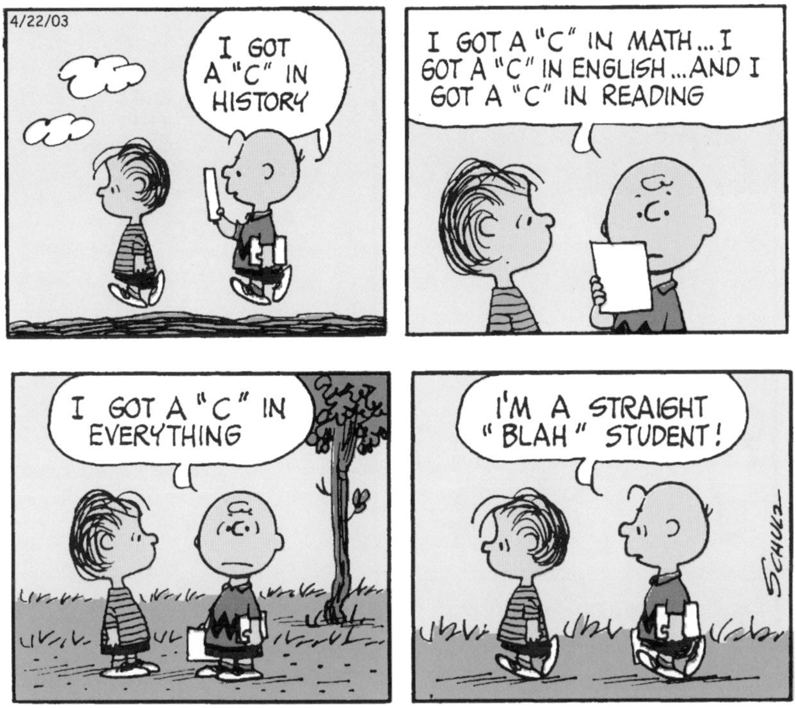
4/22/03
I GOT A "C" IN HISTORY
I GOT A "C" IN MATH... I GOT A "C" IN ENGLISH... AND I GOT A "C" IN READING
I GOT A "C" IN EVERYTHING
I'M A STRAIGHT "BLAH" STUDENT!

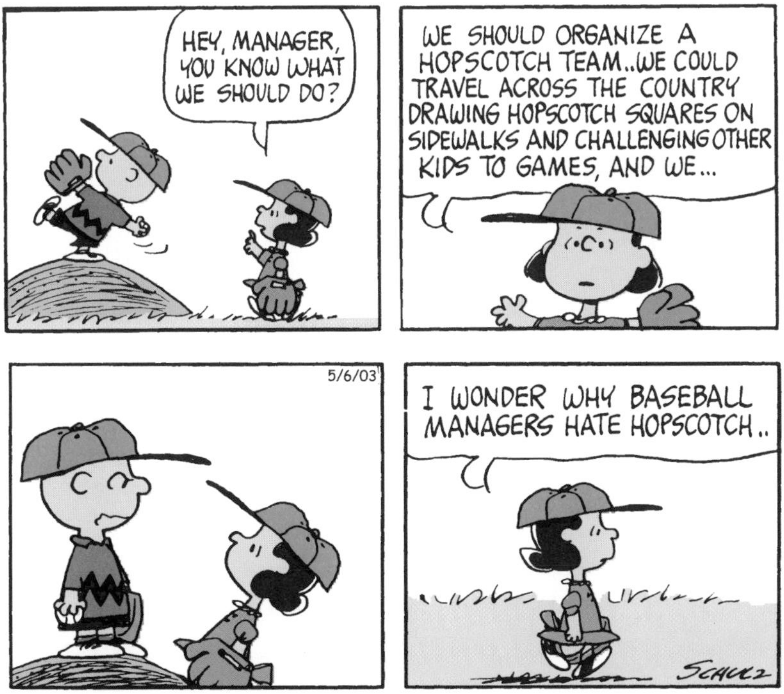
HEY, MANAGER, YOU KNOW WHAT WE SHOULD DO?
WE SHOULD ORGANIZE A HOPSCOTCH TEAM..WE COULD TRAVEL ACROSS THE COUNTRY DRAWING HOPSCOTCH SQUARES ON SIDEWALKS AND CHALLENGING OTHER KIDS TO GAMES, AND WE...
5/6/03
I WONDER WHY BASEBALL MANAGERS HATE HOPSCOTCH..

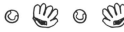

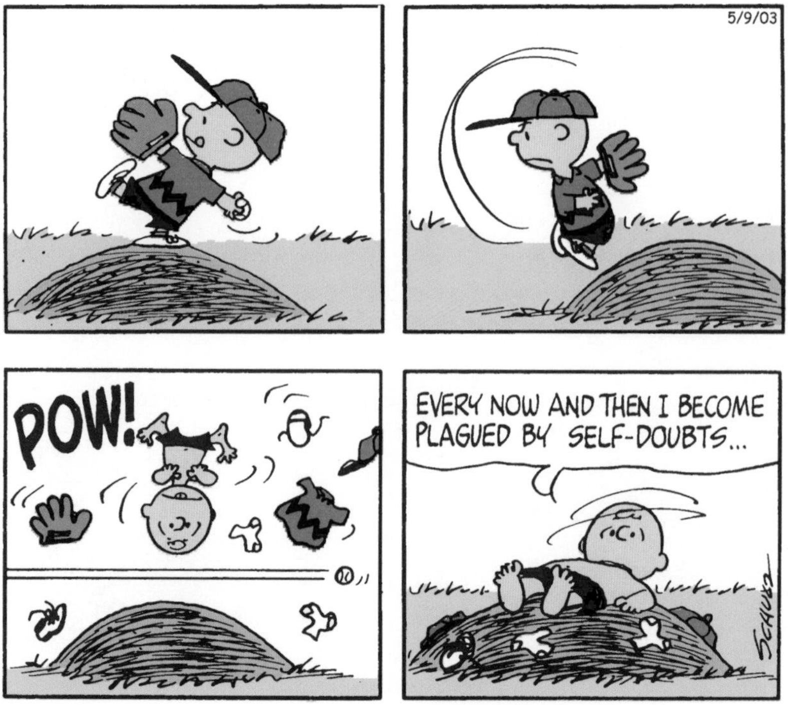
5/9/03
POW!
EVERY NOW AND THEN I BECOME PLAGUED BY SELF-DOUBTS...
SCHULZ

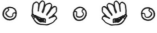

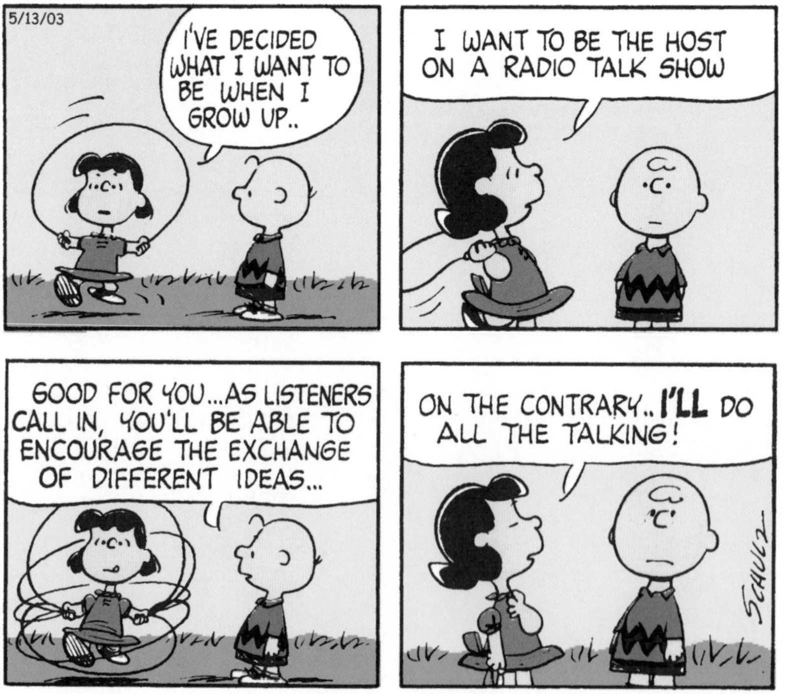
5/13/03
I'VE DECIDED WHAT I WANT TO BE WHEN I GROW UP..
I WANT TO BE THE HOST ON A RADIO TALK SHOW
GOOD FOR YOU...AS LISTENERS CALL IN, YOU'LL BE ABLE TO ENCOURAGE THE EXCHANGE OF DIFFERENT IDEAS...
ON THE CONTRARY.. I'LL DO ALL THE TALKING!
SCHULZ

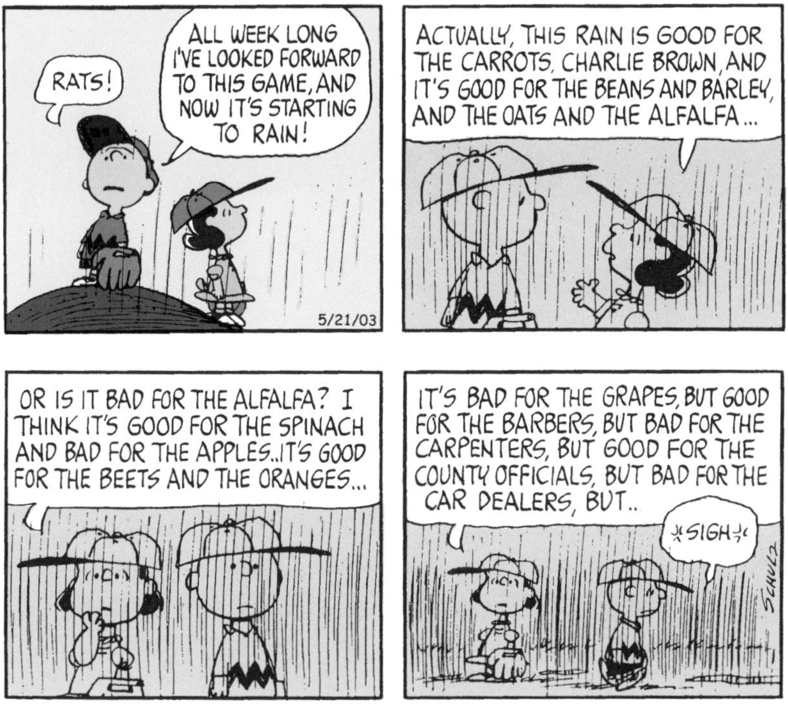
RATS!
ALL WEEK LONG I'VE LOOKED FORWARD TO THIS GAME, AND NOW IT'S STARTING TO RAIN!
5/21/03
ACTUALLY, THIS RAIN IS GOOD FOR THE CARROTS, CHARLIE BROWN, AND IT'S GOOD FOR THE BEANS AND BARLEY, AND THE OATS AND THE ALFALFA...
OR IS IT BAD FOR THE ALFALFA? I THINK IT'S GOOD FOR THE SPINACH AND BAD FOR THE APPLES..IT'S GOOD FOR THE BEETS AND THE ORANGES...
IT'S BAD FOR THE GRAPES, BUT GOOD FOR THE BARBERS, BUT BAD FOR THE CARPENTERS, BUT GOOD FOR THE COUNTY OFFICIALS, BUT BAD FOR THE CAR DEALERS, BUT..
SIGH

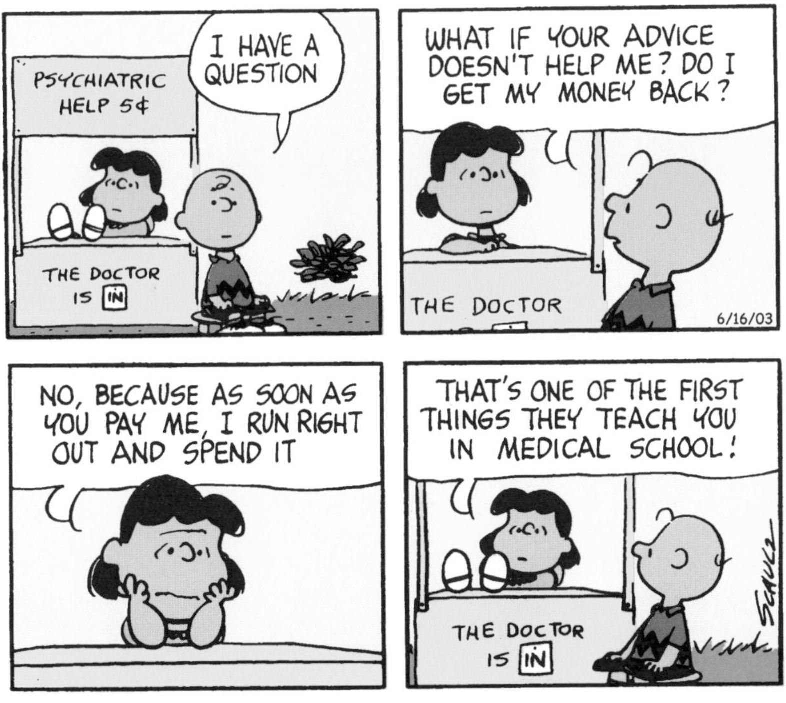
PSYCHIATRIC HELP 5¢
THE DOCTOR IS IN
I HAVE A QUESTION
WHAT IF YOUR ADVICE DOESN'T HELP ME? DO I GET MY MONEY BACK?
THE DOCTOR
6/16/03
NO, BECAUSE AS SOON AS YOU PAY ME, I RUN RIGHT OUT AND SPEND IT
THAT'S ONE OF THE FIRST THINGS THEY TEACH YOU IN MEDICAL SCHOOL!
THE DOCTOR IS IN

HA! YOU DIDN'T THINK I COULD GET MENTIONED, BUT I DID!
I DON'T KNOW WHAT YOU'RE TALKING ABOUT..
THE SCHOOL PLAY! THE PROGRAM WHERE EVERYONE GETS MENTIONED!
SEE? THEY HAVE THE NAMES OF ALL THE KIDS WHO WERE IN THE PLAY, AND THEY HAVE THE NAMES OF ALL THE ADULTS WHO HELPED WITH SCENERY AND FOOD AND THINGS...

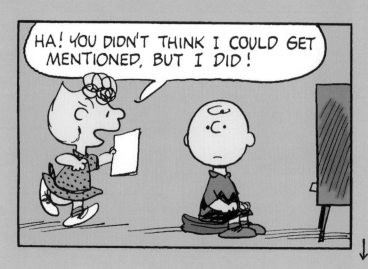

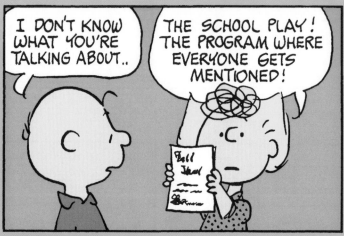

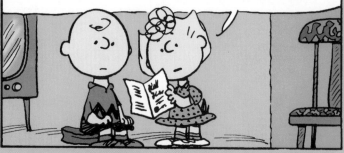

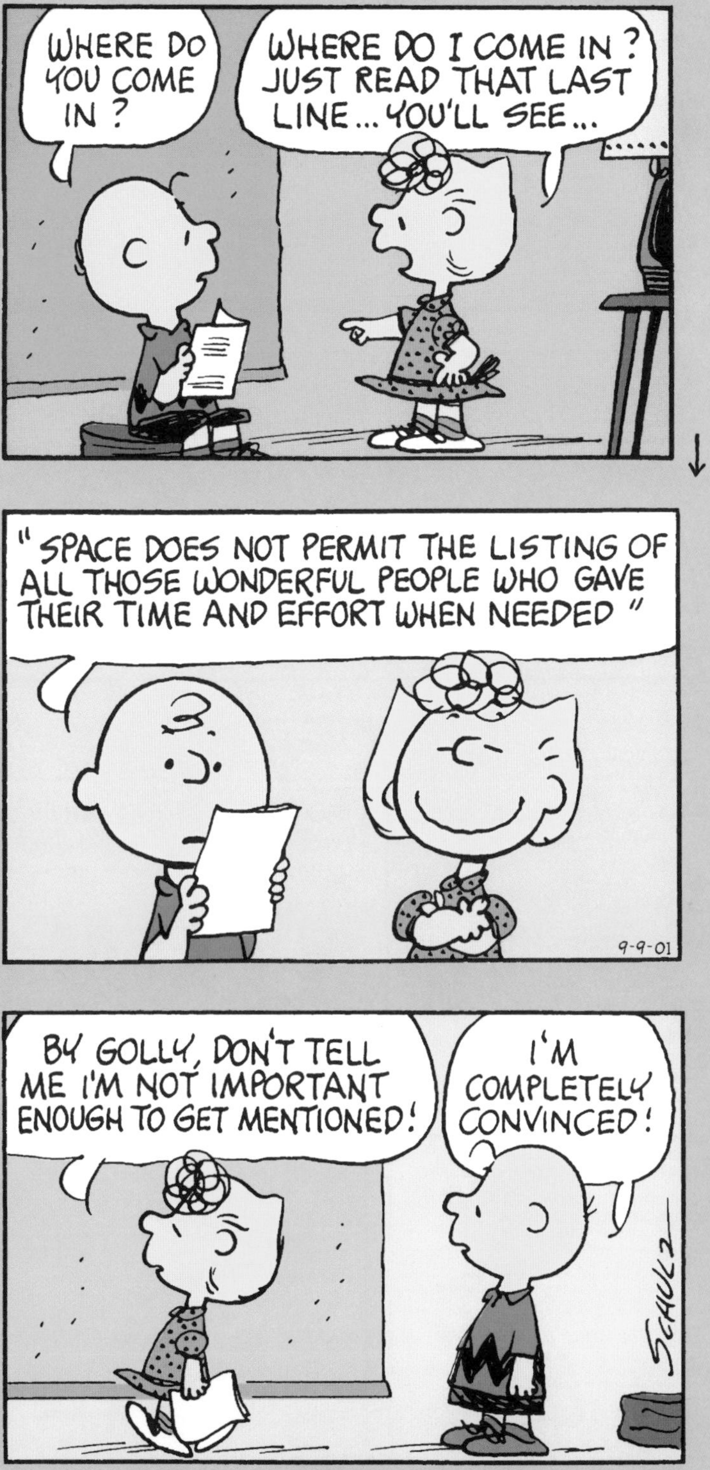
WHERE DO YOU COME IN ?
WHERE DO I COME IN ? JUST READ THAT LAST LINE... YOU'LL SEE...
" SPACE DOES NOT PERMIT THE LISTING OF ALL THOSE WONDERFUL PEOPLE WHO GAVE THEIR TIME AND EFFORT WHEN NEEDED "
9-9-01
BY GOLLY, DON'T TELL ME I'M NOT IMPORTANT ENOUGH TO GET MENTIONED !
I'M COMPLETELY CONVINCED !
SCHULZ

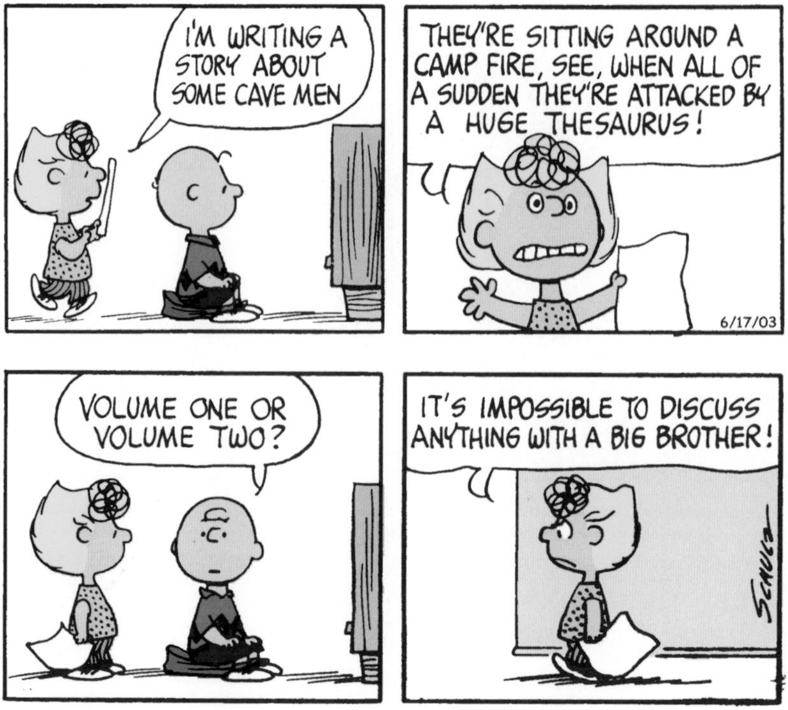
I'M WRITING A STORY ABOUT SOME CAVE MEN
THEY'RE SITTING AROUND A CAMP FIRE, SEE, WHEN ALL OF A SUDDEN THEY'RE ATTACKED BY A HUGE THESAURUS!
6/17/03
VOLUME ONE OR VOLUME TWO?
IT'S IMPOSSIBLE TO DISCUSS ANYTHING WITH A BIG BROTHER!
SCHULZ

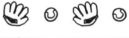

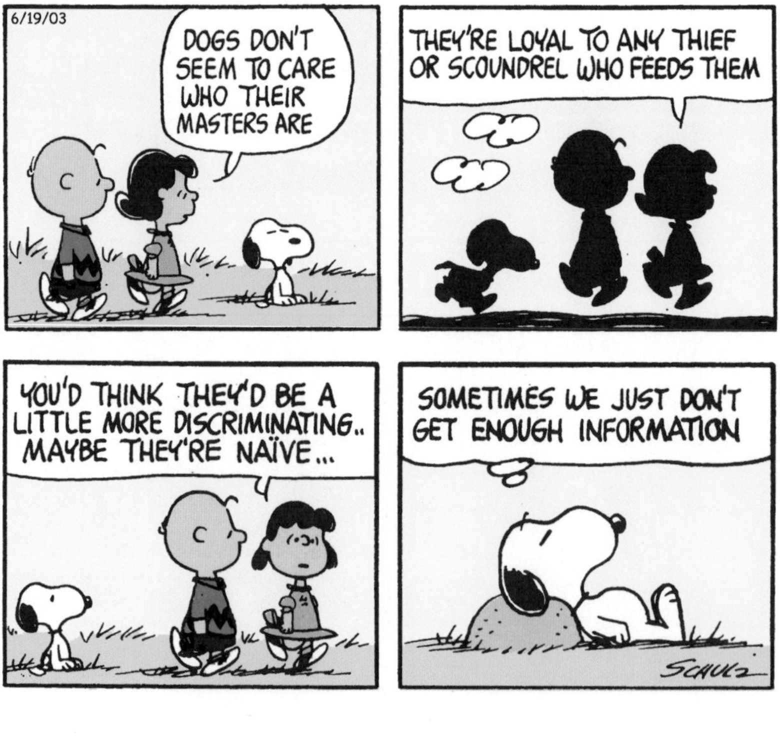
6/19/03
DOGS DON'T SEEM TO CARE WHO THEIR MASTERS ARE
THEY'RE LOYAL TO ANY THIEF OR SCOUNDREL WHO FEEDS THEM
YOU'D THINK THEY'D BE A LITTLE MORE DISCRIMINATING.. MAYBE THEY'RE NAÏVE...
SOMETIMES WE JUST DON'T GET ENOUGH INFORMATION
SCHULZ

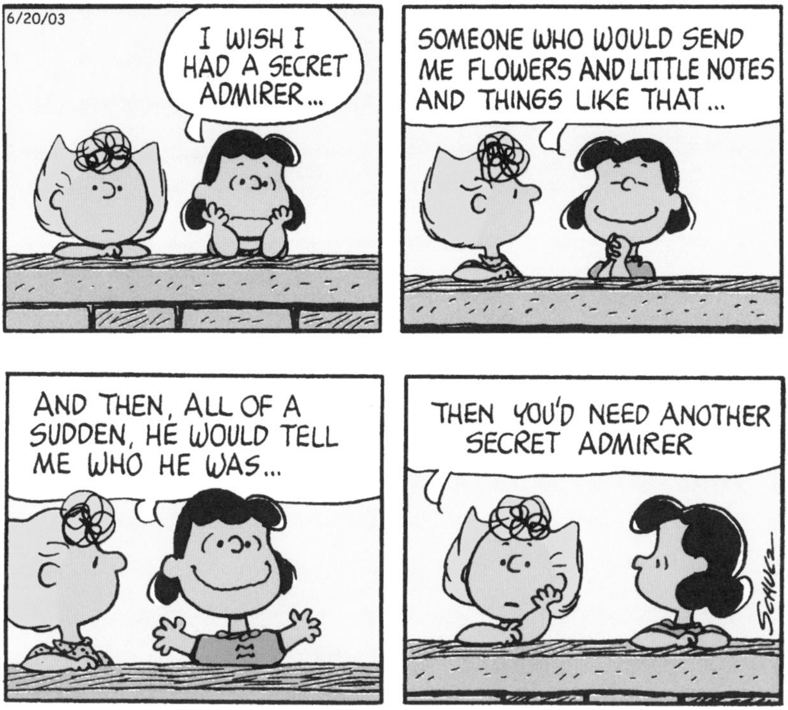
6/20/03
I WISH I HAD A SECRET ADMIRER...
SOMEONE WHO WOULD SEND ME FLOWERS AND LITTLE NOTES AND THINGS LIKE THAT...
AND THEN, ALL OF A SUDDEN, HE WOULD TELL ME WHO HE WAS...
THEN YOU'D NEED ANOTHER SECRET ADMIRER
SCHULZ

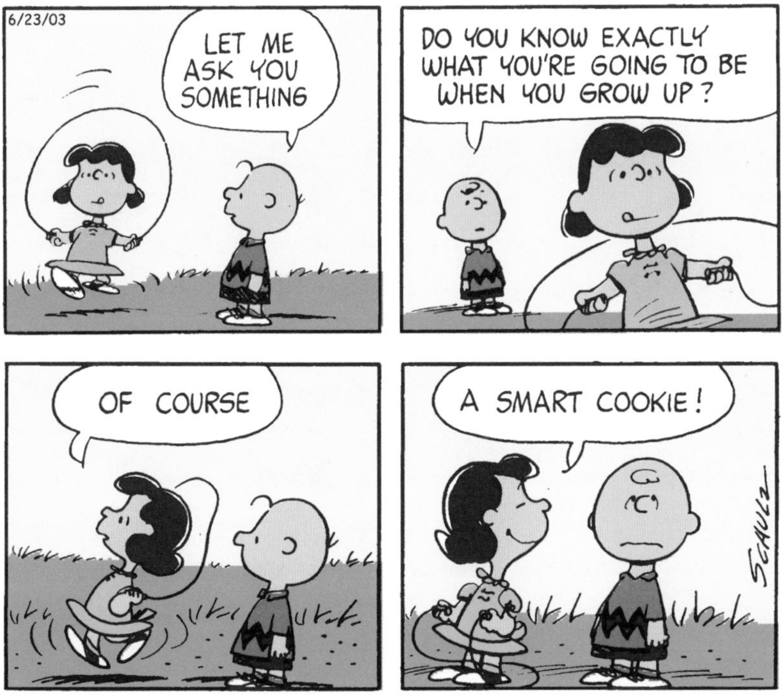
6/23/03
LET ME ASK YOU SOMETHING
DO YOU KNOW EXACTLY WHAT YOU'RE GOING TO BE WHEN YOU GROW UP?
OF COURSE
A SMART COOKIE!
SCHULZ

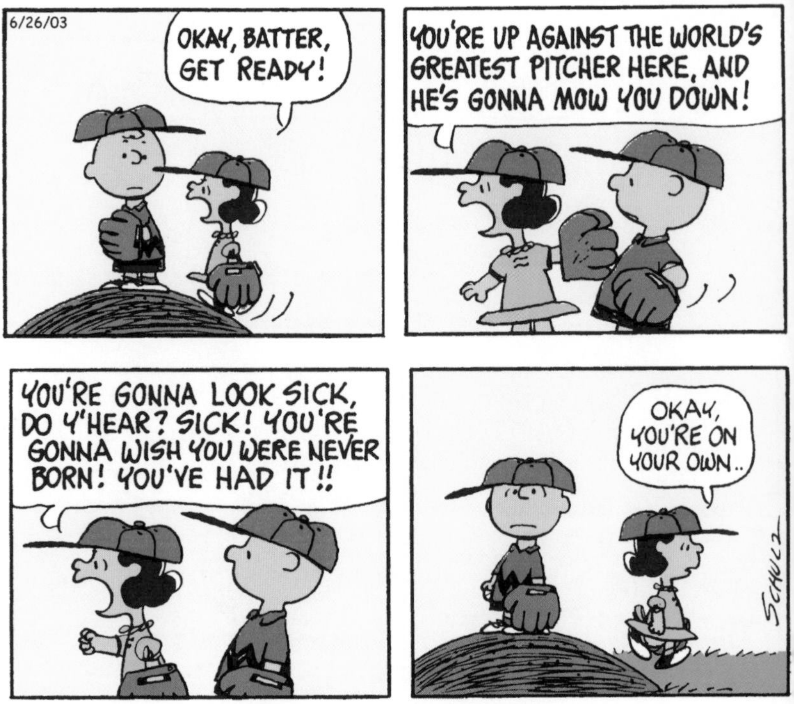
6/26/03
OKAY, BATTER, GET READY!
YOU'RE UP AGAINST THE WORLD'S GREATEST PITCHER HERE, AND HE'S GONNA MOW YOU DOWN!
YOU'RE GONNA LOOK SICK, DO Y'HEAR? SICK! YOU'RE GONNA WISH YOU WERE NEVER BORN! YOU'VE HAD IT!!
OKAY, YOU'RE ON YOUR OWN..
SCHULZ

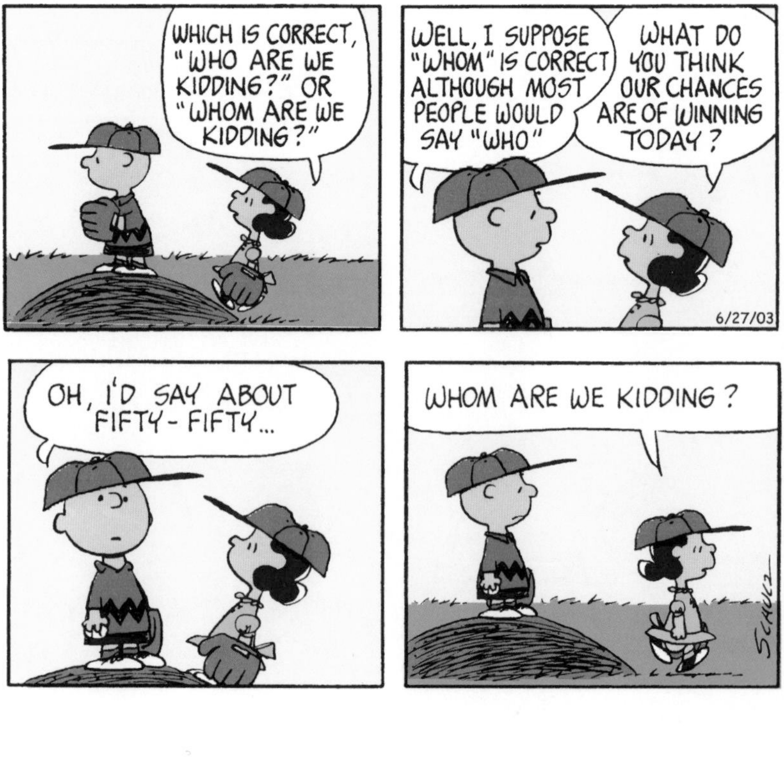
WHICH IS CORRECT, "WHO ARE WE KIDDING?" OR "WHOM ARE WE KIDDING?"
WELL, I SUPPOSE "WHOM" IS CORRECT ALTHOUGH MOST PEOPLE WOULD SAY "WHO"
WHAT DO YOU THINK OUR CHANCES ARE OF WINNING TODAY?
6/27/03
OH, I'D SAY ABOUT FIFTY-FIFTY...
WHOM ARE WE KIDDING?
SCHULZ

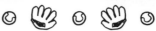

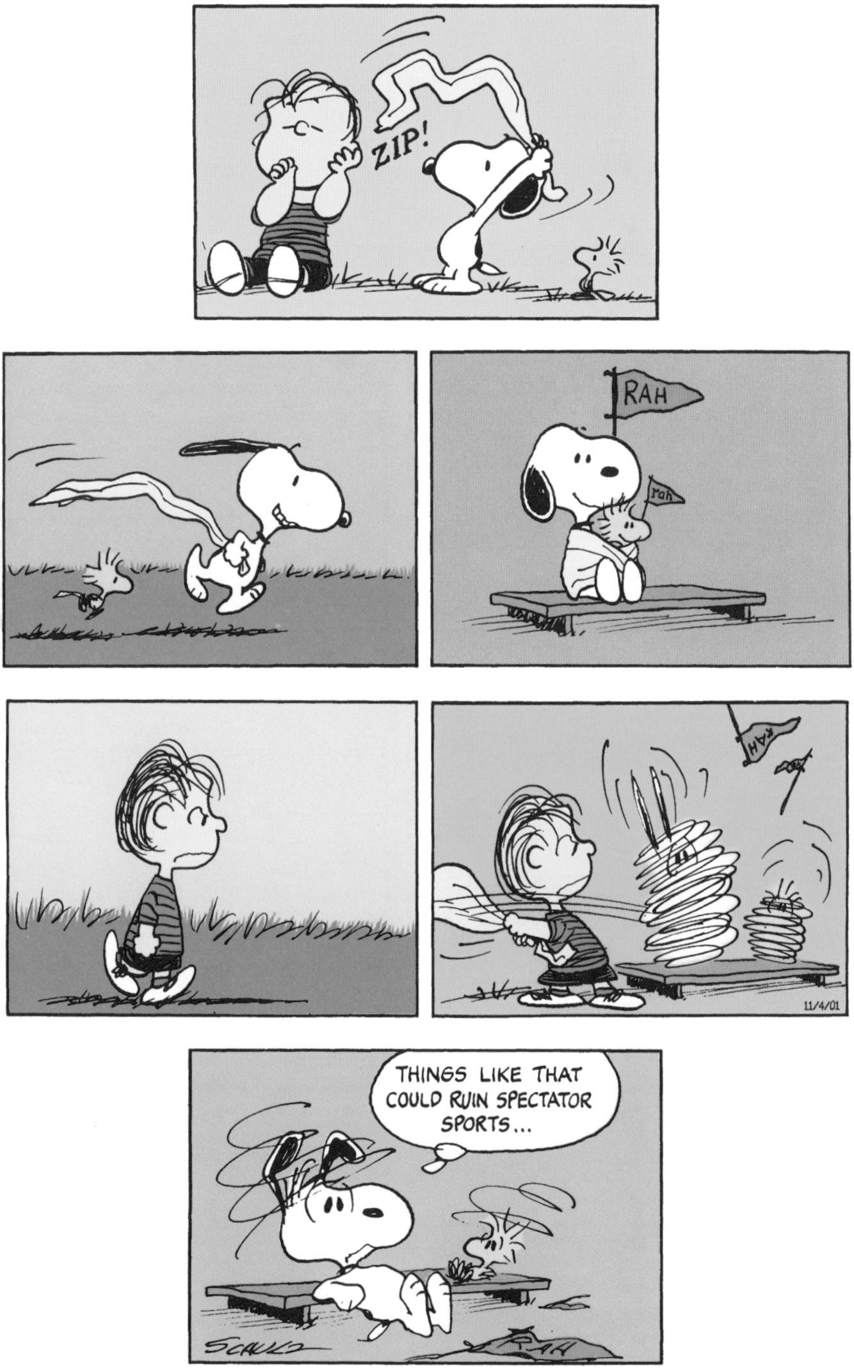
ZIP!
RAH
rah
RAH
11/4/01
THINGS LIKE THAT COULD RUIN SPECTATOR SPORTS...
SCHULZ
RAH

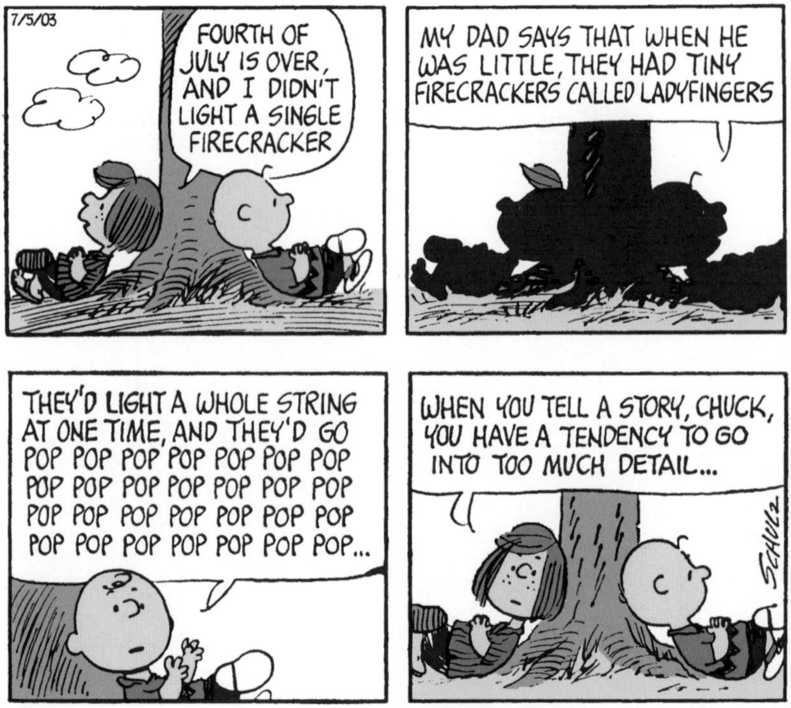
7/5/03
FOURTH OF JULY IS OVER, AND I DIDN'T LIGHT A SINGLE FIRECRACKER
MY DAD SAYS THAT WHEN HE WAS LITTLE, THEY HAD TINY FIRECRACKERS CALLED LADYFINGERS
THEY'D LIGHT A WHOLE STRING AT ONE TIME, AND THEY'D GO POP POP POP POP POP POP POP POP POP POP POP POP POP POP POP POP POP POP POP POP POP POP POP POP POP POP POP POP...
WHEN YOU TELL A STORY, CHUCK, YOU HAVE A TENDENCY TO GO INTO TOO MUCH DETAIL...
SCHULZ

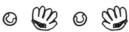

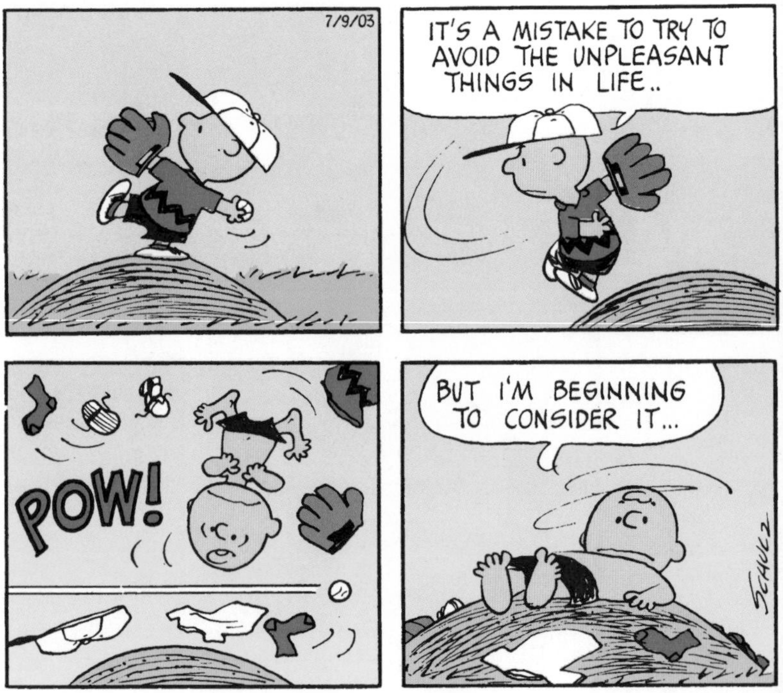
7/9/03
IT'S A MISTAKE TO TRY TO AVOID THE UNPLEASANT THINGS IN LIFE..
POW!
BUT I'M BEGINNING TO CONSIDER IT...
SCHULZ

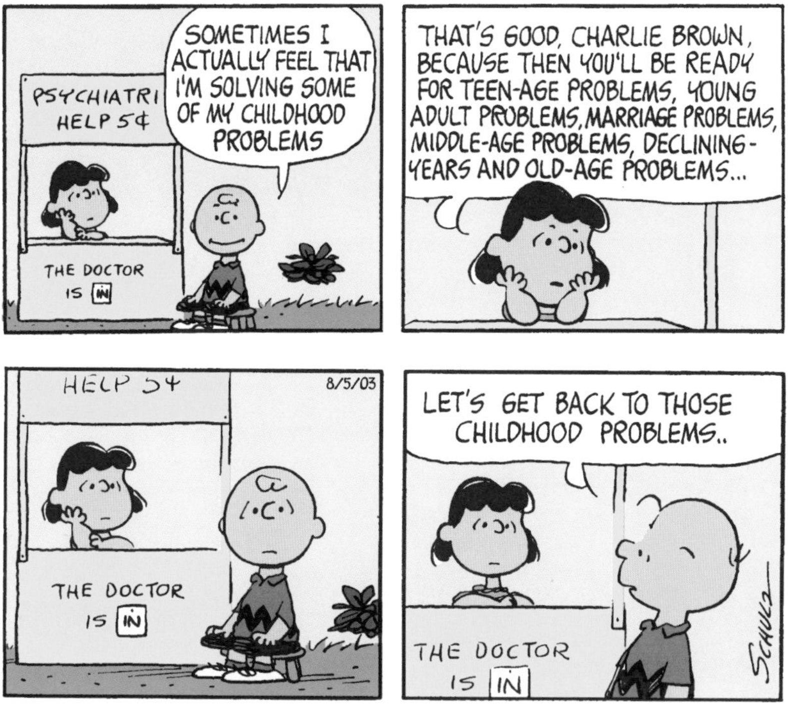
PSYCHIATRI
HELP 5¢
SOMETIMES I ACTUALLY FEEL THAT I'M SOLVING SOME OF MY CHILDHOOD PROBLEMS
THE DOCTOR IS IN
THAT'S GOOD, CHARLIE BROWN, BECAUSE THEN YOU'LL BE READY FOR TEEN-AGE PROBLEMS, YOUNG ADULT PROBLEMS, MARRIAGE PROBLEMS, MIDDLE-AGE PROBLEMS, DECLINING-YEARS AND OLD-AGE PROBLEMS...
HELP 5¢
8/5/03
THE DOCTOR IS IN
LET'S GET BACK TO THOSE CHILDHOOD PROBLEMS..
THE DOCTOR IS IN
SCHULZ

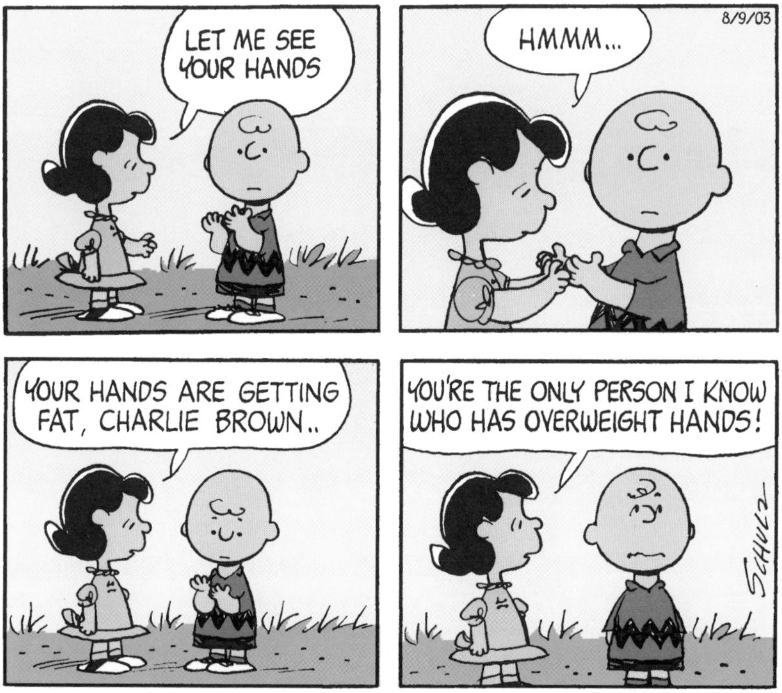
LET ME SEE YOUR HANDS
HMMM...
8/9/03
YOUR HANDS ARE GETTING FAT, CHARLIE BROWN..
YOU'RE THE ONLY PERSON I KNOW WHO HAS OVERWEIGHT HANDS!
SCHULZ

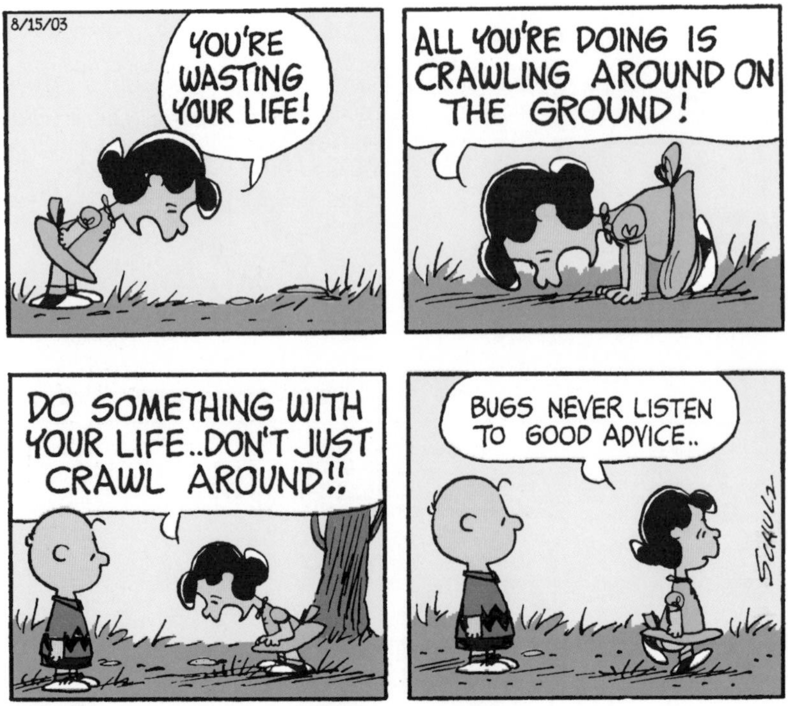
8/15/03
YOU'RE WASTING YOUR LIFE!
ALL YOU'RE DOING IS CRAWLING AROUND ON THE GROUND!
DO SOMETHING WITH YOUR LIFE..DON'T JUST CRAWL AROUND!!
BUGS NEVER LISTEN TO GOOD ADVICE..
SCHULZ

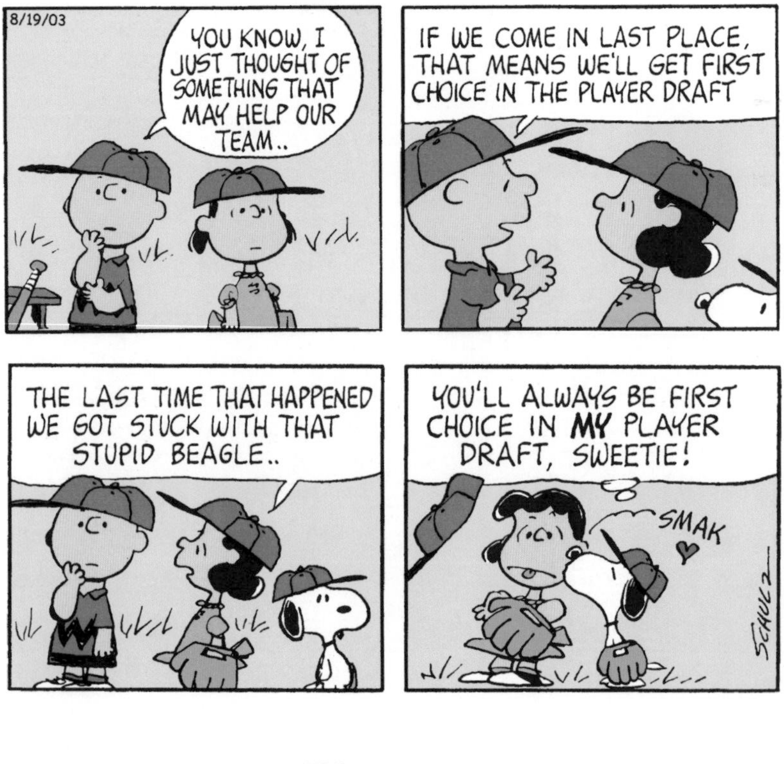
8/19/03
YOU KNOW, I JUST THOUGHT OF SOMETHING THAT MAY HELP OUR TEAM..
IF WE COME IN LAST PLACE, THAT MEANS WE'LL GET FIRST CHOICE IN THE PLAYER DRAFT
THE LAST TIME THAT HAPPENED WE GOT STUCK WITH THAT STUPID BEAGLE..
YOU'LL ALWAYS BE FIRST CHOICE IN **MY** PLAYER DRAFT, SWEETIE!
SMAK
SCHULZ

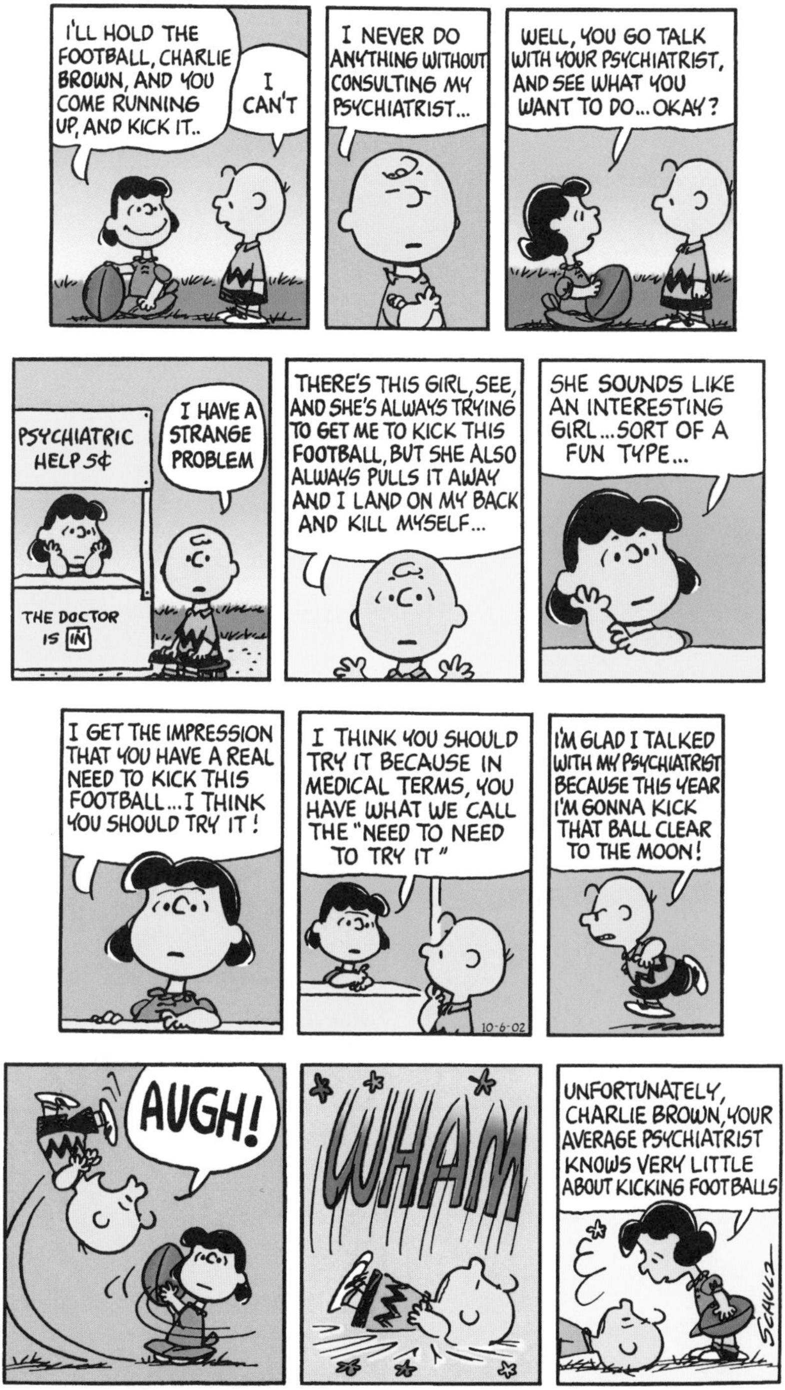
I'LL HOLD THE FOOTBALL, CHARLIE BROWN, AND YOU COME RUNNING UP, AND KICK IT..
I CAN'T
I NEVER DO ANYTHING WITHOUT CONSULTING MY PSYCHIATRIST...
WELL, YOU GO TALK WITH YOUR PSYCHIATRIST, AND SEE WHAT YOU WANT TO DO... OKAY?
PSYCHIATRIC HELP 5¢
THE DOCTOR IS IN
I HAVE A STRANGE PROBLEM
THERE'S THIS GIRL, SEE, AND SHE'S ALWAYS TRYING TO GET ME TO KICK THIS FOOTBALL, BUT SHE ALSO ALWAYS PULLS IT AWAY AND I LAND ON MY BACK AND KILL MYSELF...
SHE SOUNDS LIKE AN INTERESTING GIRL... SORT OF A FUN TYPE...
I GET THE IMPRESSION THAT YOU HAVE A REAL NEED TO KICK THIS FOOTBALL... I THINK YOU SHOULD TRY IT!
I THINK YOU SHOULD TRY IT BECAUSE IN MEDICAL TERMS, YOU HAVE WHAT WE CALL THE "NEED TO NEED TO TRY IT"
10-6-02
I'M GLAD I TALKED WITH MY PSYCHIATRIST BECAUSE THIS YEAR I'M GONNA KICK THAT BALL CLEAR TO THE MOON!
AUGH!
WHAM
UNFORTUNATELY, CHARLIE BROWN, YOUR AVERAGE PSYCHIATRIST KNOWS VERY LITTLE ABOUT KICKING FOOTBALLS
SCHULZ

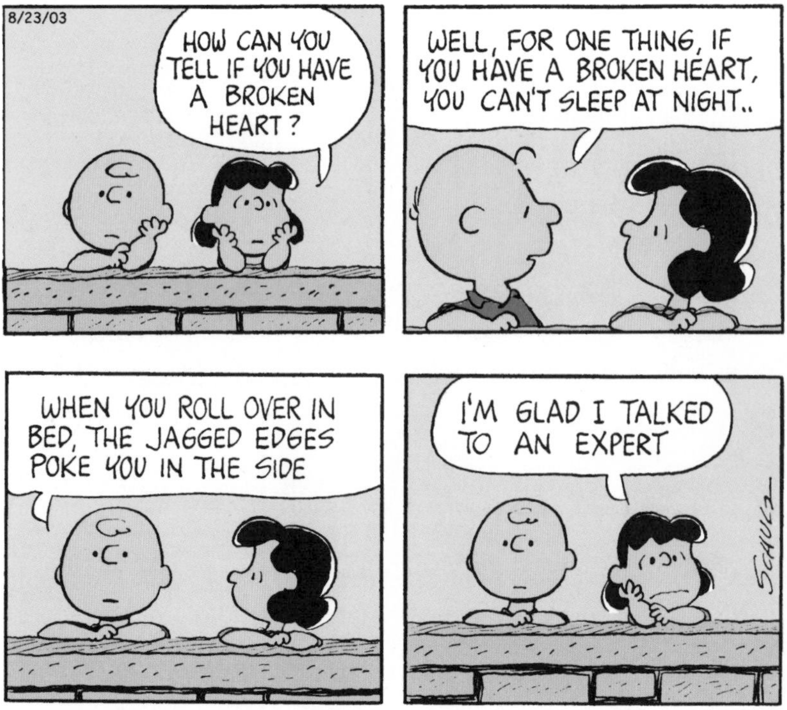
8/23/03
HOW CAN YOU TELL IF YOU HAVE A BROKEN HEART?
WELL, FOR ONE THING, IF YOU HAVE A BROKEN HEART, YOU CAN'T SLEEP AT NIGHT..
WHEN YOU ROLL OVER IN BED, THE JAGGED EDGES POKE YOU IN THE SIDE
I'M GLAD I TALKED TO AN EXPERT
SCHULZ

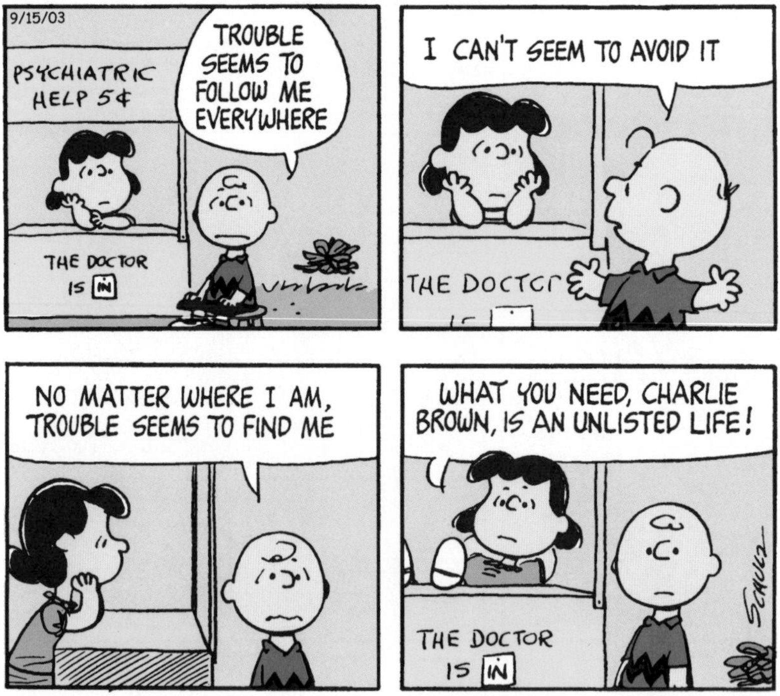
9/15/03
PSYCHIATRIC HELP 5¢
THE DOCTOR IS IN
TROUBLE SEEMS TO FOLLOW ME EVERYWHERE
I CAN'T SEEM TO AVOID IT
NO MATTER WHERE I AM, TROUBLE SEEMS TO FIND ME
WHAT YOU NEED, CHARLIE BROWN, IS AN UNLISTED LIFE!
THE DOCTOR IS IN
SCHULZ

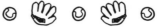

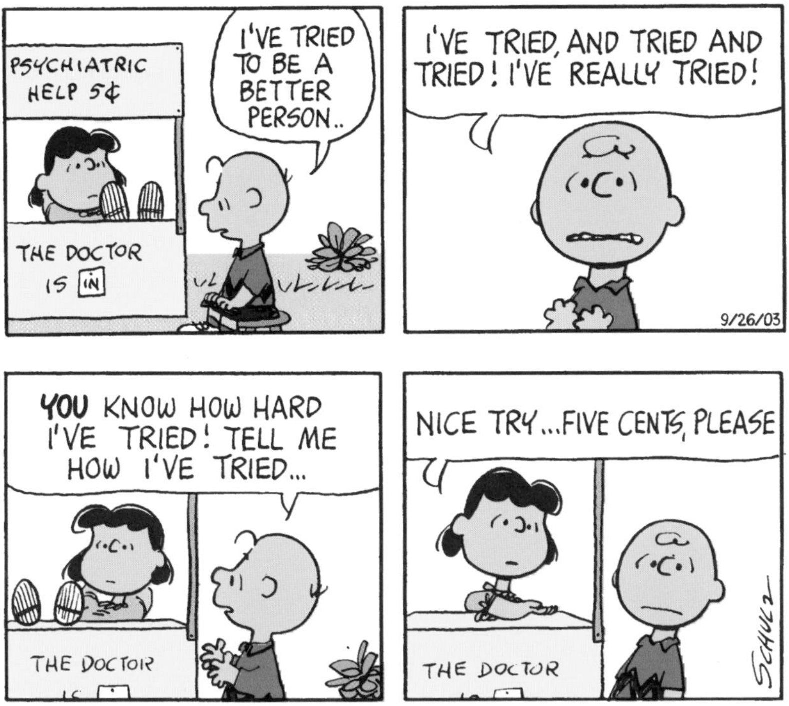
PSYCHIATRIC HELP 5¢
THE DOCTOR IS IN
I'VE TRIED TO BE A BETTER PERSON..
I'VE TRIED, AND TRIED AND TRIED! I'VE REALLY TRIED!
9/26/03
YOU KNOW HOW HARD I'VE TRIED! TELL ME HOW I'VE TRIED...
THE DOCTOR
NICE TRY...FIVE CENTS, PLEASE
THE DOCTOR
SCHULZ

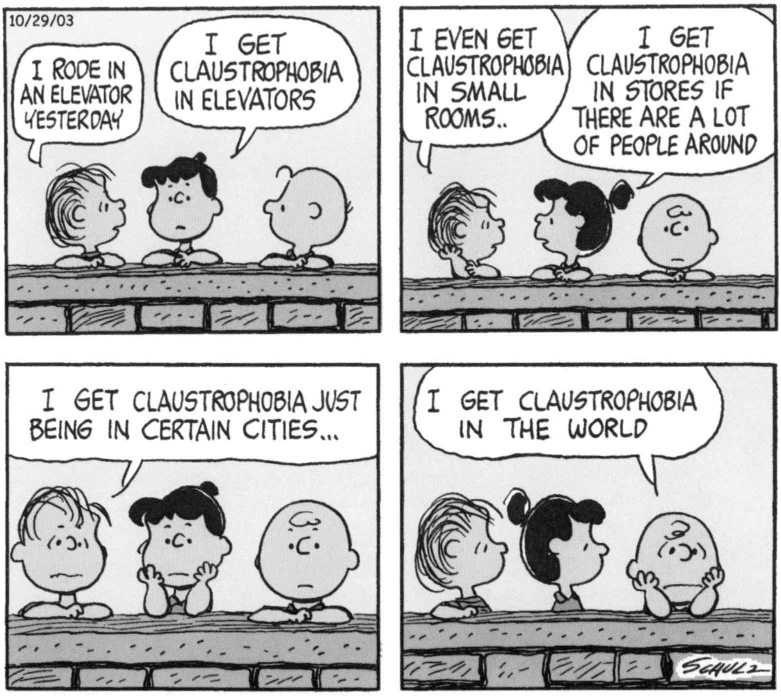
10/29/03
I RODE IN AN ELEVATOR YESTERDAY
I GET CLAUSTROPHOBIA IN ELEVATORS
I EVEN GET CLAUSTROPHOBIA IN SMALL ROOMS..
I GET CLAUSTROPHOBIA IN STORES IF THERE ARE A LOT OF PEOPLE AROUND
I GET CLAUSTROPHOBIA JUST BEING IN CERTAIN CITIES...
I GET CLAUSTROPHOBIA IN THE WORLD
SCHULZ

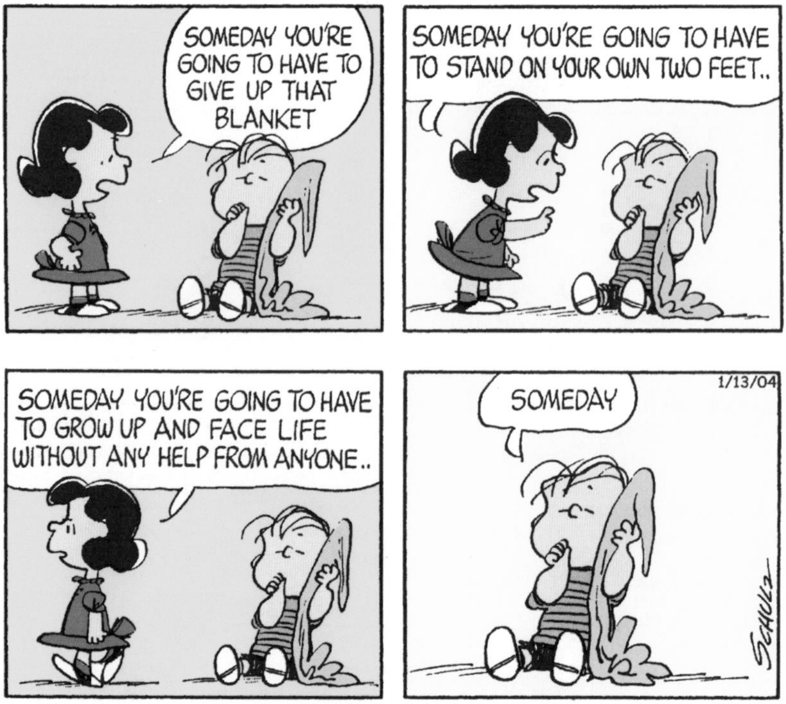
SOMEDAY YOU'RE GOING TO HAVE TO GIVE UP THAT BLANKET
SOMEDAY YOU'RE GOING TO HAVE TO STAND ON YOUR OWN TWO FEET..
SOMEDAY YOU'RE GOING TO HAVE TO GROW UP AND FACE LIFE WITHOUT ANY HELP FROM ANYONE..
1/13/04
SOMEDAY
SCHULZ

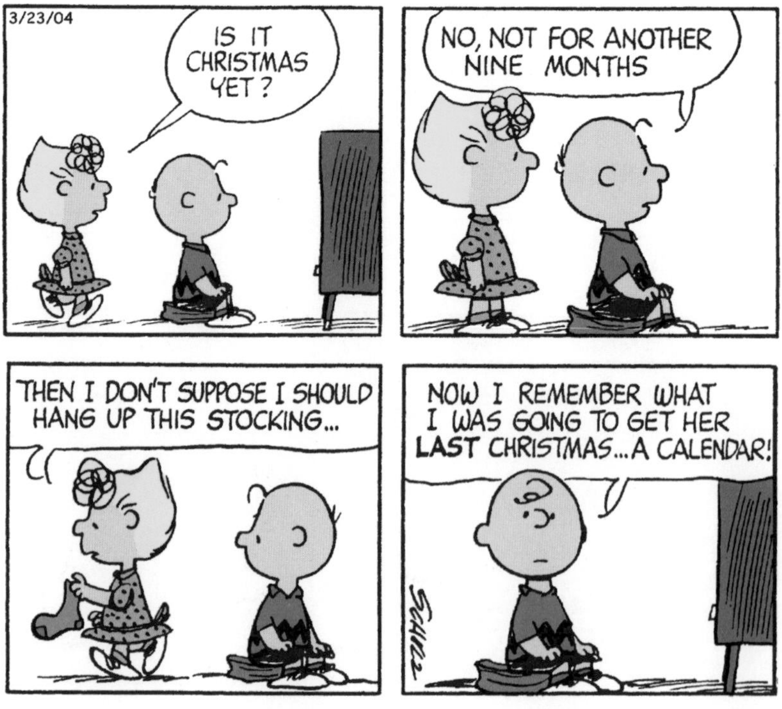
3/23/04
IS IT CHRISTMAS YET ?
NO, NOT FOR ANOTHER NINE MONTHS
THEN I DON'T SUPPOSE I SHOULD HANG UP THIS STOCKING...
NOW I REMEMBER WHAT I WAS GOING TO GET HER **LAST** CHRISTMAS...A CALENDAR!
SCHULZ

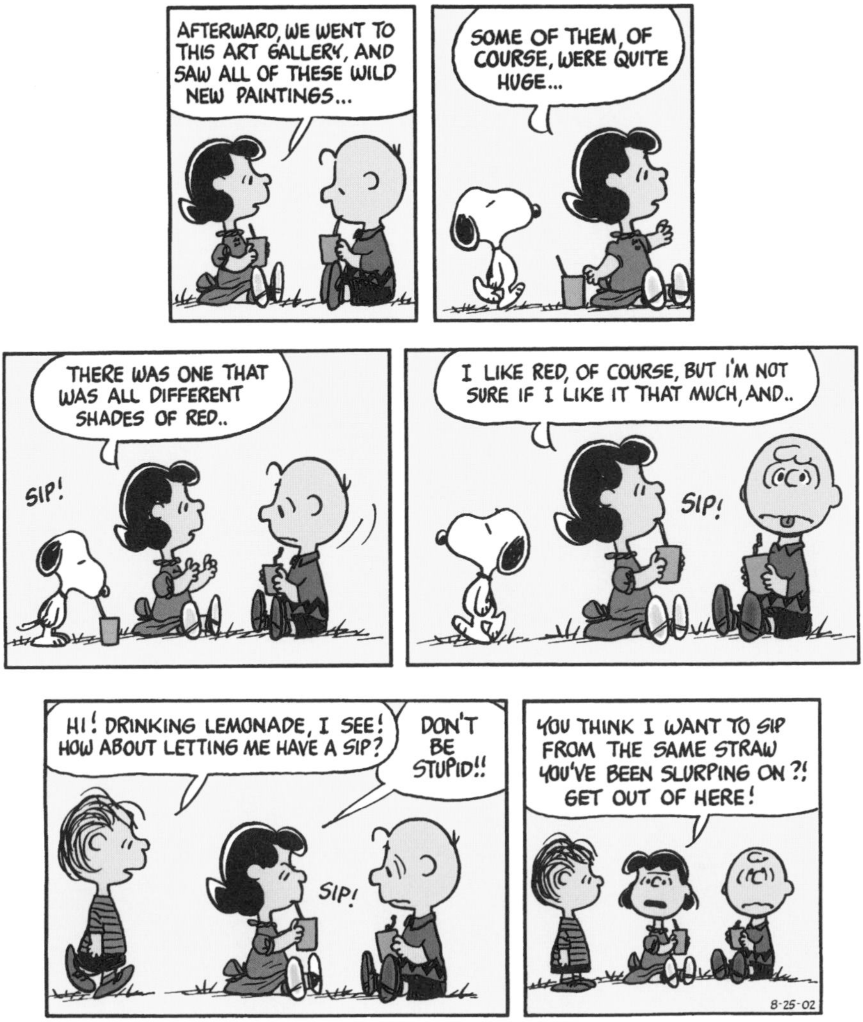
AFTERWARD, WE WENT TO THIS ART GALLERY, AND SAW ALL OF THESE WILD NEW PAINTINGS...
SOME OF THEM, OF COURSE, WERE QUITE HUGE...
THERE WAS ONE THAT WAS ALL DIFFERENT SHADES OF RED..
SIP!
I LIKE RED, OF COURSE, BUT I'M NOT SURE IF I LIKE IT THAT MUCH, AND..
SIP!
HI! DRINKING LEMONADE, I SEE! HOW ABOUT LETTING ME HAVE A SIP?
DON'T BE STUPID!!
SIP!
YOU THINK I WANT TO SIP FROM THE SAME STRAW YOU'VE BEEN SLURPING ON?! GET OUT OF HERE!
8-25-02

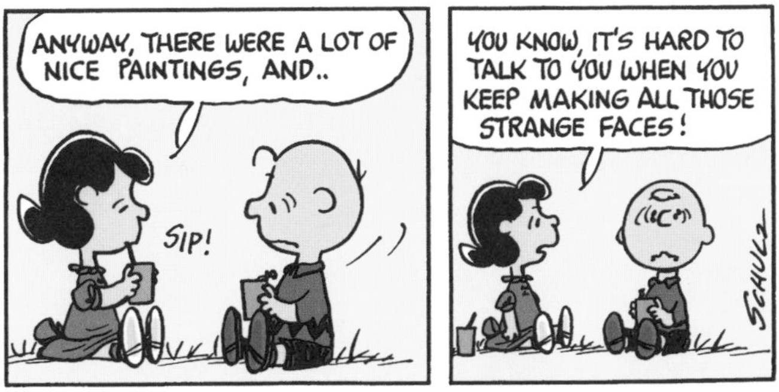
ANYWAY, THERE WERE A LOT OF NICE PAINTINGS, AND..
SIP!
YOU KNOW, IT'S HARD TO TALK TO YOU WHEN YOU KEEP MAKING ALL THOSE STRANGE FACES!
SCHULZ

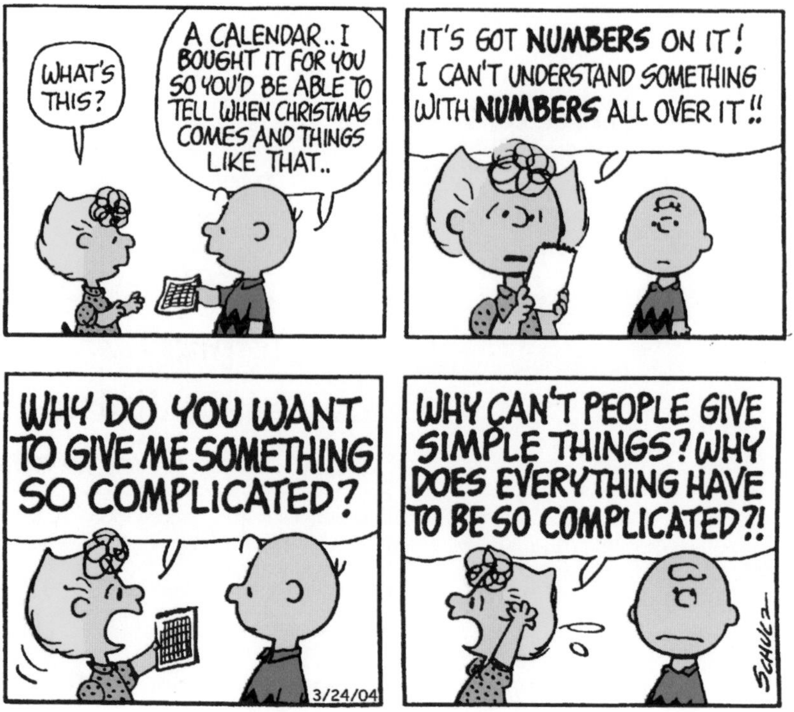
WHAT'S THIS?
A CALENDAR.. I BOUGHT IT FOR YOU SO YOU'D BE ABLE TO TELL WHEN CHRISTMAS COMES AND THINGS LIKE THAT..
IT'S GOT **NUMBERS** ON IT! I CAN'T UNDERSTAND SOMETHING WITH **NUMBERS** ALL OVER IT!!
WHY DO YOU WANT TO GIVE ME SOMETHING SO COMPLICATED?
3/24/04
WHY CAN'T PEOPLE GIVE SIMPLE THINGS? WHY DOES EVERYTHING HAVE TO BE SO COMPLICATED?!
SCHULZ

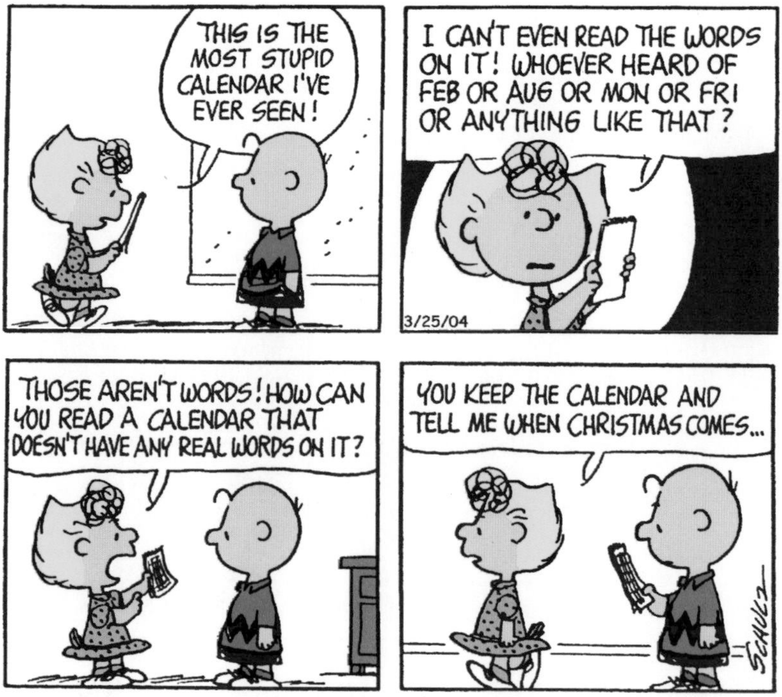
THIS IS THE MOST STUPID CALENDAR I'VE EVER SEEN!
I CAN'T EVEN READ THE WORDS ON IT! WHOEVER HEARD OF FEB OR AUG OR MON OR FRI OR ANYTHING LIKE THAT?
3/25/04
THOSE AREN'T WORDS! HOW CAN YOU READ A CALENDAR THAT DOESN'T HAVE ANY REAL WORDS ON IT?
YOU KEEP THE CALENDAR AND TELL ME WHEN CHRISTMAS COMES...
SCHULZ

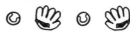

MORE TO EXPLORE!

In addition to all these great *Peanuts* cartoons, here are some cool activities and fun facts for you. Thanks to our friends at the Charles M. Schulz Museum and Research Center in Santa Rosa, California, for letting us share these with you!

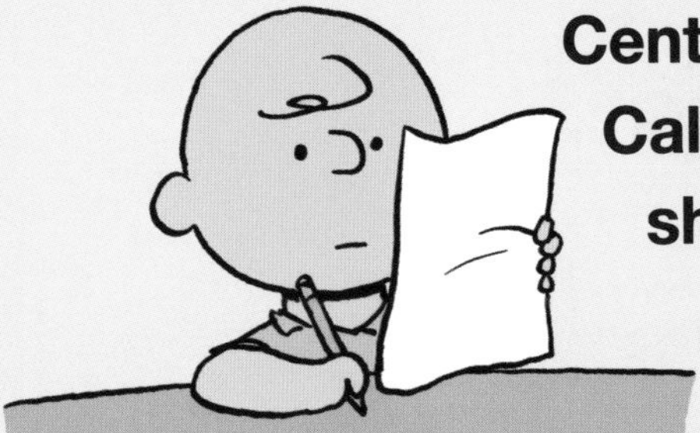

Make a Charlie Brown Mask

MATERIALS: round, white paper plate; scissors; large craft stick; black marker; tape

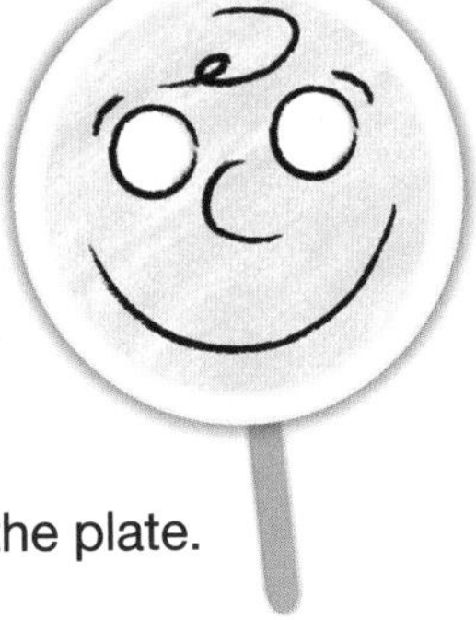

INSTRUCTIONS:

1. Cut out two holes for the eyes.
2. Draw a “C” in the middle of the plate for Charlie Brown’s nose.
3. Draw a big, long smile at the bottom of the plate.
4. Draw a curlicue on top for Charlie Brown’s hair.
5. Tape craft stick to the bottom of the paper plate for the handle.

Make an Animated Flip Book

An animator must capture a broad range of movements in order for a cartoon to look continuous. Animation is possible because of a phenomenon called "persistence of vision," when a sequence of images moves past the eye fast enough, the brain fills in the missing parts so the subject appears to be moving.

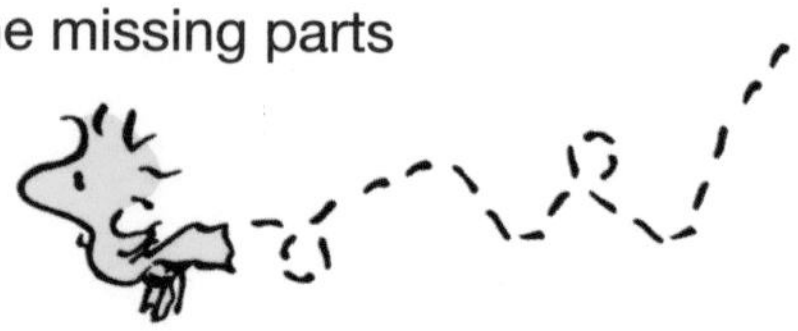

MATERIALS: paper, index cards, or sticky notes; stapler and staples, paper clips, or brads; pencil or marker

INSTRUCTIONS:

1 Cut at least 20 strips of paper to be the exact same size, or use alternative materials, such as index cards or sticky notes.

2 Fasten the pages together with a staple, brad, or paperclip.

3 Pick a subject—anything from a bouncing ball to a flying Woodstock or a shooting star.

4 Draw three key images first: the first on page one, the last on page twenty, and the middle on page ten, then fill in the pages between the key images.

1.

10.

20.

Make Snoopy's Favorite Puppy Chow

Snoopy may be a dog, but we think he'd prefer this fun puppy chow over simple dog food. With an adult's help, make this easy sweet treat for you and your friends to enjoy.

INGREDIENTS: *(for 12 servings)* 3 cups Chex® Cereal (or comparable cereal), ⅓ cup chocolate chips, 2½ table-spoons peanut butter, ½ cup powdered sugar

INSTRUCTIONS:

1. Pour cereal into a bowl.

2. Melt the chocolate over low heat, then add peanut butter.

3. Pour chocolate and peanut butter mixture over cereal and mix.

4. Put powdered sugar in a plastic bag, add cereal mixture, then shake it up! When the cereal is all coated, pour it on a sheet of waxed paper and let it cool. Store in airtight container (if there's any left!).

Go Fly a Kite that You Made Yourself

We hope you're more successful at flying a kite than good ol' Charlie Brown is!

These are directions for a diamond kite, the kind that Charlie Brown tries to fly. Kites are made of these basic parts:

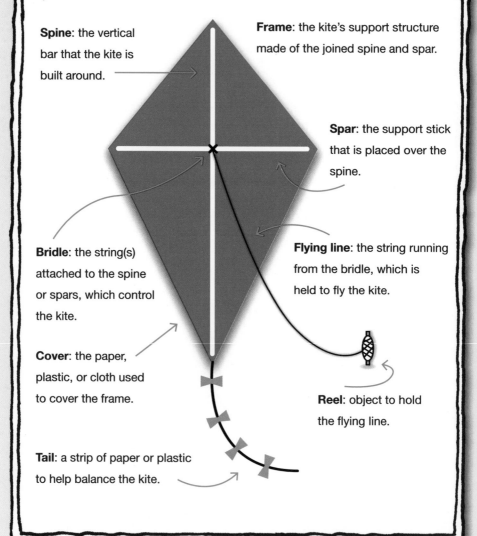

Spine: the vertical bar that the kite is built around.

Frame: the kite's support structure made of the joined spine and spar.

Spar: the support stick that is placed over the spine.

Bridle: the string(s) attached to the spine or spars, which control the kite.

Flying line: the string running from the bridle, which is held to fly the kite.

Cover: the paper, plastic, or cloth used to cover the frame.

Reel: object to hold the flying line.

Tail: a strip of paper or plastic to help balance the kite.

MATERIALS:

- One 24-inch and one 20-inch wooden dowels or bamboo sticks
- String or fishing line
- Sturdy tape
- Cover material (24 inches x 24 inches). You can use newspaper, wrapping paper, or even plastic from a trash bag.
- Scissors
- Ribbons, material, or streamers for tail
- Markers
- Ruler or tape measure

INSTRUCTIONS:

1. Tie the sticks together (tightly) with string at the center of the short stick and six inches down from the top of the long stick.
2. Lay the cover material flat and put the sticks on it. Draw a line between each point of the sticks to make a diamond, then cut the material. Tape the material securely to the sticks at each of the four points of the frame. Reinforce the center of the sticks with four pieces of tape.
3. Punch a hole in the material at the cross-section of the sticks. Attach string through this hole to the cross-section.
4. Decorate your kite and make a fun tail that you can tie to the bottom of the spine.

Be careful when flying your kite. Stay away from tall trees and power lines.

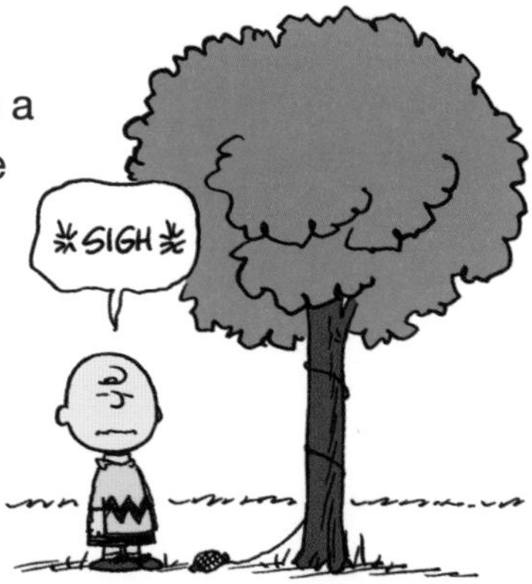
SIGH

Charles M. Schulz and *Peanuts* Fun Facts

- Charles Schulz drew 17,897 comic strips throughout his career.
- Schulz was first published in Ripley's newspaper feature *Believe It or Not* in 1937. He was fifteen years old and the drawing was of the family dog.
- From birth, comics played a large role in Schulz's life. At just two days old, an uncle nicknamed Schulz "Sparky" after the horse Spark Plug from the *Barney Google* comic strip. And that's what he was called for the rest of his life.
- In a bit of foreshadowing, Schulz's kindergarten teacher told him, "Someday, Charles, you're going to be an artist."
- Growing up, Schulz had a black-and-white dog that later became the inspiration for Snoopy—the same dog that Schulz drew for Ripley's *Believe It or Not*. The dog's name was Spike.

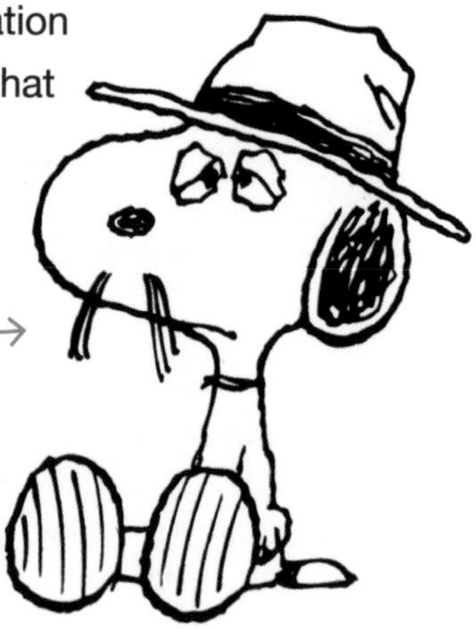

- Charles Schulz earned a star on the Hollywood Walk of Fame in 1996.

Learn How Comics Can Reflect Life

MATERIALS: blank piece of paper, pencil, markers or colored pencils

1. Make four blank cartoon panels, all the same size, on the piece of paper.
2. Look at the example below to see how Charles Schulz used his own life in his strips—even painful experiences like that of loss—and turned them into strips. Think of something that has happened to you at home or school that had a big impact on you.
3. Once you have decided on a story you want to tell, draw it in four panels. Remember, it should have a beginning, a middle, and an end.

An example from Schulz's life:

In 1966, a fire destroyed Schulz's Sebastopol studio. He translated his feelings into a strip about Snoopy's doghouse catching fire:

PEANUTS
SNIF?
I SMELL SMOKE!
SNIF SNIF
9-19
BAM! BAM!
BAM! BAM!
WHAT IN THE WORLD.....
MY BOOKS! MY RECORDS! MY POOL TABLE! MY VAN GOGH!
GOOD GRIEF!
SOB!
SCHULZ

About the Charles M. Schulz Museum

The Schulz Museum and Research Center officially opened August 17, 2002, when a dream became a reality. For many years, thousands of admirers flocked to see Charles M. Schulz's original comic strips at exhibitions outside of Santa Rosa because his work didn't have a proper home. As the fiftieth anniversary of *Peanuts* drew closer, the idea that there ought to be a museum to hold all Schulz's precious work began to grow. Schulz didn't think of himself as a "museum piece" and was, therefore, understandably reluctant about accepting the idea. That left the "vision" work to local cartoon historian Mark Cohen, wife Jeannie Schulz, and longtime friend Edwin Anderson. Schulz's enthusiasm for the museum was kindled in 1997 after seeing the inspired and playful creations by artist and designer Yoshiteru Otani for the Snoopy Town shops in Japan. From that point plans for the museum moved steadily along. A board of directors was established, a mission statement adopted, and the architect and contractor were hired. The location of the museum is particularly fitting—sited across the street from Snoopy's Home Ice, the ice arena and coffee shop that Schulz built in 1969, and one block away from the studio where Schulz worked and created for thirty years. Since its opening in 2002, thousands of visitors from throughout the world have come to the museum to see the enduring work of Charles M. Schulz which will be enjoyed for generations to come.

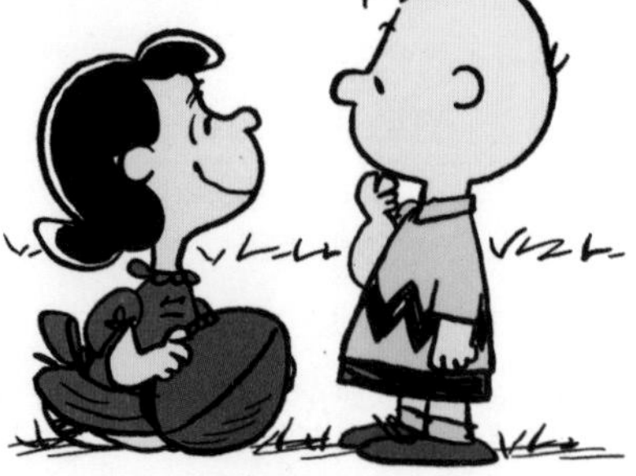

5. Type `Cats` on the next line, click the Demote button, and then press Enter.
6. Type `Birds` on the next line and then press Enter.
7. Type `Dogs` on the next line and then press Enter.
8. Type `Care and Feeding` on the next line and then press Enter.

You should have an outline similar to the one shown in Figure 13.4 (the text font size may be smaller on your actual screen).

When you promote a heading, you are moving that heading to a higher heading level where heading level 1 is the top level. For instance, if you want to move a heading at level 3 to level 1, you would place your cursor on that heading and click the Promote button. Demoting a branch or a heading works the same way except that you are moving the heading to a lower level. Now this "moving" between different levels is a little different from "moving" text around in the document. You are not actually moving text to a different section of the outline. You are just changing the level of the heading.

Microsoft Word - Document2
File Edit View Insert Format Tools Table Window Help
Heading 3
Arial
24
1 2 3 4 5 6 7 All
Outline about Pets
Household Pets
Cats
Birds
Dogs
Care and Feeding
Page 1 Sec 1 1/1 At 4.1" Ln 6 Col 17 REC TRK EXT OVR WPH

Figure 13.4.
Use the Outlining toolbar to make this outline about pets.

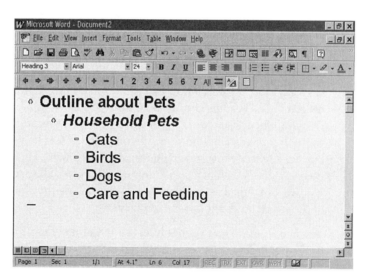

What if you find that the subheading for Care and Feeding in the previous example should be a higher heading level by itself? You can place your cursor on the Care and Feeding heading and promote it by clicking the Promote button. Your outline should then look like Figure 13.5.

+ Outline about Pets
    + Household Pets
        - Cats
        - Birds
        - Dogs
    + Care and Feeding

Microsoft Word - Document2
File Edit View Insert Format Tools Table Window Help
Heading 2
Arial
24
Outline about Pets
Household Pets
Cats
Birds
Dogs
Care and Feeding
Page 1 Sec 1 1/1 At 4.1" Ln 6 Col 17 REC TRK EXT OVR WPH

Figure 13.5.
The Care and Feeding heading was promoted to a higher level in the outline.

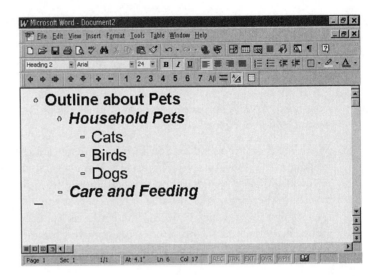

Likewise, if you find that the Care and Feeding heading should be placed back as a subtopic under the Household Pets heading, you would place your cursor on the Care and Feeding heading and click the Demote button to move that heading back to the lower heading level.

It's really that easy to promote and demote a heading. You might find that you don't want the text to be a heading after all, but rather, text in a heading. In this case, you can also select Demote to Body Text, which is where, instead of writing a new heading, you are writing body text. After typing a heading, you can press your Enter key, click the Demote to Body Text button, and type your paragraph text as you normally would. Note that for the body text, there is a dot instead of a plus or minus sign. It would be at this point that you might find yourself switching back to Normal view by clicking the Normal view button at the bottom of the screen on the horizontal scrollbar.

You may want to draft your outline first in Outline view, then switch to Normal view. You could then type your text in Normal view. When you switch back to Outline view, you would find that your paragraph text under a heading would be at the body text level.

Expanding and Collapsing the Outline

The next two buttons are the Expand (+) and Collapse (-) buttons. In Outline view, place your cursor on a heading and then click the Expand/Collapse buttons to see the subheadings under that heading. Each click expands or collapses the outline headings one level at a time.

Moving Headings Up and Down Through an Outline

Okay, you know how to promote, demote, and demote to body text. But what about moving headings and text around an outline? This is simple: Use the Move Up and Move Down buttons on the Outlining toolbar.

To move a heading, place your cursor on the heading, and click the Move Up or Move Down button to move the heading up or down through the outline.

If you want to move everything under a heading, select the heading and everything under the heading (the subheadings, the text, and so on). Start clicking the Move Up or Move Down button to move the blocked heading/subheadings/text to wherever you want.

JUST A MINUTE

You can also move headings and body text by selecting and then dragging and dropping the headings and body text from one part of the outline to another part of the outline. Similarly, you can cut and paste parts of your outline. However, for those of you who are not comfortable with dragging and dropping text (you might accidentally drop the selected headings and body text in the wrong place), you may want to use the Move Up and Move Down buttons instead.

Heading Number Buttons

The 1 through 7 heading number buttons are like Collapse/Expand buttons that let you collapse and expand your outline to the outline heading level that you specify. If you click the 1 button, you will collapse your outline to the level-1 headings. If you click the 7 button, you will expand your outline to level-7 headings.

Show All Headings, First Line Only, and Formatting Buttons

The next three buttons are the Show All Headings button, the Show First Line Only button, and the Show Formatting button. As with the other Outlining toolbar buttons, these buttons are easy to understand and use.

Click the Show All Headings button to show all headings regardless of heading level as well as all body text. If you click the Show All Headings button again, you collapse the outline.

If you want to see only the first line of each heading, click the Show First Line Only button. Click the button again to see all the lines of each heading.

If you click the Show All Formatting button, you can hide and show the special formatting (such as bold formatting, and so on) you have for text in your outline.

13

Numbering Your Outline Headings

Okay, you now know the basics of promoting, demoting, and writing body text for your outline. You know how to switch back and forth between Normal and Outline view. But how do you number the headings of your outline? You can let Word number the headings automatically for you, and you can delete and change the heading numbers as well.

In Outline view, choose Edit | Select All, select Format | Bullets and Numbering, then click the Outline Numbered tab. This should display a Bullets and Numbering panel similar to the one shown in Figure 13.6.

Bullets and Numbering
Bulleted
Numbered
Outline Numbered
None
1)
a)
i)
1.
1.1.
1.1.1.
Article I. Headin
Section 1.01 H
(a) Heading 3
1 Heading 1
1.1 Heading 2
1.1.1 Heading 3
I. Heading 1
A. Heading 2
1. Heading
Chapter 1 Head
Heading 2
Heading 3
List numbering
Restart numbering
Continue previous list
Customize...
Reset
OK
Cancel

Figure 13.6.
You can select different outline numbering formats for your outline.

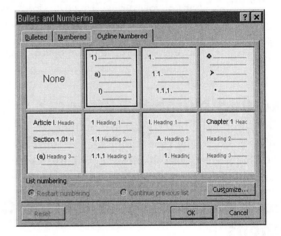

Select the numbering style you wish to use and click OK. You should then see your headings numbered. If you move or promote/demote a heading, the numbering changes.

If you make a new heading, but do not want that heading to be numbered, simply delete the number that is automatically inserted by Word 97 from the Outline Numbered tab of the Bullets and Numbering dialog box. Simply place your cursor on the heading that is to be unnumbered, then click None. You may want to set your numbering before you start writing the main text for your document. For those who are wondering whether paragraphs and other body text will be numbered, they are not supposed to be. However, if they are numbered, the numbers should disappear when you demote the paragraphs and other body text by clicking the Demote to Body Text button. The backspace key also deletes the numbers, but you should make sure the paragraph is demoted to text so there are no numbers.

You can select different numbering styles for different parts of your outline. Similarly, you can select only certain portions of your outline for numbering. Instead of selecting the entire outline, you would just select those parts of the outline that you want numbered, select Format | Bullets and Numbering, and then select the numbering style you want. Make sure the Restart Numbering option is selected.

Seeing Heading Styles in Normal View and Changing a Paragraph's Outline Level

One nice feature you will want to know about is how you can see the outline levels for parts of your document when you are in Normal view. To do this, select Tools | Options and then click the View tab. Toward the bottom in the Windows section, set the Style Area Width to .6 or .7 inches (or larger or smaller depending on how much information you want to see), and then click OK. After you have done that, when you are in Normal view you will see a Style Area column on the left side of the screen, which shows you the style of various parts of your document. To remove the column with the style information, click Tools | Options, and repeat the previous steps, setting the Style Area Width to 0.

Summary

You have learned in this chapter that using the outlining features of Word 97 is very easy. You can now switch between Normal view and Outline view. You learned how to promote, demote, and demote to body text certain parts of your outline. You also learned how to move parts of your outline around by using the Move Up and Move Down buttons. You can easily expand and collapse an outline. You also know how to show all or parts of an online. You can set up a Styles column in Normal view, and can set paragraphs to an outline level so you can see them while in Outline view when all the paragraphs are collapsed from view. Now that you know how to use outlines in Word 97, you will find yourself more organized and productive when you write your reports and other documents.

13

Q&A

Q **I don't like the fonts that I am getting in Outline view. Can I use different fonts when I am in Outline view, and will they be the same when I go back to Normal view?**

A Yes, you can. You can use the functions you use in Outline view as you would in Normal view. The fonts should stay the same when you switch back to Normal view.

Q **My Outlining toolbar disappeared. How do I get it back?**

A Click View | Toolbars | Outlining to turn the Outlining toolbar on or off.

Q **Can I print a document as an outline without printing the whole document?**

A Yes, you can print an outline. Switch to Outline view, collapse your outline so you only see the headings of your outline, and then print.

13

Hour **14**

Working with Tables

This hour explains how tables are created, modified, and enhanced. Tables are one of the most powerful features in Word 97. Tables turn Word into a spreadsheet, a database, a calendar-creator, a Web designer, or a tool to create publications. New in Word 97 is the Draw Table feature, which lets you put your artistic touches on tables. The new Tables and Borders toolbar gives one-touch access to table creation and formatting.

The highlights of this hour include

- ☐ How to insert a table
- ☐ How to use the Tables and Borders toolbar
- ☐ What AutoFormat can do to enhance tables
- ☐ How to add columns of numbers in tables
- ☐ How to use tables creatively

Inserting a Table in a Document

There are several ways to insert tables in documents. Before you start, however, you may want to turn on the Tables and Borders toolbar. The Tables and Borders icon on the Standard toolbar activates the Tables and Borders toolbar (see Figure 14.1). Drag it either to the top or bottom of the screen to move it out of the typing area. You can also use the alternate method, which is to select Toolbars from the View menu and click Tables and Borders.

Tables and Borders

Figure 14.1.
The Tables and Borders toolbar.

The Insert Table Icon

The simplest way to insert a table is to click the Insert Table button on the Standard toolbar. Insert Table lets you build a grid for the table with the number of columns and rows you want.

When working with tables, the term *cell* is important. Cells are the individual squares that make up a table. A cell is often defined as the intersection of a column and a row. A row is a group of cells running across the page, while a column is a group of cells that go down the page. For example, Figure 14.2 shows a table being inserted from the Insert Table icon that has four rows and six columns. You can tell by the text under the picture (4×6 Table).

Microsoft Word - Document3
File Edit View Insert Format Tools Table Window Help
99%
Normal
Times New Roman
12
Favorites
Go
Document3
4 x 6 Table
Page 1 Sec 1 1/1 At 1" Ln 1 Col 1 REC TRK EXT OVR WPH

Figure 14.2.
Inserting a table from the Standard toolbar.

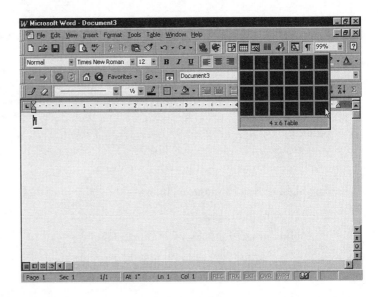

To insert a table using the Insert Table button on the Standard toolbar:

1. Position the cursor at the point in your document where you want to insert a table.
2. Click the Insert Table button.
3. Select the desired number of columns and rows by moving the mouse pointer across and down until you have a table the size you want it, then click.

One of the nice things about tables is that they are easily modified after you insert them. You can add rows, delete columns, change the sizes of columns or rows, or change the size of a single cell. Tables are as flexible as you need them to be.

Insert a Table from Menus

Inserting a table from the Table menu is a more precise way to lay out a table. Figure 14.3 displays the dialog box that comes up when you select Insert Table from the Table menu. You can specify the number of columns and rows, and set the column width to an exact size. The default column width says Auto, and this is what you get when you use the toolbar button for Insert Table. Word automatically sets the size of the columns to an optimal width to stretch from the left margin to the right margin. You can specify exact widths for the columns if you already know what size you want them.

Insert Table
Number of columns:
Number of rows:
2
Column width:
Auto
Table format: (none)
OK
Cancel
AutoFormat...

Figure 14.3.
Inserting a table from the Table menu.

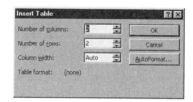

One of the buttons in the Insert Table dialog box shown in Figure 14.3 is AutoFormat. AutoFormat includes several predesigned table formats that can be applied. If you've worked with Excel's AutoFormats, these designs will look familiar. Figure 14.4 shows the dialog box that comes up when you click AutoFormat.

Table AutoFormat
Formats:
(none)
Simple 1
Simple 2
Simple 3
Classic 1
Classic 2
Classic 3
Classic 4
Colorful 1
Colorful 2
Preview
Jan Feb Mar Total
East 7 7 5 19
West 6 4 7 17
South 8 7 9 24
Total 21 18 21 60
Formats to apply
Borders
Shading
Font
Color
AutoFit
Apply special formats to
Heading rows
First column
Last row
Last column
OK
Cancel

Figure 14.4.
Using AutoFormat to add a table design.

14

You can select which of the AutoFormat design elements you want to apply to the table. If you don't like the shading, uncheck the Shading box. If you don't like the font styles Word selected, uncheck Font. These options are probably less important when you're using

AutoFormat to create a new table than when you are applying AutoFormat to an existing table. You may have gone to a lot of trouble to use special fonts or borders and don't want them replaced by AutoFormat.

The Apply special formats to options add special formatting to heading rows and the first column because these are the sections you usually use for headings. Uncheck these options if you don't want them. You can also apply special formatting to the last row and last column. These are particularly useful when you need a row or column of totals to stand out in a document.

Select an AutoFormat design from the list and watch what happens in the preview window when you apply one of the options. The font may be accented, or a line drawn to separate either the row or column from the rest of the table. Select a design you like, set the options you want to include, and click OK.

If you have already created a table and want to apply one of the AutoFormats, click the AutoFormat button on the Tools and Borders toolbar. The same AutoFormat dialog box comes up that you saw in Figure 14.4. You can apply AutoFormat options to the existing table.

Draw Table

Draw Table is a new feature that the artist in you will appreciate. We typically think of tables as cold, calculated cells of equal size, like a spreadsheet full of numbers. Draw Table would probably not be appropriate for a spreadsheet-type table. It's too difficult to make the cells equal in size using Draw Table.

Draw Table is, however, a freeform drawing tool that lets you define an outside border for the table and then draw lines inside the border for individual rows and columns. To create a table using Draw Table:

1. Activate Draw Table from the Table menu or from the Draw Table icon on the Tables and Borders toolbar (the one that looks like a pencil drawing a single line).

   If you're in another view, Word switches to Page Layout because Draw Table is a graphic tool. The mouse pointer turns to a pencil.

2. Click and hold down the mouse button on the page where you want your table. The pencil will have a square attached to it.

3. Drag the pencil down and to the right to create a box that will be the outline for your table (see Figure 14.5).

4. When it is sized about the way you want it, release the mouse button.

14

Figure 14.5.
Use Draw Table to get creative with tables.

Microsoft Word - Document3
File Edit View Insert Format Tools Table Window Help
69%
Normal
Times New Roman
12
Favorites
Go
Document3
Click and drag to create table and to draw rows, columns and borders.

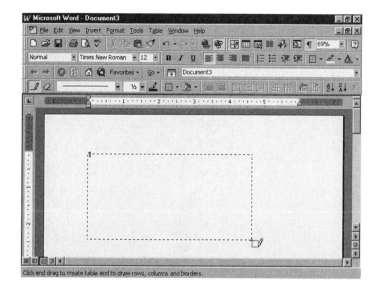

To insert a new column or a row:

1. Click the Draw Table icon if it is not already turned on (if it's turned on, it looks pushed in and lighted); the mouse pointer will still look like a pencil.
2. Click the top border of the table and start moving down with the pencil. The pencil knows where you're headed and creates a column.
3. Click the left border of the table and start moving the pencil to the right. The pencil creates a row.

As long as the Draw Table button is turned on, you can continue to draw columns and rows until you have the table looking the way you want it. You can start drawing lines from any existing edge or cell border. One of the real pluses is being able to draw a column that only goes as far as a certain row, or a row that only reaches to a particular column as in Figure 14.6. There's a lot of creative freedom in using Draw Table.

Adding Rows and Columns to a Table

You can easily add more rows or columns to any table, whether it was created with the Insert Table button or with Draw Table. First, you need to know how to select portions of a table. Table 14.1 shows the selection methods for tables.

Microsoft Word - Document3
File Edit View Insert Format Tools Table Window Help
Normal
Times New Roman
12
Favorites
Go
Document3
Drag to draw columns and rows or apply border using current linestyle.

Figure 14.6.
Fine-tune rows and columns with Draw Table.

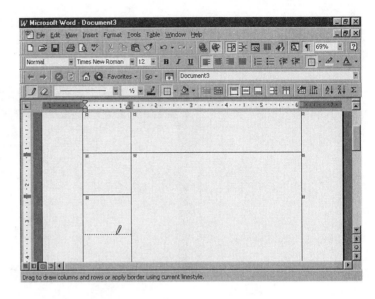

Table 14.1. Selecting parts of a table.

Selection	Selection method
A cell	Position the mouse pointer in the cell in a location where the pointer is displayed as an arrow pointing up and to the right, then click.
A row	Click in the left margin next to the row (with the arrow pointing to the right), or click anywhere in the row, and select Table|Select Row.
A column	Position the mouse pointer above the column until it turns to a dark arrow pointing down, then click (see Figure 14.7), or click in any cell in the column and select Table|Select Column.
The entire table	Position the cursor anywhere in the table and press Alt + (numeric keypad) 5 (the Num Lock key must be turned off when using this key combination to select a table). Or, click in the table and select Table|Select Table.

If you're already working in a table, the Insert Table button on the Standard toolbar changes to either an Insert Rows or Insert Columns button. If you have a row selected, the icon is used to insert rows. If you have a column selected, the icon changes to Insert Columns.

With a row selected, click the Insert Rows button to insert a row above the selected row. Keep clicking the Insert Rows button to insert more rows. With a column selected, click the Insert Columns button to insert a column to the left of the selection.

Figure 14.7.
Selecting a column.

Microsoft Word - Document3
File Edit View Insert Format Tools Table Window Help
Normal
Times New Roman
12
Favorites
Go
Document3
Page 1
Sec 1
1/1
At
Ln
Col
REC
TRK
EXT
OVR
WPH

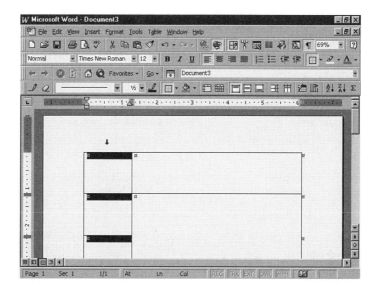

To insert a row at the end of a table, press the Tab key in the last cell of the table. To insert another column at the right edge of a table, position the mouse above the table just past the last column until you see the black arrow that points down. Click the mouse button, then click the Insert Columns button on the toolbar or select Insert Columns from the Table menu.

TIME SAVER

> If you insert a table on the first line of a document and later decide you need text above the table, you can insert a regular paragraph above a table by placing the cursor in the first cell of the table and pressing Ctrl+Shift+Enter.

Entering Text into a Table

One of the reasons you don't need to have all rows established when you create a table is because Word automates the addition of rows as you type. To begin adding text to a table, position the cursor in the first cell of the table. Type everything you want in the cell. If you type more text than the cell can handle on one line, the text wraps to a second line in the cell and the cell height is enlarged to permit the extra lines. To move to the next cell in the row, press Tab. The Tab key is the primary key for getting around in tables. When you come to the last cell in a row, pressing the Tab key advances to the first cell in the next row. If there is no row following the last cell, a new row is automatically created. Table 14.2 lists some navigational keys you'll use in tables.

14

Table 14.2. Navigational keys for tables.

Keys	Function
Tab	Moves one cell to the right; starts a new row if pressed in the last cell of a table.
Shift+Tab	Moves one cell to the left, or to the last cell in the row above if the cursor is in the first cell of a row.
Down arrow	Moves to the cell below the current cell (if the cursor is in the last line of the cell).
Up arrow	Moves to the cell above the current cell (if the cursor is in the first line of the cell).
Alt+Page Down	Moves to the cell below the current cell from any line in the cell.
Alt+Page Up	Moves to the cell above the current cell from any line in the cell.

If you are at the end of an existing table and you press the Tab key in the last cell, a new row is inserted on the next line. As you can see, you need start only with a single row. Word adds the extra rows as you need them.

Aligning Table Text

You learned about aligning text in Hour 6, "Formatting Paragraphs." The same principles apply to text in tables. Text can be left-aligned, right-aligned, centered, or justified in cells.

> **Step-Up**
>
> One of the great enhancements to Word's Table feature is being able to align text vertically within a cell. You can align text at the top, bottom, or center of a cell. Move the mouse across the Tables and Borders toolbar and you'll find selections for Align Top, Center Vertically, and Align Bottom. There is also an icon to change the direction of text (Change Text Direction).

Figure 14.8 shows some of the different alignment options. The directional text feature adds the versatility for placing text that Excel has had for a long time. If your headings are too long to fit horizontally in a table, rotating text with the Change Text Direction button provides an easy solution.

14

Microsoft Word - Document5
File Edit View Insert Format Tools Table Window Help
Normal
Times New Roman
18
Favorites
Go
Document5
Aligning Text from top to bottom from the Tables and Borders Toolbar
Align Top
Center Vertically
Align Bottom
Press the Change Direction button until you get text the direction you want it
NORMAL
UP
DOWN
Page 1 Sec 1 1/1 At 1.9" Ln 1 Col 13 REC TRK EXT OVR WPH

Figure 14.8.
Table text alignment options.

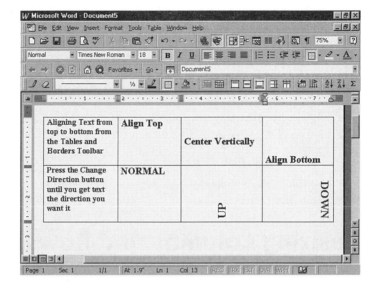

You might want text centered both vertically and horizontally in a cell and the direction of text changed to display vertically rather than horizontally. To do this:

1. Click in the table cell.
2. Click the Center button on the Formatting toolbar.
3. Click the Center Vertically button on the Tables and Borders toolbar.
4. Click the Change Text Direction button on the Tables and Borders toolbar as many times as needed to place text in the direction you want. Text will rotate between the normal, top-to-bottom, and bottom-to-top placement options as you click the button.

JUST A MINUTE

When you change the direction of the text to one of the vertical text options, the Alignment buttons change functions. For example, the Left Align button becomes the Align Top and the Align Top becomes the Left Align function. You'll notice that the toolbar icons flip directions for the alignment icons. This is because the text has a different orientation to the top and sides of the cell when it is rotated.

Using Tabs in Tables

The Tab key is used to get back and forth in a table, so it can't be used to set a real tab in a table cell. One of the primary reasons for needing a tab in a table is to set a decimal-aligned tab that lines up numbers on the decimal point. It is very hard to get lists of figures to look good without a decimal-aligned tab.

To insert a tab in a table, press Ctrl+Tab. You can also set tabs from the ruler or by selecting Format | Tabs. The easiest way to insert decimal-aligned tabs in a column is to

1. Type the text (numbers) in the column cells.
2. Select the column.
3. Select Format | Tabs.
4. Type in a number for the Tab stop position (for example, .5 inches). Click Decimal under Alignment.
5. Click Set, then click OK.

Word automatically inserts the tabs in every cell of the column. You won't even see the tab markers in the cells. Once a tab is set, you can move it on the ruler if it's not where you want it.

Resizing Columns and Rows

When you use the Insert Table button on the Standard toolbar to insert a table, the column and row sizes are preset to fit the width of the page. The columns are all the same size. You may want to alter the sizes so that they better fit the contents of the columns. For example, you may want a column containing names to be wider than a column that includes birthdays. Columns are easily resized. When you position the mouse pointer in the space between two columns on the ruler, a double-headed arrow appears with the message Move Table Column, as shown in Figure 14.9. Move the pointer right or left to resize the columns.

Microsoft Word - Document5
File Edit View Insert Format Tools Table Window Help
Normal
Times New Roman
13
Favorites
Go
Document5
Move Table Column
Name
Position
Birthday
Martha Walters
Chief Cook
May 23
April Dougherty
Assistant Cook
January 12
Amy Jones
Dietician
November 10
Page 1
Sec 1
1/1
At 1.2"
Ln 2
Col 11
REC
TRK
EXT
OVR
WPH

Figure 14.9.
Moving a column.

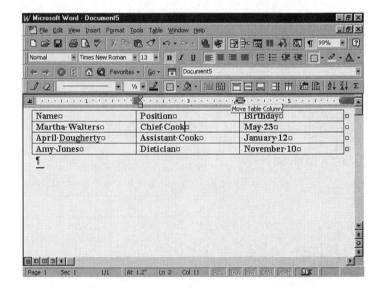

You can also move columns by positioning the mouse pointer on the line between two columns. The mouse pointer changes to a line with an arrow on either side. Click and drag the line in either direction to change column sizes. One of the problems with this method is that it's easy to grab a single cell and move the cell rather than the whole column. The column must be selected in order to move it. If a single cell is selected, only that cell will be resized.

There may be times when you actually want to move a single cell. This is particularly true when tables are used to create forms. Cells often need to be specific widths to accommodate the different kinds of information that must be entered in the form. They won't necessarily line up neatly in columns. To resize a single cell:

1. Select the cell (click in the cell with the mouse pointer pointing up and to the right).
2. Position the mouse on either the right or left border of the cell (the pointer changes to the line with an arrow on both sides).
3. Click and drag the border either to the left or to the right to resize it.

Distribute Rows and Columns Evenly

When you start dragging columns around, you are bound to get columns that don't look the way you want them. Perhaps you have two columns on the left side of the table that need to vary in width and four columns that need to be the same width. By the time you've dragged and adjusted columns, you may have altered the sizes of the four columns enough that they are not the same. The Tables and Borders toolbar has new tools to help correct these kinds of problems. To make the last four columns the same size:

1. Select the columns by positioning the mouse pointer above the first of the four columns until the dark arrow appears.
2. Click and drag the mouse pointer to the right to select all four columns.
3. Click the Distribute Columns Evenly button on the toolbar.

All four columns are proportioned equally to fit the amount of available space.

Distribute Rows Evenly works the same way for rows. Select the rows, then click the Distribute Rows Evenly button, and all of the rows will be of equal height. The capability to distribute rows and columns is a great Word 97 enhancement to the Table feature.

AutoFit

If you want to let Word figure out the size for columns, AutoFit is a handy feature. AutoFit looks at the text in the cells and adjusts the columns to accommodate the widest line of text

14

in the column. Text in the cells will wrap as needed to keep the columns within the page margins. If you want to use AutoFit for the whole table:

1. Select the table (Table | Select Table or Alt+5 on the keypad).
2. Select Table | Cell Height and Width.
3. Click AutoFit in the Column tab.

If you accidentally move a couple of single cells and they don't line up with the other cells in the columns, AutoFit will readjust the table cells to bring them back into nice straight columns. It resizes all of the columns in the process.

Split Cells and Merge Cells

Merging cells is useful when you want to center a title in the first row of a table as in Figure 14.10. The second row of the table is the only one that is formatted normally. The first row is three cells merged together to allow for the title.

Figure 14.10.
Merging and splitting cells.

Merged cells
Microsoft Word - Document6
June
To Do
Appointments
Notes
SPLIT
CELLS
Split cells

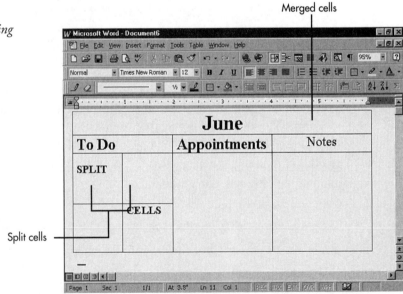

To merge cells:

1. Select the cells to be merged (combined).
2. Click the Merge Cells icon on the Tables and Borders toolbar, or select Merge Cells from the Table menu.
3. Click the Center button on the Standard toolbar (or press Ctrl+E) if you want to center text across the columns.

Splitting cells is just as easy. To create more cells within a single cell as in the first cell of the third row in Figure 14.10, select the cell and click the Split Cells button. A dialog box asks how many columns and rows you want the cell divided into. It actually creates another small table within a cell.

Deleting Rows or Columns

If you've tried using the Delete key to remove a row or column, you know it doesn't work. The Delete key removes the contents of the row or column, but leaves the cells. To delete a row, select it and choose Delete Rows from the Table menu. Similarly, delete a column by selecting it and choosing Delete Columns from the Table menu. To remove an entire table, select the table and then select Table | Delete Rows.

Sorting a Table

There are times when you will want to sort a table. If you enter the reservations for an event in a table as they are received, it may be a little hard to keep track unless the entries are ordered in some way. The table could be sorted alphabetically by the guests' last names to make it easier to reference.

You would normally include headings above the columns to indicate what information is in each column. The column headings for a reservation list might be Last Name, First Name, Phone, and Reservations.

Word tables are smarter than they used to be. A default is set to tell Word that the first row is a header row. When you sorted a table in earlier versions, it would sort the header row along with all the other rows unless you specified that the first row was the header row. Your headings always ended up in the middle of your table somewhere. Now you have to tell Word when you *don't* have a header row.

There are two ways to sort a table. The easiest is to select the column you want to sort by. In this example, the sort is by the last name, which is the first column. Click the Sort Ascending button on the Tables and Borders toolbar. The list is sorted alphabetically by last name. If you want to sort on one of the other columns, simply select another column and click the Sort Ascending button.

You can also sort in reverse order by clicking the Sort Descending button. When you're working with numeric data, this is often a preferred method for displaying facts and figures.

Businesses like to note their top salespeople and will want the big producers at the top of the list. To specify other Sort options, select Table | Sort. To sort on more than one column, specify the first sort from the selections in the Sort by drop-down list. Select a second sort from the Then by drop-down list. Figure 14.11 shows a sort by last name, then by first name. This is helpful when you're typing a phone listing or roster and need to have both parts of the name

14

sorted in the alphabetical listing. This is also where you can tell Word when you don't have a header row. Click the No header row radio button if there are no headings in your table.

Microsoft Word - Document7
File Edit View Insert Format Tools Table Window Help
Normal
Times New Roman
13
Last Name
First Name
Phone
Reservations
Jefferson
Thomas
Washington
George
Adams
John Quincy
Fillmore
Millard
Coolidge
Calvin
Grant
Ulysses
Adams
John
Sort
Sort by
Last Name
Type:
Text
Ascending
Descending
Then by
First Name
Type:
Text
Ascending
Descending
Then by
Type:
Text
Ascending
Descending
My list has
Header row
No header row
OK
Cancel
Options...
Page 1 Sec 1 1/1 At 1" Ln 1 Col 1

Figure 14.11.
Sorting a table by first and last names.

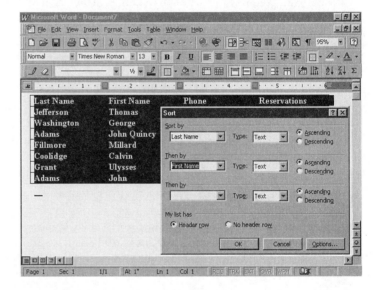

Sorting rearranges an entire table in a certain order. If you simply want to reorder a couple of rows in a table, you can use the same keyboard combination used to move text up and down. Alt+Shift+Up arrow or Down arrow moves a selected row up or down to promote or demote a row. For example, select a row and press the Alt+Shift+Up arrow to move the row ahead of the previous row.

Converting Text to a Table

Sometimes you have already typed text when you decide you want it in a table. Tables are really easier to work with than tabbed text to create manageable lists and columns of text. Text in a list is usually separated by tabs or commas, but it can be in almost any format for Word to divide it into a table. To convert text to a table:

1. Select the text you want to convert to a table.
2. Select Table|Convert Text to Table. The Convert Text to Table dialog box opens.
3. Word looks at the selected text and determines the number of columns it thinks are required. If this is incorrect, type the number of columns needed in the Number of columns box.
4. Choose one of the options for Separate text at (for example, if your text is separated by tabs, click the Tabs option).
5. Click OK.

JUST A MINUTE

> If the text being converted to a table is separated by tabs or another separator, there should be only one separator between each item. Additional separators throw off the table conversion. The Undo button does work if things don't work quite right in the conversion process.

If your text is not separated by one of the standard options (paragraphs, tabs, or commas), you can specify any other character you separated text with, including a space. Type the character in the Other box. Figure 14.12 shows a simple list with a single space between each item and a table that was created from the same list by converting text to a table. A space was entered in the Other box by clicking in the box and pressing the spacebar. Word inserts a cell division wherever there is a separator (in this case, a space).

Microsoft Word - Document8
File Edit View Insert Format Tools Table Window Help
Normal
Times New Roman
17
One·Two·Three·Four
Five·Six·Seven·Eight
Nine·Ten·Eleven·Twelve
One
Two
Three
Four
Five
Six
Seven
Eight
Nine
Ten
Eleven
Twelve
Page 1
Sec 1
1/1
At 1.5"
Ln 3
Col 23

Figure 14.12.
Creating a table from text.

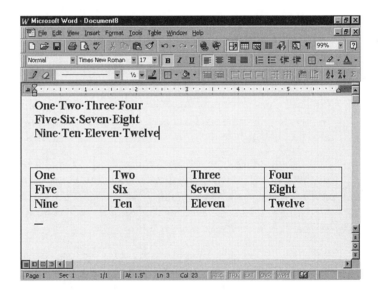

It is just as easy to turn a table into text. When you select a table, the option under Table is no longer Convert Text to Table. It becomes Convert Table to Text and gives the same options to replace cell divisions with text separators.

AutoSum

When you're working with figures in a table, it's nice to be able to add up columns of numbers without a calculator. AutoSum does the job in Word tables. Position the cursor in the cell below a column of numbers and click the AutoSum button to calculate the sum of the numbers above (see Figure 14.13).

Figure 14.13.
Calculating a column of numbers with AutoSum.

AutoSum
Microsoft Word - Document10

Unit No.	First Quarter	Second Quarter	Third Quarter	Fourth Quarter
East	35,950	22,800	39,000	28,500
West	21,200	21,500	21,800	23,200
North	32,900	43,500	23,000	43,900
South	31,900	21,400	81,700	28,500
Totals	121,950	109,200	165,500	

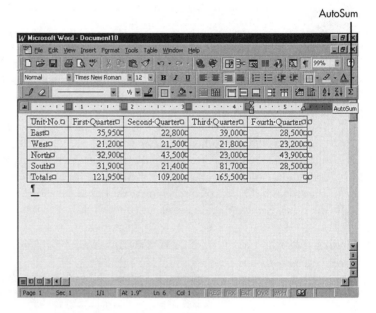

Unlike a spreadsheet program, Word does not automatically update the sums if you change numbers in the table. You will need to either use AutoSum again to repeat the calculations or right-click each of the sums and select Update field from the shortcut menu.

You can do other types of calculations using Table | Formula if you know a little about mathematical expressions and spreadsheet terminology. It's not complex, but you'll probably end up in a spreadsheet program if your figures need to be updated from time to time. Updating the fields or repeating AutoSum for each column is not only time-consuming, it can be inaccurate if you miss a column.

Cells in a table start numbering with A1 for the top-left cell—the first cell in the table. A1 is the first cell in the first column. The next cell in the row is B1, and so on. The next row starts with A2 and the numbering continues in this way. Figure 14.14 shows a table and indicates how cells are numbered. In this figure, the Formula function is being used to calculate bowling averages. To calculate an average such as the one in this table:

1. Position the cursor in the cell where you want the result to appear.
2. Select Table | Formula.

The Sum function appears in the Formula box. This is the most commonly used function, so it comes up as the suggested calculation.

1. In the Formula box, select and delete the Sum formula.
2. Type = (every formula begins with the equal sign) in the Formula box.

3. Select Average from the drop-down list under Paste (or type `Average` after the equal sign in the Formula box).
4. The range of cells must be specified for the calculation. In this example, A2:A4 is the range and the range is placed in parentheses. A2:A4 designates everything between and including cells A2 and A4.
5. Click OK to enter the calculation in cell A5.

The same method is used to calculate the average for the rest of the columns. For column 2, the cursor is placed in cell B5 and the average is calculated for cells B2:B4 and so forth.

Microsoft Word - Document2
File Edit View Insert Format Tools Table Window Help
Dick
Jane
Sally
Spot
85
45
150
5
92
108
130
7
100
79
148
12
Cell A2
Cell C4
Formula
Formula:
=AVERAGE(A2:A4)
Number format:
Paste function:
Paste bookmark:
OK
Cancel

Figure 14.14.
Calculating a bowling average.

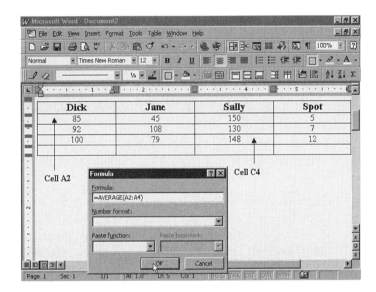

Tables as a Design Tool

Tables are not only a great tool for numbers and lists, but can be used in a variety of other ways. You might choose to do a newsletter in table format. Rather than use the standard columns, you can remove the borders so that no one knows that the publication was laid out as a table. To remove table borders:

1. Select the table.
2. Select Format | Borders.
3. Click None in the Borders tab.

You can also add or remove borders from the drop-down list of border options as shown in Figure 14.15. The last selection is grayed slightly and shows no dark lines. This is the selection for no border. The other icons are visually descriptive of the kinds of borders that can be selected.

Figure 14.15.
Using the border options to remove borders.

Microsoft Word - Document10
File Edit View Insert Format Tools Table Window Help
Normal
Times New Roman
12
99%
Unit No First Quarter Second Quarter Fourth Quarter
East 35,950 22,800 28,500
West 21,200 21,500 21,800 23,200
North 32,900 43,500 23,000 43,900
South 31,900 21,400 82,700 28,500
Totals 121,950 109,200 166,500
No Border
Page 1 Sec 1 1/1 At 1" Ln 1 Col 1 REC TRK EXT OVR WPH

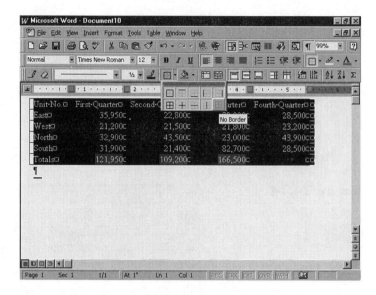

You may still see a faint gray border around the cells. These are the gridlines. To see what the table looks like without them, select Gridlines from the Table menu to turn the gridline display off.

Create a one-page newsletter using a table rather than standard columns. Be creative and use Draw Table to lay out sections of different sizes. One of the great new features is the eraser. If you want some of the lines to show but not others, use the eraser on the ones you don't want. Simply click the Eraser button and drag it over a portion of a line to make it disappear.

Figure 14.16 shows a newsletter that was created in a table (with the gridlines showing). Figure 14.17 shows the same newsletter without the gridlines visible. Only one line is really there—the one underneath the header; the others were gridlines. Gridlines don't print. They're only there so that you can see where you're working in a table. When borders are applied, the lines are dark and solid rather than faint gray and the gridlines will print.

In Figure 14.16, there is space added between the gridline and the text in the second cell of row two. To add the extra space that you normally want between columns of a newsletter:

1. Select the cell (or column if you want added space between two columns).
2. Select Format | Paragraph.
3. Type in a left indent (in Figure 14.16 there is a .3-inch left indent).
4. Click OK.

Indents can be used in table cells just as they are in paragraphs. You can also add graphics to a table. To insert a graphic in a table, it must be placed as an inline graphic. Details on inline graphics versus graphics that float above the text layer are discussed in Hour 17, "Working

with Graphics." Tables take on a whole new look when borders and shading are applied. Hour 19, "Jazzing Up Your Documents," shows how to apply borders and shading to tables and other documents.

Microsoft Word - Document11
Fine Arts Guild News
May 1997
String Concert a Big Success
Magestic Organ to be Refurbished

Figure 14.16.
Creating a newsletter in a table.

Microsoft Word - Document11
Fine Arts Guild News
May 1997
String Concert a Big Success
Magestic Organ to be Refurbished

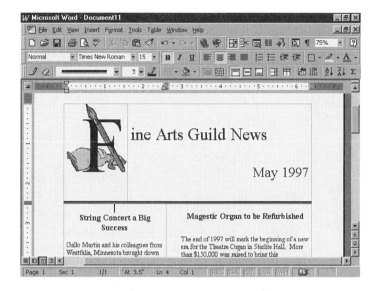

Figure 14.17.
The newsletter as it will print (without the gridlines).

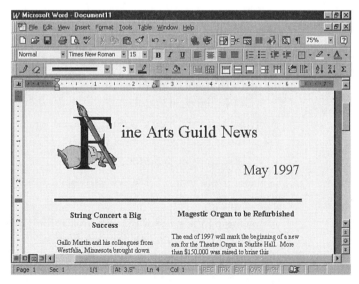

Use tables to create sidebars, calendars, menus, or any number of documents that require text to be placed in distinct areas on the page. You'll be surprised how much easier it is to work with tables than with tabs for text placement.

Summary

This hour highlights one of Word 97's greatest achievements. Tables can be sketched out with Draw Table. The options to rearrange text in tables are almost endless. One of the most significant additions to the new table features is being able to rotate text using the Change Text Direction tool. You can easily sort tables or convert tables to text—do the reverse to convert existing text to a table. Add up the columns of numbers in a table with AutoSum. Tables are feature-rich workhorses in Word 97.

Q&A

Q Is there a way to prevent a row that has more than one line of text from splitting between two pages?

A Yes. Select Table|Cell Height and Width. Uncheck the box that says Allow row to break across pages. It forces the row that would normally split between pages to move to the next page.

Q When I try to insert a table from the Insert Table icon, I can only get a table as large as five columns and four rows. Why can't I make a bigger table?

A If you click the Insert Table button, move the mouse pointer across and down, and click the last cell (lower right) to set the table size, the largest table you can create is one that is five columns by four rows. If you click the Insert Table button, click in the first cell (upper left), and move the mouse pointer across and down to set the table size, you can insert a table as large as eight columns by thirteen rows. If you want to create a table that is six columns by six rows:

1. Click the Insert Table button.
2. Click in the top-left cell.
3. Hold down the mouse button and drag the mouse to the right to select six columns and down to select six rows.
4. Release the mouse button.

The alternative is to use Table|Insert Table to specify the number of columns and rows.

Q I was changing the sizes of the columns and my table moved off the right edge of the paper. Why can't I see it to readjust it?

A You are probably in Page Layout view or another view that displays the page as it will print. Switch to Normal view and you can grab the right edge of the table and move it back. Bring it back to the right margin to be within the print range. You could also resize all the cells to bring them within the page margins by selecting Table|Cell Height and Width, select the Columns tab, and click AutoFit. This will, however, resize all the columns.

14

Q I like being able to sort a table. Is there any way to sort a list of items that isn't in a table?

A Yes. Select text you want to sort, then select Table|Sort. The same dialog box comes up that you see when you sort a table, but it says Sort Text at the top. Usually you sort by paragraph (which would be line-by-line for a list). Once in a while, you type a list with first name, then last name, and wish you'd typed the last name first so that you could get an alphabetical listing. To put the list in order by last name without retyping:

1. Select the list.

2. Select Table|Sort.

3. Select Word 2 (last name) in the drop-down list under Sort by.

4. Select Word 1 (first name) from the Then by list.

The list is sorted without requiring you to retype it!

14

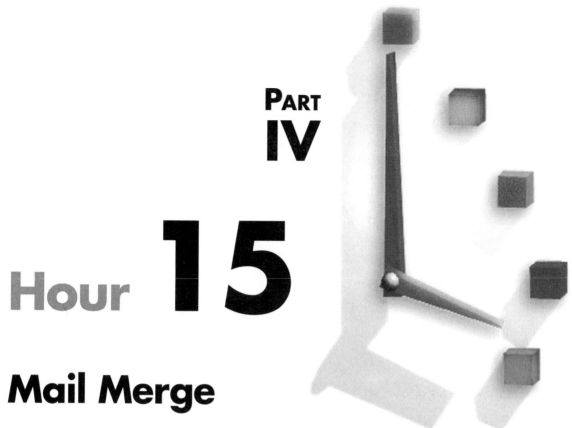

Hour **15**

Mail Merge

This hour explains how and why you would use mail merge. Today's business environment is fast paced and communications need to be timely. Employees no longer have the time to type the same letter to twenty people, nor would they want to with the kinds of tools that are available.

Mail merge used to be so complicated that instead of using it, people would type the contents of the letter and then type over the name and address to send the same letter to a different person. That works fine if you only have to do this for one or two people, but if you want to send the letter to twenty people, typing over the name and address can be time consuming. You also have no record of who the letters were sent to. Mail merge was created to expedite this process.

The highlights of this hour include

- ☐ How to set up a mail merge for form letters
- ☐ How to create a list with mail merge
- ☐ How to use mail merge for mailing labels and envelopes
- ☐ What kinds of files you can use for data sources in Word

Why Use Mail Merge?

Mail merge is not just a tool for creating form letters, but that's its primary purpose. You get junk mail every day that someone created with mail merge. It is now possible for individuals to buy a CD-ROM or a series of CD-ROMs with the names and mailing addresses of practically everyone in the country. These CD-ROMs contain data that is collected and packaged so that others can use it. A vendor can purchase one of these packages and write a letter with codes that read the information from the CD-ROMs. Your name and address can be inserted in the letter using mail merge. You've probably received letters that use your first and last names in the salutation, such as *Dear David Smith*. Most people don't call you by your first and last names.

The reason the letters are written that way is because the data was created with only one name field. We talked briefly about fields in Hour 1, "Word 97—A Multipurpose Tool." Fields are the units used to hold certain pieces of information. The pricier data sources break down the information into more fields than the ones you can buy off the shelf in many stores. That's why some letters say, Dear David Smith and some say Dear David or Dear Mr. Smith—the first and last names are separate fields you can use individually.

Mail merge can also be used to create mailing labels. You might send an organizational newsletter to a hundred people once a month. If you had to type these same labels every month, you'd probably spend at least half a day just getting the labels ready. With mail merge, you can print out the 100 mailing labels in a matter of minutes.

Why use mail merge? It's a great time saver. After you see how mail-merge documents are set up, you'll discover that it's not the complicated process it used to be.

Main Documents and Data Sources—
What's the Difference?

Mail merge has two major components. One is the main document and the other is the data source. The main document is the form letter, the mailing label form sheet, or another document that contains codes for information that comes from another file—the data source. The data source is the file that contains information such as names and addresses that will be combined with the main document to complete a merge process. You might compare it to a fill-in-the-blank form. The main document is the form. The data source contains the information that goes in the blanks.

Mail merge can be used to create a single letter that can be individualized for as many people as you wish. The main document is typed normally, but the recipient's name, address, and salutation are added to the document as fields (placeholders for information that comes from

15

another source). By connecting the main document to a data source that contains the information for many individuals, the information that was entered as fields is replaced with the information from the data source. Field names in the data source *must* match the field names in the main document.

The term *merge* is descriptive of what happens in this whole process. The main document and the data source are merged, or combined, to create a final product such as a sheet of mailing labels or a batch of letters. This all happens because of the field codes in the main document that match the fields in the data source. During the merge process, the main document field codes are replaced with the contents of the fields in the data source.

Main Documents

Figure 15.1 shows a main document. It is a letter from a fictitious Widgets company, and has what looks likes some odd codes in it. If this looks like a foreign language, don't worry. You'll soon understand the language of merge. If you can't see the codes in a merge main document, press Alt+F9 to display the field codes. The Alt+F9 key combination toggles the field code display on or off.

Figure 15.1.
A main document with merge codes.

Microsoft Word - Document2
Date field
Name and address fields
Salutation field
{DATE \@ "MMMM d, yyyy" * MERGEFORMAT}
«FirstName» «LastName»
«Address1»
«Address2»
«City», «State» «PostalCode»
Dear «Title» «LastName»:
Thank you for your recent response to our questionnaire. We are sending you a small gift in appreciation for your reply. The information from this survey will help us better evaluate our services and products. Your input and that from hundreds of other who responded to the survey give us a starting point to build our customer service department at Widgets Enterprises. We hope to better serve you in the future.

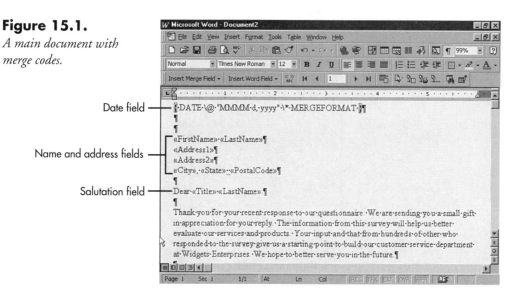

Line one contains the codes to insert the current date. Each time the letter prints, it prints the current date if this field is present. You learned a bit about inserting dates in the discussion on headers and footers in Hour 8, "Setting Up the Page." Select Insert | Date and Time from the menu, choose one of the available date formats, and check the Update automatically box. If you don't add the update automatically provision, the date will be inserted, but it will not be a field and will not change if you use the document again.

The lines following the date are the information fields for the name, address, and salutation. The body of the letter is already typed into the main document. The only thing that is needed is a source to bring in the names and addresses of the people the letter is to be mailed to. That's where the second component in mail merge comes in—the data source.

Data Sources

The data source can come from any one of a number of sources. It can be an Access database, an Excel spreadsheet, Microsoft's Address Book, or a data source that you create in Word. Figure 15.2 shows a typical data source created in Word and displayed in table form. The line at the top is called the header row, which was mentioned in Hour 14, "Working with Tables." In this case, the header row contains the field names (Title, Firstname, and so on).

The main document must have field codes that match the field names in the document source header row. In the merge process, the field codes in the main document, like the ones shown in Figure 15.1, read from the document source shown in Figure 15.2 to gather the information it needs to fill in the field codes.

Figure 15.2.
A data source in table view.

Microsoft Word - Sample data source.doc
File Edit View Insert Format Tools Table Window Help
Normal
Times New Roman
12
99%
Title FirstName LastName Address1 Address2 City State PostalCode
Mr. James Carlton 2100 Macomb Court Ardvaark MD 32490
Mrs. MaryAnn Clemonts PO Box 145 Merryville ND 35890
Mr. and Mrs. Carol and David Smith 2948 Maple Tree Lane Conway WI 49007
Mr. Dewey Jones 3900 Pendleton Heights Apt 14 Lands End MI 48008
Mr. and Charles Hockema 23 Trailway #354 Parker City CO 50091
Page 1 Sec 1 1/1 At 3.4" Ln 14 Col 6 REC TRK EXT OVR WPH

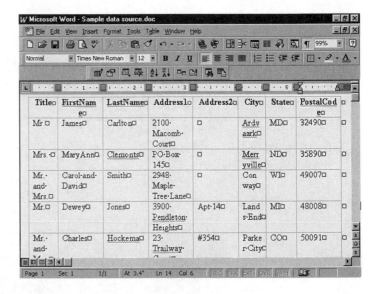

Creating a Simple Mail Merge

To set up a mail merge, two documents are needed—a main document and a data source. This example goes through the steps of a mail merge from start to finish. A new main document and a new data source are being created. You could also create a main document and use an existing data source such as an Access or a dBASE file to do a mail merge. A mail

merge always begins with the main document, and the merge itself (combining the main document and the data source) must take place within the main document.

Step 1—Setting Up the Main Document

The first step is to set up the main document. To do this:

1. Select Tools | Mail Merge. The Mail Merge Helper dialog box appears, as in Figure 15.3.

Mail Merge Helper
Use this checklist to set up a mail merge. Begin by choosing the Create button.
1
Main document
Create
Form Letters...
Mailing Labels...
Envelopes...
Catalog...
2
3
Merge the data with the document
Merge...
Cancel

Figure 15.3.
Creating a mail-merge document from a new document.

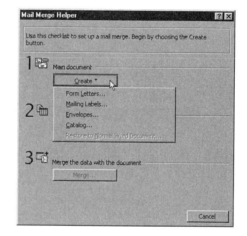

2. Select Form Letters from the Create drop-down list to create a form letter.

   A dialog box appears, asking whether you want to create the main document from the active window or from a new document.

3. Click New Document if you have another file open. (If you were in a document that you wanted to use for the mail-merge document, you would click Active Window.)

Step 2—Setting Up the Data Source

After the new main document is created, you are returned to the Mail Merge Helper dialog box. Step 2 is to set up the data source.

1. Click the drop-down Get Data list.
2. Select Create Data Source as shown in Figure 15.4.

Mail Merge Helper
The next step in setting up the mail merge is to specify a data source. Choose the Get Data button.
1
Main document
Create
Edit
Merge type: Form Letters
Main document: Document4
2
Data source
Get Data
Create Data Source...
Open Data Source...
Use Address Book...
Header Options...
3
Close

Figure 15.4.
Selecting a data source—Create Data Source.

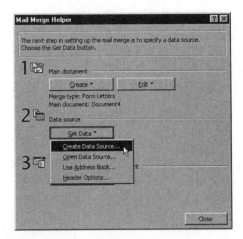

Step 3—Adding and Removing Fields from the Data Source

Word displays the Create Data Source dialog box, where you specify what the field names will be in your data source and your main document (see Figure 15.5). Word shows a list of suggested fields in the box of field names. If you don't like the ones Word has chosen, you can delete them and add your own.

Create Data Source
A mail merge data source is composed of rows of data. The first row is called the header row. Each of the columns in the header row begins with a field name.
Word provides commonly used field names in the list below. You can add or remove field names to customize the header row.
Field name:
Field names in header row:
Add Field Name >>
Remove Field Name
Title
FirstName
LastName
JobTitle
Company
Address1
Address2
Move
MS Query...
OK
Cancel

Figure 15.5.
Selecting field names for the merge document.

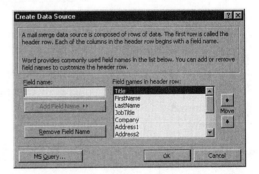

Delete field names that you don't want in your data source by selecting each field name individually and clicking the Remove Field Name button for each deletion. If, for example, you want to remove the Country, HomePhone, and WorkPhone fields:

1. Select Country from the Field names in header row list. Click Remove Field Name.
2. Select HomePhone from the list. Click Remove Field Name.
3. Select WorkPhone from the list. Click Remove Field Name.

These three field names are removed from the data source. To add a field, type a name in the Field name box and click Add Field Name.

TIME SAVER

> Adding a field for salutation offers more flexibility in the way you address people. You might have a mix of individuals in your data source. Some you would call by their first names, some you might address by nickname, and others you might address more formally by title and last name. There is no way to allow for these different types of salutations with the preset field names.

You can rearrange the order of the field names in the list by selecting a field name and clicking the move up or move down arrow buttons to move the item up or down in the list. You do not need to have fields in any specific order. They can be inserted in any order in the main document. One good reason to rearrange the order is to facilitate data entry. You will often work from a list that has the information in a specific order. It is much easier to enter the information in the data source if the fields are ordered in the same way that the information appears in the printed list you are working from.

Step 4—Naming and Saving the Data Source

After you delete, add, and move field names in the list, click OK. Word prompts you to give the data source document a name, as shown in Figure 15.6. This is sometimes a source of confusion for people. You are saving and naming the data source document at this point, *not* the main document.

Save As
Save in: Sample Docs
Name
Size
Type
Modified
Sample Agriculture.doc 22 KB Microsoft Wor... 4/1/97 9:22 PM
Sample data source.doc 19 KB Microsoft Wor... 4/30/97 5:08 PM
sample.txt.doc 19 KB Microsoft Wor... 4/5/97 9:58 PM
savetest.doc 19 KB Microsoft Wor... 4/2/97 7:01 AM
test.doc 19 KB Microsoft Wor... 4/11/97 9:07 AM
test2.doc 14 KB Microsoft Wor... 4/11/97 9:13 AM
test3.doc 19 KB Microsoft Wor... 4/11/97 ...
Save
Cancel
Options...
Save Version...
File name: Widget letter data
Save as type: Word Document (*.doc)

Figure 15.6.
Naming the data source document.

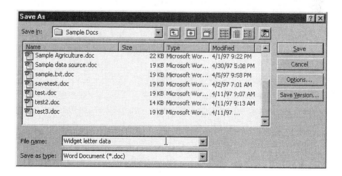

Step 5—Editing the Data Source

When you save the data source document, a dialog box opens asking whether you want to edit the data source or the main document. It really doesn't matter which you do first. You need to do both when you are creating the data source. Click Edit Data Source to fill in the information about the people the letter is to be sent to (see Figure 15.7).

Microsoft Word
The data source you just created contains no data records. You can add new records to your data source by choosing the Edit Data Source button, or add merge fields to your main document by choosing the Edit Main Document button.
Edit Data Source
Edit Main Document

Figure 15.7.
Click Edit Data Source to begin entering names and addresses.

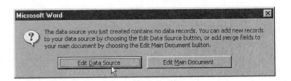

The Data Form dialog, shown in Figure 15.8, appears with boxes to enter information for each person. Working in the Data Form dialog is similar to working in a table. Press the Tab key to move from one field to the next. Press Shift+Tab to move up one field. After you enter the information in the last field of a record, press the Enter key or click the Add New button to begin a record for another person.

Data Form
FirstName: Terrance
LastName: Cantor
JobTitle: Production Assistant
Address1: 3589 LaFerny
Address2: Apt 20
City: Bay View
State: MI
PostalCode: 48848
Salutation: Terry
OK
Add New
Delete
Restore
Find...
View Source
Record: 3
First record
Previous record
Next record
Last record
Current record

Figure 15.8.
Entering information in the Data Form dialog.

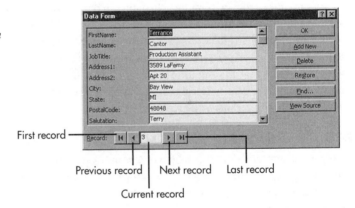

NEW TERM A *record* contains the collection of fields (individual pieces of information) that pertain to a single individual. In other types of data source documents, a record might contain related information for something other than individuals (for example, the names of items in a home inventory, or products in a catalog).

If you don't have information for a certain field, tab to the next field. You don't have to enter information in every field. For example, if you have an individual who has one line of address but not a second line, enter information in the Address1 line and skip the Address2 line. Word can handle blank lines and eliminate them from the document when you are in the printing stage. When you finish entering the information for every individual, click OK. You are returned to the main document.

CAUTION

It is important to be consistent when you enter information in a data source. People often don't consider how the information will be combined with the main document when entering data. If, for example, you decide to shortcut the process and enter all of the name information (first and last name) in the first name field and then decide you want to include the first name in the salutation, it can't be done with the data as it has been entered. If you have two contacts at the same address, you might decide to use the first name field for one contact and last name for the other contact. Imagine the mess you'll have when you try to merge this information (Dear Firstname Lastname will translate to something like Dear Mary Smith Carl Walker).

15

Step 6—Adding Fields to the Main Document

Word needs to know where you want the information from the data source to be placed in the main document. The Mail Merge toolbar is visible when you are in a merge document. The Insert Merge Field button provides the information you need to insert the fields in the main document. To add fields to the main document:

1. Position the cursor in the document where you want to insert the first field.

2. Click the Insert Merge Field button to bring up the list of all the fields that are in the data source file.

3. Select the first field to insert (FirstName).

    If you need spaces or punctuation between fields, it must be entered in the main document. In this case, press the spacebar to insert a space after the FirstName field.

4. Click the Insert Merge Field button again to select the next field (LastName).

5. Press Enter to start a new line.

6. Click the Insert Merge Field button and insert the Address1 field. Press the Enter key to start a new line, then repeat the process for the rest of the address fields. Remember to add spaces, commas, or other punctuation that should appear in the document. The comma between city and state and the punctuation after the salutation are prime examples.

7. Add the salutation field in the appropriate location, as shown in Figure 15.9.

Figure 15.9.
Inserting the Salutation field in the main document.

Microsoft Word - Widget survey letter.doc
File Edit View Insert Format Tools Table Window Help
Normal
Times New Roman
12
Insert Merge Field
Insert Word Field
FirstName
LastName
JobTitle
Address1
Address2
City
State
PostalCode
Salutation
«LastName»¶
«PostalCode»¶
Dear ¶
Thank·you·for·your·recent·response·to·our·questionnaire.·We·are·sending·you·a·small·gift·
in·appreciation·for·your·reply.·The·information·from·this·survey·will·help·us·better·
evaluate·our·services·and·products.·Your·input·and·that·from·hundreds·of·other·who·
responded·to·the·survey·give·us·a·starting·point·to·build·our·customer·service·department·
Page 1 Sec 1 1/1 At 2.7" Ln 10 Col 6

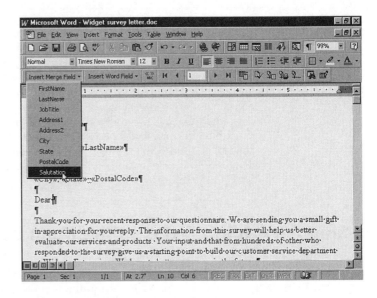

Step 7—Previewing Before Printing

After all the pertinent fields have been added to the main document, you're ready to determine whether everything is going to merge correctly before you print the letters. First, click the Check for Errors button on the Mail Merge toolbar. This feature checks to make sure there are no problems in either the main document or the data source that would prevent the document from printing properly. If there are problems, you can fix them before wasting paper.

To see what your letters will look after the letter is merged with the information from the data source, click the View Merged Data button (see Figure 15.10). Word displays the letter with the data included. Scroll through all the letters by clicking the Next Record button. You can navigate through the records using the buttons on the Mail Merge toolbar just as you do in the Data Form dialog. To move to a specific record, click in the Go To Record box and type in the record number. If things look good and you're ready to print, move to step 9 to print the letters. If not, go to step 8 to fix the problems.

Step 8—Fixing Errors Before Printing

If there are errors that need to be corrected before printing, check the main document and make any necessary changes. To make changes to the data source, click the Edit Data Source button on the right end of the Mail Merge toolbar. Edit Data Source opens the Data Form dialog, where you can make changes to the data.

Figure 15.10.
Viewing the merged letter.

Microsoft Word - Widget survey letter.doc
Insert Merge Field
Insert Word Field
View Merged Data
April·30,·1997¶
Mary·Alice·Taylor¶
37·Bay·View·Court¶
Bay·View,·MI··48848¶
Dear·Ms.·Taylor:¶
Thank·you·for·your·recent·response·to·our·questionnaire.·We·are·sending·you·a·small·gift·in·appreciation·for·your·reply.·The·information·from·this·survey·will·help·us·better·evaluate·our·services·and·products.·Your·input·and·that·from·hundreds·of·other·who·responded·to·the·survey·give·us·a·starting·point·to·build·our·customer·service·department·at·Widgets·Enterprises.·We·hope·to·better·serve·you·in·the·future.¶

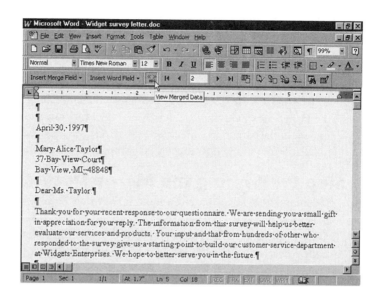

You may not have a problem with the data itself (the information you entered in the fields), but say you found errors or omissions in the field names themselves. To modify or add another field:

1. Click the View Source button in the Data Form dialog.
2. Click the Manage Fields button on the Mail Merge toolbar.

   The Manage Fields dialog box comes up. You can add or remove fields just as you did when you first set up the fields. You can also rename one of the existing fields as in Figure 15.11. The PostalCode field is renamed Zip.

Figure 15.11.
Changing a field name.

Manage Fields
Field name:
Zip
Add ▸▸
Remove
Rename...
Field names in header row:
LastName
JobTitle
Address1
Address2
City
State
PostalCode
Salutation
OK
Cancel

3. Click Rename to change the field name.
4. Click OK.

Return to the main document by clicking the Mail Merge Main Document button on the Mail Merge toolbar. This takes you to the main document.

The field names in the data source must match the field names in the main document. If you change the name of a field in the data source, you must remove the old field from the main document and insert the new field. In this case, you need to select the PostalCode field in the main document and press the Delete key to remove it.

When you click the Insert Merge Field button on the Mail Merge toolbar, you no longer see the PostalCode field name. Insert Merge Field includes only the names of fields that are present in the data source. Because PostalCode was changed to Zip, you now see Zip in the list. Insert Zip in the document where PostalCode was removed.

Step 9—Printing the Merge Documents

If you're satisfied that the letters look the way they should, you're ready to print. It's a good policy to print a sample before printing all the records. If you have 100 records in your data source, you don't want to print all 100 and then find out that something isn't working quite right. What you see onscreen may not always match what prints. To print the a test letter:

1. Click the Mail Merge button on the Mail Merge toolbar, and the Merge dialog box opens (see Figure 15.12).

Figure 15.12.
Print a sample first.

Merge
Merge to:
Printer
Setup...
Records to be merged
All
From: 1
To: 1
When merging records
Don't print blank lines when data fields are empty.
Print blank lines when data fields are empty.
No query options have been set.
Merge
Close
Check Errors...
Query Options...

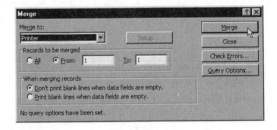

2. Select Printer from the drop-down list under Merge to.
3. Click From and type in 1 in both the From and To boxes to try a test run. You're telling Word which records to print. In this case you want Word to begin and end with record 1 to get a single page.

Time Saver

> If you don't put anything in the To box, Word assumes you want everything from the first record you specified to the end of all of the records. In this case, if you entered a 1 in the From box and left the To box empty, all of the letters would print.

If your test letter comes out correctly, you can repeat the process and select All under Records to be merged, or you can type 2 in the From box and leave the To box empty since you already printed the first letter as your test case. Leaving the To box empty means that all records from 2 to the end will print.

Mailing Labels

You can also use merge for mailing labels. To print mailing labels from the same data source you used for the letters:

1. Select Tools | Mail Merge.
2. Click Create, and select Mailing Labels.
3. Select New Main Document.
4. Click Get Data and select Open Data Source.
5. Find and select the name of the data source file from the Open dialog box that you created for the form letter. Click Open.
6. Click the Set Up Main Document button that appears. The Label Options dialog box, shown in Figure 15.13, comes up. Click on your printer type under Printer information.

Label Options
Printer information
Dot matrix
Laser and ink jet
Tray: Manual feed
Label products: Avery standard
Product number:
2160 Mini - Address
2162 Mini - Address
2163 Mini - Shipping
2180 Mini - File Folder
2181 Mini - File Folder
2186 Mini - Diskette
2660 Mini - Address
Label information
Type: Address
Height: 1"
Width: 2.63"
Page size: Mini (4 ¼ x 5 in)
OK
Cancel
Details...
New Label...
Delete

Figure 15.13.
Selecting label options.

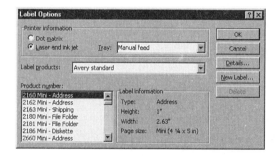

7. Select the type of label you are using from the Product number list.
8. Click OK.

The Create Labels dialog box opens. You can build a picture of the way you want the labels to print by adding fields from the Insert Merge Field list just as you did in the form letter (see Figure 15.14). Add spaces between fields where you need them and press the Enter key at the end of each line. Click OK when you have all the relevant fields added to the labels.

Word builds a page of labels that includes field codes on each label. Again, it's a good idea to go through the checking process as you did with the form letter.

- ☐ Check for errors (click the Check for Errors button).
- ☐ View merged data (click the View Merged Data button).
- ☐ Print a test page.

Create Labels
Choose the Insert Merge Field button to insert merge fields into the sample label. You can edit and format the merge fields and text in the Sample Label box.
Insert Merge Field
Insert Postal Bar Code...
FirstName
LastName
JobTitle
Address1
Address2
City
State
Zip
Salutation
OK
Cancel

Figure 15.14.
Adding fields to the label.

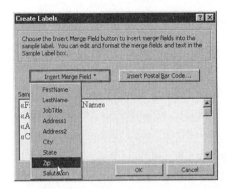

It's especially important to do a trial run for labels. Print a sample on paper before printing on labels. Labels are expensive. Put the sample in front of a label page and hold them up to the light to see if things line up properly. If everything looks good, click the Mail Merge button on the Mail Merge toolbar to set up the print specifications, or you can click the Merge to Print button that prints all of the records.

Envelopes

Creating envelopes is quite similar to creating mailing labels. To create an envelope main document:

1. Select Tools | Mail Merge.
2. Click Create and select Mailing Labels.
3. Select New Main Document.
4. Click Get Data and select Open Data Source.
5. Find and select the name of the data source file from the Open dialog box. Click Open.
6. Click the Set Up Main Document button. The Envelopes Options dialog box, shown in Figure 15.15, will appear.
7. Select an envelope size from the drop-down list. Size 10 is the normal business envelope size, but you can specify other sizes.
8. Change the font types and sizes for the delivery and return addresses if you want to use something other than the default font. Click the Font buttons to change one or both of the fonts.
9. Click OK.

Envelope Options
Envelope Options
Printing Options
Envelope size:
Size 10
(4 1/8 x 9 1/2 in)
If mailed in the USA
Delivery point barcode
FIM-A courtesy reply mail
Delivery address
Font...
From left:
Auto
From top:
Auto
Return address
Font...
From left:
Auto
From top:
Auto
Preview
OK
Cancel

Figure 15.15.
Setting envelope options.

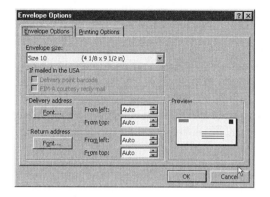

Start building the envelope as you did the mailing labels by inserting fields one at a time. You may want to add a postal barcode above the address lines to speed delivery. To add a barcode:

1. Click the Insert Postal Bar Code button.
2. You must tell Word which field contains the zip code so that it can build the barcode from these numbers. In this data source, the postal code is in the Zip field. Figure 15.16 shows the dialog box that comes up when you insert a postal barcode. Select Zip from the drop-down list at the top. The message above the box says Merge field with Zip code, showing that it builds the postal bar code from the information in the Zip field.

Insert Postal Bar Code
Merge field with ZIP code:
Zip
Merge field with street address:
FIM-A courtesy reply mail
OK
Cancel

Figure 15.16.
Adding a postal barcode to envelopes.

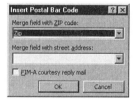

Continue to build the other lines of address as you did when you created labels.

Just a Minute

> You can also insert postal barcodes in labels, but they often take up more space than the label allows, and it can be a little trickier. Experiment with different fonts and font sizes to get a label form that works if the barcodes on the labels don't fit quite right.

After you've created the envelope, a sample envelope appears with the field names inserted. You can enter a return address in the upper-left corner if there is nothing there, or if the default return address isn't what you want. Again, run through the checking process before printing.

Using Data from Other Sources

You can attach a different data source file to a main document. If, for example, you want to send the Widgets letter (refer to Figure 15.1) to a group of people listed in an Access file:

1. Open the Widgets letter.
2. Select Tools | Mail Merge.
3. Click Get Data.
4. Select Open Data Source.
5. Select MS Access Databases in the Files of type box.
6. Locate the Access file and open it (see Figure 15.17). Note that there are many different kinds of file types that can be used as data sources for a Word main document.

Figure 15.17.
Selecting an Access file for the data source.

Open Data Source
Look in:
My Documents
Amy's Projects
Cathy's Projects
Chuck's Projects
George's Projects
Harry's Projects
Linda's Projects
Pat's Projects
Teresa's Projects
Word 97 Book
test.mdb
Open
Cancel
MS Query...
Advanced...
Select method
Find files that match these search criteria:
File name:
Text or property:
Find Now
Files of type:
MS Access Databases (*.mdb)
Last modified:
any time
New Search
MS Access Databases (*.mdb)
MS Excel Worksheets (*.xls)
MS Query Files (*.qry)
dBase Files (*.dbf)
MS FoxPro Files (*.dbf)
All Files (*.*)

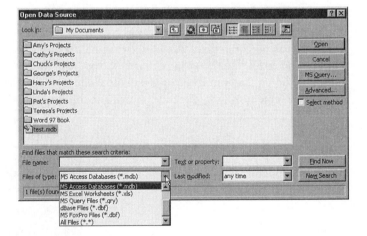

You are returned to the Mail Merge dialog box. Click Close to return to the main document. Make sure that the field names are the same in both the data source and the main document. In this case, the field for the first name in the Access file was called First and the last name was called Last. The fields FirstName and LastName must be deleted from the main document and replaced with First and Last using the fields in the drop-down Insert Merge Field list.

Using Query to Print Specific Records

If you have a large data source file, there may be times when you want to print letters for only certain groups of people. For example, say you want to send the Widgets letter to only the people who live in Indiana and Michigan. Query is a powerful tool that lets you select only the records with IN or MI in the State field. To select only these records:

1. From the main document, click the Mail Merge button on the Mail Merge toolbar.
2. Click Query Options.
3. Select State from the first drop-down Field list (see Figure 15.18).
4. Select the Equal to option from the Comparison tab.

Query Options
Filter Records
Sort Records
Field:
Comparison:
Compare to:
State
Equal to
IN
Or
State
Equal to
And
Address2
City
State
Zip
Salutation
OK
Cancel
Clear All

Figure 15.18.
Using Query to specify which records to print.

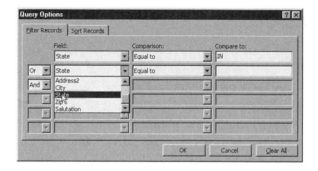

5. Type `IN` in the Compare to box.
6. Select the Or option from the drop-down list of operators in the box to the left.
7. Select the State option from the second drop-down Field list.
8. Select the Equal to option from the Comparison tab.
9. Type `MI` in the Compare to box.

Word looks for all the records that contain IN or MI in the State field and prints letters for only those records. These are called conditional statements. The conditional statement, if it were printed, might read something like this:

> If the State field contains IN or the State field contains MI, then print the letter. If it doesn't, don't print the letter. If you use the And operator, both conditions must be true. In this case no letters would print because there are no records that have both IN and MI in the State field.

You would use the And operator to narrow the records by two or more fields. For example, you might want all of the records for the people in Lansing, Michigan. Your query would include City, Equal to, Lansing—And—State, Equal to, MI.

You can also specify which Jones you want to send a mailing to by selecting Lastname, Equal to, Jones—And—Firstname, Equal to, Harry. This is helpful if you get a page jammed in the printer and need to print only a specific record. If you know the record number, it's easier to select it in mail merge and specify the record to be merged.

Summary

This hour outlines mail merge, one of the prime functions of a word processor. Merge can be used to create four kinds of documents: form letters, mailing labels, envelopes, and catalogs. Data can come from a variety of sources. You can use a data file you create in Word, one you already have stored, or one from a different source such as Access, Excel, or dBASE.

Q&A

Q I ran a query to select certain records to print, but now I can't print all the records. What should I do?

A Click the Mail Merge icon, then click Query Options. Select Clear All to remove the query.

Q I wanted to use a dBASE file as a data source, but I don't have an option in the list of file types for dBASE, and I can't use All Files to select the file. Word doesn't recognize it.

A You may not have installed the converters for dBASE when you installed Word (or Office). You need to run Setup again to add the converters. Another option is to save your dBASE files as comma- or tab-delimited files. They could then be used as data sources.

Q When I try to print my letters, Word creates another document with all the letters in it, but it doesn't print my letters. What's going wrong?

A Click the Mail Merge icon. In the Merge to box, it may say New Document. Select Printer from the drop-down list. If New Document is selected, Word merges the letter with the data and creates a new document with every letter in it. Some people like to work this way. After the letters are merged to a single document, click the Printer icon, or select File | Print from the menu to print the letters.

15

Hour 16

Automating Tasks

This hour explains how to use AutoText and macros to take care of repetitive tasks. AutoText has taken on new meaning in Word 97. Using AutoText is about as easy as using Copy and Paste to insert frequently used text or graphic elements. If you're thinking about skipping the section on macros because you've always thought of them as something only programmers can figure out, don't! If you can turn on a tape recorder to record music, you can use macros. There's nothing to it.

The highlights of this hour include

- [ ] What kinds of items you would save as AutoText
- [ ] How AutoText can save your time
- [ ] What you would use a macro for
- [ ] How to assign a macro to a toolbar button or a shortcut key combination

AutoText

AutoText has been around in some form since the very early versions of Word. It used to be called the Glossary. Word 97 has expanded the AutoText feature. You can save frequently used text or graphics to AutoText entries. After they are saved, they can quickly be inserted in a document any time you need them.

You may have noticed AutoText working and didn't even realize it. Start typing today's date. After you type the first three or four characters, a yellow screen tip appears above the text with the complete date. This is AutoComplete working in the background. If you press Enter when you see the screen tip, AutoComplete will finish typing the rest of the date. If your name is entered in the User Information under Tools | Options, start typing your name. Word recognizes you after you've typed a few letters and brings up the screen tip. Press Enter to have Word finish typing your name.

AutoComplete works with AutoText to make AutoText entries even easier to enter than in the past. There are several items that AutoComplete automatically recognizes and offers to finish for you:

- ☐ Days of the week
- ☐ Months
- ☐ Current date
- ☐ The name listed in User Information
- ☐ AutoText entries

Because AutoComplete recognizes the shortcut names you've given your AutoText entries, you will also get screen tips for these items.

Adding Entries to AutoText

You may not want the AutoText toolbar open all the time, but the quick access is helpful if you're adding several items to AutoText or using a document where you will be inserting AutoText items frequently. To activate this toolbar, select View | Toolbars and click AutoText. It's a very simple toolbar with three buttons: AutoText, All Entries, and New. Unless something in the document is selected, the New button is grayed out. Think of something you type routinely that could be added to AutoText. The first thing most people think of adding to AutoText is their signature block (the closure lines of a letter that include the sender's name). To add a signature block:

1. Type the signature block as you normally do.
2. Select the signature block.
3. Click the New button on the AutoText toolbar.

16

A dialog box comes up asking you to name the AutoText entry. Word usually suggests the first words in the selected text, but it helps to make the names short. You will see why when you learn how to insert AutoText.

4. Type in a short name for the signature block, such as `sig` (see Figure 16.1).

Figure 16.1.
The AutoText toolbar.

AutoText options
Drop-down list of entries
Add new entry
Microsoft Word - Document2
All Entries
New...
Create AutoText
Word will create an AutoText entry from the current selection.
Please name your AutoText entry:
sig
OK
Cancel
Sincerely,
Linda Jones
MIS Coordinator

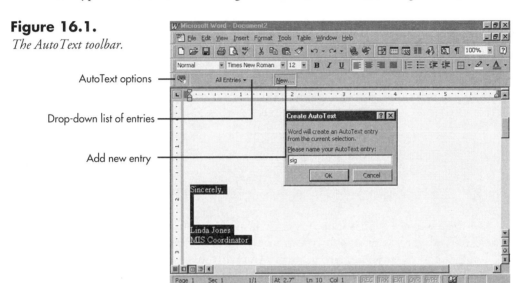

You now have an AutoText entry with the name `sig` that includes your signature block.

Inserting AutoText Entries in a Document

To insert the newly created `sig` AutoText entry in a letter:

1. Position the cursor where you want the closure to begin.
2. Type `sig`, then press the F3 key. Word automatically inserts your signature block.

Typing the shortcut name and pressing F3 is the quickest way to insert an AutoText entry, but you can also insert it from the drop-down list of All Entries from the AutoText toolbar. Word categorizes AutoText entries, and you can see in Figure 16.2 that it places the new `sig` AutoText entry under the Normal category. Word categorizes AutoText entries by the style that is applied to the first paragraph in an AutoText selection. If a selected paragraph has a Heading 2 style applied and is saved as an AutoText entry, a new Heading 2 category is created and the AutoText entry is saved in that category.

There are several entries that Word designed for you as AutoText. If you look through the other menu options, there are AutoText entries for a lot of common phrases used in correspondence. You may remember the discussion in Hour 8, "Setting Up the Page," about inserting AutoText entries in headers and footers. Header/Footer is one of the categories in the All Entries list. These categories are predefined.

Microsoft Word - Document3
File Edit View Insert Format Tools Table Window Help
Normal
Times New Roman
12
100%
All Entries
New...
Attention Line
Closing
Header/Footer
Mailing Instructions
NL
Normal
sig
PD
Reference Initials
Reference Line
Salutation
Signature
Signature Company
Subject Line
Page 1 Sec 1 1/1 At 1" Ln 1 Col 1 REC TRK EXT OVR WPH

Figure 16.2.
Adding an AutoText entry from the All Entries list.

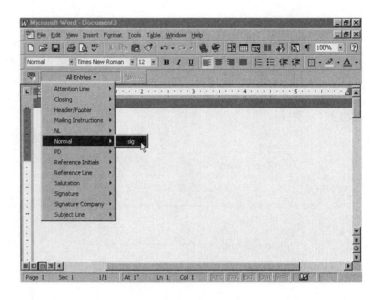

A third way to enter an AutoText entry involves AutoComplete. Rather than saving an AutoText entry with an abbreviated name like `sig`, accept the longer name that Word suggests or type an abbreviated name that is at least four characters. AutoComplete does not work with AutoText entries that have names shorter than four characters.

You might want to insert your city, state, and zip code in an AutoText entry. Type this information, select it, and click the New button on the AutoText toolbar. When the dialog box opens asking you to name the AutoText entry, give it an abbreviated name of at least four characters or accept the suggested name and click OK. The next time you start typing the city name, Word displays a screen tip with the AutoText entry as shown in Figure 16.3. Press the Enter key, and Word will complete the typing for you. This is a great new feature in Word 97.

If you've been a Glossary/AutoText user through several generations of Word, you may be so accustomed to using the shortcut names and the F3 key that AutoComplete is a nuisance to you. To turn off the AutoComplete tips, click the AutoText button on the AutoText toolbar and uncheck the box for Show AutoComplete tip for AutoText and dates.

Microsoft Word - Document3
File Edit View Insert Format Tools Table Window Help
Normal
Times New Roman
12
100%
All Entries
Indianapolis, IN 46290
Indi
Page 1 Sec 1 1/1 At 1" Ln 1 Col 5

Figure 16.3.
AutoComplete will fill in an AutoText entry when you press Enter.

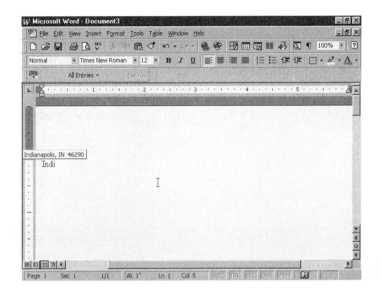

Deleting AutoText Entries

If you've set up several AutoText entries for a specific project, you might want to delete them when the project is over. There may be certain terms or elements that you use over and over—like the city and state names as mentioned previously or long technical terms. Anything that requires a lot of repetitive keyboarding could be targeted for an AutoText entry. You can also save graphics, such as an electronic signature or a company logo as AutoText entries. If you want to clean up these AutoText entries and get rid of the ones you're not using

1. Click the AutoText button on the AutoText toolbar (or select Insert | AutoText | AutoText to bring up the same dialog box).
2. Select an AutoText item from the list (see Figure 16.4). The Preview box lets you see what the complete AutoText entry looks like so you know which item you have selected. You may have several entries with similar names. In this case, Telecommunications Project Engineers, which was used for a specific document, is no longer needed.
3. Click the Delete button to remove the selected AutoText entry. You can also remove any of Word's built-in AutoText entries that you never use.

AutoCorrect
AutoCorrect
AutoFormat As You Type
AutoText
AutoFormat
Show AutoComplete tip for AutoText and dates
To accept the AutoComplete tip, press Enter
Enter AutoText entries here:
Telecommunications
Take care,
Telecommunications
Thank you,
Thanks,
tip
To Whom It May Concern:
VIA AIRMAIL
VIA FACSIMILE
VIA OVERNIGHT MAIL
Add
Delete
Insert
Show Toolbar
Preview
Telecommunications Project Engineers
Look in:
All active templates
OK
Cancel

Figure 16.4.
Deleting an AutoText entry.

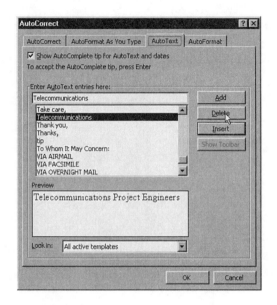

Modifying an AutoText Entry

Once in a while you may need to change an AutoText entry. Say you get a promotion and want to change your title in your signature block:

1. Type the new signature block as you want it to appear, and select it.
2. Click New on the AutoText toolbar (or use Insert | AutoText | New).
3. Type the same name you used previously for the signature block (`sig` was used in the previous example).
4. You will get a message asking whether you want to redefine the AutoText entry. Click Yes, and your AutoText entry will be changed to reflect your new job title.

As you use AutoText, you will think of terms and even whole paragraphs that you use over and over. If you type similar letters but include different paragraphs depending on your audience, you could add these paragraphs as AutoText entries. You could even name them as simply as P1, P2, P3, and so on.

To build the letter, type the shortcut name for the paragraph you want first (for example, `P2`), and then press the F3 key. Add all the paragraphs you need for a particular letter in this way, and then add your AutoText signature block. You can create a letter in a matter of minutes.

Macros

One of the greatest ways to build your efficiency quotient is with macros. A macro can record your actions step by step, save the actions, and repeat them back to you on demand. Although macros can be used for the same kinds of things you do with AutoText, AutoText takes care of those functions so efficiently that you probably don't want to use a macro simply to insert a signature block.

Instead, think of the times you access a menu to change certain settings for a particular project. You may actually change options in several different menus. Anything you do repetitively is a candidate for a macro. All you have to do to create a macro is record your keystrokes. When you want to perform these steps again, just play the macro.

Recording a Macro

The Macro Recorder is the tool that is used to memorize the steps you go through to accomplish a task. After the Macro Recorder has memorized the steps and you have given the macro a name, it can repeat back those steps time after time. To turn on the Macro Recorder, select Tools | Macro | Record New Macro or double-click the REC button on the Status bar.

Figure 16.5 shows the dialog box that comes up. You are asked to supply a name for the macro. This macro will be called `Letter`. Unlike with filenames, you cannot include spaces in a macro name. If you want to be able to use this macro in all documents, leave the setting on All Documents in the Store macro in box. You can add information in the Description box that tells what this macro does. This can be helpful if you set up two similar macros. The `Letter` macro sets the top margin to 2.5 inches, prints from the Manual Feed tray, and includes a date field, salutation, and signature block.

Record Macro
Macro name:
Letter
OK
Cancel
Assign macro to
Toolbars
Keyboard
Store macro in:
All Documents (Normal.dot)
Description:
Creates a letter with 2.5" top margin, sets print for manual feed, enters date field, includes salutation and signature block

Figure 16.5.
Naming a macro.

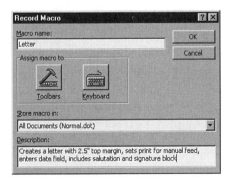

When you click OK in the Record Macro dialog box, the macro recorder starts. The pointer changes to resemble a cassette tape, and a box opens to allow you to stop the recorder when you finish or to pause during parts of the recording as in Figure 16.6. To create the `Letter` macro now that the recorder is turned on:

1. Select File | Page Setup.
2. Change the top margin to 2.5 inches in the Margins tab.
3. Change the tray setting in the Paper Source tab to Manual Feed.
4. Click OK.
5. Select Insert | Date and Time.
6. Select a date format from the list and check Update Automatically; then click OK.
7. Press Enter twice to enter two blank lines.
8. Type `Dear`, then press Enter twice.
9. Type the signature block or insert the AutoText entry for the signature block.
10. Click the Stop Recording button.

The Macro Recorder records each of your steps. When you stop the recorder, all of the steps are saved to a Macro called `Letter`. You never have to repeat those steps again. The macro does them for you.

Figure 16.6.
The Macro Recorder at work.

Microsoft Word - Document3
File Edit View Insert Format Tools Table Window Help
100%
Normal
Times New Roman
12
Stop R
Page 1 Sec 1 1/1 At 2.5" Ln 1 Col 1 REC TRK EXT OVR WPH

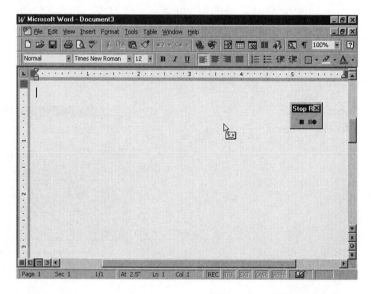

JUST A MINUTE

> The Macro Recorder will not allow you to use the mouse to position the cursor or to select text as part of the macro. You can use the keyboard combinations to position and select text.

Macros are created with a programming language called Visual Basic. If you want to edit a macro after it has been created, you probably need to know a little about Visual Basic or another similar programming language. Alternatively, you can re-record the macro with the same name as the one you recorded earlier. Word asks whether you want to replace the existing macro. Click Yes and record over the previous version.

Using a Macro

Using a macro is like using the playback feature on your tape recorder. To use the `Letter` macro:

1. Open a new document.
2. Select Tools | Macros.
3. Select Letter.
4. Click Run.

KEYBOARD SHORTCUT

Alt+F8 brings up the Macro list without going through the menus.

Running the macro gives you a letter like the one in Figure 16.7. All you need to do is fill in the text of the letter and the inside address.

Microsoft Word - Document3
File Edit View Insert Format Tools Table Window Help
100%
New
Times New Roman
12
May 2, 1997
Dear :
Sincerely,
Linda Jones
MIS Coordinator
Page 1 Sec 1 1/1 At 4.8" Ln 13 Col 1 REC TRK EXT OVR WPH

Figure 16.7.
The document created by the new `Letter` *macro.*

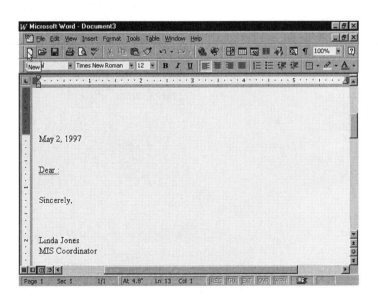

Adding a Macro to a Toolbar

You may develop macros that you use so routinely that you'd like the convenience of assigning them to buttons on a toolbar. You could add them to the new toolbar you created in Hour 11, "Customizing Word to the Way You Work." If you do a lot of work with e-mail files, for example, you might want to create a macro for the process used in Hour 7, "Manipulating Text," to get rid of extra paragraph marks. If this is a daily activity for you, you could add this macro to a toolbar by following these steps:

1. Select View | Toolbars.
2. Select the toolbar to which you want to add the macro.
3. Select View | Toolbars | Customize.
4. In the Commands tab, scroll down in the Categories list to Macros and select it.
5. Locate the macro in the Commands list, click, and drag it to the toolbar as shown in Figure 16.8.
6. Click Modify Selection to change the button. `Normal.NewMacros.FormatEmessage` makes for a very long toolbar button name. Modify the button as prescribed in Hour 11 to use one of the standard button images, or click the Name box near the top of the menu and type the word `Emessage` to replace the long name with a shorter one (see Figure 16.9).

Figure 16.8.
Adding a macro to a toolbar.

Microsoft Word - twh16or.doc
File Edit View Insert Format Tools Table Window Help
Customize
Toolbars Commands Options
Categories:
Drawing
AutoShapes
Borders
Mail Merge
Forms
Control Toolbox
All Commands
Macros
Fonts
AutoText
Commands:
Normal.NewMacros.FormatEm
Normal.NewMacros.Letter
Normal.NewMacros.NEWBULLE
Description:
Macro recorded April 25, 1997 by Linda Jones
Save in:
Normal.dot
Keyboard...
Close
My Favorites
Letter
Page 9 Sec 1 9/9 At Ln Col REC TRK EXT OVR WPH

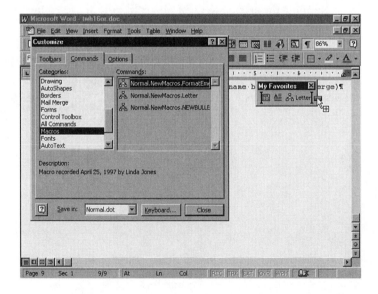

Figure 16.9.
Changing the button text for a macro.

Microsoft Word - twh16or.doc
File Edit View Insert Format Tools Table Window Help
Customize
Toolbars
Commands
Options
Categories:
Drawing
AutoShapes
Borders
Mail Merge
Forms
Control Toolbox
All Commands
Macros
Fonts
AutoText
Commands:
Normal.NewMacros.FormatEm
Normal.NewMacros.Letter
Normal.NewMacros.NEWBULL
Selected command:
Description
Modify Selection
Save in:
Normal.dot
Keyboard...
My Favorites
Letter
Normal.NewMacros.FormatEmessage
Reset
Delete
Name:
Emessage
Copy Button Image
Paste Button Image
Reset Button Image
Edit Button Image...
Change Button Image
Default Style
Text Only (Always)
Text Only (in Menus)
Image and Text
Begin a Group
Page 9
Sec 1
9/9
At
Ln
86%

16

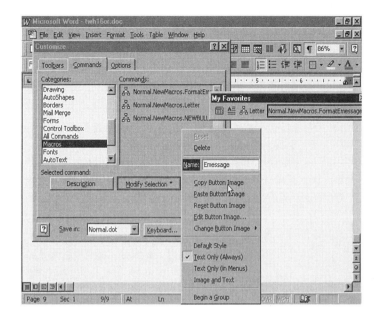

TIME SAVER

If you want to use an image for a toolbar button but none of the pictures seems to fit, Word has a great new feature to let you use any picture as a button image. To use a picture as a button image:

1. Copy the image to the clipboard (insert the picture in a Word document, select it, and click the Copy button).
2. Follow steps 1–6 of the previous instructions to add the macro to the toolbar.
3. Click Paste Button Image from the Modify Selection drop-down menu. The image from the clipboard is pasted as the button image.
4. Click Close.

Assigning a Macro to a Shortcut Key Combination

You can also assign a macro to a shortcut key combination. You use shortcuts like Ctrl+C to copy and Ctrl+V to paste. You can assign functions to any key combinations that are not already programmed. Many of the Ctrl key combinations have functions associated with them, but several of the Ctrl+Alt+letter/number combinations (such Ctrl+Alt+A and Ctrl+Alt+4) are not currently assigned. To assign a macro to keyboard shortcut:

1. Select Tools | Customize.
2. Click the Commands tab.
3. Click the Keyboard button.
4. Scroll down in the Categories list to Macros and select it.
5. Select a macro from the Macros list.
6. Click in the Press new shortcut key box and press the key combination you want to use (see Figure 16.10). The message under the Press new shortcut key box tells you whether this combination is currently unassigned. If the key combination you select is already used by a Word function, the message tells you what the keys are currently assigned to do.

CAUTION

> Figure 16.10 shows the Alt+E combination in the Press new shortcut key box. The message under the box does not indicate that this key combination is currently assigned. The Alt+letter combinations are used as shortcuts to the menus (for example Alt+E is the shortcut to the Edit menu), but the Customize Keyboard dialog box does not tell you this. It is a good idea to avoid using these combinations.

7. Click the Assign button.
8. Click Close, then click Close again to exit the Customize dialog box.

Customize Keyboard
Categories:
Borders
Mail Merge
All Commands
Macros
Fonts
AutoText
Macros:
FormatEmessage
Letter
NEWBULLET
Close
Assign
Remove
Reset All...
Press new shortcut key:
Alt+E
Current keys:
Currently assigned to:
[unassigned]
Description
Macro recorded May 2, 1997 by Linda Jones
Save changes in:
Normal.dot

Figure 16.10.
Assigning a macro to a shortcut key combination.

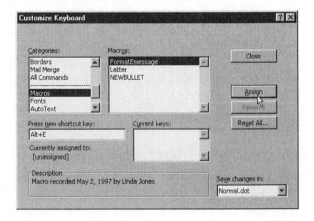

TIME SAVER

When you assign shortcut keys, look for combinations that are unassigned. For example, if you press Ctrl+E, the description under the Press new shortcut key box shows that this key combination is currently assigned to CenterPara (Center Paragraphs). You probably don't want to change the shortcuts Word already has assigned.

Sample Macros

Here are ideas for other actions you might want to save as macros:

- ☐ Insert a table, resize the columns, insert decimal tabs set for specific columns, and add a border to the table.
- ☐ Open a specific file, print it, and close it.
- ☐ Add bullets of a particular style to selected paragraphs, format the paragraphs with specific indents (for example, both right and left indents), and format the font and font style.
- ☐ Create a header and/or footer you use routinely.
- ☐ Set up a document in two sections with specific page numbering, margins, and headers and footers defined for each section.

The next time you start a task that involves several steps, turn on the Macro Recorder as you work. You'll enjoy the freedom from tedium that macros can give you.

Summary

This hour shows how to save time and effort by turning on the Macro Recorder and recording repetitive tasks so that you never have to do them again. Macros can be added and assigned to shortcut keys or toolbar buttons. AutoText is a big time saver. Save blocks of text or graphics as AutoText entries that can be quickly retrieved by using the AutoText Entries list, the AutoText entry name+F3, or AutoComplete and the Enter key.

Q&A

Q Sometimes when I click the AutoText Entries drop-down list on the AutoText toolbar or choose AutoText from the Insert menu, I see only one or two of my AutoText entries instead of the whole list. Why?

A Your cursor is probably in a paragraph that has a specific style applied that has AutoText entries associated with it. In the example earlier in the hour, an AutoText entry was created from text in a Heading 2 style. The entry was placed under a new category called Heading 2. If, for example, your cursor is positioned on a paragraph formatted in Heading 2 style, the drop-down AutoText list button and the Insert | AutoText menu will display the Heading 2 style name, and only the AutoText entries in that category are available. This will happen only if there are AutoText entries that were created in the specified style.

Q I tried to record a macro and got an Invalid Procedure Name error. What did I do wrong?

A You probably tried to save a macro with a name that included a space or another invalid character. Try again and give it a name without any spaces or punctuation.

Q Can I include another macro in the one I'm creating?

A Definitely. Insert as many as you want. Save yourself as many keystrokes as you can. You can also insert AutoText entries in a macro.

RW **4**

Word in Real Time

Creating a Catalog

Mail merge has a main document type called *Catalog*. Catalog is a useful feature for creating lists. You could always type a list into a Word document, but you may want to keep a database-type listing in a data source that includes lots of information. You can pick and choose which information to use for certain reports using mail merge and the Catalog feature.

This project involves creating an employee listing for Widgets Enterprises. It includes

☐ Creating a mail merge catalog

☐ Creating a data source for the catalog

☐ Using a table in the catalog document

☐ Inserting a header above the table with AutoText

☐ Sorting the list alphabetically

Setting Up the Catalog and Data Source Files

The first step begins like any other mail merge: Select Tools | Mail Merge. For this project, select Catalog from the list of Main document options in the Create drop-down list as in Figure R4.1.

Mail Merge Helper
Use this checklist to set up a mail merge. Begin by choosing the Create button.
1 Main document
Create
Form Letters...
Mailing Labels...
Envelopes...
Catalog...
Restore to Normal Word Document...
2
3 Merge the data with the document
Merge...
Cancel

Figure R4.1.
Select Catalog as the Main document type.

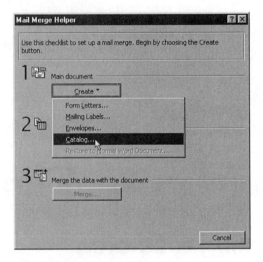

Select Active Window if you just opened Word and have a new document open. If not, select New Main Document to start a new document for the merge file.

The next step is to set up the data source. To do so:

1. Click Get Data and select Create Data Source.
2. Delete unwanted fields (Title, Address1, Address2, City, State, PostalCode, Country). FirstName, LastName, JobTitle, WorkPhone, and HomePhone should be left.
3. Add new fields that pertain to employees, as in Figure R4.2 (Room, Birthday, Spouse, EmergencyContact, HireDate, JobClass, HomeAddress, HomeCSZ). HomeCSZ is a field that combines City, State, and Zip for ease of entry.

JUST A MINUTE

HomeCSZ is not always useful. Luckily, you can keep the City, State, and Zip fields separate if you need to. But for our purposes, it's okay to combine them.

Figure R4.2.
Changing field names for the employee listing.

Create Data Source
A mail merge data source is composed of rows of data. The first row is called the header row. Each of the columns in the header row begins with a field name.
Word provides commonly used field names in the list below. You can add or remove field names to customize the header row.
Field name:
HireDate
Add Field Name
Remove Field Name
Field names in header row:
JobTitle
WorkPhone
HomePhone
Room
Birthday
Spouse
EmergencyContact
Move
MS Query...
OK
Cancel

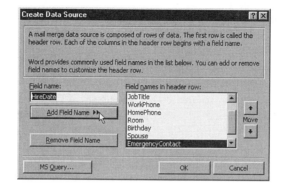

4. Use the Move Up and Move Down functions to place the fields in an order that makes sense when you're doing the data entry. For example, you may want the HomePhone and HomeAddress fields together because they are probably grouped together in the paper copy you are using for this information.
5. Click OK to exit the Create Data Source dialog box.
6. The Save dialog box opens. Name the data file and click Save.
7. Click Edit data source.

Enter the information in the data form for each employee. Use either the Tab or the Enter key at the end of each line to move to the next entry box. Notice the scrollbar to the right of the entry lines, shown in Figure R4.3. This scrollbar indicates that there is more information in each record than you can see in one screen. You can scroll down to see the other fields. At the end of each record, press Enter to start a new record. When you have the records entered, click OK.

Figure R4.3.
Adding records to the data source.

Data Form
FirstName: Marge
LastName: Binford
JobTitle: Sales Associate
WorkPhone: 484-9002
Room: 12
Birthday: 4-19-72
Spouse: Larry
EmergencyContact: Carol Smith 472-8907
HireDate: 5/96
OK
Add New
Delete
Restore
Find...
View Source
Record: 1
Scroll to other fields

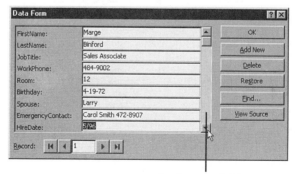

Inserting a Table

Return to the main document after you complete the entries in the data source. The main document will only include one line of field codes even though you want to list all records. Form letters are set up to print one record per page or letter, but the Catalog function creates a list with all records on the same page. If there are more records than will fit on one page, Catalog creates as many pages as necessary to complete the list.

In this sample, you'll put the field names in a table. To build the table and insert the field names:

1. Click the Insert Table button on the Standard toolbar.
2. Insert a table that is four columns wide and has only one row.
3. Position the cursor in the first cell.
4. Click Insert Merge Field and select LastName.
5. Insert a comma and a space after the LastName field, then use Insert Merge Field to insert the FirstName in the same cell.
6. Insert the JobTitle field in cell 2, the Room field in cell 3, and the WorkPhone field in cell 4 (see Figure R4.4).

Microsoft Word - Document5
File Edit View Insert Format Tools Table Window Help
Normal
Times New Roman
12
Insert Merge Field
Insert Word Field
FirstName
LastName
JobTitle
WorkPhone
Room
Birthday
Spouse
EmergencyContact
HireDate
JobClass
HomeAddress
HomeCSZ
HomePhone
«JobTitle»
«Room»
Page 1 Sec 1 1/1 At 1" Ln 1 Col 1

Figure R4.4.
Inserting merge fields in a table.

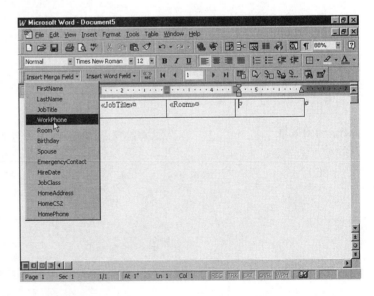

Adjusting the Table

The name and job title columns need to be wider than the room and phone columns. Use the Move Columns buttons on the ruler to adjust the column sizes, as shown in Figure R4.5.

Microsoft Word - Document5
File Edit View Insert Format Tools Table Window Help
Normal
Times New Roman
12
Insert Merge Field
Insert Word Field
«LastName», «FirstName»
«JobTitle»
«Room»
«WorkPhone»
Page 1 Sec 1 1/1 At 1.1" Ln 2 Col 2

Figure R4.5.
Adjusting columns in the table.

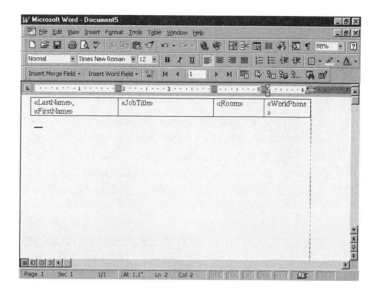

Adding a Heading

If you create a heading in the body of the document, Word inserts a heading before each record when it merges, as in Figure R4.6. Instead of using one heading to top the entire column, you have a heading for every record. This is not how you want Catalog to operate.

Microsoft Word - Catalog3
File Edit View Insert Format Tools Table Window Help
Normal
Times New Roman
12
Name Position Room Phone
Binford, Marge Sales Associate 12 484-9002
Name Position Room Phone
Stapleton, Cary Product Engineer 14 484-9003
Name Position Room Phone
Lovell, Tamara Public Relations Director 28 484-9100
Name Position Room Phone
Partridge, Michael Staples Coordinator 20 474-8900
Name Position Room Phone
Aylesworth, David Product Inspector 27 484-2415
Name Position Room Phone
Lamford, Terri Assembly Crew 55 484-3579
Name Position Room Phone
Stover, Sharon Assembly Crew 55 484-3579
Name Position Room Phone
Michaels, Bill Assembly Crew 55 484-3579
Name Position Room Phone
MacKenzie, Polly Assembly Crew 55 484-3579
Name Position Room Phone
Page 1 Sec 1 1/3 At 1" Ln 1 Col 1

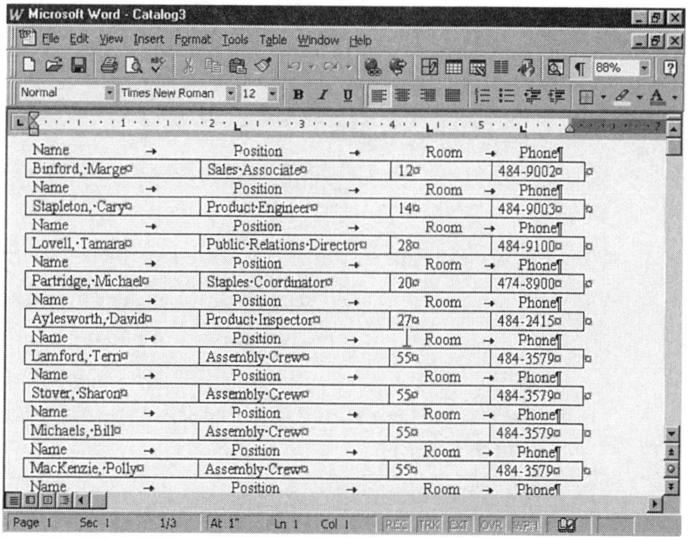

Figure R4.6.
Adding a title to a catalog produces unsatisfactory results.

One of the best solutions is to use the header area for the title. A header doesn't have to be positioned at the top edge of the page. You can move it down so it appears to be part of the document. Select View | Header and Footer and follow these steps to use the header as the title for the employee listing:

1. Select File | Page Setup.
2. In the Margins tab, change the measurement under Header to 1.2 inches. This will set the header down 1.2 inches from the top of the page rather than the standard .5 inches.

   The Widgets Enterprises employee created an AutoText entry for previous publications that can be inserted from the Insert AutoText list. Figure R4.7 displays the AutoText list and the WEL entry being inserted in the header.

Microsoft Word - Document5
File Edit View Insert Format Tools Table Window Help
Header
Times New Roman
12
75%
Insert Merge Field
Insert Word Field
- PAGE -
Author, Page #, Date
Confidential, Page #, Date
Created by
Created on
Filename
Filename and path
Last printed
Last saved by
Page X of Y
WEL
Widget Enterprises
Insert AutoText
Close
Page 1
Sec 1
1/1
At 1.1"
Ln
Col 1
REC
TRK
EXT
OVR
WPH

Figure R4.7.
Inserting an AutoText entry in the header.

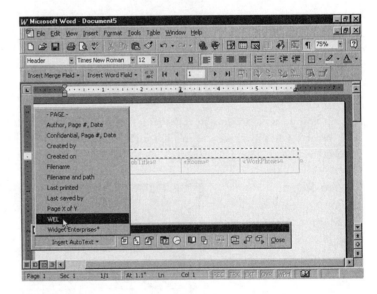

3. The Widget Enterprises title is added to the header from the WEL AutoText entry.
4. Add the date to the left section of the header by clicking the Insert Date button.
5. Tab to the right edge of the header and type the word `Page`, then a space, and then click the Insert Page Number button (see Figure R4.8).
6. If the fonts do not match the title, select the date and page line and format the font to match the title.
7. Click Close.

Figure R4.8.

Add the date and page number to the title.

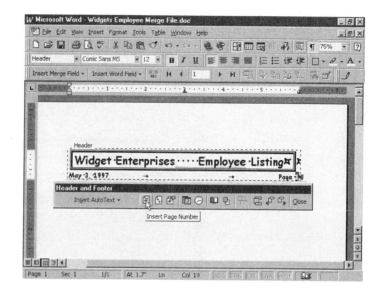

Adding Row Headers

It's helpful to know what each column contains. This information can go into the header. To add column headers, Select View | Header and Footer, and then follow these steps:

1. Position the cursor after the page number field and press Enter to add a new line.

2. Remove any tabs that appear on the ruler by clicking and dragging them from the ruler. Refer to Hour 6, "Formatting Paragraphs," for details on adding and removing tabs.

3. Type the title for the first column (Name) and press Tab.

4. Type the title for the second column (Position) and press Tab.

5. Type the title for the third column (Room) and press Tab.

6. Type the title for the fourth column (Phone).

7. The headings don't line up where you'd want them with the columns, but you can easily drag the tab markers across the ruler so that they do. The vertical line that appears down the page helps identify where the tab (and the heading that follows the tab) will be.

8. Click Close or double-click in the typing area to exit the header.

Figure R4.9 shows what the header will look like after the headings have been inserted and the tabs have been aligned with the columns.

Microsoft Word - Catalog2
File Edit View Insert Format Tools Table Window Help
Header
Comic Sans MS
12
75%
Header
Widget Enterprises Employee Listing
May 3, 1997
Page 1
Name
Position
Room
Phone
Header and Footer
Insert AutoText
Close
Page 1 Sec 1 1/2 At 1.9" Ln Col 25

Figure R4.9.
Adding column titles to the header.

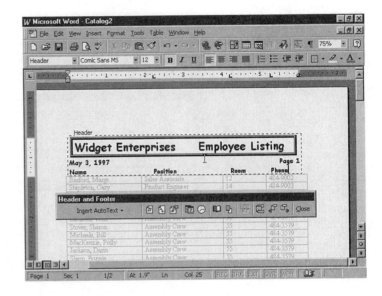

Putting It All Together

You're ready to merge, but this time merge the file to a new document. Click the Merge to New Document button on the Mail Merge toolbar. If the document is merged to a new document, the table can be sorted. In this example, it makes sense to sort the table so that the employees are listed alphabetically. To sort the table:

1. Select the first column (position the mouse above column 1 until you see the dark black arrow pointing down and click the mouse button).
2. Select Table | Sort.
3. Column 1 appears as the Sort by option because it is selected (see Figure R4.10). Click the No header row option at the bottom of the Sort dialog box if it isn't already selected. In this case, there is no header row because you have placed the headings in the header rather than in the table.
4. Click OK to start the sort.

You're ready to print your new employee listing. You could also modify this report by adding different field names and making slight changes to the header. You might, for example, create a list with employee home addresses and phone numbers or a report with the emergency contact names for each employee. One data source—many reports.

Figure R4.10.
Sorting the list alphabetically.

Sort
Sort by
Column 1
Type:
Text
Ascending
Descending
Then by
Type:
Text
Ascending
Descending
Then by
Type:
Text
Ascending
Descending
My list has
Header row
No header row
OK
Cancel
Options...

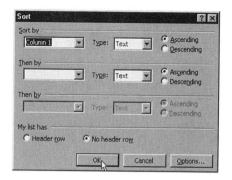

PART
V

Word the Desktop Publisher

Hour

Hour 17

Working with Graphics

This hour explains Word 97 graphics. Two major breakthroughs in Word 97 are the Web tools and the graphics functions. The new graphic capabilities have changed dramatically from previous versions. This chapter explores the new features such as custom word wraps and brightness and contrast controls that make it a whole new product in terms of images.

The highlights of this hour include

☐ How to add your own pictures to Clip Gallery

☐ How to use the Picture toolbar to enhance graphics

☐ What's new and improved in WordArt

Clip Gallery

The former ClipArt Gallery has been renamed Clip Gallery because of the new multimedia add-ins such as sounds and videos. For those who were disappointed with the scant clip art collection in the last version of Word, the new additions of clip art will be a welcome sight. The included photographic art is also a nice touch, though probably more usable in PowerPoint, where the final product is usually displayed onscreen rather than in print.

To open the Clip Gallery, select Insert | Picture | Clip Art. Figure 17.1 shows the Clip Art tab in the Clip Gallery. When you insert clip art, you are automatically switched to Page Layout view.

Figure 17.1.
The Clip Gallery.

Microsoft Clip Gallery 3.0
Clip Art
Pictures
Sounds
Videos
[All Categories]
Academic
Animals
Backgrounds
Borders & Frames
Buildings
Business
Buttons & Icons
Cartoons
Communication
Currency
Dividers & Decora
Electronics
Entertainment
Flags
Food & Dining
Frames & Borders
Gestures
Healthcare & Mec
Home & Family
Insert
Close
Find...
Help
Magnify
Clip art in this category: 3187
Scroll down to view more clip art
Edit Categories...
Clip Properties...
Import Clips...
Clip Art Keywords: Reward Accomplishment Milestone Guarantee

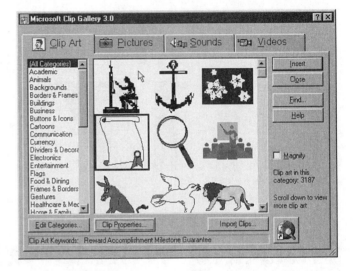

When you view the entire list (All Categories), you look through a very long list of pictures. To narrow your options, click one of the categories in the category list to see only the clips under that heading.

The clip art is indexed on keywords. If you're looking for something in particular, click the Find button and type a word in the Keywords box, as shown in Figure 17.2. Click Find Now, and Word searches through the index and brings up the pictures that are indexed on that term.

Figure 17.2.
Finding clip art on a subject.

Find Clip
Find all clips in the Clip Gallery that have:
Keywords:
child
File name containing:
[All Names]
Clip type:
[All Types]
Find Now
Cancel
Reset
The Find command looks for clips that are already in the Clip Gallery. It will not find clips that are on your hard disk that haven't been imported into the Clip Gallery.

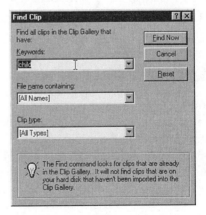

A search of clip art using the keyword Child brings up all the matches in all categories that are indexed on this word. Depending on how you install Word, you will get more or fewer clip art selections. If you installed Word from a CD-ROM, and the CD-ROM is currently in the CD-ROM drive, Clip Gallery displays the extra pictures that are included on the CD-ROM. There are more clip art selections on the Office 97 CD-ROM than the Word 97 CD. When you find a picture that fits your project, click the Insert button to bring it into your document.

More Clip Art!

If the clip art that comes with the Gallery doesn't have what you need, you can connect to Microsoft's Clip Gallery Live site on the Web at http://www.microsoft.com/clipgallerylive. You must be connected to the Web in order to grab these extra Clips and add them to your Clip Gallery. Hour 24, "Working with the Web," tells how to get connected. This involves a process of connecting and logging in.

If you are connected, you can jump directly to Clip Gallery Live by clicking the Connect to Web for additional clips button in Clip Gallery. To add a clip to your collection from the Clip Gallery Live selections, do the following:

1. Select Insert | Picture | Clip Art from the menu.
2. Click the Connect to Web for additional clips button.
3. Click the Accept button to accept the terms for using any clip art from this site.
4. Click the arrow beside the Select a category box to choose a broad category from which to search for clips.
5. Click the Go button.
6. When you find something in Clip Gallery Live that you'd like to add to your collection, click the filename beneath the clip (see Figure 17.3). The clip is automatically added to your Clip Gallery.

You can also add clip art or pictures you have gathered from other sources to the Clip Gallery. You need to know that there are two main kinds of computer graphics in order to understand what's happening when you add items to the Clip Gallery.

Vector Graphics

Vector graphics are clip art. This kind of art consists of shapes grouped together to form a larger picture. It does not lose quality when it is resized. Advanced drawing programs like Adobe Illustrator, CorelDraw, and Macromedia Freehand can create vector art. WMF files are Microsoft's clip art graphics that are created with their own program. WordPerfect does the same to create WPG files. All these real clip art formats retain their quality when resized.

Microsoft Clip Gallery Live - Microsoft Internet Explorer
File Edit View Go Favorites Help
Back Forward Stop Refresh Home Search Favorites Print Font Mail Edit
Address http://www.microsoft.com/clipgallerylive/
Links
MICROSOFT PRODUCTS SEARCH SUPPORT SHOP WRITE US
Microsoft
Browse Search
Select a category:
Weather
Go
Help Feedback
Your Browse for Clip Art returned 23 results.
Results 1 through 12 are shown below:
NATU001856_x5.WMF NATU001857_x5.WMF NATU001861_x5.WMF
39 kb 58 kb 16 kb
NATU001879_x5.WMF NATU001902_x5.WMF
288 kb 10 kb
Shortcut to NATU001874_x5.cil

Figure 17.3.
Add to your clip collection from Microsoft Clip Gallery Live.

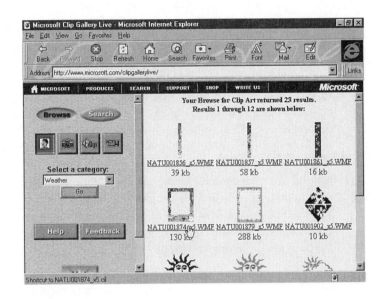

Raster Graphics

When a raster graphic is saved to a file, the program essentially looks at the individual dots (pixels) that make up the picture and saves a picture of the dots. Raster art is subject to distortion when it is resized as in Figure 17.4. Photographs, scanned images, and art created with programs such as Paint and Photoshop are raster graphics. They are not necessarily photo art. Common graphic types such as TIF, BMP, JPG, GIF, and PCX are raster graphics.

One of the reasons this is important is that Clip Gallery saves the two types of images in two different places. If you import a vector graphic, Word places it with the art in the Clip Art tab. If you import a raster graphic, Word puts it in the Pictures tab. Because all the existing art in the Pictures tab is photographic, it may be a bit confusing when your imported art ends up under pictures instead of clip art.

To add a picture to the Clip Gallery:

1. Select Insert | Picture | Clip Art from the menu.
2. Click the Import Clips button in the Clip Gallery dialog box.
3. From the Open File dialog box, locate the file you want to add to the Clip Gallery and select it, then click the Open button.
4. Type keywords to add to the clip index for this file (see Figure 17.5).
5. Click the box beside the category (or categories) that the clip would fit in, or click New Category to create one.
6. Click OK.

Microsoft Word - Document1
File Edit View Insert Format Tools Table Window Help
Normal
Times New Roman
12
100%
Page 1 Sec 1 1/1 At Ln Col REC TRK EXT OVR WPH

Figure 17.4.
Raster graphics are distorted when enlarged.

Clip Properties
File name: bubbles
File type: Windows Bitmaps
File size: 2118 bytes
File path: D:\My Documents\bubbles.bmp
Previews in: C:\WINDOWS\ArtGalry.cag
Keywords:
bubbles
Categories:
Academic
Animals
Backgrounds
Borders & Frames
Buildings
Business
Buttons & Icons
Cartoons
OK
Cancel
New Category...

Figure 17.5.
Adding your own pictures to the Clip Gallery.

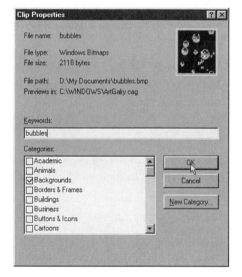

JUST A MINUTE

There are not as many categories in the Pictures tab as in the Clip Art tab, but all the categories appear when you are saving clips to the Gallery. If you import a raster graphic and select a category that doesn't exist in the Pictures tab, Word creates a new category in Pictures and places your clip in it.

Modifying Pictures

Word has a host of new graphic manipulation tools to modify not only clip art, but other graphics as well. When you're working with a picture, the Picture toolbar automatically comes up to give you access to these tools (see Figure 17.6).

Figure 17.6.

Use the Picture toolbar to alter pictures.

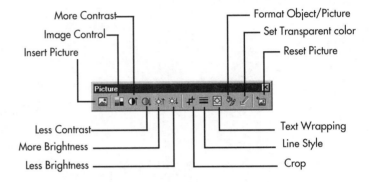

Labels (clockwise from upper left): More Contrast, Image Control, Insert Picture, Format Object/Picture, Set Transparent color, Reset Picture, Text Wrapping, Line Style, Crop, Less Brightness, More Brightness, Less Contrast

Resizing

The picture you insert in a document is often too small or too large for the space you want to use it in. To resize a picture:

1. Click the image. Sizing handles (small squares) surround the object.
2. Click one of the corner sizing handles; a double-headed arrow appears. Resizing from a corner handle keeps the width-to-height ratio the same as the original.
3. Click and drag the handle away from the object to make it bigger or toward the center of the object to make it smaller.

    A dotted outline displays the position and size that the object will be when it is resized, as shown in Figure 17.7. Release the mouse button when the object reaches the size you want.

To resize a picture to an exact size:

1. Select Format | Picture or click the Format Picture button on the Picture toolbar to display the Format Picture dialog (see Figure 17.8).
2. Click the Size tab.
3. Select Lock aspect ratio to keep the picture proportionally correct. If you need a specific width or height, change that measurement. The other measurement changes automatically when Lock aspect ratio is selected.

17

Figure 17.7.
A dotted outline shows how big the resized object will be.

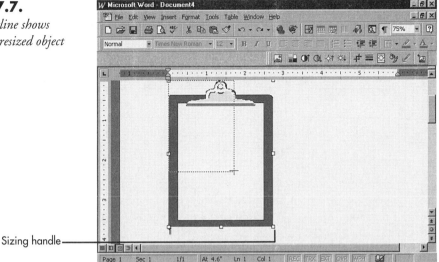

Microsoft Word - Document4
File Edit View Insert Format Tools Table Window Help
Normal
Times New Roman
12
75%
Sizing handle
Page 1 Sec 1 1/1 At 4.6" Ln 1 Col 1
REC TRK EXT OVR WPH

Figure 17.8.
Setting a picture to an exact size with the Format Picture dialog.

Format Picture
Colors and Lines
Size
Position
Wrapping
Picture
Text Box
Size and rotate
Height: 2.48"
Width: 1.83"
Rotation: 0°
Scale
Height: 100 %
Width: 100 %
Lock aspect ratio
Relative to original picture size
Original size
Height: 2.49"
Width: 1.83"
Reset
OK
Cancel

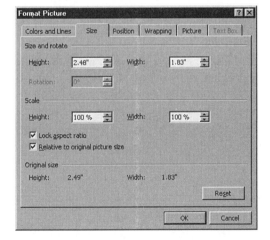

4. Click OK. If you want an exact width and height, do not check Lock aspect ratio. You can specify both the width and height measurements.

   You can also scale the picture to a certain percentage of the original. For example, set Scale to `200%` and the picture will be twice as large as the original. Again, if the Lock aspect ratio box is checked, both scales change when you change one of them.

After you've resized the picture, place it anywhere you want by clicking it and dragging it from one location to another. The pointer changes to a four-sided arrow when you select and move pictures or objects.

Step-Up

Previous versions of Word required that you put a frame around a graphic in order to move it. In Word 97, graphics inserted normally "float" over text and do not have to be in a frame to be moved. The Float over text option can be changed so that the graphic is actually on the text layer. It is called an inline graphic when it is positioned with text on the same layer. An inline graphic must be inserted in a text box that must then be converted to a frame in order to be capable of movement. It's much easier to take advantage of the Float over text option for graphics.

One of the reasons you might want to use an inline graphic is to insert it in a table. If you want to insert a graphic in a table, it *must* be an inline graphic rather than one that floats over text. If you've inserted a clip in your document and want to change it to an inline graphic:

1. Select the clip.
2. Click the Format Object button on the Picture toolbar. If a picture is one of the Clip Gallery selections, the button name is Format Object rather than Format Picture (because the clips are not all pictures).
3. Select the Position tab.
4. Uncheck the Float over text checkbox.
5. Click OK.

Crop

Cropping is a way to cut off part of a picture that you don't want (the old "cut the disfavored relative out of the picture" scenario). In earlier versions of Word, cropping was a hit-or-miss affair. You had to specify a certain amount of space to crop from an edge. If you cropped too much or not enough, you had to go back to the menu to increase or decrease the measurement until the picture looked about right. The addition of the cropping tool to the Picture toolbar eliminates the guesswork. To crop a picture:

1. Select the picture.
2. Click the Crop button on the Picture toolbar.
3. Click one of the sizing handles.
4. Drag the handle in a direction that removes the unwanted section of the picture, as shown in Figure 17.9.

17

Figure 17.9.
Use the cropping tool to eliminate part of a picture.

Microsoft Word - Document4
File Edit View Insert Format Tools Table Window Help
Normal
Times New Roman
12
75%
Position the pointer over any handle and drag to crop.
Cropping tool

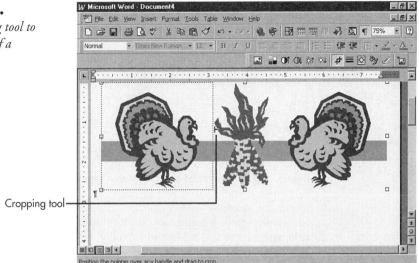

The dotted outline shows how much of the picture will be left after the picture is cropped. Release the mouse button to complete the cropping. You can crop from any edge or corner. If you crop more than you want:

1. Click the Crop button. Position the cropping tool on the sizing handle you used to crop the picture.
2. Click and drag the sizing handle back in the opposite direction to restore part of the picture. The complete picture is still there; cropping just hides part of it from view. A common misconception is that the file size can be decreased by cropping a picture. This is not the case because the entire image is really there.

Cropping is a good way to eliminate extra whitespace or unwanted portions of the graphic such as borders. For example, you might scan a signature and save it. When you try to insert it in a signature block, you may find you saved the image with too much whitespace on the top and bottom to allow it to fit nicely in the block. Cropping the picture from the top and bottom gets rid of the unwanted space. Sometimes graphics have an existing border (a picture frame effect) that you don't want to include. You can crop from all sides to eliminate the picture frame.

Brightness and Contrast

The new brightness and contrast features offer a lot more control over the image. These are features that you would expect to find in a graphic manipulation package or a desktop publishing program.

If a picture is too dark, select it and click the More Brightness button on the Picture toolbar. Click the button again to increase the brightness one step at a time. Similarly, the Less Brightness button darkens the picture.

Contrast is the ratio of dark to light tones within the picture. Decreasing the contrast eventually fades the picture to gray. Increasing contrast heightens the difference between lights and darks.

CAUTION

> Clip art in the Clip Gallery is optimally set for contrast and brightness. What you see onscreen may not be what you get in print. Try a test page before adjusting contrast and brightness settings. If you increase the brightness before printing to a color printer, you may get unsatisfactory results (for example, faded colors and annoying horizontal lines). This is a known problem that seems to affect only color printers. If you make changes to a graphic that cause distortion or unwanted results (color, brightness, cropping, resizing, and so on), select the graphic and click the Reset Picture button on the Picture toolbar to restore the original.

Add a Picture Frame

You can dress up a picture by adding a custom frame or border around the outside edge. To place a box around a picture:

1. Click the picture.
2. Click the Line Styles button on the Picture toolbar.
3. Select one of the predefined line styles, or click More Lines to vary the line width, color, and style. The Format Picture dialog box, shown in Figure 17.10, appears.

Figure 17.10.
Framing a picture with line styles.

Format Picture
Colors and Lines
Size
Position
Wrapping
Picture
Text Box
Fill
Color:
Semitransparent
Line
Color:
Style:
Dashed:
Weight:
10 pt
Arrows
Begin style:
End style:
Begin size:
End size:
OK
Cancel

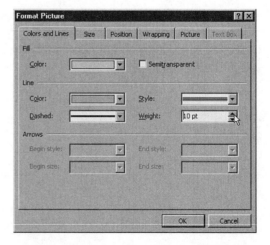

4. Select Color and Style from the drop-down lists. Add a dashed line style if you like. Weight determines how thick or heavy the line will be. Use the default or modify the point size in the Weight box.

Add or Change the Background Color

A picture can go from simple clip art to a work of art with some of Word's new custom background options. Photoshop-like background effects can bring a graphic to life. Figure 17.11 shows a piece of clip art that has one of the new gradient fills applied to the background.

Figure 17.11.

Clip art with a gradient-fill background.

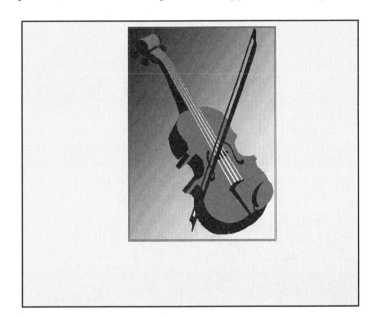

To add a special background fill to a picture:

1. Select the picture.
2. Click the Format Picture icon on the Picture toolbar or select Picture from the Format menu.
3. Click the Colors and Lines tab.
4. Click the Color drop-down list under Fill.
5. Select Fill Effects.
6. Click the Gradient tab to select fills like the one that was used to create the illustration in Figure 17.11. Figure 17.12 shows the Gradient Fill options.

Fill Effects
Gradient
Texture
Pattern
Picture
OK
Cancel
Colors
Color 1:
One color
Two colors
Preset
Color 2:
Shading styles
Variants
Horizontal
Vertical
Diagonal up
Diagonal down
From corner
From center
Sample:

Figure 17.12.
Selecting a gradient fill.

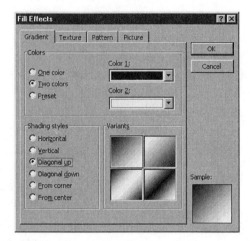

Experimenting with the different fill options is the best way to learn how they work and how they look in print. Textures and patterns also provide interesting background choices. If you'd like to use another picture as a background, select the Picture tab and open the picture. While it may sound strange to use another picture for a background, there is a wealth of clip art that has been designed especially for backgrounds.

Text Wrap

Another of the fun things about Word 97 is its capability to wrap around text in new ways. Word has always had the old standards—text on top and bottom, text to the left, text to the right, and a few other variations. Word 97's new text wrap options are much less constricting with the Edit Wrap Points feature.

Select a picture and click the Text Wrap button on the Picture toolbar to see what wrap options are available. The last item in the list is Edit Wrap Points. When you insert one of the clip art pictures and select Edit Wrap Points, Word outlines the item as shown in Figure 17.13. Text flows up to the edit points.

The wrap points are the darkened squares on the dotted line that surrounds the picture. You can click and drag any of the wrap points in any direction for some unique text-wrap effects.

The Wrapping tab in the Format Picture dialog box gives greater control over text wraps, including adding more whitespace between the graphic and the text (see Figure 17.14). Increase the measurements in the Distance from text section to provide more whitespace. Not all options are available for every wrapping style. The Distance from text and Wrap to options are grayed out and cannot be selected if they do not apply to a specified wrapping style.

Figure 17.13.
Edit Wrap Points brings text up to the picture.

Microsoft Word - Document5
File Edit View Insert Format Tools Table Window Help
Normal
JOIN.....
The Morris Community School Disk Sharing Program. If you have extra 3 ½" disks to share with the students at Foster Elementary and Morris High School, contact Mary Tyler at 899-809-7777. Students at these
Page 1 Sec 1 1/1 At 1" Ln 1 Col 1

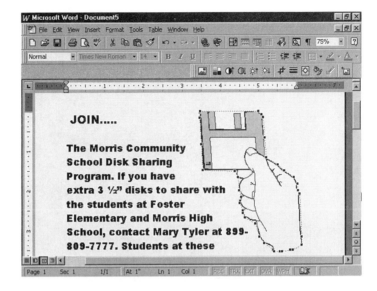

Figure 17.14.
More text wrap options from the Format Picture dialog.

Format Picture
Colors and Lines
Size
Position
Wrapping
Picture
Text Box
Wrapping style
Square
Tight
Through
None
Top & bottom
Wrap to
Both sides
Left
Right
Largest side
Distance from text
Top: 0.3"
Left: 0.3"
Bottom: 0.3"
Right: 0.3"
OK
Cancel

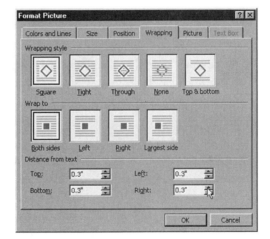

Image Control

The Image Control button on the Picture toolbar lets you change the image type, as shown in Figure 17.15. Automatic is the format the image is already in when it is added to a document. You can convert the image to:

- Grayscale—changes every color to a shade of gray
- Black and white—changes every color to either black or white (line art)
- Watermark—changes the image to a faded image that can be used behind text. The image in Figure 17.15 has been converted to a watermark.

Microsoft Word - Document9
File Edit View Insert Format Tools Table Window Help
Automatic
Grayscale
Black & White
Watermark

Figure 17.15.
Converting an image to a watermark.

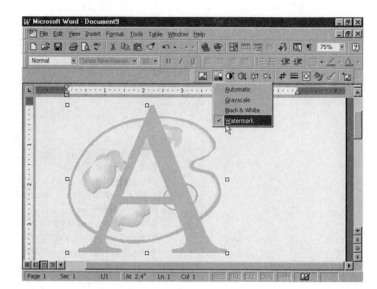

WordArt

Word 97's WordArt is strikingly different from previous versions. It has great-looking 3D effects for headings and titles. They're sharp enough to be standalone graphics anywhere in your document. To add WordArt to your document:

1. Select Insert | Picture | WordArt.
2. Select one of the WordArt designs, as shown in Figure 17.16, and click OK.

WordArt Gallery
Select a WordArt style:
OK
Cancel

Figure 17.16.
WordArt comes with a whole set of 3D designs.

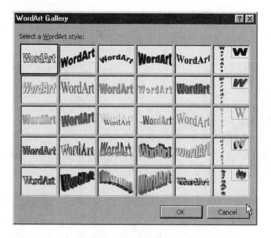

3. Type the text you want to use as a WordArt object.
4. Select a font and a font size.
5. Click OK.

Your WordArt title is created, and the WordArt toolbar opens to give you quick access to lots of editing features. Click the WordArt Gallery button if you want to apply a different style. From the toolbar, you have the following options in addition to changing the style:

- Format WordArt—gives almost the same options as Format | Picture. You can set colors and lines (and fill effects), text wrapping, position, and size.
- WordArt Shape—offers a menu of over 30 different shapes that you can apply to the WordArt (see Figure 17.17).

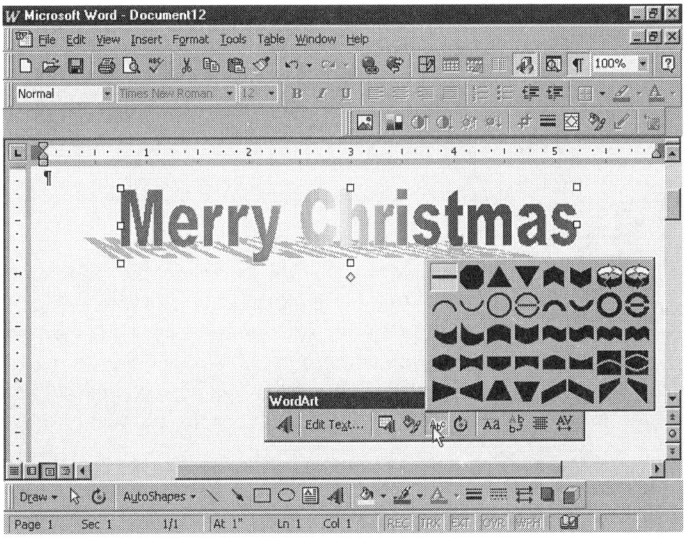

Microsoft Word - Document12
File Edit View Insert Format Tools Table Window Help
100%
Normal
Times New Roman
12
Merry Christmas
WordArt
Edit Text...
Draw
AutoShapes
Page 1 Sec 1 1/1 At 1" Ln 1 Col 1 REC TRK EXT OVR WPH

Figure 17.17.
Change the shape of a WordArt object.

- Free Rotate—lets you grab a corner of the WordArt and change its direction on the page. (Hour 18, "The Drawing Tools," explains the Free Rotate tool.)
- WordArt Same Letter Heights—makes every letter the same height.
- WordArt Vertical Text—lets you flip the WordArt on its side so that it runs vertically rather than horizontally.
- WordArt Alignment—aligns WordArt as you would other text with a couple of other special additions (word justify, letter justify, and stretch justify).
- WordArt Character Spacing—lets you increase or decrease the amount of space between letters.

Other Pictures

Many other types of graphic files can be used in Word. A huge variety of art is available on disk, CD, or through the Internet in many forms. Most of these file types can be used in Word. To insert a graphic that is not part of Word's Clip Gallery:

1. Select Insert | Picture | From File.
2. Select the source where the graphic is located from the Look in box. It might be on a CD in your CD-ROM drive, on a disk in your floppy drive, or on your hard drive.
3. Select the name of the graphic.
4. Click Insert.

   If the graphics are vector graphics, they work exactly like the pictures you inserted from Clip Gallery. Other graphic files (raster graphics) work in nearly the same way. You can't apply fills to raster graphics, and the text wrap options will be less flexible. Raster art will always be rectangular, so the only edit points will be the four corners.

CAUTION

Most art on the Internet is copyrighted. Even some of the art you purchase on disk or CD-ROM is copyrighted. A common misconception is that this art is free for the taking. Be sure to check any restrictions that apply before using any art. You will sometimes see the term *royalty free*, which means that you can use the art without charge. It is important to read the documentation to find out how you need to reference the source of the art and any other restrictions the producer has on its usage.

Summary

This hour is devoted to the way Word 97 works with art. The new and improved Clip Gallery has hundreds of pieces of clip art (over 3,000 if you have the Office 97 Professional CD) that can be inserted in your documents. New text wraps and the splashy effects added to WordArt make Word 97 well worth the investment. Hour 18, "The Drawing Tools," contains many functions that expand on what you've learned in this chapter. The drawing tools work in conjunction with clip art and other pictures to round out the Word graphics package.

Q&A

Q **Is there any way to change the colors in a clip art graphic?**

A Yes, but it takes patience. Clip art is a series of many objects and shapes that have been grouped together. We'll look at "ungrouping" these elements and recoloring along with another possible solution to recoloring clip art in the next hour.

Q **I tried both the Tight and the Through Text Wrap options. I can't see any difference. Is there anything different about them?**

A Tight goes closely around the edge of the object. Through works exactly like Tight but has an added feature to allow text to move into empty space within a graphic if you manipulate the wrap points correctly. For example, you could run text into the center of a wreath so that you have text both inside and outside of the wreath. It's probably easier to use a text box, however. Text boxes are covered in the next hour.

Q **I can't connect to the extra clip art in the Clip Gallery. When I click the button to get additional clips from the Web, Microsoft Internet Explorer opens but nothings happens.**

A You can't use Internet Explorer unless you have Internet access and go through the process to connect. See Chapter 24 to find out how you can get connected to make this function work.

Q **Should I avoid using raster art because it distorts the images when they're enlarged?**

A There are certain kinds of graphics, such as photographic art and scanned images, that are always raster art; you will probably have many occasions to use them. There may also be raster art available and suitable for your project that may not be available as vector graphics. Anyone can create raster art with inexpensive software, so there's a lot of it.

Q **When I print a WordArt object to my color printer, it works fine. I often have trouble printing to my laser printer, however. Sometimes I get a printer overrun error. I also can't get the color gradations. The text shows up as solid black. Is there some way to make WordArt work better with my laser?**

A WordArt requires a lot of printer memory when using a laser printer. The printer overrun occurs when there is not enough printer memory to complete a print job. Depending on your printer, you may be able to set an option to print graphics as raster rather than vector graphics. Select File | Print. In the Print dialog box, click Properties. If there is a Graphics tab, click it. Under Graphics mode, select the Use raster graphics option. The color gradation for WordArt seems to work in this mode.

17

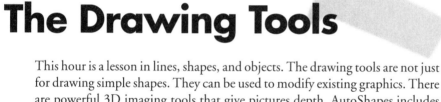

Hour 18

The Drawing Tools

This hour is a lesson in lines, shapes, and objects. The drawing tools are not just for drawing simple shapes. They can be used to modify existing graphics. There are powerful 3D imaging tools that give pictures depth. AutoShapes includes many new shapes. Create callouts, flow charts, and stylized arrows from the new collection of AutoShapes. Text boxes create moveable text. Position text on top of graphics or in a box that is independent from other text in a document.

The highlights of this hour include

- ☐ How to use layers to place graphics behind text
- ☐ How to link text boxes
- ☐ What kinds of things you would put in a text box
- ☐ How to turn a flat picture into a 3D object

Shapes

If you've ever used Paint or another simple drawing program, the primary drawing tools in Word 97 for performaing tasks such as drawing a line or rectangle will look very familiar. The main headquarters for working with the drawing tools is the Drawing toolbar. Select View | Toolbars and click Drawing to open the toolbar.

It seems there is a toolbar for every significant function. You don't need the Drawing toolbar up all the time, but when you're working with graphics, it's essential. Figure 18.1 shows the Drawing toolbar positioned at the bottom of the screen. It really helps to have the toolbar available, but out of the way while you're working.

Figure 18.1.
Placing the Drawing toolbar at the bottom of the screen for quick access.

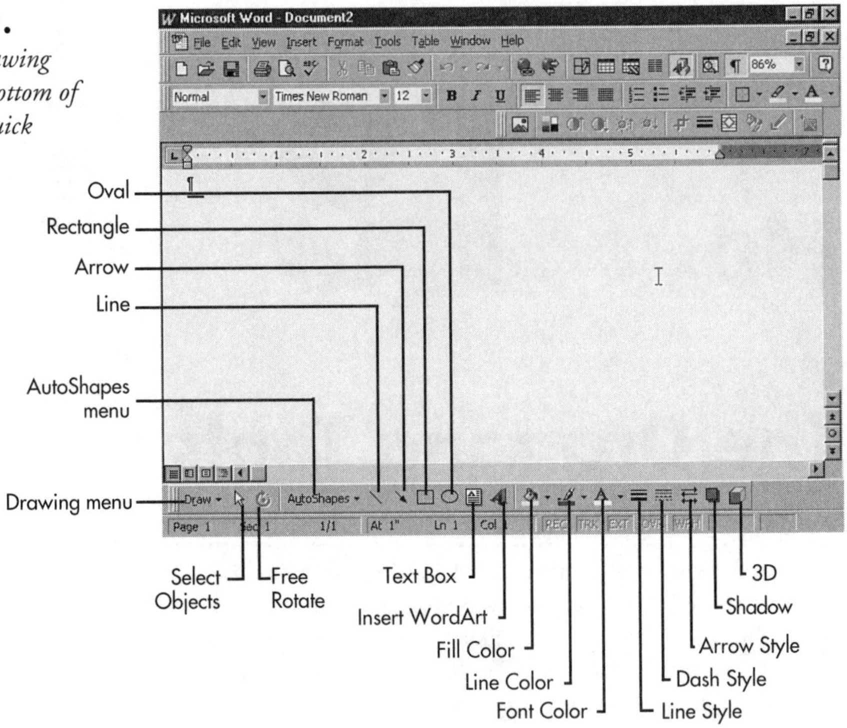
Microsoft Word - Document2
Oval
Rectangle
Arrow
Line
AutoShapes menu
Drawing menu
Select Objects
Free Rotate
Text Box
Insert WordArt
Fill Color
Line Color
Font Color
3D
Shadow
Arrow Style
Dash Style
Line Style

Rectangles, Squares, Ovals, and Circles

Rectangles and squares are created from the Rectangle button on the Drawing toolbar. To add a rectangle or square to a document:

1. Click anywhere in the document.
2. Click the Rectangle button on the Drawing toolbar.
3. Move to the typing screen; the mouse pointer turns to a crosshair. Click and drag the mouse across and down to create a rectangle (see Figure 18.2).

Microsoft Word - Document2
File Edit View Insert Format Tools Table Window Help
75%
Normal
Times New Roman
12
Draw
AutoShapes
Page 1 Sec 1 1/1 At 1.1" Ln 2 Col 1
REC TRK EXT OVR WPH

Figure 18.2.
Move the crosshair across and down to create a rectangle.

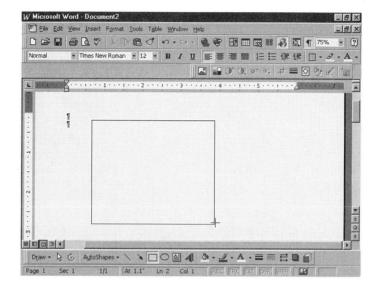

4. If you want a square, you can eyeball your rectangle and try to make it square as you click and drag, but this is not an easy task. If you hold down the Shift key while clicking and dragging the crosshair from the top-left corner to the lower-right corner, the shape will be proportionally the same height and width.
5. The same process is used to insert an oval or a circle. The Shift key in combination with the Oval tool creates a circle. Using the Shift key while clicking and dragging any of the AutoShapes maintains the width-to-height ratio.

Fills and Lines for Shapes

You don't have to settle for a plain rectangle or circle. You can fill it with color, modify the line style of the outer edge, and change the line color. The paint bucket icon on the Drawing toolbar is standard to many graphic programs. This is the Fill button. To fill an object with color:

1. Click the object.
2. Click the drop-down list beside the Fill Color button and select from one of the colors, or click the More Colors button to bring up a color wheel.
3. Click one of the colors shown in Figure 18.3 to select it, or click the Custom tab to do some color mixing to create other colors.

Figure 18.3.
Selecting a Fill Color from the color wheel.

Colors
Standard
Custom
Colors:
OK
Cancel
New
Current
Semitransparent

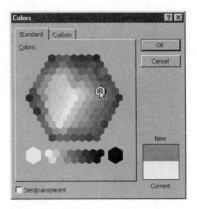

4. Click OK when you have a color that you're satisfied with.

You may have noticed the Fill Effects entry in the drop-down list of fill choices. These are the same options that were discussed in the last hour for adding backgrounds to clip art—Gradient, Texture, Pattern, and Picture Fills. Fill effects can turn a simple box or circle into a custom backdrop for a title or an accent graphic. Figure 18.4 displays three objects with different fills:

- 1 has a pattern fill
- 2 has a texture fill (woven rug)
- 3 has a gradient fill (Colors option = One color, Shading Styles option = From center)

Figure 18.4.
Using different fill effects in drawing objects.

Microsoft Word - Document2
File Edit View Insert Format Tools Table Window Help
75%
Normal
Times New Roman
12
1¶
2¶
3¶
Draw
AutoShapes

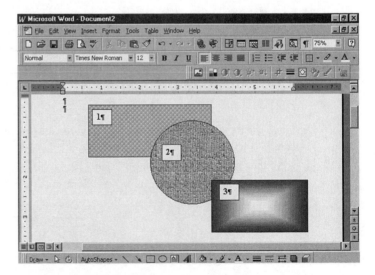

Grouping and Ungrouping Objects

If you wanted all of the objects in Figure 18.4 to act as a single object, you could group them together. Grouped objects can be moved around as though they are a single object. To group objects together:

1. Hold down the Shift key and click each object without releasing the Shift key between selections. The positioning handles appear for each selected object. This is called the multiple select method.
2. Click the Draw menu on the Drawing toolbar.
3. Click Group as shown in Figure 18.5.

Figure 18.5.
Group several drawing objects to make them one object.

Microsoft Word - Document2
File Edit View Insert Format Tools Table Window Help
Normal
Times New Roman
12
75%
Group
Ungroup
Regroup
Order
Grid...
Nudge
Align or Distribute
Rotate or Flip
Edit Points
Change AutoShape
Set AutoShape Defaults
2¶
3¶
Draw
AutoShapes
Page 1 Sec 1 1/1 At 1" Ln 1 Col 1

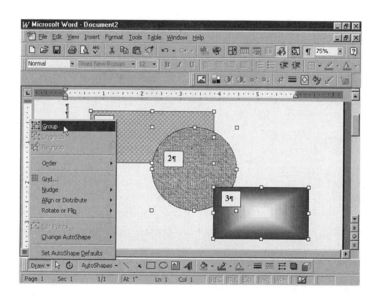

Grouped objects become a single object that can be moved as one (see Figure 18.6). Click anywhere on one of the objects and drag it to another area. The outline in Figure 18.6 shows that all three items are being moved together. You can no longer click the individual items to format or move them. Any new formatting applied, such as a background, applies to all of the objects. If, for example, you applied a gradient fill to the grouped object, the fill in all three objects would be changed.

Microsoft Word - Document2
File Edit View Insert Format Tools Table Window Help
50%
Normal
Times New Roman
12
Draw
AutoShapes
Page 1 Sec 1 1/1 At 1" Ln 1 Col 1 REC TRK EXT OVR WPH

Figure 18.6.
All of the objects that are grouped can be moved together.

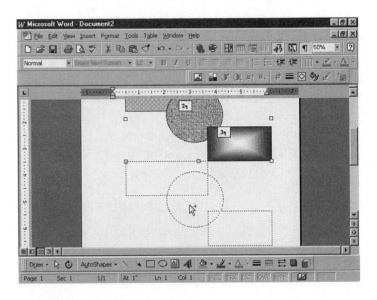

Time Saver

It can be difficult to reposition drawing objects, clip art, or text boxes in small increments with drag-and-drop. To inch the object slightly in one direction or another:

1. Select the object.
2. Select Nudge from the Draw menu on the Drawing toolbar.
3. Click the direction you want the object to move (Up, Down, Left, or Right).

Nudge moves a selected object in increments of five pixels. The arrow keys on the keyboard do the same thing. To move items more precisely (one pixel at a time), hold down the Ctrl key while pressing an arrow key on the keyboard.

If you decide you need to make changes to one or more of the objects, click anywhere on the grouped object and select Ungroup from the Draw menu. Each object can again be formatted, resized, or moved individually. Clip art is made up of a series of grouped objects. There may be dozens of small pieces in a single clip art picture. Those objects can be modified if you ungroup them. To change portions of a clip art image:

1. Click the clip art picture.
2. Select Draw | Ungroup from the Drawing toolbar.

3. Hold down the Shift key and click each object you want to include in the selection (multiple select).

4. To change the color of the objects, select a fill color from the drop-down list on the Drawing toolbar.

JUST A MINUTE

Clip art is often made of so many separate objects that it is very difficult to recolor it. PowerPoint includes a feature on its Picture toolbar specifically for recoloring. It would be much easier to insert the clip art in PowerPoint to recolor it, then copy and paste it into your Word document.

5. To move the objects, click and drag them to a new location.

6. To remove the objects entirely, press the Delete key.

Changing the Order of Objects

Word uses a layering system that lets you determine whether an object is in front or in back of another. If you have text that flows through an object, you can specify that the text is on top. Use Order from the Draw menu to change the layer a selected object is placed on. If you select Send to Back, the object is placed on a layer behind the other objects in the document. Select Bring to Front, and the item is placed on a layer above the other objects (and/or text). Use the Behind and In Front of Text options to place an object on a layer above or behind text.

You may have more than two layers. In this case, the Send Backward option sends an object back one layer at a time. If you refer to Figure 18.4, you'll see that there are three objects on the page. The rectangle labeled 3 is on the top layer. The circle is on the second layer, and the rectangle labeled 1 is on a third layer. Click the number 3 rectangle and choose Send Backward to place it behind the circle. Click the circle and choose Send Backward to place it behind the number 1 rectangle. If all three objects were touching, you could select rectangle number 3 and choose Send to Back. This would place it behind both numbers 1 and 2.

AutoShapes

Figure 18.7 displays the kinds of AutoShapes that can be inserted from the AutoShapes drop-down list under the flowchart options. You can essentially build a flowchart using flowchart AutoShapes and a series of connecting lines.

18

Microsoft Word - Fills.doc
File Edit View Insert Format Tools Table Window Help
Normal
Times New Roman
12
80%
Lines
Basic Shapes
Block Arrows
Flowchart
Stars and Banners
Callouts
Draw
AutoShapes
Page 1
Sec 1
1/1
At 1.1"

Figure 18.7.
Building a flowchart with AutoShapes.

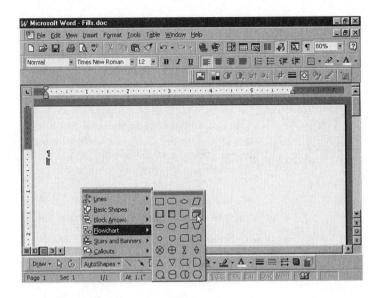

Here are some tricks for building a flowchart with AutoShapes:

- You usually want all of the same size boxes for one level of a flowchart. Instead of inserting and drawing each box, draw one box. Hold down the Ctrl key and click and drag the box to another location to make another copy of it. Continue this process until you have as many boxes as you need.
- When you draw connecting lines, it is often difficult to get the line to stop right at the edge of the flowchart box. Don't worry about making it exact. If the line is a little longer than it needs to be and spills into the box, click the line and select Order from the Draw menu on the toolbar. Select Send to Back. This places the line in back of the box so the spillover isn't visible.
- Use the Nudge feature or the Ctrl+arrow key combinations to position the flowchart boxes more precisely. Selecting and nudging an object moves it in very small intervals.
- You may have three or four boxes that are supposed to be on the same level of the flowchart, but it's hard to get them to line up exactly and Nudge can take too long. To get them evenly spaced and lined up:

    1. Hold down the Shift key and click each of the boxes (multiple select).
    2. Select Draw | Align or Distribute | Align Top.
    3. Select Draw | Align or Distribute | Relative to Page from the Drawing toolbar.
    4. Select Draw | Align or Distribute | Distribute Horizontally.

5. Use the multiple select procedure to reposition all of the boxes and keep them aligned (Shift+click the objects to select and move them as in Figure 18.8). Using multiple select is like temporarily grouping objects. When you do something to one, you do it to all of them.

Figure 18.8.
Lining up and moving boxes in a flowchart.

Microsoft Word - Document3
File Edit View Insert Format Tools Table Window Help
Normal
Director of Sales
M. Kelly
Draw
AutoShapes
Page 1 Sec 1 1/1 At 1" Ln 1 Col 1

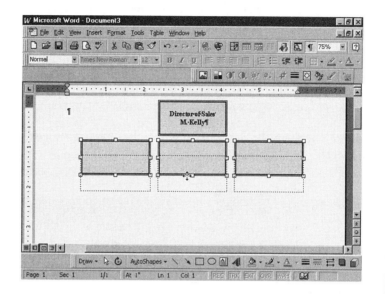

Figure 18.9 displays some of the other types of AutoShapes. When callouts are inserted, they include a text box because they were designed to hold text like the thought bubbles in cartoons. The callout in Figure 18.9 shows the outline of the text box.

Figure 18.9.
More AutoShapes to choose from.

Microsoft Word - Fills.doc
File Edit View Insert Format Tools Table Window Help
Heading 1
Times New Roman
12
Lines
Basic Shapes
Block Arrows
CALLOUTS
Stars & Banners
Draw
AutoShapes
Page 1 Sec 1 1/1 At 2.8" Ln Col 9

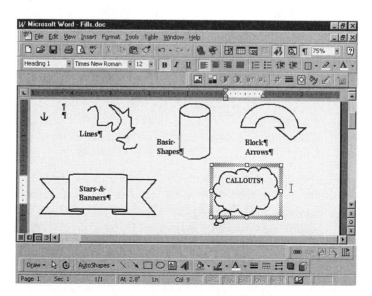

Text Boxes

You have already seen text boxes in the figures used in this hour. All of the text in Figure 18.9 was inserted using text boxes, as was the title in the top box of the flowchart in Figure 18.8. The numbers in Figure 18.4 were also included in text boxes. You can see the outline of the text boxes in Figure 18.4. This is what text boxes look like when they are inserted. The default is a thin line border with a white fill color.

Adding and Resizing Text Boxes

You have an idea what text boxes do from the examples used previously. To add and resize a text box:

1. Click the Text Box button on the Drawing toolbar.
2. Position the mouse pointer on the typing screen; it turns into a crosshair. Click and drag the mouse pointer just as you would if you were drawing a rectangle (to the right and down).
3. Drag one of the corners to resize the box proportionally or resize it vertically or horizontally by clicking a sizing handle on one of the edges and dragging it to make it smaller or larger.
4. Move the text box by clicking the box and positioning the mouse on one of the edges until the four-sided arrow appears. Click and drag the text box where you want it.

Inserting Text in a Text Box

A text box is essentially a container for text. It combines graphic elements with text. You can move both a text box and the text inside it at the same time. If you select a text box and press the Delete key to remove it, the text is gone too. This is a handy way to insert instructions within a document. When the user is finished with the instructions, it only takes a click and Delete to remove the entire text box.

Unlike using Rectangle to insert a box, a text box is created with a paragraph mark inside it so that you can add text to it. If a text box is selected, all the text can be formatted at once using Format | Font or using the Formatting toolbar. Text alignment applies to everything in the box. To apply formatting to only certain sections of the text box, select those portions individually.

If you type more text than will fit in the text box, it will seem to disappear. Click one of the edges or a corner to resize the box and make it big enough to display all the text or resize text to make it small enough to fit in the box. You can rotate the text vertically in a text box like you can with WordArt as outlined in Hour 14, "Working with Tables." To change the orientation of text in a text box:

18

1. Select the text box. The Text Box toolbar, which is available only if a text box is selected, will appear. If you don't see it onscreen, select View | Toolbars and select the Text Box toolbar.
2. Click the Change Text Direction button as in Figure 18.10. Keep clicking until you have the text orientation the way you want it.
3. Click one of the alignment buttons on the Formatting toolbar to align the text.

Microsoft Word - Document4
File Edit View Insert Format Tools Table Window Help
Normal
Times New Roman
38
75%
NEW
Text Box
Change Text Direction
Draw
AutoShapes
Page 1 Sec 1 1/1 At 0.9" Ln Col 3

Figure 18.10.
Change the direction of text in a text box.

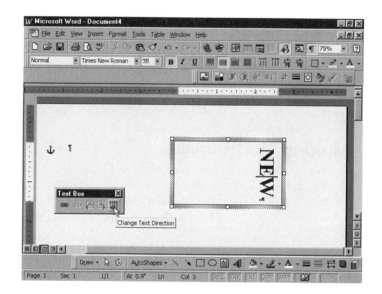

Removing or Changing the Text Box Border and Fill

You will often want to place a text box on top of another object to provide a label for the object as in the numbers that were used in Figure 18.4. You usually want to remove both the line and the fill when you're using the text as a label. To remove the line and then the fill:

1. Click the text box.
2. Select Format | Text Box from the menu.
3. Click the Fill Color drop-down list and select No Fill.
4. Click the Line Color drop-down list and select No Line, as in Figure 18.11.
5. Click OK. Both the line and the fill will be removed.

Figure 18.11.
Removing the line and fill from a text box.

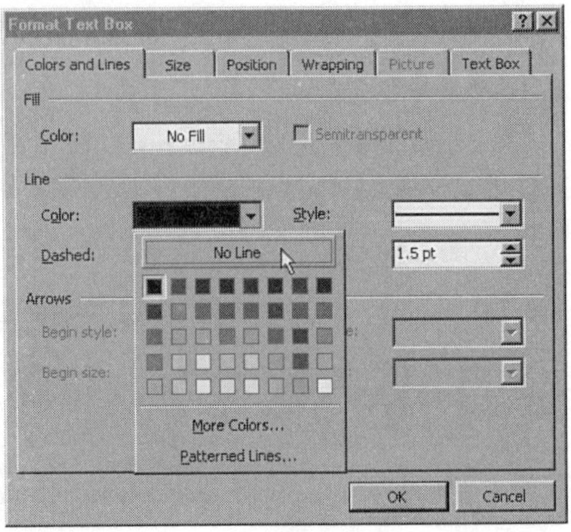
Format Text Box
Colors and Lines
Size
Position
Wrapping
Picture
Text Box
Fill
Color:
No Fill
Semitransparent
Line
Color:
Style:
Dashed:
No Line
1.5 pt
Arrows
Begin style:
Begin size:
More Colors...
Patterned Lines...
OK
Cancel

Linking Text Boxes

Linking text boxes is a great way to create newspaper-like reports that flow from one column to a section on another page. It's also a way to jump from one place to another in a document. To create a link between two text boxes:

1. Create the first text box.
2. Create a second text box elsewhere in the document.
3. Click the first text box.
4. Click the Create Text Box Link button on the Text Box toolbar. The mouse pointer will look like a water pitcher.
5. Move to the second text box and position the mouse pointer over the box. The pitcher looks like it is pouring, as in Figure 18.12. Click the text box to complete the link.

When you type text in the first text box and space runs out, the text spills over into the second text box. To jump between text boxes, use the Previous and Next Text Box buttons on the Text Box toolbar. You can lay out an entire document as you would a newspaper and have articles flow from one page to another.

CAUTION

The second text box must be empty in order for you to create the link to it.

Figure 18.12.
Linking two text boxes.

Microsoft Word - Document4
File Edit View Insert Format Tools Table Window Help
Normal
Times New Roman
12
75%
Text Box
Draw
AutoShapes
Page 1 Sec 1 1/2 At 2.5" Ln Col 20
REC TRK EXT OVR WPH

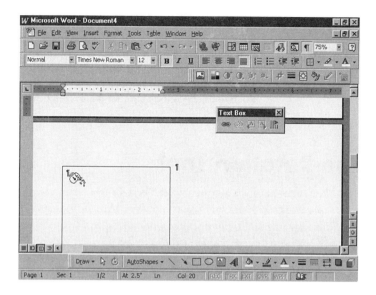

JUST A MINUTE

The Text Box toolbar is only visible when you are in a text box. It hides as soon as you move out of the box.

18

Lines and Arrows

Creating a line or an arrow is as simple as creating a rectangle or circle. To create a line:

1. Click the Line button on the Drawing toolbar.
2. Click in the document.
3. Drag the crosshair in any direction and release the mouse button when the line is as long as you want it.
4. Use the same process to create an arrow with the Arrow button. To modify either a line or an arrow, the object must be selected. The Line Style button brings up a list of line styles, the Dash Style button gives options for dashed lines, and the Arrow Style button contains the arrowhead styles. The line style of the arrow is selected from either the Line Style or Dash Style button.

JUST A MINUTE

Hold down the Shift key while dragging to draw a straight line. You can rotate the line in 15 degree increments as you move the mouse pointer, and the line will always be straight. Lines that are rotated without the Shift key may appear jagged, but they will print as straight lines. It is important to have the lines look straight if they will be viewed onscreen.

The Rotation Tool

The rotation tool is accessed via the Free Rotate button on the Drawing toolbar. Free Rotate only works with drawn objects like WordArt, AutoShapes, and other objects created using the Drawing toolbar. It does not work with clip art, text boxes, or pictures inserted from files. That's probably being held in reserve for the next version of Word.

To rotate an object:

1. Click the object.
2. Click the Free Rotate button on the Drawing toolbar or the WordArt toolbar for WordArt rotation. The sizing handles change from squares to small colored circles.
3. Click one of the circles; the pointer turns to four arrows rotating in a circle.
4. Drag the mouse in the direction you want the object to rotate. A dotted line appears as you move the mouse, showing where the object will be repositioned. Release the mouse when the text lays the way you want it (see Figure 18.13).

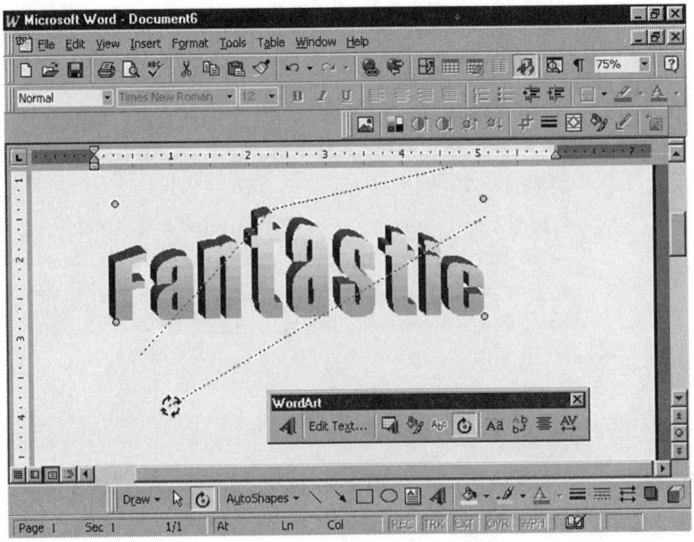
Microsoft Word - Document6
File Edit View Insert Format Tools Table Window Help
Normal
Fantastic
WordArt
Edit Text...
Draw
AutoShapes
Page 1 Sec 1 1/1 At Ln Col

Figure 18.13.
A dotted line shows where the rotated object will be.

TIME SAVER

You can rotate clip art if you ungroup it first. It then becomes a series of drawing objects. Rotate the objects, then immediately regroup them.

Special Effects

The new Shadow and 3D effects add a great touch to simple graphics. They also work with WordArt to create some dramatic effects. It will look like you spent hours on a project when you touch it up with special effects here and there.

Shadows

Add a shadow to a selected drawing object by clicking the Shadow button on the Drawing toolbar. For example, when you're creating flowcharts or titles placed in boxes, you can accent them with shadows. Figure 18.14 shows some of the standard shadow effects you can apply. When you apply a shadow style, it creates the smallest shadow possible. Sometimes it is even hard to tell that there is a shadow at all. Select Shadow Settings to nudge the shadow by small increments up, down, left, or right. The button on the right side of the Shadow Settings toolbar lets you change the shadow color. The button on the left lets you toggle the shadow on or off. You will not see the Shadow samples when you're working with the Shadow Settings toolbar. They are both shown in Figure 18.14.

18

Microsoft Word - Document2
File Edit View Insert Format Tools Table Window Help
Normal
Shadow Settings
No Shadow
Shadow Settings...
Draw
AutoShapes
Page 1 Sec 1 1/1 At Ln Col

Figure 18.14.
Adding a shadow to an object.

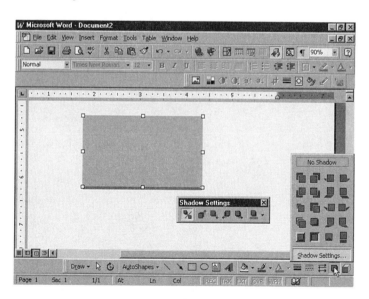

3D Effects

You can have a lot of fun with the 3D options. Figure 18.15 shows a simple rectangle with a gradient fill and a WordArt object that have 3D effects applied. Click the 3D button on the Drawing toolbar to apply a 3D style to a selected object. To further enhance or define the style, use the 3D Settings toolbar, shown in Figure 18.15; the 3D Settings toolbar can be accessed from the 3D button.

Figure 18.16 shows examples of 3D settings that have been modified. The 3D Settings toolbar lets you make these changes:

- Tilt—changes the angle from which the object is displayed. Increase the amount of tilt by clicking repeatedly on one of the Tilt buttons.
- Depth—increases the perspective or depth of the object. The higher the specified point size, the greater the depth.
- Direction—select from nine presets to display the object from different directions.
- Lighting—changes the direction the light hits the object. Also choose Bright, Normal, or Dim lighting settings.
- Surface—select from Wire Frame, Matte, Plastic, or Metal. (It may be hard to distinguish much difference other than brightness between the last three options in some objects.)
- 3D Color—changes the color of the 3D effect. This does not change the color of the original object. It only changes the color of the part of the picture that is added to make it look 3D.

Microsoft Word - Document2
File Edit View Insert Format Tools Table Window Help
Normal
FREE
3-D Settings
Draw
AutoShapes
Page 1 Sec 1 1/1 At 1" Ln 1 Col 1

Figure 18.15.
Apply 3D effects to drawing objects and WordArt.

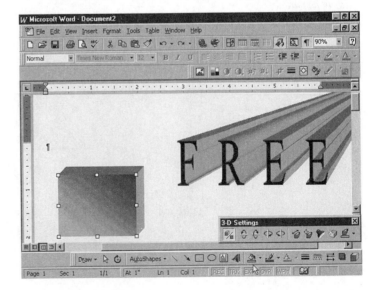

Figure 18.16.
3D settings offer many ways to modify 3D effects.

Tilt Down
Tilt Up
Depth 72 pt
Tilt Left
Tilt Right
Direction Change
Lighting Change
Wire Surface

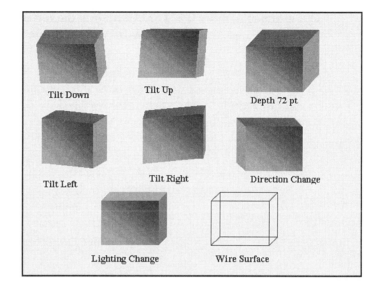

Summary

This hour offers a synopsis of the drawing tools. You can draw shapes or use AutoShapes. Enhance them with colors, shadows, and 3D effects. Label them with text boxes. Group them to move simultaneously or format them as a single object. Link text boxes to create a newspaper-like format that allows text to continue from a box on one page to a box on another page.

Q&A

Q I used linking text boxes to create a newsletter. I'd like to add a page reference in the text box such as "continued on page 3," but this shoves the text into the other box. How can I do this?

A You will probably not display the outline border for the text box in the final form. Simply type the *continued to* statement on the line below the first text box and the *continued from* statement on the line above the linked box on the other page.

Q I want to insert a rectangle and rotate it, then I want to put text in it, but I can't rotate the text in a text box. Is there any way around this?

A Instead of a text box, use one of the simple WordArt designs and position it in a rectangle. Group the rectangle and the WordArt, then rotate them as a single object.

Q **I'm trying to move the WordArt up into the rectangle, but I keep grabbing the rectangle instead. I can't get WordArt into the rectangle. Is there an easier way to do this?**

A If you have one of the drawing objects selected, pressing the Tab key allows you to move from one object to another. If there are four drawing objects on a page, you can easily toggle between them using the Tab key. Once an object is selected, it can be easily moved.

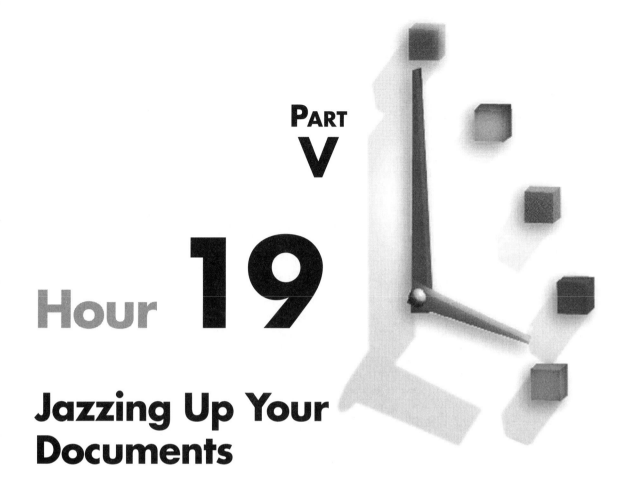

Hour 19

Jazzing Up Your Documents

This hour details some of the ways you can give your documents a cosmetic overhaul. Columns of different sizes can be applied to remodel a document and give it greater readability and eye appeal. Borders and shading can add accentuating lines, colors, and shading. They add the professional decorator's touch to documents.

The highlights of this hour include

- [ ] How to insert columns in only part of a page
- [ ] How to create columns of uneven widths
- [ ] How to apply new whole-page border designs
- [ ] How to use headers and footers for more than page numbers

Columns

Multicolumn documents can't be beat for readability. People are more likely to read the short lines they are used to seeing in newspapers and magazines. Most newsletters use some variation of columns for their basic design. Hour 5, "Working with Words," discusses the message that fonts portray. Serif fonts, for example, depict a more formal, conservative message. Likewise, column styles reflect a certain tone. A page layout consisting of two columns of equal size is seen as a conservative, formal style. A page layout with three columns of equal size, though still conservative, has a less formal, even friendly appearance. Uneven column widths portray a modern, informal tone.

Training documents with one narrow and one wide column allow for explanatory notes or definitions in the narrow column. Although the content may be very technical in nature, the layout makes it less formidable. This is an interesting format for reports of any kind. Use the short column as a sidebar with a sidelight story or explanation. The short column is often referred to as a *scholar's margin*.

You can work with columns in Normal view, but they will appear as one long column. Switch to Page Layout view to see the columns as they are actually laid out.

Placing Existing Text in Columns

The easiest method for inserting columns is to type the text first. As with many of the other Word functions, columns can be applied to text using a menu option or a toolbar button. To place text in columns using the toolbar button, perform the following steps:

1. Select the text to be placed in columns.
2. Click the Columns button on the Standard toolbar.
3. Drag the mouse across the number of columns you want, as in Figure 19.1.

As soon as you release the mouse button, the selected text is placed in columns, as shown in Figure 19.2. Notice that a double-dotted line with the words *Section Break (Continuous)* is placed between the title and the rest of the text. The title was not part of the selection that was placed in columns, so it is not formatted in columns.

Each section can be formatted differently, as outlined in Hour 8 "Setting Up the Page." For example, the title section could have .5-inch left and right margins and the other section could be set up with 1-inch margins.

If you had selected all the text and applied columns, the title would have appeared in the first column. You can correct this by selecting the title, then clicking the Columns button and selecting one column. Word will create the section break that divides the sections. You cannot mix the number of columns within a single section, but you can have different numbers of columns on the same page. When you use this method to place selected text in columns, Word inserts a continuous section break.

19

Figure 19.1.
Select the number of columns from the Columns button.

Microsoft Word - MAYOR.DOC
File Edit View Insert Format Tools Table Window Help
75%
Normal
Times New Roman
11
3 Columns
A·Message·from·Mayor·Brown¶
Boy, it sure has been a big year as your mayor, here in Bloomsburg. We have seen a lot of things happen since the floodwaters have begun to subside. Several families have moved back into their homes and have started the process of cleaning the mud off their furniture and floors. It takes a big mess like this to make us really appreciate the important things in life. As for myself, many of you may have noticed that I was pitching right in when it came to placing sandbags around the bank of the river. I placed more than 60 sandbags, so that's something to think about when it comes to electing a new mayor next month. My challenger, Mr. Veeblefinch, placed only 45 sandbags on the bank of the river. I think this clearly shows that his priorities are not entirely with this town's interests.¶
It was so rewarding to see little Timmy Smith save his puppy from imminent danger, as he grabbed the puppy from the top of his doghouse, just as the waters were cresting near the top of the doghouse roof. Mrs. Smith said that Timmy could never have accomplished this without the use of my powerboat, which I graciously loaned him that afternoon.¶
In related news, Mrs. Rebecca Lynch has announced her retirement as Assistant Librarian at the County Library. We wish her a pleasant retirement, and hope that she will enjoy the extra time she will have with her llamas at her llama ranch. She may also spend some time visiting with family members that she has not seen during her busy time as Assistant Librarian.¶
Page 1 Sec 1 1/1 At Ln Col REC TRK EXT OVR WPH

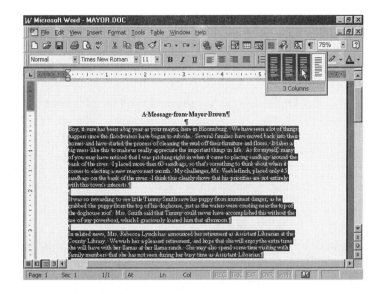

Figure 19.2.
A section break is inserted when selected text is placed in columns.

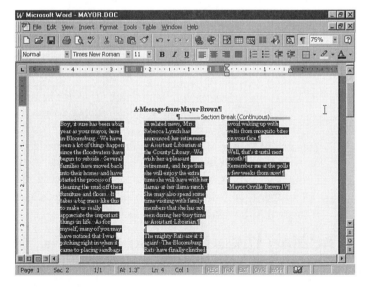

Microsoft Word - MAYOR.DOC
File Edit View Insert Format Tools Table Window Help
75%
Normal
Times New Roman
11
A·Message·from·Mayor·Brown¶
Section Break (Continuous)
Boy, it sure has been a big year as your mayor, here in Bloomsburg. We have seen a lot of things happen since the floodwaters have begun to subside. Several families have moved back into their homes and have started the process of cleaning the mud off their furniture and floors. It takes a big mess like this to make us really appreciate the important things in life. As for myself, many of you may have noticed that I was pitching right in when it came to placing sandbags
In related news, Mrs. Rebecca Lynch has announced her retirement as Assistant Librarian at the County Library. We wish her a pleasant retirement, and hope that she will enjoy the extra time she will have with her llamas at her llama ranch. She may also spend some time visiting with family members that she has not seen during her busy time as Assistant Librarian.¶
The mighty Rats are at it again! The Bloomsburg Rats have finally clinched
avoid waking up with welts from mosquito bites on your face.¶
Well, that's it until next month!¶
Remember me at the polls a few weeks from now!¶
-Mayor Orville Brown IV¶
Page 1 Sec 2 1/1 At 1.3" Ln 4 Col 1 REC TRK EXT OVR WPH

You can also add columns using the Format | Columns menu. If you want something other than the standard columns of equal width, use the menu rather than the toolbar button. There are many options that you can specify through the menu that can't be applied with the toolbar button.

Formatting Column Widths

Sometimes you'll want columns that are not all the same width. Use Format | Columns to vary the column options. Figure 19.3 shows the changes you can make from the Columns dialog box. At the top of dialog box are five presets:

- One—the standard single column used for most normal documents
- Two—two columns of equal size
- Three—three columns of equal size
- Left—two columns; the one on the left is half the size of the one on the right
- Right—two columns; the one on the right is half the size of the one on the left

The Left and Right presets use the scholar's margin layout mentioned earlier.

Columns
Presets
One
Two
Three
Left
Right
OK
Cancel
Number of columns:
3
Line between
Width and spacing
Preview
Col #:
Width:
Spacing:
1:
1.67"
0.5"
2:
1.67"
0.5"
3:
1.67"
Equal column width
Apply to:
Selected text
Start new column

Figure 19.3.
Use the Columns dialog to select column layouts.

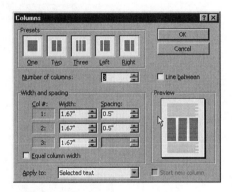

You are not limited to the preset options; you can design your own layout. Type a number or use the arrows in the Number of columns box. Specify the width of each of the columns in the Width and spacing section. Spacing is the amount of space between columns. You cannot specify any of these numbers unless the Equal column width box is unchecked. If it is checked, the columns cannot be different widths.

Adding Lines Between Columns

A nice touch is to add a line between columns. It's also a good separator between two sections of a publication. To insert a line, check the Line between option in the Columns dialog box to create a document such as the one in Figure 19.4. This document uses the Right preset, which lays out the columns with a scholar's margin on the right. Calendar information is added as a sidelight to the mayor's article on the left.

Microsoft Word - MAYOR.DOC
File Edit View Insert Format Tools Table Window Help
Normal
Times New Roman
10
75%
A Message from Mayor Brown
Boy, it sure has been a big year as your mayor, here in Bloomsburg. We have seen a lot of things happen since the floodwaters have begun to subside. Several families have moved back into their homes and have started the process of cleaning the mud off their furniture and floors. It takes a big mess like this to make us really appreciate the important things in life. As for myself, many of you may have noticed that I was pitching right in when it came to placing sandbags around the bank of the river. I placed more than 60 sandbags, so that's something to think about when it comes to electing a new mayor next month. My challenger, Mr. Veeblefinch, placed only 45 sandbags on the bank of the river. I think this clearly shows that his priorities are not entirely with this town's interests.
It was so rewarding to see little Timmy Smith save his puppy from imminent danger, as he grabbed the puppy from the top of his doghouse, just as the waters were cresting near the top of the doghouse roof. Mrs. Smith said that Timmy could never have accomplished this without the use of my powerboat, which I
Upcoming Calendar
May 14 – Next Council Meeting
May 18 – Next Lady Rats Game
June 1 – Founders Day Dinner
June 12 – Bridge Construction over Pine Creek begins
June 13 – City Budget Review
June 20 – Council Meeting
June 24 – Men Rats Baseball Game
Page 1 Sec 2 1/1 At 2.1" Ln 57 Col 17 REC TRK EXT OVR WPH

Figure 19.4.
Adding a line between columns.

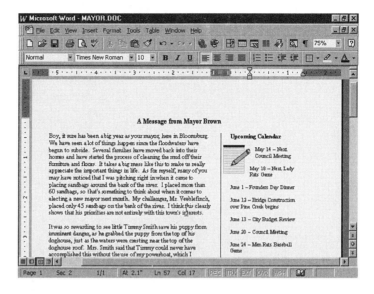

Adding Column Breaks

Sometimes the columns don't break in appropriate locations. To force a break at a certain point, position the cursor in the line ahead of the text you want to move to the next column. Select Insert | Break | Column. This forces the text from that point forward into the next column.

19

JUST A MINUTE

> Although this method is the quick and easy way to create a column break, later adjustments to text may cause some problems. Another way to ensure that text you want to keep together stays in one column is to select the text, then select Format | Paragraph. In the Line and Page Breaks tab, check the Keep lines together box. Keep lines together does not work for text that is in tables, however. You must use the Table | Cell Height and Width option. In the Row tab, uncheck the Allow row to break across pages box.

Figure 19.5 shows how the document in Figure 19.4 appeared as it was first typed. The Upcoming Calendar section needed to be placed in the second column. Placing the cursor just ahead of Upcoming Calendar and inserting a column break forced the calendar section into the second column.

Figure 19.5.
Inserting a column break to push text into another column.

Microsoft Word - MAYOR.DOC
File Edit View Insert Format Tools Table Window Help
Heading 1
Times New Roman
11
75%
Break
Insert
Page break
Column break
Section breaks
Next page
Even page
Continuous
Odd page
OK
Cancel
Don't forget that mosquito seas
Well, that's it until next month!
Remember me at the polls a few
-Mayor Orville Brown IV
Upcoming Calendar
May 14 – Next Council Meeting
May 18 – Next Lady Rats Game
Page 1 Sec 2 1/1 At 9.1" Ln 48 Col 1

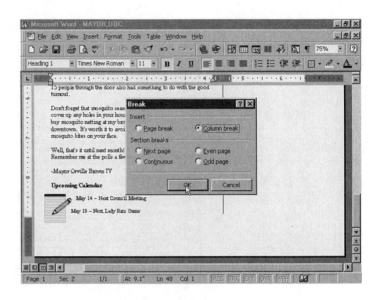

Adjusting Columns from the Ruler

The system for moving columns on a page is similar to the methods used for moving columns in a table. If the ruler is not visible, select Ruler from the View menu. If you position the mouse pointer on the ruler in the gray area between two columns, the pointer changes to a double-headed arrow that says Move Column. Click and drag the Move Column marker either to the right or the left. To see the column measurements as you drag the column marker, hold down the Alt key while you drag the marker (see Figure 19.6).

Figure 19.6.
Resizing columns from the horizontal ruler.

Microsoft Word - MAYOR.DOC
File Edit View Insert Format Tools Table Window Help
Body Text
Times New Roman
11
75%
3.36"
2.76"
1"
A Message from Mayor Brown
Section Break (Continuous)
Upcoming Calendar
May 14 – Next Council Meeting
May 18 – Next Lady Rats Game
June 1 – Founders Day Dinner
June 12 – Bridge Construction over Pine Creek begins
June 13 – City Budget Review
June 20 – Council Meeting
June 24 – Men Rats Baseball
Page 1 Sec 2 1/1 At 2.2" Ln 9 Col 62

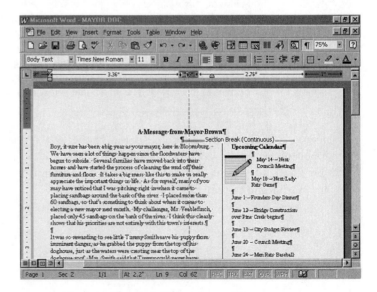

Borders and Shading

Borders are frames and lines that set off a title, divide sections, outline parts of a table, or in other ways make use of lines to create visual breaks. Shading can be used with or without borders to create similar effects of division or accent. Borders and shading are also ways to enhance tables.

Adding Emphasis Lines

When working with borders and shading, it's a good idea to bring up the Tables and Borders toolbar for quick access to many of the borders and shading features. To display the Tables and Borders toolbar, click the Tables and Borders button on the Standard toolbar or select View | Toolbars | Tables and Borders from the menu. Some of these toolbar features were covered in Hour 14, "Working with Tables."

To add a line under a heading, use the Tables and Borders toolbar or the Format | Borders and Shading menu. To insert a line using the toolbar, perform the following steps:

1. Select the paragraph that will be underlined.
2. Click the Line Style drop-down list (see Figure 19.7) to choose a line style. The pointer changes to the Draw Table pencil. Don't be confused by this. As soon as the pointer moves back to the Tables and Borders toolbar, the pointer reverts back to the selection arrow.

Figure 19.7.
Selecting a line style.

Borders
Line Weight
Line Color
Line Style
Tables and Borders

19

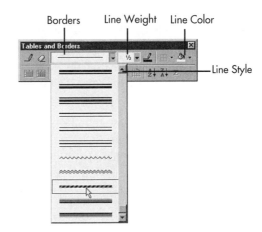

The line selected in Figure 19.7 is one of the new lines added to Word 97's expanded collection of line styles.

3. Click the arrow beside the Borders button for a drop-down list of the border choices (see Figure 19.8). Select the Bottom Border option.

Most of the line styles can be weighted or made thicker by changing the measurement in the Line Weight box. Some of the styles, like the one in Figure 19.8, are preset to a certain size and can't be changed.

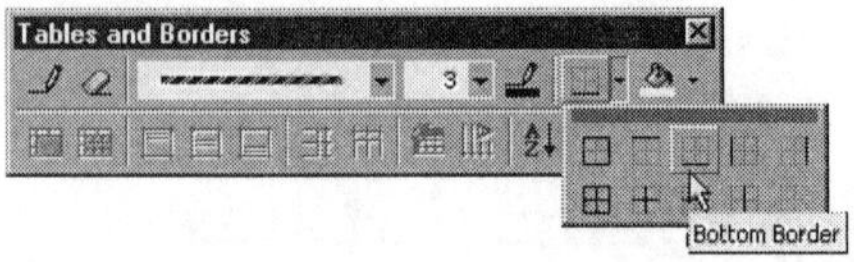
Tables and Borders
3
Bottom Border

Figure 19.8.
Selecting a bottom border.

If you have a color printer and want to add a touch of color, click Border Color to change the color of a line. If you decide you don't like the line and want to change it, do the following:

1. Select the paragraph to which the line style is applied.
2. Select a new style from the Line Style list.
3. Make changes to line weight and border color, if desired.
4. Click the Border icon to activate the new line style (in this example, the Border icon displays the Bottom Border option).

If you want to delete a line, position the cursor in the paragraph to which the line is applied and click the Borders button to remove the line. The Borders button appears lighted when a line or border is applied to a paragraph. Clicking it darkens it and removes the line from the selected paragraph.

Placing Boxes Around Text

To place a box around a paragraph, use the same technique as for creating a line, except select the Outside Border option from the Borders drop-down list. First select the paragraph. Select a line style, line weight, and color as you did for a line, then click the arrow beside the Borders button to display the drop-down list of borders. Select the Outside Border option.

If you want to place a box around the text in a title but not the whole paragraph, select the text in the line without the paragraph mark at the end. After you select a line style, weight, and color, and click the Borders button to select Outside Border, the box encloses only the text. Figure 19.9 shows an example of a border applied to the paragraph in the first line as well as an example of a border applied to the selected text in the second line.

If you don't like the way either of these options looks, you can always set the line style and use the Draw Table feature to draw a table with a single cell and type the text in it, but it would probably be easier to use a text box. Text boxes are more moveable.

Figure 19.9.
Placing a box around a paragraph or a text selection.

Microsoft Word - Document6
File Edit View Insert Format Tools Table Window Help
88%
Normal
Times New Roman
12
Tables and Borders
Chapter One
Chapter One
Page 1 Sec 1 1/1 At 1.6" Ln 3 Col 1 REC TRK EXT OVR WPH

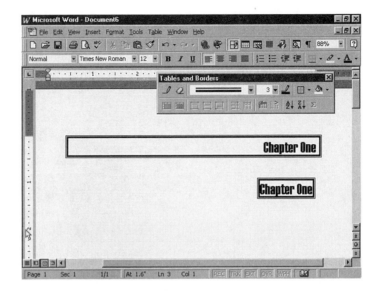

Full Page Borders

If you're responsible for the one-page flyers, announcements, and invitations for your business or organization, you probably keep looking for borders to accent the entire page. You may have even resorted to buying packaged clip art that includes borders. Microsoft must have recognized that this is one of the big things people do with a word processor. Word 97 has added a Page Borders tab to the Format | Borders and Shading options. To add a page border:

1. Select Format | Borders and Shading.
2. Click the Page Borders tab.
3. Select from any of the line styles, or choose one of the art borders (see Figure 19.10).
4. Click OK to apply the border style.

Figure 19.11 shows the art border applied to the one-page message from the mayor. Even though there are lots of border and shading options, it's always better to err on the side of too little than too much ornamentation. A little accent dresses up your document; a lot makes it look like a menagerie. A simpler border style would have been a better choice for this document. This border looks like something more appropriate for a certificate or award. It seems out of place in a newsletter from the mayor.

Borders and Shading
Borders
Page Border
Shading
Setting:
None
Box
Shadow
3-D
Custom
Style:
Color:
Auto
Width:
16 pt
Art:
Preview
Click on diagram below or use buttons to apply borders
Apply to:
Whole document
Options...
Show Toolbar
OK
Cancel

Figure 19.10.
Apply new full-page art borders.

Microsoft Word - MAYOR.DOC
File Edit View Insert Format Tools Table Window Help
Body Text
Times New Roman
11
70%
A Message from Mayor Brown
Upcoming Calendar
May 14 – Next Council Meeting
May 18 – Next Lady Rats Game
June 1 – Founders Day Dinner
June 12 – Bridge Construction over Pine Creek begins
June 13 – City Budget Review
June 20 – Council Meeting
June 24 – Men Rats Baseball Game
Page 1
Sec 2
1/1
At 1.8"
Ln 6
Col 1

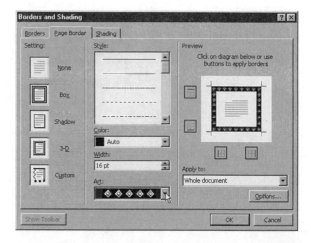

Figure 19.11.
A whole-page border added to a one-page newsletter.

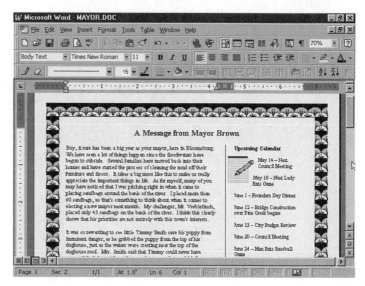

Extra Border Options

The Borders tab in the Format | Borders and Shading dialog box gives you a few extra options that don't appear in the Tables and Borders toolbar. You can apply shadow and 3D effects to borders. Click one of the icons under Setting to choose a border effect or remove an existing border. The dialog box offers options similar to those on the toolbar to apply a line style, color, and weight. Select which lines you want to apply borders to by clicking the Border buttons in the Preview box or clicking the edges of the sample picture where you want to apply lines. If a border is already applied and you want to remove specific border lines, click the Border buttons for the lines you want to delete, or click the lines themselves.

Shading

Shading can be applied with or without a border. As with most other features, you get the fast food from the toolbars, but the menus offer a full-course meal. The most common shades are available from the Shading Color drop-down list on the Tables and Borders toolbar. Select other shading options, including several patterns, from Format | Borders and Shading in the Shading tab (see Figure 19.12).

Borders and Shading
Borders
Page Border
Shading
Fill
None
Dk Grid
Dk Trellis
Lt Horizontal
Lt Vertical
Lt Dwn Diagonal
Lt Up Diagonal
Lt Grid
Lt Trellis
20%
Color:
Black
Preview
Apply to:
Cell
Show Toolbar
OK
Cancel

Figure 19.12.
Select shading colors and patterns from the Borders and Shading dialog.

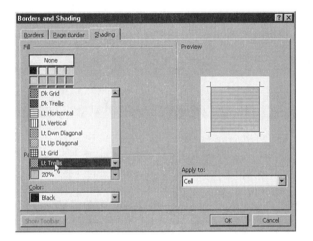

The Shading button on the Table and Borders toolbar looks like the Fill Color bucket on the Drawing toolbar. They work in the same way, but the shading color is applied to the text layer, while the fill color is applied to objects on the graphics layer. You can't use them interchangeably.

Figure 19.13 shows how black shading with white text is used in the Professional Report template to accent the chapter number and a title. These accents draw the reader to the page by creating focal points.

Microsoft Word - Document11 - Report
File Edit View Insert Format Tools Table Window Help
Close Window
Company Name
Arial Black
16
Chapter
1
Blue Sky Marketing Plan
Blue Sky's Best Opportunity for East Region Expansion
How to Modify This Report
To create your own version of this template, select File New and choose this template. Be sure to indicate "template" as the document type in the bottom right corner of the dialog. You can then:
1) Insert your company name and address in place of the text on the cover page by clicking once and typing.
Page 1 Sec 2 2/3 At Ln Col REC TRK EXT OVR WPH

Figure 19.13.
White text with black shading creates accents for the page.

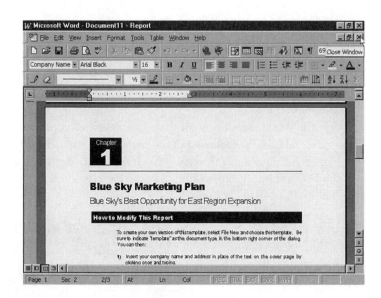

Special Effects with Headers and Footers

Use borders and shading in headers and footers to provide a sense of consistency throughout a document. Figure 19.14 shows a header that was created with borders and shading. It has a pushbutton look that is accentuated by the font that appears to be etched in the button.

First Page Header
Word 97
June 23, 1997
Header and Footer
Insert AutoText
Close
Close Full Screen

Figure 19.14.
Creating a 3D header.

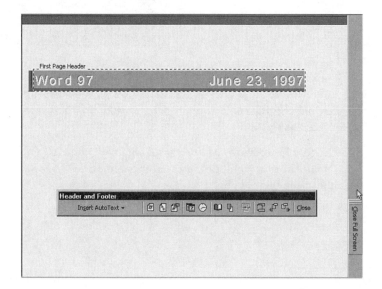

To create this special-effect header, do the following:

1. Select View | Header and Footer.

2. In the header pane, use the Tables and Borders toolbar to add medium-gray shading by clicking the Shading Color button and selecting one of the shades of gray.

3. Select one of the new shadowed lines from the drop-down list of line styles and increase the line weight to make it one or two sizes thicker.

4. Click the Borders button and select Bottom Border and Left Border. This gives the 3D appearance.

5. Add text to the header using a sans serif font such as Arial or Helvetica, and increase the font size. Use Format | Font to apply the engrave effect.

6. Select File | Page Setup. In the Margins tab, increase the Header margin to about .8 inch to bring the header down slightly.

Use the same technique to create a footer in a similar style. If you want a scaled down version of the first page header to appear on the rest of the pages of the document, do the following:

1. Select File | Page Setup.

2. In the Page Layout tab, check the Different first page box under Headers and Footers.

   Figure 19.15 shows a sample footer and second page header created to go with the first page header. There is no need to re-create the border and shading each time.

3. Copy and paste the first page header to the second page header, then replace the existing text. Do the same for the footer.

4. Add a page number to page two so that the document will start numbering on this page.

You could also use the drawing tools to dress up the header and footer. Figure 19.16 was created with a rectangle formatted with the 3D effects, a WordArt title, and a text box with no line or fill for the date. The date font was enhanced with an outline effect.

Insert your company logo or other trademarks that uniquely identify you or your organization in the header or footer.

19

Header and Footer
Insert AutoText
Close
First Page Footer
An Up-to-Speed Seminar
Close Full Screen
Header
Word 97
2

Figure 19.15.
Coordinating the footers and second page header.

Microsoft Word - Document3
File Edit View Insert Format Tools Table Window Help
Header
Times New Roman
12
Can't Redo
100%
Header
Word 97
June 23, 1997
Insert AutoText
Close
Page 1 Sec 1 1/2 At 0.5" Ln Col 1

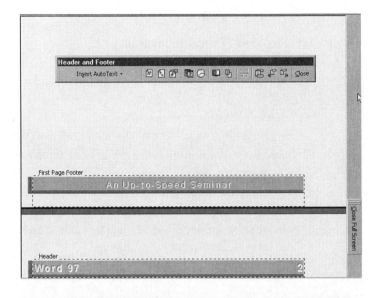

Figure 19.16.
Creating a header with the drawing tools.

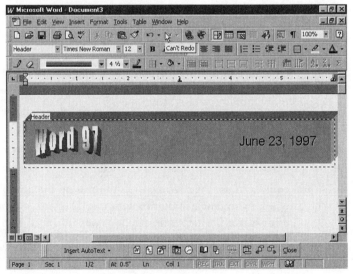

TIME SAVER

Create personalized stationery with monograms to use or give as gifts. Use Word's alphabet clip art or create your own with WordArt. Creating a single letter in WordArt usually renders a distorted image, but using two or three initials or a last name looks pretty impressive. These would not need to be placed in a header if you're printing out the stationery for gifts. It works well, however, if you are going to type the letter and print it out

> with the header at the same time. This would be a good candidate for a template.

Summary

This hour shows the functionality of columns and how they can change the look and tone of a document. With a little help from borders and shading, documents can move from plain to professional with minimal effort. Borders and shading create natural visual breaks and accents. The new page borders can frame certificates, flyers, and announcements with fun or fancy designs. Headers and footers can be used for more than inserting page numbers and dates. Use them to insert titles, borders, and graphics.

Q&A

Q **I tried to change the border around a text box, but it seems to be inside the text box. When I make the box bigger, the border doesn't move or get bigger.**

A You must have applied the border from the Tables and Borders toolbar. This formats a border only around selected text. Text box borders are applied through the Format | Text Box menu. The Format Text Box dialog box includes the options for lines that can be applied to text boxes.

Q **I like to use borders, but the lines are always too close to the text. Is there any way to get more space between the lines and the text?**

A Yes. Select the paragraph or section that includes the border. Select Format | Borders and Shading. In the Borders tab, click Options. You can specify (by point sizes) how much whitespace is placed between the border and the text. Select space for top, bottom, left, or right or any combination of the sides (for example, you may only want more space left and right but not on the top and bottom).

Q **I changed a line style using the Tables and Borders toolbar, but the line didn't change.**

A You would assume changing the style would change the selected object, but you need to click the Borders icon to reapply the new line style.

19

PART
V

Hour 20

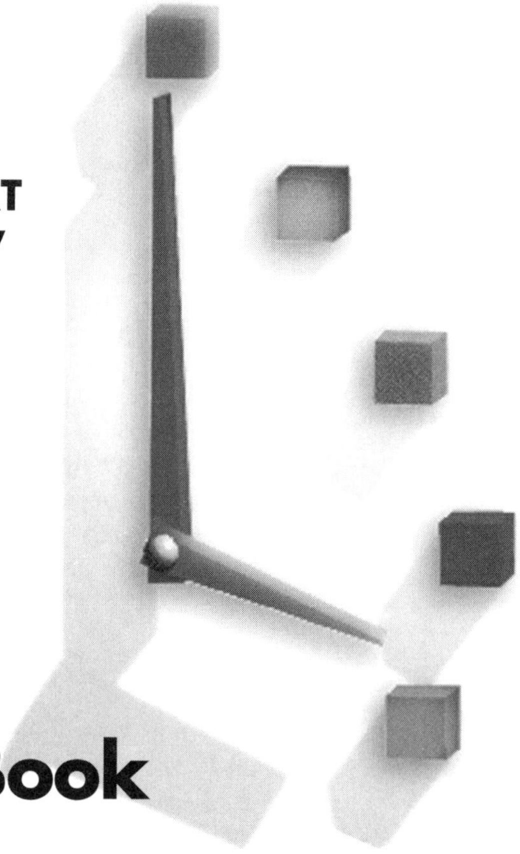

I Could Write a Book

by Ruel T. Hernandez

If you have been itching to write the next best-selling book, you can do so with Word 97. In fact, Word 97 is being used to write this book!

You may already have all the basic text written for the main part of your book or document, but now you want to set up a professional-looking table of contents, index, footnotes, and captions for pictures. Can you do all of that with Word 97? Yes, you can! And that's what I cover in this jam-packed chapter. These are the sorts of things you will need to know how to do if you are writing a book, a school thesis or paper, or some other document requiring a table of contents, index, footnotes, or captions.

So in this hour, you will learn how to do the following:

- Set up a table of contents
- Set up an index
- Set up footnotes and endnotes
- Set up captions for figures
- Set up a table of figures

Creating a Table of Contents

A table of contents will help you inform readers about how your book or document is organized. What is really nice about Word 97 is that it can build the table of contents for you.

Check the Headings

To set up the style area width so you can see the style of the headings and text in a column on the left side of your Word 97 screen, do the following:

1. Select Tools | Options.
2. On the View tab, set the Style Area Width option in the Windows section at the bottom of the dialog to .5" or .6" and click OK. (To turn off the style area, reset the style area width to 0.) You should see a column to the left with various styles listed.

Instead of viewing the style area, you can switch to Outline view to check the headings. Nevertheless, you may find viewing the style area while in Normal view to be very convenient.

To ensure that the headings in your document are correct, you should look at the heading levels listed in the style area column. Also look at the style settings for the paragraphs in your document; make sure they are set to normal or body text so they will not show up in the table of contents. You can switch between Normal view and Outline view to demote/promote the headings. If any paragraph in your document is set to a heading level, demote the paragraph to body text so the paragraph will not show up in the table of contents.

Selecting and Inserting the Table of Contents

To begin creating a table of contents, follow these steps:

1. Set up the Styles view area as discussed previously. Alternatively, you can check the headings by switching back and forth between Normal view and Outline view.
2. Move your cursor to wherever you want to place your table of contents and then click Insert | Index and Tables.

   You might want to insert a new page at the beginning of your document by going to the top of your document and pressing Ctrl+Enter to insert a page break. Place your cursor before the place where you want the page to break. You may want to press Enter a few times to put in some blank lines.

   To change the page number format for the table of contents pages, select Insert | Page Numbers and then click the Format button on the Page Numbers dialog. This invokes a Page Number Format dialog; in the Number Format pull-down selection list, you can select different page numbering formats. For instance, you can select the i, ii, iii page number format and then switch to regular numbers for the regular pages of your document after the table of contents.

3. Click the Table of Contents tab; you should then see a dialog similar to the one shown in Figure 20.1.

Index and Tables
Index
Table of Contents
Table of Figures
Table of Authorities
Formats:
From template
Classic
Distinctive
Fancy
Modern
Formal
Simple
Preview
Heading 1 1
Heading 2 3
Heading 3 5
Heading 4 7
Heading 5 10
Heading 6 12
Heading 7 14
OK
Cancel
Options...
Modify...
Show page numbers
Right align page numbers
Show levels:
9
Tab leader:

Figure 20.1.
Select a table of contents format for your book or document.

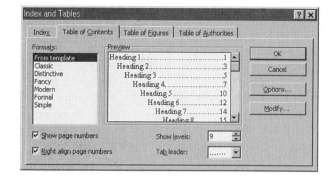

4. From this dialog, select a format, such as From template.
5. You should adjust the number of heading levels by increasing the number of levels in the Show Levels area on the Table of Contents tab. The default is three levels. If you leave the number of levels at three, your table of contents will show only the top three heading levels. Increase the number of levels shown if you want a more thorough table of contents.
6. You can then select the tab leader. A tab leader can be blank space, periods or dots, dashes, or a solid underline between a heading and the page number. A tab leader helps the reader trace the heading to the appropriate page number.
7. Click OK, and a table of contents will be inserted in your document.

There are also Options and Modify buttons on the Table of Contents tab on the Index and Tables dialog. If you click the Options button, you will get the Table of Contents Options dialog. Do so if you want to include paragraphs with styles other than the usual heading styles in the table of contents. You may wish to use the Modify button if you want to modify the table of contents format, but you will only be able to modify the From template format.

If you have the style area column enabled, you will see that elements in the table of contents are designated by the `TOC` style label with a number indicating the heading level. For instance, `TOC 1` would indicate a TOC heading with heading level 1. You can change the fonts or edit the text in the table of contents as you would any other text in your Word 97 document. For instance, you could select some text in the table of contents, select Format | Font, and then change the font.

As you can see, making a table of contents is easy! Figure 20.2 shows you a sample table of contents.

Microsoft Word - SAMPLE.doc
File Edit View Insert Format Tools Table Window Help
Normal
Courier New
10
Chapter 2 4
REGULATORY THEORY 4
Traditional Industry Capture Theory 4
Regulators Refute Industry Capture 6
Telephone Deregulation Model 9
Telecommunications in the "Public Interest" 13
Regulatory Influence Models 14
Changing Environment 18
Modified Final Judgment 18
Third Computer Inquiry 20
1987 Modified Final Judgment Review 22
COMPUTER ONLINE SERVICES AND SYSTEMS 29
Scope of Services and Systems 29
Online Activity and Political Impact 35
Enhanced Service Providers Proposal 39
Lessons of Computer III 44
Page 80 Sec 15 89/89 At 3.6" Ln 18 Col 1 REC TRK EXT OVR WPH

Figure 20.2.
A sample table of contents using the From template format.

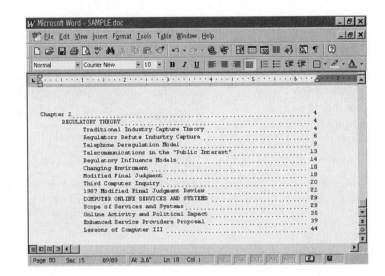

Building an Index

Using Word 97, you can set up an index to help readers find topics in your book or document. An *index* is an alphabetized list of words and phrases that includes the page numbers where each word or phrase can be found. Like a table of contents, an index can help readers find certain topics right away, but an index gives a reader more specific direction on where to find certain items.

Main Entries for the Index (and Generating a Quick Index)

To build an index for your book or document, do the following:

1. You'll probably want to begin your index on a separate page at the end of your document. Place your cursor where you want the index to appear, then press Ctrl+Enter to place a page break to start a new page. You might want to center the word *Index* at the top of the new page and press the Enter key a few times to insert some blank lines.
2. Click Insert | Index and Tables, and click the Index tab. You should see a dialog similar to the one shown in Figure 20.3.
3. Click Mark Entry to invoke the Mark Index Entry dialog (see Figure 20.4).

Index and Tables
Index
Table of Contents
Table of Figures
Table of Authorities
Type
Indented
Run-in
Preview
Aristotle 2
Asteroid belt .... See Jupiter
Atmosphere
Earth
exosphere 4
ionosphere 3
mesosphere 3–4
OK
Cancel
Mark Entry...
AutoMark...
Modify...
Formats:
From template
Classic
Fancy
Modern
Headings for accented letters
Right align page numbers
Columns:
1
Tab leader:

Figure 20.3.
Select an index format for your book or document.

Mark Index Entry
Main entry:
Subentry:
Options
Cross-reference:
See
Current page
Page range
Bookmark:
Page number format:
Bold
Italic
This dialog box stays open so that you can mark multiple index entries.
Mark
Cancel
Mark All

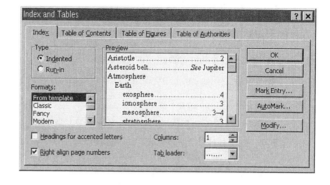

Figure 20.4.
Enter the index entries you want listed in your index.

4. In the Mark Index Entry dialog, in the Main entry blank, type or simply select the words from your document that you want indexed. (The Mark Index Entry dialog will stay open so you can also type other words or select words or phrases in your document to be inserted in the Main entry blank.)
5. Click the Mark button on the Mark Index Entry dialog. You may find that blocking words or phrases and then clicking the Mark button is an easy way to build your index. For each index entry you make, you will see an entry like the following inserted in your text after the word or phrase being indexed:

   {XE "word or phrase"}

   The words or phrase within the quotation marks is what is indexed. Onscreen, the index entry would have a dotted underline to indicate that it is a hidden font code.

20

TIME SAVER

To hide this code (and other formatting codes), click the Paragraph icon on the Standard toolbar under the menu bar. (Or you can hide the formatting codes by clicking Tools | Options and, on the View tab, unclicking Hidden Text or All in the Nonprinting Characters section of the View tab.)

6. After you have marked all the words or phrases that you want to index, close the Mark Index Entry dialog.

Subentries for the Index

You can also enter a subentry of a main entry. To do this, perform the following steps:

1. Position your cursor after the words or phrase in the text that you want to be a subentry. Do not block the words or phrase.

2. On the Mark Index Entry dialog, enter the words or phrase in the Subentry field, and enter the words or phrase for the main entry in the Main entry field. For instance, if you have a main entry for dogs and you want a subentry for show dogs, place your cursor after the words *show dogs* in your document. On the Mark Index Entry dialog, enter the word dogs in the Main entry field, then enter the words show dogs in the Subentry field.

3. Click the Mark button. Repeat these steps for other subentries you might want to make.

Cross-References

You can enter cross-references in the Mark Index Entry dialog. A *cross-reference* is used to alert the reader to similar items that are related to an indexed item. To make a cross-reference, perform the following steps:

1. Place your cursor by the words or phrase you want cross-referenced (you can block this text if you want this to be a main entry). Make sure the words or phrase show up in the Main entry or Subentry field (with the appropriate main entry typed in for a subentry).

2. After the word *See* in the Cross-reference field, type the cross-reference. Be sure the Cross-reference option is enabled.

Current Page, Page Range, and Bookmarks

The Current page option (the default) indicates that the index entry is to be on the page your cursor is currently on. The Page range option lets you specify a range of pages, such as pages 32 to 39, where a particular topic is discussed. The Page range option requires that you insert bookmarks prior to marking text for the index. A *bookmark* is a selection of text that you mark for the page range. This is how you would insert a bookmark and set up a page range:

1. Click Insert | Bookmark (you might have to click the down arrow at the bottom of the Insert menu to find Bookmark).

2. On the Bookmark dialog, type a bookmark name, and then click the Add button.

3. Place your cursor by the text you want to index (or select the text) and choose Insert | Index and Tables.

20

4. Enter the main entry (and subentry, if applicable), then click the Page range option

5. Select the bookmark.

6. Click the Mark button to insert the index code.

The Mark All Button

Think of the Mark All button as a shotgun approach to marking all the occurrences of a word or phrase in a document. If you want every occurrence of a word or phrase in a document to be listed in the index, you would use the Mark All button to insert an index entry code next to each and every instance of the word or phrase in the document. For instance, if you are writing a document about dogs and you have repeated the words *dog house* many times in the document, you can use the Mark All button to mark all of the instances of that phrase without having to search for each instance. This is probably one of the easier ways to build an index; you may find yourself using the Mark All button quite a bit. To use the Mark All button, do the following:

1. Select or place your cursor on the text you want to index.

2. In the Mark Index Entry dialog, ensure that the text is in the appropriate Main entry and Subentry fields

3. Click the Mark All button.

Page Number Format

You can set the index page number format to bold, italic, or both. To do so, simply click the Bold and/or Italic options on the Mark Index Entry dialog.

Creating the Index

To create the Index, do the following:

1. Mark all the index entries.

2. Place your cursor wherever you wish to place the index (usually at the end of your book or document).

3. Click Insert | Index and Tables.

4. On the Index tab, select the index format you want to use, such as the From template format.

5. Select how many columns you want for your index. Word 97 selects two columns as the default. You may instead want to set up the index for one column.

6. Click OK.

The index will be couched between a couple of hidden section break lines that will not print. You can change the fonts and manipulate the index as you would the rest of your Word 97 document. Figure 20.5 shows a sample index.

20

Microsoft Word - SAMPLE.doc
File Edit View Insert Format Tools Table Window Help
Normal
Courier New
12
Page Break
INDEX
Section Break (Continuous)
American Telephone, 2
Baldwin Theory, 2
Enhanced Service Provider, 2
Federal Communications Commission, 6
Industry capture, 7
Modified Final Judgment, 18
Pressure group influence, 4
Online Providers, 4
Regulatory Hearings, 10
Special interest group process, 5
Systems and Services, 29
Telephone deregulation model, 8
Third Computer Inquiry, 20
Traditional industry capture, 4
Page 63 Sec 15 72/72 At 1" Ln 1 Col 6
REC TRK EXT OVR WPH

Figure 20.5.
A sample index created using the From template format.

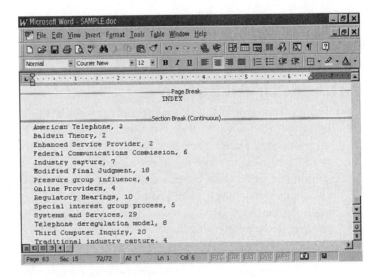

To change the formatting of the index, you must adjust the index's style. You must select the From template format to be able to make any formatting changes. This is what you do:

1. From the Index tab on the Index and Tables dialog, select the From template format and click the Modify button.
2. In the Style dialog, select the style you want to change and then click the Modify button.
3. In the Modify Style dialog, make whatever changes you desire and then click OK.
4. Repeat this for any other formatting changes you would want to make. When you are finished, click the Apply button.
5. Click the OK button to insert your index.

Creating a Concordance File

An easy way to build an index is to create a concordance file. To do so, you must create a new document and make a two-column table:

1. Start with a new blank document.
2. Select Table | Insert Table. The default is two columns by two rows, which is acceptable for our purposes. Click OK.

3. In the first box in the first column, type the words or phrase for which you want Word to search and mark index entries in your document. Press Tab to move to the next column.

4. Type the index entry to correspond with the text in the first column. This is what you want to appear in the index. Press Tab. If there is no second row of boxes, pressing the Tab key will create a new row for you.

5. Repeat the previous two steps for each index reference and entry.

6. Save your concordance file.

7. Open the document you want to index.

8. Click Insert | Index and Tables.

9. Activate the Index tab.

10. Click the AutoMark button.

11. Type the name of your concordance file (or search for and select your concordance file).

12. Click the Open button. Word will input an index entry code on each occurrence of the words or phrases you want indexed.

13. Select the place where your index is to appear, such as at the end of your document. You may want to press Ctrl+Enter to start a new page.

14. Click Insert | Index and Tables.

15. Activate the Index tab.

16. Select your index format, number of columns, and so on (as described previously), then click OK to insert your index.

Many users feel that creating a concordance file is the easiest way to build an index in Word 97. This is particularly true if you are working on a large document with numerous words and phrases you want to index. But you may want to use the other index-building techniques when you work on smaller documents.

Footnotes and Endnotes

Footnotes and endnotes are for documenting your sources for facts or quotations you have in your book or other document. *Footnotes* can be of the usual type that you find at the bottom of pages, or they can be set up as *endnotes*, which are placed at the end of your document.

Inserting a Footnote/Endnote

To insert a footnote/endnote, perform the following steps:

20

1. Place your cursor at the place where you want to indicate the presence of a footnote (usually after a quotation or a fact whose source you want to note).
2. Click Insert | Footnote and, from the Footnote and Endnote panel, click either Footnote or Endnote; your screen should then be divided into two sections (as shown in Figure 20.6). In the main text (upper) area, type your main text. In the footnote/endnote (lower) area, type your footnote/endnote text.

Microsoft Word - Document4
File Edit View Insert Format Tools Table Window Help
Normal
Courier New
20
This is where you type in the main text for your document.1
Footnotes All Footnotes
Close
1This is where you type in your footnote....
Page 1 Sec 1 1/1 At 1.3" Ln 2 Col 1 REC TRK EXT OVR WP

Figure 20.6.
Word will divide the screen so that you type your main text in the upper area and your footnotes/endnotes in the lower area.

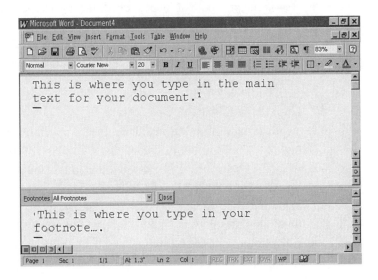

3. In the footnote/endnote entry pane area, type your footnote or endnote.
4. Click the Close button when you finish typing your footnote or endnote. A superscript footnote/endnote reference number should show up in the main body of your text.

If you are in Page Layout view, you may notice that the mouse pointer turns into a flag when passed over a footnote/endnote number. You may also see a screen tip with text of your footnote/endnote. This can be helpful if you need a quick reference to the text you have entered.

Editing and Deleting a Footnote/Endnote

To edit a footnote/endnote, double-click the reference number. The editing pane will show up at the bottom of the screen, and you can edit the footnote/endnote. Alternatively, you can click View | Footnote or View | Endnote to open up the footnote/endnote pane and then search for the footnote/endnote you want to edit.

If you have a lot of footnotes/endnotes, you can use the Go To command:

1. Click Edit | Go To (or use the Ctrl+G shortcut command).

2. Select Footnote or Endnote.

3. Type the footnote/endnote number you want to edit.

Delete a footnote/endnote by deleting the footnote/endnote reference number in the main text of your document.

Numbers or Symbols

Word 97 will automatically number your footnotes/endnotes. You can select different numbering or lettering options in this way:

1. Click the Options button on the Footnote and Endnote dialog. A Note Options dialog will pop up. The two tabs, one for All Footnotes and the other All Endnotes, are identical.

2. Select where you want to place the footnotes/endnotes by clicking the Place At pull-down selection list.

3. Select the numbering format.

4. Select whether to start your footnotes/endnotes at number 1 or at a different number.

5. Select whether to have the numbering be continuous, restart with each section of your document, or restart with each new page of your document.

6. After you finish, click OK two times.

7. Type your footnote/endnote text in the footnote/endnote entry pane area at the bottom of the screen. You may want to be in Normal view to see the footnote/endnote entry pane area. If you switch to Normal view and don't see the footnote/endnote entry pane area, select View | Footnotes to see the area where you can type your footnote/endnote.

8. Click Close after you finish typing your footnote/endnote.

You'll usually want to use numbers when creating footnotes/endnotes, but there may be times when you want to use symbols instead. You can use symbols instead of numbers, but you must change the symbols manually. That is, if you use numbers, the numbers increment automatically from footnote to footnote (or endnote to endnote). If you use a symbol such as an asterisk (*) to designate one footnote/endnote and then another symbol to designate the next footnote/endnote, you must manually select which symbol you want to use for each footnote/endnote like so:

1. Click Symbol.

2. Select the symbol you want to use.

3. Click OK.

20

If you have many footnotes or endnotes, consider using automatic numbering. If you use a random combination of symbols, you may confuse yourself or your reader.

Moving and Copying a Footnote/Endnote

Whenever you move text in Word 97, footnotes/endnotes associated with the text you are moving should move with it. If the footnotes/endnotes do not move with their associated text, locate the footnote/endnote reference number you want to move. Select that reference number and move it to the location where you want to place it. It's just as easy as moving regular text.

Similarly, you can copy an existing footnote/endnote to another location in your book or document. Again, find the reference number for the footnote/endnote, select that reference number, copy it, go to the new location in your document, and then paste it in. Word 97 will automatically give the copied footnote/endnote a new number. If you want to edit the copied footnote/endnote, do so as you would any other footnote/endnote.

Footnote/Endnote Separators and the Continuation Notice

The footnote/endnote editing pane has a pull-down menu that lets you switch between editing footnotes/endnotes, changing the footnote/endnote separator or continuation separator, and editing the footnote/endnote continuation notice. Think of these as different views. You can change the separators, but you might want to stick with the defaults. That way, you'll probably only have to edit the footnotes/endnotes and set up the footnote/endnote continuation notice. For the continuation notice, where the footnote or endnote continues on the next page, enter something like (Continued next page) in the footnote/endnote continuation notice field of the editing pane.

Captions for Pictures, Graphs, and Diagrams

Captions are for figures (such as pictures, graphs, and diagrams) in your book or document. A *caption* is like a text description of a figure to help the reader understand what the picture or diagram is and why it appears in your book or document. For instance, say you're writing a document about dogs, and you insert a picture of an award-winning show dog. You may want to use a caption to state the breed (and maybe the name) of the dog. To insert a caption, select Insert | Caption. This invokes a dialog similar to the one shown in Figure 20.7.

20

Caption
Caption:
Figure 1.1
Options
Label:
Figure
New Label...
Position:
Below selected item
Delete Label
Numbering...
AutoCaption...
OK
Cancel

Figure 20.7.
Captions help you describe a picture or diagram for your book or document.

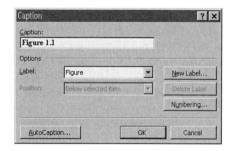

Captions and Tables of Figures

After you set the captions in your document, you can set up a table of figures, which is similar to a table of contents except that it lists only figures. You must first decide where you want to place the table of figures. You might place it after the table of contents or the index. To set up a table of figures, do the following:

1. If you want to place the table of figures after the table of contents, press Ctrl+Enter to start a new page, press Enter once or a few times, and then press Ctrl+Enter again to separate the table of figures from the subsequent text in your document.
2. Click Insert | Index and Tables from the menu bar.
3. On the Table of Figures tab, select a table style, such as From template.
4. Click OK.

Summary

In this hour, you have learned how to set up a table of contents and an index, to create footnotes and endnotes, and to assign captions for figures to illustrate your best-selling book, award-winning report, or grade A+ paper.

Q&A

Q Why can't I see all of the levels of my table of contents?

A Increase the number of levels to show in your table of contents by clicking Insert | Index and Tables and, in the Show Levels area, increasing the number of levels.

Q Can I convert footnotes to endnotes and vice versa?

A Yes. To convert only one footnote/endnote, display it in the footnote/endnote editing pane, right-click it, and then click the Convert to footnote/endnote selection. To convert all your footnotes to endnotes, select Insert | Footnote, click

Options, and then click Convert. Select the conversion you want (Convert all footnotes to endnotes or Convert all endnotes to footnotes) and then click the OK button. When finished, click Cancel until you get back to your document.

Q Can I set up a subentry of a subentry in an index?

A Yes. The trick is to use semicolons when you type the subentries. For instance, if you want a main entry of pets, then a subentry of dogs, and then a further subentry of show dogs, type `pets` as the main entry in the Mark Index Entry dialog, and then type `dogs; show dogs` as the subentry.

20

RW 5

Word in Real Time

Design a Newsletter

This project will pull together several graphic and page layout options to build a newsletter. You can always use Word's Newsletter template, but it's more fun to design your own and use it for future editions. This project will involve these features:

- ☐ Columns
- ☐ Clip art
- ☐ WordArt
- ☐ Borders

It's a good idea to lay out your ideas before you sit down at the computer to generate a publication. Create a mock-up drawing of how you want the publication to be laid out. Figure out who your audience is. Are you trying to appeal to a conservative or a liberal audience? You don't have to get political, but you need to be aware of what will be effective with the majority of your readers.

Think about readability and the visual contact points on the page. Will columns make it easier to read? Will specific fonts make the text more legible? Do text and graphics flow together in a way that draws the reader from one place to another, or does it look like little chunks pasted together?

JUST A MINUTE

A good rule of thumb is to use no more than two fonts in one publication. Newsletters usually work well with sans serif fonts for headings and serif fonts for the body of the newsletter. The best advice is to keep it simple.

Create a Heading

A good header is essential to draw the reader in. It may make the difference between whether the newsletter gets read or tossed. Figure R5.1 shows the first stages of the header. The chalkboard and apple are two separate clips from the clip art collection. The title was created in WordArt, and all three items were grouped. To group objects, do the following:

1. Hold down the Shift key and click each of the objects.
2. From the Drawing toolbar, select Group from the Draw menu.

Microsoft Word - School News.doc
File Edit View Insert Format Tools Table Window Help
Normal
Times New Roman
12
80%
Parent Partners
Happy Swallow Elementary School
May 1997
Page 1 Sec 2 1/1 At 2.8" Ln 5 Col 1
REC TRK EXT OVR WPH

Figure R5.1.
Using clip art and WordArt for the title.

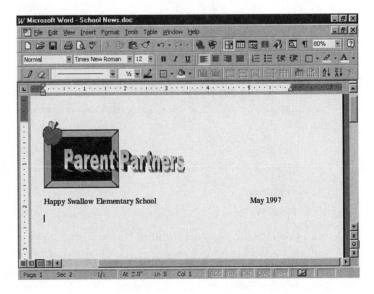

In addition to allowing you to move the objects as one unit, grouping your graphics makes it easier for you to add a text wrap. This example uses a top and bottom style text wrap so that text does not flow around or next to the graphic. To add a top and bottom text wrap:

1. Click the drawing object.
2. Select Format | Object from the menu.
3. In the Wrapping tab, select the Top & bottom option.
4. Click OK.

A line of text was added below the title and formatted with a font similar to the one used in the WordArt object.

This letter will be sent to parents of elementary school children. Give it a festive look with a decorative line beneath the last line of the heading. Figure R5.2 displays the line style that will be added. The key to remember is that the line is not applied until you make a selection from the Borders drop-down list. This tells Word where you want the line (top, bottom, and so on).

Figure R5.2.
Adding a decorative line.

Microsoft Word - School News.doc
File Edit View Insert Format Tools Table Window Help
Heading 1
Times New Roman
13
80%
Partners
y School
May 1997
Page 1 Sec 1 1/1 At 2.4" Ln 2 Col 1

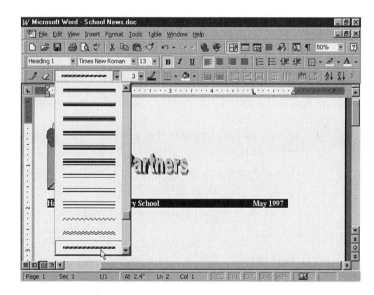

In the paragraph after the header, insert a break by selecting Insert | Break. Select a Continuous Section break. Section 1 is the heading, and section 2 is the text for page 1.

Adding Columns

A change of pace for newsletters is to use something like a scholar's margin. This example is set up with a scholar's margin on the left for page one and a mirrored image on page 2 with the scholar's margin on the right. That means you'll need a section break at the end of page 1 so that the columns can be different for page 2. To add columns to section 2 of page 1 (the section after the heading):

1. Place the cursor in section 2.
2. Select Format | Columns and choose the Left option in the Presets section (see Figure R5.3).

Columns
Presets
One
Two
Three
Left
Right
OK
Cancel
Number of columns:
2
Line between
Width and spacing
Col #:
Width:
Spacing:
1:
1.67"
0.5"
2:
3.83"
Equal column width
Preview
Apply to:
This section
Start new column

Figure R5.3.
Setting a scholar's margin for page 1.

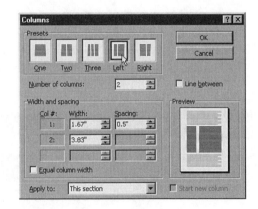

3. Leave a few blank lines and insert another section break (for page 2). Make this section break a Next page section break.
4. Place the cursor in section 3 (page 2) and use Format | Columns to set a Right option in the Presets section.

Type the articles in the larger column and use the scholar's margin (the short column) for the article titles.

Final Touch

A nice touch is to use symbols between articles to mark the end of one section and the start of another. The symbols used between the articles in this newsletter were pictures of an open book found in the Wingdings symbol set. Select Insert | Symbol from the menu and choose from the interesting symbols for fonts like Monotype Sorts or Wingdings. Increase the symbol's size by selecting it and increasing the font size from the Formatting toolbar. The newsletter is complete (see Figure R5.4).

Figure R5.4.
The finished newsletter.

Microsoft Word - School News.doc (Preview)
File Edit View Insert Format Tools Table Window Help
33%
Close
Parent Partners
Page 1 Sec 1 1/2 At 2.4" Ln 2 Col 14 REC TRK EXT OVR WPH

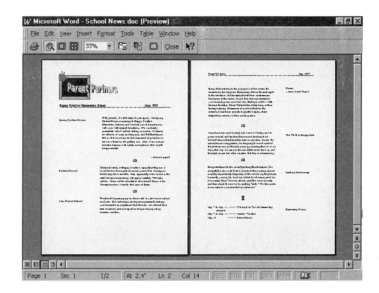

PART
VI

Word Has Connections

Hour

PART VI

Hour 21

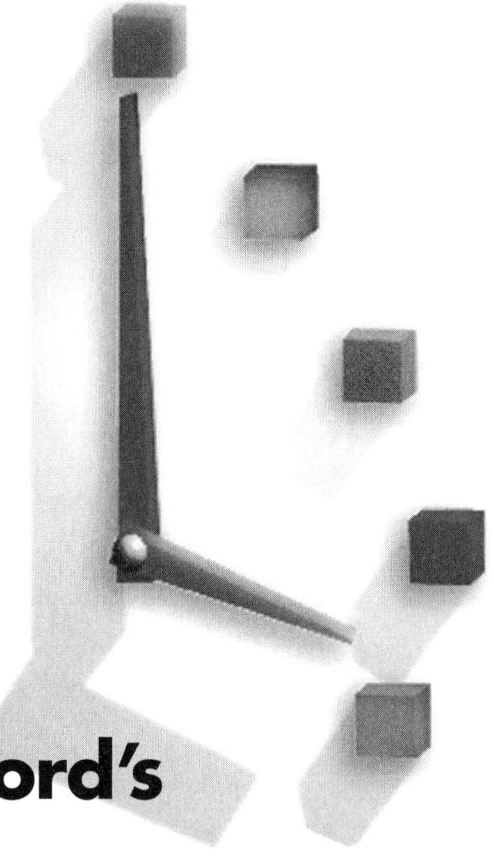

Bookshelf and Word's Editing Tools

by Ruel T. Hernandez

Word 97 has several easy-to-use editing tools that you can use to hone your documents. This hour covers the Undo/Redo command, the spelling and grammar checker, the AutoCorrect capability, and Bookshelf. The Undo/Redo command can be found under the Edit menu on the menu bar, and the other functions can be found under the Tools menu on the menu bar.

The highlights of this chapter include

- The Undo/Redo command
- The spelling and grammar checker
- The AutoCorrect function
- Bookshelf

Just a Minute

Bookshelf Basics is included with the professional edition of Office 97, but not with the standard or small business editions. Bookshelf is also not included in the standalone version of Word 97. If you wish to use Bookshelf, you will have to get the professional edition of Office 97 or get the standalone Bookshelf program.

Undo/Redo

Think of the Undo command as your "oops" function. Say you accidentally delete a word or a paragraph. You can undelete what you have deleted using the Undo command. Try it! Type something in Word, and then delete it. Then select Edit | Undo Typing or press Ctrl+Z to undelete the words you have deleted. When you select Edit | Undo, Undo may show up as Undo Clear, Undo Typing, or something similar, with the word after Undo describing the action last completed.

Undo is very useful for undoing almost anything, including typing or deletions. Word keeps track of all your actions as you type your document. For instance, if you type a whole paragraph and then decide against using it, you can press Ctrl+Z to undo what you have typed instead of deleting the paragraph. Essentially, you are going back a step, or going in reverse, to the point where you were before you typed the paragraph (you may have to press Ctrl+Z or click Edit | Undo several times to get there). Use the Redo command to redo what you have undone using the Undo command. To use the Redo command, select Edit | Redo or press Ctrl+Y.

Just a Minute

You cannot use Undo/Redo to perform multiple undelete commands. Some people cheat by using the undelete command in other word processing programs to perform a copy/move/paste maneuver. In Word 97, you must use the regular Copy/Paste commands to copy and move sections of your document.

You can also undo and redo by clicking the Undo and Redo buttons on the Standard toolbar. The Undo button is designated by an arrow going counter-clockwise, and the Redo button is designated an arrow going clockwise. To the right of each button is a pull-down list of the actions you have taken in the writing of your document that you can undo or redo. These actions generally include almost all the word-processing actions you have taken since you opened your document.

JUST A MINUTE

> You usually lose the record of your undo/redo actions when you close your document. To save those actions for the next time you open and work on your document, select File | Versions to invoke the Versions dialog box, then click the Automatically save a version on close option. This is useful if you want to see the progression of how a document was constructed. To see the undo/redo actions of a previous version of a document, select File | Versions to open the previous version of the document, and then trace the undo/redo activity that occurred in the drafting of the document.

Spelling and Grammar Checking

Word 97 has a wonderful spelling and grammar checker that can help you draft your documents. The spelling and grammar checker can be found under the Tools menu on the menu bar (listed as Spelling and Grammar); you can also activate this function by pressing the F7 key on your keyboard. When a spelling or grammatical error is found, a Spelling and Grammar dialog box similar to the one shown in Figure 21.1 pops up on your screen.

Spelling and Grammar: English (United States)
Non-standard Word:
Ain't this sentence which is wrongly drafted wrote incorrectly and erroneously.
Ignore
Ignore All
Next Sentence
Suggestions:
Non-standard Word (no suggestions)
Change
Check grammar
Options...
Undo
Cancel

Figure 21.1.
Word 97 has a spelling and grammar checker that will help you proof your document.

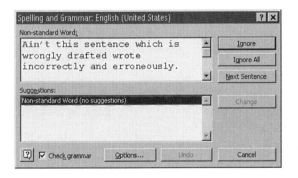

The text containing the spelling or grammatical error appears in the top part of the dialog box. The bottom part of the dialog shows suggested changes to correct the error. You can ignore the error, ignore all of the same errors, go on to the next sentence, or accept the suggested change. This floating dialog remains on the screen until the spell check is complete, at which time a Readability Statistics dialog box will appear on the screen (more on the Readability Statistics dialog later). Until you finish the spell check, the dialog remains on the screen unless you click on the Cancel button; you can continue to type your document while the dialog remains on the screen (the dialog's Ignore button will change to a Resume button that you can click to continue the spelling and grammar check). The spelling and grammar checker is very straightforward and easy to use.

Spelling and Grammar Options

You can set several spelling and grammar options. Enable the Check grammar with spelling checkbox in the Spelling & Grammar dialog box if you want the spelling and grammar checker to check spelling and grammar; leave this option unchecked if you want the spelling and grammar checker to check for spelling only. Access more spelling and grammar options by clicking the Options button at the bottom of the Spelling & Grammar dialog box or by selecting Tools|Options from the menu bar. This invokes a dialog box with a series of spelling and grammar options (see Figure 21.2).

Spelling & Grammar
Spelling & Grammar
Spelling
Check spelling as you type
Hide spelling errors in this document
Always suggest corrections
Suggest from main dictionary only
Ignore words in UPPERCASE
Ignore words with numbers
Ignore Internet and file addresses
Custom dictionary:
CUSTOM.DIC
Dictionaries...
Grammar
Check grammar as you type
Hide grammatical errors in this document
Check grammar with spelling
Show readability statistics
Writing style:
Standard
Settings...
Recheck Document
OK
Cancel

Figure 21.2.
In the Spelling & Grammar dialog box, you can set Word 97 to automatically check your spelling and grammar.

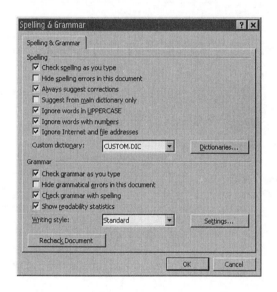

In the spelling section of the options dialog, you can set the following options:

- Check spelling as you type (Word automatically checks your spelling as you write your document)
- Hide spelling errors in document (this is so you don't see the red squiggly underline on misspelled words; you must run the spelling and grammar checker to find out about any errors)
- Always suggest corrections (Word finds correct spellings for you)
- Suggest from main dictionary only (this is useful if you want Word to point out every error without the help of a supplemental custom dictionary)
- Ignore words in UPPER CASE (this is useful in the case of proper names that you may want to type in uppercase; otherwise, Word will point them out as errors)

- ☐ Ignore words with numbers (such as ignoring F114 and similar words with numbers)
- ☐ Ignore Internet and file addresses (this is to ignore Internet addresses such as `http://www.address.com` and filenames such as `C:\MY DOCUMENT\FILENAME.EXT`)

I suggest you select the Check spelling as you type and the Always suggest corrections options, as well as the three ignore options. You can also specify the name of a custom dictionary that will be used in addition to the main dictionary included with Word 97. The default is `CUSTOM.DIC`, to which you can add your own words.

In the grammar section of the options dialog, you can set the following options:

- ☐ Check grammar as you type (Word automatically checks your grammar as you type)
- ☐ Hide grammatical errors in this document (this hides all grammatical errors; you must run the spelling and grammar checker to find the errors)
- ☐ Check grammar with spelling (if you do not check this, only spelling errors will be looked for)
- ☐ Show readability statistics (this shows you how readable your document is after you have completed a spell and grammar check)

I suggest you select the Check grammar as you type and the Check grammar with spelling options. If you are writing for a particular audience or readership, consider selecting the Show readability statistics option. This prompts a Readability Statistics dialog box to pop up on the screen after the spelling and grammar check is complete. The readability statistics include

- ☐ The number of words, sentences, and paragraphs in your document
- ☐ The average number of sentences per paragraph and words per sentence
- ☐ Readability statistics, including the percentage of passive sentences, to help you determine how readable your document is
- ☐ What percentage of your document contains passive sentences

You can set the grammar checker to one of several different writing styles:

- ☐ Casual
- ☐ Standard
- ☐ Formal
- ☐ Technical
- ☐ Custom

You can switch between these styles to tell Word how critical the grammar check will be. For instance, if you select the Formal writing style, Word will point out more grammatical errors.

21

If you select the Casual option, Word will let certain errors slide. You can edit the a writing style by clicking the Settings button, but I suggest that you edit only the Custom writing style.

Automatically Check Your Spelling and Grammar as You Write

You may want to configure Word 97 so that it checks your spelling and grammar as you type. This way, Word 97 immediately tells you when you misspell a word or write a grammatically incorrect sentence. If the misspelled word or grammatically incorrect sentence is not changed by AutoCorrect, the word or sentence will be underlined by a wavy line. A red wavy line indicates a spelling error and a green wavy line indicates a grammatical error. Right-click the misspelled word or grammatically incorrect sentence to invoke the shortcut menu. For spelling errors, that shortcut menu shows suggested changes in bold text and offers several options:

- ☐ Ignore all similar errors in the document
- ☐ Add the word to the dictionary
- ☐ AutoCorrect to automatically correct the word with a suggested word
- ☐ Spelling to run Word's spell checker on the word

For grammatical errors, the shortcut menu shows suggested changes in bold text and offers the following options:

- ☐ Ignore the error
- ☐ Run the grammar checker

For spelling errors, you may prefer to right-click misspelled words and then click one of the suggested changes as you write instead of waiting to run the spelling checker later. Likewise, for grammatical errors, you may prefer to right-click the incorrect sentence and simply rewrite it until the wavy line vanishes rather than runn the grammar checker after you finish writing. Or you can ignore the errors and wait until you finish writing, at which time you can run the spelling and grammar checker. If you prefer to make corrections later, you don't have to right-click each error that pops up. (If you like, you can even hide the spelling and grammar errors, as discussed in the "Spelling and Grammar Options" section.)

AutoCorrect

AutoCorrect automatically corrects as you type. The difference between AutoCorrect and automatic spell checking is that AutoCorrect automatically searches for and corrects predefined errors as you type. For instance, commonly misspelled words, such as *the* where the *t* and *h* are transposed, are automatically corrected as you type. You can add misspelled words or grammatically incorrect phrases to the AutoCorrect function of Word 97 by clicking Tools | AutoCorrect. You should get a dialog similar to the one shown in Figure 21.3.

AutoCorrect
AutoCorrect
AutoFormat As You Type
AutoText
AutoFormat
Correct TWo INitial CApitals
Exceptions...
Capitalize first letter of sentences
Capitalize names of days
Correct accidental usage of cAPS LOCK key
Replace text as you type
Replace:
With:
Plain text
Formatted text
(C)
(r)
(tm)
Add
Delete
OK
Cancel

Figure 21.3.
You can set Word to automatically correct commonly misspelled words or grammatically incorrect phrases.

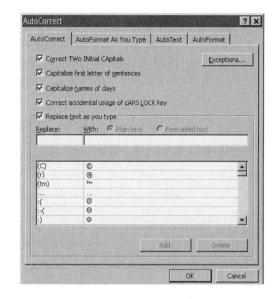

Word has about 500 preset automatic corrections built into its AutoCorrect function. If you often misspell a certain word or use a certain phrase that you know is grammatically incorrect (or that Word tells you is grammatically incorrect), add it to AutoCorrect like so:

1. Click Tools | AutoCorrect. You will get the AutoCorrect dialog box.
2. Click the AutoCorrect dialog tab if it is not the first tab showing on the dialog box.
3. Type the incorrect word or phrase in the Replace field.
4. Type the correct word or phrase in the With field.
5. Click the Add button at the bottom of the AutoCorrect dialog (if the incorrect word or phrase is already in the AutoCorrect list of automatic corrections, the Add button will become a Replace button).
6. Click OK to return to your document.

You can change or delete automatic corrections that are already in AutoCorrect. If there is an automatic correction you want to change or remove, find it in the AutoCorrect dialog and delete it by clicking the delete button on the dialog or change it to suit your needs. One automatic correction you may want to remove or edit is the one for the copyright symbol. If you type `(c)`, Word automatically changes it to a copyright symbol (©). This is a default automatic correction in Word 97. You can avoid the automatic correction by typing an uppercase `C`, or by inserting the lowercase c between the parentheses (type `()`, then insert the lowercase `c`). You can edit this automatic correction by doing the following:

1. Click Tools | AutoCorrect.

2. Click the AutoCorrect tab if it is not activated.

3. Scroll through the list of automatically corrected words or phrases. Select the correction you want to edit (in this case, (c)); it should appear in the Replace and With fields.

4. In the Replace field, change the lowercase c to an uppercase C, and then click the Replace button.

5. You will get a dialog box telling you that the AutoCorrect entry already exists and asking whether you want to redefine it. Click the Yes button.

6. Click the OK button to return to your document.

You can also make AutoCorrect ignore errors by specifying AutoCorrect exceptions:

1. Select Tools | AutoCorrect. If necessary, click the AutoCorrect tab to activate it.

2. Click the Exceptions button.

3. In the AutoCorrect Exceptions dialog that appears, you will see two tabs: First Letter and Initial Caps.

   Normally, Word capitalizes the first word that is typed after a period, but what if you want to type an abbreviation in the middle of a sentence? The First Letter tab contains a list of abbreviations for which Word is told not to capitalize the first word after the abbreviation. For instance, say you want to type John Doe lives at 123 Main St. in Springfield. If the abbreviation St. is not in the exception list on the First Letter tab, the first letter of the word after St. in the sample sentence will be capitalized (John Doe lives at 123 Main St. In Springfield).

   The Initial Caps tab contains a list of words wherein the first two letters of each word are capitalized. Although there may be few words whose first two letters are capitalized, this list is useful in other instances. For example, some businesses use a naming convention in correspondence and other types of documents that turns a first name and a last name into a single word (for instance, John Doe becomes JDoe). If your office uses this naming convention, you would enter those words/names as exceptions on the Initial Caps tab. (There is also a three-initial–caps naming convention that will not cause errors in Word.)

4. Click the First Letter tab.

5. In the Don't capitalize after field, type def. (an abbreviation for the word *defendant*).

6. Click the Add button.

7. Click the Initial Caps tab.

8. In the Don't correct field, type the first letter of your first name followed immediately by your last name (do not separate them with a space). Be sure that the first two letters of the resulting word are uppercase.
9. Click the Add button.
10. Click OK to return to the AutoCorrect dialog box.
11. Click OK to return to your document.

Type `def.` in a sentence. The first letter of the word that you type after `def.` will remain lowercase (if you typed it in lowercase). Then type your name using the two-initial–caps naming convention (as in JDoe). Word will not change the second letter to lowercase.

Using the Word 97 Thesaurus

Think of how many times you've written a word that's close, but isn't quite right for the sentence. (The night was *hot.* No, wait: *humid. Muggy? Sultry.* The night was *sultry.*) You can save yourself a lot of trouble by using the thesaurus that is built into Word 97. To use the thesaurus, do the following:

1. Place your cursor on the word you want to change.
2. Select Tools | Language | Thesaurus or press Shift+F7 (be sure to press the Shift key or you will run the spelling and grammar checker). A Thesaurus dialog box similar to the one shown in Figure 21.4 will pop up; this dialog provides synonyms and related words that you can use to replace the unsatisfactory word in your document.

Thesaurus: English (United States)
Looked Up:
drafted
Meanings:
made (adj.)
Related Words
Replace with Synonym:
made
made
designed
written
created
combined
authored
composed
compounded
forged
Replace
Look Up
Previous
Cancel

Figure 21.4.
Word's thesaurus will let you choose synonyms and related words to use in your document.

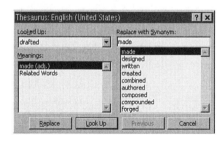

Consulting Microsoft Bookshelf

The professional version of Office 97 is packaged with Bookshelf Basics, which is a subset of the full version of Bookshelf. Bookshelf Basics consists of the American Heritage Dictionary, the Original Roget's Thesaurus, and the Columbia Dictionary of Quotations. The full version of Bookshelf offers these reference books as well as the Concise Columbia Encyclopedia, the Concise Encarta World Atlas, the People's Chronology, the World Almanac and Book of Facts, the Bookshelf Internet Directory, and the National Five-Digit Zip Code and Post Office Directory. The Bookshelf Basics version has preview versions of the additional references that come with the full version of Bookshelf. This book limits its discussion to the American Heritage Dictionary, the Original Roget's Thesaurus, and the Columbia Dictionary of Quotations.

If you have the professional edition of Office 97, you must install Office 97 as either a typical or custom installation. If you run Office 97 from the CD-ROM drive, you will not be able to run Bookshelf from the Word menu bar. You can run Bookshelf separately from the Windows Start button by selecting Start | Programs | Microsoft Reference | Microsoft Bookshelf Basics. If you are using the full version of Bookshelf and it does not integrate itself into Word 97 (for example, if you are running Office 97 from one CD-ROM drive and Bookshelf from another CD-ROM drive), you can launch Bookshelf separately from the Windows Start button by clicking the Windows Start button and then selecting Programs | Microsoft Reference | Microsoft Bookshelf 1996–1997.

Using Bookshelf with Word

After Bookshelf is installed, and assuming it is integrated into your Word Tools menu, start Bookshelf (while inside Word) by performing the following steps:

1. Be sure your Office 97 professional edition or Bookshelf CD-ROM is inserted into your CD-ROM drive.
2. Select Tools | Look Up Reference. This invokes the Lookup Reference dialog box.
3. Click Microsoft Bookshelf 1996–97 Edition or Microsoft Bookshelf Basics.
4. Type a word you want to search for in the Search Text field on the Lookup Reference dialog.
5. Click OK.

21

You may find yourself using Bookshelf to look up definitions of words. To do so, right-click a word in Word 97, click Define on the shortcut menu, and Bookshelf will provide the definition of the word according to the American Heritage Dictionary.

You will have to go separately into the Original Roget's Thesaurus and the Columbia Dictionary of Quotations, as well as the other references in the full version of Bookshelf, and use the Copy and Paste functions to use the information from those references in your Word documents. This is discussed in the next section, "Copying/Pasting from Bookshelf to Word."

Just a Minute

All the references in Bookshelf use the same interface. For instance, the Contents tab lets you see what is in the reference by alphabetical order; the Find tab lets you quickly see whether your word or topic is covered in the reference (Figure 21.5 shows the Find tab in the thesaurus); the Gallery tab helps you search for articles that contain audio, animation, video, and images.

Microsoft Bookshelf Basics - Thesaurus
File Edit Tools Books Help
Thesaurus
Contents Find Gallery
To search, type a word or phrase, then click Find.
republic
Find
Articles (5) for republic
Authority: political organization (noun)
Region: definite space: territory (noun)
Humankind: nation (noun)
Unimportance: nonentity (noun)
Celebration: special day (noun)
Thesaurus
Volition: The exercise of the will: General social volition: Authority
political organization (noun)
political organization, body politic
state, nation state, commonwealth
country, realm, kingdom, republic, city state, city, free city, polis
temple state
federation, confederation
principality, duchy, archduchy, dukedom, palatinate
empire, dominion, colony, dependency, protectorate, mandate, mandated territory, territory
free world, communist bloc, eastern bloc, Third World, region
superpower, superiority
banana republic, inferiority
buffer state, interjacency
Year in Review Preview... Address Builder Preview... Advanced Find... Outline... Back

Figure 21.5.
By using the Find tab on the Bookshelf's thesaurus, you can find words similar to the word you want to use in your Word document.

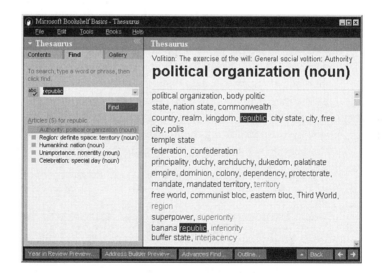

Copying/Pasting from Bookshelf to Word

You already know how to copy and paste between documents in Word or from one section of a document to another; copying and pasting between Bookshelf and Word is no different.

Say you're in the Columbia Dictionary of Quotations and you find a good one that you want to put in a Word document. If Bookshelf is integrated into your Word menu, do the following:

1. Be sure your Office 97 professional edition or Bookshelf CD-ROM is inserted into your CD-ROM drive.
2. Select Tools | Look Up Reference. This invokes the Lookup Reference dialog box.
3. Select the text in Bookshelf that you want to copy.
4. Right-click the selected text.
5. Click the Copy to option.
6. Select Word.
7. You will automatically be switched over to Word, where you will see a Copy to Word dialog box. Select New Document, Current Document, or End (of an open document that may be listed).
8. Click OK.

The text you selected and copied from Bookshelf will be pasted into your Word document. You may want to change the font of the pasted text to match the rest of your document by selecting that text in the Word document and selecting a new font from the Formatting toolbar. Notice the superscript number at the end of the text that you pasted into your document. This is a footnote. If you move your cursor above the footnote number, a flag and then a screen tip will pop up to tell you where the text came from. You can edit the footnote by selecting View | Footnotes. This invokes a footnote editing pane area at the bottom of the screen, where you can edit the footnote. Click the Close button on the footnotes divider bar when you finish editing the footnote. See Chapter 20, "I Could Write a Book," for more information about footnotes and endnotes.

If Bookshelf is not integrated into Word, do the following to copy and paste text from Bookshelf:

1. Make sure your Office 97 professional version or Bookshelf CD-ROM is in your CD-ROM drive.
2. Go to the Columbia Dictionary of Quotations by selecting Books | Quotations from the Bookshelf menu bar.
3. Find an article from which you want to copy. Copy whole articles by selecting Edit | Copy from within Bookshelf, or copy only the text you want by selecting it and then choosing Edit | Copy.
4. In Word, place your cursor in the spot in your document where you want the copied text to be placed.
5. Paste the text into your document by selecting Edit | Paste from the menu bar, or by right-clicking and then choosing Paste from the shortcut menu.

21

This method of copying and pasting from Bookshelf to Word is just like what you would do between other Windows programs. Unlike the first method, this method does not automatically create a footnote.

Summary

This chapter instructed you about how to use Word 97's editing tools. These tools include the Undo/Redo functions, the spelling and grammar checker, the AutoCorrect function, the thesaurus, and the Bookshelf references. The Undo/Redo functions are for undoing what you've written and redoing what you've undone. You can use the Undo function as a simple undelete function, but you can use the full power of the Undo/Redo functions to retrace the history of your document. The spelling and grammar checker, the AutoCorrect function, and the thesaurus are very easy to use. If you set the spelling and grammar checker to automatically check your spelling and your grammar, you will find yourself correcting your writing as you work on your document. And if you want more capabilities than are provided in Word's built-in editing, spelling, and grammar functions, you can go into Bookshelf to look at more references. It's all at your fingertips.

Q&A

Q **The Undo and Redo commands in the Edit menu sometimes say Undo Clear or Redo Clear, sometimes Undo Typing and Redo Typing, and sometimes other things. Why?**

A It depends on what activity you undid. For instance, if you were typing, the Edit menu will say Undo Typing and Redo Typing. If you were pasting, it will say Undo Paste and Redo Paste.

Q **When I type a sentence that I know is grammatically correct, Word 97 says it's grammatically incorrect. What can I do to fix it?**

A You can try changing the writing style or set up a Custom writing style to reflect your writing style. Or you can simply turn off the grammar checker by unclicking all the boxes for it in the Spelling & Grammar dialog box.

21

PART

VI

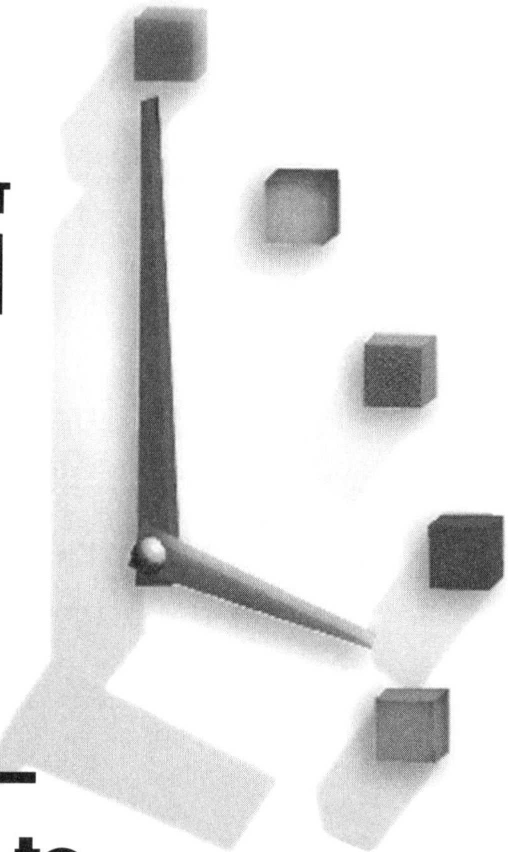

Hour 22

The Insert Menu—Adding Elements to Documents

by Ruel T. Hernandez

This chapter will show you how to add or insert several different things into your documents, including the date and time, symbols, fields, files, objects, reviewer's comments, and bookmarks. You learned about inserting graphics (clip art, WordArt, charts and graphs, and other pictures) in Hour 17, "Working with Graphics," and covered inserting tables of contents, indexes, footnotes, and captions in Hour 20, "I Could Write a Book." So you already have some experience in inserting various things into Word documents. In this hour, you will start by examining the simplest items you can insert into a Word document and progress to the more complex items (not necessarily meaning they will be more difficult). You will learn how to insert the following into your documents:

- Date and time
- Symbols
- Fields
- Files
- Objects
- Reviewer's comments

Date and Time

Inserting the date and time into your document is easy. To do so, follow these simple steps:

1. Place your cursor where you want to insert the date or time.
2. Click Insert | Date and Time. You will see a Date and Time dialog similar to the one shown in Figure 22.1.

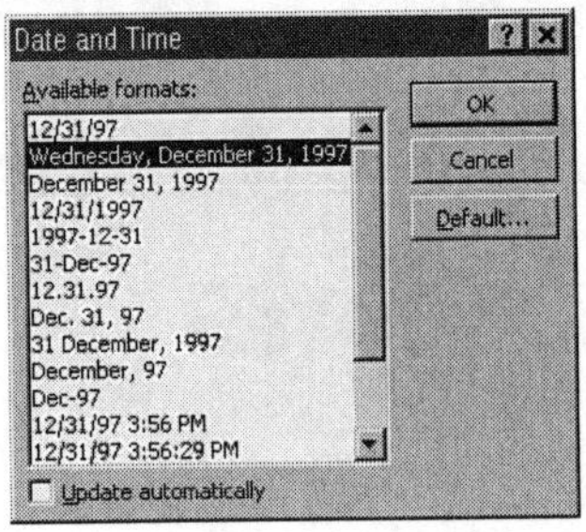
Date and Time
Available formats:
12/31/97
Wednesday, December 31, 1997
December 31, 1997
12/31/1997
1997-12-31
31-Dec-97
12.31.97
Dec. 31, 97
31 December, 1997
December, 97
Dec-97
12/31/97 3:56 PM
12/31/97 3:56:29 PM
OK
Cancel
Default...
Update automatically

Figure 22.1.
You can select different formats to use to insert the date and time into your document.

3. From the Date and Time dialog box, click one of the available formats for date and/or time.
4. Click the Update automatically checkbox at the bottom of the Date and Time dialog box.
5. Click OK.

Some of the different date formats include

- 12/31/97
- Wednesday, December 31, 1997
- December 31, 1997
- 12/31/1997
- 1997-12-31

Some of the different date and time formats include

- 12/31/97 12:12 PM
- 12/31/97 12:12:12 PM
- 12:12 PM
- 12:12:12 PM
- 20:20
- 20:20:20

If you click the Automatically update box on the Date and Time dialog, the date and/or time format that you select will be automatically printed with the current date and/or time. This is useful if you are printing form letters or similar documents and you do not want to change the date each time you print the letter or document. Some examples of documents in which you may want to insert the date and the time are memos and fax cover sheets. An example of a document in which you would only insert the date might be a letter.

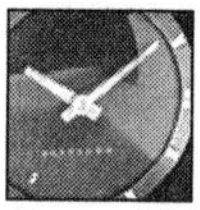

JUST A MINUTE

> Make sure that the internal clock on your computer is set correctly. Otherwise, the wrong date and time will be inserted into your document. In Windows 95 or Windows NT 4.0, right-click the time display on your Windows taskbar and click Adjust Date/Time. This invokes the Date/Time Properties dialog panel, where you can adjust the date and the time. Click OK when you are finished.

Symbols

You can insert a whole slew of typographical symbols into your document. These include mathematical, Greek, Hebrew, Japanese, and Wingdings symbols. The number of symbols available to you depends on what fonts are installed on your computer. If you have many fonts installed on your computer, you will have many symbols from which to choose. It is quite easy to insert a symbol. For example, to insert a paragraph symbol, perform the following steps:

1. Select Insert | Symbols. You should see a dialog similar to the one shown in Figure 22.2 (you may have to click the Symbols tab).
2. Click the Font drop-down list and select the normal text option.
3. Click the Subset drop-down list and pick Latin-1.
4. Find and click the paragraph symbol (¶). If you are having trouble seeing the symbols, click the symbol you want to use to view a magnified version of the symbol contained in that cell.

Figure 22.2.
You can insert different typographical symbols into your Word 97 document.

Symbol
Symbols
Special Characters
Font:
(normal text)
Subset:
Latin-1
AutoCorrect...
Shortcut Key...
Shortcut key:
Insert
Cancel

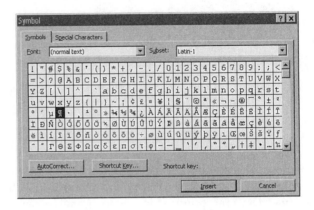

5. Click the Insert button.
6. Click Close to return to your document.

Fields

Fields are like placeholders indicating where data is to be placed in a document. This is useful if you are making form letters or address labels, as well as when you mail merge documents (mail merging is covered in Hour 15, "Mail Merge"). Some examples of fields that you might use include author name and filename. If you want your document's filename to be printed on the document, insert a filename field.

Inserting Fields

To insert a field, do the following:

1. Select Insert | Field.
2. Click a category and then a field name.

For instance, if you want use fields to insert the current date and time, do the following:

1. Click Insert | Field.
2. Select Date and Time from the Categories list.
3. Select a category, such as PrintDate, from the Field names list. Many of the categories are self-explanatory. In this case, the PrintDate field inserts a field for the date when the file was last printed.
4. Click OK.

The field will show up as text within a gray block. You may have to click the field to see the gray shading.

If you want to insert the filename of the document as mentioned previously, this is what you do:

1. Select Insert | Field.
2. Select Document Information from the Categories list.
3. Select FileName from the Field names list.
4. Click OK.

Updating Fields

If you insert a field where the information may change, as would be the case for a field for the time or file size, you can update that information by clicking the field and then pressing the F9 key. Automatically update all fields at once when you are going to print by doing the following:

1. Select Tools | Options from the menu bar.
2. Click the Print tab.
3. Click the Update fields checkbox.
4. Click OK.

Files

Inserting a file into your document is useful if you want to insert the whole file and not just a portion. This is useful if you are working with a report containing multiple documents written by different people (you may be a manager of an office or a unit and need to gather monthly reports into one single document). You would use Insert Files to insert the separate documents (the monthly reports) into one single document.

But if you only want to insert a portion of the file, this is what you do:

1. Open the file from which you want to get text as a separate document.
2. Select the portion of text from the document you wish to insert.
3. Select Edit | Copy.
4. Return to your original document.
5. Select Edit | Copy to paste the copied portion into your original document.

If you know you want to insert an entire separate file into your document, this is what you do:

1. Place your cursor at the point where you want to insert the separate file (this is the insertion point).
2. Select Insert | File.

3. Click the file you want to insert.
4. Click OK.

Objects

An *object* can be just about anything other than a Word document. An object is information created in another software program that you might want to insert into your Word document. For instance, you can insert, or *embed*, an Excel worksheet or chart as an object into your Word document (more on inserting and embedding in Hour 23, "Teaming Up Word with Other Office Applications").

You've already dealt with objects in the form of graphics and pictures that are inserted into documents. Think of inserting objects as similar, except you perform the insertion through the Object dialog box (shown in Figure 22.3) instead of through the Clip Gallery. (You can insert clip art using both the Clip Gallery and the Object dialog box.)

Why insert an object at all? Well, you can add clip art or pictures to help illustrate the point being made in your document. You can add an Excel worksheet or chart to provide numerical information to supplement the information in the text of your document.

Figure 22.3.
You can insert objects into your document using the Object dialog box.

Object
Create New
Create from File
File name:
.
Browse...
Link to file
Float over text
Display as icon
Result
Inserts the contents of the file into your document so that you can edit it later using the application which created the source file.
OK
Cancel

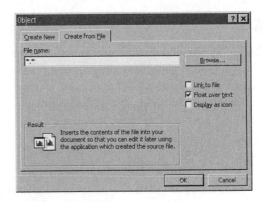

Inserting an Existing Object File

To insert an object, follow these steps:

1. Select Insert | Objects.
2. Click the Create from File tab.
3. Click the Browse button, find and click the file you want to use, and then click OK. If you know the name of the file and the directory the file is in, type it in the File name input field (you'll have to delete or overwrite the `*.*` wildcard). You might type something like `C:\MY DOCUMENTS\FILENAME.OBJ`.

When you find it, click the file and then click OK. The name of the file with the directory will appear in the File name input field in the Object dialog.

4. Click OK, and the object will appear in your document.

CAUTION

> When you insert an object, you insert into your document the entire file in which that object resides. So if you are inserting an Excel worksheet, you may wish to insert only a portion of that worksheet instead of the whole file. In this case, perform a copy-and-paste operation from the Excel worksheet to your Word document.

When you insert an object, you have three options that you can use individually or in combination with each other:

☐ Link to a file—Choose this, and you create a link to the existing object file. If you make any changes to the original object file, the changes will be reflected in your Word document. However, you will not able to make any changes to the linked object while you are in Word. You are only linked to that object; you must go to the software program in which that object was created to make any changes in the object.

☐ Float over text—Choose this, and the object will actually be in your document.

☐ Display as an icon—If you choose this, the object will only appear in Word as an icon. Displaying an object as an icon can save time in loading a text object or a graphic/picture object. Instead of text objects or graphic/picture objects, icons show up on your computer screen.

Creating a New Object

To create a new object, click the Create New tab (see Figure 22.4) on the Object dialog. You must be familiar with the software program that you want to use to create the object. For example, if you wish to create a new Photoshop object, you should have Photoshop installed on your computer and you should know how to use it.

Say you want to create a bitmap image (a BMP file). To do so, follow these steps:

1. Select Insert | Object from the menu.

2. Click the Create New tab.

3. Select Bitmap Image.

4. Pick Float over text or Display as an icon.

5. Click OK.

6. Word will display a Windows Paint program interface from which you can construct a bitmap image to be inserted into your document.
7. To get back to your document and return to the regular Word interface screen, click outside of the object's boxed area. To get back into the object, just double-click it and you'll return to the Windows Paint program.

Object
Create New
Create from File
Object type:
Adobe PhotoDeluxe Image
Bitmap Image
Cetus CWordPad Document
EasyPhoto Photograph
LiveUpdate Crescendo
Media Clip
Microsoft Clip Gallery
Microsoft Equation 3.0
Float over text
Display as icon
Result
Inserts a new Bitmap Image object into your document.
OK
Cancel

Figure 22.4.
You can create a new object to insert in a Word document.

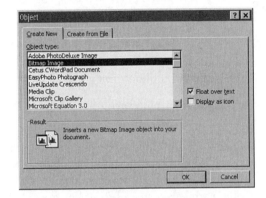

Figure 22.5 shows what the Word interface looks like when you create a bitmap image object.

Microsoft Word - Document1
File Edit View Image Options Window Help
which is wrongly drafted wrote incorrectly and erroneou
63,14
Page 1 Sec 1 1/1 At Ln Col REC TRK EXT OVR WPH

Figure 22.5.
Word changes its interface to allow you to create objects.

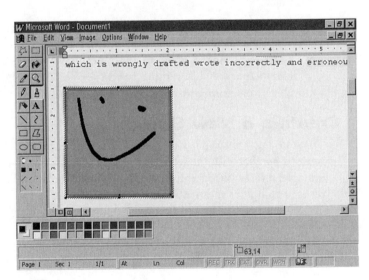

Word's interface changes according to what type of object you wish to create. Unless you know what you're doing, you may want to insert existing objects instead of creating new ones.

Reviewer's Comments

Many people insert reviewer's comments into a document to provide suggestions and criticisms they may have regarding the document. For instance, say you're required to review someone else's document before it is sent out. Word 97 allows you to insert your comments into the document; those comments are read onscreen.

Insert comments into a document that you are reviewing by doing the following:

1. Select Insert | Comments.
2. Type your comments in the Comments pane that appears at the bottom of the screen (see Figure 22.6).
3. Click the Close button on the Comments pane divider bar.

If you receive a document that contains comments, you can read them by selecting View | Comments. The Comments pane will appear at the bottom of the screen for you to read. You can see the reviewer's initials, as shown in Figure 22.6, to determine who wrote the comments.

Microsoft Word - Document3
File Edit View Insert Format Tools Table Window Help
Comment Text
Courier New
14
Comments From: All Reviewers
Close
This is a reviewers comment being written....
Page
Sec 1
At
Ln
Col 46
REC TRK EXT OVR WPH

Figure 22.6.
Type your comments in the Comments pane.

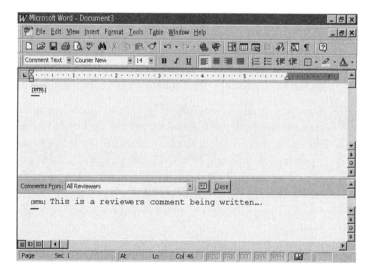

Voice Comments

It's possible to insert voice comments, but doing so requires the use of a microphone and sound card. If you have such equipment and wish to insert voice comments, and if the person who wants to listen to the comments also has the right equipment, follow these steps:

1. Select Insert | Comments.
2. Click the Insert Sound Object button (the one that looks like a cassette tape).

3. The Windows Sound Recorder pops up on the screen. Click the Record button (the one with the red dot), and then speak into the microphone.

4. When you finish speaking, click the Stop button (the button to the right of the Record button).

   You can play what you recorded by clicking the Play button (the middle button with the triangle pointing to the right).

5. When you finish recording, exit the Sound Recorder. You should see a Speaker icon in the Comments pane in Word.

6. To listen to the comments, double-click the speaker icon.

Viewing Comments

To view comments, select View | Comments. The Comments pane will appear at the bottom of the screen; here, you can read the comments. You should also see the insertion codes for the comments in the main text of your document.

If there is more than one reviewer, and if you want to see only one reviewer's comments, click the pull-down menu on the Comments pane divider with the names of all the reviewers, and then click the name of the reviewer whose comments you want to read.

You may be able to see text that is highlighted or blocked in yellow or another color. Move your mouse cursor above the text in that area. If the Comments pane is at the bottom of the screen, a little flag will pop up, and when the mouse is moved over the highlighted text, you should see a screen tip with the reviewer's name along with his or her comments.

You can also right-click the highlighted area to get a menu that will let you edit the comment. If you do not have the Comments pane at the bottom of the screen, you may have to right-click several times to get the correct menu. To make it easier for you to find and read the comments, you should have the Comments pane turned on.

Protecting Comments

Protect your comments to make sure no one deletes or edits them. To do so, follow these steps:

1. Select Tools | Protect Document.

2. Select Comments.

3. To make sure the protection is not turned off, type a password (you'll have to type it again to confirm it).

   When you select a password, pick one that only you will know. Also, you should pick a password that you will remember.

4. Click OK.

22

Printing Comments

Normally, you see the comments onscreen, not on the printed page. But if you want to print the document with comments, this is what you do:

1. Select Tools | Options.
2. Click the Print tab.
3. In the Include with document section, click disable the Comments checkbox.
4. Click OK.

The comments will automatically be printed with your document. If you decide later that you no longer want the comments to be printed, simply enable the Comments checkbox.

To print only the comments (not the document with the comments), do the following:

1. Select File | Print.
2. Toward the bottom of the Print dialog, click the Print What pull-down menu and select Comments.
3. Click OK to begin printing.

Bookmarks

Bookmarks let you quickly jump from place to place in the document. Instead of paging up or down through your document, you can simply jump to a bookmark. Think of bookmarks as reference points in your document. For a bound book, you would place a bookmark, such as a piece of paper, in the book to mark where you read an important or significant passage. You can do the same in Word by leaving an electronic bookmark in your document to mark an important or significant place in the document.

Adding a Bookmark

Inserting a bookmark is simple. This is what you do:

1. Click the point in your document at which you want to place the bookmark, or select a portion of text that you want to bookmark.
2. Select Insert | Bookmark. You may have to scroll down the Insert menu to get to Bookmark. You will then get the Bookmark dialog box.
3. Type a name in the Bookmark name area of the dialog box.
4. Click the Add button.

Repeat this for all bookmarks you want to place in your document.

Changing a Bookmark's Location

You can change the location of a bookmark that has already been inserted in your document. You might want to do this if you think a bookmark name is more appropriate for a different part of the document than where it was originally inserted. To change a bookmark's location, do the following:

1. Click the point or select a portion of text in your document where you want to place the bookmark.

2. Select Insert | Bookmark.

3. In the middle section of the Bookmark dialog, select the name of the bookmark whose location you want to change.

4. Click the Add button.

Deleting a Bookmark

If you have no use for a bookmark that you have inserted, you can delete it like so:

1. Select Insert | Bookmark.

2. Select the bookmark you want to delete.

3. Click the Delete button.

Finding a Bookmark

You can find a bookmark that has already been inserted in one of two ways: by using the Bookmark or the Find dialog box. To use the Bookmark dialog box to find a bookmark, do the following:

1. Select Insert | Bookmark.

2. Click Sort by Name to see an alphabetical listing of your bookmarks or click Sort by Location to see the bookmarks in the order they appear in your document.

3. Select the bookmark you want to go to in the bookmark list in the middle of the Bookmark dialog box.

4. Click the Go To button.

To use the Find dialog box to go to a bookmark in your document, do the following:

1. Select Edit | Find, click the Find button on the Standard toolbar, or press Ctrl+F. This invokes the Find dialog box.

2. Click the Go To tab on the Find dialog box.

3. Click Bookmark on the Go to what list.

4. Pull down the Enter bookmark name list or type the name of the bookmark to which you want to jump.

5. Click the Go To button.

22

22

Summary

In this chapter, you learned about inserting dates, symbols, fields, objects, and comments into your Word documents. These are really easy to insert; the only tricky aspect is inserting objects. I recommend that you insert existing objects instead of creating new ones unless you know what you are doing. If you only want to insert clip art and pictures, you'll most likely find the Clip Gallery easier to use.

Q&A

Q Sometimes when I'm typing a word that happens to be the name of a month, such as *May*, a little box pops up with today's date. Why?

A That is an automatic date insertion function of Word 97. Whenever you see that, just press Enter to insert today's date. That way, you don't have to type it all yourself. If you do not wish for the date to appear in your document, simply continue typing. For more information about AutoText, see Hour 16, "Automating Tasks."

Q I tried to insert a voice comment in a document that I was reviewing, but it wouldn't work. I can play sound files on my computer, so why can't I record a voice comment?

A Speak into your microphone. Be sure that the microphone is turned on and is plugged into your computer. If these suggestions yield no results, you may have a hardware problem. Consult the manual for your computer or for your sound card.

Q When I insert an object such as a picture into my document, it takes very long for the picture to show up on my computer. How can I avoid waiting so long?

A You may want to insert pictures or other objects as icons in your document to avoid waiting so long.

Q I tried to create an object in my Word document, but my computer crashed on me. Why?

A Word accepts OLE, a program integration technology standard. If the object you are trying to create is not OLE, you may not be able to create that type of object (hence, the crash). You may want to insert an existing object file instead, or create the object outside of Word 97 using whatever programs you may have.

PART VI

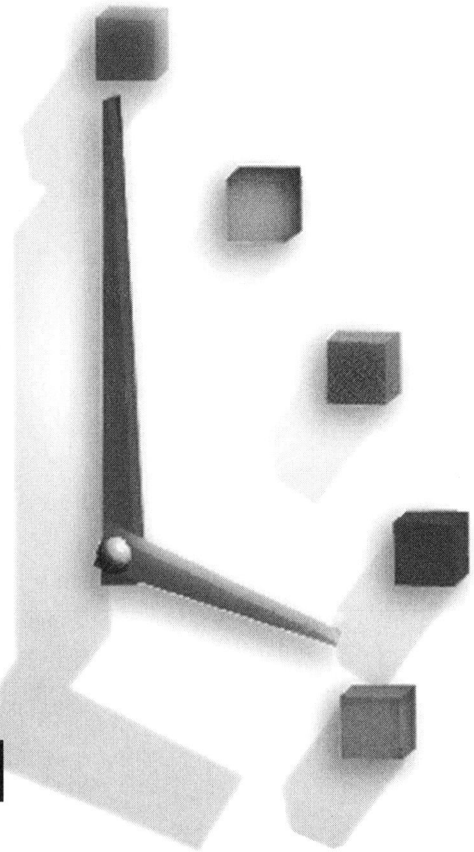

Hour 23

Teaming Up Word with Other Office Applications

By Ruel T. Hernandez

This hour shows you how to do some of the typical things you might do in an office setting. These include binding several documents together, placing spreadsheets and graphical charts in documents, setting up mailing lists of people to whom you want to send documents, and setting up office forms for people in the office to use. Luckily, Word 97 is offered as part of the Microsoft 97 package of programs that includes Word, Excel, Access, Binder, and others. In this hour, you will be introduced to some of these programs. The highlights of this hour include

- Using Word with Binder to bind documents together
- Using Word with Excel worksheets and charts
- Using Word with an Access mailing list database
- Using Word to create office forms

Using Binder to Organize Projects

Binder lets you set up an electronic computer "binder" to organize related files as separate sections of the binder. For instance, if you have several Word documents on a related topic or for a single report, you can assemble those files as separate sections into a binder using the Microsoft Office Binder program.

As with a regular binder, you can assemble an electronic binder into separate sections. You can start with a blank binder and add files, or you can use the templates that are available with Microsoft Office Binder. In this hour, you are going to place Word documents into a binder. This is what you have to do:

1. Run the Binder program by clicking the Windows Start button, selecting Programs, and then selecting Microsoft Binder.
2. From Binder's menu bar, select Section | Add from File. Binder opens the Add from File dialog (see Figure 23.1), from which you can select files to put in your binder. The dialog opens up to the `C:\MY DOCUMENTS` directory, which is the default documents directory for all Microsoft Office programs. If you changed your default directory, or if your files are not located in the `C:\MY DOCUMENTS` directory, you will have to go to the directory where your files are located.

Add from File
Look in:
My Documents
basketball.ppt
sample.doc
sample.ppt
sample2.doc
Tph02bp.doc
TPH21 multimedia.ppt
Tph21or.doc
twh13bp.doc
twh13bp2.doc
Twh13or.doc
Twh20or.doc
Twh20or2.doc
Twh21or.doc
Twh22or.doc
Add
Cancel
Advanced...
Find files that match these search criteria:
File name:
Text or property:
Find Now
Files of type:
Office Documents (*.doc; *.xls; *.ppt;
Last modified:
any time
New Search
14 file(s) found.

Figure 23.1.
You can add your Word document files to an electronic binder.

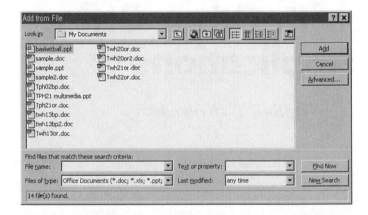

3. Click the Word document files you want to add to your binder, and then click the Add button. You can simultaneously add several files to your binder. Do so by holding down the Ctrl key and clicking each file you want to add as sections to your binder. After you have clicked the Add button, you should see the Microsoft Office Binder program load up the files as shown in Figure 23.2.

Figure 23.2.
Binder can load your Word document files as separate sections for a binder.

Microsoft Office Binder - Binder2
File Edit View Insert Format Tools Table Go Section Help
Normal
Courier New
10
TWH20OR
masters
Developm
SAMPLE
TWH13OR
twh13bp2
three institutions -- Congress, the courts, and business -- show that deregulation may have boundaries at which it cannot go beyond. Particularly in the access charge situation, the demonstration of political opposition would show that flags are being waved in an attempt to put the brakes to the FCC economic-analysis engine thereby stopping it and preserving the ESPs' protective regulatory niches. As Herwitz noted for the broadcasting industry during the telecommunications conference,
the industry and the FCC were [once] going together saying "this is great" . . . "we want competition". . . . [Then] the industry stopped and the FCC kept going and kept deregulating further to increase competition beyond the desires of the . . . industry.
This independent FCC, seemingly riding roughshod in this one instance, would certainly show there can no longer be any industry capture of the regulator. In this access charge situation, the FCC is "convinced the access charge plan is sound economic theory that will benefit the industry (Scott 1987, 7)." However, as the political situation shows, opponents would not stand for an acceleration of the deregulatory movement here.
9 section(s)
1 section(s) selected

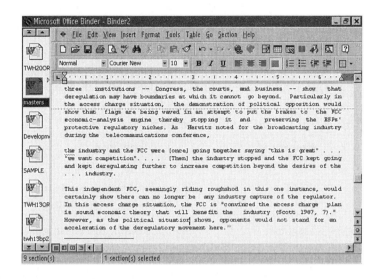

As you can see, the Binder program changes its screen to resemble the Word program's, but subtle differences between the two indicate that you are still in the Binder program. For example, the column to the left shows the separate sections of the binder. You can scroll through that column to see the binder sections. On that column, you will also see arrow buttons at the top and the bottom that you can click. If you click the arrow buttons with the lines, you will either go to the very first or the very last sections of the binder (depending on which button you click). You should also notice a few other differences. For example, the menu bar contains two pull-down menus: Go and Section (I'll discuss these in a moment). You will also notice that if you click File, the File commands refer to binders and not documents.

You can work on a binder section as you would a Word document. The difference is that you are working on a binder section that is a part of a binder. When you save any work you do on a binder section, the whole binder will be saved as an OBD binder file, which will include all of the sections of the binder.

When you save and then close your binder, the Binder program keeps your place. When you open the binder later, the Binder program returns you to the place you were in the binder when it was last saved. This is handy because a binder can become large and may have numerous sections (if you were working on separate Word documents that were not placed in a binder, you would have to wade through each document to find out where you left off).

If you click Go on the menu bar, you will see various commands for opening files or for accessing documents on the World Wide Web. By using a command under the Go selection, you can load the actual program that would normally be associated with the file you are loading. So if you load a Word document, you will actually go to the Word program to edit a document instead of integrating the document as a section into a binder. The Section pull-down menu contains several commands that are useful for working with the different sections of a binder. The commands that appear under the Section selection are listed in Table 23.1.

Table 23.1. The Section selection.

Command	Function
Add	Add a binder (using predefined binder templates)
Add from File	Add to the binder from existing file(s)
Delete	Delete section(s)
Duplicate	Duplicate section(s)
Rename	Rename a section
Rearrange	Rearrange a section (move section to another place in a binder)
Next Section	Go to the next section
Previous Section	Go to the previous section
Hide	Hide a section
Unhide Section	Unhide a section
Page Setup	Set up page formatting
Print Preview	Preview what a print job will look like
Print	Print your binder
Save as File	Save a section to a file
View Outside	View a section using outside program
Section Properties	Provide a summary of the binder
Select/Unselect All	Select or unselect all sections (for duplicating, deleting, and so on)

Binder offers predefined templates with predefined sections that you can use. You might want to explore the different binder templates by selecting Section | Add. If you choose to use the existing templates, you will see a dialog similar to the one shown in Figure 23.3. From this dialog, you can select the template you wish to use.

23

Add Section
General
Office 95 Templates
Webpages
LETTERS
MEMOS
OTHER
REPORTS
Contemporary Memo.dot
Contemporary Press Release.dot
Contemporary Report.dot
Contemporary Resume.dot
Directory.dot
Elegant Fax.dot
Elegant Letter.dot
Elegant Memo.dot
Elegant Press Release.dot
Elegant Report.dot
Elegant Resume.dot
Invoice.dot
Preview
OK
Cancel

Figure 23.3.
Binder has a multitude of predefined templates that you can use if you do not want to construct a binder from scratch.

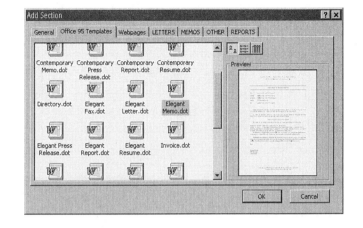

The Duplicate and Rearrange commands will help you copy or move sections around in your binder. Selecting Duplicate or Rearrange invokes the Duplicate Section or Rearrange Sections dialog box, respectively. Figure 23.4 shows these dialog boxes.

Duplicate Section
Insert after:
Cover Letter
Executive Summary
Slide Show
Analysis
Executive Summary (1)
Data
OK
Cancel
Rearrange Sections
Reorder sections:
Cover Letter
Executive Summary
Slide Show
Analysis
Executive Summary (1)
Data
OK
Cancel
Move Up
Move Down

Figure 23.4.
You can duplicate and rearrange sections in your binder.

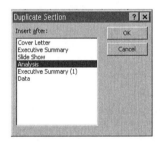

Especially with the predefined templates, you will find that binders are easy to make using your pre-existing Word documents (which you would add to a binder using the Add from File command).

Adding Excel Worksheets and Charts to Word Documents

You can embed (*insert*) a new worksheet, or you can link (*import*) an existing Excel worksheet (also known as a *spreadsheet*) into your Word document. When you embed a new worksheet, you can work with it as you would any Excel worksheet. However, if you link the worksheet, you cannot change the formulas or otherwise manipulate the worksheet.

Embedding a New Excel Worksheet

You can embed a worksheet by using the Insert Object command (this process is similar to what was discussed in Hour 22, "The Insert Menu—Adding Elements to Documents"). To embed a worksheet using the Insert Object command, do the following:

1. Click your cursor in your document where you want to embed the Excel worksheet. You might want to press the Enter key a few times to provide some blank lines between your text and the worksheet.
2. Select Insert | Object to invoke the Object dialog (shown in Figure 23.5).

Object
Create New
Create from File
Object type:
Media Clip
Microsoft Clip Gallery
Microsoft Equation 3.0
Microsoft Excel Chart
Microsoft Excel Worksheet
Microsoft Graph 97 Chart
Microsoft Map
Microsoft Photo Editor 3.0 Photo
Float over text
Display as icon
Result
Inserts a new Microsoft Excel Worksheet object into your document.
OK
Cancel

Figure 23.5.
You can embed an Excel worksheet as an object into your Word document.

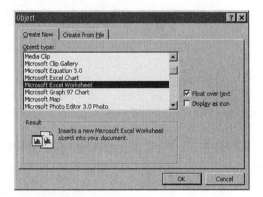

3. In the Create New tab on the Object dialog, click Microsoft Excel Worksheet.
4. Check the Float over text checkbox and click OK.

You can also click the Insert Excel Worksheet button on the Standard toolbar to embed a worksheet:

1. Click the Insert Excel Worksheet button on the Standard toolbar. You will see a 5×4 grid checkerboard.
2. Move your cursor diagonally along the checkerboard, then click when you have selected the number of rows and columns you want for the worksheet.

An Excel worksheet similar to the one shown in Figure 23.6 will be embedded into your Word document.

Double-click inside the worksheet; you will be able use it as you would any Excel worksheet. Click outside the worksheet to work on the surrounding Word document. If you click one time inside the worksheet, you can move the worksheet around your document as you would a picture or graphic object. Manipulate the size of the worksheet by moving the sides as you would with a picture or graphic object.

Microsoft Word - Document1
File Edit View Insert Format Tools Data Window Help
This is a Word document with an Excel worksheet embedded in the document as an object.
Sheet1
Page 1 Sec 1 1/1 At Ln Col

Figure 23.6.
The Excel worksheet will appear inside your Word document.

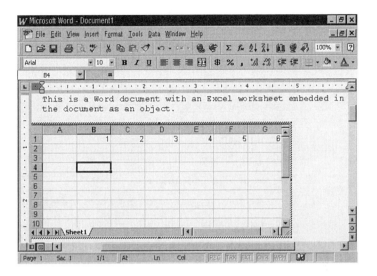

If you check the Display as icon checkbox in the Create New tab of the Object dialog when you embed a worksheet (refer to Figure 23.5), you will embed an Excel worksheet as an icon in your Word document. Double-click that icon to activate Excel so you can work with the worksheet, as shown in Figure 23.7.

Microsoft Word - Document1
File Edit View Insert Format Tools Table Window Help
Microsoft Excel
File Edit View Insert Format Tools Data Window Help
Worksheet in Document1 2
Ready
Microsoft Excel Worksheet
Page 1 Sec 1 1/1 At 4.1" Ln 7 Col 2

Figure 23.7.
You can embed an Excel worksheet as an icon. Double-click the icon work with the worksheet.

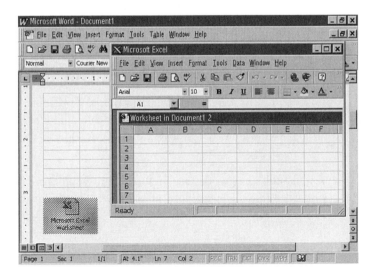

Linking an Existing Excel Worksheet

If you have Excel, you can simply copy and paste from Excel to your Word document:

1. Open the worksheet in Excel from which you want to copy.

2. Select the area in your worksheet that you want to copy. To do this, hold your mouse cursor down on the first cell that you want to start copying from and move your cursor to the end of the area. Release your mouse cursor after you have selected the area.

3. Select Edit | Copy.

4. Go to your Word document.

5. Click the point in your document where you want to place the worksheet.

6. Click Edit | Paste.

If you don't have Excel on your machine but want to import an existing Excel worksheet (perhaps one that is on your company's intranet):

1. Click the Open File button on the Standard toolbar or select File | Open.

2. Click the pull-down Files of type menu at the bottom left of the Open dialog and select Microsoft Excel Worksheet.

3. Click the Excel worksheet (XLS or XLW) file that you want to import into your Word document. Then click OK.

4. This invokes the Convert File dialog, shown in Figure 23.8. Make sure Microsoft Excel Worksheet is selected, and then click OK.

5. You should then see the Open Worksheet dialog (see Figure 23.8). Select Entire Workbook from the Open document in Workbook pull-down menu.

6. If you select anything other than Entire Workbook, you can choose a name or cell range if names or cell ranges are available. If available from the Name or Cell Range pull-down menu, specify the number or name of the range you wish to import.

7. Click OK.

You should see a worksheet imported into your Word document. You can move the worksheet around your document as you would any object, but you cannot double-click it to manipulate it as a worksheet.

Convert File
Convert file from:
Schedule+ Contacts
Personal Address Book
Outlook Address Book
MS-DOS Text with Layout
Text with Layout
HTML Document
WordPerfect 5.x
WordPerfect 6.x
Microsoft Excel Worksheet
OK
Cancel
Open Worksheet
Open document in Workbook:
Entire Workbook
OK
Cancel
Name or Cell Range:
Entire Worksheet
Format for Mail Merge

Figure 23.8.
To link a worksheet, you must convert the worksheet, then select either the entire worksheet or a part of the worksheet to be linked.

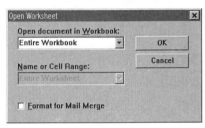

Embedding an Excel Chart

Embedding an Excel chart is very similar to embedding a worksheet. Follow the procedures for inserting an Excel worksheet, but click Microsoft Excel Chart on the Create New tab in the Object dialog (refer to Figure 23.5). You will see a sample chart (similar to the one shown in Figure 23.9) that you can change and manipulate. As you can see, there are Chart and Sheet tabs at the bottom of the worksheet that you can click to switch between the graphical chart and the regular worksheet to change how the chart looks.

Microsoft Word - Document8
File Edit View Insert Format Tools Chart Window Help
100%
Arial
10
Chart Area
Chart
Chart Area
This is a Word document with a Microsoft Excel Chart:
35
30
25
20
15
10
5
0
Food
Gas
Motel
Jan
Feb
Mar
Apr
May
Jun
Chart1
Sheet1
Page 1
Sec 1
1/

Figure 23.9.
When you insert an Excel chart into a Word document, you can manipulate it as you can any Excel worksheet by clicking between the Chart and Sheet tabs at the bottom of the chart.

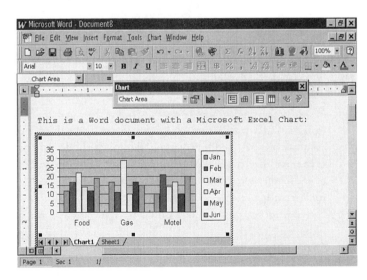

Click between the Chart and Sheet tabs to change the numbers and formulas. Double-click inside the chart to work with the chart, and click outside the chart to work with the surrounding Word document. As with any other object, you can single-click inside the chart to move the chart and change its size.

If you do not have Excel, you can insert a Microsoft Graph 97 chart (see Figure 23.10) by selecting Microsoft Graph 97 Chart from the Object dialog. As with the Excel chart, you get a sample chart with a datasheet that you can manipulate to change the chart (the chart and the datasheet would correspond with the Chart and Sheet tabs for the Excel worksheet).

Figure 23.10.
If you do not have Excel, you can insert a Microsoft Graph 97 chart.

Microsoft Word - Document9
File Edit View Insert Format Tools Data Chart Window Help
Arial
10
100
80
60
40
20
0
1st Qtr
2nd Qtr
3rd Qtr
4th Qtr
Boardwalk
Park Place
Electric Co.
Document9 - Datasheet
A B C D
1st Qtr 2nd Qtr 3rd Qtr 4th Qtr
1 Boardwalk 20.4 27.4 90 20.4
2 Park Place 30.6 38.6 34.6 31.6
3 Electric Co 45.9 46.9 45 43.9
Page 1 Sec 1 1/1

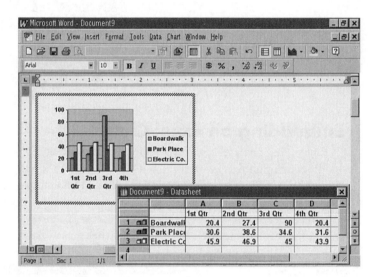

Merging Letters Using an Access Database

Word-processing programs are known for their capability to *mail merge*. In mail merging, information is drawn from a database (in this case, a database made with the Microsoft Access database program) and incorporated into a form document to create multiple copies of the document. Each copy includes information from one record from the database. To perform a mail merge, you would create a database containing records of mailing address information; each record is a collection of fields of specific address data. For instance, a database of all of the addresses of your friends would have specific records for each of your friends. In each

record, there would be even more specific fields of data for such items as first name, last name, street address, city, state, zip code, and so on.

Creating a Mailing List Database with Access

If you have Microsoft Access 97 (it is included with the Professional Edition of Microsoft Office 97 or can be purchased separately), you can build a mailing list database with Access. To do so, follow these steps:

1. Run Access 97.

2. Click the New button (or select File | New Database).

3. Select Blank Database and click OK.

4. In the File New Database dialog, give the new database a name with the .mdb extension. Access will provide a default name, such as db1.mdb. After you choose a filename, click the Create button.

5. This brings you to a database dialog that has several tabs (Tables, Queries, Forms, Reports, Macros, and Modules). Click the Tables tab, and then click the New button.

6. In the New Table dialog, you'll see several options (Datasheet View, Design View, Table Wizard, Import Table, and Link Table). Click Table Wizard, and then click OK.

7. In the Table Wizard dialog, select Mailing List from the Sample Tables list.

8. In the Sample Fields list, pick LastName, FirstName, Address, City, State, and PostalCode. Click the > button to select each field. Each field you select appears in the Fields in my new table list.

9. Click the Next button.

10. You will be asked whether Access should automatically pick a primary key for each database record (a record consists of fields). Choose Yes, and then click the Next button.

11. You will be asked how you want to enter your data. Unless you are comfortable with database programs, click the Enter data into the table using a form the wizard creates for me option. You can also click the New Object button (next to the Office Assistant button on the Database toolbar) to get a wizard-created AutoForm, where you can easily input address information.

    Click the Finish button, and you should see a Mailing List dialog similar to the one shown in Figure 23.11.

Microsoft Access
File Edit View Insert Format Records Tools Window Help
Mailing List
Mailing ListID
3
Last Name
LastName
First Name
FirstName
Address
123 Any Street
City
Any Town
State
ST
Postal Code
12345-6789
Record:
3
of 3
Form View

Figure 23.11.
With Microsoft Access 97, you can easily create and enter records into a mailing list database.

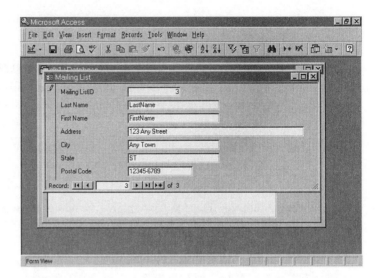

12. Enter address information into the Mailing List dialog. After you finish entering a record, click the button with the right arrow and the asterisk to advance to a blank record so you can enter a new record.
13. Click the exit button on the dialog (the *X* button in the upper-right corner). You will be asked whether you want to save your changes; if you do, click Yes. You will then be asked to provide a name under which the form will be saved. Type a name or use the default name, and then click OK.

Creating Your Mail Merge Document

To create a mail merge document, do the following:

1. Start a new document in Word.
2. Select Tools | Mail Merge.
3. In the Main document section of the Mail Merge Helper dialog (shown in Figure 23.12), click the Create button and select Form Letters.
4. Click Active Window. (If you did not start a new document in Word, click New Main Document.) Click the Edit button that appears next to the Create button, and then click Form Letter.
5. This opens a new document; a Mail Merge toolbar will appear on the screen under the other toolbars.
6. Type the text that you want to merge with your database information. Be sure to leave empty spaces and blank lines between paragraphs where you want the database information to be inserted.

Mail Merge Helper
The main document and data source are now available. Choose the appropriate Edit button to work on either one.
1 Main document
Create
Edit
Merge type: Form Letters
Main document: Document5
2 Data source
Get Data
Edit
Data: db1.mdb!TABLE Mailing List
3 Merge the data with the document
Merge...
Query Options...
Options in effect:
Suppress Blank Lines in Addresses
Merge to new document
Cancel

Figure 23.12.
Word provides a useful Mail Merge Helper dialog that you can use to merge documents.

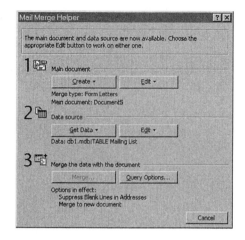

7. Again, select Tools | Mail Merge.
8. In the Data source section of the Mail Merge Helper dialog, click the Get Data button and select Open Data Source (refer to Figure 23.12). This invokes an Open Data Source dialog, which looks very similar to the Open File dialog box.
9. Click the Files of type pull-down menu and select the MS Access Databases option.
10. Go to the directory where you saved your Access mailing list database file. Click that file, and then click the Merge button.
11. You will get a Microsoft Access dialog with two tabs for Tables and Queries. The Tables tab should be active, and should show your mailing list database. If the mailing list is not highlighted, click that and then click the OK button.
12. Because there are no merge fields in your document yet, you will get a dialog box asking you to edit your main document so you can insert merge fields where the database information is to be merged. Click the Edit Main Document button to return to your document. Note that the Insert Merge Field button appears on the Mail Merge toolbar in your document.
13. Click the Insert Merge Field button to pull down the selections for all the fields you can insert into your document. Click the appropriate field to insert them into the appropriate place in your document. For instance, insert the FirstName field after the word *Dear* and before the comma (or before the colon if you use that punctuation in your salutations). Each field will look something like <<*Field*>>.
14. After you insert all the fields in your document, select Tools | Mail Merge. On the Mail Merger Helper dialog, click the Merge button.

15. This invokes a Merge dialog like the one shown in Figure 23.13. In the Merge to drop-down list, select New document. If you want specific records to be merged, specify the range. If there are blank fields in any of the records in your database, you can specify whether blanks will be printed.
16. Click the Merge button.

Merge
Merge to:
New document
Setup...
Records to be merged
All
From:
To:
When merging records
Don't print blank lines when data fields are empty.
Print blank lines when data fields are empty.
No query options have been set.
Merge
Cancel
Check Errors...
Query Options...

Figure 23.13.
You can specify the range of records to be merged into your mail merge document.

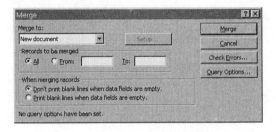

The records in the mailing list database will be merged into the document. For more information about mail merging, review Hour 15, "Mail Merge."

Word's Built-In Data Creator

If you do not have Access, you can still create a mailing list database. From the Mail Merge Helper dialog, click the Get Data button, and then select Create Data. This invokes the Create Data Source dialog, as shown in Figure 23.14.

Create Data Source
A mail merge data source is composed of rows of data. The first row is called the header row. Each of the columns in the header row begins with a field name.
Word provides commonly used field names in the list below. You can add or remove field names to customize the header row.
Field name:
Add Field Name >>
Remove Field Name
Field names in header row:
Title
FirstName
LastName
JobTitle
Company
Address1
Address2
Move
MS Query...
OK
Cancel

Figure 23.14.
You can create a data source file with fields for a mailing list in Word 97.

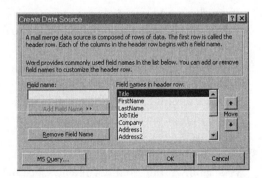

This dialog box contains the basic mailing list fields, some of which you can delete by clicking the Remove Field Name button. Click OK when you are finished; you will then be asked whether you want to edit your data document. Click the Edit Data Source button. In the Data Form dialog, enter the address information (see Figure 23.15).

Data Form
FirstName:
LastName:
Company:
Address1:
City:
State:
PostalCode:
OK
Add New
Delete
Restore
Find...
View Source
Record:
1

Figure 23.15.
Enter the mailing list address information using the Data Form dialog.

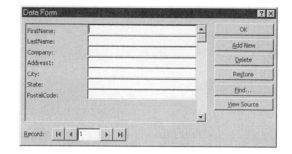

Click the Add New button if you want to add a new record. Click OK when you are finished; you will be asked to make up a name under which to save your mailing list. This mailing list will be saved as a DOC file. Insert the fields into your document and then merge the mailing list data into the document as discussed previously.

Designing Forms

You can design forms for use in your office. There are three types of form fields that you can use:

- A *text form field* allows you to insert an input area in your document where you can type text. For instance, you might use a text form field so a user can type name and address information.
- A *checkbox form field* allows a user to check a selection. Examples of checkbox form fields are Yes/No boxes that users can check to provide an answer to a question.
- A *drop-down* (or *pull-down*) *form field* gives a user a list of selections from which to choose. Drop-down form fields are good for situations where users must answer a multiple-choice question.

Text Form Fields

To insert a text form field into a document, perform the following steps:

1. Create a new document or open an existing one.
2. Click your cursor on the spot in your document where you want to insert a text form.
3. Activate the Forms toolbar (shown in Figure 23.16) by selecting View | Toolbars | Forms.

Forms
ab|

Figure 23.16.
Use the Forms toolbar to insert text, checkbox, and drop-down form fields into your document.

4. Click the Text Form Field button (the one on the far left). Double-click the gray or black field that appears on your document; this invokes the Text Form Field Options dialog (see Figure 23.17).

Text Form Field Options
Type:
Regular text
Default text:
OK
Cancel
Add Help Text...
Maximum length:
Unlimited
Text format:
Run macro on
Entry:
Exit:
Field settings
Bookmark:
Text1
Calculate on exit
Fill-in enabled

Figure 23.17.
You need to set these options when setting up text forms.

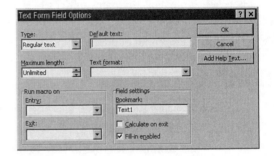

5. The Text Form Field Options dialog contains several options:
   - Type
     - Regular text
     - Number
     - Date
     - Current date
     - Current time
     - Calculation (for calculating a number from a formula that you would insert)
   - Maximum length (any number of characters up to unlimited)
   - Default text (type something or leave this blank)
   - Text format (uppercase, lowercase, first capital, and title case)
   - Fill-in enabled (check this box so the user can type something into the text form field, or "fill in the blank")

You might want to accept the default options, but you might want to type in some default text. For instance, in a text form field where you expect a first name to be entered, you might simply want to use the words `first name` as default text. You should also make sure the box for Fill-in enabled is checked. If you do not check this box, the user will not be able to type anything into the text form field (until you protect the form as described in the section titled "Protect Your Forms").

6. Click OK and repeat as necessary.

Checkbox Form Fields

You can use checkbox form fields for simple questions in your documents. This is what you do:

1. Create a new document or open an existing one.
2. Click your cursor on the spot where you want to place the checkbox form field.
3. If the Forms toolbar is not active, select View | Toolbars | Forms.
4. Click the Check Box Form Field button (the box with the check inside it). A gray box should appear in your document.
5. Double click the gray box; this opens the Check Box Form Field Options dialog (see Figure 23.18).

Figure 23.18.
When using checkbox forms, you may only need to select either the Not checked or the Checked radio button.

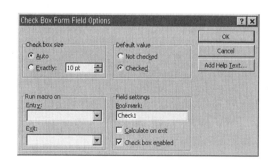

Check Box Form Field Options
OK
Cancel
Add Help Text...
Check box size
Auto
Exactly: 10 pt
Default value
Not checked
Checked
Run macro on
Entry:
Exit:
Field settings
Bookmark:
Check1
Calculate on exit
Check box enabled

6. Click OK and repeat as necessary.

In a typical Yes/No form, you might type `Yes` and then `No`, then insert a checkbox form field after each one. You might want the Yes or No option to be checked automatically as the default answer. Configure this by selecting the Checked on radio button in the Default value section of the Check Box Form Field Options dialog.

Drop-Down Forms

Insert drop-down (or pull-down) form fields into your forms document by following these steps:

1. Create a new document or open an existing one.
2. Click your cursor on the spot in your document where you want to place the drop-down form.
3. Activate the Forms toolbar (if it's not already active).
4. Click the Drop-Down Form Field button (third from the left). A gray field should appear on your document.
5. Double-click the gray field to open the Drop-Down Form Field Options dialog (see Figure 23.19).

Drop-Down Form Field Options
Drop-down item:
4th Item
Add ▸▸
Remove
Items in drop-down list:
1st Item
2nd Item
3rd Item
Move
OK
Cancel
Add Help Text...
Run macro on
Entry:
Exit:
Field settings
Bookmark:
Dropdown1
Calculate on exit
Drop-down enabled

Figure 23.19.
From the Drop-Down Form Field Options dialog, you can add items to appear on a drop-down form.

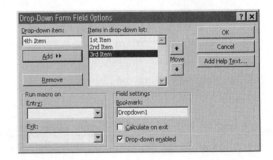

6. In the Drop-down item section, type an item (up to 50 characters) that is to appear in the drop-down form when it is pulled down. Click the Add button. Repeat to add more items.
7. Use the Move arrow keys to move items around. Use the Remove button to remove items.
8. Click OK after you finish adding items. Repeat by adding drop-down forms elsewhere in your document.

Protect Your Forms

When you finish inserting your forms, click the Protect Form button on the Forms toolbar. This will protect your forms from inadvertent changes. If you want more secure protection, add password protection; simply select Tools | Protect Document to invoke the Password dialog box. Type a password that you will remember and click OK; your password will show up as asterisks (*). You will be asked to type in the password again. Do so to confirm the password, and then click OK. To remove the password protection, select Tools | Unprotect Document. Type your password and then click OK.

Summary

This hour demonstrates how to use Word with other Microsoft Office programs such as Binder, Excel, and Access. You learned how to make a binder. You learned how to insert Excel worksheets and charts. You also learned how to make a mailing list using Access and Word's built-in data creator, as well as how to merge that mailing list into a document for mass distribution. You learned how to make office forms using text form fields, checkbox form fields, and drop-down form fields. Now you can move on to Hour 24, "Working with the Web," where you will move out of the office and onto the Web.

Q&A

Q **You didn't go into a lot of specifics of how to use the Excel and Access functions in this hour. Where can I get more information about the specifics of using Excel, Access, and other Office 97 programs?**

A You can go to the Help function in Excel and Access for more instruction. You can also use the wizards in those programs for some direction. You can also get copies of *Teach Yourself Microsoft Excel 97 in 24 Hours*, *Teach Yourself Microsoft Access 97 in 24 Hours*, and *Teach Yourself Microsoft Office 97 in 24 Hours* to learn more about how to use the other Office 97 programs.

23

Hour 24

Working with the Web

This hour explains how to create Web pages and how to use Word's Web tools. Word 97 includes features that simplify the way that Web pages are created, making it possible for anyone to develop a great-looking Web page.

The hyperlinks tool is not only valuable for creating Web pages, but can also be great for organizing groups of Word documents. Microsoft has given top priority to integrating its products with the Web, and it certainly has come a long way with Word 97's Web capabilities.

The highlights of this hour include

☐ How to use the Web toolbar

☐ How to create hyperlinks and use them effectively

☐ How to turn existing Word documents into Web pages

Connecting to the World

The Internet is a collection of interconnected computer networks that span the globe, allowing a tremendous amount of information to be shared. The World Wide Web (WWW or Web) is a user-friendly system that allows users with Web browser software to find their way through the Internet. Word 97 can open a Web browser program to give you access to information on the Web.

A *Web browser* is a software program that allows you to access the Web. Netscape Navigator and Microsoft Internet Explorer are two popular Web browsers.

You need to have Internet Explorer or another Web browser installed before you can connect to the Web. Word 97 needs to run a Web browser program to open Web pages or to preview your Web page designs.

JUST A MINUTE

If you do not have Web access, you can use some of the Web features of Word 97, such as *hyperlinks* in Word documents, but you will not be able to view anything on the Web. If you want to get connected to the Web from home, you will need a modem and an *Internet service provider (ISP)*. Here are a few of the popular ISPs:

- ☐ AT&T Worldnet (800)967-5363
- ☐ Microsoft Network (800)386-5550
- ☐ CompuServe (800)848-8199
- ☐ America Online (800)827-6364

Most ISPs charge a monthly rate of about $20 for unlimited access, and most have an hourly rate program. You may wish to find a local ISP by looking in your Yellow Pages under Computer Online Services or Internet Service Providers. If you work for an organization that has a computer network, your computer may have Web access through that network.

 A *hyperlink* is text or a picture that causes you to jump to another document or Web page when it is clicked. Text that is a hyperlink is underlined and often has a different font color. Pictures that are hyperlinks often have a colored border.

An *Internet service provider (ISP)* is a company that maintains a large computer system to which you can connect. The company has the telephone and computer resources to link to the Web. When you dial in using your modem through your phone line, you can connect to the ISP's computer systems that link to the Web. Most ISPs also have interesting resources that you can use directly from their computers (called *servers*).

Many long distance telephone companies such as AT&T and MCI are starting to offer combinations of telephone and computer services that include access to the Internet. The new trend is moving toward a combination of cable television, telephone service, and Internet access from a single provider over the same lines.

When you subscribe with an ISP, it will supply you with software that needs to be installed on your computer to link to its computers. It will provide the instructions for using the software to connect. Once you have the software installed, you go through a process called *logging in*, where you supply your computer name (or your real name) and a password (of your choosing) each time you connect. This protects you and your ISP from unauthorized use of your account.

Using the Web Toolbar

Clicking the Web toolbar button on the Standard toolbar makes the Web toolbar visible. Many of the capabilities of Microsoft Internet Explorer are included in Word 97 and are represented on the Web toolbar.

The Web toolbar interfaces with the Web browser you have on your computer. For the sake of this discussion, we will assume you are using Internet Explorer. There are similar buttons and functions in other Web browsers, and most are designed in such a way that they are easy to figure out. Figure 24.1 shows Word's Web toolbar.

Back
Forward
Stop Current Jump
Refresh Current Page
Start Page
Search the Web
Favorites
Go
Show only Web toolbar
Address

Figure 24.1.
The Web toolbar.

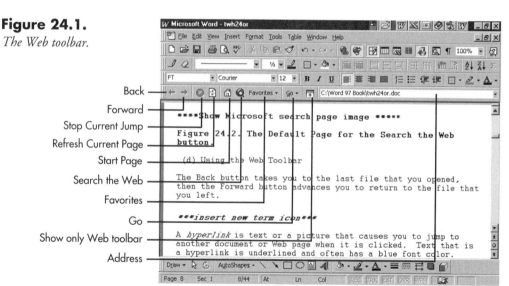

Check Your Connection

Click the Search the Web button on the Web toolbar. Internet Explorer opens with the Microsoft search page as in Figure 24.2 (unless you have changed the default search page). If the search page appeared, you are connected. If you didn't connect and you get an error message, there are a few things you can check:

- Are you still connected to your ISP through your phone line? Close Word to see whether you have a Windows message saying you are disconnected. If so, you'll need to log in again to reconnect.

Figure 24.2.
The default page for the Search the Web button.

Netscape - [microsoft.com Search Wizard]
File Edit View Go Bookmarks Options Directory Window Help
Go to: http://www.microsoft.com/search/default.asp
MICROSOFT PRODUCTS SEARCH SUPPORT SHOP WRITE US
Microsoft
microsoft.com Search Wizard
WHERE DO YOU WANT TO go TODAY
I want to search for:
Quick Tips for more effective searching.
I want to search the:
microsoft.com site
(Full Site Search)
Internet using Alta Vista
Internet using Excite
Internet using Infoseek
Internet using Lycos
Internet using Magellan
Internet using Yahoo
Document: Done

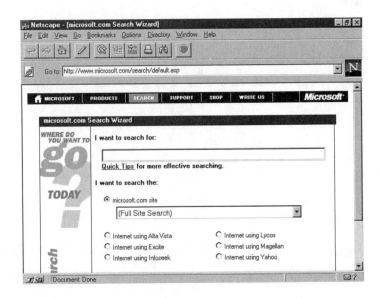

- If you don't see a disconnect message, you may need to install a browser. Internet Explorer is included with Word, but if you didn't select the Web options when you installed Word, you'll need to run Setup again to add the Web options.
- If neither of these solutions gives you access to the Web, contact your ISP and explain your situation. Your ISP should be able to help with problems specific to connecting to the Web through its service.

TIME SAVER

> If you use the same telephone line for your phone and your modem, you can only use one at a time. If you are online, a disconnection may occur when someone picks up one of the phones on this line. If you lose your connection and aren't sure why, this is probably the first thing to check. Don't be too hard on the culprit. Get in the habit of putting a sticky note on the phones to warn others when you're using the line.

The Web Toolbar Buttons

Microsoft went to a lot of trouble to design the Office 97 toolbars with consistency in mind. Word's Web toolbar mirrors closely what Internet Explorer displays. If you click the Search the Web button on Word's Web toolbar, you actually open Internet Explorer (or your browser). You will see buttons similar to those on Word's Web toolbar, like Back, Forward, and Start Page.

Back and Forward

Because of the amount of jumping from document to document that you do, the Back and Forward buttons on Word's Web toolbar are useful with documents that use hyperlinks. These buttons will only take you to files opened from:

- ☐ The Start button
- ☐ The Search the Web button
- ☐ Favorites
- ☐ A Web address you type in the Address bar

The files become part of the history list, which includes as many as ten of the last documents you opened using one of these techniques. Using File | Open opens a file, but this file is not included in the Web history list.

Stop Current Jump

The Stop Current Jump button is the button that lets you stop a jump when you are opening a Web page. Click this when the Web page is taking too long to open. This button does not work for hyperlinks to documents on your hard drive.

 A *Web page* is a document stored somewhere on a computer that others can link to through the Internet. An organization's or individual's introductory document (the Web site's first page) is called a *home page.*

Refresh Current Page

When you open a file on the Web, your Web browser makes a copy of the file for you to read. If you visited this site previously, what you see may not actually be the newest version of the file. Some sites update constantly, such as the ones that relay sports scores or stock quotes. Clicking the Refresh Current Page button gives you the most recent information.

Start Page

The Start Page button opens the default beginning Web page or document.

To change your Start page:

1. Open the file or Web page that you want to use as your Start page. This should be a document or Web page that you use frequently or one that you don't mind seeing each and every time you search the Web.
2. Select Set Start Page from the Go menu on the Web toolbar.
3. Click Yes to make the current Web page or document your new default Start page. This will now be the page that first opens in your browser if you are using Internet Explorer.

24

Search the Web

The Search the Web button can be changed in the same way as the Start page. Most people prefer to have a Start page that includes the major search engines. Internet Explorer has an excellent reference to these search engines on the default Start page, so consider carefully before changing the default to another page or document—you'll want to find your way around when you're out on the Web.

NEW TERM *Search engines* are tools Web developers have created specifically to find information on the Web. Search engines include a box where you can type what you're looking for. By clicking a Search button of some variety, you direct the search engine to look through huge databases to compile a list of places that might have the information you want.

Favorites

Use the Add to Favorites option shown in Figure 24.3 to save the location of the current document to your list of Favorites. Using Favorites from the Web toolbar is much like using Favorites in the Open or Save dialog boxes, but it also includes references to places you link to through the Web.

Microsoft Word - Hormel thank you- Mike MacLean
File Edit View Insert Format Tools Table Window Help
Normal
Times New Roman
10
Favorites
Go
C:\Jobs and Grades\Job Search\Hormel thank you- Mike MacLean.
Add to Favorites...
Open Favorites...
Annual report docs
Imported Bookmarks
schoolwork
GA resume
pasta recipes
John A. Doe
123 Sunny View Apts., Bloomington, IN 47408
(812) 555-3912
April 18, 1997
Michael MacLarson
Manager, Professional Staffing and Recruitment
Hefty Foods Corporation
1 Hefty Place
Austin, MN 55912
Dear Mike,
Draw
AutoShapes
Page 1 Sec 1 1/1 At 2.2" Ln 11 Col 1 REC TRK EXT OVR WPH

Figure 24.3.
The Favorites menu.

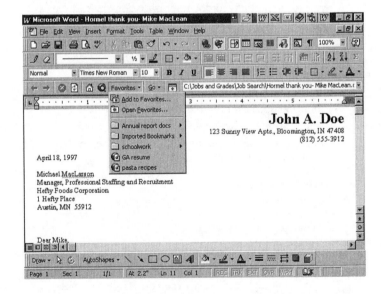

The Favorites folder is also used in Internet Explorer to save the location of favorite Web pages. It is a handy way to quickly open files and Web pages that you use often, but your favorites list can become a crowded mess if you regularly use the Favorites folder. If you put a lot of files in the Favorites menu, you may want to delete some files or create folders to organize the files.

To organize the Favorites folder:

1. Select Open Favorites from the Favorites menu.
2. Click the Configure button. This opens the Favorites folder in Windows Explorer (see Figure 24.4).

Exploring - Favorites
File Edit View Tools Help
All Folders
Contents of 'Favorites'
Windows
Command
Config
Cookies
Cursors
Desktop
Favorites
Annual report docs
Imported Bookmarks
proposals
schoolwork
Fonts
Forms
Help
History
Inf
Annual report docs
Imported Bookmarks
proposals
schoolwork
GA resume
Interview with Keith Kelley
Interview with Teresa Jones
Jobs and Grades
My Documents
spring
10 object(s)
0.98KB (Disk free space: 36.7MB)

Figure 24.4.
Organizing the Favorites menu.

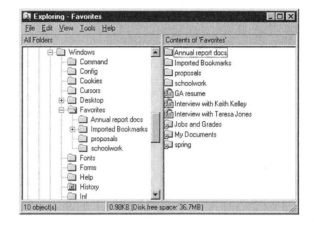

3. Delete any unwanted files by selecting the files and pressing the Delete key.
4. Click Yes if you get a message asking whether you want to send the files to the recycle bin. (You may or may not get this message depending on the way your recycle bin options have been set.)
5. Organize files into folders by selecting New | Folder from the File menu.
6. Type in a name for the folder.
7. Drag the documents that you would like to keep together into that folder.

Go

The Go drop-down menu has an option called Open, which allows you to type a Uniform Resource Locator (URL) or the location of a file on your drive. Be sure to click the Open in new window box if you are opening a file from your hard drive and don't want to close the file that is currently open.

NEW TERM A *Uniform Resource Locator* is like a mailing address. It tells the Web browser exactly where to go. For example, URLs that begin with `HTTP://` go to a site like `www.microsoft.com`, which is Microsoft's home page, and may go to a specific page or document at the Microsoft site. You can often tell what kind of site you're linking to by the three-character extension at the end of the site address. For example, `.com` denotes commercial sites, `.edu` denotes educational institutions, `.gov` denotes government sites, `.org` denotes organizations, and so forth.

If you are connected to the Web, here are some examples of URLs (Web addresses) that you can use to visit some good Web pages:

`http://www.discovery.com`—for inquisitive minds

`http://www.disney.com`—for the kids

`http://www.businessweek.com`—business news

`http://www.allapartments.com`—find an apartment

`http://www.amazon.com`—buy a book

`http://www.switchboard.com`—find the phone number, address, or e-mail address of a lost friend or relative

Address Box

The Address box shows the path and name of the document that is currently in use. Clicking the drop-down arrow to the right of the Address box gives you a list of previously used files. Files listed are limited to the ones mentioned earlier in the section on the Back and Forward buttons. Web pages that you have visited in Internet Explorer also appear in the list. You can select a file or Web page from the list, and it opens.

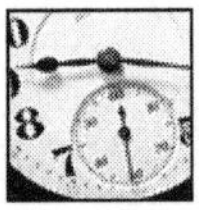

TIME SAVER

> Quickly open a Web page or document by selecting whatever filename or URL appears in the Address box and replacing it by typing a different filename or URL and pressing Enter. You may find this quicker than using the Open function from the Go drop-down menu. Also, you don't need to type the `http://`, and you can often leave off the www that starts many Web addresses. For example, you can type `microsoft.com` in the Address box instead of `http://www.microsoft.com`. Notice that the browser adds the `http://` for you.

Hyperlinks

Web pages are written in Hypertext Markup Language (HTML), which uses hyperlinks extensively. Word also uses hyperlinks. Hyperlink text in a Word document is blue and underlined, as it is on most Web pages. When you move your pointer over a hyperlink, the pointer turns into a hand. When you click the hyperlink, you jump to the file or Web page to which the hyperlink is linked.

Inserting a Hyperlink

You might have a document that includes information that can be found in another document or from a Web site. Inserting a hyperlink lets you connect to a file or Web page. This is quickly becoming a standard method of conveying information. Rather than

including myriads of text in a single document, hyperlinks provide a way to specify other locations from which to gather the information.

To insert a hyperlink:

1. Select some text or a picture. This becomes your hyperlink.
2. Click the Insert Hyperlink button on the Standard toolbar. The Insert Hyperlink dialog box appears (see Figure 24.5).

Figure 24.5.
Inserting a hyperlink in a Word document.

Insert Hyperlink
Link to file or URL:
C:\Hal\97 CSR Meetings\April 30 Meeting letter.doc
Browse...
Enter or locate the path to the document you want to link to. This can be an Internet address (URL), a document on your hard drive, or a document on your company's network.
Path: ..\Hal\97 CSR Meetings\April 30 Meeting letter.doc
Named location in file (optional):
Browse...
If you want to jump to a specific location within the document, such as a bookmark, a named range, a database object, or a slide number, enter or locate that information above.
Use relative path for hyperlink
OK
Cancel

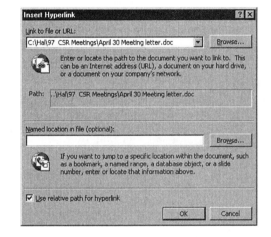

3. Type the name of a file or the address of a Web page in the Link to file or URL text box. If you want to link to a file but aren't sure of its location, click the Browse button to locate the file.
4. Click OK.

KEYBOARD SHORTCUT

Ctrl+K inserts a hyperlink for selected text or pictures.

Clicking the hyperlink automatically goes to the file or Web page that you set as the file path or URL. You do not need any kind of permission to create a hyperlink to a Web page. You only need to know the URL. If you do not have access to the Web, you can use the Insert Hyperlink function to create hyperlinks to other documents on your computer.

TIME SAVER

A quick and easy way to avoid errors in typing long URLs when making a hyperlink follows:

1. Go to the Web page to which you intend to link.
2. Select the entire URL from the Address box of your Web browser.
3. Press Ctrl+C to copy the URL to the clipboard.
4. Click the Insert Hyperlink button on the Standard toolbar.
5. Press Ctrl+V to paste the URL in the Link to file or URL box.

Another easy way to create a hyperlink is to simply type a URL. Try typing any URL in a document; Word recognizes it and turns it into a hyperlink. This is great if you want the URL you type to be a hyperlink. Of course, this feature can be maddening if you are typing URLs that you don't want to turn into hyperlinks. To change a URL to regular text, press the backspace key after you have typed the URL and it has become a hyperlink.

To disable the automatic hyperlink function:

1. Select AutoCorrect on the Tools menu.
2. Select the AutoFormat As You Type tab.
3. Uncheck the Internet and network paths with hyperlinks option, as shown in Figure 24.6.

AutoCorrect
AutoCorrect
AutoFormat As You Type
AutoText
AutoFormat
Apply as you type
Headings
Borders
Tables
Automatic bulleted lists
Automatic numbered lists
Replace as you type
"Straight quotes" with "smart quotes"
Ordinals (1st) with superscript
Fractions (1/2) with fraction character (½)
Symbol characters (--) with symbols (—)
Bold and _underline_ with real formatting
Internet and network paths with hyperlinks
Automatically as you type
Format beginning of list item like the one before it
Define styles based on your formatting
OK
Cancel

Figure 24.6.
Removing the automatic hyperlink function.

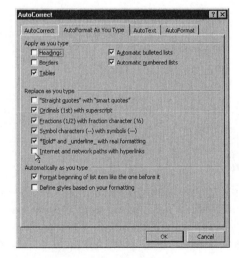

4. Select the AutoFormat tab and uncheck the Internet and network paths with hyperlink box if you plan to use AutoFormatting in the document.

You will sometimes want to make a hyperlink jump to another location within the same document. You might also want to jump to a specific place in another document. The easiest way to create these kinds of hyperlinks is by using the drag-and-drop technique.

To create a hyperlink between two documents by using drag-and-drop:

1. Open both documents and select Arrange All from the Window menu. This allows you to see both documents at the same time.
2. Find the start of the text in the document to which you want to link. Select a few words at the beginning of the segment.
3. Click the selected text and hold down the right mouse button while dragging it to the location where you want to place the hyperlink.
4. Click Create Hyperlink Here.

The hyperlink will appear with the name of the selected text. If you want to change the name of the hyperlink, simply select and type over the existing name. Changing the hyperlink name has no effect on the original text. When you click a hyperlink, the referenced document opens and you are placed at the location where you created the hyperlink. You can still access any part of the document, but this is your starting point.

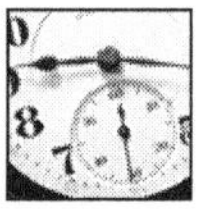

TIME SAVER

> When you select a hyperlink to change its name, be certain that the pointer is far enough from the hyperlink to display the I-bar rather than the hand. Otherwise you will activate the hyperlink rather than select the hyperlink text.

Getting Rid of a Hyperlink

If you want to remove the hyperlink attribute that has been assigned to text or a picture, follow these steps:

1. Select the entire hyperlink text or picture.
2. Click the Insert Hyperlink button. The Edit Dialog box opens.
3. Press the Remove Link button. If the hyperlink was text, the text will now be bold.
4. Select the text that was the hyperlink and click the Bold button on the formatting toolbar to remove the bold style from the text.

To get rid of a hyperlink and the representative text or graphic, simply select the hyperlink and press the Delete key.

When to Use a Hyperlink

Hyperlinks are useful in a variety of situations. For example, say you are creating a to-do list for someone who is substituting for you in your job. Using hyperlinks to files in this kind of document makes it easier for someone who is unfamiliar with your computer filing methods to locate the necessary files (see Figure 24.7).

Figure 24.7.
A document with hyperlinks.

Microsoft Word - Note for Courtney L.doc
File Edit View Insert Format Tools Table Window Help
Normal
Times New Roman
11
Courtney,
Thanks for sitting in for me today. It really helps me out that you can cover for me like this.
Here's what needs to be done:
(click on the hyperlinks to get to the files you need)
• Greg Mather needs this proposal proofread before lunch. Please print it and put it on his desk with any corrections.
• This letter about the Apr. 30th meeting needs to be sent to the following people. If Teresa Jones calls for information about the meeting, I put together an agenda that should answer her questions.
• I started an Excel worksheet that analyzes our shipping and printing costs over the past 6 months. Ray Burke in Accounting (ext. 143) said that he could help you locate some of the information that is missing.
Thanks so much for your help!
Page 1 Sec 1 1/1 At 1" Ln 1 Col 1 REC TRK EXT OVR WPH

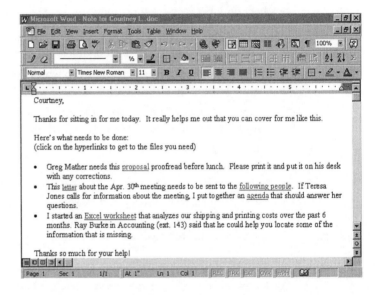

The underlined words appear in blue to signify the hyperlinks. All the substitute has to do is click the hyperlinks to get to the pertinent files.

You could use hyperlinks to interconnect sets of related documents to take the hassle out of opening each document when you work. Hyperlinks could also be used at the beginning of a large document to quickly jump to specific sections of the document. This is part of the principle behind the Master Document format.

CAUTION

Don't use hyperlinks if you are going to move any of the files and you don't want to redo the hyperlinks. When you move a linked document, the linking document can no longer find it.

Saving Documents in HTML

If you have never created a Web page, now is your chance.

1. Open any Word document.
2. Select Save as HTML from the File menu.
3. Click the Save button. You are now a Web page creator.

If you put this new file on a computer that is a Web server, it is said to be "on the Web." Your network administrator or your ISP can help you with the details on how to place your files on the server. Anyone who has Web access can read the file if he knows the address of the file (the URL). It could also be used on a company's intranet system in the same way.

 An *intranet* is like an internal Internet. People within a company or an organization have an interconnected computer system and can share information and resources through a centralized system (a server or servers).

JUST A MINUTE

> When you select Save as HTML, some parts of your Word document will not convert to HTML. Specifically, margins, tabs, columns, and page numbers do not translate. Font sizes and line spacing are also different. The differences come because HTML is incompatible with some of Word's features. For example, Word saves text in the nearest available font size that works in HTML. You will see some differences because there are fewer HTML font sizes than Word font sizes.

24

When you are working with an HTML document, three new buttons appear on the Standard toolbar: the Web Page Preview, Form Design Mode, and Insert Picture buttons, as shown in Figure 24.8.

Figure 24.8.
The Standard toolbar for HTML documents.

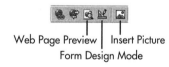

Web Page Preview | Insert Picture
Form Design Mode

Web Page Preview

Click the Web Page Preview button to see what your HTML file looks like in your Web browser. Your page might look very different when you preview it in your Web browser. It is a good idea to click the Web Page Preview button periodically while authoring Web pages with Word to see how they will actually look on the Web. You can edit your HTML file with most of the same tools that you would use to edit a Word document to clean up any conversion problems or to add to the document.

Form Design Mode

Clicking the Form Design Mode button brings up the Control toolbox, which boasts several different icons. If you have ever used Microsoft Access, the Office database tool, you'll notice a striking resemblance. You can create sophisticated HTML documents that include elements such as buttons, drop-down lists, and password requirements (see Figure 24.9).

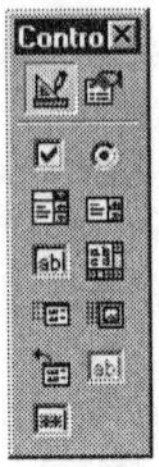
Contro

Figure 24.9.
Use the Control toolbox to add buttons and lists.

The Control toolbar is also available in a regular Word document. Some of the options are different from the ones that are available when working in an HTML document.

You can make your Web pages accept information with the use of form controls. You will be able to add these controls, but you will need to consult with your ISP or Web administrator to make them functional.

To add form elements:

1. Select Forms from the Insert menu (be sure you have an HTML document open) or click the Form Design Mode button.
2. Choose the type of form element you would like to add. The Control toolbox opens, and you can click the properties button to change the attributes of your form element.

Insert Pictures

Pictures on the Web are of two types: JPG and GIF. Word conveniently converts many types of pictures to GIF format when you select Save as HTML. This is a terrific feature for Web page authors, who generally have had to use separate software to convert files to these Web-compatible types.

If you insert a JPG in the Word document, it will not be changed to a GIF in the conversion to HTML. The two drawbacks are that there is no feature that allows you to convert to JPG format, and all converted pictures are renamed to a number, such as `image1.gif`, so you may want to rename the picture to something more descriptive. GIFs look best for drawings and icons, while JPGs look best for photos.

TIME SAVER

Graphical images add a lot to Web pages and can make them more appealing. Keep in mind that the quantity and size of graphics affect the time it takes to load your Web page. If your primary aim is to communicate information rather than to look impressive, it may be a good idea to keep graphics to a minimum. People with slower modems are likely to give up before the page loads if there is too much graphical content.

24

Web Page Wizard

The Save as HTML function is great if you already have a Word document that needs to be put on the Web. If you are starting a page from scratch, it is best to use the Web Page wizard or use a blank Web page. Starting a page this way avoids the conversion problems.

To create a Web page with Web Page wizard:

1. Choose New from the File menu.
2. Select the Web Pages tab.
3. Select Web Page Wizard (see Figure 24.10). If the Web Pages tab does not appear, you need to install Word's Web authoring tools.

New
General
Letters & Faxes
Memos
Other Documents
Web Pages
Office 95 Templates
Blank Web Page
More Cool Stuff
Web Page Wizard
Preview
Preview not available.
Create New
Document
Template
OK
Cancel

Figure 24.10.
Creating a Web page with Web Page wizard.

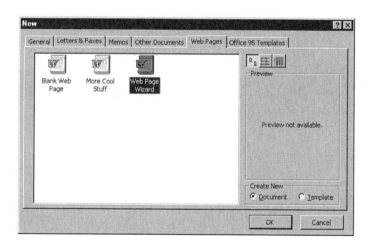

The Web Page wizard will prompt you to select a Web page type, then a visual style as in Figure 24.11. When you have completed the steps in the Web Page wizard, you type over the top of the text on the page with your own information as with other templates to create your Web page.

Web Page Wizard
What type of Web page would you like to create?
<Blank>
2-Column Layout
3-Column Layout
Calendar
Centered Layout
Form - Feedback
Form - Registration
Form - Survey
Personal Home Page
Simple Layout
Table of Contents
Cancel
< Back
Next >

Figure 24.11.
Choosing a style from the Web Page wizard.

To give your Web page the look you want, there are many ways to customize your page with Word's features. To change the font color of the document text:

1. Choose Select All from the Edit menu or press Ctrl+A to select the whole document.
2. Select Format | Font.
3. Choose a color from the Color drop-down list.

To change the background color or image:

1. Select Background from the Format menu.
2. Choose a color for your background, or if you want a textured background, choose Fill Effects and select one of the Texture designs (see Figure 24.12).

Fill Effects
Texture
Texture:
OK
Cancel
Stationery
Other Texture...
Sample:

Figure 24.12.
Choosing a textured background style.

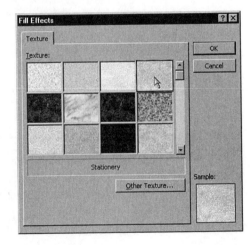

To insert pictures:

1. Select Picture from the Insert menu.
2. Select Clip Art or From File.
3. If you're inserting a picture from a file, locate the file and click Insert. If you're inserting from the Clip Gallery, select an image and click Insert.
4. Click the Web Page Preview button on the Standard HTML toolbar to see the image on your Web page. When using images on a page, be sure to keep track of where they are. If you put an HTML file on a Web server, you will also need to place all of the image files that go with it on the server.

To add a horizontal line:

1. Position the cursor where you want to insert a line.
2. Select Horizontal Line from the Insert menu (see Figure 24.13).
3. Click one of the line styles, or click the More button for additional styles.
4. Select a style and click OK.
5. Click the Web Page Preview button on the Standard toolbar to see what the line looks like on your page.

Horizontal Line
Style:
OK
Cancel
More...

Figure 24.13.
Adding a horizontal line.

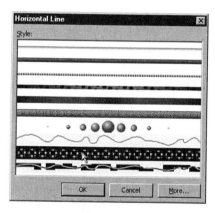

Using Tables in Web Pages

Tables are widely used in Web pages, and can be a useful way to format information on your pages. To create a table:

1. Select Insert Table from the Table menu, as shown in Figure 24.14, or click the Insert Table button on the Standard toolbar. A grid will appear that allows you to specify the size of the table you want.

2. Hold down the mouse button and move across and down to define the number of columns and rows in the table. You can readjust later if you need to add or remove cells.
3. Make any adjustments to the table by selecting the table and using the tools in the Table menu.

Microsoft Word - My Very First Home Page
File Edit View Insert Format Tools Table Window Help
Draw Table
Insert Table...
Delete Cells...
Merge Cells
Split Cells...
Table Properties...
Cell Properties...
Borders...
Select Row
Select Column
Select Table
Distribute Rows Evenly
Distribute Columns Evenly
Convert Text to Table...
Sort...
Split Table
Hide Gridlines
Normal
Times New Roman
100%
Taste tests
Links to Friends
A table of Packers Stats:
13 x 4 Table
Page 1 Sec 1 1/1 At 0.9" Ln Col 12 REC TRK EXT OVR WPH

Figure 24.14.
Adding a table to the Web page.

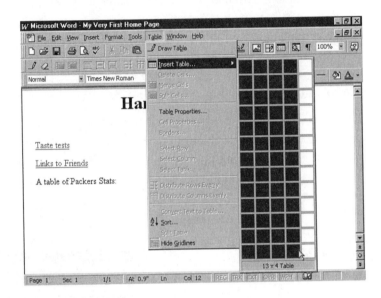

Summary

This hour discusses Word 97's Web features. Many of these features can be useful for simple document sharing without Internet access. The Web toolbar has tools that allow you to search the Web with your browser. Hyperlinks can be used in both Word documents and Web pages to allow the reader to jump to other documents or locations.

The Save as HTML option allows you to convert existing Word documents to Web pages. You can create a new Web page by using the Web Page wizard or a blank Web page.

Q&A

Q How can I work with the actual HTML programming language when making a Web page?

A Choose HTML Source from the View menu to see the source code. This is useful if you know how to program in HTML and would like more precision, or if you are curious to know what HTML is and how it works.

Q **How can I make a counter on my Web page so that I know how many people have visited my site?**

A This requires you to insert a code into your HTML source code. It also requires the help of a site that supplies Web counter services, such as `http://www.digits.com` or `http://www.nosc.mil/planet_earth/info.html`, to update your counter. This is often free unless a large number of people visit your site. The place that supplies the counter will tell you exactly what to put in your HTML source code.

Q **How do I put video clips or sound into my Web page?**

A Both of these options are under the Insert menu. Select Video or Background Sound to add these types of files to your Web page. Be aware that video and sound files load very slowly from the Web. This discourages many people from visiting a site. Until speedier video comes along, most designers avoid using it on a regular basis. Sound does not slow the process as dramatically, but may be enough to cause you to ask whether it is worth the price of deterring part of your audience.

Q **How can I make text that scrolls across the screen?**

A Select Scrolling Text from the Insert menu, then type in the text that you want to have scroll. This feature works when viewed in Internet Explorer, but not in Netscape Navigator. The text appears stationary in Navigator.

24

RW 6

Word in Real Time

Building a Web Page

This example uses some of the techniques discussed in Hour 24, "Working with the Web," to develop a simple corporate Web page.

The first step in developing a good Web site is to consider the structure of the site. Think about what information you wish to convey, and how this information could be broken down into a series of interrelated Web pages. This company wants the user to be able to see four things:

- ☐ A price list for the product
- ☐ The number to call to order the product
- ☐ The company's mission statement
- ☐ A link to the Web page of an industry association

All these items will be linked to the first page of the Web site, called the *home page*. The pages developed for each of these can be accessed from the home page.

Step 1—Create a Home Page

A company's home page is its face to the world. When users connect to the company's Web site, this is the first page they will see. A home page usually includes information about the organization and acts as a home base that leads to information on linking pages. The greatest amount of development time is usually spent creating the home page because it is the first thing that visitors to the company's site see. To create a home page for Widgets Enterprises, do the following:

1. Start a new blank Web page from the Web Pages tab in the File | New dialog box.

   You might see a message that asks whether you want to learn about new Web page authoring tools. Unless you are logged on and connected to an Internet server, click No. If you are connected, you can click Yes if you want to look for the tools; click No to move on.
2. Type, in regular text, what you want the page to look like. Use short topic descriptions such as "Order a Widget" for text that you want to use as hyperlinks (see Figure R6.1). Text can be formatted using Word's heading styles. Main headings, for example, should be formatted with the Heading 1 style.
3. Save the file as `index.html`. Most Web servers automatically look for a file called `index.html` to call up a home page. Network administrators can point to a file with any name for a home page, but using `index.html` is a standard practice. It is much easier for people to access your page when you follow this convention.
4. Click the Web Page Preview button to view the page from Internet Explorer or your browser.

Figure R6.1.
The Widget Enterprises home page.

Microsoft Word - home
File Edit View Insert Format Tools Table Window Help
100%
Normal
Times New Roman
Widget Enterprises
Welcome to Widget Enterprises! We are the largest supplier of standard-size unpadded widgets in the Northeastern United States, and have been in business since 1918. Our business is expanding rapidly, and we hope that you, too, will come to see why so many companies and individuals are choosing us for all of their widget needs.
What would you like to do?
Order a Widget
Read our Mission Statement
Go to the Widget Producers of America (WPA) home page
Page 1 Sec 1 1/2 At 2.7" Ln Col 54 REC TRK EXT OVR WPH

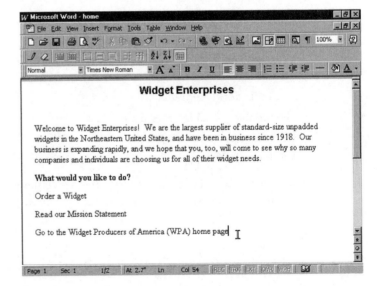

Step 2—Create a Page for Orders

It was previously determined that there would be access to the information for ordering products. To create the document that will be used for ordering purposes:

1. Create another new blank Web page, and give it the filename `order.html`. It's always a good idea to save all your linking Web pages in the same folder as your home page file.
2. Add a title to the top of the page. Again, format text using Word's heading styles.
3. Add a table to the page to use for a price list using the Insert Table button on the Standard toolbar, or by using Table | Insert Table.
4. Add the information and the toll-free number to the table.
5. Adjust the rows and columns of the table to achieve the look that you want. To add borders to tables in a Web page, you must use the Table | Borders menu. You have only two presets to choose from (with or without a grid). You can also set the line width.
6. Save the file again, and click the Web Page Preview button to see what the table looks like in your browser (see Figure R6.2).

Figure R6.2.
Preview the `order.html` *page in your default browser.*

order - Microsoft Internet Explorer
File Edit View Go Favorites Help
Back Forward Stop Refresh Home Search Favorites Print Font Mail Edit
Address C:\WE Web page\order.html
Links
Order a Widget
Widget Model Type Price
061 Circulating 20 hp $19.95
062 Circulating 40 hp $36.50
071 Compression 80 hp $49.95
072 Compression 100 hp $55.00
081 Fixed Position 500 hp $250.00
Call 1-(800) 555-2000 to order a widget or a free color brochure
Done

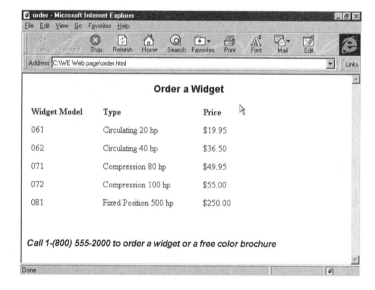

Step 3—Create a Hyperlink from the Home Page to the Order Page

A hyperlink is needed between `index.html` and `order.html` so that people can jump from the home page to the order page. To create the link:

1. Select Window | index.html to create a hyperlink from the home page to the order page.
2. Select the text "Order a Widget" and choose Hyperlink from the Insert menu or click the Insert Hyperlink button on the Standard toolbar.
3. Type `order.html` in the Link to file or URL text box (see Figure R6.3).
4. Click OK.

Insert Hyperlink
Link to file or URL:
order.html
Browse...
Enter or locate the path to the document you want to link to. This can be an Internet address (URL), a document on your hard drive, or a document on your company's network.
Path:
order.html
Named location in file (optional):
Browse...
If you want to jump to a specific location within the document, such as a bookmark, a named range, a database object, or a slide number, enter or locate that information above.
Use relative path for hyperlink
OK
Cancel

Figure R6.3.
Make a hyperlink to `order.html`.

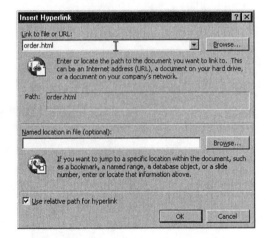

Step 4—Create a Hyperlink to the Company's Mission Statement

The company's mission statement was already created as a Word document. To use it as a hyperlink to the home page:

1. Open the document.
2. Select File | Save As HTML (see Figure R6.4).
3. Name the file (for example, `mission_statement`). Web page names should not include spaces. In this case, an underscore is used between the words. This is another common Web page naming convention.

Microsoft Word - Mission Statement.doc
File Edit View Insert Format Tools Table Window Help
New... Ctrl+N
Open... Ctrl+O
Close
Save Ctrl+S
Save As...
Save as HTML...
Versions...
Page Setup...
Print Preview
Print... Ctrl+P
Send To
Properties
1 order
2 C:\WE Web page\order
3 home
4 24twhrwx
Exit
nterprises Corporate Philosophy
he leading producer of widgets in the world, creating the
customers world-wide. We will achieve this through:
closely to what our customers need, and aggressively meet
will be fully satisfied with each widget and will have that
Customers must be delighted with the speed, color and
at they use in their own products or in use at home.
ake sure that our employees have the tools that they need to
-quality widgets to the customer. All employees will be
amily members here at Widget Enterprises. Highly
be rewarded for outstanding work.
Page 1 Sec 1 1/1 At 1.2" Ln 2 Col 1

Figure R6.4.
Turn this document into a Web page with Save as HTML.

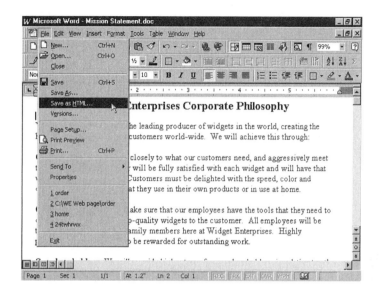

The hyperlink to `mission_statement.html` is created the same way as `order.html` was: by inserting a hyperlink where the text is that you would like to use as the jumping point to the mission statement from `index.html`. On the home page, select the words Mission Statement and create the hyperlink to `mission_statement.html`. Remember that all the files should be saved in the same folder or the path names are needed.

Step 5—Linking to the Widget Industry Association's Home Page

The final hyperlink is to the home page of the Widget Producers of America. Having been to this Web site previously, you know that the URL is `http://www.widgets.org`. To create a hyperlink from Widgets Enterprises to Widget Producers of America:

1. Select the text Widget Producers of America (WPA) on the Widgets Enterprises home page that you want to link to Widget Producers of America.
2. Click the Insert Hyperlink button (or select Insert | Hyperlink).
3. Enter the URL in the Link to file or URL text box as in Figure R6.5.

Just a Minute

> A URL must be typed exactly, including upper- and lowercase letters.

Insert Hyperlink
Link to file or URL:
http://www.widgets.org
Browse...
Enter or locate the path to the document you want to link to. This can be an Internet address (URL), a document on your hard drive, or a document on your company's network.
Path: <Link to containing document>
Named location in file (optional):
Browse...
If you want to jump to a specific location within the document, such as a bookmark, a named range, a database object, or a slide number, enter or locate that information above.
Use relative path for hyperlink
OK
Cancel

Figure R6.5.
Creating a hyperlink to another Web page.

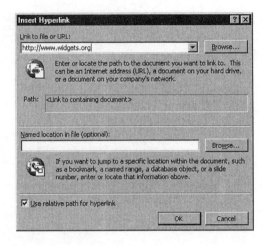

You have now created Web pages that could be put on the Web to use as a company's Web site. To add some color, you might consider adding an appropriate picture, a horizontal line, or a background to the Web pages. You get a picture placeholder when adding an image, but you can see what the page will look like by viewing it with your browser (see Figure R6.6). When all the changes have been made, be sure to save `index.html` with all the new additions.

home - Microsoft Internet Explorer
File Edit View Go Favorites Help
Back Forward Stop Refresh Home Search Favorites Print Font Mail Edit
Address C:\WE Web page\home.html
Links
Widget Enterprises
Welcome to Widget Enterprises! We are the largest supplier of standard-size unpadded widgets in the Northeastern United States, and have been in business since 1918. Our business is expanding rapidly, and we hope that you, too, will come to see why so many companies and individuals are choosing us for all of their widget needs.
What would you like to do?
Order a Widget
Read our Mission Statement
Go to the Widget Producers of America (WPA) home page
Done

Figure R6.6.
The finished home page with a horizontal bar added.

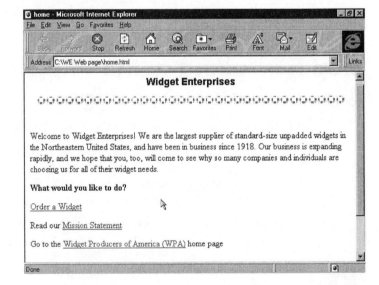

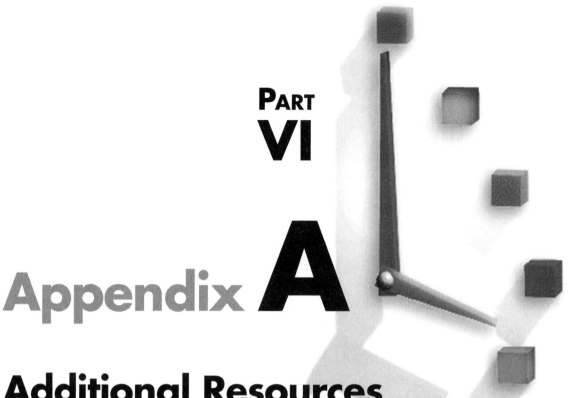

Appendix **A**

Additional Resources

Call for Help

There are many resources available when the help information provided in Word does not provide the answers you need.

Support Engineers

Microsoft offers a wide range of telephone support. A call to a Microsoft support engineer may be worth the long distance charges. These people walk you through a problem step by step in minimal time. It will probably take you more time to get hooked up to the support person than it takes him or her to solve the problem. To reach a support engineer, phone:

- ■ (206) 462-9673 6 a.m.–6 p.m. Pacific time (M–F)

Have Word up and running (unless you're having an installation problem— they can help there, too). Be prepared to give the support engineer your product ID number (this can be found in Word on the Help menu under About Microsoft Word, on the back of the installation CD-ROM, or in the printed materials that came with the floppy disks).

After the first phone call, things will go even more quickly. Microsoft puts you in its system, and you don't have to verify your license.

FastTips

Call first, and Microsoft will send you a map and/or catalog of the technical reports and help files available. It's hard to navigate through the system without the map or catalog, so make the call for these items first. Otherwise, you may go through a maze of phone menus to access the tip you need. Some items can be accessed by phone, others can be faxed or mailed to you. You can listen to recorded messages that answer many commonly asked questions or order technical reports from the FastTips line.

This is a computerized system, and you'll have to be alert to keep up with telephone instructions. To call for the FastTips map and catalog or to use the FastTips system, call:

- (800) 936-4100 (24-hour toll-free service)

Visit Microsoft's Web Site

If you have a way to connect to the Internet, there is a wealth of information on the Microsoft Web site. You can easily find your way around Microsoft's site. To save time, go straight to the Word support site at `http://www.microsoft.com/mswordsupport/` (see Figure A.1).

Microsoft Word - Technical Support - Microsoft Internet Explorer
File Edit View Go Favorites Help
Back Forward Stop Refresh Home Search Favorites Print Font Mail Edit
Address http://www.microsoft.com/mswordsupport/
Links
MICROSOFT PRODUCTS SEARCH SUPPORT SHOP WRITE US
Microsoft
Microsoft Technical Support
Site Map
Guided Tour with the Support Wizard
Knowledge Base
Troubleshooting Wizards
Frequently Asked Questions
Help Files, Service Packs, & Other Files
Newsgroups
Support Options & Phone Numbers
Submit a Question to a Support Engineer
Support Highlights
Microsoft Word
Support Highlights
To search technical support resources for this product, enter your request, then click Find.
Search Hints
Conversion
New for '97
Obtaining the Word 97 Import Converter
Use the Word 97 import converter to open Word 97 documents in Word 6.x or
Programming
New for '97
DOWNLOAD: Microsoft Word 97 Visual Basic for Applications Knowledge Base Articles
A compilation, in Microsoft
Opening picture: updatedfor97.jpg at www.microsoft.com

Figure A.1.
Word's Web site support.

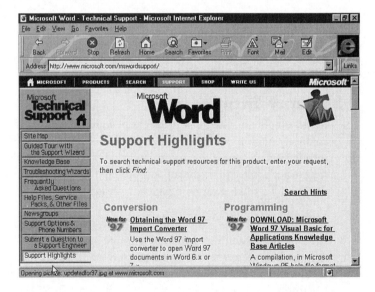

You get more than answers to questions from the Web site. You can download extra clips (art, sounds, and movies) and bug fixes (Microsoft does actually try to fix things). The Knowledge Base lets you search for information on specific topics. Troubleshooting wizards guide you through solutions to some of your Word problems. A file for frequently asked questions may include your question. Chances are if it's a common problem, the site will either tell you how to get around it or confirm that it is a known problem and you can't do anything about it until a bug fix is issued.

Newsgroups can be as helpful as any other portion of the online helps. This is the area where users post their Word problems and other users reply with solutions they've come up with. If you get into the newsgroup section, you can send your own problem to the group to see whether someone can answer it for you. It's like informal chatting, but with people who volunteer their time to post intelligent answers to questions.

Questions in the newsgroups are broken down into categories such as drawings and graphics, mail merge and fields, and page layout. You can go directly to an area where you might find answers rather than wading through a lot of topics that don't relate to your problem. Browsing the newsgroups is a good way to learn about known problems and possible solutions.

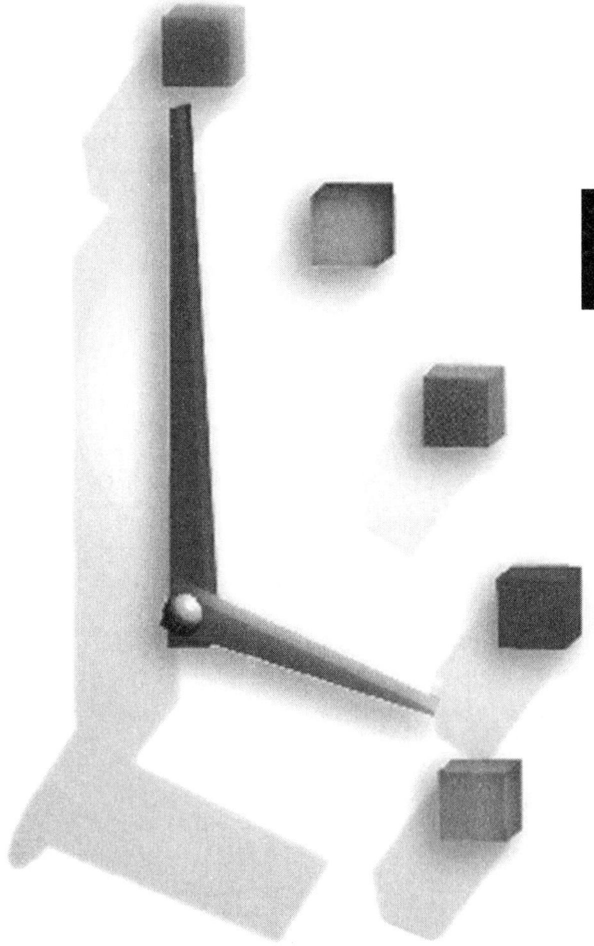

INDEX

Symbols

A

D

E

F

G

H

I

J - K

L

M

N

O

P

Q - R

S

T

U - V

W - Z

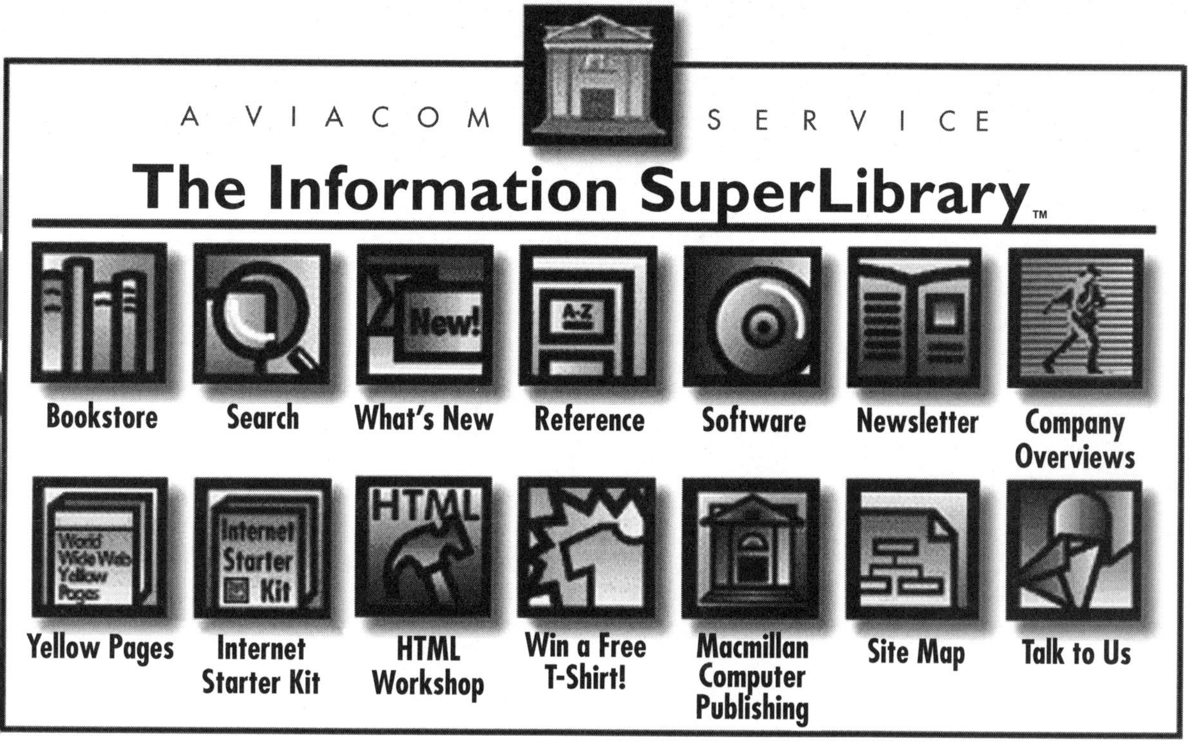
A VIACOM SERVICE
The Information SuperLibrary™
Bookstore
Search
What's New
Reference
Software
Newsletter
Company Overviews
Yellow Pages
Internet Starter Kit
HTML Workshop
Win a Free T-Shirt!
Macmillan Computer Publishing
Site Map
Talk to Us

MACMILLAN COMPUTER PUBLISHING USA

A V I A C O M C O M P A N Y

Technical ----- Support:

If you need assistance with the information in this book or with a CD/Disk accompanying the book, please access the Knowledge Base on our Web site at **http://www.superlibrary.com/general/support**. Our most Frequently Asked Questions are answered there. If you do not find the answer to your questions on our Web site, you may contact Macmillan Technical Support **(317) 581-3833** or e-mail us at **support@mcp.com**.

Teach Yourself Microsoft PowerPoint 97 in 24 Hours

Alexandria Haddad and Christopher Haddad

Teach Yourself Microsoft PowerPoint 97 in 24 Hours is an introductory tutorial that enables the reader to quickly create dynamic, captivating presentations. Beginning users will quickly learn how to utilize the new features of PowerPoint 97 with the easy, task-oriented format—the material is presented in manageable one-hour lessons. Practical, easy-to-follow exercises walk the reader through the concepts. Sections on free informational resources (templates, graphics, and so on) are included.

Price: $19.99 USA/$28.95 CDN *User level: New–Casual*
ISBN: 0-672-31117-8 *400 pages*

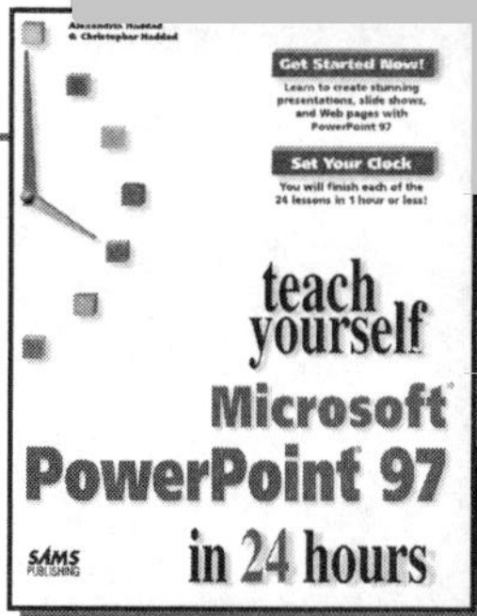
Get Started Now!
Set Your Clock
teach yourself
Microsoft
PowerPoint 97
in 24 hours
SAMS PUBLISHING

Teach Yourself Microsoft Excel 97 in 24 Hours

Lois Patterson

Teach Yourself Microsoft Excel 97 in 24 Hours uses a task-oriented format to help the reader become productive in this spreadsheet application with just 24 one-hour lessons. Many new features of Excel 97, including increased connectivity and the enhanced Chart wizard, are covered in this book, making it a tutorial for those who are upgrading from previous versions of Excel. Accomplished users will find tips to help increase their productivity. This book includes numerous illustrations and figures that demonstrate how to operate Excel's key features as well as more mathematical and scientific examples than many texts.

Price: $19.99 USA/$28.95 CDN *User level: New–Casual*
ISBN: 0-672-31116-X *400 pages*

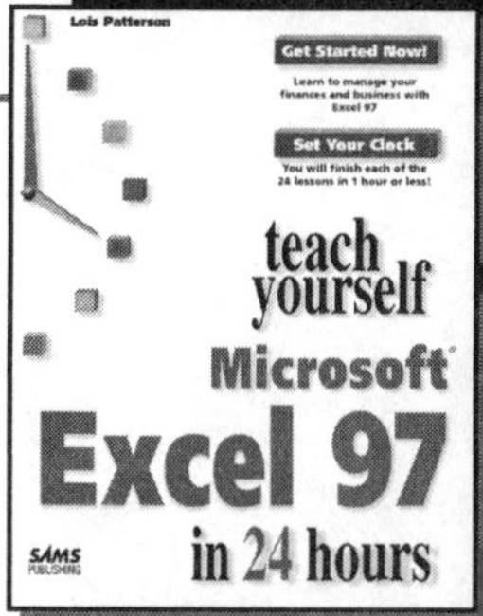
Lois Patterson
Get Started Now!
Set Your Clock
teach yourself
Microsoft
Excel 97
in 24 hours
SAMS PUBLISHING

Teach Yourself Access 97 in 24 Hours

Timothy Buchanan, David Nielsen, and Rob Newman

As organizations and end users continue to upgrade to NT Workstation and Windows 95, a surge in 32-bit productivity applications, including Microsoft Office 97, is expected. Using an easy-to-follow approach, this book teaches the fundamentals of a key component in the Microsoft Office 97 package, Access 97. Users will learn how to use and manipulate existing databases, create databases with wizards, and build databases from scratch in 24 one-hour lessons.

Price: $19.99 USA/$28.95 CDN *User level: New–Casual*
ISBN: 0-672-31027-9 *400 pages*

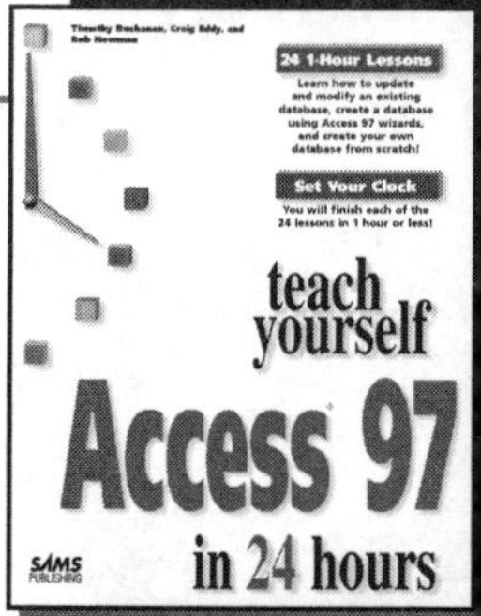
24 1-Hour Lessons
Set Your Clock
teach yourself
Access 97
in 24 hours
SAMS PUBLISHING

Teach Yourself Microsoft Outlook 97 in 24 Hours

Brian Proffitt and Kim Spilker

Microsoft Office, the leading application productivity suite available, will have Outlook as a personal information manager in its next version. Using step-by-step instructions and real-world examples, readers will explore the new features of Outlook and learn how to successfully and painlessly integrate Outlook with other Office 97 applications. Each lesson focuses on working with Outlook as a single user as well as in a group setting.

Price: $19.99 USA/$28.95 CDN *User level: New–Casual*
ISBN: 0-672-31044-9 *400 pages*

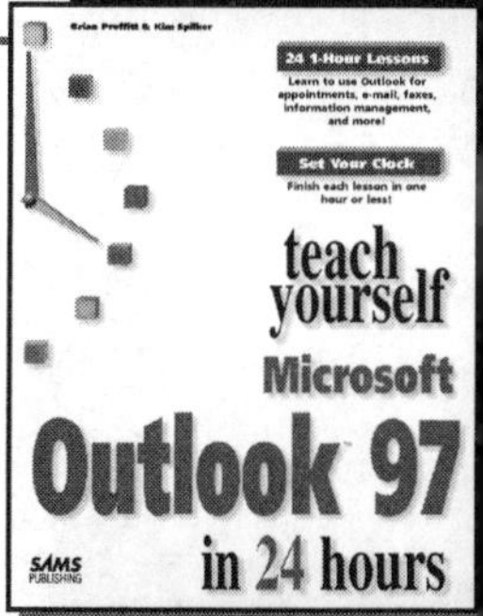
24 1-Hour Lessons
Set Your Clock
teach yourself
Microsoft
Outlook 97
in 24 hours
SAMS PUBLISHING

Microsoft Office 97 Unleashed

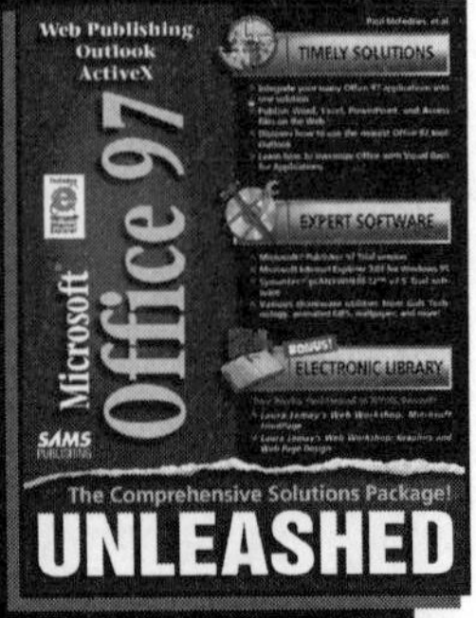

Web Publishing
Outlook
ActiveX
TIMELY SOLUTIONS
EXPERT SOFTWARE
ELECTRONIC LIBRARY
Microsoft Office 97
SAMS
The Comprehensive Solutions Package!
UNLEASHED

Paul McFedries and Sue Charlesworth

Microsoft has brought the Web to its Office suite of products. Hyperlinking, Office Assistants, and Active Document Support lets users publish documents to the Web or an intranet site. It also completely integrates with Microsoft FrontPage, making it possible to point and click a Web page into existence. This book details each of the Office products—Excel, Access, PowerPoint, Word, and Outlook—and shows the estimated 22 million registered users how to create presentations and Web documents. The CD-ROM that accompanies the book includes powerful utilities and two best-selling books in HTML format.

Price: $39.99 USA/$56.95 CDN — *User level: Accomplished–Expert*
ISBN: 0-672-31010-4 — *1,200 pages*

Paul McFedries' Windows 95 Unleashed, Professional Reference Edition

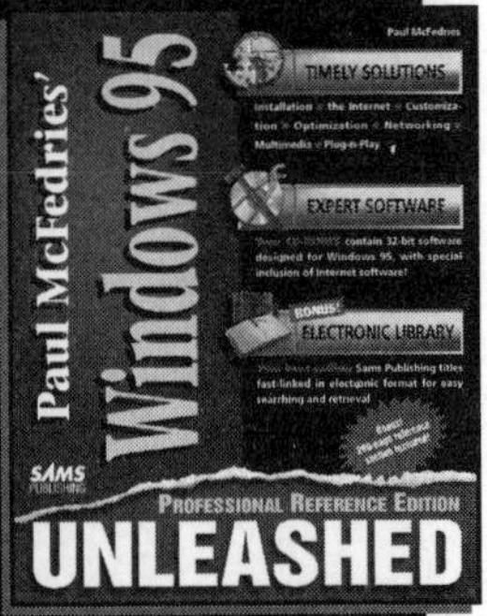

Paul McFedries'
Windows 95
TIMELY SOLUTIONS
EXPERT SOFTWARE
ELECTRONIC LIBRARY
SAMS
PROFESSIONAL REFERENCE EDITION
UNLEASHED

Paul McFedries

Paul McFedries' Windows 95 Unleashed, Professional Reference Edition takes readers beyond the basics, exploring all facets of this operating system, including installation, the Internet, customization, optimization, networking multimedia, plug-and-play, and the new features of the Windows Messaging System for communications. It includes coverage of Internet Explorer 4.0, bringing the "active desktop" to Windows 95. The accompanying CD-ROM contains 32-bit software designed for Windows 95 and an easy-to-search online chapter on troubleshooting for Windows 95.

Price: $59.99 USA/$84.95 CDN — *User level: Accomplished–Expert*
ISBN: 0-672-31039-2 — *1,750 pages*

Teach Yourself Web Publishing with Microsoft Office 97 in a Week

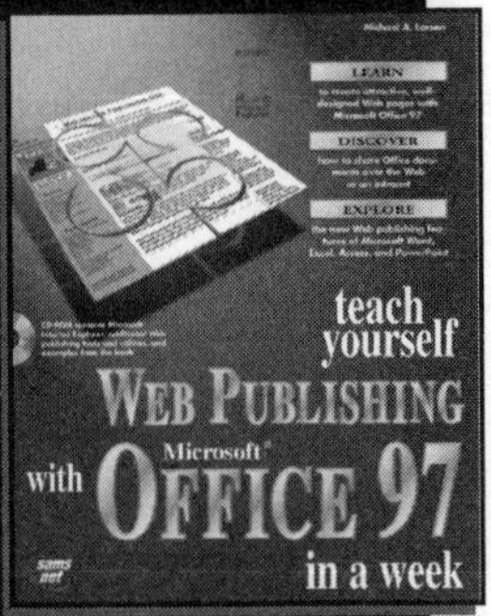

LEARN
DISCOVER
EXPLORE
teach yourself
WEB PUBLISHING
with Microsoft OFFICE 97
in a week

Michael Larson

Microsoft Office is taking the market by storm. With this book's clear, step-by-step approach and practical examples, users will learn how to effectively use components of Microsoft Office to publish attractive, well-designed documents for the World Wide Web or intranet. This book focuses on the Web publishing features of the latest versions of Word, Excel, Access, and PowerPoint, and explains the basics of Internet/intranet technology, the Microsoft Internet Explorer browser, and HTML. The accompanying CD-ROM is loaded with Microsoft Internet Explorer 3.0 and an extensive selection of additional graphics, templates, scripts, ActiveX controls, and multimedia clips to enhance Web pages.

Price: $39.99 USA/$56.95 CDN — *User level: New–Casual–Accomplished*
ISBN: 1-57521-232-3 — *464 pages*

Teach Yourself Microsoft FrontPage 97 in a Week

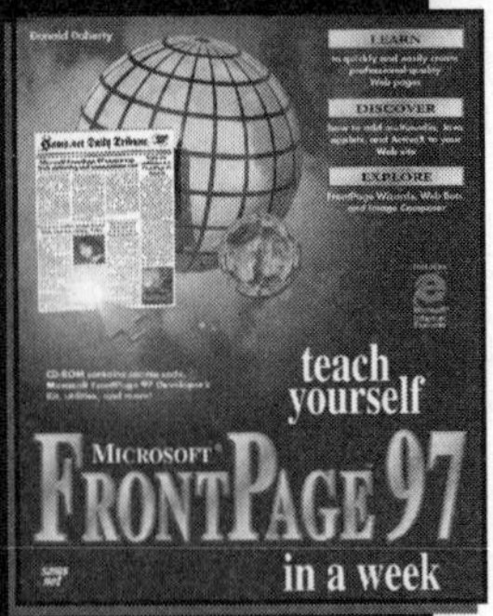

LEARN
DISCOVER
EXPLORE
teach yourself
MICROSOFT FRONTPAGE 97
in a week

Donald Doherty

FrontPage is the number one Web site creation program in the market, and this book explains how to use it. Everything from adding Office 97 documents to a Web site to using Java, HTML, wizards, VBScript, and JavaScript in a Web page is covered. With this book, readers will learn all the nuances of Web design and will have, through the included step-by-step examples, created an entire Web site using FrontPage 97. The accompanying CD-ROM includes Microsoft Internet Explorer 3.0, ActiveX and HTML development tools, plus additional ready-to-use templates, graphics, scripts, Java applets, and more.

Price: $29.99 USA/$42.95 CDN — *User level: New–Casual*
ISBN: 1-57521-225-0 — *500 pages*